Voices
of
Jewish-Russian
Literature

An Anthology

ACADEMIC
STUDIES
PRESS

Voices
of
Jewish-Russian
Literature

An Anthology

Edited, with Introductory Essays
by Maxim D. Shrayer

The editor gratefully acknowledges the support of Boston College.

On the cover: "A Blind Man with a Violin," 1926, oil on canvas, by Yehuda (Yu. M.) Pen (1854–1937). Reproduced by arrangement with the Vitebsk Regional Museum of the Republic of Belarus.

Library of Congress Cataloging-in-Publication Data

Names: Shrayer, Maxim, 1967, editor.

Title: Voices of Jewish-Russian literature : an anthology / edited by Maxim D. Shrayer.

Other titles: Jews of Russia & Eastern Europe and their legacy.

Description: Boston : Academic Studies Press, 2018.

Series: Jews of Russia and Eastern Europe and their legacy "...this definitive anthology of major nineteenth- and twentieth-century fiction, nonfiction and poetry by eighty Jewish-Russian writers explores both timeless themes and specific tribulations of a people's history"—Publisher's info. Includes bibliographical references and index.

Identifiers: LCCN 2018023268 | ISBN 9781618117922 (pbk. : alk. paper)

Subjects: LCSH: Russian literature—Jewish authors—19th century—Translations into English. | Russian literature—Jewish authors—20th century—Translations into English. | Jews—Fiction.

Classification: LCC PG3213 .V65 2018 | DDC 891.708/08924—dc23 LC record available at https://lccn.loc.gov/2018023268 ISBN 978-1-61811-792-2 (paperback) ISBN 978-1-61811-793-9 (electronic)

Book design by Kryon Publishing Services (P) Ltd.
www.kryonpublishing.com

Academic Studies Press
28 Montfern Avenue
Brighton, MA 02135, USA
P: (617)782-6290
F: (857)241-3149
press@academicstudiespress.com
www.academicstudiespress.com

Table of Contents

Acknowledgments

Like its predecessor, *An Anthology of Jewish-Russian Literature: Two Centuries of Dual Identity in Prose and Poetry, 1801–2001* (2007), this volume has been in the works for many years.

I would like to thank Boston College for its continuous support of my research.

Patricia Kolb, Editorial Director at M. E. Sharpe, stewarded the original anthology into print. Laura Stearns, Publisher at Routledge, assisted with the transition to the present volume.

Former Boston College undergraduates Elizabeth Baker and Benjamin Wilken assisted me with the preparation of the final text.

Chris Soldt of Boston College Media Technology Services generously helped with the preparation of the cover image.

The copyeditor, Dobrochna Fire, herself an accomplished translator, has done a superb job, and I very much appreciate her linguistic acumen and her tactful resistance to my authorial folly.

My thanks go to Kira Nemirovsky, Daria Pokholkova and the entire staff of Academic Studies Press for giving the anthology a loving home.

I would like to extend my gratitude to all the writers and writers' families who have responded to my queries and kindly supplied the information I requested.

Since the publication of *An Anthology of Jewish-Russian Literature* (2007), the two-volume set in which the majority of these texts originally appeared, six of the writers featured in this anthology have passed away. I would like to remember them here: Ruth Zernova (1919–2004), Bella Ulanovskaya (1943–2005), Vassily Aksyonov (1932–2009), Aleksandr Mezhirov (1923–2009), Inna Lisnyanskaya (1928–2014), and Vladimir Britanishsky (1933–2015). The departure of the historian John D. Klier (1944–2007), who wrote the outline of Jewish-Russian history included in this volume, has left a void in the field of Jewish-Russian studies.

I would never have been able to undertake this anthology without the passion and dedication of a team of gifted translators. Their contributions are labors of love and expressions of their commitment to the cause of making Jewish-Russian literature available in English translation.

I would also like to take this opportunity to remember the contributing translators who have passed away over the past decade: Richard Sheldon, Harold Shukman, Greta Slobin, Andrew Von Hendy, Daniel Weissbort.

My friend and colleague Patricia Herlihy passed away as this anthology was in the final stages of production. I owe her a debt of graditude.

* * *

My parents, David Shrayer-Petrov and Emilia Shrayer, raised me as both a Jew and a Russian in the former Soviet Union. They lived through almost nine hellish years as Jewish refuseniks between 1979 and 1987. I owe to them not only my life but also all the opportunities and freedoms I have enjoyed since we came to America in 1987.

Without my wife, Karen E. Lasser, I would never have been able to complete this anthology, and there are no words in Russian or English to express my love and gratitude.

Our daughters, Mira and Tatiana, were born and came of age in the years that I have been working on anthologizing works of Jewish-Russian literature. Mira and Tatiana inspire me every day.

* * *

I would like to dedicate this anthology to the memory of my paternal grandparents, Bella Breydo and Pyotr (Peysakh) Shrayer, and my maternal grandparents, Anna (Nyusya) Studnits and Arkady (Aron) Polyak Z"L. As young people, my late grandparents left the former Pale of Settlement and moved to great Russian cities, making Russian culture their own while always remaining Jews and never forgetting their Jerusalem.

M.D.S.

Brookline–South Chatham, Mass.

3 February–12 June 2018; 24 October 2018

Note on Transliteration, Spelling of Names, and Dates

A significantly modified (and we hope reader-friendly) version of the Library of Congress system for transliterating the Russian alphabet is used throughout the editor's general introduction, the editor's introductions to individual authors and their works, the English translations of works, and the notes to them. Exceptions are Russian words and geographical and personal names that have gained a common spelling in English, such as Maxim Gorky instead of "Maksim Gorky," Joseph Brodsky instead of "Iosif Brodsky," Osip Mandelstam instead of "Osip Mandelshtam," Vladimir Jabotinsky instead of "Vladimir Zhabotinsky," Babi Yar instead of "Babii Iar,"and so forth. Bibliographical references, including titles of Russian-language periodicals, in the main text, footnotes, and the bibliography of primary sources are rendered in the standard Library of Congress system of transliterating the Russian alphabet, without diacritical marks.

We have adopted the transliteration system established by YIVO and commonly used in English contexts for the spelling of all Yiddish words and expressions, including those using Cyrillic in the Russian originals. *The Yiddish Dictionary Sourcebook: A Transliterated Guide to the Yiddish Language* by Herman Galvin and Stan Tamarkin (Hoboken, NJ: Ktav, 1986) has been a useful resource for verifying spellings. Hebrew words and expressions have been transliterated to conform to English-language rather than Russian-language standards.

While the bibliography of primary sources lists transliterated Russian titles of all literary works, the editor's general introduction and the editor's introductions to individual authors and their works provide transliterated Russian titles or transliterated quotations from the Russian originals only where the editor has deemed it absolutely necessary. Otherwise, English translations, as literal as possible, are provided instead.

Where a Russian periodical is mentioned for the first time in a particular entry, the English translation is followed by the Russian title in parentheses. In some cases, however, major Russian periodicals, such as *Pravda* or *Novy mir*, are known in English-language scholarship by their original names and have gained common spellings. These titles have not been translated.

All quotations from the Hebrew Bible are from *A New Translation of the Holy Scriptures According to the Traditional Hebrew Text* (Philadelphia: The Jewish Publication Society, 1985); all quotations from the New Testament are from *The Revised English Bible with Apocrypha* (Oxford/Cambridge: Oxford University Press/Cambridge University Press, 1989).

In working on this anthology, the editor drew on a number of published and some unpublished sources. The following encyclopedias and dictionaries proved invaluable: *Encyclopedia Judaica,* 16 vols. (Jerusalem, 1972); *Evreiskaia entsiklopediia,* 16 vols. (St. Petersburg, 1906–13); *Kratkaia evreiskaia entsiklopediia,* 10 vols. plus 3 supplements (Jerusalem, 1976–2001); *The New Standard Jewish Encyclopedia,* new revised edition (New York, 1992); *Russkie pisateli 1900–1917: biograficheskii slovar',* 5 vols. pub. to date (Moscow, 1989–).

Unless otherwise specified, the dates in the table of contents and at the end of each individual text refer to the completion of the work; in some instances, the date of first publication follows if it differs significantly from the date of completion. Unless otherwise specified, a parenthetical date in the editor's general introduction, the editor's introductions to the individual authors and their works, or the notes refers to the first publication of a work; in some cases, the date of completion precedes if it differs significantly from the date of first publication. Parenthetical dates for nonliterary works always refer to the date of publication. Where two dates are provided for a historical event, the first refers to the Julian calendar, used in Russia prior to 1918, and the second to the Gregorian calendar.

For information about the primary sources that have been consulted and the history of the publication of all the works included in the anthology, please see the bibliography of primary sources following the Selected Bibliography at the end of this anthology.

Unless otherwise indicated, all translations from the Russian in the introductory essays, headnotes, explanatory notes, and footnotes are by Maxim D. Shrayer.

Unless otherwise indicated, all bibliographical notes, introductory essays and headnotes, explanatory notes, footnotes, and bibliographies are by Maxim D. Shrayer.

Note on How to Use This Anthology

One would certainly benefit from reading the anthology sequentially, in the order in which the eighty-one authors and their works appear in the table of contents. However, in addition to a chronological and consecutive reading, this anthology yields itself readily to selective reading in accordance with the reader's predilections, literary interests, or fascination with a specific author or a particular period of nineteenth- or twentieth-century Jewish and Russian (and Soviet) history. Individual sections of the anthology and works by particular authors can be read out of sequence or one at a time.

In addition to the editor's general introduction and introductory essays preceding each of the eight sections, the anthology includes a concise survey of Jewish-Russian history written by the historian John D. Klier. Readers less familiar with the main historical events that shaped the destinies of Russia's Jews would especially benefit from consulting Klier's outline, found in the back of the volume.

Names of the authors featured in this anthology are boldfaced throughout, except in the sections devoted to their own works. A critical essay highlighting principal biographical events, artistic contributions, and place in literary history introduces each individual author. The introductory essays focus primarily on the writers' artistic careers, while their other professional and/or social occupations are referenced only insofar as they directly pertain to their literary works. Additionally, each work or selection of works by a given author is prefaced by a headnote containing information about the work's conception and publication and outlining some of the historical and literary contexts that might help the reader understand it better.

Throughout the individual introductory essays and headnotes, efforts have been made to introduce a system of cross-references: every time another author or work featured in the anthology is mentioned or a major historical or literary event discussed elsewhere is evoked, a parenthetical reference points to its appropriate place or places in the anthology. This cross-referencing approach also emphasizes instances of dialogue among authors and of interplay among their texts. A comprehensive index of names, works, and selected subjects referenced in the anthology, located in the back of the volume, should be especially helpful to readers who wish to trace these connections.

The editor's general introduction outlines the details of the periodization of Jewish-Russian literature and the organizing principles behind the anthology's division into eight separate sections. The brief introductory essays placed before each individual section of the anthology focus on the various intersections of historical events and aesthetic developments.

The chronologically and historically oriented organization of this anthology could never achieve perfect order and transparency simply because writers' lives do not fit too neatly within external boundaries, however carefully conceived. This is why the order of writers and works in the anthology and within its individual sections is based in part on the time of a work's creation and in part on its year of publication. The latter circumstance is especially valid for the post–World War II sections of the anthology. To those writers whose works span beyond the chronological confines of a given section, such as **Genrikh Sapgir, Yan Satunovsky,** or **Boris Khazanov,** the editor has applied the notion of a critical mass of the composition dates (for example, the majority of the author's works were composed in the late 1960s) or the publication dates (such as, the works were composed in the 1970s in the USSR but published in the 1990s in emigration).

Finally, given the limited available space and a desire to feature a diversity of authors and works and to illustrate each of the historical periods with adequate and representative works, hard choices had to be made in the final selection of the included texts. It is therefore important to keep in mind that length and number of works in and of themselves do not represent a value judgment of a given author's status and contribution. Furthermore, some longer prosaic or poetic texts yield themselves poorly to abridgment and had to be included almost in their entirety. Where a selected text could be included only in extracts, ellipsis points [...] within brackets indicate the location of the abridgement. In a few cases, the editor felt that longer introductions were necessary in order to do justice to the complexity of the critical debates surrounding the career of a particular Jewish-Russian author (**Boris Slutsky,** for example). Additionally, the historical and cultural backgrounds of several individual works called for longer headnotes (such as **Lev Levanda**'s *Seething Times*). But only in three instances (**Ilya Ehrenburg, Vasily Grossman,** and **Boris Slutsky**) are the author's works represented in more than one section of the anthology. These three exceptions are the result of the special circumstances of these authors' lives and the indispensability of their works to the sections of the anthology in which they appear. In these three cases, separate headnotes introduce the works by the same author found in the different sections.

For the reader's convenience, an alphabetical index of writers included in the anthology is found in the back, with page numbers following each writer's name. Also found in the back of the volume are detailed bibliographies that reflect the history of each work's publication. In some cases, obtaining complete information on a given work's original publication, either in periodical or in book form, was an arduous task, and the editor and publisher would be grateful to readers for any additional information they might have. At the bottom of the last page of each individual author's selection, the reader will find information on copyright. In several cases we have been unable to obtain information on the present copyright owner, and we invite anyone with knowledge thereof to contact us.

In preparing this anthology, the editor was lucky to have worked with a team of excellent literary translators. A separate index of translators is found in the back of this anthology and lists all contributions of each translator by author. Faithfulness to the originals' meaning and design, precision in places bordering on literalism, and commitment to safeguarding the "strangeness" of the original texts' appearance and provenance have shaped the editor's formal expectations. This applies particularly to the efforts to rescue and preserve the originals' prosody and versification. In places going against the grain of the currently dominant practices in Anglo-American verse, the editor and the translators have sought to protect the originals' intactness, their structural accoutrements and formal vestments. At the same time, the editor has done his best to shield the translators' artistic autonomy. Where translators have introduced substitutions and accommodations, notably in some of the verse translations, they have made those choices not as acts of cultural violence but in the belief that art does stand to gain something in translation.

General Introduction: The Legacy of Jewish-Russian Literature

By Maxim D. Shrayer

DUAL LITERARY IDENTITIES

What are cultures measured by? Cultural contributions are difficult to quantify and even harder to qualify without a critical judgment in hand. In the case of verbal arts, and of literature specifically, various criteria of formal perfection and originality, significance in literary history, and aspects of time, place, and milieu all contribute to the ways in which one regards a writer's contribution. In the case of Jewish culture in Diaspora, and specifically of Jewish writing created in non-Jewish languages adopted by Jews, the reckoning of a writer's status is riddled with a set of powerful contrapositions.

Above all else, there is the duality, or multiplicity, of a writer's own identity—both Jewish and German (Heinrich Heine) or French (Marcel Proust) or Russian (**Isaac Babel**) or Polish (Julian Tuwim) or Hungarian (Imre Kertész) or Brazilian (Clarice Lispector) or Canadian (Mordechai Richler) or American (Bernard Malamud). Then there is the dividedly redoubled perspective of a Diasporic Jew: both an in-looking outsider and an out-looking insider. And there is the language of writing itself, not always one of the writer's native setting, not necessarily one in which a writer spoke to his or her own parents or non-Jewish childhood friends, but in some cases a second or third or forth language—acquired, mastered, and made one's own in a flight from home.[1]

Evgeny Shklyar (1894–1942), a Jewish-Russian poet and a Lithuanian patriot who translated into Russian the text of the Lithuanian national anthem

---

1 In the context of Jewish-Russian history and culture, the juxtaposition between a "divided" and a "redoubled" identity goes back to the writings of the critic and polemicist Iosif Bikerman (1867–1941? 1942?), who stated in 1910, on the pages of the St. Petersburg magazine *Jewish World* (*Evreiskii mir*), "Not dividedness [*razdvoennost'*] but redoubledness [*udvoennost'*]"; quoted in Shimon Markish, *Babel' i drugie*, 2nd ed., 186 (Moscow and Jerusalem: Personal'naia tvorcheskaia masterskaia "Mikhail Shchigol'," 1997).

and was murdered in a Nazi concentration camp outside Kaunas, wrote in the poem "Where's Home?" (1925; in this anthology):

> . . . In Judaism fierce, hidden strengths appear
> To nurture twice exile's flowers
> And deep within the heart's most buried bowers
> To pick amongst them and to make it clear
> You're going either where all's alien but dear
> Or where the majestic past regales the hours . . .[2]
>
> (Trans. Maxim D. Shrayer and Andrew Von Hendy)

The poem was composed at a time when dreams of a Jewish state were becoming much more than a poet's parable. The land "where all's alien but dear" is, of course, Shklyar's native Pale of Settlement, while the place where "the majestic past regales the hours" is Shklyar's vision of Israel. The duality of a Diasporic Jew's loyalties is both political-ideological and cultural-linguistic. In the poem's final line, envisioning his own life as a Jewish-Russian poet and translator of Lithuanian poets into Russian come to Israel to hear children "greet [him] with words of welcome in *ivrit*," Shklyar employs the italicized (and transliterated) Hebrew word for the ancient Jewish tongue. The poet's word choice in the final, rhyming position also underscores the shape of his identity: linguistically and culturally at home in the east European abode where "all's alien but dear" and spiritually, if symbolically, traveling to the land of Israel, "where the majestic past regales the hours," and yet, where the Jewish-Russian poet is culturally a foreigner.

"Exile" in Shklyar's poem is the Diaspora, where Jews have added Hebrew-Farsi, Ladino, and Yiddish to their Hebrew, while also translating their identities, albeit never fully or completely (but is translation ever?), into Arabic, Spanish, Italian, French, German, English, Polish, Russian, and many other languages spoken in the places of their dispersion. But Shklyar's "exile" is also the Jewish poet's exile from his literary home, his Russian tongue, and this duality renders nearly meaningless debates about the legitimacy of "Jewish" literatures in "non-Jewish" languages.

In the late nineteenth and the twentieth centuries, the torrents of history, coupled with personal artistic ambitions, thrust Jewish writers across the globe in numbers far greater than ever before. In their adopted countries, some continued to cultivate writing only in their native non-Jewish languages, while others became translingual authors. Using the Jewish languages to define the

---

2 Hereinafter, unless indicated otherwise, all translations from the Russian are the editor's own.

"religion," "identity," or "nationality" of a Jewish writer's work becomes especially knotty in the twentieth century, when a critical mass of the Jewish population shifted from the use of Yiddish to the use of modern European languages or Modern Hebrew. The Shoah then completed the undoing of Yiddish as the transnational language of Ashkenazic Jews, the undoing that the rigors of modernization, acculturation, and integration had been performing both in the USSR and in the West for almost a century.[3]

"All writers immigrate to their art and stay therein," stated the Russian-American writer Vladimir Nabokov (1899–1977) soon after having fled to America from war-stricken Europe with his Jewish wife and son aboard a ship chartered by HIAS, a Jewish refugee agency. One is tempted to ask where *Jewish* writers immigrate, whence they emigrate, and where they stay. One also wonders how the dualities or multiplicities of the Jewish writers' selves change in their travels across time and culture, and, finally, what these Jewish writers share in their comings and goings. A Jewish poetics, perhaps? Many of the answers to these questions lie in the nineteenth- and twentieth-century works gathered in this anthology of Jewish-Russian literature.

In the two centuries that followed the spread of the Haskalah (Jewish Enlightenment) in the late eighteenth century, linguistic self-expression in non-Jewish languages was central to the Jewish experience and Jewish survival in Diaspora. Two decades of curating anthologies have taught me that, especially in the nineteenth and twentieth centuries, Jewish literary culture created in non-Jewish languages increasingly served as one of the main receptacles into which the traditions of Jewish spirituality were poured. Varieties of Jewish self-awareness are channeled and transmitted through what is called, for lack of a better term, "secular literature." Quite often, while an uninformed reading of a Jewish text created and published in the literary mainstream reveals only superficially Jewish references, a rereading shows how much of the Judaic heritage is captured and preserved in its pages. A classic example of such a dual, non-Jewish and Jewish, model of (re)reading is **Isaac Babel**'s novel-length

---

3 A few examples will suffice: Abraham Cahan, born outside Vilna in 1860, died in 1951 in New York, wrote in Yiddish and English; Gertrude Stein, born in Pittsburgh, Pennsylvania, in 1874, died in Paris in 1946, wrote in English; Stefan Zweig, born in 1881 in Vienna, died by his own hand in 1942 in Petrópolis, Brazil, wrote in German; Rahel, born Rachel Bluwstein in 1890 in Saratov, died in Tel Aviv in 1931, wrote in Russian but mainly in Hebrew; Paul Celan, born Paul Antschel in 1920 in Czernowitz (then Romania, now Ukraine), a suicide in Paris in 1970, wrote mainly in German but also in Romanian in his youth; Joseph Brodsky, born in 1940 in Leningrad (now St. Petersburg), died in 1996 in New York, wrote in Russian and English.

cycle of stories *Red Cavalry* (first book edition 1926). A more recent example is Saul Bellow's novel *Ravelstein* (2000), where a dying Jewish-American gay neoconservantive intellectual finds himself truly at home only in one book, *The Book,* if in any place at all.

As I think of the ways Jewish literature transgresses and transcends boundaries of history, politics, and culture, I am reminded of an essay–testament by **Lev Levanda** (1835–1888) titled "On Assimilation." Levanda's polemical essay appeared in the St. Petersburg Russian-language *Weekly Chronicle of Sunrise* (*Nedel'naia khronika Voskhoda*) in 1885. "The Jewish nationality, that is, the universal doctrine known as Judaism, does not particularly need a strictly assigned territory: its territory is the entire wide world!" wrote Levanda. " . . . Jews do not consider themselves a living people; they consider themselves a living *nation* that lives and must live, namely, a *Jewish* nation, that is, a doctrine, an idea. As an *idea*, Judaism does not necessitate a particular territory. . . ." By implication, as it embodies aspects of Jewish spiritual life both directly and obliquely, Jewish literature is perhaps also not bound to a particular local philological terrain and retains its Jewishness in translation. While translation from a non-Jewish language into a Jewish one, or into another non-Jewish language, may either enhance or obscure a writer's subterranean Judaic references, Jewish literary culture itself is both national and transnational. One of the reasons to study Jewish literature is that it preserves and reveals aspects of the Jewish condition that a Jewish religious mind would commonly seek elsewhere and a non-Jewish mind might not at all be conscious of during the act of reading.

Among the letters between the Russian poet and thinker Vyacheslav Ivanov (1866–1949) and the Jewish-Russian philosopher of culture Mikhail Gershenzon (1869–1925), gathered in *Correspondence from Two Corners* (1920; published 1921), one of the most tragic of Gershenzon's letters underscored a survival of Jewish memory in the works that acculturated Jews address to the cultural mainstream: "How can I forget my native Jewish Kishinev of the spring of 1903!" Gershenzon cried out to his non-Jewish interlocutor. "Perhaps this Kishinev is outside of Russian history, perhaps the Krushevans are outside the history of Russian society [the journalist Pavel Krushevan incited anti-Jewish violence in the Kishinev Pogrom], but they live on in my memory, and I am their judge. . . . And my people is outside history, and its history is outside the schemas of the world historians—but I know the price of all these historical constructs by writers who do not wish to know the truth."

WITHIN RUSSIA AND WITHOUT RUSSIA

This anthology tests our conception of Jewish literature in Diaspora in what is arguably its most extreme case: Russia and the former USSR and the waves of emigration from Russia and the former USSR. In *Jewry and the Christian Question*, written in 1884, three years after Fyodor Dostoevsky's death, the Russian religious philosopher Vladimir Solovyov (1853–1900) posited three main questions about the interrelation between Christianity, and specifically Russian Orthodoxy, and Judaism. Solovyov's questions also apply to the survival of Jewish identity and culture in Russia: "1. Why was Christ a Jew, and why is the stepping-stone of the universal church taken from the House of Israel? 2. Why did the majority of Israel not recognize its Messiah, why did the Old Testament church not dissolve into the New Testament church, and why do the majority of the Jews prefer to be completely without a temple rather than join the Christian temple? 3. Why, finally, and for what purpose was the most solid (in the religious aspect) part of Jewry moved to Russia and Poland, placed at the boundary of the Graeco-Slavic and Latin-Slavic worlds?" Solovyov, who on his deathbed prayed in Hebrew for the Jewish people, did not live to see the pogroms of 1903–1906, the 1917 revolutions and the ensuing civil war, the destruction of traditional Jewish life during the first Soviet decades, and the horrors of the Shoah. With slight adjustments, Solovyov's fundamental questions still hold true: Why, despite all the misfortunes and pressures, have the Jews of the Russian Empire and the Soviet Union survived without losing their selfhood, even though so many have lost their religion and living ties to Yiddish and Hebrew? One of the most fascinating cultural paradoxes of Russian Jewry is that, against all the historical odds, even during the post-Shoah Soviet decades, it continued to nurture its dual sense of self, both Jewish and Russian, and Russian letters became its principal outlet for articulating this duality. Furthermore, through the exodus of Soviet Jewry in the 1970s–1990s, the vast majority of Soviet and ex-Soviet Jews left for Israel and North America, resulting in the depletion of the Jewish communities in Russia and the former Soviet republics and in the creation of what Zvi Gitelman calls "the New Jewish Diaspora."[4]

Russia was the last European nation to gain—through western expansion and colonization—a large Jewish minority and also the last to free its Jews of oppressive restrictions. (For details, see John D. Klier's "Outline of

---

4 See Zvi Gitelman, ed., *The New Jewish Diaspora: Russian-Speaking Immigrants in the United States, Israel, and Germany* (New Brunswick, NJ: Rutgers University Press, 2016).

Jewish-Russian History" at the back of this volume.) The Jewish question has occupied a prominent place in Russian—and later Soviet—history since the 1860s. The Jewish question in Russia involved the mostly prejudicial attitudes of both the Russian government and the general population toward the Jews but also the attempts of the Jewish community to preserve its spiritual and cultural identity as a minority without a territory of its own. The double bind of anti-Jewish attitudes and policies during the tsarist era presented a contradiction: on the one hand, the Russians expected the Jews to assimilate if not convert to Christianity; on the other, fearful of a growing Jewish presence, the Russians prevented the Jews from integrating into Russian life by instituting restrictions and not discouraging popular antisemitic sentiments.

By the early twentieth century, the Russian Empire had the highest concentration of Jews in the world: in 1897, about 5.2 million (about 47 percent of the world's Jewish population), and in 1914, at the beginning of World War I, still about 5.5 million, including 2 million Jews in Russia's Polish provinces (about 41 percent of the world's Jewish population). According to the same census of 1897, 24.6 percent of Jews in the Russian Empire could read and write in Russian, but only 1 percent considered Russian their mother tongue. In growing numbers, the nonemancipated Jews strove to enter the Russian social and cultural mainstream. Anton Chekhov (1860–1904), an astute student of the Jewish question, remarked as he sketched a southern provincial town in "My Life" (1896) that "only Jewish adolescents frequented the local . . . libraries." In the story "Ionych" (1898), Chekhov stressed again that ". . . the people in S. read very little, and at the local library they said that if it hadn't been for unmarried ladies and young Jews, one might as well close the library. . . ." The Jewish question certainly preoccupied the creator of *Ivanov*, "Steppe" (1888), and "Rothschild's Fiddle" (1894), and during his final years in Yalta, Chekhov was likely to hear from his acquaintances among the Jewish-Russian intelligentsia about the mesmeric and polarizing impacts of both Zionism and Marxism.

Russia—and the former USSR—offers the student of Jewish literature and culture a challenging case study of contrasting attitudes, ranging from philosemitic dreams of a harmonious fusion to antisemitic fabrications and genocidal scenarios. To measure the enormity of the religious, historical, and cultural baggage that the Jews brought to Russian letters would mean much more than merely to examine Jewish history through the prism of Russian literature created by Jews. And to state, in keeping with the genre of anthology introductions, that the Jews have made a major contribution to Russian literature would be to commit a necessary truism. Of the four Russian writers to have been awarded the Nobel Prize in literature, two were born Jewish: **Boris Pasternak**, whom the Soviet authorities forced to turn down the prize in 1958; and **Joseph Brodsky**, a Russian poet and American essayist banished from the USSR, who received the prize in 1987. For a Jew in Russia or the Soviet Union, the act of becoming a Russian writer often amounted to an act of identity revamping. In some cases, a Jewish-Russian writer's gravitation to Christianity and abnegation of his or her Jewish self completed the process of becoming Russian (e.g., **Boris Pasternak** [1890–1960]). In other cases, deeply devotional Judaic thinking (**Matvey Royzman** [1896–1973]) or a militantly Zionist worldview (**Vladimir** [Ze'ev] **Jabotinsky** [1880–1940]) was combined with an acute aesthetic sense of one's Russianness. Jewry gave Russia its arguably most European poet of modernity, **Osip Mandelstam** (1891–1938); its most talented and controversial mythologists of the Revolution and the civil war, **Isaac Babel** (1894–1940) in prose and **Eduard Bagritsky** (1895–1934) in poetry; its mightiest voice of the people's resistance during the years of the Nazi invasion, **Ilya Ehrenburg** (1891–1967), and its first national poetic witness to the mass murder of Jews by Nazis and their accomplices, **Ilya Selvinsky** (1899–1968); its savviest herald of the Thaw, **Boris Slutsky** (1919–1986); the great underground keeper of avant-garde freedom in the late Soviet era, **Genrikh Sapgir** (1928–1999); and even Russia's most admired literary comedian of the late Soviet decades, Mikhail Zhvanetsky (b. 1934). And Jewry also gave Russia many distinguished Jewish-Russian authors, such as **Mark Aldanov** (1886–1957), **Dovid Knut** (1900–1955), or **Friedrich Gorenstein** (1923–2002), who later became exiles and émigrés while remaining Russian writers. Others yet, such as Elsa Triolet (1896–1970), had started in Russian but in exile switched to writing in western languages. By writing in Russian, a Jew becomes a Russian writer.[5] But to what degree does she or he also remain a Jewish writer?

---

5 I am indebted to Alice Nakhimovsky's observations about Jewish-Russian writers made in connection with the career of **David Aizman**, whose work is featured in this anthology. See Alice Stone-Nakhimovsky, "Encounters: Russians and Jews in the Short Stories of David Aizman," *Cahiers du monde russe et soviétique* 26, no. 2 (April–June 1985): 175–84. I previously discussed this subject of a Jew's becoming a Russian (and/or Soviet) writer in *Russian Poet/Soviet Jew: The Legacy of Eduard Bagritskii* (Lanham, MD: Rowman & Littlefield, 2000).

SCOPE, STRUCTURE, PERIODIZATION

This anthology of fiction, nonfiction, and poetry by Jewish-Russian writers explores both the timeless themes and the specific tribulations of a people's history. This anthology investigates the dilemma of cultural duality by attempting a story, a history, and an overview of Jewish-Russian literature. It features exemplary works by seventy-nine Jewish authors, written and published in the Russian language between 1801 and 2001.

This project has been in the making for a period of almost twenty years. It began as a reconstruction of the canon, and its results appeared in 2007 as *An Anthology of Jewish-Russian Literature: Two Centuries of Dual Identity in Prose and Poetry, 1801–2001*. The original, expansive anthology showcased works by over one hundred thirty authors. The present volume is not merely or simply an abridgment of the 2007 two-volume edition. About 10 percent of the material is new, most significantly, new English translations of two short stories by **Isaac Babel**, English translations of two Shoah poems by **Ilya Selvinsky**, and a new English translation of **Vasily Grossman's** "The Hell of Treblinka." The rest of the material, including all the editor's introductions to the sections, the essays about the individual authors, and the headnotes, has been updated. Aspiring for a more reader-friendly and contemporary volume, we made a tilt in favor of human interest and accessibility in our selection and presentation.

A strong preference was given in this anthology to including works in their entirety, although in some cases larger works, such as long narrative poems or novels, are anthologized through representative excerpts. Drama yields itself very poorly to excerpting and anthologizing. Much to the editor's regret, even such major works of Jewish-Russian theater as Nikolay Minsky's *The Siege of Tulchin* (1888), **Isaac Babel's** *Sunset* (1928), or **Friedrich Gorenstein's** *Berdichev* (1975) do not appear in this volume. (A separate anthology of Jewish-Russian theater is much needed, and I hope to turn to this project at a later date.)

Historical considerations have affected the structure of the anthology. The lower historical boundary, 1801, was the year Alexander I ascended the Russian throne; the upper boundary, 2001, exactly two hundred years later, was the first year of Vladimir Putin's presidency after the Russian election of 2000. Within the glare of two hundred years, other historical boundaries serve as historical demarcation points. Some are major events of Russian and world history: 1917, the year of two revolutions, and 1920, the end of the civil war in European Russia; 1939, the beginning of World War II, and 1941, the Nazi invasion of the USSR; 1953, Stalin's death and the beginning of the

Thaw; 1964, the ousting of Khrushchev in a Kremlin coup and the beginning of Brezhnev's rule; 1991, the end of the Soviet Union. Other boundaries bear particular significance to Jewish-Russian history: 1840, the year of the imperial ukase establishing, as part of Nicholas's reforms of Russia's Jewish community, "The Committee to Develop Measures for the Fundamental Transformation of the Jews"; 1881, the beginning of the first wave of ferocious pogroms following Alexander II's assassination; 1902, the year preceding the Kishinev Pogrom and summoning the start of the second wave of pogroms; 1967, the Six-Day War and the breaking off of diplomatic relations with Israel by the USSR. The eight sections of the anthology, based on decades rather than exact years, correspond both to chapters of Russian/Soviet history (e.g., "Revolution and Emigration: 1920s–1930s") and to chapters of Jewish history (e.g., "The Jewish Exodus: 1970s–1990s"). While historically based, the structure of the anthology also reflects the major artistic periods and trends of the two centuries, from romanticism to postmodernism.

DEFINITION

In selecting materials for this anthology, I have read and considered works by as many as 350 authors. To this day, with some questions still unanswered, I fundamentally agree with Alice Nakhimovsky's definition as formulated in her *Russian-Jewish Literature and Identity* (1992): "any Russian-language writer of Jewish origin for whom the question of Jewish identity is, on some level, compelling." Through example and commentary, this anthology presents the many "levels" of the figuration of Jewishness while also highlighting the dual— multiple—identities of Jewish-Russian writers writing in the nineteenth and twentieth centuries.

From the earliest debates to the present, critics both Jewish and non-Jewish have mainly crossed swords over the definition of Jewish-Russian literature and the inclusiveness of the criteria one employs in constructing its canon.[6] A terminological diversity reflects some of the fundamental problems a student of Jewish-Russian literature still faces today. In this anthology, the transparent term of choice is "Jewish-Russian literature." In the critical literature, one commonly encounters the expression "Russian-Jewish literature."

---

6 Ruth R. Wisse offers illuminating comments about the making of the canon of Jewish literature in her book *The Modern Jewish Canon: A Journey through Language and Culture* (New York: Free Press, 2000).

The English-language term "Russian-Jewish literature" is a literal, and at that imperfect, rendition of the Russian term *russko-evreiskaia literatura,* which, in turn, comes from the expression *russkii evrei* ("a Russian Jew"), in which "Russian" is an adjective and "Jew" a noun. To the same family of terms belong such contortedly descriptive expressions as "Jewish Russian-language litera-ture" (Mikhail Vainshtein), "Jewish literature in the Russian language" (Dmitri A. Elyashevich), or even *"la littérature juive d'expression russe"* (Shimon Markish 1985). In opposition to the terms that put stock in the complex cultural stand-ing of Jewish-Russian literature, one also comes across variations on the term "Jews in Russian literature," such as "writers who are Jews [*pisateli-evrei*] in Soviet Literature" (Marc Slonim), and so forth. It is both difficult and awkward to render in English such Russian expressions as *evrei-pisatel'* (literally "a Jew who is a writer") or *pisatel'-evrei* (literally "a writer who is a Jew"), both of which stand for a writer who is Jewish or of Jewish origin and are sometimes used in contrast to *evreiskii pisatel'* (literally "Jewish writer"), commonly understood in Russian to mean a writer in a Jewish language and only to a lesser degree a writer with a manifest "Jewish" agenda. The two opposing sets of critical terms thus reflect either their user's conviction that Jewish-Russian writers constitute a bicultural canon or their user's dismissive view of Jewish-Russian literature as a cultural and critical category.

My term of choice is "Jewish-Russian literature," by close analogy with such terms (and the respective phenomena they describe) as African-American literature, French-Canadian literature, or Jewish-American literature. I prefer the term "Jewish-Russian literature" to "Russian-Jewish literature" or others because it strikes me as the most direct and transparent one: the first adjective determines the literature's distinguishing aspect (Jewishness) and the second the country, language, or culture with which this literature is transparently identified by choice, default, or proxy. Below, in the section "The Texture of Jewishness"[7] and elsewhere in this anthology, I will have more to say about my choice of the term "Jewish-Russian literature."

---

7 I am certainly not the first author to use the term "the texture of Jewishness," and I do not wish to claim having invented it. A Google search revealed one substantiative reference, in an essay by the Jewish-America writer Rebecca Goldstein. "I have found," Goldstein wrote in 1997 in the pages of *Tikkun*, "like several others linked in this suggested revival of Jewish American letters, that my Jewish dreams, at least sometimes, take me backward in time, into a past in which the texture of Jewishness was more richly felt"; see Rebecca Goldstein, "Against Logic: Jewish Author's Reflection on Her Work and Jewish Literature," *Tikkun*

This anthollogy reflects a specialist's avid interest in the possibility of elaborating a "Jewish poetics." Yet it also signals a generalist's skepticism toward the idea that seemingly universal and all-encompassing laws of artistic creation vary for the artistic imaginations of the representatives of different ethnic, national, and religious groups. Simply put, my approach rests on three premises: first, that at different stages Jewish-Russian writers displayed varying types of duality; second, that Jewish-Russian writers are by nature at least bicultural; and third, that any noninclusive and reductive approach to the selection of material is likely to result in cultural violence. My ensuing working method has been to steer clear of any advance generalizations about the canon of Jewish-Russian literature. Rather, the canon wrote itself as I gradually selected the materials while also parsing an approach to Jewish writing in Diaspora, an approach that invites complexity and evades categorization. The results of my investigation are in the texts themselves—and to some extent in my introductions and headnotes to the sections of this anthology and the individual Jewish-Russian authors and their works included here.

THE TEXTURE OF JEWISHNESS AND CRITERIA OF JEWISH-RUSSIAN LITERATURE

In 2014, responding to the editor's question, "What is that Jewish *something else* in writing?"—*something else* referring to what lies beyond Jewish themes or Jewish characters—**David Shrayer-Petrov** stated: "It's a secret, and I don't think you can isolate it the way scientists isolate a gene. Otherwise one could take this Jewish something and transfer it onto any material. Luckily, it doesn't work this way. Each writer has his or her own Jewish secret. **Babel** has his own, and we immediately feel it. Or take **Ilya Ilf** and **Evgeny Petrov** and their classic novels *The Twelve Chairs* and *The Golden Calf*. Even though most of the characters aren't Jewish, the authorial grin is very Jewish. Or consider [**Vasily**] **Grossman's** *Life and Fate* . . . the way the author mourns the Jewish fate as he sets it against the backdrop of the entire country's devastating fate."[8]

(November–December 1997): 42; http://www.trincoll.edu/~rgoldste/Tikkun_Against_logic.htm, accessed 8 June 2005.

8 David Shrayer-Petrov and Maxim D. Shrayer, "A Fictional Model of the Former USSR: Part 1 of a 3-Part Conversation," Jewish Book Council, 8 July 2014; https://www.jewishbook-council.org/_blog/The_ProsenPeople/post/maxim-shrayer-david-shrayer-petrov-inter-view-part-1/.

In this anthology, I have been guided by a vision of Jewish-Russian literature as bicultural and binational. Such a vision goes back to the pioneering work of Shimon Markish (1931–2003), the son of the martyred Yiddish classic Perets Markish (1895–1952) and the brother of the writer **David Markish** (b. 1938). Shimon Markish demonstrated a passionate commitment to the systematic incorporation of Jewish-Russian literature into the curricula of both Russian and Jewish studies. In 1995, Markish offered this definition of Jewish-Russian literature: "Jewish literary creativity (broadly conceived) in the Russian language . . . [is] one of the branches of the New Jewish letters." One of Markish's premises was the fundamental notion of a unity of Jewish culture across the languages in and of Diaspora. This premise was in many respects an application of the argument of the great Jewish historian Shimon Dubnow (1860–1941), specifically as Dubnow expressed it for the émigré audience in the essay "The Russian-Jewish Intelligentsia in Its Historical Aspect" (1939):

> We must remember that inadvertent language assimilation in Diaspora does not yet mean inner assimilation and departure from the national unity. In all epochs of our history, many of the best representatives of our people spoke and wrote in alien tongues, which had become their own, and expressed in them ideas that became the foundation blocks of Judaism [*kraeugol'nymi kamniami iudaizma*]. One cannot exclude Philo, Maimonides, [Moses] Mendelssohn, [Heinrich] Graetz, Hermann Cohen, and many other thinkers from the cohort of the builders of Judaism. Future generation will not forget the contributions of the newest Russian-Jewish intelligentsia, which has created a national literature [in Russian] alongside the literature in both languages of our people [Yiddish and Hebrew].

In the words of Shimon Markish, "A double belonging of a writer means that, among all else, his creativity belongs to two nations equally." Biculturalism is one of the key aspects of the artistic vision of Jewish-Russian writers (and, for that matter, of any Jewish writer in Diaspora who is conscious of his or her origins). In 1994 the St. Petersburg scholar and politician Aleksandr Kobrinsky illustrated this point splendidly with examples from **Isaac Babel**'s *Red Cavalry* stories.[9] For instance, in **Babel**'s story "The Rabbi's Son," much of the Judaic

---

9 Several Western scholars, including Maurice Friedberg and Ephraim Sicher, have made similar points about the place of the Judaic texts and traditions in Babel's bicultural fiction.

religious background is lost on non-Jewish readers, but the story still works well with both audiences:[10]

> Everything was dumped together: mandates of a political agitator and memos of a Jewish poet; portraits of Lenin and Maimonides lay there side by side; the nodulous iron of Lenin's skull and the dull luster of silk in Maimonides's portraits; a lock of hair was pressed into a booklet of Sixth Party Congress resolutions; and crooked lines of ancient Hebrew verse crowded the margins of Communist leaflets. They descended upon me like a dismal, scanty rain: pages of the "Song of Songs" and revolver cartridges.
>
> (Trans. Maxim D. Shrayer)

One of the central implications of the inherent biculturalism of Jewish-Russian writers is that their works should not be defined oppositionally, whether to Yiddish and Hebrew or to Russian letters. Furthermore, through the experience of perusing thousands of pages written by Jewish-Russian writers in search of both balance and representativeness, I have come to believe that only the most inclusive definitions of Jewish Diasporic literature are fundamentally indisputable.

In the cannonade of the critical debates of the 1880s through the 1920s, critics have deemed an author's language (Russian) and identity (Jewish) and the works' thematic orientation (related to Jewish spirituality, history, culture, or mores) as cornerstone criteria determining an author's assignation to Jewish-Russian literature. Two more criteria have been proposed and have met both acceptance and opposition. Some critics, going back to **Vladimir Jabotinsky**, insist on the criterion of the text's Jewish addressee, either implied or real. Other critics have argued that a work of Jewish-Russian literature constructs a unique insider's perspective on both Jews and non-Jews: "No matter what the attitude of the writer toward his material,"

Remarkably, the author of a postrehabilitation Soviet book about Babel's life and works, Fyodor Levin, had been able to signal this point; see F. Levin, *I. Babel'. Ocherk tvorchestva*, 7–9 (Moscow: Khudozhestvennaia literatura, 1972).

10   In this regard, the way non-Jewish Russian readers approach works of Jewish-Russian literature remains a fascinating subject of inquiry. Incidentally, my personal experience at teaching works by Jewish-American writers at a Jesuit university to a predominantly Catholic student audience confirms that these texts yield a bicultural model of reading. The non-Jewish American students read them in translation as native works and yet intuitively recognize in the strangeness of these texts the presence of another, Jewish culture.

Shimon Markish remarked in 1995, "his outlook is always an outlook from within, which represents the principal difference between a Jewish writer and a non-Jewish one who has turned to a Jewish subject (regardless of how they treat the subject)."

In addition to the author's identity, one looks for the textual presence of Jewish and/or Judaic aspects and attributes, such as themes, topics, points of view, reflections on spirituality and history, references to culture and daily living, and the like. And yet, one is frequently left with the impression that not everything has been accounted for, that a Jewish something is slipping through one's fingers. Aleksandr Kobrinsky has advanced the notion of a Jewish text's "mentality," although he readily admits that "calculating" it would be a grueling task. Consider Kobrinsky's argument: "When we place side by side and compare two works in the Russian language, written on a Jewish theme by a Jew and a Russian, respectively, then the main criterion would be the system of values calculated on the basis of the author's angle of vision: fluctuations of style and stylistic play, the level of the narrative subject or a poem's lyrical hero, varieties of narration, background of the action and its shifts, lyrical and philosophical digressions, and so forth. In Jewish literature, a Jewish system of values either is accepted as a given . . . , or one (traditional) Jewish system is juxtaposed with another Jewish system [of values]." The principal implication is a need for "calculable" formal criteria of judging the Jewishness of a text in Russian or another language that Jews have adopted as their own. If there is a Jewish poetics, it certainly encompasses much more than theme, subject matter, or system of textual references. Born at the intersection of the author's identity and aesthetics, a Jewish poetics is often buried in plain view. Its real measure is "not text, but texture," to borrow Vladimir Nabokov's mysterious phrase from *Pale Fire*. By this I mean not only that the Jewishness of the text may not be reduced to its author's Jewish self-awareness and the awareness of his readers or to the text's thematic and topical parameters. For example, in a text such as the poetic cycle "Kol Nidrei" (1923; in this anthology) by **Matvey Royzman**, the Judaic topos overwhelms the reader, facilitating the recognition of the texture of Jewishness:

> On the Torah these bells
> Tremble like a fallow deer.
> Held as by a knifepoint spell,
> Congregants chant pure and clear.

This is David's rising shield
Like the true new moon tonight,
And of all the fast has healed,
Freed, the shofar sings delight.

(Trans. Maxim D. Shrayer and J. B. Sisson)

Another common device of signaling to the reader the texture of Jewishness is the emulation of Yiddish speech or the introduction of Yiddish lexical items, as in the story "Sarah and Rooster" (1988) by the Philadelphia-based writer **Philip Isaac Berman** (b. 1936): "Marusya stayed in our room and paid the rent. You know what a room in Moscow means? Now one has to pay thousands and thousands to get one in the city. So when we returned [from Kazakhstan] in 1943 we had a place to live in. I had left her as much money as I could. What was money then? Nothing, *gornit!* A *shtikl* paper!"[11]

At the same time, readers frequently respond to a work by a Jewish author in a non-Jewish language, lacking apparent Jewish clues, with comments such as "I hear a Jewish intonation in this text" or "There is something Jewish between the lines." A number of works in this anthology, especially in its latter part, elicit such responses, not only in their Russian originals but also in translation. Those comments are but a reader's way of trying to put his or her finger onto something quite real. The main challenge that students of Jewish-Russian literature face, both theoretically and practically, is to develop an approach that investigates and measures the texture of a work's Jewishness. Before such an approach has been developed, the only ethical choice I have in seeking to present the canon of Jewish-Russian literature in its maximum fullness, unity, and diversity is to apply the most transparent and all-inclusive criteria.

Believing as I do that the only representative anthology of a literary canon is a full unabridged canon (and the digital revolution may soon allow for just that), I have had to make difficult, at times agonizing decisions in selecting materials for this volume. I favored transparency over obscurity and inclusivity over exclusivity. In selecting many materials for this anthology from a large pool of texts, I found quite useful the position of Aleksandr Kobrinsky, who stated in 1994, "A writer's unequivocal self-identification as a Jewish writer appears to be necessary, although not sufficient, to qualify a Russian-language writer as a Jewish one."

Two main criteria, a sufficient one and a necessary one, govern the selection of texts chosen for this anthology. First, in regard to the author's origin and/

---

11 *Gornit* (Yiddish) = nothing; *shtikl* (Yiddish) = bit.

or identity, it suffices that a given author be Jewish either in Halakhic terms (in terms of Judaic law) or in any other terms (ethnic, national, etc.) in which Jewishness was legally defined or commonly understood in the Russian Empire, the Soviet Union and its successor states, or any other country of the writer's residence either during the author's life or in subsequent periods. The fact of a Jewish-Russian author's conversion to another religion does not automatically disqualify him or her from being included in this anthology. At the same time, the fact of having been born Jewish does not automatically qualify an author, however important his or her place may be in the Russian literary tradition, for inclusion in this anthology. Here the necessary criterion must be applied: engagement of Jewish subjects, themes, agendas, or questions in the writing.

APOSTASY, ASSIMILATION, AND THE CHANGING TYPES OF DUALITY

Quite impermeable to historical and geopolitical changes, the Halakhic config- uration of Jewishness could not have changed over the relatively short span of Jewish-Russian history. At the same time, the radical political transformation of Russian society after the 1917 revolutions brought on a transition from the reli- giously based official legal definition of Jewishness to an ethnically based one. Jewish assimilation, whether real or marranic, voluntary or forced, within the context of tsarist Russia meant religious conversion, a Jew's formally ceasing to be someone of Mosaic confession.

In his model study "Jewish Apostasy in Russia: A Tentative Typology" (1987), the historian Michael Stanislawski pointed out that "in the nineteenth century more Jews converted to Christianity in the Russian Empire than anywhere else in Europe; this is not too surprising, of course, since Russian Jewry was by far the largest Jewish community in the world."[12] Treating the available statistics with a "healthy dose of skepticism," Stanislawski cited the data of the Russian Holy Synod, which "establish that 69,400 Russian Jews were baptized in the Russian Orthodox Church during the entire nine- teenth century." "Western historians of Jewish apostasy," Stanislawski noted, "have claimed in addition that some 12,000 Jews, most probably in the Polish provinces, converted to Roman Catholicism, and 3,100 to various forms of Protestantism, especially Lutheranism." The Russian Empire had gained about

---

12 See Michael Stanislawski, "Jewish Apostasy in Russia: A Tentative Apostasy," in *Jewish Apostasy in the Modern World,* ed. Todd M. Endelman, 189–205 (New York: Holmes and Meier, 1987).

900,000 Jews in 1773, following the first partition of Poland. In 1815, when the so-called Kingdom of Poland became a part of the Russian Empire, there were about 1.5 million Jews in Russia. According to 1897 census data, the Russian Empire had 5.2 million Jews, or about 41 percent of the world's Jewish population (about 4.9 million of those in the Pale of Settlement). Given these statistics, one would have to conclude that the total number of Jewish converts to Christianity (Russian Orthodoxy, Catholicism, different denominations of Protestantism) in nineteenth-century Russia (69,400) was low.

Overall, one observes a correspondence between rates of conversion and the dynamics of imperial Russia's political climate and anti-Jewish restrictions. During the reign of Nicholas I, from 1825 to 1855, and the lifetime of the institution of *kantonisty* (Jewish youths forced to become military recruits), which coercively encouraged the baptism of Jews in army schools, one sees higher rates of conversion to Russian Orthodoxy. After a period of decline during the rule of the more liberal Alexander II, from 1855 to 1881, the rates of conversion increased again in the 1880s and early 1890s, following the pogroms of the 1880s and the introduction of further anti-Jewish restrictions. Emblematic of this historical trend is the timing of conversion by members of the swelling ranks of the Jewish-Russian intelligentsia, such as the poet Nikolay Minsky, who converted to Russian Orthodoxy in 1882. Of the subsequent tsarist decades, Stanislawski writes, "While the heady years of 1905–1906 saw the number of converts decline, and the astonishing return to Judaism of recalcitrant apostates, between 1907 and 1917 a new, and even larger, wave of baptism was reported to have swept Russian Jewry." For example, the conversion of **Osip Mandelstam** to Methodism in 1911 exemplifies both a response to the post-1907 climate and a desire to circumvent anti-Jewish institutional quotas. The wave came to a halt in 1917, and in fact, soon after the February 1917 Revolution, one observed a reaffirmation of the Jewish faith by some reluctant Jewish converts to Christianity.

The imperial Russian definition of Jewish (Judaic) identity was replaced by the imperial Soviet one, in which Jews were conceived of as a national minority in ethnic, ethnolinguistic and, to some extent, in historical terms, with the religious components of Jewishness forcefully disavowed. Tsarist-era legal discrimination against Jews, epitomized by the notorious Pale of Settlement, had been abolished after the February 1917 Revolution. In the Soviet state, anti-Jewish restrictions were never given legal status, but from the 1940s they did gain a state-sponsored status. Even prior to the 1940s, the popular antisemitism, which had decreased in the first Soviet decade

but had risen again by the early 1930s, had been driving ethnic assimila-
tion. In 1936, when passports were replaced after the passage of "Stalin's"
1936 Soviet Constitution, a wave of Jews took advantage of the opportunity
to change their official nationality in the new document. Such ethnic (self-)
obliteration and assimilation was particularly manifest in mixed marriages
of Jews and non-Jews. Jewish parents and parents in mixed marriages were
likely to register their children's "nationality" not as Jewish but as Russian
(or Ukrainian, Belorussian, Armenian, and so forth) so as to protect them from
discrimination. While official papers might have eased the plight of half-Jew-
ish individuals registered as not Jewish, the Soviet-era popular antisemitism
was commonly directed at phenotypic or visible cultural markers of one's
Jewish origin. "They hit you not on the passport but on the face"—so went a
popular Soviet adage. At the Soviet crossroads of Jewish history and Russian
culture, identity scenarios such as the one of the poet **Inna Lisnyanskaya**
(1928–2014) were not uncommon. Born to a Jewish father and an Armenian
mother, Lisnyanskaya was baptized in her infancy by her Armenian grand-
mother. Raised in a Russian-, Yiddish-, and Armenian-speaking household in
Baku during the most antireligious Soviet years, **Lisnyanskaya** declared her
official nationality as Jewish in 1944, when she turned sixteen. "And I thought
. . . if I'm baptized as a Christian, then I must register myself as a Jew, because
so many have been annihilated . . . ," Lisnyanskaya explained to the editor of
this anthology in January 2000. Remaining a Christian, Lisnyanskaya treated
Jewish subjects in her lyrics. Her example illustrates how during the Soviet
years both the official rhetoric on Jewish identity and antisemitism might
have enhanced a Jewish-Russian writer's multiple self-awareness.

The official definitions of Jewishness have changed not only from epoch
to epoch but also from country to country. The latter circumstance is of some
weight, given that from the 1917 revolutions until the Soviet late 1980s emigra-
tion was a prominent feature of this twentieth-century Jewish-Russian cultural
experience. Moreover, in their lifetimes a number of authors in this anthol-
ogy have changed countries or lived in a country whose regime and geopo-
litical status changed not once but twice, sometimes even three or four times.
Characteristic is the experience of the writer Grigory Kanovich (b. 1929), who
grew up in prewar independent Lithuania, survived the Shoah by escaping to
the Soviet hinterland, returned and lived for five decades in Soviet Lithuania,
then for two more years in the newly independent Lithuania, only to make
aliyah and move to Israel in 1993. The official status of one's Jewishness would
sometimes undergo rapid and cataclysmic transformations, especially during

transition and emigration. The careers of Jewish-Russian writers provide a number of such examples.

To illustrate the polyvalent figurations of the sufficient criterion of Jewishness, I turn below to a few individual cases from the anthology. Among the authors included here, the reader will find the poet **Semyon Nadson** (1862–1887), the son of a non-Jewish mother and a father who was born Jewish but who was baptized as a child when his own father converted to Orthodox Christianity. If one takes a broad and inclusive view of the canon of Jewish-Russian literature, the prose writer **Yury Trifonov** (1925–1981), the son of a Don Cossack father and a Jewish mother, would also belong in it. Consider also two émigré examples that naturally call for a comparison: the lives of two contemporaries, the poets Anna Prismanova (1892–1960) and **Raisa Blokh** (1899–1943). Born Anna Prisman in Libava, in Courland (Kurland)Province (now in Latvia), Prismanova converted to Russian Orthodoxy at the age of eighteen and spent much of her adult life in France. Prismanova survived the roundups of thousands of Jews in occupied wartime France, partly on a technicality: she had entered France on papers listing her as Russian Orthodox. Blokh was born in St. Petersburg to the family of a Jewish lawyer who, as far as one can tell, had converted to Russian Orthodoxy so as to be able to practice law. She immigrated to Germany in 1922 and to France in 1933. Blokh perished, most likely, in a concentration camp in 1943 after Swiss border guards returned her to the Nazis.

Jewish history teaches us to be sensitive to the complexity of the architectonics of a Jewish identity. At the same time, Jewish apostasy takes on a very different meaning and significance during the late Soviet decades. As such, it is likely to have much more of an impact on one's judgment of a writer's Jewishness than Jewish conversion during the tsarist period. In assessing the phenomenon of Jewish apostasy in the postwar Soviet Union, it is important to make clear that one is dealing with a conversion by choice and without visible gain in legal status or career advancement, in contrast to either the forced conversion of Jewish teenaged recruits under Nicholas I or the unenthusiastic, frequently marranic conversion of Jews during the later tsarist years for purposes of bypassing official restrictions. Conversion to Russian Orthodoxy (and, to a much lesser degree, to Catholicism) became a notable phenomenon in the 1960s and 1970s among artists and intellectuals from urban Jewish families, mainly in Moscow and Leningrad (St. Petersburg). In contrast to the perilously inaccessible Judaic sacred texts and religious traditions, Russian Orthodox religious texts and religious practices were more easily accessible to an average

Soviet citizen. Furthermore, degrees of interest in Christian spirituality on the part of the second and third Soviet generations of acculturated Jews were part of the general shift toward God searching among the Soviet intelligentsia during the so-called years of stagnation.

Conversion to Russian Orthodoxy by choice among the postwar Jewish-Russian intelligentsia has been the subject of the research of Judith Deutsch Kornblatt.[13] Kornblatt's approach is qualitative, based on interviews with over thirty individuals, including artists and writers, whose anonymity Kornblatt has protected. Quantitative data on apostasy among Jews from the USSR (including the émigrés of the 1960s through the 1980s) would be difficult to obtain. I estimate the number of Jewish apostates in the Soviet Union of the last three decades to be in the range of several thousand. The individuals in question would have come predominantly from the middle and upper echelons of the intelligentsia and would be especially visible among the artistic milieu. They include, to take examples from different generations, the author and dissident Feliks Svetov (Fridlyand, 1927–2002); the poet and children's author **Genrikh Sapgir** (1928–1999); the "last Jewish joker" Mikhail Zhvanetsky (b. 1934; Alice Nakhimovsky's expression); the poet, translator, and prose writer Anatoly Nayman (b. 1936); the culturologist and essayist Mikhail Epstein (b. 1950); and the fiction writer and essayist **Ludmila Ulitskaya** (b. 1943), who made her mark in contemporary Russian prose with stories about the survival of Jewish-Russian memory and identity. The person who stood at the helm of the movement for Jewish conversion to Christianity in the Soviet 1960s–80s was the Jewish-born Russian Orthodox priest and theologian Father Aleksandr Men (1935–1990), who, through personal example, charisma, and proselytizing among the Jewish-Russian intelligentsia, advanced a platform of the "double chosenness" of Jewish-born Christians.

In representing in this anthology the cultural contribution of apostates among Jewish-Russian writers, I have proceeded on the premise that both an author's confession and an author's change of confession can be private matters. As one might expect, information of this sort is not always available about writ-

---

13   See Judith Deutsch Kornblatt, "Jewish Converts to Orthodoxy in Russia in Recent Decades," in *Jewish Life after the USSR,* ed. Zvi Gitelman, Musya Glants, and Marshall I. Goldman, 210–23 (Bloomington: Indiana University Press, 2003); *Doubly Chosen: Jewish Identity, the Soviet Intelligentsia, and the Russian Orthodox Church* (Madison: University of Wisconsin Press, 2004).

ers, especially those from the former USSR. While I sent no questionnaires to the living contributors to this anthology, I did request biographical information from those with whom I have had direct contact, and some writers have volunteered facts about their religious life. I have also garnered information in the course of extensive interviews and shorter conversations with some of the featured contemporary authors. The émigré fiction writer **Philip Isaac Berman** (b. 1936), one of the most overt Jewish metaphysicians in this anthology, told me in 2004 that even in the postwar Soviet years his late father used to go to shul every morning on his way to work as a Moscow civil servant, thus providing me with an important fact about his Jewish upbringing in the postwar USSR. What I learned helped explain the roots of Berman's fervent Judaism. When the émigré poet and former victim of Stalinism Naum Korzhavin (b. 1925) told me, also in 2004, of his conversion to Russian Orthodoxy in Moscow in 1992, years after he had begun to explore Christian themes in his writings, this information, too, constituted a literary fact.

While I did not deliberately seek out private information unless the fact of a Jewish-Russian writer's conversion had already been established or publicly stated, I did seek out clarification as to when, where, and under what circumstances the conversions took place. In the careers of about half a dozen authors representing the postwar Soviet and émigré years in this anthology, cultural identity and spiritual identity are much further apart than in the cases of other Jewish-Russian writers. From a cultural (bicultural, transcultural) standpoint, those writers are part of a canon of Jewish-Russian literature and an aspect of this discussion. While Jewish apostates by choice opt to remove themselves from the Judaic religious community, they are still part of the Jewish cultural patrimony, whether or not they choose to recognize it. Finally, they are a part of Jewish culture not only because one cannot fully leave one's home but also because they might still choose to return. In refusing to write off this group of writers among living Jewish-Russian authors, I was partly guided by the emblematic twentieth-century example of the composer Arnold Schoenberg and his return to Judaism. Marc Chagall was one of the two witnesses who signed Schoenberg's reaffirmation certificate in Paris in 1933.[14]

---

14 See the certificate facsimile in *Schoenberg, Kandinsky, and the Blue Rider*, ed. Esther da Costa Meyer and Fred Wasserman, 62 (New York: The Jewish Museum; London: Scala Publishers, 2003).

SELECTION, REPRESENTATIVENESS, AND EXCERPTABILITY

How many works by a given Jewish-Russian author are enough to satisfy the necessary criterion? What if, out of his entire oeuvre, an author has left only one or two Jewishly marked poems, as was the case with **Semyon Nadson**, but their presence and impact on the Russian literary mainstream has been vital? Conversely, what if a writer of the Soviet period shunned Jewish subjects throughout his successful public career and yet could not help reflecting, in the secrecy and privacy of his diaries and notebooks, on his own shedding of Jewishness, first in the Stalinist 1930s, and later, in the 1970s, during the rise of Judeophobia among the Russian cultural right? This was the case of the gifted poet and translator David Samoylov (born Kaufman, 1920–1998), especially lionized by some circles of the post-Thaw Jewish-Russian intelligentsia. Following Samoylov's death, the publications of his previously unprinted verse have confirmed that, even in what Samoylov wrote for his "desk drawer," one finds only two or three faint and tired Jewish motifs, such as a Jewish fiddler playing in the fringes of one of the poems. Yet in Samoylov's discursive reflections, which his widow published in the late 1990s–2000s, one finds seminal passages about the trauma of the poet's failed assimilation and Russianization. Samoylov's notebooks and diaries might have helped me understand the place of Jewish poems in his oeuvre—had Samoylov indeed written such poems. But he did not; he *chose* not to write them, and it is with regret that I am unable to include him in this anthology. I am certainly aware that an author's meaningful silence about a particular topic or subject may be regarded as a "minus-device," as Aleksandr Kobrinsky has suggested, applying Yury Lotman's term to the study of Jewish-Russian literature. However, when set against the background of some discussions of Jewish questions in his diaries and notebooks, Samoylov's virtual silence about Jewishness in verse amounts not to a minus-device but rather to a "plus-device." This example is hardly an exception for the Jewish-Russian writers of the postwar Soviet years. In working on this anthology, I had to draw the line based not only on the relative weight and singularity of a given work in the author's entire known oeuvre, whether published in the author's lifetime or posthumously, but also on the historical weight and recorded impact of a given work on Russian and Soviet society and the public imagination of both Jewish and non-Jewish readers.

Both the general conditions of state control over culture in the USSR and the specific situation with the post-1930s official Soviet taboo on Jewish topics complicate the study of Jewish-Russian literature because some works remained unpublished for various reasons until the period of reforms and the fall of the Soviet Union. It was common for a Soviet author, Jewish or otherwise, to go to the grave without publishing a single work in the official press, and a Jewish-Russian writer was likely to have lived most if not all of his or her life without ever publishing a single work displaying Jewish features. In some cases, such works were disseminated in samizdat (underground, unauthorized but limited circulation) or in tamizdat (abroad), both options bearing risks for their authors. In other cases, the presence of such works would not come to light until their discovery among the writers' papers. Important works still remain unpublished, unknown, and buried in archival obscurity. Such is the case of Feiga Kogan (1891–1974), whose work is not represented here. A student of the symbolist poet and philosopher Vyacheslav Ivanov, Kogan was a poet in her own right, a gifted translator, and a theorist of versification and literary declamation. Drawing on Ruth Rischin's trailblazing research, Carole B. Balin has traced Kogan's career from her first poetry collection, *My Soul* (1912), to her peerless Russian translation of all 150 Hebrew Psalms, completed in the Soviet 1950s. Kogan left a trove of unpublished materials, which include, in addition to the translations, poems and extensive diaries that chronicle what Balin has called "a Jewish life behind the scenes." Unfortunately, even knowing what I know about Kogan, I was unable to justify the inclusion of her unpublished poetry in this anthology, whereas her early, published verse does little justice to her contribution as a Jewish-Russian poet.

In the Soviet period, especially its postwar years, writers would live to be old and grey, or even pass away, before their principal works were made available in print at home, owing to censorship and a ban on their publication. **Genrikh Sapgir**, the patriarch of the Moscow poetic avant-garde of the 1960s–90s and a famous author for children, could not publish a single line of poetry for adults, including his own renditions of the Psalms, in the USSR until 1989, although his works for adults were widely circulated in the underground and abroad. During the late Soviet and post-Soviet years, **Sapgir** became one of Russia's most admired *published* poets. Much information about unpublished or underpublished works came to light during the perestroika and post-Soviet years and is still emerging, putting the anthologizer's task to the test. While the Soviet-era sections of this anthology are predominantly concerned with works disseminated through publication in the cultural mainstream, I did attempt to correct for the censorship factor and the factor of delayed cultural recognition by paying attention to works published out of the desk drawer, as it were. It is a fairly common feature of Jewish-Russian texts from the Soviet period that decades separate the date of composition and the date of first publication. Moreover, such significant delays and deferrals in publication of literary works complicate the periodization of Jewish-Russian literature during the Soviet period. As writers' lives do not always fit neatly within chronological and classificational boundaries, the approach employed here is based in part on the year of composition and in part on the year of publication. The latter is especially valid for the postwar Soviet and émigré sections, and compromises had to be made in order to accommodate the anthology's general structural principles as well as the sometimes intricate history of an individual text's publication. To use one example, the short novel *The Hour's King* (1968–69) by **Boris Khazanov** first appeared in the Russian-language samizdat magazine *Jews in the USSR* in 1975 and was reprinted in 1976 in Israel. **Khazanov** did not immigrate to and settle in Germany until 1982, and yet the featured excerpt from *The Hour's King* appears not in the section on "Late Soviet Empire" but in a different section, "The Jewish Exodus." This decision, incongruous with the chronology as it may appear, reflects Khazanov's personal view, as expressed to me, that his career best fits in the section on the legacy of the Jewish emigration.

Finally, there are the practical difficulties of excerptability. Some works simply do not excerpt well, and constraints of space have forced me to leave out not only all the works of the Jewish-Russian theater but also several very important works of prose and epic and narrative poetry. The example that comes to mind most immediately and painfully is the tale *In a Backwater Small Town* (*V glukhom mestechke*) by N. Naumov (N. Kogan, 1863–1893), which was published in 1892 in the major Russian monthly *Messenger of Europe* (*Vestnik Evropy*) and received immediate and wide recognition. Of the writers who left the former USSR, I especially regret not having been able to feature the memoir *Hellenes and Jews* (1996) by Yury Gert (1931–2003; immigrated to the United States in 1992) and the novel *Exchanged Heads* (pub. 1992) by the author and violinist Leonid Girshovich (b. 1948, immigrated to Israel in 1973 and to Germany in 1979).

THE DILEMMA OF LITERARY QUALITY

For each of the works in this anthology, in addition to the affirmative answers to the anticipated questions "Is this Jewish literature?" and "Is this Russian literature?" one should ideally be expected to answer "yes" to the question "Is this good literature?" However, and especially given the history of the bicultural canon of Jewish-Russian literature with its modest beginnings and subsequent aesthetic explosions, a constant expectation of quality is neither simple nor safe. Prior to the 1900s–1910s, when a number of writers firmly entered Russian culture, an assessment of their literary quality warrants a double reckoning. On the one hand, these works are to be regarded vis-à-vis writing that was mainly confined to the Jewish-Russian press, that served Jewish-Russian readers, and that was not known to a wider non-Jewish audience. On the other hand, they are to be construed in terms of the Russian national literary mainstream. The poetry of Simon Frug (1860–1916) serves as a telling example of such a teetering double judgment. Widely published in the Jewish-Russian press of his day, Frug, whom Shimon Markish has called the "national poet" on several occasions, was immensely popular among Russia's Jewish population. As a Russian-language poet (he also wrote Russian prose and Yiddish poetry and prose), Frug met a social need of the growing ranks of Russia's integrating Jews by bringing them accessible Russian-language lyrics at a time when the mainstream Russian poetry did not exactly converge with the Jews' dual sensibilities. If judged by the formal standards of Russian poetry of Frug's day, his unoriginal verse is of average quality, but it certainly accomplished enough to have gained recognition among readers in Russia's cultural mainstream—had this, and not writing in Russian for Russia's Jews, indeed been Frug's ambition. What distinguishes Frug's Russian-language verses is the way they exhibit an awareness of their Jewish-Russian reader. Judging by the accounts of Frug's Jewish contemporaries, including such great artists as Hayyim Nahman Bialik, Frug's Russian poems must have touched chords that would have left most non-Jewish readers indifferent. When the critic Arkady Gornfeld stated that Frug's contribution to "Jewish thought" was great and to Russian poetry "modest," he pinpointed the discrepancy between Frug's recognition by Jewish-Russian readers of his day and the place Frug the Russian-language poet has earned for posterity. At the same time, as a result of Frug's almost exclusive focus on the Jewish-Russian audience, to this day he remains practically unknown to historians of Russian poetry. Frug's poetry has not been featured even in the largest and most representative anthologies of Russian poetry, where it undoubtedly belongs, with the exception of a few specialized anthologies devoted to Jewish and Biblical themes or motifs. Even more modest was the aesthetic place of Frug's contemporary, the Russian-language poet Mikhail Abramovich (1859–1940), the son of the Yiddish classic S. Y. Abramovich (Mendele Mokher Sefarim, 1835–1917). Frug, Abramovich, and the other poets populating the pages of Jewish-Russian publications in the 1890s–1900s have not been recognized in the Russian literary canon.

I would maintain that for Jewish-Russian writers the issue of quality as we judge it today and as the Russian literary mainstream judged it at the time only became relevant around the turn of the nineteenth century, during the Russian Silver Age. The bicultural imbalance caused by almost a century of virtual isolation and both legal and cultural fencing is finally righted in the first two decades of the Soviet period. From that point, the judgment of literary quality becomes truly relevant in the assessment of the place of a Jewish-Russian writer in both canons. In the 1920s, Jewish-Russian literature finally had a prose genius of the first magnitude, **Isaac Babel**, as well as the peerless poetry of **Osip Mandelstam**, **Boris Pasternak**, and **Eduard Bagritsky**. Centered as they were in the Russian-language literary mainstream, these writers set the highest imaginable formal standards, which enabled Jewish-Russian writers to measure themselves not only against the non-Jewish Russian classics or contemporaries but also against these and other resplendent authors of Jewish origin. Not having had its Tolstoy or Dostoevsky in the nineteenth century, Jewish-Russian literature gained its uneclipseable stars in the twentieth. When Korney Chukovsky, in his polemical essay of 1908 titled "Jews and Russian Literature," lamented the dearth of genius among the Jewish contributions to Russian letters, he probably had no idea that in his own lifetime a score of major writers would become a looming cultural reality during the early Soviet years and would also enrich if not transform Jewish culture outside Russia.

IN ISRAEL

During the 1920s–40s, both before and immediately after the founding of the state of Israel in 1948, Jewish-Russian writers immigrated there. With a few exceptions, however, they were quite minor even for the context of Russian émigré writing in the *yishuv*. Such was the case of Abraham Vysotsky (1884–1949), author of *Tel Aviv* and other novels, who immigrated to the British Mandate of Palestine in the winter of 1919–20. Unlike the majority of the Russophone writers who came from Russia to Palestine in the 1920s, Vysotsky continued to write and publish in Russian. Perhaps the most famous example of the transition from writing in Russian to writing in Hebrew was the poet Rahel (Rachel Bluwstein, 1890–1931), who permanently settled on the territory of the British Mandate of Palestine in 1919 to leave Russian writing behind and become a major voice of the new Hebrew poetry. Perhaps even more fascinating was the example of Elisheva (Elizaveta Bikhovskaya, born Zhirkova, 1888–1949), "Ruth from the banks of the Volga," who became a

Zionist and a Hebrew poet after a brief but powerful career as a poet in the Russian language and a translator of Hebrew verse. "I am a Jew in my heart and soul," Elisheva wrote to a Jewish correspondent in 1919. In 1925 Elisheva moved to the territory of the British Mandate of Palestine with her Jewish husband and died there in 1949. (In today's Israeli literature, the career of the author and scholar Chava-Brocha Korzakova recalls the example of Elisheva. Born in Leningrad in 1969 in an ethnic Russian family, Korzakova converted to Judaism and made aliyah in 1991. Both Elisheva and Korzakova thus represent a scenario of a Russian author who becomes Jewish and belongs both to Jewish-Russian culture and to Israeli culture.)

In the 1920s–1950s, not very many writers remained actively bilingual practitioners of both Russian and Hebrew letters. Notable among these was Leyb Jaffe (1878–1948), who arrived in Palestine in 1920 and edited the newspaper *Ha'aretz*. Another notable example is the prose writer Yuly Margolin (1900–1971), who settled in the land of Israel in 1946 already at an advanced point in his literary career after spending the interwar and wartime years in Poland and the USSR. Featured in this anthology is poet **Dovid Knut** (1900–1955), a major literary voice of the first émigré wave, who arrived in Israel in 1949 after having lived in France for nearly three decades. Also noteworthy is the story of Batya Kahana (née Berta Shrayer, 1901–1979), who moved to the Mandate in 1920, originally wrote prose fiction in Russian, yet published exclusively in Hebrew. In the words of the Israeli scholar Yaffah Berlovitz, Kahana and some other Hebrew women writers of her generation "remain nothing more than names," even to historians of Israeli literature.[15] Finally, it is worth mentioning that young men and women who came to the British mandate Mandate of Palestine from the former Russian Empire in the 1920s formed the new Hebrew literature while remaining active translators of Russian literature. They included the poet Avraham Shlonsky (1900–1973; moved to the Mandate in 1921), who translated Pushkin's *Eugene Onegin* into Hebrew.

The real influx of numerous and diverse Jewish-Russian writers did not start until the exodus of the late 1960s and the 1970s from the USSR, when a stalwart Russian-language culture began to take shape in Israel, armed with its own literary journals, such as *Zion* (*Sion*), *Twenty-Two* (*Dvadtsat' dva*), and others. A number of Russian-language authors entered the cultural scene

---

15 See Yaffah Berlovitz, "Prose Writing in the Yishuv: 1882–1948," in *Jewish Women's Archive: Encyclopedia*, https://jwa.org/encyclopedia/article/prose-writing-in-yishuv-1882-1948, viewed on 21 November 2017.

after having moved to Israel. Consider, for instance, the intriguing career of Eli Luxemburg (b. 1940), who came to Israel from Tashkent in 1972 and incorporated into his fiction the traditions of Jewish mysticism and Judaic holy texts. Among the notable representatives of this wave are the prose writer Efrem Bauch (b. 1934), the poet Mikhail Gendelev (1950–2009), the visual artist and poet Mikhail Grobman (b. 1939), and the essayist and critic Maya Kaganskaya (1938–2011). In this anthology, six writers represent the extensive Russian-language literary community that had formed in Israel by the 1980s. This Russian-Israeli literary community included arrivals from the middle 1970s (the poet **Ilia Bokstein** [1937–1999; in Israel since 1972] and the prose writers **David Markish** [b. 1938; in Israel since 1972] and **Ruth Zernova** [1919–2004; in Israel since 1976]) and was subsequently replenished by new arrivals (the prose writer **Dina Rubina** [b. 1953; in Israel since 1990] and the poets **Sara Pogreb** [b. 1921; in Israel since 1990] and **Anna Gorenko** [pseudonym of Anna Karpa, 1972–1999; immigrated to Israel in 1989]).

Many writers came to Israel old enough to have been shaped as Russian-language authors in the USSR but young enough to change and evolve, and their careers underwent aesthetic and ideological transformations as they became Israelis. Immigrating to Israel and becoming new Israelis cannot but alter these writers' position vis-à-vis Jewish writers remaining in Diaspora. In some cases, the writers would subsequently leave Israel, usually seeking larger artistic spaces or broader horizons for self-expression, after spending there the initial or transitional years following emigration from the USSR. Three writers epitomize this trend: Henri Volohonsky (1936–2017), who lived in Israel from 1973 until 1985, when he moved to Germany; Yuri Kolker (b. 1947), who spent the years 1984–89 in Israel before alighting in England; and Felix Roziner (1936–1997), who was very active in Russian-language Israeli culture from 1978 until 1985, when he chose to emigrate again, to the United States. Does secondary immigration to Western Europe or North America immediately restore one's status as a Jewish writer in Diaspora?

During the reform era and early post-Soviet years, Jewish-Russian writers of the older generation, most notably Grigory Kanovich (b. 1929; in Israel since 1993) and **Sara Pogreb** (b. 1921; in Israel since 1990), made Israel their home. The late 1980s and early 1990s also brought to Israel younger writers who already had a voice and reputation and a body of published works. Among them was the poet Aleksandr Barash (b. 1960; emigrated 1989), the prose writer and artist Elena Makarova (b. 1951; emigrated 1990), and, most famously, the prose writer **Dina Rubina**. Finally, there is a group of young Russian-language Israeli authors whose entire careers have unfolded in Israel, such as **Anna Gorenko** (pseydonym of Anna Karpa; 1972–1999).

Can Israel's Russian-language authors be considered Jewish writers in Diaspora? Do they carry with them their Diasporic Jewish-Russian culture? Felix Roziner, a former Muscovite, said this in a 1983 interview to a Tel Aviv Russian-language magazine *Circle* (*Krug*): "[A Russian writer in Israel] begins to create Israeli culture—in terms of his belonging to the cultural environment of which he is becoming a part." Russian-language writers in Israel are a fascinating phenomenon. Not to have featured them in this anthology would have been a great mistake, but we also sought not to overrepresent them. In 1985, in a brief essay, the writer **David Markish** suggested that he and the others writing in Russian in Israel "prefer to call themselves Israeli-Russian writers." Markish also admitted that "our colleagues, Israeli writers writing in Hebrew, while not doubting that we belong to Israeli literature, call us none other than 'Russian writers,' as they marvel quietly that in our work we do not pay sufficient attention to Russian bears, gypsies, and other proverbial boners [*razvesistaia kliukva*, literally 'branchy cranberry plant']."

About a million *olim* came from the former USSR to Israel in the late 1980s–2000s. The aliyah of the 1990s transformed Israel in more ways than we have fully understood and accounted for. Roman Katsman, the leading student of Russian-language literary culture in Israel, speaks of the "demarginalization of Russophone literature" in Israel following the influx of Russian immigrants in the late 1980s and early 1990s: "The contemporary Russophone Israeli literature is no longer émigré, minor, or marginal." This new wave includes the prose writer and critic Alexander Goldstein (1957–2006), the prose writer and literary scholar Dennis Sobolev (b. 1971), the poet Gali-Dana Singer (b. 1962), who writes in both Hebrew and Russian, and the prose writers Nekod Singer (v. 1960), Mikhail Yudson (b. 1956), and Alex Tarn (b. 1955). In the words of Katsman, they imagine themselves "as an integral part of the global, decentralized, networking Russian and Jewish cultures."[16] Today's Russophone writers in Israel challenge us not only to rethink the juxtaposition between Israel and

---

16 Roman Katsman, "New Literary Geography: Demarginalization of Contemporary Russophone Literature in Israel," a lecture at the Davis Center for Russian and Eurasian Studies, Harvard University, 11 October 2017; https://daviscenter.fas.harvard.edu/events/new-literary-geography-demarginalization-contemporary-russophone-literature-israel, viewed on 21 November 2017.

Diaspora but also to account for a new fluidity of these writers' translingual lives and careers. This calls for a more detailed inquiry and, perhaps, a separate anthology.

CANON MAKING, CANON BREAKING

Canons take form slowly, which is to say that our ideas about a particular body of artistic works shape themselves over a period of time, sometimes long enough for a living canon to have become a necropolis. This sobering possibility is quite real in the case of Jewish-Russian literature, and one way of beating time, the merciless canonizer, at its own game is to anthologize.

What then is this anthology? A collection of landscapes of Jewish-Russian literature over the past two centuries, complete with its mountain peaks, crumbling hills, mounds and hummocks, dales, valleys and ravines, rivers, streams, dams and irrigation canals, lakes and ponds, forests, fields of wheat, cherry orchards, orange groves and olive gardens, swamps, deserts, steppes, and even its taiga and tundra? A record of Jewish survival? A debate about Jewish selfhood? A series of dual literary selves? A grand experiment in canon making? I hope it is all of the above and much more.

To reiterate: this anthology aims at inclusiveness but does not aspire to be exhaustive or complete. It seeks to represent many artistic movements and thematic trends, many genres and forms of prose and poetry, both traditional and experimental, both archaic and avant-garde—in a word, many different Jewish textures of the Russian verbal artistic experience. As with any anthology—and especially the first of its kind—this is not only a creation but also an interpretation of the Jewish-Russian literary canon.

Any anthology is always and inevitably a record of its compiler's predilections of various sorts, of the anthologizer's own self. In this sense, the only objective anthology would be one that includes all works by all authors, a kind of virtual library project that, as I have already suggested, may become possible in the future. If I have erred in my judgment, it is in the direction of inclusiveness.

THE FUTURE OF JEWISH-RUSSIAN LITERATURE

In 1959, there were 2,280,000 Jews in the USSR (880,000 in the Russian Federation). By 1979, largely through Jewish emigration, this number had been reduced to 1,830,000. In 1989, according to the last official Soviet census, there were 1,480,000 Jews in the USSR (570,500 in the Russian Federation), and in 1999, 544,000 remained (310,000 in Russia). Today's core Jewish population of about 160,000 puts Russia behind Israel and the United States by millions and also behind France, Canada, and the United Kingdom. When put in perspective, these numbers tell a powerful story.

Echoing the population data with a culturological commentary on the place of the Jewish question in Russian intellectual life in 1985–95, the Russian thinker Sergey Lyozov argued in 1996 that "Jews as enemies or simply as protagonists have been dropped from the central Russian myths of the 1990s." Lyozov suggested that "what one might call a 'normalization' of the Jewish question in Russian culture is taking place 'before our eyes.'" "There is," Lyozov indicated, "no direct linkage between this normalization and the level of our anti-Jewish sentiments [sic]."[17] There is perhaps some truth to such Russian-centric arguments as Lyozov's, or, at the very least, they reflect a post-Soviet picture of the Russian cultural mainstream, where openly Judeophobic and antisemitic views occupy something of a marginal and provincial niche. But the suggestion that the Jewish question captivates post-Soviet Russian culture to a lesser and lesser degree must have to do primarily with a disappearance not of the anti-Jewish myths, which tend to outlive both their subjects and their makers, but of the Jews themselves from the mainstream of Russian culture in the former USSR.

It is disheartening to observe that the xenophobic prayers of Russian ultranationalists about cleansing Russian culture of Jews might have been answered. While Jewish names will not have been erased from the Russian literary scene of the decades to come, a Russian cultural chauvinist might soon be hard pressed to speak of the alleged dominance of Jews and Judaism in Russian letters. Jewish names are disappearing from the mainstream of Russian culture and the arts. Jews are less and less known to—and knowable by—the average Russian. The effect of this trend on public attitudes is as yet uncertain, but according to the 2016 Levada Center's study of public opinion, "the majority of Russian citizens (61 percent today, up from 52 percent in 1990) do not personally know any Jews (among family, relatives, close acquaintances, or colleagues), which is why opinions about them are mostly figments of 'social imagination,' almost folklore."[18]

---

17 See Sergei Lezov, " 'Evreiskii vopros' v russkoi intellektual'noi zhizni (1985–1995)," *Znamia* 9 (1996): 182–87.

18 Quoted in Maxim D. Shrayer, *With or Without You: The Prospect for Jews in Today's Russia* (Boston: Academic Studies Press, 2017), 86–57. The book offers detailed sta-

In addition to the writers of the older generations who could not publish under Soviet conditions, the post-Soviet literary culture in Russia has gained many new authors of Jewish descent born in the 1960s–80s. While too little time has passed to draw safe assumptions, my preliminary conclusion is that Jewish-Russian writers whose careers were formed during the Soviet years continue to address Jewish topics in their works, some due to a renewed personal interest as well as the freedom to write and publish about it, others out of cultural inertia. At the same time, younger authors of Jewish origin in today's Russia have tended to be more assimilated and Russianized, resulting in a dearth of Jewish consciousness in their writing.

Commenting on the prospects of Jewish life and culture in Russia, the writer Afanasy Mamedov (b. 1960) stated in a 2016 interview:

> Where are our own Jewish writers? . . . What is being done to foster their existence? In order for us to have our own Malamuds, Roths, and Bellows, . . . we should in all sorts of ways nurture the writers we already have. . . . There are different ways of solving this problem. For instance, to institute a prize. But I haven't heard of any Jewish literary prizes [in Russia]. There isn't a single café for Jewish intelligentsia to congregate. . . . Hebrew classes at the synagogue or fitness facilities could hardly address this problem. . . .
>
> One could say, "What is 20 years of freedom? Wait, it's all on the way." But one wants it now and more of it. I think Jewish cultural life in Russia depends on direct philanthropy. We don't have our own [Jewish] Morozovs and Tretyakovs [major Russian philanthropists and patrons of the arts in the second half of the nineteenth century]. . . . I doubt the situation is going to change any time soon, and the birth of the next Kafka is unlikely here. . . . Everything is still rising from the old yeast.[19]

Only in Israel Jewish-Russian literary culture is surviving with some degree of vibrancy. In the United States and Canada, the older émigrés continue to write and publish in Russian, while the younger literary generation of Russian Jews is naturally turning to writing—and reading—in English. At the same time, Jewish-American writers born in the former USSR and

---

tistics on the Jewish population in Russia and on the worldwide presence of Russian-speaking Jews.

19 Quoted in Shrayer, *With or Without You*, 70–71.

raised in North America are becoming increasingly visible in the English-language cultural mainstream.

Jewish time in Russian culture seems to be almost over, or perhaps Jewish-Russian culture of the post-Soviet period is living on borrowed time. Celebrating almost 200 years of Jewish-Russian literature, does the upper chronological boundary of this anthology, 2001, also close the page on the canon of Jewish-Russian literature? I would not want this introduction to become either an elegy or an obituary.

In closing, I would like to turn to the work of the distinguished St. Petersburg ethnographer Natalya V. Yukhneva (1930–2013). Yukhneva has advanced the notion of "Russian Jews" (*russkie evrei*) as a "subethnic group," "with the Russian spoken language and a simultaneous belonging to two cultures: Jewish and Russian."[20] Emphasizing the bicultural, "bicivilizational" character of Russian Jewry, Yukhneva posited that "Russia at the beginning of the twentieth century saw the formation within the Ashkenazim of a subethnic group characterized by Russian as the conversational and secular language, Hebrew as the language of religion and national traditions, a combination of Russian and Jewish culture in professional and daily life, Judaism (it is quite likely that within the group one version of reform Judaism or another would eventually have become widespread), and, finally, the emergence of a group consciousness at whose foundation lies not religious but ethnic identity." It is difficult to speculate how Yukhneva's scenario might have continued to develop in the twentieth century had Soviet history not made different arrangements. The Soviet period witnessed a state-sponsored attempt at eradicating the religious aspects of the Jewish identity. The Soviet rhetoric on Jewish identity promulgated a view of Soviet Russian Jews as an ethnic group whose belonging to the community of world Jewry was severed and denied, except when it was politically and economically advantageous to the Soviet government (e.g., during World War II). And yet, in the final analysis, I find myself taking exception to the position of Yukhneva and other historians and ethnographers who speak of the predominantly ethnic self-consciousness of Russian Jews by the end of the Soviet period and of the disappearance of the Jewish religious self-awareness among Russia's Jews. In terms of the fifty-eight centuries of Jewish spirituality, the seventy Soviet years are but a flicker of time,

---

20 See, for instance, Natalya V. Yukhneva, "Russkie evrei v XX v.: osobennosti etnicheskogo razvitiia," preprint of a paper delivered at Plenary Session 4b at the Sixth World Congress of Central and East European Studies, Tampere, Finland, 2000.

and millennia of Jewish religious culture could not have been erased from the identities of Russia's Jews during the seventy Soviet years. The works gathered in this anthology of Jewish-Russian literature tell a different story, amassing a record of Jewish religious, cultural, and ethnic endurance.

Jewish-Russian writers have been the carriers of a vital Judaic culture and spirituality expressed through the Russian language. According to 2017 data, emigration from Russia to Israel was up 10 percent, and this trend is likely to continue. The great outflux of Jews from the former USSR and the post-Soviet states has taken a toll on public awareness of and public attitudes toward Jews. It has changed—and possibly transformed—the living space of world Jewry. With over 1 million Russian-speaking Jews in Israel, over 500,000 Russian-speaking Jews in the United States and Canada, and over 100,000 Russian-speaking Jews in Germany, the critical mass of Russophone Jewish intelligentsia resides outside Russia's borders. A formidable force, Russian Jews have transformed the texture of daily life in Israel and also, to a degree, in parts of the United States and Canada. This "New Jewish Diapora" is both a living memory of Jewish-Russian literature and a space for its survival and proliferation. It is up to us to embrace the rich legacy of Jewish-Russian literature and make it our own.

A SELECTED BIBLIOGRAPHY

Far from a complete or exhaustive bibliography, this list of books and articles mainly includes works referred to in the general introduction. The main purpose of this bibliography is to present a history of the study of Jewish-Russian literature from the 1880s to the present and to highlight the dynamics of the principal debates about the contents and criteria of its canon. If a work is available in the original language and in English, preference has been generally given to English versions.

Aikhenval'd, Iu[lii]. "Sushchestvuiut li pisateli-evrei?" *Segodnia* [Riga], no. 202 (9 September 1927): 2.

Alexandrova, Vera. "Jews in Soviet Literature." In *Russian Jewry 1917–1967*, ed. Gregor Aronson et al., trans. Joel Carmichael, 300–27. New York: Thomas Yoseloff, 1969.

Aronson, G[rigorii]. "Evrei v russkoi literature, kritike i obshchestvennoi zhizni." In *Kniga o russkom evreistve ot 1860-kh godov do revoliutsii 1917 g. Sbornik statei*, ed. I. G. Frumkin et al., 361–99. New York: Soiuz russkikh evreev, 1960.

———. "Russko-evreiskaia pechat'." In *Kniga o russkom evreistve*, ed. Frumkin et al., 548–73.

Balin, Carole B. *To Reveal Our Hearts: Jewish Women Writers in Tsarist Russia*. Cincinnati: Hebrew Union College Press, 2000.

Berlovitz, Yaffah. "Prose Writing in the Yishuv: 1882–1948." In *Jewish Women's Archive: Encyclopedia*. https://jwa.org/encyclopedia/article/prose-writing-in-yishuv-1882-1948, viewed on 21 November 2017.

Blium, A[rlen] V. *Evreiskii vopros pod sovetskoi tsenzuroi, 1917–1991*. St. Petersburg: Peterburgskii evreiskii universitet, 1996.

Cavaion, Danilo. *Memoria e poesia: Storia e letteratura degli ebrei russi nell'età moderna*. Rome: Carucci editore, 1988.

Chernikhovskii, S[aul]. "Russko-evreiskaia khudozhestvennaia literatura." In *Evreiskaia entsiklopediia*. Vol. 13, 640–42. St. Petersburg: Obshchestvo dlia Nauchnykh Evreiskikh Izdanii; Izdatel'stvo Brokgauz-Efron, [1906–13].

Chukovskii, Kornei. "Evrei i russkaia literatura." *Svobodnye mysli*, 14 January 1908.

Czerny, Boris. "The Russian-Jewish Fiddler: Analyzing Representations and Their Symbolic Value in Russian, Russian-Jewish, and Yiddish Literature." *Cahiers du monde russe* 2003/4. Vol. 44, 657–72.

Dolzhanskaia, Tamar, ed. *Na odnoi volne. Evreiskie motivy v russkoi poezii*. Tel Aviv: Biblioteka "Aliia," 1974.

Donat, Aleksandr, ed. *Neopalimaia kupina. Evreiskie siuzhety v russkoi poezii. Antologiia*. New York: New York University Press, 1973.

Dubnov, Simon [Shimon Dubnow]. "Russko-evreiskaia intelligentsia v istoricheskom aspekte." *Evreiskii mir. Ezhegodnik za 1939 god*, 11–16. Paris: Ob"edinenie russko-evreiskoi intelligentsii v Parizhe, 1939.

Dubnow-Ehrlich, S. [Sofia Dubnova-Erlikh]. "Jewish Literature in Russian." In *The Jewish People: Past and Present*, ed. Rafael Abramovich. Vol. 3, 257–67. New York: Central Yiddish Cultural Organization, 1952.

El'iashevich, D[mitrii] A. "Russko-evreiskaia kul'tura i russko-evreiskaia pechat'. 1860–1945." In *Literatura o evreiakh na russkom iazyke, 1890–1947. Knigi, broshiury, ottiski statei, organy periodicheskoi pechati. Bibliograficheskii ukazatel'*, ed. V. E. Kel'ner and D. A. El'iashevich, 37–78. St. Petersburg: Akademicheskii proekt, 1995.

———. "Russko-evreiskaia pechat' i russko-evreiskaia kul'tura: k probleme genezisa." In *Trudy po iudaike* 3 (1995). St. Petersburg: Peterburgskii evreiskii universitet, 1995. www.jewish-heritage.org/tp3a7r.htm, viewed on 10 February 2005.

Friedberg, Maurice. "Jewish Contributions to Soviet Literature." In *The Jews in Soviet Russia since 1917*, ed. Lionel Kochan. 3rd ed., 217–25. Oxford: Oxford University Press, 1978.

———. "The Jewish Search in Russian Literature." *Prooftexts* 4, no. 1 (1984): 93–105.

Geizer, Matvei. *Russko-evreiskaia literatura XX veka. Avtoreferat na soiskanie uchenoi stepeni doktora filologicheskikh nauk*. Moscow: Moskovskii pedagogicheskii universitet, 2001.

Gitelman, Zvi, ed. *The New Jewish Diaspora: Russian-Speaking Immigrants in the United States, Israel, and Germany*. New Brunswick, NJ: Rutgers University Press, 2016.

Gornfel'd, Arkadii. "Russkoe slovo i evreiskoe tvorchestvo." In *Evreiskii al'manakh*, ed. B. I. Kaufman and I. A. Kleinman, 178–99. Petrograd and Moscow: Knigoizdatel'stvo Petrograd, 1923.

Grinberg, Marat. *"I am to be read not from left to right, but in Jewish: from right to left": The Poetics of Boris Slutsky.* Boston: Academic Studies Press, 2011.

Grozovskii, Mikhail, comp., Evgenii Vitkovskii, ed. *Svet dvuedinyi. Evrei i Rossiia v sovremennoi poezii.* Moscow: AO "KhGS," 1996.

Hetényi, Zsuzsa. Örvényben. 2 vols. (1. *Az orosz-zsidó próza története, 1860–1940.* 2. *Az oro-sz-zsidó próza antológiája, 1860–1940*). Budapest: Dolce Filológia II, 2000.

———. *In a Maelstrom. The History of Russian Jewish Prose (1860–1940).* Budapest: Central European University Press, 2008.

Horowitz, Brian. *The Russian-Jewish Tradition: Intellectuals, Historians, Revolutionaries.* Boston: Academic Studies Press, 2017.

Katsis, Leonid. *Osip Mandel'shtam: Muskus iudeistva.* Moscow: Mosty kul'tury; Jerusalem: Gesharim, 2002.

Katsman, Roman. *Nostalgia for a Foreign Land: Studies in Russian-Language Literature in Israel.* Boston: Academic Studies Press, 2016.

Kel'ner, V[iktor] E. *Dopolneniia k ukazateliu "Literatura o evreiakh na russkom iazyke, 1890–1947."* Moscow: Evreiskoe nasledie, 1998.

Kel'ner, V[iktor] E. and D. A. El'iashevich, comp. *Literatura o evreiakh na russkom iazyke, 1890–1947.* St. Petersburg: Akademicheskii proekt, 1995.

Khazan, Vladimir. *Osobennyi evreisko-russkii vozdukh: K problematike i poetike russko-evreiskogo literaturnogo dialoga v XX veke.* Moscow: Mosty kul'tury; Jerusalem: Gesharim, 2001.

———. "Sovetskaia literatura." In *Kratkaia evreiskaia entsiklopediia.* Vol. 8, 97–142. Jerusalem: Evreiskii universitet v Ierusalime, 1996 [the entry is unsigned].

[Kheifets, Mikhail]. "Russkaia literatura v Izraile." In *Kratkaia evreiskaia entsiklopediia.* Supplement 2, 324–34. Jerusalem: Obshchestvo po issledovaniiu evreiskikh obshchin; Evreiskii universitet v Ierusalime, 1995 [the entry is unsigned].

Kisin, I. "Razmyshleniia o russkom evreistve i ego literature." *Evreiskii mir* 2 (1944): 164–72.

Kleinman, I[osif] A. "Evrei v noveishei russkoi literature." In *Evreiskii vestnik,* ed. S. M. Ginzburg, 155–66. Leningrad: Obshchestvo rasprostraneniia prosveshcheniia mezhdu evreiami, 1928.

Kobrinskii, A[leksandr]. "K voprosu o kriteriiakh poniatiia 'russko-evreiskaia literatura.'" *Vestnik evreiskogo universiteta v Moskve* 5 (1994): 100–114.

Kolganova, Ada, ed. *Menora. Evreiskie motivy v russkoi poezii.* Moscow: Evreiskii universitet v Moskve; Jerusalem: Gesharim, 1993.

Kornblatt, Judith Deutsch. "Jewish Converts to Orthodoxy in Russia in Recent Decades." In *Jewish Life after the USSR,* ed. Zvi Gitelman, Musya Glants, and Marshall I. Goldman, 210–23. Bloomington: Indiana University Press, 2003.

Kunitz, Joshua. *Russian Literature and the Jew: A Sociological Inquiry into the Nature and Origin of Literary Pattern.* New York: Columbia University Press, 1929.

Lazarev, M. N. "Zadachi i znachenie russko-evreiskoi belletristiki (Kriticheskii ocherk)." *Voskhod* 5 (1885): 28–42; 6 (1885): 24–42.

Levitina, Viktoriia. *Russkii teatr i evrei.* Jerusalem: Biblioteka "Aliia," 1988.

————. . . . *I evrei—moia krov'*. (*Evreiskaia drama—russkaia stsena*). Moscow: [Izdatel'stvo Vozdushnyi transport], 1991.

L'vov-Rogachevskii, V[asilii]. *Russko-evreiskaia literatura*. Intro. B[oris] Gorev. Moscow: Gosudarstvennoe izdatel'stvo; Moskovskoe otdelenie, 1922. Reprint, Tel Aviv, 1972; English edition, *A History of Russian-Jewish Literature*, ed. and trans. Arthur Levin. Ann Arbor: Ardis, 1979.

Markish, David. "Russko-evreiskaia literatura v Izraile." *Cahiers du monde russe et soviétique* 26, no. 2 (April–June 1985): 255–56.

Markish, Shimon. *Babel' i drugie*. 2nd ed. Moscow and Jerusalem: Personal'naia tvorcheskaia masterskaia "Mikhail Shchigol'," 1997.

————. "A propose de l'histoire et de la méthodologie de l'étude de la littérature juive d'expression russe." *Cahiers du monde russe et soviéétique* 26, no. 2 (April–June 1985): 139–52.

————. "Eshche raz o nenavisti k samomu sebe." *Dvadtsat' dva* 16 (December 1980): 177–91.

————. "O nadezhdakh i razocharovanii (usykhaiushchaia vetv')." In *Babel' i drugie* [1993], 188–93.

————. "O rossiiskom evreistve i ego literature." In *Babel' i drugie*, 194–211.

————. "O russkoiazychii i russkoiazychnykh." In *Babel' i drugie* [1990], 182–88.

————. "The Role of Officially Published Russian Literature in the Reawakening of Jewish National Consciousness (1953–1970)." In *Jewish Culture and Identity in the Soviet Union*, ed. Yaacov Ro'i and Avi Beker, 208–31. New York: New York University Press, 1991.

————. "Russkaia podtsenzurnaia literatura i natsional'noe vozrozhdenie (1953–1970)." In *Babel' i drugie*, 213–34.

————. "Russko-evreiskaia literatura." In *Kratkaia evreiskaia entsiklopediia*. Vol. 7, 525–51. Jerusalem: Obshchestvo po issledovaniiu evreiskikh obshchin; Evreiskii universitet v Ierusalime, 1994 [the entry is unsigned].

————. "Russko-evreiskaia literatura: predmet, podkhody, otsenki." *Novoe literaturnoe obozrenie* 15 (1995): 217–50.

Markish, Shimon, ed. *Rodnoi golos: stranitsy russko-evreiskoi literatury kontsa XIX–nachala XX vv.: kniga dlia chteniia*. Kyïv : Dukh i litera, 2001.

Murav, Harriet. *Music from a Speeding Train: Jewish Literature in Post-Revolutionary Russia*. Stanford: Stanford University Press, 2011.

Nakhimovsky, Alice Stone. *Russian-Jewish Literature and Identity: Jabotinsky, Babel, Grossman, Galich, Roziner, Markish*. Baltimore: The Johns Hopkins University Press, 1992.

————. "Russian Literature." In *The YIVO Encyclopedia of Jews in Eastern Europe*, ed. Gershon D. Hundert. New Haven: Yale University Press, 2008. http://www.yivoencyclopedia.org/article.aspx/Russian_Literature.

Safran, Gabriella. *Rewriting the Jews: Assimilation Narratives in the Russian Empire*. Princeton: Princeton University Press, 2000.

Sedykh, Andrei (Iak. Tsvibak). "Russkie evrei v emigrantskoi literature." In *Kniga o russkom evreistve, 1917–1967*, ed. Ia. G. Frumkin et al., 426–47. New York: Soiuz russkikh evreev, 1968. [Vol. 2 of the 1960 edition.]

Serman, Il'ia. "Spory 1908 goda o russko-evreiskoi literature i posleoktiabr'skoe desiatiletie." *Cahiers du monde russe et soviétique* 26, no. 2 (April–June 1985): 167–74.

Shklovskaia, Margarita, ed. *Orientatsiia na mestnosti. Russko-izrail'skaia literatura 90-kh godov. Antologiia.* Jerusalem: Assotsiatsiia po izucheniiu evreiskikh obshchin—"Biblioteka 'Aliia,'" 2001.

Shrayer, Maxim D. *I Saw It: Ilya Selvinsky and the Legacy of Bearing Witness to the Shoah.* Boston: Academic Studies Press, 2013.

———. *Russian Poet/Soviet Jew: The Legacy of Eduard Bagritskii.* Lanham, MA: Rowman and Littlefield, 2000.

———. *With or Without You: The Prospect for Jews in Today's Russia.* Boston: Academic Studies Press, 2017.

———. ed. *An Anthology of Jewish-Russian Literature: Two Centuries of Dual Identity in Prose and Poetry.* 1801–2001. 2 vols. Armonk, NY, and London: M. E. Sharpe, 2007.

———. and David Shrayer-Petrov. *Genrikh Sapgir: Klassik avangarda.* St. Petersburg: Dmitrii Bulanin, 2004; 3rd ed. Ekaterinburg: Ridero, 2017.

Sicher, Efraim. *Jews in Russian Literature since the October Revolution: Writers and Artists between Hope and Apostasy.* Cambridge: Cambridge University Press, 1995.

Slonim, Mark. "Pisateli-evrei v sovetskoi literature." *Evreiskii mir* 2 (1944): 146–64.

Smola, Klavdia, ed. *Eastern European Jewish Literature of the 20th and 21st Centuries: Identity and Poetics.* Munich-Berlin: Die Welt der Slaven Sammelbände, Verlag Otto Sagner, 2013.

Stanislawski, Michael. "Jewish Apostasy in Russia: A Tentative Apostasy." In *Jewish Apostasy in the Modern World,* ed. Todd M. Endelman, 189–205. New York: Holmes and Meier, 1987.

[Timenchik, Roman]. "Russkaia literatura." In *Kratkaia evreiskaia entsiklopediia.* Vol. 7, 489–525. Jerusalem: Obshchestvo po issledovaniiu evreiskikh obshchin; Evreiskii universitet v Ierusalime, 1994 [the entry is unsigned].

Tolts, Mark. "Demography of the Contemporary Russian-Speaking Jewish Diaspora." In *The New Jewish Diaspora: Russian-Speaking Immigrants in the United States, Israel, and Germany,* ed. Zvi Gitelman, 23–40. New Brunswick, NJ: Rutgers University Press, 2016.

———. "Demography of the Jews in the Former Soviet Union: Yesterday and Today." In *Jewish Life After the USSR,* ed. Zvi Gitelman, Musya Glants, and Marshall I. Goldman, 173–206. Bloomington: Indiana University Press, 2003.

Vainshtein, Mikhail. *A list'ia snova zeleneiut . . . Stranitsy evreiskoi russkoiazychnoi literatury.* Jerusalem: Kakhol'-Lavan, 1988.

Wisse, Ruth R. *The Modern Jewish Canon: A Journey through Language and Culture.* New York: Free Press, 2000.

Zhabotinskii [Jabotinsky], V[ladimir (Ze'ev)]. "Pis'mo. (O 'evreiakh i russkoi literature')." *Svobodnye mysli* 24 (March 1908). Reprinted in *Izbrannoe,* 61–68. Jerusalem: Biblioteka "Aliia," 1978.

Zinberg, Israel. *A History of Jewish Literature. Part Twelve: The Haskalah Movement in Russia.* Cincinnati: Hebrew Union College Press; New York: Ktav, 1978.

———. *A History of Jewish Literature. Part Thirteen: Haskalah at Its Zenith.* Cincinnati: Hebrew Union College Press; New York: Ktav, 1978.

Early Voices: 1800s–1850s

Editor's Introduction

(For a background in Jewish-Russian history, see the outline by John D. Klier at the back of this anthology.)

Although their population in Russia had been miniscule before the partitions of Poland, Jews created important works in the Russian language as early as the beginning of the eighteenth century. In 1817, Baron Pyotr Shafirov (1669–1739), a Russian vice-chancellor and top diplomat, the son of a converted Jew, and a close cohort of Peter I, published *Discourse Concerning the First Causes of the War between Sweden and Russia*. While it would be a big stretch to call Shafirov's book a literary text and feature it in this anthology, the *Lament of the Daughter of Judah* (St. Petersburg, 1803) by **Leyba Nevakhovich** (1776–1831) can be considered to be the first genuine work of Jewish-Russian literature. One of Russia's earliest maskilim (followers of the Haskalah, the Jewish Enlightenment movement), Nevakhovich resorted to artistic devices in his prose so as to persuade the members of the Jewish Committee, then deliberating in St. Petersburg, to "look for the human being in the Jew." For the next several decades, **Nevakhovich**'s would remain the lone Jewish-Russian literary voice among his generation of the maskilim. The Haskalah was born in the German lands in the second half of the eighteenth century, and the news about the teachings of Moses Mendelssohn (1729–1786) and his followers spread into the Pale of Settlement from Prussia. Copies of *The Gatherer* (*Ha-Meassef*), the Hebrew monthly founded in 1783 in Königsberg (now Kaliningrad) and subsequently published in Berlin and other German cities, quickly reached Courland (Kurland) and its neighboring northwestern provinces. As was to have been expected, therefore, the early maskilim in Russia looked to the German lands for inspiration, while the principal early writings by the Russian maskilim, most notably the "Russian Mendelssohn," Isaac Baer Levinson (1788–1860), were in Hebrew and occasionally Yiddish, not in Russian. Between **Nevakhovich**'s *Lament* and the year 1841, when **Leon Mandelstam** (1819–1889) published his *Poems* in Moscow, hardly anything of note by Jews appeared in Russian. Of historical interest only is the publication, in 1846 in Vilna, of *Thoughts of an Israelite*, written in awkwardly manipulated Russian by Abram Solomonov (1778–18??), a Jew of the generation of the early Russian maskilim.

In 1840, the Imperial Committee endorsed a proposal by Count Sergey Uvarov, minister of public education, addressing the question of Jewish education and calling for the creation of government elementary and secondary Jewish schools in the Pale. After Rabbi Max Lilienthal (1815–1882), Uvarov's first point man, quit in frustration and departed for America in 1844, **Leon Mandelstam** essentially took charge of Uvarov's reforms. The first Jew to graduate from a Russian university, **Mandelstam** also holds the distinction of publishing the first collection of Jewish poetry in Russian (Moscow, 1841). **Leon Mandelstam**, **Ruvim Kulisher** (1828–1896), and other members of the second, Russian-oriented generation of the Russian maskilim showed a great interest in the public education and integration of the Jewish masses. The featured writers in this section constitute the very first, still fragile and thin, layer of the Jewish-Russian intelligentsia of the 1840s–60s, for whom writing in Russian became an intellectual imperative and a great artistic ambition. For the history of early Jewish-Russian letters, the landmark year, after 1803 and 1841, will always be 1859, when a tale by **Osip Rabinovich** (1817–1869), *The Penal Recruit*, was published in *The Russian Messenger* (*Russkii vestnik*), a leading Russian review of its day. A Jewish writer had entered the Russian literary mainstream and enjoyed a favorable reception.

LEYBA NEVAKHOVICH

Leyba (Lev) **Nevakhovich** (1776–1831) was the Russianized name under which Judah Leib ben Noah published *Lament of the Daughter of Judah* (1803), arguably the first work of Jewish-Russian literature and the one that opens this anthology. Born in the Podolian town of Letichev, Nevakhovich was one of the earliest Russian *maskilim*, proponents and champions of the Haskalah, the Jewish Enlightenment movement. Proficient in several European languages, by the 1790s Nevakhovich had fallen under the influence of Moses Mendelssohn (1729–1786) and the Haskalah. He moved to St. Petersburg together with the family of his former pupil, the naval contractor Abram Perets, and became part of what John D. Klier called the "informal triumvirate" of Jews influencing the Russian policies on the Jew in the early 1800s, the other two being Perets himself and Nota Notkin, a promoter of Jewish economic reform. Nevakhovich worked as a government employee and translator from the Hebrew (e.g., preparing the materials on the arrests of Rebbe Zalman ben Baruch Shnoeur of Lyady in 1798 and 1800; Rebbe Zalman Shnoeur was finally released in 1801). As Andrey Rogachevsky recently demonstrated, Nevakhovich composed an ode in Hebrew on the ascension of Alexander I to the throne (12 March 1801), accompanied by a Russian translation. It was not published but has survived in the archives.

Nevakhovich contributed to the discussions of the Jewish Committee, which was established by Alexander I in November 1802 (see Klier's "Outline of Jewish Russian History") and to which *kahal* deputies gave testimony in the summer and fall of 1803 in St. Petersburg. He wrote his *Lament of the Daughter of Judah* specifically for the deliberations of this committee. Dedicated to Prince Viktor Kochubey, at the time the minister of internal affairs, it was printed in St. Petersburg in 1803. In 1804, an expanded Hebrew edition appeared in Shklov, Belorussia, under the title *Kol Shavat bat Yehudah*.

Disillusioned by the 1804 "Statute for the Jews," which fell far too short of his hopes and expectations and in effect confirmed the Pale of Settlement, Nevakhovich gave up writing on Jewish issues. His next work was a philosophical treatise, *Man in Nature. Correspondence between Two Enlightened Individuals* (1804). In 1804–6, he contributed to the Russian journals *Northern Messenger* (*Severnyi vestnik*) and *Lyceum* (*Litsei*), and in 1809 the Imperial Theater staged his drama *The Suliots, or Spartans in the Eighteenth Century*. Although in the *Lament* Nevakhovich did not posit conversion as a sine qua non of Jewish modernization, he was baptized around 1806. News of his apostasy, as well as of Abram Perets's baptism in 1813, contributed negatively to the spread of the Haskalah among the masses of Russia's Jewish population, who regarded the movement as a threat to Judaic traditions. Nevakhovich subsequently served as a civil servant in Warsaw in the field of finances and translated from the German. In 1832 his drama *Sword of Justice* was staged in St. Petersburg.

His descendants made contributions to Russian culture and scholarship: Mikhail Nevakhovich was a cartoonist and the founder of *Mish-Mash* (*Eralash*), the first magazine of humor in Russia; Aleksandr Nevakhovich was a playwright and a repertory director of the emperor's theaters in St. Petersburg; and Nevakhovich's daughter Emilia was the mother of Ilya Mechnikov (1846–1916). A great Russian microbiologist and a disciple of Louis Pasteur, Mechnikov shared the 1908 Nobel Prize for Physiology or Medicine with Paul Ehrlich.

* * *

In addition to the opening essay, which lent its title to the entire book, Nevakhovich's *Lament* included two other parts: "Conversation among Sinat-Hadat [Intolerance], Emet [Truth], and Shalum [Peacefulness]" and "The Feelings of a Loyal Citizen, On the Occasion of the Institution by the Highest Order of His Royal Majesty Emperor Alexander I, the Russian Monarch, of the Committee Concerning the Accommodation of the Jews in Accordance with the Needs of the State and Their Own Needs." The latter parts of the book are believed to have been composed in Hebrew and then translated into Russian. They differ stylistically from the opening essay, which is composed in the style of Russian neoclassical prose, in competent albeit aging eighteenth-century Russian. Nevakhovich advocates religious tolerance and the extension of equal civil rights to the Jews, pleading with the Russian authorities to regard them as loyal citizens and patriots. His arguments are imbued with the ideas of the European Enlightenment and the Haskalah, and he pays tribute to two cornerstone texts: Gotthold Ephraim Lessing's *Nathan the Wise* and Moses Mendelssohn's *Jerusalem*. A brief note, "From the Author," precedes the text of the *Lament of the Daughter of Judah*: "Love for the Emperor and the Fatherland, enchantment with today's enlightened times, pleasure and a certain sense of dignity and pride in being able to call the Russians my compatriots, compassion consuming my heart as I judge the fellow members of my tribe—this is the portrayal of the spirit that here guides my feeble pen!" The following excerpt (about one-third of the entire *Lament of the Daughter of Judah*) comes from the middle section of the essay.

FROM *LAMENT OF THE DAUGHTER OF JUDAH*

[...] Centuries and nations accuse the Jews—but why are these accusations not consistent? Just look at history and you will see many contradictions: one minute they are accused of sorcery,[1] the next of lack of faith, the next of superstition. The centuries had not yet had time to discover the futility of the intrigues against them before new ones were already arising. Like the links in an unbreakable chain, they have been welded together for the oppression of this nation alone, which in its lot resembles an unhappy son suffering in the bosom of a family that hates him. His brothers interpret all his acts in a bad light; and if, nay, when his innocence is revealed to them, they strive, as if ashamed of their former errors, to level new accusations against the sufferer in order to prolong his torments and stifle the reproaches of their conscience, so palpable and striking, for those acts of oppression which they have inflicted upon him hitherto. Has it been long since the beads of the innocent children of Israel ceased to fall beneath the sword of the vile libel that accused them with unshakable assurance of using Christian blood during their festival called Pesach (Passover)?

O Russians, you who love your fellow men! You would shudder from the bottoms of your kind hearts if you saw the effect of that terrible accusation which Jews who were eyewitnesses to the unjustified deaths of fellow members of their race cannot call to mind without trembling. More than once during my childhood my tears mingled with those of my mother, who used to tell me, with grief in her voice, of the terrible events that broke the nation's heart. Almost the whole world knows how many thousands of victims this unjust accusation cost.

The festival of Pesach just mentioned is that in which Jews remember the time of their forefathers' exodus from Egypt, a time that they revere as a memorial of the first era of their free existence. During this festival, they mentally share in the joy of their forefathers.

Noble children of the north! Your mild monarchs have taught you to look with a calm and impartial eye upon the rites of worship of the different nations living under your shield, upon the various festivities that make up their

---

1 A certain German book describes extremely heatedly how great a number of Christians perished through the supposed sorcery of the Jews—a hellish fabrication for simple folk, but how much blood that fabrication cost in days gone by. [L. N.]

happiness—and you do not disturb this! But in those days Jews did not yet have the good fortune to be Russia's subjects; in those days hatred, that hellish Fury, managed to convince many that Jews supposedly have need of this horrific evil on the day of that festival. Then the credulous and simpleminded were incited by cunning and wily souls to place a dead and mutilated infant surreptitiously by night beneath some house of a Jew, which malice was pleased to designate. The next morning that house is surrounded by a crowd of people demanding vengeance. A grizzled patriarch is plucked in the most contemptuous and violent manner from the circle of his innocent family; the rabbi (teacher of the law) and the most venerable of the Jews are taken; and finally, without further investigation, without the acceptance of any protestations of innocence from the victims, they are subjected to the most brutal executions. Children are robbed of a father, the wife of a husband, the brother of a brother. . . . The joy and festivity they had hoped to enjoy at that time gave way to lamentation, sobbing, and despondency. And so afterward, as this festival approached, each of them was seized by a terror that some sort of similar misfortune would descend on his house. But when this terrible lot was drawing to a close and some of the persecuted had fallen victim to the fury of the misguided plotters devoted to their devilish delight, the rest, with grief-stricken hearts, counted themselves safe for that year. What a pitiful solace! What a sorrowful comfort!

The Polish king Augustus Poniatowski of blessed memory, a wise and benevolent ruler, was moved to tremble at such inhuman outrages and through his wisdom brought them to an end. At last the dead bodies of infants ceased to be found beneath the houses of Jews, which still further demonstrated the absurdity of the past calumnies. Alone the mighty hand of Empress Catherine the Great of Russia was able to ease the lot of this nation, which had previously been the plaything of arbitrary deeds. Under the peaceful protection of Russian power, those hounded by fate found respite from earlier oppressions and began to feel to the full extent their former woes, the recollection of which even now forces whole floods of tears from their eyes. Alas! Now that the blows have ceased, these people begin to feel the pain of their wounds, which previously in their fever-like suffering they could not feel![2]

---

2 It is well known that the Jewish people were everywhere oppressed for several centuries, being driven out of Spain, France, and Portugal. . . . They were oppressed in Poland before its annexation to Russia. And to what humiliation they were brought there! Even schoolchildren had some appointed days on which they attacked Jews and their homes, beat them, and reviled them mercilessly, with no respect even for old people. Those days were known among Jews as *shiler gelauf*, that is, schoolchildren running wild, and during those days

Oh, Christians! You who live in community with them, you must know that virtue is just as sacred to them as it is to you—just look! But how do you look upon them? . . . Do you look for the Jew in the human being? No. Look for the human being in the Jew, and you will find him without a doubt. Only look. You will see among them many people who keep their word sacredly. You will see many compassionate people who give alms to the poor, not only of their own tribe but of other tribes too. You will see that many of them magnanimously pardon wrongs. You will see in them gratitude, restraint, and respect for the old. Likewise you will see with what feeling they revere those people of other faiths who show them kindness and do good to them—and with what veneration they bethink themselves of the sovereign. Lessing puts it splendidly this time: "a Christian and a Jew really first and foremost a Christian and a Jew rather than human beings?"[3] I do not doubt that there are many among you who, in having dealings with Jews, have witnessed the generosity of their behavior and their sentiments of gratitude. The trouble is, the only trouble is, that no one discloses observations of this kind. And if anyone happened to observe something repugnant in certain of them, you still cannot form an opinion about the generality of people on this basis, just as I, if I see many depraved people among Christians, similarly cannot make a judgment about all of their coreligionists.

I also make so bold as to say this to you: If you have observed depravity in some Jews close to you, take a good look at yourselves and do not be upset that I am going to ask, "Are you yourselves not perhaps the cause of it?" Forgive the Jews if the torments inflicted upon them over several centuries have given them an unfavorable opinion of the Christian nations. Might it be that a Jew of upright principles will in fact not establish close ties with you but will seek to distance himself, just as the Americans avoided the Spanish? In those close to you, then, you do not for the most part see the image of the real Hebrew but only the depraved one. Have a long hard look at yourselves, I say, do you yourselves perhaps support their outrages with your patronage? . . . So you live with

---

the Jews would take cover and not ply their trade. In some towns mayors, by then Russian appointees, still noticed such willful disturbances, but, having at their disposal the Statute of Good Order, the Constitution of the Provinces, and the Civil Command, they put a stop to them; some schoolchildren were imprisoned, and Jews saw for the first time that being cruel is not the duty of a Christian. [L. N.]

3 See *Nathan der Weise*. [L. N.] Nevakhovich is referring to *Nathan the Wise: A Dramatic Poem in Five Acts* by Gotthold Ephraim Lessing (1729–1781).

a nation without knowing its heart. I swear that a Jew who observes his religion faithfully cannot be a wicked person or a bad citizen!

I will extend further the lament of my burning heart. The religion professed by the Jews is harmless to any citizenship. This can be very clearly seen from the fact that in many well-ordered states it is not proscribed. The main purport of this religion is that each person, of whatever faith, is capable of achieving perfection, even if not well versed in the Jewish religion's rites, which, according to its canon, have been established by God solely for the Jews in commemoration of the covenant made between them in the wilderness of Horeb.[4] And in Jewish traditions it is enjoined to pray for the prosperity of the tsar,[5] it is laid down that the state law[6] is the substantive law, it is likewise forbidden to transport goods without paying duties, and so forth. If the law is honest, then the true followers of it must be honest.[7]

---

4 See Mendelssohn's *Jerusalem*. [L. N.] Nevakhovich is referring to the treatise of 1783 by the prototype of Lessing's Nathan the Wise, Moses Mendelssohn (1729–1786), a major figure of the Jewish Enlightenment, a philosopher and publicist, translator of the Pentateuch into German.

5 See the Jewish legends called *Pirke Avos*. [L. N.] *Pirke Avot* (lit. "Ethics of the Fathers") is the fourth tractate of the Mishnah in *Nezikin*, without any halakhic commentary. Containing teachings and maxims of the sages dating from the third century B.C.E., *Pirke Avot* is a part of the liturgy that is read by Ashkenazic Jews on Sabbath afternoons in the summer and by the Sephardic Jews at home on Sabbaths between Passover and Pentecost.

6 See the *Talmud* in the tractate *Bava Kama*, last *pereq* [chapter]. [L. N.]

7 For the reader's curiosity, I impart here an extract from a morning prayer offered by Jews that encompasses the whole doctrine of the Jewish faith: "Exalted is the living and most glorious God, the Being whose existence is independent of time, the One like unto whom there is none other, the Unfathomable whose Oneness has no successor, who has no likeness with beings corporeal nor yet incorporeal. His holiness is beyond investigation. He is the precursor of each created being, the First without antecedent; this Lord of all the World shows His grandeur and dominion to every creature. Part of His foreknowledge He vouchsafed to men deemed worthy of His love and loveliness. No prophet, nor any contemplator of His image, arose in Israel like Moses. God gave the true law to His people through His prophet and willing servant. God will not alter His law or replace it with another through all eternity. He sees into us and knows all that is hidden there. He foresees the end of an act even in its beginning. He dispenses grace to man according to his deeds and casts misfortune upon the unrighteous according to his iniquity. He will send us our anointed one at the end of the age for the redemption of those who rely upon His salvation. God will resurrect the dead according to the abundance of His mercy. May His name be blessed and glorified for all eternity." [L. N.] This is a literal translation of Nevakhovich's Russian-language rendition of Yigdal, the traditional Jewish hymn based on Maimonides's "Thirteen Principles of Faith"; in the Ashkenazic rite, Yigdal serves as an opening hymn of the weekday morning service.

It is indisputable that the morals and manners of nations are different and that each nation has its own particular moral propensities. Yet I cannot allow that these propensities are innate in a nation. Does Nature really produce people already glued to those things whose charm depends only on prejudices? What! A person has just been born and already understands that a piece of metal can afford him many benefits if it has upon it some image of which he is as yet ignorant! No, nurture is the cause of everything, nurture dependent on the disposition and habit of those who are responsible for it and whose disposition depends likewise on nurture. What an amazing mutual dependence: nurture on disposition, disposition on nurture! And what is the origin of this interdependence? There is in nature no effect without a cause and no cause without an effect. The morals and manners of nations are formed by a concatenation of different circumstances. The state of morals and manners is just as necessary in relation to the course of things in the moral world as are natural effects in relation to [the course of things] in the physical world.[8] When we do not feel animosity toward a person weighed down by physical ailments but only feel sorry for him, have we any reason to hate a person suffering from ailments of the heart? Moral ailments lend themselves to healing as much as physical ones; all that is necessary is to discover their true causes. And really there is no reason to feel hatred for a depraved person: after all, the punishment of lawbreakers is not an act of vengeance or malice but has as its object the averting of a greater evil; the punishments laid down for lawbreakers are necessary for keeping society within the due bounds of law and order, and in the opposite instance they deserve to be deplored. Dear compatriots! Let us kiss the divine book[9] of the immortal sovereign Empress Catherine II, in which it is

---

8 If a nation is kept under oppression for a long time, it degenerates in its morality. The Greeks, who were an example to the whole world, finding themselves under the oppressive yoke of the Mohammedans, transformed into something outlandish. . . . Jews in England, Holland, Prussia, in short, where they have more rights and freedoms, are far superior in moral behavior to those who had, or still to this day have, no such things. [L. N.]

9 Instruction for Composing the Draft of a New Law Code. [L. N.] Rus. *"Nakaz dlia sochineniia proekta novogo ulozheniia."* Nevakhovich is here referring to (and misquoting the title of) *"Nakaz Eia Imperatorskogo Velichestva Ekateriny Vtoroi o sochinenii Proekta Novogo Ulozheniia"* ("Instruction of Her Imperial Majesty Catherine II Concerning the Composition of the Draft of a New Law Code"), which Empress Catherine II presented to her celebrated Legislative Commission of 1767.

confided to us that punishment beyond the measure needed for correction is a tyrannical punishment! [. . .]

1803

Translated from the Russian by Brian Cooper

LEON MANDELSTAM

Leon (Arie-Leyb) **Mandelstam** (1819–1889), Hebraist, Jewish educator, multilingual author, was born in Novo-Zagory, Vilna Province (presently Zagare, Lithuania). Mandelstam's father, a reader of the *The Gatherer* (*Ha-Meassef*), a Haskalah journal founded in Königsberg in 1783, made sure that his son learned languages and general subjects. The teenaged Mandelstam discovered Maimonides's *Guide for the Perplexed* and Spinoza and composed his first literary opuses. Mandelstam was married at seventeen and went to live with his wife's parents. In their strictly Orthodox household, where any subject beyond the study of Talmud was regarded as blasphemous, Mandelstam suffered a nervous breakdown. Moving back home, he obtained a *get* (annulment of marriage) and pursued the study of foreign languages and literatures.

In 1839, Mandelstam petitioned Russian authorities to be allowed to take the examination for a gymnasium[10] diploma and was permitted to enter Moscow University. In his *Notes of the First Jewish Student in Russia*, Mandelstam reminisced: "Thus I stand now—a wild, strong, free son of nature, loving his fatherland and the language of his native land, but miserable with the misery of his coreligionist brothers. [. . .] The goal of my life is to vindicate them before the world and to help them earn this vindication. They are not mean nor incurably afflicted and corrupt, but they lie supine like a desperate patient with clenched teeth and do not wish to accept curative drops from the hands of the physician; but perhaps their native son, someone of their own soul, suffering with them, will succeed in persuading them" (published 1908). Mandelstam entered Moscow University in 1840, and his Russian-language collection *Poems* was published there in 1841. He transferred to St. Petersburg University, to the Faculty of Philosophy, and in 1844 was the first Jew to graduate from a Russian university, although both Derpt University and Vilna University had had Jewish students who were not apostates.

After graduating, Mandelstam went abroad to continue his philological training. Upon his return, he was appointed by Prince Sergey Uvarov, Russia's minister of education, to the post of "expert Jew" at his ministry following the departure of Rabbi Max Lilienthal (1815–1882) for the United States in 1844. Mandelstam's task was to implement a plan of Jewish education reforms. He was

---

10 Gymnasium = high school based on the classical model of liberal arts education.

also charged with preparing materials to replace the Talmud in state-sponsored Jewish schools. While in effect running the official Jewish educational program between 1845 and 1857, Mandelstam put together *A Maimonides Reader* (1848), an instruction on civic duties (*Shene Perakim*, 1852), and other texts. Of great importance were Mandelstam's *Hebrew-Russian Dictionary* (1859) and *Russian-Hebrew Dictionary* (1860), used at government yeshivas. Mandelstam also undertook to translate the Pentateuch into Russian. Inspired by Moses Mendelssohn's German translation of the Pentateuch (1783), the first Russian translation by a Jew was a major accomplishment of Mandelstam's career. The first edition of his translation was published in 1862 in Berlin. Permission was finally granted in 1869 for the publication of his translation of the Pentateuch and the Psalms, with parallel Hebrew and Russian texts, and was printed in 1872 in Berlin for distribution in the Russian Empire.

In 1857, Mandelstam left his post at the ministry. He lived abroad for a period of time, publishing books on the Bible and the Talmud and contributing to foreign and Russian periodicals. A brochure with two of Mandelstam's polemical essays was printed in St. Petersburg in 1859 under the title *In Defense of the Jews*. His tale in verse, *The Jewish Family*, which was published in Berlin in 1864, was blocked by the censors and only appeared in Russia, in expurgated form, in 1872. In 1880, a German-language volume of Mandelstam's poetry appeared in London. Initially successful, Mandelstam's publishing ventures eventually failed. Forgotten and impoverished during his last years, he died in St. Petersburg in 1889. Writing in 1944 in the New York magazine *Jewish World* (*Evreiskii mir*), the Yiddish poet and critic Y. Kisin (1886–1950) commented that "the lonely Mandelstam of the 1840s expressed a grievance that was 'eternally Jewish, eternally human,' while at the same time predicting and defining the dividedness [*razdvoennost´*] of a member of the Russian-Jewish intelligentsia."

* * *

More than half of Mandelstam's *Poems* (1841) were his own translations of what he had originally written in Hebrew. The collection was a landmark of Jewish-Russian literature, the first Russian-language poetry collection by a Jew. Compositely autobiographical for the growing numbers of Jews breaking into the ranks of the Russian intelligentsia in the 1840s–50s, the Jewish Student of the book's programmatic poem "The People" meekly dialogues with Olga, a young Russian woman or feminized Russia herself, asking for pity, understanding, and tolerance. Olga appears as a lyrical addressee in several other poems in the collection.

Pleading with the Russians to recognize the humanity of Jews, "The People" constitutes the volume's penultimate section and was probably composed directly in Russian; it exhibits the greatest formal sophistication and hints at Mandelstam's knowledge of Russian Romantic poetry. Fascinating is Mandelstam's likening of his fellow Jews to a messy poem in need of a good (Russian, perhaps even Christian) editor.

Mandelstam's patriotic and apologetic collection is the work of a gifted imitator who did not start writing in Russian until after the age of fifteen. The poems, some stilted and wan and others stylistically old-fashioned already in the 1840s, stand in vast contrast to **Ruvim Kulisher**'s punchy and zesty Pushkinian *An Answer to the Slav* (1849).

THE PEOPLE

1.

Olga
  There where you live no flower blooms,
No stream flows—all is desolation;
It must be that your hearts are numb,
Your souls devoid of aspiration . . .

Student
  In life I know no bliss or leisure—
Around me naught but emptiness;
But I do know a song's sweet pleasure,
And lofty dreams are my bequest!

In dreams I leave the plains of exile,
In dreams I join the ranks of men;
I step inside the promised temple,
The homes of brothers and of friends.
In dreams my soul keeps hope alive,
Through dreams of nation Jews survive!

2.

Olga
　　How to tame them? How to curb them?
Their savage customs breed contempt.
No matter how we teach them, spurn them—
They keep intoning "Talmud" and "Reb"!

Student
　　The wind once made the sun a wager:
Who had such might over the stranger
To take the coat from off his back . . .
And flapping its powerful wings in attack
It swooped down in thirty-two onslaughts of black:

　　Storms rushed like malevolent criminals, churning
And shrieking with frenzy, with murderous wrath,
They surged and they whirled, stirring up in their path
The water of rivers, the earth on the banks,

　　While gusts seized the arms and the legs of the stranger,
His chest and his shoulders . . . How tough was the man! . . .
He wrapped himself tight, and he walked with eyes shut;
He struggled, he fell—but held on to his coat! . . .

　　The winds die down; the sun in splendor
Sows blossoms on the gloomy track;
It soothes, it strokes the weary stranger,
Calms his suffering, warms his back . . .

　　He feels the sunshine's rich abundance
And breathes more freely in its rays.
His clothing now hangs hot upon him—
His winter coat he casts away! . . .

3.

Student
Our people in essence is much like a poem,
There are errors in form and the whole is perplexing;
Its end comes before it begins incorrectly;
Its parts are untidy, the sense does not hold! . . .
But a powerful critic, loving the heathen,
Glibly amends the disorganized verse,
Revealing the true spirit of poetic words—
Until heartrending melodies penetrate, seething . . .

Olga
Please tell me some more of your national traits,
Tell me your failings and also your strengths;
And although you alone are the rule's one exception,
For me one's sufficient—your people's redemption
From my scorn is assured; may Christ hold you all dear
And forgive you—you're worthy of genuine tears! . . .

1840

Translated from the Russian by Alyssa Dinega Gillespie

RUVIM KULISHER

Ruvim (Reuben) **Kulisher** (1828–1896), essayist, poet, and Jewish communal leader, was born in Dubno, Volhynia, in 1828. His father, a follower of the Haskalah, insisted on giving him a systematic European education along with a solid grounding in Judaism. Kulisher, therefore, studied at the Zhitomir classical gymnasium. He entered St. Petersburg University in 1848 and was, to the best of our knowledge, the third Jewish student (after **Leon Mandelstam** and Mavriky Rappoport) to graduate from a Russian university. Kulisher studied at the Medical-Surgical Academy in St. Petersburg in 1852–56, whereupon he joined the Russian army's medical corps as a physician, one of the first three Jews to be given such a position. Starting in 1860, Kulisher was on the staff of the Kiev Military Hospital, and he spent 1869–76 in western Europe on a research fellowship, specializing in public health. He published several medical articles, including an analysis of skin diseases mentioned in the Bible.

A close disciple and friend of the "Russian Mendelssohn," Isaac Baer Levinson (1788–1860), Kulisher contributed essays on Jewish history, communal living, and education to Jewish periodicals in both Hebrew and Russian. In 1892–94, the Jewish-Russian periodical *Sunrise* (*Voskhod*) serialized the first part of Kulisher's memoirs, *Summing Up. The Hopes and Expectations of Russian Jews over the Past 50 Years, 1838–1888*, expanded and published as a separate book in 1896. He died in Kiev in August 1896.

* * *

Kulisher created one of the earliest works of Jewish-Russian poetry, the polemical poem *An Answer to the Slav*. He composed *An Answer to the Slav* in November 1849 while a student at St. Petersburg University. Hand copies of this poem of nearly 400 lines circulated and were known to Kulisher's contemporaries. Attempts by Kulisher and his friends to publish the poem in the 1840s–50s failed, most likely owing to government censorship. One stanza made it to print in 1861, quoted in the Jewish-Russian weekly *Dawn* (*Rassvet*). In 1911, Saul Ginsburg (1866–1940), a Jewish historian and journalist, founder of the Yiddish daily *The Friend* (*Der Fraind*, St. Petersburg), obtained the text of *An Answer to the Slav* from Kulisher's son and published it with a biographical introduction in issue 3 of the collection *The Bygone*

(*Perezhitoe*). In *Tsar Nicholas I and the Jews* (1983), the historian Michael Stanislawski described the poem as expressing "bitter disillusionment with the basic axioms of the Haskalah's political ideology." Kulisher's poem was a daring response to the Judeophobic commonplaces of Russian literature and journalism of the 1820s–40s, where the Jewish question was habitually treated with a mixture of ignorance, antisemitic stereotyping, and crude Christian supersessionism. The writings that were likeliest to provoke Kulisher's answer were not such works as *The Avaricious Knight* (1830), the "little tragedy" by the national Russian author Alexander Pushkin, whom Kulisher mentions, but rather the works of Faddey Bulgarin (1789–1859), a popular middle-brow novelist and journalist, especially his novels *Little Esther* (1828) and *Ivan Vyzhigin* (1829) and his article "Polish Jews" (1838). What is particularly important, and especially if compared to the shyly apologetic argument of **Leon Mandelstam**'s "The People," is not only the demand for legal equality for the Jews but also the poem's attack on the Slavs' Christian, religious antisemitism. "The Jews have always treated us in accordance with the Jewish faith," the Russian religious philosopher Vladimir Solovyov would write thirty-five years after Kulisher in *Jewry and the Christian Question* (1884). "We Christians, on the contrary, have yet to learn to treat the Jews in the Christian fashion."

The Romantic-ironic detachment and the formal makeup of Kulisher's poem point to its sources in Pushkin's *Eugene Onegin* (1833). Both the iambic tetrameter of Kulisher's poem and its stanzaic structure and rhyme (quatrains in which conjoining and enclosing rhymes alternate with couplets) recall the Onegin stanza. Additionally, Kulisher includes several deliberate allusions to and borrowings from Pushkin's novel in verse. In places skillful and well tempered, in others a composition of an imitator-apprentice, *An Answer to the Slav* showcases instances of elegant versification alongside those of heavy-handed rhymestering. But it is the work of a Russian poet, and nothing in its composition and language bespeaks a Jew timidly making his entrance into the forbidden corridors of Russian literature. The unapologetic, militantly satirical Jewish-Russian voice of Kulisher's poem makes it absolutely unique for its time and anticipates **Vladimir Jabotinsky**'s feuilletons of the 1890s–1900s. Had Kulisher's poem been published soon after its composition, it would have given other aspiring Jewish-Russian authors a model to follow: learn from the Russian masterpieces and infuse your work with Jewish subject matter.

FROM *AN ANSWER TO THE SLAV*

Introduction

I hesitate to sound immodest,
So I must warn you in advance,
If you will listen now in earnest,
Then please excuse my stance.

More frightening than other words—
And I will use this startling word—
It is as novel to your ears
As were steam whistles I first heard.
Perhaps your ears are all too tender,
Unused to terrifying sounds,
Then you'll immediately consider
My speech so spitefully unbound.

Not ancient ghosts or petty demons,
Nor the old mounted wicked witch,
Nor even Satan's evil sermons
Contribute to the subject which
I wish to talk to you about:
Those themes have long since been portrayed,
And even cannibals no doubt,
To some will seem a bit too staid.
I wish to introduce the *Jew.*
Please don't be scared, I beg of you,
Oh, how you trembled, turning pale—
I'll either smash the frightening tale
Or for a time put it aside
So fragile souls can feel no fear
While those with moral strength decide,
To love the truth with hearts sincere.

[. . .]

III

In exile I was given shelter,
For loads of money, by the Pole;
My sufferings grew manifold
With wild assaults by Polish *szlachta*[11]
Beholding my incessant torments
How many times the Pole rejoiced:
His crops were watered by the torrents
Of Jewish blood upon his fields!
From Little Russia came the raids
By Cossacks threat'ning to erase me,
And for my gold the Pole repaid me
With nothing but profound contempt.

Those people had no God, although
They wanted to appease him so;
And knowing neither Faith nor Love
They sought those virtues in my blood.
And though the people have improved
And they no longer torture Jews,
We still cannot sigh with relief,
The road to peace is long and steep.
It's been my lot to stand there waiting
At Russia's still unopened gate.
For bread and salt upon a plate
In vain I stood anticipating.
I'm just allowed to share the pain
Of this vast empire and its nation:
Your brother in war and desperation,
In peace you treat me with disdain.
Enlightenment brings me only torment,
I see without any adornment:
With them enjoying naught but bliss
What misery for me exists.

---

11 *Szlachta* (Pol.) = Polish rank-and-file landed gentry.

[. . .]

Why is my lot much more ill fortuned
Than ev'n the fate of the Tatars
Whose gifts to you were yoke and torture,
Who kept you debtors from afar?
Is it because you hate and envy
The fact your Savior was a Jew?
Whatev'r may say the mob of enemies
He's mine, yet suffered He for *you.*
There is no need to force upon us
And fiercely teach the law of love:
For generations we have followed
What our forebears gained from above!

When will the freedom of our conscience—
The spirit's priceless treasury—
Be finally granted to the nation
That heeds its ancestors' decrees?
Too few still victims of coercion[12]
And violence defying reason?
Does spiritual apostasy burgeon
Amid the riches bought with treason?
Or maybe God has willed this daily
Defilement of our holy rights?
Should we blaspheme in public sight,
And abnegate our family?
A child will disavow his mother,
A father will disown his son,
And then 'til death they'll weep and suffer . . .
Behold the plight of the martyred nation!

---

12 The Jewish *kantonisty* [conscripts] and recruits are subjected—of course, without the
knowledge of the government—to treatment that hardly disposes the Jews toward fulfilling
their military service . . . [R. K.]

IV

No longer stalwart in his ways,
The Jew is subject now to changing;
So in advance I have portrayed—
And you may well find this estranging—
A previous image of my nation:

The way they had existed prior
To '46, when regulations
Compelled a change in their attire
And wearing garb of German style;[13]
Back when the trepid brides would fear
The matronly matchmakers' wile;
The Jewish girls would not come near.
The Hussar's captivating tricks;
The Jew had not discovered the theater,
And actresses and the coulisse,
And listening to a female singer
Was not a negligible sin.
His thoughts converged upon one thing:
On gaining bliss through faith and care,
On acts of goodness one has wrought,[14]
On bettering his heart through prayer,
And reaching God in lofty thought.

[. . .]

Here is for you a salient feature
Of my portrayal, and with its help
I understand the total picture,
The mystery reveals itself.
But there is yet another trait

---

13 In 1844, the government of Tsar Nicholas I abolished the *kahal* communal structure of
   Jewish life in the Russian Empire. According to the 1846 regulations that followed the
   abolishment of the *kahal*, Jews were required, among other things, to modernize their
   medieval garb.
14 *Tora u-maasim tovim* [Heb. = Torah and good deeds]. [R. K.]

My nation's everlasting fate,
The Holy Land we left behind,
The unforgettable, the cherished,
The one that never leaves our minds,
The land whose image never perished.
This high abode of dreamy visions,
Lays claim to us our whole life long;
This dream we yet again revisit,
Transported on the wings of song.
There everything heartfelt abounds,
The sky vault's nearer to the ground.

One does not seek the heavens there—
Where heav'n and earth are merged forever.[15]
The Jew has carried into exile
His feelings for the Holy Land,
He'll bear them yet through every trial,
And every hardship he'll withstand.

[. . .]

Behold his main characteristics:
My sketchy portrait of the Jew
Is a defense, and bold logistics
To show how slanders are untrue.
I know the day will finally come
When Slavs embrace us all as one.
The Russian and the Polish nation
Will offer us reconciliation.
For all their ancestors' offense
Their heirs will show me tolerance,
And having heard my tale of torments
Will willingly tear down the fences.
I hope the face that I have shown
The Jew acknowledges as his own.

---

15 Especially remarkable among the beliefs the Jews have about the Holy Land is the one that attributes to this land the capacity to purify of sins those who are buried in it. Therefore many Jews move there in old age so as to await death. [R. K.]

I hope he shows his future children,
And tells of me without chagrin.
And if he's worthier than I
And more enlightened he is made—
May he appreciate my aid
When I was fighting for his rights!

1849

Translated from the Russian by Maxim D. Shrayer

OSIP RABINOVICH

Osip (Yosef) **Rabinovich** (1817–1869), fiction writer, essayist, and editor, was born in Kobelyaki in Poltava Province and received a broad education in the home of his affluent father. After his marriage at the age of eighteen, he studied law independently before entering Kharkov University in 1840. Because of a government prohibition against unconverted Jews on the bar, Rabinovich was unable to study law and enrolled instead at the Faculty of Medicine, but he left without taking a degree after his father's affairs deteriorated. In 1845, Rabinovich settled in Odessa, where he served at the Commercial Court. He was elected a notary public in 1848 and participated as a city councilman in the drafting of Odessa's new civil code.

The publication in 1847 of Rabinovich's Russian translation of the poem *The Battle* (*Ha-Krav*) by the Hebrew poet Jacob Eichenbaum (1796–1861) showcased his impeccably perfect command of literary Russian. It was reprinted in St. Petersburg by the very popular magazine *Library for Reading* (*Biblioteka dlia chteniya*), edited by the Polish-born orientalist and author Osip Senkovsky, whose literary pen name was Baron Brambeus. Two essays published in *The Odessa Herald* (*Odesskii vestnik*), "The New Jewish Synagogue" (1847) and "Apropos the Kind Word" (1848), defined the agenda of Rabinovich the polemicist. His principled if conflicted position of "fighting on two fronts"—defending Jews from antisemitism while also exposing their own flaws—influenced a whole generation of Russianized Jewish intelligentsia.

Rabinovich's first work of fiction, *The Story of the Trading Firm Firlich & Co.* (1849), was free of Jewish thematics, but his next short novel, *Morits Sefardi* (1850), is commonly considered the first work of Jewish-Russian fiction. In terms of Russian literary history, there were many "firsts" in *Morits Sefardi*: a young maskilic protagonist; a traditional Jew rendered not through antisemitic caricature or abstract humanism but with deep knowledge and understanding; and Jewish speech represented in Russian not via imitation of accent but through Jewish sayings translated almost literally. Rabinovich's next novel, *Kaleidoscope*, published in its entirety in 1860, featured Odessa's multiethnic life and a poet as one of its protagonists. Jews in it have speaking albeit not principal parts. In the years following the ascension and reforms of Alexander II, Rabinovich gained a national reputation as a writer on Jewish issues. In 1859, his most famous work, *The Penal Recruit*, appeared in the Moscow review *The Russian Messenger* (*Russkii vestnik*). Russian Jewry hailed Rabinovich's tale, and it was read publicly in Jewish homes where no other non-Jewish books were allowed. Legends describe gatherings of Jews where makeshift Yiddish translations of *The Penal Recruit* would be improvised and read on the spot. An 1860 volume with the German translation, published in Leipzig, sold several thousand copies.

The Penal Recruit (excerpt below) was the first in a two-part work titled *Pictures of the Past*, set in the era of Nicholas I. The second part, the tale *The Hereditary Candlestick*, appeared serially in 1860 in the new magazine *Dawn* (*Rassvet*), which Rabinovich cofounded in Odessa with Yoachim Tarnopol (1810–1900; on the history of the Jewish-Russian press, see the section introduction). *Dawn* was the first Jewish-Russian weekly magazine, although several Jewish periodicals with the same title appeared subsequently. As the magazine's editor, Rabinovich contributed thirty-nine front-page articles. He was hopeful that Russia's Jews would ameliorate themselves with the government's support. However, *Dawn* was closed down after a year, both under government pressure and also due to Rabinovich's own realization that his arguments were lending wind to the sails of Judeophobes. Disillusioned with his own powers as a Jewish-Russian spokesman but also with the extent of Alexander II's liberalizing reforms (the Pale, a chief impediment of Jewish opportunities in the Russian Empire, was never dismantled), Rabinovich divided his latter years between the tasks of a journalist for the mainstream Russian press and those of a Jewish-Russian belletrist. His most formally accomplished work is *The Tale of How Reb Hayyim-Shulim Feiges Traveled from Kishinev to Odessa and What Transpired with Him on the Way* (Odessa, 1865). Rabinovich's maskilic scorn had metamorphosed into warmth and sympathy, and the narrator's Jewish perspective was no longer encumbered by the contradictions of being both an advocate for and a critic of his people. Rabinovich was seriously ill in his last years and died of consumption in Merano, Tyrol, in 1869.

* * *

Almost nothing in the style of *The Penal Recruit* betrays a nonnative Russian writer, and for a Jewish writer composing prose in Russian in 1859, this is one of its significant achievements. The subject and the narrator's outlook are deeply Jewish, though, and the tone, both dispassionate and naive, is perfectly chosen to depict the recruitment of Jews under Nicholas I. Rabinovich presented Jewish suffering neither sentimentally nor ethnographically. The Russian reader of Rabinovich's age would find Rabinovich's tale both strange and gripping, while the Jewish reader would feel the bittersweet pleasure of recognition.

FROM *THE PENAL RECRUIT*

The entire next day I couldn't get the recruit out of my mind. Taking pains to wait until evening, I then set off to see him. This time he greeted me more kindly; I could even tell that my visit gave him pleasure.

"Do you know, I've been waiting impatiently for you," he said to me. "Since the time this disaster struck me, I have not seen a friendly face to take an interest in me, a person to whom I could pour out my sorrow. I only managed to see my wife and daughter once . . . for a very short time, but now how can I see them? God Almighty! I wouldn't wish such a situation on anyone."

"When did you see them?" I asked.

"When they were putting the gray overcoat on me," he answered, "an hour before they sent me on my long journey. But that's the end of my story, and you don't yet know the beginning. Now listen to this."

We sat down across from one another; he rested his elbows on the table, crossed his hands, and in a drawn out, quiet voice began his story:

"The town where I lived, grew up, and became a man is inhabited nearly entirely by Jews and located not far from the border. We have a fairly large community. Although I was not one of the very rich men, I was still well off. I was involved in trade like the majority of our people and managed to earn enough to maintain my position thanks to hard work and thriftiness. I lived happily with my family, my wife and two daughters; God did not give me a boy. For a long time I complained, but now I see that it was for the best. In my free time, and there was quite enough of it, since my business did not demand constant work—I bought up wool and sold it to foreign merchants who came for it—I liked to read and study non-Jewish subjects. These were accessible to me thanks to a natural inclination, which had been developed in me by my late father. You know that for the most part we all study on a shoestring since we are intended to engage in trade. Actually only someone who wants to devote himself exclusively to scholarship studies seriously and systematically; the merchant class considers serious study secondary. With us in the western provinces in any case, that's the way it is. There is certainly no point in looking for scholars or highly educated men among us—that's a luxury, and we are condemned to work. We have to exist, and it isn't easy to exist, because we are crammed in large communities and restricted in most of our actions, as you know. So there is no point in looking for well-educated men among us, but at the same time, total ignorance, a lack of at least some knowledge, this, too, is a rarity among us.

Many of us have more or less studied a bit, and one doesn't feel embarrassed to meet with them, as we Jews say. That is, among us there are well-cultivated individuals, in a Jewish, limited way, of course, since they are still far from true European enlightenment, and this applies not only to them but to many others, too, who are much higher than they are on the social ladder and enjoy far better living conditions. I am speaking about civil servants and proprietors. Of course, the exceptions do not change this fact.

"I had my own small circle of friends, which consisted of what we call *autodidacts*, that is, the self-taught. We used to get together and discuss Jewish literature, which in recent years has achieved great success abroad, or new works in Polish and German. Few in our midst knew Russian well— for the most part only those who had direct contact with the government knew Russian, such as the tax farmers, their lawyers, contractors, and those who carried out official duties. I was happy, surrounded by my small family and friends. Our time was divided between our respective business affairs and the tranquil evenings spent at one of our homes, where ignorant Jewish businessmen, unknown to the world at large, sometimes discussed the latest questions of science and literature from the far corners of Europe. Our town and its outlying small towns, it seems, enjoyed as much prosperity as we could, given the periodic invasions of the municipal and rural administrations, for whom a place populated by Jews makes up a profitable source of revenue. There's no point in telling you about it since I think it must be the same where you live too, right?"

"Unfortunately, yes," I answered.

"Of course!" the old man continued with vigor. "Whether it's a fair, a dead body, a deserter, or a new ordinance concerning synagogues or private schools—all of it is turned into a pretext for bribery, making a solid source of income for certain people. The end is always the same: a sum is collected by members of the community, the representatives go off with the offering, and the drumbeat of disaster subsides until the next time. And we are used to it. You know how easily a Jew reconciles himself to his fate. A warm hearth, an onion, a piece of bread, and a piece of fish or meat on the Sabbath, and he's happy. Recalling that persecution is his fate from the cradle on, that it is predestined from above, he hums his *zemiros* (mealtime songs)[16] and wipes a random tear with his fist in expectation of a better future."

16 *Zemirot (zemiros)* = traditional Hebrew songs sung during the Sabbath meal; see **David Aizman**'s "The Countrymen."

He stopped and for several minutes sat in deep silence.

"But our community was afflicted by one misfortune from which we could never extricate ourselves," the soldier began again. "And it affected not just our community but everyone, as far as we know. It is the shortfall in our quota of military recruits. We constantly expended huge sums on bribes in the provincial capital, hired replacement recruit s from other towns, jumped out of our skin, but were always in arrears. Since I enjoyed an honorable reputation in our town and was known as a selfless man, I, among others, was chosen as a *kahal* representative and served in this position over ten years. Do you know what a *kahal* representative does? He is either a robber or a martyr; there is no in-between. He has to endure the cries of a poor man who, because of his debts, has just been deprived of his last blanket, which had served as a shield from the cold for his naked family. He has to endure the screams of a widow from whom her last son has been taken as a recruit. He has to put up with persecutions from rich Jews, if in some way he has inconvenienced their distant relatives in the effort to collect debts or meet other obligations; the rich always have defenders on call. He is vulnerable to the persecution of the authorities if, out of pity for poor Jews, he thinks of stopping the daily robbery of the tax collector, who sells meatless bones as though they were meat, and at the double price, no less. If the *kahal* representative has a heart, he is apt to experience torture daily. If he has a rock in his chest instead of a heart, he joins the oppressors and makes a sizeable profit. Either a criminal or a martyr, I tell you! Fortunately or unfortunately, I belonged to the latter group. Only God Almighty knows what I endured and experienced.

"The eviction of Jews from the countryside and villages, their restriction to a few occupations and to living in the Pale of Settlement, and other laws, coming at the same time as the growth of the population, brought on terrible poverty. You could barely count one wealthy Jew for two hundred poor ones. Pauperism and homelessness increased every year. Our custom of marrying children at an early age contributed a great deal to this poverty. This stupid custom has done a great deal of harm! If for a rich man a large family increases the number of workers and brings beneficence, for a homeless man who has no specific employment it is an absolute curse. [...]

"With each year and each recruitment selection, our community's monetary and recruitment arrears kept accumulating. Earlier selections had quite depleted us; many families ran away and disappeared without a trace, and many of those capable of working fled abroad. There was not a single middle-class family that was not short of a brother, a son, a grandson, a husband. Some went into hiding, while others had already been handed over to the recruitment. Some families had already given recruits two or three times, but soon their turn would come again, since there was no one left. Recruitments came often in our parts. If there was one in the Western Region, we gave recruits; if there was one in the Eastern Region, again we gave recruits—and each time, ten for every thousand. An impossible task! And how many among the thousand were underage, already deceased, aged, sick, or infirm? How many had run away or, in the end, had already been drafted for military service but had not been removed from the recruitment list as they should have been!

"For us, the elected representatives, this was pure torture. God is a witness how we were tortured as we tried to fulfill the government's demands. And what could we do? It was completely beyond our power. Whenever we saw an orphan, an unmarried man, a drunkard, we turned them over. Families fought with us, and they were right; they had fulfilled their quota long ago with one and even two recruits. We collected money, sent it off to various places, and hired recruits, but that was always connected with extreme difficulties and expenses and rarely was crowned with success. The government officials would nag us, threaten us. We had to go down to the capital of our province, get down on our knees, beg, give present after present, incur terrible expenses. Documents and reports flew in all directions: 'such and such urban community cannot fulfill . . . owing to cholera or recent fires' . . . or something else, and meanwhile time would pass and the storm would die down for a few months, but the costs were huge! Our strength and money perished in vain because our arrears not only did not diminish but grew larger.

"Don't even ask about the district officials and inspectors for God's sake! Whether one of them had a paper from the provincial authorities or didn't have one, if we had to send recruits or not, what business was it of his? He would roll into a small town, and the small town would shake as though in a fever. 'Close the shops . . . punish someone . . . drive everyone into the synagogue . . . light black candles . . . swear in both young and old!' Why? For what reason? God only knows! Of course, the outcome was the same: another deputation, more bows, and the usual presents.

"I must confess that this constant fear and worry made life repulsive. I implored the community to relieve me of the duties of *kahal* representative and choose someone in my place. I wanted to leave the town, even the region, so as to move far away and not see scenes that outraged my soul and occurred more and more frequently as we failed to manage.

"I've already told you that I had two daughters. One was seventeen at the time, already engaged. Her fiancé was an orphan, without money, but he had great talents. He was studying medicine at a distant university, at my expense. The end of his course of studies was still three years away, but when he got his diploma we were going to have a wedding. My other daughter was only a child of thirteen. My daughters were pretty . . . or perhaps it just seemed that way to a father's eyes. Did I see them as obligations? They were my children, my blood, my joy and consolation in this world. They made up a part of my being. It seemed impossible to separate them from me, just as it would be impossible to tear my heart from my breast . . . Oh my God, my God; they have been ripped away from me, and I am still alive! . . ."

He jumped up and in inexpressible despair began to swing his arms and hit himself in the chest, letting out hollow moans. I let him get all his crying out. Perhaps I also cried, I don't remember. After a few minutes he calmed down somewhat and sat down again.

"Excuse the tears of an unfortunate father," he began again, taking my hand. "I cannot remember my children without shedding tears. Right here, this is where I feel terrible pain!"

He pointed to his chest.

"I understand your grief," I replied, "but I—"

"—but you cannot ameliorate grief with tears," he interrupted, without letting me finish, "you cannot return the past. You're right. I'll go on with my story. My daughters had received a modest education, corresponding to my financial position. I asked the community if I could retire in order to devote the remainder of my days to the happiness of my children. Influential people in the community were prepared to grant me my wish. They took into consideration my old age and long service, which, whether you judge it good or bad, I had carried out and which, besides worry and distress, brought me nothing. But suddenly new circumstances came to the fore, and my liberation from service became entirely impossible.

"An order was received to the effect that, in order to avoid any future lapse in fulfilling the quota, we would now have to give the following: two recruits as a penalty for each no-show and a recruit for each debt of two thousand rubles. In the event that we did not fulfill these conditions, we had to yield up the *kahal* representatives and community elders as soldiers, putting them on the list as part of the penalty. They listed our debts as forty recruits, so now, imagine, we had to hand over one hundred twenty. Then add another one hundred twenty or so future recruits in the next selection, not to speak of the tens of thousands of rubles of debt, which we also had to replace with people, and you will understand the predicament. Horror paralyzed us, even more so when we realized that if we didn't manage to deliver the penal recruits, then a *new penalty* would be levied upon us, two recruits for one, and so on in a progression until our entire town turned into one huge recruitment. We couldn't have any doubt about the consequences because we had no hope of fulfilling the new order.

"What happened to us then I am incapable of describing to you. Our representatives went posthaste to the provincial capital, money flew about like useless throwaway trash. We begged for mercy, a delay . . . . Again papers were sent to various places. And we weren't napping in the meantime; we began to grab whomever we could. Whoever did not have someone to defend him was our recruit. We took children of eight as recruits; we chained them in pairs and sent them off. We were deaf to shrieking and wailing. It was a terrible time. Let God the merciful forgive those who invoked Him against us."

"But I don't understand the despair," I remarked. "Our fatherland needs soldiers; it is a sin to refuse to serve when the tsar orders it."

"Without the slightest doubt, it's a sin," answered the old man. "The tsar's will is the will of God. We are obliged to sacrifice our lives for our fatherland if need be. Who would argue with that? But our people are still not used to military service. And, moreover, there's military service and there's military service. If there was any hope of promotion, that would be something else, but a Jew cannot get promoted. In addition, look at his treatment from his ignorant fellows. On whom do they vent their anger and irritation if not on the *damn kike*? Whom should they kick for no reason at all if not the kike? To whose mug should they hold out a piece of pig fat if not to the kike's? Not to mention that the officers look at him differently, knowing that no accomplishment will propel the kike upward. There are exceptions, of course, but I'm speaking of the rule. Don't forget this was happening to adults, who sometimes can stand up for themselves, can complain to the officers; but what about the children? What can a poor child barely out of diapers do in a foreign land among boorish and cruel people who hate his religion, his tribe, among people who don't even treat their own any better and whose language he often does not understand at all? What kind of service can you expect from such a child? He is supposed to herd the military settlers' pigs and endure beatings and shoves if by chance he doesn't manage to fall into his grave quickly enough. No, real service is something else. One must serve if one is ordered to serve, and it's a shame that the treatment is not always tolerable, especially from the lower-ranking officers.

The higher officers are always well meaning and respect God's creation in every man, but one is far from the higher-ups, and the lower officers are always at hand.... Anyway, that's not the point ... back to my story.

"We wore ourselves out like fish knocking against the ice. We already began to accept those with only one eye, or no teeth, and cripples, and old men too. But the costs of each recruit! How much the doctor cost, the military recruitment committee, legal clerks! It's terrible even to speak of it. And still there was little sense to it since we didn't even get half of the full number. The recruitment arrears gradually increased and reached several hundred. I don't remember the exact figure, but even counting them up was frightening. We stopped even answering orders from the provincial capital. We couldn't fulfill them, and trying to explain that we didn't have enough recruits was futile. Then somehow it let up. Everything was quiet for a time, as though dark clouds were thickening over our heads. That illusory peace they gave us terrified us more than the former strict instructions. We felt that an unavoidable storm was gathering over us, and we weren't wrong. It soon broke out in the most terrible way.

"One morning—it was the fourth day of Hanukkah (the holiday of the Maccabees), when we were readying ourselves to celebrate the victory of our heroic ancestors, which was the capture of Antioch—the sound of many bells rang out through the town. Our hearts sank. Government officials came from the provincial and district recruitment offices. A detachment of armed soldiers entered the town. A few troika carriages rode straight to the synagogue. Our people were herded to the synagogue like sheep. They drove the old and young, women and children, drove everyone with their rifle butts. They ordered the entire population of the town to gather together. We, kahal representatives, tax collectors, and elders, all those who held a position, were immediately placed in chains and pushed along with everyone else. A lot of people were collected. Not only were the men's and women's sections filled, but so was the entire courtyard and street in front of the synagogue. An official stepped onto the podium and began to read from a piece of paper. He read for a long time and berated us for persistently disobeying the government. When he finished reading, he began to curse us. He abused everyone, everyone without distinction. Everyone silently listened with anxiety and trepidation. But when in conclusion he yelled out threateningly, 'You've picked the wrong people to trifle with! You know, you contemptuous and insignificant people, that in an instant we can wipe you from the face of the earth, crush you underfoot like a foul worm!'—when he pronounced these words, loud weeping broke out from the listeners' breasts.

And those who were in the courtyard and those in the street, hearing the sobs of their brothers in the synagogue, also began to weep, having a premonition of something terrible. Shrieks filled the air. It was terrible to see how the entire population sobbed uncontrollably. It seemed that the deaf walls of the houses were also ready to break out in tears.

"But that was still only the beginning. The order was to grab whomever they could, whoever looked at all like a suitable recruit. People ran in all directions like a frightened herd. The soldiers ran after them. There was terror on everyone's faces. Everyone scattered wherever they could, hiding in basements and in attics. All the stores were locked, all activity ceased, the confusion was indescribable. But those who were snatched up in the streets still did not come close to making up the needed number of recruits. Orders were given such that the panic could die down a bit by evening. Then at night houses were searched, and men were dragged from their beds. Scream as much as you like: 'I'm old' or 'I'm alone and can't possibly be a candidate' or 'I already have a brother and a son in the service' or 'I'm transferring to the merchant class and soon will be certified' or what have you, they didn't pay any attention to it. They shackled and sheared you in the twinkling of an eye.

"Our town could not emerge from its stupor for a long time, they say. For a long time no one dared show his face on the street, and whoever absolutely needed to would sneak by back alleys and under fences like a thief. Shops were closed for two months, markets were empty, no life, no movement could be seen. Moans and sighs, moans and sighs, this was all that you could hear. Everyone mourned someone: here there was no father, or no brother, or no son or husband, and elsewhere one and the other or all three together were gone.

"That is how it ended, the raid we brought upon ourselves because of our unintentional, unavoidable failure to provide recruits. The raid struck our town with paralysis because everyone had both hands and legs taken away, everyone lost his energy; this unprecedented event and fear for the future lay on everyone's breast like a lead weight. And those of us who held administrative positions—and there were fifteen of us—they added to the group of *penal recruits* and, placing us in chains, sent us to the capital of our province and from there to jail. Some of us couldn't take it and soon died in jail.

"You can imagine the mournful condition of my family. My wife, an old woman, who felt boundless attachment and respect for me and, according to her own understanding, considered me an untouchable person; my engaged daughter, who seemed to have the brightest future of happiness with a loving husband; the other, younger daughter, the darling of her parents, who found it difficult to imagine someone superior and more important than her father—all of this was somehow left hanging and in a single second was bereft of its leader and guardian. The entire past dissipated like fog, broke into tiny pieces. I can't even tell you anything about myself. It seemed to me that the whole thing was untrue, that it was a bad dream. But unfortunately the chains and prison reminded me that it was not a dream but merciless reality.

'My wife and eldest daughter soon followed me to the provincial capital. My wife collected as much money as she could, hoping to free me. They went everywhere together, begged and didn't spare any expense. There were good people who became involved in my case, who took money from them and promised their help. But as it turned out, they could not help. Sometimes they permitted me to see my wife and daughter in my cell. They gave me strength, consoled me, and mixed their tears with my own. Worry and sleepless nights exhausted them, but they did not lose heart and gathered all their energies to ease my situation. Nothing came of it. One morning my beard was cut off, my head was shaved, and I was led outside, where several wagons were standing. A crowd, recruits and police officers, were moving about. I didn't see anything, my mind somehow grew muddled. They took off my coat and began to put a soldier's overcoat on me. Suddenly I heard a terrible scream . . . my wife and daughter threw themselves at me . . . I stood as though turned to stone. Pity expressed itself on the faces of all those who surrounded me. Even a few soldiers and policemen said in an undertone, "Poor women!" My wife hung on my chest like a hundred-pound weight . . . another scream and she fell like a lump at my feet. An apoplectic fit struck her down.

"I asked for a delay in order to hear my wife's last breath. They gave it to me. In an hour my wife was dead, and a few minutes after her death our eldest daughter went insane."

The old man fell silent. His tears poured down his face in two streams. I felt as though my own hair was cutting into me. I was inwardly amazed that such a feeble old man, tormented by being confined in jail and tortured by the fate of two beings dear to him, a fate that befell them in his presence, could still remain alive after this. "But here I am, you see, I have not gone crazy, and I'm still alive," he continued after a short silence and as though responding to my hidden thought. "I am a useless vessel, a broken dish, and must endure all the torments of a mind that has not become muddled; but she, such a beautiful and innocent girl, who had just begun to blossom, had to say goodbye to her dreams and hopes . . . . What can one do? God is just. He gave and He took away, let His name be blessed!"

"So what happened then?" I asked, seeing that he had calmed down a bit.

"What could happen then?" he responded bitterly. "Wasn't this alone enough for me? I was sent far to the north; there I spent several months. With the help of good people I was later transferred to the garrison here and given good recommendations. With the help of these same people, my business was properly closed down, since my misfortune came upon me suddenly and my affairs were in disorder. Whatever could be collected from my property and whatever remained after my wife's last large expenditures and theft by various clerks they turned into cash and transferred into trustworthy hands. They assigned an old female relative to care for my youngest daughter and from the interest on the money give her enough for her needs. My eldest daughter, as I was informed in a letter, is at death's door in a hospital in the provincial capital. I pray to heaven to take her away quickly. I am also often sent money here, and for that reason I don't lack for funds; anyway I don't need much here. The officers treat me well. They allow me to rent an apartment and are not too concerned with the service. Let God, the patron of all unfortunates, give them their due. They are respectful toward me, the senior officials that is. The younger ones sometimes give me trouble, although I know what I have to do and to whom I should give my offerings. Anyway, nothing can be done, I endure. Sometimes I even become energetic and reconcile myself to my situation, but this does not last long. The thought of my unfortunate child, the only dear being who is left to me, torments me constantly. The girl is growing up, developing . . . what is going to happen to her, an orphan, without a mother, twelve hundred versts away from me!"

He dropped his head onto his chest and yielded to his heavy sorrow. For a long time I walked back and forth in the room, at times glancing at the penal recruit. He continued to sit in the same position and seemed to have forgotten entirely about my presence. I came up to the window and opened it. The summer evening was at the height of its charming beauty. In the dark-blue sky full of millions of stars, now sparkling with brilliant blinding light, now barely glimmering as though shaking in the unimaginable distance, there swam a barely visible full moon, which gave off a pale, calming light. The town was long since asleep. Everything in nature was quiet and triumphal.

I approached the old man and placed my hand on his shoulder. He got up. I took his hand and led him over to the window.

"Look how beautiful everything is here," I said to him. "Is even this not capable of consoling you?"

"You are speaking of the beauty of nature," he answered, "and asking whether it consoles me. No . . . You are young, you have still not encountered misfortune. Your eyes perceive differently and send their impressions to your heart in a different way. I was young, too, and I looked at the world and nature differently then . . . but not now. I remember," he added, pointing at the horizon, "I remember that there should be happiness and brightness here, but my eyes don't see it, and my heart doesn't feel it. The sky is dressed in the colors of mourning, the moon is a funeral candle for me, the stars seem to me open gaping ulcers on a tormented body from which blood is about to start pouring out, and the trees seem to be whispering about the horrors that occur in silence . . . No, whatever is visible is black for me, and what is beyond, what is ahead, what is invisible to my earthly eyes, what is covered by mystery for all of us— that is what consoles me. *There*, beyond what appears to you as bright images, beyond what appears to me as dark ghosts, there, where thought does not dare to reach—there it is, my consolation." [. . .]

1859

Translated from the Russian by Brian Horowitz

Seething Times: 1860s–1880s

Editor's Introduction

Writing of the founding fathers of Jewish-Russian literature, such as **Osip Rabinovich** (1817–1869), **Lev Levanda** (1835–1888), and **Grigory Bogrov** (1825–1885), the émigré critic Grigory Aronson suggested in 1960 that "during the initial, pioneering period, the [Jewish-Russian] writer was cognizant of the fact that his readers are not only Jews but also new readers from the Russian milieu, for whom Russian Jewry appeared as a mysterious sphinx, either in the magisterial but abstract image of the Eternal Wanderer Ahasuerus or in the rather uncouth, miserable, ugly, and repulsive image that a number of renowned Russian authors had nevertheless associated with the Jews residing in poverty, oppression, and unbearable toil in the Pale of Settlement." In the 1860s, one observes the rise of the Jewish-Russian panoramic novel, such as Lev Levanda's rutted *Seething Times* (published 1871–73), which was set during the Polish Uprising of 1863–64 and at first glance advocated a Jewish allegiance to Russia and Russianness. Writing of the aspirations of the Jewish-Russian writers and politicians in the 1860s–70s, not only of **Rabinovich** and **Levanda** but also of Leon Pinsker (1821–1891), the future author of *Autoemancipation* (1882) and founder of the Palestinophilic Hibbat Zion (Hebrew "Love of Zion") movement, the ranking historian of Jewish-Russian letters Shimon Markish noted that they "tried to tear their way, their arms thrust open, into the greater but inhospitable world, only to return to the narrow, crowded, and untidy Jewish street and limit themselves to its interests." The idea that in the 1860s–70s the early current of Jewish-Russian writing might have been too weak for the larger Russian literary mainstream and therefore carried the writers back to their limited Russian-language Jewish audience calls for a brief digression about the early Jewish-Russian periodicals, where much of the work by Jewish-Russian authors was appearing until the late 1890s. (See also the section "On the Eve: 1890s–1910s.")

Dawn (*Rassvet*), the first Jewish-Russian serial publication founded in Odessa in 1860, lasted for only a year. Two other short-lived periodicals, *Zion* (*Sion*, 1861) and *Day* (*Den'*, 1869–71), also appeared in Odessa, the unrivaled center of the Russian Haskalah in the 1860s. In the 1870s, the center of Jewish-Russian publishing shifted to St. Petersburg. According to the data of Dmitry

A. Elyashevich,[1] a total of forty-three Jewish-Russian periodicals appeared in St. Petersburg between 1871 and 1916. An important step was the founding in 1863 in St. Petersburg of the Society for the Dissemination of Education among Jews (OPE). The four principal St. Petersburg publications, where the lion's share of Jewish-Russian writing appeared in the 1870s–80s, were the magazines *Dawn* (1879–84, known as *Dawn* "2"), *Messenger of Russian Jews* (*Vestnik russkikh evreev*, 1871–79), *The Russian Jew* (*Russkii evrei*, 1879–84), and the collective volumes of *Jewish Library* (*Evreiskaia biblioteka*, altogether eight volumes between 1871 and 1880 and two more in the 1900s).

Following the government's palliative efforts at "ameliorating" the position of the Russian Jews during the period of the Great Reforms in the 1860s, Jews began to leave the Pale in larger numbers through education, military and civil service, and conversion and enter the mainstream of Russian society. The first Jewish-Russian authors to reach a position of prominence in the Russian cultural mainstream emerged from their ranks in the 1880s–90s, including Nikolay Minsky (1855–1937) and the first major Jewish-Russian woman writer, **Rashel Khin** (1861–1928), who was encouraged in her youth by the aged Russian classic Ivan Turgenev. The half-Jewish **Semyon Nadson** (1862–1887), Russia's most popular poet of the 1890s–1900s, brought into the Russian mainstream an awareness of the growing Jewish cultural presence. As early as 1880, Russian xenophobic authors and publicists began to decry an alleged Jewish takeover of the mainstays of Russian society—professional life and culture—and the paranoia has not quite subsided to this day. "The Yid Is Coming," a programmatic essay by Aleksey Suvorin, the editor of the newspaper *New Time* (*Novoe vremia*), set the tone for the antisemitic retrenchment. Emperor Alexander II was assasinated on 1 March 1881; among the populist terrorists was Gesya Gelfman, a Jewish woman. A wave of about 150 pogroms in 1881–82, among them the particularly violent pogroms in Elizavetgrad (15 April 1881) and Balta (29 March 1882), changed the course of Jewish-Russian history. The 1881–82 pogroms weaned the second-generation Russian *maskilim*, such as **Lev Levanda**, of their illusions and of their false hopes for an integration into and fusion (*slyianie*) with the Russian people.

---

1 See D. A. El'iashevich, "Russko-evreiskaia kul'tura i russko-evreiskaia pechat'. 1860–1945," in *Literatura o evreiakh na russkom iazyke, 1890–1947. Knigi, broshiury, ottiski statei, organy periodicheskoi pechati. Bibliograficheskii ukazatel'*, ed. V. E. Kel'ner and D. A. El'iashevich, 37–78 (St. Petersburg: Akademicheskii proekt, 1995).

LEV LEVANDA

Lev (Yehuda Leyb) **Levanda** (1835–1888), fiction writer, essayist, journalist, was born in Minsk to a poor family. He studied at a reformed Talmud Torah in Minsk and a government-sponsored Jewish school. In 1849, he entered the Vilna Rabbinical College, at the time a hub of maskilic thought, graduating in 1854 with a teacher's diploma and a knowledge of several languages and both Russian and Western literature. Levanda taught at a government-sponsored Jewish school in Minsk until 1860, and from then until his death he served as an "expert Jew" (*uchenyi evrei*) at the office of the governor-general of Vilna. In this capacity, Levanda submitted reports on Jewish life and education in the Northwestern Region and in the late 1860s participated in the Vilna Commission on the Organization (*ustroistvo*) of Jews.

Levanda's literary talent was most evident in his partially memoirist *Sketches of the Past* (1870), *Travel Impressions and Notes* (1873), and *Schoolfear* (1875), which invite a comparison with *Notes of a Jew* by **Grigory Bogrov**. Exciting from a historical point of view are Levanda's novels and tales *Friend Bernard* (1861), *Samuil Gimpels* (1867), and *Avraam Iezofovich* (1887). Levanda's satirical fiction, *Confession of a Dealer* (1880) and *The Great Fraud* (1880–81), betrays an influence of the dominant Russian satirical novelist Mikhail Saltykov-Shchedrin (1826–1889). The mastery of Levanda's prose grew toward the end of his career, especially in his discursive works, but Levanda's language never lost its patina of being not quite native. Some pages of Levanda's fiction read like slightly imperfect translations, exhibiting a stiffly over-correct usage, or an unwarranted Polonism, or a faint misuse of Russian verbal aspect. The Russian of his fellow pioneers of Jewish-Russian literature **Osip Rabinovich** and **Grigory Bogrov**, who were exposed to Russian under different circumstances, is more pure and elegant.

Levanda wrote for *Zion* (*Sion*), which replaced *Dawn* in 1861–62, and after *Zion*'s closing contributed articles about the Northwestern Region to the central newspapers *The St. Petersburg Gazette* (*Sankt-Peterburgskie vedomosti*) and *New Time* (*Novoe vremia*). In 1864–65, Levanda edited *The Vilna Province Gazette* (*Vilenskie gubernskie vedomosti*). In 1878, a collection of his sketches and feuilletons, previously published in *The Vilna Messenger* (*Vilenskii vestnik*), came out under the title *Vilna Life*. Levanda's best-known novel, *Seething Times*, was serialized in the St. Petersburg-based *Jewish Library* (*Evreiskaia biblioteka*, founded 1871) in 1871–73 (excerpt below). Many of Levanda's belles lettres appeared in that periodical and in the Jewish-Russian magazine *Dawn (Rassvet,* known as *Dawn "2"),* founded 1881.

While he was in Minsk, Levanda contributed feuilletons to *The Minsk Province Gazette (Minskie gubernskie vedomosti)* under the anagrammatic pen name Ladneva. Alexander II's reforms fueled Levanda's optimism about the amelioration of the Jewish condition and his desire to fight for an improvement of the Jewish civil status. He was hopeful that Russia's Jews would quickly be granted equality. Joining arms with **Osip Rabinovich**, Levanda became a leading contributor to the Odessa-based *Dawn (Rassvet,* 1860–61). Levanda's first work of belles lettres, *The Warehouse of Groceries. Pictures of the Jewish Life* (book edition Vilna, 1869; Hebrew translation 1874), which was serialized in *Dawn,* tendentiously portrayed much in Jewish life as dark, stagnant, and fanatical while presenting the mainstream Russian life uncritically.

From 1879, Levanda poured most of his energies into polemical essays. In a letter published in 1879 in the first issue of *The Russian Jew (Russkii evrei),* he advanced an assimilationist platform: "to effectuate energetically all that leads to the irrevocable rebirth of the Russian Jew into a Russian citizen with a shade of religious particularity." The pogroms of 1881–82 transformed Levanda's vision, making him skeptical of the idea of a fusion *(sliianie)* with the Russian people and putting him, as Brian Horowitz remarked in an article of 2004, "into an ideological cul-de-sac." After having been an avid proponent of the transformation of Russia's Jews into "Russians of Mosaic law," Levanda became a devotee of the Hibbat Zion (Love of Zion) movement. In his later essays, especially "The Essence of the So-Called 'Palestine' Movement (Letter to the Publishers)" (1884), Levanda discussed the emerging ideas of Jewish self-preservation *(samosokhranenie)* and self-assistance *(samopomoshch')* in keeping with the proto-Zionist position of Leon Pinsker (1821–1891) and his *Autoemancipation* (1882). Levanda's last testament was his essay "On Assimilation," published in the *Weekly Chronicle of Sunrise (Nedel'naia khronika Voskhoda,* 1885).

Levanda died in 1888, in a mental clinic. He was the best-known Jewish-Russian essayist and literary polemicist in the 1870s–80s, and his articulation of the most pressing issues made Levanda's fiction successful with Jewish-Russian readers. Shimon Markish called Levanda, along with **Osip Rabinovich**, a "founding father" of Jewish-Russian literature.

* * *

Written possibly as early as the mid-1860s, Lev Levanda's *Seething Times: A Novel from the Last Polish Uprising* was serialized in *The Jewish Library* in

1871–73; a separate revised book edition was issued in 1875 in St. Petersburg by *The Jewish Library*'s publisher, A. E. Landau. At the historical center of Levanda's colorful if artistically flawed novel lie the events of the Polish Uprising of 1863–64. Several of Levanda's other fictional works, a number of his essays, and his 1885 sketches *Wrath and Mercy of the Magnate* deal with Jewish life in the former Polish–Lithuanian Commonwealth. Recognition by contemporary Jewish historians, including John D. Klier and Brian Horowitz, underscores the novel's documentary value.

The uprising began as a protest against the conscription of Poles into the Imperial Army. The January 1863 manifesto issued by the Polish Provisional Government declared "all sons of Poland free and equal citizens without distinction of religion, condition, and estate," which theoretically applied to the Jews in the historically Polish lands. The insurgents, whose force of about 10,000 faced regular Russian troops of about 200,000, persisted with armed struggle. The uprising, in which some Jews fought on the side of the Polish rebels, was crushed by September 1864; Polish losses were estimated at 20,000 dead, with thousands of rebels deported to Siberia.

Spanning the period from the summer of 1861 through the summer of 1864, *Seething Times* is set partly in the city of G. (Grodno) and largely in the city of N., actually Vilna, both the Jerusalem of eastern Europe and a stronghold of Polish culture and national spirit. The Jews of the Northwestern Region are experiencing anxiety over their future and allegiance. One of the novel's characters, Jules Perets, wonders whether the liberated Poland would be "fairer toward us" [i.e., the Jews]. The travails of the Jewish intellectual Sarin, the privileged if schematic protagonist, reflect Levanda's opinion that Jews ought to be neutral in the Russian–Polish conflict while proceeding to acculturate after a Russian fashion. Pavel Lavrinets argued in 1999 that, in keeping with the conventions of the Russian "antinihilist novel" of the 1860s–70s, Sarin comes to realize that the future lies with Russia while seeing only "hypocrisy" in the Polish "courtship of the Jews," aimed at winning their support in the uprising against Russian rule.

In the words of Shimon Markish, despite a lack of both verisimilitude and an "organically unfolding fabula," *Seething Times* presents "a decisive answer to the question . . . what is a Jew to do who had chosen the path of enlightenment and realized his humiliating inequality." On the surface of it, the novel's thesis advocates Jewish civil and cultural allegiance with Russia, not Poland. However, there is enough polyphony and ambiguity in the novel to represent other perspectives and to show the existence of a degree of closeness among Polish-educated (or Western-educated) Jews and members of the Polish intelligentsia. As Brian Horowitz has argued, "by showing the political failures of Sarin, the author's ideological mouthpiece, and by drawing the Poles as fully developed characters as opposed to the one-dimensional Russians, Levanda subverts the positive message of Russification." Particularly fascinating is Levanda's depiction of amorous relations between Polish aristocrats and members of the Jewish intelligentsia (e.g., Vaclav Zaremba and Polina Krants; Julia Staszycka and Arkady Sarin), which serve to embody, through desire, the Jewish–Polish attraction and confrontation.

Seething Times does not yield itself well to excerpting, especially its thriller-paced sequences portraying the uprising. The excerpts below all come from the first of the novel's four parts. Titled "To the Right or to the Left?" it captures the Polish national upheaval of 1861 mainly through the eyes of the female protagonist, Sofia Aronson, and her circle of young Jewish women from privileged N. families. The narrative mode alternates between pages of Sofia Aronson's journal (chaps. 4, 7, 11, 16) and letters sent to their mutual Jewish acquaintance in N. by Arkady Sarin from G. (chap. 17) and to Sofia by her friend Mary Tidman (chap. 21). The text below follows the original serial publication of *Seething Times*, not the revised book edition.

FROM *SEETHING TIMES*

Part 1

IV

27 July

I could not have expected that the scene with Vaclav in the garden would get so deep inside my head.[2] [Vaclav's] words "Is not Panna[3] Sofia as much a Polish lady as you are?" have not left my memory now for several days. They distress me, for some reason persistently demanding my response. No matter what I apply myself to, the question is right there, waiting. It screens off everything

---

2 In this journal entry, Sofia Aronson is referring to her own birthday party, which took place six days earlier, on 21 July 1861. In addition to the members of her circle, young Jewish women and men educated after a western fashion, Sofia also invited her former Polish tutor, Izabella, who brought her cousin, Vaclav Zaremba; both Izabella and Vaclav made a philosemitic speech and a passionate, if self-serving, plea for Polish-Jewish unity.

3 *Panna* (Pol.) = Miss; *Pan* (Pol.) = Sir.

else I try to focus on. Why did this Vaclav pronounce such a phrase, which, most likely, will leave me restless for a long time? Did he know how much unrest he would introduce into my soul with this seemingly innocent phrase?

Who am I in fact? A Pole? I have received a predominantly Polish education. I studied at a Polish boarding school. My governesses were all Polish. I love Polish literature, my library collection consists of Polish books, and I am writing this journal also in Polish. But I feel that between me and a Polish lady there's a whole abyss; I have always felt that a Polish lady looks upon me as a *żydówka*,[4] and I look upon a Polish lady with the same feeling as a despised person does the one despising her, that is, with concealed malice. I have never been conscious of this feeling, but it has existed and exists nonetheless. I have had occasion to lose myself in Polish society, that is, to think and even to feel that I and *they* are the same, especially since I was also taken with their intelligentsia and understood the works of Polish literature not only no worse but actually better than many of the noble Polish ladies; but it would suffice for one word to be uttered, most likely without any unkind intention, by one of the *aristocrats*, it would suffice for one glance to be cast in my direction, one flattering but in truth tactless compliment, and I would wake up from my quick reverie only to feel, of course with pain in my heart, that I am one thing and all of them another, that, as the Jews say, I am dancing at the wrong wedding. No, I am not Polish and will never be Polish!

Who am I then, a German? But this does not make any sense whatsoever. The land we live on is not at all German land, and all our surroundings have nothing to do with things German. I know the German language, German literature, but this does not at all make me German, just as if I were to become a Chinese woman because I knew Chinese. I find Jules Perets laughable, he who has learned French and imagines himself to be a Frenchman, or John Berkovich, who has mastered English and contorts himself into a native Englishman. Messrs. Perets and Berkovich are, perhaps, good teachers of French and English, but what kind of Frenchman and Englishman are they! Just the same for me: although I know German, I find it difficult to imagine myself a German. Pretending to be one would be stupid and silly. I have always been amazed at the educated Jewish families where the entire domestic life has been fashioned after Germany. This would have made at least some sense if they themselves, or their near ancestors, had come from Germany; but no,

---

4 Żydówka (Pol.) = Jewess; Żyd (Pol.) = Jew; neither has the same pejorative as the Russian *zhidovka* or *zhid*.

they and their great-great-grandfathers were born here. Why then, on what grounds, do they make themselves into some sort of a German colony here, on Lithuanian soil? Of course one cannot blame them: there probably were, and still are, reasons for this, perhaps very important, legitimate ones. But their position is nevertheless false and at times even comical.

So then, what am I, a Jewess? Without a doubt. But day after day the meaning of this word gets narrower and narrower. Abroad, they say, this word now only refers to one's confession. In time, the same will probably happen here. But confession is only one part of life, not all of life. My mother, for instance, is a Jew, a complete, full Jew, by faith, notions, customs, feelings, hopes, and aspirations, while I am already only half, or even one-fourth of a Jew. So who am I in the remaining three-fourths of my being? Many Jewish women like me probably ask themselves the same question. We feel that the Jewish ground is getting narrower and narrower under our feet; we feel that it is becoming crowded and uncomfortable for us to stand on this ground. It will likely reach a point when we will not be able to be there. To whom should we attach ourselves?

So we attach ourselves, each of us as God allows, one to one people, another to another people. Mary [Tidman] is predominantly a German, and I am predominantly a Pole. Perets is French. Berkovich is English. Children of one tribe and one city, we have spread ourselves around different peoples. And this all happened by accident. Mary ended up in Riga by accident and came out of it a German woman; by accident I ended up at a Polish boarding school and emerged a Polish woman. Perets, I imagine, chanced upon a good textbook of French and felt that he could easily become a Frenchman, and Berkovich pretty much says that Robertson[5] and *The Vicar of Wakefield*[6] made him an Englishman.

This position is strange, abnormal, false, and unpleasant. In essence, Mary is not a German, I am not a Pole, Perets is not a Frenchman, and Berkovich is not an Englishman. In each of us there is only a fraction of that which we pretend to be. I am judging by myself. In analyzing my feelings, I discover that of all things Polish I love only Polish literature, and everything else is alien to me. I am indifferent toward the Poles, their destiny, their interests, and their homeland. Who is to blame? Is it I, who do not know how to love Poland, or they, who have not succeeded in teaching me this love? It is enough that it makes me

---

5 Perhaps William Robertson (1721–1793), prominent British eighteenth-century historian.
6 Best-known novel by Oliver Goldsmith, first published in 1776.

so sad to be asking myself the question "Who am I?" and not to be able to find a direct answer in my heart.

How happy our mothers were, who did not ask themselves such questions and wrack their brains over their resolution. They knew they were Jewish, and that was sufficient for them. . . .

VII

This morning I met Vaclav on the street.

"God himself has arranged our meeting," he continued after the usual greetings and inquiries about health. "Walking here, I thought of you."

"Might I be able to find out the reason for your thinking of me?" I asked.

"I wanted to convey to you an interesting piece of news," he replied, twisting his thin moustache.

"News, and even interesting news! That's very interesting. Speak without further delay."

"Aha! So you are curious as well!"

"Surely I am! Am I not Eve's daughter? Do please go on, do not torment me."

"Fine, I shall not. But allow me first to ask if you read newspapers."

"No," I replied. "What is the use in reading them, particularly for women?"

"You at least find out what happens in the whole wide world."

"In the whole wide world everything happens without us," I objected.

"How could it be without us?" Vaclav asked, hurt. "Not angels, but people do everything in the world, the same kinds of creatures as us. It stands to reason that we, too, can do something—and we shall do it. Please believe me that we shall do it and do it well! The sky will be feeling the heat!"

"Oh, Jesus and Mary! How terrifying!" I said jokingly, wringing my arms.

"Have you the pleasure of joking, Panna Sofia?" Vaclav remarked with reproach.

"Why then are you tormenting me? Where is the news you promised?"

"Here it is," he said, removing from his side pocket a folded issue of a Polish newspaper. "In here you will find, marked with a red pencil, an article that I recommend you read carefully."

"And who is the author of this article, not Pan Vaclav Zaremba by any chance?" I asked slyly.

"I don't know," he replied with an author's modesty. "It is unsigned."

"Never mind. I promise to read it with great attention."

"And if you like it," Vaclav added, "then please do read it to your girlfriends, and especially the ones whom I had the good fortune of meeting at your birthday party."

"And to Panna Polina Krants?" I asked suggestively.

"Naturally," he responded, blushing and starting to bid me adieu.

Upon returning home, I pored over the newspaper. The article marked with a pencil was a long contribution from our city, in which—whoever would have expected it!—the celebration of my birthday was described with all the details and in such colors! Names were not revealed, only identified with initials. Even conversations, even jokes were not forgotten. Pan Vaclav must have an excellent memory and also must be quite observant. At the forefront is, of course, Panna P.[7] He calls her now a "pearl in an eastern princess's diadem," now the "main flower in the arrangement." The correspondent comments with delight on our pure Polish pronunciation, our purely Polish *dowcip*.[8] But even more than by the article itself, I was struck by the following editorial commentary:

> In this interesting article, which, we hope, every good Pole will read with contentment, the unharmonious word *starozakonni*[9] has unpleasantly struck our ears. Does not our esteemed contributor know that we do not have and should not have *starozakonni* but only *Poles of Mosaic persuasion*? If he does not know, then be it known to him and to all *those who ought to know*, that the word *starozakonny* is as old as are those harmful prejudices that we must repudiate forever if we want to go apace with the century, if we want the enlightened world to be with us and not against us. Do you understand, brothers of ours in Poland, Lithuania, Volhynia, and Podolia? . . . If you obstinately persecute an honest man with the label "thief," he will become a thief, not because of his nature but through your doing. If you continue to call Israelites Yids, *starozakonni*, they will never become Poles. We do not intend here to enter into an inquest about which of you are right and which are wrong. Maybe they are at fault, but maybe we ourselves are even more at fault than they

---

7   Polina Krants, Sofia Aronson's friend who, in their Vilna circle of young Jewish women and men, is most taken with Polish patriotism.

8   *Dowcip* (Pol.) = wit.

9   *Starozakonny* (sing.), *starozakonni* (pl.) (Pol.; cf. Rus. *starozakonnyi*) = lit. "of the old law"; a traditional supersessionist Polish-Catholic reference to the Jews ("those of the Old Testament").

are. We nullify the old scores and extend our hands to them in *zgoda, jedność, braterstwo*.[10] Those to whom we feed our bread must not be and cannot be our enemy. Jews are a historical people, tremendously capable and energetic, not a crowd of gypsies but a civilized society with a significant culture. In them there is an abyss of patriotic feelings. The proof is their two-thousand-year-long attachment to their former fatherland, religion, customs. If we succeed in taking advantage of this feeling, we shall not lose. If we make this land a second Palestine for them, they will go through fire to lay down their lives for it, they will shed their blood for it. With what self-sacrifice, worthy of imitation, did they defend their holy city from the victorious Roman legions! Read Josephus Flavius, and you will be convinced of how much military valor, courage, and fearlessness this people had. Reaching our hands out to today's Israelites, we extent our hands not to the heirs of the despicable Russians or to the traitors of their fatherland but to the successors of brave *knights*, defeated only by the will of Providence. *Sapienti sat* . . .[11]

It is difficult for me to express in words what I felt when I read these fiery lines. My heart began to pound. . . . My head was spinning. . . . I kept reading and rereading it, and I could not believe my eyes. . . . A language completely new to me. . . . It arouses my blood. . . . I am all atremble. . . . And a Pole saying this? And he is not joking, not teasing? . . . Go away, doubts! . . . I want to believe, I want to love! . . . Cannot we indeed grow to love our motherland the way our ancestors loved Palestine? Yes we can! A thousand times we can! . . . Are we monsters of some kind? We are "successors of brave knights, defeated only by the will of Providence"! Does this mean we have not always been greedy buyers and sellers, spendthrifts, egoists? Give us a chance to love, and we will not be calculating everything in cold blood. Do you think we enjoy not loving anything, not belonging anywhere, always feeling ourselves among strangers? The old generation may have found pleasure in this, but it burdens us, the young. Belonging to our people alone does not satisfy us; we do not find in it that which our parents did. Our needs are entirely different. . . . They must be satisfied. So satisfy them! Do not push us away with words, glances, for we so morbidly understand your words and glances. Give us a fatherland, give us a nationhood! . . . We are loathe to be Germans on Polish soil. . . . I want to be, must be, and can

---

10 *Zgodna, jedność, braterstwo* (Pol.) = concord, unity, brotherhood.
11 *Sapient sat* (Lat.) = [This] will suffice for the intelligent.

be a Polish woman. A Pole just like my fellow countrywomen! . . . Do you hear what your elder brother is telling you? "If we succeed in taking advantage of this feeling, we shall not lose. If we make this land a second Palestine for them, they will go through fire to lay down their lives for it, they will shed their blood for it." Yes. We shall show you that a Jewess can be no less of a patriot than an aristocratic Polish lady. And woe be unto you if you take away from us the chance to love our fatherland the way you love it! . . .

My hand trembles . . . I cannot go on . . .

XI

14 August

The city has put on mourning. This, as they say, is mourning for our fatherland. In cathedrals they sing hymns. The Poles demand that the Jews also wear mourning, which means we have a common cause. Poland is our common fatherland. All of us are called to its defense. We shall all go, we must go. We must not spare any sacrifices. How sweet it is to have a fatherland, to love it, to worry about it, to shed tears and blood for it. Our old ones never knew this feeling, but they also did not know many other things; times were different. The old ones say things used to be better, but I believe they were worse. A meaningless attitude toward life might be healthier, but it humiliates one. Yes, such an attitude toward life is actually impossible, unimaginable in our times. Our times push us forth; they do not let us lose track of time or meaninglessly stare around. Thank God, the wheel of time has caught us Jews at last. We cannot stay forever behind the onward-moving procession. Where the Poles go, we go also. In a society of living beings, we might be resurrected, especially since we are not quite dead yet. . . .

I have just received a note from Polina. She writes: "Poland, enslaved and oppressed, stretches out to us her motherly embrace. Let us hasten to press ourselves to her love-giving breast. She is crying; let us dry her tears, rejoice along with her, our wet nurse! Have you read the proclamation addressed to us? Today we received it in the mail. Father, after reading it, wanted to rip it up, but I did not let him.[12] It is in my possession. Tomorrow I will bring it to you. Tomorrow my dress will be ready. Today I shall not go out—I do not want to

---

12 In earlier chapters, Levanda describes how the fathers of these young Jewish women, especially Sofia Aronson's and Polina Krants's fathers, reacted with skepticism and hostility to the Polish overtures toward the Jews. "Let them do what they want, but we are not their companions," Sofia's father says in chapter 11. "We shall pray to God for our present tsar [Alexander II], who is merciful to us, and Poland . . . Let it rebel, to its own detriment."

appear in the streets in colorful garb. It is uncouth for us to lag behind our sisters of Catholic persuasion. By the way, invite over all our girlfriends and close acquaintances tomorrow. We shall read to them the paper and the proclamation. We must now act in concord.

Out motto: "Long live Poland!"

XVI

31 August

The whole city has not stopped talking about the great honor Countess Staszycka bestowed upon us in the public garden.[13] Acquaintances have been congratulating us and asking about details of that stroll [in the garden]. Many cannot believe that Countess Staszycka, that proud Polish aristocrat, would forget herself to such an extent as to stroll in public almost arm in arm with young Jewish women. Many see in this most significant fact a great change for the better for us Jews. Yet many treat this fact with skepticism. "Deception! Fakery!" they say. "Poles will not love us; all this fraternization with Jews is but a comedy, politics. They seek our friendship because they have been ordered to do so from Warsaw and Paris. In their hearts they still hate us and detest us as always. Poles are very cunning and adept at pretending."

On whose side is the truth? O God! Can people really be so false? What good would it do for the Poles to deceive us? Why cannot they love us sincerely? What good would it do for them and for us to hate each other? . . . No, this is not deception, not fakery! . . . Go away, you miserable thought!

Many of our other girlfriends, on whom the honor of Countess Staszycka's graces has not been bestowed, envy and disparage us. M-lle Zakman, for example, is beside herself and is acting sulky. Such a fool! How can she not understand that the countess has shed her grace through us onto all of Jewish youth, which includes her as well?

What is good in this whole occurrence is that M-lle Zakman and many other young Jewish women have finally understood a need to know Polish, the study of which they have now seriously taken up. Thank God! They have finally heard reason. To be Polish women at least of some kind in our region [i.e., the Nothwestern region] makes much more sense than to contort ourselves into Germans. I have recently referred five new students to Panna

---

13 Countess Julia Staszycka, a wealthy and influential aristocrat and one of the leaders of the city's pro-independence movement.

Izabella. Yesterday, when we met, she informed me that her new students are making incredibly rapid progress in the Polish language. She cannot praise their diligence, their intelligence enough. If it were up to me, I would make it obligatory for all Jews to learn Polish. Without the Polish language we shall never understand and come to love each other. Language is the first step in the rapprochement of peoples.

It is strange that Jews do not understand this or do not wish to understand. Even my father has a very strange perspective on the Polish language. The other day he put it to me directly that he was very sorry I had been taught Polish, and he would be very happy if I did not know this language. He said this to me in connection with my account of the encounter [with Countess Staszycka] in the public garden. I thought he would be glad for me, but it turned out the other way around. He furrowed his eyebrows and advised me to try to avoid Polish company, as such company, in his opinion, would not lead to anything good.

And Polina has had to endure a more tempestuous scene with her father and even her brother. There they could not do without screaming, threats, and even tears. "You want to bring yourself down and me as well!" old Krants screamed. "I will put you on a chain; I will banish you to a small town," and so on.

Even intelligent old people sometimes hold very strange beliefs.

I have just received a note from Izabella, who has invited Polina and me to her birthday party. I have almost forgotten that her birthday is the day after tomorrow. I must prepare a present.

XVII

Arkady Sarin to Morits Mozyrsky[14]

G., 2 September 1861

. . . So, where you are, everything is sleeping like the dead and no trumpet's blare has managed to awaken you? Does this mean that everything is well with all of you? Lucky you! It is as though you were living in Arcadia. And we, for some reason, have been unable to sleep, and how can we sleep now? Everything around us is stirring, bustling, making noises. All across

---

14 Arkady Sarin, a teacher and a charismatic leader of a circle of young Jewish people, advancing a program of cultural Russification in G. (Grodno), is writing to his friend Morits Mozyrsky in N. (Vilna), where Sarin is soon to be transferred. This letter is one of the novel's most famous and programmatic episodes.

the expanse of Russia a general breakage is taking place, from above and from below. A breakage of old ideas, obsolete principles, petrified institutions and customs eroding the flesh. Noise, cracking sounds, and rattling. Everything hurries to renew and purify itself, everything strives ahead, toward something new, heretofore unseen, almost unexpected. Even our coreligionists have gotten on their feet and are ready to go. . . . Except they still do not know where. Are the pleasing calls of the trumpet reaching you from the south? It appears not, because from your city no response has followed. Please tell me, for God's sake, could it be that the incredible noise of all that is happening has not reached your ears? Have the past five years really rushed over your heads completely without a trace? Could it be that your thirty-thousand-strong community is still the same disorganized, unflustered, and lazy mass we knew five, ten years ago?[15] Are the activities of your sated ones still limited to nothing more than their afternoon walk? Do your hungry still expect manna to fall from the sky—or yet another Old Testament miracle? Do your petty capitalists still consider themselves candidates to succeed Rothschild and your mean bankrupts, clever entrepreneurs? Do your learned still think they are unrecognized geniuses, and do your littérateurs still dream of resurrecting the Jewish tongue through their rhymed gibberish? Do your women still imagine themselves to be Germans by origin and marquises by manner? Do your maidens still dream of ardent love and marry in keeping with a no less ardent attraction to pockets stuffed full of money? Is your newly fashionable prayer house, which held so much promise at its founding, still as rich in promises alone? Do your progressives still stand in the rear, waiting for a bomb of some sort to push them forward? In a word, is your community still dwelling in munificence, as the Israelites did in the days of Solomon, not worrying about anything and not knowing anything?

But please know that the times are coming, *seething times*, when your vineyards and fig trees will no longer offer shade and relief to those resting beneath them. A time is coming when they will demand of us, with a knife pressed to our throats, a categorical answer to the questions: "Who are you? What are you? Who do you stand for? Whose side are you on?" In the Polish camp something serious is in the making, and it smells of blood. For a year now some fermenting has been visible in it. It was just not known what it would burst into. Now this

---

15 Sarin's number is fairly accurate for Vilna's Jewish population; at the time of the novel's publication, Vilna's Jews constituted about 38,000, or about 46 percent, of the city's total population.

fermenting is making itself clearer and clearer. The centuries-old domestic quarrel enters the stage again. We do not know when the battle will begin, but we do know that this battle will be to the death. This battle will, one way or another, touch us as well. We have been getting rather transparent hints in this regard. The Poles have been sniffing around, courting us, perchance we could be tempted, since we have also not been living too freely under the Russian law. They sense in us or presuppose a spirit hostile to Moscow, and this is why we come handy to them. A population of two million with a significant economic position is indeed no joking matter. They have sized us up pretty well. What is silly is that they have come to their senses too late. But we know that *Polak mądry po szkodzie....*[16] Therefore, it is not our fault that reason only paid them a visit a few days ago. And do you know what is going on in Warsaw? Since 1831 we have grown older by thirty years.[17] They now regard us as adults. They count on us, appeal to us. And so, have you figured out already where we should turn, *to the right* or *to the left*? Do not forget that the future of our tribe rests on this decision. This means that it would be worth your while to wrack your brains over this decision.

We here have thought and decided to go to the right, to stick to Moscow. Our instinct, considerations, and, finally, sense of gratitude lead us there. We must never forget that *barbaric* Russia, not *civilized* Poland, first started to concern itself with our education and upbringing. We owe to Russia, not Poland, the awakening of our self-consciousness. Emperor Nicholas I was for us Jews in some ways what Peter I was for the Russians. What has Prince Czartoryski[18] done for our education? For him we did not exist at all. But we did exist for Count Uvarov;[19] he selected us for Russian education; he did a lot for us, and he *wanted* to do even more. We must not forget it and shall not forget it.

---

16 Sarin, whose knowledge of Polish might be less perfect than his command of Russian, seems to misquote slightly the expression "*Mądry Polak po szkodzie,*" which may be translated as "A Pole is wise after the damage is done."

17 Sarin is referring to the Polish Uprising of 1830–31 (the November Uprising) against Russian rule.

18 Prince Adam Czartoryski (1770–1861), a descendant of Polish-Lithuanian royalty, was a prominent associate of Tsar Alexander I during the early years of his rule and served as the Russian foreign minister in 1803–1806. Czartoryski was intrumental in obtaining the 1815 Polish Constitution at the Congress of Vienna. After the Polish Uprising of 1830–31, during which he headed the Polish Provisional Government, Czartoryski fled to France, where his Paris home became a center of the Polish independence movement.

19 Count Sergey Uvarov (1786–1855)—Russia's minister of education in 1833–49; see introductions to **Lev Levanda** and to **Leon Mandelstam**.

Poland has given us neither fatherland nor nationhood—what should we love in her? Having given us shelter, Poland has turned us into a horde of petty traders, which she badly needed, so let her now look for patriotism in this horde. She will not find it? Of course not, and it would be odd if she were to find it. What you have not sown, you will not reap. We will perhaps have more luck with Russia. Having received from her the key to education, we shall, God willing, unlock Russian nationhood, a Russian sense of citizenship, a Russian fatherland with this key. . . . True, they do not much favor us in Russia either. But my heart tells me that in time the Russians will love us.[20] We shall *force* them to love us! With what?—With love itself. The Russian nation is a healthy, happy nation, and in a healthy nation there is more love, more benevolence, and, finally, more intelligence than in a languishing, miserable, dying tribe. The Poles *cannot* love us:

> That heart will never learn to love,
> Which has grown tired of loathing and hating.[21]

Poland has done nothing but hate: the aristocracy hated the common folk; the common folk, the aristocracy; and both hated other Slavs, Russians, Swedes, Germans. Why should she start to practice loving on us Jews? . . . History moves in mysterious ways. It is quite possible that the Poles will emerge victorious from the upcoming struggle. In that case we who have not sided with their banner will have it tough. I suppose they would not be opposed to annihilating us completely. Well, so be it: this way we shall once and for all end our impossible existence. I experience hellish torments each time I think that I am like a dog without a master, forlornly wandering the streets without anybody to love, to be loyal to, to show tenderness for. Such a dog, have you noticed, has even lost the habit of barking, because he has nothing to guard, nobody to protect. He walks silently and indifferently by a nighttime thief creeping into a sleeping peasant hut. "Let him steal, what do I care? Whereas if I find a bone, I will gnaw on it and be sated. I need no more than that."

I am sick and tired of being such a stray, free-roaming dog, and that is why I am very happy to decide once and for all who we are and with whom we are.

---

20 Compare the ending of **Ruvim Kulisher**'s *An Answer to the Slav* (1849) in this anthology.

21 The last two lines of the fifth and final quatrain of the poem "Grow quiet now, Muse of revenge and sorrow . . ." (1855) by the major Russian poet Nikolay Nekrasov (1821–1877). Concluding Nekrasov's 1856 collection of poetry, this poem was perceived by his contemporaries as being both a new manifesto and a boundary marker in Nekrasov's life and creative work.

In determining the centuries-long strained relations between the Poles and the Russians, this struggle will also determine our ambiguous position amid these two peoples. Neither the Poles nor the Russians will let us get away with such phrases as "we do not know, we do not understand," because now we must *know*, we must *understand*.

Do you know, do you understand, my dear Morits, and you, my treasured comrades in arms? . . . Beware that approaching events do not catch you by surprise. Stand guard, be vigilant. The education we have received, and our calling of the people's mentors and therefore leaders of the young generation, commit us to go consciously where we ought to go and not where the blowing wind would push the senseless crowd . They look at us as at the vanguard, and thus we must go onward, to a specific goal, firmly, consciously; they will not forgive us any spineless deviations to the side.

XXI

[Mary Tidman to Sofia Aronson][22]

G., 12 September 1861

Just imagine, chére Sophie, I have been taking Russian lessons. You did not expect it? I also did not expect it. And this is, indeed, strange: I wear mourning for the *Polish* fatherland and study the *Russian* language! But what else was I supposed to do? Sarin insisted, coaxed, and so did Mrs. Lipman; I could not refuse and agreed to acquaint myself with the Russian language, which, as you know, until recently I had not been able to bear. Sarin reassures me that in due time I will grow to love both the Russian language and Russian literature. Do you hear this, *literature*? The Russians have literature! A completely new discovery for us, is it not? From translations we know that Spanish literature exists, even Swedish literature, even Persian, but to suppose that there is Russian literature—this we never suspected, or at least I had never heard of it in Riga. If I did not know Sarin to be a very serious person, one who does not allow himself to say something untrue, even jokingly, I would think he was making a joke in order to mystify me. But since Sarin is talking about Russian literature, then such a thing must exist in the world, and now I am burning with impatience to get to know this thing as quickly as possible. This impatience of mine slightly

---

22 After her father lost his fortune, Mary Tidman left N. (Vilna) to live with her aunt's family in G. (Grodno).

sweetens the tedium of the first lessons. My God, what words! What letters! My teeth start aching from pronouncing them, as if I were nibbling on rocks. Sarin says this is from unfamiliarity. Perhaps, but that does not make me feel any better. But without the Russian language, as Sarin says, I would not be of use to the circle of which I have the honor to be a part, since all the business, all the correspondence of our circle is conducted in Russian. Besides, since I live here, I cannot lag behind the locals—*mit den Wölfen muss man heulen*.[23] All the local young Jewish women know Russian and gladly use this language. I cannot just sit with them and stare with incomprehension.

A few days ago I had the following conversation with Sarin:

"To whom are you handing over command?" I asked, half-seriously, half-jokingly.

"In our circle there has never been and can never be a command," he replied. "Besides the idea we serve, we do not accept any power over us, any personal will. We, all of us, are fellow workers at the same factory: one does one thing, another does something else, and from our common work something whole emerges, more or less in keeping with the plan we put together. Even as I depart I do not cease to belong to the local artel. I am only changing my place of residence, not my mode of operation."

"So this means you will not cut off your ties with us?"

"So this means you have not familiarized yourself enough with the spirit of our circle if you can ask me such a question. No matter where destiny casts me or any one of us, we will not stop working for as long as we have strength, in the spirit of our defined program."

"What is this program?" I asked.

"Our program is to pull our coreligionists from the bewitched circle into which unfavorable circumstances have thrust them and to place them on a course toward becoming citizens of Russia. In a word: our program is to make Jews into Russians."

"Why Russians and not Germans?" I asked, a bit frightened by the circle's program. "Do you not acknowledge that German civilization is incomparably higher than Russian?"

"We could not care less which civilization is higher," he replied. "For now we are talking not about civilization but nationhood, that is, spirit and language. We live in Russia, and therefore we must be Russians."

---

23 (Ger.) = literally: "When with wolves, one must howl," meaning that one must learn to adapt to a hostile environment.

"What will the Poles say?"

"The Poles have already had their say. Their entire past policies toward us have proved that it is not desirable to them that we be Poles."

"But are they not singing a totally different song now?" "What they sing now they should have sung at least one hundred years ago. Then it would have made sense. And now we have no use for their swan song; it touches us like the voice of a dying man, but it does not compel us to lie down into the grave next to Poland as it passes away into eternity. Destiny has ordained for us to live, and this is why we must and shall live. We shall live and sing: Do we want to be Russians?"

"But what happens if your new song does not find a response with the Russians as well?" I asked.

"This cannot be," he replied firmly.

"Why?"

"Because the Russian nation is no fool, and also we should not jump too far ahead of ourselves. Let us try—trying is not a crime."

"But what if your attempt fails, that is, what if it proves that the Russians also do not want to know you? What then?"

"Then . . . ," Sarin began, slightly pensively, "then we know what will happen. But why such skepticism? If you think it will shake our determination, you are mistaken. We are very firm in our hopes and convictions, firmer than you think, especially since we have had no reason to doubt them. We are convinced that we can become Russians, and therefore we must strive for it with all that is in our power. We are doing our job, so you do the job you have been entrusted with: learn Russian! We have so far not asked more of you, but not for anything in the world would we free you of the little you have already promised us. Study Russian—and *basta!*"

How do you like such despotism? They have simply enslaved me. I do not have a choice now: I *must* study Russian because I gave them my word.

P.S. Sarin is leaving in a few days. I shall give him a letter for you. This will give you the opportunity to meet him. I hope you two will get along well.

1860s

Translated from the Russian by Maxim D. Shrayer

Lev Levanda, *Goriachee vremia*. English translation, introduction, and notes copyright © by Maxim D. Shrayer.

GRIGORY BOGROV

Grigory Bogrov (Beharav, Bagrov) (1825–1885), fiction writer, memoirist, and essayist, was born in Poltava, a Ukrainian provincial capital, to a rabbi's family. His father, revered by the local Jewish community as a tzaddik, left scholarly notes on astronomy. From childhood, Bogrov received rigorous Talmudic training, while at the same time developing a passion for Russian, which he taught himself, hiding Russian books from his parents because he feared punishment. After his marriage at the age of seventeen, Bogrov lived separately and pursued the study of Russian, German, and French as well as music. Bogrov spent the 1850s–60s serving as a government tax farmer, underwhelmed intellectually, surrounded by provincial civil servants and businessmen, and unhappy in his first marriage.

In 1863 he composed the three opening chapters of what would become his famous memoir, *Notes of a Jew*, set in the 1830s–40s. Bogrov unsuccessfully sought a publisher for a number of years, until Nikolai A. Nekrasov (1821–1878), editor of the esteemed review *Notes of the Fatherland* (*Otechestvennye zapiski*), opted to print the chapters. Sharing some of the populist rhetoric on the Jewish question of the 1860s, the poet, nobleman, and liberal Nekrasov was given to imagining ubiquitous Jewish tentacles on the innocent communal body of the Russian people. Nekrasov serialized Bogrov's entire memoir—about one thousand pages total—in his journal in 1871–73. It was the first time that a Jewish author had contributed such a vast text to a leading mainstream Russian publication, a text that provided not only a broad panorama of Jewish life in the Pale of Settlement but also a wealth of anthropologically valuable explanations and footnotes. *Notes of a Jew* was favorably received by the Russian press and public and was known in western Europe through the 1880 German translation, *Memorien eines Juden*. An English translation of the entire memoir would be a welcome edition. Following the success of his memoir and the novel *The Captive* (1873), Bogrov moved to St. Petersburg and devoted himself to writing. Among his other works of the 1870s, besides *The Captive* (Hebrew trans., *Hanilkad*, 1877), were the historical novel *Jewish Manuscript: Before the Drama* (1876; Hebrew trans., *Ketav-Yad Ivri*, 1900), set in Ukraine during the Bohdan Khmelnitsky rebellion (1648–54), and several shorter works, such as the short stories "The Mad Woman," "The Vampire," and "Who Is to Be Blamed?"

In St. Petersburg Bogrov came in contact with Jewish-Russian authors and participated in the editing of the Jewish-Russian periodicals *The Russian Jew* (*Russkii evrei*) and *Dawn* (*Rassvet*) and in his latter years served as a contributor to—and one of the coeditors of—the magazine *Sunrise* (*Voskhod*). His complex position was powerfully expressed in an 1878 letter to Lev Levanda: "In the broad sense of the term, I am an *emancipated* cosmopolitan [Bogrov's italics]. If Jews in Russia were not subjected to such abuse and systematic persecution, I would perhaps cross over to the other shore, where alternative sympathies and alternative ideals smile at me. But my fellow members of the [Jewish] nation, actually four million people, suffer without guilt—can a decent person wave off such an injustice?" Bogrov spoke out against anti-Jewish discrimination while advocating the abandonment of Talmudic mores and favoring rapid acculturation. In his novel *Maniac* (1884), he even crudely satirized the proto-Zionist Hibbat Zion (Love of Zion) movement. Yet in his novel *Scum of the Century* (1879–81), he wrote compassionately of traditional Jewish values and derided "superficial assimilation" (Shimon Markish's expression). Not long before his death, Bogrov published the essay "Of Mixed Marriages," adumbrating his own apostasy. Several months prior to his death, he converted to Russian Orthodoxy in order to marry a Christian woman with whom he had been living. He died in Derevki, Minsk Province, in 1885.

Jews have accused Bogrov of contempt for centuries-old Jewish life; Russian antisemites have quoted Bogrov's *Notes of a Jew* in support of their arguments. Bogrov's belletristic recollections of his childhood and youth may strike a vigilant Jewish reader as bordering on hatred of one's past self and origins. At the same time, blaming the Jewish victims for their own victimization hardly seems to have been an objective of Bogrov's work. In his dry and analytical prose, Bogrov superbly articulated the anxieties of acculturated Russian Jews of the 1860s, who were suspended between past and present, tradition and modernity, the forbidding Talmud and the slithery promises of conversion.

FROM *NOTES OF A JEW*

Childhood Sufferings

Part 1, Chapter 2*

There is nothing duller than attending the birth of the hero of a story and fussing over him until the commencement of his conscious life. Not wishing to bore my readers for no special reason, I will pass over my first seven years and turn immediately to the time when I became dimly conscious of myself and of the bitter fate that has burdened me my entire life. If Jews attain moral maturity unusually early, they owe that unnatural precociousness to the merciless blows that fortune deals them from their earliest youth. Misery is the best instructor.

My first seven years are not particularly interesting. I suppose my mother loved me a great deal, although I often felt the weight of her heavy hand on my feeble body. My father was always strict and serious; he almost never hugged me, though at the same time he never hit me. [. . .]

We lived in the countryside, in a deep forest. Some cottages, some huts, the ever-smoking distillery in the distance, a rivulet winding through tall pines, horned cattle, boars grown fat on the waste from the distillery, eternally grimy peasant men and women—that picture is etched in my memory and has not faded to this day. [. . .]

Once I turned five, an assistant of my father's, a gangly Jew, began to teach me the Hebrew alphabet. How I hated my teacher and his notebook! But I was afraid of my strict father and sat at my writing for hours, although the sun shone so brightly in the yard, the pretty little birds chirped so merrily, and I so wanted to run away and dive into the thicket of tall, succulent grass!

I turned seven. I was already reading the language of the Bible fairly fluently. My gangly teacher had passed on almost all that he knew. I was proud of my learning and very happy. But what happiness is ever solid or long-lasting?

One truly beautiful summer day, my father returned from town. Seeing him from afar, I grew suddenly bold and ran to meet him. He ordered the young coachman to stop.

"Srulik! Do you want to ride up to the house with me?"

Instead of answering, I clambered onto the wagon. My father's tenderness surprised and delighted me—it was so rare.

---

*   The text has been slightly abridged

"And Srulik, I brought you a new outfit and shoes!"

Knowing nothing of the custom of thanking people for attention, I just looked at my father and smiled joyously.

How happy I was that day! I was free of the teacher, I had a new outfit, my father was paying attention to me, my mother kissed me so often, and no one kicked me that whole long day! [...]

Three days later, they put me sobbing into the wagon. My father sat down next to me. The boy Tryoshka, in his ill-fitting deep astrakhan hat, made a smacking sound, shook his long stick, and we were off on our long journey. "Don't cry, my poor Srulik," my mother, sobbing no less than me, repeated for the hundredth time. "Soon I'll come to you, or I'll bring you home!"

My father did not even try to comfort me. He knew what he was doing, and that was enough for him. How I hated him then!

Nothing amused me during the journey. My father was deep in thought or else dozing, and I tried to divine my future. Where was I going? And why? What would I do there? And as for the old dragon, the witch—as my mother called her—would she beat me often? My thoughts were heavy and sad. My childish mind imagined a new, unknown world, full of sorrow, sadness, boredom, suffering. And the instinct of a child did not betray me.

Shaken up, spent, and exhausted, we arrived one cloudy evening in P. For the first time in my life, I saw a series of straight streets, bordered with wooden sidewalks and tall poplars, through which I saw big, clean, beautiful houses. For the first time I saw well-dressed people sauntering back and forth. I felt frightened in this new world; I suppose I felt like a country dog brought to a market square bustling with a crowd of unfamiliar people: it thinks each of these people is busy only in order to hit it as deftly as possible.

Eventually we turned from one of these wide streets onto an alley and finally stopped at a broken-down gate. My father went into the courtyard. Right past the gate, a small clean house stood out facing the alley. Could it be, I wondered, that an old witch lives in that pretty house? [...]

However modestly my parents lived in the country, however little I was used to luxury and every comfort, at least at home I was used to cleanliness and order, to unbroken if simple pieces of furniture. Here I saw something completely different.

The room was fairly big and irregularly shaped. Two wide-open doors on the sides, leading into dark spaces, reminded me of the open mouths of toothless old men. The room was lit by a single tallow candle end placed in a tall dusty copper candlestick. The furniture consisted of a simple table, three or four unpainted chairs, and a low cupboard. In the eastern corner was a small ark covered by a faded brocade cloth.

A stooped old Jew sat at the table in front of an enormous open book. When we entered, he slowly lifted his head and lazily turned it toward us. I met his eyes meekly and was startled by his face. Under a pair of bushy gray brows I saw gray eyes. Almost his whole face was covered by his long thick *peyes*[24] and beard; what was not covered by growth was ashy yellow. Innumerable wrinkles traced his flat brow. A faded, soiled, velveteen yarmulke on the back of his head made a greasy, dirty spot on his bald skull.

"Well, sit down, Reb Zelman, you are welcome here," he greeted my father in a hoarse, guttural voice. "Ah, so this is your kid? Looks like a weak little thing ... What has he been taught at home?"

"He can read the Bible a bit, but nothing else yet."

"That's very little, very little; you'll have to work hard, kid! You can't be lazy here; I don't spoil anyone."

I kept quiet, but a sob caught in my throat. It took all my child's willpower not to start wailing. I would undoubtedly have failed but for another person who darted in through one of the side doors and caught my attention. I saw a stooped, wrinkled, small old woman with a face like a soaked apple, eyes small and black like thorns, no trace of eyelashes, and a nose like the beak of the most bloodthirsty bird of prey.

"There you are, Zelman! Thank God!" the old woman said in an unpleasant treble. "I'd already concluded that you changed your mind about bringing your little boy?"

"Why did you think so, auntie?" my father asked.

"God knows what kind of people you are! Your Rebecca is such a fashion plate that she may have decided it's not necessary to have her son educated." [...]

"My dear auntie," my father said with a conciliatory smile, "let's not quarrel the first time we all meet."

During this whole unpleasant scene, I seemed not even to exist; they had completely forgotten about me. Finally, the nasty old woman noticed me, seemingly by accident.

"Aha! That's your son? He looks so delicate! He must have been raised on gingerbread! If I'd known he was so sickly, I'd never have agreed to take on such

---

24 *Peyes* (Yiddish) = sidecurls.

a burden. He could get sick and die, and I'll be held responsible. Come here, kid," Leah called me in the most commanding of tones.

I went to her unwillingly and timidly. She took my chin in her dry wrinkled hand and roughly raised my head.

"Are you spoiled? Huh? Tell the truth, kid. You watch out here . . . By God, I don't spoil anyone; I don't tolerate any nonsense around here." [. . .]

The reception we were given presaged nothing good. It was hard to sleep, but physical and emotional exhaustion brought me into that deep slumber that children attain after crying for an hour.

The next morning my father turned over my few belongings, gave me a few silver coins, said an unusually tender farewell, and left. I was now alone.

From that day I began to go to the heder (school), where my stern guardian and teacher ruled despotically. The heder was in a shack that my uncle rented from a poor Jewish woman. We studied in a low, dim room with sooty walls and a gigantic stove with a shelf on top. That shelf was our oasis in the desert: there we huddled in the dim light and rested; there we ate the provisions that each of us had brought; there we told frightening tales about dead people and witches; there we made merry. As soon as the thin one-kopeck tallow candle was lit and a light pierced the darkness of the shelf, we jumped down; the light was a signal to gather around the table and bend again threefold over our books until late at night. We followed this same routine every day. The numbing monotony lay on our souls like a dead weight, with no distraction, not a minute of rest during the entire day; how nice it would have been to run around, how we wanted to stretch our aching limbs!

There were about fifteen of us students. We lived more or less in harmony and friendship. The Jewish heder is an unusual kind of school, where all the students are equally intimidated, equally timid, equally scared, equally suffocated by the dreadful power of the teacher, who punished us at whim and was partial to no one. A kind of fellow feeling developed among the heder students, as among prisoners taken together to captivity and put in the same cell. The more the melamed (teacher) persecuted any one of the students, the more affinity the other students felt for this student. Then again, the lucky one who was the teacher's favorite and suffered less from his cruelty would awaken envy, expressed in open enmity, from his classmates. This trait is so deeply etched into the Jewish character from childhood that it does not leave him even when he and his fellow heder students enter adult society. A Jew would give his last shirt to his suffering fellow, share his last piece of bread with him in a time of trouble but is suffused with poisonous envy and malice when his fellow Jew succeeds. He is prepared to destroy the other's happiness with his own hand, at no benefit to himself, just to bring him down to the same level. For the Jew, fate is just such a vile, fickle melamed.

My teacher was pleased with me: I did my lessons dutifully and, thanks to my fair memory, could translate the Bible into Yiddish[25] fairly fluently. I acknowledged, however, that I understood nothing at all of what I was saying: I was a parrot. It didn't matter, so long as he was satisfied. I did get the occasional kick, pinch, or slap, which I soon learned to endure stoically. In our heder we thought it dishonorable to cry over such trifles. There were stoics among us who smiled with tears in their eyes after being dealt a deafening slap. Contempt for the teacher's bony hands was our revenge.

Of all my fellow students I became closest to a poor, pale, blue-eyed boy named Erukhim. I was charmed by his kindness, tenderness, and sincerity. I loved him as my own brother, and we shared everything that weighed on our hearts. My life became much more bearable once we had become close. Now I had a modest, understanding, and kind friend to whom I related all my feelings and complained about the fate that deprived me so early of my mother's affection and placed me in the hands of a cruel old dragon.

Erukhim told me all about his parents, whom he loved dearly. He described his father as a pious and legendarily honorable person. In spite of his poverty and his large family (my friend had several brothers and sisters), he never sent a hungry person away without food, and whenever he could help a poor family he would go around untiringly night and day, taking time away from his own work, gathering kopecks for those in need. My friend's mother, he said, was a beautiful and quiet woman who worshipped her children and gave all her energy to them, and she loved and cosseted Erukhim the most. Erukhim told her of our friendship and about me and my sad position in the home of my mean relatives.

One day, one of our classmates was not in heder. The teacher was furious and planned one of his special punishments, casting frequent glances at the three-pointed whip that hung in a place of honor. Suddenly the door opened and a synagogue official entered with a tin collection box in his hand.

"Charity saves from death," he said through his teeth in a monotonous, apathetic voice.

"Who died?" the teacher asked, just as unconcerned.

"Shmul, the shopkeeper."

This was the father of our missing friend

---

25   In Bogrov's Russian original, "into Jewish jargon" ("*na evreiskii zhargon*").

The teacher pulled on his hat and sped to the home of the dead man to attend him on the journey to that place from which no one returns.

This event saddened all of us. Erukhim and I climbed to our beloved stove shelf. We sat in silence for a long time, lost in sad thoughts of death and its consequences.

"Erukhim! What would happen to you if your mother died?" I asked suddenly.

Erukhim started and paled. Clearly I had voiced his very thought.

"Don't say that, Srulik, for God's sake don't! If they buried my poor mother, I'd jump into her grave and die there. What about you?" he asked after a silence.

"Me? I don't really know. I'd cry, for sure, but as for dying—I wouldn't want to."

The gloomy autumn with its fogs, rains, and morning frosts was long over. Winter had been raging for a long time, with hard frosts and sharp winds that froze my ears and hands. My life continued monotonously: prayers and the old woman's curses in the mornings, the walk to heder, there cramming, the teacher's kicks and scolding, the walk home, prayers, a scanty lunch, the old woman's curses, prayers, the walk to heder, cramming, shoves, evening prayers, a rest on the shelf, cramming, prayers, the return home, prayers, a scanty cold supper, prayers, the old woman's curses at bedtime, a last prayer before bed, and then sleep on a buckled trunk. That routine varied only on the Sabbath with the addition of a garlicky dish to our meal, extra prayers, and attendance at synagogue. [...]

In my free moments at home—if my teacher, who wanted to turn me into a scholar at the age of eight, wasn't torturing me by making me repeat the lessons I hated—my favorite occupation was sitting at the window, looking at the deserted yard covered in snow, and thinking. I can no longer remember what I thought about with such concentration, but I know that unchildish questions and reveries stirred within me. The harsh school of life was obviously forcing me to develop, setting my immature mind in motion. My teacher was not only a scholar but a well-known kabbalist. He owned some ancient, thick, strange books in a reddish binding. Jewish men and women frequently asked him to heal them from the evil eye or toothache. He possessed some trick and occult remedies for epilepsy; he could charm away toothache and stop bleeding by casting a spell on the wound. Sometimes he would make wax figures, murmuring incessantly. While this secret work went on, which was always in the evenings, the shrewish old woman would keep quiet, following the movements of the old man's hands with her frightened eyes. I was always sent to my bedroom and ordered to sleep. The mystical atmosphere of the old couple always terrified me. I trembled on the trunk in my dark empty room. There was no one to hear my complaints. I would pull my little coat over myself and press my face into the pillow; fortunately I always fell asleep quickly and slept soundly till morning. My teacher, in a talkative moment, told me that among his books was one that guarded him against fire by its presence alone. Another unprepossessing book could be touched only by a person who had prepared himself by fasting, prayer, and righteous living. He assured me that he who took the name of a certain spirit in vain risked death. He insisted that there was no miracle that could not be performed by Kabbalah. For instance, one could expose any theft, see whomever one wanted to in a dream, tap wine from a wall, and even make oneself invisible.

While I looked distractedly at the snowdrifts adorning our yard, importunate thoughts would fill my young mind. Why does the government waste money on fire companies? Why doesn't every householder keep books that guard against fire? Then there would be no more fires. Why did my teacher buy watery wine every Friday when it would cost him nothing to get it from a wall? How I wanted to become invisible! Then . . . of course, first of all I would run away from this accursed house, I would get on the first carriage that passed—after all, no one would see me!—and go far, far away. If I got hungry, I'd go into the first house I saw and eat whatever I wanted. If I needed money I'd go to a money changer and take as many shiny ten-kopeck coins as I wanted! My thoughts went on in this vein God knows where; I lived in a world of fantasy, and time passed without my noticing. In those moments I was very happy. [. . .]

On Fridays we were released fairly early from heder so that they could prepare for the approaching Sabbath. On one of those relatively free days I sat before evening at my dull window, looking at the yard, admiring the matte golden disk of the setting sun, which gave the winter scene a special, enchantingly soft color. A boy of about twelve shot out of the back door of a pretty house and began to run around, executing various jumps as he went. I admired this lively boy. His full fair face, flushed from the cold, was enlivened by two big blue eyes, and his pretty mouth wore a happy smile. His every movement, every jump expressed strength, suppleness, and health. He was well proportioned; a broad, prominent chest made it seem that he would become a very strong man.

His clothing was plain: thick knee-high boots, a lined sheepskin coat, a gymnasium uniform cap with a red band, wool gloves.

"Mitya!" I heard a long-drawn-out, sweet female voice.

The boy stopped in midjump and whirled in the direction of the voice. I, too, looked that way. On the porch that faced the yard stood an attractive middle-aged lady, a short-sleeved jacket carelessly tossed over her shoulders.

"Mitya dear, come here!"

The boy bounded toward her.

"Naughty boy!" the woman reproved him, a smile on her lips. "Look, your jacket's undone, and you're running around as if nothing's wrong!"

With those words the woman bent toward the boy and began to fasten his jacket, but the boy spun out of her hands with a ringing laugh.

"Mama," he said, "I want to make a snowman, a really tall one!"

"Then make one, darling."

"But Mama, don't tell Olya about it until I'm ready."

"All right, dear."

Mitya rushed into the yard, lifted a shovel that was lying there, and started to dig up the very deepest snowdrift.

"What did he want to do? What's a snowman?" I wondered and began to watch him with special interest.

Meanwhile, Mitya's strong arms were at work. He dug out a pile of snow, then began to carve away the sides of the pile, throwing some snow aside. [. . .] Within fifteen minutes the pile of snow looked like a human figure without legs or arms, like the crudest ancient stone idol. A round head of the same sort appeared on the snow figure's shoulders. Mitya finished his work, ran a few steps back, and, checking his results, stood for a moment, clearly satisfied with his work. Then he ran back into the house.

"Why has that foolish boy been working so hard?" I thought. I had barely finished formulating that question when Mitya was back in the yard clad in a gymnasium student's gray overcoat with its red collar and metal buttons. He looked around and dashed to his snowman, quickly threw the overcoat on it, took off his cap, and adroitly put it on the snowman's head. In such respectable clothes, the snowman resembled Mitya himself, standing there and seeming to look at the sunset. Mitya stood for a few minutes with his head bare, rubbing his ears with his hands, which were red from cold and work. It was clear that he was quite chilled. He kept looking at the door, clearly expecting someone, and then back at his snow twin, but no one came. Mitya impatiently stamped his foot, turned decisively, and ran straight to our cottage. I was so interested in his movements that I jumped from my observation point and ran to the hall. Mitya arrived at the same moment.

"Olya isn't coming," he said in a voice quivering from excitement, "and I'm cold. Please run to our place and call Olya. Tell her Mitya wants her as soon as possible."

I understood very little Russian and could barely speak at all, except for a few Ukrainian words. The only thing I understood of what Mitya said was that he was cold. Not thinking long, I took off my inelegant fur hat and offered it to Mitya.

"Yuck!" he yelled, pushing the hat away with loathing. "I don't need your beanie. Go over to our house and call Olya. I can't . . ."

At that moment a girl appeared in the door of the house where Mitya had been steadily looking. Without finishing his sentence, Mitya fell silent, hid behind the door, and eagerly, barely breathing, watched the girl's every movement.

Shading her eyes with her hand, the girl looked around the yard and paused when she saw what seemed to be Mitya. She stood for a few seconds, smiled, and then carefully, soundlessly, went down the three steps of the low porch and toward the snowman, walking in the funniest way, rolling from one foot to the other, making faces, worried that her feet would make a sound by scraping against the snow. Meanwhile, behind the door, Mitya was overcome by irrepressible, soundless laughter, and in the passion of amusement grabbed my hand and squeezed hard. Wearing a big black hood and snugly wrapped in a fur, Olya crept two paces away from the snowman and, wanting to scare what she took for Mitya, suddenly threw herself and grabbed him from behind.

"Oh!" she cried in a frightened voice when she felt that she was holding a pile of snow under the gymnasium student's overcoat. She jumped away awkwardly and fell face forward in the snow.

I ran headlong toward her, Mitya behind me, but I got there first and lifted her up. She looked at me with fear and then, seeing the frightened Mitya behind me, burst into ringing childish laughter.

"Oh, you're so bad, Mitya! I'm not hurt. But I thought it was you, and I wanted to scare you."

"You're so brave! But then you got scared yourself and fell down."

"That's not true! I wasn't scared, I just stumbled."

I was silent during this whole conversation and stared at Olya. I can't account for what I saw in her young face, but I know that it charmed me. There was so much kindness and tenderness in the girl's dark blue eyes, her delicate mouth, and her round, dimpled chin.

"Mitya, put on your cap!" called the frightened voice of the woman who had been fastening up his jacket half an hour ago. "Mitya! Olya! Come inside!"

"We're coming, Mama, we're coming," Olya answered. Grabbing the cap off the snowman, she put it on the boy's head, seized his hand, and playfully pulled him along. Then she stopped abruptly, released Mitya's hand, and ran to me.

"Thank you for lifting me up," she said, looking me warmly in the eyes. I felt that I was blushing up to my ears; I lowered my eyes and did not answer.

"Will you come and visit us?" Mitya in his turn asked remarkably tenderly. "Come over, brother, we'll play together."

Hand in hand, the children ran off and disappeared behind the door of the house. I stood where I was for a long time. Something fresh and kind emanated from these children. Could these really be Christian children? Could it really be that they did not despise me? Why was I so afraid of Russian boys? And I would perhaps have stood for a long time asking myself these kinds of questions if the old hag's shrill voice hadn't roused me from my thoughts with a harsh call.

"Why are you standing there like a stone idol? What are you doing trying to strike up an acquaintance with the *goyim?*[26] Get away, you moron, before you get a beating! He takes every opportunity to hang around and gape. Good boys have already been in synagogue for a long time, and he's hanging around with all sorts of scum."

I hung my head and went back into our quarters. I had long since ceased to be affected by my tormenter's insults and threats, but her abuse was especially unpleasant at this unusually sweet moment. In my mind I compared the joyful life of those happy, playful, free children, bursting with health, and my tormented existence, full of degradation, deprivation, and confinement. With an inexpressibly bitter feeling of envy and dissatisfaction, I went into my room. Without meaning to, I glanced into the fragment of unpolished mirror glued to the wall: I saw my own reflection and started. My inordinately long, irregular, pale yellowish face, with sunken cheeks and prominent cheekbones, shadowed by long, lank, thin *peyes* that looked like worms, my ridiculously gangly neck

26 The word *goyim* translates as *tribe*, but since almost all the tribes in ancient times were idol worshippers, the word became an insult. [G. B.]

with no tie, my whole thin, bent body on my skinny legs, and my clumsy shoes filled me with such overwhelming disgust that I turned away and spat, but I did this so awkwardly that the spittle landed on the old woman's cheek. She turned green with anger and slapped my cheek so hard with her dry hand that I saw sparks.

"Go to synagogue, you scoundrel!" she screamed, pushing me out and slamming the door loudly behind her.

"To synagogue again," I whispered with a deep moan. "God! When will this ever end?"

Covering my burning cheek with one hand, I went off to synagogue. On the porch of his house Mitya was whimsically jumping around. I came even with him.

"Where are you going?" he asked. I heard teasing in his voice and walked by silently.

"Fool!" he called at me. I began sobbing and, to hide it, ran away without looking back.

It is painful to bear an insult, but to be insulted by a happy person is unbearable.

1863

Translated from the Russian by Gabriella Safran

RASHEL KHIN

Rashel (Rachel) **Khin** (1861–1928), belletrist and playwright, was born in Gorki, Mogilev Province. Khin enjoyed opportunities that were denied to the vast majority of Russia's Jews; her father, a wealthy entrepreneur, moved his family to Moscow and gave his children a first-class European education. He may have financed his children's acculturation, but Khin's father was adamant about remaining Jewish. In Moscow Khin attended the Women's Third Gymnasium in 1877–80 and went to St. Petersburg in 1880 to train as a midwife; her brief medical studies informed the novella "From Side to Side" (1883). In a career change, she moved to Paris to study literature and history at the Collège de France. In Paris Khin met Ivan Turgenev (1818–1883), who became her mentor. She would later dedicate her collection of seven tales, *Downhill*, published in Moscow in 1900, to Turgenev's memory.

Khin debuted in 1881 in the magazine *Friend of Women* (*Drug zhenshchin*) and during the next two decades published fiction in mainstream journals, such as *Messenger of Europe* (*Vestnik Evropy*), and in the Jewish-Russian review *Sunrise* (*Voskhod*), some under the pen name R. M-khin. Her fiction, while stylistically timid, articulated the anxieties of the Jewish-Russian intelligentsia and one-sidedly critiqued the Jewish nouveaux riches. Her most fascinating work is the short novel *The Misfit*, which was published 1886 in *Sunrise* and was included in Khin's collection *Silhouettes* (Moscow, 1895). Her other notable Jewish fiction is "Makarka," published in *Sunrise* in 1889 and reprinted in 1895 in the same "cheap edition" as the short novel *In a Backwater Small Town* by N. Naumov, the pen name of the important Jewish-Russian writer Naum Kogan (1863–1893).

In the mid-1880s, unhappy in her marriage and unable to obtain a divorce from her Jewish husband, Solomon Feldshteyn, who was the father of her young son, she converted to Catholicism, which under Russian law at the time resulted in the dissolution of her marriage. She later married Onisim Goldovsky, a lawyer and a convert like herself. Goldovsky was involved in a number of Jewish causes and rendered financial assistance to the writer **Semyon Yushkevich**. In the late 1890s, she became acquainted with leading Russian writers and intellectuals, including Vladimir Solovyov and Anatoly Koni. In addition to being a "salon Jewess of sorts," as she was called by her American student Carole B. Balin, Khin also distinguished herself in the 1890s–1900s as a playwright. Two of the five plays she wrote, *Young Sprouts* and *Heirs,* were staged by the Maly Theater in Moscow. *Young Sprouts* (1905), the better known of the two, deals with women's emancipation. In 1905, Khin moved to France, returning to Russia in 1914. Her fifth play, poignantly titled *Ice Drifting* (1917), appears to have been her last published work. Little is known about her latter years in Russia and her death in 1928. Forgotten during the Soviet period, Khin was the best-known Jewish woman in nineteenth-century Russian letters. The publication, in 2017 in St. Petersburg, of a large volume of Khin's writings, introduced by the critic Lev Berdnikov and titled *The Misfit* (after one of Khin's best tales, excerpt below), made the work of this neglected writer available to the Russian reading public.

* * *

Several of Khin's works, among them the tales "Makarka" and "Dreamer," address burning Jewish issues. In *The Misfit*, written in 1881, Khin fictionalized her sister's, and perhaps her own, story of conversion. In 1881, Khin's sister, a governess with an aristocratic family, converted to Orthodoxy. The novel's protagonist, Sara Berg, finds herself on the verge of apostasy and is helped by a French teacher who suggests Gotthold Lessing's *Nathan the Wise* as a model of Jewish dignity. She is determined to help poor Jews, but too much separates her from them. Abandoned by her Jewish husband, she loses a daughter to death. A double outsider, she eventually experiences the love of a wealthy aristocrat who wants to marry her—but she refuses.

Included below is the opening scene of Khin's novel, which depicts a painful confrontation between eleven-year-old Sara Berg and her father. A reader of Fyodor Dostoevsky will note a likely allusion to the problematic discussion of blood libel (*krovavyi navet*) by Liza Khokhlakova and Alyosha Karamazov, which occurs in chapter 3, book 11, of part 4 of *The Brothers Karamazov* and was written in May 1880. Published as a book in 1881, *The Brothers Karamazov* appeared serially in *Russian Messenger* in 1879–80, not long before Khin wrote *The Misfit*. In the scene in question, which has bewildered many a Dostoevsky student, Liza asks Alyosha, "Alyosha, is it true that at Easter [in Russian the same word, *paskha*, is used for both Easter and Passover] Yids [*zhidy*] steal children and kill them?" And Alyosha replies, "I don't know." A possible allusion to this discussion in *The Brothers Karamazov* makes it so much more difficult to regard Khin's novel merely as a Jewish "fathers and daughters" tale of the times. *The Misfit* was one of the very first works by Jewish-Russian writers to negotiate Jewish self-hatred.

FROM *THE MISFIT*

Chapter 1

Pavel Abramovich Berg paced angrily up and down his lavish study, which was crammed with all kinds of fine objects and resembled a fancy haberdashery store. He finally stopped, put his hands in his pockets, and, frowning, turned to his wife:

"So now you don't want to send *her* to a boarding school?"

His wife, a beautiful pale brunette with timid dark eyes, about thirty years old, sighed, looked down, and in confusion began to run her fingers over the fringe on a silk pillow.

"This is intolerable!" Pavel Abramovich fumed. "Not only do I run around from morning to night, bustle about trying to make a living, wear myself out, I still have to take care that my children don't grow up to be shopkeepers. Do you really think that love for one's children consists of stuffing them with food from morning to night? I'm telling you that you don't love your children, you hate them, you're ruining them, you . . ."

Seeing his wife sniffle, Pavel Abramovich lost his temper completely.

"Tears again!" he cried. "What the devil is this? I can't say a word. It's as if I'm a beggar come in from the street. You'll all be the death of me, I'm leaving the house . . ."

"But I'm not saying a word," said Berta Isakovna, quickly wiping away her tears. "Do as you wish."

The cause of this domestic scene was a very small person, the Bergs's daughter, Sara, a delightful girl of about eleven, with fiery dark eyes, a dark complexion, and perfect features. The girl was hot tempered, playful, and impressionable and caused her parents—that is, her father (her mother was always able to win her over with kindness)—no end of trouble. But Pavel Abramovich! He was the embodiment of a type of wealthy Jewish autodidact that appeared in Russia about thirty years ago. Quite intelligent, proud, and capable, he had borne since birth the heavy burden of poverty, even penury, had encountered people of the most varied disposition and social status and got on well with everyone. Gradually, he turned from Peysach into Herr Paul and from the latter to Pavel Abramovich and, passing, as they say, through fire and water, had reached that ideal state when it's no longer the Jew who obsequiously looks into the policeman's eyes but the policeman who sweetly murmurs to the Jew, "How may I help you?" But Pavel Abramovich had not forgotten the bitter days of his youth. His dream, his ambition, his *idée fixe* was his children. His main goal was that no one should "recognize" them, and, at the same time, he would not allow even the thought that they might formally convert to Christianity. In general, all his actions were ruled precisely by a hidden desire for revenge—to prove to *them,* that is, Russians, that "look at us, we're no worse than you," a natural desire, characteristic of a slave who has gained his freedom. And now what! A child, a girl is hindering his plans. Told to recite poetry for guests, she clams up, while in the nursery she declaims to her nurse with such fervor that the nurse's head pounds. Sara had a new governess almost every week. She usually bombarded them with questions—what for, why, how come—and, when not satisfied with the answers, she abandoned her books and, instead of learning her lessons, played with her favorite poodle, Valday, for hours on end. The only thing that attracted her was music. One of her governesses was a thin, old, almost illiterate Russified Englishwoman. One evening, as usual, Sara had quickly deserted her for her poodle, but when she heard her abandoned governess playing some passionately pensive Scottish ballad, she left the dog and quietly sat down next to the piano.

"What are you playing, miss?" she asked.

The governess began to explain.

"Play some more," the girl said peremptorily.

The governess obeyed.

When she finished, the girl was silent and seemed to continue listening.

"I want to play like that, too. Teach me," she announced at last.

Thanks to her music, the governess lasted about a year with the Bergs. Sara learned to chatter fluently in English, and she played the ancient ballads with such inexpressible and deep feeling that tears came to the eyes of the elderly miss when she listened to her. Still, Sara did not betray Valday, her favorite, and he became the unintentional cause of her removal from her parents' home.

Pavel Abramovich had a servant, a crafty, sneaky fellow, a fop and a tattletale, who enjoyed the unlimited trust of his master. There was no one in the house, beginning with the mistress, for whom Aleksey (that was the servant's name) did not cause trouble. Sara hated him so much that she wouldn't take anything from his hands. The servant took revenge on her in his own way. One day he stepped on Valday's paw right in front of her. The unhappy poodle began to yelp. Sara burst into tears and ran to him. The dog limped for several days. The girl cared for him tenderly, bandaged his paw, brought food to him herself, and then, one day, when she was making her way to Valday carefully so as not to spill his bowl of soup, through the half-opened door she saw Aleksey, who had tied the poodle to the leg of the sofa and was whipping his injured leg with a hunting whip. Valday just howled and tried helplessly to jump out of the way. Sara felt faint. Beside herself, she dropped the bowl, dashed into the room, tore the whip from the hands of the terrified lackey, and began to whip his face with it in some kind of frenzied rage. . . . A week after this incident, she was taken to the aristocratic boarding school of Mme. Roget in Moscow to "change her character."

The boarding school was no better and no worse than other institutions of this type, but it differed from them in its extreme seclusion, which the girl's lively nature found impossible to accept. She loved her mother passionately, missed her terribly, and suffered from her absence, reviving only on Sundays, when her mother visited the school. As soon as she saw her carriage approach the porch, she would run into the reception room as fast as her legs would carry her, throw herself onto her neck, kiss her pale hands and cheeks and beautiful dark eyes, and complain that "Ugly Puss"—Mme. Roget—gave them nothing to eat and had not let her have dinner three times that week.

"She was stingy with her 'slop' so I stole two hunks of bread and cheese," she would say about her exploits.

Her mother would shake her head reproachfully, and her daughter would begin to justify herself.

"Oh, mother, I know myself it's not right, but why don't you want me to live at home? If you sent me to the gymnasium I would be an excellent student, while here it's so revolting that I can't do anything except think of how to make someone mad. Take me back home."

"It's impossible, my angel," her mother would usually reply to this pestering. "You know papa doesn't want that."

But then vacations were such a joy! On Christmas Eve, Mme. Roget had a Christmas tree and gave presents to all the pupils. The pupils, in turn, had to show their solicitude with various surprises—and how angry she would get if the surprise was not on the expensive side. Classes ended about three days before the holiday. The baking of meat pies from sweet dough began early in the morning; the girls would steal it right out from under Mme. Roget's hands and eat it raw in the dormitory. But now, thank God, the last candle on the tree has gone out . . . the pupils begin to leave for home. Sara's heart sinks at the thought that they might come for her tomorrow instead of today.

Finally Amalia Karlovna, the housekeeper, arrives.

"On vient te chercher," Mme. Roget says to Sara, "*mais il faut tard; veux tu pas aller demain, petite?*"[27]

Such thoughtfulness makes Sara's temples throb.

"Oh, madame, il ne m'arrivera rien, bien sûr,"[28] she mumbles and, without waiting for a reply, runs off; in a minute, already dressed, she runs down the stairs, skipping several steps and stumbling in her hurry. Amalia Karlovna keeps her from falling, but she does not calm down until she's in the sleigh. "Now they won't leave me," she thinks aloud, and almost throws herself on the coachman's neck and begs him to go "faster, for God's sake." "There are four streets left, three, two," she says to Amalia Karlovna, who shares her impatience rather calmly.

The horses stop at a gray stone house with an imposing cast-iron awning. Sara almost knocks over the servant, bursts right into her mother's room in her coat and boots, and throws her arms around her neck. The laughter and horseplay of the girl—who is trying to enjoy her freedom as fully as she can, bothering and nagging everyone she encounters, from her mother to her five-year-old sister Lidochka, who bursts into tears from her caresses—sounds strange in the quiet, decorous house. The two weeks of vacation seem infinite to her, the boarding school disappears in some kind of hazy distance; who knew what can happen in two weeks: maybe they would keep her at home for good. But the hours fly by, and the last evening comes. Sara's father, who usually leaves for his club after dinner, stays home purposely to be with his daughter, but she, knowing that *he* was the one who was forcing her to stagnate at "Ugly Puss's," reacts to his kindness rather coldly. She even has an irresistible desire to anger him.

"Papa, we're Jews, right?" she says.

"Of course," answers her father, "as if you didn't know."

"And is it true that all Jews are such vile swindlers that after death every single one of them burns in hell?"

"Who told you that, Sara? Not Mme. Roger, I hope."

"No, not her; I've heard it from a lot of people."

"It's pure rubbish. I advise you not to repeat such nonsense," says her father.

---

27 "They've come for you . . . but it's late; wouldn't you like to go tomorrow, my little one?" (Fr.)
28 "Oh, of course I'll be fine." (Fr.)

"I've also heard," continues Sara, unruffled, "that Jews drink human blood with matzah on Passover."[29]

"Have you ever drunk it on Passover?" her father asks angrily.

"There you are," the daughter replies resentfully, "we're not real Jews."

"And what kind are we?"

"I don't know what kind, only not real ones; real ones are all dirty."

"Jews, like Russians, are dirty when they are poor and uneducated. If you don't want to be dirty, study. I spare nothing for your education, as you must realize."

"And I can't stand kikes and will certainly get baptized when I grow up," Sara blurts out, vexed that she's unable to make him angry.

"Get out of here, you nasty girl. You'll stay at the boarding school all summer."

She leaves but pauses in the corridor. She hears her mother's meek voice.

"Those are the fruits of bringing her up away from home, in someone else's house," she says. "It had to end like this."

"Leave it alone, please," says her father. "I know what I'm doing. She has to stay at the boarding school for at least three years. I want her to know languages fluently and to have manners fit for society. She can't get that at home. And as for her philosophy, I don't give a damn about it. We just have to tell Mme. Roget to keep a stricter watch over her."

Upon hearing this verdict, Sara threw herself on her bed and cried until she fell asleep.

1881

Translated from the Russian by Emily Tall

---

29 Sara Berg here invokes the blood libel, the charge that Jews allegedly use the blood of Christian babies to make matzos, of which the Jews of Europe had been accused from the twelfth century (the William of Norwich affair) by their persecutors in order to justify anti-Jewish violence and restrictive measures. The accusation had a history in Russian in the Velizh affair of 1823, for example, and others.

SEMYON NADSON

Semyon Nadson (1862–1887), poet and essayist, was born in St. Petersburg in 1862. His father, a civil servant who came from a Jewish family and was baptized after his own father had converted to Russian Orthodoxy, died in a lunatic asylum when Nadson was two. His mother, a private teacher descended from the Russian nobility, died of consumption in 1873, whereupon his uncle, I. S. Mamontov, became the boy's guardian. In his autobiographical notes, written in 1880 and published in 1902, Nadson described the humiliation of being a ward in the household of his antisemitic uncle, who called the impressionable, sensitive boy "kikish ninny." After graduating from a military high school in 1879, he entered a cadet school and then, in 1882, the 148th Caspian Regiment as a lieutenant. In 1884, the consumptive Nadson retired and left for European resorts with his companion Maria Vatson, who abandoned her husband to be with him. Returning to St. Petersburg in 1885, Nadson soon went to live in Ukraine. He died in Yalta in 1887 and was buried in St. Petersburg. A large crowd turned up for Nadson's funeral; students carried his casket to the Volkov Cemetery, where it was laid to final rest next to Nikolay Dobrolyubov (1836–1861), a leading "civic" critic of his time, who also died young of consumption.

Nadson's first poem was published in 1878 in the magazine *Light* (*Svet*). In 1881, he met the prominent poet Aleksey Pleshcheev, who published Nadson's poems in *Notes of the Fatherland* (*Otechestvennye zapiski*), a leading journal, forging Nadson's literary reputation. Nadson later referred to Pleshcheev as his literary "godfather." Nadson's essays of 1882–86 were gathered in the volume *Literary Sketches* (1887). In 1886 Nadson was awarded half the Pushkin prize for his *Poems*, a tremendous distinction in and of itself, and all the more so when accorded to a poet of Jewish origin. In the last two years of his life, Nadson enjoyed phenomenal popularity, yet these years were also poisoned by ostracism, especially in the implicitly xenophobic feuilletons of Viktor Burenin.

Semyon Nadson was Russia's most popular poet throughout the three decades preceding the 1917 revolutions. His first collection, *Poems* (1885), was reprinted twenty-nine times before 1917 and sold over 200,000 copies—a bestseller by any account. Nadson was the first Russian poet of Jewish descent to achieve national fame, emerging as a "captor" of the souls of younger readers in the period of Alexander III's rule following the defeat of the populist revolutionary movement of the 1870s. In the decades that followed Nadson's death, educated Russians were very likely to know one or two of his poems by heart.

Oscillating between the poetry of "pure art" (e.g., Afanasy Fet) and the poetry of social reflection, Nadson was a link between the civic poetry of Nekrasov and early Russian Symbolism. A number of critics and poets were condescending toward him, due in part to his Jewishness, yet such major Russian writers as Lev Tolstoy, Mikhail Saltykov-Shchedrin, Vsevolod Garshin, and Anton Chekhov thought very highly of his gift. When he was starting out in literature, Dmitry Merezhkovsky (1865–1941), one of the founders of the Russian Symbolist movement, regarded Nadson, his senior by only three years, as his literary master. Metrically quite traditional, narcissistically melodious and sonorous, many of Nadson's verses showcase a disillusioned poet's quest for an enduring liberal ideal of humanity. A central theme in a number of his poems is the poet's place in society. Nadson's love lyrics speak with verve and affectation of lost or unrequited love.

In the late 1880s–90s, Nadson was a cult figure among young adults and university students, and his influence is distinctly notable in the early verses of such original poets as Ivan Bunin (1870–1953, the first Russian writer to win the Nobel Prize for Literature for his fiction in 1933). Russian composers—Anton Arensky, Ceasar Cui, Anton Rubinstein, and Sergey Rachmaninoff among them—have set Nadson's lyrics to music, and to this day they remain a solid part of the repertoire of Russian classical *romansy*.

* * *

Semyon Nadson wrote one poem with an explicit Jewish theme ("I grew up shunning you, O most degraded nation . . .") and also a poem ("The Woman") where the autobiographical motifs of a Jewish child's loneliness and alienation are entertained, albeit never quite explicitly. However, the relative importance of Nadson's "Jewish poem" is tremendous, as he, being Russian Orthodox, openly identified with the people of his father and their plight at the time of the pogroms and the new antisemitic restrictions of the 1880s. Composed in 1885, "I grew up shunning you, O most degraded nation . . ." first appeared in the famous collection *Aid to the Jews Devastated by Poor Crops* (1901).

FROM "THE WOMAN"

(Part 2)

I grew up all alone. No family's gentle care
Gave shelter from early storms or first misfortune.
My mother did not kneel beside me giving prayer,
Nor nanny whisper meekly into my sleeping ear,
Making the cross above me, her passionate devotion . . .
. . . .
I recall an ancient temple, glittering with lights,
I remember, too, my mother: all bestrewn with flowers,
With clenched and bloodless lips and hands clenched tight she lies,
So silent, in her coffin above our timid height—
Beside her bier, in tears and disbelief, we cower.
My little sister's hand I take in my hand firmly . . .
Dressed in her mourning gown, she's doubly sad and pale,
She presses close against me, so trusting and so small,
Unchildlike anguish floods her eyes as she observes me . . .
We are afraid . . . Death's grisly silences appall,
As do the murky shadows gathering in corners,
The staircase draped in black, and black uncommon garments,
And mother in her coffin, so mute, and cold, and frail.
We want to fly away, into the deepening azure,
Where heaven arches wide and cloudlets gently sift,
Where on the garden path the fragrant green is lavish,
And moths with gaily patterned wings winnow and drift . . .
But yet we do not dare escape, and, hardly knowing
Why we are here amidst the stern and alien crowd,
We listen as the chorus's last hymn resounds
And fades, then solemnly swells again to overflowing . . .

1883

* * *

I grew up shunning you, O most degraded nation,
'Twas not to you I sang when inspiration called.
The world of your traditions, the scourge of lamentation
Are alien to me, as are your laws.
And were you, as in times of yore, robust and thriving,
And were you not humiliated everywhere,
But warmed and animated by other, cheerful striving,
I would not hail you then, I swear.

Yet in our times, when, humbled by the weight of sorrow,
You bow your head, await salvation all in vain,
These times when just the name "Jew" keenly harrows,
Or hangs in the mouths of masses like a symbol of disdain,

And when your enemies, a pack of rabid dogs, endeavor
To tear you all to pieces—snarling, wroth with greed—
Then let me also join the ranks of your defenders,
O nation scorned by destiny!

1885

Translated from the Russian by Alyssa Dinega Gillespie

On the Eve: 1890s–1910s

Editor's Introduction

During the next several decades, five principal factors defined the thematic thrust of Jewish-Russian writing: the outburst of Russian antisemitism in the 1880s–1900s, punctuated by pogroms and blood libels; the introduction of further discriminatory regulations and quotas, which were not abolished until 1917; the massive flight of Russian Jews to North America; the rise of the Jewish worker's movement, especially after the founding of Bund, the Jewish Socialist party, in 1897 in Vilna; and the growth of political Zionism in Russia and abroad.

Census data indicate that, of about 5.2 million Jews in the Russian Empire in 1897, 24.6 percent could read and write in Russian, but only 1 percent considered it their mother tongue. These data, combined with the data on the Jewish-Russian periodicals, help quantify and qualify the still small but growing readership of those Jewish-Russian writers who, like the popular belletrist **Ben-Ami** (1854–1932), targeted the audience of Russian-reading Jews. The emergence of Jewish-Russian lyrical poetry, exemplified by the ascent of Simon Frug (1860–1916), who was celebrated by Russia's Jews and unknown to the general Russian reader, occurred as a response to an elemental need for accessible Russian-language Jewish poetry. Frug and his lesser contemporaries and epigones published in the Jewish Russian-language press of the 1880s–1900s.

One should also note the publication of the major monthly *Sunrise* (*Voskhod*, 1881–1906) and its weekly supplement. After 1884, *Sunrise* would remain the only regular Jewish-Russian periodical for fifteen years, its print run growing, according to Dmitry A. Elyashevich's 1995 survey, from 950 copies in 1881 to 4,397 at its peak in 1895. This information gives us a sense of the dimensions of the immediate audience of Jewish-Russian writers in the 1860s–90s. Perhaps the commanding Jewish-Russian journal of the late tsarist era was *Dawn* (known as *Dawn* "3"), founded in St. Petersburg in 1907 as the official Zionist weekly and widely consumed by Jewish-Russian educated circles. With a print run of 10,000 copies, *Dawn* "3" was certainly the most read and the most influential of the periodicals; its publication stopped in 1915 in the atmosphere of wartime censorship. Finally, I should mention the rise of provincial and local Jewish-Russian publications in the Pale and the south of Russia in the 1900s–1910s. For instance, the young **Samuil Marshak** (1887–1964) published his early, Zionist verse in the Yalta-based magazine *Young Judea* (*Molodaia Iudeia*, 1906).

By the 1890s, Jewish-Russian authors had come to the Russian national mainstream; one of these was **David Aizman** (1869–1922), the "Jewish Chekhov," who published in such leading magazines as the populist *Russian Wealth* (*Russkoe bogatstvo*). The pogroms of 1903 to 1906, especially the 1903 pogrom in Kishinev, Hayyim Nahman Bialik's "city of slaughter," brought Russia's Jewish problem to the world's attention while propelling masses of the Jewish population to emigrate. For Jewish-Russian writers, **S. An-sky** (1863–1920), for example, the 1900s were a time of greater involvement in Russian politics and revolutionary activity. Both the wave of pogroms and the failed 1905–7 Russian revolution pushed Jewish-Russian writers, notably such neorealists as Aizman or **Semyon Yushkevich** (1869–1927), to depict anti-Jewish violence and the daily lives of the Jewish working masses. Zionism and revolutionary ideology (Marxism and other types of radical thought, such as agrarian socialism and anarchism) were the two gravities that pulled apart Russia's Jewish community, leaving major imprints on the lives and works of Jewish-Russian writers. In the words of Shimon Markish, whose contribution to the study of Jewish-Russian literature is discussed in the general introduction, Zionism gave Jewish-Russian literature "a new generation of literary polemicists [*publitsisty*] and a new polemicist style. The unrivaled primacy in this field . . . belongs to **Vladimir Jabotinsky** [1880–1940]." A gifted author and subsequently a Zionist leader, **Jabotinsky** particularly excelled at the literary feuilleton in the 1900s. The Jewish question had become so vital to Russian life and culture in the first decade of the twentieth century that Jewish-Russian authors articulated it in the pages of mainstream newspapers and magazines. A telling example is the special "Jewish" 1909 issue of *Satyricon*, a leading highbrow magazine of humor, where **Sasha Cherny** (1880–1932) published his sharp and witty poem "The Jewish Question." This was also the time when both Jewish and non-Jewish writers started arguing on the pages of popular publications about the status and criteria of Jewish-Russian literature, as is particularly evident from the so-called "debates of 1908," which is also considered in the general introduction.

The 1900s–1910s, known as the Silver Age of Russian culture, witnessed the emergence of a number of talented Jewish-Russian poets, prose writers, playwrights, translators, and critics. This period also set the stage for an explosion of Jewish-Russian creativity during the first Soviet decade. For the first time during the Silver Age, Jews were visible in all the principal Russian literary and artistic movements, first in symbolism and then in futurism, acmeism, imagism, and other groups and trends. At this time, the ranks of acculturated or partly acculturated Jewish families gave Russian culture the "Russian Sappho," **Sofia Parnok** (1885–1933; in this section), and two of its most important twentieth-century poets: **Osip Mandelstam** (1891–1938; in the section "Revolution and Emigration: 1920s–1930s") and **Boris Pasternak** (1890–1960; in the section "War and Shoah: 1940s").

Finally, in the late 1900s and then again in the late 1910s, one observes the beginning of a brief but fascinating cultural dialogue, to crescendo in 1917–18, between Hebrew and Russian authors, in which Jewish-Russian authors such as Leyb Jaffe (1878–1948) were the bicultural harbingers of cross-pollination and translation.

BEN-AMI

Ben-Ami (1854–1932), fiction writer, journalist, and Zionist activist, was born Mark Rabinovich in Verkhovka, near the town of Bar, Ukraine, presently in Vinnitsa Province. In Hebrew, "Ben-Ami" literally means "son of my people"; in Genesis 19:30–38, Lot's daughters lay with their father and later gave birth, the elder to Moab, the younger to Ben-Ami. The writer chose the latter as his *nom de plume* to sign his fiction.

Ben-Ami attended a yeshiva in Odessa. There he experienced the powerful influence of Peter (Peretz) Smolenskin (1842–1885), the Hebrew-Russian novelist and essayist who founded the Vienna-based *The Dawn* (*Ha-Shahar*) and advocated eastern Jewry's rapprochement with the west. Becoming a maskil on Smolenskin's model, Ben-Ami studied at a Russian gymnasium and later Novorossiysk University. He debuted in 1881 in *Sunrise* (*Voskhod*) with the essay "On the Necessity of Special Textbooks of the Russian Language for Jewish Schools." During the 1881–82 pogroms, Ben-Ami took part in organizing Jewish self-defense. He subsequently journeyed to Paris seeking assistance for the pogrom victims from the Alliance Israélite Universelle. Ben-Ami contributed "Letters from Paris" to *Sunrise* under the pen name "Reish-Geluta," a term that, first, referred to the leader of the ancient Jewish semiautonomous government in Babylonia and Persia and, second, must have been a bilingual phonetic pun on the Russian *rech' galuta*, meaning "speech of exile." Ben-Ami here voiced a profound admiration for enduring Jewish values and a critique of assimilationism. After moving to Geneva in 1882, Ben-Ami began a series of Russian-language stories and tales celebrating the spirit of Jewish festivals and legends, including "The Tzaddik's Arrival" (1883) and "Baal Tefila" (1884). Appearing regularly in *Sunrise*, his stories were in great demand, and Ben-Ami was the first major Jewish writer of popular fiction in Russian for the growing ranks of Russianized professionals and businessmen.

In 1887, Ben-Ami returned to Odessa, remaining there until the eruption of the first Russian revolution in 1905, when he moved back to Geneva. He published Russian fiction, such as the cycle *Stories for My Children*, and essays, decrying governmental antisemitism while also condemning the Jewish intelligentsia for its abnegation of the oppressed Jewish masses and its assimilationist tendencies. Remaining one of *Sunrise*'s principal authors until its termination in 1906, Ben-Ami also published a collection of Russian-language *Biblical Stories for Jewish Children* (Odessa, 1903) and a cycle of stories in Yiddish, one of which appeared in the second issue of Sholem Aleichem's *The Jewish Popular Library* (*Die Yiddishe Folksbibliotek*) in 1889. Several of his works have been translated into Hebrew by Hayyim Nahman Bialik. Written in Yiddish, Ben-Ami's short novel *A Night in a Small Town* (*A nacht in a kleyn shtetl*, 1909) stemmed from his Russian-language "shtetl" fiction of the 1880s. Ben-Ami's literary output dwindled after his return to Geneva in 1905.

Ben-Ami was a member of the central committee of Hovevei Zion (Lovers of Zion) in Odessa from its founding in 1890 and a delegate to the First Zionist Congress and to the subsequent congresses presided over by Theodor Herzl. In 1923, Ben-Ami moved to Palestine, where he died in Tel Aviv in 1932. Except for Laura Salmon's Italian-language monograph of 1995, modern scholarship about Ben-Ami remains scarce.

* * *

Narrated in the first person, Ben-Ami's Russian fiction is set in the 1860s. One wonders if Ben-Ami's idealization of his childhood and youth did not betray some nostalgia for the epoch when the majority of the Jewish masses in Russia had not fully confronted the problems of modernization and acculturation. Sentimental and free of authorial irony, Ben-Ami's narratives minimize dramatic conflict and underrate structures of desire; many are not stories but actually long sketches or pseudoautobiographical recollections. In contrast to the maskilim who are the heroes in the works of his contemporaries, Ben-Ami's characters are run-of-the-mill Jews in the Pale. A typical example is "A Little Drama" (1893), in which the protagonist, a righteous but poor bookbinder, manages to scrape together enough money to buy his son a pair of new boots. On the eve of Passover, as the father and son wash themselves in the communal bathhouse, the new boots are stolen and the boy's heart is broken. In its dramatic collision, the story recalls the well-known tale of a poor Baltic-German musician in the St. Petersburg of the 1830s, "A Story of Two Galoshes" by Vladimir Sollogub (1813–1882).

There is reason to believe that Ben-Ami was keenly aware of both his dominant reader's expectations and level of linguistic and cultural preparation. His mission was to depict the beauty of the Jewish past and to lift his reader's spirits, and shorter fiction was just a convenient medium, not his form of choice. Ben-Ami's achievement as an essayist eclipses his own contribution as a fictionist; his essays were punchier and tighter, displaying a greater degree of authorial self-reflection. Romanticizing as it does the "soul of the *Jewish* folk," the following preface to a volume of his Russian fiction was a credo of Ben-Ami the Russian writer and a testament of Ben-Ami the Jewish activist.

PREFACE TO COLLECTED STORIES
AND SKETCHES (1898)

The Jewish reading public is more or less familiar with the stories that follow[1]—I am referring, of course, to Jewish readers who are interested in the life of their people.

In these stories I have tried, to the best of my strength and ability, to reproduce the life of our national masses or, to be more precise, those sides of this life with which I am more familiar and the way I know them—to reproduce them not as an indifferent outside observer but as a coparticipant who has experienced it all and suffered along with others. This, however, does not mean in the least that the author actually appears throughout these stories as a character. If the story is told for the most part in the first person, that is because such a form seems to me the most straightforward and natural.

Actually, I am imprecise in speaking about the "life of the national masses," for the overwhelming majority of Jews live their lives without knowing a division into estates.

Woven of woe and privations, this life is sorrowful and joyless. But the severe, impossible struggle to earn one's daily bread, which gets harder and more ruthless every day, every hour, has not murdered the people's soul, which is still alive and receptive to anything lofty and noble. The ancient national ideals still linger at the bottom of the people's soul, the ancient hopes and aspirations still live—the great heritage of our nation's great grievers, the prophets.

And that is the only solace, the bright light that shines in the life of Jewry, bright in the realm of the spirit, in the realm of ideals. A dark fathomless ocean of suffering, over which up on high, here and there amid thick black storm clouds, little stars sparkle . . .

---

1 With the exception of the story "At Night on the Eve of Goshano Rabot," which previously appeared in a general-interest magazine, all the other stones were originally published to *Sunrise*. Of the three stories included in this volume, only "Baal Tefila" has undergone substantial reworking. [B-A.] The third story included in vol. 1 was "A Little Drama."

At a time when different individuals and groups are prepared to make various "adjustments" of their selves, supposing thus to ease their lives and in doing so pretend to be now zealous Germans, now flaming Poles, Czechs, Magyars— in a word, whatever they need to pretend to be—our people in its vast majority continues to live its *own* life. And it does not even think about or care to know whether its existence is pleasing to anybody else. Quite the contrary, it is fully conscious of the fact that it is not pleasing. And this, I believe, serves as a significant stimulus for the people to value its own existence. For the people's instinct is in general nobler than all the premeditated and deliberate punditry, nobler just by virtue of being an *instinct*—that is, a natural phenomenon, inborn and not something artificial, devised for a particular occasion.

It is common for the Jewish writer, if he devotes his literary work to Jews, to regard himself for the most part as a "defender" of the Jews. No matter to what area of literature he contributes, he above all has such a "defense" in mind. And even when he addresses an exclusively Jewish audience, often even when he writes in a language that is completely inaccessible to the non-Jewish world, in Hebrew for instance, even then his spiritual gaze inadvertently remains shackled to "them," these visible and invisible "enemies" of Israel. And in nearly every passage can be seen the clear intention to persuade "them," to prove to "them," to vindicate in "their" eyes, to solicit "their" compassion, and so forth.

I confess that in me all these types of "defense," these strivings to "prove," and so on, have always elicited the heaviest, most unpleasant feelings. I know nothing more insulting to or more humiliating for a person's dignity than the sense that everyone for whatever reason believes it his duty to vindicate or defend the person before whomever, almost apologizing for the person's unforgivable desire to exist. The thought of appearing as a "defender" is therefore not only alien to me but also antithetical to my beliefs. I think least of all about proving or demonstrating something to someone. I decisively do not believe that we are guilty before anyone, and I could not care less what somebody thinks of us.

What opinion people have about us does not depend on us, and even less on our obsessive explanations and appeals.

If I really sought to instill sympathy for the deeply miserable masses of our population, which alone bear the oppressive burden of Jewish sorrow and Jewish dire need, that would be above all and mainly in the Jews themselves, those numerous "cultured" Jews who have suddenly become the keepers of the vineyards of others while leaving their own to the cruel mercy of fate.

I am not speaking of those vile reptiles from the ranks of our own gilded house servants who, out of pitiful, despicable vanity, and expecting to receive the master's patting or the master's smile, thrust themselves as benefactors upon those who need them the least. They can shell out tens of thousands for the publication of works they do not understand and hundreds of thousands for the establishment of various schools, homes, shelters, and so forth, which can well be organized without the help of the Jewish Derunovs.[2] They will not blind anyone, nor deceive anyone with their rich offerings. These offerings belong to the sort that in ancient times were not admitted to the Temple . . . Everybody knows perfectly well that it is not nobleness but rather the baseness of their souls that motivates them, for nobleness makes its sacrifices for the weakest, not the strongest.

I speak not of the renegades who are a subject of contempt both by the ones they have abandoned and the ones upon whom they force themselves.

I have in mind those who have dedicated themselves to the vineyards of others because they do not suspect the existence of their own or else do not know of its woeful state.

Yes, may the Jews themselves be filled with a genuine love for the Jewish people and for Jewry—and that would be perfectly sufficient.

Not from the others must we expect salvation.

This eternal anticipation of the mercy of others, this eternal standing on our hind paws before the table of others and awaiting their crumbs is what completely paralyzes our moral strength and corrupts our character, developing in us so many lowly, unworthy traits.

Our help, our salvation is in ourselves. We can and must help ourselves. And only such help, coming from within ourselves, is capable of strengthening us morally and spiritually, elevating us both in our own eyes and in those of others, and making us equal to other nations.

---

2   Osip Derunov is the protagonist of "Pillar" ("Stolp"), a chapter in *Speeches of a Loyal Citizen*, a cycle of essays that the novelist, satirist, and essayist Mikhail Saltykov-Shchedrin (1826–1889) published in *Notes of the Fatherland* in 1872–76. The subject of "Pillar" is the post-1860s reform for the development of capitalism in Russia. A small-time trader prior to the abolition of serfdom in 1861, Osip Derunov becomes, by hook or by crook, a wealthy businessman and major power broker in his province, making his capital off the impoverished peasants and ruined gentry. Derived etymologically from the Russian verb *drat'* ("to rip"), Derunov became a name in Russian culture that denoted a ruthless individual who would stop at nothing to increase his capital and power.

Only those rights are valid and valuable that accord a nation the opportunity to develop its spirit freely and independently and that by their very nature alone cannot be offered as a gift.

1897; 1898

Translated from the Russian by Maxim D. Shrayer

Ben-Ami, "Ot avtora," *Sobranie rasskazov i ocherkov,*
vol. 1 (Odessa, 1898). English translation, introduction, and notes
copyright © by Maxim D.Shrayer.

DAVID AIZMAN

David Aizman (1869–1922) was born in Nikolaev, a coastal city in Ukraine where **Isaac Babel** spent his childhood. Aizman spent most of his adult life as a perpetual wanderer. In an autobiographical note penned in January 1914 in Odessa and reminiscent of the tearful laughter of Sholem Aleichem's Tevye, Aizman wrote: "What else can I say? To this day I have no certain place of residence. . . . A nomad, I live in hotels and paltry furnished apartments. I suffer a great deal from the absence of a residence permit. . . . I would like to be able to visit my native city of Nikolaev, but I cannot: it is now also outside the 'Pale.' . . . It is unethical to give bribes. I give bribes. It is dishonest to bypass the law. I bypass the law. I am a writer. I pass myself off as a shop assistant. It is only as a shop assistant that I can legally stay in Petersburg, if only temporarily."

Aizman left Odessa and went to Paris in 1896 to study painting. In 1898, he and his wife, a Jewish-Russian physician, moved to the French countryside, to the Haute-Marne region. While living in France, Aizman gained his own literary voice and made his debut in *Russian Wealth* (*Russkoe bogatstvo*), then a leading Russian monthly with a *narodnik* (populist) stance. Two of David Aizman's most original works of fiction, "In a Foreign Land" (published 1902) and "The Countrymen" (published 1903), were composed and set in France. Aizman returned to Russia in 1902. Despite two lengthy stays, first in France (1896–1902) and later in Italy (1907–9), he never became an émigré and died in Russia in 1922. During the 1900s–1910s, Aizman's stories and novellas appeared regularly in the leading Russian periodicals, and major theaters staged his plays; Maxim Gorky's Znanie was among his publishers. An eight-volume edition of Aizman's works was released in 1911–19. As unknown today as he was famous then, Aizman was characterized by the writer Aleksandr Amfiteatrov in 1908 in the following terms: "After Dostoevsky and also partly [Vsevolod] Garshin, we have not had a verbal artist who would know how to 'strike hearts with an unprecedented force' more poignantly, consistently, and effectively than David Aizman." From his early stories, notably including "In a Foreign Land" and "The Countrymen," a Chekhovian power of understatement distinguishes Aizman's best works. In his other well-known works, especially in "Ice Breaking" (published 1905), "Anchl's Morning" (published 1906), and "The

Bloody Deluge" (published 1908), with its harrowing account of a pogrom, Aizman succumbed to the osmotic pressures of Gorky's and Leonid Andreev's neorealist fiction of social upheaval. In 1907, Gorky himself reproached Aizman for writing of the anti-Jewish violence with "much screaming and no wrath."

The open and naturalistic portrayal of Russian and Ukrainian antisemitism and the anti-Jewish violence of 1905–6 made Aizman too unpalatable for the Soviet literary canonizers. Starting with the early 1930s, his books went out of print in the Soviet Union, and he was chiefly remembered there as a playwright (his most significant play is the 1907 *Thorny Bush*) and in connection with Gorky's circle of writers. Neither a Zionist nor a Jewish revolutionary writing about both Zionists and revolutionaries, Aizman has fallen prey to cultural amnesia by both Russian and Jewish readers. In 1985, in a passionate reassessment of his career, Alice Stone Nakhimovsky described Aizman's early stories as works of "a Jewish Chekhov." Despite the efforts of the past two decades, by Alice Nakhimovsky, Claudia Colombo, Shimon Markish, and Mikhail Weinstein, David Aizman remains vastly forgotten by the reading public both in the former Soviet Union and outside of it. No books by Aizman are in print in Russia or available in English translations. If distant echoes of Aizman's acclaim have reached the ears of the American public, these would be through *Sima* (1976), Leonard J. Lehrman's opera based on Aizman's novella "The Krasovitsky Couple," and the 2003 publication of his story "The Countrymen" in *Commentary* in English translation.

* * *

Written in 1902 in Paris, Aizman's "The Countrymen" is a poignant story of the Jewish-Slavic unburdening of guilt in exile, indeed a gem of Jewish writing in Diaspora. Of "The Countrymen" and "In a Foreign Land," Shimon Markish wrote in 1985 as he replied to an antisemitic Russian émigré journalist, "I do not know a more penetrating and heartfelt depiction of the irrational, obsessive love for the land, the people who, it would seem, have done everything to instill [in the Jews] hatred for them."

THE COUNTRYMEN*

I

For the first week, Varvara Stepanovna Klobukova[3] felt simply splendid in her new surroundings. Above all, she was tickled by the knowledge that a miracle had occurred and she was abroad, in France. Making her no less happy was the thought of her salary: 700 francs a month, plus room and board—more than she would have earned in a year at home in Mertvovodsk.[4] Finally, there was pleasure to be had from living in luxury and comfort of a kind she had never known.

Varvara Stepanovna had been given two wonderful rooms and a *cabinet de toilette* with a bath, a shower, and a very large three-section mirror in which one could admire oneself from every angle.

The furniture was all truly "royal," and what astonished Klobukova most of all was the bed, an edifice with carved rosewood columns, silk covers, and lace curtains.

Her chambermaid was "a thousand times" more elegant than that "faker" Oberemchenko—Mertvovodsk's first social lioness—and at dinner a stately footman in stockings and white gloves served her innumerable dishes of the most refined taste.

Varvara Stepanovna had gotten her job in the following way.

Count de Saint-Blin[5] was a rich and enterprising French industrialist who owned shares in a number of Russian factories and visited Russia several times a year. His wife, a heavy, rotund woman, famous in her youth for parties and wild sprees, usually stayed home, either in Paris or at their castle in the provinces, giving herself over to pious exercises such as knitting jerseys for the poor or subjecting herself to treatments for illnesses she did not have. But it so happened one day that the countess took it into her head to tour her Russian properties, and off she went.

---

*   The text has been slightly abridged

3   Varvara Stepanovna Klobukova—Varvara is the Russian equivalent of Barbara, and it points directly to "barbarian" (*varvar*). Klobukova derives from *klobuk*, referring to the headgear of an Orthodox monk.

4   Mertvovodsk—a fictitious name, literally, "[Town] of Dead Waters." Varvara's home town of Mertvovodsk possibly hints at the town of Zheltye Vody (literally, "Yellow Waters") in the upper western corner of Kherson Province and some thirty miles north of Krivoy Rog.

5   Saint-Blin—the name of a French village in the Haute-Marne region where Aizman and his wife, a physician, lived from 1898 to 1902.

Naturally she was accompanied by a whole staff of servants: chamber-maids, footmen, coachmen, and a secretary for her philanthropic activities, as well as two lady's companions and a Swedish masseuse, Mlle. Norcelius.

The countess spent two weeks in Ekaterinoslav[6] Province and a month in Kherson Province, visited St. Petersburg, and stopped for a while in Moscow before, excited and enchanted by everything she had seen, in particular our people—"*ils sont si soumis, les russes*"[7]—she started making arrangements to return home.

All of a sudden, the Swedish masseuse announced she was staying. In Mertvovodsk she had met a compatriot who owned a fish store, and she was marrying him.

The countess gasped.

So shaken was she by the girl's untoward behavior that for a whole week she could not knit a single charitable jersey. But somehow she managed to calm down and initiated a search for a replacement.

Varvara Stepanovna was chosen.

The countess immediately took a strong liking to her. First, she was *soumise* and second, she excelled in her work. Or at least so the countess said. She declared that no one had ever given her as good a massage as this *petite russe*. When the moment came to pack for home, she found she could not part from Varvara Stepanovna, not for anything in the world; trebling her salary, she took her back to her castle.

Varvara Stepanovna's duties occupied her for exactly one hour each day, from nine to ten in the morning. The rest of her time was hers to dispose of as she would. But how to spend it, she did not know.

She had brought with her a few issues of *Virgin Soil* magazine and a volume of Vonlyarsky's[8] writings, and though she was no lover of books, she now spent long hours reading. But that could hardly fill up an entire day, and when the writings had been read, Klobukova quickly became bored.

She strolled in the park, vast and strikingly beautiful; she took long walks to neighboring villages; she spent hours feeding the swans in the village pond and the rabbits in their sheds. All the while, she never ceased being bored.

She could more or less understand French—she had studied it back home at her progymnasium, where her education had safely ended—but she spoke

6   Ekaterinoslav—now Dnepropetrovsk, in Ukraine.
7   *Ils sont si soumis, les russes* = They are so pliant, the Russians.
8   Vonlyarsky, Vasily (1814–1852)—a popular Russian belletrist of the 1840s–50s.

it very badly. Still, when she had to, she was capable of expressing herself and making some sort of conversation, and the countess had made her solemnly swear not to engage in conversation with any of the castle's servant staff. "Mlle. Norcelius used to chat with everyone," the countess complained. "She was a socialist, and I'm very happy she's finally gone . . . You, I hope, are not a socialist?"

Klobukova reassured the countess.

Her father, she said, was a retired captain and prison warden, her brother was a police officer, and she herself professed quite moderate beliefs.

"*Je vous en félicite*," the countess responded, adding that in November her grandchildren with their two governesses would be arriving, and then Klobukova would have people to talk to, for they would all have breakfast and lunch together.

But in the meantime, Varvara Stepanovna had to sit at the table alone, and she was unbearably lonely from having nobody to talk to. Nor did she find palatable the *suprême de volaille à l'Elysée* or the aromatic fine wines she was served. She longed for the sweet taste of cabbage, for dried salty fish.

At home in Mertvovodsk, she had known how to fill her day—visiting clients, doing things around the house, mending, embroidering, knitting doilies and other totally useless objects; on summer evenings, she would walk to the main boulevard where officers and post-office clerks courted her; in winter she would go skating or visit friends or attend balls at the club.

Never before had she been away from her hometown or her family. Now she languished in the grip of sadness.

The alien French faces, so different from the Russian type; the quick, nasal speech, which made it hard to discern what was being said; the cheery beauty of the landscape; the strangeness of the peasants' garb—all this made Klobukova uncomfortable and sometimes angry. . . .

"The devil only knows why they need wooden shoes!" she would exclaim crossly.

Day by day, she grew more sullen and grim. She lost weight and became pale. She even wept a few times.

"I'm such a fool," she would say, trying to stop herself. "A twenty-two-year-old crying like a school girl . . . ."

But admonitions did not help. Tears streamed down her face as she climbed into her huge rosewood bed a little after nine in the evening, thinking angrily and bitterly how lousy her life was. For the sake of a few hundred francs she had left her native land and all of her loved and dear ones, parted with all her old habits and customs, gone God knows where to live with God knows whom, sold herself into servitude.

In her dreams, when she would finally fall asleep, she would see Mertvovodsk—the market square littered with horse manure; a soldier standing in the watch tower; pigs strolling on the boulevard; the tipsy sexton, Lavrenty; the firm, oak-brown legs of Gorpyna, the dishwasher; and other people, vistas, and objects close to her heart. . . .

If, of a nighttime, Russia or things Russian failed to fill her dreams, she would arise in the morning more subdued and somber than ever. . . .

Everything around her was more beautiful, more graceful, more fanciful, more costly, and more cheerful than in Russia, and still they elicited only vexation, ennui, and longing. "When the governesses come I'll feel better, happier," she tried to console herself. But she knew that the governesses could not help and that the longer she stayed, the more acute and unbearable her yearnings would become. Every day she wrote lengthy letters—even to people she wasn't close to—counting the days ahead and marking down when she should expect a reply.

"I should leave everything, run away!" would sometimes flash in her head.

But then she would immediately recall her family's dire finances, soon to worsen when her brother Vasya went to university, and her parents' little old house, mortgaged and remortgaged and upon the very point of foreclosure. . . .

And, gathering all her strength and courage, Varvara Stepanovna would chase away the enticing thought of escape and go on bearing her cross with ever increasing anguish.

II

One day after breakfast, she was taking a walk in a meadow along the bank of a stream. It had just rained, and tousled scraps of storm clouds, blackish-blue and softly silver, rushed across the sky, ceaselessly changing shades and shapes. Now the sun hid away, now it emerged, causing light effects that followed each other in sharp rapidity. First the poplars lining the stream's banks sparkled in the bright sunshine, while the pine forest behind them was enveloped in gloomy, listless shadow; a moment later, hot rays of light fell upon the forest, while the poplars grew dusky and almost black. But the landscape's brighter and happier hues escaped Varvara Stepanovna's notice; her longing soul was fixed on the gloom of the cold shadows.

"God, how unbearable," she said with a sigh. "A penal colony . . . worse than any penal colony."

"*Comment?*" someone unexpectedly spoke up from the other side of some tall blackberry bushes girding the stream.

Varvara Stepanovna raised her head.

Sitting on the bank, angling, was a decrepit old man wearing brown satin trousers and a navy blue shirt. Klobukova muttered something and made as if to continue on her way. Removing his hat, the old man greeted her.

"*Bonjour, mademoiselle!* Taking a walk? Well, the weather today isn't too shabby. Would you care to do some fishing? Please, have a seat next to an old man."

He spoke rapidly, mumbling and lisping as old people do, and Varvara Stepanovna was unable to follow what he was saying.

"*Sit down, mademoiselle!*" The old man ran his hand along the grass next to him.

"If only this were old Nikanorych!" she thought. Neither sitting down nor leaving, she stared with distaste at his foreign face, beardless as an actor's.

"Here, I'll set up a rod for you," said the old man merrily. "It's a rather amusing thing, fishing. You, I suppose, are pretty bored here, right?"

"*Vee,*" Varvara Stepanovna replied with a sad smile.

"Sure! A foreign place . . ." The old man glanced quickly at the water before lifting his eyes to Klobukova. "You see, I think this: our country isn't bad, but if one isn't from here, one has got to be pretty bored."

Varvara Stepanovna stood in silence. . . .

"Yes. I, for instance, am about to be eighty-three years old, and I've never been farther than fifty kilometers from my village. The town of Chaumont[9] is only six kilometers away, and yet I haven't been there more than ten times. You know, home's best."

The old man moved his lips and fell silent.

Varvara Stepanovna still did not walk away from him.

"But tell me please, *mademoiselle*, how does one get to your country? By way of Spain?"

Varvara Stepanovna explained the route from there to Russia.

---

9   Chaumont—a town in the Haute-Marne region of France.

"Oh, I see! Well, Austria is okay, too. A nice place. What isn't good is being away from home. My son Ernest has been abroad—in Prussia, as a prisoner of war. And what do you think? He wants some grape vodka, and he cannot say 'grape vodka' to a Prussian. A Prussian wouldn't get it; he has a totally different word for it. And fish, for instance, isn't fish to him but something else. Everything's different."

A bitter smirk twisted Varvara Stepanovna's mouth. The gentle words of this compassionate oldster had given her a surge of warmth but also pain.

"*Mademoiselle*," he started again. "Have you met your countrymen in town?"

"*Comment?*" Varvara Stepanovna asked, listening more closely.

"Your countrymen, in Chaumont. Have you met them already?"

"What's he saying?" Klobukova thought, alarmed. "Are there Russians in Chaumont?"

"Ah, you don't know?" the old man sang out. "I can't believe they haven't told you. Oh, those people at the castle! They don't even know what to tell a person. Of course, you have fellow countrymen living in Chaumont, Russians."

"*Pas possible!*" Varvara Stepanovna exclaimed. "Are you sure?"

The old man made a face and shrugged his shoulders.

"*Parbleu*! On Sunday I was in their shop buying hats for my grandchildren. Why don't you go see? Go to the square where the prefecture is, and there on your left is Rue Sadi Carnot. Walk up the street, past a dozen houses or so, and there, opposite the lycée, there's a millinery shop."

In agitation Varvara Stepanovna stared at the old man. Russians? she thought. In Chaumont? Oh, my God! This cannot be true. What would they be doing in Chaumont, a nothing little town in central France? No, this is nonsense. The old man has it all wrong.

"Yes, and the hats are splendid, too. Expensive but very good, real felt. These countrymen of yours were banished from Russia," grunted the old man, stretching his legs, which had fallen asleep. "They were banished, and they came to live here. From your country they chase away the Israelites. They don't want them, but we don't mind. We let them stay."

Oh, they're kikes! Varvara Stepanovna drew it out in her mind.

And suddenly taking umbrage, she started to walk away.

"We let them stay," the old man repeated, studying the surface of the water. "Nothing wrong with it, selling hats. Why should we kick them out? Real felt. They charged me an arm and a leg, but they gave me real felt, shiny. When I sell them fish, I'll charge *them* an arm and a leg."

Having taken five or six steps, Varvara Stepanovna composed herself. She felt that she had acted discourteously. Turning toward the fisherman and, trying to sound friendly, she yelled out, "*Au revoir!*"

One could not say that Varvara Stepanovna hated Jews. She had never had a significant encounter with one, never observed them closely, did not associate them with anything specifically bad, could not justly feel any animosity toward them. But she found them ridiculous and deserving of contempt, if not revulsion: they were repulsive, chafing creatures. Along with her father—and probably all of Mertvovodsk—she knew and could explain to you that Jews cared about nothing but commerce and moneylending, that they ate garlic and something called kugel, that they gave off a foul smell and had crooked noses, and, finally, that the Russian people suffered on their account. If she ever saw a ragged Jew on the street, she would hold her nose and think "dirty Jew"; and when she came across smartly dressed Jews promenading on the boulevard or at the club, she would mock their lack of taste and remind herself that their silks and velvets had been paid for with stolen cash.

And now, under the label of fellow countrymen, she was to be served up these same stinking Jews? . . . For the rest of the day Klobukova felt a depressing mixture of chagrin, bitterness, and a gnawing disappointment. It was as if she had read in the newspaper that she had won the lottery and then it turned out to be a misprint, she hadn't won anything at all. . . .

Still, she thought, what if there really were Russians living there? Yes, a remote corner of the world, the sticks, the middle of nowhere—but didn't she, Klobukova, end up here? So why couldn't others? And how good that would be, how fortunate! She would have someone to talk to, to give her heart a rest. She could visit these Russians in town, and they would come to see her in the castle. Life would assume a totally different course! She could stay longer with the countess then: a year, even two. After all, no matter how you looked at it, life here was comfortable and the pay was excellent. She could order books on embroidery, study French, subscribe to a Russian magazine. Sure, Klobukova concluded, I could arrange my life here better if there were people, Russians, even a single family. Otherwise I'll die of longing.

Up until today it had never even occurred to her that there might be Russians in Chaumont; now, the lack of them struck her as strange, almost unfair. She was getting angry. Now Jews are all over the place; you find them everywhere. But Russians? They're so inert, afraid to move; they sit by their stoves and never take so much as a step anywhere.

At night, before falling asleep, Varvara Stepanovna sat on her bed and cried. She was thinking about her family, who just like that had let her go off to a foreign land. They should have struggled, suffered, borrowed money, done anything, but they should never have sent her so far away, to this cursed castle. They had acted greedily, selfishly.

It took a letter six days to reach Russia, crossing three borders and all of Switzerland and Austria. What if she were to die here? It could happen—no one was insured against death—and there would be no one to bury her. "I'll go to town, to see those kikes!" Klobukova suddenly decided. She was overcome by a desire to spite someone, to have revenge. "What's the big deal! I swear I'll go. By God, I'll go."

The windows of her bedroom lay open to the park. The moon shone brightly; listless shadows fell along the winding paths and across the lawns. The pond slept, as did the trees and birds, and a deep, untroubled silence reigned all around.

Like a cemetery, Klobukova thought, and I'm all alone. She got down from the bed, put out the candle, and sat by the window.

"The town lies just beyond this forest. On foot, I could get there in an hour and a half." She sat still, her eyebrows raised, and stared out at the forest and at the road to Chaumont that flanked it like a magical, shining stripe. Varvara Stepanovna could not take her eyes off that stripe. "*Zdravstvuyte*," she suddenly said in Russian, smiling softly. And then, changing the pitch and tone of her voice, she responded to herself, "Hello . . ."

Tomorrow she might hear somebody else say this same word to her. And, "What good fortune brings you here!" And many other such things. And she would speak Russian, a lot, and for a long time! "Why shouldn't I go see them?" she asked herself. "Why not? Of course I'll go."

In the morning, when she awoke, her first thought was that today she would be going to town to see the Jews. "So what if they are kikes? They are still almost my own people. And what if they turn out to be decent? There are occasionally decent Jews. Take Dr. Morgulis—all of Mertvovodsk receives him, the best homes; he even gets invited to General Skripitsyn's Christmas party. A very decent person, no worse than your average Russian."

From nine to ten in the morning, she gave the countess her massage. Immediately thereafter, she started to ready herself for her journey. But since the mailman did not make his second round of the day until two in the afternoon, and since she had marked in her notebook that today, 18 October, two letters were due—one from Semyon Ivanovich and one from her Aunt Anfisa—she decided to wait. She ate her lunch with appetite, her face considerably less gloomy than before. She couldn't stop thinking about the Jews who lived in Chaumont, whom she envisioned looking exactly like Dr. Morgulis—neatly dressed, not misrolling their *r*s too badly, their noses not at all crooked.

The mailman came at the usual hour, but there were no letters. This small misfortune, which recurred almost daily and customarily plunged her into a black mood, left Klobukova unmoved. "No problem. Tomorrow I'll have three letters, including one from Vasya."

Hurriedly she put on her hat and veil and headed to town.

III

The road traversed several hamlets. The peasants were threshing grain, and the rumbling whistle of the machines could be heard everywhere. Every so often huge carts clattered by carrying loads of straw or bags of grain. The fat, strong horses harnessed in teams of four, sometimes six, stepped slowly, tranquilly, effortlessly. Along the way, the peasants bowed to Varvara Stepanovna and struck up a conversation. She spoke to them cheerfully, bravely, although she did get confused and befuddled at every phrase, and she laughed aloud when, failing to comprehend something or other, she answered them at random.

She was in a strange mood.

She felt happy, and she knew that the best and most interesting part was yet to come. But at the same time, she was still vaguely offended at the idea that here she was, going to see Jews.

She was doing something wild, unbecoming, and somehow it humiliated her in her own eyes.

"If I have to associate with kikes, I wish they'd come to see me first. But there they are, sitting at home, happy as clams, and I'm running after them."

Her thoughts unsettled and confused her, but she brushed them away and with all her strength tried not to give in to the anger that flared up in her.

"What can you do," she asked herself. "No wonder the Ukrainians have a saying: 'In a foreign city, seeing a dog is almost as good as seeing your own father.' And besides, they couldn't really have come to see me. How would they have known I'm here? Besides, they wouldn't dare. And anyway, it's only me who's such a ninny as to need fellow countrymen. Someone else in my place wouldn't even *want* to see them." As she approached the town, her offense gave way to a pleasant rush of anticipation. "Funny, isn't it," she thought, an involuntary smile appearing on her lips. "How strange! How terribly strange!" And then, entering the town, crossing a railroad bridge, she had a new and jarring idea. "What if the Jews refuse to see me? What if they treat me coldly or even rudely? Didn't they emigrate from Russia because things were bad for them there, because they were oppressed? That must mean they don't like Russia and Russians. They could, perhaps, insult me, offend me."

"They wouldn't dare!" Varvara Stepanovna was becoming angry again, though she realized her anger was misplaced. "Why shouldn't they, after all? What's to prevent them? Here they have nothing to fear." And suddenly she herself was overcome by fear. More than ever before, she felt lonely, abandoned, forgotten. Aunt Anfisa wasn't writing, . . . and Vasya wasn't either.

She stopped.

Her eyes filled with sadness and self-pity as they fixed on the tall building of the police prefecture, which was where she was to turn onto Rue Sadi Carnot. For a couple of minutes she stood stock still. "No, it's okay. I'm going!" She shook off her stupor. "I'm going. What will be, will be!"

She hastened across the square in front of the prefecture, her heart trembling as she saw a dark blue sign, Rue Sadi Carnot, on the yellowish wall of the tall corner building. She stared at the white letters, which seemed to smile and bow to her. "Strange," she thought, walking up the street, "so strange."

Having taken about a hundred steps, Varvara Stepanovna stood in front of the lycée. The building was set back from the street, surrounded by a large garden, and she could see only heavy gates and an ornate fence. Klobukova walked along the length of the fence as shadows from its wrought-iron ornaments swam across her face and bodice. At the end she saw a large gray house with balconies. Next to it stood another house, a white one. Across the road, in a squat brick building, there was a glass door and over the door a sign: *Chapellerie moderne.*

"Of course, it's here," Varvara Stepanovna said out loud. "Here!"

She ran across the street and, after climbing the front steps, peered inside. A short, stooped, scrawny man with completely gray hair stood behind the counter, staring sorrowfully at the street through the window. He had only one eye, a blemish that was imperfectly concealed by the big round spectacles placed athwart his short, fleshy nose. His left hand was gripping a shelf cluttered with hat boxes, while his right hand drummed lazily on the counter.

"Well, isn't this strange?" Varvara Petrovna said to herself. "It's as though he were Uncle Afanasy Petrovich, and I'm about to surprise him by turning up."

She pushed open the door and, hardly over the threshold, called in a resounding voice, "*Zdravstvuyte!* Well, hello!"

The gray-haired man behind the counter made a strange, jerking motion. His glasses jumped, the large round lenses sparkling.

"*Oy* . . . what's this?" he exclaimed, startled.

And for a moment he froze.

Then he swiftly turned his face to the dark-red curtain behind the counter and yelled for all he was worth, "Dvoyra! Dvoyra! Come here right away, Dvoyra! *Oy*, look what's happening here!" He was speaking in Yiddish, and Varvara Stepanovna's heart smiled at the guttural sounds that she could not understand but recognized so well.

"You're Russian? You're from Russia? When did you come from Russia?" The old man threw himself at Klobukova. "Oh, how wonderful! So you're from Russia! Where from? What province? Taurida? No? From Kherson? Oh, my God! That's incredible! That's so rare!"

With both hands he shook Varvara Stepanovna's small hand, still shouting in agitation, "You know, we've been here eleven years now, and this is only the third time I've seen a Russian person. Only the third time. In eleven years! Well? What do you say to that? Dvoyra! Come now! Come, look, just look who's here!"

"Well, no, they won't hurt me," Varvara Stepanovna thought, smiling gently at the agitated Jew. "How excited he is to see me! What a funny little fellow!" The red curtain fluttered, and Dvoyra entered, a short plump woman wearing a dark-brown dress. Hers was a typical Jewish face, with a large curved nose and big beady eyes. With composure, carrying herself with cold pride, she bowed to Klobukova and stood by the counter.

"A Russian, you see! She's Russian!" the excited old man pointed to Varvara Stepanovna.

Dvoyra made a wry face. "What are you so happy about?" she asked him in a halfwhisper, in Yiddish. "Did you get an inheritance or something?"

The old man cast a baffled look at his wife, then turned again to Varvara Stepanovna and began to jabber, "My name's Shapiro. We're from Russia . . . Why, we're from Krivaya Balka.[10] Oh yes! We used to live in Krivaya Balka.

---

10 Krivaya Balka—like Varvara's Mertvovodsk, the Shapiros' Krivaya Balka is an invented name. Most likely it refers to Krivoy Rog, a town in Kherson Province of the Russian Empire, presently in Ukraine, where anti-Jewish violence took place in 1883. At the turn of the nineteenth century, Krivoy Rog had a Jewish population of almost 3,000 out of a total of about

And you? Permit me to ask, are you here visiting? Passing through town? And how much longer will you stay? Oh, what a wonderful thing! Simply incredible! But please pass through into the parlor. Why are we standing here? Please, please come in!"

"She's fine where she is," Dvoyra grumbled in Yiddish, angrily pursing her lips. "She can go back where she came from."

Bewildered, Shapiro glanced at his wife. "Ah, you'd better be quiet," he mumbled softly but very dramatically. "My God, what's come over you?"

"Please, come into the dining room," he called out to Varvara Stepanovna, dashing to the curtain and pulling it open with an energetic motion. "Oh, how did it all happen, that you went so far from home? Here, please, sit here, in the armchair, by the light, by the window, please! Dvoyra, invite her, *nu!*"

"Well, sit down," Dvoyra said gloomily as if forcing herself to speak. "I guess we can sit for a while."

All three entered the dining room and sat, and Varvara Stepanovna started to tell them the story of where she was from and how she ended up in France. "Ah, forgive me, please," Shapiro suddenly jumped up from his chair. "Forgive me for interrupting . . . Just one moment . . . I should call for a samovar."

"Why a samovar?" Dvoyra confronted her husband in a deep low voice. "No need, the water boils faster on gas."

"Oh no, Dvoyrochka! Gas? Don't you understand? This is a Russian person. She needs tea from a samovar!"

"We don't have any coal," Dvoyra muttered.

"No coal?" Shapiro grabbed his head with both hands and made a comically pitiful face. "*Oy*, what a misfortune! Can there be any coal in this town? Is this possible? In the whole town they've burned up all the coal? Georgette! Georgette!" he dashed to the door. "Georgette, run quick to Monsieur Petitjean's shop and bring some coal. And put on the samovar, quick! And do it in one minute, in one second!" He was speaking in some extraordinary, homegrown, French-Russian-Yiddish dialect. Varvara Stepanovna couldn't help smiling.

"This little old Jew is all right," rushed through her head. "He seems to be hospitable and kind." But her feelings were moving faster than her thoughts, and her feelings did not care for her mind's condescending tone. Her entire

---

15,000 residents. The name also evokes Balta, a town in the former Podolia Province, where a well-documented pogrom erupted in 1882. Shapiro's further comments betray Aizman's detailed knowledge of the region, as the village of Starye Krinitsy, which Shapiro mentions, most likely alludes to Belaya Krinitsa, halfway between Kherson and Krivoy Rog.

being was drawn to this noisily bustling Jew and even to his gloomy, pouting wife. Happy and excited, she continued her tale about life at the castle, speaking with complete openness, concealing nothing, and all the while feeling as though she were addressing members of her own family or people she had known for a long time. . . .

Dvoyra maintained her harsh expression, but her husband could not tear his eyes away from Varvara Stepanovna, nor, like her, could he stop smiling. At times he lost his self-control, exclaiming, "Oh, my God," "*Nu! Nu!*" or "That's wonderful!" And these exclamations reflected not so much the stories Varvara Stepanovna was telling as the marvelously delightful and joyful state that had suddenly gripped his heart and soul.

Turning to the subject of her loneliness and longing, Klobukova tried to sound humorous, but Shapiro, it seemed, knew well the bitterness and anguish that lay beneath this humor. Sorrowfully he looked at Varvara Stepanovna, sighing with compassion and rocking his head. "Of course, of course," he said under his breath. "What do you expect, being so far from home. And besides, it's your first time. And you are still a child. Just a child. When a person is thrown like this into a foreign place, surely he is the most miserable individual in the whole wide world. . . ."

IV

Then Shapiro, in turn, started telling her about his business and his children. Their son Solomon worked as a *chef d'atelier* at "the biggest" hat factory in Lyon. Their daughter was doing well in school and, God willing, would become a doctor. Dunechka was now visiting her brother in Lyon, but in a few days she was coming back, "and you'll see for yourself what a beauty she is and how well educated." As he talked about their children, his wife Dvoyra's face became less gloomy, and she even put in a few words. Cheered, her husband brightened still more and began to speak even more openly and loudly.

"Why did you leave Russia?" Varvara Stepanovna asked.

Shapiro became flustered. "It just turned out that way." An embarrassed, guilty smile appeared on his face. "Do I know why? Silliness. I got it into my head, and I left."

"Did you have a hard life in Krivaya Balka?"

"Hard?" Shapiro lifted his eyebrows. "Not hard, but you know . . . We lived the way everybody does. But you know, well, how could I explain this to you? Well, for instance fish seek deeper waters, and man . . ."

"Why are you telling tales?" Dvoyra suddenly interrupted, noisily pulling up her chair and planting both elbows on the table. "'Fish seek deeper water . . .' Did she ask you about fish? We escaped from Krivaya Balka because of the pogroms. There's the answer for you!"

"Please, Dvoyra. Leave it be!" Shapiro said in a shrill, almost frightened voice. "Leave it be. This isn't the right time."

"It's always the right time! What kind of secrets are these? Why leave it out? You think we had a sweet life there? We suffered, we endured, our entire life we were just trying to survive. And then came the good people—your Russian people—and made a pogrom, and everything we had in the house they destroyed instantly."

"Well, they destroyed it. Well, well, what's to be done about it now?" Shapiro beseeched his wife. "Please let's not talk about it."

"And they whacked him in the eye with an iron," Dvoyra raised her voice. "And he's been blind ever since. He lost his eye. Why would we stay there after that? Tell me, please. So they could torment us some more? You think it wasn't enough? I think we'd had plenty. So that's why we left. We were going to America, but on our way my brilliant husband's other eye started to hurt—the eyes are connected, and when one hurts, the other responds—and he nearly went totally blind. So we couldn't go any further, and when we got to Chaumont he had to be hospitalized. And my two children and I were left on the pavement. And it looked like our only option was to lie down and die or else throw ourselves under a train. Well? What were we to do? But let me tell you, maybe the people here aren't as nice as in Russia . . . don't interrupt!" Dvoyra yelled, casting a furious glance at her husband. "Don't interrupt, I'm telling you, be quiet! I, thank God, haven't gone mad yet! I, too, am allowed to say a few words!

"Here the people didn't take out our eyes, you know," she went on, turning toward Varvara Stepanovna. "And they didn't rob us either. They gave us shelter and a job—sewing visors on hats. My Solomon and I, we worked day and night, first visors, then ribbons, and when this president of mine left the hospital, not only did we have food on the table but we also had an apartment and had managed to save up seventy francs. You see?"

Dvoyra sat with her arms akimbo and proudly nodded her head. "Could we possibly have had all this in Russia? What do you think? And so we settled here, and thank God, we're happy here."

"Happy, eh?" Shapiro moaned in a quiet voice, looking sadly at the plush frames with pictures of Chaumont hanging on the wall in front of him.

"Yes, happy! Just so you should know, we're happy. In Russia he was a tailor. There we were always hungry. And now, look at our store. This is no small thing! And no one abuses us or hurts us, and no one makes our life miserable, no one yells 'stinking kike!' at us. We're treated like people here, so there!"

And Dvoyra spread her arms in an expressive gesture and leaned back against her chair. Having gotten everything off her chest in front of Varvara Stepanovna, she evidently felt relieved. Her face had lost its gloomy pout, and instead she shone with an air of independence and proud contentment.

Varvara Stepanovna was looking at the Jewish woman timidly, out of the corner of her eye.

For the first time in her life, she had had occasion to have a conversation with Jews; for the first time, she had listened carefully and seriously, without a desire to mock. Dvoyra's seething words made her feel quietly sad and vaguely selfreproachful.

"But tell me, please," Shapiro asked in a small voice. "Do you happen to know how the crops are now in our Kherson Province?"

"Bad, I think. Everything got scorched."

"Scorched again!"

Dvoyra shrugged her shoulders contemptuously.

"So what's going to happen now?" the old man continued, as if thinking out loud. "Well, in Krivaya Balka they do have some retail stores, although now, of course, what sort of sales can they expect? But what's going to happen in the villages? In Korenikha, for instance? Or in Chervonnoe, in Starye Krinitsy?"

He grew silent for a minute. Then he sighed. "People are going to die," he answered his own question.

"*Vey*!" Dvoyra burst in, derisively pressing her lips together. "What's the great sorrow? Let them . . ."

Shapiro swiftly raised his head. "Dvoyra!" he moaned, folding his hands on his chest. "Why are you doing this? Why, I ask you?" And turning to Varvara Stepanovna, he said, "You know, this is all a show. You're sitting here, a Russian, and she wants to show you that she's angry with the Russians and cannot stand them. But actually," Shapiro glanced at his wife with a sad smile, "actually, she's the one who thought of calling our daughter Dunya, Dunechka."[11]

"That means nothing," Dvoyra said, taken aback.

---

11 Dunya, Dunechka—diminutives of the Russian Christian name Evdokiya (Avdotya).

"In Russia we called our little girl by her Jewish name, Branka. And the Russian kids would yell 'banker,' 'wanker,' 'tanker,' and other rhymes they'd come up with."

"When a Russian needs to offend a Jew, he knows how to find good rhymes," Dvoyra added.

"But no matter how much they insulted our little girl, we paid no heed and continued to call her our way—Branka. But since we went abroad, my wife started calling her Dunya . . . What? Isn't it true?"

Dvoyra was silent. A sorrowing smile played faintly on her full lips. Varvara Stepanovna looked at Shapiro, then at his wife. She wanted to say something nice, tender, warm, but for some reason she felt awkward, and the words would not come.

But then Georgette rolled into the room, a round old French lady in a white apron and bonnet, and set a samovar and glasses on the table.

"*Nous voici à Moscou maintenant,*" she burbled in a kindly voice. "*Du thé, le samovar, une belle demoiselle russe . . . Ah, que j'aime la jeunesse!*"[12]

Dvoyra started pouring tea.

No doubt she was tired of being dour, and her husband's words had knocked the wind out of her sails. . . . Gradually her face lost its final traces of grimness, and she was becoming more and more friendly. Ceremoniously, with a certain affectation, she waited on Varvara Stepanovna, insisting that she take four—no fewer than four—lumps of sugar with her tea and diligently spooning first sour cherry and then apricot preserves onto her plate, followed by brown pastries with honey that she had baked herself. As the conversation grew livelier, they jumped from topic to topic, but no matter what they talked about— people, buildings, weather, hat making—everything was connected with Russia and Russians. Dvoyra's tongue was finally untied, and she jabbered loudly in a singsong. Varvara Stepanovna's face, a typical, good Russian face, white with rosy cheeks, clear blue eyes, and a fresh, affectionately smiling mouth, was an invitation to open up, and within half an hour Dvoyra no longer held back any secrets from her guest. She was pouring out her whole heart.

And Varvara Stepanovna also talked, talked, and smiled, listening to her own voice and her words in quiet wonderment. How unexpected this all was! How strange! How unusual! And how long it was since she had been in such pleasant and entertaining company!

---

12 *Nous voici à Moscou*, etc. = "Now here we are in Moscow. Some tea, the samovar, a young Russian beauty . . . Oh, how I love youth!"

Now Shapiro was the only one with little to say. Three times he went back to the store to wait on customers, and when he returned he sat quietly and listened to the women talk. His expression had grown pensive, gently doleful, and now and then a quiet, forgiving smile surfaced on his bloodless lips.

Dvoyra took Klobukova to look at Dunechka's room, showed Klobukova her daughter's photograph, her books and notebooks, and then started taking her trousseau out of the closets and trunks. She had already put away four eiderdown comforters, and a fifth was in the works; there were dozens of different chemises and blouses, cuts of silk and satin. "She says she doesn't need all this," Dvoyra said. "All she worries about are her studies. Does a child understand? She wants to be a doctor. With pleasure! But a down comforter cannot hurt."

"Haven't you had enough?" Shapiro stopped his wife. "Put away the rags, why don't you talk of something else?"

"No, about this, about this," Varvara Stepanovna yelled playfully, digging into a new pile of lingerie. "If you would please not interrupt us. This is women's business."

"That's right!" Dvoyra agreed. "Women's business. And you—sit here and listen, philosopher!"

For a while longer, the women went through clothes and chatted away. Varvara Stepanovna liked Dvoyra more and more. She now thought that, both in appearance and in character, this new acquaintance resembled her cousin twice removed Vasilisa Efremovna, the wife of the rural deacon from Novopokrovsk. Her cheeks, too, were chubby and red, and her waist started under her shoulder blades, and she laughed just the same way, raucously and heartily. A little funny, but dear, very dear.

V

About an hour and a half later, Klobukova picked up her hat and announced she was leaving. But Dvoyra, bowing ceremoniously and pulling a face, tried to take the hat out of her hands.

"Let's say," she said in a sugary falsetto, "let's say we won't let you go, and you'll stay for supper. Today, by the way, is Friday."

The invitation both gladdened and confused Varvara Stepanovna. She had no desire whatsoever to hurry back to the castle, but she didn't want to take advantage of her new acquaintances' hospitality. "It will be too late to return," she objected indecisively.

"And why should you return late when you can return early?" Shapiro asked with a sly smile.

Varvara Stepanovna thought she knew what he meant, but it only added to her embarrassment. "Yes, exactly," the old man went on. "Your countess gets up at nine, so if you sleep over and leave here bright and early, you'll surely make it back in time."

"Oh, how wonderful!" Dvoyra splashed the air with her hands. "That's the best thing to do. Makes the most sense. You'll sleep in Dunechka's room."

A half-hour later, all three settled around the festively set table. Six candles stood lit in new nickel-plated candlesticks, and in front of them, under a starched, snowwhite napkin, loomed two large challahs. Customarily the Shapiros' Friday-evening meal was accompanied by solemn rituals, but this time, for the sake of their guest, Shapiro simplified matters considerably, and after a brief prayer he sat down at the head of the table. A fish course—stuffed carp—was served, followed by a traditional broth with noodles, then chicken and compote.

"And where's the kugel?" Varvara Stepanovna inquired.

Dvoyra explained that one ate kugel on Saturday, at midday, and that the tasty dish in question was still baking in the oven. "There's no kugel for you," Shapiro chimed in, "but you will get to sing *zemiros.*"

"What's that, *zemiros?*"

"They're Sabbath songs. We sing them between courses, in Hebrew, the ancient Jewish tongue."

"Oh, please sing, please!"

"Will you help with the high notes?"

"Yes, yes. Please start."

Shapiro cleared his throat, rubbed the outside of his windpipe with a finger as if to clear it, and started singing an ornate oriental-sounding song in a trembling, goatish voice:

> He who sanctifies the Sabbath properly,
> He who observes it unprofaned,
> Will have a great reward . . .[13]

---

13 "He who sanctifies"—the opening of the first of the melodies traditionally sung at the Sabbath meal.

"Sing along, go ahead," said Dvoyra, nudging Klobukova, although she herself did not understand a single word of her husband's Hebrew song. Varvara Stepanovna opened her mouth and sang with an expression of timidity and reverence. For a minute or two, a wondrous cacophony filled the room. Then the old man's voice climbed somewhere very high and, halting suddenly, he started to laugh.

"We don't have a conductor, that's why," he explained.

They rose late from the table—it was after nine. Varvara Stepanovna felt both tired and almost intoxicated from all these new and unexpected impressions. She was pleased, amused, and also a bit melancholy. She thought of her own family, of her longing to see them, and of her recent despair. "Dear, dear," she thought, looking at the shortish Dvoyra, so wishing to pour tenderness upon her, to hug and kiss her.

VI

Georgette put out the candles, wished her employers good night, and retired.

Dvoyra lay in bed, stretching with pleasure. It was quiet. The dense white curtains swallowed the moonlight, and a transparent, pale green dusk permeated the room. "Well? What do you say to this whole business?" she asked in a halfwhisper.

Shapiro sat on an ottoman by the window. Light fell on him from behind; his expressive, sorrowful face was covered in thick shadow. "All sorts of encounters happen," he replied vaguely, "so this one had to happen too."

"Such a remarkable person," Dvoyra put in, speaking with passion but without raising her voice. "So gentle, so polite. Just like our own child, I swear!"

"She must be well educated," Shapiro said. "You know, they torment us, but their young people, when they're well educated, they're so good, so good, there are none better in the whole world."

"So modest, so tender!"

"Remember, in Krivaya Balka, Vasyl Ivanovich, the priest's son . . . he was later exiled to Siberia?"

"When she saw Dunechka's corsets, the ones embroidered in silk and lace, she sighed with awe," Dvoyra recalled, dreamily staring at the ceiling. "That's okay. It's good for her to know."

Shapiro didn't reply. He sat, his hands resting on his knees, his head tilted to the side. Several minutes passed in silence. At the lycée across the street, the clock tolled the eleventh hour, slowly, with long pauses. The final beat was especially long and sad, as if sighing after the somber place of its birth even while slipping from the narrow and suffocating clock tower and flying up toward the bright moon and the free sky. . . .

"You know, Dvoyrenu, what I'm thinking right now?" Shapiro lifted his head.

"What?"

"This is what I'm thinking: Suppose back then, you and I had suffered through everything and never left Krivaya Balka. Then, say, for instance, our grandchildren, or even our great-grandchildren—would they have been able to live there safely, like human beings?"

Startled, Dvoyra stirred in bed. "Oh, that old tune!" she said in vexation.

Shapiro didn't reply. "Sure, it's old," he acknowledged after a pause. "Old is right." He continued to sit without moving, his head tilted toward his left shoulder.

"In front of the little house where our heder stood, there was always a swampy patch," he spoke again, unhurriedly, smiling a quiet, clumsy, pained smile. "And whenever it rained, a sort of pond would form there, and the boys used to go wading. They would roll up their trousers to the groin and roam around in it. Me, too. And my grandmother would drag me out and beat me. I would weep, and my grandmother would weep, and she would give me a cookie. I had scrofula on my legs, and it got inflamed when I waded in that water. I wonder if the little house is still there, and that swamp."

"Please, go to bed already," Dvoyra whispered with irritation. "Sleep!"

Shapiro didn't move. Something knocked against the ceiling. Upstairs, in Dunechka's room, Varvara Stepanovna was throwing off her boots.

"Fifty years we lived and worked there," the old man went on sorrowfully. "Our fathers, grandfathers, great-grandfathers are all buried there . . . and four of our children."

Dvoyra turned noisily to the wall. "So what do you want? Why all this now? Now he's going to drag it out and drag it out. Go to bed, I'm telling you!" Strangled tears could be heard in her trembling voice.

Shapiro sighed loudly. "If a time came . . . if only for our grandchildren, our great-grandchildren," he muttered.

Dvoyra no longer responded. "They'll get hit on the head with a log," her heart cried out. But she suppressed the words and lay without moving, with the blanket pulled over her head.

Shapiro looked over at his wife. He wanted to say more, but he took pity. Quietly he got up and went out into the yard. There, near the cellar, in a broad band of shadow, stood a large planter with a short, stocky boxwood tree. The French are fond of these shrubs, which are in leaf throughout the year and provide green branches for decorating headstones. The little tree had been watered earlier in the evening, and now, under the bright rays of the moon, the green drops on its dark branches sparkled like fireflies.

Shapiro sat on the edge of the wooden planter and turned his face to the sky. With his lone eye he gazed mournfully at the clear, docile moon pouring its light on this alien Chaumont as well as on that distant, sorrowful country where they had taken out his eye, where his dear ones were buried, a country to which he felt such a solid, such a sacred claim. He gazed, and the same old, old tune sounded in his sad heart: if only for our grandchildren, if only for our great-grandchildren, if only one day . . .

1902

Translated from the Russian by Maxim D. Shrayer

SEMYON YUSHKEVICH

Semyon Yushkevich (1868–1927), fiction writer and playwright, grew up in Odessa in an affluent family of Russianized Jews. Odessa's multiethnic population remained as a background in Yushkevich's literary imagination throughout his life, and assimilated urbanized Jews were his characters of choice and figures of verisimilitude. Yushkevich attended a Jewish government school and later a gymnasium, which he did not complete. He left home after marrying at seventeen and supported himself by working as a pharmacist's assistant and contributing prose to *The Odessa Sheet* (*Odesskii listok*). From 1893 to 1902, Yushkevich lived in Paris, graduating from the medical faculty of the Sorbonne. In 1897, Yushkevich's story "The Tailor. From Jewish Daily Life" appeared in the *narodnik* journal *Russian Wealth* (*Russkoe bogatstvo*); some critics consider the publication of this story to be the start of a new period in Jewish-Russian literature. The most famous—or infamous—Jewish-Russian author of the prerevolutionary period, Yushkevich is credited with making the Jewish question a piece of the thematic repertoire of mainstream Russian prose and drama in the 1900s–1910s.

Written in 1895, the short novel *Disintegration* appeared in *Sunrise* (*Voskhod*) in 1902 and made Yushkevich famous; his 1904 collection of stories sold a record 6,000 copies in one year. In the 1900s–1910s, Yushkevich published numerous works of fiction, including the short novels *Ita Gaine* (1901), *Our Sisters* (1903), *The Jews* (1904), and *Street* (1908, published 1911), and the three-volume satirical novel *Leon Drei* (1908–19). The Jewish literary historian Sergey (Israel) Zinberg (1873–1943) labeled Yushkevich the "assimilated chronicler of the disintegration" of the traditional Jewish petit-bourgeois family. While the products of this "disintegration"—the Jewish haute bourgeoisie and working class—sometimes interacted in Yushkevich's works in a rehearsed quasi-Marxist dialectic, in his best works history's footlights paled when compared to the blazing and often physical individuality of his characters. Yushkevich focused unabashedly on the urban extremities of abject poverty, crime, and prostitution. While less charismatically portrayed, Yushkevich's Jewish criminals anticipate the legendary Odessan gangsters of **Isaac Babel**. Yushkevich described his characters' sexuality and bodies with naturalistic and at times vulgar openness. His obsession with eroticism and carnality signaled a covertly modernistic orientation and reflected his aesthetic allegiance with such fashionable non-Russian authors of his age as the Austrian Jews, Hugo von Hofmannsthal and Arthur Schnitzler, and the Pole, Stanisław Przybyszewski, all three of whom were popular in turn-of-the century Russia. In his artistic imperative to push forward the chaste boundaries of Russian literature, Yushkevich anticipated the later works of his great contemporary and friend Ivan Bunin (1870–1953).

Through the writer Nikolay Teleshov, Yushkevich entered the "Wednesday" circle of neorealist writers and became affiliated with Maxim Gorky's Znanie publishing house; in 1903 through 1938, Znanie released the first five volumes of Yushkevich's eight-volume *Collected Works*. After the Kishinev Pogrom (1903), Yushkevich moved to Berlin and turned to playwriting. He wrote a total of fifteen dramas and comedies, which were staged by major theaters in Moscow and St. Petersburg and in the Russian provinces. His plays included *In the City* (1905), *The King* (1905, cf. **Isaac Babel**'s eponymous story of 1921), *Hunger* (1906, cf. the title of Knut Hamsun's 1890 novel), *Miserere* (1909, staged by the Moscow Art Theater), *Comedy of Marriage* (1909), *Mendel Spivak* (1914), and others.

Jewish readers took pride in Yushkevich's achievement but also voiced anxiety about some of the aspects of his works. In an article in *The Jewish Encyclopedia* published in Russian in 1906–13, Zinberg spoke of Yushkevich's "anti-artistic works" such as *In the City* and *Leon Drei*. Some felt that by airing dirty Jewish laundry Yushkevich gave ammunition to antisemites. Russian critics praised his "courage" and "honesty," albeit not always out of their love for Jews. Uneven and perhaps at times lacking in artistic taste and refinement, the talented Yushkevich did not appear either self-conscious or apologetic about his treatment of Jewish characters.

Yushkevich emigrated in 1920. In 1921, he went to the United States, where his works appeared in print in American Yiddish periodicals and in book form, and his plays were staged in Yiddish translation. Yushkevich remained prolific, publishing several books and contributing to Russian émigré periodicals. In 1924, he settled in Paris, where he died in 1927.

* * *

Dedicated to Gorky as a gesture acknowledging both a literary affinity and Gorky's numerous philosemitic statements, Yushkevich's famous novel *The Jews* (1903, published 1904) originally appeared, as Ruth Rischin demonstrated in her monumental study of 1993, in the Znanie (Knowledge) *Miscellany 2* (1904), with many censorial omissions.

The novel showcases the strength as well as the limitations of Yushkevich's literary gift. Compared to David Aizman's account of a pogrom in "The Bloody Deluge" (1908), which is harrowing in its controlled presentation, Yushkevich's graphic, shocking portrayal of anti-Jewish violence seems less than nuanced, even if in places it does reach the explosive intensity of Bialik's *The City of Slaughter* (1903). But just how much room is there for nuance and understatement when one writes of the enraged victimizers mutilating and raping their powerless and defenseless victims?

FROM *THE JEWS*[*]

Chapter 12

The pogrom began . . .

On Sunday, the sixth of April, precisely at two o'clock in the afternoon, bands of rabble, drunken and enraged, with a group of youths in the vanguard, let forth the whistles and catcalls that were to stifle within them the final remnants of compassion for others and of an understanding of their own actions. The sounds of rocks shattering glass were the first noises to break the bar of tension and terror of the moment. This was the initiating communication of an incitement to violence, a secret, mighty, persuasive, and commanding language. . . . And the truly menacing, the horrific cries of "Kill the Yids!" carried throughout the city.

The pogrom began. . . .

Surrounded by a festive crowd of onlookers and directed by invisible instigators, the violators burst into the first Jewish hovels they came upon, and the lament and bowl of people disoriented by terror filled the streets with all manner of human moans. And this lamentation, like an oath of weakness, sounded as a signal, and so the pogrom began to rage. . . .

Like those crazed by hatred, like those retaliating for long years of felt grievances, the violators ran into the homes of the poor, where blinded by rage, by joy, by excitation, they threw themselves on domestic possessions . . . . They battered down doors, smashed windows, broke apart furniture, threw dishes to the floor, tore open pillows and scattered the feathers, and after seizing everything that they could carry away—whether money or dresses—they

---

[*]   The text has been slightly abridged

dashed on amidst the approving crowd. They dashed like demons in their tattered clothing, frightful, carrying within them a thirst for destruction, for the eradication of those in whom they saw the unclean ones, the enemy, whom they now considered to be truly guilty for their own miserable lives. Some drunk and others sober, with faces breathing malice and conquest, they already seemed to sense that they held in their hands the dream of the good life, calm and secure, that would reign once they annihilated the Jews. They forgot about the amity in which they had lived with the Jews; they forgot about their own oppressive existence, about the ones who truly were guilty of imposing the yoke under which they lived. They saw only the enemy that was pointed out to them: the Jew, the Jews. And feeling only hatred toward the Jews, inculcated in them since childhood, and also a pitiless rage, they ignored their own unfortunate lives side by side with the Jews, they barbarically, fiendishly destroyed everything that fell into their hands as if the last day of the world had come and no other would ever be. They spared nothing, and neither pleas nor cries touched them. With each hour this madness of destruction escalated, and now the violators perseveringly stayed inside the houses of the Jews and with crowbars and axes unhurriedly chopped up, crushed, and destroyed the piteous goods of their unfortunate victims. . . .

The pogrom raged, the pogrom spread. . . . With astonishing speed, like a flame in a storm, the frightful news swept throughout the city, and the Jews, abandoning their dwellings, with cries and wringing of hands, embracing and making their farewells, tried to save their own lives. They hid in cellars or among Christians, if the latter accepted them, in attics, in outhouses, on rooftops, in stables; submissive as always, not daring to think about resistance, they ran out onto the streets. . . . And a heavy, tormenting anger beat in their hearts at the thought of this outrageous injustice that was being visited upon an innocent people. . . . Living walls, silent and submissive! By means of them, the current evil validated itself, and this evil presently gave them up to the people's anger in order to assuage their thirst for real vengeance, so terrible, so justifiable. Who could protect the Jews when they had been sacrificed in advance? And the city presented an astonishing aspect: given over to the rule of mindless violators, it was left without rule, and all that happened in it happened as if it had been sundered from the life of the rest of the country. The book of human law lay at its feet, and a drunken, maniacal populace trampled on it with disdain.

The pogrom continued. . . . It grew, spread, enveloping new layers of the city, and like a heaven-sent misfortune, resembling an ever more rapidly swinging chain, it beat in every direction, creating calamity among the population. The fiendishness of the violators intensified, and the joy of victory over a defenseless enemy soon attracted the crowd. In threatening handfuls, like Cossack chieftains, well-dressed people ran, bustled about, motioned, directed the violators, whipping up their anger to an even higher pitch. Feathers and down hung in the air and then fell to the ground, covering the city streets with a mask of innocence. . . . Everywhere piles of belongings and furniture that had been tossed out of windows and doors were lying about, some heavy and cumbersome, others light, and a well-dressed crowd of rapacious men, women, and children, without repugnance or horror, with the thirst of cowardly robbers, sorted through them, hid things under their clothes and left, innocently blinking their eyes and shaking their heads. . . .

The moans and wails carried throughout the city. . . . But the hunting rage did not abate, and the more completely the violators felt themselves to be masters of the situation and the more piteously the Jews begged to be spared, the more the anger of the violators increased. It was as if until this moment they had been deceived but only now ripened and clearly saw who their enemy was. The Jews prayed, the Jews wailed in fear, the Jews ran away—they were culpable— and those who were fleeing had to be caught and killed, the submissive had to be tortured, tormented, and beaten. . . . Wild rumors spread, passed from mouth to mouth, confusing minds, and the mayhem intensified. And what was most odd in this massive attack was the sense that it seemed to be directed by some kind of conscious will; not a single instance of indecision had been observed among the violators, and no gratuitous moves had been made. Everything took place as if it had been orchestrated. . . . From night to morning—and this was later noted— the gates of all Christian homes had been marked with a cross, while icons and cruciforms had been placed in windows; the holy images, as if in mockery, served as pointers for the violators, showing them where they should not and where they should plunder and kill. And there was something truly frightful and inhuman in this conspiracy of conscious will and elemental force. . . .

The bands rushed about amidst the din and encouragement of bystanders, and so long as the moans of those being tortured and killed did not resound, the pogrom resembled a created nightmare. But with the first killing, the last sluice gates seemed to have been thrown open, inundating the city in a bloody wrath in bloody waves. No one had ever heard such mad prayers, such cries of pain and terror; no one had ever seen such refined means of torture to which the defenseless victims were subjected. Inflamed by the instigators, by a previously unknown wild freedom, by popular approval, the violators went haywire with their victory. The wildest plans of vengeance were born in a flash, and the entire horror of the barbarism that resides in a person burst to the surface. The Jews tried to save themselves, but they were found everywhere. They were hunted on city streets with howls, with roars, with outcries. They were pushed from dray carts, from horse-drawn trains. They were stopped at train stations or captured outside train cars, dragged out of churches, seized in churches, and immediately beaten, murdered, fleeced pitilessly, without regard for gender or age. Nothing could soften the instincts of the violators, and this time the entire catechism of torment had to be exhausted. They burst into houses, sought out the Jews in cellars and in attics; they killed, defiled, raped young girls, beat them, or ripped open their bellies, or cut off their breasts, or strangled their babies, and when they ran off they left behind a pile of unconscious bodies or corpses. They bashed in heads with clubs, crowbars, or axes; men who resisted had their tongues torn out, their hands sawed off, their eyes gouged out, or their noses or heads pinned with nails. . . .

The slaughter began earlier in the outskirts than in the city. Nakhman and Natan, surrounded by Meita and Feiga, still did not believe what was happening. The gates of their house were locked; the men were walking around in the courtyard, and although they were pale and scowling and the women were wringing their hands and mumbling, still for some reason it seemed that the threat would pass them by. Old Sima and Chama hid under their beds, Mikhele stayed close to his mother, and Blyumochka, standing at the window, kept asking:

"What are those cries, Mother Chama, why are they crying in the yard?"

And Chama would reply, "They're crying because the city is burning, Blyumochka, hush! . . ."

"I'm frightened, Nakhman," resounded Meita's voice. "Let's run away from here."

"There are many men in the courtyard," Nakhman persisted in his determination to stay. From the moment the pogrom began, he became somehow disoriented. His replies were not to the point, he was lost in thought, he paced the room incessantly, while a great sorrow was growing in his soul. It was as if that enormous something that had been kindled inside of him and that had blinded him suddenly began to flicker out, to be destroyed, and because it had flamed up for nothing, because it had beckoned and now was going out, his eagerness for life was being extinguished along with it. A pogrom? Indeed, would the ground hold beneath his feet? Where was the great dream [...] about the coming equality of all peoples? Where was the truth that just yesterday had been so palpable? Where was the belief that Jews and Christians were brothers? They had been slaves of one life, of one suffering, but something enormous divided them, and it was turning out that the stronger slaves were attacking the weaker. ... And each time the torment of spiritual upset possessed him, he would run over to Meita and feverishly ask her, "Do you still believe in it, Meita, do you, at least, still believe?"

But Meita, forlorn and frightened, replied with a question:

"Why are they killing us, Nakhman?"

Only Natan remained calm. He did not pray, he did not ask questions, but in each word, in each glance thrown to Feiga, as ever, lay the force of his conviction.

"You aren't afraid, Feiga," he said, not letting go of her hand. "Tell me that you're not afraid. . . ."

But on the second day, it began. Around 10 o'clock in the morning, the sounds of the first blows against the gates rang out.

"They're here," cried someone in a strained voice. . . .

Screams were heard. Suddenly the gates were broken apart, with a groan they were thrown onto the ground, and a crowd of forty or so people with the cry "Kill the Yids!" burst into the courtyard. Their leader was the carpenter, a man of forty or so years, with a curly beard and a flat nose. He ran in front in peculiar, ungainly little jumps, and the red shirt he was wearing waved like a banner of blood lust. Behind him came a mob armed with crowbars, bludgeons, and axes, and their threatening shrieks "Kill the Yids!" sounded like striking cymbals. . . . Wailing, cries, and entreaties went round immediately. The man in the red shirt stopped, barked some commands, gasped, and completely unexpectedly bludgeoned the head of a Jew cutting across his path. The fall and cry of the Jew at once turned into a signal to plunder and slaughter. The pogromists scattered among the flats, and right away came the ugly sound of glass, furniture, doorframes, and doors being broken. Men, women, and children ran through the courtyard trying to save their lives. They threw themselves on their knees before the pogromists coming toward them, beseeching them. They were beaten, then they got up and flew to the side wall in order to jump into the houses of strangers, but they were pursued, beaten on the head, wounded. . . . The howls and shrieks became unbearable. In a single moment the spacious courtyard was transformed into a field of infamous battle.

The great moment of suffering was nearing. Natan and Feiga managed to hide in the cellar, but Nakhman, Meita, Blyumochka, and Chama had not been able to hide on account of the little girl, and so they returned to their own flat and bolted the door. Sima all the while remained under the bed protected by Mikhele.

At the window appeared the face of the red-shirted carpenter, peering into the room for a long time.

"Oho, lads, so many Yids!" echoed his raucous voice. "Lean on the door!"

Out of fear, Chama crawled under the bed and imploringly called to the children,

"Hide, my children, hide, my darlings, Blyumochka come to me!"

A strong blow with the crowbar shook the door. . . . The face of the carpenter appeared at the window again, and now the glowering gaze and the graying mustache splayed against the glass presented a terrifying image.

"Break down the door!" he commanded, having espied Meita.

Blyumochka crawled under the bed. She lay next to Chama and embraced her, and all her movements and prayers were so quiet that it would have been impossible to guess whether she was preparing to suffer or simply going through meaningless motions. Meita, pressing herself to Nakhman and as if foreseeing her own fate, quietly moaned.

"Oh, Nakhman. Oh, my Nakhman!"

Suddenly a handful of voices filled the room. Now the door yielded to the pressure, and eight men in torn shirts burst into the foyer. An inhuman cry was heard, and it fell into the choir of those who had been tortured in the yard. It was Mikhele who shouted. Like a small dog he did not leave the bed under which Sima was lying, whispering tender words to her and not daring to start crying so as not to frighten her. Upon seeing the hefty pogromist wagging a threatening finger at him, he shouted wildly, and immediately Sima's gray head appeared from under the bed. The pogromist, wielding a piece of iron, breathed heavily and looked at the head of the old woman. His nostrils began to quiver. Then he turned his glance to Mikhele, who was shouting with his mouth open, suddenly drew in his breath, frowned awkwardly, took aim straight at the center of his forehead, and with all his might, as if lashing a whip, struck him with the piece of iron. The old woman turned her head with her cheek upward and started piteously wailing. Clutching at the air with his hands, blood pouring from his head, Mikhele soundlessly toppled over.

"Help!" wailed Sima, and with difficulty and torment she began to crawl out from under the bed. "They killed my little boy, my little boy!"

The pogromist seized the old woman by the hair, and wrapping her gray tresses in his hand, he pulled her toward him and yelled in a thick, oily voice, yanking her hair, "Give me money, you maggot, give me money!" She whimpered in fright, while he pounded her face and her back with his fists.

In the second room, two men were smashing everything that fell into their hands, another two were gathering up all the valuables they could find, while a youngish pogromist pulled Blyumochka out by the legs and, not heeding her shrieks, carried her into the next room, while Nakhman, using the legs of a stool, was defending himself against the last two men, and, in a hoarse, half-crazed voice, he roared:

"Do not touch the girl!"

But the flat-nosed carpenter in the red shirt had already overpowered Meita, who in vain tossed and yelled in the strong hands of the pogromist while Nakhman was being dragged out of the room.

"Nice little Jew girl," the carpenter's ragged voice could be heard, and to Nakhman it seemed that they were tearing off his skin. "Oho, so you bite, do you? Shut up, scourge of mankind!! That's right, lie still and don't kick!"

"Nakhman, oh, my Nakhman!" he could hear her piteous shriek. . . .

Nakhman dashed toward her and drew the two robbers after him, not feeling the blows they were now inflicting upon him. And when he reached the threshold of the door, wounded, beaten, his own blood pouring from his face, and saw what was happening there, with a hurried, small cry, choking on his sobs, he wailed:

"Meita, I'll be right there, Meita . . . I'll help you!"

The pogromists threw themselves at him, and seeing how they were beating him, she cried, "Nakhman, oh, my Nakhman!"

She lay on the floor, naked to the waist, in only the sleeves from her blouse—her blouse had been ripped off of her. Her face, piteous and disfigured, was blue from the bruises, but the carpenter, sitting next to her, struck her when she fought back and gradually overpowered her. . . . Nakhman stopped, sensing again what he had experienced in the first moment when the violators burst in, that somehow something had gone out in him, that he had been twirled around, had turned into a mouse, a cow, a bear, and that his head was now filled with darkness. And suddenly he noticed the old woman on all fours. She crawled like a big dog whose legs had been broken, with imploring eyes, howling or calling out. She crawled from the bed straight to the man in the red shirt and, when she reached him, raised herself on her knees and standing behind his back prayed to him loudly, louder, and then quietly, more quietly, humbly:

"Don't touch my girl, don't you dare touch her. . . . She's honorable, she's a virgin, she's good. . . . Don't touch my girl, she's little. I beg of you, I implore you. . . . Here I am, I can take it all, please, I ask you, I implore you . . ."

And she beat her hands against her head, licked Meita's dear braids, which lay spread on the ground, kissed the carpenter on the back of his head, his back, his hands. But with malice he pushed her off with his fists. Meita extended her arms to Nakhman, to her mother, but she had no strength to utter a word. One of the violators could no longer stand Chama's supplications, and he struck her on the head with his club. She fell silent. Nakhman was already shivering and writhing. . . . Blood rushed to his head, something began to jump before his eyes, perhaps a bear, or a little bird, or a fly, and suddenly, throwing off the violators, all covered in the blood flowing from his nose and his head, he ran over to the carpenter who had overpowered Meita and suddenly sank his teeth into his hairy arm and immediately raised his face with a bloodied mouth. A long, hoarse howl sounded. . . .

The pogromists became confused. But then someone figured out what had happened and snuck up behind Nakhman and cleaved his skull. In the next room old Sima was lying unconscious from the blow to her head. The young- ish lad had already overpowered Blyumochka. Agitated by her cries and her moans "Mama, Mama!" he raped her and then at once silenced her with a club. . . . Now Meita was alone in the room with the carpenter. . . . She lay immo- bile, exhausted and tormented by the impure caresses. It was not Meita who lay there but something that had been humiliated to the last degree, a miserable creature with a dark swollen face, with tooth marks on her shoulders, on her hands, on her breast, bare and bloody. She lay unmoving and indifferent; and both this poor body, insulted and spat upon, and this poor soul, insulted and spat upon, prayed for death. . . .

The pogromist got up. He looked at the girl's body and spat upon it. Then slowly turning from her, as if asking himself what else to do. . . . With a strange, lost glance, he looked at the room in which all had been destroyed, the murdered Nakhman, the bludgeoned Chama, and not hurrying began to pull a knife from the back of his high boot. As if drunk, he went up to Meita and got down on his knees as if preparing to pray, and turning the blade sharply toward her breast, with a gesture as if he wanted to free himself from something, he plunged it into her body from the blade to the handle. Her cry and the movement of her hands, as if for an embrace, touched him, and he stabbed the body again, on the other side, twisted it, pulled it out, and he stabbed again and for a long time stared at the black and red blood that ran down her stomach. And again be rose, having heard at the door the call of his fellow murderers, who were already on their way out of the courtyard, and again he dropped to his knees, entirely in the power of this fresh body, which still demanded something from him. The high bare breast of the girl caught his eye, and he pressed himself to it passionately, not understanding what was happening to him.

And, as if breaking some chains, he rose and ran to his accomplices. . . .

The pogrom continued to rage. . . . The pogrom did not quiet down; it did not want to quiet down, and the whole day bloody rain poured on the ground of the accursed city. The patrols walked along the streets picking up bodies and dispatching them to the cemetery, to the morgue. And there in a row lay the innocent victims of a created slaughter, of invented hatred. . . .

[. . .] Impotent warriors, nursed in slavery, in fear, in suffering—with what shameful submission they gave up their lives. Who could defend them?

Night was falling. . . . The windows of destroyed houses and apartments peered out like eyes without eyeholes. Filled with an alien suffering, lulled by the subsiding growls of the thugs, the accursed city was falling asleep sweetly and peacefully. And only in cellars and ditches, on the field beyond the city, the Jews did not sleep but moaned and cried over their dear martyrs; they cried over their murdered fathers, mothers, brothers, and sisters, and the blind night echoed them with all of its sorrows. . . . And the moans did not die down: a holy, bloody rain poured down on the earth.

It poured down innocently. . . .

1903

Translated from the Russian by Ruth Rischin

VLADIMIR JABOTINSKY

Vladimir (Ze'ev) **Jabotinsky** (1880–1940), writer, literary translator, and Zionist leader, was born to an affluent Jewish family in Odessa. In 1898, Jabotinsky was expelled from a gymnasium and soon went abroad, pursuing the study of law at the University of Berne and later the University of Rome. He became a published author at sixteen. In 1898–1901, under the pen name Altalena ("swings" in Italian), he published regular "Italian Letters" in the *Odessa News* (*Odesskie novosti*). As a newspaperman, he learned from the celebrated Russian feuilletonist Vlas Doroshevich (1864–1922). After Jabotinsky returned to Odessa in 1901, his dramas *Blood* and *So Be It* were staged at the Odessa City Theater. A number of his books were published in Odessa in the 1900s.

Jabotinsky's first Zionist poem, "City of Peace," appeared in 1899 in *Sunrise Voskhod*. The Kishinev Pogrom (April 1903) truly changed his life. Jabotinsky joined Jewish self-defense, formalized in the wake of this pogrom, and became an active Zionist. In August 1903, Jabotinsky attended the Sixth Zionist Congress in Basel, where he heard Theodor Herzl speak. Jabotinsky moved to St. Petersburg in 1903 and wrote for both the Jewish-Russian and the mainstream Russian press. A fabulous speaker, he lectured in 1905–7, traveling across the Pale. In 1910, his play *Alien Land* premiered in St. Petersburg, calling on Jewish-Russian youth to abandon the revolutionary movement and devote themselves to serving Jewish national goals. A volume of Jabotinsky's selected feuilletons appeared in St. Petersburg in 1913 (third, corrected, edition in Berlin in 1922); another collection, *Causeries*, came out in Paris in 1930. Unapologetic about their Jewish-centric political agenda, Jabotinsky's feuilletons presented the day's reader with gems of intellectually witty and brilliantly feisty literary prose.

Jabotinsky first visited Palestine in 1908. He left for the front in 1914 as a correspondent of *The Russian Gazette* (*Russkaia gazeta*), remaining a Russian journalist until 1917. That year, in Alexandria, he met Joseph Trumpeldor and poured his energies into the newly created Jewish legion, going through a sergeant's training and later taking a commission. Following the dismantling of the Jewish legion, Jabotinsky organized the first regular units of Jewish self-defense (*Haganah*) in Jerusalem. During the 1920 Passover pogrom by an Arab mob, he tried to break into the Old City with a unit. Sentenced to fifteen years of hard labor by the British Mandatory Government, Jabotinsky was released under international pressure. He became a member of the Zionist Executive in 1921 but resigned in 1923 over profound political and strategic differences.

As part of his publishing activities, Jabotinsky prepared the first Hebrew-language atlas of the world. In 1922–34, he stood at the helm of the émigré Jewish-Russian periodical *Dawn* (*Rassvet*), which appeared in Berlin and later in Paris. Jabotinsky contributed essays on Jewish subjects in several languages to a number of periodicals and published the novels *Samson* (1927) and *Five* (1936; English translation 2005), a collection of stories, and a volume of poetry in Russian. After *Dawn* ceased to exist in 1935, Jabotinsky stopped writing in Russian; he wrote his autobiography in Hebrew. As an adult, Jabotinsky, whom Michael Stanislawski called "the most cosmopolitan Zionist leader," had an excellent working command of seven languages besides Russian.

Jabotinsky headed the Jewish military-nationalist youth movement Betar from its creation in 1923. He established the Union of Zionists-Revisionists (Hatzohar) in 1925 and the New Zionist Organization (NZO) in 1935. The principal political goals of the NZO were to press for free immigration to Palestine. Jabotinsky settled in London in 1936; he organized and became the commander of the Irgun Tzvai Leumi (IZL), the military branch of his tripartite movement. Jabotinsky and his organizations were instrumental in delivering to the British Mandate of Palestine tens of thousands of Jews on the eve of the Shoah.

In February 1940 Jabotinsky left for the United States to create a Jewish army to fight the Nazis on the side of the Allies. He suffered a heart attack on 4 August 1940 and died at a Betar camp in upstate New York. He had requested in his will that he be buried in Israel, and in 1964 the remains of Jabotinsky and his wife Jeanne were reburied on Mount Herzl in Jerusalem.

* * *

A number of Jabotinsky's Russian oratorical political poems, including Gonta's monologues in the play *Foreign Land* (1907; published 1922) and "In Memory of Herzl" (1904), belong to the best in the genre. Also remarkable are some of his translations of Hayyim Nahman Bialik, especially *Tale of the Pogrom* [*The City of Slaughter*], and some of his love lyrics. (First published in St. Petersburg in 1911, Jabotinsky's translation of Bialik's *Songs and Poems* had gone through six editions by the time of its 1922 publication in Berlin.) "In Memory of Herzl" appeared in the St. Petersburg monthly *Jewish Life* (*Evreiskaia zhizn'*) in

June 1904 and later in *Dr. Herzl* (1905), a slender volume consisting of the poem and two essays. In the original publications it bore the title "Hesped," which refers in Hebrew to the mitzvah of eulogizing the deceased and to the traditional funeral oration.

In 1926, Jabotinsky wrote in the New York Yiddish paper *The Morning Journal* (*Der morgn jurnal*): "For most of us Russia has long since become foreign. [. . .] But the Russian Language [. . .] has sentenced us to a life-long bond with a people and a country whose destiny concerns us no more than last year's snow." Compare Jabotinsky's sobering comments with the remarks of the émigré writer Mikhail Osorgin on the occasion of Jabotinsky's fiftieth birthday (1930): "I congratulate the Jewish people that they have such an activist and such a writer. But this does not prevent me from being most sincerely angry that Jewish national affairs have stolen Jabotinsky from Russian literature. . . ."

IN MEMORY OF HERZL[14]

He did not fade, like Moses long ago,
right at the margin of the promised land;
he did not shepherd to the motherland
her children longing for her far-off song.
He burned himself and gave his whole life
and didn't "forget you, O Jerusalem,"[15]
but fell too soon and in the desert died,
and on the finest day to our dear Palestine
we shall conduct the tribune's ashes home.

---

14 Herzl, Theodor (1860–1904)—born in Budapest and educated in Vienna, founder of modern political Zionism, journalist and publicist, author of *The Jewish State* (*Judenstaat*, 1897) and other works; presided over six Zionist congresses (1897–1903). After the formation of Israel, Herzl's remains were moved from Vienna to Israel, where he was reburied on Mount Herzl in Jerusalem in 1949, fifty-two years after the meeting of the First Zionist Congress.

15 Paraphrase of Psalm 137 ("By the rivers of Babylon . . ."): "If I forget you, O Jerusalem, let my right hand wither . . ." (Psalm 137:5).

I've understood the riddle of the phrase
that Bar-Hanina[16] relates in Aggadah:
that buried in the silent desert are
not just the house of craven runaways,
the lowly line, onto whose hearts and backs
Egyptian whips once seared a burning brand,
but next to them, amid the voiceless tracts,
the mighty ones lie buried in the tracks—
their hearts of steel, their bodies copper strands.

And yes, I've grasped the sage's ancient writ:
we've left our bones throughout the world's reaches,
not forty years, but forty jubilees—
we've wandered endlessly across the desert;
and not a single slave who fed on scourges
we've buried in the arid alien land:
he was a titan who had granite shoulders,
an eagle he was, with eagle-eyed insurgence,
an eagle's sorrow on his noble forehead.

And he was proud and lofty and fearless,
his call would rumble forth like metal stakes,
his call goes out: no matter what it takes!
and leads us all ahead and to the east,
and sings amazingly of light-filled life
in a far country—free, majestic, ours.
He slipped away just when his purpose thrived,
the thunder crashed, the song of his life died—
but we shall finish his song in Eretz.[17]

---

16 Jabotinsky most likely is referring to Bar-Hanina (Hanina [Hinena] Bar Papa), the fourth-
    century Palestinian *amora* (a special title given to Jewish scholars in Palestine and Babylonia).
17 From *Eretz Israel* (Heb.) = Land of Israel.

Let us rot beneath a yoke of pain,
let whirlwinds mutilate the holy Torah,
let our sons become nocturnal robbers
and our daughters enter dens of shame,
let us become instructors of smut and vice
at that black hour, on that worst of days
when we forget your song and all your ways
and so disgrace the one who died for us.

Your voice was just like manna from the clouds,
without it we are bowed with grief and hunger:
you dropped your all-commanding hammer,
but hammers we will lift—a hundred thousand—
and grief will fade beneath their crashing clamor,
our hunger die amid all their uproar
of triumphs in the land where we belong.
We'll gnaw the granite cliffs to lay our roads,
we'll crawl just when our legs cannot endure,
but, *Chai Ha Shem*,[18] we'll finish his whole song.

Thus long ago our father Israel
came near the threshold of his native home,
but God himself stood waiting in the road
and wrestled him,
but Jacob still prevailed.
Like leaves, a storm has tossed us through the world,
but we are your descendents, you who grappled
with God, and we shall win against all odds.
And if the road is guarded by God's sword
we still shall move ahead and wrestle.

---

18 *Chai Ha Shem* (Heb.) = I swear by God; literally, I swear by the Name.

Sleep, our eagle, sleep, our regal tribune,
the day will come—you'll hear our celebration,
the squeak of carts, the footsteps of our nation,
the flap of banners, and our ringing tune.
And on this day from Ber Sheva to Dan
a grateful nation will acclaim its savior,
and singing songs of our independence
our maidens will perform a circle dance
before your crypt in our beloved Zion.

1904

Translated from the Russian by Jaime Goodrich and
Maxim D. Shrayer

SASHA CHERNY

Sasha Cherny (1880–1932) is the pen name of Aleksandr Glikberg, arguably the most celebrated Russian satirical poet of the pre-Revolutionary era. Born to a pharmacist's family in Odessa, Cherny was baptized at the age of ten in order to bypass the *numerus clausus*. In 1895, he ran away from home to St. Petersburg, and the following year, after he was expelled from a gymnasium in St. Petersburg for poor grades, his parents disowned him. Cherny was taken in by the family of K. Roshe, a civil servant in Zhitomir, a provincial capital in Volhynia. In Zhitomir, due to a conflict with the headmaster, Cherny was later expelled from a local gymnasium, without the right to enter a university. After serving in the military in 1900–1902, Cherny worked as a customs officer in Bessarabia. Living in Germany in 1906–7, he audited courses at Heidelberg University.

In 1904, Cherny debuted as a feuilletonist in the Zhitomir newspaper *Volhynian Messenger* (*Volynskii vestnik*). In 1905, his poem "Gibberish" appeared in the satirical magazine *The Viewer* (*Zritel'*) under the pen name Sasha Cherny, and his first collection of poems, *Sundry Motives* (or *Sundry Tunes*), came out the following year. Cherny himself later scorned the volume and considered the next one, *Satires* (1910), to be his true entrance into literature; it was followed in 1911 by *Satires and Lyrics*. Each volume subsequently went through five editions, with revised versions reprinted in Berlin in the 1920s. In 1908, Cherny joined the staff and quickly became the leading poet of the weekly magazine *Satyricon*, gaining a vast audience, national fame, and the admiration of many writers. The great Russian poet Vladimir Mayakovsky (1893–1930) readily acknowledged Cherny's influence. Cherny left *Satyricon* in 1911 to become an "unemployed humorist" and freelance contributor to such periodicals as *Contemporary World* (*Sovremennyi mir*) and *Sun of Russia* (*Solntse Rossii*), as well as newspapers in Kiev and Odessa. He also translated the works of the great Jewish-German poet Heinrich Heine and others from the German. Cherny's next collection, *The Living Alphabet*, was published in 1914 and included the long poem *Noah*. Cherny's lyrical poetry is suffused with existential pessimism.

During World War I, Cherny was called into active duty and served in military hospitals. In 1918, he made his way from Pskov to Vilna, then to Kovno, and eventually to Berlin, becoming an émigré. Settling in Charlottenburg, a suburb where many Russians lived at the time, Cherny was active in Russian émigré publishing, which in the 1920s had its main center in Weimar Berlin. He headed the literary department of the review *Firebird* (*Zhar-Ptitsa*) and edited the émigré "Children's Library 'Word.'" His collection *Thirst*, more lyrical than satirical, was published in 1923. Soon after emigrating, Cherny slightly altered his pen name to A. Cherny. His satirical poems became staunchly anti-Bolshevik. In 1924, he moved to Paris and in 1927 became a regular contributor to the leading Russian daily *The Latest News* (*Poslednie novosti*). Still, in exile Cherny's artistic talons did not twitch nearly as much as they had in Russia, especially as compared to those of the other famous émigré satirists Nadezhda Teffi (1876–1952) and Don-Aminado (1888–1957).

Cherny's first collection of children's verse, *Knock-Knock!* appeared in 1913, and in emigration he devoted much energy to writing for children, producing about twenty books for young émigré readers. Soon after moving to La Favière in Provence in 1932, Cherny died of a heart attack while helping to extinguish a fire. His *Soldier's Tales* appeared posthumously in 1933. In an obituary published in Berlin in *The Rudder* (*Rul'*), Vladimir Nabokov thanked Cherny for having shown him kindness when he was starting out as a poet in the early 1920s. More importantly, Nabokov pointed out a salient feature of Cherny's poetics: "It seems there is not a poem by [Cherny] where one would not find at least one zoological epithet. [. . .] A little animal in the corner of the poem is Sasha Cherny's trademark. [. . .]"

* * *

Cherny's best satirical poems are unforgettable: irresistibly hilarious, biting, and politically poignant. They mock things laughable and worthy of derision, from corrupt and stupid politicians to provincial Russian philistines trying hard to be Europeans. Cherny's redoubled attitude to Jewishness was rather typical of assimilated and some converted Jews of his age: while embarrassed by "shtetl Jews," he was hypersensitive to even the most minute hints at antisemitism. His two best-known Jewish poems, "The Jewish Question" and "Judeophobes," appeared in 1909 in the special "Jewish" issue of *Satyricon*. "Judeophobes" was signed "Heine from Zhitomir," Cherny's alternative pseudonym, which alone said so much. Cherny had translated the works of the Jewish-Austrian humorist Moritz (Moses) Saphir (1795–1858) into Russian, including his story "Judeophobe," which may have informed the poem included in this selection.

THE JEWISH QUESTION

There are four Jewish questions, not one:
Among gentleman cardsharps and whores of the pen,
Among monsters whose hearts are harder than leather,
Among half-starved police spies with the souls of bellwethers
An axe is the answer, again and again:

"Thump those Jews to a pulp! They suck people's blood!
Who got Russia beaten? Why, it was the yids!
We'll grind up their bones into stinking manure.
They're vermin! They're Judases! Killers! They're dogs!"
Black facts, not my fancy, be sure.
> For others, fine ladies and toffs,
> It's all such rib-tickling stuff:
> Policemen are baddies, but a Jew is quite good
> Provided his fat nose is hooked.
> "Hi Moshe, hi Abe! The lads with pig's ears!"[19]
> Yes, that's what they're waiting to hear.
> Earlocks and box-pleated jackets,
> Anecdotes to send you crackers.

> "On the way—I came by train—
> I saw a funny Jew again,
> Saying his prayers next to the door.
> The carriage jolted—to the floor
> From off the rack, via his nut
> Fell his filthy case—and what
> Was it made of? Just imagine: PIG SKIN!"

For others again,
Those deserving the name of men,
> The question's settled once and for all:
> There *is* no "Jew" or "Finn," or "Negro" or "Greek,"[20]
> But only men. That's it.

---

19 A form of mocking Jews was to fold the corner of a jacket flap to resemble a pig's ear and thus to allude to the Judaic prohibition against eating pork.

20 Likely an allusion to Galatians 3:28: "There is no such thing as Jew nor Greek, slave and free man, male and female; for you are all one person in Christ Jesus."

Such people deserving the name of men
Sense and will always sense
    The most burning shame at those who pour
    Life-blood in the dirt, on the forest floor,
    To the sound of mad-dog guffaws.

And the Jewish question for Jews?
    Such defeat, damnation, and inner pain:
Forgive me if I refuse
    To touch on *that* with my sullied pen.

1909

JUDEOPHOBES

Roll up, roll up for the latest excursion
Round the *cloaca maxima* of chewed-over lies!
"Jewboys and Jewgirls. Earlocks and onion.
Good people, save Russia! Sharpen your knives!"

Donning surgical gloves and gripping my nostrils—
The stench of that puke is too much to bear—
I politely request you might stop being hostile
And answer this question—it's pointless, but clear:

I see very well you're as pure as the driven
January snow, and as wise as the grave:
So could you please tell me why six in a dozen
Jew-haters are scoundrels, and six have no brains?[21]

1909

Translated from the Russian by Catriona Kelly

---

21 The last two lines of the original literally read, "So why is it that in a hundred Judeopbobes/
Fifty are scoundrels, fifty are asses?" The "hundred" may be an allusion to the antisemitic
Black Hundreds.

S. AN-SKY

S. An-sky (1863–1920), prose writer, playwright, and folklorist, was born Shloyme (Solomon) Rapoport in Chashniki, in Vitebsk Province (presently in Belarus) and received an Orthodox Jewish education in the family of an affluent broker. He learned to read and write in Russian between the ages of sixteen and seventeen and became interested in the ideas of the Haskalah. An autodidact, he studied rigorously while also learning bookbinding and blacksmithing. In 1881 An-sky wrote his first Russian story, "History of One Family," which was published in *Sunrise* (*Voskhod*) in 1884.

In the early 1880s, An-sky was taken with the ideology of the Russian populist revolutionary movement and resided among Russian peasants, teaching their children and working at coal and salt mines. Upon the advice of Gleb Uspensky (1843–1902), a leading representative of *narodnik* literature, An-sky moved to St. Petersburg and adopted a pen name derived from the name of his mother, Hanna (Anna). An-sky's *Sketches of Popular Literature* appeared serially in *Russian Wealth* (*Russkoe bogatstvo*) and as a separate edition in 1894. From a sociological perspective, his collection *The People and the Book* (Moscow, 1913–14) remains illuminating to this day.

In 1892, An-sky left Russia and in 1894 settled in Paris after a brief stay in Germany and Switzerland. In Paris he became personal secretary to Pyotr Lavrov (1823–1900), a philosopher and a prominent figure of the international socialist movement living in permanent exile. In Paris, An-sky composed in Russian stories of traditional Jewish life in the Pale. His sketches memorialized the aspirations of the Haskalah-minded Jewish youth of the 1870s. He mainly wrote in Russian until 1904 but then transitioned partially to Yiddish. In Yiddish he composed the one-act play *Father and Son* and the long poem *Ashmedai*. In 1905, An-sky took advantage of the October 1905 Manifesto and returned to Russia, where he joined the Socialist-Revolutionary Party (SR). He contributed to periodicals, both *narodnik* (*Russian Wealth*) and Jewish-Russian (*Sunrise*), published a collection of Russian-language stories in 1905, and wrote, notably, the lyrics for the Bund anthem "Di Shvue" (The Oath).

In the late 1900s, An-sky developed a strong interest in Jewish folklore and Hasidic legends. This interest led to his ethnographic research and publications and to the gradual creation of his world-renowned play *The Dybbuk*.

In 1911–14, An-sky headed the Jewish Ethnographic Expedition, funded by Baron Horace Günzburg, collecting oral materials in Volhynia and Podolia. During World War I, An-sky organized relief committees for Jewish refugees, and in 1917 he was elected to the All-Russian Constitutional Assembly as a deputy from the Socialist-Revolutionary Party.

The archeology of An-sky's famous play originally titled *Tsvishn tsvei veltn* (Between Two Worlds) is ponderous. He began it in Russian around 1911. In 1916 an excerpt from act 1 appeared in Russian in the Moscow Zionist newspaper *Jewish Life (Evreiskaia zhizh')*, An-sky then sought to have it staged at the Moscow Art Theater by Konstantin Stanislavsky, who made valuable suggestions but passed on it, and then by Dovid Herman at the Vilna Theater, where it was also rejected. Hayyim Nahman Bialik translated it from Yiddish into Hebrew, and it appeared in *The Epoch (Ha-Tekufah,* vol. 1, 1918). While relocating to Vilna in 1919, An-sky lost the original Yiddish text and had to retranslate the play from Bialik's Hebrew, introducing changes. In Vilna, Ansky founded a Jewish ethnographic society. He moved from Vilna to Warsaw, where he died in 1920. The second Yiddish version of *The Dybbuk*—a palimpsest of the Russian, first Yiddish, and Bialik's Hebrew versions—was staged by the Vilna troupe only a month after An-sky's death. In1922, the visionary director Evgeny Vakhtangov (1883–1922), a Russified Armenian who did not know Hebrew but identified with An-sky's play, gloriously staged *The Dybbuk* in Hebrew at the Habimah Theater in Moscow.

A posthumous fifteen-volume edition of An-sky's *Collected Works* appeared in Yiddish in 1920–25. Inspired by Jewish folklore and the modernist theater of Henrik Ibsen, Anton Chekhov, and Maurice Maeterlinck, *The Dybbuk* remains a prominent part of the world theatrical repertoire.

* * *

Dated "Minsk, 1910," An-sky's story "The Book" differs from the earlier stories of the Pale for which he is well known, such as "In a Jewish Family" (1900) and "Mendel the Turk" (1902). Of particular interest here is the setting: Königsberg, the capital city of East Prussia, Immanuel Kant's city and an early center of the Haskalah. Here in Königsberg, the Hebrew monthly *The Gatherer* (*Ha-Meassef*) was founded in 1783, spreading its influence not only across central Europe but also eastward, into the Russian Empire.

An-sky's autobiographical storyteller is both an observer of and a witness to the "fruits of Enlightenment." Himself an acculturated Russian Jew, he is anxious about the survival of Jewish identity in the face of both external and internal assimilation. Coming from An-sky, the student of popular readership and reading, the story's title is doubly significant. While Jewish culture, broadly conceived, is one of the sources of Jewish endurance, a different source—an indispensable one—is reaffirmed at the end of An-sky's story.

THE BOOK

A few years ago I had occasion to be in Königsberg.[22] I went there on business, thinking it would just be for a few days, but as it turned out I had to stay there much longer. It was sad to be in an unfamiliar town, without acquaintances, without my usual routine, and in extremely uncertain circumstances. In addition, it was autumn, rainy and slushy. To escape the oppressive loneliness, I often sat all evening in a big, noisy, brightly lit cafe, looking through newspapers, writing letters, and spending hours watching some skillful billiard players at their game.

One evening I sat at a small table in that cafe and read a Yiddish newspaper that had come in the mail that day along with my letters. Lost in my reading, I sensed rather than noticed that someone was right next to me. I lifted my head and saw that a man who had been sitting at the next table over a mug of beer was leaning close and peering at my paper. He was about thirty, a typical Prussian, fleshy, with a short fat neck, an angular face, a shaven blunt chin, slightly glassy eyes, and an arrogant, self important expression. Not at all disturbed by my startled, questioning look, he pointed his short fat finger at the paper and asked hoarsely, "What kind of newspaper is that?"

"An antisemite. He wants to start a fight," went through my mind. But I answered him in a dry, calm tone, "It's a Jewish newspaper."

"I see it's a Jewish paper," he answered, not at all confused by my tone. "I'm asking what the title is. I've read the first three letters, but I don't know the rest." He jabbed his finger at the title.

I was very surprised. Could he really be a Jew? I looked at him again carefully. I saw nothing Jewish either in his features or in the expression of his eyes.

"How do you know Jewish letters?"

---

22 Königsberg—formerly the capital city of East Prussia; a part of Prussia and Germany until the end of World War II; presently Kaliningrad, capital of Kaliningrad Province of the Russian Federation.

"I learned them as a child. I even read well then, but now I've forgotten," he answered coolly.

"You're a Jew?"

"No . . . My father's Jewish, but I'm a freethinker and . . . a German!" he added meaningfully, thrusting out his chest.

In order to prolong our conversation, I threw out a phrase: "One can be a freethinker and remain a Jew."

He leaned against the cushion of his seat and chuckled in a self-satisfied way. "Ha, ha! I've heard that already . . . It's an old tune! . . . I see you're from Russia? Everything is barbaric in Russia, and the Jews are barbarians, too. They don't understand what *Vaterland* is."

The arrogant, self-important tone with which he pronounced these words was so unpleasant that I decided to cut our conversation short and buried my head in the newspaper. However, my neighbor paid no attention and spoke up again, "Do you know someone in Russia, in Petersburg, named Alekseev or Eliseev? I think he's a count. He has a big stud farm. Last year he sent two horses here, Naddai and Igor, to compete at the races. He hoped to win first prize, but he failed."

"You like horse racing?"

"I'm a jockey!" he answered proudly. "I've won prizes seventeen times. Twice I took first prize, and I've never let a foreigner outrun my horse. Germans always have to be ahead!" he concluded with some feeling.

I became intrigued by this horsey German patriot, and I began to ask him about who he was. He willingly told me that his father had come to Königsberg from Poland about forty years ago. The old man was still alive, worked as a broker at the exchange, and had remained a pious Jew to this day, going to synagogue, observing all the rituals, and often sitting over religious books until late at night. He read German books but only those about Jewish religious matters.

"What's his attitude about the fact that you don't consider yourself a Jew?" I asked.

He burst out laughing. "What kind of attitude could he have? He used to scold me, but now he's calmed down and keeps quiet . . . And what's wrong with me? After all, I haven't converted. My two sisters, you see, both converted. One married a traveling salesman and the other a civil servant. And he didn't break off relations with them either. He visits them sometimes. But he doesn't like to talk to them or to me. He's always quiet, or he sits with his books . . . After the second daughter converted, though, he decided to go back home to Poland . . .

My interlocutor either clicked his heels in some special way or made some kind of sound with his lips and then told the waiter to bring him another mug of beer.

I imagined the father of this freethinking jockey, an old Jew coming from some small Jewish town, living his whole life in a strange land, losing all his children here, and now returning, alone and foreign, to his home country—and I began to feel sorry for this unknown old man.

The jockey sat for a while, leaning back with his legs stretched out, slowly drinking his beer. Clearly, he somehow grasped my mood and, putting the mug down, said briskly, "You know what? You should come over and meet my father. He'll be awfully happy to speak with someone from his country! Whenever he meets a Jew from Russia, he sits with him, sometimes for whole evenings, and talks about metaphysical subjects. It's true! Really, you should come! And it will be interesting for you to talk with him. He's a clever old fellow."

Seeing that I was wavering, he added, "You should come over to my place—I live with my father—and I'll introduce you!"

I agreed.

The next evening, I arrived promptly. My new acquaintance met me, brought me into a big, well-furnished room, and introduced me to his father. "Here, Father, is the man I spoke of yesterday."

And he went out.

A short, very stooped, but seemingly still strong old man with a small gray beard and a weary, thoughtful, patient gaze arose from the desk and came toward me. He held out his hand, asked me to sit down, and sat down across from me.

"You're from our parts? Have you come here for long?" He began to ask the usual questions, looking at me coldly and distrustfully.

I satisfied his curiosity.

"My son told me that you'd like to look at Jewish books. I have rather a lot of them." (He pointed toward a big bookcase full of books). "But except for me, there's no one in the house to use them," he added with a sad smile.

"I admit that I'm more interested in a live Jew than in books," I answered. "I don't know a soul here."

"And I know half the city, but I also rarely encounter a live Jew," he answered with the same sad smile.

I went up to the bookcase and began to look at the books. Along with the thick volumes of the Talmud and other religious books, I noticed some German books on Judaism.

"What do you do?" my host asked.

"I'm a writer," I answered and turned back to the desk, sensing that my answer would provoke a whole series of questions.

"A writer? What do you write about?"

"A lot of things. Mostly issues that affect Jews."

"What do you write? What do you argue in your writings?" the old man continued his questioning calmly and persistently, a note of distrust in his voice.

"It's hard to say briefly. In general, I argue that it's important to stay Jewish."

The old man was not satisfied with this answer. His eyes expressed even more distrust, and he asked again, "To stay Jewish? . . . Su-u-ure! . . . And how do you argue that? And what do you call 'staying Jewish'?"

The old man's endless interrogation and his distrustful tone began to annoy me, and I decided to give him my *profession de foi* once and for all. Everything that Jewishness once depended on—religion, the Torah, the Talmud—has fallen away, is lost. So here we representatives of the new Jewry are trying to create something new, aside from religion, to bring the people together and unify them. That's what we write about.

The old man listened to me very carefully. But as soon as he got my basic idea, he raised his wide-open eyes, where I saw a severe protest and barely restrained indignation. "You think the old fence has been destroyed?" he said in a dry, hostile tone. "Don't worry, it's still strong, and we don't need a new one!"

"But look at what's happening around us, not just here, but in Russia as well!" I couldn't help exclaiming.

"And what's happening?"

"What do you mean, what? The religion has fallen away completely, Jewish schools are empty, yeshivas are closing, nobody studies the Talmud."

The old man's face froze with its stem expression. Looking fixedly into the distance like a sleepwalker, be said coldly and calmly, "That doesn't mean anything!"

"But what else do you need?" I continued. "Jews are forgetting their native language, they're forgetting that they're Jews, they're denying their own people, they're converting . . ."

I broke off, remembering that my words touched at the most painful spot in the life of an old man whose children had converted. But he didn't even pay attention to that and continued as persistently as before.

"Tha-a-at doesn't mean anything!"

"So what in your opinion would mean something?"

The old man stood up, silently went to the bookcase, took out a German book, returned to me, and, pointing at the title, spoke slowly and very deliberately, "Read this! Do you see? Here it says, '*Zurück zum Talmud*.' Do you understand? *Zurück zum Talmud*,"[23] he drew the words out. "Read this book, and you'll see that the old fence is not yet destroyed. Jews must return to the Talmud—it can't be otherwise!"

I looked at the old man silently and could not decide what I was seeing: an old madman who can't see or understand what is happening around him, or a sage who, through blatant facts, through generations, through his own tragedy, has looked into the future . . .

1910

Translated from the Russian by Gabriella Safran

---

23 *Zurück zum Talmud* (Ger.) = Back to the Talmud.

SAMUIL MARSHAK

Samuil (Samuel) **Marshak** (1887–1964), poet, children's author, and translator, was born in Voronezh in 1887. His father worked at soap-making factories as a foreman. The philanthropist and scholar Baron David Günzburg (1857–1910) took an interest in the gifted Jewish youth and in 1902 introduced him to the influential critic Vladimir Stasov (1824–1906). Stasov was impressed by Marshak's "masterful command of our language," helped arrange his transfer to a gymnasium in St. Petersburg, and served as his mentor.

Marshak's poems first appeared in 1904, in the St. Petersburg monthly *Jewish Life* (*Evreiskaia zhizn'*). While in Yalta in 1906, he became active in the illegal Poalei Zion ("Workers of Zion") movement and helped organize its branch and distribute *The Jewish Workers' Chronicle* (*Evreiskaia rabochaia khronika*), publishing his Russian translation of "Di Shvue" (The Oath) by **S. An-sky**. In the middle to late 1900s, Marshak created a body of Zionist verse, some of which appeared in periodicals and collectives such as *Young Judea* (*Molodaia Iudeia*, Yalta) but never in a separate book. Marshak and his Soviet students and censors later obliterated their existence. His Zionist connections, including those with Poalei Zion activist Ber Borochov (1881–1917), continued into the early 1910s. In 1908, Marshak became a contributor to *Satyricon* (see **Sasha Cherny**) and in the 1910s published satirical verses and sketches in provincial and central newspapers. In 1911, Marshak and the poet Yakov Godin (1887–1954) journeyed to Palestine and Syria. In 1912, unable to enter a university in Russia, Marshak went to England and Ireland. While in England he studied at the University of London, traveled, and worked on translations of English poets, including Shakespeare, Blake, Robert Burns, Coleridge, and Wordsworth, and English folk ballads.

Marshak and his wife worked with Jewish refugee children in Voronezh after returning to Russia in 1914. The death of Marshak's young daughter the following year directed him toward children's literature. In 1917, Marshak moved to Ekaterinodar (now Krasnodar), where he headed the province's section of orphanages. His first book, *Satires and Epigrams*, appeared in 1919 in Ekaterinodar under the pen name Dr. Friken. After the Reds captured Ekaterinodar, Marshak coorganized the first Soviet children's theater with Elizaveta Dmitrieva (Cherubina de Gabriak, 1887–1928) and cowrote plays, collected in *Theater for Children* (Krasnodar, 1922; later reprinted).

Marshak moved to Petrograd in 1922 to join the new Theater for Young Spectators. In 1925, he became head of the children's literature section of the State Publishing House in Leningrad. In the 1920s to early 1930s, he also edited several children's magazines. Many of Marshak's books for children became classics, including *Kids in the Cage* (1923), *Fire* (1923), *Story of the Silly Little Mouse* (1923), *Baggage* (1926), *So Absentminded* (1930), and others. In 1930, when Marshak became the butt of ideological criticism, Maxim Gorky declared him the "founder of our children's literature." When the Children's State Publishing House was established on Gorky's initiative, Marshak became its editor-in-chief. He worked in this capacity until 1937, when a number of his staff were purged; to escape a possible arrest, Marshak fled to Moscow.

Marshak's popular anti-Nazi feuilletons in verse appeared during World War II, along with cartoons by Kukryniksy (the collective composite pen name of three artists), in *Pravda* and military papers. Marshak's translations were gathered in several volumes, and his later verses were published in *Collected Lyrics* (1962). His greatest achievement as a translator was his renderings of Shakespeare's sonnets. Marshak also translated from the Yiddish, including the work of Itsik Fefer, Shmuel Halkin, Dovid Hofshteyn, and Leyb Kvitko. In his latter years, he continued to write occasional Jewish poems, which were not published in the USSR. In 1961, Marshak published *At the Beginning of Life*, a tender memoir featuring scenes of a childhood and hinting at an Orthodox Jewish life. A beloved Soviet children's author, Marshak died in Moscow in 1964.

* * *

Although never published as a separate collection, Marshak's verse of the 1900s–1910s presents the Jewish historian with arguably the most accomplished body of Zionist verse written at the time in Russian. The thematic repertoire of Marshak's Jewish poetry encompasses not only his inspirational verses about young Zionists but also Biblical legends and dramatic historical events, such as the Spanish Inquisition. His translations of Hayyim Nahman Bialik, Zalman Shneour, and David Shimonovitz (Shimoni), which appeared in *Young Judea* (Yalta, 1906), *The Jewish Anthology* (Moscow, 1918; see **Vladislav Khodasevich**), and other Jewish-Russian publications of the late 1900s–1910s, are linked to his early poetry both thematically and formally.

Marshak was a talented if unadventurous poet in the classical vein. The powerful Zionist energy of his early poems was clad in the perfectly starched shirts of his classical prosody. The five-part poem "Palestine" (1916) apparently appeared in the Moscow Zionist weekly *Jewish Life* in 1916 and was later included in the landmark collection *By the Rivers of Babylon: National Jewish Lyrics in World Poetry* (1917) edited by Leyb Jaffe.

PALESTINE

1.

Now when my eyes grow dark from grieving
I conjure up our fathers' lands:
The stormy sea's expanse where weaving
Boats full of oarsmen's rhythmic hands

Tilt on the crest, then finely diving
Speed on toward town, the lazy hum,
The ringing shouts of vendors' striving,
The coffeehouse where those who come

Will find a game, a hookah ready
Beneath low vaults and cool, bare walls,
Where nearby, dusty, slow but steady,
A caravan of camels crawls.

The Bedouin who walks behind them,
Dark skinned, free, and dignified,
Need make no gesture to align them;
Their straight procession warms his pride.

Unbothered by the flow of gritty
Life, the uproar of the town,
Now near the gates of the Holy City
He lets his camels hunker down.

And now, beneath a peaceful wonder,
An olive grove's discovered shade,
His camels sleep, their legs bent under,
Till the morning call must be obeyed.

Long ages past Jacob's descendants
Took to their mournful exiles' ways,
But still the nomads' independence
Preserves the charm of far-off days.
They move like dreams of past devotion
That modern city dwellers scan;
You cannot watch without emotion
Their slender, filing caravan.

2.

How strange that in the cyclic flowing
Of peoples, centuries, events,
The past's not washed away, that, growing
Upon our country's soil, the sense

Of names survives, of sacred places.
In a poor village of fellahin
Called Anotot, in this oasis,
The prophet lived who learned to keen

The fate of Israel's exiled nation . . .
Eyeing the speechless stones around,
I sought what tied my pained sensation
So closely to this rugged ground.

It was not forbears' graves, the gashes
That mark the sites of their last retreat,
But Jeremiah, born from ashes,
Standing there in the village street.

The *Lamentations*, slow and swelling
 As father read on the Ninth of Ab,[24]
Sound near an Arab's modest dwelling;
From Prophet's holy lips they throb.

3.

I trail the caravan: the cunning
Bells are ringing, singing, the sand
Emits a sound that's low and running
As if gold ocean moved on land.

My midday hour I spent by dreaming
Through spineless ecstasies of heat,
But I recall a cool spring streaming
And rustling leaves; that hour was sweet.

The spring runs out from nearby boulders,
Innocent as in paradise;
Whoever drinks with bending shoulders
Will gaze upon reflected eyes.

The Bedouins' way through once granted,
An Eastern girl, dark-skinned and slight,
Stands at the spring, her jug down-slanted.
She's gorgeous in the blazing light.

And still more sudden, one sees showing
Beyond the fences' green confines
A fragrant lemon grove and glowing
Clusters of grapes on arbor vines.

---

24 The Ninth of Ab (*Tisha b'Av*), the ninth day of the Jewish month of Ab (corresponds to July–
   August), is a day of mourning and fasting for Jews. It memorializes several mournful events in
   Jewish history: the burning of the city of Jerusalem by King Nebuchadnezzar of Babylon, the
   destruction of the Temple in Jerusalem in 70 CE by Emperor Titus's forces, and others. The
   same five activities prohibited on Yom Kippur are prohibited on the Ninth of Ab: eating and
   drinking, bathing, anointing, wearing (leather) shoes, and engaging in sexual relations.

O Happy land! Longing, privation,
I'm ready still to bear the load
For one such hour of meditation,
Of perfect peace along the road.

When will you come through torments' welter,
Nomads across the world's wide span,
Home to the welling source, the shelter,
As did this swaying caravan?

4.

But those today who have come questing,
Who did return to their promised land,
Have found, not long-awaited resting,
But fates in struggle never planned.

Belligerent and wily neighbors
Disturbed their dreams of peaceful life;
Their years of stubborn, honest labors
Were stained with bloody civil strife.

And as they sowed the desert, sinking
Their blessed, healing stands of trees
Fever crept in, unnoticed, slinking,
Killing their youth by slow degrees.

Yet now in the desert one oasis
After another rises fast,
The fighting spirit at their basis
Uncrushable from first to last.

There the guards, on foot or mounted,
Throughout the watches of the night
Preserve the vineyards times uncounted,
Alert in the dark's unnerving spite.

The sky rains stars on those who listen,
Thick as the leaves that autumn scrapes,
Mild drops of condensation glisten
On bunches of the blue-black grapes,
And out beyond the fence, where cooling
Sands stretch endlessly away,
The sly night jackals, weeping, drooling,
In fits of fear and longing, bay.

5.

We lived in crowded camps, in tenting.
A ring of hills ran all around;
Great tangles of dry bushes, venting,
Smoked and burned on the scorching ground.

My old comrade, upon arrival,
Picked out on nearby slopes in haze
A wretched village's survival—
Zorah of Samson's infant days.

Now here's where we need Samson 's service;
From dawn till nearly round the clock,
We're chasing scorpions and serpents,
Burning the brush and hauling rock.

How patiently the crew is thronging
To build the valley's well today.
The scream of a donkey made with longing
Disturbs the silence, dies away.

But now night breezes waft and hover;
Large wreaths of sunset roses blaze;
A flock of goats, quick to recover,
Runs easily downslope to graze.

Moonrise comes brighter than expected;
Each constellation claims its place;
With curtains of our tent rejected
We gaze upon the night sky's face.

As if a bubbling spring's insistence
Were caught in song upon the air,
Our Arab watchman in the distance
Intones his verse of nighttime prayer.

He stands there white in moonlight, glowing,
As in the realm of nearing dreams
The spell of droning prayer is growing
Along with the orb's increasing beams.

The night's mysterious candescence
Floats my soul till it drinks its fill.
A luminous angelic presence
Alights upon the selfsame hill

On which he stood when times were other,
When angels visited the earth,
And told to Samson's humble mother
The good news of his coming birth.

1916

Translated from the Russian by Andrew Von Hendy and Maxim D. Shrayer

SOFIA PARNOK

Sofia Parnok (1885–1933), the "Russian Sappho," was born to an educated Jewish family in Taganrog, Anton Cheknov's birthplace. Parnok's father ran a pharmacy, and her mother was a physician. Parnok's mother died in 1891 soon after giving birth to twins, both of whom became writers: Valentin Parnakh (1891–1951) and Elizaveta Tarakhovskaya (1891–1968). The family name was spelled "Parnokh," but Sofia Parnok and her brother both spelled it slightly differently, Sofia electing the more Slavic-sounding "Parnok." The Parnokh children received no Jewish religious upbringing but were given a solid European education.

Parnok attended the Taganrog Empress Maria Gymnasium and studied piano in 1904–6 at the St. Petersburg Conservatory and the Geneva Conservatory of Music. She later studied law at the Bestuzhev Higher Academy (*kursy*) for Women at St. Petersburg University. Her first poems, sustained by symbolist aesthetics, were published in 1906. Parnok's first long-term relationship, with Nadezhda Polyakova, lasted from 1902 to 1907. She married the playwright Vladimir Volkenshtein (1881–1974) in a Jewish ceremony in 1907, but they divorced two years later; in a letter to her friend Mikhail Gnessin (1883–1957), the founder of the Society for Jewish Music, Parnok later acknowledged, "I have never, unfortunately, been in love with a man." In 1913, Parnok converted to Russian Orthodoxy, perhaps believing, as some others among the Jewish-Russian artistic intelligentsia have believed, that conversion would accord her greater harmony with Russian culture—without a disavowal of her Jewish self.

A poet outside literary movements, in the 1910s Parnok participated in the literary life of St. Petersburg. An affair with the great poet Marina Tsvetaeva (1892–1941) entranced Parnok in 1914–16; Tsvetaeva dedicated to her the cycle "Girlfriend" (1915). Prior to 1917, Parnok's poetry appeared in *Messenger of Europe* (*Vestnik Evropy*), *Russian Thought* (*Russkaia mysl'*), and other periodicals. Parnok's first collection, *Poems* (St. Petersburg, 1916), displayed her fine mastery of versification. Parnok published perceptive criticism and reviews under the pen name Andrey Polyanin as a staff critic for *Northern Notes* (*Severnye zapiski*) in 1913–17.

Parnok lived in the Crimean town of Sudak in 1917–21 with her second major partner, actress Lyudmila Erarskaya (1890–1964). Having fallen under the spell of the ancient lesbian poet in 1914, Parnok consumedly read—and rewrote—Sappho. Her Sapphic stylizations appeared in her collection *Roses of Pieria* (Moscow-Petrograd, 1922). Parnok settled in Moscow in 1922. She became a member of the Lyrical Circle—an informal literary group whose members included **Vladislav Khodasevich**, Leonid Grossman, and Vladimir Lidin; the members of this group emphasized literary clarity and harmony.

Parnok had an increasingly difficult time making a living and publishing. In the 1920s, she managed to publish three collections with small print runs: *The Vine* (1923), *Music* (1928), and *In a Half-Whisper* (1928). In 1926–28, Parnok poured her energies into the publishing cooperative "The Knot" (Uzel). The premier scholar of Parnok, Diana Lewis Burgin, described Parnok's Soviet years as a "double poetic isolation"; Parnok was alienated from the Soviet literary environment both as an apolitical poet and as a lesbian writing lesbian lyrics. To support herself, Parnok worked for publishing houses translating Henri Barbusse, Marcel Proust, Romain Rolland, and others from the French. After 1928, she was unable to publish poetry. In 1929, she completed the libretto for the opera *Almast* by Aleksandr Spendiarov (1871–1928). Based on an Armenian legend shaped by the Armenian classic Ovanes Tumanyan (1869–1923), *Almast* premiered in 1930.

Starting in 1925, Parnok lived with the mathematician Olga Tsuberbiller (1885–1975). In her late poetry, Parnok shed her ornamental richness of diction and prosody for the sake of conversational lyrical simplicity couched in undexterous meters. Her love for the physicist Nina Vedeneeva (1882–1955) precipitated *Ursa Minor* (1932) and *The Useless Good* (1932–33), two cycles of startling lyrics. Parnok died of a heart attack outside Moscow in 1933. Her first *Collected Works* appeared in the United States in 1979, edited by Sofia Polyakova. Parnok editions and scholarship on Parnok finally appeared in Russia in the post-Soviet period.

* * *

As early as 1903, in the poem "To the Jews," Parnok expressed faith in the renascence of the Jewish nation. A number of Parnok's poems drew from the stories of the Old and New Testaments. In her poetry, Parnok continued to ask controversial, and occasionally Judaic, questions even after her conversion to Russian Orthodoxy.

All three poems chosen here were written between 1913 and 1922 and gathered in "Green Notebook," gifted by Parnok to her friend, the writer Evgeniya Gertsyk (1878–1944). "My anguish does the Lord not heed . . ." and "Not for safekeeping for awhile . . ." appeared in the group collection *Lyrical*

Circle (Moscow, 1922); Parnok included "My anguish does the Lord not heed..." in her third collection, *The Vine* (1923).

* * *

My anguish does the Lord not heed,
And does not gladden me with coldness,
My tired flesh He does not lead
From out a fevered, flaming vortex,

And people still drink up my lips,
Undrunk yet their last drops of fever.
Like age-old mead, my blood is thick,—
Oh, sultry servitude! My Egypt!...

But still I dream, a light-blue current
Flows upward from the hollow deep
And I ascend,—and all alone—
I'm standing face to face with Thee.

1913–22

HAGAR

So Hagar sits in obloquy
And gushing piteously
The spring pours out a threnody
Beer-lahai-roi.[25]

Yon lands belong to Abraham,
But this expanse—to none:
In front of her, the wilderness
To Shur itself does run.

---

25 *Beer-lahai-roi* (Heb.) is usually translated as "the well/source of the Living One Who sees me"; see Gen. 16, esp. 16:13–16, where the Angel of the Lord speaks to Hagar near a drinking source on the road to Shur: "And [Hagar] called the Lord who spoke to her, 'You Are El-roi,' by which she meant, 'Have I not gone on seeing after He saw me!' Therefore the well was called Beer-lahai-roi; it is between Kadesh and Bered.—Hagar bore a son to Abram, and Abram gave the son that Hagar bore him the name Ishmael. Abram was eighty-six years old when Hagar bore Ishmael to Abram."

Despair, despair instinctual!
In her Egyptian eyes,
Disconsolate, elongated,
A nascent teardrop cries.

The frigid torrent's shimmering,
A dagger's cutting edge,—
O, terrifying, childless,
O, dread proprietress!

"Hagar!"—And her countenance
Dark-skinned did drain of blood.
She looks,—her eyebrows lifted at
The angel of the Lord . . .

1913–22

* * *

Not for safekeeping for awhile,—
For the altar, not donation,—
For the fire, the fire, its oblation
Rapt Israel brought in times gone by!

And pleasing to the Lord's own nostrils
Was smoke from sacrificial fires,
Because a consecrated offering
In truth cannot be taken back . . .

You, pastors of the flocks of Christ,
Merchants of patristic bearing!
What is your gift? A simple price:
Deposit and withdrawal banking!

And Israel, your ancient torch
Shall shine above the world again,
The cross atop the church is stained
And God is not inside that church!

1913–22

Translated from the Russian by Diana L. Burgin

LEONID KANNEGISER

Leonid Kannegiser (1896–1918), the Jewish-Russian poet who earned a place in history by assassinating a major Jewish-Russian Bolshevik official, was born in St. Petersburg to an affluent Jewish family. His father, Akim (Joakim) Kannegiser, a brilliant engineer, was granted hereditary nobility (a great exception for a Russian Jew who was not a convert to Christianity) and in 1907 became chairman of the board of Nikolaevsky Shipyards in St. Petersburg. Because of his father's prominent position, Kannegiser grew up in an exceptionally privileged social environment that few Jews enjoyed at the time. Tsarist generals mingled with radicals and artists in the Kannegisers' St. Petersburg house; several writers, notably Georgy Ivanov and Marina Tsvetaeva, later reminisced about the Kannegisers' salon. In 1915–17, Kannegiser studied at the Petrograd Polytechnic Institute, where he was an active member of an organization of Jewish students. Kannegiser participated in literary events and readings and had several poems published in *Northern Notes* (*Severnye zapiski*) and *Russian Thought* (*Russkaia mysl'*). He aligned himself most closely with poets of the acmeist movement.

After the February 1917 Revolution, which Kannegiser welcomed, he entered the Mikhailovsky Artillery Officers' Cadet School and soon became chairman of the Union of Socialist Cadets. While not initially hostile to the October Revolution, Kannegiser's view of the new Bolshevik regime turned negative after the signing of the peace treaty of Brest-Litovsk in March 1918. In the summer of 1918, a group of cadets and officers from Kannegiser's circle was arrested by the Cheka and executed; among them was Viktor Pereltsveig, an officer and Kannegiser's intimate friend. On the morning of 30 August 1918, Kannegiser entered No. 6, Palace Square, where the offices of the Interior Department of the Northern Commune and the Petrograd Cheka were located. The Northern Commune incorporated Petrograd and the vast surrounding regions, and its interior minister was Mikhail (Moisei) Uritsky (1873–1918); Uritsky doubled as chairman of the Petrograd Cheka. When Uritsky arrived in the office, Kannegiser pulled out a gun and shot him. He fled but was arrested and charged with Uritsky's murder. The official published account of the investigation indicated that after his arrest Kannegiser admitted he killed Uritsky not by order of a party or organization but on his own, to avenge the execution of his friend Pereltsveig by the Bolsheviks.

The best-known account of Kannegiser's life and a version of the assassination story were offered in "The Assassination of Uritsky" (1923) by the émigré **Mark Aldanov** (in this anthology). In the post-Soviet decades, Aldanov's heroic-romantic version was questioned by historians and journalists. Conspiracy theorists are tickled by the fact that on the same day, 30 August 1918, Lenin was wounded by gunshots outside the Mikhelson Factory in Moscow. The person charged with the assassination attempt was Fanny Kaplan (1890–1918), a Socialist-Revolutionary who had served a sentence of hard labor for her revolutionary work and was half blind. Kaplan allegedly stated that she wanted to kill Lenin for his "betrayal of the revolution." Like Kannegiser, Kaplan was Jewish, and both were executed on the same day, 3 September 1918. Suggestions have been made that Kannegiser was set up by forces within the Bolshevik regime that were trying to get rid of Uritsky. Others have suggested that both the murder of Uritsky and the attempt on Lenin's life were orchestrated to give the Bolshevik regime the justification to unleash the Red Terror in early September 1918.

In his *Book of Life*, the great Jewish historian Shimon Dubnow (1860–1941) characterized Kannegiser's assassination of Uritsky as a "heroic deed." Émigré anti-Bolsheviks and Jewish apologists alike have capitalized on Kannegiser's story to stress that not all Jews were pro-Bolshevik and that Kannegiser's loyalties to Russia—and to justice—outweighed his Jewish national self-interest. At the same time, one still hears today from the ultranationalist Russians that the murder of one Jew (Uritsky) by another (Kannegiser) "did not stop the Jewish Cheka from murdering thousands of Russians."

* * *

Both poems chosen for the anthology appeared in the memorial volume *Leonid Kannegiser* (Paris, 1928). In addition to a selection of the poet's verses, the volume contained essays by émigrés **Mark Aldanov**, Georgy Ivanov (1894–1958), and Georgy Adamovich (1894–1972).

Initially a poet of acmeist orientation as a result of his friendship with Sergey Esenin, Kannegiser also composed stylizations with elements of peasant folklore. Thematically, his poems fall into two groups: religious and political. While no direct evidence points to Kannegiser's conversion to Christianity, his religious poems feature Catholic ("Poems about St. Francis," 1915), Russian Orthodox ("Yaroslavl," 1916; "Snowy Church," 1918), and Judaic motifs. "A Jewish Wedding" (1916) possibly refers to the wedding of Kannegiser's brother Sergey, who committed suicide in 1917.

Through passing the 20 March 1917 ukase "The Abolition of Restrictions Based on Religion and Nationality," the Provisional Government abolished all forms of legal inequality for Jews in Russia. One of Kannegiser's last poems, "Regimental Inspection" (1917), registers an enthusiasm shared by educated assimilated Jews in the first months of the February 1917 Revolution.

A JEWISH WEDDING

Seven melting candles are burning,
With another held in His hand,
While an organ surges with yearning
For the ancient Jewish homeland.

Oh, the rabbi, stern with deep feeling,
Raised his hand, the ring, to rejoice,
To the drowsy synagogue ceiling,
Like a soaring falcon, his voice.

Adonai! Adonai! Dread power!
Do you hear that keen wailing whine?
Under scythes, the rose, softest flower
Of Your gardens in Palestine.

1916

REGIMENTAL INSPECTION

The sun makes their bayonets glisten—
Foot soldiers. Don Cossacks in force
Beyond, at attention to listen:
Kerensky astride a white horse.

His eyes are fatigued with endeavor.
Long silence in corps upon corps.
His voice, to remember forever,
Of Russia, of freedom, of war.

Fire, iron—the heart alchemizes,
The spirit —green oak against threats,
And the eagle, *Marseillaise*, arises
Aloft from our silver cornets.

To arms! And the demons will cower.
As darkness descends over all,
Archangels of limitless power
Will envy our cavalier fall.

If rasping my racking death rattle,
O Mother, O land I love best,
If after defeat in some battle,
In agony, shot in the chest,

Near death, with a dream of pure pleasure
In bliss at that entrance and source,
With Russia and freedom, I'll treasure
Kerensky astride a white horse.[26]

1917

---

26 Alexander F. Kerensky (1881–1970) was a Russian political leader in the 1900s and 1910s.
In the short-lived Provisional Government (1917), he was, in turn, minister of justice, min-
ister of war, and later both prime minister and supreme commander of the Russian army.

Revolution and Emigration: 1920s–1930s

Editor's Introduction

Russia was the last major European country to grant its Jews equal rights and freedoms. One of the great accomplishments of the February 1917 Revolution was the 20 March 1917 ukase "Abolition of Restrictions Based on Religion and Nationality": "All the laws and statutes are abolished, whether in effect throughout all Russia or in its various parts, which establish—on the basis of the adherence of citizens of Russia to a particular religious denomination or sect or by reasons of nationality—any restrictions."[1] For the Jews of the former Russian Empire, this meant abolition of the Pale of Settlement and of official discrimination at all levels of society, including *numerus clausus* at institutions of learning. For Jews worldwide, November 1917 brought not only the Bolshevik Revolution but also the Balfour Declaration, which made the Zionist dream of a Jewish state in Israel a foreseeable possibility. In the years following the 1917 revolutions, as the social and cultural life of European Russia stabilized after the end of the civil war, Jewish-Russian artists expressed their sense of liberation by shaping the early Soviet cultural landscape. At the same time, the destructive official campaign against Judaism and traditional Jewish life proceeded at a fast clip.

The 1920s and early 1930s were a fascinating and turbulent time in the history of Jewish-Russian culture; indeed, these years saw an eruption of Jewish-Russian creativity. Anti-Jewish restrictions had been temporarily removed both de jure and de facto. Thousands of Jews born in the 1890s–1900s poured into the Russian cultural mainstream. They came from Yiddish-speaking and Yiddish- and Russian-speaking multilingual households of the former Pale, as well as from the already thoroughly Russianized Jewish families of such large urban centers as Kiev, Odessa, or Kharkov. While the former Pale gave early Soviet culture the majority of its Jewish writers, all areas of the former Russian

---

1   See *The Russian Provisional Government*, ed. R. Paul Browder and Alexander F. Kerensky, vol. 1, 211–12 (Stanford: Stanford University Press, 1961).

Empire where Jews had been allowed to live, including the Urals and Siberia, contributed their young and initially enthusiastic Jewish authors (e.g., Iosif Utkin [1903–1944]). So many remarkable literary Jewish-Russian figures burst onto the Soviet literary scene in the early Soviet decades that it has been impossible to do them all justice even in an anthology of this scope and ambition. At the same time, the Jewish-Russian authors already active on the literary scene in the 1910s wrote and published some of their greatest works of poetry and prose in the Soviet 1920s. This includes **Osip Mandelstam** (1891–1938), who is featured in this section, and **Boris Pasternak** (1890–1960), whose work appears in the section "War and Shoah: 1940s."

The 1920s were a time of openness in the discussion of antisemitism and Jewish identity by Soviet authors writing in Russian and Yiddish. Some of the most penetrating fictional treatments of the parallel dynamics of swift Soviet assimilation of the Jews and the persistence of popular antisemitism appeared in the 1920s. The names of **Andrey Sobol** (1888–1926) and Mikhail Kozakov (1897–1954) readily come to mind in this connection. Writing with astounding linguistic power, often in a language that was not that of their parents, Jews made countless and peerless contributions to the Russian poetry, prose, and drama of the 1920s–30s. Jewish-Russian writers were represented in every corner of the early Soviet literary scene. They included **Lev Lunts** (1901–1924), **Veniamin Kaverin** (1902–1989), and **Elizaveta Polonskaya** (1890–1969), members of the Serapion Brothers group. Among these Jewish-Russian writers were inveterate avant-gardist poets, such as the imagist **Matvey Royzman** (1896–1973) and the jazz-poet Valentin Parnakh (1891–1951). They also counted among their ranks the most gifted literary representative of the Russian formalist movement, author and theorist **Viktor Shklovsky** (1891–1984). Jewish-Russian writers betoken much of the political and aesthetic spectrum of the literary groups of the Soviet 1920s: the constructivists **Ilya Selvinsky** (1899–1968; in the section "War and Shoah: 1940s"), **Vera Inber** (1890–1972), and **Eduard Bagritsky** (1895–1934); **Semyon Kirsanov** (1906–1972) from the Left Front of Art (LEF); Yury Libedinsky (1898–1959) from the Russian Association of Proletarian Writers (RAPP); and others. Some of the best Jewish-Russian writers of the early Soviet decades, including one of the strongest Jewish-Russian geniuses, **Isaac Babel** (1894–1940), came from Odessa and the Black Sea area and collectively formed, in the eyes of their readers and critics, the so-called Southwestern school (Victor Shklovsky's expression). Jewish-Russian literature gave the early Soviet readers their most beloved satirical writers, the Odessans **Ilya Ilf** (1897–1937) and his (questionably) non-Jewish coauthor **Evgeny Petrov** (1903–1942). By the early 1930s, after the relatively independent literary and artistic groups of the 1920s had been suppressed and dismantled, Jewish-Russian writers keenly participated in the formation of the Union of Soviet Writers and the institutionalization of Soviet literature.

The First Congress of the Union of Soviet Writers convened in Moscow in 1934. The statistics of its officially published stenographic report are revealing.[2] Of the 597 Soviet delegates, 201 were Russians and 113, or about 19 percent, were Jews. While Jews made up only about 1.8 percent of the country's population, Jewish delegates outnumbered Georgians (28), Ukrainians (25), Armenians (19), Tatars (19), Belorussians (17), and so forth. There were 57 Jews in the Moscow delegation (second after 91 Russians) and 11 Jews in the Leningrad organization (second after 30 Russians). Twenty-four Yiddish writers were delegates at the congress (holding the fourth place after Russian-, Ukrainian-, and Georgian-language writers), but the vast majority (about 70 percent) of all the Jewish delegates were writing in Russian, and only a few of the Jewish delegates were writing in other languages, such as Ukrainian or Belorussian, or in more than one language.[3]

One of the most telling aspects of these statistics for the story and history of Jewish-Russian literature was that Jews from the former Pale, whether or not they physically migrated to Russia from where they had grown up, were almost exclusively (im)migrating to Russian literature, although they might have been linguistically equipped to become Ukrainian or Belorussian authors. This movement was to have been expected, so powerful was the draw of the expanses of Russian literary culture. Only a small minority of Jews from the former Pale born in the 1890s–1900s, such as Leonid Pervomaisky (1908–1973), became Jewish-Ukrainian writers, that is, Jews writing in Ukrainian as opposed to Jewish-Russian or Yiddish writers from Ukraine. And even fewer followed the earlier example of the older Zmitrok Biadulia (Samuil Plavnik, 1886–1941) and joined the ranks of the Jewish-Belorussian *pismenniki* during the early Soviet decades.

---

2 See Yehuda Slutsky, "Jews at the First Congress of Soviet Writers," *Soviet Jewish Affairs* 2.2 (1972): 61–70.

3 See "Prilozhenie 5" in *Pervyi vsesoiuznyi s"ezd sovetskikh pisatelei, 1934, Stenograficheskii otchet*, 697–708 (Moscow: Khudozhestvennaia literatura, 1934).

Writing about **Isaac Babel** and the early Soviet decades, the great historian of Jewish-Russian writing Shimon Markish proposed that the works by Jews "represent the first in time . . . and the most significant other-national branch [*inonatsional'naia vetv'*] in Russian-language Soviet literature." While the report and activities of the First Congress of Soviet Writers made very obvious the omnipresence of Jews in Soviet literature, neither the congress nor Soviet literary criticism, more generally, acknowledged the existence of a bicultural Jewish-Russian literature as such. The only "Jewish" (*evreiskaia*) literature that fit the mold of the Soviet policy on nationality and of national cultures was Yiddish literature, at the time still enjoying the official green light. Yet one should be mindful of the fact that, despite the significant presence of Jewish delegates and of Yiddish writers, the First Congress of Soviet Writers did not feature a separate speech about or presentation on Jewish literature. As Vladimir Khazan pointed out in 1996, "the Jewish theme was being tendentiously provincialized, shifted to the peripheral spaces of Soviet culture." The congress also made clear that an unspoken taboo on Jewish topics was already in place in Soviet Russian letters. The Israeli-Russian critic Khazan has argued that as early as the 1930s this resistance to the presentation of the Jewish experience in Russian literature stemmed from "the official Soviet political line, based on the idea that the 'Jewish question' does not exist, as it has been completely and finally resolved in the Soviet Union." In the famous satirical novel *The Little Golden Calf* (1931; excerpt in this section) by **Ilya Ilf** and **Evgeny Petrov**, a Soviet journalist tells an American Jewish activist visiting the USSR, "We no longer have this question." "How can there be no Jewish question? . . . But aren't there Jewish people in Russia?" the American presses on. "There are Jews, but no question," the propagandizing journalist replies.

It was the position of Shimon Markish that Jewish-Russian literature "was suffocated and ceased to exist on the eve of World War II. . . . Babel's literary generation . . . turned out to be the last one; after it was a desert." The quality and volume of the material gathered in the latter sections of this anthology do not empirically support Markish's view. What is tragically true is that the Jewish-Russian periodicals and editions had disappeared in the USSR by the early 1930s, not to be resuscitated until the late 1980s. The Jewish-Russian samizdat of the 1970s–80s is another story, to be discussed in the introduction to the section "Late Soviet Empire and Collapse: 1960s–1990s." As Dmitri Elyashevich put it, Jewish-Russian print culture in the 1920s "for a short time agonized in the ugly forms of OZET [acronym for the Society for the Settlement of Jewish Toilers on Land] publications, becoming an ersatz of the same sort as was the politics of 'Birobidzhanism.'" Continuing into the 1930s, the propaganda publications of the "Jews on the land" movement and the Birobidzhan project produced little of literary value in Russian, a notable exception being *Jews on the Land* (1929) by **Viktor Fink** (1888–1973), featured in the pages to follow.

In the 1930s, a group of lesser writers (e.g., Lev Fridland, David Khait, Lina Neiman, Leon Ostrover, Lev Vaisenberg) treated Jewish themes within the prescribed guidelines of the Soviet—and Stalinist—rhetoric on Jewish history and identity. (The poem "To a Jewish Girl," written by the young Margarita Aliger [1915–1992] in connection with the annexation of eastern Poland after the Soviet-Nazi Pact of 1939, well illustrates such ideologically faithful Jewish-Russian works.) In selecting materials for the section on the early Soviet decades, an anthologist faces special challenges. We have not included, for instance, the artistically wanting but historically and ideologically fascinating novella *The Nose*, its title recalling Nikolai Gogol's famous St. Petersburg tale, by the Warsaw-born author and Communist activist Bruno Yasensky (Polish spelling Jasieński, born Wiktor Bruno Zysman, 1901–1938). In 1929, Yasensky made his way from western Europe to the USSR and soon transitioned from Polish to Russian. Serialized in *Izvestia* in 1936, Yasensky's *The Nose* employed Gogolian phantasmagorical realism to expose the absurdity of Nazi racial anthropology. We have also left out such nationally renowned authors for young readers as Lev Kassil (1905–1970) and Ruvim Fraerman (1891–1972), who entered the literary scene in the 1920s and early 1930s.

Despite the various degrees of revolutionary and Soviet enthusiasm among many Jewish-Russian authors in the 1920s and early 1930s, by the late 1930s echoes of a growing anxiety over the future of Jewishness in the USSR began to register in the works of Jewish-Russian writers (in this anthology, see **Eduard Bagritsky**'s *February*, **Elizaveta Polonskaya**'s "Encounter"). Alarming was not only the rise in popular antisemitism, still discussed in the Soviet press and vociferously opposed by the Bolshevik Party, but also the realization that the Soviet rhetoric on Jewishness was, perhaps, more harmful to the survival of Jewish identity than the tsarist-era policies. And yet, until the early 1930s, **Babel, Bagritsky, Ehrenburg**, and many other writers who had been born in the 1890s and 1900s and experienced the horrors of anti-Jewish violence during the 1902–6 pogroms and the civil war felt that Bolshevism was still a better alternative for the three million Soviet Jews. The seizure of power by the

Nazis in Germany in 1933 brought the anxiety of many Jewish-Russian writers to a new level as they now faced the reality of Europe's Jews being collectively placed by history between Stalin and Hitler.

A prominent feature of this anthology is its coverage of literature by Jewish-Russian émigré authors. Featured in this section are works by five émigrés of the so-called First Wave, who left Russia during and in the aftermath of the Russian revolutions of 1917 and the civil war of 1918–22. There were not many Jews and even fewer authors of Jewish origin among the émigrés of the so-called Second Wave—the exiles who left the Soviet Union during and in the aftermath of World War II, many of them as so-called displaced persons (DPs). Works by Jewish-Russian writers of the so-called Third Wave and Fourth Wave appear in the section "The Jewish Exodus: 1970s–1990s."

Up to 15 percent of the émigrés who left Russia following the 1917 Revolution and the civil war must have been Jewish. To translate that into real numbers, as many as 120,000 Jewish-Russian exiles lived in Europe between the two world wars. Not surprisingly, a number of Jewish-Russian authors of the older generation ended up abroad, among them **Semyon Yushkevich** and **Sasha Cherny** (both in the section "On the Eve: 1890s–1910s"), and by and large they did not take too well to the new cultural climate. Several of the authors of the middle generation became leaders of the émigré literary community: **Vladislav Khodasevich** (1886–1939) and **Mark Aldanov** (1886–1957) in this anthology, but also, notably, the poet and satirist Don-Aminado (1888–1957). The careers of a number of younger Jewish-Russian authors took shape or unfolded entirely in exile. For those among them who came from provincial areas of the former Pale, such as **Dovid Knut** (1900–1955), originally from Bessarabia, becoming a Russian writer abroad was a profoundly self-conscious and multicultural experience. Consider this dimly antisemitic joke of émigré Paris in the 1930s: "Who are those old Jews?" one émigré asks another as they pass a café on the Montparnasse. "Oh, those are young Russian poets."

Jews were very visible in the Russian-language émigré press both in some of the cultural capitals of the Russian Diaspora (Berlin, Paris, Riga, New York, and Shanghai) and in smaller communities with a significant Jewish-Russian readership, such as *The Libava Russian Word* (*Libavskoe russkoe slovo*) in Libava (Liepāja), Latvia. The émigré press was dominated in the interwar period by pre-Revolutionary liberal and left-of-center politicians (Constitutional Democrats, Socialist-Revolutionaries, and Mensheviks), and some of the leading periodicals had Jewish editors and coeditors. Those included Iosif Gessen of Berlin's daily *The Rudder* (*Rul'*) and Mark Vishnyak, Ilya Fondaminsky (Bunakov), and Mikhail Tsetlin (Amari) of the Parisian quarterly *Contemporary Annals* (*Sovremennye zapiski*). *The New Review* (*Novyi zhurnal*), a direct heir of the Parisian *Contemporary Annals*, was founded in New York in 1942 by the novelist **Mark Aldanov** and the poet Mikhail Tsetlin (Amari). By contrast, the few émigré publications that targeted the Jewish readership were mostly inferior from a literary point of view. S. D. Zaltsman's publishing house, active in Berlin in the 1920s, was the only prominent firm specializing in Russian-language Jewish books, and attempts to launch major Jewish-Russian journals were not successful. The weekly *Dawn* (*Rassvet* or *Dawn* "4," 1922–34), relaunched in Berlin by **Vladimir Jabotinsky** and subsequently appearing in Paris, was the only authoritative and lasting Jewish-Russian periodical of the First Wave. Established in Paris in 1939, the excellent annual *Jewish World* (*Evreiskii mir*) moved to New York and published only one more edition in 1944. (In 1992, a middlebrow Jewish-Russian weekly by the same name started appearing in New York.)

Unlike their colleagues in the USSR, émigrés were free to practice Judaism and the Jewish traditions. Yet Jewishness as a topic was understated in the 1920s–30s émigré literary mainstream; rather, the cosmopolitan spirit of the Russian intelligentsia reigned supreme in the principal émigré editions. The most important writers among the exceptions were **Dovid Knut**, perhaps the "national poet" of the Jewish-Russian emigration, and the historical novelist Abraham Vysotsky (1883–1949).

For the overloaded identities of many of the educated Jewish émigrés in the interwar years (e.g., Russian, Jewish, and German or Russian, Jewish, and French), nurturing a Russian self-consciousness seemed a higher priority. (Vladimir Nabokov, who was married to a Jewish woman and lived in Berlin until 1937, noted this in the short story "Perfection," where a Jewish-Russian family in Weimar Berlin hires an émigré tutor for their son David, who is already thoroughly Germanized and regards Russian as a useless commodity.) At the same time, some Jewish-Russian authors withdrew from Russian-language publishing activities. In 1930, **Jabotinsky** (see his poetry in the section "On the Eve: 1890–1910s") inscribed a book to the writer and journalist Andrey Sedykh (1902–1994) as follows: "from the late author." Responding to Sedykh's surprised reaction, **Jabotinsky** reportedly remarked: "For Russian literature I am now only a 'late' author." Similarly, in the late

1930s, **Knut** devoted himself to Jewish activism in France and to Jewish-French journalism.

Nazism was a rude awakening for many of the émigrés, and by the end of the 1930s, the very map of the Jewish-Russian Diaspora had narrowed. World War II and the Shoah claimed the lives of a number of Jewish-Russian authors (in this anthology, **Raisa Blokh** [1899–1943] and **Evgeny Shklyar** [1894–1942]). Some of the survivors had managed to escape to America, where they continued their literary activity. In postwar Europe, only France had a considerable community of Jewish-Russian authors, whereas the center of Jewish-Russian émigré writing had shifted to New York. In addition to *The New Review*, several other First Wave "thick journals" of literature and culture sprang up in the Russian New York of the 1940s. Among them, *Housewarming* (*Novosel'e*, 1942–50), edited by Sofia Pregel (1894–1972) had a manifest interest in Jewish writing. In the 1940s and early 1950s, some of the survivors of the First Wave settled in Israel (e.g., **Dovid Knut** and the prose writer Yuly Margolin [1900–1971]).

The legacy of the First Wave of Russian émigré literature was kept alive by some of its last Mohicans, such as **Sofia Dubnova-Erlich** (1885–1986; in the section "War and Shoah: 1940s"), into the final decades of the twentieth century. Some of the émigré survivors lived long enough not only to reflect in their works the growth of the state of Israel and the successes of the Jewish-American community but, in the 1970s and early 1980s, to pass the baton to writers of the new, predominantly Jewish, Third Wave of emigration from the USSR (see the section "The Jewish Exodus: 1970s–1990s").

LEV LUNTS

Lev Lunts (1901–1924), fiction writer, playwright, critic, and translator, was born in St. Petersburg to an affluent family and received a Jewish education in his childhood. He studied at Petrograd University in 1918–22, staying on to do graduate work and to teach Spanish and French (Lunts knew eight or nine languages). Both Maxim Gorky and Evgeny Zamyatin were taken with his literary talent, and Lunts's essays, stories, and plays made him a celebrity in the early 1920s.

Lunts became the guiding spirit behind the Serapion Brothers literary group in 1920–21. Active until 1929, the group included the prose writers Konstantin Fedin (1892–1977), Vsevolod Ivanov (1895–1963), Mikhail Zoshchenko (1895–1958), Nikolay Nikitin (1897–1963), Mikhail Slonimsky (1897–1972), and **Veniamin Kaverin** (1902–1989); the poets **Elizaveta Polonskaya** (1890–1969) and Nikolay Tikhonov (1896–1979); and the critic Ilya Gruzdev (1892–1960). The poet Vladimir Pozner (1905–1992) and the writer and critic **Viktor Shklovsky** (1893–1984) were initially close to the group, as was the playwright Evgeny Shvarts (1896–1958). Lunts proposed the group's name after E. T. A. Hoffmann's collection *The Serapion Brethren* (1819–21). Hoffmann's hermit Serapion and his brothers became an allegorical model of literary salvation. The Serapions used coded names: Lunts's was "Brother Buffoon"; **Kaverin**'s, "Brother Alchemist"; and so forth. In addition to camaraderie, humanistic values, and a penchant for fantasy, the Serapions shared a commitment to narrative fiction. Lunts's manifesto, "Why We Are Serapion Brothers," appeared in 1921. "It is high time to say that a non-Communist short story can be mediocre, but it can also be a work of genius," he stated. "And we do not care with whom [meaning "on whose side"] Blok the poet, the author of *The Twelve* [1918 epic poem about the Revolution] was, or Bunin the writer, the author of 'The Gentleman from San Francisco' [1915 novella about the death of a wealthy American on Capri]. [...] We are with hermit Serapion. [...] We write not for propaganda." Lunts responded to the barrage of official Marxist criticism in the essay "On Criticism and Ideology." He spelled out his orientation in the second manifesto, "Go West," published in 1923 in Gorky's Berlin-based magazine *Conversation* (*Beseda*).

Living at the Petrograd House of the Arts in harsh conditions with his health deteriorating, Lunts remained prolific, writing short stories ("Native

Land," "In the Desert," "Reference No. 37"). The Moscow-based Habimah Theater (see **S. An-sky**) asked Lunts to join its staff (he was unable) and commissioned from him a translation of *Saul* from the Italian of Vittorio Alfieri (1749–1803; Lunts completed it in 1923). Lunts's first play, *Outside the Law* (1920), was accepted for production in Petrograd in 1923 but was banned. It was published in 1923 in *Conversation* and staged in several European cities. Luigi Pirandello thought it "the best play to come out of Russia in recent years." Lunts's other dramatic works include the one-act absurdist play *Here Come the Monkeys* (1920; published 1923), *Bertran de Born* (1922; published 1923), and the dystopian *City of Truth* (1923; published 1924).

In 1921, Lunts's family immigrated to Germany; Lunts joined his parents in June 1923. He died in Hamburg in 1924, probably of a congenital heart condition that resulted in a brain embolism. Inscriptions in Russian, German, and Hebrew on his gravestone pay tribute to his Russian and Western literary selves and his Jewish soul. In the words of Gary Kern, "fate spared Lunts from compromises but also kept his imaginative works from their intended public."

Wiping Lunts's name out of literary history, Soviet officialdom never forgave him his declarations. Launching the postwar campaign against "cosmopolitanism" in 1946 and vilifying Mikhail Zoshchenko, Andrey Zhdanov remembered the Serapion Brothers and cited Lunts's "preaching of rancid apoliticism." Lunts's works circulated in the 1970s in Soviet samizdat, including in the underground magazine *Jews in the USSR* (*Evrei v SSSR*). Although collections of his works have appeared in the West, both in Russian and in translation, his literary return to Russia has been slow: a volume of Lunts's works, edited by the Israeli-Russian critic Mikhail Weinstein, finally came out in St. Petersburg in 1994.

* * *

In her notebook, **Elizaveta Polonskaya** wrote about Lunts's death: "He was the best of the Jewish boys who came to Russian literature" (in her "Shop of Splendors," written in commemoration of Lev Lunts). More Jewish than his Jewish-Russian literary peers raised in Russianized families, Lunts expressed doubts about being a Jew in Russian literature. In 1922, Lunts wrote but never sent a letter to Maxim Gorky: "But I am a Jew, convinced, faithful, and I rejoice at that [. . .]. But I am a Russian Jew, and Russia is my native land, and I love Russia more than any other country. How can I reconcile these things?"

Two of Lunts's best stories draw parallels between Jewish life in ancient times and in Soviet Russia. "In the Desert" (1923) focused on the return of Jews from Egyptian bondage; composer Sergey Slonimsky, the son of Lunts's friend Mikhail Slonimsky, likened the story's "unique expressionism" to that of Arnold Schoenberg's *Moses and Aaron* (1932; 1957). Dated 1922 and included below, "Native Land" was published in Moscow in *The Jewish Almanac* (1923). To quote Efraim Sicher's commentary on Lunts's story, "Petrograd is decadent Babylon, and it is to ancient Babylon—the Jews' first exile, where they prayed to the West (the direction of Jerusalem) and where they forgot their fathers' names—that [Lunts] dream-travels dressed in his ancient Hebrew-Yiddish name Yehuda[h]-Leib, together with Binyamin ([Benjamin]-Veniamin-Kaverin), who, like the other Serapion Brothers, also turns to the West." The dedication to **Veniamin Kaverin**, who came from a much more assimilated family than Lunts, hinted at the Jewish questions that galvanized the two young Jewish-Russian writers. Both published in 1923, **Kaverin**'s two early Jewish stories, "The Purple Palimpsest" and "Shields (and Candles)," represent his entries in his interrupted dialogue with Lunts.

NATIVE LAND

To V. Kaverin

I

"You do not know yourself, Venya,"[1] I said. "Just take a look at yourself."

---

1 "Venya" (Venia) is a common affectionate diminutive of Venyamin (Veniamin), the first name of the writer V. Kaverin, to whom L. Lunts dedicated the story. Venyamin is the Russian equivalent of the Biblical name "Benjamin," youngest son of Jacob by Rachel, born on the road between Bethel and Bethlehem. The smallest of the Jewish tribes at the time of the Exodus from Egypt, the Benjaminites later gave the Jews their first king, Saul. Having formed a close alliance at the rule of King David, the tribes of Benjamin and Judah formed the body of the Jewish nation after the return from Babylonian captivity (see Ezra 1).

"Lyova" is a common affectionate diminutive of Lev (literally: lion), Lunts's first name. The latter explains the story's (ironically tragic) identification of the modern character of the Russian Jew Lyova with the ancient Judean Yehudah (Judah). In Genesis 49:8–10, Jacob bestows this blessing upon Judah: "You, O Judah, your brothers shall praise/Your hand shall be on the nape of your foes;/Your father's sons shall bow low to you./Judah is a lion's whelp;/On prey, my son, have you grown,/He crouches, lies down like a lion,/Like the king of beasts—who dare rouse him?/The scepter shall not depart from Judah,/Nor the ruler's staff from between his feet;/So that tribute shall come to him/And the homage of people be his." Commentators commonly interpret Jacob's blessing of Judah to mean that he is destined to rule over the Jewish people (lion as the king of animals) and to have the

A mirror. And in the mirror, a tall man with a powerful face. Black locks lash about his stem forehead, and savage, deep, desertic eyes shine passionately under his calm, clear brows.

"Venya, you do not see yourself. Thus you came out of Egypt to Canaan, remember? You lapped water from the Cheron, like this, with your belly on the ground thirstily and quickly. And remember how you overtook the hated one when he caught his hair in the foliage and hung over the ground? You killed him, and you screamed, and he screamed, and the cedar screamed . . ."

"Silly guy," answered Venya. "Why do you pester me? I don't like Jews. They're dirty . . ."

"Sure, Venya. But in every Jew, even in you, there exists—how can I put it?—an ancient prophet. Have you read the Bible? Look, I know what is in me, I have a high forehead . . . but then, I am small and puny, my nose peers down at my lip. Lev they call me—or Yehudah—but where is the lion in me? I want to, but I cannot squeeze it out of myself; I cannot summon forth what is austere and beautiful. . . . Pathos, Venya. But you can, you have the face of a prophet."

"Leave me alone, Lyova, please. I don't want to be a Jew."

On a summer evening in Petersburg, my friend and I are sharing homebrew. In the next room my father, an old Polish Jew, bald, with gray beard and peyes, prays to the east; and his soul mourns that his only son, the last scion of the ancient line, drinks homebrew on the holy eve of the Sabbath.[2] And the old Jew sees the blue sky of Palestine, where he has never been, but which *he has seen, now sees, and will always see.* And I, not believing in God, I also mourn. For I want to, but I cannot see the distant Jordan and the blue sky, because I love the city in which I was born and the language I speak—a foreign language.

"Venya," I say, "do you hear my father? Six days a week he trades, deceives, and grumbles. But on the seventh day he sees Saul, who threw himself on his own sword. You too can see, you should see, in you there is rapture and frenzy—and cruelty, Venya."

"I'm coarse and hardened," he answers. "I don't like Jews. Why was I born a Jew? Still, you are right. I am foreign to myself. I cannot find myself."

---

courage of a lion in fighting the enemies of the Jews. At the end of the Torah, Moses "lion-blesses" two tribes: Gad (Deut. 33:20) and Dan (Deut. 33:22).

2   The writer's father, Natan Lunts, originally from Lithuania and a pharmacist by training, was an educated man with a strong flair for European languages and literatures. Not a traditional Orthodox Jew in his adulthood, he did honor Judaic rituals and raised his children to do the same.

II

"Well, I am going to help you," I said. "Let's go, Venya."

Behind the wall my father stopped praying. They sat down at the table: father, mother, sister. They did not call me, for three years they had not called me; I lived like a Philistine in their home. Their home stood under an eternally blue sky, surrounded by vineyards, on a Bethlehem[3] mountain. But my home faced Zabalkansky Prospekt[4]—straight, foreign, but beautiful. And my sky was dirty, dusty, and cold.

The Revolution: empty streets. A white evening. The street swims along like a railway track, receding in the distance. Streetcar posts fly by like a flock of birds.

"Venya, when I look at this city it seems to me that I've seen it before: it was hot, straight, and monstrous. And it was there we met; you were the same, only in different, strange clothing. You're laughing at me . . ."

But he is not laughing. On Obukhovsky Bridge, he is black and savage, he stands up taller, stretching his hands out over the river. His gray cloak flies up behind his shoulders, and his desertic, passionate eyes see:

"Yes!" he shouts, his voice singing like a violin string, long and powerfully. "I remember. We sailed on a boat together. It was round as a ball. And we poled it with boat hooks. It was hot . . ."

"It was hot!" I answer with a shout. We exchange frenzied looks, standing taller, feverish, and we recognize each other. Then suddenly we bend down humbly and laugh.

"What an odd one you are," says Venya. "Even I couldn't hold out. Such nonsense."

A white summer evening. The choral synagogue stands surrounded by dry stone houses. We go up the broad steps, and the puny custodian, an old shammes, comes out toward us. He says: "Ach, so it's you again? Not today. Today is Sabbath."

This is directed at me. It is not the first time I have come to him. And it is not the first time I have turned my back on him in disgust.

---

3 The city of Bethlehem (*Bet Laham* in Hebrew) stands within the boundaries of the territory assigned to the tribe of Judah; see Joshua 15, esp. 15:20–63.

4 Zabalkansky Prospekt—old name of a street in St. Petersburg, renamed Mezhdunarodny Prospekt in 1922 and renamed Moskovsky Prospekt in 1956.

Looking aside, I thrust some money into his hand, and he slips away like a mouse, leading us noiselessly through an entryway into a gigantic sleeping hall.

Venya, bored, walks along and looks lazily about. But I take small, mincing steps, lowering my eyes.

"This vay," says the shammes.

A barely noticeable door screeches open, and we are seized by the bitter cold. Slippery stairs lead downward. The lamp flickers. And the door closes behind us.

"Listen!"

Far below—a rumbling.

"I have been here three times already, Venya. I was afraid . . . but with you I am not afraid."

"I also am not afraid," he says. "But I don't want to go. I don't want to."

He says, "I don't want to," and heads down the slippery stairs. "I don't want to," he says and keeps going.

The descent is long and stifling. And the further we go, the louder grows the rumbling. The lamp flickers as before.

The stairs end. A wall. Behind the wall sounds a loud, heavy rumble, the roar of wheels and the cracking of whips. And the lamp goes out.

"Lev," says Venyamin, "come on!"

"There's a wall here, Venyamin. I've been here many times. There is no exit."

And again in the dark his voice sings out like a violin string, long and powerfully.

"Yehudah! Here! I know the way!"

The stone door heaved open, and the blazing gold of the sun struck us furiously in the face.

1

The first thing Yehudah remembered: The street, straight as the royal way. The heavy, sleepy sun dazzles the great city, and a white transparent dust floats over Yehudah. Yehudah—a boy in a dirty flaxen mantle and a dirty tunic—sits on the roadway and swallows the dust. A chariot flies by. The powerful horses, spread out like a fan, run snorting and tossing their stupid snouts in the sky. Toward them speeds another chariot, and with a dusty rattle the two chariots cross in the narrow street, maintaining their firm pace. Yehudah sits between them, and the sonorous Lydian whips whistle over his head.

The first thing Yehudah loved: The great city, the straight and precipitant streets, straight, precise angles and the huge, quiet houses. In Babylon was Yehudah born. He was short and fast, and his spirit was weak, like that of a senseless but cunning bird. He had no father, no mother, no grandfather, no friend; and no one knew his family or tribe, but he was a Judean.

Yehudah knew: far to the west, beyond the desert, lay a beautiful land, from which came his mother, whom he did not know, and his father, whom he did not remember. Yehudah saw his tribesmen praying to the west, praying to the mysterious and terrifying Yahweh to return them to the land of their ancestors. But Yehudah did not pray. For he lived in the street, and he loved the white, translucent dust of the city in which he was born, Babylon.

2

But when the wind blew from the west, the transparent dust turned yellow and stung the eyes. Then Yehudah arose and ran until the wind abated. Like a wild Nysaean horse, he flew along the straight streets. Babylonians lay on the ground, basking in the sun and swallowing the dust. Yehudah jumped over them, outstripping the chariots, and his red Judean hair fluttered in the wind like the mane of a lion. The wind blew from the west, across the desert, from the land of his father, whom he did not know, and his mother, whom he did not remember. And the yellow dust of the desert lifted Yehudah and swept him through Babylon like a grain of sand.

Babylon spread out over the Euphrates with straight streets and straight intersections. Straight as sunbeams at noon, the streets dropped to the river, proceeding in under the high embankments, tearing through the brass gates, and descending in steps to the river. Like a stone from a sling, Yehudah ran beneath the gates, plunged into the rapid river, and swam. The river was mottled with boats, and more than once boat hooks struck the Judean, and more than once they called to him coarsely and painfully loud. But Yehudah neither heard nor saw. After crossing the river, he ran up the steps and flew on, not stopping to shake the cold, bright drops from his mantle, pursued by the western wind.

He was weak and sickly, but when the wind blew from the desert, he ran from sunrise to sunset to sunrise—faster than the angars,[5] footmen of the king.

---

5   The word *angar* is apparently of Persian origin and entered modern European languages via the Greek *aggaros* (king's courier or messenger); its main imprint in English is the word "angariate" ("mounted courier") and its derivations.

He ran past the old palace on the right bank and under the bright new palace on the mountain.

Eight times he circled the temple of Bel Marduk, eight times according to the number of towers standing one on another. Four times he circled the mound of Babil, where the mysterious gardens hung in four stories, high over the city. The guards beat him with the blunt ends of the lances, and the archers drew a thick bowstring to see if an arrow would overtake him. The arrow did overtake him. But Yehudah, tireless as the yellow wind blowing from the desert, ran on and on through the city.

Around the city crept Nilitti-Bel, the great wall. It looked out on all four sides of the earth, and all four sides were equal in handbreadths. A hundred gates cut into the wall, and at the hundred gates the Bactrian trumpets trumpeted at sunset. The rampart was as wide as a street, and there was a street on the rampart. Toward evening Yehudah climbed the western wall and ran along its edge, looking out into the desert from where the wind blew. And when the wind abated and the dust again became white and transparent, the Judean lay down on the wall and looked to the west where there lay a mysterious, beautiful, foreign land.

3

And when the wind blew from the swamps, a damp stench crept into Babylon. Then the people went inside, and the horses, slowing down, lowered their heads. And then despair floated into Yehudah's soul. He got up and walked solemnly across the bridge to the right bank, where the Judeans lived in low, gloomy houses. He walked along heavily, swaying like a youth returning from a woman's bed for the first time. And coming up to his fellow tribesmen, he listened avidly to the ringing and cruel words of a prophet who told of a marvelous distant land. But Yehudah did not believe the prophet, and despair grew in his soul.

And it came to pass that once as he heard the prophet his gaze fell on the youth standing afar. He was a tall youth with a powerful face. Black locks lashed about his stern forehead, and savage, deep, desertic eyes shone passionately under his calm, clear brows. Yehudah recognized the youth but could not recall where he had seen him. And incomprehensible words spoke in his soul. He saw a gray, unfamiliar, cold sky, and a cold wind whistled in his ears.

And the youth looked at Yehudah and recognized him. His stern forehead tensed painfully, his eyes looked deeply: they saw a gray, unfamiliar, cold sky.

Yehudah went up to him and asked: "Who are you, boy?"

And the youth answered: "I'm Benjamin, but my father's name I do not know. And who are you, boy?"

And Yehudah answered: "I'm Yehudah, a Judean, but my father's name I do not know."

Then Benjamin said: "I have a longing, Yehudah. I'm a stranger in Babylon. Where is my native land?"

And Yehudah repeated: "Where is my native land?" And both fell silent. They breathed quickly and lightly, and incomprehensible words arose from their souls. Then suddenly Yehudah noticed that on the youth's left arm, just below the shoulder, there were three white spots like the marks of an ulcer in the form of a triangle. And the two youths cried out in a strange foreign tongue.

And Benjamin said: "I know you."

And Yehudah said: "I know you."

For a long time they stood looking in confusion. But then the prophet shouted that deliverance was at hand, that Yahweh was coming with the forces of Koresh,[6] king of Persia, to return the Judeans to the promised land.

4

The first thing that Benjamin recalled: the dark and strange itch on his left arm beneath the shoulder. On the left arm beneath the shoulder were the white porous spots. They itched like a salted wound. Benjamin fell to the ground like a wounded Epirusan dog, rubbed his arm in the sand, tore at it with his fingernails, and kissed the spots with his burning lips, pushing back the skin with his right hand. But the pain did not abate. And only when the northern wind blew from the swamps did Benjamin arise and breathe in the cold, and with cold—peace.

The first thing Benjamin loved: a hot and consuming hatred. Eman the goldsmith, who was called his adopted father, found him as a baby in Babylon. Benjamin was very handsome, and Eman loved him as his own son, but Benjamin hated him and left him. And Benjamin went to Amasai the Levite and left Amasai the Levite. He changed many homes and fathers, for everywhere the blessings of Yahweh lay upon the home of his master, and upon his deeds, and upon his family. But Benjamin left. He had the soul of a beast, wise, silent,

---

6   Koresh—the Hebrew transliteration of Cyrus (559–529 B. C. E.), the Persian king who permitted the Jews previously held captive in Babylon to return to Judah in 538 B. C. E.

and hating. He hated Babylon, the city in which he was born, and the beautiful land from which came his father, and where there once lived the father of his father, and the father of the god Yahweh, mysterious and foreign.

5

And the years flowed on like the waters of the Euphrates plunging into the Erythraean Sea. New days rolled behind the old, Yehudah grew, a beard grew on his face, and love grew in his heart for Rimat the Babylonian girl, daughter of Ramut the engraver. Rimat was small and dark and uncomely, but she had blue eyes like a northern slave girl. Yet Yehudah was poor and naked. He had the soul of a bird and he lived like a bird: senselessly and clearly. But when a beard grew on his face and love grew in his heart, he arose and went through the city seeking work. But he found none.

Every day Yehudah met Benjamin, and he shivered with fear and joy, seeing the gray, cold, native sky, which he did not recognize. The two youths looked long at each other and parted without a word.

But once Benjamin came up to Yehudah and said: "Yehudah, you are hungry."

And Yehudah said: "I am hungry."

And Benjamin said: "Come with me. I know a boat which has no boatmen."

And Yehudah asked: "Where shall we take it?"

And Benjamin answered: "To Ur."

And Yehudah said: "So be it."

6

From Babylon to Ur they floated skins of Chiosian wine, Maltese fabrics, Cyprian copper, and Chalcedonian bronze artifacts. Thus was it done: the vessel was made of Armenian willows joined together and covered by skin; it was round and deep and filled with straw. Yehudah and Benjamin poled it downstream with long boat hooks. The wares lay on the straw, and an ass stood on the wares. And when they came to Ur, they sold the wares, the vessel, and the straw, but the skin they removed and packed on the ass. Then they returned along the bank to Babylon, for the Euphrates was rapid, and no man could master its current.

More than once the youths coursed the Euphrates from Babylon to Ur, and more than once they measured the road from Ur to Babylon. Their old master Abiel had already died, and now they bought and sold the wares and the boats by themselves. Yehudah now had three changes of clothes and a pair of low Boeotian shoes. The girls began to look at him. And once while returning from Ur they were met on the road by some women. And Yehudah said: "I love you, girl." And she answered: "All right." And she lay down in the sand. But Benjamin stood off and looked to the west. There in the west were sesame fields lined with canals, fig orchards, and the yellow desert beyond, but beyond the desert lay a beautiful and unknown land, from which came Benjamin's father, and where there once lived the father of his father.

And Yehudah began to love Benjamin, and Benjamin began to love Yehudah. But they loved each other in silence. Several times they made the journey without saying a word to each other. But once, as they neared the brass gates of Babylon, the western wind arose from the desert, stirred up Yehudah's spirit, and Yehudah exclaimed: "Is my native land not there?" His hand pointed to the west. And Benjamin exclaimed: "No!" And again he exclaimed: "No! I hate you, Yahweh, cruel and malicious one. Our sins lie upon your head, and your crimes lie upon your heart." And Benjamin fell to the ground, and his body was seized with writhings, and foam sprayed from his mouth. And he exclaimed: "Thus says Yahweh, who created you, a Jacob! Fear not: for I have redeemed you, you are mine. When you pass through the waters, I will be with you; and through the rivers, they shall not overflow you. For I am Yahweh, your God, the Holy One of Israel!

"I will bring you seed from the east and gather you from the west; I will say to the north, Give up; and to the south, Keep not back: bring my sons from afar and my daughters from the ends of the earth. I am Yahweh, your Holy One, the creator of Israel, your King."[7]

And Yehudah understood that the spirit of Yahweh had descended upon Benjamin, and he prostrated himself. But off in the distance, beyond the dust, he perceived the great wall, the eighth tower of the temple of Bel Marduk, and the hanging gardens on the mound of Babil; and he recalled the straight streets and the white, transparent dust, and said: "I do not believe!"

And on the following day Benjamin the prophet arose, took his knife, and stripped the skin from his left arm beneath the shoulder. But when the wound

---

7 Here and below, Lunts presents a compressed and freely retold rendition of Isaiah 43–44, which the translator rendered more or less literally, although in keeping with the diction of the King James Bible.

healed and the new skin grew out, once again there showed the three white spots in the form of a triangle.

7

And it came to pass that Yahweh took Koresh king of Persia by the hand to subdue the nations before him, and he loosed the loins of kings to open the gates before him. He went before Koresh and smoothed out the mountains, broke the gates of brass, and cut in sunder the bars of iron.

Then Koresh king of Persia diverted the waters of the Euphrates into a lake; and when the star Tishtrya arose, he set out for Babylon along the dry bed. There he slew the king of Babylon and all those close to him. The king's treasures he took for himself, but the wives he distributed among his soldiers.

And that very night, when the Tishtrya arose, Bai-baiul, the bird of love, sang in Yehudah's heart. For Ramut the engraver was on the wall defending the city from its enemies, and Rimat his daughter let down a thick cord from her window. Yehudah climbed up the cord, and on that great night he knew Rimat and he knew happiness.

But in the morning, Habiz, a Persian, came to tell Rimat that he had killed her father and that henceforth she would be his slave.

8

Thus says Yahweh through the lips of Benjamin the prophet:

"Fear not, O Jacob, my servant, whom I have chosen. For I will pour water upon that which thirsts and streams upon that which has dried up, I will pour my spirit upon your seed and my blessing upon your offspring; and they will spring up as among the grass, as willows at the watercourses. Remember these things, O Jacob and Israel, for you are my slaves. I will blot out, as a fog, your transgressions, and, as a cloud; your sins. Rejoice, O ye heavens, for Yahweh says this; shout for joy, ye depths of the earth; break forth into singing, ye mountains and forests. Thus says Yahweh, your redeemer and he that formed you from the womb. I am Yahweh, who made all things, who stretched forth the heavens alone, who spread abroad the earth by myself, who destroyed the tokens of liars and revealed the madness of diviners, who turned wise men backwards and made their knowledge foolish; who says to Jerusalem, You shall be inhabited; and to the cities of Judah, You shall be rebuilt; who says to the deep, Be dry; who says of Koresh, He is my slave."

And alone from all the crowd of Judeans, Yehudah spoke: "I do not believe!" And Benjamin the prophet said: "Be accursed!"

9

Along Aibur-shabu the processional way, across the canal Lilil-Khegalla, across the bridge to the Western Gate—crept the Judeans. The neighing of horses and the lowing of mules, the shouting of singers and the ringing of Judean harps and cymbals: all these glorified Yahweh and Koresh king of Persia. The horsemen in high hats held the crowd with whips. And all of them together were forty-three thousand six hundred people; from Bethlehem, Netophah, Azmaveth, Kiriath, Shaaraim, and other places. All were going to the land from which came their fathers, and where once there lived the fathers of the fathers. They went in tribes, in families, with wives, with children, with cattle, with utensils. And Sheshbazzar the son of Jehoiakim led them. And so they went out of Babylon.

Babylon spread out over the Euphrates with straight streets and straight intersections. Straight as sunbeams at noon, the streets were flying, and under the cruel, sleepy sun, the huge, quiet houses were burning. A white, transparent dust arose over Babylon.

Around Babylon crept Nilitti-Bel, the great wall. On its western side by the large gates lay Yehudah. And when the sons of all the tribes walked by, a congregation of men who didn't know the names of their fathers came out onto the road. Ahead of them went Benjamin the prophet. He was straight and tall, and he looked to the west. And Yehudah shouted to him: "Benjamin!" And Benjamin answered: "Be accursed! One day you will come to me and tear off your clothes and sprinkle your head with ashes and, say, 'Take me with you!' But you shall be repaid for your deeds, and for a traitor there is no forgiveness. Be accursed!"

And it was evening. The wind blew from the swamps. Then Yehudah arose and went to Habiz the Persian, saying: "Give me your slave Rimat for a wife." And Habiz asked him: "What will you give me in return?" And Yehudah said: "Myself!" And they shaved off his beard, and he bowed down to Ormuzd, and so he became a slave of the Persian and married the slave girl Rimat.

10

On the fourth day Yehudah the slave went out in the street and lay down in the middle, as once he had lain as a boy. And he inhaled the white transparent dust of his native city, breathing quickly, deeply, and joyfully. Passersby stepped over him, chariots flew past him, cracking Lydian whips over his head.

But it came to pass when the sun stood in the west that a yellow wind arose from the desert. And the wind lifted up Yehudah. And Rimat the Babylonian girl asked him: "Where are you going?" But he did not answer.

And the wind bore Yehudah toward the western gates, toward the road which led through Circesium and Riblah to Jerusalem. It was hot, and Yehudah ran snorting like a horse, tireless as a horse, or an *angar*, footman of the king. The road was firm and sonorous, and Yehudah ran. His body was torn and bleeding, his head hung heavily on his shoulders, and he ran. He breathed loudly and with hissing, striking his heels soundlessly on the firm road; he ran during the day and he ran at night. Blood flooded his eyes, foam covered his body, his soul grew weak, but the western wind blew as before, and he ran.

On the third day toward evening he saw the Judeans away in the distance. He shouted and stretched his arms out to them, and he kept on shouting and stretching his arms, but he could not catch up with them. Then he fell on the ground and crawled along the road like a snake. His body was torn and bleeding, his soul was dripping with blood, and he crawled. The sun went down and came up again, and came up again; dust arose in the distance, the Judeans were walking to their native land, and Yehudah crawled. Behind Yehudah a bloody track crawled on the road. The wind blew from the west as before.

On the sixth day he reached the Judeans. Behind the others walked men who did not know the names of their fathers, and Benjamin the prophet was leading them. And when they stopped to rest beside a wrecked wayside house, Yehudah crawled up to them.

And Benjamin said: "He has betrayed his people and shaved off his beard. Kill him, Judeans!" And Yehudah said: "Brother!" But Benjamin answered: "You are not my brother." Then Yehudah got up. His knees were bent, his body was dripping with blood, his arms were covered with blood, but on his left arm beneath the shoulder there showed three white spots in the form of a triangle. Blood spurted from his mouth, and together with the blood he spit out unfamiliar words, foreign and cold. And the slave grabbed Benjamin by the left arm, and the Judeans saw the three white spots beneath the shoulder in the form of a triangle. And the prophet trembled and screamed in a foreign, sonorous tongue, thrusting his left arm out to Zaccai, a soldier, and saying: "Cut it off!" And Zaccai the soldier severed his left arm from the collarbone, and the arm fell onto the ground. And the Judeans saw the three white spots on the arm, just like the marks of a sore.

With his right hand Benjamin lifted it up and threw it at Yehudah. Yehudah fell, and the Judeans stoned him. The stones landed loudly and deliberately, collecting in a great heap.

Without a sound the door heaved closed, and a gray gloom peered silently at me. But the gold of a desertic, sleepy sun lingered in my eyes.

"Venyamin!" I cried. "Take me with you Venyamin!"

A steady rumble answered me from behind the wall, like stones falling on stones. And suddenly a voice rang out, long and powerfully, like a violin string: "Be accursed!"

And the clatter of numberless feet pressed against the damp wall, scratching it frantically. My wounded body, covered with blood, cried out in pain. The clatter died out in the distance. Then there was silence.

"Venyamin!" I cried. "Brother! Why have you left me?"

And again silence.

Minutes, perhaps days passed. I do not know how long I remained standing there: unmoving, without thought, in pain. And I do not know why suddenly I hunched over and went up the stairway. The ascent was difficult and stifling. My torn feet slipped, my knees touched the stairs and suddenly I stumbled. At that moment the lamp flickered, and I saw on the step before me my clothes, Venyamin's clothes, and Venyamin's left arm. Blood, still warm was oozing from the shoulder, and standing out whitely and triumphantly in the form of a triangle were three *pock marks*: the eternal stamp of sapient Europe.

III

I went out in the street. My beloved old pea jacket, my beloved old pants covered a ragged tunic and ragged body. I was no longer in pain; the clothing stopped up my wounds like a plaster. Only a golden, hot sun still roamed in my eyes.

A store. In the window, a mirror. And in the mirror, a little man, bald, with a narrow forehead and moist, cunning eyes; he is dirty and abominable. It is I. I recognize myself. And I understood: everything beautiful and ancient in me, my high forehead and enraptured eyes, everything remained there on the road which runs through Circesium and Riblah to Jerusalem. The Judeans are walking along that road to their native land; Sheshbazzar the son of Jehoiakim leads them, and behind them walks Benjamin the one-armed prophet.

Petersburg spread out over the Neva with straight streets and straight intersections. The streets precipitant as sunbeams and the huge, quiet houses. And over Petersburg lay a gray, cold sky: a native but foreign sky.

1922

Translated from the Russian by Gary Kern

VENIAMIN KAVERIN

Veniamin Kaverin (1902–1989), fiction writer, playwright, and memoirist, was born to an assimilated Jewish family and grew up in Pskov, where his father, a military musician, was stationed. Their family name was Zilber, and "Kaverin" later became the writer's Russian pseudonym and permanent name. At the age of sixteen, Kaverin left Pskov to finish a gymnasium in Moscow. In 1920, he transferred from Moscow University to Petrograd University. The literary theorist and writer Yury Tynyanov (1894–1943) became his mentor; Kaverin later married Tynyanov's sister. Giving up poetry, Kaverin turned to prose as he trained with the people who redefined literary and cultural studies in the name of formalism—Tynyanov and Boris Eikhenbaum (1886–1959). After graduating from Petrograd University in 1924, Kaverin stayed on to do graduate work.

In 1920, Kaverin joined a group of writers formalized in 1921 called the Serapion Brothers (see entries on **Lev Lunts** and **Elizaveta Polonskaya**). His first published story appeared in a 1922 Serapion collective volume. Kaverin belonged to the western wing of the group, as reflected in his published statement of 1922: "Of the Russian writers I love [E. T. A.] Hoffmann and [R. L.] Stevenson above all else." Kaverin's debut collection *Masters and Apprentices* (1923) contained his most experimental fiction. His novel *The End of a Gang* (1926) marked a shift from un-Russian realms toward contemporary life. Kaverin's novel *The Troublemaker, or Evenings at Vasilievsky Island* (1929) dealt with academic and literary politics; his professors and colleagues, including the Serapion "Brother Troublemaker" **Viktor Shklovsky**, served as the prototypes for this novel.

Kaverin's "Speech not Given on the Eighth Anniversary of the Order of the Serapion Brothers" (1929)—unpublished at the time but preserved—underscored the disintegration of the group. His novel *Artist Unknown* (1931), a defense of artistic freedom from collectivist and utilitarian aesthetics, was attacked as "a battle call of bourgeois restorationism." This attack pushed him toward the salutary formula of his next four decades: masterfully crafted novels that satisfied official ideological demands while also leaving room for the eternal ethical dilemmas of art and science. The novel that propelled Kaverin toward national fame, official acclaim, and prosperity was *Two Captains* (1938–44), awarded the Stalin Prize in 1946. A hit with both adolescents and adults, a romantic-heroic adventure tale with a double plot, *Two Captains* underwent over fifty editions in Russian alone.

Kaverin served as a war correspondent in 1941–45, reporting from several fronts. Among his wartime books were *House on the Hill* (1941), *Leningrad. August 1941* (1942), and *We Became Different* (1943). Kaverin wrote about Israel Fisanovich (1914–1944), the heroic Jewish submarine officer, for the Jewish Antifascist Committee (JAC); his writing about Fisanovich appeared as a book in Yiddish. With the poet **Pavel Antokolsky**, Kaverin coauthored "Sobibor Uprising" for the **Ehrenburg–Grossman** derailed *Black Book* (see introductions to **Ilya Ehrenburg** and **Vasily Grossman**); in 1945, they managed to publish the essay in the magazine *Banner*.

Kaverin's trilogy *Open Book* (1949–56) fictionalized the careers of Zinaida Ermoleva (1898–1974) and her husband, Kaverin's brother Lev Zilber (1894–1966), both major microbiologists. Ermoleva headed the group that created Soviet penicillin in 1942; Alexander Fleming's discovery and Howard Florey's laboratory production of penicillin had preceded Ermoleva's. The novel's subject was advantageous as Soviet science was under great pressure to make advances "independently" of the West.

Searches and Hopes, the third part of *Open Book,* depicted the darkest years for Soviet biological sciences and appeared only after Stalin's death, bridging Kaverin's middle and latter periods. Kaverin's anti-Stalinist works included *Piece of Glass* (1960) and *Seven Pairs of the Unclean* (1962). A leading Soviet author of the liberal camp, Kaverin, who remained prolific, was more restrained in his published works than in his support of dissident writers. One of Kaverin's best novels, *A Two-Hour Walk* (1979), elegantly dissected a scientist's moral undoing. The memoir *Illuminated Windows* (1970–75) was Kaverin's compromise with the Brezhnevite reality. Kaverin finished *Epilogue* in 1979; the last in a series of memoirs, it was written for the desk drawer. It was published in Moscow in 1989, the year of Kaverin's death, summing up his life of limited artistic cooperation with—and measured resistance to—Soviet ideology.

* * *

Jewish characters appeared in many of Kaverin's works, but Jewish topics were confined to his early works, including *Masters and Apprentices* (1923) and the novel *The End of a Gang* (1925). Still, in his later works Kaverin made the point of manifesting Jewishness, sometimes unexpectedly, as in the scene of a Jewish funeral in siege-stricken Leningrad (*Two Captains*).

The collection *Masters and Apprentices* showcased two of Kaverin's most Jewish stories, "Shields (and Candles)" and "A Purple Palimpsest" (both 1922); they were never reprinted after 1930. In "A Purple Palimpsest" (not included in this anthology), Diaspora in Western Europe represents the top layer of history's parchment, beneath which one can glean Jewish life in ancient Israel. In "Shields (and Candles)," which is found below, young Kaverin allegorically described the place Jews held in European history. Kaverin's stories share their metahistorical exploration of the Jewish past with the early fiction of **Lev Lunts** (in this anthology).

SHIELDS (AND CANDLES)

> *The game isn't worth the candle.*
> —A well-known [Russian] saying

I

All three preserved silence or spoke briefly.

The cobbler's workroom—small, square, with a little oblong window looking out on a yard—was lit by a candle. The candle burned and crackled. Shadows crept behind it, and in its light three faces appeared in sharp outline: the first with a low brow and a heavy chin, the second redbearded and blunt, and the third the face of Birheim the cobbler.

They were playing.

The jack of diamonds was expending his worthless fate in an unequal squabble with the queen and king of clubs. The hearts calmly followed the course of the battle.

"There's the shadow," said Birheim. "There's the shadow of your head, carpenter."

The carpenter glanced at the cards, smiled in his beard and spoke:

"Keep your mind on the game, Birheim."

"There is no sorrow in the world," said Birheim again. "Carpenter, do you agree with me? There is no sorrow in the world."

"Maybe so," answered the carpenter. "I'm discarding the jack of spades, what do you say to that?"

And so the game continued. But late that night, after a fixed period of time had elapsed, Birheim arose, removed the decree from the table drawer and said:

"Lay down your cards."

And he threw his own down on the table.

The mute lowered his hands and cautiously unclasped them, but the carpenter only glanced at Birheim expectantly.

"Silence," repeated Birheim. Then he placed a tabouret at the table and sat down on it, stretching out his long and bony legs.

The mute removed the snuff from the candle, walked off and leaned against the wall, crossing his arms.

Birheim read:

The decree of Landsknecht,[8] the ancient game invented in Germany.

We, the game of Landsknecht, bearing in mind both honor and faith, hereby inform our faithful servants: preserve our merits.

By edict of the king and the heretics, We, Landsknecht, are henceforth outlawed on penalty of death. Our servants are beset by unexampled persecutions. Many have paid with their lives for opposing this edict.

Yielding to the protracted prayers of Our faithful subjects and wishing to safeguard the life of Our people, We direct:

To change the symbols and names of the suits in the deck: hearts are shields, diamonds—banners, spades—lances, and clubs—swords.[9]

"So then," said Birheim, "listen, both of you, mute and carpenter."

"Someone's knocking," answered the carpenter. "Birheim, can you hear."

In order that the new suits be fixed in the hearts of Our subjects, We deem it appropriate to institute and effect a game on the night of Saturday, month

---

8   Landsknecht (from Ger. Land = "land, country, state" and Knecht = "servant, helper, slave")—a wagering card game for two or more players, wherein one player acts as a dealer/banker, covers all the bets, and usually remains a dealer throughout the entire game. The game is believed to date back to the sixteenth century.

9   The substitution is based on the French national symbols of card suits, which became international and were adopted in Russia: hearts (*coeur*); diamonds (*carreau*); spades (*pike*); clubs (*trefle*); in the Russian language, the terms for the four suits are *chervi* (hearts); *bubny* (diamonds); *piki* or *vini* (spades); and *trefy* or *kresti* (clubs). The mysterious substitution in the "decree of Landsknecht" possibly takes into account the German suit symbols: *Herz* (hearts); *Schellen* (bells, corresponds to diamonds); *Grun* or *Blatt* (green or leaf, corresponds to spades); and *Eichel* (acorn, corresponds to clubs); as well as the Italian and Spanish decks, where the suits are cups, coins, swords, and clubs, and the cups are sometimes drawn like chalices or candle holders.

of August, year of 17—, using the new suits. But since the masters, as yet unaware of Our edict, were unable to print the aforesaid, the carpenter, mute and Birheim will serve as the suits for Our game.

"You are lances," said Birheim to the carpenter, "I am swords and the mute is banners, the merry suit."

"Listen," said the carpenter, "someone's knocking. Do you hear it? Or are you deaf, Birheim?"

"Someone's knocking," answered Birheim, "but in the edict there is no fourth person for hearts. The game cannot take place; there are only three of us, carpenter."

He continued reading:

At the conclusion of the game to notify us how the game was effected and in what way it ended.

Proclaimed in the year 17—, month of August, on the 7th day.

Signed on the original in His Majesty's own hand:

Landsknecht

"Birheim, you have been mad from the day of your birth," laughed the carpenter. "But I will obey the edict."

"Quiet," answered Birheim, "we lack the fourth suit."

"Night will pass quickly and we will fail to enact the king's edict."

The mute moaned indistinctly. His eyes blazed, while he himself, firmly clasping both elbows, shook from the terrible strain.

"An awl will serve as a sword," said Birheim, "needles as lances, scraps of leather as banners. But where will we get the shields?"

"When did you write that decree?" asked the carpenter. "Haven't I spent the whole day with you?"

The skin on Birheim's forehead gathered into creases and his eyebrows rose up toward his knotted hair.

"Someone's knocking," said the carpenter again, "I'll open the door."

He took a knife from the table and held it near the candle.

The light slid along the sparkling blade, formed a point and disappeared behind the folds of clothing.

The carpenter went to the door.

"Who knocks?" he asked, raising his hand to the bolt.

No one answered.

"Silence," said Birheim and tossed back his head, baring to the light a chin overgrown with coarse stubble.

The carpenter ran the tip of his finer along the blade and began to unfasten the bolt. The door flung open.

The flame of the candle tossed to the left, to the right, and again to the left.

The wind coursed through the room, and the mute, freeing his firmly clinched arms, breathed deeply and noisily.

A man stepped slowly through the door. The carpenter closed it and refastened the bolt.

"Who here is Birheim the cobbler?" asked the man. "The Jew Birheim, damn his soul!"

"His Majesty, the King," announced Birheim. "Landsknecht, I see. The fourth suit is shields."

He pursed his lips slyly and raised a finger to his brow.

"The Jew Birheim," repeated the soldier, sitting down at the table. "Hell's spawn. Are you Birheim, you with the red beard?"

The carpenter remained silent.

"We will enact the king's edict," screamed Birheim, and laughed: "Four suits: swords, lances, banners, shields—and the heretics will not touch us."

"He abducted my sister," said the soldier wearily. "Which one of you is Birheim, speak up."

The mute walked up close to him and raised his hands to the level of his shoulders. But then as if fearing something, he pressed his lips tightly and hurried back.

"Sister?" said Birheim, trying to recollect. "Your sister, Landsknecht? My memory has been rather vague of late."

"The Jew Birheim abducted her," repeated the soldier. "And stop calling me by that blasted name. I must kill him and return my sister to our home. Our home is burned down and destroyed."

"The devils dance on its ruins," said the carpenter sympathetically. "You're too late to return."

"Night fell long ago," observed Birheim. "Time to start the game."

His hands flicked away the cards and they landed on the table in a disordered heap.

The mute removed a bundle of candles from his pocket and began to light them slowly, one by one.

The workroom splintered into sharp angles under Birheim's unwavering gaze.

He lifted his eyelids with his fingers and looked around smiling: the window grating had weaved itself solidly into iron fingers and the gloomy night had fused into one mass behind the window.

"Where is my sister?" repeated the soldier. "I cannot find her anywhere."

"Birheim is anxious," said Birheim, placing his hand over his heart. "It is time to begin the game."

"Let us begin," prompted the carpenter, and the mute nodded in approval. And they began.

II

"May I have your attention," said Birheim, raising his hand. "May I have your attention. *Ching tsze tung*[10] says that our game was created in 1120 and that its origin is divine."

"I do not remember," answered the carpenter, "are the diamonds banners, or the clubs? The decree was vague on that point. And if I am lances, why don't you give me a shoe needle?"

"I will give you a needle," said Birheim, "and the mute a scrap of leather."

He separated the four suits from a deck of colored cards and threw one suit before each player. The black fell to the carpenter and Birheim; the mute and the soldier got red.

"Landsknecht, Your Majesty," said Birheim, "pick up your cards, you are delaying the game."

The soldier stood up and rattled his weapons. Instantly the mute's eyes blackened and his eyelids slightly flared. The carpenter fingered the knife in his pocket.

"Just a minute," said the soldier hoarsely and wearily, "I do not wish anyone ill. The Jew Birheim abducted my sister. I wish only to kill him. Nothing more."

"This may be so," replied Birheim, "but you are delaying the game. Please begin, Your Majesty."

The soldier sat down and moved the candle to the center of the table.

The jack of lances and the ten and ace of banners were dealt to Birheim.

He threw down the ace and gathered in the low cards. The soldier calmly discarded the queen of shields.

Landsknecht, the king of banners, was still far away.

---

10 *Ching tsze tung* (1678)—Chinese encyclopedic dictionary compiled by Eul Koung; historians of playing cards often cite this dictionary's entry on the origins and history of the game.

"Your beret is crumpled," said the queen of clubs to the jack, "and your face reveals expectation."

"Silence," rustled the jack, bending over in the hands of the soldier. "The people are in a peculiar mood today. The hands of that one sitting at the end of the table are trembling."

"Trembling?" repeated the queen derisively. "They are exchanging some frayed pieces of paper, and the hands of the one who is losing them are beginning to tremble."

"The hands of the hook-nosed man are trembling," answered the jack. "But don't you love it when they play with those round pieces of yellow and white? They ring gloriously when they fall and it's so pleasant to cover them with jacks' clothing."

"Their minutes are centuries to us," rustled the king of spades. "The senate must be convened; we will perish this night."

"That cannot be done until a new game begins," responded the jack. "Your Majesty, we will take every measure to safeguard your precious life. Take care, Your Majesty, not to scratch the dotted line on the uneven surface of the table."

"Seven years ago you left her a marvelous maiden," said Birheim. "But now you have not found her and you have not even found your own home."

"Home is burned down," answered the soldier. "Enough said about that. I recall with perfect clarity that her tresses were fair."

"The sister of His Majesty, King-Landsknecht, cannot disappear without a trace," said Birheim again. "You need only intensify your search and you will find her. But you have forgotten her face."

"Birheim killed the maiden," said the carpenter, beginning to tremble, but the mute squeezed his arm firmly and he fell silent.

"In the course of seven years I have forgotten her face," said the soldier. "Nothing wrong with that. But why do you keep calling me by the name of a king?"

And he threw down the ace of shields. The carpenter and the mute threw down low cards, Birheim—jack of banners.

The first hand was coming to an end. The candles had burned down halfway and long streams of bright wax had poured down from the flames.

Landsknecht, the king of banners, a fair-headed man in a blue beret with a scepter in his hands, lay on top of the deck. The crossed insignia of the game, the sign of Landsknecht, had been cut by Birheim into blue ribbon which was strung across his shoulder. He fell to the soldier, who noisily pushed away the tabouret and stood up.

"Landsknecht?" said Birheim, glancing at the soldier's cards. "His Majesty, the King. Just look, carpenter, how pale his face is."

"Noble senate and loyal subjects," said the soldier, standing up to full height and raising his hand, "we have summoned you here today in order to discuss in the most sagacious manner the many difficulties which we have encountered at the very source of our lofty responsibilities."

"Madness, madness," screamed the carpenter, covering his face with his hands. "Birheim killed the maiden. Why play on any further?"

The soldier rose up from behind the table and waved his hands furiously. "Play!"

They played.

III

"In the name of our King-Landsknecht," announced the king of clubs, when all the kings had gathered in the center of the deck, "I declare this session of the senate open. The following questions require deliberation: First, an attack on His Imperial Majesty by those persons commonly termed the people."

All present startled and reached for their swords.

"Second," continued the king of clubs, "the replacement of our sacred suits by others. And third, the threat to the whole happy family of our subjects presented by the distressing condition of those persons who direct our fate."

"The people are our fate," grumbled the king of spades with contempt, "and we are the fate of the people. Who can make sense out of it?"

"I request a guard at the doors of the senate," he said loudly. "A crowd is rumbling at the windows. The fires on the squares have gone out."

"As regards the first question, it behooves me to state the following," said the third king, raising his scepter: "From whom came the information of the assassination attempt? In my domain all is quiet."

"The information came to us from the province of diamonds," answered the king of clubs. "During the last hand the mood of the people became unusually alarming."

"I have every basis," declared the king of hearts, arising from his place and holding high his scepter, "to confirm the aforesaid information. Our firm decision, taken in a recent session of the senate—"

"—I beg your forgiveness, Your Majesty," interrupted the king of the clubs, "the guard has snapped to attention. It appears that the king is approaching the senate chamber."

The doors flung open and Landsknecht entered, jangling his weapons. His face twitched with a fierce spasm, his lips trembled.

"Who among you is Birheim the cobbler?" he screamed, going up to the table and casting his weary eyes about. "Home is burned down. My sister has vanished."

The kings glanced around in confusion.

"Your Majesty is ill," prompted the king of clubs, bowing low and blanching, "the events of recent days have taken a heavy toll on Your Majesty's health."

"Nonsense," answered King-Landsknecht, breathing heavily and attempting to draw his sword, "disloyalty pursues me, death snaps at my heels."

"He's falling, my God, he's falling," screamed the king of clubs, extending his arms.

Night passed and the quick rays of dawn rushed in through the chinks of the windows.

"It seems to me," said the soldier, after the second hand had ended, "that games of chance were outlawed by an edict of the king. I will play no more."

"One more hand," answered Birheim. "Landsknecht, pick up your cards, we will continue the game."

"No," said the soldier again. "I will play no more. Night has passed. I came here to kill Birheim.

"You will kill him at the end of the game," insisted Birheim. "I beg you to pick up your cards."

"Nonsense," said the soldier, arising. "You see that morning has come, it's time to snuff the candles."

The mute pushed from the tabouret and stood up. Then he began to snuff the candles.

"He is executing the king's order," laughed the carpenter. "His Majesty gives orders."

"I will not play," repeated the soldier, breathing heavily and drawing the shiny steel of a cutlass from its scabbard. "You have a hooked nose. Are you Birheim, tell the truth?"

"Indeed I am," said Birheim, "you are not mistaken. But look at your shadow. Does it not seem to be falling?"

All the candles but one had gone out. And this last one rested in the hands of the mute.

He walked slowly from one man to the next. Coming up to Birheim, he stopped and peered into his eyes.

"The maiden was killed by me," said Birheim. "Night has passed, the candles have gone out, it is time to end the game."

And all three threw themselves on the soldier. He tried to lean forward and swing the cutlass but suddenly fell and lay still.

"We shall continue the game without the fourth suit," said Birheim. "We shall enact the king's edict."

And he wrapped a white rag around the teeth marks on his hands and outlined the soldier's profile with an awl on the edge of the table.

1922

Translated from the Russian by Gary Kern

VLADISLAV KHODASEVICH

Vladislav Khodasevich (1886–1939), poet, critic, and translator, was the son of an impoverished Lithuanian-Polish nobleman. Khodasevich's mother was the daughter of Yakov Brafman, convert to Russian Orthodoxy and author of the nefarious *Book of the Kahal* (1869); she was born Jewish but brought up Catholic by a zealous Polish-Catholic family. Born in Moscow, Khodasevich studied at Moscow's Third Classical Gymnasium and attended lectures at Moscow University in 1904–5 without taking a degree. In 1905 his poems appeared in print, and his first collection, *Youth*, came out in 1908 as Khodasevich began to translate from Polish and French and work as an editor.

Khodasevich's second collection, *The Happy Little House*, was published in 1914. Sickly from birth, in 1916 Khodasevich developed tuberculosis of the spine, and for the rest of his life he was plagued by poor health. In late 1916, Khodasevich befriended Leyb Jaffe (1878–1948) and worked with him on *The Jewish Anthology: A Collection of Young Jewish Poetry* (the first two editions appeared in Moscow in 1918, the third edition in Berlin in 1922). Jaffe and Khodasevich coedited the volume, and each translated some of the poems. Jaffe selected the Hebrew poems while Khodasevich did the editing of the Russian translations. The prominent critic Mikhail Gershenzon (1869–1925), a friend of Khodasevich's, wrote the preface.

Khodasevich's third collection, *By Way of Grain*, appeared in Moscow in 1920 and was reprinted in Petrograd in 1922. Khodasevich left Russia in June 1922 in the company of the young Russian poet of Armenian descent, Nina Berberova (1901–1993); in emigration Berberova developed into a prominent prose writer. His fourth collection, *The Heavy Lyre*, was published in Moscow in 1922 and reprinted in 1923 in Berlin. Khodasevich published *From the Jewish Poets* in 1922, also in Berlin, taking his translations of six Hebrew poets from *The Jewish Anthology*: two by David Frischmann (1861–1922), four by Saul Tchernichovsky (1875–1943), two by Yaakov Fichman (1881–1958), one by Zalman Shneour (1887–1959), two by David Shimonovitz (Shimoni, 1886–1956), and one by Avraham Ben Yitzhak (1883–1950). He removed a poem by Judah Katzenelson (1847–1917) but supplemented the selection with a poem by Hayyim Nahman Bialik (1873–1934) and an additional one by Tchernichovsky ("Dumplings"; Heb. "Levivot")—a gem of the new Hebrew poetry and of Russian literary translation.

After wandering around Europe in 1924–25, Khodasevich and his common-law wife Berberova settled in Paris. Although he was a leading émigré critic and major poet, Khodasevich did not have an easy time making a living. His *Collected Poetry* (Paris, 1927) included poems from *By Way of Grain* and *The Heavy Lyre* and, as its last section, Khodasevich's fifth collection, *European Night,* which gathered his émigré verses. After 1927, Khodasevich wrote only about fifteen poems. In 1932, Berberova left Khodasevich, and in 1933 he married Olga Margolina (he had been married twice in Russia). In 1939, *Necropolis,* a volume of his literary memoirs, was published in Brussels. Khodasevich died in Paris the same year. His wife, Olga, perished in a Nazi concentration camp in 1942. As Donald Rayfield remarked, "[Khodasevich's] death [. . .] spared him from the Nazi extermination camp."

Khodasevich gained his own voice in the 1910s after shaking his symbolist affinities. To quote John Malmstad, "In poem after poem between 1916 and 1920, Khodasevich clarified his vision in a language resistant to subjective overstatement and capable of dealing with a world of actualities." Starting from his third collection, *By Way of Grain* (1920), Khodasevich's best poems derived their intonation from a distillation of the lyrical impulse that is buttressed by dissonant prosaic details and often framed by irony and even absurdity. Few Russian poets have been able to strike chords of confessionalism and ruthless introspection—and communicate a sense of a poet's physical and metaphysical alienation—with the doomful clairvoyance that marks Khodasevich's best love poems.

* * *

Manifest in Khodasevich's biography, Jewish questions occasionally pulsated in his poetry. His principal contribution to Jewish letters was as a translator of Hebrew poets into Russian and as a critic who wrote profoundly about Jewish literature (Tchernichovsky, whom he favored, Bialik, and **Semyon Yushkevich**). To a believer in the mutually mirroring relationship between life and art, his early poems with Jewish themes, such as "Evening" (1913) and "Rachel's Tears" (1916), may signal an identification with a Jewish mother that expands the boundaries of both Gospel narratives and Jewish Biblical history.

In June 1922, Khodasevich left Russia and arrived in Berlin to spend the last seventeen years of his life as a Russian émigré in interwar Europe. The most important Russian émigré poet of the First Wave, Khodasevich was more hopeful than many of his émigré contemporaries about the prospects of Russian literature in exile. Of the two poems in this selection, the first was dated in man-uscript "12 February 1917–2 March 1922": Khodasevich started it in Moscow and completed it in Petrograd, four months before his emigration. This liminal poem was included in his fourth collection, *The Heavy Lyre*, which came out in Moscow the year he emigrated; the second edition appeared in Berlin in 1923. The son of a Jewish mother who was raised Catholic (and who raised him Catholic) and a Polish Catholic father, in this major poem Khodasevich articulated his anguished sense of never being completely a native in the pas-tures of Russian culture.

The second poem in the selection is properly an émigré poem, com-posed in the German resort of Saarow in 1923. A literary critic and a stu-dent of the literary culture of the late eighteenth to the early nineteenth centuries, Khodasevich published two books about Pushkin, *The Poetical Estate of Pushkin* (Moscow, 1925) and *On Pushkin* (Berlin, 1937). While he identified with Pushkin the man and the poet, the identification here might have something to do with the strangeness of Pushkin's origins. Alexander Pushkin (1799–1837), who inherited his phenotypic characteristics from his great-grandfather, A. P. Gannibal, "the Blackamoor of Peter the Great," was his whole life preoccupied with his African and Semitic origins. Abducted at a young age, Pushkin's legendary great-grandfather was, according to the version still prevalent in the 1920s, an Abyssinian prince, a descendant of the royal dynasty founded by Menelik I, the son of the King Solomon and Makeda, the Queen of Sheba.

* * *

Not my mother but a Tula peasant woman,
Elena Kuzina, nursed me. It was she
Who hung my swaddlings on the stove for warming,
And made the cross above me to chase away bad dreams.

She knew no fairytales, she didn't sing,
But she always saved for me some special treasure
In her cherished trunk encased in shining tin:
A minty horse or a Vyazma[11] cake of ginger

---

11 Vyazma—town in Smolensk Province, Russia, about one hundred fifty miles west of Moscow, famous for its *pryaniki* (ginger cakes).

She never taught me to say my prayers[12]
But gave ungrudgingly, without reserve,
That wistful, bitter motherhood of hers
And simply everything that she held dear.

Just once, when I had tumbled from the window
But didn't die (how clearly I recall!)
At the Iberian Madonna she lit a penny candle
For my miraculous salvation from the fall.[13]

And that was how, O Russia, "glorious dominion,"[14]
In pulling at her suffering teats
I sucked out the excruciating privilege
Of loving thee and cursing thee.

In that honorable exploit, that joy of singing
To which I am a servant all my days,
My teacher is thy wonder-working genius,
My field—they language, with its magic, lilting ways.

And so before thy weaker songs and lieges
At times I still can pride myself, and not in vain,
That this majestic tongue, bequeathed by all the ages,
I guard more lovingly, more jealously than they . . .

The years rush by. The future does not lure me.
The past is burnt away within my soul.
But still a secret joy lives on and reassures me
That I, too, have one refuge from the creeping cold:

---

12 The nurse was Russian Orthodox; Khodasevich was raised Catholic.

13 Destroyed in 1929 and restored in the post-Soviet years, the chapel with the famous Iberian Madonna icon stands in Moscow in Red Square.

14 Quote from Aleksandr Pushkin's long poem *Gypsies* (1824): "Thus the destiny of your sons/O Rome, O glorious dominion." Pushkin, Russia's national poet, is the "wonder-working genius" in the next stanza.

It's there, where love for me that never perishes
Is harbored in a heart all gnawed by worms:
She sleeps close to the tsar's Khodynka[15] revelers,
Elena Kuzina, my faithful nurse.

1917; 1922

* * *

In Moscow I was born. I never
Saw smoke rise from a Polish hearth;
My father left to me no treasured
Locket filled with native earth.

Stepson to Russia, and to Poland
I hardly know what I am to her.
But eight slim volumes—and all my homeland
In them is perfectly preserved.

The rest of you choose exile, suffer,
Or bend your necks beneath the yoke.
But I will cart away my Russia
In a traveling case packed tight with books.

You need the homeland's dusty vistas,
But I, wherever I am, can hear
The sacred moorish[16] lips that whisper
Of fabled kingdoms far and near.

1923

Translated from the Russian by Alyssa Dinega Gillespie

---

15 Reference to Khodynka Field (*Khodynskoe pole*) in Moscow, where the coronation of
Nicholas II and Alexandra took place on 7 November 1894. The coronation proved a calamity since peasants and workers flooded Khodynka Field when they did not receive the gifts of
food and trinkets they had been promised. As a result, over 1,300 people died; the police tried
to cover up the disaster, although eventually the new emperor and empress were informed.

16 That is, Pushkin's lips. The "eight slim volumes" in the second stanza refer to the eight-volume
edition of Pushkin's works edited by P. Efremov and published in St. Petersburg in 1903–8.

ANDREY SOBOL

Andrey Sobol (1888–1926), fiction writer, playwright, memoirist, and trans-
lator, was born Israel Sobel; he Russianized his name to Yuly Sobol. The pen
name Andrey Sobol, which in English would be Andrew Sable, was proba-
bly fashioned after Andrey Bely's ("Andrew White" in English). Left without
means after the death of Sobol's father, Sobol's mother moved the family from
Saratov to Shavli (Šiauliai, Lithuania), where Sobol studied at a government
Jewish school. A fourteen he left home for a life of wonderings. In Perm he
joined a Zionist socialist group and composed verses in the manner of Simon
Frug, publishing some. In response to the Kishinev Pogrom (1903), Sobol
wrote militant poems, kindred in message to Hayyim Nahman Bialik's *The City
of Slaughter*. (Sobol would publish a powerful essay on Bialik in 1916 in the
Moscow-based Zionist newspaper *Jewish Life* [*Evreiskaia zhizn'*].) Sobol joined
the Socialist-Revolutionary (SR) Party in 1904 and was arrested in 1906. He
served part of his four-year sentence of hard labor at the construction site of
the Amur Railroad. (In the 1920s, Sobol depicted his convict's experience in
memoir and drama.) Penal servitude interrupted his creative work.

Sobol escaped from Siberian exile to Europe in 1909. A prosaist of life's
shifty gray, he contributed fiction to Russian periodicals in the 1910s. The novel
Dust, published in 1915 in *Russian Thought* (*Russkaia mysl'*), was a landmark in
Sobol's early prose. Featuring Jewish SR terrorists, the novel argued that even
within the revolutionary movement Jews felt alienated. Sobol also created heroic
images of Jews in contrast to the doubly estranged Jewish intellectuals. Of special
interest is his story "The Gentle Current" (1918) about Jews in Siberia.

Sobol returned to Russia illegally in 1915 and reported from the Caucasian
front under an assumed name. Five books by Sobol appeared in 1916–17. In the
late 1910s and early 1920s, Sobol contributed to Jewish-Russian publications,
among them *Collection Safrut* 1 (1918), edited by Leyb Jaffe, and coedited the
volume *Jewish World*, published in Moscow in 1918. Sobol enthusiastically
received the February 1917 Revolution and served as an army commissar of
the Provisional Government. The Bolshevik coup had a sobering effect on him,
however, and he spent the civil war in the south. Unwilling either to support
Bolshevism or to oppose it, he was in turn arrested by the Whites and the Reds,
and as a prisoner of the Odessa Cheka in 1921, he barely escaped execution. In
1922, Sobol returned to Moscow and, in 1923, published an open letter admit-
ting his political "errors."

Responding to the chaos and violence of the revolutionary years, Sobol embraced an expressionist style. Characteristic of Sobol's narrative aesthetics of that time is the short novel whose Russian title, *Bred* (1917–19), means delirium, gibberish, and nonsense. In the 1920s, Sobol published a number of books. Two different editions of his *Collected Works* appeared, in 1926–27 (four volumes) and in 1928 (three volumes), respectively. Some critics cite the short autobiographical novel *Salon Car* (1922) as Sobol's best work.

In spite of the negative reception of Sobol's work by party-minded critics deeming him a "right-wing fellow traveler," Sobol enjoyed popularity. In several questionnaires of the mid-1920s, readers identified Sobol as their favorite prose writer, alongside the beloved poet Sergey Esenin (1895–1925). Sobol's success did not stop the onset of depression as he continued to defend artists' autonomy from official control. Sobol shot himself in the center of Moscow in 1926. In his suicide letter, Sobol wrote, "My entire life is a story about things turning out in the opposite way. A real story. And I'm ending it fittingly."

The Lethean waters of Stalinism rushed Sobol's name into oblivion. No works by him were reprinted until 1989, but contemporaries conjured up Sobol's image in their memoiristic fiction. In *The Golden Rose* (1955), Konstantin Paustovsky described a 1921 encounter with Sobol in Odessa. Valentin Kataev (whose brother, **Evgeny Petrov**, co-author of **Ilya Ilf**, is in this anthology), mockingly portrayed Sobol, disguised as Serafim Los, in the short novel *Werther Has Been Written* (published in 1980). Two volumes of Sobol's prose appeared in 2001–2 in Moscow. In 2017, the Russian-Israeli scholar Vladimir Khazan published the first English-language book-length study of Sobol's life and legacy.

* * *

In her 2002 dissertation, Diana Gantseva suggested that in depicting Jewish characters Sobol created a "drama of a personality with a split [. . .] consciousness." Throughout his career, Sobol highlighted the liminality of Jewish characters while pondering the limits of assimilation (his 1916 novella "Inadvertently" scorned apostasy).

Among Sobol's greatest Jewish works was "When Cherry Trees Bloom" (published in 1925), which dialogues with **Isaac Babel**'s *Red Cavalry*. The novella's bespectacled "Yid," who introduces himself as Marat (after Jean-Paul Marat), wins in a confrontation with the chieftain Dzyuba, who evokes the anarchist leader Nestor Makhno (1888–1934).

Sobol included "The Count" in his *Book of Little Stories, 1922–25* (1925), where two other stories, "The Cellar" and "Pogrom," offered haunting footage of Jews caught in the meat grinder of the revolution and the civil war and of the genocidal violence against Jews during the years 1919–20.

THE COUNT

His fingers burning, raising himself up only to fall down again, Lipman crawled toward the fence that remained unscathed—to seek shelter.

If only for a moment, for just one brief moment, to reach that patch of land where it was damp and cool, where the suffocating black smoke does not blind the eyes.

And on that patch of earth of his—to die, to fall asleep.

There was shooting in the distance . . .

Or is all the earth reduced to fiery coals? Or is all the earth breathing fire?

And through all the days and nights—endless nights and endless days—without cease, without abatement, without respite, will these smashed and scorched human mouths moan, scream, and wail?

And will today be yesterday? And tomorrow, today?

The synagogue still smoldered.

Meanwhile, to the left a new fiery whirlwind had leapt up, and Lipman with his clouded eyes still managed to make out that it was Monozon's house that was burning, that the wind was gusting to the right and that he should crawl not to the fence but to the well.

And—on all fours, on all fours, his palms against the flaming earth, his knees against cinders, his face turned slightly toward the sky, silent and shut tight (thus the eternal circle closes over a man's tiny life)—Lipman started to crawl along the fence.

And at the end of it—where the fence adjoins the post office—he saw around the bend the top row of lighted windows and close by, right by his ear, spurs jingled—one, two, three.

And when the last pair of spurs—maybe the fifth—stumbled against his leg and, after stumbling, immediately became still, he only had time to reflect that he was not to lie upon the damp cool earth.

Is all the earth reduced to burning coals?

Is all the earth to end in fire?

The shot at so close a range did not even flash.

A chuckle—and a young voice, slightly hoarse from the night air.

"You're lucky, Romka. How many does that make today?"

"I'm not counting. Nine, I think. But it's all crap—they're all old geezers. Give me some young ones, some Bolsheviks. Don't bother to check, he's a goner. I don't miss."

The spurs began to jingle again, as they set off to catch up with those who'd gone on ahead.

Behind the well, hunched up, Shaya nudged Gdalevich:

"Another one. Did you hear? Did you hear?"

"Quiet," wheezed Gdalevich. "I'm counting. Quiet. I know the count. Quiet." And he lay face down in the puddle.

And the dark water, screened from the treacherous, terrible flashes of light by the shell of the well, washed his cracked, swollen lips and the bloody scar on his forehead.

And the dark water lightened the pain.

But his eyes, swollen tight, it could not pacify—and they will remember everything, and they will register everything, and they will take everything with them, within them.

Rivers flow, they merge together, they wash their banks, they know a quiet, even current, they know the murmur of a rolling wave, but the dark water of the puddle by the well will never flow anywhere, and it will preserve the blood spilled in the night and return it to the earth: from the earth it came—into the earth the blood will be restored.

And the swollen eyes know: this blood must not be forgiven.

And the eyes bend toward the puddle—and the heart drinks the smell of blood, and the heart will not return this smell, will not give it back to the earth, for all the old commands and the old laws are dead, they lie, and the earth, the old cheat, lies too.

For the earth does not wish to keep the great count.

"Quiet. I know the count. Quiet. I'm counting."

They will carry away everything with them, those eyes, which have become determined, penetrating.

Everything: the horses' distinct clatter, and the unit commander's moustache, and the cart loaded with smashed boxes of tobacco, and the children's toys on the steps of the house, and next to the toys a slate with some scribbling, and a lit cigarette stuck in the dead teacher's mouth. Everything: the carriage with the woman dressed in a sealskin coat and an officer's cap over her blond curls—the cap jauntily perched, her ringed fingers holding the reins tight, and the red-haired little girl with her naked, bloody legs spread wide apart and the waltz from *Pupsik*[17] in the plundered house to the accompaniment of gunshots, the tread and clatter of horses' hoofs, a woman's screams, and the crackle of burning roofs.

"Quiet . . . Quiet. I know the count."

Shaya merged with the well, Gdalevich with the earth.

He felt his way in the direction of where the shot had just sounded—blindly, with his stomach in the puddles, toward the broken glass, his chin level with the filth, dung, and his restive eyes turned toward the fresh fire.

With his hand he groped for the body; hugging the ground even more tightly, he dragged the corpse, and, without getting up, he labored to turn the dead man's head toward him.

The roof of Monozon's house collapsed, a wild and fiery rocket slashed the sky; in the light the slain man bared his teeth.

"Lipman," Gdalevich said, upon returning to the well. "That's the seventeenth today."

And, like Shaya, he merged with the well.

Flashing crimson for a moment, the bloody puddle again became dark—the earth reclaimed that which it had given up.

The cavalrymen departed from Monozon's house, the horses' rumps shining in the light.

They were moving the tables in the postmaster's apartment. Olimpiada Petrovna was ransacking the drawers of her dresser: the napkins had disappeared somewhere; Semyon Grigovievich had just brought some six dozen, but nobody knew where they'd gone to.

She was panicking, flinging things around, until she found them. But she found only three dozen. Where were the rest—all of the household goods seem to get lost little by little, and the Monozons were known for their linens.

Semyon Grigorievich trailed behind and begged that he be allowed to count them again, perhaps a mistake had been made.

Meanwhile, on the staircase, spurs were already ringing; the good officers had arrived for the banquet.

---

17 *Pupsik*—Russian title of Püppchen (1912), an operetta by the German composer and conductor Jean Gilbert (pseudonym of Max Winterfeld, 1879–1942). The operetta was reworked for the Russian stage in 1914–15. (Trans.)

In nervous haste, Anichka primped her curls with a pencil stub.

Three or four houses down from the post office, Mendel Shmerts said distinctly, for the last time:

"I gave a thousand. There's nothing left," and he closed his eyes: the gray eyebrows met, as if they had drawn the final line.

"Give him a treat," Valitsky nodded to Yevtushenko.

Without a word Yevtushenko methodically struck a match, lit the cigar, took a long pull, coughed a few times, then took another puff.

And when the circle of the tip had grown wider and turned red, Yevtushenko pinched the cigar between two fingers and bent down toward Shmerts.

Valitsky raised his hand.

"Well, are you going to cough it up? One . . . two . . . three."

The old man was silent.

Tearing open the collar of Shmerts's shirt, Yevtushenko thrust the cigar into Shmerts's hairy gray chest.

The smell of singed hair filled the room.

The bed creaked under Schmerts, his legs, bound with ropes, jerked and fell still again; the gray brows met even more tightly. Valitsky, holding his saber, stooped down toward the old man:

"Will you talk, you shit? Damn you, you tight-fisted bastard! You going to talk?"

Yevtushenko stooped down as well, but he had trouble keeping his balance and started to sway; the cigar slipped from his fingers and fell on the exposed body.

The cigar lay there and smoldered. Bluish smoke wafted over the old man's face, toward his eyebrows.

"I'll give it to you, I'll give it to you," shouted Basya from the doorway; she was trying to get up, but her crooked fingers kept slipping down the door jamb. "I know. I'll give it to you." "She's lying," Yevtushenko muttered without turning around. "She's the maid."

"No. No," Basya choked. "His very own sister. Oy . . . oy, his sister."

"Maid," Yevtushenko repeated.

"Sister," her mouth spat out its bloody drool.

"Maid. The dirty whore's lying. She's wearing an apron . . . Plain as day."

The cigar smoldered.

The clatter of horses' hoofs—Valitsky glanced out the window: in the purple light horses with sacks thrown across their saddles glided by; the ends of the saddlecloths fluttered.

"Hey! Hey!" barked Valitsky, leaning out the window.

The men on horseback did not stop.

Valitsky darted down the stairs with his saber, boots and a balalaika thrown over his shoulder clattering behind him.

Yevtushenko unsteadily hurried after him, after crushing the old woman Basya by stamping on her legs.

"Stop! Hey!" Valitsky hollered, as he jumped into the stirrups.

"Ho-ho!" answered the cheerful fading voices. The strings of a balalaika twanged; Yevtushenko tumbled down the stairs; from afar the beams of Monozon's house crackled.

The fire crept on in all directions, embers shot up in the sky like flares and sparks, like stars; both embers and sparks vanished in the darkened half of the shtetl. While on the illumined side a cross burst forth, sharp and bright, from the church, as crimson as though bathed in blood from top to bottom.

The cigar smoldered; the torn white shirt did not stir beneath the ropes. The old woman lay stretched out on the floor, writing and bellowing.

Behind the well there is darkness and mud.

In the mud and darkness are two figures: maybe people or perhaps shadows, begotten of the night, the flames, the smoke, and the blood.

"Quiet, Shaya. Quiet. I know the count."

They crawl—from night to night, from fire to fire, from smoke to smoke. They crawl, holding their breath. But when they come to the house with the illumined windows, their fingers and mouths dig into the earth: figures could be glimpsed in the illumined windows.

Service jackets and uniforms rushed past, curved sabers dragged behind, and the piano jangled with spirit: the good officers, having finished their dinner, were dancing.

1922–23

Translated from the Russian by Natalia Ermolaev, Sergey Levchin, Ronald Meyer,
Jonathan Platt, and Timothy Williams

ILYA EHRENBURG

Ilya Ehrenburg (1891–1967), fiction writer, poet, and journalist, was born in Kiev to a family of Jewish-Russian intelligentsia. His father, an engineer, moved the family to Moscow in 1894. Ehrenburg later studied in Moscow's First Gymnasium. In 1908, Ehrenburg was arrested for his involvement with Bolshevik activities and spent almost a year in Moscow jails. In December 1908 his father arranged for him to travel abroad, and Ehrenburg spent the next eight years as an expatriate, soon distancing himself from Bolshevik activities. In the 1910s, Ehrenburg forged connections with members of the artistic avant-garde, including a lifelong friendship with Pablo Picasso. He started out as a poet in 1910, publishing six collections in the pre-1917 period. His first story, "In November," appeared in 1911. Richly equipped to absorb artistic innovations from the air of culture, Ehrenburg treated style as a means and not an end of expression. Formal aspects of writing served to underscore Ehrenburg's principal métier: a polemicist and a witness to his torrid times.

Ehrenburg wrote poetry his whole life and also translated French and Spanish poets into Russian. As was the case with other prominent prose writers who also write poetry, such as Vladimir Nabokov, Ehrenburg treated his poems as public diaries or sketchbooks filled with studies for future fiction. Formally diverse and lacking a signature intonation, some of Ehrenburg's poems are very accomplished, especially his lyrical poems of soul-searching.

In 1911, Ehrenburg went through a phase of fascination with Catholic medieval mysticism and with the poetry of Francis Jammes (1868–1938). He planned to enter a Benedictine monastery but had a crisis and changed his mind. Two notable poems with Jewish themes, "To the Jewish Nation" and "Jews, I haven't strength to live with you. . . ," appear in Ehrenburg's early collections *I Live* (1911) and *Dandelions* (1912) and reflect the poet's strained identity. They bring to mind the words of Morris Feitelzohn in Isaac Bashevis Singer's novel *Shosha* (1974; in English, 1978): "I love Jews even though I cannot stand them."

During World War I, Ehrenburg served as European correspondent for *Morning of Russia* (*Utro Rossii*) and *The Stock Exchange News* (*Birzhevye vedomosti*) and wrote about the war in *Verses about the Eves* (1916). Following the February 1917 Revolution, Ehrenburg returned to Russia. He did not accept the Bolshevik coup and moved to Kiev, where he witnessed civil-war violence, including a Jewish pogrom. Ehrenburg's poetry of the time echoed the anti-Bolshevik sentiments of his articles. In Kiev, Ehrenburg met and married Lyubov Kozintseva, who would remain his wife despite Ehrenburg's extramarital affairs.

In 1921, Ehrenburg was allowed to travel abroad with a Soviet passport. He headed for Paris but was not permitted to stay. At the Belgian resort of La Panne, he composed his first (and best) novel, *The Extraordinary Adventures of Julio Jurenito and His Disciples* (published in Berlin in 1922; excerpt in this anthology); the Jewish theme played a significant role in the novel. Ehrenburg spent the next two years in Berlin (see excerpt from **Viktor Shklovsky**'s *Zoo*) before moving to Paris in 1924. Between 1921 and 1927, he published seven novels, several of them interspersing European and Russian (Soviet) settings and characters. Ehrenburg also published collections of essays, poems, and stories, including *The Thirteen Pipes* (1923). In the opinion of Shimon Markish, Ehrenburg's novella "Shifscard" from the collection *Six Novellas about Easy Endings* (1922) was the worker's "first Jewish prose." Ehrenburg's 1927 novel *The Stormy Life of Lazik Roitshvanets* was not reprinted in the USSR until 1989 as it flew in the face of the Soviet rhetoric on the Jewish question.

Stalin's rise to absolute power in the late 1920s signaled a change in Ehrenburg's orientation. In 1932, he became a special correspondent of *Izvestia*. Making a prominent appearance at the First Congress of Soviet Writers in 1934 and drawing on the impressions of a perfunctory tour of Soviet industrial sites, Ehrenburg concocted *The Second Day of Creation*, a production and construction novel praised by Stalin. In the mid-1930s, Ehrenburg increasingly turned his energies to writing and lobbying against Fascism and Nazism. He reported on the events of the Spanish Civil War from the trenches of the Loyalists. He visited the USSR briefly in 1936 but went back to Paris and waited out the Great Purges. Following the defeat of the Loyalists in 1939 and the Soviet–Nazi pact, Ehrenburg continued to dispatch to Moscow vitriolic articles that did not get printed while he remained an *Izvestia* correspondent. In July 1940, Ehrenburg was evacuated from Paris to Moscow with the Soviet embassy staff.

Right after Nazi Germany invaded the Soviet Union, Ehrenburg became staff war correspondent for *Red Star* (*Krasnaia zvezda*), the Soviet army's central newspaper. He wrote daily articles during World War II. Ehrenburg's impact on the morale of the Soviet troops was paramount. Ehrenburg was one of the principal cultivators of popular hatred against the Nazi invaders, which he famously summed up in his article "Kill!" published in *Red Star* on 24 July 1942 as the Nazi armies pushed ahead toward the Caucasus and Stalingrad. Largely responsible, along with the writer Aleksey Tolstoy, for the "Kill the German" wartime rhetoric, Ehrenburg sensed, despite his own internationalism, that the Soviet people needed a visceral anti-Nazi message. His writings were personally targeted by Adolf Hitler and Joseph Goebbels in their speeches. In 1942, Ehrenburg's novel *The Fall of Paris* was published and awarded a Stalin Prize in literature.

From the very beginning, Ehrenburg wrote and published about the Shoah—in nonfiction, poetry, and fiction—more openly than any Soviet writer of his official status and magnitude. One of his wartime projects, *The Red Book*, memorializing Jewish heroism in battle, was derailed. The second was *The Black Book*, documenting Nazi atrocities against the Jews. Ehrenburg led this collective project in 1943–44 under the auspices of the Jewish Antifascist Committee (JAC), working closely with a team of Soviet writers that included, of the authors featured in this anthology, **Pavel Antokolsky**, **Vasily Grossman**, **Vera Inber**, **Veniamin Kaverin**, and **Viktor Shklovsky**. Toward the end of the war, Ehrenburg had a falling-out with the JAC (several interpretations of his conduct have been advanced), resigning as head of *The Black Book* project, and **Vasily Grossman** took over. *The Black Book* was scheduled to appear in the USSR in 1947, with Ehrenburg and Grossman listed as coeditors. Its publication was banned, and a reconstructed text appeared in Israel only in 1980 (English translation, *The Black Book*, 1981; *The Complete Black Book of Russian Jewry*, 2002). Ehrenburg's novel *The Storm* described the murder of Soviet Jews at Babi Yar and the destruction of European Jewry. It was awarded a Stalin Prize in 1948.

The end of World War II and the late 1940s constituted the peak of Ehrenburg's favor with Stalin. He was sent on official foreign missions as a propagandist for the Soviet state. His tour of the United States and Canada in 1946 produced starkly negative and distortional essays in the spirit of cold-war Soviet rhetoric. Despite the raging "anticosmopolitan" (read: antisemitic) campaign of 1948–53, Ehrenburg was unharmed, although at the time he constantly feared arrest. On the occasion of Stalin's seventieth birthday, Ehrenburg published in *Pravda* an embarrassing dithyramb. In 1949, he was one of the few Jews elected to the Supreme Soviet, and in 1953, he was awarded a Stalin Peace Prize.

Soon after Stalin's death in 1953, accustomed as he was to recognizing the winds of history, Ehrenburg quickly wrote and published the novel *The Thaw* (1954), which lent its title to the period of de-Stalinization and temporarily expanded artistic freedom in the middle to late 1950s and early 1960s. *The Thaw* gave impetus to greater anti-Stalinist works and placed Ehrenburg in the camp of liberalizers. One of the main characters, Vera Sherer, is a Jewish doctor; both the Doctors' Plot and the Shoah were depicted. From 1960 until his death in 1967, Ehrenburg worked on his great memoir, *People, Years, Life*. Even in its expurgated published form, it amounted to a large window onto fifty years of western and modernist culture and played a major role in the aesthetic education of the postwar generations.

Helen Segall wrote that Ehrenburg "felt a strong obligation to his fellow Jews to make the world aware of what had befallen them during the Holocaust." A man of "tangled loyalties" (the title phrase of Joshua Rubenstein's 1996 biography of Ehrenburg), a survivalist by profession but never a conformist by conviction, Ehrenburg was a unique creation of his personal predilections, Jewish history, and Soviet ideology. Ten million copies of his books were published in the USSR in thirty languages. While not the most talented of the Jewish-Russian writers of the twentieth century, Ehrenburg was the most visible and audible champion of Jewish causes.

(See Ehrenburg's wartime essay and poems in the section "War and Shoah.")

* * *

The complete title of Ilya Ehrenburg's novel excerpted below is *The Extraordinary Adventures of Julio Jurenito and His Disciples: Monsieur Delet, Karl Schmidt, Mr. Cool, Aleksey Tishin, Ercole Bambucci, Ilya Ehrenburg, and Aysha the Negro, in Days of Peace, War, and Revolution, in Paris, Mexico, Rome, Senegal, Kineshma, Moscow, and Other Places, as well as Diverse Opinions of the TEACHER about Pipes, about Death, about Love, about Freedom, about the Game of Chess, about the Tribe of Judah, about Constructivism, and about Numerous Other Matters.*

The prototype of the novel's charismatic protagonist was the great Mexican muralist Diego Rivera (1886–1957), whom Ehrenburg befriended in Paris. Oddly enough, despite a controversial episode of Jurenito's visit with Lenin in the Kremlin, Lenin and Boris Kamenev (1883–1936), a major Bolshevik leader, both liked the book. Originally published in Berlin in 1922, *Julio Jurenito* was reprinted in the USSR in 1927–28 and subsequently included there in Ehrenburg's collected editions. Jurenito, an anarchist, seeks to bring the world to the brink of self-destruction so as to summon a better new world. Jurenito dies under banal circumstances, his prospects unfulfilled. In the novel told by Jurenito's "disciple" Ehrenburg, Jewish questions keep popping up, and the chapter included here famously presents Ehrenburg's vision of Jewish history and his prophesy of the Shoah. The prophesy is crowned by a replaying of the famous Grand Inquisitor "poem" from Dostoevsky's *The Brothers Karamazov*, where structurally Ehrenburg assigns himself the place of Christ and Jurenito, that of the Grand Inquisitor.

FROM *THE EXTRAORDINARY ADVENTURES OF JULIO JURENITO AND HIS DISCIPLES*

Chapter XI

The Teacher's Prophecy Concerning the Destinies of the Tribe of Judah

On a lovely April evening, we forgathered once again in the Teacher's Paris studio on the seventh floor of one of the new buildings in the Grenelle quarter. We stood for a long time by the large windows, admiring the beloved city with its unique, insubstantial, unreal twilight. Schmidt, too, was with us, but I tried in vain to convey to him the beauty of the dove-gray houses, the stony groves of the Gothic churches, the leaden reflections in the slow Seine, the chestnut trees in flower, the first lights in the distance, and the touching song of a hoarse-voiced old man with his barrel organ underneath the window. Schmidt said that all this was excellent for a museum but that he had detested museums from childhood; one thing that did enchant him was the Eiffel Tower, so light, so slender, swaying in the wind like a reed, the indomitable iron bride to another age silhouetted against the tender blue of an April night.

Amid such peaceful talk we awaited the Teacher, who was dining with some important military supplier. He soon came in and, after putting away in a small safe a pile of documents that had been thrust untidily into his pockets, said to us cheerfully:

"Tonight I've done good work. Things are looking up. Now we can rest and chat for a while. But first, before I forget, I must draw up the text of the invitations, and you, Alexey Spiridonovich, will take them tomorrow to the Union Printing Works."

Five minutes later he showed us the following:

To Take Place Shortly
Solemn Performances
of the Destruction of the Tribe of Judah
in Budapest, Kiev, Jaffa, Algiers
and many other places.
The program will include, apart from the traditional pogroms—
a public favorite—a series of historical reconstructions in the
spirit of the age, such as burning of Jews,
burying same alive, sprinkling of fields with Jewish blood, as well as
modern methods of "evacuation," "removal of suspicious
elements," and so on and so forth.
This invitation is extended to
cardinals, bishops, archimandrites, British lords, Roman noblemen,
Russian liberals,
French journalists, members of the Hohenzollern family, Greeks regardless of pro-
fession or trade, and all others wishing to attend.
Time and place to be announced later.
Entrance free.

"Teacher!" Alexey Spiridonovich cried in horror. "This is unthinkable! The twentieth century and such vile doings! How can I deliver such a notice to the Union—I who have read Merezhkovsky!"[18]

"You are wrong to think that the two are incompatible. Very soon, in two years' time perhaps, or in five years, you will be convinced of the contrary. The twentieth century will turn out to be a very jolly and frivolous age, without any moral prejudices whatsoever; and the readers of Merezhkovsky will be the most enthusiastic audience at the performances. The diseases of mankind, don't you see, are not the measles of infancy but old, deep-seated attacks of gout, and certain habits have been formed in the course of time concerning their cure. You don't break a habit in your later years.

---

18 Merezhkovsky, Dmitry (1865–1941)—Russian writer and Christian religious philosopher, major representative of the symbolist movement; emigrated in 1919 with his wife, the writer Zinaida Gippius (1869–1945), and spent most of his émigré years in Paris. In the mid-to-late 1930s, Merezhkovsky's anti-Bolshevism (conjoined with his religious and political antisemitism and a degree of opportunism) pushed him to express enthusiasm for European Fascism and pay homage to Mussolini. To Ehrenburg's Aleksey Spiridonovich, the Merezhkovsky of the early 1920s embodies a Russian modern cultural prophet of Christian love. Unlike his character, Ehrenburg displays unerring intuition regarding the trajectory of Merezhkovsky's career.

"When, in ancient Egypt, the Nile went on strike and drought set in, the wise men would remember the existence of the Jews, who would be summoned and slaughtered to the accompaniment of prayer; and the earth would be sprinkled with fresh Jewish blood: 'May famine pass us by!' Naturally this could not replace either rain or the Nile in flood, but nevertheless it gave some satisfaction. Even at that time, it is true, there were some cautious people of humane views who said that killing a few Jews wouldn't do any harm, of course, but sprinkling the earth with their blood was a bad idea because this blood was poisonous and would produce thistles instead of wheat.

"In Spain, whenever there was an epidemic—of the plague or the common cold—the Holy Fathers would solemnly proclaim forgiveness for the 'enemies of Christ and mankind' and, shedding profuse tears (not, however, profuse enough to put out the pyres), would burn a couple of thousand Jews. 'May the pestilence pass us by!' The humanists, fearing the high temperature of the fire and ash that the wind wafted everywhere, would whisper guardedly in each other's ears—lest they be overheard by some stray Inquisitor—'Wouldn't it be better just to starve them to death?' . . .

"In Southern Italy, during the earthquakes people would at first run away to the north, then come back cautiously, one by one, to see whether Mother Earth was still shaking. The Jews would also run away—in fact before anyone else—and also come home—later than anyone. Naturally, the earth shook either because they, the Jews, had wanted it or because it, the earth, had not wanted the Jews. In either case, it was advisable to take representatives of the tribe and bury them alive, which was done with all speed. What did the progressive folk say? Oh, yes: they were very much afraid that the buried Jews would make the earth shake still more.

"There, my friends, is a short excursion into history. And since humanity is to experience both famine and pestilence, as well as a goodly amount of earth shaking, I am merely looking ahead in a commonsense way by having these invitations printed in advance."

"But Teacher," Alexey Spiridonovich retorted, "aren't the Jews men like ourselves?" (During Jurenito's "excursion," he had sighed loud and long and wiped his eyes with his handkerchief but moved to a place fairly far from my side, just in case.)

"Of course not! Are a football and a bomb one and the same thing? Do you think the tree and the axe can be brothers? You can love the Jews or hate them, you can regard them with dread as fire-raisers or with hope as saviors, but their blood is not yours, nor is their cause your cause. You don't understand? You refuse to believe? Very well, I'll try to make it clear to you. The night is calm and cool; let us amuse ourselves with a rather childish game over a glass of Vouvray. Tell me, my friends, if you were asked to keep just one word from the whole of human language—namely, 'yes' or 'no'—and discard the rest, which would you choose? Let us begin with the oldest. You, Mr. Cool?"

"Of course I'd choose 'yes': the affirmation and the basis. I don't like 'no'; it's immoral and criminal. Even when a workman I've just sacked entreats me to take him back to work, I do not say to him that harsh and bitter word, 'no'; I say 'wait a while, my friend; you'll be rewarded for your sufferings in the next world.' When I show my dollars, everyone says 'yes' to me. Destroy any words you like, but leave the dollars and the little word 'yes,' and I'll undertake to cure humanity of all its ills."

"I'd say that both 'yes' and 'no' were extremes," said Monsieur Delet, "whereas I like moderation in all things: the golden mean, you know. But still, if the choice must be faced, I'll say 'yes.' 'Yes' is joy, élan, what else? Everything! Madame, your poor husband is dead. A fourth-class funeral, n'est-ce pas? Yes! Garçon, a Dubonnet! Yes! Zizi, are you ready? Yes, yes!"

Alexey Spiridonovich, still shaken by what had gone before, could not collect his thoughts, made mooing noises, jumped up several times, sat down again, and finally yelled: "Yes! I believe, O Lord! Communion! The sacred 'yes,' the 'yes' of Turgenev's pure young girls! O, Liza! Come, sweet dove!"

Schmidt, who found the whole game completely ridiculous, declared briefly and in a businesslike manner that the dictionary should really be revised with a view to expunging certain unnecessary, archaic words such as "spirit," "sacred," "angel," and so forth; "yes" and "no," however, must be retained, being serious words. Last night, if he had had to make a choice, he would have chosen "yes" as a word having an organizing function, something like a good river.

"Yes! Si!" replied Ercole. "On all pleasant occasions in life they say 'yes'; you only hear 'no' when you're being thrown out on your ear."

Aysha, too, preferred "yes." When he begged Krupto (the latest god) to be kind, Krupto said "yes." When he asked the Teacher for two sous to spend on chocolate, the Teacher said "yes" and gave him the money.

"Why aren't you saying anything?" the Teacher asked me. I had not replied earlier, afraid of vexing him and my friends.

"Teacher, I cannot deceive you. I would keep "no." Candidly speaking, I'm always rather pleased when something goes wrong or breaks down. I'm very fond of Mr. Cool, but it would give me pleasure if he were suddenly to lose all his dollars; yes, simply lose them like a button, down to the last one. Or if Monsieur Delet's clients mixed up all the categories. Imagine what would happen if the man with a class-sixteen burial—three years' tenure, you remember—suddenly got up and cried, 'Bring out your scented handkerchiefs, I want the luxury class!' When the purest young girl who has been running round this dirty world picking up the hem of her skirt, making a great to-do of her virginity, meets a resolute tramp in a little wood outside the town, that's not bad either. Or when the waiter slips and drops a bottle of Dubonnet: I love that. Of course it's as my great-great-grand-father, that clever fellow Solomon, said, 'There is a time to gather stones and a time to cast them aside.' But I'm a simple man, I've got only one face, not two. No doubt someone'll have to gather them, maybe Schmidt. As for me, believe me I'm not trying to be original if I say in all conscience: destroy 'yes,' destroy everything in the world, and then 'no' will remain of its own accord."

While I was speaking, all my friends who had been sitting next to me on the sofa moved into the opposite corner. I was left by myself. The Teacher addressed Alexey Spiridonovich:

"Now you see that I was right. A natural division has taken place. Our Jew is left alone. You can destroy all the ghettoes, wipe away all the Pales of Settlement, dig up all the frontiers, but there's nothing to fill those ten feet that separate you from him. All of us are Robinson Crusoes, or convicts if you prefer; the rest is a matter of personality. One man will tame a spider, study Sanskrit, and lovingly sweep the floor of his cell. Another will bang his head against the wall: crack! a bump; another crack! and another bump; and so on. What will prove stronger: the wall or his head? The Greeks came along and looked around—the place could have been more comfortable to live in, it's true; without disease, or death, or suffering, something like Olympus. But it couldn't be helped; this was where they had to live. And so, to keep their spirits up, they decided to proclaim every discomfort, including death (you couldn't abolish the discomforts anyway), as the greatest boon. The Jews came along and crack! it's the head against the wall at once. 'Why is this place the way it is?' You have two men, why shouldn't they be equal? But no, Jacob finds favor, Esau's out in the cold. And so it begins: the undermining of heaven and earth, of Jehovah and the kings, of Babylon and Rome. The ragged beggars who spend their nights on the steps of the temple work away, concocting a new reli-gion of justice and poverty, as though mixing an explosive in a cauldron. Now just watch unconquerable Rome go flying head over heels! The poor, ignorant, dull-witted sectarians come out against the beautiful order and wisdom of the ancient world. Rome trembles. The Jew Paul has conquered Marcus Aurelius.

Yet ordinary people, who prefer a cozy little house to dynamite, begin to settle down in the new faith, making the bare hut homely and pleasant. Christianity is no longer a well-beating machine; it has become a new fortress. Terrible, naked, destructive justice has been replaced by human, comfortable, india-rubber mercy. Rome—the world—has withstood the onslaught. But seeing this, the tribe of Judah repudiated its child and started undermining once again. At this moment there's undoubtedly someone in Melbourne sitting alone, sapping away, not in deed but in thought. Again they're mixing something in cauldrons, again they're preparing a new faith, a new truth. Forty years ago the gardens of Versailles shivered with the first access of fever, just like the gardens of Hadrian long ago. Rome prides itself on its wisdom, the Senecas write their books, the brave cohorts stand ready. It trembles again, 'Rome the unconquerable!'

"Israel has borne a new child. You will behold its wild eyes, red hair, and little hands that are as strong as steel. Having given birth, Israel is ready to die. A heroic gesture: 'there are no more nations, I am no more, but we are.' Oh, naïve, incorrigible sectarians! They'll take your child, wash it, dress it, and it'll become exactly like Schmidt. Once more they will say 'justice,' but they'll replace it by expediency. Once more you'll go away to hate and wait, beat your head against the wall, and moan 'how long?'

"I will tell you: until the day of your madness and theirs, until the day of infancy, a distant day. Meanwhile the tribe will be drenched once more in the blood of parturition in the squares of Europe, giving birth to another child that will betray it.

"But how should I not love that spade in the thousand-year-old hand? It digs the graves, but does it not turn up the soil of the fields too? It will be shed, the blood of Judah, the invited guests will applaud, but (remember the whispers of long ago?) the blood will only make the earth still more poisonous. The world's great medicine!"

And the Teacher came up to me and kissed me on the forehead.

1922

Translated from the Russian by Anna Bostock in collaboration with Yvonne Kapp

Ilya Ehrenburg, *Neobychainye pokhozhdeniia Khulio Khurenito i ego uchenikov.*
Copyright © by the Estate of Ilya Ehrenburg. Introduction and note
copyright © by Maxim D. Shrayer.

VIKTOR SHKLOVSKY

Viktor Shklovsky (1893–1984), literary theorist, critic, fiction writer, memoirist, and screenwriter, was born in St. Petersburg. Shklovsky's Jewish father converted when he was a student and married Shklovsky's mother, who was half-Russian and half-German-Latvian.

Shklovsky studied philology at St. Petersburg University and sculpture at Leonid Shervud's studio. During World War I, he was a noncommissioned officer in an armored-car unit, and after the war, in 1917–18, he was active in the right wing of the Socialist-Revolutionary (SR) Party. After announcing that he was ceasing political work, Shklovsky returned to Petrograd and in 1920 was elected professor of the Russian Institute of Art History. In 1922, after the extent of his previous involvement in the SR anti-Bolshevik underground was disclosed in a book by the former head of the SR military faction, Shklovsky fled abroad through Finland. In 1922–23, he stayed in Berlin.

The year 1914 marked the publication of two slim books by Shklovsky—the first two of many to appear over his seven prolific decades. Shklovsky's *Resurrection of the Word* (1914) was instrumental in pulling together a group of young theorists collectively bent on replacing the traditional notions of creativity, textuality, and literary dynamics that were prevalent at the time with radically new approaches. In 1916 the group called itself OPOYAZ, the Russian abbreviation for Society for the Study of Poetic Language. Fondled by the winds of neo-Kantianism wafting in from Germany and inspired by the literary experiments of the Russian futurists, Shklovsky and his colleagues laid the foundation of Russian formalism in 1916–21. Influential and stimulating to this day, this movement constitutes an indispensable part of university courses on literary theory. Among the principal formalists were Yury Tynyanov (1894–1943) and Boris Eikhenbaum (1888–1959). A Jewish background was dominant among the members of the formalist movement; in the 1970s–90s, the ultranationalist Russian critics, Vadim Kozhinov most vociferously, charged them with promoting allegedly alien and destructive ideas about (Russian) culture.

One of Shklovsky's most influential essays, "Art as Device" (1917), postulated that new styles and forms came into existence not to express new contents but to oust previous ones. It also introduced the powerful concept of estrangement. Shklovsky published a number of books blending theory and philosophy of culture with criticism of contemporary works and analyses of such iconic texts as Cervantes's *Don Quixote* and Sterne's *Tristram Shandy.* They included *The Articulation of the Plot* (1921), *On the Theory of Prose* (1925, expanded edition 1929, where his major early essays were gathered), *The Hamburg Reckoning* (1928), *Pro and Contra. Notes on Dostoevsky* (1957), *Artistic Prose. Thoughts and Analyses* (1959), *The Bowstring: On the Incompatibility of the Compatible* (1970), and others. In the post-Stalinist years, Shklovsky repackaged his formalist works in revised and expanded volumes, such as the 1985 edition of *On the Theory of Prose.* As a theorist, Shklovsky was increasingly self-referential, writing about himself reading and writing. As a literary historian, he coined a number of seminal formulations, including the term "Southwestern school" (1933) after the title of **Eduard Bagritsky**'s collection *Southwest* (1928); Shklovsky used it in reference to the constellation of writers, originally from Odessa and the Black Sea area, who entered the mainstream in the 1920s (**Isaac Babel**, **Eduard Bagritsky**, both in this anthology, and Yury Olesha, and others). Lev Tolstoy preoccupied Shklovsky, from "Art as Device" (1917) to the monograph *Material and Style in Tolstoy's Novel "War and Peace"* (1928) to his 1963 Tolstoy biography.

To return to Shklovsky's years abroad: in Berlin he completed his two best works, both of which were published in 1923. Shklovsky's *Sentimental Journey: Memoirs. 1917–1922* took its title from Laurence Sterne's antinovel *A Sentimental Journey through France and Italy* (1768). Shklovsky's epistolary novel *Zoo, or Letters Not about Love, or the New Héloïse* negotiated the terms of his "surrender" and return to Soviet Russia. Letter twenty-nine, the last in the first edition, was titled "Declaration to the All-Russian Central Executive Committee." "I cannot live in Berlin," Shklovsky wrote. "I am bound by my entire way of life [. . .] to the Russia of today. I am able to work only for her" (trans. Richard Sheldon).

In 1923, Shklovsky returned to Soviet Russia. He continued to write memoiristic nonfiction; *The Third Factory* (1926) and *Daily Work* (1930) subtly chronicled the evaporation of artistic freedom. In 1930, Shklovsky published in *Literary Gazette* (*Literaturnaia gazeta*) the article "Monument to a Scientific Error," both "scientific" and "error" referring to formalism. (In the late 1930s and early 1950s, the term "formalist" acquired more and more ominous tones in official Soviet lingo.) Shklovsky's literary "professionalization" in the USSR followed several directions. He turned to the safety of historical belles lettres, churning out a number of books; in 1958, some were gathered in the hefty *Historical Tales and Stories*. Having previously made a contribution to film theory (for example, his 1923 *Literature and Cinematography*), Shklovsky now produced film criticism and screenplays. In the 1920s, he wrote screenplays for prominent Soviet directors, among them *By the Law* (1926, screenplay with director Lev Kuleshov), *Traitor* (1926, director Abram Room, screenplay with Lev Nikulin), and *Meshchanskaya 3* (1927, screenplay with director Room, *Bed and Sofa* in English). Shklovsky's work in cinema continued through the 1960s.

Feeling doubly vulnerable because of his SR and formalist past, Shklovsky felt the need to prove his loyalty by taking part in such notorious cultural events as a team of thirty-six who coauthored, in 1934, a volume about the construction of the White Sea–Baltic Sea Canal (the Belomor Canal), built by prison labor. The volume featured, among others, Evgeny Gabrilovich, **Vera Inber**, and Mikhail Kozakov. During World War II, Shklovsky lived first in Almaty, Kazakhstan, doing film work, then in Moscow reporting for periodicals.

A skillful survivalist, Shklovsky never shunned magazine and newspaper "daily" work. Such article titles as "The Time of Maturity—Communism" (1961, about German Titov's flight into space) captured the absurdity of Shklovsky's Soviet literary life while subverting his formalist tenets. Shklovsky privately helped many victims of Stalinism and Soviet totalitarianism, earning the gratitude of such a harsh judge as Nadezhda Mandelstam (see chapter about Shklovsky in her *Hope against Hope*). The apogee of Shklovsky's *sui generis* prose, both shrewd and lyrical, transcending boundaries of genres and forms, was the publication in 1964 of *Once Upon a Time*, which included *Zoo, About Mayakovsky*, and tales about Isaac Babel, Sergey Eisenstein, Yury Tynyanov, and others. About Babel—but also about himself—Shklovsky wrote in *Once Upon a Time*: "I saw him for the last time at Yasnaya Polyana [Lev Tolstoy's estate in Tula Province, now a museum]. [. . .] Babel walked forlornly, calmly, talking about cinema; he looked very tired, calmly describing and unable to tie together, to complete that which he already understood. [. . .] We strolled together on soft green grass; a river that was not wide shot blue in front of us; it was like a line drawn in blue pencil in an accounting book, so as to write under that line the word 'thus.' We were not old at the time; the year 1937 had begun."

One of the most metafictional of Soviet authors, endowed with artistic gifts comparable to Vladimir Nabokov's, Shklovsky might have achieved so much more if he had stayed in Berlin—as he knew better than anyone else.

*   *   *

Given Shklovsky's origin and sensibility, his Jewish half expressed itself mainly in reflections on antisemitism, presented from the sidelines and with doubly ironic distancing, as in *Sentimental Journey*, as well as in his memoirs of Jewish cultural figures.

In his review of Aleksandr Granovsky's 1925 film *Jewish Happiness* (*Yiddishe Glikn*), based on Sholem Aleichem's writings, Shklovsky wrote skeptically of Zionism. In 1926, on the commission of OZET (the Society for the Settlement of Jewish Toilers on Land), he cowrote with Vladimir Mayakovsky the screenplay for Abram Room's 1927 documentary *Jew on the Land* (see also **Viktor Fink**'s *Jews on the Land* [1929]). Ever the master of subtlety, Shklovsky managed to signal his Jewish interests in rather unexpected places. For example, one of his tales about Peter the Great, published in 1941, was titled "Jester Lacosta" and portrayed one of the several Sephardic Jews at the tsar's court (see **David Markish** and *The Jesters*). Shklovsky contributed an essay on the Nazi atrocities in Kislovodsk to the derailed Ehrenburg–Grossman *Black Book*.

Selected below are three letters from Shklovsky's great novel *Zoo* (1923). Disguised as "Alya," the novel's romantic heroine was Elsa Triolet (1896–1970), then a young Russian writer of Jewish descent living abroad. Shklovsky included six of Triolet's own letters in the text of *Zoo*. In 1928, Triolet married the French writer and left-wing activist Louis Aragon; later she became a prominent French author, explicitly addressing Jewish subjects in her novel *Le Rendez-vous des étrangers* (1956). While writing about **Ilya Ehrenburg**, Shklovsky coined one of his enduring aphorisms, "Pavel Savlovich" (literally, Paul the son of Saul), thus mapping the extreme boundaries of a Jewish-Russian identity. *Lekhaim* (*To Life*), a post-Soviet Jewish magazine published in Moscow, features a column about Jewish-Russian writers that is titled "Pavel Savlovich."

FROM *ZOO,* OR *LETTERS NOT ABOUT LOVE*

Letter Seven

About Grzhebin on canvas, about Grzhebin in the flesh. Since the letter is written in a penitent mood, the trademark of the Grzhebin Publishing House is affixed. Here too are several fleeting remarks about Jewry and about the attitude of the Jews toward Russia.

What to write about! My whole life is a letter to you.

We meet less and less often. I've come to understand so many simple words: yearn, perish, burn, but "yearn" (with the pronoun "I") is the most comprehensible word. Writing about love is forbidden, so I'll write about Zinovy Grzhebin, the publisher.[19] That ought to be sufficiently remote.

In Yury Annenkov's portrait of Zinovy Isaevich Grzhebin, the face is a soft pink color and looks downright delectable.

In real life, Grzhebin is pastier.

In the portrait, the face is very fleshy; to be more precise, it resembles intestines bulging with food. In real life, Grzhebin is more tight and firm; he might well be compared to a blimp of the semirigid type. When I was not yet thirty and did not yet know loneliness and did not know that the Spree is narrower than the Neva and did not sit in the Pension Marzahn, whose landlady did not permit me to sing at night while I worked, and did not tremble at the sound of a telephone—when life had not yet slammed the door to Russia shut on my fingers, when I thought that I could break history on my knee, when I loved to run after streetcars . . .

"When a poem was best of all
Better even than a well-aimed ball"—

(something like that)

. . . I disliked Grzhebin immensely. I was then twenty-seven and twenty-eight and twenty-nine.

I thought Grzhebin cruel and rigid for having gulped down so much Russian literature.

Now, when I know that the Spree is thirty times narrower than the Neva, when I too am thirty, when I wait for the telephone to ring—though I've been told not to expect a call—when life has slammed the door on my fingers and history is too busy even to write letters, when I ride on streetcars without wanting to capsize them, when my feet lack the unseeing boots they once wore and I no longer know how to launch an offensive . . .

---

19 Greatly indebted to Richard Sheldon's notes accompanying his English translation of Shklovsky's *Zoo*, the editor assumes responsibility for the information provided below.

An artist and well-known editor and publisher, Zinovy Grzhebin (1877–1929) ran several major literary and arts publishing houses, including Shipovnik (Sweetbriar) and Panteon (Pantheon); *Sweetbriar* was also the name of the series of collections and annuals that Grzhebin published in Russia. In 1920, he left Russia and soon settled in Berlin. Taking advantage of the economic situation in Germany at the time and hoping to distribute his Russian-language books outside the émigré communities, mainly in Soviet Russia, he started a large and highly ambitious publishing venture. By 1926, Grzhebin's publishing ventures had completely failed.

. . . now I know that Grzhebin is a valuable product. I don't want to ruin Grzhebin's credit rating, but I fervently believe that my book won't be read in a single bank. Therefore, I declare that Grzhebin is no businessman, nor is he stuffed either with the Russian literature gulped down by him or with dollars.

But, Alya, don't you know who Grzhebin is? Grzhebin's a publisher; he published *Sweetbriar*, he ran the publishing house Pantheon, and now he seems to have the most important publishing house in Berlin.

In Russia, between 1918 and 1920, Grzhebin was buying manuscripts hysterically. It was a disease—like nymphomania.

He was not publishing books then. And I frequently called on him in my unseeing boots, and I shouted in a voice thirty times louder than any other voice in Berlin. And in the evening I drank tea at his place.

Don't think that I've grown thirty times narrower.

It's just that evening has changed.

I hereby give the following testimony: Grzhebin is no businessman.

Grzhebin is a Soviet-type bourgeois, complete with delirium and frenzy.

Now he publishes, publishes, publishes! The books come running, one after another; they want to run away to Russia but are denied entry.

They all bear the trademark ZINOVY GRZHEBIN.

Two hundred, three hundred, four hundred—soon there may be a thousand titles. The books pile on top of each other; pyramids are created and torrents, but they flow into Russia drop by drop.

Yet here in the middle of nowhere, in Berlin, this Soviet bourgeois raves on an international scale and continues to publish new books.

Books as such. Books for their own sake. Books to assert the name of his publishing house.

This is a passion for property, a passion for collecting around his name the greatest possible quantity of things. This incredible Soviet bourgeois responds to Soviet ration cards and numbers by throwing all his energy into the creation of a multitude of things that bear his name.

"Let them deny my books entry into Russia," says he—like a rejected suitor who ruins himself buying flowers to turn the room of his unresponsive beloved into a flower shop and who admires this absurdity.

An absurdity quite beautiful and persuasive. So Grzhebin, spurned by his beloved Russia and feeling that he has a right to live, keeps publishing, publishing, publishing.

Don't be surprised, Alya. We are all capable of raving—those of us who really live. When you sell Grzhebin manuscripts, he drives a hard bargain, but more out of propriety than greed.

He wants to demonstrate to himself that he and his business are real.

Grzhebin's contracts are pseudo-real and, in that sense, relevant to the sphere of electrification in Russia.

Russia dislikes Jews.

All the same, though, Jews like Grzhebin are a good remedy for high fever.

It's nice to see Grzhebin, with his appetite for the creation of things, in idle, skeptical Russian Berlin. [...]

Letter Twelve

Written, it would seem, in response to a comment apparently made by telephone, since the dossier contains nothing in writing along these lines; the comment had to do with table manners. Also contained in the letter is a denial of the assertion that pants absolutely must be creased. The letter is liberally garnished with Biblical parallels.

So help me, Alya, pants don't have to be creased!

Pants are worn to thwart the cold.

Ask the Serapions.[20]

As for hunching over one's food, maybe that ought to be avoided.

You complain about our table manners.

We hunch down over our plates to minimize the transportation problem.

We will no doubt continue to surprise you—and you us.

A great deal surprises me about this country, where pants have to be creased in front. Poor people put their pants under the mattress overnight.

In Russian literature, this method is well known; it's used—in Kuprin—by professional beggars of noble origin.

This whole European way of life provokes me!

Just as Levin was provoked (*Anna Karenina*) when he noticed how preserves were being made in his house—not his way, but the way it had always been done in Kitty's family.

---

20 On the Serapion Brothers, see introductions to **Lev Lunts**, **Veniamin Kaverin**, and **Elizaveta Polonskaya**.

When Judge Gideon was gathering a guerrilla band for an attack on the Philistines, he first of all sent home all the family men.[21]

Then the Angel of the Lord commanded him to lead all the remaining warriors to the river and to take into battle only those who drank water from the palms of their hands, and not those who hunched over the water and lapped it like dogs.[22]

Are we, by any chance, bad warriors?

Well, when everything collapses—and that will be soon—we will leave two by two, with our rifles on our shoulders, with cartridges in the pockets of our pants (not creased); we will leave, firing at the cavalry from behind fences; we will head back to Russia, perhaps to the Urals, there to build a New Troy.

But it is preferable not to hunch over one's plate.

Terrible is the judgment of Gideon the judge! What if he refuses to take us into his army!

The Bible repeats itself in curious ways.

Once the Jews defeated the Philistines, who fled, fleeing two by two, to seek safety on the other side of the river.

The Jews set out patrols at the crossing.

On that occasion, it was difficult to distinguish a Philistine from a Jew: both were, in all likelihood, naked.

The patrol would ask those coming across, "Say the word '*shibboleth*.'"
But the Philistines couldn't say "sh"; they said "*sibboleth*."[23]
Then they were killed.

In the Ukraine, I once ran across a Jewish boy. He couldn't look at corn without trembling.

He told me this: When the killing was going on in the Ukraine, it was frequently necessary to check whether the person being killed was a Jew.

They would tell him, "Say '*kukuruza*.'"
The Jew would say "*kukuruzha*."[24]
He was killed.

---

21 See Judges 7, where, in assembling his army against the Midians, Gideon reduces his large force to three hundred men and wins.
22 Paraphrase of Judges 7:5–7.
23 See Judges 12:5–6, where the Gileadites conduct a pronunciation test to identify the Ephraimites. *Shibboleth* (ancient Heb.) = ear of corn.
24 *Kukuruza* (Rus.) = corn; Shklovsky relates a well-known historical anecdote, versions of which continued to circulate throughout the Soviet period. In the anecdote, people were asked to pronounce words such as *kukuruza* in order to identify Jews by their Yiddish ("Jewish") accent, especially audible in words containing the Russian *r* and *z*; see also **Semyon Kirsanov**'s "R" in this anthology.

Letter Twenty-Five

About spring, the Prager Diele, Ehrenburg, and pipes. About time, which passes, and lips, which renew themselves—about a certain heart that is being worn to a frazzle while the lips in question are merely losing their paint. About my heart.

It's already forty-five degrees outside. My fall coat has become a spring coat. Winter is passing, and, come what may, I won't be forced to endure a winter like this again.

Let's believe in our return home. Spring is coming, Alya. You told me once that spring makes you feel as if you've lost or forgotten something and you can't remember what.

When it was spring in Petersburg, I used to walk along the quays in a black cape. There the nights are white and the sun rises while the bridges are still drawn. I used to find many things on the quays. But you will find nothing; all you know is that something has been lost. The quays in Berlin are different. They're nice, too. It's nice to follow the canals to the workers' districts.

There, in some places, the canals widen into quiet harbors and cranes hover over the water. Like trees.

There, at the Hallesches Tor,[25] out beyond the place where you live, stands the round tower of the gasworks, just like those at home on the Obvodny Canal. When I was eighteen, I used to walk my girlfriend to those towers every day. Very beautiful are the canals—even when the high platform of the elevated train runs along their bank.

I am already beginning to remember what I've lost.

Thank God it's spring!

The little tables in the Prager Diele[26] will be carried outdoors, and Ilya Ehrenburg will see the sky.

Ilya Ehrenburg promenades in Berlin as he promenaded in Paris and in other cities full of émigrés—always bent over, as if looking on the ground for something he's lost.

However, that's an incorrect simile. His body is not bent at the waist: only his head is bent, his back curved. Gray coat, leather cap. Head quite young.

---

25 Hallesches Tor—an area in the Kreutzberg section of Berlin known for its very busy traffic with street and canal transportation, long-distance trains, and an elevated railway built there in 1902. The cemetery at Hallesches Tor is a major cultural site in West Berlin; the writers E. T. A. Hoffmann and Adelbert von Chamisso are buried there.

26 Prager Diele—café where Berlin's Russian writers and intellectuals liked to congregate in the 1920s.

He has three professions: (1) smoking a pipe; (2) being a skeptic, sitting in a cafe, and publishing *Object*; (3) writing *Julio Jurenito*.[27]

Later in time than *Julio Jurenito* is the book called *Trust D. E.* Rays emanate from Ehrenburg; these rays bear various names; their distinctive feature is that they all smoke a pipe.

These rays fill the Prager Diele.

In one corner of the Prager Diele sits the master himself, demonstrating the art of smoking a pipe, of writing novels, and of taking the world and his ice cream with a dose of skepticism.

Nature has endowed Ehrenburg lavishly—he has a passport.

He lives abroad with this passport. And thousands of visas.

I have no idea how good a writer Ilya Ehrenburg is.

His old stuff isn't any good.

But *Julio Jurenito* gives one pause. It is an extremely journalistic affair—a feuilleton with a plot, stylized character types, and the old Ehrenburg himself, garnished with a prayer; the old poetry functions as a stylized character. The novel develops along the lines of Voltaire's *Candide*—though with a less variegated plot.

Candide has a nice circular plot: while people look for Cunégonde, she is sleeping with everybody and aging. The hero winds up with an old woman, who reminisces about the tender skin of her Bulgarian captain.

This plot—more accurately, this critical orientation on the idea that "time passes" and betrayals take place—was already being processed by Boccaccio. There the betrothed woman passes from hand to hand and finally winds up with her husband, assuring him of her virginity.[28]

The discoveries she made during her travels were not limited to hands. This novella ends with the famous phrase about how lips are not diminished but only renewed by kisses.

But never mind, I will soon remember what I've forgotten. Ehrenburg has his own brand of irony; there is nothing Elizabethan about his short stories and novels. The good thing about him is that he chooses not to

---

27 About **Ilya Ehrenburg**, see above. In 1922, **Ehrenburg** and the artist El Lissitsky (1890–1941) published three issues of the international constructivist trilingual magazine *Veshch'* (*Object*). *Trust D. E.: A History of the Demise of Europe* is the title of **Ehrenburg**'s novel, published in Berlin in 1923, a year after the publication of *Julio Jurenito* (1922), by A. Vishnyak's Gelikon, which in 1923 brought out **Shklovsky**'s *Zoo*. Part of the print run of Gelikon's books was distributed in Soviet Russia.

28 The reference is to the seventh story of the second day in *The Decameron* by Giovanni Boccaccio (1313–1375).

continue the traditions of "great" Russian Literature; he prefers to write "bad stuff."

I used to be angry with Ehrenburg because, in transforming himself from a Jewish Catholic or Slavophile into a European constructivist, he failed to forget the past. Saul failed to become Paul.[29] He remains Paul, son of Saul, and he publishes *Animal Warmth*.[30]

He is more, though, than just a journalist adept at organizing other people's ideas into a novel: he comes close to being an artist—one who feels the contradiction between the old humanistic culture and the new world now being built by the machine.

Of all these contradictions, the most painful to me is that, while the lips in question are busy renewing themselves, the heart is being worn to a frazzle; and with it go the forgotten things, undetected.

1923

Translated from the Russian by Richard Sheldon

---

29 Shklovsky is here alluding to 1913–15, when Ehrenburg, under the influence of French mystic authors Francis Jammes and Léon Bloy and his friendship with Max Jacob, was on the verge of conversion to Catholicism and planned to enter a Benedictine monastery. Ehrenburg then went through a spiritual crisis and changed his mind.

30 *Animal Warmth* (*Zverinoe Teplo*, 1923) is the title of Ehrenburg's volume of poetry, published in Berlin by the same publisher (Gelikon) that also published Shklovsky's *Zoo* and the first edition of Ehrenburg's *Julio Jurenito*.

MATVEY ROYZMAN

Matvey Royzman (1896–1973), poet, fiction writer, and translator, was born in Moscow to a traditional family of a Jewish tradesman. The principal source of Royzman's understanding of Judaism was his grandfather, a former *kantonist* and "Nicholas's recruit" (see John D. Klier's "Outline of Jewish-Russian History"). As a teenager, Royzman participated in many amateur theater productions; in 1916–18, he appeared on stage in Moscow's drama studios. He entered the Law Faculty of Moscow University in 1916.

Serving as a translator in a Red Army office, Royzman debuted as a poet in 1918. In the late 1910s and early 1920s, he worked on the staff of several newspapers and magazines in Moscow. In 1920, he aligned himself with the imaginists (*imaginisty*), a postsymbolist movement whose members included Sergey Esenin, Ryurik Ivnev, Anatoly Mariengof, and others. The imaginists were completely independent of the imagists in Anglo-American poetry, the name entering Russian from the Italian *immagine*. Visible on the Moscow literary scene in the 1920s, Royzman directed the publishing house of the All-Russian Union of Poets. He contributed to the collections *Horse Garden* and *Imaginists* and other publications of the imaginists. Jointly with the group's leading theoretician Vadim Shershenevich, Royzman published two volumes of poetry, *Red Alcohol* (1921) and *With This We Repent* (1922). His first solo collection, *The Wine of Hebron* (1923), included several long poems divided into shorter, numbered parts: "Kol Nidrei" (included below), *Passover* (in Russian, the same word, *Paskha*, refers to both Passover and Easter), *The Garden*, and *The New Year* (referring to Rosh Hashanah, the Jewish New Year). The arrangement of texts in *The Wine of Hebron* corresponds to the Jewish calendar. Royzman's second collection, *The Palm Tree* (1925), showcased his shorter poems of 1922–23, the lyrical "Sabbath" among them. Weaving Biblical and Talmudic motifs into a fabric of metaphorically colorful and exuberantly rhymed modernist verse, poems in *The Wine of Hebron* and *The Palm Tree* amounted to one of the strongest manifestations of Jewish-Russian poetry. In addition to original verse, Royzman also published translations from Yiddish and Belorussian poets. In the late 1920s, Royzman put together a volume of Yiddish poets in translation, which was never published.

The mid-1920s marked Royzman's double shift: to prose and to safer ideological pastures. Set during the years of the New Economic Policy (NEP), Royzman's first novel *Minus Six* (1928; second, corrected edition 1930), tendentiously "exposed" the Jewish bourgeoisie. Having jumped on the self-hating wagon carrying Jewish writers around the Soviet antireligious racetrack, Royzman portrayed the Jewish private entrepreneurs as unethical and hypocritical. The novel's inferred authorial worldview stood in grave contrast to the proud, self-consciously Judaic self of Royzman's earlier poetry. Essays and sketches in two collections of nonfiction, *Good Acquaintances* and *Gold Hands* (both 1931), presented Jewish life in the Soviet Union according to the prescribed Soviet rhetoric on the Jewish question. In his second novel, *These Landlords* (1932), about Jewish settlements in the Crimea, Royzman signaled an outgrowth of popular antisemitism in the lower echelons of Soviet bureaucrats. He was criticized for "nationalism" and never again attempted anything even mildly controversial. Formulaically depicting Jews and Belorussians working side by side in a small town near the Polish border, the novel *Frontier* (1935) was the last of Royzman's published works to treat Jewish topics.

Royzman worked as an editor at a film studio in Moscow in the late 1930s. He discovered a thematic niche, detective-adventure tales about Soviet law-enforcement organs and spies. His first book on the subject, *Friends Risking Their Lives* (1943), was followed by *Wolf* (1956), *Berlin Azure* (1961), and others. Toward the end of his life, Royzman turned to the genre of memoirs. His last book, *Everything I Remember about Esenin*, appeared shortly before Royzman's death in Moscow in 1973. Unlike the poetry of his friend, the famous Russian poet Sergey Esenin, who killed himself in 1925, Royzman's poetry was unavailable in print and remembered by few.

* * *

Royzman's collection *The Wine of Hebron* (1923), where "Kol Nidrei" appeared, was quite unique for its fusion of avant-garde poetics with Judaic motifs. Blazingly metaphoric, Royzman's language in "Kol Nidrei" and other poems celebrated the ecstasy of being alive after the millennia of Diaspora, alive and astride in several cultures. As a Jewish participant of the Russian Imaginist movement writing and publishing in the Soviet 1920s, Royzman deserves more attention by students of Jewish culture.

KOL NIDREI[31]

1

Ashes on my hair
After centuries flaming,
In my heart the seeds of prayer
In Your hand a sling,
Sent out on the prophets' path
In the footsteps of their wrath.

Neither for Romanov's song
Nor the *Marseillaise* do I care,
Someone else's wrong
If to mimic snowy air
Feathers spilled and floated
From the pillows of my sky?

And the sunset is a bloated
Belly slashed and wrenched awry,
Blood, intestines over brick,
Over crosses, over roofs,
Where the headlong wind will scream,
Fling its arms, and kick:
Oy, el malei rahamim!"[32]

You will, if you listen,
Hear the distant gravestones,
Executioner's blocks,
Whispering as witnesses
Of the murdered children.
Israel, arise!

---

31 Kol Nidrei—the solemn public breaking (annulling) of all commandments (vows) read at
the beginning of the evening service of Yom Kippur. The first two words of the prayer, *kol
nidrei*, mean "All commandments." Here and after, the commentary draws on Royzman's
own notes to the text as well as the commentary by Eduard Shneiderman in his splendid
anthology *Poety imazhinisty* (St. Petersburg, 1997).

32 *El malei rahamim*—opening of the traditional Jewish mourning prayer: "God filled with mercy!"

Blow your burnished golden horn
So that dusk creeps into town
Like the weevils in the corn,
Eating deeply down
In the greedy killers' eyes.

2

O Reb Yeshua, great-grandfather of my grief,
Adamantine bolt in Israel's door,
O forefather, whipped for your belief
And wounded while besieging Turks in the war,
The wine of your memory, my brave,
Is more fragrant and far stronger,
And may this elegy grace your grave
Like falling leaves of myrrh.

True to Savaof, firstborn son,
I'm imbued with Torah learning.
Does the fathers' bloodline run
Through the stanzas of my yearnings?

Aren't I in the book[33] since I,
On a Yom Kippur abroad,
Exiled, was the first to cry
Vengeance on their pogrom squad?

Was not my shell of heartache
Circumcised[34] for Him, so I've
Been reflected in fate's lake
And my rooster is white, alive,
As a sacrifice of joy
For my brother and my God.

---

33 Book of Life, see Daniel 12.
34 Cf. Jeremiah 9:24–25: "Lo, days are coming—declares the Lord—when I will take note of everyone circumcised in the foreskin [. . .]. For all those nations are uncircumcised, but all the House of Israel are uncircumcised of heart."

Land! Now in the name of Adonai
Cities and groves are overawed,
And by my spell let that horde submerge
In our slaughtered people's blood,
And on the crimson waters of that flood
My white heart will surge
Out of the wound like an ark.

3

Ah, my Tishrei, Tishrei,[35]
Wandering and wearing out your shoes,
You should stride more quietly
Along the city avenues.

Here the sun will never clip those
Curls of almonds, delicately gray,
With shining scissors of gold,
Nor has a groggy lily ever tolled
Its gentle bell to sway
To the rhythm of whispering meadows.

Here olives are never meant
To shed onto the dry sand
Their black embossed earrings, nor
Will a grapevine ever pour
Its fragrant autumnal scent
Into the goblets of a forestland.

Here only lindens overfill
Themselves with so much blood
Aortas of leaves burst and spill,
And onion domes are whipped by an ill
Wind that's pouring evening ashes
On coppery bald spots.

---

35 Tishrei–seventh month of the Biblical year, first month of the civic year; corresponds to
    September.

Ah, sempiternal Tishrei,
Savaof summoned me to say,
Would I light the candles of our ancestry
In the Old Testament way?

4

Oh, my star, well may you stare
In the lap of the ancient East:
I'll reply the cruel nightmare
And its visions have increased.

Seven withered ears of wheat
Have devoured the seven full ears.[36]

So, North, rend your clothes.
Sackcloth, South, for evermore.
Soon your world will decompose,
Sifted through revengeful sieves,
All your people fugitives
Scourged with internecine war.

Drought will give the fields a shave
And manure instead of dates,
Urine, not the finest wines.

Spades to dig a grave,
And a wind that mutilates
Flags like branches off dead pines.

---

36 Cf. the dream of the Pharaoh in Gen. 41:20–30: "Immediately ahead are seven years of great
abundance in the land of Egypt. Immediately ahead are seven years of famine, and all the
abundance in the land of Egypt will be forgotten."

Grass throughout this land will hiss,
Rustling with funereal words
Of the pogroms' prejudice,
In a dirge to birds.
So the naked earth

Opens jaws of iron wide.
Some man in a pitch-black womb
Lies like grapes crushed in a winepress,
Blind and bloody eyed,
In the city's rubble tomb
Buried deep, skull smashed.

5

And in the windows of the synagogue here
The spreading branches of a palm tree
Are glowing crimson in the sunset.

And here a gray rabbi,
The oak of Bassan[37] won't falter in fear
In the cherished *Shmoine Esrei*[38]

Borukh, Ato, Adonai[39]

O Yahveh's Marranos most true,
I stand in your bonfire's flame,
And I, ever trampled anew,
Renounce every promise and claim.

---

37 The oaks that grew in the Bassan area on the east coast of Jordan; mentioned in the Bible as
   particularly sturdy.
38 *Shmoine Esrei*—eighteen praises, liturgical prayer.
39 *Borukh, Ato, Adonai*—"Blessed Be You, Lord."

And seven times sprinkling away
The blood from my fervent heart thus,
Like Aaron my keen Kol Nidrei
I give as an offering for us.

Shema, Isroel!

On the Torah these bells
Tremble like a fallow deer.
Held as by a knifepoint spell,
Congregants chant pure and clear.

This is David's rising shield
Like the true new moon tonight,
And of all the fast has healed,
Freed, the shofar sings delight.

This is Savaof lifting high
Faithful souls above the land,
This the dove that gives her sigh
Gently in his blessed hand.

Shema, Isroel,
Adonai Eloheinu
Adonai Ehod.[40]

1923

Translated from the Russian by J. B. Sisson and Maxim D. Shrayer

---

40 Words of the Shema: "Hear, o Isreal, the Lord Our God, the Lord is One."

MARK ALDANOV

Mark Aldanov (1886–1957), novelist and essayist, was born in Kiev to an affluent Jewish family. He graduated in 1910 from the Law and Physics-Mathematics Faculties of Kiev University, moved to Europe where he studied at the Collège des Sciences Politiques et Économiques, and then returned to Russia in 1914 to work as an industrial chemist. (Aldanov authored papers on organic chemistry; chemists appeared as characters in his fiction.) He made his literary debut in 1915 with the study *Tolstoy and Rolland*. In 1918 in Petrograd, Aldanov published the essay *Armageddon* about early lessons of the revolution. Being a liberal, Aldanov remained a staunch anti-Bolshevik for the rest of his life.

Aldanov emigrated and settled in Paris in 1919, becoming an active contributor to the émigré press. Written in French, his *Lenin* (1919; German translation, 1920; English translation, 1922) was followed by *Two Revolutions* (1921), a comparison of the Russian and French revolutions. Aldanov was equipped to become a French author but remained a Russian émigré writer. Turning to fiction, Aldanov produced sixteen novels and philosophical tales. His subject of choice was political cataclysm. The thinker, a gargoyle on the roof of Notre Dame de Paris sticking his tongue out to the world, embodies Aldanov's discomfort with determinist explanations. Centering on the Napoleonic era, Aldanov's tetralogy *Thinker* included *The Ninth Thermidor* (1923; English, 1926); *Saint Helena, Little Island* (1923; English, 1924); *The Devil's Bridge* (1925; English, 1928); and *Conspiracy* (1927).

Aldanov's second cycle of novels was a trilogy about the Russian Revolution and the émigré community: *The Key* (1930), *The Escape* (1932), and *The Cave* (1934). In 1939, Aldanov published part 1 of *The Beginning of the End* (complete English translation, *The Fifth Seal*, 1943), a novel about the members of a Soviet embassy in a small European country on the eve of World War II. The end of "Russia Abroad" was imminent, so Aldanov and his wife escaped to the United States in 1941.

Aldanov regrouped with Mikhail Tsetlin (1882–1945, pen name Amari) and founded the émigré journal *The New Review* (*Novyi zhurnal*) in New York. In the 1940s and early 1950s, before the *Lolita* explosion, Aldanov was the most successful Russian writer in America. Translations of his books included the story collection *A Night at the Airport* (1949), and he continued to write fiction and political-philosophical nonfiction in Russian, including the novel *Live as You Wish* (1952) and the treatise *A Night at Ulm: The Philosophy of Chance* (1953). In addition, Aldanov played a prominent role in organizing relief aid for émigrés stranded in wartime Europe. "I trust this man more than anyone on this earth," the often cynical Ivan Bunin said of Aldanov. Testifying to Aldanov's distinguished status, chapter 5 of Vladimir Nabokov's *Pnin* (1957) presented a gathering of Russian émigrés in America, "sitting on rustic benches and discussing émigré writers—Bunin, Aldanov, Sirin [Nabokov's own Russian pseudonym]."

America never became Aldanov's true home; he returned to Europe in 1947 and died in Nice in 1957. Aldanov's works were banned in the USSR until 1989, but his six-volume *Works*, edited by Andrey Chernyshev, appeared in Moscow in 1991 (reprinted 1994–96).

Some critics judge Aldanov's novels about contemporary historical events less successful than his Napoleonic tetralogy, while others deem Aldanov's nonfiction altogether superior. Aldanov was a superb plot maker but not a wizard of verbal style and not very compelling as a writer of complex character psychology, perhaps knowing in advance that free will was but an illusion. Yet Aldanov refrained from overt metaphysics, and as C. Nicholas Lee remarked, "the prominent place of philosophical discussion in his novels bears witness that rabbi and *philosophe* both coexist in his nature." The doubly ironic perception of history in Aldanov's novels offered the post-Soviet reader an antidote to much of the historical pulp fiction that had flourished—and continues to flourish—in Aldanov's former homeland.

* * *

Owing to Aldanov's background and his sense of historical verisimilitude, Jews received speaking parts in his works. This is not to say that Aldanov the fictionist was interested in Jewish themes but rather to suggest that Aldanov shared his worldview with his principal Jewish characters, an old Jew interpreting the French Revolution in the tetralogy and a Jewish journalist in the trilogy. One aspect of modern Jewish history preoccupied Aldanov: the Jews' participation in the Russian Revolution. A case in point was his investigation of the life of Evno Azef (1869–1918), head of the Socialist-Revolutionary Combat Organization and agent for the tsarist secret police.

Aldanov's memoir-essay "The Assassination of Uritsky" appeared in 1923 in the Warsaw-based émigré newspaper *For Freedom* (*Za svobodu*) and the leading Parisian émigré quarterly *Contemporary Annals* (*Sovremennye zapiski*). The version that follows appeared in *Leonid Kannegiser* (1928), a memorial collection consisting of essays by Aldanov, Georgy Ivanov, and Georgy Adamovich and poems by **Leonid Kannegiser**.

On 30 August 1918, **Kannegiser** assassinated Mikhail (Moisey) Uritsky, chief of the Petrograd Cheka and the interior minister of the Northern Commune. Kannegiser was executed by the Bolsheviks. Aldanov was cognizant of the perceived ironies of an assimilated Jewish-Russian author's account of an anti-Bolshevik Jew killing a Bolshevik Jew. (See also **Leonid Kannegiser** in this anthology.)

Both yesterday's right-wing émigrés and today's Russian ultranationalists cite "The Assassination of Uritsky" as an objective work by a Jew and an exception to what they regard as the Jews' refusal to deal with their alleged responsibility for the Russian Revolution. This was hardly Aldanov's sole intention.

THE ASSASSINATION OF URITSKY

I

Socrates. *Or in your opinion was there no merit in those divine men who fought beneath the walls of Troy and the first among them, the fearless son of Thetis? After all, it was to him that the goddess said, "If you take vengeance for Patroclus, inevitable doom awaits you." But he answered her, "I scorn death and despise danger. It is worse for me to live without having avenged my friend."*

Plato [*Apology*, 28, b–d]

The pages that follow have to do with a young man who perished tragically five years ago.[41] I knew him well. As impartially as possible, I have collected information about the man whom he killed. What I write is not history but a

---

41 This article was written in 1923. [M. A.] Here and hereafter, Mark Aldanov's notes have been expanded and supplemented by C. Nicholas Lee and Maxim D. Shrayer. Unless noted otherwise, all notes are those of the translator and the editor. Aldanov's text has been slightly abridged. In the English translation, the passages Aldanov quotes from Kannegiser's diaries have been abridged.

source for it. A historian will have materials that I do not. But I have also had materials that he will not have, since he will never have seen either Kannegiser or Uritsky.[42]

For various reasons I am not taking upon myself the task of characterizing Leonid Kannegiser. This is a subject that could tempt a great artist; it may be that some day a Dostoevsky will be found to treat it. Truly Dostoevskian also is the city where Kannegiser lived and died: the terrible St. Petersburg of the 1910s.

I shall say only that the young man who assassinated Uritsky had exceptional natural gifts. A talented poet, he left behind several dozen poems. Six or seven of them—far from the best—were published in *Northern Notes* and *Russian Thought*.[43] He recited many others to me at one time or another.

I do not know just how many "proletarian poets" were spawned by the Bolshevik Revolution—for some reason or other nobody hears about their masterpieces. Here is another, very incomplete list: Gumilyov, one of the most significant talents of the last decade, was executed; nineteen-year-old Prince Paley, in whom a competent judge, A. F. Koni, saw the hope of Russian literature, was executed;[44] Leonid Kannegiser was executed.

But when I speak about the exceptional talents of Uritsky's assassin, I have in mind not only his poetry. His entire nature was unusually gifted.

Fate placed him in very favorable circumstances. The son of a famous engineer with a European reputation, he was born to wealth and grew up in a highly cultured milieu, in a house frequented by all St. Petersburg. In his parents' drawing room, imperial ministers rubbed shoulders with German Lopatin[45] and affected young poets met with distinguished generals.

Fortune's favorite, endowed by fate with brilliant gifts, good looks, and a noble character, he was the unhappiest of men.

I was recently given extracts from the diary he left behind. The man who wrote the diary was shot by a firing squad; the same fate also befell the man who safeguarded it in the days following Uritsky's murder.[46] These diary entries,

---

42 This, by the way, is not such a disadvantage for the historian. He will at least have full freedom of judgment and evaluation. I do not have *full* freedom. [M. A.]

43 *Severnye zapiski* and *Russkaia mysl'* in the original.

44 He was thrown down a mine shaft for being related to the ruling dynasty—there was no other reason. [M. A.]

45 Lopatin, German (1845-1918)—Russian revolutionary and socialist, close to Karl Marx and Nikolay Chernyshevsky in the 1870s. After 1905, he retired from political life.

46 Incidentally, this diary would have had nothing to offer a Bolshevik investigating commission. It breaks off at the beginning of 1918 and does not touch upon Kannegiser's terrorist activity at all. [M. A.]

connected with the memory of people who have died, have miraculously survived and made their way abroad.

I recall it was Mikhailovsky[47] who remarked that a diary can be kept only by very solitary people. It would be more accurate to say: only by very solitary or very unhappy people. It can certainly not be said that Marie Bashkirtseff,[48] for example, lived in solitude. But she could not remember a single day in her life without torments. Why? She also asked why:

> Pourquoi, pourquoi dans ton oeuvre céleste
> Tant d'éléments si peu d'accord![49]

I will not speak in detail of Leonid Kannegiser's diary, which is truly remarkable in many respects. He began his diary entries in 1914—the first is dated 29 May. The war found him—in Italy—a sixteen-year-old boy. He passionately wanted to go to the front as a volunteer. His parents did not let him. Like all boys, he was attracted to war by what does not exist in war. But there was also something else.

I quote almost at random several diary entries:

"I have a room, a bed, dinner, money, coffee, and no pity for those who do not. If I am killed in the war, then there will undoubtedly be some higher meaning in it . . ."

"I interrupted my writing, walked back and forth around my room, reflected, and, I think, for the thousandth time decided: 'I'm going!' Tomorrow morning, perhaps, when I wake up, I'll think: 'What nonsense! Why should I go? We have an enormous army!' And in the evening I'll change my mind again. Then I'll settle for a compromise: 'It's better to go as a medical orderly.' It's the same thing every day: I hesitate, I try to decide, I despair—and I don't do a thing.

"Others at least work for the good of the wounded. I also went once to the railway station. One wounded man had to be taken into the dressing station. As I watched, his bandage was removed, and I saw on his leg a shrapnel wound half the size of the palm of my hand; I saw his whole blue, mutilated, pitted body, thick drops of blood. A doctor had shaved off the hair around the wound. An army

---

47 Most likely Aldanov is referring to Nikolay Mikhailovsky (1842–1904)—Russian author and social thinker, one of the theoreticians of *narodnichestvo*.

48 Marie Bashkirtseff (1858–1884)—Russian artist and diarist, best known for her extensive journal, *Le Journal de Marie Bashkirtseff*, first published in France in 1887.

49 (Fr.) = "Why, oh why, in your celestial work,/Are there so many elements so little in agreement with each other?"

nurse was preparing the dressing. Two students walked quietly out. One came up to me, pale, smiling in embarrassment, and said, 'I can't stand to see it.' The wounded man was groaning. And suddenly he asked plaintively, 'Please be more careful.' I felt a shudder, it didn't seem to be anything, and I continued to look at the wound, but I couldn't stand it. I felt my head spinning, everything went dark before my eyes. I was going to be sick. I was on the point of falling, but I pulled myself together and went out into the fresh air, staggering like a drunk.

"And that could happen to—me. To know that that wound is 'on my leg . . .' And when suddenly, as if in response, an irresistibly glad-sweet feeling rises in my soul: 'I'm in no danger,' then I know, 'I am a scoundrel.'"

"[. . .] I am setting myself no external goals. It is all the same to me whether I am the Pope of Rome or a shoe-shine boy in Calcutta—I don't associate any specific emotional states with these circumstances—but my single goal is to lead my soul to marvelous enlightenment, to inexpressible sweetness. Whether by religion or by heresy—I do not know." [. . .]

I make no commentary on anything. All diaries are somewhat alike. Even Tolstoy and Amiel were not exceptions to this rule. But I am struck by the extracts from Kannegiser's diary, even with their naïveté of style and thought. It would be futile to look for logic in them: The decision to go off to war alternates with the decision to go off to a monastery; pages of pure metaphysics are followed by pages that are terrible to read; enthusiasm for the monuments of Ferrara and for the paintings of [Paolo] Veronese gives way to enthusiasm for the Soviet of Workers' and Soldiers' Deputies.[50] And from every page of the diary you can see raw nerves and hear, "My soul is ripping itself away from my body . . ."[51]

I made his acquaintance in the home of his parents on Saperny Lane and often met him there. He also came around to see me sometimes. I could not fail to see that there was a tragic side to his nature. But nothing in him gave any inkling of a future terrorist.

One characteristic scene, however, has stayed in my memory. It was in the spring of 1918. He and I had been playing chess for a long time. I lived in the house on Nadezhdinskaya Street where the Petropolis bookstore was located.

---

50 Kannegiser's enthusiasm clearly predates the October 1917 Bolshevik coup; on the changes in his attitude toward the Bolsheviks, see below.

51 Aldanov is quoting from a poem by the Decembrist Kondraty Ryleev, composed in 1826 in the Fortress of Peter and Paul during the inquest and dedicated to a fellow Decembrist insurrectionist, Prince E. P. Obolenskii. Ryleev and four other Decembrists died on the scaffold, hence the parallel with Kannegiser.

At that time Petropolis was offering for sale the magnificent old library of Prince Gagarin, which consisted principally of French books of the eighteenth and beginning of the nineteenth centuries. I had made a few purchases there, and the books I had acquired were lying on my desk in my study. My guest began to leaf through them. I started talking about books and hazarded the guess (which I had not verified and based solely on their character) that this library belonged at one time to the same Prince Gagarin who was rumored— groundlessly, it appeared—to have written the anonymous letters that were the cause of Pushkin's death.

The expression on Leonid Akimovich's face changed, and he even dropped a book onto the desk.

"What sort of person would you have to be," he said, turning pale, "to write such a letter—about Pushkin . . ."

And he fell silent. Then suddenly, in a low voice, he began to recite the verses:

> The secret guardian of freedom, the punishing dagger,
> The final arbiter of disgrace and offense,
> For the hands of immortal Nemesis
> The god of Lemnos forged you . . .[52]

In general he was poor at reciting poetry, like all Russian poets, I think (with the exception of I. A. Bunin, an amazing elocutionist): he recited poetry without any expression, in an unnatural monotone, as if to show that no expressiveness or oratorical art could add anything to the beauty of the verses themselves. If I am not mistaken, this style of recitation was introduced by Aleksandr Blok. But this time the young man recited these verses differently from the way he always did—or does it only seem that way to me now?

"Note," said Kannegiser after breaking off the declamation at the first quatrain, "note that Pushkin slipped up here: in this stanza the second line should not have been rhymed with the third. If the third line is put in place of the fourth, the result is much more powerful. . . . Pushkin slipped up," he repeated with an ironic smile. "This is the way I would have written it . . ."

And he recited the quatrain in his redaction. His tone was amusing—the ironic smile, of course, was to suggest the presumption of this "correction" of

---

52 Here and hereafter, a literal, unrhymed and mostly unmetered, translation of Pushkin's "The Dagger" (*Kinzhal*) is provided.

Pushkin. I thought to myself that he was right: that way it really was more powerful.[53]

He was silent for a little and then recited in a completely changed voice the end of "The Dagger":

O righteous young man, fateful chosen one,
O Sand, thy life was extinguished on the executioner's block,
But the holy voice of virtue
Has remained in the dust of the young man who was executed.
Thou hast become the eternal shadow of thy Germany,
Threatening criminal force with disaster—
And on the solemn grave
A dagger burns without an inscription.

I see him in front of me at that moment as if it were now. He was sitting in a deep armchair, his head bowed low. His fine sensitive face had completely changed . . . I feel awestruck when I remember those lines of "The Dagger" now—as Uritsky's assassin recited them. Art is a frightening thing! Was Pushkin perhaps one of those responsible for the death of the chief of the Petersburg Extraordinary Commission?

I remember that I called the young man's attention to the rare technical perfection of these amazing lines, to the sobbing sound of the second line ("O Sand"), which consisted of short monosyllables, and to the effect achieved by the sound *a*. Pushkin, although he never studied in a poets' guild, had the ear to grasp all the tricks of contemporary prosody. André Chénier, in an ode that, although not as good as "The Dagger," served as a model for it, used a similar dramatic effect, the sound *ar*:

Le poign*ar*d, seul esp*oir* de la terre,
Est ton *ar*me sac*ré*e . . .[54]

---

53 The question of whether Pushkin "slipped up" turns out to be rather complex, however. The fair manuscript copy of Pushkin's "The Dagger" was thought to be lost; the famous poem did not begin to appear in print in Russia until 1876. [. . .] Now, in the first volume of *Voices of the Past* (*Golosa minuvshego*) for 1923, M. A. Tsyavlovsky has for the first time published Pushkin's fair copy. [. . .] In this text the second line rhymes not with the third but with the fourth (just as Kannegiser required), but the third and fourth lines (of the usual redaction) also precede the first two lines: "The god of Lemnos forged you/For the hands of the immortal Nemesis,/The secret guardian of freedom, the punishing dagger,/The final arbiter of disgrace and offense!" [M. A.]

54 (Fr.) = "The dagger, sole hope of the earth, is thy sacred weapon . . ."

But the young man was not listening to me (although he could talk for hours about poetry). He began to question me about Sand.[55] I do not wish to say that I might have begun to suspect something that evening. At the time, probably, nothing had as yet even been planned.

Leonid Kannegiser took no part in politics before the spring of 1918. The February Revolution bowled him over—who wasn't carried away by it for the first two or three weeks or so?

He was the chairman of the Union of Socialist Cadets. I cannot guarantee—however strange this may seem—that he did not also feel some enthusiasm for the ideas of the October Revolution. Lenin made a very strong impression on him on 25 October—I have spoken about this elsewhere. The events of 1918, the peace treaty of Brest-Litovsk, soon changed Kannegiser's opinions. It is not my task to give an account of his political evolution (I'm not really familiar with that evolution). But in April (or May) 1918, he already hated the Bolsheviks with a burning hatred and took some part in conspiratorial work directed to their overthrow. The death of his friend (Pereltsveig) made him a terrorist. . . .

IV

Le président du tribunal: *Qui vous a inspirée tant de haine?*
Charlotte Corday: *Je n'avais pas besoin de la haine des autres.
J'avais assez de la mienne.*[56]

Court interrogation of Charlotte Corday

The brief and complex process that rent the soul of Uritsky's assassin in the days preceding the drama is not clear to me: Why did Kannegiser's choice fall on Uritsky? I do not know. His assassination cannot be justified even from the viewpoint of an inveterate advocate of terror.

---

55 Sand, Karl Ludwig (1795–1820)—German nationalist student executed for assassinating German playwright and Russian official August Friedrich von Kotzebue (1761–1819). Kotzebue was an intermittent Bonapartist, and Sand became a martyr to anti-Napoleonic Europe, but Pushkin, in the poem "The Dagger," depicted him more generally as a tyrant's assassin who pays for his heroism with his life.

56 (Fr.) = Presiding judge: *Who inspired such hate in you?* Charlotte Corday: *I didn't need the hatred of others. I had enough of my own.*

Kannegiser apparently had no accomplices. The Bolshevik inquest was unable to uncover any despite the extraordinary desire of the authorities to do so. The official document says this about it:

"On being interrogated, Leonid Kannegiser declared that he did not assassinate Uritsky in accordance with the decision of a party or any organization but from personal motives, wishing to avenge the arrests of officers and the military execution of his friend Pereltsveig, whom he had known for about ten years. The interrogation of prisoners and witnesses of this affair revealed that Pereltsveig's military execution had strongly affected Kannegiser. After this execution by firing squad had been made public, he left home for a few days—where he was at this period could not be established."

The [Bolshevik] inquest admitted that "it was impossible to establish by means of direct evidence that the assassination of Comrade Uritsky was organized by a counterrevolutionary organization." The investigation nonetheless remained of the opinion that such an organization existed—and was inclined, as usual, to suspect "the imperialists of the Entente."[57] The Entente at that time—the summer of 1918—had other things to do. Besides, it is difficult as a matter of general principle to imagine Lloyd George as an instigator of political assassinations. His representative in Russia did not inherit the terrorist views of his predecessor, the famous George Buchanan, the sixteenth-century antimonarchist. As for Clemenceau, although he can hardly be numbered among those opposed to terror on principle, of course he did not busy himself in organizing attempts on the lives of Chekists.

I am inclined to think that the evidence Leonid Kannegiser gave at the inquest corresponds to the truth. He carried out Uritsky's assassination alone. No organization—neither the one whose members he and Pereltsveig had been, nor any other organization of any kind—would have entrusted him with the task of assassinating the chief of the Petrograd Extraordinary Commission. Probably the immediate reason for what he did was indeed the desire to avenge the death of his friend (only this can also explain why he chose Uritsky). The psychological basis for it, on the other hand, was of course very complex. I think the psychological motivation consisted of the noblest and most exalted feelings. A great deal went into it: the ardent love of Russia that filled his diaries; the hatred of those that enslaved her; the feeling of a Jew who wanted his name

---

57 In Soviet circles, somebody came up with the absurd theory that, escaping after the assassination, Kannegiser rode his bicycle along Millionnaya Street to the English embassy, where he wanted to find asylum. [M. A.]

set off against the names of the Uritskys and the Zinovievs[58] before the Russian people and before history; the spirit of self-sacrifice—the same old feeling of "but I haven't been in the war"; the craving for strong, agonizing sensations— he was born to become a Dostoevskian hero; and more than anything else, I think, the thirst for the "all-cleansing fire of suffering"—the feeling conveyed by this reverberating figure of speech was not fabricated by poets.

I repeat, he probably had no accomplices, but he may have had a living model. He admired the personality of G. A. Lopatin, and I believe he made Lopatin an example for himself—it was far from a bad example. Of course, Lopatin took no part in their circle: in that last year of his life, he was no longer capable of any work. Besides that, in the midst of such conspirators, he would have felt a little the way Achilles felt dressed up as a girl among the daughters of King Lycomedes. But Lopatin, who kept his stormy temperament to the end of his days, did not mince his words when he talked about the Bolsheviks and the mean of doing battle with them. I also remember this from my own conversations with the late Lopatin.

I also know this. On the very same day that Leonid Kannegiser's mother was released from prison, she was informed by telephone from the hospital that German Lopatin was dying and would like to see her. R. L. Kannegiser [Kannegiser's mother] went immediately to the Hospital of Sts. Peter and Paul. Lopatin, fully conscious, told R. L. that he was happy to see her before he died.

"I thought you were angry with me . . ."

"For what?"

"For the death of your son."

"In what way were you guilty of that?"

He kept silent and said nothing more. A few hours later, Lopatin died.

He can hardly have had any cause to accuse himself of anything except the passionate words that he could blurt out in conversation with Leonid Kannegiser; he was very fond of the young man.

The same official document contains the following:

"The Extraordinary Commission was unable to establish precisely when the decision to assassinate Comrade Uritsky was made, but Comrade Uritsky himself knew that an attempt on his life was being prepared. He was forewarned repeatedly, and Kannegiser was definitely indicated as the prime suspect, but Comrade Uritsky did not take these warnings seriously enough.

---

58   Zinoviev, Grigory (Radomysl'sky, 1883–1936)—major Bolshevik leader, born in Ukraine to a family of Jewish dairy farmers.

He was already well informed about Kannegiser from the intelligence information at his disposal."

This is a truly astonishing assertion. It is totally improbable. If Uritsky was warned about preparations for an attempt on his life, with the name of the terrorist indicated, then it must indeed be assumed that the assassination was the work of some organization (or at least had some connection with it). But this contradicts the words quoted earlier from the same summary of the investigation: "it was impossible . . . to establish." Besides that, what grounds could Uritsky have for being skeptical about the warning? And why did he not order Kannegiser to be arrested ahead of time? It was very simple to track him down: he spent most of the day at home, in the apartment of his father, who was well known to all St. Petersburg.

Yet all the same there is something mysterious and sinister in this assertion. Was Uritsky well informed about Kannegiser? . . . I have a strange feeling when I read this part of Mr. Antipov's investigative summary.[59]

This is what I heard not so long ago. Some time before the assassination, Kannegiser said ironically to his friend, "NN, do you know whom I talked to on the phone today?"

"Whom?"

"Uritsky."

And that was all. At that time NN paid no attention to what the young man had said. There were plenty of reasons for St. Petersburg residents to phone the Extraordinary Commission in those days! NN, like the present writer, learned about the assassination of Uritsky while he was away from St. Petersburg, from the newspapers, and he was just as astonished as I. That was when he remembered Kannegiser's enigmatic remark.

There really were plenty of reasons for telephoning Uritsky . . . But all the same this is very strange. It is highly unlikely that, even at that time, the chief of the Extraordinary Commission himself could be summoned to the phone to answer a simple inquiry or to put in a good word for an ordinary citizen of

---

59 Antipov, Nikolay (1894–1941)—Bolshevik official, who served as the deputy chief and then the chief of the Petrograd Cheka in 1918–19.

Here and above, Aldanov quotes Antipov's "Sketches of the Activities of the Petrograd Extraordinary Commission," published in the Soviet newspaper *Petrograd Pravda* (*Petrogradskaia Pravda*). However, Aldanov does not provide more information about his source. He may be referring to Antipov's report of the Kannegiser investigation printed in *Petrograd Pravda* on 4 January 1919. The editor is indebted to Gleb Morev's research on Kannegiser. Also see editor's introduction to Kannegiser in this anthology.

St. Petersburg, completely unknown to anyone. In any case, whoever made the phone call had to give his name. Or did Kannegiser use an assumed name as a cover? In that case, why did Uritsky come to the phone to talk to somebody he didn't know? And why did he need to? And just what was it that his future assassin said to the people's commissar?

I cannot understand—and yet I do not doubt for a minute that what NN told me is true. I do not doubt because I knew Leonid Kannegiser. That was his *style* ... No, style is not the right word for it. But I feel that independently of what he might be about to do (he was capable of dreaming up much more than that!), he needed this terrible, frightening sensation. Why, after the murder, did Raskolnikov go to *listen to the bell* in Alena Ivanova's apartment? Why, before the murder, did Charlotte Corday have a long talk with Marat? ...

I had left St. Petersburg even before Pereltsveig was arrested. I saw Kannegiser for the last time in July 1918 in his parents' apartment on Saperny Lane. He was animated and in high spirits. I advised his father to send the young man off to the south somewhere: St. Petersburg was a wretched hole ...

After the execution of his comrades, which profoundly shook him, Kannegiser no longer stayed at home at night. At that time almost half the city tried to spend the night away from home (for some reason arrests were carried out in the dead of night). His relatives suspected nothing and asked about nothing. He said nothing about himself.

On 16 (29) August (the day before Uritsky's assassination), he came home, as always, toward evening. After dinner he offered to read aloud to his sister—this was their custom. Up to then they had been reading a book by Schnitzler and had not yet finished it. But this time he had come supplied with something else: a one-volume French edition of *The Count of Monte Cristo*, recently acquired from a second-hand bookseller. Despite protests, he began to read from the middle of the book. Was it a coincidence, or had he chosen the pages on purpose? It was the chapter about a political assassination that had been carried out in his youth by an old Bonapartist, the grandfather of one of the female characters in the famous novel.

He read enthusiastically until midnight. Then he took leave of his sister. She was fated to see him yet once more from a distance from the window of her cell on Gorokhovaya Street: he was being led for interrogation under escort.

He spent the night, as always, away from home. But early the next morning, he came back to his parents' apartment for tea. At about nine he knocked on the door of his father's room. His father was unwell and was not working.

Despite the inappropriate early hour, he proposed a game of chess. His father agreed—he never refused his son anything.

Apparently Leonid Kannegiser connected something else with the outcome of this game: the success of his plan? Success in escaping? An hour before the assassination the young man played for all he was worth and did his best to win. He lost, and this made him extremely upset. Chagrined at his success, his father proposed another game. The young man looked at his watch and refused.

He said goodbye to his father (they never saw each other again) and hurried out of the room. He was wearing the sporty leather double-breasted jacket of military cut that he had worn as a cadet and that I had often seen on him. He left the house, got on a bicycle, and headed off in the direction of Winter Palace Square. In front of the Ministry of Foreign Affairs he stopped: Uritsky, who was also in charge of the Northern Commune's foreign policy, received petitioners in this building.

It was twenty minutes after ten.

V

Death had not been invited . . .

From an old legend

He went in through the entrance located in the middle of the half of the semicircular Rossi palace that goes from the Arch of the General Staff to Millionnaya Street.[60] Uritsky always came into the ministry from this entrance. How had Kannegiser found this out? Or had he been following the people's commissar during the preceding days? I am also prepared to accept the hypothesis, by the way, that he could have simply asked the first staff member who turned up at what time, by what means, and by what entrance Comrade Uritsky came in. The fascination with the risk that asking such questions involved, the craving for acute sensations—"Will they suspect me? Will they arrest me? I must ask in an offhand way, God keep me from turning pale"—all these impulses were part of his nature, just like the telephone call to Uritsky.

---

60 Some details of the account in this chapter came to me from an absolutely reliable source connected to Soviet ruling circles, which it is impossible for me to name. [M. A.]

A stairway and the cage of an elevator are located opposite the door into the room where the assassination was carried out, a large room directly overlooking the street. A hard wooden sofa, several chairs, and pegs for wraps that hung along the white-washed walls—those are the furnishings of this room, which stood out because of how miserable it looked in the magnificent ministry palace. In it there was always a hall porter, who had served in this position for about a quarter of a century. This old man, stunned by the new way of doing things, like most of the household servants in the imperial palaces, called Uritsky "Your Exalted Excellency."

"Is Comrade Uritsky in?" Kannegiser asked.

"He has not yet arrived, sir . . ."

He walked over to the window looking out onto the square and sat down on the windowsill. He took off his cap and laid it down next to him. He looked out the window for a long time.

What was he thinking? That it was still not too late to renounce this terrible business—that he could still go back to Saperny Lane, have tea with his sister, make up for the chess game he had lost to his father, or continue reading *The Count of Monte Cristo*? That there were only a few minutes left for him to live, that he would never again see this sun, this square, this Rastrelli palace? That maybe it was time to release the safety catch on his revolver and cock it to "fire"? That the hall porter was squinting in a strange way, that he suspected? His sensations in those minutes could have been rendered by Dostoevsky, whom he so loved . . .

He waited. People passed by on the square. His heart was pounding. Twenty minutes passed like an eternity that was too short. At last, in the distance, he heard the approaching soft, terrible roar that meant *the end*.

The imperial automobile slowed down and stopped at the entrance.

Uritsky had come from his private apartment on Vasilievsky Island.

How many death sentences was he supposed to sign on that fateful day? Another sentence had been drawn up.

"Death had not been invited."

It appeared without an invitation.

The young man in the double-breasted leather jacket had put his hand into his pocket and was already getting up from the windowsill.

The chief of the Extraordinary Commission came in the door and walked toward the elevator.

The visitor made several quick steps in his direction.

Did their eyes meet? Did Uritsky read: *death?*

A shot rang out. The People's Commissar collapsed without making a sound, killed on the spot. At a distance of six or seven paces, a moving assassin shot a man who was walking briskly. Only the sure hand of an experienced marksman could have aimed the bullet like that—if I am not mistaken, Kannegiser had no idea of how to shoot.

At that time there was nobody nearby.[61]

The assassin rushed for the exit.

If he had put on his cap, placed the revolver into his pocket, and calmly walked to the left, he would probably have easily been able to hide by turning under the arch onto Morskaya Street and mixing in with the crowd on Nevsky Prospekt. The chase did not begin until two or three minutes later. That was plenty of time for him to walk along the square to the arch. But he was unable to walk calmly. Of course he lost his self-control at that point. He must have imagined to himself a thousand times at night the way it would happen. But *it* didn't *turn out that way. It* never does *turn out that way.*

Without his cap, which he had left on the windowsill, not letting go of the revolver, he ran out into the street, jumped on his bicycle, and sped off to the right—toward Millionnaya Street.

A minute later, an uproar erupted in the room where the historic assassination had taken place. Employees of the People's Commissariat heard the shot on the second floor. Several people ran down the stairs and stopped dumbfounded in front of Uritsky's dead body. Not yet understanding clearly what had happened, they picked the commissar up and carried him over to the wooden sofa by the wall.

The man who was the first to remember about the assassin and rush off in pursuit of him was not an ordinary policeman. He was a peculiar fellow, fanatically devoted to the Revolution, poor, illiterate, selfless—even then already soaked in blood from head to foot. He is a fit subject for a work of literature. He still awaits the author of "Loopy Ears" to portray him.[62] He dashed out into the street shouting. Others ran after him. It was easy to decide which way to go: a young man speeding along on a bicycle, without a

---

61 The hall porter must have been opening the door to the elevator for "His Exalted Excellency." Uritsky's office was on the third floor. [M. A.]

62 "Loopy Ears" (1916) is a famous short story by Ivan Bunin, whose protagonist is a megalomaniacal murderer.

cap, with a revolver in his hand, could not remain unnoticed on thinly populated Winter Palace Square.

The automobile flew off in pursuit at terrible speed.

Once he was on his bicycle, the assassin apparently recovered his self-control. Eyewitnesses said that he seemed to be zigzagging along the streets—trying to avoid a bullet in his back.

When he heard the rumbling of the speeding automobile behind him, he understood that he was done for. At Number 17 on the left side of the street, very close to the Marble Palace, he braked the bicycle, jumped off, and dashed into the courtyard. The enormous architectural complex of the English Club, like all the buildings on that side of Millionnaya Street, looks out onto the Neva Embankment.

If the entrance gates in the courtyard had been open, the assassin would still have been able to escape.

Fate was against him:

The gates were closed.

In despair, he ran in through the door in the right half of the building and quickly began to climb the back stairs. On the third floor, the door to the apartment of Prince Melikov was open. He dashed into it, ran through the kitchen and several rooms, in front of the stupefied servants in the entrance hall put on somebody else's coat, which he had grabbed from the hall coat rack, opened the outside door, and went down the main staircase.[63] [...]

VI

The villain maintained complete composure. He bragged about his crime, asserting that he had avenged his friends who had perished. The attempts of the law court to force Anckarström to name his accomplices, despite the efforts of the executioners, were unsuccessful. The criminal kept his hellish calm even on the scaffold. He said he was dying for Sweden . . .

---

63 I may be mistaken in the details. The future Lenotre [Théodore Gosselin (1857–1935), French historian who wrote extensively about the French Revolution] of the Russian Revolution will be able with greater accuracy and in greater detail to reconstruct this terrible act of the drama that played itself out in the space of a few minutes on the property of the English Club if he has access not only to the stories I have used but also to the testimony of eyewitnesses that has been collected in the archives of the Extraordinary Commission. What I have said is sufficient to appreciate the remarkable self-control of the twenty-year-old terrorist. [M. A.]

During the night after the execution, unknown people secretly penetrated to the place where Anckarström's body was displayed and covered the ignominious remains of the regicide with flowers and laurel leaves. The investigating commission was unsuccessful in bringing the guilty to light.

The Case of the Assassination of King Gustav III[64]

I can add nothing to the epigraph of this chapter . . .

What sustained this youth, this boy, in the inhuman sufferings that fell to his lot? I do not know. I want to understand—and I cannot.

Johan Anckarström's "tempestuous soul" had been tempered by passions and trials. Ravaillac and Damien were firmly convinced that on the other side of the torments of earthly death there awaited them the eternal blessedness that they had purchased at a terrible price. To the scaffold of Karl Sand, erected on a meadow that to this day is called "Karl Sand's Himmelfahrtswiese,"[65] there flocked tens of thousands of people who regarded him as a German national hero and craved the chance to moisten their kerchiefs in the blood of the holy martyr. The Russian terrorists of the tsarist period who died *without an audience* in the courtyard of the Shlisselburg Prison were at least sure that only they, not their wives or their fathers, would suffer for their acts. Leonid Kannegiser did not have even that consolation. He knew that the relatives he tenderly loved had been arrested. From his dealings with the Bolsheviks, he could have expected up to the end that execution awaited his whole family. In actual fact, they were saved. It was a miracle: St. Petersburg in those days was awash with torrents of blood. "Revolutionary terror" had obviously set about terrorizing the population so as to protect its Zinovievs from new attempts on their lives— what was more "expedient" than to shoot the families of political terrorists!

He also realized that he was the target of blind curses from totally innocent people who were being murdered as hostages for what he had done. Instead of

---

64 King Gustav III of Sweden (1746–1792) was shot at a masked ball in the Stockholm opera house by Captain Jacob Johan Anckarström (1762–1792) as part of an antiroyalist aristocratic conspiracy. Gustav died two weeks later, and a month after that Anckarström was beheaded. The allusion to his "tempestuous soul" may be partly connected with the free rendering of the events in Verdi's opera *Un Ballo in Maschera* (1859), where the character representing Anckarström falsely suspects the king of a liaison with his wife.

65 (Ger.) = "The meadow where Karl Sand ascended to heaven."

Uritsky, it was Boky,[66] ten times worse than his predecessor and chief, who carried out the reprisals.

It is not for me to speak about Leonid Kannegiser's fate. It is recounted in black words in the three-volume "Case of the Assassination of Uritsky." Will that case ever see the light?

He behaved and died like a hero.

His whole short life was spent in search of tormenting sensations. He drained that cup to the dregs, and I do not know another to whom fate gave such a cup. He spent long weeks draining it without the consolation of faith, without the triumph of victory over death before a crowd of many thousands of spectators, without Taras Bulba's "I hear!"[67] Nobody heard. Nobody was listening. Will his grave ever be found? Will Russia erect a monument over it? That probably no longer meant anything to him by the time he had reached the level of estrangement from the world to which he ascended in his last days.

There something else was to by revealed:

Happy is he who falls down on his head:

For him, if only for a moment, the world's different . . .[68]

1923

Translated from the Russian by C. Nicholas Lee

Mark Aldanov, "Ubiistvo Uritskogo." English translation and notes copyright © by C. Nicholas Lee. Introduction © by Maxim D. Shrayer.

---

66 Boky, Gleb Ivanovich (1879–1937)—prominent Soviet party official who succeeded Uritsky and worked as the chairman of the Petrograd Cheka and the Union of Communes of the Northern Region until November 1918.

67 Taras Bulba—protagonist of the tale by Nikolay Gogol (1809–1852), which bears its protagonist's name. A Ukrainian Cossack leader, Taras Bulba yells, "I hear" from a crowd of onlookers at his son Ostap's public execution by Polish authorities, after Ostap cries out: "Father, where are you? Can you hear me?"

68 The last two lines of a 1922 poem from *European Night* by **Vladislav Khodasevich**.

OSIP MANDELSTAM

Osip Mandelstam (1891–1938), poet, prose writer, and translator, was born in Warsaw and grew up in and around St. Petersburg in a secularized middle-class Jewish family, receiving no systematic Jewish upbringing. Mandelstam studied at the private Tenishev School from 1900 to 1907, lived in Paris attending lectures at the Sorbonne during 1907–8, and studied in Heidelberg in 1909–10. In 1911, he was baptized at a Methodist Church in Vyborg. No longer subject to *numerus clausus*, he entered St. Petersburg University, where until 1915 he read Old French without taking a degree. Mandelstam's first, civic poems were composed in 1907 under the spell of **Semyon Nadson**. He debuted as a poet in 1910 in the review *Apollo* (*Apollon*) and in 1912 joined the acmeists, developing a lifelong friendship with Anna Akhmatova. His manifesto "Morning of Acmeism" dates to 1913, and his first collection, *Stone*, was printed in that same year (second edition, 1916; third edition, 1923).

Mandelstam's attitude to the revolution was contradictory. Initially enlivened by the revolutionary events, he regarded the destruction of the Russian monarchy as historically justified. At the same time, Mandelstam abhorred bloodshed and reportedly responded to the 1918 assassination of Mikhail (Moisey) Uritsky by **Leonid Kannegiser** with the words "Who appointed him judge?" In 1917–18, Mandelstam worked on the staff of the Socialist-Revolutionary newspaper *Banner of Labor* (*Znamia truda*). He moved south in 1919 and lived in Kiev, the Crimea, and Georgia. It was in May of that year that he met Nadezhda Khazina, who would become his wife. With the assistance of **Ilya Ehrenburg**, Mandelstam returned to Russia in the fall of 1920. In 1922, his second collection, *Tristia*, appeared in Berlin (second edition, 1923).

Mandelstam published twenty books of translations, including the prose of Franz Werfel and Arthur Schnitzler. In the 1920s, he turned to prose, writing (semi)autobiographical nonfiction and fiction. In 1928, Mandelstam's publishing difficulties mounting, *Poems*—his last collection—was helped into print by Nikolay Bukharin. A 1928 scandal, resulting from false charges of plagiarism, was conveniently used to ostracize Mandelstam. A feuilleton by the odious critic and journalist David Zaslavsky (1880–1965) was printed in Moscow's *Literary Gazette* (*Literaturnaia gazeta*) on 7 May 1929; in 1958, the Jewish-born Zaslavsky was one of **Boris Pasternak**'s official detractors.

A letter in support of Mandelstam appeared there on 13 May 1929, signed by Leopold Averbakh, **Eduard Bagritsky**, Aleksandr Fadeev, Mikhail Kozakov, Leonid Leonov, Yury Olesha, Boris Pasternak, Boris Pilnyak, and others, a total of sixteen writers representing different backgrounds and different parts of the Soviet literary spectrum. Mandelstam traveled to the Caucasus to escape the nerve-wrecking scandal, but the publication of his politically uncommitted prose about Armenia bred further controversy in 1933.

Mandelstam's growing dissent exploded in November 1933 in his anti-Stalinist poem "We live without feeling our country beneath ourselves . . . ." After his arrest in May 1934, Mandelstam was exiled for three years to Cherdyn in the northern Urals. After attempting to take his life, he was allowed to settle in Voronezh, where *The Voronezh Notebooks* were composed. The Voronezh exile lasted until May 1937, when, hoping to rectify his position, Mandelstam composed a Stalinist panegyric. It did not help him. Unlike such contemporaries as Pasternak or Ehrenburg, Mandelstam was remarkably unsuccessful in his tortured attempts to collaborate with the regime. For instance, while conveying an anti-Fascist message, the poem "Rome" (1937, in the *Third Voronezh Notebook*) was far too complex and riddled with nonformulaic Mandelstamian questions about art, power, and religion to fulfill an ideological commission. Evoking motifs from both the Hebrew Bible (David, Moses) and the gospels (the birth of Jesus in Bethlehem: "the gates are opened before Herod"), Mandelstam denounced the poem's new Herod, the "dictator-degenerate" Mussolini and his Fascists ("Italianate blackshirts"). The poem first appeared in New York in 1961 and not until 1967 in the Soviet Union. Mandelstam was rearrested several months after his return from the Voronezh exile and sentenced to five years of labor camps. He is believed to have died in December 1938 in a transit camp near Vladivostok in a state of mental distress. Mandelstam's widow, Nadezhda Mandelstam (neé Khazina), preserved his legacy and memorialized his life.

Mandelstam's posthumous rehabilitation began in 1956. His return to Soviet print was perilous, and an incomplete and expurgated edition of his poetry appeared—in the Poet's Library series in Moscow—only in 1973, edited by the literary scholar Nikolay Khardzhiev. However, his texts circulated widely in the underground. In 1995, a comprehensive edition of Osip Mandelstam's poetry, edited by the scholar Aleksandr Mets, finally came out in St. Petersburg in the New Poet's Library. Still, Mandelstam's impact on postwar Russian poetry was tremendous. In the West, the first postwar collection of Mandelstam's verse appeared in 1955, followed by extensive efforts to publish his heritage, efforts that culminated in a four-volume Russian-language academic edition (1967–81). Outside Russia, Osip Mandelstam is perhaps the best-known twentieth-century Russian poet.

* * *

A handful of Mandelstam's poems, including the two included here, address Jewish and Judaic questions. An impressive number of his prose works, among them *The Noise of Time* (1925), *Theodosia* (1925), "Kievan Sketches" (1926), *Egyptian Stamp* (1927), and *Fourth Prose* (1928–30), discuss Jewish topics and showcase Jewish fictionalized characters (most brilliantly in *Egyptian Stamp*, set in 1917 Petrograd; the protagonist of this short novel was partly based on Valentin Parnakh) as well as real-life Jews such as mathematician Veniamin Kagan.

Multiple incongruities characterize Mandelstam's self-awareness as a Jew and as a Jewish writer. Mandelstam's career exhibits a Judaic-Christian dynamic that is far more complex than what the poet's Jewish and Christian apologists would like to believe. Those who speak of his rejection of Orthodox Judaism probably overstate the case for Mandelstam's knowledge of Judaic traditions. At the same time, even Russian ultranationalist critics fail to agree on Mandelstam's place in their Judeophobic fantasies of Russian culture. In the 1970s, Pyotr Palievsky reportedly spoke of Mandelstam as a "kikeish boil on the pure body of [Fyodor] Tyutchev's poetry." In the 1990s, Stanislav Kunyaev sermonized in print that "it is impossible to chase Mandelstam back into 'Judaic chaos' [. . .] he has irreversibly entered the wide Russian expanses."

The apostasy of the twenty-year-old Mandelstam, however low-key or even opportunistic, was only part of his emblematic story. Over the years, his self-awareness as a Christian changed as his interests ran the gamut from Catholic universalism to Russian Orthodoxy, to a Hellenic-Christian outlook. Christian references are prominent in his poetry and prose of the early and middle periods. To suggest that Christianity was largely a cultural category for Mandelstam is to do the poet's sensibility an injustice. During the earlier part of Mandelstam's career, Hellenism ousted Judaism as a spiritual and ethical foundation for his version of Christian civilization. Furthermore, Mandelstam's response, in his prose of the mid-1920s, to contemporary un(der)assimilated Jews was predominantly that of embarrassment. Reproduced below, "Judaic Chaos" (from the memoir *The Noise of Time*) illustrates what Maurice Friedberg described as Mandelstam's "painfully neurotic self-hating awareness of his Jewish antecedents." Not surprisingly, Mandelstam was receptive neither to Zionism nor to the early Soviet rhetorics on the Jewish question.

Mandelstam made his most positive discursive statements about Jewish culture in 1926, notably in his essay about the great Jewish actor Shloyme (Solomon) Mikhoels (1890–1948). Due in large measure to Mandelstam's misfortunes of the late 1920s, the years 1929–30 were marked by a reassessment of Jewishness. (Mandelstam reportedly likened his ostracism to the Dreyfus affair.) Critics cite chapter 12 of *Fourth Prose* as evidence that Mandelstam had re-embraced his Judaic roots: "The profession of a writer, as it has evolved in Europe and especially in Russia, is incompatible with the honorable title of a Judean, of which I am proud. My blood, burdened by the heritage of shepherds, patriarchs, and kings, rebels against the thievish gypsiness of the tribe of writers." Earlier in the same text, Mandelstam spoke about the charges of plagiarism that had been brought against him by Arkady Gornfeld (a Jew and a respected litterateur who had been used to instigate the scandal) and the scandal itself, which David Zaslavsky (a Jew who was a scoundrel and vilified Mandelstam in print) had spun into the public's eye: "At a certain year of my life, adult men from the tribe that I detest with all my heart and soul and to which I do not want to and will not belong intended to perform upon me collectively a repulsive and vile ritual. The name of this ritual is literary circumcision or dishonorment, which is performed according to the custom and calendar needs of the tribe of writers, while the victim is selected by the choice of the elders." Elsewhere in *Fourth Prose*, Mandelstam described the House of Writers as a building with "twelve lit Judas's windows" and his ostracism as a "ringing of [thirty] silver coins." One can only speculate what precisely the hurt and hunted Mandelstam had in mind, but it is doubtful that his stance in *Fourth Prose* is that of a proud Jew embracing his roots.

Seeking spiritual nourishment not in Judaism but in the more accessible Christianity, some members of the Jewish-Russian intelligentsia in the Soviet 1960s–80s identified with Osip Mandelstam. What makes the Jewish-born Mandelstam unique and worthy of admiration and further study is not his relationship to either Christianity or Judaism, which was symptomatic of his time and milieu, but his peerless poetic genius.

FROM *THE NOISE OF TIME*

Judaic Chaos

Once, a foreign character came to visit, a spinster in her forties in a crimson bonnet and with a sharp chin and dark vicious eyes. Claiming to hail from the small town of Shavli,[69] she demanded we find her a husband in Petersburg. She stayed a week before we managed to send her on her way. Every so often wandering writers would turn up: bearded men in long coats, Talmudic philosophers, peddlers of their own printed quotations and aphorisms. They would leave signed copies behind and complain of persecution by mean wives. Once or twice in my life, I was taken to a synagogue as though to a concert, following lengthy preparations, all but buying tickets from scalpers; and I would return in a heavy fog from all that I had seen and heard there. In Petersburg there is a Jewish quarter: it begins just beyond the Mariinsky Theater, where the scalpers freeze, behind the prison angel left over from the Lithuanian Castle that burnt down in the time of the revolution. Scattered throughout market streets were Jewish signs with a bull and cow, women with marriage wigs peering out from beneath headscarves, and worldly child-adoring old men mincing in their floor-length caftans. The synagogue, with its conical hats and onion spheres, is lost among the wretched buildings like a luxuriant, alien, exotic fig tree. Velvet berets with pompons, tired attendants and choristers, menorah clusters, tall velvet headdresses. The Jewish vessel, with its balcony full of ringing altos, with a choir of overwhelming children's voices, is gliding full sail, split by some ancient tempest into male and female halves. Lost in the women's balcony, I sneaked around like a thief, concealing myself behind the beams. The cantor, like mighty Samson, brought down the leonine building—the velvet headdresses responded, and the wondrous equilibrium of vowels and consonants, in clearly enunciated words, communicated an unvanquishable force to the chanting. But what an insult— the rabbi's banal, albeit literate, speech. What vulgarity when he pronounces "His Majesty the Emperor," how vapid is everything he says! And suddenly two gentlemen in top hats, splendidly dressed, gleaming with affluence, approach the heavy book with the elegant gestures of high society, leaving the circle to

---

69   Shavli is the Russian name of Šiauliai, a district capital in northern Lithuania, also known as Schaulen in German and Shavl or Shavl in Yiddish; Mandelstam mistakenly (or condescendingly) refers to Šiauliai as *mestechko* ("small town," "shtetl"); in 1902, it had a Jewish population of about 9,900 out of a total of about 17,000.

perform in our place, on behalf of everyone, something honorable and most important. "Who is he?"—"Baron Günzburg." "And he?"—"Varshavsky."[70]

As a child I absolutely never heard Yiddish, only later on did I get my fill of that crooning, ever surprised and disillusioned, questioning speech with its sharp accents on the semitones. The speech of my father and the speech of my mother—doesn't our language feed all its life on the confluence of the two? Do they not form its character? Mother's speech is clear and shrill, not the slightest foreign additive, with its somewhat widened and overly open vowels—grand literary Russian. Her vocabulary is meager and compressed, her phrases repetitive, but this is a language in which there is something rooted and confident. Mother loved to talk and enjoyed the stems and sounds of proper Russian speech, impoverished slightly by the way the intelligentsia used it. Was she not the first of our kin to obtain pure and clear Russian sounds? Father had no language at all; it was hotchpotch, tongue twisting, languagelessness. The Russian of a Polish Jew? No. The speech of a German Jew? Not that either. Perhaps a particular Courland accent? I've never heard one like his. A totally detached, invented language, a weave of words, the embellished and tangled talk of an autodidact, where ordinary words interlace with the obsolete, philosophical terms of Herder, Leibnitz, and Spinoza, the wondrous syntax of a Talmudic scholar, artificial, often incomplete locutions—anything but a language, be it Russian or German.

In essence, my father would transport me to a completely unfamiliar epoch, to surroundings that were remote but in no way Jewish. If you like, it was the purest eighteenth or even seventeenth century of an enlightened ghetto somewhere in Hamburg. Religious interests had been completely scratched out and dissolved. Enlightenment philosophy was transformed into intricate Talmudic pantheism. Somewhere in the vicinity Spinoza is breeding his spiders in a jar. There is a general anticipation of Rousseau and his natural man. All is detached, intricate, and schematic to the outer limits of possibility. A fourteen-year-old boy, raised to be a rabbi and forbidden secular books, runs away to Berlin, finds himself in a Talmudic academy alongside equally stubborn, brainy youths from backwater small towns, who regard themselves as geniuses;

---

70 Günzburg, Baron Horace (1833–1909)—banker, diplomat, philanthropist, and major spokesman for the Jewish-Russian community; Varshavsky, Mark S. (1853–1897)—attorney, prominent Jewish-Russian public figure and author, and nephew of the railroad builder and philanthropist Abram Varshavsky (1821–1888); M. S. Varshavsky was close to Baron Günzburg and shared in his efforts on behalf of Russian Jewry.

instead of the Talmud, he reads Schiller and, note, reads it as though it had just come out. After sticking with it for some time before falling out of this strange university, he dives back into the boiling world of the 1870s, where he learns about the conspiratorial dairy stand on Karavannaya Street from which a mine was planted under Alexander [II], and he preaches the philosophical ideals of the eighteenth century to flaccid and bemused clientele in a glove shop and a leather factory.

When they were taking me to the city of Riga, to my Riga grandfather and grandmother, I resisted and nearly wept. It seemed to me they were taking me to the homeland of my father's unfathomable philosophy. We set out with an artillery of boxes and baskets with padlocks, our bulging, cumbersome household belongings. Winter clothes were sprinkled with the coarse salt of naphthalene. Armchairs stood like white horses in the horse-blankets of their covers. The preparations for the trip to the Riga coast depressed me. At the time I collected nails: the most peculiar collector's fancy. I would run my fingers through my piles of nails like the avaricious knight,[71] rejoicing as my prickly treasure trove grew. Now they took my nails and used them for packaging.

The trip was disquieting. At night in Derpt,[72] some *Vereins*[73] stormed our dimly lit train car, singing their loud Estonian songs; they were returning from a big song festival. The Estonians pounded and endeavored to break through the door. It was very frightening.

Grandfather was a blue-eyed old man in a yarmulke covering half his forehead, with prominent, rather solemn features, of the sort very esteemed Jews sometimes possess. He smiled, happily greeting us—he wanted to be affectionate but didn't know how—his thick brows lifted. He wanted to take me into his arms; I was on the verge of tears. My kindly grandmother, with a black wig over her gray hair, in a housecoat with yellowish flowers, shuffled with tiny steps across the squeaky hardwood floors and continuously tried to treat me to something or other.

---

71 Reference to the title of Aleksandr Pushkin's "little tragedy" *The Avaricious Knight* (*Skupoi rytsar'*, 1830).

72 Derpt (Germ. Dorpat; orig. Rus. Yuriev)—German name of present-day Tartu, the location of Estonia's oldest university.

73 Mandelstam uses the German word *Verein* (organization, society, association), probably in reference to members of a society or union of ethnic Estonians, perhaps a student brotherhood.

She would ask, "Hungry? Hungry?"—the only Russian word she knew. But I didn't like the spiced old people's delicacies, their bitter almond taste. My parents went out to town. My disappointed grandpa and sad and frantic grandmother try striking up a conversation, then frown like old ruffled birds. I tried to explain that I wanted my mother, but they didn't understand. Then I used my fingers on the table to depict my desire to leave, making a walking motion with my middle finger and pointer.

Suddenly grandfather drew a black-and-yellow silk shawl from the drawer of a commode, put it over my shoulders, and made me repeat after him words made up of unfamiliar noise; dissatisfied with my mumbling, he became angry and shook his head with disapproval. I felt suffocated and afraid. I don't remember how my mother came to my rescue.

Father would often refer to grandfather's honesty as a spiritual virtue. For a Jew, honesty is wisdom and almost sanctity. The further back in the generation of these somber, blue-eyed old men, the more honest and serious they were. Great-grandfather Benjamin once said, "I'm through with my business and trade—I need no more money." He had exactly enough to last him until the day he died. He did not leave a kopeck.

The Riga coast might as well be an entire country. It's famous for its viscous, incredibly fine and pure yellow sand (only an hourglass had such sand!) and for the fenestrated little walkways, one or two boards wide, spanning the twenty-verst resort Sahara.

No other resort can compare with the vacationland of the Riga coast. The walkways, flowerbeds, palisades, and glass spheres form a never-ending settlement, all on the kind of yellow stone—ground flour of the canary—tinted sand that children play with.

In their backyards, the Latvians dry and string out flounder, a one-eyed, bony fish, flat as a wide palm. Children crying, piano scales, countless dentists' moaning patients, the clang of dishes in small resort *table d'hôte*, singers' trills, and peddlers' cries never wane in the labyrinth of kitchen gardens, bakeries, and barbed wire; and along horseshoe rails on a sand foundation, as far as the eye can see, run toy trains filled with fare dodgers who jump aboard while the trains are moving, from the meticulous German Bilderlingshof to the overcrowded Jewish Dubbeln, which smells of diapers. Through the sparse pine groves wander traveling musicians—two pretzel-shaped trumpets, a clarinet, and a trombone—and, emitting their unforgiving brass out-of-tune notes, are cast out at every stop, here and there regaling listeners with the cavalry march of the lovely Karolina.

The whole territory was owned by a monocled baron by the name of Firks. He had partitioned his land into "clean of Jews" and "not clean." On the clean land sat the German students, ironing little tables with their beer mugs. On the Judaic land, diapers were hanging and scales gagged their way up and down. In Majorenhof, on the German side, there was music—a symphony orchestra in a garden shell, Strauss's "Death and Transfiguration." Elderly fraus with flushed cheeks, in fresh mourning, found comfort there.

In Dubbeln, where the Jews were, the orchestra gagged on Tchaikovsky's "Pathétique." And one could hear the two-stringed nests calling to each other.

It was at that time that I fell in love with Tchaikovsky, with a sickly nervous tension reminiscent of the desire of Dostoevsky's Netochka Nezvanova[74] to hear a violin concerto playing behind a flame of silk curtains. I would glean the broad, smooth, purely violin phrases in Tchaikovsky from behind a barbed-wire fence, and more than once I would tear my clothes and scratch my hands while trying to sneak up to the orchestra shell. I would fish fragments of strong violin music from the wild gramophone of the resort cacophony. I don't remember how this awe for the symphony orchestra grew in me, but I think I correctly understood Tchaikovsky, sensing in him a particular feeling for the concertesque.

How convincing they sounded, these violin voices, softened by Italian lack of will but still Russian, in this dirty Jewish cloaca! What a thread extended from those first squalid performances to the silk fire of the Assembly of Noble Deputies and the puny Scriabin, who might be squished any minute by the still mute semicircle of singers and the violin forest of "Prometheus" surrounding him from all sides, over which, like a shield, hangs the sound receiver, a strange glass apparatus.

1925

Translated from the Russian by Amelia Glaser and Alexander Zeyliger

---

74 Netochka Nezvanova—protagonist of Fyodor Dostoevsky's short novel of the same name (1849).

* * *

One Alexander Herzovich,
A Jewish pianist,
Played Schubert songs with perfect pitch,
Clear as an amethyst.

From dawn to dusk he would perform
The pure immortal art
Of one sonata, light and warm
And splendidly by heart.

What, Alexander Herzovich?
Dark is the street below?
Dear Alexander Schmerzovich,
So what! On with the show!

That beautiful Italian girl
On snowy afternoons
Brings out her little sled for a whirl
To your Schubertian tunes.

When we hear music sweetly played,
We don't mind death's sour notes,
And afterward we're not afraid,
Hung like crow-feather coats.

This, Alexander Herzovich,
Began long, long ago.
Dear Alexander Scherzovich,
So what! On with the show![75]

1931

---

75 An individual by the name of Aleksandr Gertsevich was a neighbor of O. Mandelstam's
brother, Aleksandr Mandelstam. *Herz* (Ger.) = heart; *schmerz* (Ger.) = pain; *serdtse* (Rus.)
= heart; *scherzo* (Ital.) = musical form, from the Italian "joke."

* * *

Say, desert geometer, shaper
Of Arabic sand into form,
Can lines that you scribble on paper
Be stronger than wind in a storm?

To me his convulsions don't matter—
Judaic upheaval and strife.
He charters a life out of chatter
And laps up the chatter of life.

1933

Translated from the Russian by Maxim D. Shrayer and J. B. Sisson

DOVID KNUT

Dovid Knut (1900–1955), poet, prose writer, and journalist, was born David Fiksman in the Bessarabian town of Orgeev (Orheyev, Orhei) and grew up in Kishinev (now Chişinău, Moldova). Knut's father kept a dry-goods store and supported a large family. Knut attended a government Jewish school and debuted as a poet at age of fourteen in Kishinev periodicals. In 1918, he edited the magazine *Young Thought* (*Moladaia mysl'*). In adopting his pen name, Dovid Knut followed the Yiddish (Ashkenazic Hebrew) orthoepic norm (Dóvid, not Davíd) and used the maiden name of his mother, Perl Knut. The linguist M. J. Connolly has suggested to the editor that the poet chose a word (*knut* = standard Russian and Yiddish for "whip, lash") that in both languages has connotations of oppression and slavery/serfdom.

In 1920, Knut left Kishinev, then in Romania, and settled in France, where he engaged in a wide variety of activities: he studied chemical engineering in Caen; he ran an eatery in the Parisian Latin Quarter in the 1920s and later operated a dyeing shop; and he worked as a tricycle delivery courier in the early 1930s. Additionally, the gregarious Knut stood at the helm of cultural initiatives in émigré Paris. In July 1922, he coorganized the "Exhibition of Thirteen," whose participants included Vladimir Pozner, a former Serapion Brother, and Aleksandr Ginger, the future husband of the poet Anna Prismanova. In 1925, Knut joined the Union of Young Poets and Writers, and in 1925–27, he coedited the émigré magazine *New Home* (*Novyi dom*).

Knut contributed to a variety of periodicals in Russia Abroad, including the reviews *Will of Russia* (*Volia Rossii*, Prague), *Numbers* (*Chisla*, Paris), *Contemporary Annals* (*Sovremennye zapiski*, Paris), and *Russian Annals* (*Russkie zapiski*, Kharbin), as well as the newspapers *Latest News* (*Poslednie novosti*) and *Days* (*Dni*), both in Paris. Knut's first and most Jewish book, *Of My Millennia* (1925)—published in Paris, as were all five of his lifetime Russian collections of poetry—was well received for its Biblical intonation and verbal vibrancy. Leading senior critics, including Georgy Adamovich (mentor to younger Parisian poets), Alfred Bem, and Zinaida Gippius, gave Knut high marks, yet one sensed a patronizing encouragement of a "Jewish" poet by some Russian authors. Along with Boris Poplavsky (1903–1935),

Knut was a star on the pale horizon of younger Parisian émigré poetry. **Vladislav Khodasevich** remarked in a letter to Mikhail Froman in December 1925: "There are quite a few young and not so young poets here, but I do not see major talents. Better than others is D[o]vid Knut, writing some rather interesting verses very much in the Jewish spirit."

The ruthless Vladimir Nabokov (1899–1977) gave Knut's *Second Book of Poems* (1928) a somewhat sympathetic review in *The Rudder* (*Rul'*, Berlin), appreciating Knut's "energetic verses," his "slightly overdone Biblical coarseness," and a "healthy thirst for all earthly things." Faulting Knut for abusing overloaded terms such as "bread" or "manliness" and for sloppy rhyming, Nabokov rather correctly identified lapses of taste in Knut's treatment of sexuality and the body. In part 2 of the cycle "'The Ark," one finds the line "Where [is] the memory of friendships, [of] beloved legs and breasts!" ("Gde pamiat' druzhb, liubimykh nog i grudei!")—and this is not self-parody.

After the 1929 chapbook *Satyr* came *Paris Nights* (1932; cf. **Khodasevich**'s book-length cycle *European Night*), which some critics consider Knut's best collection. Bearing a bitterly ironic title, Knut's collection *Daily Love* (cf. "daily bread") included his best love lyrics and the long poem *The Journey*. World War II undercut plans for the publication of a volume of Knut's rich stories about Bessarabian Jews originally printed in periodicals.

Knut and his first wife, Sarra (Sofya) Groboys, the mother of his son Daniel, parted in the early 1930s. His growing interest in Jewish activism— and his transition to Jewish-French journalism—paralleled his rapprochement with Ariadna Scriabin (1905–1944), the daughter of the composer Alexander Scriabin (1872–1915). In April 1934, Knut participated in the evening of the Tel Hai Fund, where **Vladimir Jabotinsky** gave a speech. Knut and Ariadna Scriabin sailed to the British Mandate of Palestine in August 1937, returning in December of the same year. While they were there, in October 1937, *Ha'aretz* published a Knut poem in a Hebrew translation by Avraham Shlonsky (1900–1973). Despite a realistic assessment of the limited literary opportunities in Eretz Israel, Knut was enthusiastic about moving there. On the basis of his visit, he composed the cycle "Foremotherland," weaving its Biblical motifs around King Solomon and Ecclesiastes. Knut completed "Foremotherland" in 1939; apparently, no later Russian poems by him survive.

Knut edited the Jewish-French newspaper *Affirmation* (*L'Affirmation*) from January 1938 to September 1939. He had no illusions about the impending catastrophe and attacked authors and intellectuals who professed antisemitism. His essay about L.-F. Céline's *Bagatelles for a Massacre* (1937) appeared in Hebrew in *Ha'aretz*. In 1939, Knut and Ariadna Scriabin attended the Twenty-first Zionist Congress in Geneva. In September 1939, Knut was mobilized into the French Army. He and Ariadna officially registered their marriage in March 1940, and she converted to Judaism in May 1940, taking the name Sara. The Knuts reached Toulouse in June 1940, and at the end of 1941, Knut wrote the pamphlet *What Is to Be Done?* (published 1942) about armed resistance to Nazis and collaborators. In December 1942, with the Gestapo on his trail, Knut escaped to Switzerland. Ariadna gave birth to Yosi, Knut's son, in May 1943. A hero of the French Resistance, she was killed in July 1944, two weeks before the liberation of Toulouse.

Knut returned to Paris in the fall of 1944. He worked at the Centre de Documentation Juive Contemporaire, editing its bulletin (as Dovid Knout) and, from August 1946, the newspaper *The Jewish World* (*Le Monde Juif*). Knut's book *Toward a History of Jewish Resistance in France in 1940–1944* (Paris, 1947), the first documentary testimony about the Shoah in France and in some respects a Jewish-French equivalent of **Ilya Ehrenburg** and **Vasily Grossman**'s *The Black Book* (see introductions to **Ilya Ehrenburg** and **Vasily Grossman** in this anthology), was reticent about the prominent role he himself had played in the Jewish Resistance.

Knut translated into French the play *The Hill of Life* by Max Zweig (1892–1992), about the 1920 Arab attack on Tel Hai in Upper Galilee. During production in the summer of 1947, Knut met the actress Virginia (subsequently Leah) Sharovskaya, who became his wife. They traveled to Israel at the end of 1948 and vacationed in Tiberias, returning in January 1949. Knut made further contacts with Israeli poets from Eastern Europe, including Leah Goldberg (1911–1970), as he hoped to have a book published in Hebrew. Some poems appeared in Israeli periodicals, but book plans did not materialize.

Knut's *Selected Poems* appeared in Paris in May 1949. An exitgesture, the Russian-language volume got a lukewarm reception in Europe and a favorable one in the United States. Vladimir Khazan, Knut's biographer and the editor of his two-volume *Collected Works* (Jerusalem, 1997–98), suggested that the Russian Montparnasse was not sympathetic to Knut's Zionist views and no longer regarded him to be a Russian author but rather a Jewish journalist. A 16 February 1939 entry in Zinaida Gippius's diary dispels all illusions: "We took a late walk and ran into Knut with his repulsive wife (the former Scriabina)[...]. She converted to kikery [*zhidovstvo*] because Knut became not so much a poet as a militant Israelite. 'His blood be on us and on our children.'" (Gippius is quoting Matthew 27:25.)

In the fall of 1949, the Knuts settled in Tel Aviv with his family. They experienced difficulties finding housing and work and studied Hebrew at an *ulpan* (absorption and immersion center) in Kiryat Motzkin. Leah eventually found work as an actress at the Cameri Theater in Tel Aviv, and in 1951, the Knuts settled in a suburb of Tel Aviv. Knut wrote memorial essays about Russian literature and culture, which appeared in Hebrew translation in *Ha'aretz*. He died of a brain tumor in February 1955.

Knut's verse struck émigré readers with the vitality and vigorous rhetoric of the lyrical self. Critics noted an emphasis on the Hebrew Bible erotic, on the metaphysics of sex, and on the cultural codes preserved in Jewish Diasporic memory and everyday living. According to Vladimir Khazan, "[...] in twentieth-century poetry it is hard to name another poet who perceived his national origin as erotically."

The Israeli-Russian scholar Dmitri Segal observed an intriguing dynamic of Knut's career: starting out as a passionate Judaic poet, by the 1930s Knut wrote less about Jewishness in poetry while moving into Jewish-French journalism and activism. Indeed, Knut's voice lost much of its unique "Jewish" accent as his Russian lyrical poetry of the 1930s (in *Daily Love*) closed ranks with the Parisian émigré mainstream.

Knut was influenced by a number of Russian poets, including Ivan Bunin, Aleksandr Blok, Anna Akhmatova, **Vladislav Khodasevich**, Marina Tsvetaeva, and Sergey Esenin. He dialogically responded to the Soviet modernism of the 1920s (e.g., Nikolay Tikhonov, Nikolay Aseev in *Paris Nights*) and his émigré contemporaries ("Parisian Note" in *Daily Love*); futurism and constructivism left traces in his versification. The uniqueness of Knut's poetry lies in its articulation of Jewish motifs and its Jewish intonation. A number of émigré poets of his generation were born Jewish: Lidia Chervinskaya, Leonid Gansky, Mikhail Godin, Lazar Kalberin, Vera Lurie, Boris Zakovich, and others. Yet only a few (Anna Prismanova, Sofia Pregel, and, in this anthology, **Raisa Blokh** and **Evgeny Shklyar**)—and especially as compared to their Soviet coevals—addressed Jewish topics; fewer yet experimented with the texture of Jewishness in their verse. Knut towered over his generation as the most important and self-conscious Jewish-Russian poet of the First Wave, and this position resulted in an inflation of his literary reputation.

The Russian émigré philosopher Georgy Fedotov (1886–1951) wrote: "Dovid Knut is one of the most prominent poets of the Russian Paris, but the Russian form might perhaps be a matter of chance for him. This is his difference from many Jewish poets in Russian culture, of which at least one—Osip Mandelstam—has every chance of becoming a Russian classic. But Knut will not fit in Russian literature. In him sounds the voice of millennia, the voice of Biblical Israel and its limitless love, passion, longing." Knut's earlier poems, where Jewish motifs abound, might be regarded as either Russian poetry marred by slight errors of accentuation and idiom betraying a native speaker of a Jewish-Ukrainian-Bessarabian-flavored Russian or as Russian poetry deliberately spoken in a Jewish "voice." This complex issue goes back to the critical discussions of earlier Jewish-Russian poets and the quality of their verse (e.g., Simon Frug), and students of Jewish writing will inevitably confront it in the years to come.

* * *

The following selections represent Knut's most exemplary Jewish poems. Knut included them in *Selected Poems* (1949) and opened *Of My Millennia* (1925) with "I, Dovid-Ari ben Meir . . . ." Praised by G. Adamovich as the best twentieth-century Jewish-Russian poem, "A Kishinev Burial" appeared in *Contemporary Annals* in 1930 under the title "Recollection." In *Parisian Nights* (1932), Knut published it without a title, whereas in *Selected Poems* he added the title "A Kishinev Funeral." In the "Jewish-Russian air" of Knut's Kishinev, the traumatic memories of the 1903 Kishinev Pogrom (and of Jewish poets, Bialik among them, who condemned this "city of slaughter") are mixed with blissful memories of Pushkin, who in 1821–22, during his "Southern exile," had strolled where Knut spent his childhood. Published in émigré periodicals in 1938–39, "The Land of Israel," come from Knut's cycle "Foremotherland."

* * *

I,
Dovid-Ari ben Meir,
Son-of-Meir-Enlightener-of-Darkness,[76]
Born by the foothills of Ivanos,[77]
In a plenteous land of plenteous, hominy,
Of sheep cheese and sharp *caciocavallo*,[78]
In a land of forests and strong-loined bulls,
Of bubbling wines and bronzy breasted women;
Where midst the steppes and ruddy fields of corn
Still roam the smoky fires of gypsies making camp;

I,
Dovid-Ari ben Meir,
The boy who soothed the angry Saul with song,
Who gave
The rebel line of Israel
A star's six points as shield;

I,
Dovid-Ari,
Whose sling and stone
Brought bellowing oaths from the dying Goliath—
The one whose steps sent tremors through the hills—
I've come into your camp to learn your songs
But soon, I'll tell you
Mine.

---

76 The editor is indebted to Vladimir Kazan's commentary in his two-volume edition of Dovid Knut's works (Jerusalem, 1997–98). Knut simultaneously offers a literal translation and an interpretation of the Hebrew "ben Meir," which literally means "son of Meir," but the word *meir* means "he who enlightens/illuminates." Given that later in the poem Knut identifies himself with the future King David soothing King Saul with music and song. (cf. I Kings 16) and slaying Goliath (cf. I Kings 17), the name "Ari," which in Hebrew means "lion," should not be overlooked.

77 The Ivanus (Ivanos) is one of the left tributaries of the Reut, a river in Moldova and itself a right tributary of the Dniester; Orgeev, Knut's native town, is located in the Ivanus (Ivanos) valley.

78 *Caciocavallo* (from the Italian for "horse muzzle")—type of hard cheese made out of sheep's or cow's milk; Knut uses a Russian corruption, *kachkaval*.

I see it all:
The deserts of Canaan,
The sands and date trees of parchèd Palestine
The guttural moan of Arab camel trains,
The cedars of Lebanon, and bored ancient walls
Of my Holy Yerushalaim.

And the awesome hour:
The crack, crumble, and roar of Sinai,
When fire and thunder sundered the Heavens,
And in the cauldron of wrathful clouds
Arose the knotted eye of Adonia-The-Lord
Staring in anger through the haze
At the lost creatures in the sand,

I see it all: the grieving Babylon rivers,
The creaking of carts, the tinkling f cymbals,
The smoke and stench of father's grocery—
Its quince, halvah, garlic, and tobacco sheaves—
Where I guarded from roving Moldavian fingers
The moldy half-moon cakes, fish, dried and salted.

I,
Dovid-Ari ben Meir,
Whose wine has wandered some thousands of years,
Stop now at this crossing in the sands
To sing you, brothers, my song—
My heavy burden of love and longing—

The blessed burden of my millennia.

1925

A KISHINEV BURIAL

It was a dismal evening in Kishinev:
We rounded the bend from Inzov Hill,[79]
Where Pushkin once had lived. A sorry knoll
Where the short, curly-haired clerk had lived—
The celebrated rake and scapegrace—
With those hot, those blackamoor eyes
Set in a swarthy, thick-lipped, lively face.

Beyond dusty, sullen, still Asia Road,
Along the hard walls of the Maternity Home,
They were carrying a dead Jew on a stretcher.
Beneath the unclean funeral cover,
Protruded the bony features
Of this man gnawed to death by life.
Of this man so gnawed to the bone that
Afterward there was nothing left on which
The thin worms of the Jewish cemetery might feed.

79 The great Russian poet Aleksandr Pushkin (1799–1837), whose great-grandfather, A. P. Gannibal, godson of Peter the Great, was born an Abyssinian prince (according to the version prominent source at the time of the poem's composition), lived in Kishinev in 1821– 23, serving under the auspices of the Bessarabian governor, General Ivan N. Inzov, before being transferred to Odessa, where he spent the last year of his so-called "Southern exile." Inzov Hill is a neighborhood of Kishinev where General Inzov's house was located; Pushkin stayed there from the spring of 1821 to the spring of 1822. Today the streets and buildings of Knut's native city bear the memories of Pushkin and his era, and a Pushkin Museum still functions in Chişinău (formerly Kishinev), now the capital of independent Moldova. Inzov Hill was a place in Knut's Kishinev that one passed on the way to Aziatskaya (Asia) Road, a Jewish area to which Knut's family moved around 1903.

Behind the elders carrying the stretcher
Walked a handful of Jews Mané-Katz might paint,[80]
Greenish-yellow and with big sunken eyes.
From their moldering gabardine caftans
Came a compounded odor of holiness and fate,
The Jewish odor of poverty and sweat,
Of moths, salt herring, and fried onion,
Of sacred books, soaked diapers, and synagogues.

Great grief gave simple cheer to their hearts,
And they walked with an unheard step,
Submissive, easy, measured, unhurried,
As if they had walked behind the corpse for years,
As if there were no start to their procession,
As if there were no end to it . . . With the step
Of Zion's—of Kishinev's—sages and elders.

Between them and their sad black freight
Walked a woman, and in the dusty falling darkness
We could not see her face.
But how excellent was her high voice!
Under the knocking step, under the faint rustle
Of fallen leaves, of rubbish 'neath her cough
Flowed another, an as yet inconceivable song.
In it were tears of sweet submission
And eternal devotion to the will of God,
In it was the rapture of humility and fear . . .

O, how excellent was her high voice!

---

80 Katz, Mané (Mané-Katz, Ohel Emmanuel, 1894–1962)—Jewish painter, famous for his
portrayal of Jewish life in eastern Europe; born in Russia and settled in the west in 1921.
Knut was personally acquainted with the painter.

Not of the thin Jew on the stretcher
Bobbing up and down, did she sing but of me,
Of us, of everyone, of vanity, of dust
Of old age, of grief, of fear,
Of pity, of vanity, of bewilderment,
Of the eyes of dying children . . .

The Jewess walked, almost stumbling,
And each time that the cruel stone
Tossed up the corpse on sticks, she
Threw herself on him with a cry, and her voice
Suddenly broadened, grew strong, resonant,
Solemnly gonged a threat to God,
And it grew livelier from her furious cries.
And the woman threatened with her fists
The One Who Floated in the greenish heaven
Above the dusty trees, above the corpse,
Above the roof of the Maternity Home,
Above the hard, uneven road.

But here, the woman became frightened of herself,
And she beat her breast and froze,
And repented, hysterically and long.
Frightened, she praised God's will,
Shouted frenziedly of forgiveness,
Of faith, humility, of faith,
Started up and huddled to the ground
Under the heaviness of the invisible eyes
That gazed down from the skies sadly and sternly.

… … … … … … … … … … … … … … … … …

What had taken place? Evening, quiet, a fence, a star
Heavy dust . . . My poems in *The Courier*.
The trusting gymnasium student, Olya,
A simple rite of Jewish burial,
And a woman from the Book of Genesis.

But I'll never be able to tell in words
What hovered over Asia Road,
Over the lampposts of the city outskirts,
Over the laughter suppressed at back alleys,
Over the boldness of an unknown guitar,
Rocking from where, God only knows—over the baying
Of melancholy, snarling dogs.

. . . That peculiarly Jewish-Russian air . . .
Blessed are those who have ever breathed it.

1929

THE LAND OF ISRAEL

To Eva Kirshner

I was walking along the shore of Tiberias
And joyously, divinely sullen (As if my heart was glad and was not glad),
I picked my way among the stones of Capernaum
Where once . . . Listen and just think
In the shade, in the dust of the olive grove.

All the while, the same voice in the universal bar,
Sleepless, international, irrevocable,
On the subject of the unslaked desire of the flesh
And those (For all! For a farthing! Indefatigable!)
Faces off of film ads
On the walls of the City—of Jerusalem.

What's there to tell you about Palestine?
What's there to recall? The unpopulated Sedjera,
The orange cloud of the hot desert wind,
The staid voice of the convert from Astrakhan,
Or the slim insulted back
Of the boy shot while keeping watch?

The haughty camel over the trough,
The mute tzaddiks in *peyes* from Tsfat?
The dry sky unsaturated with eternity
Over the childhood of the world in death's embrace?
And the obliterate numerous slabs
Of the senseless dead, men of Josaphat.

Or a young woman named Judith
Who waved her swarthy hand long after I had passed.

1938

Translated from the Russian by Ruth Rischin

EVGENY SHKLYAR

Evgeny Shklyar (1894–1942), poet, translator, and essayist, was born to an engineer's family in Druya (Druja), a shtetl in the Disna District of Vilna Province, presently in Belarus's Vitebsk Province. He later attended a gymnasium in Ekaterinoslav (Dnepropetrovsk) in Ukraine, and studied at Warsaw University following evacuation to Rostov-on-Don during World War I. Shklyar began to contribute poetry to periodicals in the south of Russia in 1911. After being drafted into the army, Shklyar trained at a cadet school, served at the Caucasus front, and was decorated with a St. George's Cross. Shklyar fought the Reds during the civil war in several armies and edited the SR (Socialist-Revolutionary) newspaper *Free Daghestan* (*Vol'nyi Dagestan*).

Shklyar immigrated to Lithuania in 1919, settling in Kaunas (Kovno) in 1921. He worked at the Kaunas newspaper *Echo* (*Ekho*) and in 1924–25 at the Riga-based *People's Thought* (*Narodnaia mysl'*), as well as serving as the Kaunas correspondent of *Today* (*Segodnia*), a major émigré newspaper based in Riga. The three independent Baltic states, especially Latvia and Lithuania, had an active Russian émigré press, and, regularly journeying to Riga and Tallinn, Shklyar contributed to Russian periodicals in Latvia, Lithuania, and Estonia, while enjoying a reputation in the émigré world outside the limitrophes.

In 1923, Shklyar founded *The Baltic Almanac* (*Baltiiskii al'manakh*), advancing a platform of intercultural exchange across the Baltic region. He edited *The Baltic Almanac* in 1923–28 and published it in 1928–29 and 1937. His other ventures included *The Lithuanian Market* (*Lietuvos rinka/Die litauische Markt*, 1928), *Our Echo* (*Nashe ekho*, 1929–31), *The Lithuanian Courier* (*Litovskii kur'er*, 1932–33), and *The Lithuanian Messenger* (*Litovskii vestnik*, 1935–39). Shklyar lived in Paris in 1926–27, returning to Kaunas in 1928.

Shklyar considered Lithuania his home. He wrote with passion about Lithuanian culture and the Lithuanian countryside. More importantly, along with the prominent symbolist Russian poet turned Lithuanian diplomat Jurgis Baltrušaitis (1873–1944), Shklyar was a conduit between Lithuanian and Russian letters. A principal translator of Lithuanian poets into Russian during the interwar independence, Shklyar translated authors from different generations and movements, including Kazys Binkis, J. A. Herbačiauskas, Liudas Gira, Jonas Maironis, Pranas Morkus Putinas, Teofilis Tilvytis, Petras Vaičiūnas,

Vydūnas, and others. In 1927, he published *Lietuva, the Golden Name*, a Russian-language collection about Lithuania, which appeared in Lithuanian translation in 1931.

Shklyar published eight books of Russian poetry: *Cypresses* (Kaunas, 1922), *Caravan* (Berlin, 1923), *Lights on Mountain Tops* (Berlin, 1923), *Evening Steppe* (Berlin, 1923), *The Staff* (Riga, 1925), *Lietuva, the Golden Name* (Paris, 1927), *Eliyahu, Gaon of Vilna* (Riga, 1929), and *Poeta in Aeternum* (Riga, 1935), this last including dedications to Lithuanian poets and translations.

Writing in *The Lithuanian Voice* (*Litovskii golos*) on 19 August 1935, the critic Boris Orechkin polemicized with Liudas Gira's view of Shklyar as a "fellow-traveler of contemporary Lithuanian writers and poets." "Evg. Shklyar is both a poet and a citizen," Orechkin observed, invoking the dictum by Nikolay Nekrasov that a poet must be committed to civic duty. "[Shklyar] is both a Russian and a Lithuanian poet, and a Lithuanian citizen," Orechkin continued. "Can there be such a combination and can a Russian poet be Lithuania's trou-badour [*sic*] and her loyal son?" Although Orechkin did not mention the third key component of Shklyar's identity, his Jewishness, he alluded, conspicuously, to "arguments of 'racists,'" concluding: "[...] Shklyar's ties to the Lithuanian land extend far back. He is a Lithuanian, if not by blood, then at least by birth." In 1928, Shklyar published in *The Baltic Almanac* his Russian translation of the Lithuanian national anthem from the lyrics by Vincas Kudirka (1858–1899): "Lithuania, my homeland, land of heroes!/Let your sons draw strength from the past [...]." Evgeny Shklyar perished in a concentration camp outside Kaunas in 1942.

* * *

A covert modernist and not an original talent, Shklyar addressed ancient Judaic motifs and aspects of modern Jewish history. The theme of religious pluralism and interfaith dialogue manifested itself throughout Shklyar's career, as evidenced by "Shield of David, crescent or icon ..." from *Lights on Mountain Tops* (1923). The second poem in the selection, "Where's Home?" appeared in *The Staff* (1925) as part of the cycle "White and Blue," dedicated to **Vladimir Jabotinsky**.

The nine poems of Shklyar's cycle "Names" (*Cypresses*, 1922) focus on female names that bear religious and cultural significance for Muslim (Persia, Turkey, Azerbaijan, Central Asia), Catholic (Lithuania, Poland), and Orthodox (Georgia) regions and for the Judaic civilization. In Shklyar's collections one also finds poems that stylize or imply a genuinely Christian authorial sensibility. The 1931 poem "At Easter" (*Poeta in Aeternum*, 1935) expresses nostalgia for a

Russian Orthodox childhood and makes one wonder about Shklyar's Christian leanings. Yet Shklyar's long poem *Eliyahu, Gaon of Vilna* (1927–29), dedicated to the memory of the poet's mother, Lyubov-Rashel Shklyar-Vilinskaya, glorifies the career of the great Rabbi Eliyahu of Vilna (1720–1797), thus testifying to Shklyar's enduring Judaic spirit.

* * *

Shield of David, crescent or icon,
In the grip of prayer I'll implore:
"Russia, dear God, is many nations,
How *can* I not love her the more?"

I shall plead with Him loudly; urgent, ardent,
I shall bow my head to the sand:
"Righteous Lord, will you please save and pardon
Russia, the suffering land!"

1923

WHERE'S HOME?

For "home," that cherished word, there's no exchange;
The ways of exile press you down like rocks.
A native corner full of memories, old crocks,
Even straw-roofed peasant huts, or grange
Are dearer than a beauty foreign, strange.
You're almost there, now you see the oxen,
The rows of carts, the yellow fields, the riverside,
And then the sunset: red hot, molten, overflowing,
A herd of purple huts above the river glowing,
And ripening crops extending far and wide;
You lose yourself, then scream with pain inside
As the last enchanting visions flutter, going.
O how, when your heart is split, will you ever come
To love, not these accustomed days and nights,
Nor springtime Dnieper's rushing, golden light,
But Jericho's noise of time, its ancient hum,
How to compare the steppe to Hebron's desertdom,

Thatched roofs to tops of Bedouin tents pulled tight?
In Judaism fierce, hidden strengths appear
To nurture twice exile's flowers
And deep within the heart's most buried bowers
To pick amongst them and to make it clear
You're going either where all's alien but dear
Or where the majestic past regales the hours.
To you, to you, land of the endless years,
The spirit of Israel again is lit
And nothing shall extinguish ancient writ,
My life is full of promise, full of cheer
When olive-skinned, cavorting children there
Greet me with words of welcome in *ivrit*.

1925

Translated from the Russian by Maxim D. Shrayer and Andrew Von Hendy

ISAAC BABEL

Isaac Babel (1894–1940), fiction writer, playwright, essayist, and screenwriter, was born to a Jewish mercantile family in Odessa and grew up in Nikolaev and Odessa. Babel's last name, an Ashkenazic corruption of Bavel, embodies the Diaspora and its greatest text, the Babylonian Talmud. At home Babel received private instruction in Hebrew and Jewish law. He attended the Nicholas I Commercial School in 1905–11 and then studied at the Kiev Commercial Institute in 1911–15. Babel wrote his first stories in French at the age of fifteen. His first published story, "Old Shloyme," about the suicide of an old Jewish man faced with his family's conversion, appeared in 1913 in Kiev. After arriving in St. Petersburg in 1915, Babel was encouraged by Maxim Gorky. Two of Babel's stories were published in Gorky's *Chronicle* (*Letopis'*), earning Babel a charge of pornography. Babel published short sketches in 1916–17 under the pen name Bab-l (Hebrew for "Gates of God"), promising the arrival of an "Odessan Maupassant."

In the fall of 1917, after serving on the Romanian front, Babel returned to Petrograd and worked for the Cheka (earliest incarnation of the Soviet secret police), using his knowledge of languages. His first nonfictional reflections on the new Bolshevik state appeared in 1918 in Gorky's paper *New Life* (*Novaia zhizn'*), which was soon shut down. These reflections anticipated some of the controversial aspects of his *Red Cavalry*. While endorsing the revolution and repudiating tsarism, Babel questioned the use of terror and violence and the destruction of the old culture. Refracted through the Jewish consciousness, the confrontation of the old and the new took the shape of a clash between a traditional Judaic mentality, both constricted to and preserved by the Pale, and the revolutionary rhetoric of Jewish liberation.

In the spring of 1920, during the Polish campaign, he was attached to the First Red Army as a correspondent. Under the assumed Russian name *Kirill Lyutov*, literally Cyril the Ferocious, Babel traveled with the troops, contributing to the newspaper *Red Cavalry Soldier* (*Krasnoarmeets*). He kept a diary (part of which has survived), graphically recording the antisemitic violence of Semyon Budyonny's Red Cavalry units. Babel returned to Odessa in November 1920 to recuperate from typhus. Fictionally transmogrified, the war events found their way into the stories of his *Red Cavalry*, which were published in the periodicals of Moscow, Leningrad, and Odessa in 1923–26 to become a cornerstone of Babel's reputation. From the very beginning, Babel's great success was laced with controversy. In 1924, General (later Marshal) Semyon Budyonny rancorously attacked Babel in the magazine *October* (*Oktiabr'*). Titled in Russian "Babism Babelia," a play on the Russian word *baba* ("peasant woman" or pejorative "woman"), Budyonny's title might be translated as "Babel's Babism" and interpreted as the "womanish hysteria of babbling Babel." The first edition of *Red Cavalry* came out in 1926 in Moscow; by 1933, it had gone through eight editions.

In 1921–23, Babel wrote and published four pieces from the cycle of "Odessa Stories": "The King," "How It Was Done in Odessa," "Father," and "Lyubka Kazak." The stories mythologized Benya Krik, a gangster whose fictitious name, in vintage Babelesque fashion, encodes Judaic and Slavic meaning: "Ben Zion the Scream." Babel's fascination with the Odessan underworld betrayed a fantasy of "strong" self-empowered Jews who would feel adequate to Gentiles in every way. In "How It Was Done in Odessa" one reads: "You can spend the night with a Russian woman, and the Russian woman will be satisfied with you. You are twenty-five years old. If heaven and earth had rings attached to them, you would seize hold of those rings and pull heaven down to earth . . . And that is why [Benya Krik] is the King, while you are nothing" (trans. David McDuff). Babel composed two other stories with the subtitle "from Odessan stories," and all six constitute a strand of his fiction. Additionally, Babel used gangster material as the basis of the screenplay *Benya Krik* (1926) and a stage play *Sunset* (1928), which Sergey Eisenstein called "the best . . . post-October play in terms of the mastery of drama."

The third distinct unit in the corpus of Babel's short fiction (about eighty altogether) is composed of the "autobiographical" childhood stories. Spanning fifteen years of Babel's writing and set in Nikolaev and Odessa, they feature an autobiographical protagonist-narrator, aged nine to fourteen. Babel composed the first, "Childhood. At Grandmother's," in 1915. The most famous of the childhood cycle, "The Story of My Dovecote," was dated 1925. Babel referred to these stories as his "cherished labor," returning to his childhood in 1929–30 and hoping to have a book ready in 1939. Finally, there are Babel's stories unconnected to cycles. They include such metafictional masterpieces as "Guy de Maupassant" (1920–22; published 1932), a favorite of American creative writing workshops, and "Line and Color" (1923), Babel's manifesto about art and ideology with a glimpse of Trotsky's speech.

Odessa constitutes an overarching text in Babel's life and art, figuring prominently not only in his fiction and drama but also in his discursive writings. Babel identified with a group of writers from Odessa and the Black Sea coast, most of them Jewish, who poured onto the literary scene in the late 1910s–early 1920s. Termed the Southwestern school by **Viktor Shklovsky**, the constellation included **Eduard Bagritsky, Ilya Ilf** and **Evgeny Petrov**, Valentin Kataev, Yury Olesha, Zinaida Shishova (Brukhnova), Konstantin Paustovsky, and others. In a preface to a 1925 collection by Odessan writers that never appeared, what Babel wrote of his friend's vibrancy and *joie de vivre* fully applied to his own writings: "Bagritsky is full of purple moisture like a watermelon that in the remote days of our youth he and I would break open against the bollards of Pratique Harbor [in Odessa]."

By 1925, most of the Southwesterners had migrated to Moscow, which became Babel's home literary base. Evgenia Gronshtein, whom Babel had married in 1919, moved abroad in 1925. For over a year, in 1927–28, Babel stayed abroad. His daughter Nathalie, who later edited his publications in the West, was born in Paris in 1929. Babel once again joined his family in 1932, returning to Russia alone the following year. In 1935, Babel made his last visit abroad, attending the Anti-Fascist International Congress of Writers for Peace in Paris. His peregrinations, and especially the fact that he returned when he could have stayed abroad, puzzle his students. In 1934, Babel started a second family in Moscow with the engineer Antonina Pirozhkova, who bore Babel a daughter, Lidia, in 1937.

Babel's work in the cinema began in the late 1920s, when he did the intertitles for a movie based on Sholem Aleichem's *Wandering Stars*. In 1936, he and Sergey Eisenstein coauthored the screenplay for *Bezhin Meadow*; the film was banned and destroyed. Babel also wrote another stage play, *Maria* (1935), inferior to *Sunset*. Babel published a small number of new stories in the 1930s, as his previous ones were reprinted in various collections. "The Trial," the last short story published in Babel's lifetime, appeared in 1938. Although at the First Congress of Soviet Writers Babel referred to himself as a "master of silence," he never stopped writing. After visiting areas of so-called "total collectivization" of agriculture in 1930–31, Babel worked on a novel under the provisional title *Velikaya Krinitsa* (fictionalized name of Velikaya Staritsa, a village outside Kiev). The manuscript apparently disappeared after Babel's arrest in 1939. Only one chapter, "Gapa Guzhva," was published in 1931; another chapter, "Kolyvushka," survived and appeared in 1963 in New York.

In 1969, A New York–based émigré journal published a fragment from another unfinished work, "The Jewess," in which a widow leaves a decaying small town to live in Moscow with her son, a Red Army commander. Like this story, several other works published in the 1930s placed the theological and ideological gaps between Jewish parents and their Sovietized children at center stage. Babel's gentle authorial humor helped surmount the courtroom confrontation in "Karl-Yankel" (1931), in which a Jewish infant, circumcised by his grandmother against his father's will, receives a hyphenated name, after *Karl* Marx and *Jacob* the Patriarch. More problematic is the message of "The Journey," an autobiographical, if fictionalized, story Babel published in 1932. Dated 1920–30, it sets the protagonist's service at the Cheka, portrayed as a joyful camaraderie, against the virulent antisemitic violence that he encounters en route from the Pale to Petrograd. As usual, the difficulty with Babel is to ascertain the degree of fictionalization as well as the extent of his romantic-ironic authorial detachment. He was also contemplating an entire novel about the *chekisty*.

Babel, who had had ties to former NKVD chief Nikolay Ezhov (1894–1940) and other officers of the Soviet secret police, was arrested in Peredelkino on 15 May 1939. A number of unfinished works apparently disappeared after the arrest. (The fate of Babel's confiscated papers continues to fuel the imaginations of scholars and writers alike; as Carol J. Avins demonstrated in 2003, the protagonist of *Vast Emotions and Imperfect Thoughts*, a 1988 novel by the Brazilian writer Rubem Fonseca, is obsessed with the prospect of possessing a Babel manuscript stolen from Soviet archives.) Babel was executed in Moscow on 27 January 1940 on charges of espionage and conspiracy. During the Thaw, **Ilya Ehrenburg** steered Babel's works back to print and wrote an introduction to the 1957 Soviet edition of Babel's *Selected Works*. Only a few book editions of Babel's works had appeared in the USSR by 1990, when a two-volume edition was prepared there by his widow Antonina Pirozhkova. It came out in 1991–92.

The first English translation of *Red Cavalry* appeared in 1929. Furnished with Lionel Trilling's introduction, Walter Morrison's 1955 translation of *Collected Stories* made Babel a household name in Anglo-American letters. Maurice Friedberg, Shimon Markish, and Efraim Sicher wrote poignantly in the 1970s–90s about the "Jewishness" of Babel. David McDuff's Penguin volume of Babel's *Collected Stories* appeared in 1995. Babel's popularity with the Anglo-American reader is likely to continue now that *The Complete Works of Isaac Babel* (2002), edited by Nathalie Babel, translated by Peter Constantive and introduced by Cynthia Ozick, are available in English, and also with the recent publication of new books of Babel's translations by Val Vunokur and by Boris Dralyuk. Babel's genius continues to elude English translators as his legacy continues to attract new translators, scholars, and biographers. Among the recent smattering of publications about Babel is the book *Between Walls of Fire* (2017) by the Russian-Israeli author Michael Weisskopf. Also noteworthy is the 2014 comprehensive German edition of Babel, translated by Bettina Kaibach and Peter Urban and edited by Urs Heftrich.

* * *

The Odessan Jew Isaac Babel was an incomparable master and manipulator of the Russian language. His short stories are structured and textured like highly self-conscious poetic texts; a single object, reference, or trope often builds up and unfolds into a narrative entanglement. In "The Story of My Dovecote," the dove, both a shared universal (also Judeo-Christian) symbol of peace, hope, and renewal (e.g., Noah's dove) and a specifically Christian symbol (the Holy Spirit), becomes an instrument of antisemitic violence. In "First Love," the patronymic of the Russian woman, Galina Apollonovna, signals connections with both Greek mythology and Nietzschean thought. Babel was in some ways an embodiment of the rich heritage of both classic Yiddish storytelling (S. Y. Abramovich and Sholem Aleichem, both of whom he translated) and Hasidic folklore. His texts sparkle with subtle Hebrew and Yiddish verbal play.

A grand European belletrist, Babel is also one whose works concentrated most profoundly on the parameters of the Jewish experience: violence and antisemitism; Jewish-Christian relations; Jews and the revolution; and recastings of the Jewish identity. A witness to the destruction of the Pale in the areas that had fallen under Soviet control, Babel recounted the uprooting of communal Jewish life, in both rural and urban settings. His humor, ranging from the hilariously hysterical (reciting Julius Ceasar in the story "In the Basement") to the lyrically perverse (earned love lessons from a prostitute in "My First Honorarium"), teeters on the brink of tears. Babel wrote some of the greatest tales about the psycho-sexual, ideological, linguistic, and religious trauma of the Jewish youths who discover "that world" and seek an "escape."

Until the seventh, expanded edition of *Red Cavalry*, where the story "Argamak" was added to uplift the tone of the ending, "The Rabbi's Son" (1924) was the book's final story. Both the title of Babel's story and the last name of its young Jewish protagonist reveal Babel's dialogue with one of the most famous tales by the Hasidic leader Rabbi Nahman of Bratslav (1772–1811), recorded by his disciple Rabbi Nathan Sternharz.

Composed in 1930 and published in 1931, "Awakening" belongs to the cycle of Babel's "autobiographical" stories.

THE RABBI'S SON

. . . Vasily, do you remember Zhitomir?[81] Vasily, do you still remember the Teterev and the night when the Sabbath, the maiden Sabbath, stole along the sunset, squashing the stars with her little red heel?

The thin crescent moon bathed its arrows in the black water of the Teterev. Comical Gedali, the founder of the Fourth International, led us to evening prayers at Rabbi Motele Bratslavsky's.[82] Comical Gedali fanned the cockerel feathers of his top hat in the evening's red smoke. The predatory eyes of candles blinked in the Rabbi's room. Bent over prayer books, broad-shouldered Jews moaned sonorously, and the old jester of Chernobyl tzaddiks jingled copper coins in his shredded pocket. . . .

. . . Do you remember that night, Vasily? . . . Outside the window, horses neighed and Cossacks hooted. The desert of war was gaping outside the window, and Rabbi Motele Bratslavsky, his withering fingers clutching his talles, prayed at the eastern wall. Then the curtain of the cabinet was pulled back, and the funereal glow of candles revealed the Torah scrolls, wrapped in mantles of purple velvet and blue silk, and also the lifeless, acquiescent, beautiful face of Ilya, the Rabbi's son, the last prince of the dynasty, drooping over the Torah. . . .

And then, Vasily, just two days ago, regiments of the Twelfth Army opened the front at Kovel.[83] The victors' contemptuous cannonade rattled through the town. Our troops caved in and were trapped. The train of the Political Department started crawling away across the lifeless back of the fields. The typhus-stricken peasantry moved forward, trundling the customary hump of soldiers' death. The peasants jumped onto the footboards of our train and fell back, knocked down by the strikes of rifle butts. They huffed, were scraped,

---

81 Zhitomir—provincial capital in north-central Ukraine, on the river Teterev; center of Jewish Hebrew book printing in nineteenth-century Russia; site of a 1905 pogrom; in 1897, about 31,000 Jews lived in Zhitomir, or 47 percent of the population.

82 The name Bratslavsky is derived from Bratslav, a town in Ukraine that became a major center of Hassidism after the famous tzaddik Nahman of Bratslav (1772–1811) settled there in 1802 and lived there until 1810.

83 Kovel—town in western Ukraine, forty-three miles west of Lutsk, the capital of Volhyn Province; in 1897, about 8,500 Jews resided in Kovel, or 48 percent of the population.

flew forward, and kept silent. And at the twelfth verst[84] mark, when I had run out of potatoes, I flung a pile of Trotsky's leaflets at them. Yet only one of them extended a dirty dead hand to grab a leaflet. Then I recognized Ilya, the son of the Zhitomir Rabbi. I recognized him immediately, Vasily. And it was such a torment to see the prince—he'd lost his pants and was broken in half by a soldier's duffel bag—that we broke regulations and pulled him into our train car. Bare knees, as clumsy as those of an old woman, knocked against the rusty metal of the steps; two buxom typists clad in sailor's robes dragged the dying man's long, timorous body along the floor. We laid him down in the corner of the editorial office, on the floor. Cossacks in wide red trousers straightened his undone clothes. The young ladies, pressing the crooked legs of unsophisticated females into the floor, soberly perused his sexual parts—that shrunken, curly masculinity of an expiring Semite. And I, who had seen him during one of my vagabond nights, I began to arrange all the scattered belongings of the Red Army soldier Bratslavsky in a small trunk.

Everything was dumped together: mandates of a political agitator and memos of a Jewish poet; portraits of Lenin and Maimonides lay there side by side; the nodulous iron of Lenin's skull and the dull luster of silk in Maimonides's portraits; a lock of hair was pressed into a booklet of Sixth Party Congress resolutions; and crooked lines of ancient Hebrew verse crowded the margins of Communist leaflets. They descended upon me like a dismal, scanty rain: pages of the "Song of Songs" and revolver cartridges. The sunset's dismal rain washed the dust from my hair, and I said to the young man dying in the corner on a torn pallet:

"Four months ago, on a Friday night, the used-goods dealer Gedali brought me to see your father, Rabbi Motele, but you weren't in the Party then, Bratslavsky."

"I had already joined the Party," the boy answered, scratching his chest and writhing with fever. "But I couldn't abandon my mother . . ."

"And now, Ilya?"

"In a Revolution, a mother is but an episode," he whispered and quieted down. "My letter, the letter B, came up, and the organization dispatched me to the front . . ."

"And you ended up in Kovel, Ilya?"

---

84   Verst—an old Russian measure of distance, equivalent to about 1.66 miles or 1.1 km.

"I ended up in Kovel!" he screamed in despair. "The kulak horde opened a front. I assumed command of a joint regiment, but too late. I ran out of artillery . . ."

He died before we reached Rovno.[85] He died, the last prince, amid verses, phylacteries, and footwraps. We buried him at a forsaken junction. And I, barely containing the storms of imagination in my ancient body, I received my brother's final breath.

1924

Translated from the Russian by Maxim D. Shrayer

AWAKENING

All the people in our circle—brokers, shopkeepers, bank clerks, and steam-ship office workers—taught their children music. Our fathers, seeing no future for themselves, came up with a lottery. They played it out on the bones of little people. More than any other city, Odessa was possessed with this madness. And it's true—for decades our city supplied the con-cert halls of the entire world with wunderkinds. Mischa Elman, Zimbalist, Gabrilowitsch came from Odessa, and Jascha Heifetz started out in our city.[86]

When a boy turned four or five years old, his mother took this puny, feeble creature to see Mr. Zagursky. Zagursky ran a factory of wunderkinds, a factory of Jewish dwarfs in lacy collars and little patent-leather shoes. He sought them out in the slums of Moldavanka,[87] in the stinky courtyards of the Old Bazaar. Zagursky offered the initial direction, and then the children were sent to Professor Auer in St. Petersburg. A powerful harmony lived in the souls of these starvelings with blue bloated heads. They became renowned

---

85 Rovno—provincial capital in western Ukraine; in 1897 about 14,000 Jews, or 56 percent of the total population, were living there.

86 Elman, Mischa (1891–1967), born in Kiev and raised in Odessa; Zimbalist Efrem (1889–1985), born in Rostov on Don; Heifetz, Jascha (1901–1987), born in Vilna (Vilnius)—Russian-American violinists. Elman Zimbalist and Heifetz studied in St. Petersburg with Leopold Auer. Gabrilowitsch, Ossip (1978–1936)—Russian-American pianist, born in St. Petersburg of Odessan ancestry.

87 Moldavanka—a historic section of Odessa; in the early twentieth century, Moldavanka was still a low-income area with workers' tenements; the site of Babel's cycle of stories about Odessa's Jewish gangsters.

virtuosi. And so my father decided to follow in their stead. Even though I had long since exceeded the age of wunderkinds—I was over thirteen—my height and puny physique made it possible for me to pass for an eight-year-old. That was the hope.

I was taken to see Zagursky.[88] Out of respect for grandfather, he agreed to charge one ruble per lesson—a cheap rate. My grandfather Leivi-Itskhok was the city's laughing stock and its adornment. He walked around the streets in a top hat and decrepit cut-off boots and helped resolve some of the most opaque arguments. He was asked to explain what a tapestry was, why the Jacobins betrayed Robespierre, how artificial silk is produced, how a cesarean section is performed. My grandfather could answer all these questions. Out of respect for his learnedness and madness, Zagursky charged us one ruble per lesson. And in fact, he made an effort with me, only because he feared my grandfather, because in fact there was nothing to make an effort with. Sounds slipped off my violin like metal shavings. These sounds sliced even my heart, but my father wouldn't give up. At home all they talked about was Mischa Elman, whom the tsar himself had released from military service. Zimbalist, according to my father's information, was introduced to the British king and played at Buckingham Palace. Gabrilowitsch's parents bought two houses in St. Petersburg. Wunderkinds brought wealth to their parents. My father would have reconciled himself to poverty, but he craved fame.

"Impossible," whispered those who ate dinner at his expense, "it's impossible that the grandson of such a grandfather . . ."

But I had something different in mind. While playing through some violin etudes, I placed books by Turgenev or Dumas on the music stand, and while sawing away, I devoured page after page. During the day, I told tall tales to the neighborhood kids, and at night I transferred them onto paper. Composing fiction was a hereditary occupation in our family. Leivi-Itskhok, having gone off his rocker in his old age, had for years been writing a tale titled *Man without a Head*. I took after him.

Three times a week, encumbered by my violin case and music sheets, I dragged myself to Witte Street, the former Dvoryanskaya,[89] to Zagursky's.

---

88 Fictitious name—Zagursky's prototype was P. S. Stolyarsky (1871–1944), violinist and violin teacher in Odessa; Stolyarsky was a student of Leopold Auer (1845–1930), violinist and conductor, a professor of the St. Petersburg Conservatory of Music.

89 The name of Dvoryanskaya Street literally refers to *dvoryanstvo*, the Russian nobility, hence a certain symbolism in the story of a Jewish boy's awakening in a country where Jews were

There, along the walls, awaiting their turn, sat Jewesses, their hysteria flaring. They pressed violins that exceeded the size of the children who were expected to perform at Buckingham Palace to their weak knees.

The sanctuary door would open. Brainy, freckled children would emerge from Zagursky's office—unsteady on their feet, necks thin as flower stems, a manic fervor burning on their cheeks. The door would slam, swallowing the next dwarf. Behind the wall, straining himself, the teacher would sing and conduct with a bow, reddish curls, and frail legs. The director of a monstrous lottery, he populated Moldavanka and the black cul-de-sacs of the Old Bazar with specters of pizzicato and cantilena. Later old Professor Auer would propel these tones to a diabolical brilliance.

There was nothing for me to do in this sect. Though a dwarf like the rest of them, I detected a different calling in the voice of my ancestors.

The first step was the hardest to make. One day I left home, saddled with the violin, its case, music, and twelve rubles in cash—the monthly payment for my lessons. I was walking down Nezhinskaya Street, and I should've turned onto Dvoryanskaya in order to get to Zagursky's place, but instead I went up Tiraspolskaya Street and found myself in the port. I was allotted three hours, and they passed swiftly in Practique Harbor.[90] Thus began my liberation. Zagursky's anteroom never saw me again. More important matters took hold of all my existence. My classmate Nemanov and I now took to visiting an old sailor by the name of Mr. Trottyburn on board the steamship *Kensington*. A year my junior, Nemanov had been engaging in the most elaborate commerce in the world since the age of eight. He was a genius of commercial operations, and he fulfilled all his dreams. He's now a millionaire in New York, director of General Motors, a company as mighty as Ford. Nemanov dragged me around with him because I obeyed him without a word. He bought contraband tobacco pipes from Mr. Trottyburn. The old sailor's brother in Lincoln handcrafted these pipes.

"Gentlemen," Trottyburn would say to us, "mark my words. One should make babies with one's own hands . . . To smoke a factory-made pipe is the same as putting an enema into your mouth . . . Do you know who Benvenuto Cellini was? . . . Now that was a great master. My brother in Lincoln could tell you about him. My brother doesn't get in other people's way. But he's convinced

---

legally disenfranchised. The street was renamed Witte Street to honor Count Sergey Witte (1849–1915), Russia first prime minister and one of Russia's most influential politicians, who had a strong connection to the city of Odessa.

90 Practique Harbor (Rus.: *Prakticheskaya gavan'*).

that one should make babies with one's own hands, not other people's . . . We cannot but agree with him, gentlemen."

Nemanov sold Trottyburn's pipes to bank directors, foreign consuls, rich Greeks—with a hundred percent mark up.

The Lincoln master's pipes breathed poetry. Each of them was invested with thought, that small drop of eternity. A yellow eye shone through their mouthpieces; their cases were lined with lustrous silk. I tried to imagine the life of Matthew Trottyburn in old England, the life of the last master of tobacco pipes, he who opposes the progress of things.

"We cannot but agree, gentlemen, that one should make babies with one's one hands . . ."

The heavy waves breaking against the sea wall separated me further and further from our home, redolent with onion and Jewish destiny. From Practique Harbor I relocated to the breakwater. There, on a scrap of a sandy bar, kids from Primorskaya Street hung out. From morning till night they refused to pull on their pants, diving under the scows, stealing coconuts for lunch, and waiting for the time of year when flat-bottomed vessels loaded with watermelons would start coming in from Kherson and Kamenka, and you could break the watermelons open against the moorings right there in the port.

Knowing how to swim became my dream. I was ashamed to admit to those bronzy boys that I, even though born in Odessa, hadn't even seen the sea until the age of ten and at fourteen still couldn't swim.

I had to learn such necessary things so late! As a child, nailed to the Gemara,[91] I led the life of a sage; having grown up, I started climbing trees.

Knowing how to swim turned out to be unattainable. Fear of water on the part of all my ancestors—Spanish rabbis and Frankfurt moneychangers—pulled me down to the bottom. Water didn't hold me up. Whipped up and down, soaked with salt water, I would return to the shore—to my violin and music. I was tied to the weapons of my crime and lugged them around with me. The battle of the rabbis with the sea lasted until the moment when a local water God took pity on me. He was the proofreader for the *Odessa News*, Efim Nikitich Smolich. Empathy for Jewish boys lived in this man's athletic chest. He reigned over swarms of rickety starvelings. Efim Nikitich collected them in the bedbug-infested cellars of Moldavanka, led them to the sea, buried them to the neck in the sand, did calisthenics with them, took

---

91 Gemara—integral component of the Talmud, both a commentary on and a supplement to the Mishnah.

them diving, taught them songs, and while they were roasting in direct sunlight, told them stories about fishermen and animals. Smolich explained to adults that he was an adherent of natural philosophy. Smolich's stories made Jewish children explode with laughter; they squealed and nuzzled up to him like puppies. The sun sprinkled them with creeping freckles, freckles the color of lizards.

The old man silently observed my struggle with the waves from the sidelines. After seeing that there was no hope and I wasn't meant to learn how to swim, he added me to the permanent residents of his heart. All of it was there with us; his merry heart never condescended, was never greedy or anxious . . . With his copper shoulders, the head of an aged gladiator, with his bronze, slightly bandy legs, he would lie among us behind the breakwater like a lord of those watermelon and kerosene waters. I grew to love this man the way only a boy suffering from hysterics and headaches could love an athlete. I stayed by his side and tried to ingratiate myself to him.

He said to me:

"Don't worry . . . Work on strengthening your nerves. Swimming will come to you naturally . . . What do you mean the water doesn't hold you up . . . Why shouldn't it hold you up?"

Seeing how I felt, Smolich made an exception only for me among his disciples. He invited me to his clean, spacious attic covered in jute rugs, showed me his dogs, his hedgehog, his tortoise, his doves. In exchange for these treasures, I brought him a tragedy I had just composed.

"I just knew you dabbled in writing," said Smolich. "You have that look . . . More and more you're looking nowhere . . ."

He read my compositions, shrugged a shoulder, ran his hand through his tight grey curls, walked across the attic.

"I wouldn't be surprised," he drew out, growing silent after each word, "if you had a divine spark within you . . ."

We went out onto the street. The old man stopped, struck the pavement with his stick, and set his gaze on me.

"What is it that you lack? . . . Youth isn't a problem, you'll get over it with time . . . What you lack is a feeling for nature."

He pointed his walking stick at a tree with a reddish trunk and low crown.

"What kind of tree is that?"

I didn't know.

"What's growing on that bush?"

I didn't know that either. The two of us were strolling through a little park on Alexandrovsky Prospect. The old man aimed his stick at every tree, he grabbed my shoulder when a bird flew by and made me listen to different birdcalls.

"What bird is singing now?"

I couldn't answer his questions. Names of trees and birds, their division into genera, where birds flew, from which direction the sun rose, when dew was heavier—all of that was unknown to me.

"And you have the audacity to write? . . . A person who doesn't live in nature, the way a stone or an animal does, won't come up with two decent lines in his entire life . . . Your landscapes resemble descriptions of set designs. For God's sake, what have your parents been thinking about for fourteen years? . . ."

What have they been thinking about? . . . Disputed IOUs, Mischa Elman's mansions . . . I never said this to Smolich; I held back.

At home, during supper, I didn't touch my food. It wouldn't go down my throat.

"A feeling for nature," I was thinking. "My dear God, why hadn't I thought of it before? . . . Where would I find a person who would interpret birdcalls and names of trees for me? . . . What do I know about them? I might have been able to identify lilacs, and only when they were in bloom. Lilacs and acacias. Deribasovskaya and Grecheskaya Streets[92] were lined with acacias . . ."

Over supper, my father told a new story about Jascha Heifetz. Before he got to Robin's, he ran into Mendelsohn, Jascha's uncle. The boy, it turns out, takes in eight hundred rubles for each appearance. Calculate how much it comes to with fifteen concerts every month.

I calculated—it came to twelve thousand a month. Multiplying and carrying the four in my head, I looked out the window. Striding across the narrow cement courtyard, his Inverness coat gently fluttering in the wind, reddish ringlets jutting out from under his soft fedora, strode Mr. Zagursky, my music teacher, leaning on a cane. One couldn't say that he discovered my absence too early. More than three months had already passed since the day my violin had been deposited on the sand beside the breakwater . . . Zagursky approached the front door. I dashed to the back entrance, which had just the day before been nailed shut as a protection against burglars. Then I locked myself in the water

---

92 Deribasovskaya Street—one of Odessa's most famous central streets, much of it closed to traffic and lined with stores and cafés. Grecheskaya (literally: Greek) Street—one of Odessa's oldest streets, where historically members of the city's Greek community settled.

closet. Half an hour later, the entire family gathered outside the door. Women cried. My aunt Bobka rubbed her fat shoulder against the door and burst into a fit of sobbing. My father was silent. Then he spoke more quietly and distinctly than he had ever spoken in his life.

"I'm an officer in the army," said my father. "I have a country estate. I go hunting. The peasants pay me rent. I placed my son in a military boarding school. I don't need to worry about my son . . ."

He stopped. Women were sniveling. Then a terrifying blow shook the water closet door. My father slammed his whole body against the door; he kept throwing himself at it.

"I'm an officer," he wailed. "I go hunting . . . I'll kill him . . . The end . . ."

The hook snapped off; there was also a latch, but it held by one nail. Women rolled on the floor. They clung to my father's legs; enraged, he pulled away. My father's elderly mother heard the noise and got there just in time.

"My child," she said to him in Yiddish, "our sorrow is great. It is boundless. The last thing we need is bloodshed in our home. I don't wish to see bloodshed in our home . . ."

My father groaned. I heard his departing steps. The latch barely hung by the last nail.

I sat until nightfall in my fortress. When everything settled, my aunt Bobka took me to grandmother's. It was a long walk. Moonlight froze in unfamiliar bushes, in trees without names . . . An invisible bird whistled and expired, perhaps falling asleep . . . What bird was that? What's it called? Is there dew in the evening? . . . Where's the Big Dipper in the sky? From which direction does the sun rise? . . .

We walked along Pochtovaya Street. Aunt Bobka firmly gripped my hand so I wouldn't run away. She was right. I was thinking of escape.

1931

Translated from the Russian by Maxim D. Shrayer

Isaac Babel, "Syn rabbi" and "Probuzhdenie." English translation © by Maxim D. Shrayer. Introduction and notes copyright © by Maxim D. Shrayer.

VERA INBER

Vera Inber (1890–1972), poet, prose writer, translator, and playwright, was born in Odessa. Her father, Moisey Shpentser, operated the Methesis publishing house, and her mother ran a school for Jewish girls. Leon Trotsky (1879–1940), her father's cousin, had been raised in their home; this connection later haunted Inber. Inber took the last name of her first husband, with whom she had a daughter, the writer Zhanna Gauzner (1912–1962).

After graduating from a gymnasium, Inber entered Odessa's Higher Women's Courses but soon left for Europe, spending four years there. From her early poems, Inber's writing was marked by what the Moscow critic Inna Rodnyanskaya identified as "stylish, sober irony" and by elegance of form. In 1914, Inber's first collection, *Melancholy Wine*, appeared in Paris in Russian. Critics pointed out the influence of Anna Akhmatova (1889–1966) on Inber's lyrical personae. Acmeist—and symbolist—influences aside, Inber's early poems testified to her authentic poetic sensibility. *Bitter Delight* (Petrograd, 1917) and *Wasteful Words* (Odessa, 1922) signaled a developing interest in description and landscape and a growth of narrativism.

In 1922, Inber moved to Moscow. After joining the Literary Center of Constructivists (LTsK; see **Ilya Selvinsky**), she incorporated into her verses the constructivist emphasis on the "semantic dominant." Political and industrial themes entered Inber's writing in the mid-1920s. Her *Goal and Path* (1924) contained a poem dedicated to Trotsky, as well as verses about Lenin's funeral. To the constructivist collective *The State Plan of Literature* (1925), Inber contributed the long poem *Black Coal*; she also contributed to *Business* (1929), the third and final LTsK collective. Inber's poems of 1924–26 were gathered in *To the Son I Don't Have* (1927). Although Inber is commonly remembered as a poet, her greatest achievement was not in poetry but in fiction. Collections of her stories included *Nightingale and Rose* (1925), *Stories* (1926), *Catcher of Comets* (1927), and others. *Place under the Sun* (1928), her autobiographical "lyrical chronicle," enjoyed success. The 1920s were Inber's most prolific decade, as evidenced by her six-volume *Collected Works* (1928–30).

Shifting gears, Inber wrote with romantic enthusiasm about socialist construction (e.g., her 1932 *Poems*). She participated in the 1935 collective volume about the Belomor Canal (see also **Viktor Shklovsky**). Safely Soviet,

Inber's 1935 collection *Lane of My Name* preserved nuggets of talent, as did her long poems *Travel Diary* (1939, a Stalinist overture about Georgia) and *Ovid* (1941).

Staying in Leningrad during the nine-hundred-day Nazi siege, Inber wrote about the city and its defenders. She worked at the Soviet Information Bureau and joined the Communist Party in 1943. Inber's wartime books included *The Soul of Leningrad: Poems 1941–42* (1942) and *Diary: Almost Three Years* (1946; English: *Leningrad Diary*). Her famous long poem *The Pulkovo Meridian* (1942) received the Stalin Prize in 1946; a Hebrew version soon appeared in Israel, translated by Avraham Shlonsky (1900–1973), founder of the symbolist school in Hebrew poetry. To the derailed *Black Book* (see **Ilya Ehrenburg** and **Vasily Grossman**), Inber contributed a section on the Nazi and Romanian atrocities in her native Odessa.

After the war, Inber continued to publish poetry (e.g., *April: Poems about Lenin* [1960]) and essays about writing. She held positions of prominence in the Union of Soviet Writers, behaving ignobly during the Pasternak affair (1958; see **Boris Pasternak**). Inber's four-volume *Works*, both censored and self-censored, came out in 1965–66.

* * *

Jewish characters and themes took center stage in Inber's stories of the 1920s. Endurance of antisemitism was the subject of "Garlic in the Suitcase" (1926; title story of Inber's 1927 collection), and memories of pogroms informed "Parallel and Essential" (1929). Four Jewish stories stand out: "The Nightingale and the Rose" (1924; text below; title story of a 1925 collection), "Hayim Egudovich's Liver" (1924), "Exceptions Do Occur" (1925; title story of a 1927 collection), and "Equation with One Unknown" (1926; title story of a 1926 collection). With representatives of the Southwestern school, Inber's prose shared a sensation of being blissfully alive in language. While Inber's stories of the 1920s may remind today's readers of **Isaac Babel's** irony and of Yury Olesha's crystalline keenness, they were original and deserve to be read anew.

Set during the NEP (New Economic Policy), Inber's "The Nightingale and the Rose" appeared in the Moscow magazine *Searchlight* (*Prozhektor*) in 1925. In addition to the prominence of the motif in classical Persian poetry (Hafiz, Rudaki, Saadi) and its imitations by Aleksandr Pushkin, Afanasy Fet, and other nineteenth-century Russian poets, the title brings to mind Oscar Wilde's "The Nightingale and the Rose" (1891).

The story's Russian title is "Solovey i Roza." "Solovey" (literally "nightingale"), both the name of the bird and the last name of the Jewish tailor, is familiar to readers from Sholem Aleichem's novel *Yossele Solovey* (1889). "Roza" (literally "rose") is both the name of the flower and the first name of Nightingale's wife. The first name of the tailor, Emmanuel (Immanuel), means "god will us" in Hebrew (see Isaiah 7).

THE NIGHTINGALE AND THE ROSE

1

Here's my recipe for spring: fresh, sharp leaf buds, with sun poured over them, left to open slowly on an old black poplar (breathe the scent in deeply—could anything be more wonderful?). Then have a slender new moon rise above the whipped-cream clouds: it looks vast, far larger than the roundest full one. Just at that moment, stir in a heavy warm rain, falling slowly, no more than a drop a minute. The bundle of small, round, dark-blue domes over the little centuries-old church on Uspensky Lane[93] will start shining, reflecting the starlight. And in the herb-scented churchyard, the sound of kisses will ring out: one long note and two short ones. And there you have it: city springtime in the 1920s.

Spiced by accordion music from a basement bakery and the roar of distant trams like surf on a seashore, spring like that goes down a treat. The problem is, once you've swallowed it, it's hard to digest, and you get heartburn. Southern countries have their own kinds of spring, much more imposingly luxuriant: real classical springs, with roses and nightingales. But there are roses and nightingales in this town, too, if you know where to look for them. And the nightingales sound just as yearning under a pallid northern sky, and the thorns on the rose are just as sharp. It's the classic recipe for spring.

If you know where to look, you can find a nightingale on Uspensky Lane as well. See the house opposite the church with the dark-blue onion domes, the one with the bakery in the basement, where the accordion music comes from in the evenings. On the ground floor is Emmanuel Nightingale's tailoring workshop, "Orders taken for military uniforms and gentlemen's suits. Repairs also carried out."

Nightingale the tailor is put together this way: long skinny legs, stooped shoulders, balding gingery hair, and bright blue eyes with a slightly absent look

---

93 Uspensky Lane = literally "Assumption" Lane.

in them. You won't often see a Jew from Minsk with eyes that bright blue color, but if it happens, you can be sure they'll have exactly that other-worldly expression. They're the eyes of someone who's still afloat in Noah's Ark, who's still looking down on the earth from the height of Mount Ararat.

People ordering suits from tailor Nightingale who didn't know the man very well sometimes took fright when they saw his eyes. This bodes no good, they'd think; you can tell what kind of suit you'll get here: the lines down the sides of your trousers will be skewed, your jacket lapels will be as wide as the runners on a car, and the collar will be jibbing you in the neck like no one's business.

But only people who didn't know tailor Nightingale well thought that.

The man was transfigured by his work. His eyes narrowing like a snake charmer's, chalk held fast in his hand, pins in his mouth, and a tape measure around his neck, he'd get going on his magic. And the cross-grained cloth would submit to his creative powers, the swirling chaos of suiting turn into a smooth linear flow.

As he worked, tailor Nightingale, undaunted by his mouthful of pins, would sing select passages of the Song of Songs, set to tunes of his own devising. His favorite place was Shulamith's fragrant verse: "Sustain me with raisin cakes, refresh me with apples, for I am faint with love."[94] And, hearing his rising descant, the tailor's wife Rose (every Nightingale must have his Rose, as you see) would say to five-year-old Izzie, a born hooligan if ever there was one:

"Izzie, put the hammer down, for heaven's sake! Do you hear me? You know perfectly well your father's singing 'I am faint with love.' He must be working on the sleeves then. He needs quiet."

"Don't wannoo," Izzie would say, driving yet another nail into the croup of his long-suffering toy horse.

Rose the tailor's wife was full blown and had plenty of thorns. She loved Nightingale and was violently jealous of all the other flowers in the world. And especially the baker's wife, Klavdiya Makarovna, who was as circular and plump as a fresh currant bun, with a deep dimple on her chin like the cicatrix of a dropped-out raisin.

"Why does that hussy Klavdiya always look at you in that funny way, out of the corner of her eyes?" she would say, as they lay down together on their big goose feather bed. "Why does she look at me in that funny way too? She's got something on her conscience, Emmanuel. Mannie, Mannie, I can tell you like her really."

---

94 See Song of Songs 2:5.

"Rosie my dear," Nightingale would object from under the big puffy comforter.

"How could you even think such a thing?"

"Well then. And so what was you saying to her this morning, while you was ironing that gray weskit, eh?"

"Rosie, I didn't say nothing to her, she just said to me it looked like the cold would be lasting into May, Rosie."

"Well then, the cold would be lasting would it, Emmanuel. So what did you say to her then, Emmanuel?"

"I said to her, Rosie, just that same way, dead cold—and how could you suppose anything else, for heaven's sake? I said to her, and even little Izzie could hear what I was saying, it was that loud . . . Rosie, my honeybunch, move up a little, will you? I can't hardly breathe. That's it, my sweetheart . . ."

And Rose would hide her thorns and turn, fragrant with love, toward her Nightingale. An hour or two. Afterward, Rose would sleep gently, but Nightingale would lie awake. In the corner of the bedroom, which also served as the workshop, stood a wooden dummy, almost always with an unfinished jacket hanging on it. With a crafty wink of its top button, the jacket would start a telepathic conversation with Nightingale:

"What, mate," the jacket would say, "not sleeping again? It's high time you was getting some rest. There's lots to do tomorrow. I dropped you a heavy hint yesterday when you was doing the fitting: those darts aren't in the right place."

"Never mind the darts," Nightingale would answer, with a thoughtful flash of his bright blue eyes. "Never mind them, I say. It's my heart that's not in the right place."

"What do you mean?" the jacket would ask, the top of its pocket dropping open in surprise. "What do you mean? Hang on, I've got to hear this . . . Rose and you . . ."

"My Rose, Rosalia Abramovna, and me, we're just fine together! And little Izzie's a wonderful boy; there his is, sleeping in his cot now, still as a thimble. But what does Shulamith say about all that, eh? Upon my couch at night I sought the one I love—I sought him, but found him not."[95]

"I don't get this," the jacket would say, wrinkling its lapel. "Emmanuel, you shock me. Do you really mean to say family life don't make you happy?"

"Shut your face, you no-good lounge lizard," Nightingale would snap, annoyed. "You double-breasted scoundrel, you. You're trying to push me into

---

95 See Song of Songs 3:1.

saying something I'll regret. I can see straight through you. You've got white stab-stitching all over you, you have, and a cheap shiny lining."

And turning his back on the jacket, Nightingale would fall sound asleep.

2

One snowy morning, there was a ring at the door.

"That'll be someone to collect the uniform jacket you made for that shady type Well-Yessabut," Rose says. (This wasn't, of course, the man's surname. It was just that this client had the habit of starting every sentence with the phrase "Well, yes sir, but . . . ," a habit that for some reason made Rose think he must be suspicious.)

"That"l be someone to collect Well-Yessabut's jacket," said Rose. "Got it ready, have you, Mannie?"

"Yes, Rosie," said Nightingale, "but the problem is that it might be someone to pick up the trousers I was supposed to make over for Leybovich before New Year's. I haven't quite got round to those yet, you see."

A second ring interrupted these thoughts.

Rose opened the door with its covering of oilcloth and felt and stepped back in silence. On the doorstep, dressed in a snow-covered fur coat, stood a beautiful woman, asking for tailor Nightingale.

"He's right here," said Rose, "but first tell me what exactly you want. Have you come for Leybovich's trousers?" She looked suspiciously at the woman's fur coat and long eyelashes.

"No, I've got nothing to do with Leybovich. I'm here on my own account. I want to order a suit. A suit with a uniform jacket and riding breeches."

"You? For yourself?"

"I do. For myself."

"'Sustain me with raisin cakes, refresh me with apples,'" Nightingale whispered with shaking lips and took hold of the tape measure around his neck to stop himself from keeling right over. "Some Well-Yessabut," Rose thought, looking at the woman's felt bootees. "This is a real Well-Yessabut."

Well-Yessabut sits herself down on the holey wicker chair that Izzie generally used as a stable for his wooden horse. Well-Yessabut flutters her eyelashes at Nightingale and repeats that she needs a uniform jacket and breeches, made in blue cheviot (and here she hands over the cheviot) to wear in a play, that she's an actress, and that she got citizen Nightingale's name as a nightingale whose work's good quality and well priced. And that she'd like a fitting right now, if he can manage, as she's in a tearing hurry.

She's in a tearing hurry, yes. She rips off her fur coat. Underneath she's got long dangly earrings on and a necklace of green stones. She goes and stands in front of the mirror and lets Nightingale measure her arms, her shoulders, her knees—whatever he says he needs to. And Rose, silent and fuming, thorns bristling, takes down the measurements.

"Waist, twenty-four, Rose, my dear," says Nightingale. "Your waist is so supple," he adds, turning to Well-Yessabut, "that I really don't know how I'm going to fit it properly."

Rose gives a meaningful cough, and Nightingale nearly swallows a pin.

"Bust, thirty-six, Rosie, dear," says Nightingale very faintly.

Rose notes this down in silence. Not a peep out of her, but her silence is so oppressive that Izzie starts bawling his eyes out and wailing that his toy horse just bit him.

Well-Yessabut gets back into her fur, makes an appointment for her fitting, and, having dipped her eyelashes in the blue radiance of Nightingale's eyes, vanishes into the snow.

"'Thou hast ravished my heart with one of thine eyes, with one chain of thy neck,'"[96] Nightingale sings to himself soundlessly as he marks up the blue cheviot with chalk. "Bust, thirty-six. And her eyelashes must be a full quarter-inch long. Staggering." And although the blue cheviot is cheap, coarse stuff, his shears fly over it, twittering gently, like swifts.

The suit is finished: Rose takes it off to the address the client gave. The suit is finished, delivered, and forgotten. While it was being measured and made, a cloud hung over the Nightingale house like a lead weight. Rose faded and drooped; she was so desperate she even made friends with Klavdiya, the baker's wife. Izzie got hardly any attention and managed to pick up scabies somewhere. But Nightingale's blue eyes shone so fiercely that when he went into the district housing office to pay his rent for January, they forgot to charge him for heat and light.

And the suit is delivered and forgotten . . .

3

Six months have gone by. It's spring in Uspensky Lane.

Tailor Nightingale, worn out by his long working day and the heady mood of spring, sits at the window in the falling light, listening to the kisses in the churchyard: one long one and two short. A beautiful plump cloud covers the

---

96 See Song of Songs 4:9.

western sky. But it's not going to rain: or not more than a warm drop or two, one every minute. The new sickle moon is slender. His heart is so full it hurts. And Nightingale says to Rose:

"Rosie, dear, suppose we go to the pictures?"

The Electric Wonder cinema house is crammed with loving couples. The lights go down. Whispers go through the rows like breezes. The lovers sit hand in hand, cheek to cheek, watching the adventures on the screen. They gallop wildly along with the heroes, plunge into foaming waterfalls, bring nests of criminals to book. The thin air of spring pours in through the singing ventilators. And a fireman in the back row feels uneasy, sensing all the smoldering conflagrations around him.

The movie showing today in the Electric Wonder is *The Deluge in Mine No. 17B*. The lights go down. A wedge of light strikes the screen. The action flies along. An evil-doer has planned a dreadful accident. He has bored a hole into the mineshaft, and soon water will pour in to flood the shaft. But the wicked plot has been discovered. And now, crawling over strange airy bridges and walkways, along a spider's web of scaffolding, hanging in the air itself, scrambles the woman who is going to avert disaster.

Squashed up as tightly as autumn swallows on telegraph wires, the lovers freeze, hearing a loud cry:

"My breeches, my breeches! Hey, hang on, hang on . . ."

Mine No. 17B vanishes from the screen. The lights go up, and a policeman looms menacingly over the man with bright blue eyes.

"Emmanuel," Rose whispers, "you've disgraced me now for good and all."

"Beg pardon," a trembling Nightingale says to the policeman. "Beg pardon. I didn't mean it that way at all . . . But they really are my breeches, you see. I made them. The ones on the rescuer in Mine No. 17B. And when I saw them hanging in the air like that, I kind of took fright. Seeing her so high up, taking such risks . . . I even thought the side seams might give way."

"It wasn't the side seams you were worried about, Emmanuel," Rose sobs. "You were worried about that wretched woman. Pity she didn't break her neck, I say. Ought to be ashamed of yourself, and you a family man!"

Rose has cried herself to sleep. But Nightingale, stung by love, can't sleep at all. For the first time in his life, he leaves the family nest at night and flutters off into the streets.

It's midnight outside, but people are up and about. Spring is so short. There's a scattering of stars over the central square. Emmanuel Nightingale makes his way there by back lanes, hardly realizing where he's going.

He's seen the woman with the quarter-inch-long eyelashes only twice. The first time was when she brought round the blue cheviot, the second when he did the second fitting. And now he's seen her gain, in the air, hair streaming above the mineshaft, collar unbuttoned, eyelashes wide.

Nightingale walks into the night alone. There are two people ahead of him. They're walking hand in hand, cheek to cheek, in loving harmony, like one being not two, but there are two of them all the same, and they're happy. Nightingale, slowly coming to himself after the flood in the mineshaft, is able to look and listen again. A dark woman—a Gypsy, maybe—is selling flowers.

"Buy some nice flowers," she accosts the couple walking ahead of Nightingale. "Buy a lovely rose for your beauty," she says to the young man, "buy it for your airy beloved."

But it's Nightingale who buys one, in delirium, in electric wonder, bewitched by the woman from the mineshaft, the one hanging in the air. He buys it for his beauty, for his airy beloved. He buys her a red rose without thorns, a beautiful night-dark rose of love. He takes it to the address she gave. He gives it to the janitor and tells him to give it to so-and-so without delay. There's a note attached to the rose. "I saw you yesterday evening in that movie. My name doesn't matter, but I'll never forget you."

Afterward he feels weak and shaky, as though he'd been carrying a steam iron, not a rose. His mouth goes dry; it longs for moisture, it is feverishly hot. And on Sadovaya Street, Nightingale walks up to the first Mosselprom[97] kiosk he sees and whispers softly through scorched lips:

"I beg of you, refresh me with apples, for I am faint with love."

1925

Translated from the Russian by Catriona Kelly

Vera Inber, "Solovei i roza." English translation copyright © by Catriona Kelly. Introduction and notes copyright © by Maxim D. Shrayer.

---

97 Mosselprom—abbreviation for Moscow Association of Establishments for Processing Products of the Agricultural Industry; Mosselprom kiosks sold soda water by the glass. Since Sadovaya Street means "Garden Street," there is additional play on the word "apples" in the last line.

ELIZAVETA POLONSKAYA

Elizaveta Polonskaya (1890–1969), poet, translator, and children's author, was born Elizaveta Movshenzon in Warsaw, in the assimilated family of a Jewish-Russian engineer; she subsequently took the last name of her husband, Lev Polonsky. Living in Łódź until 1905, Polonskaya learned both Polish and Yiddish. After a 1905 pogrom, her family fled to Berlin, later moving to St. Petersburg. Taking part in the revolutionary movement, Polonskaya fell under police surveillance. In 1907, she went to France, where she studied medicine at the Sorbonne. Polonskaya served with the Russian Red Cross during World War I and continued practicing medicine after the Bolshevik Revolution, working in various Soviet healthcare institutions until 1931.

Leslie J. Dorfman, Polonskaya's biographer, wrote of her literary pedigree: "Having passed through Symbolism and Acmeism, she returned to her own particular brand of civic verse, written in a rhetorical, often Biblical style sometimes described as masculine, yet with a distinctly feminine point of view." A participant of the legendary literary studio at the World Literature publishing house, in 1921 Polonskaya became the only "sister" of the literary group that called itself the Serapion Brothers (see **Lev Lunts** and **Veniamin Kaverin**). Her early poetry was gathered in *Omens* (1921) and *Under Stone Rain, 1921–1923* (1923). Among Polonskaya's controversial poems of the early 1920s was "Carmen" (1924), in which a Russian Bolshevik woman was portrayed as both a zealous revolutionary and a passionate and sexual female. *A Trip to the Urals*, Polonskaya's 1927 volume of essays, already signaled the ideological compromise that she and most of her fellow travelers probed in the mid-to-late 1920s. Polonskaya's collection *The Stubborn Calendar* featuring some of her best lyrical and epic verses from the 1920s, appeared in 1929. Polonskaya published a dozen children's books in the 1920s–30s.

In 1931, Polonskaya gave up medicine for the next ten years, earning a living solely as a writer. She traveled as a reporter for *Leningrad Truth* (*Leningradskaia pravda*), earning the kind of mileage that filled the pages of her next four books. The volume of essays *People of the Soviet Working Days* (1934) was followed by three poetry collections: *Years. Selected Poems* (1935), *New Poems, 1932–1936* (1937), and *Times of Courage* (1940), including many unremarkable verses tired of their own formal and ideological concessions. Her "Song of Youth" (1936) ended with the lines "Long live Stalin!/Long live

May!" During World War II, Polonskaya served as a front-line military doctor. Some of her wartime poems were gathered in *The Kama Notebook* (1945) and her prose in *On Our Own Shoulders* (1948).

Polonskaya published virtually no original verse in 1946–56, the shadow of Zhdanovshchina (the postwar onslaught of reaction known by this name after Stalin's henchman Andrey Zhdanov) and the anticosmopolitan campaign hanging low over her shoulders. She concentrated on translations and in the 1950s served as the head of the Translators Section of the Leningrad branch of the Union of Soviet Writers. Polonskaya included few of her early poems in *Selected Poems* (1966). Her contorted introduction pledged allegiance to the "spirit of her people" (here she meant "Soviet people") and to "the wide road of October." And yet, the mere remembrance of her poetry mentor Nikolay Gumilyov and her Serapion brother **Lev Lunts**, both forbidden in the USSR, said more about Polonskaya's past and her poetry than most of the verses in the volume. Toward the end of her life, Polonskaya worked on *Encounters*, a memoir of the 1920s and 1930s, which she left unfinished. Polonskaya died in Leningrad in 1969, a survivor and circumspect witness whose "rebellious" early poetry (L. Dorfman's expression) was almost unknown to the postwar generations of Russian poets.

* * *

Jewish and Judaic motifs are visible in Polonskaya's early poems, including "February 1" and "Shylock," both in *Omens*. Russian and Christian readers cringed at her poem "I cannot stand the infant Jesus. . . ," also included in *Omens*, where the poet unapologetically identified with the Jewish God of the Hebrew Bible and called Jesus of Nazareth a "forger." While exhibiting ample Judaic pride, Polonskaya's declarative poem betrayed insensitivity to the beliefs of the Christians. Polonskaya's early Jewish poems were never reprinted in her subsequent Soviet editions.

In the poem "A Shop of Splendors," Polonskaya mourned the prematurely deceased writer **Lev Lunts**. An early version of the poem was published in 1925 in the magazine *Leningrad*; the full text appeared in Polonskaya's collection *The Stubborn Calendar* (1929). In Polonskaya's last free-spirited collection, the poem memorialized much more than **Lunts**. For Polonskaya, **Lunts**, and their literary brothers and sisters, the departing 1920s had been the artistic "shop of splendors."

Polonskaya included the intriguing poem "To a Friend" (1932) in *New Poems* (1937). Referring to both herself and the "friend," presumably a western Jew, as having "inherited" "the Arian word" and a "Judaic childhood" and alluding to Nazism, she offered to show the "friend" "her home and her country." Was this a thinly veiled invitation addressed to Jewish Socialists and Communists in the West? Polonskaya translated the anti-Nazi poets Johannes R. Becher and Eric Weinert, who found themselves in the USSR in the 1930s. Also included in *New Poems* was "Gold Rain" (1936), an embarrassing piece of Birobidzhan propaganda. Occasional echoes of the Shoah were heard in Polonskaya's writings.

"Encounter," Polonskaya's poem included below, appeared in *The Stubborn Calendar*. Reprinted in *Years. Selected Poems* (1935), this poem deserves special attention for the clarity and courage with which it articulated the impossibility of assimilation.

ENCOUNTER

Morning flew by in the usual way,
Up and down streets, it raced,
Unwinding the spring of an ongoing watch
That the night would wind up again.

A coat was fastened over the chest
With a clasp and a little chain,
Then a voice from the gut: "*tayer yidish kind,*[98]
Give to a beggar, Jewish daughter."

From under her rags she studies me
With a tender, cunning old face,
A sentinel's eye and a hookish nose,
And a black wig, parted smooth.

An ancient, yellowish hand
Grabs my sleeve, and the words
Of a language I don't comprehend
Sound out, seizing my heart.

---

98 "Dear Jewish child" (Yiddish).

And there I stop, I cannot go on,
Though I know—I shouldn't, I shouldn't,
And drop a small coin in her open palm
And lift a thirsty heart to her face.

"Old woman, how did you, half-blind,
Pick me out among these strangers?
After all, your muttering is odd to me,
After all, I'm like them, the same as those—
Dull, alien, strange."

"Daughter, dear, there are things about us
That no one can mistake.
Our girls have the saddest eyes,
And a slow, languorous walk.

And they don't laugh like the others—
Openly in their simplicity—
But beam behind clouds as the moon does,
Their sadness alive in their smiles.

Even if you lose your faith and kin,"
A id iz imer a id![99]
And thus my blood sings in your veins,"
She says in her alien tongue.

That morning flew by in the usual way,
Up and down streets, it raced,
Unwinding the spring of an ongoing watch
That the night would wind up again.

1927

Translated from the Russian by Larissa Szporluk

Elizaveta Polonskaya, "Vstrecha." English translation copyright ©
by Larissa Szporluk. Introduction and note
copyright © by Maxim D. Shrayer.

---

99   "A Jew is always a Jew" (Yiddish).

VIKTOR FINK

Viktor Fink (1888–1973), fiction writer, essayist, and memoirist, was born and grew up in Odessa in a family of Jewish-Russian intelligentsia. In 1906, Fink entered the Law Faculty of Novorossiysk University in Odessa. After moving to Paris in 1909, Fink studied law at the Sorbonne. He fought in the French Foreign Legion during World War I, returning to Russia after the February 1917 Revolution.

Fink's first book, *Buzya Lipak*, appeared in 1927, followed by *Jaurès* (1928), a short book about the famous French socialist, a defender of Alfred Dreyfus. Fink became well known for his nonfiction after the release of *Jews on the Land* (1929; excerpt below) and *Jews in the Taiga* (1930; second, expanded edition, 1932). His best-known fiction, *Foreign Legion*, appeared in 1935. A novel-length cycle of thirteen novellas set during World War I and narrated by a Russian legionnaire fighting for France, *Foreign Legion* has been compared, generously, to the war tales of Guy de Maupassant and Alphonse Daudet. Unsparing and unsentimental, Fink's tale of service sometimes resorts to humor and lyrical characterization.

The 1930s were the peak of Fink's official prominence. In 1937, he lived in Paris, contributing to Soviet periodicals, and was a member of the Soviet delegation at the Second International Congress for the Defense of Culture in Spain. In the late 1930s, Fink turned to the subject of Moldavian (Moldovan) history. His short novel *Death of the World*, set in a Moldavian village, appeared in 1938–39. The theme found further treatment in Fink's formulaic novel *Moldavian Rhapsody* (1966), spanning 1917–44 to end with the defeat of the Romanian fascists. During World War II, Fink worked in the French branch of Moscow Radio world service. His *In France. Writer's Sketches* appeared in 1942, and his novel *The Fate of Henry Lambert* came out in 1948, when the anticosmopolitan campaign was gaining full speed. After having rebounded from a hiatus in publications in the late 1940s–early 1950s, Fink saw *Foreign Legion* and *Moldavian Rhapsody* reprinted several times in the 1950s–early 1960s.

From the Thaw until his death in Moscow in 1973, Fink enjoyed the status of "one of the oldest Soviet writers." First published in 1960, Fink's *Literary Memoirs* went through several editions—a pale, tame peer of **Ilya Ehrenburg**'s *People, Years, Life.* Some chapters were set abroad (Paris; Spain) and focused on meetings with left-wing European intellectuals and writers (e.g., Romain Rolland), yet Fink did succeed in planting occasional Jewish references, in safe contexts, such as mentioning the word "antisemitism" in a discussion of the Dreyfus Affair; evoking the Shoah in connection with the death of Jean-Richard Bloc's family members; recalling Isaac Babel's love for Jewish cuisine in the 1930s; including the "Jewish poet from Haifa Isaac Ioffe [Jechok Joffe]" in a list of writers who perished in the Spanish Civil War; identifying the Jewish origins of Grigory Iolos and Mikhail Gertsenshtein, members of the Duma assassinated by "monarchists"; and so forth. At the same time, Fink avoided even the most hushed references to his research for *Jews in the Taiga* as he described a 1929 expedition to the Far East. In 1967, Fink's memoir appeared in German under the unduly sensationalist title *Zwischen Paris und Moskau* (Between Paris and Moscow).

* * *

Owing to tsarist-era restrictions, by 1917 only 2 percent of the Jewish population was engaged in agriculture. Among the chief concerns of the Jewish Section (*Evsektsiya*) of the Bolshevik Party was to battle massive Jewish poverty. In 1919, the Jewish Section helped organize the first Jewish agricultural cooperatives in Belorussia and Lithuania, and, starting with 1924, it poured its energy into placing Jews in industry and in agriculture. The elemental drive of Jews on the land was already underway, the Jewish agricultural population increasing from about 53,000 in 1917 to about 76,000 in 1923. In August 1924, KOMZET (KOMERD in Yiddish), the Committee for the Settlement of Jewish Toilers on Land, was founded under the auspices of the Council of Nationalities of the TsIK (Central Executive Committee). Led by Pyotr Smidovich, KOMZET was in charge of the "Jews on the land" program. In 1924, new Jewish settlements were founded in Ukraine, where by the late 1920s three Jewish national districts operated: Kalinindorf, Novozlatopol, and Stalindorf. By 1925, the number of Jewish peasants had grown to about 100,000. While the state provided concessions to the settlers, a large part of the aid came from abroad, from the American Joint Distribution Committee (which incorporated Agro-Joint to distribute assistance), ORT ([Jewish] Association for the Promotion of Skilled Trades), the JCA (Jewish Colonization Association), and other agencies.

To abet KOMZET, the Society for the Settlement of Jewish Toilers on Land (OZET) was created in 1925 and was headed by Yury Larin. It was a citizens' organization, but leaders of the Jewish Section in effect controlled it starting in

1926. OZET assisted with the logistics of creating Jewish agricultural colonies and concentrated on fundraising and propaganda work. Enlisting the support of the Jewish intelligentsia, OZET engineered such appeals for help as the 1926 declaration "To the Jews of the World," whose signatories included Soviet Yiddish writers Shmuel Halkin, Dovid Hofshteyn, Itsik Fefer, and others. OZET had branches in the Soviet republics and regions and groups of support abroad. At the First Congress of OZET in 1926, Mikhail Kalinin, tutelary head of the Soviet state and champion of the "Jews on the land" program, spoke strongly against Jewish assimilation (the so-called "Kalinin Declaration"), lending temporary support to the previously rejected idea of a Jewish national enclave (or enclaves) in the USSR. The late 1920s marked the height of OZET propaganda and cultural-education work, which included publications in a number of languages. In 1927, Abram Room directed the documentary *Jew on the Land*, based on a screenplay that OZET commissioned from Vladimir Mayakovsky and **Viktor Shklovsky**.

By the mid-1920s, a grander program of Jewish settlement was introduced, targeting the north and northeastern parts of the Crimea, with vacant lands and difficult conditions for agriculture; in 1930, the Freidorf Jewish national district was established there. Some settlement work proceeded in Belorussia, in Smolensk Province, Russia, and in Uzbekistan and the Caucasus. In 1928, KOMZET introduced its five-year plan, forecasting the number of peasant Jews to increase from 100,000 to 250,000 in 1933, and eventually to one-half million. In 1936, there were about 200,000 "Jews on the land" in the USSR, and it is estimated that there were still about 100,000 Soviet peasant Jews on the eve of the Nazi invasion in 1941. The program of Jewish agricultural settlement was never realized on a scale as ambitious as declared. The collectivization of Soviet agriculture harmed and in many cases devastated Jewish agricultural colonies. Be that as it may, the "Jews on the land" program did produce, if temporarily, some impressive results. The shortcomings of the program hardly justify a comparison to the Birobidzhan fiasco.

Jewish agricultural colonies in Ukraine and Crimea represented efforts to battle some real socioeconomic problems of the Jewish population. At the same time, the prospects of solving the Jewish question in the USSR in the 1920s through the "Jews on the land" program—and especially through the Birobidzhan project—offered the Soviet leadership a politically advantageous alternative to Zionism. The plan for the creation of a Jewish enclave in the Far East, in the Amur River basin near the Soviet-Manchurian border, was put forth in 1927. The first 654 settlers-pioneers arrived in Birobidzhan in the spring of 1928 to find themselves in severe climactic conditions, surrounded by the taiga (boreal forest), with insufficient logistical and equipment support. The population grew slowly, many Jewish settlers returning after temporary stays. In 1930, a Jewish national district was incorporated with 2,672 Jews out of the Birobidzhan area's total population of 38,000. By 1934, the Jewish population of the Birobidzhan area was a little over 8,000 instead of the projected 50,000. Yet the Soviet leadership pushed on with its plan, making the area a Jewish Autonomous Province in 1934. While the Birobidzhan project initially stirred enthusiasm among Soviet Jews, it existed primarily as an ideological tool of the Soviet leadership, attracting support and even enlisting settlers among Jewish Communists abroad. (According to Soviet data for 1959, 14,289 Jews, or about 9 percent of the total population, were living in the Birobidzhan area, and fewer than 2,000 people called Yiddish their native language.) Both KOMZET and OZET were liquidated in 1938, and many of their leaders were purged.

* * *

The propagandistic, socioeconomic, and educational literature that emerged from the "Jews on the land" and Birobidzhan projects was significant. Several books and brochures with virtually the same title were published, including Fyodor Veitkov and B. Polishchuk's *Jews on the Land* (Moscow, 1930) and I. Geller's *Jew on the Land* (Smolensk, 1930). A number of Jewish-Russian litterateurs wrote about Jewish peasants and Birobidzhan, among them Iosif Kleinman, Semyon Bytovoy (Kogan) (1931 collection *Roads. On Jewish Collective Farms of the Crimea*), and others. **Matvey Royzman** devoted the novel *These Landlords* (1932) to Jewish settlements in the Crimea.

Most extensive and stimulating from a literary point of view was Viktor Fink's dilogy *Jews on the Land* (1929) and *Jews in the Taiga* (1930; 1932); two sections of *Jews on the Land* follow below. Derivative editions and brochures, such as *On the Way from Egypt* (1929), *Jews in the Field* (1930), and *The Taiga Region* (1931), were issued. *The Taiga Region* appeared in Yiddish translation in Kharkov (*A kant a taygisher*, 1932) and in Warsaw (*In Biro-Bidzshaner tayges*).

Critics in the 1930s noted Fink's skill at rendering with precision and humor the minutiae of life in Crimean and Belorussian agricultural settlements and in Birobidzhan. While Fink's ideological position is in line with that of the Party circa late 1920, his sketches are particularly interesting where they capture an intertwining of old traditions and new, of religion and technology, of ancient Hebrew and Soviet-infused Yiddish. In addition to prose efforts, Fink devoted a play, *New Motherland* (1933), to the collectivization of Jews in Birobidzhan. It was criticized for its lack of the "typical" and the "epochal."

In the December 1938 issue of *Red Virgin Soil* (*Krasnaia nov'*), Fink published the essay "The Jewish Question." Probably rushed to print, the essay makes reference to the events of Kristallnacht (November 1938). Fink described a recent visit to the Stalindorf Jewish national district in Ukraine, situated between Dnepropetrovsk and Krivoy Rog. Fink slapped together truths about the persecution of Jews in tsarist Russia and Nazi Germany, half-truths about life on the Jewish collective farms and communities in Stalindorf, and lies about the "solving of the Jewish question" in the USSR. Reading Fink's ideological commission is a painful experience for a number of reasons, and less so because of the loyalism with which Fink pounded the chords of Marxist-Leninist rhetoric on the Jewish question and established Stalin, the People's Commissar of Nationalities in 1918, as the founder of the first Jewish agricultural colonies in the Soviet Republic. Despite—or perhaps because of—its glorification of Jewish life in Stalindorf, Fink's essay reads today like a eulogy for the Jewish national districts in Ukraine and Crimea. Devastated by World War II and the Shoah, some Jewish settlements were taken over by non-Jewish neighbors; the Soviet authorities liquidated Jewish national districts soon after the victory over the Nazis.

FROM *JEWS ON THE LAND*

3. The Preachers

Hand-written posters appeared in the neighborhood of the synagogue to the effect that on Friday evening a preacher would be making a presentation. The program: (1) on the divinity of Lenin (the word "divinity" had been scratched out and replaced by the word "greatness"); (2) on the significance of the Sabbath; and so forth.

"Actually, this very expression 'and so forth' is the most important part of the sermon, because the first two points are only the introduction," said my host to me. "Go see what he has to say."

Onto the pulpit strode an emaciated man with a fiery gaze. Clearing his throat and swaying as if he were intoning a prayer, he began in a singsong voice to relate a parable.

"Listen, Jews, to the story of what happened, *oy*, happened to me . . . Once I had a horse, yes, a horse! It was a sickly nag, a sickly nag for sure, which I was disgusted to ha-a-a-arness! It was blind, and its ribs showed to such an extent that the harness wouldn't stay in place on them, *oy*, just wouldn't stay in place! And poverty reigned in my house from the fact that my nag was weak, and no matter how much I rode her, I had a hard time earning any money with her for the Sabbath.

"Then came market day. Yes, market day did come, and I traded my nag for a steed. The steed was beautiful and smooth. Smooth he was and beautiful, and his eyes were sighted, and my soul rejoiced when I looked at him! I thought—this marks the beginning of a new life for me, fast and easy.

"But, *oy oy oy oy oy oy*, Jews! *Oy oy oy oy oy*! Hardly had I handed over my nag and taken possession of the reins pulled by my new steed when I saw, *oy*, Jews, what did I see?

"I saw that my steed was colicky and lame. I could not ride him a single step! . . . So there I sat, exclaiming: 'Why did this have to happen to me? I would have been better off keeping my old nag. She at least had the use of her legs. What use to me is this gorgeous beast everyone admires? What use to me is this beauty if I cannot ride him?'"

That's it, the whole parable. The audience consisted entirely of small tradesmen. Their wretched lives under the tsars had been like the feeble nag, so they had traded it for the steed of the Revolution. And their "souls rejoiced."

But then it all ended when private enterprise was eliminated.

"So what use to me is this beauty if I cannot ride him!"

There are other good parables—for example, the parable about the ladder:

"I entered a courtyard overshadowed by an enormous new building. And I see, *oy*, what do I see: I see a ladder lying there among the trash.

"And having seen me, it called out:

'Man! Man! See how wretched is my fate! You see this marvelous building? Know, then, that I took part in its construction. I stood upright. The builders went up me and down me; they carried materials up me, and I served as a support for many activities. But now that the building is completed, I have been thrown into a trash heap, and no one so much as looks in my direction—oy, in my direction no one so much as looks!'

"And I answered it:

'Ladder! Ladder!' I answered it, 'don't lose hope! No building on earth is permanent. The time will come when this building, too, will collapse and you will once again be needed and they will pull you out of the trash! Oy, out of the trash will they pull you, and you will once again stand upright . . .'"

In this case, too, the dots will not be put over the *i*'s with too much precision. But that doesn't matter. The audience consists of people for whom the concept of class has been drowned in the concept of nationality. The audience believes that it has actually taken part in the Revolution. Hasn't this small town produced revolutionaries? And now that the building is completed, it turns out that trade has been taken over by the co-ops, while they, the audience, are lying in the garbage, being trampled by the tax assessor . . .

Of course, the sermon from the pulpit of the synagogue is not always constructed so wittily. Sometimes it's hysterically coarse.

In Mogilev, on the day of the Jewish New Year, the blast produced by the shammes from a ram's horn was barely sounded when the preacher bellowed:

"Jewish women! It is better to lead your children to slaughter than to hand them over to the Young Pioneers."

Sometimes the sermon is insultingly naïve and obtuse. The town of Orsha found a smart fellow:

"Jews!" he proclaimed. "I will explain to you, Jews, why there's such a decline in trade. In the old days a Jew sat day and night poring over the holy books in search of virtue and wisdom. This irritated Satan the tempter, so he sent to the Jew some Christians in order to lure him away from the holy books on the pretext of trade. And the Jew traded. And now Satan saw that the Jew, on his own, no longer pored over the holy books; that he, on his own, had fallen away from the faith of his fathers; that he, on his own, no longer sought virtue and wisdom. What else did Satan need? He was satisfied! There was no longer any need to tempt Jews. Therefore he no longer dispatched Christians to the Jew under the pretext of trade."

But the audience cleverly distinguishes between professional wailers and subtle political propagandists. It demonstrates a clear preference for worldly motifs. They demand of the cantor at the synagogue—the *hazzan*—that after the service he provide songs on secular topics born of anonymous folk creation during the years of the Revolution. Here we find both satire aimed at old-style Jews, and a sharp comment or two for the Jewish commissar, and complaints about life's hardships, sometimes directed at the hope for a better future, sometimes frittered away in endless grief.

A certain *magid*[100] of the erstwhile merchants wandered through Belorussia. He at one time had possessed a second-class license, but that

---

100 *Magid* (Heb., Yiddish) = preacher; used in Poland and Ukraine in reference to a popular, charismatic preacher.

document had vanished by the time an armful of subpoenas arrived from the tax collector. The merchant didn't give a good goddamn about anything, so he went off "to burn the hearts of men with the word."[101] He was a strapping burly fellow about thirty years of age, with a well-oiled tongue. In the old days, that tongue had helped him speculate in textiles; now he speculated in the thirst of those former merchants to hear a word of sympathy . . .

His speeches were witty and laced with humor. Those same parables about the horse and the ladder he would deliver without hysterical lamentations—as cheerfully and playfully as he had once sold the "best calico in the world." He would invariably end as follows:

"Jews! Keep in mind that there are three possibilities, Jews!" After a pause came an enumeration:

"It can happen that everything is fine. Kopeck chases kopeck, and ruble chases ruble. Then the Jew has no need of a preacher. Or it can happen the other way around—that everything is bad, and you've lost all hope. Then kopeck is in no hurry to chase kopeck, and ruble simply lies in place, and it's not clear just what place that is. In that case, too, the Jew has no need of a preacher. Yet there is a third possibility—the one in which the Jew has no need of a preacher. For example, the preacher hasn't a half-kopeck to his name; he isn't reimbursed for his board and room; he hasn't had a bite to eat or a drop to drink. He needs the Jews to remember that the support paid to the wise man is pleasing to God. So I ask you: have you thought to collect several rubles for the *magid*, or haven't you? . . ." [. . .]

7. The New Culture

The Revolution put forward powerful weapons against small-town squalor. Let's put aside for now the Jewish schools, the Jewish workers' organizations, the Jewish athletic societies. Take the recognition of Yiddish as an official state language! . . . How hard is it to penetrate the soul of a Jew who finds himself at a railroad station? Only a few years ago, he would have slid through the railroad station in order not to be noticed by a policeman, a stationmaster, even a switchman or a porter. Now all the station names are written in Russian, Belorussian, and Yiddish, and a Jew feels in this an unprecedented recognition of the fact that he is not a stranger but a real citizen just like everybody else.

---

101 In Russian, "*Glagolom zhech' serdtsa liudei*" is the last line of Pushkin's famous poem "The Prophet" (1826), based in part on Isaiah 6.

Or take, for example, the Jewish courtroom! . . . The judge, the members of the jury, the clerk, the parties to the lawsuit, the witnesses, the lawyers—they all speak Yiddish. Court records, summonses, court orders—all of it is written in Yiddish.

It seems to me that there's not a single Jew whose heart doesn't stop, if only for a minute, when he sees with his own eyes a Jewish courtroom. For Jews, especially for the Jewish poor who hang around courtrooms, having a legal proceeding in their own language is not just a question of convenience. These days all Jews speak Russian, so Jews could be tried in a Russian court. Even, I must confess, the participants in the pleadings, unbeknownst to themselves, lapsed into the sort of Yiddish in which the indictment is called "der indictment" and the subpoena is called "die subpoena."

"The malice smells mit denunciation!" was said, for example, by a Jewish defense attorney. But the very existence of a Jewish courtroom, even with the occasional "die subpoena," encourages in the Jewish masses an awareness of their legal and civic value, which is precisely those elements of the Jewish national psychology that various governments always tried in vain to destroy by every possible means.

A Jew who can come to a Jewish courtroom clearly feels his value as a human being and his significance as a citizen, and this is enormous for him, and new. The Institute of Belorussian Culture in Minsk has a Jewish section. Several young researchers sit there pouring over their books with the same fanaticism that their fathers and grandfathers displayed in poring over the Talmud. Bit by bit, brick by brick, letter by letter, they collect the scholarship pertaining to Jewish culture.

Working in the Jewish section are the following groups: (1) a historical commission, which has already succeeded in collecting extremely interesting new data on the history of world Jewry; (2) a literary commission, which is studying both old and new Jewish literature, elaborating questions of literary form, Jewish theater, and collecting folklore; (3) a linguistics commission, studying questions of Jewish lexicology, composing a Jewish-Belorussian, Belorussian-Jewish dictionary, an academic dictionary, and a linguistic geographic atlas, elaborating questions of orthography and terminology; (4) an economic and demographic commission studying the economy of the small town and the colony.

This is the germ of a future Jewish Academy of Sciences . . .

Someone may say, I suppose, but this isn't such a big deal: people are paid a salary, and they work up a sweat, but who needs it? . . . But therein lies the whole unexpected crux of the matter. The labor of these young scholars cannot keep up with the demands of a reawakened Jewish culture. The Proceedings of the Jewish Section are hefty editions of some 400 to 800 pages. One volume costs five rubles, and the edition is sold out—two thousand copies of each book have been distributed. A vast amount of research on the history of Jewry, on literature, on socioeconomic and cultural-social issues, detailed elaborations of the colossal statistical data on the past and the current life of Jewish towns, on the collection of folklore, on area studies—to all this information gravitate not only assiduous workers but also readers, obviously extremely eager readers, because five rubles to a member of the Jewish intelligentsia is a lot of money.

But if it is necessary to demonstrate the enormous cultural growth of the Jewish masses, its vital creative connection to the institutions of culture, it is worth acquainting oneself with the Letters to the Editor section of *The Proceedings*. It turns out that a rigorous study of the culture is going on not only here, in the halls of the research institutions—here it is being systematized—but out there, in the small urban centers and remote little towns.

"We have gotten involved in the collection of folklore," I am told by one of the researchers. "We published an appeal. More than 250 correspondents have responded."

Someone else says, "We began to compile a dictionary. Unpaid volunteers have helped us. We now have 200,000 index cards."

"From where?" I ask. "How did all this happen?"

We were chatting as we sat by a window. My companion made a motion with his hand, pointing toward the street beyond the window. All kinds of folk were darting about—toilers.

"That's where they come from! . . ."

You can already discern the face of the new Jew—the Jew who is passionate about culture. In the turmoil of the historical breakage, his life still unsettled, he struggles against poverty; he overtaxes himself in the artels The Red Baker and The Red Lathe Operator, where he haggles over meat pies or uproots tree stumps on his land allotment. In his struggles, he is already creating his culture and is being drawn to the organizing cultural center.

There you have it—what the Revolution has done with him, the small-town Jew. He flies head over heels out of the demolished small town. The flight is uncomfortable, but the course is true. In the final analysis, he arrives at spiritual liberation and converts his flight into productive labor.

1929

Translated from the Russian by Richard Sheldon

Viktor Fink, *Evrei na zemle*. English translation
copyright © by the Estate of Richard Sheldon. Introduction and notes
copyright © by Maxim D. Shrayer.

SEMYON KIRSANOV

Semyon Kirsanov (1906–1972), poet and translator, was born in Odessa to the family of a Jewish tailor. Kirsanov organized the Southern Association of Futurists in 1921, and his first publications appeared in 1922–23 in Odessa's newspapers. In 1924, Kirsanov founded *Yugo-LEF* (Southern Left Front of the Arts, modeled after *LEF* in Moscow). The same year Vladimir Mayakovsky visited Odessa, deciding the young poet's lot. Mayakovsky published two of Kirsanov's poems in *LEF* 3 (1925). After graduating from the Odessa Institute of People's Education in 1925, Kirsanov moved to Moscow. He captured the readers' attention with his robust, verbally inventive, mercurial poems revealing both his natural talent and an apprenticeship with Mayakovsky and Nikolay Aseev (1889–1963). Kirsanov toured the USSR with Mayakovsky in the 1920s, giving readings.

Kirsanov's first collection, *Backsight* (1926), subtitled "rhymed stories," was followed by many more in the 1920s–30s, among them *Essays, 1925–26* (1927), *The Last Contemporary* (1930, illustrated by Aleksandr Rodchenko), and *Notebook* (1933). Kirsanov published long poems as separate editions: *My Nameday Poem* (1928), *Conversation with Dmitry Furmanov* (1928), and others.

Following Mayakovsky's death in 1930, Kirsanov carried his teacher's torch. His *Five-Year Plan* (1931) continued Mayakovsky's last long poem, *At the Top of My Voice*, and incorporated bits of Mayakovsky's text. Kirsanov's long poem *Comrade Marx* (1933) dialogued with Mayakovsky's *Vladimir Ilyich Lenin* (1924). Kirsanov lent his talent to the Soviet industrial effort by visiting construction sites, contributing verses to factory newspapers, and authoring "agit-posters" such as "The 14th of October" (1933). His incessant verbal artistry hardly suffered from propagandistic commissions.

The mid-1930s marked a shift toward the lyrical, triggered by the death of Kirsanov's wife, whom he mourned in the stunning *Your Poem* (1937). Among his finest works are the lyrical cycles "A Groan while Sleeping" (1937–39) and "The Last of May" (1940). In 1936, Kirsanov visited Europe with a group of Soviet authors and later published a strong anti-Fascist poem, *War to the Plague!* (1937). Kirsanov spent the war years as a newspaper correspondent at several fronts; his wartime poems were gathered in *Poem for the War* (1945).

Creating the poetic persona of a charismatic soldier, Kirsanov chronicled the war in *The Cherished Word of Foma Smyslov* (1942–43), printed as leaflets in millions of copies. He reported on the Nuremberg Trial; he composed the poem *Aleksandr Matrosov* (1946) in the postmortem voice of the soldier-hero, conflating patriotism and formal estrangement. During the anticosmopolitan campaign, Kirsanov scored an official victory with his "production" poem *Makar Mazay* (1951 Stalin Prize).

In the postwar years, Kirsanov turned increasingly to philosophical poetry: *The Peak* (1954), *Once Tomorrow* (1962), and *Mirrors* (1967); and the cycles "Footprints in the Sand" (1950) and "The World" (1962). In *Eden* (1945), he treated the creation of the world in Biblical terms. During Khrushchev's Thaw, Kirsanov published the anti-Stalinist long poem *Seven Days of the Week*, attacking Soviet bureaucracy; it was deemed "politically immature." The late 1950s and early 1960s witnessed the second peak of Kirsanov's popularity.

Kirsanov's poetry showcased an astonishingly wide spectrum of generic and stylistic modes, from futuristic and expressionistic verse to folkloric poetry (e.g., *The Tale of King Maks-Emelyan*, 1962–64). Separate mention should be made of Kirsanov's enduring interest in poetic science fiction and fantasy, displayed in *Cinderella* (1934), *Poem about a Robot* (1934), *The Dolphiniad* (1971), and other works. Kirsanov also translated modernist left-wing poets, including Louis Aragon, Bertold Brecht, Nazim Hikmet, and Pablo Neruda.

Kirsanov called himself a "circusman of verse," and both admirers and detractors took to heart this *profession de foi*. Diehard Soviet critics charged Kirsanov with "verbal trickery" and "formalism," but the shadow of Mayakovsky guarded Kirsanov. Much of his poetry was spoken in the first person and exhibited brilliant puns and sound orchestration and exceptional compound rhyming. A living legacy of the formal achievements and ideological compromises of the 1920s "Left Art," Kirsanov was a Soviet modernist par excellence.

Kirsanov died in Moscow in 1972 after a battle with larynx cancer. Echoing Mayakovsky's *The Backbone Flute* (1915), Andrey Voznesensky wrote in "Kirsanov's Funeral," "A flute that hadn't cried itself out/fell into its red case."

* * *

Kirsanov never shunned his Jewishness, nor did he deliberately seek out Jewish questions. Published in the collection *The Floor* [literally "the word"] *is Given to Kirsanov* (1930), "R" vertiginously captures through its wordplay and sound orchestration the travails of a Jewish young man, an aspiring Russian poet, who rolls his *r*'s differently. In using Russian, native speakers of Yiddish and their children would display a characteristically uvular (grunted) *r* instead of the lingual (tongue-trilled) Russian consonant. This would make them targets for taunting, and anecdotes about identifying a Jew by his misrolled *r*'s belonged to the common repertoire of anti-Jewish jokes. In this anthology, other Jewish writers address the subject of ethnic, cultural, and religious markers of speech (see **Victor Shklovsky** in *Zoo*).

R

Trouble
with rolling your *r*'s
       can be painfully torturous.
Everyone
cuts you
       disdainfully.
Me, as a kid,
I had problems
       with *r*'s.
Talk about torture—
my larynx
       has scars.
I've had a serious inhibition.
    See, young lovelies
       mock this
       r deficiency.
Rasping *r*'s
       made my throat and neck sick.
So closemouthed,
    I was anorexic.

I'd start a lai:
"O Rus! O Rus!"
But I would say,
"O Ghoose! O Ghoose!"
And here would come,
    alackaday,
a neighbor's loose

misshapen goose.
Kids would whistle
    and smirk:
"Hey, yellow quitter,
    homework jerk,
        homework jerk,
say
    Rotten corn fritter!"
And not "Officer Carl,"
    I'd croak, "Officegh Caghl."
In some medical books
    I would mull it.
Where, oh, where are you, R?
    I beseech you, dear R.
Can't you reach
    to my rickety gullet?

And an actor
    at the wretched Roc Theater would come,
and he'd splatter my mispronounced *r*'s
    with his curses,
and he made me recite,
    "Rumty-tum, rumty-tum,
rumty-tum, rumty-tum
    rerehearses!"

Corridor!
    Frame!
        Carborundum!
          Overrun!
Like a pea from its pod,
    that *r* struggled.
Like the seed of a grape trying to grow,
    how it guggled,
till it burst out and glowed in the sun.

Then that letter would roll
    like a lustrous black pearl
from my larynx
    as if I were cured of catarrh.
And I swaggered around
    as if gargling
        with fire,
with that sound, that miraculous
                R!

And three times I exhorted
    Muscovites, everybody,
mouth contorted
    in trumpet-like shapes:
"Up on Mount
    Ararat
      grow
        great
          ruddy
grapes,
    GRAPES,
      GRAPES!"

1929

Translated from the Russian by Maxim D. Shrayer and J. B. Sisson

EDUARD BAGRITSKY

Eduard Bagritsky (1895–1934), poet and translator, was born Eduard Dzyubin (Dzyuban) to an Odessan family where Judaic traditions were respected but the life style was that of the secularized petite bourgeoisie. He began publishing in 1913 using a nom de plume that was derived from *bagrovyi*, the Russian for "crimson," and sounded both decadent and revolutionary. Bagritsky was a contributor to Odessa's literary publications in 1915–17 and lived the life of a bohemian. After the February 1917 Revolution, he served briefly in law enforcement for the Provisional Government and joined the Red Army in 1919. He moved to Moscow in 1925 and by the time of his death had achieved wide admiration. A number of books followed his collection *Southwest* (1928): *The Lay of Opanas* (1932), *Selected Poems* (1932), *Victors* (1932), *The Last Night* (1932), and others. Bagritsky never shed the skin of an Odessan Jew from Market Street and retained a strong bond with Jewish culture until his death, splendidly translating Yiddish poetry (Itsik Fefer, Perets Markish). Bagritsky was hailed second only to Vladimir Mayakovsky himself in the Soviet literary pantheon and given an official funeral.

Owing to his unique talent, the epoch, and the brevity of his career, Bagritsky cuts a most controversial figure among the Jewish-Russian poets of the Soviet period. Facets of his colorful personality survive in the accounts of his contemporaries: in the story "Idler Eduard" (1925) and later the fictional memoir *My Diamond Crown* (1980), where Bagritsky is called Birdcatcher, by Valentin Kataev, the brother of **Evgeny Petrov** (see Petrov and Ilya Ilf); in the memoir-novel in verse *The Merry Stranger* by Mark Tarlovsky; and others. A former cocaine addict and a fabulous fictionalizer and mystifier, Bagritsky hardly compels his students to rely on his writings as a source of information about his ideology.

In many respects, his career mirrors that of his friend and coeval **Isaac Babel** (1894–1940). Bagritsky's short life typifies the destinies of Russia's Jewish artists born in the late 1890s and early 1900s, and his career betokens several emblematic facts for his generation of Jewish-Russian writers: upbringing in a mercantile Jewish family and some exposure to Judaic traditions; cultural Russianization through reading and group literary activities; enthusiastic endorsement of the February Revolution and engagement in the events of the civil war on the side of the Reds; assimilation through marriage to a non-Jewish woman; move from the southwestern provinces to Moscow; and a major literary success after the move to the Soviet capital in 1925. Following Bagritsky's premature death, the Soviet ideological machine quickly contrived Bagritsky's legacy into a convenient literary legend. A forbidden subject even at the height of Khrushchev's Thaw, Bagritsky's Jewish themes were engaged head on only when he became the object of virulent attacks by official critics. Bagritsky was a symbol of the alleged Jewish destruction of Russian culture for the Judeophobic Russian ultranationalists gaining a voice in the Soviet 1970s.

A profusely talented transgressor of boundaries—Jewish, Russian, and Soviet—Bagritsky has influenced several generations of Russian poets, including such major postwar figures as **Joseph Brodsky** and **Evgeny Reyn**. In spite of the efforts of various critics to pigeonhole him as a "bourgeois nationalist" (Zhdanovites in the late 1940s and early 1950s), a "revolutionary Romantic" (conformist Soviet moderates in the 1960s–70s), or a Zionist and Russophobe (Russian ultranationalists in the 1970s–80s), Bagritsky's beliefs and loyalties are difficult to negotiate. Bagritsky may have occasionally trumpeted allegiance to the Bolsheviks—consider his opportunistic verses about the Industrial Party trial of 1930—yet his texts cannot be said to provide reliable information about his allegiance to the regime. Bagritsky agonized over the status of his Jewishness during the years of the ferocious campaign against traditional Jewish life. Up until the early 1930s, Bagritsky—like **Babel**, **Ehrenburg**, Grossman, and other Jewish-Soviet writers of his generation—must have believed that Bolshevism was a better alternative than tsarism for the three million Soviet Jews. In 1931, in "Conversation with My Son," Bagritsky wrote both about the virulent pogromists of his childhood and about marching units of "blackshirts" and "black fascist signs" marking the wings of (Italian) fighter planes. (Bagritsky's son, the poet Vsevolod Bagritsky, was killed in World War II.) The severely ill Bagritsky spent his last two years mainly confined to his apartment in the center of Moscow; he died in 1934. In 1936, **Isaac Babel** said of his deceased friend: "The fame of François Villon from Odessa earned [Bagritsky] love but did not earn trust [...] he was a wise man, conjoining a Komsomol member with Ben Akiva" (Akiva ben Joseph, ca. 40–135 CE, great Talmudic scholar, Jewish leader, and martyr).

*　*　*

Jewish topics and characters figure prominently in about a dozen of Bagritsky's shorter and longer works. But in both "Origin" (1926) and his last poem, *February* (1933–34; published 1936), Bagritsky produced definitive poetic statements about the making of a Jewish-Russian identity and the boundaries of Jewish-Soviet assimilation. "Origin" is a militant (and self-hating) monologue of a Russian Jew at odds with his familial past and upbringing.

ORIGIN

I can't recall the exact night
When I felt the ache of a life to come.
The world rocked and swayed.
A star stumbled on its way,
Splashing into a sky-blue basin.
I tried to grab the star . . . Slipping through my fingers
It darted off, a carp with blazing fins.
Over my cradle rusty Jews
Crossed rusty blades of crooked beards.
And everything was upside down.
And nothing was ever right.
A carp pounded on the window;
A horse chirped; a hawk dropped into my hands;
A tree danced.
And my childhood went forth.
They tried desiccating it with matzos.
They tried deceiving it with candles.
They pushed its nose into the tablets—
Those gates that couldn't be opened.
Jewish peacocks on upholstery.
Jewish cream that always turned sour,
Father's crutch and mother's headscarf—
All muttered at me: "Scoundrel! Scoundrel!"
And only at night, only on my pillow
Did a beard not split my world in two;
And slowly the water fell,
Like copper pennies from the kitchen faucet.
The water dripped. Descending like a storm cloud
It sharpened the crooked blade of its jet . . .
—Tell me, how could my Jewish disbelief
believe in this ever-flowing world?
They taught me: a roof's a roof.
The chair's hard. The floor dies under your feet,
You must see, comprehend, and hear,
Leaning on this world, as on a counter.
But the watchmaker's precision of a woodworm

Already hollows the beams of my existence.
—Tell me, how could my Jewish disbelief
Believe in this solid world?
Love?
But what about lice-eaten braids;
A jutting collar bone;
Pimples; a mouth, greased with herring,
And a horsey curve of the neck?
Parents?
But aging in the twilight,
Hunchbacked, knotty, and wild
Rusty Jews fling at me
Their stubbly fists.
The door! Fling the door open!
Outside the stars have chewed all the leaves
From their branches,
The moon's crescent smokes in the middle of a puddle.
A rook screams not knowing his kin.
And all that love,
Rushing at me,
And all the self-deprecation
Of my fathers
And all the nebulae
Creating the night,
And all the trees
Tearing through my face—
All this stood in my way,
Wheezing in my chest through my ailing bronchi:
—Pariah! Take your poor belongings,
Your cursedness and rejection!
Run away!
I'm abandoning my old bed
—Should I leave?
I'm going!
Good riddance!
I don't care!

1930

Published posthumously in 1936 and banned for long periods of time in the Soviet Union, the long narrative poem *February* is set in Odessa in the 1900s and 1910s. It depicts the traumatic formation of its protagonist's Jewish-Russian self at the time of historical cataclysms. While the main events of *February* unfold in Bagritsky's native city of Odessa between the autumn of 1916 and the autumn of 1917, the first excerpt found below contains a flashback to the protagonist's childhood. The second excerpt takes place in September or October 1916, as is evident from an earlier reference to the Stokhod operation of July–August 1916, in which the protagonist has participated. Tsar Nicholas II abdicated on 15 (2) March 1917. In Odessa, the power of the Provisional Government was established on 25 (12) March 1917. On 17 April 1917, a permanent militia was created by an edict of the Provisional Government. The third excerpt, in which the Jewish protagonist describes his activities as a deputy commissar of the militia, takes place in the spring and summer of 1917 and definitely prior to the Bolshevik coup d'état of 7 November (25 October) 1917. The local soviet assumed power in Odessa only in December 1917, and the Bolshevik takeover as well as the events of the civil war remained outside Bagritsky's historical focus in *February*.

Since its posthumous publication in 1936, *February* remained a thorn in the sinewy side of Clio the Commissar, and the post-Soviet years have not made it less controversial.

FROM *FEBRUARY* (THREE EXCERPTS)

[...]
I never loved properly ...
A little Judaic boy,
I was the only one around
To shiver in the steppe wind at night

Like a sleepwalker, I walked along tram tracks
To silent summer cottages, where in the underbrush
Of gooseberry or wild blackberry bushes
Grass snakes rustle and vipers hiss,
And in the thickets, where you can't sneak in,
A bird with a scarlet head darts about,
Her song is thin as a pin;
They've nicknamed her "Bull's eye" ...

How did it happen, that born a Hebrew
And circumcised on the seventh day,
I became a fowler—I really don't know!

I loved Brehm better than Mayne Reid![102]
My hands trembled with passion
When I opened the book at random—
Birds would leap out at me from chance pages
Looking like letters of foreign alphabets,
Sabers and trumpets, globes and rhombuses.

I imagine the Archer once paused
Above the blackness of our dwelling,
Above the notorious Jewish smoke
Of goose-fat cracklings, above the cramming
Of tedious prayers, bearded faces
In family pictures . . .
[. . .]

---

102 Brehm, Alfred Edmund (1829–1884)—world-renowned naturalist. Brehm's books, including *The Animals of the World; Birdlife, Being a History of the Birds*, and others, written in German and translated into many languages, including Russian, were extremely popular among Russian teenagers. Reid, Mayne, a.k.a. Main Rid (1818–1883)—American author. His novels of adventure, including *Adventures among the Indians: or the War Trail and the Hunt of the Wild Horse* (1853); *Afloat in the Forest* (1866); *The Headless Horseman* (1866); and *Chris Rock, a Lover in Chains* (1889), were translated into Russian and enjoyed much popularity—especially *The Headless Horseman*—in both tsarist and Soviet times.

* * *

I evaded the front: I tried everything . . .
How many crumpled rubles
Escaped from my hands to the clerks'!
I bought my sergeants vodka,
I bribed them with cigarettes and pork fat . . .
From ward to ward,
Coughing in a paroxysm of pleurisy,
I roamed.
    Puffing and gasping,
Spitting into bottles, drinking medicine,
Standing naked, skinny, unshaven
Under the stethoscopes of all and every doctor . . .

When I was lucky enough by truth
Or lie—who can remember?—
To get a liberty pass,
I would shine my boots,
Straighten my blouse, and sharply
Walk to the boulevard, where an oriole sang
In the treetops, its voice like baked clay,
Where above the sand of the path
A green dress swayed
Like a slender strand of smoke . . .

Again I dragged on behind her,
Dying of love, swearing, stumbling into benches . . .
She would go into a movie theater,
Into the rattling darkness, the tremble
Of green light—in a square frame,
Where a woman beside a fireplace
Wrung her alabaster hands,
And a man in a granite vest
Was shooting from a silent revolver . . .

I knew the faces of all her admirers,
I knew their habits, smiles, gestures,
How their steps slowed down, when on purpose,
With chest, hip, or palm,
They would feel through a dainty cover
The anxious tenderness of a girl's skin
[...]
The girl had already approached the square,
    And in the dark-gray circle of museums
Her dress, flying in the wind,
Looked thinner and greener ...

I tore myself from the bench
With such effort, as if I had been
Bolted to it.
    And not turning back
Rushed after her toward the square.
All the things I used to read at night—
Sick, hungry, half-dressed—
Birds with non-Russian names,
People from an unknown planet,
A world where they play tennis,
Drink orangeade and kiss women—
All that was now moving before me,
Dressed in a woolen dress,
Flaming with copper locks,
Swinging a striped satchel,
Heels running over cobblestones ...

I'll put my hand on her shoulder,
"Look at me!
        I am your misfortune!
I'm dooming you to the torment
Of incredible nightingale passion!
Wait!"
        But there, around the corner,
Twenty steps away her dress shows green . . .
I am catching up with her.
        A little farther on
And we shall stride abreast . . .

I salute her like a soldier—his superior,
What shall I tell her? My tongue
Mumbles some nonsense,
        "Will you . . .
Don't run away . . ..
        May I
Walk you home? I was in the trenches! . . ."

She is wordless.
        Not even a look
In my direction.
        Her steps
get faster.
        I run beside her, like a beggar,
Bowing respectfully.
        How on earth
Can I be her equal!
        Like a madman
I mumble some ridiculous phrases . . .

And suddenly a halt.
    Silently
She turns her head—I see
Her copper hair, her blue-green eyes
And a purplish vein on her temple,
Pulsating with anger.
"Go away. Now." And her hand
Points to the intersection . . .
    There he is—
Placed to guard the order—
He stands in my way like a kingdom
Of cords, shiny badges, medals,
Squeezed into high boots,
And covered on top by his hat,
Around which whirl in a yellow
And unbearably torturous halo
Doves from the Holy Scriptures,
And clouds, twisted like snails;
Paunchy, beaming with greasy sweat,
A policeman,
    from early morning pumped
With vodka and stuffed with pork fat.

* * *

[...]
I stayed in the area . . .
    I worked
As deputy commissar.
    At first
I spent many nights in damp sentry boxes;
I watched the world passing by me,
Alien and dimly lit by crooked streetlamps,
Full of strange and unknown monsters
Oozing from thick fumes . . .

I tried to be ubiquitous . . .
    In a gig
I churned rural roads, searching
For horse thieves.
    Late at night
I rushed out in a motor boat
Into the gulf, curved like a black horn
Around rocks and sand dunes.
I broke into thieves' lodgings,
Reeking of overfried fish.
I appeared, like the angel of death,
With a torchlight and a revolver, surrounded
By four sailors from the battleship . . .
(Still young and happy. Still rosy cheeked.
Sleepy after a night of reckless fun.
Cocked caps. Unbuttoned pea jackets.
Carbines under their arms. Wind in their eyes.)

My Judaic pride sang,
Like a string stretched to its limit . . .
I would've given much for my forefather
In a long caftan and fox fedora,
From under which fell gray spirals
 Of earlocks and clouds of dandruff
Flushing over his square beard,
For that ancestor to recognize his descendant
In this huge fellow, rising, like a tower,
Over flying lights and bayonets,
From a truck, shaking off midnight . . .

1933–34

Translated from the Russian by Maxim D. Shrayer

MARK EGART

Mark Egart (1901–1956), fiction and nonfiction writer, was born Mordekhay Boguslavsky in Krivoy Rog, Ukraine; Egart based his pen name on his mother's maiden name, Elgart. His father was a teacher at the town's Jewish elementary school. In 1922, Egart left home with a group of *Ha-Halutz* members. He spent a year in Poland, working and recruiting *halutzim*.

Egart spent three years in the British Mandate of Palestine, arriving there in 1923. He experienced unemployment and hunger and conflicts with the Arab population and the British authorities. Disillusionment with the merciless realities of the marketplace and class division among Jews, coupled with the economic crisis of 1926–28 in Palestine, resulted in Egart's decision to return to the USSR. According to the writer's daughter Frida Egart, the crucial factor was his progressing illness, tuberculosis of the bones.

While living in Moscow in 1928, Egart turned to writing and joined a proletarian-oriented literary group. After traveling with a group of writers to the Altai Mountains in 1930, Egart wrote *The Crossing: Altai Sketches*. Describing collectivization in Altai Region, *The Crossing* appeared in 1932 in the series "New Works of Proletarian Literature"; it came out in English and German in Moscow that same year. In 1932, Egart published his most important literary work, the novel *Scorched Land,* about the struggles of young Jewish settlers in Palestine. Book 1 was serialized in *October* (*Oktiabr'*), numbers 9–12 (1932), overlapping in one issue with Mikhail Sholokhov's *Quiet Flows the Don*; Egart's entire novel appeared in book form in two separate volumes (book 1 in 1933 and book 2 in 1934). Miraculously, Egart survived the Great Terror unscathed. In 1937, the year when a "corrected" version of *Scorched Land* came out in one volume, Egart published the factory novel *Marusya Zhuravleva*. Reprinted in 1948, *Marusya Zhuravleva* was supplemented by an equally formulaic sequel, *Friends* (1950).

In January 1940, Egart published the short novel *Talisman,* about a Soviet careerist, in *Novy mir*. Like *Scorched Land, Talisman* was never reprinted after World War II. Despite poor health, Egart served as a fiction editor at Navy Publishing House during the war, and subsequently he worked for many years as head of the Commission for Young Authors at the Soviet Writers' Union. After the war, Egart mainly wrote for adolescents. Some of Egart's works, especially his "adventure tale" *Bay of Mists,* remained in print into the 1980s.

* * *

In addition to *Scorched Land*, Egart addressed the Jewish experience in the tale "Sinner Khet and Righteous Lot," composed for the desk drawer in the summer of 1953. A Biblical allegory reminiscent of **Lev Lunts**'s "Native Land" (1922, in this anthology), it was printed in 1997 in the Russian-American magazine *Messenger* (*Vestnik*).

Told in the agonistic first-person voice, *Scorched Land* followed Egart's autobiographical protagonist, Lazar Dan, from the former Pale to Palestine. Egart presented Dan's life in his home town in Ukraine, Gnilopol (from the Russian word *gniloy*, "rotten"), as one plagued by poverty and disemboweled by pogroms and one his idealistic *halutz* left behind. In many Soviet literary works (e.g., Yury Libedinsky's *The Commissars* [1925] and Iosif Utkin's *The Tale of Red-Headed Motele* [1925]), historical logic brought Jewish characters to the revolution. Egart's Soviet novel is unprecedented for outlining an alternative, if broken, trajectory: to emigration and building a Jewish enclave in Palestine. In the words of Vladimir Khazan, "in *Scorched Land*, it seems, for the first and last time in Soviet literature, was sounded an unhidden sympathy for Zionism, naturally paling in comparison with the novel's overall concept." Part 1 of book 1 opened with an epigraph from Theodor Herzl's *The Jewish State*. Politically advantageous in the early 1930s, the novel's tendentious narrative logic clamored for a Marxist-Leninist conclusion: only in the USSR—and not in Palestine—can the Jewish question be "solved." Book 2 ended with the departure of the Soviet-bound Dan from Tel Aviv and included no scenes of life in the USSR. The coarse texture of Egart's prose captured the prosaics of the daily lives of *halutzim*, the harshness of physical work, the malarial swamps, and the rough-hewn hills of Galilee. The emasculated 1937 edition could not erase all of Egart's admiration for the *halutzim*, although it did its best to obliterate the lyrical-authorial pathos of the Palestinian parts while making the anti-Zionist narrative argument unambiguously clear. Still, even the revised edition stands in contrast to the schematic, simplistic treatment of the subject by Semen Gekht (1903–1963). In Gekht's novel *The Steamship Sails to Jaffa and Back* (Moscow, 1936), the protagonist reached Palestine *only* to return to the Soviet Union.

Egart's major novel was deleted from Soviet and post-Soviet literary history. But its copies have survived, mainly in libraries outside the USSR, and a section of book 2 follows below. Part 2 of book 2 bears the bitterly ironic title "Song of Songs."

FROM *THE SCORCHED LAND*

Book 2, Part 1, Chapters 7–8*

Chapter 7

The waters of Lake Kinnaret gently lap at the decrepit boat. The green trans-
parent waters melodiously babble against its beat-up nose; the rowlocks squeak
in unison, and the tall sky languidly lowers its sunset sails. The mountains of
Transjordan rise up in the smoke of distant fires. Their purple tails crawl over
the faraway pale-blue wadi.[103]

Kopl hoists the mast made from the grip of a big pitchfork. The tarpaulin sail
swells with the wind catching up to us to us from the hills of Galilee. The night
paints the lake pale blue and violet. It moves the mountains closer and makes
the air transparent and hollow. Somewhere to the right, the horses are stomping
across a wooden bridge over the Jordan, the bells of a caravan jingle, and on the
left the yellow towers of Tiberias rise out of the water. The resourceful Niakha
lights a fig-tree branch. I steer my way around Tiberias toward Migdal. There
must be a suitable place there, in a narrow cove concealed by a cliff. The night
sails over Kinnaret, the fishermen sail through it, and our song sails along with us.

Early in the morning we return with a full catch and pull in to the shore
at the wooden gangway of the town bazaar. A canopy made of ripped canvas
sacks blankets the marketplace with latticed shadows, and the sun bursts like
golden fountains through the holes. The hot sunbeam reflections chase each
other over the wide chests, dive in between barrels filled with olives and figs,
between vats steaming with meat and greasy pitas, and flash like rainbows on
rugs, abayas, and colorful fabrics.

It's still that early hour when the coffeehouse on the shore is closed,
the merchants of *charbar*, *sabra*, and grapes are still putting out their tables,
and the water carriers are driving the donkeys down the crooked slopes to
the lake. The embankment laid out in green tiles is empty, and only the fish-
ermen who've just returned from nighttime fishing are drying and mending
their nets.

---

*   This text has been slightly abridged
103 Wadi (Arabic) = bone dry—usually a narrow riverbed in the desert that occasionally flash
      floods at times of heavy rain; equivalent of *arroyo* in the southwestern United States;
      compare also "ravine," "canyon."

A tall, hook-nosed fisherman [. . .] is gawking at us. He's munching olives, and his greasy mustache trembles with a threat. Who ever saw *yehudim* bringing fish to the marketplace? Really, there are no sneakier people than the *yehudim*. All strewn with large pockmarks, his olive face glitters with sweat like the olives he's holding in his cupped palm. He makes a loud noise as he spits out the pits, wipes his hands on his wide yellow trousers, and looks back at his mates.

The fishermen are sitting beside their nets—their lace-thin decrepit nets that must be mended daily—staring at their competitors. Dozens of eyes are mockingly examining our catch. Under the stares of the Tiberias fishermen, we sort the catch and put it in buckets. With our buckets, Zelig and I climb the mountain to the new part of town where the Jews live. Kopl and Niakha stay behind, waiting for the stores to open.

We walk along the old Turkish wall, past the tower where there's now a barbershop. We stop by the brand new building of the power plant. Zelig indecisively walks around the dressy flowerbed in front of the plant and looks in from the back door. He returns in a minute. They don't need fish here—the electricians board at Antebi's. There is meat and fish there, and everything else. But they don't recommend asking Antebi—the Bukharan is stingy [. . .] and buys everything cheap from the Arabs.

Zelig lifts his bucket, and we move on. In one house they buy crucians from us but then return them—in summer, crucian carp may carry tapeworms. At the hospital, in the hospital kitchen, they ask us to supply them meat: "If you could only get fresh meat for the patients, we'd gladly take it. Every day even. But fish . . . Soon the stench will make it impossible to pass through the town."

We looked in on the secretary of Histadrut,[104] the doctor, the teacher at the Jewish school, and finally the owner of the bookshop. But the secretary wasn't home, and his wife turned out to be a vegetarian. The doctor didn't let us past the doorstep, mistaking us for patients. "Tell them to go to the hospital!" he passed word through a servant. "Hope he gets sick himself!" I yelled into the open door. The teacher hadn't gotten paid for three months. Besides, he doesn't like it when young people, young farmers, engage in trade. If you really think about it, if you compare . . . In his time, people found other ways to start out . . . A stooping man in tussah pants and a shirt tied with little blue

---

104 Histadrut (Heb.)—acronym for the General Federation of Workers in Israel: trade-union federation of Israel founded in 1920.

pompons had some spare time and didn't mind talking about starting out back in his day.

Only the owner of the bookshop, also the librarian, who loaned books to me, buys three tenches. He'll pay later, better yet, count it toward the subscription fee. True, we owe more, but it's okay, no strangers here—we'll square accounts. The librarian, a sickly looking obese man with a brown beard that looks black on his pale face and glasses with very thick lenses, has a strange last name: Bass. Bass is a member of Histadrut, Ahdut Ha-Avodah, Tarbut,[105] and the society for the support of physical renaissance. He likes saying that he would gladly abandon his business and join our commune. But his family . . . his wife . . . "Never get married," he tells me every time and looks through his thick glasses as through vitrines. "A wife is . . ." He sniffs his fingertips but can never say what a wife is.

Bass left Russia before the war, but he still loves Russian books and Russian newspapers, and he's the only person in town who dares subscribe to *Nakanune*.[106] Bass believes the best writers are Russians and the best literature is Russian. When people ask him for advice on what to read, he tells them with conviction to "read real literature" and shoves them something from his Russian stocks. This time he shows me a book by some Ehrenburg[107] and clicks his tongue with pleasure.

Zelig offers the bookseller a commission if he refers some buyers, in response to which Bass remarks, offended, that his business is books, and "fish . . . fish is for the bazaar." Zelig looks at me, I look at Zelig. We lift our buckets and walk toward the bazaar.

The unsold crucians splash in our buckets. Our damp pants stick to our tired knees. The sun hangs right over our heads.

The hook-nosed Galilean women in wide calico trousers and skirts hiked up at their wastes walk toward us with pitchers. Their bracelet-like earrings and the piasters plaited into their braids, tinkle to the beat of their steps. Eyebrows purple with dye, fingernails red with henna, little violet stars on their lips. They bare their magnificent teeth and walk by. The water carriers haul their

---

105 Ahdut Ha-Avodah (Heb.) = labor unity—Socialist Zionist movement founded in Israel in 1919; in 1930 it was merged with Ha-Poel ha-Tzair to form the Mapai Party; Tarbut (Heb.) = culture—interwar Hebrew educational-cultural organization in Eastern Europe, with strongholds in Poland and Lithuania.
106 *Nakanune* (*On the Eve*)—Russian-language periodical published in Berlin in 1922–24.
107 **Ilya Ehrenburg**, see this section and the section "War and Shoah."

full waterskins. Donkeys bawl, turning their sly little muzzles toward the sun. Fanners, young boys, pull on thin ropes. And the fans, which look like brooms made of cane and palm leaves, drive the flies away from the merchants playing Syrian dominos.

It's noon already. It's already hot. Arab youths moan in the madrassa.

When we return to the dock, Niakha Liam is sitting in the boat by himself, and Kopl, with half a dozen fish strung on a stick, is walking around the marketplace in search of buyers. He greets us with looks of mockery—he wouldn't have come back with a full bucket. Kopl is beginning to get angry, cursing the Arabs who won't let him past the dock. It's obvious he is looking for someone on whom to take out his vexation. We sit in the full blaze of the sun, sleepy, tired, and silent.

Two fishing boats dock in, then three more, and then still more. They must have gone all the way to Transjordan and are just now returning. Huge nets shake out onto the dock's hot boards fluttering fish shiny with metallic luster. Mountains of shiny fish rise in front of our eyes.

We've been wasting our time, even Niakha understands that now. But Kopl doesn't want to admit it. He gets into the boat and turns it sideways, so that nobody could moor here. The fishermen look at him and continue unloading. Soon their fish block off our boat. Then Kopl starts shoving them off with his feet. The hook-nosed guy [. . .] shakes his fist at Kopl.

"It's our marketplace and our livelihood," yells the hook-nosed guy.

"Lazar," Niakha bugs me, "what's he doing?" . . . Niakha looks like he is about to run away. The nook-nosed guy points at Niakha with his finger and laughs. Kopl picks up an oar. In an instant, a crowd gathers.

"Make them leave! Make them get out of here! . . ."

The boys jump out of the water and cheerfully slap themselves on their wet bellies in anticipation of a fight. The police show up. They fine us for selling fish without a permit and tell us to get lost. Histradrut pays the fine for us—on the condition that we'll work it off later.

Kopl spent the entire day mending the torn net and yelling at the frightened Binka. This was the first time Kopl yelled at his wife, and it was the first time she listened to him. Wrapped to the waist in the net, he looked like someone not mending it but trying to untangle himself from its tight embrace. That evening, Kopl went out fishing again. Nobody wanted to accompany him.

Sender Kipnis, who was transporting pebbles from the shore that day, recognized him from a distance. Ignoring the warnings of the convoy, he limped toward Kopl. Who knows, maybe he wanted to see his sister, and maybe he wanted to learn about his old comrades. But Sender didn't ask about his sister or his friends.

"*Haydamaki!*"[108] Sender yelled out and laughed. He turned around and saw me. "Prospectors!" he laughed even louder. The night was approaching, the prisoners were in a hurry to break camp, and Sender had to run pushing his wheelbarrow. And yet he was still laughing.

But I no longer cared. I looked at my bare, scratched feet, my ripped shirt mended many times over, and glanced at the shore, where my mangy comrades toiled in labor and scarcity. Through the dark night, I looked over at all those who bent their backs on the rough earth of Galilee, Samaria, and Judea, and I couldn't find words of hope for them. I remembered the town, the swaggering and ragged town, where there were many people, many words, and not enough joy, and I was indifferent to that as well. The wind threw splashes of water in my face. A gust of tirelessly humming wind passed over the lake. I turned my back to the wind. Back to the wind and the life of which I expected nothing.

I found Kopl by the little cove overgrown with oleanders that had shed their flowers; both boat and net were missing. The wind lifted his shirt, the waves came up to his knees, and he was throwing stones at someone unknown, struggling against the wind.

I turned around and walked away. "Manure for the land," I whispered. "Manure for the land of Israel . . ."

And maybe because the night was dark, or because now I was completely alone, I kept stopping and looking back. I seemed to have lost my tremulous home in this hapless night.

Chapter 8

Summer loomed over the lake like an inextinguishable bonfire. The cliffs would get sizzling hot; tufts of scorched grass shot red and rusty along the slope. The lake, exhausted with heat, lay motionless down below, and yellow scummy foam stirred like a spreading pestilence along the shores. And thousands of mosquitoes and midges buzzed all day and all night.

---

108 *Haydamaki*—plural of *Haidamak*. The term *Haidamaki* refers to paramilitary bands or troops composed of Ukrainian Cossacks and peasantry in the eighteenth-century Polish-Lithuanian Commonwealth. Outside Ukraine, the term was frequently used negatively, and here Sender uses it with a mixture of derision and admiration.

Our tents now stood at the edge of the water. And still it was stuffy. It was so stuffy that in the middle of the night Binka would wake up and start tearing her nightshirt. I could hear how she tossed under the clingy mosquito net, gasping, like a fish out of water. She would push herself out of the mosquito net in the darkness, lean over the suffocating Zevulan, and look over his sunken face. Unable to bear it, Binka would take the child into her arms and, careful not to wake him, carry him to the shore. She would hold him right over the water until his breathing grew slower and deeper. He would open his tiny mouth, all dried up from the ghastly heat, wake up and cry. He had been crying a lot recently.

Sometimes during these night hours I would approach Binka. With a bandage over my eye (I got a black eye at the Tiberias marketplace), I would roam along the shore and stare at the lake. I just couldn't sleep. I would come up to Binka, and she would cautiously retreat, glancing at the tent where Kopl slept.

She would go back to the tent with the child, and I would remain on the shore, staring at the moon's path that ran from my feet toward Transjordan. The silvery path would escape from me, and I couldn't hold on to it, just as I couldn't hold on to the past. [. . .] My book of exodus hadn't materialized, the Jewish truth hadn't risen up, and the cherished notebook was being used to roll smokes.

I would climb a cliff that looked like a stone embrace. The stone shoulders shuddered, and the stone lips, illuminated by the moon, longed for each other but couldn't connect.

A fat pelican sleeping on the cliff would heavily dart off into the darkness. He would circle over my head, and I tried to drive him away, but he only clanked his scissor-like beak. He knew that I'd tire off and leave and the cliff would be his again.

Woken up, Kopl Farfel would come out of his tent and yell angrily that it was time to sleep. Before us lay the lake, terrible in its taciturn beauty. Speechless and indifferent mountains surrounded us. Kopl would quiet down. He would gaze at the lake as if hoping to see his boat and slowly drag his feet back to the tent. Who knows, maybe he though of the happiness that he had searched for so long and finally found at these shores. He asked himself: Was he happy? And couldn't find the answer.

And I just laughed.

Little by little, Kopl began to replace me in everything. A notice arrived from the bank, informing us that for every overdue day a fine would accumulate. The prices on wheat in Tiberias still held firm, but in Haifa and Jaffa they fell by 20 percent. There was talk that the government intended to import even more flour from Australia than in the previous year. Cheap flour, cheap bread, is beneficial to everyone. But what are the farmers supposed to do?

On his days off Kopl now went to town to get the news. They didn't promise anything good—prices on flour kept falling, and nobody knew when they would bottom out. Dgania, Kinneret, and Melhamia were managing. They had previous supplies, vegetable gardens, milk farms. They could ride it out. But what could the newcomers do? What were we to do, who had neither vegetable gardens, nor vineyards already turning a profit, nor feed—and the only cow had to be sold to pay off the debts? Binka never got to tend the calf. Moreover, we had to send Niakha to town to earn money. An old bathhouse attendant had died in Tiberias, and Niakha once again resumed his old trade.

He earned pretty decent money—the people of Tiberias couldn't praise their [new] bathhouse attendant highly enough. And Niakha was also happy. And so was my father. He prayed in the town synagogue on the Ninth of Ab, and the rabbi promised to keep him in mind. The melamed no longer did anything except dispense advice.

"The land is rough here, of course, but the Jews must endure; the Jews have endured things that are much worse..." Sholom-Gersh would take off his yarmulke, glossy from years of wearing, and wipe with a handkerchief the bald spot that reflected the Galilean sky. He would run his fingers through his gray beard and pull out his lip. In his faded pants of faux leather and patched-up discolored *tallit katan*[109] worn over his old Gnilopol suspenders, sitting on a rock by ancient Lake Kinnaret, he seemed so lost, so out of place that even the [...] sly pelican would click his beak-scissors with surprise and mockery, circling over the head of the learned melamed.

"Well," I would say to my father, "well, o wise one, the Cossacks on one side, the *haydamaki* on the other, and on the third . . . on the third . . ." And I would go over to Nekhama's, who dressed my wound and gave me advice about insomnia.

"She's kind," I would say to myself, "it's easy to get along with her." Without noticing it, I got used to visiting Nekhama. Her tent was really clean and cool, maybe because she lived alone. I listened to her stories about what guys used to be like in the past and how things used to be done. And now everyone had been

---

109 *Tallit katan* (Heb.) = little *tallit*—four-cornered garment worn by very observant Jewish men; the shape of a *tallit katan* resembles a poncho.

scattered all over the place, and not a word from anyone. Guralnik had turned into a "commie," and Khaya Ber had gone back home to Kholm,[110] and Tsaler, Ben-Tsur, and Shoshana had moved to Tel Yosef. That's how life had turned out . . . Nekhama looked at me, and in her eyes were sadness, exhaustion, and submission to the inevitable fate.

One time I overheard a conversation. ". . . One can never escape what's intended for him," Kuntsia Liam was saying [. . .] to Binka. "Nekhama is an honest girl . . ." Kuntsia pronounced the word "honest" with that special meaning with which married women who have never known great love and joy try to convince themselves that there is no other, better life than the one they live. I noticed how Kuntsia pursed her pale flat lips and recalled that she didn't approve of Binka's relationship with Kopl, considering it shameful for a wife to go swimming with her husband and kiss after they've had a baby. Binka probably remembered the very same thing, and from the thought that Kuntsia can— and probably does—judge her love, she turned bright red and went back to her place without saying anything.

"Binka," I called, but she didn't hear me. And Kuntsia weightily repeated, "Whatever's meant for a person . . .".

In the course of a few days Nekhama changed radically. She got hold of a light dress. It had probably been lying in some trunk for a long time, awaiting its hour. Nekhama cut off her short thin braids. It was funny and touching to look at her "Bubi Kopf" hairdo, which revealed a sharp helpless dimple on the back of her head; venturing to look younger than her age, the unmarried girl applied powder and tried to cover up her freckles.

But the freckles—huge, brown—mercilessly came back on her flabby cheeks and long desiccated arms. And yet they couldn't bring Nekhama down. Her eyes, which had been muddy-brown and despondent, now shined with the joy of fulfilled hopes, the hopes she had mourned on her long virginal nights. And this joy had straightened her skinny back, bent from constant work. Joy filled Nekhama's entire being and made her face almost pretty. A truly genuine love had entered her heart. In her withering days of maidenhood, the poor Nekhama had really fallen in love. And I didn't know what to do.

Nekhama used to work from morning until night, carefully peeled potatoes, washed the dishes, patiently busied herself in the cattle shed or the

---

110 Kholm (Yiddish; Pol. Chełm)—Edart is referring to the town (45 miles east of Lublin in Poland) that historically had a large Jewish population.

vineyard. Now, as soon as it got a little dark, she already got dressed up by her cot in front of a broken mirror, as if she was going out.

I stopped visiting her. I would take the road toward Tsemah, but Nekhama invariably found me under the pretense of having to go to the store, or to Dgania, or else as if by accident. As if it was possible to meet by accident on a deserted shore where only very few people lived.

Women already considered us husband and wife. They became even more convinced of this when Nekhama, stopping by to see Binka in the dusk and not finding Kopl there said that it's not good for a husband to leave his wife alone in the evening—Lazar never leaves her by herself. Nekhama laughed, and Binka felt even in the dark that Nekhama was blushing.

Binka told Batsheva, Batsheva told Zelig, and Zelig told me. "Why is she making this up?" I wondered. I felt sorry for her. And Zelig kept sighing that even Lazar got himself ensnared [...].

"No matter what you say, being a bachelor is better. And why were you so impatient, should have waited until the fall . . ." With small-town simplicity, Zelig used to think out loud and pour over the minute details of my affairs . . .

In the morning, I went to work. I turned and cultivated the soil in the orange plantation, reattached and reinforced the tents, made a new feeder for the mules, then went with them far into the mountains and found a secluded wadi, from which I brought back two huge bales of grass. And when everything was done, I started carrying water for the plantings.

[...]

Once I yelled at my father, who decided to instruct little Khaimka in his discipline. The *melamed* sat the boy down before a thick volume, which he had brought from Gnilopol, and rocking to and fro, as in a heder, drew out: "And . . . and . . . what did Rabbi Akiva[111] say . . . ?"

"Listen, sage," I yelled, "wrap up your wares, the market's closed."

That evening, Kopl Farfel came to see me in my tent.

"He's your father," said Kopl. "He's an old man."

"I'm old, too."

"You are going to have children, think about it, Lazar.'"

"I'm thinking."

"And Nekhama . . ."

"What do you want?"

---

111 Rabbi Akiva—Akiva ben Joseph, ca. 40–135 CE, great Talmudic scholar, Jewish leader, and martyr.

Kopl left.

Zelig got up from the cot and leaned toward me. In the darkness, I saw his puzzled eyes and his neck overgrown with hair like a goat's. Zelig stared at me for a few minutes.

"Why am I here?" I asked loudly.

Zelig was silent.

"You don't know? . . . I don't know either. What do you all want?" I yelled.

But Zelig didn't want anything. He got scared.

At first, Nekhama took my estrangement as a joke. She continued to strike up light conversation and flirt with me, powder her freckles, and spend hours in front of the little mirror. But the joke had lasted for too long, and the joy was draining out of the girl's face. Like the flowers and grasses losing color and luster on the slopes of the nearby mountains, her short-lived joy was fading away from her face. And Nekhama's face became even yellowier, older, and uglier. A morning came when Nekhama put on the old dress with caked balls of manure, rolled her sleeves up to her shoulders, once again parading all her freckles to the world. She now exhibited these big, red freckles as her shame, just as her fallen love was drowned in shame. But now I no longer felt sorry for her. And things went back to how they used to be.

One day after dinner, Nekhama approached me as though she wanted to tell me something. But Nekhama's eyes, counter to her will, counter to what her comrades expected of her, suddenly shone with such power, such anguish, such desperation, such joy appeared in her muddy eyes with thin, whitish eyelashes—and there was more joy than anything else—that I shuddered. But immediately Nekhama's face grew dim. She looked back, met Kuntsia's greedy stare, touched the bare back of her head helplessly and sorrowfully, as if trying to defend herself, and ran out. In the evening she was at work, as usual, then went to sleep, and we never saw her again.

We searched all around, went to Tiberias, Tsemah, and Dgania. [. . .] But Nekhama was nowhere to be found. Again, for entire days I roamed around the shore and threw stones into the water. No, I wasn't tormented by remorse. After all, how was it my fault that she's crazy. And what was so special in me that she had to throw herself at me, get a fashionable haircut, and powder her nose?

I examined my reflection in the water and saw a familiar, narrow-chested, gray-eyed fellow, unshaven for quite some time, with eyebrows unevenly grown together, as if clinging to each other, and a swollen right eye. I shrugged my shoulders in bewilderment and so did my double in the water. No, my conscience didn't demand that I answer for it.

On the fourth day, we found Nekhama. I found her, when I went to the stone pool to get water. The water in the pool was transparent, motionless; it looked like a square block of green glass. Only the edges of the block were embroidered by a fluffy fringe of algae and seaweed, and tadpoles darted around it. Nekhama lay on the very bottom, face up and arms spread. She lay so calmly and her body swayed so rhythmically that it looked as if she were breathing.

"Nekhama!" I called out. And hearing my hoarse voice, I suddenly realized that Nekhama was dead.

Everybody gathered around the stone pool. Kopl and Zelig undressed and got in the water. But they couldn't pull out the drowned girl right away. Somehow her hair caught on the rocks, and her feet in thick English boots were pressed against the opposite wall of the reservoir. Binka had to run back down and get scissors. Kopl cut off a braid, and the girl, as if she were still alive, stood up on her heels, and popped her swollen, freckled face out of the water. Her wide mouth was smiling dolefully, and in that smile I once again read Nekhama's desperate last love.

Nekhama was buried the following day, after the necessary formalities, not far from the place where her short-lived happiness had taken its course. On the hill, from where the lake, Transjordan, and Hermon could be seen, we interred the girl's body and wrote on the marker: "Nekhama Grille. Died of great love." I made the inscription myself, and nobody objected.

After that, I packed my rucksack and announced that I was leaving. Father had gone over to Tsfat and would probably remain there, the cot could be sold—it's worth money after all, and so farewell.

"Farewell," I said. Nobody responded.

Only Kuntsia—her personality hadn't changed a bit—asked whether I intended to order a *matseva*[112] in Haifa for Nekhama [. . .]. Niakha, who had come home for the funeral, pulled at his wife's sleeve, but Kuntsia spoke up once again about the *matseva* and about, see, Lazar, who'd ever have thought . . . oh, trouble, trouble. Kuntsia blew her nose loudly and went to prepare supper, Binka remembered she had to check on Zevulan, and Kopl took the mules to drink their evening fill. He didn't say a word.

Zelig saw me off. In front of the cliff he said goodbye. He put out his hand and wanted to say something. But he didn't. He just tapped me on the shoulder and turned back.

---

112 *Matseva* (Heb.) = sepulchral stone, gravestone.

I walked toward the sunset amid the cold mountains that turned their backs on me. Like the Wandering Jew, I roamed through life and was everywhere a stranger.

1932

*Translated from the Russian by Margarit Tadevosyan, in
collaboration with Maxim D. Shrayer*

ILYA ILF AND
EVGENY PETROV

Ilya Ilf (1897–1937) was born Ilya Fainzilberg to a lower-middle-class Odessan Jewish family. Despite pressure from their father, an accountant, to pursue business careers, two of Ilf's three brothers became artists and Ilf, a writer. In Odessa, Ilf worked for the Southern Russian Telegraph Agency, where the poet Vladimir Narbut (1888–1938) employed Odessan writers. Ilf contributed to the Odessan newspaper *Seaman* (*Moriak*) and edited the satirical magazine *Syndetikon*. After migrating to Moscow in 1923, he landed a proofreader's job at *Whistle* (*Gudok*), the railroad workers' newspaper and a hub for members of the Southwestern school. In 1925 in Moscow, Ilf, a writer of sketches, essays, and feuilletons, met Evgeny Petrov, a fellow Odessan. Together they became (arguably) the greatest Soviet satirical writers.

Evgeny Petrov (1903–1942), born Evgeny Kataev, was the younger brother of the famous Soviet writer Valentin Kataev (1897–1986). The Kataev brothers enjoyed a sheltered childhood in Odessa. Their father taught at the Women's Diocesan High School; some evidence indicates that their mother, Evgeniya Bachey, was of Crimean Karaite stock, although she was apparently born Russian Orthodox. Not only their Odessan upbringing but also a link to the Karaites, a Judaic sect that rejected the Talmud, may explain the penchant of both Kataev brothers for friendships with and marital and family ties to Jews. Prior to moving to Moscow in 1923, Petrov had a stint at the Odessa Criminal Investigation Department. After running the satirical magazine *Red Pepper* (*Krasnyi perets*), Petrov joined *Whistle* in 1926. In the 1920s, he published a number of story collections, including *Accident with a Monkey* (1927).

Ilf and Petrov's collaboration began in 1927 "by accident," as they later stated: "When we started writing together, it turned out that we were a good fit, as they say, complemented each other." After joining forces, Ilf and Petrov continued to publish some work of single authorship. Valentin Kataev apparently gave his brother and Ilf the idea for their debut, the satirical novel *Twelve Chairs* (1928), and intended to be the third author. Set during the NEP, *Twelve Chairs* relates the travails of Ostap Bender, a charismatic rogue identified as the "son of a Turkish subject." Bender had his prototype in Osip (Ostap) Shor (1899–1978), a younger brother of Anatoly Fioletov (pseudonym of Natan Shor, 1894–1918, an Odessan

Jewish-Russian poet). Ilf and Petrov's novel appeared serially in the magazine *Thirty Days* (*Tridtsat' dnei*), which Vladimir Narbut edited, and came out in book form in the publishing house Land and Factory, which Narbut had founded. (As Nadezhda Mandelstam remarked in *Hope Abandoned*, "Odessan authors ate bread" from Narbut's hands.) In the novel, Bender chases after the dispersed chairs from a set of twelve, in one of which a general's widow had hidden her diamonds. Bender's partner, the former nobleman Vorobyaninov, murders him on the eve of possessing the last chair, only to learn that the diamonds had already been discovered and a workers' club built with the funds. To this day *Twelve Chairs* remains a beloved read owing to its hilarious mock-adventure plot coupled with witty language. In Russia, Bender's aphorisms became popular adages (e.g., "key to the apartment where the money is"). Ilf and Petrov popularized the Yiddish-influenced and Yiddish-infused Odessa-speak (compare **Isaac Babel**'s Odessa stories), while also cleverly underplaying Ostap Bender's Jewishness.

Nikolay Bukharin's endorsement of *Twelve Chairs* might have backfired, and critics attacked it. However, prompted by Stalin's positive response, *Literary Gazette* (*Literaturnaia gazeta*) printed an affirmative assessment in 1929. Taking advantage of the official literary policy, which deemed satire a potent ideological weapon, Ilf and Petrov mocked corrupt officials, lazy bureaucrats, and potboilers in the feuilletonistic cycles *1001 Days, or the New Scheherazade* and *Extraordinary Stories from the Life of the Town of Kolokolamsk*, both signed "Tolstoyevsky." As Alexandra Smith noted, the cycles "were written in the spirit of the Sixteenth Communist Party Conference, which took place in April 1929."

Resurrecting Ostap Bender, the writers completed a sequel, *The Little Golden Calf*, by early 1931. It appeared in *Thirty Days* and was published in book form by émigré houses in Berlin and Riga; the first Soviet book edition was delayed until 1933. Ilf and Petrov coauthored more stories in the early to middle 1930s; their collections included *How Robinson Was Written* (1933). In the 1930s, they wrote for the cinema and the stage. With Valentin Kataev, Ilf and Petrov created the show *Under the Dome of the Circus*, basing upon it their script for *Circus* (1936), a musical comedy by Sergey Eisenstein's disciple Grigory Aleksandrov; in the film's conclusion, which portrayed the USSR as an internationalist society free of bigotry, Shloyme Mikhoels sang in Yiddish while holding a child of an African-American man and a white American woman; the biracial child is played by the would-be Russian poet Dzhems (James) Patterson.

In 1935–36, Ilf and Petrov undertook a road tour of the United States. Their book of nonfiction, *One-Storey America* (1936), garnered criticism, mainly for not being hostile enough toward capitalism. (Ilf and Petrov showed enthusiasm for some aspects of American life, including football.) Their last work, "Tonya," appeared in 1937, the year Ilf died of tuberculosis. "Poor Ilf died," Vladimir Nabokov wrote his wife from Paris in 1937. "And, somehow, one visualizes the Siamese twins being separated."

Ilf's quotable *Notebooks, 1925–37* were published in 1939 in expurgated form (a complete edition by Ilf's daughter Aleksandra appeared in 2000). Following Ilf's death, Petrov wrote scripts and the political comedy *Island of Peace* (first staged in 1947). He reported on the Soviet-Finnish war, after joining the Communist Party in 1940, and visited Germany as a *Pravda* correspondent in the spring of 1941. He died in a plane crash while returning to Moscow after reporting on Nazi-besieged Sebastopol.

During the anticosmopolitan campaign, after Soviet Writer Publishers reprinted Ilf and Petrov's *Twelve Chairs* and *The Little Golden Calf* in 1948, the secretariat of the Writers' Union issued a resolution deeming the publication a "severe political error" and the two novels about Ostap Bender a "slander of Soviet society." The novels were rehabilitated during the Thaw and later canonized as a model of Soviet satirical literature. A five-volume edition of Ilf and Petrov's works was printed in 1961 in a run of 300,000 copies. Both novels were translated into numerous languages, and their film versions have been produced both in Russia and abroad.

Following perestroika, uncensored editions of the novels appeared, including Yuri Shcheglov's edition of *Twelve Chairs* (1995) and Mikhail Odessky and David Feldman's edition of *The Little Golden Calf* (2000). Ilf and Petrov have remained popular among post-Soviet readers.

* * *

In a number of works, both those authored jointly with Petrov and those written solo, Ilf satirically examined Jewish topics. Ilf's story "The Prodigal Son Returns Home" appeared in the mass-produced illustrated magazine *Little Flame (Ogonyok)* in 1930. Ilf and Petrov used the same title (from the parable of the prodigal son in Luke 15:11–32) for chapter 17 (part 2) of *The Little Golden Calf*. Free of the tenderness of Ilf's autobiographical voice, echoes of the antireligious campaign in the Soviet Union resurfaced in Ilf and Petrov's novel: "The great schemer [Ostap Bender] did not like Catholic priests. He was equally negative about rabbis, dalai-lamas, Orthodox priests, muezzins, shamans, and other servants of the cult."

THE PRODIGAL SON RETURNS HOME
by ILYA ILF

Sometimes I dream that I'm a rabbi's son.

I'm seized with fear. What can I do about it—I, the son of a servant in one of the most ancient of religious cults?

How did it happen? Surely not all my ancestors were rabbis. Take my great-grandfather. He was a coffin maker. Coffin makers are classified as craftsmen. So without going overboard, I can tell the Purge Commission[113] that I'm the great-grandson of a craftsman.

"All right," the commission will say, "but that's your great-grandfather. What about your father? Whose son are you?"

I'm a rabbi's son.

"He's not a rabbi anymore," I whimper. "He long since cast off his . . ."

What did he cast off? His robes? No, rabbis don't cast off their robes. It's priests who cast off their robes. Then what did he cast off? He cast off something or other, he abdicated, he renounced his bearded ways, with hew and cry he served his ties with the almighty and refused him entry into the house.

But I can't explain exactly what my father cast off, and my explanations are deemed unsatisfactory. I'm fired.

I walk along the indigo snowy street and whisper to myself:

". . . Comrade Krokhky was completely right when he . . . Tell me who you are friends with, and I'll tell you who you are . . . The apple doesn't fall far from the tree . . ."

Commission Chairman Krokhky was completely right. I have to stamp it out. Really, it's high time.

I'll go back home, back to my father, the rabbi who cast off something or other. I'll demand an explanation from him. How inconsiderate can you get? Aren't there lots of other professions? He could have become a gravedigger like my grandfather, or in the final analysis he could have made himself into a white-collar proletarian, a bookkeeper. Would it really have been so awful to work at a high desk, sitting on a revolving stool? What made him pick rabbi?

---

113 Operating at a place of employment and study, "purge commissions" in the Soviet 1920s and 1930s sought to identify and weed out members of families who were considered disenfranchised outcasts (*lishentsy*) based on their social background; the outcasts commonly included descendants of the "bourgeoisie" (defined rather loosely) and of clergy.

And couldn't he see that it was totally unethical to have sons who are rabbi's sons? I'll go back home to see him. We'll have a major conversation.

The prodigal son returns home. The prodigal son in a Tolstoyan peasant shirt and cannibal tie returns to his father. His heels echoing, he runs up the Varenna marble staircase to the fourth floor. In a melancholy voice he mutters:

"I live on the fourth floor, where the staircase ends."

He's pretending. He's not melancholy, he's nervous. The son hasn't seen his father in ten years. He forgets about the impending major conversation and kisses his father on his mustache, which smells of gunpowder and saltpeter.

Father asks anxiously:

"Do you need to wash up? There's the bathroom."

The bathroom is dark, as dark as it was ten years ago when the knocked-out windows were replaced by a piece of plywood. Nothing in father's apartment has changed in a decade.

In the dark I raise my hand overhead. There used to be a shelf there with soap in an enamel dish. My hand meets the shelf and finds the soap.

Shutting my eyes, I can make my way through the whole apartment without stumbling, without bumping into furniture. Memory saves me from colliding with a chair or the little table with the samovar on it. Maneuvering with closed eyes, I can pass into the dining room, take a left, and say:

"I am standing in front of the chest of drawers. It is covered with a linen runner. On it is a mirror, a blue porcelain candlestick, and a photograph of my brother whose schoolmates called him Jumbo. He was a chubby boy, and at that time all chubby boys were called Jumbo. As for the real Jumbo, that was an elephant."[114]

Opening my eyes, I see the chest of drawers, the runner, the candlestick, and the photograph . . .

The apartment is like a ship. The furniture seems riveted into the floor, placed there once and forever. Father stands beside me, stroking his gunpowder mustache.

Why does his mustache smell of gunpowder? Because he's not a captain and not a hero of battle—he's a rabbi, an unethical servant of a cult, and

---

114 Evgeny Petrov's brother, Valentin Kataev, referred to an actual elephant by that name, a celebrity of one of Odessa's menageries, who went berserk and held the city captive for a whole week before he was shot down.

a duplicitous hypocrite to boot. Did he stop believing in god? Not at all. He apparently came home one day, let out a sigh, and said:

"Taxes are killing me. Seventeen rubles a month for electricity. It's robbery."

And he cast off his robe, that is, not a robe but something like that. A simple matter: electricity won out over religion.

But that didn't help me. I remained a rabbi's son. The victory of the light bulb in the toilet over the Almighty did not help me in the slightest.

A father like that should be despised. But I feel that I love him. So what if his mustache smells of saltpeter? Ham also smells of saltpeter, and nobody demands that it lead troops into battle.

My father has sixty-year-old amethyst eyelids and a scar on his cheek, an immobile ship's scar.

Shame—I love a rabbi!

The heart of a Soviet citizen, a citizen who believes in the building of socialism, trembles with love for a rabbi, the former instrument of a religious cult. How could this have happened? Comrade Krokhky was right. Apple, apple, tell me who your friends are, and I'll tell you who'll eat you up.

Horror: my father is an apple tree, a rabbi with a leafy beard. I have to renounce him, but I can't. No, there won't be a major conversation; I love my father too much. And I only ask:

"Why, why, did you become a rabbi?"

Father is surprised. He looks at me with tender anxiety and says: "I never was a rabbi. You dreamed this. I am a bookkeeper, a hero of labor."

And sadly he strokes his gunpowder mustache.

The dream ends with a motorcycle revving up and firing. I wake up, joyful and excited.

How good to be a loving son, how pleasant to love your father if he's a bookkeeper, if he's a white-collar proletarian and not a rabbi.

1930

Translated from the Russian by Alice Nakhimovsky

* * *

The title of Ilf and Petrov's second novel hints, diminutively, at the episode in Exodus 32 where the wandering Jews, weary of waiting for Moses, ask Aaron to make them a golden calf to worship. Aaron acquiesces and has an idol made from the molten gold jewelry collected from women and children. Returning from the mount, the wrathful Moses destroys the idol (see also 1 Kings 12 and 2 Chronicles 10 and 11 on Jeroboam and the schism of the Jewish tribes).

The Little Golden Calf depicts a scheme that Ostap Bender and his cohorts mastermind so as to "relieve" the "underground" Soviet millionaire Koreyko of his wealth. Bender's associates include the Jew Panikovsky, whose name suggests "panic"; the name of the profiteer Koreyko signals *treyf* (non-Kosher), derived as it is from *koreyka*, Russian for "cured pork." Through a series of road adventures, Bender succeeds in obtaining Koreyko's money but fails to cross the border. After the riches are confiscated by Romanian border guards, Bender is sent back to the USSR.

In addition to featuring major and minor Jewish characters, The Little Golden Calf reflected a moment in Jewish-Soviet history, as it appeared to Ilf and Petrov in 1929–30. While paying lip service to what was at the time the official campaign against antisemitism, Ilf and Petrov restricted the Jewish problem to individual antisemites, anachronisms of the pre-Revolutionary tsarist past. At the same time, the positioning of Hiram Burman, an American newspaper correspondent and a Zionist, in the opening chapter of part three, is meaningful. With a group of newspapermen, Burman takes a "special-charter train" bound for the construction of the Turkestan-Siberia Railroad (Turksib). Completed in 1931 as a major project of the First Five-Year Plan, Turksib ran from the Trans-Caspian Railroad to the Trans-Siberian Railroad, linking Central Asia and Siberia. In 1930, a measly Jewish district was incorporated in Birobidzhan (see introduction to **Viktor Fink**), the Soviet ideological machine trumpeting to the world the "success" of a Jewish national enclave in the Far East. Both the direction of the connected railroads and Burman's skepticism toward the Soviet rhetoric on the Jewish question prompt a reading of Ilf and Petrov's satire not only along but also against its Soviet grain. In the chapter that follows the one reproduced below, Ostap Bender narrates the "Story of the Wandering Jew," in which the ancient Jew (in Russian, literally "Eternal Yid") meets his death in 1919 at the hands of Simon Petlyura's Ukrainian troops. An Austrian journalist "sells" Bender's "story" to Burman, who prints it in his

American newspaper. The inserted "Story of the Wandering Jew" is supposed to betoken the annihilation of traditional Jewish (Judaic) living, which in the Soviet Union has been replaced by a society in which there are Jews but no Jewish question. Still, one detects double irony in Ilf and Petrov's treatment of the Jewish question. In 1930, were Ilf and Petrov laughing about the future of Soviet Jews as they peeked out the window of the train taking them to the Turkestan-Siberian Railroad?

FROM *THE LITTLE GOLDEN CALF* by ILYA ILF and EVGENY PETROV

Part 3, Chapter 26

Passenger of the Special-Charter Train*

A short special-charter train stood in the asphalt bay of the Ryazan Station[115] in Moscow. It had only six cars: a luggage car, which, contrary to the usual, stored not luggage but a supply of food on ice; a restaurant car, from which a chef in white kept peeking out; and a governmental lounge. The other three were couch cars, and their berths, clad in coarse striped covers, were waiting to accommodate a delegation of shock workers,[116] as well as foreign and Soviet correspondents.

The train was headed for the linking of the tracks of the Eastern Railroad. [117]

The trip ahead of them was long. The shock workers were shoving into the car vestibules their travel baskets with little black padlocks dangling on metal rods. The Soviet journalists were dashing about the platform, swinging lacquered plywood cases.

The foreigners kept an eye on the porters who were moving their big leather suitcases, trunks, and hat boxes with the colorful stickers of travel agencies and steamboat companies.

---

*   The text has been slightly abridged.
115   Presently Kazan Station in Moscow.
116   "Shock worker" is a less than perfect albeit accepted literal translation of the Soviet Russian term *udarnik*. *Udarniki* were initially Soviet overachieving workers who "overfulfilled" their quotas and targets; the term eventually came to designate any Soviet employees who achieved high records of output; they were rewarded by the system and given special privileges.
117   Ilf and Petrov are referring to the Turkestan-Siberia Railroad (Turksib).

The passengers had already managed to procure copies of the booklet *The Eastern Railroad*, the cover of which depicted a camel sniffing a rail. Copies of the booklet were sold on the spot, off a luggage cart. The author of the book, the journalist Palamidov, had already walked by the cart several times, casting vigilant glances at the buyers. He was considered an expert on the Eastern Railroad and was going there for the third time.

The departure time was nearing, but the parting scene didn't at all resemble the send-off of a regular passenger train. There were no elderly women on the platform, and nobody was sticking a baby out the window so that it could cast one last look at his grandfather. Nor was there a grandfather, whose dim eyes usually reflect a fear of railroad draughts. Needless to say, nobody was kissing. The delegation of shock workers was accompanied to the train station by trade-union leaders who hadn't yet worked out the protocol of goodbye kisses. Members of editorial staffs had come to see off their Moscow correspondents, and on such occasions they were used to limiting themselves to handshakes. As to the foreign correspondents, all thirty of them were traveling to the opening of the railroad in full order, with wives and gramophones, so they had no one to see them off. [. . .]

Ukhudshansky,[118] a correspondent of a trade-union paper, arrived at the station well before anybody else and was leisurely strolling along the platform. He was carrying with him *The Turkestan Region, Being a Full Geographical Description of Our Fatherland, a Reference and Travel Book for the Russian People,* compiled by Semenov-Tian-Shansky[119] and published in 1903. Now and then he would stop next to a group of departing passengers or ones seeing someone off and say with something of a sarcastic note in his voice, "Departing, ha? Well, well!" or "Staying, ha? Well, well!"

In this manner he walked up to the head of the train, looked at the locomotive for a long time, his own head pulled back, and finally said to the engineer, "Working, ha? Well, well!"

Then the journalist Ukhudshansky went into his compartment, unfolded the most recent issue of his union paper, and surrendered himself to reading

---

118 The humorous last name Ukhudshansky is actually derived from the Russian verb *ukhud-shat'*, which means "to make things worse."

119 Ilf and Petrov are referring to *Rossiia polnoe geograficheskoe opisanie nashego otechestva. Nastol'naia i dorozhnaia kniga dlia russkikh liudei,* ed. V.P. Semenov-Tian'-Shan'skii, under the general supervision of P. P. Semenov-Tian'-Shan'skii and V. I. Lamanskii (St. Petersburg, 1899–1913), incomplete; vol. 19, *Turkestanskii krai* (1903). Petr Semenov-Tian'-Shan'sky (1827–1914) was a famous Russian explorer of Central Asia.

his own article titled "Improve the Work of Small Business Commissions" and subtitled "Commissions Are not Being Sufficiently Restructured." The article contained a report on some meeting, and the author's attitude toward the event being described could have been defined by a single phrase, "Convening, ha? Well well!" Ukhudshansky read on until the departure. [...]

In the meantime, the train, rushing out of Moscow-in-scaffolding, had already started its deafening song. Its wheels banged, sending hellishly laughing echoes under the bridges, and only after entering the wooded area of country homes did the train settle down a bit and go at high speed. The train was going to make an impressive curve across the globe, traverse several climate zones, travel from the cool of central Russia to the hot desert, leave behind many large and small towns, and beat Moscow time by four hours.

Toward evening of the first day, two heralds of the capitalist world made an appearance in the car of the Soviet correspondents: a representative of a free-thinking Austrian paper, Mr. Heinrich, and an American, Mr. Hiram Burman. They came to introduce themselves. Mr. Heinrich wasn't very tall. Mr. Hiram was wearing a trilby. Both spoke rather clean and correct Russian. For some time everybody stood in the corridor silently, curiously looking each other up and down. At first, they talked about the Moscow Art Theater. Heinrich praised the theater, and Mr. Burman evasively remarked that as a Zionist he was mainly interested in the Jewish question in the USSR.

"We no longer have this question," said Palamidov.

"How can there be no Jewish question?" marveled Hiram.

"There just isn't. Doesn't exist."

Mr. Burman was beginning to feel agitated. He had spent his whole life writing articles on the Jewish question for his newspaper, and he would have found it painful to part with the subject.

"But aren't there Jewish people in Russia?" he asked cautiously.

"Sure," replied Palamidov.

"Then the question is there also?"

"No. There are Jews, but no question."

The tension that had accumulated in the corridor of the train car was released by the arrival of Ukhudshansky. He was walking to the washroom with a towel over his neck.

"Talking, ha?" he said, rocking from the quick run of the train. "Well, well!"

By the time he was walking back, clean and energetic, with droplets of water on his temples, the argument had consumed the entire corridor. Soviet journalists had left their compartments, several shock workers had showed up from the next car, and two more foreigners had arrived: an Italian correspondent with a Fascist badge depicting a bundle of lictor's rods and a mace, and a German professor of oriental studies who had been invited to the celebration by the All-Union Society of Cultural Ties. The front line of the argument was very long—from building socialism in the USSR to the men's berets that were becoming fashionable in the West. And on all topics, whatever they were, disagreements arose.

"Arguing, ha? Well, well," said Ukhudshansky, retiring to his compartment.

Only separate exclamations were audible in the overall noise.

"If that's the case," said Mr. Heinrich, pulling the Putilov Factory worker Suvorov[120] by his Russian shirt, "then why is it that you've just been blabbing about it for thirteen years? Why don't you organize the world revolution that you talk so much about? Because you can't? Then stop blabbing!"

"We aren't even going to make a revolution for you! You do it yourself!"

"Me? No, I won't be making a revolution."

"Well, then they'll do it without you and won't even ask your permission."

Mr. Hiram Burman stood leaning against the embossed leather partition and listlessly looking at the arguing sides. The Jewish question had fallen through some discussionary crack at the very beginning of the conversation, and the other topics didn't spark any emotions in his heart. A poet-feuilletonist who used the pen name Gargantua[121] separated himself from the group in which the German professor was making positive remarks about the advantages of Soviet matrimony over the ecclesiastical one. He approached the pensive Hiram and started explaining something to him with great passion. Hiram listened at first but was soon convinced that he couldn't make out a single thing. In the meantime, Gargantua kept fixing things in Hiram's outfit, tightening his tie, taking lint off him, buttoning and unbuttoning his coat, and all the while speaking very loudly and even distinctly. But there was some imperceptible defect in his speech that turned his words into mulch. The problem was aggravated by the fact that Gargantua liked to talk and kept asking for confirmation from his interlocutor.

"It's true, isn't it?" he would say, twisting his head, as if he were going to peck some birdfeed with his nice big nose. "It's true, isn't it?"

---

120 A rather comical juxtaposition of the name of St. Petersburg's largest machine-building factory (Putilov, later renamed Kirov) and the last name of Russia's legendary military commander Field Marshal Aleksandr V. Suvorov (1729–1800).

121 Protagonist of François Rabelais's *Gargantua et Pantagruel* (1532-64), an enormous man.

These were the only comprehensible words in all of Gargantua's speech. Everything else blended into a marvelous, convincing rumble. Mr. Burman kept agreeing out of politeness but soon ran off. Everybody kept agreeing with Gargantua, and he considered himself a person capable of convincing anybody of anything.

"See," he said to Palamidov, "you don't know how to talk to people. I persuaded him. I just proved it to him, and he agreed with me that we no longer have any sort of a Jewish question. It's true, isn't it? Isn't it?" [...]

The evening conversation was burning out. The clash of the two worlds had ended peaceably. Somehow, a fight didn't result. The coexistence on the charter train of the two systems—capitalist and socialist—would have to continue, willy-nilly, for about a month. The enemy of world revolution, Mr. Heinrich, told an old road-trip joke, after which everyone proceeded to the restaurant car for dinner, walking from one train car to the other over shaking metal shields and squinting from a windy draught. In the restaurant car, however, the two sides sat separately. It was right there, over dinner, that the bride show took place. The "abroad," represented by the world's correspondents of the largest newspapers and telegraph agencies, decorously applied itself to the grain spirits and looked with terrible politeness at the shock workers in jackboots and the Soviet journalists who, after a homey fashion, showed up in slippers, wearing only shirtsleeves and no neckties.

A wide range of people sat in the restaurant car: the provincial Mr. Burman from New York City; a Canadian girl who had arrived from the other side of the ocean only an hour before the departure of the charter train and who for that reason was still discombobulated, twirling her head over a cutlet in a long narrow metal dish; a Japanese diplomat and also another, younger Japanese man; Mr. Heinrich, whose yellow eyes twinkled with a derisive smile; a young English diplomat with the thin waist of a tennis player; a German orientalist, who rather patiently listened to the conductor's account of the existence of a strange animal with two humps on its back; an American economist; a Czech; a Pole; four American journalists, among them a pastor who wrote for the newsletter of the YMCA; and finally a blue-blooded American lady with a Dutch last name from an old pioneer family, who had abandoned a train in Mineralnye Vody[122] and for purposes of self-promotion had spent some time hiding in the station cafeteria (this event raised havoc in the American press, and for

---

122 Mineral'nye Vody (literally "Mineral Waters")—a resort of curative waters in the Stavropol Region of Russia in the foothills of the North Caucasus.

three days the papers published articles with such sensational titles as "Girl from Venerable Family in Clutches of Wild Hill Tribesmen of the Caucasus" and "Death or Ransom"); and many, many others. Some of them felt animosity toward anything Soviet, others hoped to figure out—as soon as possible—the enigmatic souls of the Asians, yet others diligently tried to comprehend what was really going on in the land of the Soviets.

The Soviet side made lots of noise at its tables. The shock workers brought food in paper bags and applied themselves to tea with lemon in glass holders made of shiny Krupp metal. The wealthier journalists ordered schnitzels, and one Lavoisian,[123] overcome by a sudden paroxysm of Slavophilia, decided to put on a show in front of the foreigners by ordering sautéed kidneys. He didn't eat the kidneys because he had disliked them since childhood, but he was all puffed up with pride nevertheless and kept casting defiant looks at the foreigners. The Soviet side likewise included different sorts of people. There was a worker from the Sormov Shipyard, voted to go on the trip by a general factory meeting, and a construction worker from the Stalingrad Tractor Factory who ten years earlier had lain in the trenches fighting Vrangel's[124] troops in the very same field where the tractor-building giant now stood; and a textile worker from Serpukhov who was interested in the Eastern Railroad because it was supposed to speed up the delivery of cotton into the textile regions. [. . .]

Later on, when even Ukhudshansky was already asleep, the car door opened, making audible the unrestrained thunder of the wheels but for a moment, and Ostap Bender entered the empty shining corridor, staring around. He hesitated for a second then sleepily waved his hand and opened the door of the first compartment. Gargantua, Ukhudshansky, and the photographer Menshov were sleeping by the light of a blue night lamp. The fourth berth, an upper one, was empty. The great master plotter didn't give it much thought. Feeling weak in his legs after all his wanderings, irreparable losses, and the two hours he had spent riding on the steps of the train car, Bender climbed up.

---

123 This seemingly Armenian name ("Lavuazian" in exact transliteration) is a pun on the name of Antoine Laurent Lavoisier (1743—1794), one of the founders of modern chemistry.

124 Vrangel, Pyotr (1878–1928)—baron, general, and commander of the Volunteer Army (the White Army) from early 1920 until its defeat and evacuation from the Crimea in November of that year.

From there, a miraculous vision appeared to him: a white-fleshed boiled chicken was lying on the table by the window, its legs stuck in the air like two shafts. [. . .] He picked up the chicken and ate it without bread or salt. He stuck the bones under the hard sackcloth mattress. He fell asleep happy, to the squeaking of the partitions, inhaling the inimitable smell of railway paint.

1931

Translated from the Russian by Margarit Tadevosyan Ordukhanyan, in collaboration with Maxim D. Shrayer

RAISA BLOKH

Raisa Blokh (1899 [1898 in some sources]–1943), poet and translator, was born in St. Petersburg to a lawyer's family. Her father, Noah (Noy) Blokh, apparently converted to Christianity pro forma, so as to be able to practice law under pre-Revolutionary anti-Jewish restrictions; her mother apparently did not convert. In the autobiographical poem "Remember, father would stand . . ." (1933; translation below), Blokh would remember her father praying, a *talles* over his head. Blokh majored in medieval studies at Petrograd University and also participated in Mikhail Lozinsky's translation seminar. Blokh was accepted to the Union of Poets in Petrograd in 1920. She was encouraged by her brother, Yakov Blokh, who later founded the Berlin branch of publishing house Petropolis.

Blokh moved to Berlin in 1922 with her brother's family and continued her studies. In 1928, she completed a dissertation on Pope Leo IX at the University of Berlin and took a job at a German academic publishing house, working there until the spring of 1933. Her research interests included the female German poet Hrosvit von Gandersheim (ca. 935–ca. 975). Blokh's first poetry collection, *My City*, appeared in Berlin in 1928. Operating in Berlin and later in Brussels, Blokh's brother published her lifetime collections.

In Berlin, Blokh was part of an informal group, "Circle of Poets," whose members included Yury Dzhanumov, Essad-Bey, Evgenia Kannak, Sofia Pregel, and others, which often convened at the apartment of its chairman, Mikhail Gorlin (1909–1942). They published three collectives: *Housewarming* (later the title of Sofia Pregel's American-based journal), *The Grove*, and *Dragnet*. The titles inadvertently reflect the contributors' insecurity about their place in Russian letters.

Blokh's junior by over ten years, the St. Petersburg-born Gorlin had come to Berlin by way of Poland. His farther, a timber merchant, was able to transfer some of his assets abroad. A student of Russian literature, in 1933 Gorlin defended a dissertation, "Gogol and E. T. A. Hoffmann," under the distinguished Slavist Max Vasmer. Gorlin published original German poetry, which exhibited Jewish themes. In 1936, his Russian-language collection *Journeys* appeared in Berlin. The Blokh–Gorlin relationship developed over the years from a platonic friendship to romance and marriage. Together they translated Sergey Esenin and Anna Akhmatova into German and composed children's tales, some of them published under the joint pen name D. Mirajew.

The poetry of Blokh and Gorlin, who were known as "a pair of doves" in emigration, exhibited signs of cross-fertilization.

After the Nazis came to power, the Gorlins left Germany, settled in Paris, and were married in 1935. Both did some research work at the Sorbonne and Bibliothèque nationale and never felt well adjusted socially in émigré Paris (they were friendly with **Vladislav Khodasevich**). Blokh's second collection, *Quietude: Poems, 1928–1934* (Berlin, 1935), was well received. In 1939, Blokh's poems appeared in the volume *Testaments* along with poems by the medievalist Myrrha Lot-Borodine (1882–1957). One of Blokh's poems was made popular by Aleksandr Vertinsky (1889–1957), the famous émigré poet-chansonnnier, who returned to the USSR in 1943. Vertinsky brought with him to the Soviet audience a repertoire that included "Alien Cities," a modified version of Raisa Blokh's nostalgically bitter poem "A snatch of speech came floating on the air, . . ." which recalls St. Petersburg's Summer Garden (Letniy Sad) and rivers and canals (translation below).

Gorlin was arrested by the Nazis in May 1941 and sent to the Pithiviers transit camp. Blokh mobilized many colleagues to rescue him, but all efforts failed. On 17 July 1942, Gorlin left Pithiviers as part of "Convoy No. 6" and on 19 July 1942 reached Auschwitz-Birkenau, where he was murdered on 5 September 1943. The Gorlins' six-year-old daughter, Dora, died in October 1942. Living under an assumed name, Blokh attempted to cross the Swiss border in November 1943 but was returned by the Swiss border guards to the Nazis. Blokh was sent to Drancy concentration camp and deported to Auschwitz on 20 November 1943. She managed to drop a note from the train car, and that note has survived. The exact circumstances of Blokh's death are unknown. After the war, the couple's friends published a volume of their essays, *Literary and Historical Études* (Paris, 1957) and a volume of their *Selected Poems* (1959). Anna Prismanova dedicated her poem "Shine" to Raisa Blokh's memory. The research of the Vienna-based émigré scholar Fedor Poljakov has shed new light on the life and legacy of Raisa Blokh.

* * *

Both of the selected poems appeared in Blokh's collection *Quietude* (1935) and in *Selected Poems* of Raisa Blokh and Mikhail Gorlin, posthumously published in Paris by the publishing house Rifma (Rhyme), directed by the émigré poet and philanthropist Sofia Pregel (1897–1972).

Reviewing Blokh's *My City* (1928) in the Berlin daily *The Rudder* (*Rul'*), Vladimir Nabokov wrote, "Thus in the end all this [poetry]—golden, lite, and slightly permeated with [Anna] Akhmatova's cold perfume (something almost unavoidable in women's poetry)—may give the undiscriminating reader the impression of something pleasant, simple, birdlike." Nabokov, who had known both Blokh and Gorlin in Berlin and who left Germany in 1937 with a Jewish wife and son, later regretted the harshness of his review. His remorse, coupled with Nabokov's deep understanding of Jewish victimhood, might have led him to the discovery of the character of Mira Belochkin in the novel *Pnin* (1957). Mira's death in a Nazi concentration camp gives the novel's non-Jewish protagonist, Timofey Pnin, reasons to live and remember.

* * *

A snatch of speech came floating on the air,
Brought me words I didn't need to hear:
Letniy Sad, Fontanka, and Neva.

The words flew by, like swallows on the wing:
Blocked out by foreign towns, withal their din,
And foreign water gurgling through the drains.

I cannot grasp, I cannot hide, or drive
Those words away: I won't recall! I'll live,
Suppress my pain, exist, hang on, survive.

All this was real, but years and years ago
The path I walked is covered by thick snow
Which muffles sounds and makes a blank white glow.

1932

* * *

Remember, father would stand,
And pray, hour by hour on end?
Black against white, the fringe
On the shawl that covered his head.

The sun stared in from outside,
Shone brightly, enjoying the scene:
The mud you picked up rolling round
In the street just wouldn't scrub clean.

1933

Translated from the Russian by Catriona Kelly

War and Shoah: 1940s

Editor's Introduction

This section showcases exemplary works created by Jewish-Russian writers in the Soviet Union (and abroad) during the 1940s. In these works, World War II, the Nazi invasion of the Soviet Union, and the Shoah are the main topics. In different ways, their authors lamented both Soviet and Jewish losses as they pondered the survival of Jewishness: first in the face of the Nazi threat from without and then of the Stalinist threat from within during the postwar repressions. The early Soviet decades had been a time of massive migration of Jews from the former Pale to large Soviet cities, where many received university and advanced degrees and joined the widening ranks of the intelligentsia. In 1939, when there were about 3.3 million Jews in the USSR, over 6 percent of the total populations of both Moscow and Leningrad were Jewish (about 250,000 in Moscow and about 200,000 in Leningrad).[1]

Following the Molotov–Ribbentrop pact and the annexation of eastern Poland (western Ukraine and western Belarus), the Baltic states, Bessarabia, and northern Bukovina, the total Jewish population of the USSR had reached about 5.3 million by the time of the Nazi invasion in 1941.

The war was a time of colossal suffering and loss of life. It was also a time of great heroism and sacrifice. In the words of Zvi Gitelman, "In the course of the war, some 30 million men and women of all nationalities served in the Soviet military. About 8–9 million died in the conflict, and another 18 million civilians, including 2.5 million Jews, fell victim of the Nazis, their allies and local collaborators. Between 350,000–500,000 Jews served in the armed forces, over 300 of them rising to general/admiral rank. A very high proportion of Jews—well over a third—were killed in combat."[2]

---

1   See Mikhail Beizer, *Evrei Leningrada, 1917–1939. Natsional'naia zhizn' i sovetizatsiia* (Moscow-Jerusalem: Mosty kul'tury-Gesharim, 1999), 360.

2   Zvi Gitelman, "Soviet Jews in Peace and War," in *Lives of the Great Patriotic War: The Untold Stories of Soviet Jewish Soldiers in the Red Army during WWII*, ed. Julie Chervinsky et al., vol. 1 (New York: Blavatnik Archive Foundation, 2011), 8.

The vast majority of the murdered Jewish civilians were living in the Nazi-occupied Soviet territories encompassing the former Pale and the south of Russia (over 50 percent of the Jewish population of Belorussia [Belarus] and over 90 percent of the Jews of Lithuania were murdered by the Nazis and their local accomplices). From a cultural standpoint, this meant a further severance of Jewish roots in the former Pale of Settlement. A large proportion of the Soviet Jews annihilated during the Shoah were the less assimilated Jews still living in small towns, whereas the survivors were more likely to have been living in big Soviet cities that were not occupied during the war and were more likely to have been integrated and Russianized. Moreover, the wartime evacuation of Jewish civilians fleeing the occupied territories to the remote interior of the USSR (the Urals, Siberia, and Central Asia) placed them in a Soviet melting pot, where Russian was the *lingua franca*.

Even before Hitler's armies invaded the USSR, some Jewish-Russian writers who had already witnessed the suppression of Judaism and of the culture of the small Jewish town (shtetl) and had endured the Soviet assimilationist policies of the 1920s–30s responded to the looming Nazi threat as a call to action. **Boris Yampolsky** (1912–1972) composed his short novel *Country Fair* (excerpted in this section of the anthology) in 1940 as a valediction of the Jewish culture of the Pale; the miracle of its publication in book form in 1942 resulted from the temporarily broadened opportunities for Jewish self-expression. Serving as military journalists during the war, Jewish-Russian writers such as **Vasily Grossman** (1905–1964) became voices of the Soviet people fighting both at the war front and at the home front. The chief voice of anti-Nazi resistance was **Ilya Ehrenburg** (1891–1967), whose wartime speeches and newspaper articles were read and heard by millions, as was his coverage of Nazi atrocities with specific mention of both Jewish martyrdom and Jewish military valor. The triple consciousness of Jewish-Russian poets—Russian, Soviet, and Jewish—was nowhere as explicit as their mournfully militant lyrics about the Shoah. In the poem "I Saw It," written and published in early 1942 and subsequently reprinted a number of times in 1942–43, the poet **Ilya Selvinsky** (1899–1968) became the first national witness to the mass murder of Jews in the occupied Soviet territories. Jewish-Russian authors traveled, embedded with the troops, or were part of the regular military forces, when the Soviet army began to liberate the large swaths of occupied territories in Ukraine and Belarus and then crossed into the pre-1939 border with Poland. They witnessed and described the aftermath of the Shoah by bullet and the liberation of the Aktion Reinhard death camps in eastern Poland. Published in 1944, **Vasily Grossman**'s "The Hell of Treblinka" became the first lengthy literary treatment of the daily torment of a Nazi death camp.

A modicum of mourning for the victims of the Shoah was tolerated in wartime and postwar lyrical poetry (in this anthology, "Death Camp" [1945] by **Pavel Antokolsky** [1896–1978] and the long poem "Babi Yar" [1944–45] by **Lev Ozerov** [1914–1996]). By bearing witness to the immediate aftermath of the murder of Jews by Nazis and their accomplices in the occupied Soviet territories, **Selvinsky**, **Antokolsky**, **Ozerov**, and other early Jewish-Russian literary witnesses openly challenged the emerging official taboo on discussing both Jewish losses and Jewish military valor. In doing so, they simultaneously committed acts of civic courage and Jewish zealotry. Their contribution to Shoah literature is all the more significant because their works appeared in the Soviet mainstream during and immediately after the Great Patriotic War and were available in print during the most destructive years for Soviet Jewish culture. The wartime surge of Jewish-Soviet patriotism even engendered a curious blend of Soviet and Judaic rhetoric in such works as the epic poem *Your Victory* (1945) by Margarita Aliger (1915–1992).

The brief interlude of Jewish self-expression came to a halt by 1947. *The Black Book: The Ruthless Murder of Jews by the German-Fascist Invaders Throughout the Temporarily Occupied Regions of the Soviet Union and in the Death Camps of Poland During the War of 1941–1945*, edited by **Ilya Ehrenburg** and **Vasily Grossman** and featuring contributions by **Ehrenburg** and **Grossman** and a number of other authors in this anthology (**Viktor Shklovsky**, **Vera Inber**, **Pavel Antokolsky**, and **Veniamin Kaverin**), was scheduled to appear in the USSR in 1947. The ban on its publication sent an ominous warning to the Jewish cultural community. The years of late Stalinism brought yet another test for the Jewish survivors of the war and the Shoah. During the Party's so-called anticosmopolitan campaign (late 1940s–early 1950s), even the mere fact of having a Jewish name (or having had a Jewish name) made one vulnerable. Just as conversion to Christianity did not safeguard Jews from Nazi race laws (and a number of émigré Jewish-Russian authors who had taken baptism did perish alongside their unconverted brothers and sisters), the absence of any expressed Jewishness in the works of writers of Jewish origin did not mean they would not fall prey to charges of "rootless cosmopolitanism" from the Soviet brownshirts. Writers whose work was overtly Jewish (such as **Ilya Selvinsky** and **Eduard Bagritsky**, the latter in the section "Revolution and

Emigration: 1920s–1930s") were now condemned for "bourgeois nationalism," some of them posthumously. Few Jewish members of the cultural intelligentsia escaped scrutiny, and the unearthing of real Jewish names behind Slavic pen names became a prominent feature of the anticosmopolitan campaign.

In the postwar period, as Maurice Friedberg so passionately stated in 1984, "Soviet Russian literature was to deny the Jews their one specifically Jewish 'aspiration'—to honor their heroes and martyrs." And in fact, it would fall to several non-Jewish authors of the Thaw, notably Viktor Nekrasov (1911–1987), Yevgeny Yevtushenko (1933–2017), and Anatoly Kuznetsov (1929–1979), to tell the mass Soviet reader parts of the story of the wartime Jewish martyrdom. The de facto taboo on writing about the Shoah and about Jewish heroism and valor at the war front was already evident in the well-publicized case of **Yury German** (1910–1967) and his novel about a Jewish doctor in the Soviet Navy, *Lieutenant Colonel of the Medical Corps*, which was derailed in 1949. In the late 1940s and early 1950s, another author of Jewish origin, the great poet **Boris Pasternak** (1890–1960), was also writing a novel about a doctor. The Shoah must have further convinced the self-fashioned Christian **Pasternak** that Jews ought to assimilate completely and without a trace, and in his novel *Doctor Zhivago* (1946–55; pub. 1957), he spoke about it through his non-Jewish doctor-protagonist, Yuri Zhivago.

Against the backdrop of mounting troubles at home, the formation of the State of Israel in 1948 gave the persecuted Soviet Jews a boost of self-pride while also soon making them doubly suspect as the alleged agents of world Zionism. The late 1940s and early 1950s were, arguably, the darkest years for Soviet Jewry. This period of Stalinism culminated in the so-called Doctors' Plot and was interrupted by Stalin's own death in 1953. The destruction of Yiddish literary culture, concluding with the execution in 1952 of leading Yiddish authors by Stalin's regime, meant that it was left to Jewish-Russian writers, whether they realized it or not, to carry the torch of Jewish self-awareness into the postwar Soviet decades.

Introduction copyright © by Maxim D. Shrayer.

BORIS YAMPOLSKY

Boris Yampolsky (1912–1972), fiction writer and essayist, was born in Belaya Tserkov', a center of commerce located about thirty-five miles southwest of Kiev. In the annals of Jewish history, Belaya Tserkov' is remembered, among other acts of anti-Jewish violence, for the 1648 massacre by Khmelnitsky's troops. In 1897, there were 18,720 Jews in Belaya Tserkov', that is, 54 percent of the entire population. Yampolsky's father was a miller, and his mother ran a small shop. Yampolsky was exposed to a multilingual stream of languages growing up: Russian, Ukrainian, Yiddish, and Polish. ("Do you know the language?" asked Yampolsky in *Dialogues*, referring to Yiddish. "Only the accent.")

Yampolsky left home in 1927. Trying to obliterate his "petit-bourgeois" origins while pursuing a writer's career, he spent several years in Baku, Azerbaijan, and later in Novokuznetsk (Stalinsk), Central Siberia, writing for local newspapers. Yampolsky's first books were the propagandistic tale *They Treasure Hatred* (Tiflis [Tbilisi]) and the collection *Ingilab. Socialist Construction in Azerbaijan* (Moscow-Leningrad, 1931). After moving to Moscow in the 1930s, he attended the Literary Institute in 1937–41. Published serially in 1941, just months before the Nazi invasion, Yampolsky's first short novel (*povest'*), *Country Fair* (excerpt below), a peerless work of Jewish-Russian literature, was virtually unnoticed. During World War II, Yampolsky was a military correspondent for *Red Star* (*Krasnaia zvezda*) and *Izvestia*; he spent over five months with guerilla units in Belorussia. His essays and fiction from that time focused on events of the war.

Yampolsky's short novel *The Road of Trials* (1955; Ukrainian translation 1956) contains no Jewish characters or themes to speak of, featuring a Red Army fighter whose unit is trying to break out of the enemy circle near Kiev. Yampolsky turned to the subject of the Shoah in the 1960s in works that could not be published in the USSR, such as the powerful short story "Ten Midgets on One Bed." During the Thaw, Yampolsky published the autobiographical short novel *The Boy from Dove Street* (1959), its title gesturing at **Isaac Babel**'s masterwork of Jewish childhood, "The Story of My Dovecote." While the narrative logic of the novel fitfully reflected the Soviet formula of Jewish "liberation" through revolution, Yampolsky managed to depict with poignancy the familial aspects of Jewish communal life (a Passover seder, a heder, and so forth), as well as a pogrom witnessed by a Jewish boy. Yampolsky's published fiction of the 1960s included the short novels *Three Springs* (1962) and *Young Man* (1963) and, alongside his stories and vignettes, the short novel *Merry-Go-Round* in his collection *Magic Lantern* (1967). Even in Yampolsky's published—and (self-)censored—stories, readers detected elements of Yiddish folklore and Sholem Aleichem's melancholy humor.

Yampolsky wrote a number of works for the "desk drawer" in the 1960s–70s. They included some of his best Jewish short stories: "Twins," "Miracle," and "A Kiev Story." Some of his works circulated in samizdat and appeared abroad in émigré periodicals. Finished in 1971 and published in the Israeli Russian-language magazine *Twenty-Two* (*Dvadtsat' dva*) in 1978, Yampolsky's short novel *Gypsy Camp* (1971) memorialized the destroyed Jewish communal life as it echoed **Vasily Grossman**'s essay "Ukraine without Jews" (1943): "There are none and there will never again be in the Ukraine: choral synagogues, heders, brises, engagements under a velvet canopy, gold and diamond weddings, fasting until the first star of the day of atonement, Yom Kippur, and the merry, heady holiday Simchas Torah."

Unmarried and without heirs, suffering from kidney disease and fearful of the confiscation of his manuscripts (as had happened to his friend **Vasily Grossman**), Yampolsky distributed them among his friends. He died in Moscow in 1972. During perestroika, the keepers of Yampolsky's manuscripts made possible the publication of his novel *Arbat, a Classified Street* (1960; published in 1988 in *Banner* [*Znamia*] as *Moscow Street*) and other works of fiction and memoirs in magazines and in book form.

* * *

Country Fair appeared in the March 1941 issue of *Red Virgin Soil* (*Krasnaia nov'*); in 1942 it came out in Moscow, in book form in the small run of 5,000 copies, of which not many copies survive. It is Yampolsky's best work and his principal contribution to Jewish-Russian literature.

Set between the Russo-Japanese War and the 1905 Revolution and depicting various social tensions in the Jewish community, the short novel *Country Fair* consists of chapters, each a story in its own right, loosely unified by the quest of a Jewish aunt and her nephew to find the nephew a home and a position. At the end of this tragicomic novel, the Jewish boy ends up where he began: in his native small town.

In this novel about Jewish roots, created amid the tempest of Soviet uprootedness, Yampolsky mythologized the small Jewish town (shtetl) as a stronghold of Jewish and Judaic traditions. As Vladimir Prikhodko observed in the 1997 volume of Yampolsky's prose, which he edited: "*Country Fair* laid bare that which [Yampolsky's] tales of the 1940s–early 1960s obfuscated while at the same time revealing the pathos of origins."

In all of Jewish-Russian literature, there is hardly anything to compare with Yampolsky's (Rabelaisian but also Gogolian) depiction of a Jewish feast, found in the pages to follow. Although Yampolsky's intonation is sharply ironic and grotesquely humorous, his scene of the feast recalls the epic catalog of Jewish names and viands in "The Feast" section of Saul Tchernichovsky's Hebrew-language "Brit Milah: An Idyll from the Life of Jews in Taurida" (1901, which Yampolsky probably knew best in **Vladislav Khodasevich**'s Russian translation), thus emphasizing a unity and continuity of Jewish literature across time, places, and languages.

FROM COUNTRY FAIR

Mr. Dykhes and Others*

The small town resounded with whistling and shouting. The smell of stewing, the smell of frying, the smell of boiling.

Mr. Dykhes had sold all his defective soap to the army. Musicians, go play! Fifers, go dance! Butchers, cut your meat! Bakers, carry your challahs! Cooks, burn in the fire! Bake and fry! Mr. Dykhes is having a good time.

The Dykhes house stands on the river bank—the tallest, most beautiful one in the whole town, with a white zinc roof that sparkles in the sun like silver. The house has a big gilded balcony, curved windows, and a wide front door as in a synagogue. Over the entrance is an emblazoned lion, as if standing watch over the Dykhes gold.

Every morning, when Mr. Dykhes stepped out onto the gilded balcony in his astrakhan, he looked upon the whole small town as his own property. And there was reason to think so. If you looked straight ahead, you saw a five-story windmill leased from the Countess Branitsky, a mill famous throughout all of Kiev Province. When people saw bread as white as snow, they all said, Dykhes flour! If you looked to the left, you saw black smoke over the Jerusalem neighborhood—that was Dykhes tar smoking and Dykhes soap boiling. If you

---

* The text has been abridged.

looked to the right, you saw in the sky the red plume of the sugar factory. Are the old people trudging to the synagogue? It's thanks to Dykhes. He built the town a golden synagogue. Is a corpse being transported? Once again, it's thanks to Dykhes, the honorary head of the local funeral society.

But today is the county fair—the mother of all fairs. Never before has Mr. Dykhes sold so much soap. And what soap it is! Never before have people bought so much flour, so much sugar, so much tar! Gold was flowing in streams.

In Mr. Dykhes's yard, a fragrance of fine cooking filled the air. The carcasses of sheep hung on hooks. Steam coiled around the mountains of hot noodles. Gigantic pies, filled with grated apples, were baking in ovens, and the lame baker was keeping an eye on them. The pastry cook in a pink cap was twisting pretzels with his white hands and sprinkling them with poppy seeds and ground nuts. An old woman covered in down and chicken blood was filling the belly of an enormous goose with nuts, apples, and all sorts of good stuff, continually repeating, "That's how Dykhes likes it!" Several ducks craned their necks to get a better look at the proceedings. It probably seemed to them that the goose had been put to sleep so that surgery could be performed, so they guffawed, asking when it would be their turn for the operation.

The old cooks stood beside the ovens with their arms akimbo, looking boldly at the fire as if they were challenging the pots and pans to a fist fight as they discussed how much pepper and how much vinegar suits Mr. Dykhes. More than anything else, the young cooks were terribly afraid of using too much salt, or not enough, and they were discussing among themselves various incidents involving too little salt or too much salt. On various bonfires, copper basins were seething with jam. The sweet smoke wafted heavenward. Birds flying over the yard stopped in their tracks.

Meanwhile the yard witnessed the arrival of the merry Jew Kukla in his straw Panama hat—a wedding jester.[1] No matter where you wanted to sit down and have something to eat, Kukla would already be sitting there. No matter where you wanted to drink, Kukla was already standing there with a glass. No matter where music was coming from, Kukla was already running there in his

---

1 Yampolsky has given a number of his characters "speaking" last names based on the peculiar and often parodic ways in which Russian/Slavic roots enter Jewish last names. Here's a partial list: *kukla* (Rus.) = doll; *kolokolchik* (Rus.) = little bell or bluebell; *kukharchik* comes from the Russian root for "cook" and "kitchen"; *piskun* = little squealer, from the Russian *pisk*; *kanareika* (Rus.) = canary; *kozliak* comes from *kozel* (Rus.) = male goat, and can also mean an edible forest mushroom with a crooked leg; *gul'ka* comes from *gulia* (Rus.) = pigeon, dove, but can also mean "shank bone."

silly Panama hat. And a wedding without Kukla was not a wedding: Who would sing and shout? And a bris without Kukla was not a bris: Who would make a speech to the baby? Who would pour into the baby's mouth its first drop of wine? And the chicken that was eaten without Kukla was not a chicken. What kind of chicken was it anyway if Kukla had not eaten the gizzard? If someone said to him, "Kukla, it's impossible to be cheerful all the time," Kukla would reply, "You're taunted by pride; I'm contorted by laughter. You drink tears and I, vodka. What I see on the bottom of a bottle, a sober person will never see. What I have eaten at funerals, you will not get to eat at a wedding." Kukla swore they had bought out the whole fair, slaughtered a bull, stuffed its guts with kasha, killed a hundred of the fattest geese and a hundred of the meanest tom turkeys. Kukla said, "We'll eat, we'll drink."

Auntie beseeched the cooks to let me soak in the smoke: "What does a Jewish boy need? Aroma."

The musicians entered. In front were the fat-faced trumpeters; behind them came the tall flautist, then the little drummer boy with a drum on his belly which was itself like a drum. They entered and stood in a row, and the drummer hit the drum twice with a drumstick, "Pay attention! See what cheeks they have!" The cooks started to laugh and gave him a lamb's leg, and each of the fat-faced trumpeters got a chicken gizzard and the trumpeters said, "God give you health," upon which they swallowed their gizzards and started to play a ceremonial flourish.

The guests were assembling.

"Hey," shouted the coachman, "get out of the way!"

In a lacquered phaeton sat Mr. and Mrs. Prozumentik and three screaming little Prozumentiks in yellow silk breeches. They stood up and stuck out their tongues at everybody. Seeing no one and hearing nothing, with a finger on his temple, a member of the bank board of directors walked by with calculations dancing in his head. Waving their arms, Kolokolchik and Kukharchik came running—two rich Jews with flushed cheeks, trying to prove something to each other along the way. When they reached the front porch, Kolokolchik spat in the direction of Kukharchik: "The conversation is over."

Now there appeared a gentleman known to no one, with a big paunch and a mustache. He carried his paunch like a precious vessel. Although he didn't have a penny to his name, everyone looking at the paunch and the mustache and said that he must have a lot of money. No one had invited him yet, but the sight of that paunch was enough to make doors open wide and, although no one knew him, everyone pretended that they had known him for a long time and went so far as to ask, "How do you feel after the party last night?" Everyone walked around him and looked at him, but if they looked only at his paunch, he would clear his throat, showing so that everyone would know he had a mustache, too, and he would smooth out his mustache and blow on it. Cripples, beggars, and hired mourners crowding around the high front door argued as to how much money he had in his pockets: in the side pocket and in the back, where he kept a red handkerchief. "Have you forgotten the vest pocket?" said a dwarf. Some calculated in rubles, some in kopecks, adding even a *grosh*[2] or two.

Along came Mr. Glyuk in his top hat; skipping along behind him was Tsalyuk in a bowler. Glyuk owned an important business with gold signs, and Tsalyuk avoided looking him in the eye.

Mrs. Ratsele in a gauzy dress, proprietress of an establishment where they drink tea with jam,[3] flew into the room on tiptoe, greeting everyone and smiling at everyone, inviting everyone over to drink tea with jam.

Everyone kept coming and coming: the rich Gonikshtein, and Syusman, and Efraim—all the very best families, and Piskun, who also considered himself a good family; and Madame Purl, a woman with a bony neck and a chin like a shovel; and Madame Tori, with a fat neck and a triple chin—one desiring the death of the other; both Madame in the turban and Madame in a burnoose—and one was ready to tear the other to pieces. This group was now joined by a Jew dressed to the hilt like a padishah; after him ran a boy with a gaping mouth and protruding ears. Suddenly new names were announced: Vasily Sidorovich Yukilzon and Pavel Ermilovich Yukinton.[4] Absolutely everyone was here: swindlers in beaver hats and girls in crimson chapeaux and dandies in starch.

The last to arrive was Madame Kanareyka—last so that everyone could see her arrive. She smiled only at the portrait where Dykhes was depicted in his astrakhan with a gold chain across his belly. She smiled as if no one except the portrait were in the hall, as if everything that stood along the walls consisted of dressers and candleholders. Everyone was bursting with envy: Why hadn't they contrived to be last? Then everyone would now be looking not at Madame Kanareyka

---

2   *Grosh* (Yiddish; Pol. *grosz*) = penny, small change.
3   Teahouse—a euphemism for bordello.
4   The humor, most likely lost on the Anglo-American reader, consists in the clash of their non-Russian, suggestively Jewish-sounding last names (Yukilzon, Yukinton) and their equally marked Russian, non-Jewish, Christian first names and patronymics; the owners of these names may be Jewish converts and/or former *kantonisty*.

but at them, and they, too, would have walked slowly by and would have taken Madame Kanareyka for a candleholder or a dresser. Behind Madame Kanareyka came Monsieur François, mincing along on his slender legs as if he were carrying Madame Kanareyka's train, although her dress had no train. Everyone was whispering, "Monsieur François!" "At whom did Monsieur François smile?" Kozlyak, a dentist in orange trouser cuffs, looked at everyone as if he wanted to pull their teeth. He was dying of envy. He, too, wanted everyone to whisper: "Kozlyak smiled!" or "Kozlyak doffed his hat!" or "Did you notice Kozlyak doffing his hat?"

Everyone rushed to walk past the mirror and to start up a conversation with those who were standing by the mirror, but, having seen themselves in the mirror, only to smile as if it were not themselves but an acquaintance whom they hadn't seen for a long time.

And so people walked back and forth, to and fro, displaying who had a gold tooth, who had a false bust, who had a padded rear end, who had an astonishing wig, who had a belly draped with a gold chain. One individual went by with a drooping mustache; he simply had nothing more to show, and the only people who paid any attention to him were those who had not as yet grown a mustache.

Someone's four scrawny daughters with ribbons in their hair glued themselves to the walls, and their faces said, "Not for anything in the world will we get married!" And they took umbrage at everyone, saying that all anyone could think about was getting married. Here came a pharmacist with the face of a lamb, looking them over, beginning with the first, then the second, then all together: "Is it possible that you don't understand why we have ribbons in our hair?" But he was a lamb, and the last thing he wanted was to offend anyone.

The man with the belly and the mustache kept exercising his bass voice, not allowing anyone to get near him, and around him whirled some smart aleck in velvet pants with an insane need to speak. The smart aleck showed the man with the belly the silver charm bracelet on his waist and the chain on his watch and the crown on his teeth and the half-silver cigarette holder and the patent leather boots, but nothing helped, and, when the man with the belly started fanning his mustache, the smart aleck jumped over to the wall.

At one end of the hall, Madame Kanareyka was speaking through her nose as she talked to the ladies about something; and the ladies paid no attention to what she was saying, but they did want to know how she talked through her nose, and some even started examining her mouth, wanting to find out how she did it, where she hid her tongue. At the other end of the hall, a lady with a blue feather held forth. Whenever she turned, the feather turned. It was visible from every angle as she turned. It was visible from every angle as it floated over all the ladies, and some started running ahead in order to have a good look.

A matchmaker passed herself off as the baker's wife, and the baker's wife as the wife of the pastry cook, and the wife of the pastry cook as the musician's wife, and the musician's wife herself had no idea what to pass herself off as. And the madam could talk only about kolaches,[5] and the baker's wife asserted that she had seen no kolaches only pretzels, and from the wife of the pastry cook could be heard only "do-re-mi-fa-so!" and the musician's wife kept silent, showing that she knew very well what was best left unsaid.

In the center stood the barber, but with such a mustache and such eyebrows, and he argued so extensively and bolstered his arguments with his index finger: a doctor, there's no other word for it. Any minute he would take out his pen and write a prescription! And when people spoke with him, they seemed to take him for a doctor, and on everybody's face was written, "Please prescribe some medicine for us." But just as soon as he gave them the cold shoulder, they didn't even want to recognize him as a barber but said that he was a dog fancier; and they even jerked their feet to show how one catches dogs.

Everyone was mean, flushed, sulky, just waiting for someone to cross them. And only the pharmacist who resembled a lamb, equipped with his little bowler hat, his cane, and his evening slippers, wandered politely among them, inquiring whether he might have stepped on someone's corn or whether anyone was bothered by the smell of the medicine. The thin ones in the assemblage hissed, the fat ones huffed, and the thin ones who wanted to seem fat puffed up their cheeks and also huffed until they drove him into a corner, hurling after him the sound "Ba-a-a."

Now a new contingent insinuated itself: a noisy shammes in a soiled robe who, more than anything else, was afraid that not everything was clear to everyone, and therefore he explained everything at length; the melamed Alef-Beiz, with red *peyes*,[6] saying "Eh!" before each and every word; then a midwife with a bow on her bosom, signaling that today everyone was to refrain from talking to her about midwifery. Also Menka, a quarrelsome Jew who would run errands, spread news, and do favors for everyone. The expression on his face always

---

5   Kolaches—Anglicized spelling of Russian *kalachi* (pl. of *kalach*), a traditional Slavic wheat bread made into round shapes by braiding dough.

6   Melamed (Heb., Yiddish)—teacher in a Jewish elementary school. *Peyes*—the Yiddish Ashkenazi pronunciation of the Hebrew *payot*—sidelocks or sidecurls worn by some Orthodox Jewish boys and men.

indicated that he had just arrived with the latest news. There was also a spiteful woman named Shprintsa and one Tsatsel, who went around all the time on tiptoe as if he feared that they would say he was making too much noise. And among them were the three salesmen from Diamant's shop, all the while looking at their master, who was in the middle of a discussion, smiling meaningfully in order to show that they knew what was being discussed and that it was extremely important. The oldest of them would pull out his watch with the chain every minute and, with an important expression, would press it to his ear and then look to see what time it was. The two junior salesmen had only chains, which they didn't pull out, but just the same they assumed important expressions whenever the senior salesman looked at his watch.

"Akh," the midwife suddenly said in a dreamy voice, "what I wouldn't give right now for a fine chicken drumstick."

Everyone seemed to light up at the memory alone.

"Do you know what I would like right now?" said Mr. Prozumentik mysteriously, not even looking at the midwife but turning to Kolokolchik and Kukharchik. "Do you know what would be interesting to eat right now?"

People held their breath, listening closely to find out what Mr. Prozumentik would like to eat right now.

"I would take a goose and would remove the stuffing . . . stuffing . . ."

The midwife looked at him with her eyes bugging out. Diamant's salesmen froze with sweetening on their faces. Menka stood as if he had just arrived with the latest news but didn't know how to tell it.

"Ah, a goose with nuts, that would hit the spot!" confirmed the midwife so that even her bow swelled with pleasure. "And how do you feel about goose with apples. Not bad, eh?"

"Ah, then there's sweet red beans," was heard on all sides.

"Ah, radishes with chicken fat," shouted the shammes in the soiled robe as he began to explain to the assemblage what radishes with chicken fat are.

"Gefilte fish," said others.

"And with horseradish."

"And with sauce, and a nice peppery sauce."

Everyone named his favorite food and sighed over his favorite food. Wishes were running rampant. And only Tsatsel kept walking around on tiptoe, afraid to say what he liked to eat.

"There's nothing better than kishke with kasha," the gentleman with the belly and the mustache suddenly said, and he said it in such a way that no one would have dared to suggest that there was something better than kishke with kasha, which the gentleman with such a belly loved so dearly. "I would open the kishke," he said, demonstrating with two fingers how he would open it and carefully eat the fried skin and then the kasha, only then."

And everyone agreed that only then would one eat the kasha, only later.

"Do you really not know how to eat?" he continued, and they all stretched out their faces, acknowledging that they really didn't know how to eat.

"First of all, you have to try it on one tooth and then, only when all your teeth start to ache, do you try it on them."

"Eh!" melamed Alef-Beis suddenly made up his mind to say something, and he was himself terribly frightened by his own "Eh!" but all the same people were all ears: would a Jew say "Eh!" in vain?

"Eh!" repeated Alef-Beis, "if you take it, rub it, pop it into the oven and sear it ever so slightly, a-a-a, then you have it."

"Yeah!" Tsatsel suddenly spoke up.

"And then add a bit of cinnamon," said Alef-Beis with growing excitement, "but you have to know how to add the cinnamon!"

"Yes, of course, the cinnamon," assented the midwife, not even hearing that you had to take it, rub it, pop it into the oven, and sear it ever so slightly in order to achieve the a-a-a.

"But I like parsnips," was suddenly heard from the quarrelsome Jew Menka, but no one paid any attention to his preferences. No one was the least bit interested in the likes and dislikes of such a Jew.

In the midst of all this frenzied commotion, Auntie suddenly sneezed loudly so that everyone could see that we were there, too. But they didn't see us, and, what's more, they didn't want to see us. The lady with the feather sat on her haunches more and more frequently. The wife of the pastry cook still more loudly repeated: "do-re-mi-fa-so." In more of a drawl than usual, the melamed said "Eh," indicating that he was about to say something.

But here came Mr. Dykhes, who resembled a pig. In spite of such a mug, about which he must have been aware, he, evidently on purpose, stuck out his nose and lips, which made him look even more like a pig. His face said plainly, "I don't have to look like a human being; you'll have to like me as a pig."

No one seemed to have noticed that Mr. Dykhes looked like a pig. No one smiled; no one cried out, "Scram!" On the contrary, they all had such faces as though they were expecting that he would shout "Scram!" at them. But Mr. Dykhes looked around at everybody and suddenly hiccuped as if to say,

"Hello, everybody." And as it happened, they all understood the hiccup to mean "Hello" and started to shout in all directions:

"Good health, Mr. Dykhes. How did you sleep?" But Mr. Dykhes didn't want to say how he had slept, so he looked around at everyone and once again hiccuped.

Mr. Dykhes always hiccupped. Even on Atonement Day, when Mr. Dykhes had eaten woodcock the night before and then fasted till the first star—even on that day he would suddenly hiccup in the synagogue, and everyone would be distracted from God and would think, "Dykhes hiccupped. What was it that he ate today?" And even Dykhes would blush as if he had in fact eaten something.

How everything had changed! Glyuk, who had just been walking on the parquet like a heron, was now twisted into a pretzel. The man with the mustache carried off his paunch so that the entryway would be wider, and Mr. Prozumentik pushed forward the little Prozumentiks, urging them to smile. Even the Diamant's salesmen stopped looking at their master and looked at Dykhes instead. People didn't mind the fact that Dykhes looked like a pig. It was actually appealing; it was somehow touching. Someone even whispered that the lump under Mr. Dykhes's nose was not a simple lump but a lump of wisdom, and that if that lump had been a little closer to the nape of his neck or—better still—on the top of his head, he would certainly have been a cabinet minister.

When Dykhes looked at the ceiling and said, "Hmm," they all gathered into a circle and discussed what that might mean. What had he wanted to say and how was one to understand that sound? Everyone found ten solutions, with commentaries, and even the commentaries generated commentaries, and that "hmm" was being deciphered to mean a whole long speech.

"You, too, will eat from silver platters," Auntie whispered to me.

She was edging me nearer and nearer to Mr. Dykhes. Mr. Dykhes had so much money that all the self-respecting mamas and papas would bring him their children in fancy little Circassian costumes or in sailor suits with gold anchors or lacy pantaloons, and they would stick out a leg and raise an arm as they recited poetry or sang or sawed away at the violin or solved little problems that Mr. Dykhes proposed. But Mr. Dykhes never made an error of judgment: the child in question would be a cantor or a thief, a first violinist or a water carrier. And if Mr. Dykhes said, "Water carrier," then that was that—and you might as well let him grow a beard, because what kind of water carrier would he be without a beard.

At the moment, a boy was standing in front of Mr. Dykhes with a violin. Around him revolved the mama and the papa, not to mention the grandma and the grandpa! Mama provided advice on how to stick out his leg, Papa showed him how to hold his head, Grandma rubbed the bow with rosin, and Grandpa showed him how to handle the bow. Now the boy took the violin, touched it with the bow as if he were asking it about something, and suddenly began to cry, and the violin also began to cry, and the boy ran over it with his bow: "Cry, cry." And no one knew any longer who was crying, the boy or the violin, and Mama and Papa and Grandpa and Grandma were also crying, and now it was perfectly clear that they didn't know the right way to stick out a leg, to hold your head, to handle a bow; their advice was useless and, if you had asked them, they themselves would have said—useless. Everyone was crying. Only Dykhes didn't bat even an eye. He looked at the boy for a long time and suddenly said, "His tooth is somehow not quite right," and he turned away.

At this point Auntie pushed me right up against Mr. Dykhes and said, "This is a golden boy!"

Mr. Dykhes glanced at me and felt my head in such a way as if he wanted to find out whether it contained brains or straw. And everyone wanted Dykhes to say Straw. But he said "Brains!" though with a grimace and a qualification: "Brains that still need to be twisted and turned so that they're in the right place."

Mr. Prozumentik pushed forward the oldest Prozumentik so that Dykhes could feel his head and ask without fail the kind of question to which he might give a clever answer. He even advised Dykhes, "Ask him the name of his papa . . ."

Mr. Dykhes picked up a thick Russian book with a velvet binding and silver clasps and, after opening it, began to leaf through it, murmuring all the while, "What a smart book."

Mr. Dykhes stopped at a certain page and put the book before me; it lay there as Mr. Dykhes held it—upside down. But when I looked at his face and wanted to turn the book right side up, Auntie gave me such a pinch that I understood: the book was lying properly; it had always lain that way since people began to read. And so, looking at the upside-down letters, I started to read, and he, smiling, ran his finger over the lines and repeated in a singsong voice what I was reading, and his face reflected such pleasure as if he had authored the book. The letters, like ants, ran in all directions and then came together again, and suddenly one of the letters turned a somersault and flew away and right after it went the other letters. I stopped peering at them and started to think up words of my own and about my own self, but Mr. Dykhes ran his finger over the line and, in a singsong voice, repeated everything that I had thought up. Moreover, he looked around at everyone with a smile. "What a smart book!" And Mr. Prozumentik said that such a boy should never be given such a smart book. It should be given to the little Prozumentiks and then—there is so much intelligence in that book that, when they add their own intelligence, it will come out so intelligent that no one will be able to understand a thing.

"Say ah-ah-ah!" was suddenly heard from Mr. Dykhes as he raised a finger. "Ah-ah-ah!"

"Ah well, ah well, repeat!" exclaimed Mr. Dykhes, holding a finger that resembled a tuning fork and listening for all he was worth.

"Ah-ah-ah!"

"No, he will never be a singer," declared Mr. Dykhes. "It's actually funny— just imagine him in an opera! Isn't that hilarious?"

And the papas in their bowler hats and the mamas in their lace and the cultured grandmas and the pink grandpas all said, "Of course, hilarious!"

"He's a lazybones," said Mrs. Gulka, who had sprung from God knows where as she pointed her walking stick at me.

"Contagious!" exclaimed Madame Kanareyka.

"A thief!" said "Diamant and Bros."

"What is he good for anyway?" they began to wonder. "Let him be a rag-picker," piped up a small boy in a sailor's jacket, upon which they all immediately started shouting, what a smart boy, and asking who his papa was. It was suggested that I be handed over as an apprentice to the dog fancier, or else to the sauna to make birch rods, or to haul buckets, to drive out the flies, to grate horseradish. But Auntie continued to say that I was a singer, and such a singer had never been and never would be.

"When he sang at a wedding, angels in seventh heaven rejoiced," she said. "Don't you want to be in seventh heaven?"

Mr. Dykhes did want to be in seventh heaven. He sat down in a comfortable chair, put one fat leg over the other, took a piece of candy from a nearby vase, hiccupped and started to suck the candy and to listen, now picking his teeth, now wagging his leg—especially during the modulations. And they all sighed: how he feels the singing, what a connoisseur!

There I was singing my heart out while Mr. Dykhes was sucking candy, smacking his lips, and slurping. But suddenly he bowed his head, grew quiet, and even stopped sucking his candy. He didn't move a muscle, he didn't hiccup, and he even bugged out his eyes. Auntie, having folded her arms in emotion, stood and listened and continually looked around to see if they had all folded their arms in emotion.

Suddenly Mr. Dykhes began to shout, "Ai-yai-yai!"

Immediately everyone began to whisper in agitation, "That note was too loud," said some. "On the contrary, too soft," said others.

"Ai-yai-yai!" repeated Mr. Dykhes and, pointing to his heel, began to laugh. It turned out that Mr. Dykhes had a tickle in his heel.

"I was listening and waiting: Would my heel start tickling or wouldn't it," said Dykhes, unusually excited.

And they were already discussing what kind of omen that was and relating to one another various historical anecdotes involving ticklish heels.

Music began to play, gramophones began to belt out their tunes, doors opened, and in came the triumphant cook, carrying a stuffed pike, which was welcomed by the approving whisper of the guests.

"Guests!" said Dykhes in a gruff voice. "Can it be that you are interested by that pike?"

"The pike is already exciting them," said Madame Kanareyka as she looked through her glasses, wishing to see the excitement with her own eyes.

The guests smiled timidly, as if they wanted to say that this might well be improper and a character flaw, but the pike really did excite them. Dykhes put out his leg and grabbed Madame Kanareyka, who was already standing beside him, knowing that he would now grab someone, and headed toward the pike. And after him came Monsieur François, as if holding the train of Madame Kanareyka, Glyuk and Tsalyuk, Madame Puri and Madame Turi, the lady with the turban and the lady in the burnoose, and the member of the bank board of directors, still holding a finger to his temple.

The din increased as the guests took their seats, smiling at the pike.

"When I sit down at the table," said Mr. Dykhes as he tied his white napkin, "I like everything on the table to be as red as a scraped dog and as fat as a pig." And the tips of his napkin began to move along the edges of his pink face like two pig's ears.

Mr. Dykhes drank some pepper vodka and, turning his head, looked at his guests: "U-u-u, bitter," and then proceeded to eat a honey cake; then he poured some lemon vodka. After he drank it, he also turned his head and, once again, peered at his guests: "Sour," and ate some almonds. At this point he moved the carafe with raspberry vodka toward him and, looking at his guests, gruffly asked, "Well, my guests? I suspect that you want some, too."

The guests started to shake and tremble.

"Fortunately," shouted Mr. Dykhes, drinking a glass of raspberry vodka, and, after eating some giblets, he passed the following judgment: "I love giblets!"

Fortunately, the guests began to eat, some washing it down with pepper vodka, others with lemon, and still others with raspberry, eating honey cake or almond or giblets, and all the while repeating, "Dykhes has good giblets."

"Hail to him who gave us the happiness of living to see this day," with tears in his eyes exclaimed the gentleman with the belly and the mustache, alluding to God but looking at Dykhes, and while the others drank a glass of pepper, lemon, or raspberry vodka, he drank a shot of each one: the pepper, the lemon, and the raspberry.

They were starting to divide up the fish.

"Mr. Dykhes gets the head, because he is the head!"

"The head for Mr. Dykhes," repeated several voices, and Ratsele smiled at the head of the fish as if hoping that the head would report to Dykhes that Ratsele had smiled at it.

"And Mr. Menka gets the tail, because he is a tail!" trumpeted Kukla in a spiteful voice.

"The tail for Mr. Menka, because he is a tail!" everyone began to shout, exulting in the fact that he was the tail and not they.

"And I get all the rest," said Kukla, "because I love all the rest."

Everyone started to laugh, seizing all the rest as they did so and leaving Kukla the nastiest piece, way up by the tail. And the shammes, who had just explained that the pike is the fish of all fishes, got not a single piece, and melamed Alef-Beis, no matter how many times he enunciated "Eh," also got not a single piece, and he looked at his empty plate with his mouth wide open, enunciating "Eh." And Tsatsel, not daring even to sit down at the table, went around on tiptoe, constantly afraid that they might accuse him of hindering people from eating their pike.

Just then the air was filled with shrieks as the hall where people were eating and drinking was invaded by a band of shaggy women from the soap-boiling factory. The guests began to twitch their noses. Some even hiccupped, and Monsieur François promptly began to wave his pink handkerchief, at which point the air began to smell of violets, lily-of-the-valley, and cypress.

"I want to know why they've come," shouted Dykhes. "I ask you what is the meaning of this? Do I not have locks on my doors? Have I no bouncers? Have I no swine?" shouted Dykhes as he looked with hatred into the red mug of the creature standing on the threshold with a log in its hand. "Am I not allowed the peace and quiet to drink a glass of vodka? And a second glass and a third!"

"Don't shout, Mr. Dykhes," said one of the women. "Let the Jews speak out."

"What's up? Does it smell bad in there?" he asked in such a tone that it was clear that he already knew why they had come.

"It smells of dog fat," said a woman with a child in her arms. "Even the baby already smells of dog fat and so does his bagel." The woman began to cry.

"Well, what do you expect? Perfume would no doubt smell better?" Dykhes asked once again.

"Better, Mr. Dykhes, better," replied the woman as she wiped away her tears.

"Well, if it smelled of perfume, I would go there to sniff the air and so would my guests. Right, guests?"

And the guests started to laugh and said that they certainly would.

"We're coughing up blood, we're exhaling blood," whispered the woman.

But no one was listening to her. The guests were laughing, washing the laughter down with vodka, and swallowing the pike and meat with thick smears of mustard, not to mention horseradish and brine. [...]

Now Dykhes was shouting, "Anyone who wants a raise should stay away from me. Hush! Go home! Lie down with your stomach on the stove and let our great God give you a raise. What do you want anyway—to tear out my guts?" Suddenly he started roaring and started jumping on a chair. "Sit down, drink, gnash your teeth, tear Dykhes apart."

"Drop dead," shouted the woman, and her baby started to cry. "But we want to eat, too. And we're going to exit through the front door and break open all the doors! ..."

Mr. Dykhes even jumped in surprise.

"You, the masters, are a bunch of villains," said the woman. "Your glasses are filled not with wine but with our blood. Look at how red and sweet it is. You drink it and still you laugh! Is life sweet for you? Do you think there will always be war and you will always be happy and you will always sleep on soft mattresses?"

"Master," all the women began shouting. "We will burn out your red eyes with sulfuric acid."

"Oy, people," shouted Dykhes. "I no longer have any eyes!"

"Oy, we no longer have any eyes," repeated the guests.

"Who is insulting my guests? Where is my wine? Where is my vodka?" bellowed Dykhes when the women had been driven out. Out of the cellar, as if from under the ground, the servants rolled a barrel of vodka; it whistled with a whistle; it boiled with boiling water.

Ten cooks, with the grease of the ovens on their faces, carried in on their extended arms big platters of smoking meat, Jewish meat, smothered in fiery sauces—some burning with pepper, others sweetened with raisins.

The geese floated like swans.

"Guests, let's eat, let's drink!" Dykhes blared out like a trumpet.

Throwing back their heads, the guests poured the sauce down their throats and questioned one another: Is it sour or is it sweet? They unexpectedly snagged the wings with near effortlessness, but some, having noticed the gizzard, smoothed out their mustaches and, with their mouths, fished out the gizzard and, after swallowing it, gazed at the host with gratitude.

"Down the hatch, guests!" said Dykhes.

Veal breasts, smoked tongue, pâtés, meat casseroles, chopped herring with potatoes and onions, meat dishes of all kinds, and vegetable dishes of all kinds, some baked on coals, others soaked in steam.

The man with the belly and the mustache, who had been advising people to try it first on one tooth, now wolfed the food down using all his teeth. In his hands he carried a leg of mutton, which he ate with gusto. He had already choked twice.

The neighbors had already pounded on his back with their fists. Having caught his breath, he once again went to work on that leg of mutton. I was looking at him, but he continued to eat, driving me away with his eyes. When he had finished devouring the leg of mutton, he heaved a sigh and went to work on a side of mutton.

The salesmen were sitting politely at the table and, when their employer was looking at them, they, like birds, pecked at the nuts and berries but when their employer lowered his eyes to his plate, they went to work on the most greasy pieces and packed them first in one cheek, then in the other. If their employer suddenly looked up, they pretended that they were pecking at the nuts and berries. And they had already taken off their bowler hats twice to wipe the sweat from their bald spots.

And the guests were served cold dishes and hot dishes, fish in aspic and stews. When it came to the goose with sweet nuts—what work it was for the jaws, trouble for the belly when they began to crunch against their teeth. The guests could not express enough joy, so they said, "This goose is a goose beyond compare!" And several even shouted, "Thank you, Dykhes, for the goose!"

Then there was noodle kugel with raisins, noodle kugel with honey, noodle kugel with cottage cheese, flour kugel with chicken fat—not to mention honey cakes, egg cakes, and almond cakes, strudels with raisins, strudels with grapes, and strudels with poppy seeds. And they ate every bit of it.

Madame Kanareyka, cautiously nibbling on a burned piece, looked at those of us who were standing in the corner, and she said, "How those beggars want to eat! How they're looking at the table! They would gladly eat us. If, in your opinion, we let them in, would they eat us up?"

Mrs. Prozumentik and Madame Puri and Madame Turi and the lady with the turban and the lady in the burnoose—all those whom Madame Kanareyka had admitted to her presence—replied that yes they would eat us up, and Ratsele in the pink scarf, whom Madame Kanareyka had not admitted to her presence, also said, "Of course, they would eat us up."

The musicians, having hiccupped for the last time, picked up their trumpets, and the guests began to sing, banging the serving dishes. Then a group of guests with deep nasal voices started shouting and loudly sniffling. The women at the door started to scream their heads off. Everything was going around in circles, rushing in all directions, flapping their coat tails, chasing after happiness.

Mr. Glyuk, with his top hat in hand, Madame Kanareyka with the shawl over her head, Madame Puri and Madame Tori, the lady with the turban and the lady in the burnoose were all going around, and the lady with the blue feather did also—when she came galloping up, she was followed closely by the galloping feather. When she took a seat, the feather took a seat, at which time the people outside would say, "She's taken a seat!"

On their heels came Mr. Prozumentik, with his fingers in the armholes of his vest, then the smart aleck in velvet trousers. On their way, Kolokolchik and Kukharchik were offering each other a shipment of baby powder that they had bought up from Dykhes. Ratsele, all puffed out in her gauzy dress but managing a big smile, invited everyone to be her guests for tea and jam. And the lamb with the walking stick was using the stick to depict the condition of his soul. Doffing their bowler hats, the firm of Fayvish and Suskind met the firm of Yukinton and Yukilzon. Suddenly between the firms, materializing out of nowhere, appeared Menka with his informative face and red handkerchief. He proceeded to dance, smiling at one and all, but no one even looked at him.

They made a circle around him, raising their arms higher. So Menka stayed by himself, with his red handkerchief and his foolish nose, hiccupping from the sweet vodka and sneezing from the strong tobacco as he ecstatically reported the news, not noticing that he was alone and that everyone had forgotten him and that no one even wanted to look at him.

The matchmaker with a smile was heading toward the baker's wife, but the baker's wife turned away and, with a smile, headed toward the pastry cook's wife, but the pastry cook's wife turned away with a smile and headed for the musician's wife, who turned away but without smiling at anyone, and so it went, round and round.

They bowed to one another and bragged to one another as they went up to one another on heels and moved away from one another on tiptoe, teasing one another, hissing at one another, spinning around in front of one another like a wheel or a top, crawling around on all fours—everyone shouting: a-a-a! The musicians because they were musicians, the insane man because he was insane, Glyuk because he was rich, and Menka because he wanted to do some shouting next to a rich man. Mr. Dykhes stood in the middle, fiery from all that he had eaten and drunk, and only moved his paunch up and down a few times as if saying, "That will do it for me."

ca. 1940

Translated from the Russian by Richard Sheldon

ILYA EHRENBURG

(See the introductory essay and an excerpt from Ehrenburg's novel *Julio Jurenito* in the section "Revolution and Emigration: 1920s–1930s.")

During World War II, while Ehrenburg worked tirelessly as a journalist and anti-Nazi propagandist, he continued to compose lyrical poetry and also to translate from the French of François Villon, sometimes at night when he was unable to sleep.

"To the Jews," the wartime essay chosen for this anthology, illustrates Ehrenburg's commitment to writing about Nazi atrocities and Jewish heroism. Two days prior to its publication in *Izvestia* on 26 August 1941, Ehrenburg read "To the Jews" at a rally of the representatives of Jewish people in Moscow. In the words of Mordechai Altshuler, "the theme of the Shoah had come to occupy the thoughts and feelings of Ehrenburg. In 1942 or 1943 while [...] he visited the areas liberated from the Nazi occupation, Ehrenburg began to gather material about the annihilation of the Jews, both by bullet and in death camps. He used some of this material in his newspaper articles." While describing the total annihilation of Jews and Roma in the occupied territories, Ehrenburg subtly alluded to the tabooed subject of collaboration by the local populations. In light of everything we know today, it is even more difficult to imagine that in the official Soviet conditions of de-Jewifying the Shoah and silencing the valor of Jewish soldiers, partisans, and ghetto fighters, Ehrenburg succeeded in having his openly Jewish essays printed in the central Soviet periodicals and thus reaching an audience of millions of his fellow Soviet citizens. In the article "On the Eve" (*Pravda*, 7 August 1944), Ehrenburg devoted a paragraph to the Nazi atrocities in the Trostinets (Trostenets) area in Belarus (see Maly Trostinets): "Half-charred corpses, stocked up like firewood, racks of corpses were still smoking. Children were neatly placed at the end of each row. . . . This was the last shipment [*partiia*], which they had not finished burning. All around I saw dug up soil and a field of skulls. [...] There they killed Soviet prisoners of war, Belarusians, Jews from Minsk, Vienna, Prague." Beneath Ehrenburg's article describing Nazi "factories of death" was a harrowing photograph of a field of corpses; the photograph, like the article, bore Ehrenburg's byline, adding to the totality of his eyewitness account.

One of the most remarkable things about Ehrenburg's poems about the Shoah is the very fact of their publication in the Soviet Union, in his collections and in central periodicals. For example, Ehrenburg's poem "Rachels, Hayims, and Leahs wander..." was originally published in his collection *Loyalty (Spain, Paris). Poems* (Moscow, 1941). In January 1945, Ilya Ehrenburg published a cycle of six poems about memory, mourning, and artistic response to catastrophe in the flagship Moscow literary monthly *Novy mir*. Ehrenburg's January 1945 *Novy mir* cycle constitutes a high point in the history of Jewish-Russian Shoah poetry created and published in the USSR. These poems spoke of the Shoah to a mass and diverse audience of Soviet readers. They owed their publication mainly to the historical context of the war moving beyond Soviet borders in 1944–45 and of the liberation of the Nazi death camps.

Of the six poems published in *Novy mir* in January 1945, Ehrenburg composed at least two in 1944 and the rest in early January 1945. Originally, the cycle that Ehrenburg submitted consisted of at least seven poems, the earliest of which was composed in 1943. As of early January 1945, Soviet troops had not yet liberated Auschwitz-Birkenau. They would approach the complex in the middle of January and liberate the camp on 27 January 1945. On 16 January 1945, *Novy mir*'s editorial board decided to publish six of the seven poems originally included in the cycle. Among the six short poems in the cycle was Ehrenburg's poem about Babi Yar ("What use are words and quill pens..."), indispensable to students of Shoah memory.

Kiev and Babi Yar occupied a special place in Ehrenburg's wartime writings. It was with great difficulty that Ehrenburg was able to speak in print about the fall of Kiev to Nazi armies, in a short *Red Star* article published on 27 September 1941: "We will liberate Kiev. The enemy's blood will wash the enemy's footprints" (trans. Joshua Rubenstein). Kiev—and Babi Yar—was also a personal wound for Ehrenburg. Over 33,000 Jews were murdered on 29–30 September 1941 at Babi Yar outside Kiev, and altogether as many as 100,000 people, about 90,000 of them Jews, were killed there throughout the Nazi occupation. As one of the best informed Soviet figures, Ehrenburg had known of Babi Yar early on. But he had to wait two years before he was able to visit Kiev and bear witness—soon after Soviet troops liberated it on 6 November 1943.

In the essay "Nationkillers," published in *Banner* in early 1944, Ehrenburg conjured up the famous image of a little Kievan girl, thrown by the Nazis into a grave: "'Why are you pouring sand in my eyes?' I hear this child's scream at night. All the people hear it. Our conscience is filled with indignation, and our conscience would not leave us be. It demands: Death to the nationkillers." Echoes of Babi Yar resound through the text of Ehrenburg's article

"To Remember!" published in *Pravda* on 17 December 1944, only weeks before the completion of the January 1945 *Novy mir* cycle: "In the countries and areas that they occupied, the Germans murdered all the Jews [even] old people and infants. Ask a captured German, why his countrymen annihilated six million innocent people, and he will answer: 'They are Jews. They are black (or red-haired). They have different blood.' This started with vapid jokes, with street urchins' yelling, with graffiti on the fences, and it led to Majdanek, Babi Yar, Treblinka, to ditches filled with corpses of children. . . ." As early as December 1944, Ehrenburg put an accurate number on the toll of the Shoah, presented the murder of Jews in the occupied Soviet territories and in the death camps in Poland as part of the same genocidal Nazi plan and thus steeped the Shoah in the long history of antisemitism.

During the Soviet period, some but not all of the individual poems in the *Novy mir* cycle were subsequently reprinted. Even though Poem 1 of the cycle appeared—in modified form and under the title "Babi Yar"—in several of Ehrenburg's poetry collections and editions of his works and became one of his most famous texts, the cycle has never since been reprinted in its entirety, either during Ehrenburg's lifetime or subsequently. Both circumstances attest to the cycle's paramount significance in the canon of Shoah literature.

TO THE JEWS

When I was a child, I witnessed a pogrom against the Jews. It was organized by tsarist police and a small group of vagabonds. But individual Russians hid Jews. I remember how my father brought home a letter by Leo Tolstoy that had been copied onto a slip of paper. Tolstoy lived next door to us. I often used to see him and knew he was a great writer. I was ten years old. My father read "I Cannot Be Silent" out loud; Tolstoy was outraged by pogroms against the Jews. My mother broke out in tears. The Russian people were not guilty of these pogroms. The Jews knew this. I never heard a malicious word from a Jew about the Russian people. And I will never hear one. Having gained their freedom, the Russian people have forgotten the persecution of the Jews as if it were a bad dream. A generation has grown up that does not know even the word "pogrom."

I grew up in a Russian city. My mother tongue is Russian. I am a Russian writer. Like all Russians, I am now defending my homeland. But the Hitlerites have reminded me of something else: my mother's name was Hannah. I am a Jew. I say this with pride. Hitler hates us more than anything. And this adorns us.

I saw Berlin last summer—it is a nest of criminals. I saw the German army in Paris—it is an army of rapists. All of humanity is now waging a struggle against Germany, not for territory but for the right to breathe! Is it necessary to speak about what these "Aryan" swine are doing with the Jews? They are killing children in front of their mothers. They are forcing old people in their agony to behave like buffoons. They are raping young women. They cut, torture, and burn. Belostok, Minsk, Berdichev, and Vinnitsa will remain terrible names. The fewer words the better: we do not need words, we need bullets. They are proud to be swine. They themselves say that Finnish cattle mean more to them than Heine's verses. They insulted the French philosopher Bergson before his death; for these savages, he was just a *Jude*. They ordered the books of the late Tuwim to be used in soldiers' latrines.[7] *Jude!* Einstein? *Jude!* Chagall? *Jude!* Can we speak about culture when they rape ten-year-old girls and bury people alive in graves?

My country, the Russian people, the people of Pushkin and Tolstoy, are standing up to the challenge. I am now appealing to the Jews of America as a Russian writer and a Jew. There is no ocean to hide behind. Listen to the sound of weapons around Gomel! Listen to the cries of tormented Russian and Jewish women in Berdichev! Do not block up your ears or close your eyes! The voices of Leah from the Ukraine, Rachel from Minsk, Sarah from Belostok will intrude on your still comfortable dreams—they are crying over their children who have been torn to pieces. Jews, wild animals are aiming at you! Our place is in the front line. We will not forgive the indifferent. We curse anyone who washes his hands. Help everyone who is fighting this rabid enemy. To the assistance of England! To the assistance of Soviet Russia! Let each and every one do as much as he can. Soon he will be asked: What did you do? He will have to answer to the living. He will have to answer to the dead. He will have to answer to himself.

1941

Translated from the Russian by Joshua Rubenstein

Poems (The January 1945 *Novy mir* cycle)

---

7   Tuwim, Julian (1894–1953)—great Polish poet, a Jew who escaped to the United States during World War II and returned to Poland after it ended; in referring to Tuwin's death, Ehrenburg must have been relying on uncorroborated information.

POEMS (THE JANUARY 1945 *NOVY MIR* CYCLE)

1.

What use are words and quill pens
When on my heart this rock weighs heavy?
A convict dragging his restraints,
I carry someone else's memory.
I used to live in cities grand
And love the company of the living,
But now I must dig up graves
In fields and valleys of oblivion.
Now every *yar* is known to me,
And every *yar* is home to me.
The hands of this beloved woman
I used to kiss, a long time ago,
Even though when I was with the living
I didn't even know her.
My darling sweetheart! My red blushes!
My countless family, kith and kin!
I hear you calling me from the ditches,
Your voices reach me from the pits.
I speak for the dead. We shall rise,
Rattling our bones we'll go—there,
Where cities, battered but still alive,
Mix bread and perfumes in the air.
Blow out the candles. Drop all the flags.
We've come to you, not we—but graves.

2.

Rockets, fireworks. The blacker the skies,
The darker the passion of those ravaged days.
They fly and they burn. And the sky stays black.
And if you don't survive an attack,
Then just for a minute, like this rocket steadfast,
You light someone else's path with yourself.

3.

Someone else's woe—like a gadfly;
You wave it off, but it gets right back at you,
You'd like to go out but it's late already,
The woe's hot and muggy air,
No matter how you breathe, suffocating.
The woe doesn't hear, a nagging hysteric,
It comes at night, moaning, aching,
And what to do with it—someone else's.

4.

Sunshine, downpour, or snow, on that day
Silence astounds. A person comes to stay.
Everything starts in silence. Like a dream
Of a person returning to silence, yet again.
O, victory's last fireworks! Not words
Will tell us of happiness—water and grass.
Not guns will mark the conclusion of battles,
But the beating of bird hearts, those tiniest of bells.
We'll hear the quietness of moth wings in flight,
If the wind has subsided and young is the night.

5.

The day will come, the warblers' loud chirps
Will sound in chorus, praising birdsome quirks,
Merrily, a dragonfly will don
Her brightest weekend eyes and keep them on.
Once again the skies will be for birds,
And the honey meadows—for lungworts.
Only those will be dimmed at noon,
Who are moonlit even without the moon,
There will be hands to hold and embrace,
There will be lips to kiss and taste.
Even the wind, after reciting poetry,
Will fall asleep under its alder tree.

6.

I beg you not for me, but those
Who lived in blood, whose mirrors froze,
Who hadn't heard love's violins
The longest, who forgot the smell
Of roses and the lilt of sleep—
Beneath them no floor will tilt.
I beg for them: both color and singing,
Please give them ringing, motley sounds,
So that the dying day, like a cygnet,
Will drop tongue-trilling silver sighs.
I beg you senselessly, my heart
Approaching, stopping, crossing again,
For just a bit of tremulous art
Behind a dainty curtain of rain.

1944–45

Translated from the Russian by Maxim D. Shrayer

ILYA SELVINSKY

Ilya Selvinsky (1899–1968), poet, dramatist, memoirist, and essayist, was born in Simferopol, where his family suffered during the 1905 Simferopol pogrom. A descendant of both Ashkenazi Jews and Krymchaks (Crimea's indigenous, rabbinate non-Ashkenazi Jews), Selvinsky grew up in Evpatoria (Eupatoria) in the family of a furrier merchant. In 1919, Selvinsky graduated from a gymnasium in Evpatoria, spending his summers as a drifter and trying his hand at different trades, including sailing, fishing, and acting in an itinerant theater. A man of great physical prowess, the young Selvinsky also worked as a longshoreman and circus wrestler.

Selvinsky published his first poem in 1915 and in the 1920s experimented with the use of Yiddishisms and thieves' lingo in Russian verse. He is credited with innovations in Russian versification, including the proliferation of *taktovik*, a Russian nonclassical meter. Extensive travel and turbulent adventures fueled Selvinsky's longer narrative works and cycles, "loadified" (term used by the Russian constructivists) with local color. Selvinsky first joined the anarchist troops in the Russian Civil War but later fought on the side of the Reds. In 1919, he entered the medical faculty of Taurida University. He moved to Moscow in 1921 and studied law at Moscow University, graduating in 1922.

The wreath of sonnets *Bar Kokhba* (1920, pub. 1924) occupies a special place among Selvinsky's works. While Selvinsky was probably influenced by the widely performed Yiddish drama *Bar Kokhba* (1887) by Abraham Goldfaden (1840–1908), as well as by **Vladimir Jabotinsky**'s "In Memory of Herzl," the formal sophistication of the twenty-year-old poet's wreath of sonnets is astonishing. Literally, it is a wreath laid in memory of the Jewish zealot; figuratively, it is a form that textually embodies might, power, resistance, and strength of conviction. One could well imagine Selvinsky's art in *Bar Kokhba* as sculpting words. Bar Kokhba, the leader of the second Jewish revolt against Rome (132–35 CE), was for Selvinsky a symbol of Jewish resistance and spiritual endurance. Against the backdrop of a growing campaign against traditional Jewish life and Judaism in the Soviet Union, Selvinsky's *Bar Kokhba* remained a powerful monument to Jewish—and Judaic—survival.

Selvinsky was the leader of the Literary Center of Constructivists (LTsK), an early Soviet modernist group, from 1924 until its dismantlement in 1930 and edited several landmark anthologies by constructivist authors (e.g., *The*

State Plan of Literature). In the late 1920s, the LTsK counted among its members the poets **Eduard Bagritsky**, **Vera Inber**, and Vladimir Lugovskoy, critic Kornely Zelinsky, prose writer Evgeny Gabrilovich, and others. In the middle to late 1920s, after the publication of *Records*, *The Ulyalaev Uprising* (1924, pub. 1927), and the narrative poem *Notes of a Poet* (1927, with a cover by EI Lissitsky), Selvinsky achieved fame and acclaim. In 1929, his tragedy *Army 2 Commander* was staged by Vsevolod Meyerhold. In 1930, trying to redeem himself after the dismantlement of the independent literary groups, Selvinsky composed the opportunistic poem "From Palestine to Birobidzhan" (1930, pub. 1933; on Birobidzhan, see **Viktor Fink**). "Portrait of My Mother" (1933) contains a constructivist's bitter comment about Jewish-Soviet assimilation: "Henceforth her son's face will remain defiled/Like the Judaic Jerusalem,/ Having suddenly become a Christian holy site."

Through a combination of personal bravery, political navigation, and luck, Selvinsky weathered the storms of Stalinism and was a major literary figure of the post-Stalinist years. He remained a proud Jew during the most antisemitic of the Soviet years, the late 1940s–early 1950s, despite direct official ostracism. In addition to *Bar Kokhba*, Selvinsky's major early Jewish works include "Anecdotes about the Karaite Philosopher Babakai-Sudduk" (1931), "Motke Malechhamovess [Motke the Angel of Death]" (1926), and *The Ulyalaev Uprising*. The first Soviet poet to publish an eyewitness account of the mass extermination of Soviet Jews in the Nazi-occupied Soviet territories, Selvinsky wrote about the Shoah in a number of wartime works (see below). Shortly before his death, he published the autobiographical novel *O My Youth* (1966), where Jewish themes figured prominently. Ilya Selvinsky was a poetic virtuoso. His literary records (note the title of his 1926 collection, *Records*) include the epic poem *The Ulyalaev Uprising*, the novel in verse *Fur Trade* (1928), and his wartime poems of witnessing the Shoah.

* * *

Soon after the Nazi invasion of the USSR, Selvinsky volunteered for the war front and was sent as a staff military journalist to his native Crimea. He joined the Communist Party in 1941; he was decorated for valor and promoted to lieutenant colonel. Selvinsky was profoundly affected by the Nazi atrocities he witnessed at the easternmost part of Crimea in and around the city of Kerch in January 1942, when the area was temporarily liberated by Soviet troops during the Kerch-Feodosia Landing Operation. Most significant for Selvinsky's experience as a poetic witness to the Shoah are the poems "I Saw It" (1942) and "Kerch" (1942), both included in this anthology. Selvinsky wrote "I Saw It," his best-known Shoah poem, in January 1941, after having seen the immediate aftermath of the executions of thousands of Jews by the Nazis and their accomplices, which were carried out in November–December 1941 at the so-called Bagerovo antitank ditch west of the city of Kerch. During the second week of January, Selvinsky made the first entry in his diary for 1942: "But near the village of Bagerovo in an antitank ditch—7,000 executed women, children, old men, and others. *And I saw them.* Now I do not have the strength to write about it in prose. Nerves can no longer react. What I could, I have expressed in verse (see 'I Saw It')." (The Shoah in Crimea and Selvinsky's career as a Shoah witness are treated extensively in Maxim D. Shrayer's book *I SAW IT* [2013]).

First printed on 23 January 1942, "I Saw It" was reprinted in the main newspaper of the Red Army, *Red Star*, on 27 February 1942 and a number of times subsequently. Selvinsky became the first national literary witness to the Shoah in the occupied Soviet territories. In the summer of 1943, Selvinsky was present at the Krasnodar Trial, to which he responded with the poem "A Trial in Krasnodar" (pub. 1945). In November 1943, a dramatic rupture occurred in Selvinsky's career, resulting from his removal from the frontlines and repressions against him, the latter ranging from his punitive dismissal from the army to party resolutions targeting the poet. The beginning of Selvinsky's wartime troubles may be traced to the summer of 1943, when Soviet troops went on a broad offensive and started to liberate occupied Soviet territories with sizeable prewar Jewish populations, in Ukraine and elsewhere, and came upon ubiquitous evidence of the Shoah. Indeed, the timing of Selvinsky's troubles concords with a final shift in the official, if not publically enunciated, Soviet attitudes to writing about both specified Jewish losses and Jewish valor. One of the palpable results of this shift was a systematic substitution of the unspecified "Soviet people" or "civilians" for "Jews." The repressions against Selvinsky were likely aimed at intimidating Soviet writers into silence about Nazi crimes against the Jews.

In April 1945, his rank and status finally restored, Selvinsky was dispatched to the Kurland (Courland) Peninsula. Outside Riga, in June 1945, Selvinsky composed his last principal Shoah work, the long poem *Kandava* (pub. 1946), which unfolds around a nightmare in which he imagines himself and his wife "somewhere in Auschwitz or Majdanek." *Kandava* holds a special place in Selvinsky's career as a poetic witness to the Shoah because it bridges what the poet saw and witnessed in Crimea, North Caucasus, and Kuban in 1941–43 and what he learned about the Nazi camps in the spring of 1945. Selvinsky poignantly brought together the Shoah by bullet and the so-called "Final Solution" into a single history.

I SAW IT

Germany, now we weave you a shroud,
And into it we weave a threefold scourge.[8]

Heine, "The Silesian Weavers"

One may choose to dismiss people's tales
    Or disbelieve printed columns of news.
But I saw it! With my own eyes.
    Do you understand? I saw it. Myself.
Here—the road. Over there—a higher plain.
    Between them, just there—a ditch.
From the ditch rises boundless pain
    And sorrow—without end.
No! About this one cannot—with words . . .
    One must sob. Roar.
7,000[9] murdered ones—in a wolf's hollow,

---

8   "Deutschland, wir weben dein Leichentuch, / Wir weben hinein den dreifachen Fluch" (Heinrich Heine, "Die schlesischen Weber," 1844).

9   The number 7,000 was apparently first cited in the news dispatches of TASS, the Telegraph Agency of the Soviet Union, on 5 January 1942. On 5 January 1942, an unsigned report, "Bloody Atrocities of Germans in Kerch," appeared in *Pravda*, stating, "According to preliminary data, altogether in Kerch the fascist scumbags killed up to 7,000 people. Many children were poisoned by German brutes." In fact, the *Pravda* report appeared one day before the issuing and two days before the publication of a note by Vyacheslav Molotov, then People's Commissar (Minister) of Foreign Affairs. Distributed worldwide, Molotov's note of 6 January 1942 cited the number of Kerch victims as 7,000, and this number was subsequently repeated in numerous publications. To this day the exact number of civilians murdered at the Bagerovo ditch is a matter of some debate. Lower estimates of the number of Jews murdered in Kerch in November–December 1941, around 2,500, have been arrived at, in part via questionable math. While some data support the presence of over 10,000 Jews in Kerch at the time of the first Nazi occupation (November–December 1941), it is difficult to speak conclusively about accurate numbers and especially about the methods by which these numbers have been subsequently revised. Some of the victims, especially Jewish-Polish refugees who ended up getting stuck in the bottleneck of the Kerch peninsula in the autumn of 1941, will probably never be accounted for. Nor will we know whether the number 7,000 is inclusive just of the Jews murdered at the Bagerovo ditch during the 29 November 1941 action or encompasses those killed throughout the first occupation of the

A hollow rusty like ore . . .
Who are these people? Soldiers? Hardly.
    Perhaps partisans? No.
Here lies the pug-nosed Kolka—
    He's eleven years old.
His kin is all here, Merriment Homestead,
All the Samostroy[10] houses—120 of them,
So dear . . . so scary . . . Like new residents,
Their bodies have moved into the ditch.
Lying, sitting, sliding onto the breastwork,
Each one—his own inimitable pose.
Winter froze in the dead ones
What the living felt at their death.
And corpses wander, menacing, abhorring . . .
Like a rally, this dead silence rumbles.
No matter how they looked when they had fallen—
With eyes, bared teeth, shoulders, necks—
They wrangle with their executioners,
They cry out "You will not triumph!"
    Over the gully there dangles a cripple,
His black crutch still juts out.
A young hawk bows his little curved beak,
Then jumps on the chest—and the corpse groans.
An old woman in a tattered nun's habit.
The wax has hardened, sealing her left eye.
But her right one gazes deep into the heavens
    Through clefts in this cloudy sky.
And such crow-calls fill her gullet,
Such words rage in her throat cavity,

Kerch Peninsula up until 30 December 1941. In writing of the victims murdered outside Kerch in late 1941, Selvinsky had to cite what had quickly become the official Soviet data.

10 Some evidence suggests that following the murder of the Jews of Kerch, Soviet prisoners of war and members of the local Roma community may also have been executed at the Bagerovo antitank ditch. Evidence also suggests that at the very end of December, with the Kerch-Feodosia Landing Operation already under way, the Nazis rounded up several hundred male residents of the workers' settlement of Samostroy near the town of Kamysh-Burun and subsequently executed them at the Bagerovo ditch in retaliation for actions by local guerilla fighters. As late as 29 December 1942, Jews were still being taken from the city jail to the ditch and killed.

Just touch it—and out, with seething sounds,
    A disavowal of divinity.
This means: through this ancient, mossy, overgrown
Black-crow mysticism—light has burst,
"If fascists live in this world,
    Then there is no god . . ."
Nearby, a mauled Jewish woman,
And a small child with her. Is he awake?
The mother's grey shawl is wrapped with such care
Around the babe's neck.
O maternal, o ancient strength!
Walking to the execution, just before she was killed,
An hour, half an hour, before the grave,
Mother was saving child from a chill.
And even death has not pried them apart.
Over them the enemies have no power.
An auburn trickle from the child's ear
Seeps into the mother's cupped palm.
Go now. Brand them! You have seen the blood bath.
You have caught them red-handed—an eyewitness.
You see how with armor-piercing bullets
The executioners decimate us.
So thunder now, like Dante, like Ovid,
Let nature itself weep and moan,
      If
        you
           saw
                all of this,
    And did not go mad.
But silent I stand over the burial pit.
What words? The words have turned to rot.
There was a time: I wooed a sweetheart,
    I praised a nightingale's chant.
One might have thought—so what?
    Same old tune. And yet,

Try finding the right word,
    Even for a familiar event.
And here? Here the nerves are like taut bows,
But the strings . . . are deafer than boiled sturgeon sinews.
No, for this unbearable torment
    No language has been devised.
To do this, one would have to call a council
Of all tribes, flagpole to flagpole,
And from each one take all that is personal—
Over the centuries everything bewailed—
And if all tribes were to give to this chorus
One word each, one word we all shared,
Then the great Russian sorrow
    To each word would add seven.
But no such language has been devised.
Even if in unheard-of stanzas
I have failed to mourn your blood-soaked sunset,
We do have just the kind of speech,
More scorching than any verbal artistry:
Canister shots, *r*'s misrolled, keep
Rattling the larynx of the battery.
Can you hear this blast at the boundary?
The avenging fire . . . Murderers grow pale!
But they will have nowhere to flee
    From your blood-soaked burial.
Now relax your muscles. Lower your eyelids,
Rise like grass over these heights.
He who saw you, henceforth forever
Shall carry your wounds in his heart.
The ditch . . . Tell about it in meter?
7,000 corpses . . . Jews . . . Slavs . . .
No! About this one cannot—with words:
Fire! Only with fire.

1942

Translated from the Russian by Maxim D. Shrayer

KERCH

In high school we divided the Crimea
Into Hellenic and Wild. The coast
From Eupatoria down and all the way to Kerch
Was called Hellas. And then, if one should happen
To steal across the mountains and descend
Onto the steppe, we used to call this:
"Going to Scythia," although in jest
We called our towns and cities
By their Greek names, as in days of yore.
I had long forgotten all about this.
But suddenly when our landing forces
Traversed the strait and took their position
On the Crimean shore, when I saw
Not far ahead of me the city of Kerch,
My voice then whispered "Panticapaeum."[11]

In lilac and orange fog, above the sea
An amphitheater of a resplendent city
Soared, while some white and lofty temple
Rose from a mountain into the sky
Amid smoking clouds. A distant cape
Shone black over the bay of chrysolite.
And silhouettes of buildings at daybreak
Suggested porticoes and columns
And statues in the forum, while Hellas
Breathed in her deep slumber. Only the fog,
Like reveries, encircled colossal sails,
A horde of billy goats or a crowd of satyrs,
And I was older by five thousand years.
Enveloped by the dozing centuries,
In my thoughts I roamed the square,
Where the Hellenes bargained like old birds

---

11   The ruins of the ancient Greek city of Panticapaeum are located within the modern city of
     Kerch. Founded in the sixth century BCE, Panticapaeum was destroyed by Huns around
     370 CE.

And fish scales passed locally for silver.
Here bread and cheese were traded for horse mackerel;
A copper shield filled to the brim with mullet,
Was an apposite payment for an ode;
And if with a spindly sturgeon they paid
For a young lady of matching shape and form—
The same aqueous sheen, the very same
Body contours and flowing curves,
The sturgeon wouldn't be offended.
(And what about the young lady? Of her offence
They hardly thought in those ruffian days.
A terrible age!) And suddenly upon this city,
Like Furies dispatched by Zeus,
Airplanes! And when out of the smoke
The city once again appeared over the bay,
And tanks with red flags rolled in, one after another
Along the embankment, then encountered a ditch
And drove through a bank's façade into a side street—
By now Kerch was lying there by the shore.
Thus, in one day I got to see two faces
Of the same city. But the war
Held a third one in store for me. That night
To the office of the army newspaper, very quietly—
Like a somnambulist, as though before him
The same vision stood incessantly, forever
Stuck on the same unceasing thought—
Came someone not pale, but simply white,
A man who was in some ways unimaginable.
In a faraway voice (so faraway
That we felt it wasn't he who spoke,
But someone else spoke for him)—he told us
In caveman's speech of Stone Age intonations,
Incising the full stops: "Six miles from here.
There's Bagerovo.[12] A small town.

---

12 The so-called Bagerovo anti-tank ditch received its name from the small town of Bagerovo
    (known in the postwar Soviet years for its classified military airfield) because in 1941, when
    the ditch was dug, Bagerovo was the town nearest to it west of Kerch, even though the village

Before you get there, to the right there's a ditch.
Anti-tank. They took over there
Seven thousand folks. Myself included. But I
On purpose threw myself down a second earlier.

I didn't even get hurt. On top of me
Mother fell. They—in the head. Then . . .
Then my wife. And after that—both my daughters . . .
One was still moaning. I dug myself out
And carried her in my arms. But in vain.
She's in the well, for now. Each time
I see her little eyes beneath the water.
Her little mouth. When the water surges,
It looks like my daughter's swimming . . .
                              So then . . .
What was it I was telling you about?
Oh right, about Bagerovo. So then:
About five hundred yards before you get there, turn right."

---

of Skasiev-Fontan (presently the district of Michurino within Kerch) was only about 2 kilo-
meters east of the ditch. The name is therefore a bit misleading. The ditch, 4 meters wide and
2 meters deep, extended for 1.5 kilometers from south to north, perpendicular to the tracks
of the Dzhankoy–Kerch Railroad and the Vokzalnoe Highway (which runs from Kerch to
Bagerovo and Chistopolie). At the present time, the ditch is located about 1 kilometer west of
the city boundary of Kerch, and about 6 kilometers east of the town of Bagerovo.

We set out right away. The writer Romm.
The photographer, myself, and the critic Goffenshefer.[13]
By sunrise we had come upon a valley
All covered in some dappled cotton fabric. Those were
The dead who had crawled out during the night.
I have described this very hazily
In the poem "I SAW IT"
And I cannot add even a single word.
Kerch . . .
There are cities whose significance lies
Not in their landscape, nor in their culture,
Nor in the aura of their everlasting glory,
But in that lightning bolt of verity,
When the smoldering mystery of the epoch
Would suddenly be revealed, like a ditch in morning fog.
Who were we before our meeting, Kerch?

The writer seems nervous. He strikes
One match, then another, while forgetting
That his own jaws are clenched with anger—
And not from the sensation of the cigarette.
"What beastliness!" the writer slowly says.
And then the critic echoes: "Beastliness."
Language is their trade. Their element—speech.
They have rummaged through the whole dictionary
To choose the selfsame word: "Beastliness."

---

13 All the witnesses described in the scene are Jews. Aleksandr Romm (1898–1943), poet, liter-
ary scholar, literary translator, and brother of the famous Soviet film director Mikhail Romm,
served in the Black Sea Navy in 1941–43. Veniamin Goffenshefer (1905–1966), well known
as a critic in the 1930s–1960s, was the author of the study *Mikhail Sholokhov* (1940) and other
works. Selvinsky's close colleague, Goffenshefer was a staff writer at the military newspaper *Son
of the Fatherland* (*Syn otechestva*) throughout the war. Romm, a writer for the *Red Black-Sea
Navyman* (*Krasnyi chernomorets*), was in Kerch on an assignment to cover the landing oper-
ation and the liberation of the Kerch Peninsula. Romm's writings about the Bagerovo ditch
massacre, if any, have not been found. The photographer Selvinsky refers to without naming
him was also a Jew, most likely Leonid Yablonsky or Mark Turovsky. After the Nazi invasion,
Turovsky, who had been based in Crimea and knew the area well, was assigned to cover the
Crimea for TASS. Yablonsky was a staff photographer for *Son of the Fatherland*, where Selvinsky
headed the literary section at the time described in the poem "Kerch."

But wild beasts under cover of night approached
The morgue so vast it covered the horizon,
And felt with all the senses of wild beasts
The elemental horror standing silently
Before them. Magpies and crows
Taking off, flying over each other, wouldn't dare
Cross over that line of hillocks.
The karagan fox, though following the scent
Along the rabbit tracks beyond the deep ravine,
All of a sudden veered off the path,
Scurried away, yelping and howling in terror,
As if a thunderous pack of hounds were chasing her.
And even the shadow of a wolf amongst the dead
Whirled around anxiously . . . Then froze . . .
And trotted back to his remote barrow,
From there the wolf's shadow turned despondently,
Lingered, then quietly vanished from sight.
Kerch,
You are the mirror in which the abyss has been reflected.

1942

Translated from the Russian by Maxim D. Shrayer

SOFIA DUBNOVA-ERLICH

Sofia (Sophie) **Dubnova-Erlich** (1885–1986), poet, essayist, translator, and memoirist, was born in Mstislavl (Mogilev Province in what is now Belarus), the oldest daughter of the great Jewish historian Shimon Dubnow (1860–1941). In 1903, she enrolled in the Bestuzhev Higher Academy (*kursy*) for Women in St. Petersburg; in 1904, she was expelled after a student political protest. In Odessa, where Dubnova-Erlich's family was living at the time, she observed, among her father's interlocutors, the philosopher of spiritual Zionism Ahad Ha'am (1856–1927) and the writers **Ben-Ami**, Simon Frug, Sholem Aleichem, and Hayyim Nahman Bialik. In 1910–11, Dubnova-Erlich studied at the Sorbonne. In 1906, her father became chair of Jewish history at the soon-to-be closed Free University of St. Petersburg, and her parents stayed there until 1921.

Dubnova-Erlich debuted with poems in the Jewish-Russian periodicals *The Futureness* (*Budushchnost'*) and *Sunrise* (*Voskhod*). Her literary activity occurred on a sociocultural orbit, which only partially intersected with her involvement in the Russian Social-Democratic Labor Party (RSDRP) and the Jewish Labor Party (Bund, founded in 1897 in Vilna). Dubnova-Erlich wrote and translated for the newspaper *Jewish World* (*Evreiskii mir*), the Bundist organ *Our Word* (*Nashe slovo*), and other periodicals. Her first collection, *Autumn Reed-Pipe*, appeared in St. Petersburg in 1911, the year she married Henryk (Genrikh) Erlich (1881–1942), one of the leaders of the Bund. They had two sons, Alexander Erlich (1912–1985), subsequently an economics professor at Columbia University, and Victor Erlich (1914–2007), later a Yale University professor and prominent Slavist.

During World War I, Dubnova-Erlich contributed to Maxim Gorky's antimilitarist *Chronicle* (*Letopis'*) and the Bundist daily *Jewish News* (*Evreiskie vesti*). Her poetry chapbook *Mother* appeared in St. Petersburg in 1916 (reprinted in Tel Aviv, 1969). Focusing on the anxieties of motherhood in cataclysmic times, it established a continuous theme of Dubnova-Erlich's poetry. Dubnova-Erlich supported the February Revolution but opposed the Bolshevik takeover. In 1918, the Erlichs moved to Warsaw and spent twenty-two years in Poland, where Dubnova-Erlich contributed to Yiddish and Russian émigré publications. She conducted research in the Bund Archives in Berlin in 1925–26.

The Erlichs fled to eastern Poland in September 1939. Henryk Erlich and fellow Bundist leader Viktor Alter (1890–1941) were detained by Soviet authorities in Brest-Litovsk. Dubnova-Erlich and her family made it to Lithuania. She last saw her father in November 1940 in Vilna; he returned to Riga, refusing to emigrate. In Kovno, Dubnova-Erlich obtained a transit visa to the Dutch Caribbean island of Curaçao, which allowed her to travel to Moscow, then to Vladivostok in the Russian Far East, Japan, and subsequently Canada. Reaching New York City in 1942, Dubnova-Erlich learned of her father's death in the Riga ghetto in 1941. In 1943, she heard that her husband and Viktor Alter were executed by the NKVD, and it was not until the post-Soviet era that the KGB archives revealed that Henryk Erlich had actually taken his life in a Kuibyshev jail in 1942.

In America, Dubnova-Erlich had a rich career as a contributor to the Russian émigré and Yiddish press. In 1950, her biography, *The Life and Work of S. M. Dubnow*, appeared in Russian in New York (Yiddish translation, 1952; English translation, 1991). Her contributions included the monograph *The Social Aspect of the Magazine "Chronicle"* (New York, 1963) and one of the earliest American overviews, "Jewish Literature in Russian," published in a 1952 volume. Dubnova-Erlich's memoir, *Bread and Matzos*, was partially serialized in the 1980s in the Third-Wave émigré review *Time and We* (*Vremia i my*). Over her long career, Dubnova-Erlich translated into Russian from Yiddish, Hebrew, German, and English the works of Sholem Asch, Thomas Mann, Kate Boyle, and others. Her translation of Dovid Bergelson's Yiddish novel *When All Is Said and Done* (*Nokh alemen*, 1913) appeared in 1923 in Berlin. Her Russian poetry was collected in *Poems of Various Years* (New York, 1973). The legacy of Dubnova-Erlich found dedicated American students in Carole B. Balin and Kristi A. Groberg.

A committed civil-rights activist, Dubnova-Erlich marched in antiwar protests and prochoice demonstrations. She died at age 100 in New York. Dubnova-Erlich's memoir appeared in 1994 in St. Petersburg, with an introduction by her son Victor Erlich. Despite her losses and peregrinations—and the intricacies of her multicultural identity—Dubnova-Erlich insisted she was a *peterburzhanka*.

* * *

Dubnova-Erlich's finest poems, lyrical and confessional, speak of motherhood and living apart from Russia: "An émigré? No, simply a daughter separated from her mother." Her verse aesthetic was nurtured by her love of Russian symbolist poetry. Notes of social protest align her with such Jewish-Russian poets as Dmitry Tsenzor.

Dubnova-Erlich's wartime essays made a prominent contribution to Russian literature about the Shoah. The essays chosen below appeared in 1943–44 in the New York–based émigré magazine *Housewarming* (*Novosel'e*), edited by Sofia Pregel. Given Dubnova-Erlich's knowledge of Jewish life in eastern Europe, the factographic precision of her prose, and the timing of the publication of her essays, they were an émigré equivalent of the wartime non-fiction of **Vasily Grossman** and **Ilya Ehrenburg**.

TWO WARTIME ESSAYS

Shtetl

The shtetl, lost here among Polish fields and groves, might be called Turek or Przasnysz, Konin or Maków, yet what one remembers is not the name but the old marketplace reeking of tar and dung where a rickety, mud-splattered bus would laboriously grind to a stop. What has stayed in my memory is an old town hall with a blackened clockface, a movie house resembling barracks with crude posters at the entrance, and a herd of coarse small houses with tiny blinking windows, all bunched together.

Getting off the bus onto the square, where left-over patches of straw from market day lay rotting between jagged cobblestones, I would step straight into the seventeenth century. Left behind was the frivolous, light-hearted capital, Warsaw, with the defiant clatter of cavalry spurs and the shrill, drunken screech of jazz trying to drown out the somber grumble of the poverty-stricken outskirts and the threatening rumble of oncoming historical storms. Here, in the provincial backwaters, poverty reigned openly and implacably; it was solid, familiar, passed on from father to son, reeking through and through of stove smoke, yesterday's warmed-up borsch, unaired comforters; a poverty firmly rooted in narrow strips of land among the shops, the synagogue, the heder, and the mikvah. The days passed by inaudibly. Every morning the water carrier would bang with his whip handle on sleepy shutters, and the ice-cold cloudy water would slop into the tubs in dark entryways; people, groaning, would crowd together in the half-darkness, like chickens under a roost. Sura-Dvosya, the shopkeeper, would push aside the creaking bolt and with a serrated knife start slowly cutting a bluish herring into five pieces; and a bow-legged boy, standing on tiptoe, opening his little fist to place his sweaty *grosik*[14] on the counter, would carefully pick up the wrapped package—two pieces of herring, topped by a yellowish half-moon of onion.

Usually I arrived in the shtetl on Fridays, late in the afternoon, when shop bolts were beginning to clank, the pathetic stalls were emptying, and sales-women, lazily winding down their bickering, would deftly tighten their heavy checked kerchiefs about their waists and disperse homeward. A holiday sadness, treacley thick, would slowly envelop the shtetl. Here and there, half-blind tiny windows warmed with candlelight illuminated the tangled fringes of wash-worn tablecloths and a challah's round golden crust.

I'd rather not end my contemplation of these meager comforts through small, low-set windows: the family's polished brass candlesticks and the timid light flickering through work-worn fingers folded in prayer. But already at the far end of the square, lights have been turned on over the entry to the Volunteer Firemen's Hall, the place for all meetings and town festivities. Skinny, dark-faced David, carpenter and member of the local Jewish socialist youth association, softly reminds us: it's time . . .

We walk to that gloomy barracks along a narrow, wood-planked sidewalk, misstepping time and again into the mud; it doesn't seem easy to make the transition from this centuries-old life to the world of Maxim Gorky, Romain Rolland, and Soviet literature. The hall, however, is already abuzz like a bee-hive, and I struggle to make my way between benches made of rough boards to a dusty and squeaky stage. Figures and faces merge, but hot currents flow toward me from the back of the hall, I feel a quickened breathing, and I would like to find true and real words to match my listeners' rapt intensity, impatience, and demands born of the depths of a harsh life. I grope to find words borrowed from those seekers of truth, passionate, impatient, and imbued with the gift of clairvoyance. I feel almost physically how invisible wires touch, how sparks of understanding and acceptance flare up, how the idea that not only social conditions but also man himself must be recast—how this idea turns for all of us into Ariadne's thread in this labyrinthine world. These young women with their berets aslant and these young fellows relegated to the stinking back lots of life because of their patched, worn-out jackets will not be satisfied with just a little: they are resolved to jump from the seventeenth century straight into the twentieth and maybe even the twenty-first . . .

---

14 *Grosik* (Polish; Yiddish: *groshik*)—diminutive for a penny.

By the glass of cloudy, overly sweet tea on the table, a pile of notes mounts—some poorly written, naïve, and clumsy, others surprisingly well phrased, bold, and concise. All the questions could be reduced to one: how to restructure the world.

My interchange with the audience did not stop when a somber custodian began turning out the lights—we just regrouped to a tighter circle. In an attic space, reached by a narrow winding staircase, wooden tables were covered with crude wrapping paper, and smooth pine needles dropped from aromatic branches that hung from low beams. Excited young voices crisscrossed; suddenly singing flared up in a corner, little tongues of flame leapt up from person to person, and the whole attic was humming and sizzling like dry birch bark set aflame, throwing into the dark, dense night of the shtetl the voices' challenge and yearning . . .

My meeting with the shtetl wasn't over yet. The most important thing is often not expressed or understood directly, face to face. Early in the morning, in the small room of the coaching inn where I had spent the rest of the night behind a wooden partition, there came a timid knocking. It was a watchmaker, with stooped shoulders and the distraught look of someone who lives among variously ticking clocks. He had a hollow cough and reddened eyes; he explained that he had spent a sleepless night thinking about the problem I had touched upon in Romain Rolland: the tragic contradiction between the aims and the methods of revolution. We bravely plunged together into the depths of history, disturbing the shadows of Hugo and Anatole France. But again a knock came on the partition, and Rakhil and Simon, from last night's audience, entered hand in hand. She was thin, quick, beautifully dark, her small head covered with dark curls, tight like the twirling petals of a chrysanthemum; he was rough and alert, all gathered together, as if invisibly protecting her from an impending woe. Rakhil, it turned out, was an artist, had been painting for some years, had tried to get to Łódź to study but didn't have the means. Now she does piecework sewing linen and lives in an unheated room, trying hard to earn enough money for paint.

Again I climb to a dovecote occupied by people and stop on the threshold in astonishment: the walls reverberate and shout in deep-brown hues, changing to crimson, wind rattles the shutters of huts clinging to the ground, the air is heavy with an oncoming storm. Her technique is weak and naive, but the genuine anxiety permeating these images is infectious, a stubborn sense that the world is approaching some sort of decisive boundary . . .

On the square, by the bus, I say goodbye to my new friends. Here are Simon and Rakhil, clear-voiced and rosy-cheeked Hannah, the public-school teacher, and David, the carpenter with the sternly Biblical face of a zealot or martyr. Hannah squeezes my hand meaningfully, "I will write you . . ."

A letter arrived after a few days. Hannah wrote that she was pregnant, the child's father was far away, and difficult days lay ahead for she would have to break with her family and her surroundings but was unafraid of the future and happy to take on the hardships . . . That was early spring, 1939.

That fall sirens began howling like hyenas. Bombs and fires, hunger and famine descended on the rough little dwellings gathered together like a frightened herd. The fearful shtetl wailed and surged out onto the road—carrying prayer books in old stiff covers, children in arms, old things grabbed on the run—some headed for the capital, some further away to the east. A hurricane had dispersed the life that centuries had shaped.

I'm thinking now of those who, in those irretrievable and by now inconceivable times, came close to me, face to face. Hannah's child, I am imagining, may have turned up in the kindergarten of a Kazakhstan kolkhoz; David may have been seized by Gestapo spies at an underground printing press and hung in the market square of some district town; Rakhil and Simon, holding hands as at our meeting, may have mounted the barricades on Miła Street[15] and, watching the German troops advance, poked the muzzles of their guns through the slit between the boards. I'm thinking of all the suffering for which there are no words in human language and of the heroism that we just cannot measure by any measure, cannot put into any epic poem, the heroism of impatient and passionate people whom history has marked for greatness.

And you, Shtetl, can it be that you have fallen silent for centuries to come, that your strangled gasp will not arouse this dulled world, a world no longer able to wonder at anything? Are you destined, with your impoverished coziness and your yearnings, your acquiescent prayers and your insolent songs, simply to become a silent tract of land, ploughed by history's bloody course for a new sowing?

1943

---

15 Miła Street—one of the main streets in Warsaw's historic Jewish quarter. Dubnova-Erlich hints at the Warsaw Ghetto Uprising of 1943; for details, see below, in the essay "Scorched Hearth," and **Aleksandr Aronov** in the section "Late Soviet Empire and Collapse: 1960s–1990s."

Scorched Hearth

I have before me a list of the victims of last year's uprising in the Warsaw ghetto—a belated echo from out there, from the last circle of the infernal regions.

Human imagination is weak: the monstrous image of thousands of deaths in gas chambers does not make you shiver since the brain cannot accommodate it. But news of the death of a person whom we remember alive, as worried or smiling, suddenly pulls the curtain aside: before us rises what now has turned into a cemetery—that fragment of a vibrant, red-hot life named the Warsaw Jewish quarter.

Untamed, frenzied hate encircled it with walls fated to turn into the walls of a cemetery. In peaceful years too. An invisible border separated this quarter from "Aryan" streets, shabbily genteel, boasting plate-glass showcases, spacious sidewalks, and a "pure" public. This is the way it was from way back: hounded by dull-wittedness, prejudice, and cunning calculation, in the course of hundreds of years Jews huddled close together, settled in warm, tight spots, in stuffy air.

The Jewish quarter was old, somber, crowded, oddly built: as if someone from above had angrily thrown into the backyards of a second-rate European capital a heap of slovenly stone boxes, drilled narrow slots for windows, houses stuffed to bursting with people, so that in the cold of winter as in the swelter of summer they would spill out into dank gateways, onto smooth-worn, bespattered sidewalks, onto jagged cobblestones. And if an inhabitant of the central streets—"Aryan" or Jew—turned up there, he would be stunned by the crush, the bustle, the excited voices and gestures, by the gaudy, cheap Oriental goods crying out from hawkers' trays and stalls.

It was far from idyllic, this motley, hard life. Standing over the ruins, we don't want to insult them by adding a gilded, confectionery veneer. "A pair of twins, inseparably fused," mourned over by a poet,[16] became a solid part of that life: "the satiety of the satiated" was considerable here, reeking of fatty food and overgrown with featherbeds and tasteless heavy furniture; and "the hunger of the hungry" was incredible in its nakedness, an absolute king in dwellings whose windows looked out onto the outhouses; in cellars where people multiplied like rabbits on mattresses that, full of holes, were spread on the floor;

---

16 Dubnova is referring to the sixth line of the poem "Esli dusha rodilas' krylatoi . . ." ("If your soul was born winged . . . ," 1918) by the Russian poet Marina Tsvetaeva (1892–1941).

around courtyard wells and cesspools and woodsheds, where olive-dark kids with pale gums and skinny bowlegs spent their childhood.

People lived in this stuffy and crowded place without pausing for breath, as if sensing an impending catastrophe. A quicker pulse beat in the municipal parochial schools in houses of worship and newspaper editorial offices, in political, professional, and cultural organizations. And everywhere one could hear the guttural Yiddish, loud in squabbles, tender in a heart-rending song. The Jewish quarter was a special kingdom, and in the greatest heat of antisemitic bacchanalia the hoodlums of different stripes—"idealistic" volunteers from the intelligentsia or tramps paid for beating up Jews—did not dare plunge into the thick of it: for a long time they remembered how an attempted pogrom was met by some hefty, ruddy-faced Jewish porters. The most astounding fact was this: through stupefying satiety as much as decimating hunger; through feverishly chasing after huge wealth or pitiful penny earnings, fountains of a genuine spiritual life sprang high. This life was particularly intense at two ends: in the grandfathers who preserved tradition and in their grandchildren who destroyed it impudently. The ecstatic melodies of those who, half saints and half holy fools, called themselves "the dead Hassids" and lived in mystical contact with the spirit of their dead *Rebbe* had something in common with the rebellious songs of the young who were demanding truth and justice for the whole world, from one end to the other.

Himmler's henchmen who stormed Warsaw cut the arteries of the Jewish quarter: drop by drop live blood began running out of it. The "satiety of the satiated" vanished: a greedy belly devoured the remnants of corpulent daily living. The "hunger of the hungry" grew to incredible proportions. But the ghetto did not succumb: squeezed between its stone walls, it boiled more than ever as underground, hot springs of rebellion and faith beat forth. Then the conqueror's crazed anger demanded hecatombs. Dejected, the doomed people marched into the jaws of the apocalyptic beast. The Hassids with their long black robes and high fur hats—those who in the autumn holidays filled the sumptuous country houses of the miracle-working tzaddikim and those who mortified the flesh—in the death trains they sang hymns about the Messiah. The young no longer sang: gritting their teeth, they stored up arms. And when the last martyrs were led out of the ghetto, there remained only the fighters.

The list of the victims of the revolt contains almost exclusively names of the young. I knew many personally—through study groups, meetings, literary evenings, heart-to-heart talks at the desk in my small study. But how they have all grown over these four years of climbing Golgotha, four years in the ghetto!

Among those who perished is a thirteen-year-old boy. On the eve of the war he was nine. His satchel hung down his back, he played hide-and-seek with his schoolmates in the dark doorway, and his mother used to stuff his pockets with tasty, crisply roasted nuts. How terrifying life must have been in the ghetto, when instead of nuts the boy found bullets in his pockets and had to stand watch in that very doorway where he used to hide behind the yardman's wheelbarrow.

Another familiar name. A young man who graduated from a foreign university and came to Warsaw as an engineer; yet hundreds of people called him simply Abrasha. He was one of the most spirited enthusiasts among young Jewish socialists—and remained that way during the years of underground work. By chance we met many times, and I remember him especially in the setting of a young workers' summer camp nestled among green hills. A cool dewy evening was settling in, from a homemade stove rose smoke of pine branches, and agile young hands gathered needles for the fire. When the dry branches began crackling, Abrasha started singing softly, his face lighting up as if in prayer, pure and stern; something childlike and monk-like came through in his expression . . . This is the way he must have gone to his death.

Michał Klepfisz, called by the London radio a "pillar of the uprising"— him I remember as a boy and a bully, mop-headed, stubborn, awkward in his movements. The boy grew into a young man, a student, silent and bashful; one felt a controlled power in him, tempered steel. I remember that during the floods in the Tatra Mountains that inundated mountain villages, he calmly and bravely saved from the raging elements dozens of peasant children. With the same calm courage, he plunged into the wild elements of the uprising.

The girl in the photograph has tender, motherly eyes and a firm chin. She graduated from public school, from teach-yourself workshops, summer youth camps. In the first months of the war, she declined to leave the ghetto for a calmer Lithuania. Later she wrote her father across the ocean: "You've traveled halfway around the world, seen wonderful things. But if we should ever meet, I'll tell you even more remarkable things." Death caught up with her when she was nineteen.

The people's struggle against the tanks, which had conquered all of Europe, endured for a whole month before suffocating in the smoke of the fires. There remain skeletons of houses, dug up roads, a cemetery stillness.

Will these skeletons of houses ever be overgrown with stone and glass, will steps again ring out along the jagged sidewalks? Will fugitives hidden in the dwellings of the Polish poor, and guerilla soldiers in the woods burned by gunpowder, and those whom fate has sent over the ocean, will these come back to their scorched hearths? And how will they come—with tears and curses alone or with a firm resolve to rebuild their city, their country, their world?

Now, above the scorched hearth are flocks of crows, a raw April wind, low clouds. But beyond the Wisła in the east there is a distant glow. Soon will come a rumble of victorious arms, sweeping away the enemy's filth. The hour of vengeance is near.

1944

Translated from the Russian by Helen Reeve with Martha Kitchen

VASILY GROSSMAN

Vasily Grossman (1905–1964), writer of fiction and nonfiction, was born Iosif Grossman in Berdichev (in Zhitomir Province of Ukraine), once known as "the Jerusalem of Volhynia." According to the 1897 census, 80 percent of the total population of Berdichev (41,617 people) was Jewish; by 1926, the number fell to 30,812 (about 56 percent), remaining about the same until 1939. Grossman came from the Russianized Jewish intelligentsia; his father was a chemical engineer and his mother, a teacher of French. Growing up, Grossman was not exposed either to Yiddish or to Judaic traditions at home. A revolutionary-minded youth, Grossman attended the Kiev Institute of Higher Education and transferred to Moscow University in 1924. After graduating in chemistry in 1929, Grossman worked in the Donbas mining region as a chemical engineer and college instructor. He was diagnosed with tuberculosis and left Donbas in 1932.

Grossman's story "In the Town of Berdichev" appeared in *Literary Gazette* (*Literaturnaia gazeta*) in 1934. This civil war story of a Jewish family harboring a pregnant Russian commissar earned the praise of Maxim Gorky and **Isaac Babel**. (Aleksandr Askoldov's 1962 film *The Commissar*, based on Grossman's story, was shelved until 1988.) Encouraging Grossman, Gorky gave him suggestions for revisiting a short novel about Soviet miners, *Glück Auf!* (1934; third edition 1935). Three collections, *Happiness* (1935), *Four Days* (1936), and *Stories* (1937), established Grossman's reputation as a short fictionist. His first long novel, *Stepan Kolchugin*, about a working-class lad's path to Bolshevism, featured descriptions of small-town Jewish life and an array of Jewish characters. Parts 1–3 of *Stepan Kolchugin* were published in 1937–40; a Stalin Prize nomination was withdrawn after Stalin labeled it a "Menshevik" novel. The war interrupted the writing of *Stepan Kolchugin*, and its four finished parts were not published until 1947 (reprinted in 1951, 1955). Dithyramb did not come easily to Grossman, and the absence of extolment of the Soviet leaders did not earn Grossman the love of Stalin and his henchmen.

The war against Nazism was not only a time of both Soviet and Jewish national woe and of personal trauma; Grossman's mother was murdered in Berdichev in September 1941 along with about 20,000 Jews. The war was also Grossman's time of glory—literary, civic, and military. In August 1941, Grossman volunteered for the armed forces, becoming a correspondent for *Red Star* (*Krasnaia zvezda*), the largest newspaper of the Soviet military, and gaining wide acclaim for his reportage and essays. Grossman's novel *The People Is Immortal* (abridged edition 1942; full edition 1943, 1945) chronicled the beginning of the Nazi invasion. Alongside **Ilya Ehrenburg**, Konstantin Simonov, and Aleksey Tolstoy, Grossman was one of the principal voices of wartime anti-Nazi journalism and literary propaganda. A number of his pamphlets, including "The Direction of the Main Strike" (1942), appeared in mass editions. "And once again, a feeling of superstitious terror took hold of the enemy: Were the ones attacking them human beings, could they be mortal?" In a slightly modified form, these and other words from Vasily Grossman's "The Direction of the Main Strike" are engraved on the Mamaev Kurgan memorial complex in Volgograd, formerly Stalingrad. Grossman's words, not identified as his on the monument, referred to the shock of Nazi troops as they faced the unimaginable heroism of Soviet soldiers fighting at Stalingrad under Stalin's sacrificial order, "not a step back." Grossman's thirteen essays about Stalingrad hold a special place. They were originally published in *Red Star*, and several were reprinted in *Pravda*, with the title *Stalingrad: September 1942–January 1943*, and appeared in book editions. Grossman may have already become a thorn in the side of the Soviet ideological machine when, at the very peak of his wartime fame, at Stalingrad, he was removed from coverage of the final stages of the Stalingrad battle and replaced with another stellar wartime correspondent, Konstantin Simonov, who was not Jewish and who stuck much closer to the official Stalinist song sheets. During the final weeks of Stalingrad, Grossman found himself in what was then the recently liberated region of Kalmykia south of Stalingrad. There, in a prelude to what he would come to witness, first during the liberation of Ukraine and later in what remained of the Aktion Reinhard death camps in Poland, Grossman encountered evidence of Nazi atrocities, including those committed in the autumn of 1942 by the SS Sonderkommando Astrachan.

His emergent view of the war as a war of both Soviet and Jewish liberation resulted in a ruthless imperative to tell the world about the Shoah and the Nazi atrocities. As a fictionist, Grossman articulated this double perspective in the story "The Old Teacher," which was printed in *Banner* (*Znamia*) in 1943, was included in a slim volume (Magadan, 1944), and was reprinted in two postwar volumes (1958 and 1962). Grossman's story offered a detailed description of the murder of the Jewish population of an occupied small town, presumably in eastern Ukraine, by a Sonderkommando assisted by regular Wermacht troops. From late 1943 to 1945, Grossman worked with **Ehrenburg** on *The Black Book: The Ruthless Murder of Jews by German-Fascist Invaders throughout the Temporarily Occupied Regions of the Soviet Union and in the Death Camps of Poland during the War of 1941–45*. In April 1944, Grossman was elected a member of the Jewish Antifascist Committee (JAC); he took over the *Black Book* project after Ehrenburg's resignation. Grossman wrote the preface sections on "The Murder of Jews in Berdichev" and "Treblinka" and prepared "The History of the Minsk Ghetto" and other sections. (The writer Andrey Platonov was not credited but apparently contributed to the Minsk Ghetto section.) Grossman and **Ehrenburg** were listed as coeditors of *The Black Book*. Set in type in 1946, *The Black Book* was derailed: a partial copy appeared in Bucharest as *Cartea Neagră* in 1947; it was published in Israel in 1980; and a complete text was discovered in Lithuania and printed there in 1993. A new edition appeared in Moscow in 2014. Grossman also wrote the powerful essay "Ukraine without Jews," published in Yiddish in the Jewish Antifascist Committee's newspaper *Unity* (*Einikait*) in 1943 but not in Russian. Teetering on the brink of the forbidden even during the war, this essay, as well as the short story "The Old Teacher," sought to open the public's eyes to the Soviet population's collaboration with the Nazis in occupied territories. Grossman published the essay "The Hell of Treblinka" (in this anthology), the first literary account of the legacy of the Nazi death camps based on research and eyewitness accounts, in *Banner* in 1944. Printed as a pamphlet in 1945, it was distributed at the Nuremberg Trials and included in Grossman's extensive volume *Years of War* (1945; reprinted 1946).

The postwar years put Grossman in confrontation with the regime. His prewar play *If You Believe the Pythagoreans*, not published until 1946, was attacked for its non-Marxist interpretation of history. Grossman had started an epic novel back in 1943 under the working title *Stalingrad*. Accepted for publication as *For a Just Cause*, it ran into difficulties in 1949. Parts 1–3 of the novel went through twelve versions of proofs until finally appearing in *Novy mir* in 1952. Mikhail Bubennov, author of the Stalinist potboiler *White Birch*, savaged Grossman's novel in *Pravda*, unleashing a campaign of antisemitic ostracism. Stalin's death eased the situation; *For a Just Cause* appeared in expurgated form in 1954, and the full text appeared in 1956. In both book editions, the subtitle was "Book 1." *Life and Fate* would form book 2 of Grossman's dilogy.

World War II and the Shoah, followed by the postwar anticosmopolitan campaign with its collective vilification of Jews, transformed Grossman. By 1952, he had completed a significant portion of *Life and Fate*—an antitotalitarian novel of Tolstoyan ambitions. By drawing parallels between Stalinism and Hitlerism—and by questioning the trajectory of Soviet history—Grossman went much farther than Vladimir Dudintsev, Aleksandr Solzhenitsyn, and other Soviet authors of the principal anti-Stalinist works that were published during the Thaw.

In 1960, Grossman submitted *Life and Fate* to *Banner*. The journal's editor, Vadim Kozhevnikov, forwarded it to the KGB. In February 1961, the KGB searched Grossman's apartment and "arrested" manuscripts of *Life and Fate*. Grossman appealed to Khrushchev but was received by Mikhail Suslov, the Party ideology secretary, who called *Life and Fate* more "anti-Soviet" than **Boris Pasternak**'s *Doctor Zhivago*. Grossman was devastated. Two copies of *Life and Fate* did survive, and it appeared in the West in Russian in 1980 and subsequently in translation. Its publication in reform-era Moscow in 1989 created a sensation.

"They strangled me in the back alley," Grossman had said to **Boris Yampolsky**, author of the fabulous *Country Fair*. From 1956 until his death at the age of fifty-nine, Grossman worked on *Forever Flowing,* an essayistic novel written for the desk drawer and uncompromising in its assessment of Stalinism and Soviet history. A key text predating fictional and discursive works by the 1960s–70s political dissidents, *Forever Flowing* appeared in Germany in 1970. Of *Forever Flowing* and *Life and Fate*, Grossman's American biographer John Garrard wrote in 1994: "Grossman's two major works constitute a thorough-going indictment of the Soviet Union and at the same time a challenge to Russian readers to face their own responsibility for what happened [. . .] the indictment and challenge were issued by a man enmeshed within the very system he autopsied; a man who in his youth believed in the promise of revolutionary change [. . .]." Grossman died in Moscow of cancer in 1964. A volume of shorter fiction, *Autumn Storm,* came out in Moscow, followed in 1967 by an expurgated version of *Goodness Be to You!* (the Shoah is a central theme of this long essay about Armenia).

Forever Flowing appeared in a number of languages abroad, including in Eastern bloc countries (for example, Poland in 1984). The hiatus in Soviet publications of Grossman ended in 1988. A number of volumes have since appeared in the former USSR, including one of shorter prose, *A Few Sorrowful Days* (1989), and a four-volume *Collected Works* (1994), edited by Grossman's longtime friend **Semyon Lipkin**.

In the words of Shimon Markish, who edited *On Jewish Themes* (1985), an anthology of Grossman's writings published in Russian in Israel, "no one had written about [the Shoah and Stalinist antisemitism] with as much poignancy and emotion." Boris Lanin, Grossman's post-Soviet student, stated, "Grossman's main philosophical contribution to Soviet literature is the rehabilitation of the concept of freedom."

"They say there are people who are born under a lucky star. Pablo Neruda may be deemed such a darling of destiny. But the star under which Grossman was born was a star of misfortune," **Ilya Ehrenburg** wrote in book 5 of *People, Years, Life*. In his afterlife, Vasily Grossman became one of the best-known and frequently taught Russian writers outside Russia. His popularity in the Anglophone world is owed in part to the work of Grossman's dedicated biographers John and Carol Garrard and his tireless translator Robert Chandler. Displaying a propensity for epic proportions, Grossman did not possess a golden pen. The power of Grossman's greatest works came from their intellectual honesty, the Promethean thrust of their authorial voice, and their commitment to the overwhelming questions. (Also see an excerpt from Grossman's novel *Life and Fate* in the section "The Thaw.")

* * *

The Treblinka Nazi extermination camp, known as Treblinka II, operated from 23 July 1942 to 19 October 1943 as part of so-called Operation Reinhard along with two other killing centers established in eastern Poland, Sobibór and Bełżec. Prior to the opening of the Treblinka death camp, a labor camp (Treblinka I) had been operating nearby since November 1941. The Treblinka camp was situated 50 miles northeast of Warsaw, about 65 miles southwest of Białystok, and about 40 miles south of Łomża. Treblinka lies about 2.5 miles south of the Małkinia Górna station on the Warsaw–Białystok railway line and over a mile south of the Boug (Bug) River. Carbon monoxide, supplied through pipes from engine exhaust fumes, was used as the killing agent in gas chambers. About 870,000 Jews and about 2,000 Sinti and Romani were murdered at Treblinka, making it the second only to Auschwitz-Birkenau, where about 1.1 million Jews and about 20,000 Sinti and Romani were murdered and where Zyklon B, a cyanide-based substance, was used as the killing agent. Three commanders were in charge of Treblinka: Irmfried Eberl, Franz Stangl (who had previously served at Sobibór), and Kurt Franz. Gassing ended at Treblibka in October 1943 after a revolt of members of the Jewish slave-labor units that were tasked with burying the gassed bodies in mass graves. As Soviet troops quickly advanced from the east, the camp was dismantled in July 1944 to conceal the evidence.

Grossman discovered an inner source of artistry when, in the summer of 1944, he came to the death camps in Poland, first Majdanek, then the Aktion Reinhard camps. *Red Star* assigned the Majdanek report to Konstantin Simonov, who, in a three-part series titled "Death Camp" ("Lager' unichtozheniia") and printed in August 1944, did his best not to deny Jewish victimhood while also paying lip service to the "do not divide the dead" Soviet doctrine. Grossman was with the Soviet troops in August 1944 when they came upon the fields of powdered bones on the site of the Treblinka death camp. His lengthy report, written in September 1944 and titled "The Hell of Treblinka," is a work that defies conventional generic forms and stylistic categories. It ran in the November 1944 issue of *Banner* to reach a wide Soviet audience. Grossman stood at the peak of his wartime artistic powers during the writing of "The Hell of Treblinka." It was as though a Jewish muse of suffering and witnessed truth read into Grossman's ear as he typed his report. Twice in "The Hell of Treblinka," Grossman emphatically draws a line between Dante's *Inferno* and Treblinka. Yet Grossman's guides are the survivors and eyewitnesses; in sight of the ashes and bones of the murdered Jews, he does not need a Virgil to lead him through the circles of Treblinka. Grossman revised "The Hell of Treblinka" in 1958, and this translation follows the revised text.

"The Hell of Treblinka" not only constitutes Grossman's greatest contribution to Shoah literature. Details of Grossman's reportage also anticipate and inform the Shoah pages of *Life and Fate* (excerpt in the section "The Thaw"). Grossman's commentators, chiefly John and Carol Garrard and Robert Chandler, have detailed some of the errors he made in reporting about Treblinka. Grossman estimated that "2.5 to 3 million" Jews were murdered there, whereas the death toll was about 870,000. Grossman had to do his own calculations based on what he believed to be the number of transports. His errors amount to a moving testament to Grossman's unsupported enterprise of documenting the Shoah in its immediate aftermath.

THE HELL OF TREBLINKA

1

To the east of Warsaw, along the Boug River, sandy areas and swamps stretch for many miles, and thick pine and deciduous forests stand tall. These places are empty and dejected, with only a few villages here and there. Travelers, whether by foot or riding, avoid the narrow, sandy rural roads, where legs get stuck and wheels go down to the very axle in the deep sand.

Here, on the Siedlce railroad branch, sits the small, backwater Treblinka station, some sixty odd kilometers from Warsaw, not far from the Małkinia station, where the railroads going from Warsaw, Białystok, Siedlce, and Łomża intersect.

It's likely that many of those who were brought to Treblinka in 1942 had occasion to pass through here in peaceful times, their absent gazes tracing the boring scenery: pine trees and sand, sand and again pine trees, heather, dry shrubbery, bleak station buildings, railroad crossings . . . And maybe the passenger's bored gaze would catch sight of the single-track railwayo, branching off at the station and disappearing into the forest amid encroaching pines. This branch leads to the quarry, where white sand was mined for industrial and urban construction.

Four kilometers separate the sandpit from the station; it is located on a wasteland, surrounded on all sides by pine forest. The soil here is meager and infertile, and farmers don't work it. The wasteland thus remained a wasteland. In some places the ground is covered in moss; in others, feeble pine trees lift their heads. Occasionally a jackdaw or a colorful crested hoopoe flies by. This miserable wasteland was selected and approved by the German Reichsführer of the SS, Heinrich Himmler, as the location of a world slaughterhouse; humankind had never before known such a slaughterhouse, not from the time of primordial barbarianism to our cruel days. Perhaps not even the entire universe had known such a slaughterhouse. The SS built their principal slaughterhouse here, exceeding and outdoing Auschwitz, Sobibór, Majdanek, and Bełżec.

There were two camps in Treblinka: forced labor camp I, where prisoners of various nationalities, mainly Poles, worked; and the Jewish camp, Treblinka II.

Treblinka I, a labor or penal camp, was located directly next to the sand quarry, not far from the edge of the forest. It was a typical camp, similar to the hundreds of others that the Gestapo built on occupied eastern territories.

It was founded in 1941. Elements of the German character, all reflected and perverted in the terrible mirror of Hitler's regime, were evident in the camp. This is how, in a rave of delirium, the thoughts and feelings a sick person had prior to his disease are revealed in an ugly and perverted way. This is how a crazy person, acting in a state of dark madness, distorts the logic of a sane person's behavior and motivations through his behavior. And this is how a criminal carries out his deeds with an inhuman cold-bloodedness, striking the bridge of his victim's nose with a mallet, and in doing so conjoins developed skills—eyesight trained to measure precise distance and a blacksmith's powerful grip.

Frugality, orderliness, deliberateness, pedantic cleanliness—these are all decent traits characteristic of many Germans. When applied to agriculture or industrial production, they can bear fruit. Hitler usurped these traits and applied them to a crime against humanity, and in this labor camp in Poland, the SS leadership acted as though they were doing nothing more than cultivating cauliflower or potatoes.

The camp's area was carved into precise rectangles, the barracks stood in straight formation, the paths were lined with birch trees, neatly sprinkled with sand. Concrete pools were built for domestic waterfowl, pools for laundry with convenient steps, services for the German personnel—a bakery, a barbershop, a garage, a gas pump with a glass globe, warehouses. The Lublin camp at Majdanek was built according to more or less the same plan, with little gardens, drinking fountains, and concrete paths; dozens of other forced-labor camps were established according to this same plan in eastern Poland, where the Gestapo and the SS intended to settle for the long haul. The design of these camps exhibited some German traits: organization, petty calculation, a pedantic propensity for order, the German love for schedules, for schemes developed and worked out to the smallest point and detail.

People were sent to the labor camp for a specific term, sometimes not long at all: four, five, or six months. Poles who broke the laws of the General Governorate would be sent here, and most of the violations were, as a general rule, insignificant, since you weren't sentenced to work in the camp for serious crimes but were immediately executed. A denunciation, false evidence, or an accidental word overheard in the street, a supply shortfall, a refusal to yield a cart or a horse to a German, a young woman's audacity in refusing the romantic advances of an SS man, merely the suspicion of possible sabotage not even actual sabotage at the factory—all this brought hundreds and thousands of Poles to the penal labor camp—workers, peasants, members of the intelligentsia, men and young women, the elderly and teenagers, family matriarchs. Altogether, around 50,000 people passed through the camp.[17] Jews found themselves in that camp only if they were eminent, famous masters of their trade—bakers, shoemakers, woodworkers, stonemasons, tailors. All kinds of workshops were set up here, including a sophisticated furniture workshop that supplied the headquarters of the German armies with armchairs, tables, and regular chairs.

Treblinka I existed from autumn 1941 to 23 July 1944. It was being completely liquidated when the prisoners heard the dull boom of Soviet artillery.

Early in the morning on 23 July, the *Wachmänner*[18] and SS personnel fortified themselves with a bottle of schnapps then proceeded with the liquidation of the camp. By evening, all the prisoners had been killed and buried in the ground. The Warsaw carpenter Max Levit managed to save himself: wounded, he lay beneath his comrades' corpses until dark and then crawled away into the woods. He later recounted how, lying in the pit, he heard thirty boys singing "Song of the Motherland" before the shots rang out; he heard how one of the boys shouted "Stalin will avenge us!"; he heard how Leyb—the boys' leader and everyone's favorite at the camp—fell on top of him in the pit, then pushed himself up a little, saying, "*Panie Wachman*, you didn't get me. *Proszę pana,* shoot me again, shoot again!"

We can now describe in detail the German order in this labor camp, as there is an abundance of testimonies from dozens of witnesses, Polish men and women who escaped or were released at one time or another from Treblinka

---

17 Treblinka I held about 2,000 inmates at a time; throughout its existence, about 10,000 inmates passed through the camp. Here and hereafter the editor relies on the work of previous commentators, including Robert Chandler and Ilya Lempertas, as well as on his previous publications on Grossman and the information gathered by the editor during his trip to Treblinka in April 2017. See Il'ia Lempertas [Notes to "Treblinka" by Vasilii Grossman], in *Chernaia kniga*, ed. Vasilii Grossman and Il'ia Erenburg (Moscow: Corpus; ACT, 2015), 570–93; Vasily Grossman, "The Hell of Treblinka," tr. Robert Chandler, in *The Road: Stories, Journalism, and Essays*, ed. Robert Chandler, tr. Elizabeth Chandler, Robert Chandler, and Olga Mukovnikova (New York: New York Review of Books, 2010), 116–62; Maxim D. Shrayer, "Grossman's Resistance," in *Holocaust Resistance in Europe and America*, ed. Victoria Khiterer with Abigail S. Gruber (Cambridge: Cambridge Scholars Publishing, 2017), 134–63.

18 *Wachmänner* were camp guards usually drawn from the ranks of the so-called Trawniki men (*Trawnikimänner*), collaborators recruited from among Soviet POWs and conscripted civilians and trained by the SS. They include Slavs, Balts, and members of other nationalities from the occupied Soviet territories; *Volksdeutche* (ethnic Germans living outside the Reich) usually served as squad leaders.

I. We know about the work in the sand quarry and how those who didn't fulfill their quota were thrown from the quarry's edge into the pit; we know about the food ration of 170–200 grams of food and a liter of some swill that was called soup. We know about the deaths from hunger and about those swollen from starvation who were taken out in wheelbarrows beyond the barbed wire and shot there; we know about the wild orgies that the Germans had, how they raped young women and then shot their enslaved lovers; we know about people who were thrown from a six-meter tower, how at night a drunken band snatched ten to fifteen prisoners from the barracks and then leisurely demonstrated methods of killing on them, shooting the doomed in the heart, the nape of their necks, their eyes, mouths, temples. We know the names of the camp's SS officers, their characters and idiosyncrasies. We know about the camp's director, van Eupen, a German of Dutch origin, an insatiable murderer and insatiable lecher, a lover of good horses and fast riding. We also know about young officer Stumpfe, a hunk of a person who would be overcome with involuntary fits of laughter each time he killed one of the prisoners or when an execution occurred in his presence. They nicknamed him "Laughing Death." The last one to hear him laugh was Max Levit on 23 July of the year the *Wachmänner* were shooting the boys on Stumpfe's order. Levit was lying at the bottom of the pit after they had failed to execute him. We know about Sviderski, the one-eyed German from Odessa whom they used to call "Master Hammer." He was considered an unsurpassed specialist in "cold" killing, and it was he who, in the span of a few minutes, used a hammer to murder fifteen children aged eight to thirteen designated unfit for work. We know about Preifi, the skinny SS man who looked like a gypsy; nicknamed "Old Man," he was grim and taciturn. He would dispel his melancholy by lying near the camp kitchen's trash heap, waiting for prisoners who would sneak over to eat potato peelings, then forcing them to open their mouths and shooting them in their open mouths.

We know the names of the professional murderers Schwarz and Ledecke. They were the ones who amused themselves by shooting prisoners as they returned from work at dusk, killing twenty, thirty, forty people every day.

All of these creatures didn't have anything in them that was human. Distorted brains, hearts, and souls; words, actions, habits, like a terrible caricature, hinted at human traits, thoughts, feelings, habits, or actions. The camp order, the documentation of the murders, the love of monstrous jokes somehow bringing to mind the jokes of drunk brawlers from German university fraternities, the choral singing of sentimental songs amidst pools of blood, the speeches continuously delivered before the condemned, the lecturing and the pious locutions carefully typed on special pieces of paper—all this came from monstrous dragons and reptiles that evolved from the embryo of traditional German chauvinism, arrogance, selfishness, and narcissistic self-confidence; from the pedantic, slavering care for one's own little nest and an iron-clad, cold indifference to the fate of all other living things; from fierce blind faith that German science, music, poetry, speech, lawns, toilets, sky, beer, houses are all better than and more beautiful than the whole universe.

The camp lived this way, like a little Majdanek, and it might have seemed that there was nothing more terrifying in the world. But those who lived in Treblinka I knew well that there was something much scarier, a hundred times more terrifying than their camp. In May 1942, three kilometers from the forced labor camp, the Germans started building the Jewish camp, the camp of slaughter. Construction progressed quickly, with more than one thousand people working on it. In this camp, nothing was designed for life; everything was designed for death. Himmler intended for this camp's existence to be kept in the deepest secrecy, not a single person was to be allowed to leave it alive. And not a single person was allowed to get near this camp. Anyone who happened to come within one kilometer of it was shot without warning. German airplanes were forbidden to fly over this area. The victims, brought by special trains along a special railway branch, didn't know the fate awaiting them until the last minute. The security guards accompanying the special trains were not even allowed through the camp's outer gates. When the train cars arrived, SS camp staff took over. The special train, usually consisting of sixty cars, would be split into three parts in the woods on the approach to the camp, and the locomotive would push twenty cars at a time up to the camp platform. The locomotive pushed the cars from the back and stopped at the perimeter, so that neither the driver nor the stoker crossed into the camp's territory. Once the cars had been unloaded, the on-duty SS *Unteroffizier* would whistle for the next twenty cars, which were waiting two hundred meters away. When all sixty cars were completely unloaded, the camp's headquarters telephoned for a new special train from the station, and the empty train went further down the branch, to the quarry, where the cars were loaded with sand and went on to the Treblinka and Małkinia stations with their new loads.

Here one can see how well placed Treblinka was: the special trains brought the victims here from all four directions—from the east and west, from the north and south. Special trains came from the Polish cities of Warsaw, Międzyrzec, Częstochowa, Siedlce, and Radom; from Łomża, Białystok,

Grodno, and many cities in Belarus; from Germany, Czechoslovakia, Austria, Bulgaria, and Bessarabia.

Trains came to Treblinka for thirteen months; each train had sixty cars,[19] and each car had the numbers 150, 180, or 200 written on it in chalk. These numbers showed how many people were in each car. Railway workers and farmers secretly kept track of these special trains. A farmer in the village of Wólka[20] (the closest to the camp), 62-year-old Kazimierz Skarżyński, told me that sometimes there were days when six special trains from the Siedlce branch alone would pass by Wólka, and in all of these thirteen months there were practically no days when at least one special train didn't pass. And the Siedlce branch was only one of the four railroads supplying Treblinka. A railroad repair worker, Lucjan Żukowa, drafted by the Germans to work on the branch leading from Treblinka to Camp II, says that from the time he started his detail on 15 June 1942 until August 1943, between one and three trains arrived on the branch from the Treblinka station every day.[21] Each train contained sixty cars, and each car had no fewer than 150 people. We collected dozens of testimonies like this. Even if we take the data on the special trains' arrivals to Treblinka as provided by witnesses and cut them in half, the number of people brought there over the thirteen months of the camp's existence would still be at about 3 million.[22]

The camp itself—with its outer fence, its warehouses for the executed people's possessions, its platform, and its other auxiliary facilities—occupies a fairly small space: 780 by 600 meters. If, for even a moment, there was any doubt about the fate of the millions brought here, and if, for even a moment, we suppose that the Germans didn't kill them immediately upon arrival, then the question arises: Where are they, the people who could make up the population of a small country or a large European capital city? For thirteen months, 396 days, the special trains left here, loaded with sand or empty, but not one person from those who arrived returned from Camp II. The time has come to ask the dreaded question: "Cain, where are they, where are the ones you brought here?"

Fascism wasn't able to keep its greatest crime a secret. But not because thousands of people unwillingly became witnesses to this crime. Hitler, confident of impunity, made the decision to exterminate millions of innocent people

---

19 The number of cars per train varied, although usually there were fifty-eight freight cars for the victims and two passenger cars for the guards.

20 Wólka Okrąglik—a village 1.2 miles south of Treblinka.

21 The first death transport arrived from the Warsaw ghetto on 23 July 1942.

22 See editor's introduction to "The Hell of Treblinka."

in the summer of 1942, at the time of the fascist troops' greatest success. We can now prove that the Germans carried out their highest volume of murders in 1942. Convinced of their impunity, the fascists showed the world what they were capable of. Oh, if Adolph Hitler had won, he would have been able to hide all traces of all the crimes; he would have silenced all the witnesses, even if there were tens of thousands of them, rather than thousands. Not a single one of them would have uttered a word. And once again, we must artlessly bow down before those who, in the fall of 1942—while the whole world, now so boisterous and victorious, stood silent—fought in Stalingrad on the Volga's steep bank against German troops, with rivers of innocent blood smoking and seething behind the enemy's back.

The Red Army—this is who prevented Himmler from keeping the secret of Treblinka.

Today witnesses have started to speak out, the stones and the earth to cry out. And today, before the world's public conscience, before the eyes of humanity, we can gradually, step by step, pass through the circles of the Hell of Treblinka, compared to which Dante's Hell is simply one of Satan's harmless and empty games.

Everything written below is based on stories told by living witnesses and on the testimonies of people who worked in Treblinka from the first day of the camp's existence until 2 August 1943, when the condemned rose up, set the camp on fire, and escaped into the woods, and on the testimonies of arrested *Wachmänner*, who confirmed, word for word, and in many cases supplemented the witnesses' stories. I personally saw these people, I talked with them at length and in detail; their written testimonies are on the desk before me. And these numerous testimonies, from various sources, agree in all details, starting from a description of the habits of the commandant's dog Barry and ending with details on the technology for murdering victims and the design of the conveyer of slaughter.

Let us now walk through the circles of the Hell of Treblinka.

Who were the people taken to Treblinka on the special trains? For the most part Jews, then Poles and Roma. By the spring of 1942, almost the entire Jewish population of Poland, Germany, and the western regions of Belarus had been herded into ghettos. In these ghettos—in Warsaw, Radom, Częstochowa, Lublin, Białystok, Grodno, and many dozens of other, smaller places—millions of Jewish people were gathered: workers, craftsmen, doctors, professors, architects, engineers, teachers, artists, entertainers, white collar workers, all with their families, wives, daughters, sons, mothers, and fathers. Around 500,000 people were contained in the Warsaw ghetto alone. Apparently, this imprisonment in the ghetto was the first, preliminary stage of Hitler's plan to exterminate the Jews. The summer of 1942, the heyday of fascism's military success, was deemed an appropriate time to implement the second part of the plan—physical extermination. We know that Himmler came to Warsaw at this time and gave the corresponding orders. Day and night preparations were made for the Treblinka slaughterhouse. In July, the first special trains had already left Warsaw and Częstochowa for Treblinka. People were informed that they were being taken to Ukraine to work in agriculture. They were allowed to take 20 kilograms of luggage and also some food. In many cases, Germans forced their victims to buy train tickets to the "Ober-Maidan" station. This was the German's code name for Treblinka. In fact, rumors about a horrid place soon spread all over Poland, and SS officers stopped using the word "Treblinka" when loading people onto the special trains. However, the way passengers were treated when they were being loaded onto the special trains was such that it no longer raised any doubts about the fate awaiting them. No fewer than 150 people were jammed into one freight car, usually between 180 and 200. For the entire duration of the trip, which lasted sometimes two to three days, the prisoners weren't given any water. People suffered so much from dehydration that they drank their own urine. Security guards demanded 100 złoty for one gulp of water, and, once they received the money, they usually didn't even deliver the water. People were traveling pressed against each other, sometimes even standing up, and in each car, by the end of the trip, especially on stuffy summer days, several of the elderly and people with heart problems died. Since the doors were never opened until the end of the journey, corpses would begin to decompose, poisoning the air inside the train cars. If one person among the passengers lit a match at night, the security guards would shoot through the walls of the car. The barber Abram Kon told me that in his car many people were wounded and five killed as a result of the guards shooting through the walls.

The trains from west European countries arrived at Treblinka in a completely different fashion. Here, people hadn't heard anything about Treblinka, and until the last minute they believed they were being taken to a work site; moreover, the Germans had described in every imaginable way the comforts and charm of the new life awaiting the travelers. Some special trains arrived with people who were convinced they were being taken across the border, to neutral countries: they had paid the German authorities a lot of money to obtain exit visas and foreign passports.

Once, a train arrived at Treblinka carrying Jews from England, Canada, America, and Australia who had been stranded in Europe and Poland during the war. After considerable efforts involving large bribes, they managed to get permission to travel to neutral countries. All the trains coming from European countries arrived without security guards, with regular service personnel on them; these trains had sleeping cars and restaurant cars. The passengers had bulky trunks and suitcases, large reserves of food. The passengers' children would run out at intermediate stops and ask how much longer till Ober-Maidan.

Special trains occasionally arrived from Bessarabia and other regions with Roma. A few times special trains arrived filled with young Poles—peasants and workers who had participated in revolts and guerrilla troops.

It's hard to say what's more terrible: to travel to your death in complete agony, knowing that it's approaching, or in complete ignorance, to look out the window of the soft sleeper right at the moment when the official at Treblinka station is already calling the camp and reporting on the arriving train and the number of people on it.

As a final was of tricking the people arriving from Europe, the bay plat-form itself at the death camp was made to look like a passenger station. At the platform, where the next twenty cars in line were being unloaded, they had erected a railway building with ticket offices, luggage storage, a restaurant with a dining area, and signs all over the place with arrows: "Board for Białystok," "To Baranovichi," "Board for Wołkowysk," and so on. When the special trains arrived at the railway buildings, a band played, and all the musicians were well dressed. A porter clad in a railroad worker's uniform collected tickets from the passengers and steered them toward the square. Three to four thousand people, loaded down with bags and suitcases, supporting the elderly and sick, walked into the square. Mothers carried children in their arms, older children pressed close to their parents, inquisitively scanning the square. There was something threatening and terrifying about this square, trampled on and leveled by mil-lions of human feet. People's sharpened gazes quickly grasped the threatening details—on the ground, hastily swept probably just a few minutes before, dis-carded objects could be seen: a bundle of clothes, opened suitcases, shaving brushes, enamel pots. How did these items get there? And why did the railroad end immediately after the station platform, and beyond it there was only yellow grass and a three-meter fence? Where were the tracks to Białystok, Siedlce, Warsaw, Wołkowysk? And why were the new guards smirking like that, staring at the men straightening their ties, the tidy old ladies, the boys in little sailor's jackets, the skinny young women, who found a way to keep their clothes neat and clean on this journey, the young mothers, lovingly tucking blankets around their babies. All these *Wachmänner* in black uniforms and SS *Unteroffiziere* were like drovers at the entrance to a slaughterhouse. For them, yet again, the newly arrived party were not living people, and they couldn't help grinning as they looked at the display of bewilderment, love, fear, or concern for loved ones and for personal belongings; they were amused when mothers scolded children for running a few steps away, when they straightened the boys' little jackets, when the men wiped their foreheads with handkerchiefs and lit up cigarettes, when the young women fixed their hair and anxiously clutched their skirts against a gust of wind. The guards were amused that the elderly tried to perch up on their suitcases, and that some of them held books under their arms, and that the sick wrapped scarves around their necks. Up to twenty thousand people passed through Treblinka every day. Days when six or seven thousand arrived from the train station were considered slow days. Four, five times a day, the square filled up with people. And all these thousands, tens of thousands, hundreds of thousands of people, these probing, frightened eyes, all these young and old faces, the beauties with curly black hair or golden locks, the hunched and stooped bald old men and timid teenagers—all of them merged into a single stream, consuming reason, beautiful human knowledge, maidenly love, childish bafflement, an elderly cough, and a human heart.

Again the newcomers trembled as they sensed the strangeness of this controlled, sated, mocking look, the look of a live beast's superiority over a dead man.

And once again, in these brief moments, the newcomers walking onto the sorting square caught sight of the little things, incomprehensible things that infected them with anxiety.

What was that there, behind that huge, six-meter wall that was completely covered with blankets and pine needles that had started to turn yellow? The blankets also caused unease: quilted, parti-colored, made from silk and covered in calico, they seemed like the blankets that used to belong to recent arrivals. How did they get there? Who brought them here? And where were they, the owners of these blankets? And who were those people with pale blue armbands? It made you remember everything you thought about recently, the warnings, the whispered rumors. No, no, it can't be. And you chase away the terrible thought. Anxiety grips the people in the square for a brief moment, maybe two or three minutes, until all the new arrivals have had time to get off the platform. This unloading always entails some delays: in every group there are invalids, cripples, elderly and sick people, who can barely move their feet. But now everyone's in the square. The *Unterscharführer* (a junior SS *Unteroffizier*) loudly and clearly instructs the newcomers to leave their things in the square and go to the "bathhouse," bringing only personal papers, valuables, and a very small bag with toiletries. The people standing there have dozens of questions: should we take a change of underwear, should we untie our bundles, won't the things left in the square get mixed up, won't something go missing? But some strange force makes them keep silent and tread fast, without asking questions or looking around, toward the gap in the six-meter wire fence covered over with branches. They go past antitank hedgehogs, past tall barbed wire, three times a person's height, past a three-meter deep antitank ditch, again past thin tangles of steel wire that would trap an escapee's feet, like the legs of flies in a spider web, and once again past many-meter-high walls of barbed wire. And a dreadful feeling, a feeling of impending doom, a feeling of helplessness overcomes them: there's no escaping, no turning back, no fighting—the muzzles of heavy machine guns are watching them from the short and squat wooden towers. Call for help? But there's just a circle of SS officers and *Wachmänner* with machine guns, hand grenades, pistols. They rule. They have the tanks and the aircraft, the lands, the cities, the sky, the railroads, the law, the press, the radio. The whole world is silent, subjugated, enslaved by the brown-shirted gang of bandits that have seized power. And it is only far away, someplace many kilometers from here that Soviet artillery roars on the banks of the Volga, stubbornly proclaiming the Russian people's mighty will to fight to the death for freedom, rousing the peoples of the world and calling them to battle.

And on the square in front of the train station, two hundred workers with sky-blue armbands (the "sky-blue group")[23] silently, quickly, skillfully untie knots, open baskets and suitcases, take belts off valises. The sorting and assessment of the belongings left by the people who have just arrived is under way. Items are tossed to the ground: carefully packed darning materials, spools of thread, children's underclothes, dress shirts, sheets, V-neck sweaters, penknives, shaving kits, bundles of letters, photographs, thimbles, bottles of perfume, hand mirrors, sleeping caps, shoes, felt boots sewn from quilted blankets for cold temperatures, women's shoes, stockings, lace, pajamas, wax paper bags with butter, coffee, tins of cocoa, prayer shawls, candlesticks, books, crackers, violins, children's blocks. It takes certain qualifications to be able to sort through these thousands of items in a matter of minutes, to appraise them—to set aside items to be sent off to

---

23 The color of the armbands indicated the tasks performed by the inmate workers.

Germany, while other items, the old, damaged, nonessential things, were to be burned. And woe to any worker who made a mistake, putting an old, fraying suitcase in the pile of leather travel bags to be sent to Germany, or the mistake of tossing a pair of Parisian stockings with a factory stamp into the pile of old, darned socks. Workers were allowed only one mistake; two mistakes were not allowed. Forty SS men and sixty *Wachmänner* worked on the "transport detail," as the first stage of arrival in Treblinka was called, the one we just described: the arrival of the special trains, ushering the new party into the "train station" and square, and supervising the workers as they sorted and appraised the possessions. During this work, the workers would surreptitiously, unnoticed by the guards, bite off a bit of bread, sugar, candy that they found in bags with food. This wasn't allowed. After the job was finished, workers were allowed to wash their hands and faces with cologne and perfume; there wasn't enough water at Treblinka, and only Germans and *Wachmänner* used water. And while the people, still alive, were getting ready for the "bathhouse," the job of sorting their things was nearing completion: valuable items were taken to a warehouse, while letters, pictures of newborns, brothers, brides, yellowed wedding announcements—all these thousands of precious items, so infinitely dear to their owners but simply trash to those in charge at Treblinka—these were all gathered into a pile and taken to huge pits, on the bottoms of which were hundreds of thousands of similar letters, postcards, business cards, pictures, children's scribbles and first awkward attempts of drawing with colored pencils. The square was hurriedly swept and was ready to receive the next group of condemned people. But the arrival of new groups didn't always go as we've just described. When the prisoners knew where they were being taken, mutinies broke out. The farmer Skarżyński twice saw a group of people burst out of the train after breaking open the doors, overpower the guards, and escape to the woods. In both cases, everyone, down to the last person, was shot and killed by machine guns. Men carried four little kids with them, aged four to six. The kids were also killed. The farmer Marianna Kobus also described fights with the guards. Once, when she was working in the field, sixty people who were escaping from the train into the forest were killed before her eyes.

Now the party moves into a second square, already within the camp's second fence. There is a huge barracks in the square and three more barracks to the right, two of which are used for storing clothes, the third for footwear. Further down, in the western section, are the barracks for the SS officers, barracks for the *Wachmänner*, food warehouses, and an animal house; there are also cars and trucks, an armored car. You get the impression that it's an ordinary camp, just like Camp I.

In the southeast corner of the camp's courtyard, there's a space enclosed with tree branches and in front of it, a booth with the sign "Infirmary." All the frail, gravely ill people are separated from the crowd waiting for the "bathhouse" and are taken on stretchers to the "infirmary." A "doctor" in a white coat with a Red Cross armband on his left sleeve comes out of the booth to greet the sick ones. We'll tell you later about the "infirmary."

The second phase of sorting the newly arrived people consists in suppressing people's will through a ceaseless string of short and fast orders. These commands are issued in the tone of voice that the German army is so proud of, the tone that is supposed to be one of the proofs that Germans are the master race. The letter "r," simultaneously guttural and hard, sounds like a whip.

"*Achtung!*"[24] sweeps over the crowd, and in the leaden silence, the voice of the *Scharführer* recites his memorized lines, repeated several times a day, many months in a row:

"Men should stay where they are; women and children will change in the barracks on the left."

According to witnesses, this is usually when terrible scenes start. A great feeling of maternal, spousal, filial love prompts these people to believe that they were seeing each other for the last time. Handshakes, kisses, blessings, tears, short, quickly spoken words into which people pour all their love, all their pain, all their tenderness, all their despair . . . the SS psychiatrists of death knew that these feelings needed to be quickly extinguished, severed. The psychiatrists of death knew the simple laws that apply to slaughterhouses all over the world, and the beasts in Treblinka applied these laws to human beings. This is one of the most critical moments: separating daughters from fathers, mothers from sons, grandmothers from grandsons, husbands from wives.

And once more the words ring out over the square: "*Achtung! Achtung!*" This is precisely the moment when, once again, people's logic needs to be distracted by hope, the rules of death must be presented as the rules of life. The same voice slices word after word:

"Women and children take off your shoes when entering the barracks. Place your stockings in your shoes. Children's stockings should be put in their sandals, boots, and shoes. Keep everything tidy." And once again, right after this: "Head into the bathhouse, take your valuables, papers, money, towels, and soap . . . I repeat . . ."

---

24 "Attention" (Ger.).

There's a barbershop inside the women's barracks; naked women's hair is cut with clippers, wigs are removed from elderly women. It's a strange psychological state: according to the hairdressers, more than anything this near-death haircut convinced the women that they really were going into a bathhouse. Younger women, touching their heads, would sometimes plea, "It's uneven here. Could you even it out, please?" Usually the women calmed down after the haircut, almost all of them left the barracks holding a piece of soap and a folded towel. Some of the younger ones cried, regretting the loss of their beautiful long braids. Why did they cut women's hair? To trick them? No, the hair was needed for consumption in Germany. It was raw material . . . I asked many people what the Germans did with these heaps of hair taken from the heads of the living dead women. All the witnesses describe how huge mounds of black, golden, and light hair, loads of curls and long braids underwent disinfection, were pressed into sacks, and were shipped to Germany. All the witnesses confirmed that the hair was shipped in sacks to locations in Germany. How was the hair used? No one can answer this question. Only Kon's written testimony states that the Naval Office used this hair to stuff mattresses, for various technical devices, and to weave rope for submarines.

It seems to me that this claim requires further confirmation; it was given to humanity by Grossadmiral Raeder, who was commander of the German Navy in 1942.

Men undressed in the yard. Between one hundred fifty and three hundred men were chosen from the morning's first group of arrivals—men of greater physical strength, whom they used to bury the dead and usually killed the next day. The men were supposed to undress very quickly, yet in an orderly fashion, neatly folding their shoes, socks, undergarments, jackets, and pants. A second team of workers, the "red group," sorted the personal effects; this group was distinguished from the "transport" group by red armbands. Items deemed worthy of being sent to Germany were immediately moved to storage. All metal and cloth labels were carefully removed from them. The remaining items were burned or buried in pits.

This whole time, anxiety grew. There was a tormenting smell in the air, and now and then the smell of bleach would break it up. The huge number of fat, obnoxious flies was baffling. What were they doing here, among the pine trees and trampled earth? People inhaled anxiously and loudly, shuddering, examining every tiny detail that could explain, give them a hint, lift the curtain of secrecy over the fate awaiting these doomed people. And why were giant excavators rumbling there, to the south of them?

The next step in the procedure began. The naked people were ushered to a ticket window and asked to turn in their documents and valuables. And once again, the terrifying, hypnotic voice shouted, "*Achtung! Achtung!* The penalty for concealing valuables is death! *Achtung!*"

The *Scharführer* sat in a small booth made of boards hammered together. SS officers and *Wachmänner* stood beside him. There were wooden boxes near the booth, and the valuables were thrown in there: one box for paper money, another for coins, a third for wrist watches, for rings, for earrings and brooches with precious stones, for bracelets. But documents—documents were tossed on the ground, no longer of any use in this world, documents of the living dead, who within the hour would already be lying, rammed together, in a pit. But gold and valuables were carefully sorted; dozens of jewelers tested the metal, determined the value of the stones, the purity of the diamonds.

Here's a surprising thing: the beasts were able to use everything—leather, paper, textiles, anything that served people, anything that was needed and could prove useful to the beasts; the only thing they didn't use was the most precious value in the world—human life, which they trampled. And what great, powerful minds, what honest souls, what endearing childish eyes, what sweet faces of old ladies, what maidenly heads proud in their beauty . . . nature labored for many thousands of centuries to create this, and now all of this was relegated in a silent stream to an abyss of nothingness. Just a few seconds was all it took to destroy what nature and the world had created in the tremendous and torturous making of life.

The "ticket windows" were a turning point: this was the end of the torment of lies that held people in a hypnotic state of ignorance, in a fever that in the span of a few minutes flung them from hope to despair, from visions of life to visions of death. This torment of lies was just one of the characteristics of the conveyer belt of death; it helped the SS officers in their work. And when the moment came to rob the living dead for the last time, the Germans radically changed the style of treating their victims. Rings were torn off hands, breaking women's fingers; earrings were ripped off, tearing through earlobes.

In order to work rapidly, this last stage on the slaughterhouse conveyer belt required a new approach. Therefore, the word "*Achtung*" was replaced with a new one, the slapping, hissing words: "*Schneller! Schneller! Schneller!* Faster, faster, faster, run into nonexistence!"

From this cruel practice of recent years, we now know how a naked man immediately loses the strength to resist; he stops fighting fate, he loses his instinct to live at the same moment as he loses his clothes; he accepts his fate as doomed. Someone with an unquenchable desire to live becomes passive and indifferent. But to make sure that things went as planned, the SS added another monstrous method of stunning people on this final stage of the conveyor belt of slaughter, driving people into a state of psychological and spiritual shock. How was this done?

It was accomplished by the sudden, riveting introduction of senseless, illogical cruelty. Having already lost everything, the naked people continued to be people, a thousand times more so than the brutes in German army uniforms who surrounded them. They still breathed, looked around, and reflected, their hearts were still beating. Bars of soap and towels were knocked out of their hands. They were put in rows of five.

"*Hände hoch! Marsch! Schneller! Schneller!*"[25]

They entered a straight alley lined with flowers and fir trees, 120 meters long, 2 meters wide, which led to the execution site. Barbed wire ran on both sides of this alley, and *Wachmänner* stood shoulder to shoulder in their black uniforms and SS men in their grey ones. The road was covered with white sand, and those who went in front with their hands up in the air could see fresh footprints in the loose sand: women's small footprints, tiny children's ones, the heavy imprints of elderly feet. These fragile tracks in the sand were all that remained of the thousands of people who had recently walked down this road, who had walked just the same way as the new four thousand people were now walking, as the next four thousand would do in two hours after these, and as the thousands more would soon walk, the ones now awaiting their turn on the forest branch of the railroad. They walked down the alley the same way as others had done the day before, and ten days ago, and as they would walk down this alley the next day and in fifty days, and as other people walked down this alley over the entire thirteen-month existence of the Hell of Treblinka.

The Germans called this alley "the road of no return."

A grimacing human-like creature by the name of Sukhomil contorted itself and screamed, purposefully mangling the German words:

"Hey kiddies, *schneller, schneller*, the water's getting cold in the bathhouse! *Schneller*, kiddies, *schneller!*" Then the creature sniggered, bent over, pranced around. People with raised hands walked silently between two rows of guards who hit them with rifle butts and rubber truncheons. Children ran, barely able

---

25 "Hands up! Go! Faster! Faster!" (German). See **David Shrayer-Petrov**'s story "Hände Hoch!' in this anthology.

to keep up with the grown-ups. During this last, sorrowful passage, all witnesses singled out the brutality of another human-like creature, the SS officer Zepf. He specialized in murdering children. Endowed with extraordinary physical strength, this creature would unexpectedly grab a child from the crowd, then either swing the child like a mace, bashing its head against the ground, or rip the child in half.

When I heard about this creature, which was supposedly born to a woman, the things being said about him seemed inconceivable and unbelievable to me. But when I personally heard these stories repeated by eyewitnesses, I realized that they were describing it as just one more detail, nothing out of the ordinary for the Hell of Treblinka. And I believed in the actuality of such a vile creature.

Zepf's actions were essential, for they contributed to the psychological shock of the condemned; they were an expression of illogical cruelty overwhelming mind and will. He was a useful, necessary cog in the enormous machine of the fascist state.

Should we be horrified that nature gives birth to such degenerates when all sorts of deformities occur in the natural world—there are cyclops and also beings with two heads, with the corresponding spiritual deformities and perversions. What's terrifying is something else: creatures that should have been put in isolation and studied as psychiatric phenomena were in some other political order given a life as active and functioning citizens. Their delusional ideology, their pathological mentality, their phenomenal crimes became necessary elements of the fascist state. Thousands, tens of thousands, hundreds of thousands of these vile creatures are the pillars of German fascism, the basis, the foundation of Hitler's Germany. Dressed in uniform, armed, decorated by the empire, these creatures owned and ruled the lives of Europe's nations for a number of years. It's not the creatures themselves we should be horrified by but the state that enticed them out of their lairs, from the darkness and the underground, and made them needed, useful, indispensable in Treblinka near Warsaw, in Majdanek near Lublin, in Bełżec, in Sobibór, in Auschwitz, in Babi Yar, in Domanevka and Bogdanovka near Odessa, in Trostinets near Minsk, or in Ponary in Lithuania, in dozens and hundreds of other prisons, labor camps, penal camps, and camps for exterminating life.

A certain kind of state doesn't just fall onto people out of the sky; people's *material* and *ideological* relationships give birth to a certain type of government structure. And this is where we should really stop and think, where we should really be terrified . . .

The route from the "ticket windows" to the site of death took only a few minutes. Urged on by blows, deafened by shouts, people came to the third square and stopped for a moment—in utter shock.

In front of them was a beautiful stone building, decorated with wooden paneling, erected like an ancient temple. Five wide, concrete steps led to low but very wide, massive, beautifully decorated doors. Flowers grew in stone pots near the entrance. But all around them chaos reigned: mountains of newly dug earth were everywhere; the steel jaws of a huge, gnashing excavator threw tons of sandy yellow soil in the air; the dust caused by this work hung between the earth and the sun. The thunder of the colossal machine, digging huge ditches— mass graves—from morning till night, mixed with the frantic barking of dozens of German shepherds.

On both sides of the house of death were narrow-gauge tracks along which people in baggy overalls rolled self-dumping carts.

The wide doors of the house of death slowly swung open, and Schmidt, the chief of the slaughter, had two of his henchmen appear in the entrance. Those two were sadists and maniacs—one tall, about thirty years old, with massive shoulders, a swarthy, smiling, and happily excited face and black hair; the other a bit younger, not very tall, with brown hair and cheeks so pale yellow that he resembled a patient who had been taking strong doses of an antimalarial drug. We know the names of these traitors to humanity, motherland, and military oath.

The tall one held a huge, meter-long gas pipe and a leather whip in his hands. The second one was armed with a saber.

At this point, the SS officers released the trained dogs, which threw themselves into the crowd and tore at the naked bodies of the condemned with their teeth. The SS officers shouted; with the butts of their guns they hit and urged on the women, who were frozen as if in a stupor.

Schmidt's other henchmen took action inside the building itself, herding people through the open doors of the gas chamber.

By this time, one of Treblinka's commandants, Kurt Franz, would have made his way to the building, leading his dog Barry on a leash. Franz had specially trained Barry to attack the condemned and tear out their genitals. Kurt Franz had made a good career in the camps, starting as a young SS *Unteroffizier* and making it all the way to the relatively high rank of *Untersturmführer*.[26] This tall, thin, thirty-five-year-old SS man didn't just

---

26 SS rank, equivalent to second lieutenant in regular military structures.

possess organizational talents, didn't just adore his work at Treblinka, unable to imagine his place anywhere else than there, where everything occurred under his tireless supervision. He was also to some extent a theoretician and loved to explain the meaning and significance of his work. It would be very good if, in these awful minutes, the most humane defenders of Hitlerism were to stand in front of the "gassing" building—as spectators, of course. They would be able to enrich their compassionate humanitarian sermons, books, and articles with new arguments. Incidentally, the Holy Father, who has stood by—silently and reverently—as Himmler disposed of humankind, would be able to estimate how many rounds it would take for the Germans to process his entire Vatican staff through Treblinka.

Great is the power of humanity! Humanity doesn't die until the human being dies. And when a short but terrible time in history comes, a time when beasts triumph over human beings, the human beings whom the beasts are slaughtering retain, until their very last breath, the strength of their souls, the clarity of their thoughts, and the passion of their love. And having killed a human being, triumphant beasts still remain beasts. A grim martyrdom lies in the immortality of people's souls, a triumph of the dying human being over the living beast. In this, during the darkest days of 1942, was the dawn of reason's victory over savage madness—the victory of good over evil, light over darkness, forces of progress over reactionary forces. A terrible dawn over a field of blood and tears, over an abyss of suffering; dawn breaking to the wails of dying mothers and babies, the death wheezes of elderly people.

The beasts and the philosophy of beasts portended the sunset of the world, of Europe, but this red blood wasn't the color of sunset—it was the blood of humanity dying but victorious through its death. People remained people; they didn't accept the morals and laws of fascism; they fought them in every way, fought them with their own human death.

I was stunned to the depth of my soul, unable to sleep or find peace of mind when I heard the accounts of how, until their last moments, the living dead at Treblinka preserved not only the image and likeness of humanity but human souls! Stories of women trying to save their sons and thus committing hopeless feats of bravery; young mothers hiding their babies in piles of blankets and shielding them with their own bodies. No one knows the names of these mothers, and no one will ever know. Ten-year old girls with god's wisdom comforting their weeping parents; a boy who stood at the entrance to the gas chambers and shouted, "The Russians will avenge us, Mama, don't cry!" No one knows these children's names, and no one will ever know them. We heard stories about dozens of condemned people who took up the fight—alone against a huge pack of SS officers armed with automatic guns and grenades—and died where they stood, their chests riddled with dozens of bullets. We were told of a young father stabbing an SS officer with a knife, of a youth brought here from the rebellious Warsaw ghetto who miraculously managed to conceal a hand grenade from the Germans—naked, he threw it into a crowd of executioners. We heard about a battle that lasted all night between a rebellious group of the condemned and units of *Wachmänner*. Shots and grenade blasts rang out till morning, and when the sun rose, the whole square was covered with the corpses of dead fighters, and next to each fighter lay his weapon: a post ripped out of the fence and used as a mace, a knife, a razor blade. No matter how long the earth endures, no one will ever know the names of those who perished. One hears of a tall young woman who yanked a carbine from a *Wachman* while she walked on the "road of no return" and then fought against dozens of SS men all firing at her. Two beasts were killed in this fight, and a third had his hand shattered. One-armed, he returned to Treblinka. The girl was subjected to agonizing abuse and punishment. No one knows her name, and no one honors it.

But is it really so? Hitlerism took from these people their homes, their lives; it wanted to wipe their names from the world's memory. But all of them, the mothers who covered their children with their own bodies, and the children wiping tears from their fathers' eyes, and those who fought with knives and tossed grenades and fell in the nighttime slaughter, and the naked young woman, like a goddess from Greek mythology, who fought alone against dozens—all of them, these people who have passed into nonexistence, have preserved for eternity the very best of names, a name that no pack of hitlers-himmlers could trample into the earth: the name of a human being. History will write on their epitaphs, "Here rests a human being!"

Residents of the village closest to Treblinka, Wólka, tell how sometimes the cries of the women being murdered were so awful that all the villagers, going out of their minds, ran into the distant forest just to get away from those earsplitting cries, cries that drill through logs, sky, and earth. Then the cries would suddenly stop, only to start up again later just as suddenly, the same awful, earsplitting cries, drilling through bones, skulls, souls . . . This happened three or four times a day.

I asked S., one of the captured executioners, about these cries. He explained that the women cried out when the dogs were unleashed and the whole crowd of the condemned was herded into the house of death: "They saw death. Moreover, it was very crowded in there, and the *Wachmänner* beat them savagely, the dogs ripped at them."

The sudden silence descended when the gas chamber doors were closed. The cries of the women started up again when a new group was brought to the gas chamber. This happened two, three, four, sometimes even five times a day. The Treblinka slaughterhouse was no ordinary executioner's block. It was a conveyor belt of execution, organized in the flow method, borrowed from modern large-scale industrial production.

And like any other real industrial complex, Treblinka didn't spring out of the ground fully formed, as we have described it. It grew gradually, developed, added on new facilities. First they built three smaller gas chambers. A few special trains arrived while these chambers were still being constructed, and since the chambers weren't ready yet, everyone who arrived was killed with cold weapons—axes, hammers, clubs. The SS didn't want to shoot people and thus reveal the purpose of Treblinka's work to those who lived in the area. The first three concrete chambers were on a smaller side, 5 by 5 meters, that is, each an area of 25 square meters. The chambers were 190 centimeters high. Each chamber had two doors—one for letting in living people, the second for dragging out the corpses after they had been gassed. This second door was very wide, around 2.5 meters. The chambers were constructed on the same foundation.

These three chambers didn't meet Berlin's capacity requirements for conveyor belts of slaughter.

Construction on the buildings described above began immediately. Treblinka's leading officials took pride in the fact that they far outpaced the power, capacity, and production floor space of many Gestapo death factories, including Majdanek, Sobibór, Bełżec.

Over the course of five weeks, 700 prisoners worked on building the new death factory. At the peak of construction, a master builder and his crew arrived from Germany and began the assembly. The new chambers, ten in total, were symmetrically situated along both sides of a wide concrete corridor. Each chamber, just like the three previous iterations, had two doors—the first on the corridor side for living people, the second located across from it on the opposite wall, so that corpses could be dragged out after the gassing. These doors led onto one of two special platforms, symmetrically installed on both sides of the building. Narrow-gauge lines went up to the platform. This way, the corpses were dragged onto the platform and from there immediately loaded onto carts, then taken to the huge grave ditches that giant excavators dug day and night. The chamber floors sloped down a bit from the corridor towards the platform, which considerably facilitated the task of clearing out the chambers. In the old chambers, corpses were removed inefficiently: they were carried on stretchers and dragged out on straps. Each new chamber was 7 by 8 meters, or 56 square meters. The total area of the ten new chambers was 560 square meters, and taking into account the area of the three old chambers, which continued to be used for small transports, all together Treblinka's total production area of death was 635 square meters. One chamber could hold 400–500 people at a time. This means that when all ten chambers were at full capacity, 4,000–6,000 people were annihilated at once. On average, the chambers in the Hell of Treblinka were filled at least two to three times a day (there were days when they were filled six times). Through the most conservative estimations, we can calculate that when the chambers were filled twice a day, that is, only the ten new big chambers, that would be around 10,000 people killed in one day in Treblinka and around 300,000 in a month. Treblinka was in daily operation for 13 months, but even if we eliminate ninety days for maintenance, routine repairs, or problems with the timely arrival of special trains, we are left with a solid ten functioning months. If 300,000 people went through Treblinka in an average month, then in ten months Treblinka killed 3 million people.[27] We have once again arrived at the number 3 million, at which we first arrived through a deliberately low estimate of the number of trains.

The process of murdering in the chambers took from ten to twenty-five minutes. Initially, when the new chambers had just been put into operation and the executioners hadn't immediately figured out the gas supply and were conducting experiments to determine the dosage of various killing agents, the victims were subjected to terrible torments, taking two to three hours to die. In the first few days, the delivery and exhaust systems worked poorly, so the torments of the victims were prolonged, lasting for nine to ten hours. Various ways of killing were employed. These included flooding the room with exhaust fumes from the heavy tank engine used to generate power in Treblinka. Such exhaust fumes contained 2 to 3 percent carbon monoxide, which binds with hemoglobin in the blood to form a stable compound, known as carboxyhemoglobin. Carboxyhemoglobin is much more stable that oxyhemoglobin, the substance formed in the alveoli when pulmonary blood interacts with oxygen from the atmosphere. The hemoglobin in human blood binds firmly with carbon

---

27 See the introduction for the death toll at Treblinka.

monoxide within fifteen minutes, and the person breathes "in vain"—oxygen no longer reaches the organism, and it begins to show signs of oxygen starvation: the heart beats furiously, pumping blood into the lungs, but this blood is poisoned with carbon monoxide and is incapable of absorbing oxygen. Breathing becomes ragged, there are signs of painful asphyxiation, consciousness fades, and the person dies as if he had been strangled.

A second method used most commonly in Treblinka was to employ special pumps to remove air from the chamber. Death occurred in much the same way as from carbon monoxide poisoning: the person was deprived of oxygen. And finally, a third method, used less commonly, but still used, was killing with steam. This way, too, was based on depriving the organism of oxygen as steam expelled air from the chambers. Various killing agents were also used, but on an experimental basis; the industrialized mass murder was performed by the two methods described above.

Treblinka's conveyor belt of death came down to this: the beasts systematically robbed the human beings of everything human beings were entitled to since the beginning of time, according to the sacred law of life.

First people were robbed of their freedom, their homes, their motherland and were taken away to a nameless wasteland in the woods. Then, in the station square, people were robbed of their possessions, letters, pictures of loved ones. Then, beyond the camp's fence, people were robbed of their mothers, wives, children. Then documents were taken from the naked humans and thrown in a fire: people were robbed of their names. They were herded into a corridor with a low stone ceiling—they were robbed of the sky, the stars, the wind, the sun.

And then came the last act of this human tragedy—entering the last circle of the Hell of Treblinka.

The doors of the concrete chamber have slammed shut, doors that were secured by sophisticated locking mechanisms, held by massive bolts, clamps, and hooks. There was no breaking them down.

Can we find the strength in ourselves to imagine what these people felt in the chambers, what went through their minds in the last minutes of their lives? We know that they were silent . . . In the terrible closeness, pressed together so tightly that bones were broken and rib cages could barely expand to breathe, they stood one against another, covered in a last, sticky, deathly sweat; they stood like one person. Someone, maybe a wise old man, gathers his strength to utter, "Console yourselves, this is the end." Someone screams a terrible curse . . . And can it be that this holy curse will not come true . . . Can it not turn out to be a holy curse . . . A mother, with superhuman effort, tries to get just a bit more space for her babe—let his last breath be at least a tiny bit easier by the ultimate force of maternal love. A young woman asks, her tongue ossifying, "Why are they suffocating me? Why can't I just love and have children?" People's heads spin, they choke. What images pass before people's glassy, dying eyes? Images of childhood, of happy, peaceful days, of their last, arduous trip? Someone may see the smirking face of the SS man on the first square by the train station. "Oh, so that's why he was laughing." Consciousness fades and then comes the moment of terrible, final torture . . . No, it is impossible to imagine what happened in those chambers . . . Dead bodies stand there, turning cold. Witnesses say that children kept breathing longer than anyone else. After twenty or twenty-five minutes, Schmidt's assistants looked into the peepholes. It was time to open the doors of the chamber that led to the platform. Prisoners in overalls began to clear out the chambers, hurried along by the loud hollering of SS officers. Since the floors sloped toward the platform, many bodies fell out on their own. People who unloaded the chambers told me that the faces of the dead were a saturated yellow, and about 70 percent of them had a little bit of blood oozing from their noses and mouths. Physiologists can explain that. SS men, talking amongst themselves, examined the bodies. If someone turned out to be alive, moaning or moving, this person was finished off with a pistol. Then teams with dental pliers would remove the platinum and gold teeth from those lying on the platform, waiting to be loaded onto carts. The teeth were sorted according to their value, then packed in boxes and sent to Germany. If it had been more advantageous or easier for the SS to pull teeth from living people, they undoubtedly would have done it without hesitation, just as they removed the hair from living women. But, apparently, it was easier and more convenient to pull teeth from the dead.

The corpses were loaded onto carts and taken to huge grave ditches. There they were laid in rows, tightly, one next to the other. The ditches remained uncovered, waiting. And at this point, when they were just starting to clear out the gas chambers, the *Scharführer* working in transport got a short command over the phone. The *Scharführer* blew his whistle, signaling the train operator, and twenty new train cars slowly pulled up to the platform of the decoy Ober-Maidan train station. A new party of 3,000–4,000 people carrying suitcases, bundles, and bags of food got off the train and entered the station square.

Mothers carried children in their arms, older children pressed close to their parents, warily looking around. There was something threatening and scary about the square, its ground flattened by millions of human feet. Why do the railroad tracks end immediately after the station platform, and beyond—just yellow grass and a three-meter fence . . .

Processing new parties of arrivals went according to a strict timetable, so that the condemned set off on the "road of no return" at the exact moment when the last corpses from the gas chambers were transported to the ditches. Uncovered, the ditch waited.

And some time later, a *Scharführer* would blow his whistle again, and once again twenty cars would emerge from the forest and slowly pull up to the platform. Thousands more, carrying suitcases, bundles, and bags of food, would get off the train and enter the square, eyes wandering. There was something threatening, something scary about the square, its ground flattened by millions of human feet . . .

And the camp's commandant, sitting in his office, encircled by stacks of papers and charts, would telephone the Treblinka station, and a sixty-car train, surrounded by SS guards armed with submachine guns and assault rifles, would pull out of a siding, scraping and rattling as it moved along, and crawl down the narrow track between two rows of pine trees.

The huge excavators worked, rumbled day and night digging huge new ditches, hundreds of meters long and many dark meters deep. And the ditches stood uncovered. They waited. They didn't wait long.

2

Himmler came to Treblinka at the end of winter in 1943, accompanied by a group of high-ranking Gestapo officials. Himmler's party flew into the area of the camp, then drove into the camp gates in two vehicles. Most of those who arrived were wearing military uniforms, but a few people, maybe experts of some sort, were civilians dressed in fur coats and hats. Himmler personally inspected the camp, and one of the eyewitnesses told us how the minister of death went up to a huge ditch and silently looked at it for a while. The accompanying persons stood a small distance away from him and waited while Heinrich Himmler beheld the colossal grave, already half filled with corpses. Treblinka was the biggest factory in Himmler's operation.[28] The SS *Reichsführer's* plane flew back the same day. As he was leaving Treblinka, Himmler issued an order to the camp leadership that perplexed them all, *Hauptsturmführer* Baron von Pfein, his deputy Karol, and Captain Franz: to

---

28 The second biggest after Auschwitz-Birkenau.

begin burning the buried corpses immediately and to burn all of them, every single one, take the ash and cinders out of the camp, and spread them across the fields and roads. There were already millions of corpses in the ground, and this task seemed inordinately complex and difficult. Moreover, they were ordered not to bury anyone gassed in the future but to burn the corpses immediately. What was the reason for Himmler's inspection and his personal categorical order, which was deemed most significant? There was but one reason: the Red Army's victory at Stalingrad. Apparently the force of the Russian strike on the Volga was terrifying to the Germans, if only a few days later Berlin was thinking for the first time about responsibility, retribution, and punishment, if Himmler himself flew to Treblinka and issued urgent orders to obliterate all traces of the crimes that were being committed sixty kilometers from Warsaw. This was an echo of the mighty blow the Russians dealt the Germans on the Volga.

Initial efforts at burning the corpses weren't successful—the corpses didn't want to be burned; it was noted, though, that women's bodies burned better ... Large amounts of gasoline and oil were used in trying to ignite the corpses, but this was expensive and didn't have much of an effect. Things seemed to be at an impasse. But then a solution was found. An SS officer arrived from Germany, a burly man of about fifty, a specialist and expert. Hitler's regime had given birth to all sorts of "experts"—specialists in murdering young children, in strangulation, in building gas chambers, in the scientific destruction of big cities in the course of one day. An expert in exhuming and burning millions of human corpses was also identified.

Under his supervision, furnaces were being constructed. This was a special type of furnace-pyre, for neither the Lublin crematorium[29] nor any of the world's other major crematoria would be able to burn such an immense number of bodies in such a short time. The excavator dug a ditch 250–300 meters long, 20–25 meters wide, and 6 meters deep. Three rows of equally spaced reinforced concrete pillars were placed along the bottom of the ditch, each of which rose 100–120 centimeters above the bottom of the ditch. These pillars were the foundation for steel beams that were placed along the length of the pit. Rails were laid across these beams, about 5–7 centimeters from each other. Such was the design of giant broiler grates in what was essentially a cyclopean grill furnace. New narrow-gauge tracks were laid leading from the grave ditches to the ditch of the grill furnace. Soon a second, then a third furnace

---

29 Grossman is referring to the Majdanek camp outside Lublin.

was built according to the same scale. Each grill furnace could be loaded with 3,500–4,000 corpses at once.

A second Bagger, a colossal excavator, was delivered, and a third was soon added. Work continued day and night. People who were assigned to burn the corpses said that these furnaces were like huge volcanoes; the terrible heat burned workers' faces; flames erupted to the height of 8–10 meters; columns of black, thick, greasy smoke reached the sky and stood in the air like a heavy, motionless blanket. Residents of nearby villages saw this flame at night even 30 or 40 kilometers away; it rose above the pine forests girding the camp. The smell of burning human flesh filled the area. When the wind blew in the direction of the Polish camp located three kilometers away, people there choked from the stench. Eight hundred prisoners were assigned to burn corpses; this was more workers than would be assigned to a blast furnace or an open hearth of any large metal factory. This monstrous factory operated day and night for eight months straight but still couldn't handle the millions of human bodies. Admittedly, new groups of people arrived all the time to be gassed, and this also added to the furnaces' volume of material.

Trains arrived from Bulgaria;[30] the SS officers and *Wachmänner* were in high spirits: deceived by both the Germans and then the fascist Bulgarian government, not knowing the fate that awaited them, these people brought large quantities of valuables, lots of delicious food, fine white bread. Then trains began to arrive from Grodno and Białystok, and after that trains from the rebelling Warsaw ghetto; then came a train full of Polish rebels—peasants, workers, soldiers. A party of Roma arrived from Bessarabia, about two hundred men and eight hundred women and children. The Roma came on foot, with their horse-drawn carts trailing behind them; they had also been deceived, and only two guards escorted this group of a thousand people, and even the guards had no idea they were leading these people to their deaths. Witnesses state that the Roma women clapped their hands in admirations when they saw the beautiful building housing the gas chambers; up until the very last minute, they had no idea of the fate awaiting them. This especially amused the Germans. The SS men were especially brutal to those who arrived from the rebellious Warsaw ghetto. They separated out the women and children and took them not to the gas chambers but to where the corpses were

---

30 Grossman is referring not to Bulgarian Jews, whom Bulgaria spared from deportation to the death camps, but to about 11,000 Jews of Greek Thrace and Eastern Macedonia, who were under Bulgarian administration. They were rounded up in March 1943 and sent to their death at Treblinka.

being burned. Mothers going mad with horror were forced to walk with their children amid the red-hot grids, where thousands of dead bodies writhed in the flames and smoke, where corpses tossed and turned as if they were alive again, where the bellies of pregnant women burst open from the heat and the babies killed before birth burned in their mother's open wombs. Seeing this would be enough to cause anyone to lose their mind, even the most hardened, but the Germans were correct in their calculation that it would be a hundred times worse for mothers trying to cover their children's eyes with the palms of their hands. Children clung to their mothers and shrieked, "Mama, what are they going to do to us? Are they going to burn us?" Dante couldn't have seen scenes like this in his Hell.

After amusing themselves with this spectacle, the Germans really did burn the children.

Even just reading about this is endlessly difficult. I hope the reader will believe me when I say it isn't any easier to write about it. Someone may ask, "Why write about it, why should we remember all of this?"

It's a writer's duty to tell the terrible truth, and it's the reader's civic duty to learn about it. Anyone who turns away, who closes his eyes and walks past, insults the memory of those who perished. Anyone who doesn't learn the whole truth will never understand what kind of enemy, what monster our great, sacred Red Army has been fighting in mortal battle.

The "Infirmary" was also refitted. Before, the sick were taken behind a space enclosed by tree branches, where they were met by a so-called "doctor" and killed. The dead bodies of the elderly and sick were transported on stretchers to the mass graves. But later, a round pit was dug. Low benches stood around the pit, as if around a stadium, so close to the edge that those sitting on them were just above the pit. A grate was built at the bottom of the pit, and corpses were burned there. The sick and the frail old people were carried into the "Infirmary," then "orderlies" sat them on the benches, facing the fire of human bodies. After amusing themselves with the spectacle, the cannibals shot the grey haired in the napes of their necks or the sick in their stooped backs, and the dead and wounded bodies fell into the fire.

We have always known about the German's heavy-handed sense of humor and never really appreciated it. But could anyone in the world have imagined the SS sense of humor in Treblinka, SS entertainment, SS jokes?

They held soccer competitions among the condemned, forced them to play tag, organized a choir of the condemned. A little menagerie was set up near the quarters of the German staff, and harmless forest animals were kept in cages there—wolves and foxes—while the most abominable swinish killers to ever walk the earth were free to roam around, to sit on birch-wood benches and listen to music. There was even a special hymn written for the condemned, and it contained these lyrics:

> Für uns giebt heute nur Treblinka,
> Das unser Schicksal ist.... [31]

A few minutes before their death, bleeding people were forced to sing idiotic German sentimental songs as a choir:

> ... Ich brach das Blümelein
> Und schenkte es den Schönsten
> Geliebten Mädgelein.... [32]

The camp's chief commandant selected several children from one group of arrivals, had their parents killed, dressed the children in their best clothes, fed them unlimited sweets, played with them, and then, a few days later, when he was bored with this lark, he ordered the children killed.

One of the main amusements was to rape and torture the beautiful girls and young women who were chosen from each party of the condemned. In the morning, the rapists themselves would bring their victims to the gas chambers. This is how the SS officers had fun at Treblinka, that stronghold of Hitler's regime and the pride of fascist Germany.

Here we should note that these creatures weren't just mechanically executing someone else's will. All the witnesses note common features among these creatures: they loved to engage in theoretical discussions, to philosophize. They had a penchant for delivering speeches before the condemned, for boasting in front of them, explaining the great meaning and the future significance of what was happening at Treblinka. They were all deeply and utterly convinced that what they were doing was right and much needed. They explained in great detail how their race was superior to all others; they delivered tirades about German blood, the German character, the Germans' mission. Their beliefs

---

31 "Now there is only Treblinka for us, that is our fate . . ."
32 "I plucked a little flower and gave it to the lovelies of my beloved girls . . ." Editor's note: modified lines from the first stanza of "Es war ein Edelweiss" (1941), march of the Nazi land forces.

were outlined in books by Himmler and Rosenberg, in Goebbels's pamphlets and articles.

After working and amusing themselves, as we have just described it above, they slept the sleep of the righteous, undisturbed by dreams and nightmares. They weren't ever tortured by their consciences, at the very least because none of them had a conscience. They did calisthenics and obsessively took care of their health, drinking milk in the morning; they took great care of their daily conveniences, planted little gardens and lush flower beds, built gazebos around their living quarters. Frequently, several times a year, they went on leave to Germany, since the administration thought their "workshop" was very harmful, and they were careful to protect their workers' health. At home they went around with their heads held high and kept silent about their work, not because they were ashamed but simply because, being disciplined, they didn't dare to break their nondisclosure agreement and their solemn oath. And when, wives on their arms, they went to the movies in the evening and laughed raucously, stomping their hobnailed boots on the floor, it was difficult to tell them apart from the most ordinary philistines. But they were beasts in the greatest sense of the word—SS beasts.

The summer of 1943 was unusually hot in these parts. There was no rain, no clouds, no wind for many weeks. The work of burning the corpses was still in full swing. The furnaces had been blazing day and night for about six months already, but only a little over half the dead had been burned.

The prisoners who burned the corpses couldn't endure the horrible moral and physical suffering; every day fifteen to twenty people committed suicide. Many sought death, deliberately violating disciplinary rules.

"Getting a bullet was a *luksus* (luxury)," a baker from Kosów who had escaped the camp told me. People said that being condemned to live in Treblinka was far more terrible than being condemned to die.

Cinders and ash were taken outside the camp territory. The farmers of the village Wólka, conscripted by the Germans, loaded the ash and cinders onto drays and emptied them along the road leading from the death camp to the Polish penal camp. Using spades, child prisoners spread the ashes out more evenly along the road. Sometimes they found melted gold coins or melted crowns in the ashes. They called these children "children from the black road." The road turned black from the ash, like a funeral ribbon. Car wheels made a distinct swishing noise along this road, and when I traveled along it, I could hear a mournful swooshing from under the wheels the whole time, faint, like a timid supplication.

Running amid the woods and fields from the death camp to the Polish camp, this black funeral ribbon of ash was akin to a tragic symbol of the terrible fate that united all nations that had fallen under the ax of Hitler's Germany.

Farmers transported the ash and cinders from the spring of 1943 to the summer of 1944. Every day, 20 drays came to work, and each one of them was filled 6–8 times a day with 7–8 poods of ash.[33]

The song "Treblinka," which the Germans forced the 800 people working at burning the corpses to sing, contained lyrics encouraging the prisoners to be humble and obedient; for this they were promised a "tiny, tiny happiness/that flickers for one single moment." And here's the incredible part: in the life of the Hell of Treblinka, there really was but one happy day. The Germans, however, had miscalculated: it was neither humility nor obedience that made this day possible for those condemned to die. The madness of the brave gave birth to this day. They had nothing to lose. They were all condemned to death; every day of their lives was one of suffering and torment. The Germans wouldn't have spared a single one of them, these witnesses to horrible crimes—only the gas chambers awaited them. And indeed they would be sent there after a few days of work, replaced by new arrivals from the next party. There were only a few dozen people who lived not hours and days but weeks and months: the skilled craftsmen, the carpenters and stonemasons, and those who served the Germans, the bakers, tailors, and barbers. They were the ones who formed a committee to plan an uprising. Of course, only those condemned to die, possessed by a thirst for ferocious revenge and a feeling of all-consuming hatred, could have conceived of such a mad plan for rebellion. They didn't want to escape until they had destroyed Treblinka. And they destroyed it. Weapons began to appear in the workers' barracks: axes, knives, clubs. What cost, what mad risk was involved in procuring each ax and knife. What phenomenal patience, cunning, and dexterity it must have taken to conceal these things in the barracks and hide them from the searches. Stores of gasoline were set aside to douse and burn the camp buildings. How did they manage to accumulate gasoline, and how did it manage to disappear without a trace as if it had simply evaporated? This required a superhuman effort, extreme mental exertion, force

---

33 Editor's note: 1 pood = 16 kg.

of will, sheer audacity. Eventually they were able to dig a large tunnel underneath the German arsenal. In this, too, audacity helped them, and the god of courage was behind them. They took twenty hand grenades, a machine gun, carbines, and pistols from the arsenal. All these items were stored in secret hiding places dug out by the conspirators. The conspirators broke into groups of five. They devised a large-scale, complex plan for the uprising, taking into account every last detail. Each group of five had its own precise assignment. And each mathematically precise assignment was madness. One group was to storm the watch towers, where *Wachmänner* sat with machine guns. The second group was to attack and overwhelm the sentries who patrolled the paths between the camp squares. The third group was to attack the armored vehicles. The fourth group was tasked with cutting the telephone wires. The fifth group was to attack the barracks. The sixth group had to cut passages in the barbed wire. The seventh group was supposed to make bridges across the antitank ditches. The eighth was to pour gasoline on camp buildings and set them on fire. The ninth group was to destroy anything that was easily destructible.

They even had anticipated supplying escapees with money. A Warsaw doctor, who was tasked with gathering the money, almost gave the whole thing away. One day a *Scharführer* noticed a big stack of banknotes sticking out of the pocket of the doctor's pants —this was the next batch of money that had been stolen from the "ticket officer," and the doctor was getting ready to stash it away. The *Scharführer* acted as if he hadn't noticed anything and then reported it directly to Kurt Franz. This was, of course, a real emergency. Franz personally set out to interrogate the doctor. He immediately suspected something was going on—why, after all, would a condemned man need money? Franz began the interrogation slowly and steadily—there likely wasn't anyone in the world who was as good at torture as he. And he was sure that there wasn't anyone on earth who could withstand the methods of torture known to Hauptmann Kurt Franz. But the Warsaw doctor outwitted the SS Hauptmann. He took poison. One of the participants in the uprising told me that never before in Treblinka had such zealous efforts been taken to save a man's life. Evidently Franz intuitively knew that the dying doctor had an important secret. But the German poison acted without fail, and the secret remained a secret.

At the end of July, stifling heat set in. When graves were opened, steam billowed out as if from gigantic boilers. People died from the monstrous smell and the heat of the furnaces. The workers, exhausted from hauling corpses, fell dead into the furnaces themselves. Billions of fat, overfed flies crawled over the ground, buzzing through the air. The last hundred thousand corpses were being burned.

The uprising was scheduled for 2 August. A revolver shot signaled the start. A banner of success was unfurled over the sacred cause. A new flame rose in the sky, not the heavy flame, full of greasy smoke, not the flame of burning corpses, but the bright, scorching, and furious flame of a real blaze. The camp buildings had caught fire, and it seemed to the rebels that the sun itself, ripping apart its body, burned over Treblinka, reigning over this feast of freedom and honor.

Shots rang out; sputtering, machine guns came to life in the towers taken over by the rebels. Hand grenades boomed solemnly, like bells of truth. The air vibrated from crashes and detonations, buildings collapsed, the whistle of bullets drowned out the buzzing of corpse flies. In the clear and fresh air axes gleamed, red from blood. On the day of 2 August, the evil blood of the SS men flowed onto the ground of the Hell of Treblinka, and the blue sky bursting with light celebrated and triumphed on this day of retribution. And here history, as old as the world, repeated itself —once again, creatures that acted like representatives of a higher race, creatures that thunderously shouted "*Achtung! Mützen ab!*"[34] creatures that ordered the residents of Warsaw to come out of their homes to their deaths with the earth-shattering, roaring voices of almighty rulers "*Alle r-r-r-raus unter-r-r-r!*"[35]—these creatures, so confident of their power when it came to executing millions of women and children, turned out to be despicable, pathetic cowards, reptiles groveling and begging for mercy when they had to face an actual life-or-death fight to the death. They lost their heads, they scurried around like rats, they forgot about Treblinka's diabolically elaborate defense system, about the all-annihilating defenses they had prided themselves on; they forgot about their weapons. But is it worth bringing this up, and is anyone in the least surprised to hear it?

Two and a half months later, on 14 October 1943, there was an uprising at the Sobibór death factory, organized by the Soviet prisoner of war Aleksandr Pechersky, a political officer from Rostov. And there, what had happened at Treblinka was repeated: people half dead from hunger were able to overpower several hundred SS reprobates heavy with the weight of innocent blood. The rebels were able to overcome the butchers using home-made axes that they had

34 "Attention! Take off your hats!"
35 "Everyone come out, now!"

forged in the camp's smithies; many of them were armed with fine sand, which Pechersky had ordered them to fill their pockets with ahead of time and throw into the guards' eyes . . . But should we be surprised by this?

As Treblinka blazed, as the rebels silently bid farewell to the ashes of the people and escaped through the barbed wire, SS and police units were rushed in from all over to pursue them. Hundreds of police dogs were put on their scent. The Germans mobilized the air force. Fights took place in the woods, in the swamps—and very few people who took part in the uprising are still alive today.

After 2 August, Treblinka ceased to exist. The Germans burned the remaining corpses, dismantled the stone buildings, took down the barbed wire, and burned down the wooden barracks the rebels hadn't already burned. The equipment from the building of death was blown up, loaded up, and taken away; the furnaces were destroyed; the excavators were removed; the countless vast ditches were filled in with earth; the train station building was demolished down to the last stone, until finally, the railway tracks were dismantled, the cross-ties were taken away. Lupines were planted on the camp's site; a colonist by the name of Streben built himself a cottage there. Now that cottage is no longer there. It was burned. What did the Germans hope to accomplish by this? To obliterate the traces of having murdered millions of people in the Hell of Treblinka? Did they think that was even conceivable? Is it conceivable to force thousands of people into silence, people who witnessed how the special trains of death came from all over Europe to the conveyor belt of slaughter? Is it conceivable to hide the heavy flame of death and the smoke that stood out in the sky for eight months, visible night and day to the residents of dozens of villages and small towns? Is it conceivable to tear the terrible wails of women and children from people's hearts, to force people to forget these awful cries, which to this day ring in the ears of Wólka's peasants? Is it conceivable to force into silence the peasants who for a year transported human ash from the camp to surrounding roads?

Is it conceivable to force the surviving witnesses of Treblinka's slaughterhouse to be silent? Witnesses who survived from its first days until 2 August 1943—the last day of its existence? Witnesses who report the exact same information about each SS officer and *Wachmann*? Witnesses who have been able to reconstruct—step by step, hour by hour—the diary of Treblinka? No one can shout "*Mützen ab*" at them; no one can force them into a gas chamber. And Himmler no longer has any authority over his henchmen, who, their heads lowered and their trembling fingers nervously pulling on their jackets, recount in a low, coarse, measured voice the history of their crimes, which may seem like a history of madness and delirium. A Soviet officer wearing the green ribbon of the medal For the Defense of Stalingrad writes down page after page of the murderers' testimonies. A sentry stands at the door, his lips pressed together, the same Stalingrad Medal pinned to his chest; his lean, weather-beaten face is stern. This is the face of the people's justice. And is it not an astonishing symbol that one of the victorious armies of Stalingrad came here to Treblinka near Warsaw? It's no wonder that Heinrich Himmler panicked in February 1943, no wonder he flew to Treblinka, no wonder he ordered furnaces built, all evidence burned, all traces destroyed. But his panicking efforts were for naught! The Stalingrad fighters came to Treblinka, the trek from the Volga to the Vistula turned out to be short. And now the very earth of Treblinka does not want to be an accomplice in the villains' crimes; it is disgorging bones, ejecting the belongings of the dead, which the Hitlerites tried to hide in it.

We came to Treblinka in the beginning of September 1944—that is, thirteen months after the day of the uprising. The slaughterhouse was active for thirteen months. And for thirteen months the Germans tried to hide evidence of its operation. It's quiet now. The tops of the pine trees lining the railroad barely move. These pine trees, this sand, that old stump were what millions of human eyes saw as the train cars slowly pulled up to the platform. The ash and split cinders rustle softly along the black road neatly lined, in German fashion, with white painted stones. We enter the camp, walk on the earth of Treblinka. The lupine pods burst open with just the slightest touch; they burst open with a light ringing sound, spilling millions of little beans onto the ground . The sound of falling beans and the ringing of bursting pods merge to form a continuous, plaintive, and quiet melody. It seems as though the ringing of tiny funeral bells is emerging from the very depths of the earth, a sound barely audible, plaintive, deep, serene. And the earth sways beneath our feet, plump, rich, as if overly saturated with flax oil, the bottomless earth of Treblinka, as unsteady as the abyss of the sea. This wasteland, fenced off with barbed wire, has consumed more human lives than all the earth's oceans and seas since the existence of the human species.

The earth disgorges split bone fragments, teeth, possessions, papers—it doesn't want to keep deep secrets.

And things crawl out of the cracked earth, from its never-healing wounds. There they are—half-rotted shirts that belonged to the murdered victims, pants, shoes, cigarette cases with greenish patina, little wheels from wrist watches, penknives, shaving brushes, candlesticks, children's shoes with red pompoms, towels with Ukrainian embroidery, lace lingerie, scissors, thimbles, corsets, elastic waist belts. And further, from another crevice in the earth, piles of kitchenware sprout to the surface: pans, aluminum mugs, teacups, pots, saucepans, casserole pans, canisters, containers, children's plastic mugs. Still further, emerging from the bloated, bottomless earth, as if someone's hand has been pushing into light everything the Germans had buried, are half-rotted Soviet passports, notebooks with Bulgarian writing, photographs of children from Warsaw and Vienna, children's chicken-scratch letters, a small volume of poetry, a prayer written on a yellow scrap of paper, ration cards from Germany ... And everywhere, hundreds of vials and tiny faceted bottles that once held perfume—green, pink, dark blue ... The awful smell of decay hangs over everything; neither fire, nor sun, nor rain, nor snow, nor wind has been able to eliminate it. And hundreds of little forest flies crawl over the half-rotted possessions, papers, photographs.

We keep walking on and on over the bottomless, swaying earth of Treblinka and then we suddenly stop. Thick, wavy blond hair, gleaming like copper, a young woman's lovely, fine, weightless lovely hair, trampled into the earth, and next to it more locks of blond hair, and further ahead thick black braids on the light sand, and further ahead more, and then more. This, apparently, is the contents of one—just one!—unshipped, forgotten sack of hair. It's all true! Gone is the last, desperate hope that all of this is a dream. And the lupine pods tinkle, tinkle, and the falling beans patter, just as if a funeral knell from countless little bells were ringing from beneath the ground. And it feels as if your heart will stop now, arrested with such sadness, such grief, such anguish as no person should be able to bear ...

Scholars, sociologists, criminologists, psychiatrists, philosophers wonder: What is this? What was behind this—innate traits, heredity, upbringing, environment, external conditions, historic predetermination, the leaders' criminal will? What was it? How did it happen? The embryonic traits of racism that sounded comical when they were voiced by Germany's second-rate charlatan professors or pathetic provincial theorists in the last century; the Germans' philistine contempt for the "Russian pig," the "Polish cattle," the "garlic-stinking Jew," the "depraved Frenchman," the "money-hungry Englishman," the "strutting Greek," the "moron Czech"—this dime-a-dozen bouquet of the Germans' pompous, cheap superiority over every other race on earth, good-naturedly satirized by columnists and humorists—all of this unexpectedly, within the span of a few years, went from being "childish" to being a mortal threat to mankind, its life and freedom; it became the source of unbelievable and unprecedented suffering, blood, crimes. There's much here to think about!

Wars such as the current one are horrid. Vast amounts of innocent blood have been spilled by the Germans. But today it's not enough to talk about Germany's responsibility for what happened. Today we need to talk about the responsibility of every nation and every citizen of the world for the future.

Today, all people are bound by our conscience, by our sons and mothers, by our motherland, and by humanity to use the whole power of our minds and souls to answer the question: What gave birth to racism? What needs to be done so that Nazism, Hitlerism never rises again, on this or on the other side of the ocean, never, for all eternity?

The imperialist idea of national, racial, or any other kind of exceptionalism logically led the Hitlerites to build Majdanek, Sobibór, Bełżec, Auschwitz, Treblinka.

We must remember that racism, fascism, will walk away from this war not only with the bitterness of defeat but also with sweet memories of the ease of committing mass murder.

This must be remembered daily and adamantly by everyone who values honor, freedom, and life for all nations, for all of humanity.

September 1944

Translated from the Russian by Molly Godwin-Jones and Maxim D. Shrayer

LEV OZEROV

Lev Ozerov (1914–1996), poet, critic, and translator, was born Lev Goldberg in Kiev to a pharmacist's family. Ozerov worked as a turner, draftsman, book designer, and violinist before joining the staff of *Kiev Young Pioneer* (*Kievskii pioner*) in 1932. Ozerov wrote poetry from the age of fifteen, admiring the early Soviet modernists (**Eduard Bagritsky, Ilya Selvinsky**, and Nikolay Zabolotsky); he was mentored in Kiev by the poet Nikolay Ushakov. By the early 1930s, **Boris Pasternak** had enthralled Ozerov.

Ozerov studied philology at the Moscow Institute of Philosophy, Literature, and History (MIFLI) in 1934–39. While pursuing a graduate degree at MIFLI in 1939–41, Ozerov worked at *Pravda*. Peers identified his aesthetics with the Lake School of English romanticism (*ozernaia shkola*), hence his flight in 1935 to the (illusive) safety of the non-Jewish pseud-onym Ozerov (literally "of the lakes"). Ozerov's first collection, *Environs of the Dnieper*, appeared in Kiev in 1940. Soon after the Nazi invasion, Ozerov was dispatched to the northern Caucasus with a Komsomol "brigade." He contributed to the army newspaper *Victory Shall Be Ours* (*Pobeda za nami*). Recalled to Moscow to defend his candidate's dissertation in 1943, Ozerov stayed to teach creative writing and in 1946 became poetry editor of the monthly *October* (*Oktiabr'*). Ozerov's wartime poems were gathered in *Rainfall* (Moscow, 1947; edited by **Pavel Antokolsky**. The collection bore a daring epigraph—the last two lines of the long poem *February* by **Eduard Bagrtisky**: "There'll be rainfalls, southern winds will blow,/ Swans will make again their calls of passion." In 1948, during the so-called anti-cosmopolitan campaign, Ozerov was fired from his teaching and editorial positions.

He resumed teaching at the Literary Institute in 1956, and his collection *Confession of Love* appeared in 1957. Shaken by the close call of 1948, Ozerov established himself as a liberal in the official camp of literature during the Thaw. He knew how to navigate the straights of post-Stalinist Soviet culture. A founder, in 1964, of the Oral Poet's Library at Moscow's Central House of Actors, Ozerov featured some poets with limited publishing opportunities. "One must help talents/mediocrities will make it on their own," stated his classic aphorism. While assisting poets and helping return deleted names to print, he distanced himself from dissident activity.

Ozerov published many books of verse, including *Chiaroscuro* (1961), *Unearthly Gravity* (1969; book design by Ozerov), *Evening Mail* (1974), *Selected Poems* (1974), *Behind the [Film] Shot* (1978), *Axis of the Earth* (1986), *Emergency Supply* (1990), *Life's Abyss* (1996), and others. He was a prominent translator of poetry, especially from Lithuanian (he headed the Council on Lithuanian Literature at the Writers' Union) and Bulgarian, and produced such anthologies as *Song of Love* (1967; several reprints), coedited with Svetlana Magidson.

A professor at the Literary Institute and the author of a number of books of criticism, Ozerov also edited important literary works. He prepared the academic edition of **Boris Pasternak**'s *Shorter and Longer Poems* (1965); the following year Ozerov escaped unscathed in another close call, when Andrey Sinyavsky, who wrote the introduction, was sentenced to hard labor along with his codefendant, **Yuly Daniel**, for "anti-Soviet activity" in connection with their publications in the West. Ozerov was active as an author and editor until his last days. He died in Moscow in 1996. Following his death, Ozerov's unfinished memoirs in free verse, *Portraits without Frames*, appeared in Moscow; the fifty chapters include verse portraits of the Yiddish writers Dovid Hofshteyn, Leyb Kvitko, Perets Markish, Shmuel Halkin, and a number of Jewish-Russian authors.

Formally elegant, entering in dialogue with other poets (such as Anna Akhmatova, **Boris Pasternak**, and Goethe, whom Ozerov translated), Ozerov's poetry displays a nature-philosophical current. He summed up his poetic predilections in a subtle, exemplary lyric about a nightingale (cf. "God Nachtigall" in the poem "To German Speech" [1932] by **Osip Mandelstam** and Ozerov's and **Mandelstam**'s German Romantic antecedents in the poetry of Goethe, Heine, and Theodor Storm), an "improviser," a poetic instrument of the universe, which Ozerov himself was not. Here is the last stanza in a literal translation: "We listened to him with bias/While thinking in thick darkness,/That he possessed night space/The way we couldn't possess ourselves." "We" collectively stands for the Soviet poets of Ozerov's generation.

* * *

Babi Yar (Rus.; literally "women's ravine") is the name of what used to be a wooded ravine in the outskirts of Kiev. Over 33,000 Jews were murdered at Babi Yar on 29–30 September 1941, and altogether as many as 100,000 people, about 90,000 of them Jews, were killed at Babi Yar throughout the Nazi occupation.

Jewish-Soviet authors turned to the subject of Babi Yar as early as 1943–44, the earliest examples including the Ukrainian poem "Abraham" (1943) by Sava Holovanivskyi (1910–1989), a 1944 article and a subsequent 1947 story in Yiddish by Itsik Kipnis (1896–1974), episodes in the Yiddish-language epic *War* (*Milkhome*, 1948, complete edition) by Perets Markish (1895–1952), **Ilya Ehrenburg**'s January 1945 *Novy Mir* cycle (in this anthology) and a scene in his novel *Storm* (1947). In the postwar years, the commemoration—or, rather, the official non-commemoration—of the Babi Yar massacre became a cause célèbre of Soviet culture, while in the West the public awareness of Soviet artists' response to Babi Yar still tended to be limited to the poem "Babi Yar" (1961) by Yevgeny Yevtushenko (1933–2017) and Dmitry Shostakovich Symphony No. 13 (1962), based in part on Yevtushenko's poem, and, to a lesser degree, to the docunovel *Babi Yar* (1966) by Anatoly Kuznetsov (1929–1979). Other Soviet writers wrote about the Babi Yar massacre in the post-Stalinist years, but none with Ozerov's mournful power and piercing lyricism.

Ozerov contributed the essay "Kiev, Babi Yar" to the **Ehrenburg–Grossman** derailed *Black Book*. He composed his poem "Babi Yar" in 1944–45, and it appeared in the April–May 1946 issue of *October*, and in 1947 in his *Rainfall*. Reprinted for the first time twenty years later in Ozerov's 1966 *Lyric: Selected Poems* (and again in 1974, 1978, and 1986), it remains the most profound treatment of the topic in Russian poetry. Ozerov revisited the topic in "Once again at Babi Yar," a short lyric against unremembrance.

BABI YAR

I have come to you, Babi Yar.
If grief were subject to age,
Then I would be too old by far.
Measure age by centuries?—too many to gauge.

Pleading, here at this place I stand.
If my mind can endure the violence,
I will hear what you have to say, land—
Break your silence.

What is that rumbling in your breast?
It makes no sense to me—
Either the water rumbles under the land
Or the souls lying in the Yar.

I ask the maple trees: reply.
You are witnesses—tell your story!
But all is quiet,
Only the wind—
Soughing in the leaves.

I implore the sky: speak your piece.
But its indifference is painful . . .
There was life, there will be life.
But your face gives no guidance.
Perhaps the rocks will have an answer.
No . . .

All is quiet.
In the coagulating dust—August.
A nag grazes in the sparse grass.
It chews a faded rusty-red blanket
—Perhaps you will answer me.
No . . .

But the nag kept its eye away from me.
A squirrel flashed by with its bluish whiteness,
And all at once—
My heart was filled by the quiet . . .

And I felt:
Twilight entering my mind
and Kiev on that autumn morning—
Before me . . .

* * *

Today they keep coming down Lvov Street.
The air is hazy.
On and on they come. Packed together, one against the other.
Over the pavement,
Over the red maple leaves,
Over my heart they go.

The streams merge into a river.
Fascists and local *Polizei*
Stand at every house, at every front yard.
Turning back? Impossible!
Turning aside? Not a chance!
Fascist machine gunners bar the way.

The diaphanous autumn day is riddled with sunlight.
The crowd flows—dark against the light.
Quietly quivering are the last candles of the poplar trees.
And in the air:
—Where are we? Where are they taking us?
—Where are they taking us? Where are they taking us today?
—Where?—ask their eyes in final supplication.
And the procession, long and relentless,
Plods along to attend its own funeral.

Beyond Melnik Street are hillocks, fences, and vacant land.
And the rusty-red wall of the Jewish cemetery. Halt . . .
Here the gravestones erected by death are parsimoniously dense,
And the exit to Babi Yar,
Like death, is simple.

It's all clear to them now. The pit gapes like a maelstrom,
And the horizon is brightened by the light of final minutes.
Death, too, has its dressing room.
The Fascists must get down to business.
They divest the newcomers of their clothes, which they arrange in piles.

And reality suddenly shatters
When assailed by a still greater reality:
The thousands frozen in their tracks,
The life of cherishing eyes,
The evening air,
And the sky.
With eyes boring into the land,
They look at that which we are given to see only
Once . . .

Now shooting, shooting, stars of sudden light,
As brother embraces sister one last time—
While a scuttling SS man snaps pictures of all this with his Leica.
Volley after volley.
The heavy gasps of those lying in the Yar.

People approach and fall into the pit like rocks . . .
Children tumbling on women, old people on kids—
Like tongues of flame, with arms clawing at the sky,
They grasp for air,
And, their strength failing, they gasp curses.

A girl, from below:—Don't throw dirt in my eyes—
A boy:—Do I have to take off my socks, too?—
Then he grew still,
Embracing his mother for the last time.

In that pit, men were buried alive.
But suddenly, out of the ground appeared an arm
And gray curls on the nape of a neck . . .
A Fascist struck persistently with his shovel.
The ground became wet,
Then smooth and hard . . .

* * *

I have come to you, Babi Yar.
If grief were subject to age,
Then I would be too old by far.
Measure age by centuries?—too many to gauge.

Here to this day lie bones,
Skulls turning yellow in the dust.
And lichen infecting the ground with its whiteness.
At that place where my brothers have laid themselves down.

In this blighted place grass refuses to grow.
And the sand is as white as a corpse.
And the wind's whistle is ever so slight:
That's my brother gasping for air.

It is so easy to fall into that Yar.
As soon as I step on the sand—
And the ground partly opens its maw.
My old granddad will ask for a drink of water.

My nephew will want to get up.
He will awaken his sister and mother.
They will want to work loose their arms,
And beg life for just a minute.

The ground gives beneath my feet:
Either bending or writhing.
Beyond the sacramental quiet
I hear a child saying:
—More bread please.

Where are you, little one—show yourself.
I am deafened by a dull pain.
I will give you my life, drop by drop—
I, too, could have ended up with you.

We could have embraced one another in the final sleep.
We could have fallen together to the bottom.
That thought will haunt me to my dying day.
That we did not share death.

I shut my eyes for a minute
And perked up my ears.
I heard voices:
—Where did you want to go? There?!

A beard jerked angrily.
Words reverberated from the empty pit:
—No, don't come here!
—Stay where you are!

Stop!
You have a future.
You must live out your life—and ours.
You don't hold grudges—start holding them.
You're forgetful—don't you dare forget!

And a child said, Don't forget.
And a mother said, Don't forgive.
And the earthen breast swung shut.
I was no longer at the Yar but on my way.

It leads to vengeance—that way
Along which I must travel.
Don't forget . . .
Don't forgive . . .

1944–45

Translated from the Russian by Richard Sheldon

PAVEL ANTOKOLSKY

Pavel Antokolsky (1896–1978), poet, translator, and essayist, was born in St. Petersburg to a lawyer's family. His grandfather's brother was the great sculptor Mark Mordechai Antokolsky (1843–1902), one of the first unconverted Jews to rise to the top of Russian culture. Living in Moscow since 1904, Antokolsky entered the Law Faculty of Moscow University in 1915 but left after two years. Starting in 1915, he acted on stage, and in 1920 he became a codirector of the theater studio of Evgeny Vakhtangov (see **S. An-sky**). Initially called the Third Studio of the Moscow Art Theater, it was renamed the Vakhtangov Theater in 1926. Antokolsky remained with the Vakhtangov Theater until 1934.

Antokolsky began to publish in 1918. His first collection, *Poems* (1922), and his second, *The West* (1926), were built around a 1923 trip to Sweden and Germany with the Vakhtangov troupe and featured Antokolsky's best poems. The texture of the verse in *The West* betrays the impact of Vladimir Mayakovsky and Marina Tsvetaeva and also the influence of **Boris Pasternak**'s *Themes and Variations*. A German expressionist atmosphere unites Antokolsky's "western" poems with the cycle *European Night* by **Vladislav Khodasevich**. Although artfully constructed (the rhyming is especially masterful), Antokolsky's poems often lack lyricism.

A number of Antokolsky's histrionic poems—*Robespierre and Gorgona* (1930), *The Commune of 1871* (1933), and others—presented events in western history with revolutionary-romantic pathos. His collection *Dramatis Personae* (1932) marked a transition to poetry of ideological commission. Including such texts as "A Materialist's Catechism," it presented as a foreground the image of a stage of history where socialism was winning. Turning to the topics of Soviet daily life, Antokolsky published *Longer and Shorter Poems* (1934) and *Great Distances* (1936). He began to teach poetry at the Literary Institute and in 1938–39 served as poetry editor of *Novy mir*. His last prewar collection, *Poems 1933–1940*, features the unabashedly loyalist "October Poems," which end in the following manner (quoted in literal translation): "[. . .] But the boy finishes [playing the bugle]. And the red/Silk flutters. And Stalin/Smiles at him." It also includes the tasteless "If I Believed in God": "If I believed in God/I would tell him this evening: Lord, O Lord, how wretched is/ Everything you can help me with!"

A correspondent for *Komsomol Truth* (*Komsomol'skaia pravda*) during World War II, Antokolsky headed a front-line theater and composed patriotic ballads and long poems. His wartime collections include *Iron and Fire* and *Half a Year* (1942). In 1943, Antokolsky joined the Communist Party. He responded to the death of his son, a junior lieutenant, in battle with the moving and mournful long poem *Son* (1943; 1946 Stalin Prize). Antokolsky's postwar collections, including *The Third Book of War* (1946) and *Ten Years Later* (1953), treat the theme of memory and loss. His writings of the last Stalinist years include the long poem *Communist Manifesto* (1948). The conformist epic poem *In a Lane beyond Arbat Street* (1955) unfolded a collective biography of Antokolsky's generation, coming of age during World War I and (dialectically) embracing socialist construction.

During the Thaw, Antokolsky assumed the position of a minor Soviet classic. His collections include *Studio* (1958), *West-East* (1960), *High Voltage* (1962), *The Fourth Dimension* (1964), *A Cradle of Russian Poetry* (1976), *End of the Century* (1977), and others. His four-volume *Selected Works* appeared in 1971–73.

A translator from a number of languages, Antokolsky edited, with Leon Toom, *Estonian Poets of the Nineteenth Century* (1961) and other anthologies. His translations from the French were collected in *Civic Poets of France* (1955) and *From Beranger to Eluard* (1966).

A professor of poetry so much more than a "poet by God's gift" (as they say in Russian), Antokolsky was a mentor to several generations of Soviet poets and a living link with both the Silver Age and the seething Soviet 1920s.

* * *

Pavel Antokolsky coauthored with **Veniamin Kaverin** "The Uprising in Sobibór" for *The Black Book* (see **Vasily Grossman** and **Ilya Ehrenburg**). In doing research for the essay, **Kaverin** and Antokolsky interviewed Aleksandr Pechersky (1909–1990), who had been one of the organizers and leaders of the uprising of inmates at the Sobibór death camp; notes in Antokolsky's handwriting have survived.

As was the case with other Soviet writers of Jewish origin otherwise disinclined to discuss Jewishness, the war and the Shoah compelled Antokolsky to turn to Jewish themes. In 1943, he wrote with piercing lyricism of the death of his son, "half-Russian, half-Jew." (Antokolsky's personal tragedy resonates through chapter 13 of Margarita Aliger's epic poem *Your Victory.*) Before the introduction of a virtual ban on the discussion of the Shoah in Soviet culture, Antokolsky memorialized the victims of Nazism in several poems. One of them, "Death Camp," appeared in the Moscow magazine *Banner* (*Znamia*) in October 1945 and in his 1946 *Selected Works* and was reprinted in the USSR in Antokolsky's later volumes; its translation follows below. By calling the old

Jewish-Polish woman Rachel and her murdered "boys" Joseph and Benjamin, Antokolsky evokes the Biblical story of Jacob and his sons in the context of the Shoah. He also most likely references Biblical Rachel, the mother of Joseph and Benjamin, "weeping for her children" (Jeremiah 31:14–16). In the 1946 *Selected Works*, "Death Camp" is sandwiched between a poem that ends with "long live Stalin" and another one, "Glory," where one finds the lines "Stalin! Stalin! To you/We give the oath of loyalty again!" Was that the price Antokolsky paid for being able to include his Shoah poem?

In the same period, Antokolsky also wrote about the memory of the Jews murdered in the Shoah. Antokolsky's three-part poem "No Memory Eternal" was published in the July 1946 issue of *Banner* and mourned the destruction of much of Jewish civilization. The third, most memorable part of Antokolsky's "No Memory Eternal" functions as a Jewish lamentation for the victims of the Shoah. Here Antokolsky throws "hanging bridges" of memory across millennia of Jewish history and Judaic spirituality. The disappearing, "bitter" tracks or traces of European Jewry become a leit-motif of the poem. Despondently, Antokolsky chants about the absence of "tracks" in the "cities of Europe." He begins to address the collective Jewish victims as personified by a young woman with a child at her breast. Here Antokolsky's poem recalls the opening part of **Ilya Ehrenburg**'s "Six Poems" (the 1945 *Novy mir* cycle, also in this anthology). Antokolsky identifies the murdered Jewish woman with the Biblical Shulamit of the Song of Songs. Just as in "Death Camp," where the word "Jew" is also nominally absent, Antokolsky builds up poetic momentum for the poem's finale: "Wake up, child of the people of the Bible!/ Gas or whip or a gulp of lead,/ Get up, you young one! In such matters,/ In such love there can be no end." Through the evocation, in the poem's last stanza, of the opening of the *Shema* (Hear, O Israel [Sh'ma Yisrael], spelled in Russian transliteration and furnished with an explanatory footnote), Antokolsky called on the survivors to remain Jewish against all odds. After 1945, Antokolsky's "Death Camp" was reprinted a number of times during the Soviet years with small emendations, whereas "No Memory Eternal" was not reprinted in the USSR until 1966. When it was next published in 1971, the poem's Judaic references were either omitted or completely obfuscated, changing and confusing the meaning of the poem. Having borne poetic witness to the Shoah in 1944–46, Pavel Antokolsky would never again speak to the world about Jewish victimhood.

DEATH CAMP

And then that woman came, distressed,
Eighty, with lemon-sallow skin,
Wearing a shawl and quilted vest—
A feebly hobbling skeleton.
Her bluish wig of straggly strands
Must have been made before the Flood.
She pointed her thin blue-veined hands
Down at a ditch of oozing mud.

 "Excuse me. I've walked very far
Through shtetls burnt down to the ground.
Sir, do you know where my boys are,
Where their dead bodies may be found?

"Excuse me. I've gone deaf and blind,
But maybe in this Polish glen
Among these broken skulls
I'll find my Joseph and my Benjamin,

"Because your feet aren't crunching stones
But blackened ashes of the dead,
The charred remains of human bones,"
Rachel, that ancient woman, said.

We followed, grievously aware
These were the fields of her despair.
The golden woods glowed bright and fair
In the late autumn Polish air.
A swath of grass was scorched and bare.
No scythes or sickles lingered there
But voices, voices everywhere,
Voices that whispered to declare,

"We're dead. We lie still and embrace.
To these loved ones and friends we cling,
But we tell strangers of this place.
To strangers we tell everything.

"You see how many hopes are dead
By counting ruts in this crushed grass,
How much they stole our sun and bread,
Here in these ashes, shards of glass,
A twisted toy, a shred of shirt,
And children's eyes covered with dirt,

"How much they sheared off the black hair
The girls had braided with such care,
Blood, phosphorus, and protein found
What value in this Fascist lair,
As the wind chased and whipped around
Our skirts and stockings along the ground.

"We are these stars, we are these flowers.
The killers hurried to be done,
Becoming blinded by the powers
Of naked lives, bright as the sun.

"The killers used their cans of gas.
Death in its beauty would soon pass
Down the highway from this morass,
Because in the new waving grass,
In evening dew and in birdsong,
In gray clouds over the world's grime,
You see, we are not dead for long
We have arisen for all time."

1945

Translated from the Russian by Maxim D. Shrayer and J. B. Sisson

YURY GERMAN

Yury German (1910–1967), prose writer, screenwriter, and playwright, was born in Riga to an educated Jewish-Russian family. His father, a lieutenant in the tsarist army, had apparently taken baptism; his mother taught Russian at a gymnasium. Throughout World War I, German accompanied his mother, who became a military nurse to follow German's father to the front. After the revolution, German lived in Kursk, where he began to contribute to *Kursk Truth* (*Kurskaia pravda*) at the age of sixteen. In Dmitrov, a town north of Moscow, he headed an amateur drama studio and wrote his first novel, *Rafael from the Barber Shop* (Moscow, 1931), set during the NEP and featuring a Jewish theme.

In 1929, German enrolled at the Leningrad College of the Stage Arts. Unhappy with the course of study, he left and worked at a metal factory. German got to know *spetsy* ("specialists," usually engineers) from Germany working in the USSR, and they became the subject of his novel *Introduction* (1931). German's novel *Poor Heinrich* (1934) also focused on western characters. In 1932, Maxim Gorky encouraged the twenty-one-year-old German in an article published in *Pravda*.

Becoming a full-time author, German composed the novel *Our Acquaintances* (1936), about a young Soviet woman's transition from a loveless marriage to a happy union with a security policeman. *Our Acquaintances* exemplifies German's prewar fiction, which avoided crude tendentiousness while constructing a Soviet prosaics "with a human face." Conservative Soviet critics nevertheless accused German of advocating "petit-bourgeois" virtues. German's tales about law-enforcement officers, *Lapshin* and *Aleksey Zhmakin*, appeared in a 1938 book; German worked the tales into the novel *One Year*, published in 1960. Starting with *The Iron Feliks* (1938), German published books about the founder of the Soviet security police (Cheka), Feliks Dzerzhinsky (1877–1926), helping to poison the minds of young Soviet readers. In 1939–40, mixing half-truths and half-lies, German published prose about his visit to the annexed eastern Poland; they included the essay "On Liberated Land," the short story "In the Shtetl," and the powerful novella "Hotel 'Voldemar'" about the "liberated" Jews of what the Soviets reinterpreted as "western Belorussia" and about Jewish-Polish relations. During World War II, German was a TASS and Sovinformburo correspondent with the Northern Fleet. His experiences informed the short novels *The Chilly Sea* (1943) and *The Far-Away North* (1943) and other works.

On 8 July 1946, German published a positive article about Mikhail Zoshchenko, a talented satirist. The 14 August 1946 Resolution of the Communist Party, "About the Journals *Star* [*Zvezda*] and *Leningrad*," vilified Zoshchenko and Anna Akhmatova; singling out several other writers, it commented on German's article: "*Leningrad Truth* committed an error in permitting a disgraceful laudatory review by Yury German about the writings of Zoshchenko [...] ." Zhdanovshchina, the postwar onslaught of reaction known by this name after Andrey Zhdanov, party secretary for ideology, flooded Soviet culture, and German was among its first victims. A year later, German published a pledge, "To Serve the Millions," in *Leningrad Truth*, but that was not enough to deflect further attacks.

In January 1949, the magazine *Star* printed the first part of German's novel *Lieutenant Colonel of the Medical Corps*. The protagonist of the novel, a Jewish physician, was deemed too preoccupied with existential and personal issues. In the climate of the mounting antisemitic campaign, the serialization of German's novel was interrupted. German was forced to denounce his novel in a brief open letter, published in March 1949 in *Star*, followed on the same page by a denunciation of the novel by the editors. A complete version of *Lieutenant Colonel of the Medical Corps* did not appear until 1956, the turning-point year of the Thaw, in the relatively small print run of 30,000 copies.

Set in Petrine Russia, German's novel *Young Russia* (1952; revised 1954) suggested parallels with the suffering of the people in Stalinist Russia. Regaining faith in the Soviet system, German joined the Communist Party in 1957, following the Twentieth Party Congress. German's trilogy *The Task You Serve, My Dear Fellow*, and *I'm Responsible for Everything* (late 1950s–early 1960s) was suffused with the Thaw's post-Stalinist historical optimism.

German also wrote for screen and stage. Among his screen credits were *The Bold Seven* (1936, dir. Sergey Gerasimov), *Pirogov* (1947, dir. Grigory Kozintsev), *Belinsky* (1953, dir. Kozintsev), and *My Dear Fellow* (1958, dir. Iosif Kheifits). German's son, the filmmaker Aleksey German (1938–2013), adapted his father's works *Operation Happy New Year!* (1971; released 1986 as *Trial by Road*) and *My Friend Ivan Lapshin* (1984). German died in 1967 in Leningrad.

* * *

The generation of Soviet Jews who came of age after the revolution was well represented in Yury German's prose. The naval physician Lieutenant Colonel (Commander) Aleksandr Levin, the protagonist of German's ill-fated novel of 1949, serves in the Northern Fleet during the war. In other works of fiction, German endowed fictional medical doctors with a Chekhovian humanism. A Jewish doctor was a cultural cliché in Soviet society. When German's novel finally appeared in 1956, the image of a Jewish physician evoked recent memories of the terror, lies, and humiliation of the so-called Doctors' Plot (see John D. Klier's "Outline of Jewish-Russian History"). The episode that follows occurs in the middle of German's novel and did not appear in the opening section published in 1949 in *Star*; it appeared for the first time in the 1956 edition of the novel. Of particular importance is the dramatic dialogue about "Judaic blood" between one of Levin's comrades-in-arms, the naval surgeon Barkan (presumably a Ukrainian), here representing Soviet internationalism, and the German pilot Stude, whose mind is infected with Nazi ideology.

FROM *LIEUTENANT COLONEL OF THE MEDICAL CORPS*

(Excerpt from Chapter 17)

This time they drew out the search, flying low over the water, with two fighter planes, sent by the commanding officer, patrolling above. The sea lapping below them was very gray, angry, with whitecaps; visibility got worse; then the fighter planes left—they were out of fuel. Bobrov kept flying and flying over the assigned squares, searching and searching, squinting his tired, teary eyes, and finally saw a figure in the water.

"All right," he said to himself and turned the plane.

A tiny boat sped beneath the plane; its crew let out wild yells and shot off a flare pistol. The green flare, curving, scattered into a shower and disappeared behind.

"All right," Bobrov repeated and righted the plane for landing.

The boat sped by close and again disappeared.

It turned dark suddenly. Large, soft snowflakes started adhering to the Plexiglas in front of Bobrov. Water spray instantly washed the snow away. The plane landed.

"Over to you, Comrade Lieutenant Colonel," shouted the medic, and with his long arms Aleksandr Markovich Levin caught hold of a lieutenant smiling in confusion. Then he took two more. One was shivering and groaning; Levin injected him with morphine. The other two he gave cognac, then returned to the first. Meanwhile Bobrov hadn't taken off; the plane was coasting along the water like a launch.

In a few minutes, a reconnaissance plane came along, humming like a bumblebee, and fired off a red flare. Bobrov banked his plane and kept coasting along the water.

"We better get to the base soon," said Lednev. "See that lightning again— we'll have snow squalls."

"With Bobrov at the helm," said Levin, "we're better off than in Tashkent. No problem. Let me have the probe and stop talking nonsense."

The navigator let out a yell.

"Stop yelling, my friend," said Levin. "That shrapnel of yours has almost worked itself out. You'll live to be a hundred and fifty, and each day you'll be embarrassed to recall how you yelled."

The gunner again scrubbed the upper hatchway clear and lowered himself by the outside companionway down to the water. Large snowflakes immediately clung to his face. A moderate swell was running, lapping along the side of the plane. Up above, the mechanic ran to the tail and, balancing there, threw down the line and called to the gunner:

"Lift slowly! Stepan! Lee-ee-ft!"

Lednev poked out of the hatchway up to his waist and suddenly said to those down below, in a whisper, like a secret:

"They got a German out of the water; honest to God, don't you believe me? A fritz, a fritz!"

No one could make out his words at first, but all, except for the wounded man, raised their heads. The medic climbed out. A few more moments went by, and water started pouring in from above. Then legs appeared, from which rivulets of water streamed down. Then a German with a thin face silently straightened out to attention before Levin.

The German wore an inflated vest, a yellow helmet blackened by the water; a pistol attached only by a cord hung down below his knee. The mechanic cut the cord with a penknife and stuck the pistol inside his jacket. The motors were already wailing, reaching the higher notes, as always before takeoff.

"*Sind Sie verwundet?*"[36] asked Levin very loudly.

---

36 (Ger.) = "Are you wounded?" In the original's footnotes, Yury German supplies translations from the German to Russian. These translations from German into English are

The pilot mumbled something.

"*Wie fühlen Sie sich?*" said Levin still more loudly. "*Verstehen Sie mich? Ich frage, wie Sie sich fühlen? Sie sind nicht verwundet?*"[37]

The pilot kept staring at Levin. "This man may be mentally deranged," thought Levin, "maybe in a psychic trauma?"

And he reached out to take the German's pulse, but the latter jerked back and said he wished no services from a "*Jude.*"

"What?" Levin asked, flushing. He knew what the man had said, had heard everything word for word, but could not believe it. Over the years of Soviet power he had forgotten about this curse; he saw only in his nightmares how they squeezed "fat out of the little Yid"; he was a Red Army Lieutenant Colonel, and here this despicable creature reminded him again of those hateful times of the pogroms.

"What did he say?" asked the assistant medic.

"Oh, just some nonsense!" Levin answered, turning away from the German.

The pilot's mouth was quivering. Glancing around, he found a place on deck by the companionway and sat down, afraid that they would suddenly kill him. But no one intended to kill him; they just looked at him—how he sat down, how he drank water, and how he began to take off his wet clothes.

They gave him cognac; he drank it and moved all the available hot-water bottles closer to him. He could not get warm enough and could not take his eyes off the large white-faced Russian pilot who looked over his neighbor attentively, calmly, and seriously, every once in a while wincing with pain.

"Comrade Doctor!" the burly Russian called.

Levin bent down to him.

"We learned German in school," the pilot said. "The language of Marx and Goethe Schiller and Heine, as our teacher Anna Karlovna told us. I understood what he . . . said to you . . . this . . . bastard . . . But don't you take offence, Comrade Doctor. To hell with him, with the vermin. Remember Korolenko and Maxim Gorky . . . how they fought against such filth. And I tell you another thing—let's shake hands, Lieutenant Shilov here . . ."

---

by Helen Reeve. In the Russian original, German consistently translated the German adjective "Jüdisches" (as in Jüdisches Blut) as "Judaic" (iudeiskaia) rather than "Jewish" (evreiskaia). In Russian, Colonel Barkan also refers to blood as "Judaic" rather than "Jewish."

37 "How do you feel? . . . Do you understand me? I am asking how you feel. Are you not wounded?"

He raised his hand with difficulty. Levin pressed it.

"I figure that you need to forget this insult. Don't give a damn and forget it. This way . . . You see—he is looking at me. He's afraid I might shoot him dead. No, I won't shoot, the setting isn't right . . ."

Licking his dry lips, he slowly turned toward the other and began putting together German phrases, alternating with some Russian words:

"You better about this Jude *vergessen! Verstanden? Immer . . . Auf immer . . .* Forever . . . *Er ist . . . für dich Herr doktor. Verstanden? Herr* Lieutenant Colonel! *Und wirst sagen das . . . noch, werde schiessen dich im hospital*—I'll shoot you dead, you s.o.b.! *Das sage ich dir—ich,* Lieutenant Shilov Pyotr Semenovich. *Verstanden?* Got the picture?"[38]

"*Ja, ich habe verstanden. Ich habe es gut verstanden!*"[39] the German answered, barely moving his lips.

. . . Shilov was moved to room five, the German got a separate room, number eight. During the night, he had a massive hemorrhage. Angelika, and Lora, and Vera, and Varvarushkina, and Zhakombai heard from Shilov how the Fascist had insulted the lieutenant colonel on the plane. They also told Barkan about it.

Frowning angrily, he entered number eight, where the prisoner lay.

"*Ich verblute,*" softly, and with fear, said Lieutenant Kurt Stude. "*Ich bitte um sofortige Hilfe. Meine Blutgruppe ist hier angegeben.*" He pointed to his bracelet. "*Aber ich bitte Sie aufs dringlichste, Herr Doktor, Ihr Gesicht sagt mir, dass sie ein Slave sind, ich flehe Sie an: wenn Bluttransfusion notwendig ist . . . dass nur kein jüdisches Blut . . .*"[40]

Vyacheslav Viktorovich Barkan looked at the German sternly.

"*Verstehen Sie mich?*" asked Lieutenant Stude. "*Es geht um mein kuenftiges Schicksal, um meine Laufbahn, schliesslich um mein Leben. Keineswegs jüdisches Blut . . .*"[41]

Barkan frowned.

---

38 "Forget this 'Jew' stuff! Got that? For good . . . once and for all. That's . . . *Herr Doktor,* Sir! to you. Got that? Lieutenant Colonel, Sir! And if you come out with that . . . again, just once more, I'll shoot you when we get to the hospital. This is me, telling you . . . me . . . Got it . . . ?"

39 "Yes. I understand. I understand very well."

40 "I am bleeding to death. I request immediate treatment. My blood type is written here . . . But I most urgently request, Doctor, Sir, by your face I see that you are a Slav. I implore you: if a blood transfusion is necessary—no Judaic blood . . ."

41 "Do you understand me? We're talking about my future, about my career, about my life, really. No Judaic blood, no matter what."

"Haben Sie mich verstanden, Herr Doktor?"[42]

"Ja, ich habe Sie verstanden!" in a hoarse voice answered Barkan. *"Aber wir haben jetzt nur jüdisches Blut. So sind die Umstände. Und ohne Transfusion sind sie verloren..."*[43]

The pilot fell silent.

Barkan fixed him with a hard, unwavering gaze. He was seeing for the first time a genuine Fascist: my God, how shameful it was, how stupid, how crazy, how ugly. As if one could divide blood into Slavic, Aryan, Judaic. And this in the middle of the twentieth century...

"Ich hoffe, dass solche Einzelheiten in meinem Kriegsgefangenenbuch nicht verzeichnet werden. Das heisst, die Blutgruppe meinetwegen, aber nicht, dass es Jüdisches..."[44]

"Ich werde mir das Vergnuegen machen, alle Einzelheiten zu verzeichnen," said Barkan. *"Ich werde alles genau angeben."*[45]

"Aber warum denn, Herr Doktor? Sie sind doch ein Slave!"

"Ich bin ein Slave, und mir sind verhasst alle Rassisten. Verstehen Sie mich?" asked Barkan. *"Mir sind verhasst alle Antisemiten, Deutschhasser, mir sind verhasst Leute, die Neger lynchen, sind verhasst alle Obskuranten. Aber das sind unnuetze Worte. Was haben Sie beschlossen mit der Bluttransfusion?"*

"Ich unterwerfe mich der Gewalt!" said the pilot and pursed his lips.

"Nein, so geht es nicht. Bitten Sie uns um Transfusion beliebigen Blutes, oder bitten Sie nicht?"

"Dann bin ich gezwungen darum zu bitten."[46]

Barkan left the ward. In the hallway he said to Angelika:

"This scoundrel needs a transfusion. If he should inquire what kind of blood this is, tell him it's Judaic." Angelika raised her eyebrows in wonder.

---

42 "Do you understand me, Herr Doktor?"

43 "Yes, understood! . . . But right now we have only Judaic blood. That's the situation. And without the transfusion, you'll die . . ."

44 "I hope the details won't get written down in my POW record. Well, the blood type of course, but not that . . . it's Judaic . . ."

45 "I'll take pleasure in writing down every detail! I'll write it all down exactly."

46 "But why, Herr Doktor? You're a Slav, after all!" "I'm a Slav, and I hate racists. Do you understand me? . . . I hate all antisemites, German-haters; I hate those who lynch Negroes. I hate reactionaries. However, there is no point talking. What have you decided about the blood transfusion?" "I submit to coercion!" . . . "No, that won't do. Are you asking for a transfusion of any kind of blood whatsoever, or not?" "Well then, I am being forced to ask for one."

"Yes, yes, Judaic," repeated Barkan. "I am in my right mind and firm memory, but this will cut him down to size once and for all."

"You are doing this for Levin!" Angelika exclaimed in her deep voice. "Yes, don't deny it. That is splendid, Vyacheslav Viktorovich, that is wonderful. You are a marvel. I'm delighted . . ."

"Glad to hear it!" growled Barkan.

That night Bobrov showed up in the clinic to see Levin.

"Plotnikov's plane didn't come back from the mission," he said, "the crew went down, and our Kurochka too."

"That's not possible!" said Levin.

His face turned gray.

Bobrov told him what details he knew. Many pilots saw the burning plane. No one managed to bail out. But still they had torpedoed the transport, and not a small one either—about ten tons, no less.

The phone on the table rang. A controlled voice warned:

"Lieutenant Colonel Levin? The general wishes to talk to you."

"Lieutenant Colonel Levin here," he said.

A tear slid down his cheek; embarrassed, he wiped it off with the sleeve of his lab coat and said again, "Lieutenant Colonel Levin here."

Over the line came scratches and clicks. Then the general coughed and said in a very tired voice:

"I congratulate you, Lieutenant Colonel. You and your pilot Bobrov are awarded the Order of the Great Patriotic War, First Class. You accomplished a great deed, a great one."

Levin was silent. Another tear ran down from under his glasses.

"Ah, yes," said the general. "Well! Good night!"

"Thank you," answered Levin, and quickly hanging up, he turned away. Bobrov was looking at him, but Levin didn't want the pilot to see him crying.

They were quiet for a while, and then Levin went to his room and brought a book that Lednev had been reading recently. It was *War and Peace*. Over the cover, very worn and very dirty, spread a large ink stain.

"Your book?" he asked Bobrov.

The pilot's eye glistened avidly . . .

"For this I thank you," Bobrov said, "many thanks. Now, really, you've made me very happy . . . Well, get some rest, Aleksandr Markovich; I believe you're tired after today."

"Yes," Levin agreed, feeling guilty, "I'm very tired."

But Bobrov did not leave immediately; he sat around a bit, told Levin how the battle ended. The Fascist caravan, over all, was defeated. Four transports were sunk, a large barge with soldiers, and two escort ships.

Levin kept wiping off his tears.

1949

Translated from the Russian by Helen Reeve with Martha Kitchen

BORIS PASTERNAK

Boris Pasternak (1890–1960), poet, translator, and novelist, was born in Moscow, where his parents had moved from Odessa in 1889. A refined artistic milieu enveloped Pasternak and his three siblings: from his father, the painter Leonid Pasternak (1862–1945), Pasternak inherited a gift for seeing; from his mother, Rozalia Kaufman (1867–1939), a gifted pianist, Pasternak received his musical talents. The Pasternaks traced their lineage back to Sephardic Jews, to Don Isaac ben-Yehudah (1437–1508). Although conversion to Christianity would have made things much easier for Pasternak's father at the beginning of his career, he never took the step on moral grounds. In 1894, Leonid Pasternak was invited to teach at the Moscow School of Painting, Sculpture, and Architecture; later the rank of Academician of Painting was bestowed upon him. In 1923 Leonid Pasternak's book *Rembrandt and Jews in His Work* appeared in Berlin in Russian and was later published in Hebrew translation. Bialik wrote admiringly of Leonid Pasternak as a Jewish artist.

The young Pasternak studied music theory and composition in 1903–9. Alexander Scriabin himself encouraged him, but the absence of perfect pitch hindered the future poet. In 1913, Pasternak was graduated from the Historical-Philological Faculty of Moscow University. His thesis dealt with Hermann Cohen's philosophy, and in May–August 1912 he attended summer school at the University of Marburg. Hermann Cohen asked him to stay for graduate work; Pasternak turned down the attractive offer.

In a letter to Jacqueline de Proyart dated 2 May 1959, Boris Pasternak spoke of having been baptized as an infant by his nanny in the Orthodox Church. Pasternak's leading biographers Lazar Fleishman and Christopher Barnes both suggest that the unconfirmed story of the infant Pasternak's conversion was a fantasy that the adult Pasternak cultivated in the 1940s–50s. As late as 1912, in his matriculation papers from Marburg University, Pasternak indicated his faith as "Mosaic." In 1922, when he married his first wife, the artist Evgenia Lurie, the marriage was certified by a Moscow rabbi. Although no evidence points to Pasternak's conversion at a later time, in the 1940s–50s he regularly went to Orthodox Church. Be all this as it may, the argument in negotiating the Judaic–Christian— and Jewish–Russian—boundaries in Pasternak's worldview should not hinge on whether or not he was converted (a compensatory myth for the adult Pasternak) but on the Christian supercessionist beliefs and assimilationist convictions expressed in his writings, above all in *Doctor Zhivago* (1944–55; published 1957). Pasternak regarded his Jewish origin an unfortunate complication. In a letter to the Judeophilic Maxim Gorky dated 7 January 1928, he wrote, "With my place of birth, with my childhood circumstances, with my love, instincts, and inclinations, I should not have been born a Jew" (trans. Lazar Fleishman).

Pasternak's poems first appeared in 1913; his first collection, *Twin in the Clouds*, came out a year later. With fellow poets Nikolay Aseev and Sergey Bobrov, Pasternak joined Centrifuge, a group of moderate Moscow futurists. His second collection, *Over the Barriers*, appeared in 1917, and that summer he finished *My Sister—Life*, which he considered his *first* book. Published only in 1922, Pasternak's astounding *My Sister—Life* was widely admired and vastly influential. Together with Pasternak's fourth collection, *Themes and Variations* (1923), *My Sister—Life* laid the foundation for his reputation as a great Russian poet.

One of the most famous fellow travelers in the 1920s, Pasternak encountered criticism from official Bolshevik critics. Responding to the charges that he was an apolitical contemplator, Pasternak sought to inscribe vestiges of class struggle into his work. In the second, 1928, edition of the volume *Lofty Malady* (first edition 1923), he patched on a bit about Lenin. The epic poems of the 1920s, *1905* (1925–26) and *Lieutenant Schmidt* (1926–27), faired better as works by a sympathetic observer of revolutionary events. Yet Pasternak's best narrative poem, *Spektorsky* (1931), with a semiautobiographical protagonist-narrator who is a half-Jewish *intelligent*, communicated an ironic detachment from history. The year 1931 was an eventful time for Pasternak: he was attacked in connection with his autobiographical prose work *Safe Conduct* (1929; book edition 1931); he left his first, Jewish wife for the non-Jewish Zinaida Neigauz (née Eremeeva); and he journeyed to the Caucasus. By 1929–30, the metaphorical fireworks and lexical and syntactic complexity of Pasternak's poetry had yielded to plainer verbal texture. Pasternak's 1932 collection *Second Birth* delivered topical poetry with details of the USSR going through five-year plans; this collection earned Pasternak official approval.

Nikolay Bukharin (1888–1938) was appointed editor of *Izvestia* in 1934 and recruited major talent for his paper; Pasternak was his favorite. In the summer of 1934, after turning to Bukharin for help following Osip

Mandelstam's first arrest, Pasternak received a telephone call from Stalin. Nadezhda Mandelstam reported the episode in a chapter of her *Hope against Hope*, along with Pasternak's cowardly response—both to Stalin's question about Mandelstam as a poet and to Mandelstam's poem against Stalin.

At the First Congress of Soviet Writers in September 1934, Pasternak was hailed a leading *living* Soviet poet (the suicide Mayakovsky topped the official Soviet poetic pantheon). In the second edition of Pasternak's *Second Birth*, the poem "Waves" bore a dedication to Bukharin, the only time Pasternak dedicated anything to a Soviet leader. (Bukharin was arrested in 1937 and executed in 1938.) On 1 January 1936, *Izvestia* ran Pasternak's poem praising Stalin without naming him. The poem constituted the first part of the four-part cycle "The Artist," in which Stalin appeared as an "artist" of history; the loftiness of Pasternak's allegory and the quality of his verse had the potential to lend more aesthetic validity to the tyrant than hundreds of cultist hymns. The Great Purges of 1937–38 plunged Pasternak into despair. He wrote few original poems, focusing instead on translation work. The contributions of Pasternak the translator are numerous; his most celebrated translations included Shakespeare's *Hamlet* (1941), Goethe's *Faust* (1953), Schiller's *Maria Stuart* (1958), and the works of Georgian poets. After the Nazi invasion, Pasternak was evacuated to Chistopol in Tatarstan; in 1941–44, he contributed occasional poems, suffused with pressurized Russian patriotism, to Soviet periodicals. While he was not a deliberate target of the postwar anticosmopolitan campaign, he was chastised in print for being "alien to Soviet reality." Following his wartime patriotic upheaval, the collection *The Expanse of the Earth* (1945), and a volume of *Selected Poems* (1945), no collections of Pasternak's appeared in the USSR until after his death.

With interruptions, Pasternak worked on the novel *Doctor Zhivago* throughout 1946–55. In 1946, Pasternak met Olga Ivinskaya (1912–1995), who became his last love. Rejecting *Doctor Zhivago* in 1956, the *Novy mir* editor, prominent Soviet writer Konstantin Simonov, and his staff wrote in a letter to Pasternak, "The spirit of your novel is the spirit of the nonacceptance of Socialist revolution." Published in Italian in 1957 and in Russian in 1958 by Feltrinelli Editore, *Doctor Zhivago* made Pasternak a world celebrity. In 1958, it competed with Vladimir Nabokov's *Lolita* on the American bestseller charts (Nabokov later described it as "melodramatic and vilely written"). Pasternak was awarded the Nobel Prize in Literature in 1958. In the Soviet Union, the award brought forth an official campaign against him. The ostracism in the media began in Moscow's *Literary Gazette* on 25 October 1958. Pasternak was expelled from the Union of Soviet Writers on 27 October, and a number of writers, including several in this anthology (such as **Boris Slutsky**), dirtied their hands in connection with the Pasternak affair. Calls, some laden with antisemitism, were made to expel Pasternak from the USSR. Harassed into turning down the Nobel Prize, Pasternak wrote a penitent letter to Khrushchev on 31 October (published 2 November) and an open letter to *Pravda*. He died in May 1960 in Peredelkino outside Moscow. A representative, albeit censured, edition of his poetry edited by **Lev Ozerov** came out in 1965 in the Poet's Library (Biblioteka poeta) series. Andrey Sinyavsky (1925–1997), himself about to go on trial for anti-Soviet activity alongside fellow writer **Yuly Daniel**, wrote the introduction to the volume.

* * *

Pasternak's direct artistic response to the Shoah was absent in prose and very limited in poetry. The two poems below were inspired by the main Soviet offensive launched in March 1944 in the south of Russia, Ukraine, and Belorussia. The Soviet forces began an operation on 8 April 1944 aimed at the liberation of the Crimea and the surrounding areas, including Odessa. Dealing the Nazi and Romanian force a powerful blow, the Soviet troops retook Sevastopol and had accomplished the operation by 13 May 1944. By the summer of 1944, the Soviet troops had crossed the pre-1941 western frontier and moved into eastern Europe. Pasternak wrote both "In the Lowlands" and "Odessa" in the spring of 1944; they were published in the newspaper *Red Navy* (*Krasnyi flot*) in March–April 1944. "In the Lowlands," dated 24 March 1944 in manuscript, was part of Pasternak's fifteen-poem cycle "Poems about the War" and appeared in Pasternak's *The Expanse of the Earth* (1945), in which Pasternak apparently forgot to include "Odessa."

Nostalgically, if faintly, the poems paid tribute not only to the victims of the Nazi and Romanian atrocities during the occupation but also to the destruction—by Soviet history and by the war—of the Jewish-Russian Odessa that had nurtured Pasternak's parents and numerous other artists. Pasternak's "Odessa" appeared under the title "The Great Day" on 12 April 1944, just two days after the liberation of Odessa. The sixth stanza of the poem, which metaphorically evokes the faces of murdered Jews, was missing in the original publication.

IN THE LOWLANDS

Silted salt marsh's amber glare,
Black soil's glories,
Locals repairing tackle and gear,
Ferryboats, dories.
Nights in these lowlands, nights are rapt,
Dawns enter glowing.
Foam of the Black Sea glides over sand,
Swishing, slowing.
Quail in the swamps, cusk in the rivers,
Crawfish all over;
This way by shore the Crimea shimmers,
Ochakov[47] the other.
Beyond Nikolaev[48] the salt marches stretch.
Westward presses
A swell of fog-surges over the steppe
Toward Odessa.[49]
Did it happen, ever? Wrought in what style?

---

47 Ochakov—Black Sea port and district center presently in Ukraine, about 40 miles south
    of Nikolaev. Founded in the late fourteenth century, Ochakov had been a Turkish fortress
    and major military outpost until 1788, when it was captured by the Russian fleet during the
    Russo-Turkish war of 1787–91 and permanently ceded to the Russian Empire.
48 Nikolaev (Mykohaiv)—city and Black Sea port, major industrial center, and capital of
    Nikolaev Province in Ukraine. Isaac Babel's birthplace and site of a major 1905 pogrom (see
    Babel's "Story of My Dovecote"). Prior to World War II, Nikolaev had a Jewish population
    of 30,000 people, of which about 25,000 escaped to the Soviet interior and 5,000 were mas-
    sacred by the Nazis in 1941. Nikolaev was occupied by Nazi troops on 16 August 1941 and
    liberated by Soviet troops on 28 March 1944.
49 From 10 August 1941 to 16 October 1941, Soviet troops defended Odessa against an attack
    force consisting of sixteen Nazi divisions. Although the Soviet troops were outnumbered
    five to one, the siege lasted for seventy-three days before the city fell. By the time Odessa
    was occupied by Romanian and Nazi forces, about 90,000 Jews, including Odessan Jews
    and Jewish refugees from Bukovina, Bessarabia, and western parts of Ukraine, had been con-
    centrated in the city. In the first days of the occupation, over 8,000 Jews were murdered by
    Nazi and Romanian units. By February 1942, about 30,000 Jews remained in Odessa. In the
    course of the occupation, tens of thousands of Jews were murdered in and on the outskirts
    of Odessa and transported to Transnystrian death camps. Odessa was liberated on 10 April
    1944. Historians estimate that about 2,000 Jews survived the occupation and remained in
    Odessa at the time of its liberation.

Where are those years?
Can they be returned? Legends revived?
That freedom be ours?
O how the ploughshare longs for the tilth,
Earth for the tillage,
The sea for the Boug,[50] south for the north,
All for each village.
Peace, long awaited, is visibly near,
Round the bend of the bay.
Outlying landscapes promise—this year
The navy will have its say.

1944

ODESSA

The land was a birthday girl, unsparingly
Kept waiting for that week's arrival
When the rescuer would break in daringly
As dusk set in or dawn was rising.

The tide roared out its gibberish, thundering
Among the splintered cliffs' recesses,
When, from above, we all heard suddenly
The rolling news, "We've won Odessa."

Down streets long empty of vehicular
Noise gushes the merry Russian humming,
Past sappers focused in particular
On doors and window frames' debugging.

Foot troops striding, cavalry cantering,
Long, horse-drawn carts, machine-gun mounted.
Midnight's still full of talk and bantering.
No one sleeps till the day's recounted.

---

50 The Boug (Bug)—Pasternak is referring to the Southern Boug River in the southwestern
    region of Ukraine, originating in the Volhynian-Podolian elevation and falling into the
    Dnieper–Boug firth (*liman*) of the Black Sea.

But all's not well; a skull expressively
Leers from a nearby gulch. A savage
Cudgel here has mauled aggressively;
It's a waste Neanderthals have ravaged.

Small heads of immortelles[51] peer cheerily
Through empty sockets, nod and caper,
Inhabit the air with faces eerily,
Those of the dead mowed down last April.

Evil must be avenged with doubled blows
And the victim's widows and relatives
Eased in the moment of their family woes
By some new word that truly lives.

With all our Russian ingenuity
We swear, inspired by the great event,
To build the martyrs in perpetuity
A worthy peacetime monument.

1944

Translated from the Russian by Andrew Von Hendy and Maxim D. Shrayer

* * *

Pasternak had completed parts 1–4 of book 1 of *Doctor Zhivago* by the summer of 1948, and the two excerpts that follow represent two of Pasternak's three main statements on Jews and Judaism found in the novel. The first appears at the very beginning of the novel; the episode describes Misha Gordon's journey

---

51 Immortelle (Lat. Helichrysum)—also known as curry plant. Intent on alluding to the literal meaning of the flower's name, Pasternak opts for the foreign "immortelle" over the native Russian *bessmertnik* (lit. "deathless one = immortal one"), which to a native speaker's ear would invoke "death" and "immortality" much more prominently than the French *immortelle*.

to Moscow in 1903 in the course of which he witnesses the suicide of Yury Zhivago's father (chap. 7, part 1, book 1). The second, taking place in Galicia in the summer of 1915, depicts Gordon's visit to the eastern front, where his friend Zhivago is serving as a military doctor (chaps. 11–12, part 4, book 1). The third discussion of Jews and Judaism takes place in the middle of the novel, in two adjacent but not consecutive sections (chap. 15, part 9, book 2; chap. 3, part 10, book 2).

In October 1946, in a letter to his first cousin Olga Freidenberg, Pasternak wrote of his novel in progress: "In it I will square accounts with Judaism, with all forms of nationalism (including that which assumes the guise of internationalism), with all shades of anti-Christianity and its assumption that there are certain people surviving the fall of the Roman Empire from whose undeveloped national essence a new civilization could be evolved" (trans. Elliott Mossman and Margaret Wettlin). In addition to the sixteen prose parts of *Doctor Zhivago*, Pasternak included, as the novel's final, seventeenth part, "The Poems of Yury Zhivago." Whether or not "Zhivago's" poems, such as "Magdalene," treat the Gospel narratives with the freedom that the Jewish-born Christian Pasternak might have enjoyed is a question for a different forum. In *Doctor Zhivago*, Pasternak spoke openly of the Jews, exploring both the theological and the historical parameters of antisemitism and offering his authorial remedies.

The fact that Zhivago, who defends a Jew from a Cossack soldier, would be sympathetic to Jewish suffering proves nothing. How could Pasternak's idealized protagonist, doctor and poet, not defend a powerless old man? In this episode, the experience of anti-Jewish—and anti-Judaic—violence right in the heart of Hasidic Galicia adumbrates Pasternak's statement on the place of Judaism after the advent of Jesus of Nazareth. Writing after the Shoah and on the eve of the worst years for Jews of the Soviet Union (1948–53), Pasternak designates the Jewish-born Misha Gordon his spokesman; the Russian Yury Zhivago listens silently. Gordon's assimilationist—and supercessionist—beliefs are later echoed in Lara's monolog to Zhivago (chap. 15, part 9, book 2), who replies that he "had not thought about it" and that his friend Gordon is of "the same views." (Parts 9 and 10 of the novel were both composed in 1949.) At the beginning of part 10, through the words of a tertiary character, Pasternak slipped in a further comment on the Jewish question. Returning home on the eve of "Great Thursday, the day of the Twelve Gospels" (the Orthodox equivalent of Holy Thursday), shopkeeper Galuzina thinks habitually antisemitic thoughts in connection with the town's small Jewish population but also acknowledges to herself that the Jewish question is hardly as central to Russian history as her fellow Russians tend to regard it. There is, perhaps, reason to suspect that Galuzina's confusion casts doubt on Lara's breathless call for Jews to "rise above themselves and dissolve without a trace among all the rest, whose religious foundation they themselves had laid and who would be so close to them, if only they knew them better."

The angle brackets in the text below indicate corrections to the translation made by the editor.

FROM *DOCTOR ZHIVAGO*

Book 1, Part 1

7

In a second-class compartment of the train sat Misha Gordon, who was traveling with his father, a lawyer from Orenburg.[52] Misha was a boy of eleven with a thoughtful young face and big dark eyes; he was in his second year of gymnasium. His father, Grigory Osipovich Gordon, was being transferred to a new post in Moscow; <the boy was transferring to a Moscow gymnasium>. His mother and sisters had gone on some time before to get their apartment ready.

Father and son had been traveling for three days.

Russia, with its fields, steppes, villages, and towns, bleached lime-white by the sun, flew past them wrapped in hot clouds of dust. Lines of carts rolled along the highways, occasionally lumbering off the road to cross the tracks; from the furiously speeding train it seemed that the carts stood still and the horses were marking time.

At big stations passengers jumped out and ran to the buffet; the sun setting behind the station garden lit their feet and shone under the wheels of the train.

Every motion in the world taken separately was calculated and purposeful, but, taken together, they were spontaneously intoxicated with the general stream of life which united them all. People worked and struggled, each set in motion by the mechanism of his own cares. But the mechanisms would not have worked properly had they not been regulated and governed by a higher

---

52 Orenburg—provincial capital on the Ural River; founded in 1735 as a military fortress, by the early twentieth century Orenburg had about 75,000 residents, including a Jewish community of about 1,300.

sense of an ultimate freedom from care. This freedom came from the feeling that all human lives were interrelated, a certainty that they flowed into each other—a happy feeling that all events took place not only on the earth, in which the dead are buried, but also in some other region which some called the Kingdom of God, others history, and still others by some other name.

To this general rule, Misha was an unhappy, bitter exception. A feeling of care remained his ultimate mainspring and was not relieved and ennobled by a sense of security. He knew this hereditary trait in himself and watched with an alert diffidence for symptoms of it in himself. It distressed him. Its presence humiliated him.

For as long as he could remember he had never ceased to wonder why, having arms and legs like everyone else, and a language and a way of life common to all, one could be different from the others, liked only by few and, moreover, loved by no one. He could not understand a situation in which if you were worse than other people you could not make an effort to improve yourself. What did it mean to be a Jew? What was the purpose of it? What was the reward or the justification of this impotent challenge, which brought nothing but grief?

When Misha took the problem to his father he was told that his premises were absurd, and that such reasonings were wrong, but he was offered no solution deep enough to attract him or to make him bow silently to the inevitable.

And making an exception only for his parents, he gradually became contemptuous of all grownups who had made this mess and were unable to clear it up. He was sure that when he was big he would straighten it all out.

Now, for instance, no one had the courage to say that his father should not have run after that madman when he had rushed out onto the platform, and should not have stopped the train when, pushing Grigory Osipovich aside, and flinging open the door, he had thrown himself head first out of the express like a diver from a springboard into a swimming pool.

But since it was his father who had pulled the emergency release, it looked as if the train had stopped for such an inexplicably long time because of them.

No one knew the exact cause of the delay. Some said that the sudden stop had damaged the air brakes, other that they were on a steep gradient and the engine could not make it. A third view was that as the suicide was a prominent person, his lawyer, who had been with him on the train, insisted on officials being called from the nearest station, Kologrivovka, to draw up a statement. This was why the assistant engineer had climbed up the telegraph pole: the inspection handcar must be on its way.

There was a faint stench from the lavatories, not quite dispelled by eau de cologne, and a smell of fried chicken, a little high and wrapped in dirty wax paper. As though nothing had happened, graying Petersburg ladies with creaking chesty voices, turned into gypsies by the combination of soot and greasy cosmetics, powdered their faces and wiped their fingers on their handkerchiefs. When they passed the door of the Gordons' compartment, adjusting their shawls and anxious about their appearance even while squeezing themselves through the narrow corridor, their pursed lips seemed to Misha to hiss: "Aren't we sensitive! We're something special. We're cultured. It's too much for us."

The body of the suicide lay on the grass by the embankment. A little stream of blood had run across his forehead, and, having dried, it looked like a cancel mark crossing out his face. It did not look like his blood, which had come from his body, but like a foreign appendage, a piece of plaster or a splatter of mud or a wet birch leaf.

Curious onlookers and sympathizers surrounded the body in a constantly changing cluster, while his friend and traveling companion, a thickset, arrogant-looking lawyer, a pure-bred animal in a sweaty shirt, stood over him sullenly with an expressionless face. Overcome by the heat, he was fanning himself with his hat. In answer to all questions he shrugged his shoulders and said crossly without even turning around: "He was an alcoholic. Can't you understand? He did it in a fit of DTs."[53]

Once or twice a thin old woman in a woolen dress and lace kerchief went up to the body. She was the widow Tiverzina, mother of two engineers, who was traveling third class on a pass with her two daughters-in-law. Like nuns with their mother superior, the two quiet women, their shawls pulled low over their foreheads, followed her in silence. < . . . > The crowd made way for them.

Tiverzina's husband had been buried alive in a railway accident. She stood a little away from the body, where she could see it through the crowd, and sighed as if comparing the two cases. "Each according to his fate," she seemed to say. "Some die by the Lord's will—and look what's happened to him—to die of rich living and mental illness."

All the passengers came out and had a look at the corpse and went back to their compartments only for fear that something might be stolen.

When they jumped out onto the track and picked flowers or took a short walk to stretch their legs, they felt as if the whole place owed its existence to

---

53 DTs—medical abbreviation = *delirium tremens*; type of delirium typically experienced by alcoholics after rapid reduction or termination of alcohol consumption.

the accident, and that without it neither the swampy meadow with hillocks, the broad river, nor the fine manor house and church on the steep opposite side would have been there.

Even the sun seemed to be a purely local feature. Its evening light was diffident, a little timid, like a cow from a nearby herd come to take a look at the crowd.

Misha had been deeply shaken by the event and had at first wept with grief and fright. In the course of the long journey the suicide had come several times to their compartment and had talked with Misha's father for hours on end. He had said that he found relief in the moral decency, peace, and understanding which he discovered in their world and had asked Grigory Osipovich endless questions about fine points in law concerning bills of exchange, deeds of settlement, bankruptcy, and fraud. "Is that so?" he exclaimed at Gordon's answers. "Can the law be as lenient as that? My lawyer takes a much gloomier view."

Each time that this nervous man calmed down, his traveling companion came from their first-class coach to drag him off to the restaurant to drink champagne. He was the thickset, arrogant, clean-shaven, well-dressed lawyer who now stood over his body, showing not the least surprise. It was hard to escape the feeling that his client's ceaseless agitation had somehow been to his advantage.

Misha's father described him as a well-known millionaire, <Zhivago>, a good-natured profligate, not quite responsible for his actions. When he had come to their compartment, he would, unrestrained by Misha's presence, talk about his son, a boy of Misha's age, and about his late wife; then he would go on about his second family, whom he had deserted as he had the first. At this point he would remember something else, grow pale with terror, and begin to lose the thread of his story.

To Misha he had shown an unaccountable affection, which probably reflected a feeling for someone else. He had showered him with presents, jumping out to buy them at the big stations, where the bookstalls in the first-class waiting rooms also sold toys and local souvenirs.

He had drunk incessantly and complained that he had not slept for three months and that as soon as he sobered up for however short a time he suffered torments unimaginable to any normal human being.

At the end, he rushed into their compartment, grasped Gordon by the hand, tried to tell him something but found he could not, and dashing out onto the platform threw himself from the train.

Now Misha sat examining the small wooden box of minerals from the Urals that had been his last gift. Suddenly there was a general stir. A handcar rolled up on the parallel track. A doctor, two policemen, and a magistrate with a cockade in his hat jumped out. Questions were asked in cold businesslike voices, and notes taken. The policemen and the guards, slipping and sliding awkwardly in the gravel, dragged the corpse up the embankment. A peasant woman began to wail. The passengers were asked to go back to their seats, the guard blew his whistle, and the train started on.

Book 1, Part 4

11

In this area the villages had been miraculously preserved.[54] They constituted an inexplicably intact island in the midst of a sea of ruins. <Gordon and Zhivago were on their way home in the evening. The sun was going down.> In one village <they passed through> they saw a young Cossack surrounded by a crowd laughing boisterously, as the Cossack tossed a copper coin into the air, forcing an old Jew with a gray beard and a long caftan to catch it. The old man missed every time. The coin flew past his pitifully spread-out hands and dropped into the mud. When the old man bent to pick it up, the Cossack slapped his bottom, and the onlookers held their sides, groaning with laughter: this was the point of the entertainment. For the moment it was harmless enough, but no one could say for certain that it would not take a more serious turn. Every now and then, the old man's wife ran out of the house across the road, screaming and stretching out her arms to him, and ran back again in terror. Two little girls were watching their grandfather out of the window and crying.

The driver, who found all of this extremely comical, slowed down so that the passengers could enjoy the spectacle. But Zhivago called the Cossack, bawled him out, and ordered him to stop baiting the old man.

"Yes, sir," he said readily. "We meant no harm, we were only doing it for fun."

Gordon and Zhivago drove on in the silence.

"It's terrible," said <Zhivago> when they were in sight of their own village. "You can't imagine what the <miserable> Jewish population <has been going> through in this war. The fighting happens to be in the <pale of their forced settlement>. And as if punitive taxation, the destruction of their property, and

---

54   The military background of the scene was the spring 1915 campaign in Galicia, the Russian capture of Przemyśl, and advances in Austria followed by the German and Austrian counter-offensive, which, by October 1915, had undone most of the Russian gains. General Aleksey Brusilov's breakthrough in Austrian Poland did not occur until June 1916.

all their own sufferings were not enough, they are subjected to pogroms, insults, and accusations that they lack patriotism. And why should they be patriotic? Under enemy rule, they enjoy equal rights, and we do nothing but persecute them. This hatred for them, the basis of it, is irrational. It is stimulated by the very things that should arouse sympathy—their poverty, their overcrowding, their weakness, and this inability to fight back. I can't understand it. It's like an inescapable fate."

Gordon did not reply.

12

Once again they were lying < . . . > on either side of the long low window, it was night, and they were talking. Zhivago was telling Gordon how he had once seen the Tsar at the front. He told his story well.

It was his first spring at the front. The headquarters of his regiment was in the Carpathians, in a deep valley, access to which from the Hungarian plain was blocked by this army unit. At the bottom of the valley was a railway station. Zhivago described the landscape, the mountains overgrown with mighty firs and pines, with tufts of clouds catching in their tops, and sheer cliffs of gray slate and graphite showing through the forest like worn patches in a thick fur. It was a damp, dark April morning, as gray as the slate, locked in by the mountains on all sides and therefore still and sultry. Mist hung over the valley, and everything in it steamed, everything rose slowly—engine smoke from the railway station, gray vapors from the fields, the gray mountains, the dark woods, the dark clouds.

At that time the sovereign was making a tour of inspection in Galicia. It was learned suddenly that he would visit Zhivago's unit < . . . >. He might arrive at any moment. A guard of honor was drawn up on the station platform. They waited for about two oppressive hours, then two trains with the imperial retinue went by quickly one after the other. A little later the Tsar's train drew in.

Accompanied by the Grand Duke Nicholas, the Tsar inspected the grenadiers. Every syllable of his quietly spoken greeting produced an explosion of thunderous hurrahs whose echoes were sent back and forth like water from swinging buckets.

The Tsar, smiling and ill at ease, looked older and more tired than on the rubles and medals. His face was listless, a little flabby. He kept glancing apologetically at the Grand Duke, not knowing what was expected of him, and the Grand Duke, bending down respectfully, helped him in his embarrassment not so much by words as by moving an eyebrow or a shoulder.

On that warm gray morning in the mountains, Zhivago felt sorry for the Tsar, was disturbed at the thought that such <anxious> reserve and shyness could be the essential characteristics of an oppressor, that a man so weak could imprison, hang, or pardon.

"He should have made a speech—'I, my sword, and my people'—like the Kaiser. Something about 'the people'—that was essential. But you know he was natural, in the Russian way, tragically above these banalities. After all, that kind of theatricalism is unthinkable in Russia. For such gestures are theatrical, aren't they? I suppose that there were such things as 'peoples' under the Caesars— Gauls or Svevians or Illyrians and so on. But ever since, they have been mere fiction, which served only as subjects for speeches by kings and politicians: 'The people, my people.'

"Now the front is flooded with correspondents and journalists. They record their 'observations' and gems of popular wisdom, they visit the wounded and construct new theories about the people's soul. It's a new version of Dahl[55] and just as bogus—linguistic graphomania, verbal incontinence. That's one type—and then there's the other: clipped speech, 'sketches and short scenes,' skepticism and misanthropy. I read a piece like that the other day: 'A gray day, like yesterday. Rain since the morning, slush. I look out of the window and see the road. Prisoners in an endless line. Wounded. A gun is firing. It fires today as yesterday, tomorrow as today and every day and every hour.' Isn't that subtle and witty! But what has he got against the gun? How odd to expect variety from a gun! Why doesn't he look at himself, shooting off the same sentences, commas, lists of facts day in, day out, keeping up his barrage of journalistic philanthropy as nimble as the jumping of a flea? Why can't he get it into his head that it's for him to <do something new and> stop repeating himself—not for the gun—that you can never say something meaningful by accumulating absurdities in your notebook, that facts don't exist until man puts into them something of his own, a bit of <free-ranging> human genius—of myth."

"You've hit the nail on the head," broke in Gordon. "And now I'll tell you what I think about that incident we saw today. That Cossack tormenting the poor patriarch—and there are thousands of incidents like it—of course it's an

---

55 Compiler of the remarkable *Reasoned Dictionary of the Living Russian Language* (1863–66), the writer Vladimir Dahl (Dal') (1801–1872) was behind the authorship of the notoriously antisemitic *Investigation of the Murder by Jews of Christian Infants and the Use of Their Blood* (St. Petersburg, 1844).

ignominy—but there's no point in philosophizing <about it>, you just hit it out. But the Jewish question as a whole—there philosophy does come in—and then we discover something unexpected. Not that I'm going to tell you anything new—we both got our ideas from your uncle.[56]

"You were saying, what is a nation? . . . And who does more for a nation—the one who makes a fuss about it or the one who, without thinking of it, raises it to universality by the beauty and greatness of his actions, and gives it fame and immortality? Well, <of course>, the answer is obvious. And what are the nations now, in the Christian era? They aren't just nations, but converted, transformed nations, and what matters is this transformation, not loyalty to ancient principles. And what does the Gospel say on this subject? To begin with, it does not make assertions: 'It's like this and like that.' It is a proposal, naïve and timid: 'Do you want to live in a completely new way? Do you want spiritual <bliss>?' And everybody accepted, they were carried away by it for thousands of years. . . .

"When the Gospel <said> that in the Kingdom of God there are neither Jews nor Gentiles, <did> it merely mean that all are equal in the sight of God? No—the Gospel wasn't needed for that—the Greek philosophers, the Roman moralists, and the <Old Testament> prophets had known this long before. But it said: In that new way of living and new form of society, which is born of the heart, and which is called the Kingdom of Heaven, there are no nations, there are only individuals.

"You said that facts are meaningless, unless meanings are put into them. Well, Christianity, the mystery of the individual, is precisely what must be put into the facts to make them meaningful.

"We also talked about the mediocre <public figures> who have nothing to say to life and the world as a whole, of petty second-raters who are only too happy when some nation, preferably a small and <suffering> one, is constantly discussed—this gives them a chance to show off their competence and cleverness, and to thrive on their compassion for the persecuted. Well now, what more perfect example can you have of the victims of this mentality than the Jews? Their national idea has forced them, century after century, to be a nation and nothing but a nation—and they have been chained to this deadening task all through the centuries when all the rest of the world was being delivered from it by a new force which had come out of their own midst! Isn't that

---

56 Who raised Yury Zhivago after his father's suicide.

extraordinary? How can you account for it? Just think! This glorious holiday, this liberation from the curse of mediocrity, this soaring flight above the dullness of a humdrum existence, was first achieved in their land, proclaimed in their language, and belonged to their race! And they actually saw and heard it and let it go! How could they allow a spirit of such overwhelming power and beauty to leave them, how could they think that after it triumphed and established its reign, they would remain as the empty husk of that miracle they had repudiated? What use is it to anyone, this voluntary martyrdom? Whom does it profit? For what purpose are these innocent old men and women and children, all these <sensitive>, kind, humane people, mocked and <massacred> throughout the centuries? And why is it that all these literary friends of 'the people' of all nations are always so untalented? Why didn't the intellectual leaders of the Jewish people ever go beyond facile *Weltschmerz* and ironical wisdom? Why have they not—even if at the risk of bursting like boilers with the pressure of their duty—disbanded this army which keeps on fighting and being beaten up nobody knows for what? Why don't they say to them: "<You are the first and best Christians in the world.> Come to your senses, stop. Don't hold on to your identity. Don't stick together, disperse. Be with all the rest. You are the very thing against which you have been turned by the worst and weakest among you."

1946–(55)

Translated from the Russian by Max Hayward and Manya Harari; corrected by Maxim D. Shrayer

The Thaw: 1950s–1960s

Editor's Introduction

In the post-World War II conditions, the issue of Jewish cultural memory became acutely significant. Both the émigré critic Vera Alexandrova (originally in 1968) and the post-Soviet scholar Aleksandr Kobrinsky (in 1994) have emphasized that, for the second and the later Soviet generations of Jewish-Russian writers, the cultural memory of the past and the traditions of Jewish literature would display themselves with subtlety but would never disappear. In contrast to some of their elders, the later generations of Jewish-Russian authors experienced less or no euphoria over the prospects of a harmonious Soviet assimilation and Jewish-Russian fusion.

As the materials gathered in the postwar and late Soviet sections will demonstrate, Jewish-Russian authors born in the late 1910s–early 1920s (the generation of **Boris Slutsky** [1919–1986]) and in the late 1930s–early 1940s (the generation of **Joseph Brodsky** [1940–1996]) could never shake the burden of otherness even while attempting to escape the Soviet-prescribed boundaries of their own Jewish selves. Among the historical events that shaped the self-awareness of Soviet Jews in the postwar period, Stalin's maniacal Judeophobia of the 1940s and early 1950s and the persecution of the Jewish intelligentsia left an indelible print in memory. For the vast majority of Soviet Jews, writing in Russian after World War II ceased to be a choice, further complicating what Alice Stone Nakhimovsky so aptly described in 1985, on the example of the still bilingual **David Aizman** (see the section "On the Eve: 1890s–1910s"): "By *choosing* [emphasis added] to write in Russian and about Jews, a writer is taking on a tradition that runs counter to the kind of unconscious self-identification that others working in their national literatures take for granted. Working in Russian, he becomes both Russian and Jew; a revisionist, a sympathizer, a self-hater." Over the years of the Thaw and the late Soviet period, degrees and shades of Jewish self-expression—and of Jewish self-suppression—determined many a writer's place not only in the official landscape of Russian Soviet literature but consequently in the underground and in emigration.

The Thaw, named after a trend-setting novel of 1954, which **Ilya Ehrenburg** (1891–1967) quickly composed after Stalin's death, was the time of the dismantling of Stalin's cult of personality. The rehabilitation of the victims of Stalinism began, including the victims of anti-Jewish cultural genocide. Jewish-Russian writers stood at the forefront of cultural politics during this period of partial and temporary liberalization, which first peaked ideologically with Nikita Khrushchev's anti-Stalin "secret speech" at the Twentieth Congress of the Communist Party in 1956 and had its final de-Stalinizing crescendo at the Twenty-Second Congress in 1962. As a member of the generation of writers who came of age during the Great Terror and World War II, **Boris Slutsky** (1919–1986) emerged as a principal literary exponent of the Thaw. Jewish-Russian authors of different generations and backgrounds met in the camp of liberalizers, among them the former Yiddish writer **Emmanuil Kazakevich** (1913–1962). Some of the older writers found windows of limited opportunity for Jewish creativity within the Thaw-era official press. **Kazakevich**, for instance, used a relatively safe political pretext to sound a Jewish note in his story "Enemies," about Lenin and two Jewish revolutionaries. Authors such as the poet Naum Korzhavin (b. 1925) wove together the recent histories of Stalinism, Hitlerism, and the Shoah in texts they managed to push past the censors. Some older writers sought greater safety in autobiographical and memoiristic writings, revisiting their prerevolutionary childhood and youth. Guardedly Jewish recollections, such as *At the Beginning of Life* (1961) by **Samuil Marshak** (his poems are in the section "On the Eve: 1890s–1910s"), meant the world to the Jewish reader in the USSR. Writing about the impact of officially published works on the Jewish self-awareness of the Soviet reader, Shimon Markish stated, perhaps too emphatically, that "not one book in Russian Soviet literature in the fifteen years after Stalin's death did as much for the Jewish awakening as did [Ehrenburg's panoramic memoir] *People, Years, Life*," published mostly in 1960–65.

For the younger generation of Jewish-Russian authors born in the late 1930s and early 1940s and entering the literary stage during the Thaw (primarily featured in the sections "Late Soviet Empire and Collapse: 1960s–1990s" and "The Jewish Exodus: 1970s–1990s"), elements of Jewish self-expression were enmeshed with notes of protest. Poems such as "Jewish graveyard near Leningrad…" (1961) by **Joseph Brodsky** (1940–1996) could not be published in the official press but circulated in the underground and first appeared in the West. Others, such as "A German Girl" (1957–58) by **Vladimir Britanishsky** (1933–2015), were not published until the years of perestroika.

During the Thaw, the literary underground became a prominent feature of cultural life in the USSR, attracting some of the Jewish-Russian authors who were unable (or unwilling) to break into the official literary mainstream. The limited opportunities available in the official Soviet culture pushed writers into the underground throughout the 1960s–80s. Jewish topics were central to the works of some authors who could not publish officially (in this anthology, the 1960s poems by **Yan Satunovsky** [1913–1982] and also poems by **Genrikh Sapgir** [1928–1999], in the section "Late Soviet Empire and Collapse: 1960s–1990s"). In *This Is Moscow Speaking* by **Yuly Daniel** (1925–1988)—an anti-Soviet novel smuggled out of the USSR and published in the West—motifs of antisemitism are treated with an articulate absence of the Thaw-era illusions that permeated officially published works. Liberating as the Thaw was for both Soviet letters and Soviet society, openly Jewish works were modestly represented in the Soviet literature of the post-Stalinist 1950s and 1960s, which explains their limited selection in this anthology.

Finally, in connection with the culture and politics of the Thaw, it bears remembering that streaks of "chill" and periods of "frost" accompanied the more liberal seasons of the Thaw from the outset. Very telling was the destiny of **Vasily Grossman**'s *Life and Fate* (1960)—the most important work about the Shoah completed during the Thaw. Seized by the KGB in 1961, the novel did not appear until 1980 in the West and at home not until the reform years of perestroika. Selective targeting and persecution of Jewish artists and writers, such as the harassment and trial of **Joseph Brodsky** in 1963–64, marked the latter years of Khrushchev's rule. Nikita Khrushchev was ousted during the bloodless coup of October 1964 and the installment of Leonid Brezhnev as the new Soviet leader.

BORIS SLUTSKY

Boris Slutsky (1919–1986), poet, translator, and essayist, was born in Slavyansk (now Donetsk Province of Ukraine) and grew up in Kharkov. Slutsky attended the literary studio (*lito*) at the Kharkov Palace of Young Pioneers. Succumbing to pressure from his father, who had trouble imagining (Russian) poetry as a career (for a Jew), Slutsky entered the Moscow Institute of Law in 1937. The following year, Slutsky was accepted to the Moscow Literary Institute on the recommendation of **Pavel Antokolsky**. He combined reading law with the study of creative writing. Slutsky joined the seminar of **Ilya Selvinsky** and became a leading member of a circle of young poets that included Semyon Gudzenko, Pavel Kogan, Mikhail Kulchitsky, Sergey Narovchatov, and David Samoylov (Kaufman); poets Kogan and Kulchitsky perished in World War II. In 1941, a poem of Slutsky's appeared in the monthly *October*; he waited twelve years for his next publication of poetry.

Slutsky volunteered right after the Nazi invasion, serving initially as a military jurist and in 1942 switching to the track of a political officer. Slutsky spent 1942–44 at the southern fronts; in 1943, he learned about the murder of his family members in the Kharkov ghetto. Slutsky joined the Communist Party in 1943 and was promoted to deputy head of the Fifty-Seventh Army political department. Slutsky wrote virtually no poetry during the front years. He completed a book of documentary prose about his experiences in 1944–45 in Romania, Bulgaria, Yugoslavia, Hungary, and Austria. In the chapter "The Jews," Slutsky interspersed authorial observations with survivors' testimony. Lacking the pathos of **Ilya Ehrenburg**'s essays about the Shoah published in the 1940s, Slutsky's book combined harsh truths about marauding Soviet troops with ideological window dressing and remained unpublished until the post-Soviet years. The complete text appeared in *Notes about the War* (2000), edited by Slutsky's longtime friend Pyotr Gorelik.

Slutsky ended his service in August 1946 as a decorated Guards major. Having been twice seriously injured, Slutsky spent two years in and out of hospitals. He returned to Moscow during the darkest years for Soviet Jewry. Receiving a small disability pension, he did hack literary work. An avant-gardist writing at the time when experimentation was deemed "formalist," "decadent," and "bourgeois," Slutsky had a perilous time. "Memorial," apparently his second published poem for adult readers, appeared in August 1953, after Stalin's death.

In July 1956, **Ilya Ehrenburg** lauded Slutsky in *Literary Gazette* (*Literaturnaia gazeta*). Slutsky became an icon of the Thaw, an enemy of the entrenched Stalinists, and a hero of the liberal intelligentsia then overcome with the palliative optimism of the Twentieth Party Congress. Slutsky's first collection, *Memory*, selected by Vladimir Ognyov from a "suitcase of manuscripts," appeared in 1957 to include elegantly rough-hewn, street-smart, colloquial, factographically lyrical poems about the war and the shedding of illusions. Slutsky bridged "the generation of 1940" and the one entering the Soviet literary scene during the Thaw. Poets as different as **Joseph Brodsky**, **Genrikh Sapgir**, or Yevgeny Yevtushenko acknowledged Slutsky's impact. Slutsky's Thaw poems, such as "Horses in the Ocean" (published 1956; text below) and "Physicists and Lyricists" (published 1959), gained national fame. Speedily accepted to the Writers' Union, in 1957 Slutsky traveled to Italy with a delegation of Soviet poets that included, as a calculated gesture, Jews (Slutsky and **Vera Inber**) and victims of Stalinism (Nikolay Zabolotsky).

In the poem "I grew up under Stalin . . ." (pub. 1965), Slutsky articulated a transformation from faith to questioning to outright rejection of Stalin: "With sadness over his [i.e., Stalin's] having croaked/I didn't soil my soul./I took off, like a rumpled shirt/Him, who ruled and severely punished." A Jew, a Communist, and a war veteran, an "official dissident," and heir-designate to the 1920s Left Art, Slutsky solidified his position as a leading anti-Stalinist poet with the publication, in 1962 in *Literary Gazette*, of the poems "God" and "The Boss" (or "The Master"). Some critics pidgeon-holed Slutsky as a "frontline poet," but he and his poetry were always about more than war or Stalinism: a Janus-like visionary, whose actions enforced the official Soviet rhetorics that many of his poems subverted.

G. S. Smith, whose book of Slutsky's translations with commentary, *Things that Happened* (1999), introduced Slutsky to the Anglo-American reader, called Slutsky "the most imporant Soviet poet of his generation." Given the magnitude of his talent and influence, a reckoning of Slutsky's career can be frustrating. The episode that most tarnished Slutsky's reputation was his speech against **Boris Pasternak** during a meeting of Moscow writers on 31 October 1958, which "unanimously" passed a resolution to "expell" Pasternak from the Union of Soviet Writers. Smith characterized Slutsky's opprobrious conduct as "an act that was honest and sincere but that tormented Slutsky for the rest of his life." Apologism does no justice to the complexity of Slutsky's nature and ambitions. Referring to the pressure that the Party's central committee exerted upon him, Slutsky claimed that he spoke with "the least indecency." In agreeing to attack the author of *Doctor Zhivago*, Slutsky apparently regarded Pasternak as a sacrifical lamb—"the price"—of the Thaw. The translator of Italian writers into Russian Lev Vershinin related in his 2002 memoir how after his speech Slutsky "rushed to Peredelkino to see Pasternak [. . .] and not figuratively but literally fell on his knees and begged forgiveness [. . .]."

In the post-Soviet mythology, Slutsky has emerged as both a calculating idealist and a romantic realist. The lives and oeuvres of such Western left-wing avant-gardists as Pablo Picasso, Louis Aragon, and Bertold Brecht loomed before Slutsky's eyes, but he was living in a Soviet totalitarian state. Slutsky attempted to intercede on behalf of undergound writers and visual artists, arguing that revolutionary art demanded radical experimentation. He promoted gifted Russian poets, among them Igor Shklyarevsky (b. 1938), and openly helped Jewish-Russian poets and encouraged them to fight antisemitism using official Soviet means. Yet the fact that one of his closest Russian protégés, poet and essayist Stanislav Kunyaev (b. 1932), in the late 1970s became a leader of the then emergent Russian ultranationalist literary movement suggests that Slutsky had deluded himself into believing he could rear poet-disciples in his own, as he may have hoped, internationalist image.

Few poets of the postwar Soviet era were Slutsky's equals in making lofty poetry out of the polluted idiom of Soviet daily living. During two decades of peak form, 1957–77, Slutsky published a new or selected volume nearly every other year. Titles of his collections augment a penchant for both philosophical lyricism and inflation of prosaisms: *Time* (1959), *Today and Yesterday* (1961), *Work* (1964), *Contemporary Stories* [or *Histories*] (1969), *The Year* [*Clock*] *Hand* (1971), *Day's Kindness* (1973), *Unfinished Debates* (1978), *Hand and Soul* (1981), *Terms* (1984), and others. Slutsky published many translations from languages of the Soviet republics and the Eastern Bloc. He produced exemplary renditions of Nazim Hikmet (1902–1963), the Turkish poet living in exile. Slutsky translated Yiddish poets, including Shmuel Halkin, Aron Kushnirov, Leyb Kvitko, and Aron Vergelis. In 1963, when the USSR still had diplomatic relations with Israel, the anthology *Poets of Israel* appeared in Moscow and comprised Russian translations, some expurgated, of the works by Hebrew, Yiddish, and Arabic poets living in Israel, a number of whom were identified in the biographical notes as "Communists" or "progressives." Slutsky was listed as the volume's editor but not the author of the tendentious introduction, signed "From the Publisher."

In February 1977, Slutsky's wife, Tatyana Dashkovskaya (1930–1977), died of cancer. They were childless, and Slutsky loved his wife beyond any words—and any poems. Slutsky wrote for three months after his wife's death, creating piercing love poems and several texts with Jewish themes, but then severe depression set in. After spending some time in mental institutions, Slutsky moved to Tula, a city south of Moscow, where he lived in his brother's family. He wrote no poetry for the rest of his life and died there in 1986.

Pyotr Gorelik reported that in 1975 Slutsky had told him he had about five hundred unpublished poems—and this turned out to be a conservative assessment. Party functionaries and the KGB kept a watchful eye on Slutsky, especially in respect to his treatment of the Shoah and antisemitism, and his poems printed in the 1950s–70s reveal censorial corruptions. Largely through the devotion of Slutsky's executor, the critic Yury Boldyrev (1934–1993), numerous magazine publications and a number of books appeared during the reform and the post-Soviet years, including Slutsky's three-volume *Collected Works* (1991). In 2013, Marat Grinberg published a study of Slutsky's poetics.

* * *

Some of Slutsky's earliest Jewish poems (1938–40) have been lost. In 1938, he wrote "The Story of an Old Jew (Story from Abroad)," his first known response to Nazism; it appeared fifty-five years later in Israel. After witnessing the immediate aftermath of the Shoah in 1944–45 and writing nonfiction about it, Slutsky returned to poetry as the anticosmopolitan campaign gained speed. Memories of the destruction of European Jewry became enmeshed in Slutsky's acutely political imagination with the antisemitic crimes of late Stalinism, giving rise to a conflation of Jewish questions that Slutsky put in verse in the 1950s and 1960s and later revisited in the 1970s.

The most outspoken of Slutsky's poems about the Shoah and antisemitism did not appear in the USSR until the reform years, although several circulated in samizdat and appeared in the West, some anonymously. (Pyotr Gorelik included a selection in Slutsky's volume *Now Auschwitz Often Appears in My Dreams* . . . [St. Petersburg, 1999].) Some of Slutsky's poems published in the USSR treated Jewish themes by employing Aesopian language and allegory. In his memoir "A Jerusalem Cossack" (1991), **David Shrayer-Petrov** called Slutsky's "Horses in the Ocean" (see below) a "requiem for the murdered Jews." In the 1950s–70s, Slutsky steered into print more poems where the Shoah was memorialized, the Jewish question was explicitly debated, and the word "Jew" was used unabashedly than any of his

Soviet contemporaries. Slutsky the legalist proceeded as though the official rhetoric on the Jewish question and antisemitism protected Soviet Jews. A tetrade of Slutsky's Jewish poems appeared in Soviet magazines as the second Thaw peaked and entered its downward spiral. Three of them, "Birch Tree in Auschwitz" (published 1962), "How They Killed My Grandma" (published 1963), and "Burdened by familial feelings . . ." (published 1964), following in the footsteps of **Ehrenburg**'s wartime writings and **Vasily Grossman**'s story "The Old Teacher," transgressed the unspoken taboo on singling out the Shoah.

In this selection of Slutsky's Jewish poems from the 1950s, only two, "Horses in the Ocean" and "Prodigal Son," appeared in the USSR in Slutsky's lifetime (see bibliography of primary sources). Of the other four, two ("Oh, but we Jews had all the luck . . ." and "Of the Jews") circulated as a pair in the Soviet underground and appeared abroad in the 1960s–70s. The other two, "These Abrám, Isák, and Yákov . . ." and "Puny Jewish children . . ." (cf. the opening of **Isaac Babel**'s "Awakening" in this anthology), languished in Slutsky's desk drawer until 1989 (see additional poems in the section "Late Soviet Empire and Collapse: 1960s–1990s").

* * *

These Abrám, Isák and Yákov
Have inherited little or none
From Messrs. Abraham, Isaac,
and Jacob—
Gentlefolk of worldly renown.

In esteem travels the father of nations,
Wise Abraham; at the same time,
Goes Abram like a poor relation.
Praise to Abraham—a plague on Abram.

They sing hallelujas for Isaac
From the generous altars on high.
But they scrutinize Isak through the eyehole
And don't let him inside their homes.
Since the time Jacob wrestled with God
Since that time,

when God had prevailed,
Jacob's known as Yakov.
This wretched Yakov
Always stands in everyone's way.

1953

* * *

Oh, but we Jews had all the luck.
With no false banner to mask its presence,
Plain evil threw itself on us,
Seeing no need in noble pretense.

The loud disputes had not begun
Across the deaf, triumphant country.
But we, pressed to the corner with a gun,
Discovered solid ground.

before 1955

OF THE JEWS

The Jews don't push on a plow,
The Jews, as a rule, are loud,
The Jews rip you off at the market,
The Jews take a good thing and muck it.

The Jews are dangerous people,
Don't ask a Jew to do battle;
Ivan lies down for his country,
Abram stands behind the counter.

I've heard this since childhood,
Now my hair is graying.
"Jews! Jews!" the incessant holler
Will hound me into the grave.

I never stood behind a counter,
I've never stolen anyone's purse,
But I carry this race like a curse:
And I'm quartered according to quota.

The Nazi bullet had spared me,
So neighbors could truthfully intone:
"None of the Jews perished!
All of them returned home!"

1952–56

HORSES IN THE OCEAN

for I. Ehrenburg

Horses weren't made for water.
They can swim but not too far.

"Gloria" means the same as "glory"—
You will easily remember this part.

Braving the sea, a transatlantic vessel
Raised its flag above the stormy waves.

In its hold stood a thousand horses,
Four thousand feet stamping night and day.

A thousand horses! Four thousand horseshoes!
Not a single one could bring good luck.

In the middle of the stormy ocean
A torpedo tore the plates apart.

People piled into rafts and lifeboats,
Horses had to swim as best they could.

Boats and dinghies weren't made for horses—
What else could the poor creatures do?

A floating herd of reds and bays, a real
Island in the blue-green sea.

And at first they thought it was a river,
And it wasn't difficult to swim.

But the river before them was unending.
As they reached the limit of their strength

The horses raised a neigh, protesting
Against those who pulled them into the depths.

Horses neighed and drowned and drowned,
All went down, to the very last.

That's all. But I often think about it:
Drowning red horses, far away from land.

1956

PRODIGAL SON

In the ragged robes of need,
In the exhaustion of toil,
The prodigal son finds his childhood home.
He taps at the windowpane softly:
"May I?"
"Son! My only one! Certainly!
Please, come in! Do whatever your heart desires.
Wet your father's old cheek, chew the calf's fragrant meat.
It's a blessing to have you around!
Oh, son, won't you settle down and stay here a while?"
With a thick wooly beard he's wiping his mouth
As he puts away the stew,
As he drinks the cold clear water,
Beads of sweat glittering on his brow
From such unfamiliar labors.
Now he's eaten as much as he could,

And he goes
To the room where the clean bed awaits him.
How long has it been since he rested!
Then wakes up and puts on his clothes,
Finds his staff,
And without a word, goes.

1956

* * *

Puny Jewish children,
Bespectacled and bookish,
Who triumph on the chessboard
But can't do a single push-up,

Consider this suggestion:
Kayaking, boxing, sailing;
Take on the barren glacier,
Run barefoot in the grasslands.

The more you come to punches,
The fewer books, the better.
Keep turning where the wind blows,
Keep marching with the ages,
Try not to break formation,
Leave the boundaries in place.

The terrible twentieth century
Still has a few more years.

1957–58

Translated from the Russian by Sergey Levchin and Maxim D. Shrayer

VASILY GROSSMAN

(See the introduction to Vasily Grossman and the complete text of Grossman's "The Hell of Treblinka" in the section "War and Shoah: 1940s.")

The main historical currents of *Life and Fate*—Stalingrad and the Shoah—set the stage for the dilemmas of the novel's protagonist, Viktor Shtrum, a talented physicist working on the Soviet nuclear program.

In February 1961, the KGB seized Grossman's manuscripts. A microfilm of a surviving copy of *Life and Fate* was smuggled abroad with the help of fellow writers **Semyon Lipkin** and Vladimir Voinovich. Edited by émigré scholars Shimon Markish and Efim Etkind, it appeared in Switzerland in 1980 and later in Great Britain, in Robert Chandler's English translation (London, 1985). The novel was first published in the Soviet Union in 1988.

The details recounted in Grossman's 1944 essay "The Hell of Treblinka" (in the section "War and Shoah: 1940s") furnish authenticity to Grossman's fictional treatment of the same subject in his novel *Life and Fate*. It is likely that the character of Sofia Levinton is based upon a real person. The narrator identifies her as a friend of the Anya Shtrum's—a character who is, as John and Carol Garrard demonstrated in *The Bones of Berdichev: The Life and Fate of Vas[s]ily Grossman* (1996), a portrait of Grossman's own mother. Grossman's mother had been massacred, along with 20,000 other Jews, in his hometown of Berdichev in 1941. Grossman does not name the camp where Sofia and David are murdered, but many details link it with the same Treblinka described in his wartime essay. One minor exception is that Sofia Levinton and David are said to die by Zyklon B gas, whereas Treblinka killed its victims with carbon monoxide. It is probably safest to see the camp as a representative of all the death camps (Auschwitz-Birkenau, Sobibór, Treblinka, Chelmno, Bełżec) that the Nazis built in Poland to murder Jews. Grossman did, however, retain horrific identifying features of the Treblinka murder machinery.

David, the teenaged protagonist of the excerpt, was born on 12 December, just like Vasily Grossman, and is a projection of the author as a boy into the horrors of the Holocaust. In 1941, when David is twelve, his mother leaves him for two months with his grandmother in Ukraine (in a fictionalized Berdichev) for summer vacation because he begs her not to send him back to summer camp. She then returns to work in Moscow. David never sees his mother again. He hides in an attic with other Jews, but they are discovered and put in a cattle car. Their final days are described in the following sections.

The above introduction to *Life and Fate* is by John Garrard and Maxim D. Shrayer, as are the notes below.

FROM *LIFE AND FATE*

Chapter 47

Sofia Osipovna Levinton walked with a measured, heavy tread, with the little boy holding onto her hand. His other hand was in his pocket, fingering a matchbox, which contained a dark brown chrysalis wrapped in dirty cotton wool. The chrysalis had emerged from its cocoon a little earlier in the cattle car. Next to them was the locksmith Lazar Iankelevich, muttering as he strode along, and his wife, Debora Samuilovna, carrying a baby in her arms. Beyond them was Revekka Bukhman, muttering "My God, my God, my God" over and over. Fifth in the row was the librarian Musya Borisovna . Her hair was combed up revealing her white collar. Several times on the train journey she had exchanged her bread ration for half a mess tin of warm water. Musya never begrudged anyone anything, and in the cattle car the others considered her a saint. The elderly women on the train, good judges of character, kissed her dress hem. The row in front of them consisted of four people. At the selection point an officer had immediately waved aside two people from this row, the father and son Slepoy. When questioned about their professions, they had shouted out, "*Zahnarzt*,"[1] and the officer had nodded. The Slepoys had guessed right and saved their lives. Of the remaining four in the row, three walked with their arms, no longer of any use, dangling at their sides. A fourth man strode along independently with a spring in his step, the collar of his jacket turned up, hands thrust into his pockets, and his head held high. Up ahead, perhaps three or four rows, Sofia could see an old man in a Red Army winter hat.

Right behind Sofia Levinton was Musya Vinokur, who had turned fourteen during the train journey.

Death! He had become a part of them. He had become their daily companion. He stopped by to call on them in their backyards, their workshops. He met a housewife at the market and took her away with her string bag of potatoes. He joined in kids' games. He looked in at the dressmaker's shop, where ladies' tailors hummed to themselves as they hurried to finish a cloak for the

---

1 *Zahnarzt* (Ger.) = dentist.

wife of a *Gebietskommissar*.[2] Death stood in line for bread or sat down beside an old woman darning a sock.

Death carried on his daily business as people went about their own. Sometimes he let people finish off a cigarette or eat a meal. Sometimes he would run to catch up with a man and slap him roughly on the back, laughing coarsely and stupidly.

Finally, it seemed, people understood how mundane and childishly simple Death was. Crossing over was really not difficult at all; it was like taking five or six steps over wooden planks thrown across a narrow stream to an open meadow where the chimneys of peasant huts were smoking. And that's all there was to it! What was there to be afraid of? Look! There goes a calf—clattering with its hooves over the bridge of planks. There go some boys—slapping the planks with their bare feet as they cross.

Suddenly, Sofia Levinton heard music playing. She first heard this music when she was a child, and then when she was a university student, and then as a young physician. The music always stirred her with its vivid premonition of the future.

This time the music deceived her. Sofia had no future. She only had her past. And the feeling of her own individual separate past, for a moment, shielded her from the present—from the edge of the abyss.

It was the strangest feeling! You couldn't convey it to anyone; you couldn't share the feeling even with those dearest to you—your wife, mother, brother, son, friend, or father. It was a secret in your soul, and your soul could not betray its secret however passionately it might want to do so. Each person will carry this secret feeling without sharing it with anyone. The miracle of a unique individual in whose conscious and subconscious is collected everything good and everything bad, everything funny, sweet, morbidly pitiful, embarrassing, tender, timid, bewildering—all that the individual experienced from childhood to old age is fused and united in the secret, private feeling of this one life.

When the music started playing, David wanted to take the matchbox out of his pocket and open it a little just for a moment so that the chrysalis would not catch cold while it looked at the musicians. But after a few steps, he stopped noticing the people on the bandstand and instead only saw the red glow in the sky and heard the music. The mournful, mighty theme filled his soul to the brim with longing for his mother. She had been neither strong nor calm and always felt

---

2   *Gebietskommissar* (Ger.) = area commissioner.

ashamed that her husband had abandoned her. She sewed a shirt for David, and the neighbors laughed because it was made of calico with flowers on it and the sleeves were not sewn in straight. His mother had been his only protection and hope. He had relied on her totally and foolishly. But perhaps it was the music: now he stopped relying on his mother. He loved her, but she was helpless and weak, just like the people who were now walking alongside him. And the music, sleepy and quiet, flowed like the tiny waves he dreamed of when, delirious with high fever, he would crawl off his hot pillow onto warm, damp sand.

The orchestra wailed on like an enormous, husky throat. The dark wall of waves, which used to rise out of the water when he had strep throat, now loomed over him filling the whole sky.

Everything that had ever terrified his young heart now flowed together. United, it became one terror, the same terror that he had felt looking at the painting in which the little goat failed to notice the wolf's shadow among the fir trees, the blue-eyed heads of slaughtered calves in the market, his dead grand-mother, Revekka Bukhman's strangled baby girl, and the first irrational night terror that had made him scream out desperately and call for his mother. Death stood as huge as the whole sky and watched little David walking on little legs toward him. All around him there was nothing but the music, and you couldn't hang onto that; you couldn't even crack your head by banging against it.

As for the chrysalis, it had no wings, no feet, no antennae, no eyes; it just lay in the box, dumb, trusting, expectant.

David was a Jew, and that was that.

He was hiccupping and choking. If he could, he would have strangled him-self. The music stopped. His little legs and dozens of other little legs ran and hurried along. He thought of nothing; he couldn't shout or cry. His sweating fingers squeezed the matchbox in his pocket but he had already forgotten the chrysalis. All he knew was that his little legs were moving, hurrying, running. If the horror that gripped him had lasted a few minutes longer, he would have fallen to the ground, his heart stopped.

When the music ceased, Sofia wiped away her tears and said angrily, "We'll see, said the blind man to the deaf man."

Then she glanced at the little boy's face; even there its terrified expression made it stand out. "What is it? What is the matter with you?" Sofia cried out and grabbed his hand. "What is it? What is the matter with you? Come on—we're just going to the bathhouse."

When the German selectors had called out for doctors, she had remained silent, fighting against their hateful force.

The machinist's wife continued walking alongside carrying in her arms her pitiful baby with an overly large head, who looked at the surrounding world with an innocent, thoughtful expression. This was the woman who the previous night in the cattle car had stolen for her baby a handful of sugar from another woman. The woman she stole from was too weak to protest, but an old man by the name of Lapidus had stood up for her. No one wanted to sit next to him because he kept urinating on the floor where he crouched.

Now this same Debora, the machinist's wife, walked deep in thought, holding her baby in her arms. The baby, who had cried night and day, was now quiet. The woman's melancholy, dark eyes diverted attention from the ugliness of her dirty face and roughened lips.

And Sofia thought, "A Madonna."[3]

Once, about two years before the war, she had watched the sun rise beyond the pine trees of the Tyan-Shan Mountains. The sun caught the snow-covered hills in its rays while the lake still lay in shadow, as though chiseled out of a single sheet of intensely dark blue rock. At that time she had thought that there was nobody in the world who would not have envied her. But now, with an intensity that burned her fifty-year-old heart, she felt that she would have given it all up if only, in some grubby, dark room, she could be hugged by the arms of a child.

Little David evoked in her a special tenderness she had never felt for children before, though she loved children. In the cattle car, whenever she gave him some of her bread and he turned his face toward her in the half-light, she felt like crying and hugging him and showering him with the quick kisses that mothers love to plant on the cheeks of their babies. She kept whispering, so low that he couldn't hear, "Eat, my darling son, eat."

She hardly talked to the boy, overcome by a strange sense of shame that made her want to conceal her maternal feelings. But she noticed that the boy always watched her anxiously when she moved to another part of the train car, and he calmed down when she was near him. She did not want to admit to herself why she hadn't responded when they called for doctors, why she had remained in the column, and why at that moment she had been seized by a feeling of exaltation.

---

3   Grossman saw *The Sistine Madonna* in 1955 in Moscow, in a big exhibition of works taken by Soviet troops from Dresden in World War II. They were later returned to Dresden's Gemäldegalerie. In that same year, Grossman drew a parallel between the Madonna and child in Raphael's painting and a Jewish mother and child being led into the gas chamber in his essay "The Sistine Madonna" (Sikstinskaia Madonna).

The column marched along beside barbed-wire fences, concrete towers with mounted machine guns, and ditches. The people who had long since forgotten what it was to be free imagined that the barbed wire and the machine guns were not there to prevent prisoners from escaping but to prevent the condemned from hiding inside the camp.

The column was now led away from the barbed-wire fence toward low, squat buildings with flat roofs. From a distance these windowless rectangular structures with gray walls reminded David of oversized toy building blocks from which the pictures had been stripped off.

Through a gap, as the rows of people turned, the little boy saw some buildings with wide open double doors. Without knowing why, he took the matchbox with the chrysalis out of his pocket and threw it to one side, not even saying goodbye. Let it live!

"Wonderful people, these Germans," said a man ahead of her in the column as though the guards could hear him and would appreciate the flattery.

Sofia could see the man with the raised collar shrug his shoulders in a peculiar way and glance to the right and then the left; he now looked bigger and taller. Then suddenly he leapt forward like a bird spreading his wings and punched an SS guard, knocking him to the ground. Sofia, shouting angrily, rushed after him but stumbled and fell. Immediately, several hands grabbed her and helped her get to her feet. The people behind pressed them forward and David, looking around fearfully, worrying that they would knock him down, caught sight of guards dragging the man away.

In the brief moment when Sofia tried to attack the guard, she had forgotten about the little boy. Now she again took him by the hand. David noticed how clear, fierce, and beautiful the eyes of a person could become when she sensed freedom, if only just for a fraction of a second. By now the first ranks of the column had already reached the asphalt square in front of the entrance to the bathhouse. The people's steps walking through the wide open doors made a different sound now.

Chapter 48

It was quiet and dark in the damp, warm undressing room, which was lit only by small rectangular windows.

Benches made of thick, unfinished planks with painted numbers on them stretched on into the darkness. In the middle of the room, from the entrance to the far wall, a low partition separated two changing areas: men were undressing on one side, women and children on the other. This separation didn't cause any alarm because people could still see each other and talk over the divider. "Manya, Manya, are you there?"—"Yes, yes, I can see you." Someone shouted, "Matilda, bring the sponge over here and scrub my back!" A feeling of calm enveloped almost everybody.

Serious-looking people in white coats walked up and down the rows, maintaining order and giving sensible advice about the need to put socks, stockings, and foot wrappings inside boots and about the vital importance of remembering the number of your row and your place within the row.

People spoke in quiet, muffled tones.

When a man is naked, he is closer to his essential self. Lord, how wiry and thick the hairs on my chest have become and how many gray hairs there are. What ugly fingernails I have. A naked man, looking at himself, draws only one conclusion, "This is the real me." He recognizes himself and defines his "I"—it's always the same. A little boy crossing his thin arms over his skinny ribs looks at his froglike body and says, "This is me." And fifty years later this same boy, looking at the knotted, blue veins in his legs and his fat, flabby chest, recognizes himself again. "This is me."

But Sofia was struck by a strange feeling. The naked bodies of young and old revealed that beneath the rags lay hidden the collective body of a whole people. There was a skinny boy with a big nose about whom an old woman, shaking her head, said, "Oh, poor little Hasidic kid," and there was a fourteen-year-old girl who attracted, even here, hundreds of admiring eyes. There were ugly and feeble old men and women who aroused pious respect. There were men with strong, hairy backs and women with sagging breasts and legs covered with veins. Sofia felt that the expression "This is me" referred not just to her but to all of them. This was the naked body of a people: at one and the same time it was young, old, vigorous, mature, strong, sick, with curly, healthy hair or thinning, gray hair, beautiful and ugly, powerful and weak. She looked at her own broad, white shoulders, recalling that no one had kissed them, except her mother when she was a child; then she gazed tenderly at the little boy. Had she really forgotten about him a few moments ago and rushed in crazed anger at the SS guard? "That hopelessly naïve young Jew," she thought, "and his old Russian disciple, both preaching nonresistance to violence.[4] But there was no Fascism in their times." No longer ashamed of the maternal feelings in her virginal body, Sofia bent down and took David's

---

4   Sofia Levinton is making a rueful reference to Jesus of Nazareth and to Lev Tolstoy.

narrow face into her large, calloused hands, and it seemed to her that she had embraced his warm eyes and kissed them.

"Yes, yes, my dear child," she said. "Now we've reached the bathhouse."
[...]

The machinist's wife wanted to show her husband their baby boy, but she couldn't see him on the other side of the partition. She held the baby out to Sofia, still half wrapped in swaddling clothes, and said proudly, "I've only just undressed him, and he's stopped crying right away."

A man with a thick, unkempt black beard, wearing torn pajama bottoms instead of longjohns, his eyes and gold teeth flashing, shouted, "Manya dear, someone wants to sell a swimsuit here. Shall I buy it then?"

Musya Borisovna, covering her breasts, which could be seen through a wide tear in her slip, smiled at the joke. Sofia knew very well that the wit of the condemned did not display strength of spirit. But terror is not so terrible for weak and timid people when they laugh at it.

Revekka Bukhman, her beautiful face exhausted and pinched, turned her huge and fevered eyes away and unbraided her thick hair, trying to hide in it the rings and earrings she had concealed.

A blind, cruel instinct possessed her. Yes, she was miserable and powerless, but Fascism had reduced her to its own level, and now nothing could hold her back from trying to save her life at all costs. As she hid the rings, she tried not to remember that with her own hands she had throttled her baby out of fear that its crying would reveal her hiding place in the attic.

But just as Revekka Bukhman gave a deep sigh, like an animal that had reached the safety of a thicket, she caught sight of a woman in a smock cutting Musya's hair with a pair of scissors. Next to her, another reaper of hair was scything the head of a little girl, and silky, black waves fell noiselessly onto the concrete floor. The hair covered the floor, and it looked as if the women were washing their feet in rivulets of dark and glossy water.

The woman in the smock unhurriedly pulled away Revekka's hand shielding her head and grabbed her hair at the nape of her neck. The scissor tips caught a ring hidden in her hair. Without pausing, the woman scooped the rings with practiced skill from Revekka's hair, then leaned over and whispered in her ear, "You'll get it all back." Then, quieter still, she breathed, "Germans are present. You must stay *Ganz ruhig*."[5] For Rebecca, the woman in the smock no

---

5   *Ganz ruhig* (Ger.) = completely quiet.

longer had a face with eyes or lips; she was nothing but a yellowish hand with blue veins.

At that moment, a gray-haired man approached the partition. With his glasses askew on his crooked nose, he looked like a sick, melancholy gnome. He searched the women's benches; then, clearly enunciating each syllable with the voice of a man accustomed to talking to the deaf, he asked, "Mama, Mama, Mama—how do you feel?"

A wrinkled little old lady, suddenly catching the voice of her son in the drone of hundreds of voices, smiled tenderly; then, guessing the customary question, she replied, "Fine, fine—regular pulse. Don't worry!"

Someone next to Sofia said, "That's Gelman, the famous internist."

A naked young woman, holding by the hand a little girl with cherubic lips who was wearing white underpants, screamed, "They're going to kill us, they're going to kill us, they're going to kill us!"

"Quiet, quiet. Calm that crazy woman down," several women said. They looked around and saw there were no guards nearby. They could rest their ears and eyes in the silence and semi-darkness. What a huge pleasure it was, one they had not experienced for many months, to take off their filthy clothes, stiffened with dirt and sweat, and their half-rotted socks, stockings, and foot wrappings. The women in smocks finished cutting hair and left, and so people could breathe even more freely. Some dozed off, others examined the seams of their clothes, still others talked among themselves quietly.

Someone said, "Pity we don't have a pack of cards. We could play a few hands."

Simultaneously, elsewhere at the camp, the head of the *Sonderkommando*, smoking a hand-rolled cigarette, was picking up a telephone receiver; the store man was loading a mechanized cart with containers of Zyklon, which looked like tins of fruit preserves with their red labels; the *Sonderkommando* sentry, sitting in the service building, kept a close eye on the wall—any moment the red signal light would go on.

Suddenly, the order "On your feet!" sounded from different corners of the undressing room.

At the end of each of the benches, Germans now stood in black uniforms. The people were moved into a wide corridor lit by dim ceiling lamps covered with thick, oval glass. The slowly and smoothly curving concrete now took on a muscular force that sucked along the human flow. It was quiet; all that could be heard was the slapping of bare feet.

At one time before the war, Sofia Levinton had remarked to her friend Eugenia Shaposhnikova: "If one person is destined to be killed by another, it would be interesting to trace the paths by which they gradually draw closer and closer. At first perhaps they might be terribly far apart. For example, I could be in the Pamir Mountains collecting Alpine roses, clicking away with my Contax camera, while at that moment my killer is eight thousand kilometers away, fishing for perch after a day at school. I might be getting ready to go to a concert, and on the very same day he might be buying a train ticket to go and visit his mother-in-law. But all the same, we will meet, and the deed will be done." Sofia recalled that strange conversation now. She glanced up at the ceiling: the thick concrete above her head would no longer allow her to hear thunder or see the upturned dipper of Ursa Major. She walked on bare feet toward a bend in the corridor that silently and stealthily floated toward her. She glided along effortlessly, in a kind of semi-conscious daze, as though everything all around, inside and out, was smothered in glycerin.

The entrance to the gas chamber opened gradually and yet suddenly. The flow of people slowly glided through. An old man and an old woman who had been together for fifty years and had been separated in the undressing room, again walked side by side. The machinist's wife carried her baby, who had now woken up. A mother and son looked over the heads of the column, scanning not for space but for time. The face of the internist flashed by, followed closely by Musya's kind eyes, then the terrified stare of Revekka Bukhman. There was Lyusya Shterental—nothing could suppress the beauty of those young eyes, her lightly flaring nostrils, her neck, her half-open mouth. Next to her came old Lapidus with the crushed blue lips. Sofia hugged the little boy's shoulders. She had never before felt in her heart such tenderness for another human being.

Revekka Bukhman, who was walking next to Sofia, started screaming—her screams were unbearable, the screams of a person who is turning into ashes.

A man with a length of metal piping stood beside the entrance to the gas chamber. He was wearing a brown, zippered shirt-jacket with short sleeves.[6]

---

6   As Grossman knew from his 1944 interviews with surviving eyewitnesses and reported in "The Hell of Treblinka," two men stood at the door to the gas chamber. The man described here was identified as Ivan Demjanjuk, nicknamed "Ivan the Terrible" by the Jewish slave workers because of his vicious beatings of victims. Armed with a lead pipe, he beat the condemned as they crossed the threshold of the gas chamber. He was arrested and convicted of war crimes in Israel but later released to return to his home in the United States. See Tom Teicholz, *The Trial of Ivan the Terrible: The State of Israel vs. John Demjanjuk* (New York: St. Martin's Press, 1990).

It was the sight of his mindless, childish, crazy, drunken smile that had caused Revekka Bukhman to scream so terribly.

The man slid his eyes over Sofia's face. Here he is, my death; we have met at last!

She felt her fingers itching to seize the neck that bulged out of his open jacket. But the smiling man swung his metal pipe in a short and quick blow. Through the ringing of bells and the crunching of glass inside her head, she heard, "Back off, you lousy bitch."

She barely managed to stay on her feet; then with a heavy, slow step, together with David, she crossed the steel threshold.

Chapter 49

David passed the palm of his hand over the steel doorframe and felt its cold smoothness. He saw reflected in the steel a light gray blurred spot; it was his own face. The soles of his bare feet told him that the floor of the chamber was cold, colder than it had been in the corridor—it had recently been washed and rinsed.

Taking short, steady steps he entered a concrete box with a low ceiling. He could see no lamps, but there was a gray light in the chamber as though the sun was shining through a concrete-covered sky. But this stone light did not seem designed for living creatures.

People who had been together the whole time were now scattered and lost touch. David caught sight of the face of Zhenya Shterental. Whenever he looked at her during the train ride, he had been overcome by the sweet sadness of young love. But a moment later, a short neckless woman appeared in her place. Immediately, that woman's place was taken by a blue-eyed old man with fluffy white hair. Then a young man with a fixed stare swam into David's vision.

People in the gas chamber moved in a way that was not natural to human beings; it wasn't natural even to the lowest form of animal life. It was unnatural because it had no sense or purpose; there was no living will motivating it. The stream of people flowed into the chamber, and again those coming behind shoved those ahead, and they in turn pushed the ones in front of them. These countless, small pushes of elbows, shoulders, and stomachs in no way differed from the movement of molecules discovered by the botanist Robert Brown.

David sensed that he was being led somewhere and that he needed to move. He reached a wall, touched its cold simplicity with his knee, then his chest; then he couldn't move any further. Sofia Levinton stood there already, leaning against the wall.

For a few moments they both watched people moving away from the doors. The entrance itself seemed far away, and one could only tell where it was by the especially dense whiteness of the human bodies as they were squeezed and compressed through the entrance. After passing through it, people could spread out across the open floor of the gas chamber.

David looked at people's faces. In the morning, after their train was unloaded, he had only seen people's backs; but now he felt that all the people advancing toward him had only faces. Sofia Levinton suddenly looked strange to him; in the flat, concrete chamber, her voice sounded different. As soon as they entered the chamber, she had changed. When she said, "Hold on tight, my boy," he felt that she was afraid to let him go, worrying that she would be left alone. They weren't able to stay by the wall; they were pushed away from it and began shuffling in tiny steps. David felt that he was moving faster than Sofia. She held on to his hand, tugging him toward her. But some soft, growing force started pulling David away, and Sofia's fingers began to lose their grip.

More and more people packed into the chamber; their movements became slower and their mincing steps shorter and shorter. There was no one to control people's movement inside the concrete box. The Germans didn't care whether people stood still in the gas chamber or moved about in nonsensical zigzags and semicircles. The naked little boy kept taking tiny, shuffling, meaningless steps. The circle traced by his slight, small body ceased to coincide with the circle traced by Sofia's large, heavy body, and soon they were parted. She shouldn't have held him by the hand; she should have held him cheek to cheek, breast to breast; they should have become one indivisible body, like those two women over there, mother and daughter, clasped together in the anguished obstinacy of love.

Still more people crowded in, and as the density and compression increased, their molecular movement no longer obeyed Avogadro's law. As he lost his grip on Sofia's hand, the little boy cried out. But instantly Sofia became part of David's past life; only the present, the here and now, existed. All around him, mouths were breathing, bodies were touching one another, feelings and thoughts were fusing together.

David fell in with a group of the rotating crowd that, after rebounding from the wall, then moved toward the entrance. He saw three people linked together, two men and an old woman. She was protecting her children, and they were supporting their mother. Suddenly, a completely new movement began right next to David. The noise was also new, distinct from the shuffling and muttering he'd heard before.

"Move aside!" shouted a man with powerful bulging muscles and a thick neck, his head bent forward as he thrust his way through the solid mass of bodies. He was struggling to escape the hypnotic rhythm of the concrete chamber; his body rebelled blindly, mindlessly, like a live fish flopping on a kitchen table. Soon though, he slowed down, gasping for breath, and began again to shuffle along just like everybody else.

The disturbance the man had produced altered the curved patterns the people traced, and David found himself next to Sofia Levinton once more. She hugged the boy to her with the amazing strength that had been discovered and acknowledged by the workers in extermination camps. When they were clearing the death chamber of corpses, they never even tried to separate the bodies of loved ones locked in such a tight embrace.

There were screams from near the entrance; when people saw the solid human mass that filled the chamber, they refused to move through the wide open doors.

David watched the doors close: as though drawn by a magnet, they moved smoothly and softly toward their steel frame, then fused and became one. David noticed on the upper part of the wall that something live was stirring behind a rectangular metal grid. At first he thought it was a gray rat, but then he realized it was a ventilator blade beginning to turn. He sensed a faint, rather sweet smell.

The shuffling of feet stopped; you could hear occasional indistinct words, groans, and cries. But speech was no longer of any use to people; action made no sense either. Action would have been directed toward the future, and in the gas chamber there was no future. David turned his head, but Sofia felt no desire to look in the same direction as any other living being.

Now she no longer needed her eyes—eyes that had read Homer, the *Izvestia* newspaper, *Huckleberry Finn*, the novels of Mayne Reid, Hegel's *Logic*; eyes that had seen good people and bad, the geese in the green meadows of Kursk, stars through the telescope at the Pulkovo Observatory, the luster of surgical steel, the *Mona Lisa* in the Louvre, tomatoes and turnips in market bins, the dark blue of Lake Issyk-Kul. If someone had blinded her at that moment, she would have felt no sense of loss.

She was able to breathe, but breathing had become hard work, and the effort was exhausting. In spite of the bells ringing inside her head, she tried to formulate one last thought, but the thought wouldn't come. Sofia stood mute, her unseeing eyes still open.

The boy's movements filled her with pity. Her feelings for him were so simple—she no longer needed words or eyes. The half-dead boy was still breathing, only the air he breathed did not prolong life but stole it away. He twisted his head from side to side, still wishing to see what was happening. He saw people sinking to the ground; he saw open mouths, some without teeth, some with white teeth, some with gold teeth; he saw a thin trickle of blood flowing from a nostril. He saw curious eyes looking into the gas chamber through the glass [...]. He still needed his voice; he could have asked Sofia about those wolf-like eyes. And he still needed to think. He had taken only a few steps in the world. He had seen traces of children's bare feet on the hot, dusty ground; his mother lived in Moscow; the moon shone down from above, and you could look up at it from below; a teakettle was boiling on the gas stove. His world, where a headless chicken ran around, where he made frogs dance by holding onto their front feet, where he drank fresh milk in the morning—that whole world still preoccupied him.

All the while, warm arms embraced David. He did not realize that his eyes were dimming, that his heart was becoming empty and hollow sounding, and that his brain was going dull and blind. He had been killed; he ceased to be.

Sofia Levinton felt the little boy's body go limp in her arms. Again, she had lagged behind him. When coal-mine shafts are filling with poison gas, the first warning is that birds and mice die because they have small bodies. And so it was here: the boy with the little, bird-like body had died before her.

"I've become a mother," she thought. That was her last thought.

But her heart still had life: it sank, contracted, ached, and felt pity for you, the quick and the dead. As a wave of nausea overcame her, Sofia continued to hug David in her arms. He was a rag doll, and now she had died and become a rag doll too.

1960

Translated from the Russian by John Garrard

JOSEPH BRODSKY

Joseph (Iosif) **Brodsky** (1940–1996), poet, essayist, translator, and play-wright, was born in Leningrad (now St. Petersburg). His Biblical first name also belonged to the Soviet dictator Joseph Stalin. After Brodsky's death in New York, contemporaries felt "in his fate," to quote **Genrikh Sapgir**, "the lot of Biblical Joseph, who was sold into bondage by his brothers and later rose up and was revered in a strange land, which he made his own."

Brodsky's father was a photojournalist; his mother was trained as a transla-tor and worked as an accountant. Brodsky left school at fifteen, never to return to formal education, and changed jobs many times between 1956 and 1962. His earliest poems, written in 1957–59, exhibited overtly modernist influ-ences, but in the 1960s he transitioned back in time, engaging in a fusion of baroque and neoclassical poetry with the poetry of the Silver Age and early Soviet modernism. In 1959–60 Brodsky appeared on the Leningrad literary scene and quickly gained acclaim and notoriety, his works still unpublished. The Leningrad poetic peers he was close to at the time included **Evgeny Reyn**, Anatoly Nayman, Dmitry Bobyshev, **David Shrayer-Petrov**, and Vladimir Uflyand. In the early 1960s, he fell under the profound personal influence of the great Russian poet Anna Akhmatova (1889–1966). Brodsky taught him-self English and Polish. When Akhmatova and **Osip Mandelstam**'s widow Nadezhda Mandelstam first heard Brodsky read, they responded, "it [sounds] so much like **Osip [Mandelstam]**."

In 1962, Brodsky fell in love with the artist and book designer Marina Basmanova, who was not Jewish. They were never married; their son, Andrey Basmanov, was born in 1967. Brodsky subsequently collected his poems for Basmanova in *New Stanzas to Augusta: Poems to M. B., 1962–1982* (1983).

A denunciatory article titled "A Paraliterary Drone" appeared in *Evening Leningrad* (*Vechernii Leningrad*) on 29 February 1963, signed "A. Ionin, Ya. Lerner, M. Medvedev." Brodsky's main detractor, the Jewish opportun-ist Yakov Lerner, commanded a Komsomol Youth Brigade; he was subse-quently convicted for corruption. Brodsky was arrested in February 1964 and was charged with "social parasitism" because he did not have a full-time job (he had been doing literary work on a free-lance basis). He set a new standard for literary martyrdom during his trial on 18 February 1964 and was sentenced to five years of administrative exile, which he served in a remote village in

Archangelsk Province. Some of Brodsky's greatest lyrics, including the cycle "A Part of Speech" (1975–76), emerged out of a poetic distillation of his northern exile. Brodsky's sentence was commuted after eighteen months.

Brodsky returned to Leningrad in the fall of 1965, and a Russian-language volume, *Longer and Shorter Poems*, appeared that same year in Washington, DC. His poems also appeared in translation, including volumes in German (1966), English (1967), and Hebrew (*Akedat Yisak* [Sacrifice of Isaac], trans. Ezra Zusman, 1969). His second Russian collection, *A Halt in the Wilderness*, appeared in New York in 1970. Brodsky had developed a unique voice by the late 1960s.

Brodsky managed to publish a handful of poems and some translations in the Soviet Union, his poems already widely circulating in Soviet samizdat. Yet he refused to compromise with the Soviet authorities. In May 1972, the authorities insisted that Brodsky fill out an application to immigrate to Israel although Brodsky expressly did not wish to be a statistic of Jewish emigration. He arrived in Vienna on 4 June 1972 and met his hero, W. H. Auden (1907–1973), who wrote a foreword to Brodsky's *Selected Poems* (1973), translated by George L. Kline. In 1981, after nine years at the University of Michigan at Ann Arbor, Brodsky moved to a professorial position at Mount Holyoke College, dividing his time between New York City and Massachusetts.

Between 1972 and 1996, a number of collections and volumes of Brodsky's Russian verse appeared in the West, among them *A Part of Speech: Poems 1972–1976* (1977), *The End of a Beautiful Epoch: Poems 1964–71* (1977), *Urania* (1987), and *Landscape with a Flood* (1996). Several books of Brodsky's poetry came out in English during his lifetime; Brodsky's poems were collected in the posthumous *Collected Poems in English* (2000). In the 1970s, Brodsky began to write essays in English. They were collected in *Less Than One: Selected Essays* (1986) and *Of Grief and Reason: Essays* (1995). Brodsky composed a book-essay about Venice, published in English as *Watermark* (1992). Simultaneously a memoir and a treatise on time, exilic memory, and beauty, *Watermark* shows that fascism and antisemitism are aesthetically incompatible with true art. W. H. Auden is Brodsky's idealized protagonist, and Ezra Pound, the antihero. An American citizen since 1977, Brodsky was the fourth writer in Russian— and the second Russian Jew—to receive the Nobel Prize in Literature (1987). In 1991–92, Brodsky was a United States Poet Laureate.

By the mid-1980s, Brodsky was a cult figure in the USSR, but an official return of his poetry to the USSR, in 1987, was poisoned by some xenophobic statements in the Soviet press. Brodsky's books were first published in the USSR in 1990. Many more followed, including a 1998 eight-volume edition. Brodsky never visited Russia.

In 1990, Brodsky married Maria Sozzani, a half-Italian, half-Russian Catholic. Their daughter, Anna, was born in 1993. Brodsky died in New York of heart failure on 28 January 1996 and was buried in Venice.

"By most accounts," wrote David M. Bethea, "[Brodsky] is the greatest poet to have been born in Soviet times [. . .]." Brodsky drew inspiration from Russian eighteenth-century poets and from English and Polish metaphysical poets. Among the Russian poets who played formative roles in Brodsky's development were (listed alphabetically) **Eduard Bagritsky**, Nikolay Klyuev, **Osip Mandelstam**, Vladimir Mayakovsky, **Boris Slutsky**, and Marina Tsvetaeva. "[Tsevetaeva] was the only poet [. . .] with whom I decided not to compete," Brodsky told Sven Birkerts in 1979.

When people try to bring [Brodsky's 'immense verbal brilliance'] into English, what you often get is almost pyrotechnics, and almost brilliance, so partly you read his poetry in English as an act of faith [. . .]," stated Robert Haas in 1996. Given the circumstances under which Brodsky mastered the English language, as a writer in English he lacked perfect pitch. He treated English prosody as though it were Russian in translation. Brodsky's Anglo-American critics often fail to acknowledge how much he had done for the preservation of poetry as an art form.

* * *

Jewish references are not numerous in Brodsky's poems. Three poems of the Soviet period deserve consideration. Shimon Markish singled out "Jewish graveyard near Leningrad . . ." (1958) as an example of a direct influence of **Boris Slutsky** (see Slutsky's "Of the Jews" in this section). "I'm not asking death for immortality . . ." (ca. 1961, also included below) has received less attention. Brodsky's third overtly Jewish poem is "Liejyklos," part 2 of "Lithuanian Divertissement" (1971). "Liejyklos" (name of a street where Jews used to live in Vilna) sketches two scenarios of Jewish-Russian history, one of which is emigration. (In America, the motif of Brodsky's Litvak ancestor pushing a cart across Vilna resurfaced in his "Lithuanian Nocturne" [1974].)

Given Brodsky's manifest metaphysical interests, can one agree with Lev Loseff's conclusion that "[. . .] Jewishness [. . .] was for [Brodsky] primarily an anthropological quality"? Much more than an expression of ethnic markers of identity, "crow, the Jewish bird" in Brodsky's poem "Afterword to the Fable"

(1993) harkens back to Schwartz the "Jewbird" in Bernard Malamud's 1963 tale of Jewish-American self-loathing and assimilation. At the same time, the versification of the poem suggests an homage to **Osip Mandelstam**'s "Say, desert geometer, shaper . . . " (1933; in this anthology).

Brodsky followed in Osip Mandelstam's footsteps by coopting into his Judeo-Christian heritage the world of (pagan) classical antiquity. Many of Brodsky's poems, especially the "Nativity" cycle, project a Christian outlook comparable with that of **Boris Pasternak**, although devoid of self-hating complexes. Shadows of Pasternak's (apostatic) devotionalism hover over Brodsky's poems, giving them dramatic power but also a greater distance from the Gospel narratives as compared to many poets who were reared Christian (e.g., part 10 of Brodsky's 1971 "Nature Morte"). Some of Brodsky's readers scorn his less than reverent attitude toward Russian Orthodoxy (e.g., Brodsky's 1986 "Performance"). Loseff conceded that Brodsky's "[. . .] treatment of Christian subjects was tinged with agnosticism, being irreverent, even blasphemous." Brodsky regarded with mocking irony the converts to Russian Orthodoxy among Soviet Jews of his generation.

The title of Shimon Markish's essay about Brodsky—"'Jew and Hellene'? 'Neither Jew nor Hellene'?: Of Brodsky's Religiosity"—captured the Jewish critic's hesitancy. Brodsky's discursive attitudes toward his Jewishness are ambivalent and self-contradictory, in places betraying his irritation with attempts to assign him a predictable identity. "I have not exactly been mishandled, but I've had my cup to drink with the Jews since I came to the West, and I resent this," Helen Benedict reported Brodsky saying in a 1985 profile. "Westerners can't really swallow properly that in Russia, Christianity and Judaism are not divorced that much. Whatever happened to Jesus is somehow prefigured by the prophets. In a sense, we are more scholars of both testaments than worshipers—or, at least, I am." "On the whole, I'd rather not resort to any formal religious rite or service," Brodsky told Sven Birkerts. "I'm a little bit opposed to that kind of grocery store psychology which underlies Christianity. [. . .] I would go for the Old Testament God who punishes—[Birkerts interrupts:] Irrationally—No, arbitrarily [. . .]. In that respect I think I'm more of a Jew than any Jew in Israel." "And how did you, author of [. . .] 'Jewish graveyard near Leningrad . . . ,' come to Christianity?" the Parisian Russian émigré journalist Vitaly Amursky asked Brodsky in 1990. "Everything depends on how narrowly or broadly one understands Christianity [. . .]," Brodsky responded. Brodsky's knowledge of Judaism hardly extended beyond reading the Hebrew Bible in

Russian and English translations. After having lived and taught in the post–Vatican II West for many years, Brodsky seemed undeterred in his statements by centuries of Christian supercessionism.

The question of Brodsky's penchant for Christianity comes up in Solomon Volkov's *Conversations with Joseph Brodsky* (English publication 1998). "In conversation with [Anna Akhmatova], or simply drinking tea or vodka with her, you became a Christian, a human being in the Christian sense of that word, faster than by reading the appropriate texts or attending church." What did Brodsky mean when he said "you became a Christian"? In 1989, Anatoly Nayman told Valentina Polukhina, "In the words 'Christian culture' I stress 'Christian,' because in Christianity there are matters more important than culture. And I say '*Christian* culture.' At the same time, it seems to me, Joseph says: 'Christian *culture*.'"

Consider a fascinating published conversation between Isaiah Berlin and Diana Abaeva-Myers: Berlin asked, "Did [Brodsky] believe in God or not?" Myers answered, "I think not, in the conventional sense. [. . .] In Christ, in that which stands behind it, he believed absolutely." Berlin asked, "But he did not take baptism, did he?" Myers answered, "No. But he inscribed a book for me 'from a Christian by correspondence.' [. . .] But taking baptism for him would have been violence over nature [. . .]." "And why, do you think, did he avoid Israel?" Myers asked Berlin. "He simply did not want to belong to any community," Berlin replied. "[. . .] he didn't want to be a Jewish Jew. To be surrounded by Jews, tormented by Jewish thoughts, to be thinking about Jewish problems—that was not for him."

* * *

Two prominent Jewish references in Brodsky's early poems are concerned with death. The first occurs in "Jewish graveyard near Leningrad . . ." (1958, pub. abroad in 1965), where Brodsky described the Jewish Preobrazhenskoe Cemetery, built in the early 1900s outside St. Petersburg. A number of Jewish men and women who had glorified Russian culture were buried there, including the Vilna-born sculptor Mark (Mordechai) Antokolsky (1843–1902). The second Jewish reference, in the poem "I'm not asking death for immortality . . ." (ca. 1961, pub. 1992), brings to mind the ending of Alexander Pushkin's "As I wander down noisy streets . . ." (1829), with its intimation of mortality: "And where will fate send me death?/In battle, in my wanderings, among waves?/Or will the neighboring valley/Receive my cold dust? // And although it is all the same to the unfeeling body/ Wherever it may rot,/Yet nearer to my dear haunts/I would like to rest. // And at the entrance to the grave/ I want young life to be at play,/And let indifferent nature/Shine with everlasting beauty." Reading young Brodsky's unfulfilled prophesy about his "Jewish grave" brings unwanted tears to the eyes of his many Jewish readers.

* * *

Jewish graveyard near Leningrad.
Crooked fence of rotten plywood.
Behind the fence lie side by side
lawyers, merchants, musicians, and revolutionaries.

For themselves they were singing.
For themselves building savings.
For others they were dying.
But first they paid taxes,
respected policemen
and, in this hopelessly material world,
interpreted Talmud, remaining idealists.

Maybe they saw more.
Or perhaps their faith was blind.
But they taught their children to be tolerant
and to be persistent
And they did not sow grain.
They never sowed grain.
They simply laid themselves
in the cold soil like grain.
And went to sleep forever.
They were covered with soil,
candles were lit for them,
and on the Day of Remembrance
hungry old men wheezing from the cold
were shouting in high voices about eternal calm.
And they achieved it
in the form of decaying matter.

Remembering nothing.
Forgetting nothing.
Behind the crooked fence of rotten plywood
two and a half miles from the end of the tram line.

1958

* * *

I'm not asking death for immortality,
Frightened, beloved, beggarly,
but with every day I live, I breathe
with greater pluck, warmth, and purity.

How broad the embankments seem to me.
How cold, windy, and eternal.
And the clouds gleaming in the window
are broken, airy, and ephemeral.

And I won't die in summer or fall—
the winter sheet won't stir.
a mere thread burns between me and life.
look, my love, there in the sunlit corner.

And something like a spider who has been stepped on
runs curiously in and out of me,
but my exhalations and my gestures
hang in the space between time and me.

Yes. I shout about my fate to time
louder and louder in sad defiance.
Yes. I make myself aware of time
but time answers me with silence.

Fly in through the window and quiver in flame!
fly down to the wick of the greedy candle.
Whistle for me, river! Bell, toll for me,
my Petersburg, my firebell.

Let time be silent about me.
Let the sharp wind weep easily.
and over my Jewish grave,
let young life shout persistently.

ca. 1961

Translated from the Russian by Joanna Trzeciak

VLADIMIR BRITANISHSKY

Vladimir Britanishsky (1933–2015), poet, translator, and prose writer, was born in Leningrad (now St. Petersburg), the son of a Jewish father, the painter Lev Britanishsky, and a Polish mother. Evacuated from Leningrad, Britanishsky spent the war in Siberia and the Urals, where he began to write. In 1946, his poem "Rocks" won a contest and appeared in *Campfire* (*Koster*), a magazine for teenagers.

In 1951–56, Britanishsky studied at the Leningrad Mining Institute, which had an active literary seminar (*lito*), its poet-members including geology and mining students Leonid Ageev, Aleksandr Gorodnitsky, and Oleg Tarutin, as well as Gleb Gorbovsky, **Aleksandr Kushner**, and Nina Korolyova, who were students elsewhere. The seminar leader, appointed by the Leningrad branch of the Union of Soviet Writers, was the poet Gleb Semyonov (1918–1982), who preached a rhetoric of compromise with Soviet ideology. By romanticizing professional experiences (e.g., travel to remote geological sites), a number of Semyonov's mentees successfully published during Khrushchev's Thaw, whereas some of their Leningrad peers had a hard if not impossible time breaking in. (In Thaw-era Moscow, the poet Grigory Levin [1917–1994], leader of the "Magistral" *lito*, played a role similar to Semyonov's.) Britanishsky remembered Semyonov as a "unique Teacher" and "spiritual father." "This Be the Verse" (1971) by Philip Larkin comes to mind in connection with the role Semyonov played in the careers of his disciples: "They fuck you up, your mom and dad./They may not mean to, but they do./They fill you with the faults they had/And add some extra, just for you. // But they were fucked in their turn [. . .]." It is hard to judge postfactually how Britanishsky's career would have turned out had he, as a young poet, not learned to harness his own talent.

Britanishsky's poems appeared in the Leningrad monthly *Star* (*Zvezda*) in 1955 and in the Moscow review *Young Guard* (*Molodaia gvardiia*) in 1956, alongside poems by other "geologists." Considered one of the most promising young Leningrad poets in the mid- to late 1950s, Britanishsky benefited from the patronage of the poet-translator David Dar and his wife, the well-known novelist Vera Panova, and from the support of **Boris Slutsky** in Moscow. Still, when Britanishsky's first collection, *Searches* (1958), came out, it was harshly criticized in *Leningrad Pravda* (*Leningradskaia pravda*) as a warning to other liberalizing poets.

In 1958, Britanishsky married Natalia Astafieva (1922–2016), a Warsaw-born Russian poet and translator from the Polish, whose remarkably original voice is yet to be discovered in the west. Astafieva's poems first appeared in 1956, through the efforts of **Ilya Selvinsky**. The daughter of prominent Polish Communists (her father, Jerzy Czeszejko-Sochacki, was purged in the USSR in 1933; her mother survived the gulag and returned to Poland in 1959), Astafieva has remained faithful to her parents' ideals—both in life and in her poetry.

In 1956–60, Britanishsky worked as a geologist in Siberia, where Astafieva joined him; their daughter Marina was born in 1959. Settling in Moscow, Britanishsky was accepted into the Union of Soviet Writers in 1961, the year his second collection, *Natasha*, was published. The third, *Ways of Transportation* (literally "ways of connection"), appeared in 1966. Britanishsky participated in geological expeditions until 1973. His book of fiction, *Environs of Last Summer*, appeared in 1969. A hiatus of twelve years reflected difficulties Britanishsky experienced with his fourth collection, *Open Space* (Moscow, 1980). The verses in *Open Space* signal an underlying passive aggressiveness, as though the poet is clenching his teeth while composing and "correcting" under pressure from Brezhnevite censors. Britanishsky's other poetry books include *Movement of Time* (Moscow, 1985) and *Old Photographs* (Moscow, 1993). In 2003, a large volume of his poetry, fiction, and essays appeared in his native St. Petersburg. Britanishsky edited and cotranslated two anthologies: *Contemporary Polish Poetry* (1979) and *Polish Poets of the Twentieth Century* (with Natalia Astafieva, 2000). His collected essays on Polish poetry, *The Words of Polish Poets*, and a bilingual volume of Britanishsky and Astafieva's poems in Russian and in Polish translation, *Two-Voice* (*Dwugłos/Dvuglas*), were published in 2005. A translator of American poetry since the early 1950s (Langston Hughes), Britanishsky has splendidly rendered Wallace Stevens in Russian. A volume of Britanishsky's selected works, *One Hundred Poems*, came out in 2013 in Moscow.

Time and silence have preserved Britanishsky's verse—a museum of the late 1950s through the early 1960s. Britanishsky's recent poems are nostalgic lamentations: "I rarely visit Nowaburg,/Thengrad I visited more often . . . ." His peers, notably **Evgeny Reyn**, who had difficulty publishing in the Soviet period, had overtaken Britanishsky, who acknowledged his displacement in post-Soviet history: "In the middle of the night phone, just returned from Jerusalem,/my pal, a poet, he flies, he's a laureate./Night has diminished the heat, but it didn't promise cool,/it was stuffy in Moscow, I was old and winged no more. // And where can I fly! Not southward, to Holy Land./Nor to Warsaw [. . .] My beloved sleeps near me. She's all I'm not sick of/ In this life. She and also Petersburg-Leningrad [. . .]." Vladimir Britanishsky died in December 2015 in Moscow. His beloved wife and muse, Natalia Astafieva, outlived him by less than a year.

* * *

A half-Jewish, half-Polish Russian poet, Vladimir Britanishsky examines his identity through two lenses: internationalism and autobiographical truth. In the poem "Mixed Marriage" (1990), he reminisces about the 1940s: "'Anyone in a mixed marriage will be spared,' my father said, about the Poles, as I overheard./ My mother, ready for the camps, never despaired./ I didn't ask what he meant but marked his word,/ those eight words he so confidently declared. // That time we got by: they didn't touch us in Leningrad./ My mother, a Pole from Gatchina, was left alone./ Poles, I beg your forgiveness, in the name of God,/ that in that year of disaster I was safe on my own. // 'Anyone in a mixed marriage will be spared,' my mother said, about the Jews, as I apprehended./ My father, ready for the camps, never despaired/ but was almost eager: sooner started, sooner ended. // That time we got by, they spared him: Stalin died [. . .]" (trans. Shrayer & Sisson). The poem included below, "A German Girl," dates to Britanishsky's youth and the Thaw and was not published until the 1990s. Britanishsky included it in his collection *Old Photographs* (1993), a post-Soviet family album with poems and photos preserved and printed—side by side.

A GERMAN GIRL[7]

The poster ordered, "Kill a German!"
A German, yes. Hate. Plain as day.
When you're exterminating vermin,
hatred is morally okay.

The village wolf-wind howled at night.
The prowling wolves were fierce and cruel.
A Volga girl faced a rough plight,
a German in a Russian school.

---

7   The "German girl" in Britanishsky's poem comes from a family of the so-called Volga
    Germans. The ancestors of the Volga Germans, thousands of them, moved to the Russian
    Empire from Germany in the 1760s during the rule of Catherine the Great. They founded
    agricultural settlements in the lower Volga basin. They left Germany in the wake of the
    Seven-Year War, fleeing the devastated countryside. The Volga German settlers sought
    religious freedom and better economic opportunities. They became part of Russia and
    regarded it as their true home while retaining their language and traditions much the way
    the Amish have in the United States. (In the 1780s, the Mennonites from West Prussia
    moved to Russia and founded "colonies" in Taurida Province on the Black Sea coast; in the
    1890s, as land in the Volga region became scarce, German settlements were also founded in
    Turkmenistan and Siberia.) Following the Bolshevik Revolution and the civil war, in 1924,
    an autonomous Volga-German Republic was founded, with Engels, a city across the Volga
    from Saratov, as its capital and German as its official language. Another major Volga-German
    city, upstream from Engels, was renamed Marks. In the 1930s, during the period of collec-
    tivization, private farms, the backbone of the Volga Germans' economic and social life, were
    rooted out. By the end of the 1930s, most of the Volga German clergy had been purged and
    the churches closed. Soon after Hitler's Germany invaded the Soviet Union in 1941, an offi-
    cial decree of banishment of the Autonomous Republic of the Volga Germans was issued.
    About 400,000 Volga Germans were rounded up in September 1941 and deported in train
    convoys to remote areas of Kazakhstan and to West Siberia, many of them dying en route to
    exile. (Soviet textbooks said nothing about the mass deportation, a tragedy whose American
    parallel is the internment of Japanese-Americans during World War II.) In the 1970s, the
    descendants of the Germans of the Soviet Union, now mainly living in Kazakhstan and also
    in West Siberia, began to apply for exit visas to Germany, in accordance with Germany's Law
    of Return, and the numbers of the ethnic Germans "returning" to Germany from the former
    USSR had reached massive proportions in the 1990s, peaking in 1995 at about 210,000.

Her eyes were always clear and steady.
She walked at a deliberate pace.
Whatever happened, she was ready,
and we could see her stubborn grace.

She was so dignified and frank
and calm yet firm, a German trait,
that any silly schoolboy prank
would suddenly evaporate.

In '42 and '43,
during the second and third grade,
we pondered that authority
and self-possession she displayed.

And I admired in later years
this German girl I hardly knew,
when hassled by my teenage peers
after they learned I was a Jew.

That slap in the face was a shock . . .
So from that time I'd always care
about the way she used to walk,
about the way she'd braid her hair.

1957–58

Translated from the Russian by Maxim D. Shrayer and J. B. Sisson

YULY DANIEL

Yuly Daniel (1925–1988), fiction writer, translator, and poet, was born in Moscow. His father was the Yiddish writer M. Daniel (Mark Meirovich, 1900–1940). Daniel was drafted in 1943 but was then injured and discharged in 1944. He entered Kharkov University in 1946. In Kharkov, Daniel met the would-be dissident Larisa Bogoraz, and their son Aleksandr was born in 1951. (The marriage disintegrated in the late 1960s.) After graduating from the Moscow Regional Pedagogical Institute in 1951, Daniel taught language and literature in schools in Kaluga Province and Moscow.

In 1956, Daniel devoted himself full time to literary work. His short novel *The Flight* was published by Detskii mir Publishing House in Moscow but was banned from being sold. Daniel's translations, chiefly from the languages of the Caucasus, Slavic languages, and Yiddish, appeared in the 1950s and 1960s. In the 1950s, Daniel befriended Andrey Sinyavsky (1925–1997), a critic who worked at the Institute of World Literature. In the 1950s–60s, Sinyavsky wrote anti-Soviet fiction (e.g., *The Trial Begins* [published 1960] and *Lyubimov* [published 1964]) and criticism (e.g., *What Is Socialist Realism?* published 1959), which appeared abroad under the pen name Abram Terz. Between 1956 and 1964, Daniel composed four works of fiction, which Sinyavsky helped smuggle out of the USSR to be published abroad. Abram Terz, the pen name of Andrey Sinyavsky, who was not Jewish, was deliberately Jewish, whereas Nikolay Arzhak, the pen name Yuly Daniel had chosen, sounded expressly non-Jewish. Subverting cultural stereotypes, the two writers had committed a partial identity trade.

Daniel paid a heavy price for a small corpus of fiction. The short story "Hands" (1956–57, published 1963)—a precursor of several works by the Third-Wave émigré writer Yuz Aleshkovsky (b. 1929)—tells of a former proletarian working as a secret-police executioner. The novella *A Man from M.I.S.P.,* Daniel's most humorous work, betrays the influence of Mikhail Zoshchenko and **Ilya Ilf–Evgeny Petrov**. The abbreviation M.I.S.P. stands for "Moscow Institute for Scientific Profanation," and Daniel's protagonist claims he can determine the sex of his offspring by concentrating, during intercourse, on the image of either Karl Marx or Clara Zetkin (notably, both German revolutionaries of Jewish descent). Excerpted below, Daniel's *This Is Moscow Speaking* appeared in book form in 1962, in Washington, DC. His short novel *The Atonement* (1964) explored the problem of collective responsibility—and complicity—of the generation that had lived through Stalinist political terror. The political significance of Daniel's (and Sinyavsky's) fiction of the 1950s–60s exceeded its artistic merits.

Identified as Abram Terz and Nikolay Arzhak, Sinyavsky and Daniel were arrested in September 1965 and tried on 10–14 February 1966 in Moscow. The smear campaign in the press and the trial itself were striated with antisemitism, not only because of Sinyavsky's Jewish pen name and Daniel's Jewishness but also because both wrote about the Jewish question. Accused of anti-Soviet propaganda, Sinyavsky and Daniel pleaded not guilty, insisting they were constitutionally guaranteed a right to free speech. Sinyavsky was sentenced to seven and Daniel to five years of hard labor. Protests against the trial and the verdict sprung up abroad and in the USSR. A letter of sixty-two Soviet writers was submitted to the presidium of the Twenty-Third Congress of the Communist Party and the presidium of the Supreme Soviet. The signatories included **Pavel Antokolsky, Ilya Ehrenburg, Veniamin Kaverin,** and **Viktor Shklovsky**. Two years after the **Joseph Brodsky** trial, the Soviet authorities used the trial of Sinyavsky and Daniel to dispatch a clear message to the artistic community.

Daniel served his sentence in the Dubravlag labor camp in Mordovia and at the Vladimir prison. Arnold McMillin described Daniel's prison poems, published in the West in 1969–71, as a "combination of conventional Russian strophic forms with typically Jewish barbed humorous cadences." Daniel was released in September 1970, lived in Kaluga, and was later permitted to return to Moscow. (After being released in 1971, Sinyavsky emigrated in 1973. Sinyavsky enjoyed a successful career while living in France; he died in Paris in 1997. In their duet, Yuly Daniel played the part of Art Garfunkel to Sinyavsky's Paul Simon.)

Daniel's translations, signed Yu. Petrov, began to appear in the USSR in 1972–73; the new pen name was a condition set by the KGB. In November 1988, the Moscow magazine *Youth* (*Iunost'*) published *The Atonement*, legitimizing Yuly Daniel a month before he died in Moscow. Daniel's prose, poetry, translations, and prison letters have appeared in post-Soviet Russia.

* * *

"You asked me why I wrote the short novel *This Is Moscow Speaking*" Daniel said at the trial. "[. . .] Because I felt a real threat of a rebirth of [Stalin's] cult of personality [. . .]." In 1962, Daniel made the Jewish question a dimension of his absurd(ist) similacrum of Soviet reality, because a decade after the events of the Doctors' Plot, visions of state-sponsored pogroms continued to loom in the historical imagination of Soviet Jews.

FROM *THIS IS MOSCOW SPEAKING*[*]

1

When I now try to reconstruct in my mind the events of the past year, I find it very difficult to put my memories in order or to give a coherent and consistent account of everything I saw, heard, and felt; but the day when *it* began I remember very well, down to the minutest detail, down to the merest trifle.

We were sitting in the garden at the *dacha*. We had all arrived the night before to celebrate Igor's birthday; we had drunk a great deal, made a lot of noise into the early hours, and finally gone to bed in complete certainty that we would not wake up until midday; the suburban tranquility, however, woke us up at seven o'clock. We got up and all began doing all sorts of absurd things: we ran about the lanes in our boxers, did exercises on the beam (no one was able to pull himself up more than five times), and Volodya Margulis even doused himself with water from the well, although everyone knew that he never washed in the mornings, making the excuse that he would be late for work.

We sat around and argued vehemently on the best way to spend a Sunday. Swimming, volley-ball, and boating were naturally among the activities mentioned, and one misguided enthusiast even suggested a cross-country walk to the church in the next village.

"It's a very nice church," he said. "A very old one, I don't remember which century..."

But everybody laughed at him—no one felt like dragging their feet five miles in the heat.

We probably looked rather strange—men and women in their thirties undressed as though for the beach. We tactfully tried not to notice all sorts of unexpected things about each other, both amusing and depressing: hollow chests and incipient bald spots in the case of the men, and hairy legs and no waists in the case of the women. We had all known each other for a long time, and were familiar with each other's suits, ties, and dresses, but no one had imagined how we would look without clothes, in a state of nature [...].

We sat with our backsides glued to the chairs, which looked so pathetic on the grass, and talked about our forthcoming athletic feats. Suddenly Lilya appeared on the terrace.

---

[*]   The text has been abridged.

"Guys," she said, "I just don't understand it."

"And what exactly are you supposed to understand? Come and join us."

"I just don't understand it," she repeated, smiling plaintively. "Over the radio . . . they broadcast it over the radio . . . I only heard the end . . . it will be broadcast again in ten minutes' time."

"The latest reduction—the twenty-first so far—in the prices of horsecollars and harnesses," said Volodya, mimicking an announcer's low-pitched voice . . .

"Let's go inside," said Lilya. "Please."

We all trooped into the room where a square plastic loudspeaker was hanging modestly on a nail. In reply to our puzzled questions Lilya did nothing but sigh.

"Steamboatlike sighs," joked Volodya. "That's a good metaphor, isn't it? As good as something out of Ilf and Petrov."[8]

"Lilya, stop pulling our legs," began Igor. "I realize you find it boring washing the dishes by yourself . . ."

At this moment the radio began speaking.

"This is Moscow speaking," it said. "We are now broadcasting a Decree of the Supreme Soviet of the Union of Soviet Socialist Republics, dated July 16, 1960. In view of the increased well-being . . ."

I looked around. Everybody was standing quietly listening to the reverberating baritone of the announcer; only Lilya bustled about like a photographer trying to take a picture of children, and made beckoning signs in the direction of the loudspeaker.

". . . in response to the wishes of the masses of working people . . ."

"Volodya, please give me a match," said Zoya. They all hissed at her. She shrugged her shoulders and, dropping the unlit cigarette into the palm of her hand, turned away toward the window . . .

". . . Sunday, August 10, 1960, is declared . . ."

"Here it comes!" cried Lilya.

". . . Public Murder Day. On that day all citizens of the Soviet Union who have attained the age of sixteen are given the right of free extermination of any other citizen with the exception of persons mentioned in the first paragraph of the addendum to this Decree. The Decree comes into force on August 10, 1960, at 6 A.M. Moscow time, and expires at midnight. Paragraph

---

8 Famous Soviet satirists, in this anthology.

one. Murder of the following categories is prohibited: (*a*) children under six-
teen; (*b*) persons dressed in the uniform of the Armed Forces or the Militia;
and (*c*) transport workers engaged in the execution of their duties. Paragraph
two. Murders committed prior to or subsequent to the above-mentioned
period and murders committed for purposes of gain or resulting from sexual
assault on a woman will be regarded as a criminal offense and punished in
accordance with the existing laws. Moscow. The Kremlin. Chairman of the
Presidium of the Supreme . . .”

Then the radio said:

“We will now broadcast a concert of light music . . .”

We stood and looked at one another in a daze.

“Extraordinary,” I said, “most extraordinary. I can’t see the point.”

“They’ll explain it,” said Zoya. “The newspapers are bound to have an
explanation.”

“Comrades, it’s a trick!” Igor was prancing around the room looking for his
shirt. “It’s a trick. It’s the Voice of America broadcasting on our wave length!”

He hopped up and down on one foot, drawing on his pants.

“Oh, sorry!” he ran out into the terrace and buttoned up his fly. No one
was amused.

“The ‘Voice of America,’” said Volodya thoughtfully. “No, it’s not possible.
It’s not technically possible. After all,” and he looked at his watch, “it’s half past
nine. There are broadcasts going on. If they were operating on our wave length
we’d hear both broadcasts . . .”

We went outside again. Half-naked people began appearing on the ter-
races of neighboring *dachas*. They huddled together in groups, shrugging their
shoulders and waving their arms in confusion.

Zoya lit her cigarette at last. She sat down on a step resting her elbows on
her knees. I looked at her hips in the tight-fitting bathing suit, and at her breasts
half revealed by the low-cut top. Despite her plumpness, she was very attrac-
tive. More so than any of the other women. As always, her expression was calm
and rather sleepy. Behind her back they used to call her “Madame Phlegmatic.”

Igor was fully dressed and, contrasted with the rest of us, looked like a mis-
sionary among Polynesians. Ever since Volodya had categorically asserted that
the radio announcement could not have been a trick played by transatlantic
gangsters, he had become subdued. He evidently regretted the fact that he had
dismissed the broadcast so lightly, but in my opinion he had nothing to worry
about. There were not supposed to be any stooges among us.

"What are we getting excited about, anyway?" he said cheerfully. "Zoya is right. There'll be an explanation. Tolya, what do you think?"

"Damned if I know," I mumbled. "There's still almost a month left before this, what's it called, Public..."

I broke off. We stared at each other again in dismay.

"I know," said Igor with a shake of the head, "it's all connected with international politics."

"With the presidential elections in America, is that what you mean, Igor?"

"Damn it, Lilya, you just keep quiet about the whole thing. You're talking God-knows what!"

"Let's go for a swim," said Zoya, getting up. "Tolya, could you bring me my bathing cap?"

It seemed that the confusion had shaken even her, or she wouldn't have called me "Tolya" in front of everyone. But apparently no one noticed.

As we were going toward the river, Volodya came up to me, took me by the arm, and said, looking at me forlornly with his Biblical eyes:

"You know, Tolya, I think they're plotting something against the Jews..."

2

And so here I'm writing all this down and wondering exactly why I needed to make these notes. I shall never be able to have them published here; there's no one to whom I can even read them or show them. Should I send them abroad? No: first, it's practically next to impossible, and second, what I intend to describe has already been reported in hundreds of newspapers abroad, and the radio has filled the air with it for days and nights; no, they've already done it to death abroad. Anyway, to tell the truth, to be printed abroad in anti-Soviet publications is not so good.

I'm pretending. I know why I'm writing. I want to find out for myself what happened. And, more important, what happened to me. Here I am, sitting at my desk. I'm thirty-five. I'm still working in this ridiculous technical publishing house. My appearance has not changed. Nor my tastes. I like poetry just as much as ever. I like to have a drink. I like chicks, and on the whole they like me. I fought in the war; I killed. I was nearly killed myself. Whenever women suddenly reach out to touch the scar on my hip, they draw back their hands and say in a shocked whisper: "Good heavens, what's that?" "It's a wound," I say, "from a dumdum bullet." "Poor boy," they say, "did it hurt very much?" Generally speaking, everything is as before. Any one of my acquaintances, friends, or colleagues might easily say: "Well, Tolya, you haven't changed a bit!" But I know only too well that Public Murder Day grabbed me by the scruff of my neck and made me look into myself! I know that I had to get to know myself all over again!

And there's another thing. I'm not a writer. In my youth I wrote poetry, and I still do on special occasions; I've written a few reviews of plays. I thought that I would gain a foothold in the literary world that way; but nothing came of it. Nevertheless, I still write. No, I don't suffer from graphomania. Those who do (and in my profession I often come across them) are convinced of their own genius, but I know I have little or no talent. But I really want to write. After all, what is the great thing about the position I'm in? It's that I know in advance that no one will read me, and I can write without fear whatever comes into my head! If I want to write:

And like black Africa the piano
Bares its negroid teeth,

I do. But no one will accuse me of expressing pretentious or colonialist ideas. If I want to write and say that in the government they're all rabble-rousers, phonies, and mostly, sons of bitches, I do so . . . I can afford the luxury of being a communist when alone with myself.

If I'm to be completely frank, however, I still hope that I'll have readers—not now, of course, but in many, many years' when I shall no longer be alive [. . .]. Well, now that I have revealed myself to my imaginary readers, I can continue.

We just weren't able to have any fun that day. Our jokes fell flat, we got bored playing games, didn't have anything to drink, and broke up early. The next day in Moscow I went to work. I knew in advance that there would be an inevitable commotion about the Decree and that some would express their opinions while others would keep quiet. But to my surprise almost everyone kept quiet. True, two or three people asked me what I thought about it all. I muttered something to the effect that I didn't know and we would have to wait and see, and the conversation ended there.

A day later a long editorial entitled "In Preparation for Public Murder Day" appeared in *Izvestia*. It made very little mention of the reason for the measure, but repeated the usual jumble of expressions, such as "increased well-being" . . . "tremendous advances" . . . "true democracy" . . . "only in our country" . . . "all our aspirations" . . . "for the first time in history" . . . "visible signs" . . . "bourgeois press" . . . It further stated that no damage should be done to public property and that therefore arson and bombing were prohibited. The Decree, moreover, did not cover persons serving sentences in jail. So there you are. The article was read and reread, but no one understood it any better, although people became somehow calmer. The actual style of the article, its routine solemnity and prosaic pomposity, probably reassured people. There was nothing special about it. After all, we had "Artillery Day" and "Soviet Press Day," so why not "Public Murder Day"? . . . Public transportation would be operating and the police were not to be harmed—that meant everything was in order.

Ten or so days passed like that. Then something began which is difficult to describe in words. There was a kind of strange agitation and unrest. No, I can't find the right words! Everyone became fidgety and began rushing around. In the subways, in movie houses, and on the streets people kept going up to each other, smiling obsequiously, and striking up conversations about their ailments, fishing, the quality of nylon stockings—in short, about anything at all. And provided they were not suddenly interrupted by their listeners, they shook their hands for a long time, looking gratefully and searchingly into their eyes [. . .].

An absolutely astronomical number of jokes went around; Volodya Margulis hurried from one friend to another, telling them and hooting with laughter. Having exhausted his entire supply on me, he reported that Igor had said at a meeting in his college that August 10th was the result of the Party's wise policy, that the Decree reconfirmed the development of the creative initiative of the popular masses, and so on, and so on in the usual vein.

"You know something, Tolya?" he said. "I knew Igor was a careerist and all that, but I didn't expect this of him."

"Why not?" I asked. "What's so special about it? He was told to make a speech, and he did. If you were a Party member like Igor, you would have reeled one off, too."

"Me? Never! First, I wouldn't join the Party for anything, and, second . . ."

"First, second! Stop shouting! Are you really any better than Igor? Didn't you jabber about nationalism at school during the Doctors' Plot?"

I said it, and was immediately sorry I had. It was a sore point with him. He couldn't forgive himself the fact that he had believed the newspapers for a while.

"I'd rather hear how you're getting along with Nina," I said more amiably. "How long since you've seen her?"

Volodya brightened up.

"You know, Tolya, it's not easy to love," he said. "It's not easy. I called her yesterday and said I wanted to see her, but she answered . . ."

And Volodya began describing in detail what she had answered, what he had said to her, and what they both said.

"Tolya, you know me; I'm not the sentimental type, but I almost burst into tears..."

I listened to him and wondered how people manage to create problems out of nothing. Volodya was married and had two children. He taught literature in a school better than anyone in his district and was in every way a bright fellow. But oh, his love affairs! It's true his wife was a bitch; you'd leave a wife like that for any woman. Well, O.K., who cares how often he did it? But what was the point of all the suffering, the transports of passion, and the small-town Hamlet act? And such expressions as "moral obligations," "divided loyalties," and "she believes in me"... Besides, "she believes in me" is said both of this wife and the latest heartthrob [...].

Volodya talked for another half hour about his complicated love life and went away. I showed him out, but he immediately rang the bell again, put his head through the half-open door, and said in a whisper so the neighbors wouldn't hear:

"Tolya, if there is a pogrom on August tenth, I'm going to fight. This isn't going to be another Babi Yar for them. I'll shoot the swine. Just wait and see!" And opening his jacket, he showed me the butt of an officer's TT pistol sticking out of his inside pocket; he had kept it since his army days.

"They won't take me easily..."

When he had finally left, I stood for some time in the middle of the room. Who were "they"? [...]

1961

Translated from the Russian by John Richardson

EMMANUIL KAZAKEVICH

Emmanuil Kazakevich (1913–1962), poet, fiction writer, essayist, and translator, was born in Kremenchug (now in Poltava Province, Ukraine), a commerce and trade center about half of whose residents before the Shoah were Jewish, and grew up in Kiev. Kazakevich's father was the Yiddish author Khenekh (Genrikh) Kazakevich (1883–1936), a Bolshevik since 1919, who edited the Soviet Yiddish magazine *The Red World* (*Di royte velt*) and later the Jewish-Ukrainian daily *The Star* (*Der Shtern*). As a young man, Kazakevich met Yiddish writers, including Perets Markish, Dovid Hofshteyn, and Leyb Kvitko, in his father's house. Kazakevich debuted as a Yiddish author in Kharkov, where he graduated from a technical college in 1931. Kazakevich moved to the Soviet Far East with his parents (on the Jewish Autonomous Region, see **Viktor Fink**). At a young age he held administrative positions in Birobidzhan, including the chairmanship of the collective farm Valdhaim and the directorship of the Birobidzhan Drama Theater. Kazakevich wrote for *The Birobidzhan Star* (*Der Birobidzhaner Shtern*), which his father edited, and the publication, in 1932 in Birobidzhan in Yiddish, of Kazakevich's *Birobidzhanboy* (*Birobidzhan Construction*, with a possible play on the Russian word *boy* = battle, which would also suggest *Birobidzhan Battle*) established his reputation. A volume of Kazakevich's translations of Vladimir Mayakovsky appeared in 1934; he also translated into Yiddish works by Pushkin, Lermontov, Heine, Balzac, and Soviet authors. Kazakevich moved to Moscow in 1938 and published several other books in Yiddish, including *Large World* (1939—songs, poems, and tales) and *Sholem and Khave* (1941, a novel in verse), all released by Moscow's publisher Der Emes ("Truth").

Kazakevich volunteered for the front in July 1941. He was decorated for valor and rose from private to captain, finishing the war in Berlin in 1945 as deputy chief of the Forty-Seventh Army Intelligence Unit. In 1942, he joined the Communist Party. Kazakevich switched to Russian (the leading Soviet-Yiddish writers would be executed in 1952). Published in 1947 in *Banner*, the short novel *Star* (about military intelligence) put Kazakevich on the larger literary map, earning him a Stalin Prize (1948). The Yiddish version, titled *Grine shonts* (Green Shadows), appeared in 1947 in Moscow. In 1948, *Star* appeared in Hebrew as *Ben kokhav la-hadamah* (literally *The Son of a Star of the Earth*), translated by Shimshon Nahmani, the translator of **Ilya Ehrenburg**'s *The*

Storm. Kazakevich's short novels *Two in the Steppe* (1948, his personal favorite) and *Heart of a Friend* (1953) were criticized, "naturalism" being one of the charges. Yet for the novel *Spring on the Oder* (1949), Kazakevich received his second Stalin Prize, in 1950.

A prominent figure of the Thaw, in 1956 Kazakevich founded *Literary Moscow* (*Literaturnaia Moskva*), which Margarita Aliger coedited, but after two volumes the publication was derailed. Kazakevich's perfunctorily anti-Stalinist novel *House on the Square* (1956) depicted the overwrought postwar atmosphere in the Soviet military. Kazakevich's fame continued to spread across the Yiddish-speaking world, and in 1957 *House on the Square* appeared in Yiddish in Buenos Aires. (In 1950, *Spring on the Oder* had been published in Yiddish in Montevideo, Uruguay.)

During the Thaw, Kazakevich turned to what he called his "main theme": Lenin. Kazakevich's short novel *The Blue Notebook* (1958) appeared in the April 1961 issue of *October*, only after Kazakevich appealed to Khrushchev. Waxing sentimental about the founder of the Soviet state, *The Blue Notebook* depicted, with poetic license, the period following the "July days" in 1917, when Lenin took refuge in Razliv outside Petrograd, before fleeing to Finland in August 1917. What made *The Blue Notebook* popular during the Thaw was the inclusion, in its historical cast of characters, of Grigory Zinoviev (Radomyslsky, 1883–1936). A leading Bolshevik, Zinoviev returned to Russia in 1917 in the same "sealed car" as Lenin. After Lenin's death in 1924, Stalin, Zinoviev, and Lev Kamenev (Rozenfeld, 1883–1936) formed the so-called "triumvirate." Zinoviev and Kamenev, former members of the defeated Left Opposition, were executed following a 1936 public trial; they were not rehabilitated in the USSR until 1988. While Kazakevich's depiction of Zinoviev was less than flattering, this was, as compared to a complete erasure of this "enemy of the people" from memory, a liberating and restorative gesture.

In his latter years, Kazakevich worked on the unfinished novel *Scream for Help*, about a Jewish ghetto during the Shoah. Returning to Yiddish, in the late 1950s–early 1960s, Kazakevich contributed nonfiction to the Polish-based newspaper *Voice of the People* (*Folksshtime*) and the magazine *Jewish Writing* (*Yidishe shriften*). Kazakevich died in Moscow in 1962, without having witnessed the subsequent crackdown on both Yiddish-Polish periodicals. *Listening to Time*, a volume of Kazakevich's diaries and notebooks, appeared in 1990 in Moscow, edited by his widow Galina Kazakevich.

* * *

Kazakevich's short story "Enemies" (1962) belonged thematically with *The Blue Notebook*, and both appeared a number of times under the same covers, including a 1963 French volume. In "Enemies" (1962), Kazakevich employed the model he had developed in *The Blue Notebook*. Yuly Martov (Tsederbaum, 1873–1923) took Zinoviev's place vis-à-vis Lenin. Martov started his political career as a Bund activist. In 1895, he cofounded, with Lenin, the Union of Struggle for the Liberation of the Working Class. In Switzerland, Martov coedited *Spark* (*Iskra*) with Lenin and Georgy Plekhanov. After developing major differences with Lenin in 1903, in 1905–7 Martov led the Menshevik faction of the Russian Socialist-Democratic Workers' Party. Martov opposed the Bolshevik usurpation of political power, left Soviet Russia in 1920, and died abroad.

According to the critic Anatoly Bocharov, Kazakevich's story fictionalized the circumstances of Martov's emigration by drawing on the experience of a historical Old Bolshevik, S. Shtern-Mikhailova. "Enemies" appeared in *Izvestia* on 21 April 1962, on the eve of Lenin's birthday, in the same issue as Khrushchev's "Leninist" speech at the Fourteenth Congress of the Komsomol. Kazakevich added a clarification in the subsequent editions (the translation below follows this revised text), justifying a degree of poetic license and historical inaccuracy. Martov was not in hiding, as described in the story, and he openly spoke out against the Bolsheviks in April 1920. In July 1920, the Central Committee of the Bolshevik Party allowed Martov and another Menshevik (and former Bund) leader Rafail Abramovich (1880–1963) to leave Soviet Russia; they departed for Berlin in October 1920.

Maurice Friedberg characterized "The Enemies" as a "thinly disguised appeal for tolerance." Indeed, in the context of the Thaw, the story betokened officially sanctioned liberalism, to the extent that Kazakevich mythologized Lenin as a strong leader who had retained a degree of (personal) attachment to Martov, a former comrade turned adversary. One should not overlook the fact that, in light of Lenin's own philosemitism and Jewish roots (his maternal grandfather was born Jewish) and of Martov's own Jewishness, Kazakevich also made the female protagonist of the story Jewish.

ENEMIES

From the author. This story describes a true event. The author merely took the liberty to interpret freely the life of the communist woman who carried out

Lenin's mission, and in so doing he hopes he has not sinned against the spirit and customs of the time.

Yuly Martov did not go abroad in April 1919 but later, in the summer. Apparently, for some of his own factional-Menshevik considerations, he did not want to take advantage of Lenin's offer and left only after he had put in a request for permission to leave, formally addressed to the Comintern but submitted to the Central Committee of the Russian Communist Party (RKP).

I can imagine Lenin's sardonic laugh when he received this "official" request. The applicant knew it would be approved. And it was approved by a decision of the Central Committee taken upon Lenin's insistence.

1

Early one April morning the secretary who had brought Lenin several papers to sign was puzzled by his absent look. Contrary to habit, he did not respond to her greeting, he gave an illogical answer when questioned about some business matter, and only as she was leaving did he seem to snap out of it and stop her by exclaiming, "One moment."

She returned and stopped near the desk, on the left side of which lay a small pile of pages filled with small handwriting, part of an article Lenin had begun the previous day—"'Left-Wing' Communism: An Infantile Disorder," and, on the right, the minutes of the State Commission for the Electrification of Russia, a department of the Supreme Council of the National Economy (VSNKh). The papers she had just brought in for Lenin to sign were in the center of the desk.

Lenin tapped his fingers on the desk in a state of apparent indecisiveness. Then suddenly he asked, "You didn't by chance become acquainted during your years abroad with a certain Sofia Markovna, who I'm told works in the Narkomsobez?"[9]

The secretary vaguely remembered some Sofia Markovna, perhaps from Geneva, perhaps Paris.

"I don't know if she's the same one," the secretary said uncertainly. "Is she a Menshevik?"

"A Menshevik, a Menshevik," Lenin answered quickly. "Precisely. A former one."

"Former?"

---

9   The People's Commissariat for Social Welfare.

"Yes. I was told that half a year ago she joined the RKP. Please ask her to come and see me. This evening, after the meeting of the Sovnarkom,[10] when they're all gone." Then he pleaded with her, "Please don't let anyone see her with me. Do you promise?"

The secretary nodded, a bit more reserved than usual. She was somewhat offended by the secrecy of Lenin's forthcoming meeting with a mysterious person.

That evening, the "person" appeared.

Sofia Markovna was a plump, squat woman, about forty-five years old, who suffered from the early stages of asthma and had short cropped dark hair that stuck up with a slight curl that, along with her thick lips, dark complexion, and coal-black lively eyes, gave her the look of an African. She wore an old beret, which she took off but did not put down, a long black dress, and over that a shabby leather jacket, once black but now practically white.

When she learned that Lenin had sent for her, she had become extremely anxious. She sat down on a chair and every few minutes fired off words of incomprehension and whole tirades of reminiscences aimed at the high ceiling of the secretary's room:

"What's this all about?

"Why does he need to see me?

"Who would have thought it?

"I've known Vladimir Ilich since '02. Maybe '03. Or '02.

"Where did we meet? In Geneva! No, in London. Or maybe in Rome. He attacked me crudely several times in his speeches. And, just imagine, I answered him back the same way. Who could have known that Lenin was— Lenin? It would have taken someone smarter than me to have understood that at the time. And if I had been smarter I would not have wasted the best years of my life with the Mensheviks.

"I wonder what he wants from me? Didn't he tell you anything? In any event, I brought some statistics, a short report on the work of my social-welfare department at the Commissariat. My work is with invalids, you know, provisions for their safety, crutches, wheelchairs, eyeglasses. If you only knew how hard it is. But someone has to do it."

The secretary went out into the reception room and waited by the window. The session had ended. Those asked to attend had rushed off in a mass. Then

---

10   The Council of People's Commissars—then the Soviet cabinet of ministers.

the people's commissars began to leave. Chicherin made an old-fashioned bow to the secretary and minced off toward the exit in a funny and endearing way. Right after him, Stalin came out of the meeting hall. He walked by, morose, without greeting anybody. His tall boots left a smell of leather in the reception room. Next came Tsyurupa and Kursky, who were engaged in a heated conversation, both carrying thick briefcases crammed full of papers. Trotsky, reserved and arrogant, walked past quickly without greeting anyone, his eyes looking straight ahead. Lunacharsky still stood in the doorway, quarreling with Semashko. When he saw the secretary, he remembered he had promised her a complimentary ticket to the Moscow Art Theater, and he immediately wrote the manager a note. Dzerzhinsky had lingered around Lenin longer than the others. When he left, he silently shook the secretary's hand and quickly walked on. The noise died down. One of the guards turned off the light in the hall. It was immediately semidark and deserted. There was a smell of old paper, bay leaves, and mice. The door of the meeting hall opened slowly, and Lenin stood in the doorway.

"Well?"

"She's here," the secretary said, and, returning to her office, she signaled Sofia Markovna to follow her. They walked through the meeting hall; the secretary opened the door to Lenin's office and showed her in.

2

When Sofia Markovna saw Lenin behind the brightly lit rectangle of his desk, she blushed with excitement, and, perhaps in order to conceal this, instead of a normal greeting she blurted out, "Why am I suddenly needed?"

Lenin laughed.

"Are you surprised?" he asked, rising and extending his hand. "I do need you, as you shall see. Have a seat."

After she was seated in a leather chair, he started pacing the room for a while and then sat down at his desk again. The light from the lamp was focused on the desk, and Lenin sat in shade, but Sofia Markovna could still not help noticing how pale and exhausted his face was. It was hard to hold back her dismay, but she didn't speak—quite the opposite—she tried to put on an aloof and even slightly ironic expression.

In the meantime, Lenin leaned back in his chair, fixed his eyes on Sofia Markovna, and asked, "Do you ever see Yuly, Sofia Markovna?"

It was so unexpected that she closed her eyes and, feeling slighted, immediately began to rattle like a cart on a cobblestone road.

"What do you mean, Vladimir Ilich? Don't you know that I've joined the RKP? And that I have nothing to do with the Mensheviks? That I consider Menshevism a stage of the workers' movement that has run its course and one that is over in my own life as well? Do you doubt my sincerity? What am I to think?"

"I don't doubt it in the least," Lenin responded gently. "Please calm down. I would like to entrust you with one matter. You must find out where Yuly is, see him, and give him this message from me. No, no, don't write it down. Memorize it. After all, you're an old revolutionary. A conspirator. And now you and I are taking part in a conspiracy. On Friday at eleven o'clock in the evening, the last—take note, the last—passenger train to Minsk and Warsaw will leave from platform one of Aleksandrovsky Station. The last, because we expect a war with Poland to begin literally in the next few days. That's right, the Poles will begin military actions any day. Our information, unfortunately, is extremely accurate. Needless to say, you should not talk about this to anyone—for now it's a state secret, but that is the situation precisely. Our breathing space has come to an end. So that's the way things are, Sofia Markovna."

He grew silent and then, as if dismissing painful thoughts and even making a dismissive gesture with his hand, he continued.

"So if Yuly wants to, he can board that train, in car number six, seat fifteen. People in the train car will know. And if he doesn't want to, let him stay, that's his business. The Mensheviks are legal here; but—you know this, of course–they are moving at full speed toward establishing an anti-Soviet underground. They've been hiding Yuly, their leader. Under the condition of war and ruin, however, we cannot tolerate an anti-Soviet underground. We will never allow that. In Russia there can only be dictatorship of the proletariat or dictatorship of the capitalists and landowners. With or without the tsar. Whoever comes out against the dictatorship of the proletariat now is coming out for that other dictatorship. Martov is an enemy because he stands against the dictatorship of the proletariat. Don't tell him any of this, of course. It's useless. Just tell him about the train."

Sofia Markovna sat quietly, like a mouse. When Lenin stopped talking, she took the black hat from her lap, put it on, regally pinning it to her hair with a long pin, and stood up.

"Two questions," she said, very businesslike. "First. Why aren't you entrusting this matter to Dzerzhinsky?"

"Because he would need time for that and the train leaves the day after tomorrow. Second question?"

"The second question," she repeated. "I hope it won't be my duty to report to anyone afterward . . ."

Lenin threw up his hands.

"Of course not!" he said. "That goes without saying. Under no circumstances will you tell me or anyone else where you saw Yuly. No matter what. I simply forbid you to report to me. Even the people's commissar will not be advised of our conversation. Consider this my personal mission."

"Very well," she said and drifted toward the door. She had at once become untalkative and her coal-black sharp eyes gazed pensively. She stopped at the door, however, and turned back to Lenin.

"Vladimir Ilich, you need to rest. You are very tired."

"Is it so obvious?" Lenin asked with interest, as if he had just heard a curious piece of news.

"Oh, yes, it's quite obvious," Sofia Markovna uttered energetically. "Take care of yourself."

"All right. Without fail."

"One more thing," Sofia Markovna said, her hand on the door. "I know Polish fairly well and may be of use in the army. In connection with the current situation. Well? Should I go apply to the Narkomvoenmor?"[11] She left without waiting for an answer.

3

Sofia Markovna woke up very early; lying with her eyes still closed, she was struck by the feeling that something fine and terribly important had occurred and had revitalized her life. This feeling did not go away even later, when the grave day appeared in full force and Lenin's mission necessitated calm thoughts and carefully considered actions.

The thoughts connected with this mission distracted her from her everyday life of hunger, her small hole of a room, which was unheated and in need of repair—she hardly lived in it, spending entire days and nights in her office in

---

11 The People's Commissariat for Military and Naval Affairs at the time headed by Leon Trotsky.

the Social Welfare Commissariat or traveling to small factories and shops where crutches, artificial limbs, and wheelchairs were made. She did not have an immediate family since her husband had left her at the beginning of the Revolution; a quiet man, a doctor who graduated from the university in Zurich, he had suddenly discovered in the bright light of the Revolution's glow that there were more interesting and attractive women around than his wife. She had never known how to create domestic comfort or to look after herself. She gave all her time to the Russian émigrés in Switzerland, to everyone who needed it, regardless of party or faction: she found them work and a place to live, she straightened out their affairs, and she settled troubles. In Switzerland she felt at home, having a perfect command of all three "Swiss" languages—French, German, and Italian.

After she was dressed and had determined that she had no firewood or bread, Sofia Markovna set out for the commissariat. There she dropped in to see Alexander Nikolaevich Vinokurov, the people's commissar, and told him that she could not attend the numerous meetings scheduled for the day. She pleaded ill, and her lively dark eyes assumed a piteous expression for a moment.

Leaving her office, she came out into the spring air of the street and walked aimlessly, not knowing where she was going at all. Rapid, muddy streams flowed beside the sidewalks. A narrow street took her to Vorontsovo Field. There were lots of jackdaws on the boulevards. The down on the tree branches was no longer green but purple. Sofia Markovna walked on and on, lightheaded from hunger and thoughts of her conversation of the day before. After that conversation, the aroused, warm, spring world seemed so full of miracles that she would not have been surprised if the first passerby had stopped her and asked, "Do you need Martov? Let's go, I'll take you to him." But in spite of her strange state of excitement, which was almost blissful, she never stopped thinking, considering, or weighing things over. And when she saw the jackdaw nests, she said to herself, "Ah! The main Menshevik nest is at the Supreme Council of the National Economy." She immediately set out for Varvarka Street, to Delovoy Dvor, where the council was located.

The echoing hallways of Delovoy Dvor were dirty and noisy. The elevators did not work. Sofia Markovna barely made it to the top floor; she was out of breath and had trouble lifting her feet. Once there she inquired about an acquaintance, a former member of the central committee of the Menshevik faction of the Social-Democratic Workers Party. He had gone to work for the Soviet regime and formally broken with the Mensheviks, but Sofia Markovna doubted his sincerity.

She entered a large office. He was sitting at a desk, absorbed in writing. His pince-nez lay before him on the page. When he heard the door creak, he brought the pince-nez to his eye and seemed startled but said nothing, simply gesturing for her to take a seat.

"I need to see Yuly," she said.

"Why are you asking *me* about him?" His eyes blinked.

"Because you know where he is."

"Who told you that?"

"Calm down, not Dzerzhinksy. I guessed it myself."

"And if I do know? Then what?"

"Then you must take me to see him."

He grew thoughtful. She began asking questions.

"You know me?"

"Yes."

"Do you know me well?"

"Yes."

"Do you trust me?"

"I do. But you . . ."

"Yes, I joined the RKP. But do you trust my word?"

"Suppose I do."

"Then I'll give you my word that no one will follow me to him. You hear? I'm giving my word."

"What do you need him for?" he asked, picking at his small black beard mercilessly.

"I have a message for him."

"From whom?"

"I can't say. I'll only tell him."

"Is it important?" he asked, staring directly at her.

"Why do you think I walked all the way up to the fifth floor?"

"Wait here."

He stood up and walked out of the office.

She waited patiently for half an hour, sitting in a deep armchair and drumming with the green ball-shaped head of her hat pin on her hat which she had taken off and put on her lap. Finally, the door opened, and the official returned along with Sukhanov.[12]

---

12   Sukhanov, Nikolay (1882–1940), born N. N. Gimmer—Menshevik leader and close political associate of Martov's at the time described in the story.

Sukhanov did not greet Sofia Markovna but looked at her intently and said caustically, "I see you're doing well under the one-party system. You look fine, no worse than on Swiss cheese and milk in Geneva."

"They hand out chickens every day to immigrants to the RKP from other parties," Sofia Markovna replied with a smile. "If you want to be fat, come over to the RKP. Though you'll always be skinny since you feed on yourself."

"I don't feed on myself, but the one-party system is devouring me," Sukhanov said gravely.

Sofia Markovna laughed provocatively.

"Like it needs you," she said, "when it has more nourishing food to chew on—Denikin, Kolchak, Yudenich."[13]

"Enough of your squabbling," the official said sullenly.

"So you need Yuly," Sukhanov said after a period of silence. "But you know, he's just gone into seclusion. He's writing a paper."

"Gone into seclusion. Ha!"

"In any case, I think there's no point in giving you a warning."

"No, there's no point. The one who sent me gave every assurance that he is not interested in Yuly's whereabouts."

"The one who sent you," Sukhanov said with a laugh. "Very solemnly stated."

Sofia Markovna was quiet, but she gave him a meaningful look from her chair, from which her short legs dangled over the floor.

"So what did you decide?" she finally asked.

"All right. They'll take you to him."

4

At four o'clock in the afternoon near the monument to the heroes of the Battle of Plevna at the Ilyunsky Gate, a man approached Sofia Markovna. He held an umbrella with a mother-of-pearl handle, and she followed him in silence.

The man with the umbrella did not take Sofia Markovna to an outlying region of Moscow as she had expected but directly to the Cheka building at the Lubyanka,[14] where he turned right and entered the courtyard of a large building at the very beginning of Myasnitskaya Street.

---

13 White Army generals and leaders.

14 Lubyanka Square in the center of Moscow was subsequently the location of the headquarters of the GPU, the Soviet secret police, and its later incarnations, including the KGB and the present-day FSB.

Sofia Markovna was amazed to see that the conspirators' apartment was located right next to the Cheka, and she laughed when she thought what Lenin would say if she reported it to him.

The man with the umbrella halted in the courtyard. He stood in the shadows, stared straight at Sofia Markovna, and asked in a hoarse voice if anyone had tailed them.

"Not me, at any rate," Sofia Markovna snapped.

They climbed up five flights of stairs to the top floor and then even higher, taking a wooden ladder to an attic. It all took a long time, since Sofia Markovna walked slowly, resting at each landing and breathing heavily. The man with the umbrella would stop one flight higher and look down at her impatiently and with what seemed to be disapproval.

The attic was inhabited. There were rooms along both sides of a long hall, and posters had been pasted between the doors: "Proletariat, to arms!" "Did *you* join the Volunteer Army?" "Stand up for the defense of Petrograd," and others.

The man with the umbrella stopped at one of the doors and knocked twice. The door opened and the man disappeared behind it. A few minutes later he came out and let Sofia Markovna into the room while he remained in the hall.

Sofia Markovna had actually thought that she would be seeing not Martov but another prominent Menshevik who, after first talking with her, would take her to Martov. She was astonished to see Martov himself in a small garret with the tiniest window. The room had only an iron cot covered with a yellow hospital blanket and a stool on top of which a primus stove burned. Martov was sitting on the cot, hunched over the primus, stirring something in a pot with a wooden spoon.

He was pale and thin, and his eyelids were puffy. The narrow face, narrow beard, and narrow body were transfixed by the soup simmering in the small pot, and it seemed that he didn't care about anything else in the world. But just then he put the spoon down on the stool, stuck his thin arms into the narrow sleeves of the tattered jersey over his shoulders, and looked up at Sofia Markovna.

For a moment they stared at each other tensely and in silence.

"Well?" Martov finally asked. "From him?"

"Yes."

Martov's face looked angry and helpless.

"What does he want?" he asked.

He listened quietly to Sofia Markovna's report. Red spots appeared on his face. After stirring the soup again, he asked with a wry smile, "Is he taking pity on me?"

"Perhaps."

"No, he isn't taking pity," he countered. "He wants to stay clean. He doesn't want to dirty his hands with my blood."

"Probably," Sofia Markovna agreed calmly, and just as calmly she asked, "Is that bad? Would it really be better if he wanted to dirty his hands with your blood?"

His eyes began blinking in dismay; he faltered and turned aside.

There must have been something in the curve of his stooped spine and in the whole pitiful state of the room that made Sofia Markovna's heart contract. She remembered the entire course of the friendship and enmity between Martov and Lenin. Sometimes Martov had been friendly with Lenin, but he always kept within bounds. What restrained him? Some flaw in his thinking or a feeling of jealousy, an unwillingness to acknowledge his own errors, the error of his entire life? Or a horror before the approaching storms, a horror that was the consequence of a weak political will but that he saw as prophetic foresight?

With these thoughts in mind, she suddenly had a perfectly clear vision of the face of the other man, the man who had spoken with her the night before at the Kremlin. She was overcome with a mysterious feeling of joy and at once said, "It's very hard for him."

"And for me it's easy?" Martov growled, turning to look at her again. He composed himself quickly, however, and asked with the curiosity of a small boy, "Why? I suppose he looks bad?"

His unexpected worldly question did not interfere with her state of joy. She answered seriously,

"It's harder for him."

Her words made Martov jump up and start shouting.

"Harder? You think so? Perhaps. But he himself . . . He took the whole burden upon himself. What arrogance! What thoughtlessness! Did he really think he could hold out? Where? In Russia? In three years' time Russia, like China, will be torn up into pieces, into provinces, spheres of influence. In three years' time the most complicated machine in Russia will be a well sweep."

She continued to speak in a serious tone.

"You're mistaken, Yuly. You don't understand; you're not able to understand the strength of the working class. You are wrong. He knows better. You don't understand him. You never have understood him. Believe me. I didn't understand either. We perceived him from an everyday perspective. As an intelligent, educated, charming, and determined man, our good friend and eternal opponent. We didn't take into account the extent of his understanding of the masses or his influence on them, his union with the masses."

Martov was quiet for a long time. Then he put out the primus and in the ensuing silence began to whisper furiously and with conviction.

"I don't want him to pity me. I hate him as much as I used to love him. I hate his face and his hands and his manners, and everything he talks about, and his conviction and modesty, and the fact that he sent you here, and everything he says and that others say about him. We're enemies. And if I leave I will remain his enemy. But I won't leave. I won't up and leave."

He began coughing, and he coughed for a long while, finally coughing up a clot of blood into a handkerchief. He quieted down and looked up bitterly at Sofia Markovna.

"Don't tell him what you've seen."

"All right."

"When is the answer needed?"

"The answer will be when you leave. Or don't leave."

She offered her hand, and after some hesitation he extended his own, limp and sweaty, and said goodbye.

"Do you have anything for me to pass on to him?" she asked, prolonging their talk.

After a moment of silence he replied,

"No."

5

Several months later, one of the officials invited to attend a government session turned to Lenin before it began.

"Vladimir Ilich, look what's going on!" he exclaimed sadly, poking a finger at a crumpled newspaper. "Martov's appearing at a Social-Democratic assembly in Germany. How was he able to get over the border?" He shook his head. "The Cheka slipped up."

Narrowing his eyes slyly, Lenin turned to Dzerzhinsky.

"Well? Did you hear what they're saying about you?"

"So we're not perfect either," Dzerzhinsky said, and his face remained a puzzle.

One of the people's commissars remarked, "It's all right. Maybe it's even good that the Chekists slipped up. One more enemy in Berlin isn't as dangerous as a martyr in a Soviet prison."

This conversation reminded Lenin of Sofia Markovna. After the session, as he hurried to get to the plenary session of the Moscow Soviet where he had to give a speech, he asked the secretary in passing, "Do you remember Sofia Markovna? Did you happen to run into her after that evening? Does she need anything?"

The secretary smiled sadly.

"No, she no longer needs anything. She left for the Polish front soon after her meeting with you. There she died of typhus."

Lenin froze for a minute.

"I see, I see," he said and quickly put on his coat.

1962

Translated from the Russian by Mary Ann Szporluk

YAN SATUNOVSKY

Yan Satunovsky (1913–1982), poet, children's author, and essayist, was born Yakov Satunovsky in Ekaterinburg (Dnepropetrovsk, Ukraine). While attending technical college in Moscow, Satunovsky met the members of the Literary Center of Constructivists (LTsK; headed by **Ilya Selvinsky** and shut down by 1930, along with other independent literary groups). Satunovsky returned to Dnepropetrovsk in 1931 and in 1936 graduated from the Chemical Faculty of Dnepropetrovsk State University. In 1936–41, he combined working as a chemical researcher with contributing light poetry, feuilletons, and cartoons to Dnepropetrovsk's *Evening Paper* (*Vecherniaia gazeta*). Soon realizing that his poems were too controversial in their formal orientation and in their nonconformist voice, Satunovsky did not seek their placement. "I'm not a poet. I haven't been in print since 1938," Satunovsky stated about himself in the 1970s.

An artillery company commander at the beginning of World War II, Satunovsky was seriously injured in 1941. After recuperating, he spent the rest of the war writing journalism and political poetry for *Patriot of the Motherland* (*Patriot Rodiny*), the newspaper of the Sixty-Sixth (Fifth Guard) Army. After the war, Satunovsky settled in Elektrostal, a suburb of Moscow, where he worked as a research chemical engineer for twenty years before taking retirement. He contributed occasional journalism and essays, as, for instance, the essay "Inventor Pavel Zarubin," published in the popular magazine *Technology for Youth* (*Tekhnika—molodezhi*) in 1951, coauthored with **Victor Shklovsky**. As was frequently the case with formally sophisticated poets who had difficulty placing their "adult" work in the USSR (cf. **Genrikh Sapgir**), Satunovsky found refuge in children's literature, publishing over two dozen books for children.

Around 1961, Satunovsky joined the underground Lianozovo group of free-spirited writers and visual artists centered around the family of the multi-talented Evgeny Kropivnitsky (1893–1978). A number of the group's principal members (**G. Sapgir**, Vsevolod Nekrasov, Oskar Rabin) were Satunovsky's juniors by a whole generation. "Call me old man Yan," he told them, overjoyed that he had finally found an artistic community that shared his distaste for the officially prescribed Soviet aesthetics. In 1974, without hoping to see his "adult" work published at home, Satunovsky put together his *Selected in Three Volumes* (seven typewritten copies), and in the late 1970s he began to dispatch his poems for publication abroad. Satunovsky died in Moscow in 1982, without seeing books of his serious poetry in print.

Having circulated in Soviet samizdat, Satunovsky's texts were independently collected and published, in Russia and in Germany, in the 1990s. The poet's brother Pyotr Satunovsky coedited with the poet Ivan Akhmetiev, a student and collector of Soviet samizdat, the volume *Do I Want Posthumous Fame* (after a line of Yan Satunovsky's poetry), published in Moscow in 1992 and passionately introduced by **Genrikh Sapgir**. Two years later the German Slavist Wolfgang Kasack published the much more substantial *Chopped Prose* (Satunovsky's term of choice for his nonclassical verses; Munich, 1994), based on one of the seven copies prepared by Satunovsky himself in 1974 and two subsequent additions, the total number of texts exceeding one thousand. Other editions have since appeared in Russia, among them *In Broad Daylight* (Moscow, 2001).

In the post-Soviet words of **Genrikh Sapgir**, "Yan Satunovsky is one of the greatest poets of modern times. This is becoming clear today [. . .]. He wrote remarkable verses, which at first glance didn't even look like verses. [. . .] In essence, it was what they call a poet's diary, which suddenly shined through the chaos of everyday living [. . .]. A refined lyrical poet, a partial witness to his own life and its contemporary events, to everything that was happening with him and with Russia, and to everything they did to him and to Russia, Yan Satunovsky is absolutely necessary to contemporary poetry." Exhibiting sophisticated sound orchestration and marked by freedom from metrical and rhyming conventions, Satunovsky's abundantly talented short locutions capture the raw consciousness of the postwar Soviet poetic counterculture.

* * *

The extensive corpus of Satunovsky's poetry presents a student of Soviet Jewry with a historically representative, concise commentary on the key political and cultural events of the 1930s–70s, starting with the rise of Nazism and the Shoah and ending with stagnant Brezhnevism. Satunovsky's verses, laconic and written for the desk drawer, attest to the dynamics of Jewish-Soviet identity in the most organically fitting, self-consciously unfinished, flung-open form.

The following selection chronologically showcases Satunovsky's Jewish poems dating to the late 1930s. Because Satunovsky quickly ceased to regard the publication of his adult poetry as a feasible or safe option, these poems are unique in the degree of their self-awareness of their author's own Jewish identity. Yan Satunovsky's poems, articulating within the constricted space of underground Soviet culture the anxieties of a Soviet-Jewish subject, offer a manifest alternative to the official career of his coeval **Boris Slutsky**.

* * *

In the country that has nearly forgotten
how to beat on its Jews,
what has turned my heart loose?

The old pogromists are buried,
The Black Hundreds are now a black memory.
A Jew in a Ukrainian shirt, your friend,
has just received a medal,
and a Russian woman has married you,
so what else can you ask for, Jew?
Why do you sigh, Jew? Speak!
Why do your narrow bones squeak?

So how can I tell my country,
how can I explain this
to her, to my mother,
and with what Russian words,
about the horror of living,
about the pain of being a miserable Jude-kike
in Berlin?

1939

* * *

Who are you,
Repatriated widows?
I wanted to make a caustic joke
at their expense, but
I choked.

Mortally tired after Hitler's raids,
atrocities, killings, bombings, and rapes,
they come to the officers' club
not to be lectured but loved.

ca. 1943

* * *

—Girls
with golden eyes,
where did you get
gold for your
eyes?
—At the church:
we have wasted
the icons,
breaking
gilded frames apart
to steal their gold.
—Girls with dark eyes,
How about you?
—At the synagogue.

1960

* * *

You're mistaken,
they are not
antisemites,
all these people:
Kochetov,
Krechetov,
Markov A.,
Markov G.,
the cheerful Sofronov
and the others,
all of them are members
of the Union of Soviet Writers,
members of the guild,
engineers of human souls.

But I cannot vouch for Eichmann.
Eichmann's not from our union.[15]

1961

* * *

It's the end of our nation.
Eaten alive by discrimination.
All Hayims
are now called Efim,
and Sruliks
have changed their names to Seraphim.

One no longer hears even
a hushed singing
in synagogues.
Markish is gone.
And Mikhoels is no more.[16]
And I'm feeling pretty low.

1962

---

15 Kochetov, Vsevolod (1912–1973), Markov, Georgy (1911–1991), and Sofronov, Anatoly (1911–1990)—Soviet Russian writers and well-known members of the Soviet literary nomenclature. In 1955–59, Kochetov was editor-in-chief of the weekly *Literaturnaia gazeta*; in 1953–86, Sofronov was editor-in-chief of the leading mass-market magazine *Little Flame* (*Ogonyok*); Krechetov is possibly referring to Sergei Krechetov (1878–1936), Russian poet of the Silver Age who emigrated after the Revolution and died in exile. Satunovsky places him in the same row with the Soviet Russian authors after Kochetov not because of his ideology but because both last names derive from names of birds: Kochetov from the noun *kochet* (cock); Krechetov from the noun *krechet* (gerfalcon); Kochetov and Krechetov, "cock and gelfalcon," thus form something of a metonymic (satirical) pair. Markov, Aleksei (1920–1992)—Soviet Russian poet who in 1961 published a scandalously ultranationalistic poem in response to Yevgeny Yevtushenko's "Babi Yar"(on "Babi Yar," see **Ilya Ehrenburg**, in this anthology, and **Lev Ozerov**, in introduction to the section "War and Shoah: 1940s"). Eichmann, Adolf (1906–1962)—Nazi official in charge of the Final Solution; for more information, see introduction to **Lev Ginzburg** in the section "Late Soviet Period and Collapse: 1960s–1990s." Dated 15 December 1961, Satunovsky's poem appears to have been inspired by the evens of the Eichmann trial (2 April–14 August 1961), as well as by the scandal surrounding the publication of Yevtushenko's "Babi Yar" and A. Markov's response to it.

16 Markish, Perets (1895–1952)—major Yiddish poet, executed in Moscow as part of a group of Jewish writers; father of **David Markish** (in the section "The Jewish Exodus: 1970s–1990s" in this anthology); Mikhoels, Shloyme (1890–1948)—major Jewish actor, assassinated in Minsk in 1948.

* * *

My Slavic language is Russian,
my people are from Smolensk, Kursk,
Tula, Penza, Velikie Luki.
They'll twist my arms behind my back,
knock me over to the ground,
break my head with a vodka bottle.
I expect
nothing else
from my people.

1963

* * *

I'm Moyshe from Berdichev.

        I'm Móyzber.[17]

Or maybe Rayzman?

        Gintsburg, maybe?

I spat in the face

        of the Nazi vermin who occupied me.

I was buried alive in clay.
I'm Vaynberg.
I'm Vaynberg from Pyatikhatki.[18]

I'm Vaynberg.

        Why was I executed?

I'm a stinking kike stuffed with rot and dung.
A monument to me stands tall in Rotterdam.

1963

---

17 In the opinion of Gennady Estraikh, a leading expert on Soviet Yiddish literature, communicated to the editor on 28 March 2005, Moyzber could be decoded as "moys" (Yiddish "mouse") plus "ber" (Yiddish "bear") while also being a play on the Yiddish name Moyshe-Ber.

18 Pyatikhatki—town in Satunovsky's native Dnepropetrovsk Province, Ukraine.

* * *

Eve,
a civilized Jewess,
a lover of
concrete chamber music
and abstract painting,
a poetess from the College of Furniture,
you are all I'm missing in life, oh Eve,
only you . . .

1964

* * *

Expressionism-Zionism.
Impressionism-Zionism.
But if they try, they will discover that REALISM
is also conspiring with ISRAEL.

1965

* * *

Blessed be the ill fate
That chose us among other tribes on earth.

To the streets!
To the streets!
Now we dancing!
Now we singing!
And e raise us from the dead!
Gut yontev![19]

Gut yontev!
Gut yontev!

1967

---

19   *Gut yontev!* (Yiddish) = Happy holiday!

* * *

Gate slamming,
shelter closing,
snail hiding,
a flimsy Jewish soul.

From birth to grave
Hayim won't escape
from beasts,
from thunder,
from pogromist boors,
from windows,
from doors.

1967

* * *

There are antisemites, and antisemites.
Nowadays they value
active antisemitism.
An active antisemite—
He's both an agitator and a propagandist.[20]

1974

---

20 Cf. "A newspaper is not only a collective propagandist and collective agitator but also a collective organizer," from V. I. Lenin's essay "Where to Start?" (1901).

* * *

Some say:
in Solzhenitsyn's time
antisemites are countless.
Other say:
in Solzhenitsyn's time
antisemites are worthless.
I don't know who's right, who's wrong,
in Solzhenitsyn's time.[21]

1974

Translated from the Russian by Maxim D. Shrayer

---

21 Dated 6 February 1974, this poem probably owes its composition to the official campaign of ostracism against Aleksandr Solzhenitsyn following the publication in the West of the first parts of *The Gulag Archipelago* and preceding his arrest and banishment from the USSR on 12 February 1974.

Late Soviet Empire and Collapse: 1960s–1990s

Editor's Introduction

Nikita Khrushchev's ouster by Leonid Brezhnev in October 1964 marked the beginning of the longest uninterrupted stride of Soviet history. The latter years of this period—lasting into the 1980s—became known as the period of "stagnation." For Soviet Jewry, the central historical development of this Soviet period was the massive emigration to Israel and North America (creative achievements of the Jewish-Soviet emigration are featured in the section "The Jewish Exodus: 1970s–1990s").

Israel's decisive victory in the Six-Day War of 1967 gave the Soviet Jews a new boost of pride. It also summoned in a period of open animosity toward the Jewish state (and, concomitantly, to things openly Jewish), indeed, a ubiquitous campaign in the Soviet media. (In the wake of the Six-Day War, the USSR broke off diplomatic relations with Israel.) Emigration and the rise of the Jewish refusenik movements gave Soviet Jews a new potent means for political and cultural self-expression. Jewish emigration split the Soviet Jewish community into the ones "leaving" (or struggling to leave) and the ones "staying" (or intending to stay). The renewed antisemitism, both ideological and cultural, of the late Soviet Empire, particularly as represented by the emergence of the official Russian cultural right and the grassroots ultranationalist movement Pamyat' (Rus. "Memory") in the early 1980s, dispelled some of the last false hopes to which the ones "staying" had clung.

The delusions of assimilation and the challenges of emigration permeated the writings of Jewish-Russian authors during in the 1970s and prereform 1980s. It would have been unrealistic to expect most Jewish-Russian writers, at the time still quite numerous in the official Soviet culture, to protest openly against the antisemitism of the late Soviet decades and the official persecution of Jewish refuseniks. Such very public voicing of protest led to repressions and to a writer's break with the official cultural mainstream, as was the case with the poem "My Slavic Soul" (1975) by **David Shrayer-Petrov** (b. 1936), a public performance of which led to official ostracism and pushed the writer toward emigration. Works created in the 1970s and 1980s, prior to their authors' emigration and first published in the émigré Russian press in Israel, Western Europe, and North America, are deliberately featured in the section devoted to "The Jewish Exodus: 1970s–1990s."

Some of the most important works treating the subjects of Jewish identity, ideological and cultural antisemitism, and Jewish emigration, such as *A Society Chronicle* (1975–79) by Iuliu Edlis (1929–2009), *Life of Alexander Zilber* (1974–75) by **Yury Karabchievsky** (1938–1992), and *Summer in Baden-Baden* (1981) by Leonid Tsypkin (1926–1982), wrote themselves for the desk drawer, with the authors' knowledge that they could only be published in samizdat or abroad. **Osip Mandelstam**'s widow, Nadezhda Mandelstam (1899–1980), completed her epochal memoirs in the Brezhnevite 1960s and 1970s, and at the time they could only appear in the West.

During this period, use of allegory, conceit, and Aesopian language occasionally enabled Jewish-Russian poets to swivel a small number of their works with Jewish themes and motifs into print (notably, poems by **Semyon Lipkin** [1911–2003] and Yunna Morits [b. 1937]). Very occasional Jewish notes warbled in the officially published lyrical poetry (such as poems by **Aleksandr Kushner** [b. 1936]) and in memoiristic prose by older writers reminiscing about their beginnings (such as Evgeny Gabrilovich [1899–1993]). Timid Jewish motifs surfaced in the fiction of such "official liberals" as Iosif Gerasimov (1922–1991) and Daniil Granin (1919–2017). Perhaps to outweigh the Jewish exodus and the refusenik movement and its culture unsanctioned by the regime, several works of the late 1970s and early 1980s, most notably *Heavy Sand* by **Anatoly Rybakov** (1911–1998) and *Only My Heart Was Broken . . .* by **Lev Ginzburg** (1921–1980), offered powerful if ideologically tempered treatments of the Shoah, an otherwise tabooed topic. Overall, instances of Jewish-Russian writers being allowed to speak with openness about the Jewish experience are so few in the cultural mainstream of the 1970s and prereform 1980s that it would not be too difficult to compile a finite list of such publications. The novel *O, Saturday* (1980; "Saturday" [*subbota*] in Russian refers both to the day of the week and to the Jewish Sabbath) by Dina Kalinovskaya (1934–2009) and the story "The Lady's Taylor" (1984; turned into a play) by Aleksandr Borshagovsky (1913–2006) are frequently cited as examples of such late Soviet works in the official culture, and they do not appear in this anthology.

In the conditions of a growing spiritual quest among the ranks of the Brezhnevite intelligentsia, a lack of passed-on Jewish knowledge offset by a dearth of opportunities for "above-ground" Judaic learning brought some

Jewish writers to Christianity (I discuss this in the general introduction). The Jewish self-consciousness of some writers safely hibernated during the years of stagnation, imploded during the late 1980s, and came to the surface as the Soviet state expired. Such was the case of the long poem *Blizzard* by **Aleksandr Mezhirov** (1923–2009), where the shock of reading in print rabidly antisemitic statements by a fellow Russian writer compels the Jew's bottled-up and conflicted biculturalism to shriek out a farewell to Russia.

The ascent of Jewish samizdat in the Soviet 1970s and the culture of the refusenik movement call for a brief digression. In 1970, the underground Jewish-Russian magazines *Iton* (Heb. for "newspaper") and *Iskhod* (Rus. for "exodus") were founded in Riga and Moscow, respectively. The Moscow-based samizdat *Jews in the USSR* (*Evrei v SSSR*) appeared in 1972–79 and was reprinted in Israel. Its last editor, the refusenik activist Viktor Brailovsky, was persecuted by the KGB and sentenced to a jail term. Founded in 1975, the magazine *Tarbut* (Heb. for "culture") challenged the image of an underground Soviet publication and unsuccessfully sought entrance into the mainstream under the motto "A nation's [people's] culture cannot be underground." Most compelling from a literary point of view were some of the materials disseminated through *Leningrad Jewish Almanac* (*Leningradskii evreiskii al'manakh*), which was founded in 1982 and coedited by the poet and critic Yury Kolker (b. 1947), then a refusenik struggling to emigrate. Two forces, the *politiki* and the *tarbutniki* (or *kul'turniki*), shaped Jewish samizdat: the political activists stood on the platform of Zionism and aliyah, whereas the cultural ones sought legal cultural autonomy and the reinvigoration of Jewish life in the USSR. Some editors of Jewish underground periodicals were granted exit visas before the reform years, immigrating to Israel and continuing their work as Jewish-Russian littérateurs abroad. Jewish-Russian authors who sought publishing outlets outside the official Soviet narrows turned to the numerous Jewishly unmarked samizdat channels of the 1970s and 1980s or smuggled their works abroad (or pursued both unsanctioned options). This anthology did not seek to represent Jewish samizdat as a separate and self-sufficient segment of the Jewish-Russian literary canon even though several works originally appeared in Jewish samizdat and were reprinted in Israel and the West (and subsequently in post-Soviet Russia). The number of original literary works written in Russian and published in Jewish samizdat periodicals (as opposed to translations from Hebrew or reprints of older Jewish-Russian works) was not very significant. The most notable exception, the fiction of **Boris Khazanov** (b. 1928), is featured in the section "The Jewish Exodus: 1970s–1990s." Other Jewish-Russian authors, including those from the ranks of refuseniks, sought publishing opportunities abroad by illegally sending their manuscripts to *tamizdat* Russian-language publications based in Europe, Israel, the United States, and Canada. This often incurred the wrath of Soviet authorities and led to the writers' persecution (consider the case of David Shrayer-Petrov and the publication of sections of his refusenik saga in Israel). In this connection, the career of the medical scientist and fiction writer Leonid Tsypkin (1926–1982) calls for a quick stop. Tsypkin's prose oeuvre is small, and it was his last work, the short novel *Summer in Baden-Baden*, which he wrote in 1977–80, that stands out as his best achievement. A refusenik since 1979, Tsypkin had the manuscript of his novel smuggled out of the country to the United States, where it was serialized in a New York–based Russian newspaper. On 20 March 1982, just a few days after learning of the publication by telephone from his son, Leonid Tsypkin died of a heart attack in Moscow. His novel finally gained a wide audience in 2001, after its English translation was reprinted in New York.

In the early 1980s, the persecution of refuseniks and Jewish activists was exceptionally severe and the official conditions for Jewish self-expression especially horrendous, inviting a comparison with the postwar years preceding Stalin's death. Repeated official calls were made to "Soviet writers, artists, and journalists" to "expose in their works and performances even more fully the antinational [read: anti-Soviet] and antihumanist character of [. . .] Zionism."[1] To the best of my knowledge, not one Jewish-born writer of literary merit demeaned himself or herself in this fashion. For whatever such a comment is worth, anti-Israeli, anti-Judaic, and antirefusenik rhetoric is absent from *literary works* even by such ideologically committed Jews of the Soviet literary establishment as Margarita Aliger (1915–1992). The Jewish sell-outs who did lend their pens to the regime's persecutory campaign (such as Tsezar Solodar and Yury Kolesnikov) bear comparison with such abominable tsarist-era personages as Yakov Brafman, the author of the venal *Book of the Kahal* (1869).

It might be instructive to compare statistics from the Eighth Congress of the Union of Soviet Writers (June 1988), the last, which occurred during Gorbachev's perestroika, with the statistics for the First Congress (1934; see details in the introduction to the section "Revolution and Emigration: 1920s–1930s"). While a representative number of Jews born in the 1910s–1930s

---

1   See the "Appeal" to the public to "form" a "voluntary Anti-Zionist Committee of the Soviet Public," printed on 1 April 1983 (no joke) in *Pravda* and signed by a number of Soviet Jewish dignitaries, headed by World War II hero Army Colonel-General David Dragunsky: "Obrashchenie," *Pravda* (1 April 1983): 4.

still populated the official space of Soviet culture, their relative weight in the official apparatus by the end of the Soviet Empire was very low. Out of 572 Soviet delegates to the 1988 congress, there were twenty Jews writing in Russian, one Jew writing in Ukrainian, two Yiddish writers, and one Bukharan Jew writing in Uzbek, a total of twenty-five Jewish delegates, or about 4 percent, while the Jewish population constituted about 0.5 percent of the total population of the USSR. At the First Congress in 1934, when the Jewish population of the USSR constituted about 1.8 percent of the total Soviet population, there were one hundred thirteen delegates, or about 19.0 percent, with the nationality "Jew."[2] Only three writers featured in this anthology (**Veniamin Kaverin, Aleksandr Mezhirov**, and **Anatoly Rybakov**) were among the delegates to the 1988 congress, as compared to eighteen at the 1934 congress. And only **V. Kaverin** was a delegate to both the 1934 and the 1988 congresses. No matter how much— or how little—stock one puts in such data, and no matter how much one tries to correct for the official cultural antisemitism of the late Soviet decades, the data corroborate the view that the Jewish public presence in Russian literature had greatly decreased toward the end of the Soviet period.

During the last few Soviet years, a growing political and cultural openness about Jewishness and the lifting of censorship and official taboos on Jewish and Judaic topics permitted the appearance of works by Jewish-Russian writers completed in the preceding decades and previously unpublished. Toward the sunsets of their careers, several officially established writers, such as **Israel (Izrail') Metter** (1909–1996), enjoyed the publication and international acclaim of their principal works with manifest Jewish themes. At the same time, a number of authors, notably the ones born in the 1940s and 1950s and previously kept off the mainstream literary arena (such as **Evgeny Reyn** [b. 1935] and **Bella Ulanovskaya** [1943–2005]), finally received recognition. Furthermore, the last Soviet years chimed in the beginning of a literary legitimation of émigré authors, including those who had left in the 1970s and 1980s.

For Jewish-Russian writers still living in the USSR by 1991, the collapse of the empire and the end of official restrictions on emigration transformed the meaning and significance of both leaving Russia and staying in Russia.

---

2   In contrast to the published statistics from the First Congress of Soviet Writers, where both nationality and literary language(s) were reported, there are my own assessments, based on available statistics from the Eighth Congress of Soviet Writers and probably needing further verification. See *Vos'moi s"ezd soiuza pisatelei SSSR. 24 iiunia–28 iiulia 1986. Stenograficheskii otchet* (Mosow: Sovetskii pisatel', 1988), 498–504.

The post-Soviet freedom of the press—and of being able to write and openly publish on Jewish topics in the literary mainstream—also altered the Jewish-Russian writers' relationship with their origins, a relationship that some of them had previously suppressed. Recent students of Russian emigration sometimes use the term "Fourth Wave" (perhaps sardonically) in referring to those who left after 1989, when emigrating from the Soviet Union became easy but gaining entry to western countries grew increasingly difficult (Germany being a notable exception). During the 1990s, a massive influx of Soviet Jews to Israel transplanted there a group of older Jewish-Russian writers (e.g., **Sara Pogreb** [b. 1921] or Grigory Kanovich [b. 1929]). Israel's new Jewish-Russian writers also include a sizeable group of those who came of age in the 1960s (in this anthology, **Dina Rubina** [b. 1953]), the 1970s, and even the 1980s (**Anna Gorenko** [1972–1999], both featured in the section "The Jewish Exodus: 1970s–1990s"). A number of Jewish-Russian writers who emigrated in the early 1990s (e.g., Michail Bezrodnyj [b. 1957] or Vladimir Gandelsman [b. 1948]) have become familiar literary names in Russia—and throughout the Russian literary world—while living abroad. Being part of the Russian literary mainstream no longer requires living in Russia.

In the early 1990s, explicit Jewish topics propelled several Jewish-Russian writers born in the 1940s and 1950s, most notably **Ludmila Ulitskaya** (b. 1943), into critical acclaim both in Russia and abroad. For others, the limited publication of their major Jewish works by small publishers did not change their marginal status. Jewish subjects seem to have fallen into a decline in Russia's literary mainstream by the 2000s, while Jewish cultural autonomy accords Jewish-Russian writers publishing opportunities in the press directed almost exclusively toward Jewish readers. Both the prospect of living as members of a dwindling ethnic and religious Jewish minority and the presently available ample opportunities to practice Judaism hold little appeal for the majority of the younger writers of Jewish origin bent on staying in Russia.

VASSILY AKSYONOV

Vassily Aksyonov (1932–2009), fiction and nonfiction writer, dramatist, translator, and poet, was born in Kazan, Tatarstan, the son of Pavel Aksyonov, a Bolshevik functionary, and Evgenia Ginzburg (1904–1977), a Jewish-born journalist and Communist educator. Aksyonov's parents were purged in 1937, survived lengthy gulag sentences, and formed new families. Aksyonov was sixteen when he was reunited with his mother following her release from the camp into exile, and he spent part of his high-school years in Magadan Region of the Russian Far East. Rearrested in 1949, Evgenia Ginzburg was rehabilitated in 1955. In 1962, at the peak of the Thaw, Ginzburg completed volume one of her memoir about Stalinism, written, on the surface of it, from the perspective of restored "Leninist truth." Ginzburg decided to have her memoir published abroad only after all efforts in the USSR had failed by 1966. First released in Russian in Milan in 1967–69 (and not published in the USSR until 1989), Ginzburg's two-part memoir has appeared in many languages (in English: *Journey into the Whirlwind* [1967] and *Within the Whirlwind* [1981]).

Aksyonov graduated from the Leningrad First Medical School in 1956 and practiced medicine until 1960. At the medical school, his classmates included **David Shrayer-Petrov** and the future film director Ilya Averbakh. Aksyonov's prose appeared in central periodicals in 1959–60, and he gained popularity as a leading author of the Moscow monthly *Youth* (*Iunost'*). One of the key young official liberals of the Thaw, a Westernizer, and an anti-Stalinist, Aksyonov rapidly published a series of short novels, including *Colleagues* (1960), *A Starry Ticket* (1961), and *Oranges from Morocco* (1963); several were adapted for the screen. Aksyonov's stories were collected in *Catapult* (1964), *Halfway to the Moon* (1965), *Sorry You Weren't with Us* (1969), and so forth. His jazzy 1960s short stories became a literary sensation. The short novel *Surplussed Barrelware* (1968) marked a watershed in Aksyonov's career, weaning him of his youthful (Soviet postmodern?) optimism. Aksyonov explored a course of ideological compromise in works of the 1970s, notably in *Love of Electricity* (1971). In 1975, he spent time in the United States on a visiting professorship, producing *Around the Clock Nonstop* (1976), a travelogue. Aksyonov's last book published in the USSR, *In Search of a Genre* (1978), anticipated his creative and ideological explosion of the late 1970s.

Aksyonov's works began to appear in Russian in the West (for example, *Our Golden Ironburg* [1979]). Aksyonov coedited the literary collective *Metropol* with Andrey Bitov, Viktor Erofeev, Fazil Iskander, and Evgeny Popov. Published in the United States in 1979 in Russian (in 1982 in English), *Metropol* featured works by both official and unofficial authors (in this anthology, Aksyonov himself, **Friedrich Gorenstein, Yury Karabchievsky, Semyon Lipkin, Inna Lisnyanskaya, Evgeny Reyn, Genrikh Sapgir**) and became the main literary scandal of the late Brezhnev era. In December 1979, Aksyonov resigned from the Union of Soviet Writers, protesting the punitive measures against his *Metropol* cocontributors, and in July 1980 he emigrated. Eventually settling in the United States, he held a number of teaching positions in American universities and was an active contributor to the Third-Wave émigré press.

Composed in 1969–75, Aksyonov's best novel, *The Burn*, appeared in the West in 1980. A fictional manifesto of Aksyonov's generation—comparable in its impact and its explicit presentation of sex (as the author's and the characters' protest against totalitarianism) to Milan Kundera's *The Unbearable Lightness of Being* (1984)—*The Burn* features a composite protagonist: five fascinating characters whose shared autobiographical past is informed by the same half-Jewish teenager, the son of a purged Jewish female Communist (parts reveal parallels with Evgenia Ginzburg's memoir). Although Aksyonov remained prolific as a Russian-American writer and enjoyed some success in translation, his subsequent works of fiction, including *Paper Landscape* (1982) and *Say Cheese!* (1985), never eclipsed the records of either *The Burn* or *The Island of Crimea* (1981), a historical fantasy of a novel. Aksyonov's *In Search of a Melancholy Baby* (1987), with its saccharine descriptions of Orthodox churchgoing in America, rang false coming from the former irreverent star of funky Soviet prose.

Aksyonov made his literary return to the USSR in 1990, and his works have been reprinted in Russia in various editions, including the five-volume *Works* (Moscow, 1994–95). Since 2003, Aksyonov made his home in Biarritz, France, dividing his time between France and Russia. Among Aksyonov's post-Soviet fiction is the disappointing trilogy *The Moscow Saga* (1993–94), as well as the novels *The New Sweet Style* (1997), *My Caesarean Scintillation* (2001), and *Voltariens and Voltariennes* (2004; received the 2004 Booker–Open Society Prize). Aksyonov, who continued to surprise his admirers, died in Moscow in July 2009. His last completed work, the autobiographical novel *Secret Passion: A Novel about the Shestidesyatniki* [the 60's generation], was posthumously published in Moscow. Some of the principal cultural figures of the Thaw, among them the writers Yevgeny Yevtushenko, Bella Akhmadulina, and Bulat Okudzhava, appear as principal characters in Aksyonov's novel, thinly disguised under fictionalized names.

As evident from his best American work, such as the story "Around Dupont" (*The New Yorker*, 1995), Aksyonov's forte lies in an authentic unraveling of the ideological, ethnic, religious, and sexual parameters of the identity of his post-Soviet—or former Soviet—characters.

* * *

In an interview published in July 1994, Aksyonov, a Russian writer born to a Jewish mother and a keen student of mixed identities and creeds, spoke about his own ideological sense of Jewishness: "In general, I must say that only this past winter did I feel a closeness to my own Jewish roots. I was visiting Israel for the first time, and when I approached the Wailing Wall and pressed my hand to it, I felt my belonging to these roots, this world. Although there is in it, I would say, a lot of ridiculousness: all these people with waving *peyes* who do not even speak in their historical language, but say, *bekitzer, bekitzer* [Yiddish: *in short, quick*]—in the language of Belarusian ghettos. All this actively disagrees with me. But in Israel one realizes that Jews are not only the yellow star, which is alive in each one, as a memory of suffering. It is also the blue star, embodying a colossal energy against the background of a desert landscape; the blue star of the modern Israel inspires optimism."

Jewish and partly Jewish characters are a common feature of fiction that chronicles the postwar Soviet intellectual and artistic elite. Assimilated, even converted, but still victimized by antisemites, Aksyonov's Jewish characters in *The Burn, The Island of Crimea,* and other works cannot conceal their origins and integrate. One of Aksyonov's best stories, "Victory: A Story with Exaggerations," was composed and originally published in *Youth* magazine in 1965. "Victory" betrays Aksyonov's early familiarity with Vladimir Nabokov's novel *The Defense* (1930), which was banned in the USSR along with Nabokov's other works until perestroika. Although Nabokov's protagonist, the émigré chess genius Luzhin, is not Jewish, he is often perceived as such. It is hardly gratuitous that, along with a chronic inability to resist his opponents' vulgarity, in "Victory" Aksyonov endows his own non-Jewish grandmaster with life circumstances that make him a victim of stereotypical treatment by a xenophobic Soviet everyman.

VICTORY

A Story with Exaggerations

In a compartment of an express train a grandmaster was playing chess with a chance companion.

The man had recognized the grandmaster right away when the grandmaster had entered the compartment, and he was immediately consumed by an unthinkable desire for an unthinkable victory over the grandmaster. "So what," he thought, casting sly knowing glances at the grandmaster, "so what, a little nerd, big deal."

The grandmaster immediately understood that he had been recognized and sadly resigned himself: two games are unavoidable. He immediately recognized the man's type. He had often seen the hard, pink foreheads of people like that through the windows of the Chess Club on Gogol Boulevard.

Once the train was moving, the grandmaster's companion stretched with an expression of naïve cunning and asked indifferently:

"How about a little game of chess, comrade?"

"Oh, I suppose so," the grandmaster muttered.

The man stuck his head out of the compartment, called the conductress, a chess set appeared, he grabbed it with an eagerness that belied indifference, scattered the pieces, selected two pawns, clenched them in his fists and showed the fists to the grandmaster. On the bulge between the thumb and the index finger of his left hand there was a tattoo: "G.O."

"Left," said the grandmaster and cringed slightly, imagining blows of these fists, either the left or the right.

He drew white.

"We've got to kill time, right? . . . A game of chess is the best thing on a trip," G.O. muttered as he arranged the chessmen.

They quickly played the Northern Gambit, then everything became confused. The grandmaster carefully studied the board making small, insignificant moves. Several times, various checkmate moves of the queen appeared like lightning before his eye, but he extinguished these flashes by lowering his eyelids slightly and submitting to the weak inner drone of an annoying plaintive note, like a mosquito buzz.

"Khas-Bulat, you are bold, but how poor is your hut . . . ,"[3] G.O. hummed tunelessly on the same note.

The grandmaster was the embodiment of neatness, the embodiment of classic simplicity of dress and manner, so characteristic of insecure and vulnerable people. He was young; he wore a grey suit, a light shirt and a tie with a simple pattern. No one but the grandmaster himself knew that his plain ties bore the label of the House of Dior. This small secret had always been, somehow, a source of comfort and warmth for the young, reticent grandmaster. His glasses, too, had served him often, hiding the uncertainty and timidity of his gaze from strangers. He was unhappy with his lips which had the habit of stretching into pitiable little smiles or else to quiver. He would gladly cover them from the eyes of strangers but this, alas, was not accepted in society as yet.

G.O.'s game dismayed and upset the grandmaster. The pieces on the left flank were crowded together forming a bundle of cabalistic charlatan symbols. It was rather like the tuning of a lousy wind band before a last-minute gig, like yellow-grayish compressed snow, thick fences, cement works. The whole left flank stank of the latrine and of chlorine, of the sour smell of barracks and wet kitchen rags, also bringing back from the early childhood a whiff of castor oil and diarrhea.

"You are the grandmaster So-and-So, aren't you?" G.O. asked.

"Yes," confirmed the grandmaster.

"Ho-ho-ho, what a coincidence!"

"What coincidence? What coincidence is he talking about? This is just incredible! How could this have happened? I refuse, accept my resignation," the grandmaster thought, panicking; then he guessed what was the matter and smiled.

"Yes, of course, of course."

"You're a grandmaster, and I'm forking your rook and queen," said G.O. He raised his hand. The knight-provocateur hovered above the board.

"Pitchfork in the bum," thought the grandmaster. "Nice little fork! Grandfather had his own fork and nobody was allowed to use it. Ownership. Personal fork, spoon and knife and a personal phial for phlegm. Also remember

---

3   "Khas-Bulat udaloi, bedna saklia tvoia . . ." is a line from "Elegy (Khas-Bulat)," a popular song with lyrics by Aleksandr Ammosov and music by O. Kh. Agrenova-Slavyanskaya (1858). Here and hereafter, G.O. hums lines from this song.

the "lyrebird" coat, the heavy coat lined with "lyrebird" fur, it used to hang at the entrance; grandfather hardly ever went out. Forking grandma and grandpa. It's a shame to lose the old folks."

While the knight hovered over the board, the phosphorescent lines and dots of the possible preemptive checkmate raids and victims flashed again before the grandmaster's eyes. Alas, the dirty-lilac flannel sticking out on the knight's neck was so convincing that the grandmaster just shrugged his shoulders.

"Giving away the rook?" asked G.O.

"What's one to do?"

"Sacrificing the rook for the advantage, right?" asked G.O., still hesitating to place his knight on the desired square.

"Simply saving the queen," muttered the grandmaster.

"You're not tricking me, are you?"

"Oh, no, you are a strong player."

G.O. executed his cherished "fork." The grandmaster hid the queen in a quiet corner behind the terrace, behind the crumbling stone terrace with the slightly rotted carved little pillars, with a pungent smell of fermenting maple leaves in autumn. Here one can sit it out, squatting comfortably. It's nice here; in any case, the ego does not suffer. He got up for a moment, peeked from behind the terrace and saw that G.O. had removed the rook.

The intrusion of the black knight into a senseless crowd on the left flank and his occupation of b4, in any case, demanded further thought.

The grandmaster understood that in this variant, on that green spring evening, the myths of youth alone would not suffice. It is all true, there are jolly fools wandering round the world—young sailor Billy, cowboy Harry, the beautiful Mary and Nelly, and "the brigantine is raising all its sails . . .";[4] but there comes a moment when one feels the dangerous and real proximity of the black knight in the square b4. Ahead was the fight—complicated, intricate, entrancing and calculating. Ahead was life.

The grandmaster took a pawn, got out a handkerchief and blew his nose. The few moments of complete solitude, when both lips and nose were hidden by the handkerchief, put him in a banal-philosophical mood. "So you keep

---

4 "The brigantine is raising all its sails . . ." ("Brigantina podnimaet parusa . . .") is a line recurring three times in "Brigantina: Pesnia" (1937), a popular romantic poem (also lyrics of a well-known Soviet song) by Pavel Kogan (1918–1942). Kogan, killed in World War II, composed "Brigantine" at the age of nineteen.

striving for something," he thought, "and what then? All your life you strive for something; victory comes but it does not bring happiness. Take, for example, the city of Hong Kong. It's distant and quite mysterious, but I've already been there. I've already been everywhere."

"In his place Petrosian would have already surrendered," said the grandmaster under his breath.

The loss of a pawn did not upset G.O. much; after all, he had just won a rook. He responded to the grandmaster by the move of the queen, which brought on heartburn and a sudden attack of migraine.

The grandmaster surmised that there were still some joys in store for him. For example, the joy of the prolonged moves of the bishop along the whole diagonal. Dragging the bishop lightly across the board could substitute, to a degree, for a headlong glide in a skiff along the sunlit and greenish stagnant water of a pond in the Moscow countryside: from light to shade, from shade to light. The grandmaster felt an overwhelming, passionate desire to conquer square h8, that square, that mound of love, with transparent dragonflies hanging above it.

"That was clever, the way you got my rook and I totally missed it," said G.O. in a deep voice. Only the last words betrayed his irritation.

"Forgive me," the grandmaster said quietly, "perhaps you should return the moves?"

"No-no, no favors, I beg of you," said G.O.

"I will give you my sword, and my horse, and my gun . . ." G.O. began to hum, deep in considerations of strategy.

The tempestuous summer holiday of love in the field h8 both gladdened and unnerved the grandmaster. He felt the externally logical but internally absurd forces would converge upon the center very soon. As before, he would hear cacophony and smell chlorine as in that damned memory of the distant corridors on the left flank.

"I wonder: why are all the chess players Jewish?" G.O. asked.

"Why all?" said the grandmaster, "for example, I'm not Jewish."

"Really?" said G.O. with surprise and added: "Please, don't think that I mean anything. I have no prejudices on this account. Just curious."

"Well, take you, for example, you are not Jewish," said the grandmaster.

"How could I be? . . ." muttered G.O., sinking back into his secret plans.

"If I do this, he'll do that," thought G.O. "If I take one here, he'll take one there, then I go here, he responds like this. . . . No matter, I'll finish him off, I'll break him down, I will. Big deal, grandmaster-cheatmaster, your muscle still can't match mine. I know your championships: all prearranged. I'll squash you anyway, I'll give you a bloody nose."

"Well, I've lost my advantage," he said to the grandmaster, "but that's O.K., it ain't over yet."

He began the attack in the center and of course, as expected, the center immediately turned into an arena of senseless and terrible actions. This was non-love, non-meeting, non-hope, non-greeting, non-life. The chills of influenza and, again, the yellow snow, the postwar confusion and domestic disarray, the itching all over the body. In the center, the black queen kept croaking like a crow in love, yes, crow love and, besides, the neighbors were scraping a tin bowl with a knife. Nothing proved the senselessness and the elusiveness of life as definitely as this center position. It was time to end the game.

"No," the grandmaster thought, "there is still something besides this." He put on a long tape of Bach's piano pieces, calming his heart with sound, pure and even, like the splashing of waves. Then he went out of the summer cottage and down to the sea. The pines were rustling above him and there was a slippery springy floor of pine needles under his feet.

Remembering the sea and imitating it, he began to analyze the position harmonizing it. His heart suddenly felt pure and light. Logically, like a Bach coda, came the checkmate to the black. A dim and beautiful light lit the opaque checkmate, now complete, perfect like an egg. The grandmaster looked at G.O. He was silent, staring like a bull into the deepest rear of the grandmaster. G.O. did not notice the checkmate. The grandmaster was silent for fear of disrupting the magic of the moment.

"Check," said G.O. quietly and carefully, moving his knight. He could barely contain his inner bellow.

... The grandmaster let out a scream and fled. After him, stamping and whistling, ran the owner of the summer house, the coachman Eurypides and Nina Kuzninichna. Ahead of them all, catching up with the grandmaster, leapt the unchained dog, Duskie.

"Check," repeated G.O., putting down his knight and swallowing air with painful lust.

... The grandmaster was being led along a passage in the midst of a silenced crowd. The one walking behind him barely touched his back with some hard object. A man in a black greatcoat with SS lightnings on the lapels was ahead of him, waiting. One step-half-a-second, another step-a-second, another step-two. . . . Steps going up. Why up? Such things ought to be done in a ditch. One must be brave. Must one? How long does it take to put a stinking burlap sack over one's head? Now, it got completely dark and difficult to breathe, and only somewhere far away an orchestra was playing with bravura "Khas-Bulat, you're bold . . . ."

"Checkmate," G.O. shrieked like an old copper horn.

"So, you see," muttered the grandmaster, "congratulations!"

"Ugh, ugh, umph, I'm all sweaty, just incredible, God damn it, I can't believe it happened! Incredible, slapping a checkmate on a grandmaster! Incredible, but a fact!" G.O. broke out laughing. "I'm quite a guy, ain't I!" He patted himself jokingly on the head. "Oh, you grandmaster, my dear little grandmaster," he buzzed, putting his hands on the grandmaster's shoulders and squeezing them with familiarity. "My dear young man .. . . The poor little nerves gave out, didn't they?"

"Yes, yes, I broke down," the grandmaster confirmed hurriedly.

G.O. swept the pieces off the board with a wide free gesture. The board was old and cracked, the varnished surface was chipped off in places exposing yellow tired old wood, with fragments of round stains left long ago, here and there, by glasses of railroad tea.

The grandmaster stared at the empty board, at the sixty-four absolutely dispassionate squares which were capable of absorbing not only his personal life, but an infinite number of lives. And this endless pattern of light and dark squares filled him with adoration and quiet joy. "It seems," he thought, "that I haven't committed any major acts of ignominy in my life."

"Suppose I were to tell about this, nobody would believe me," G.O. sighed.

"But why shouldn't they? What's so incredible about this? You are a good player with strong will power."

"No one will believe it," G.O. said. "They will say I'm lying. What proof do I have?"

"Allow me," said the grandmaster, a little hurt by G.O.'s words, staring at his hard, pink forehead. "I shall give you convincing proof. I knew that I would meet you."

He opened his briefcase and took out a gold medallion as large as the palm of his hand. Handsomely engraved upon it were the words: "The bearer of this defeated me at a game of chess. Grandmaster So-and-So."

"It remains only to add the date." He removed a set of engraving tools from his briefcase and neatly engraved the date in the corner of the medallion. "This is pure gold," he said, presenting the medallion.

"You aren't serious?" G.O. asked.

"Absolutely pure gold," repeated the grandmaster. "I ordered a lot of these medallions and I shall keep replenishing my stock."

1965

Translated from the Russian by Greta Slobin

ALEKSANDR KUSHNER

Aleksandr Kushner (b. 1936), poet, essayist, critic, and translator, was born in Leningrad to Jewish parents; he was evacuated to Syzran on the Volga during the war. After graduating in 1959 from the Herzen State Pedagogical Institute in Leningrad, Kushner taught Russian language and literature in high school; his poems appeared in 1956–57 in Leningrad collectives and periodicals. As a member of Gleb Semyonov's literary seminar *lito* at the Mining Institute (see **Vladimir Britanishsky**), Kushner took to heart his mentor's main lesson in liberal conformism: noble poetic subjects are eternal, and it is better to be in print than to dwell in the underground. This is not to say that Kushner shunned samizdat; Kushner's poems were featured in the Leningrad issue of the unsanctioned magazine *Syntax* (*Sintaksis*) in April 1960 and reprinted in the émigré review *Facets* (*Grani*) in 1965, including the programmatic "In Defense of Sentimentality," and were equally suitable for the official and unofficial Soviet publications of the Thaw.

In the 1960s, Kushner published three collections, *First Impression* (1962), *Night Watch* (1966, cf. the title of Rembrandt's 1642 painting), and *Omens* (1969), which established him on the Soviet pantheon. He was accepted to the Writers' Union in 1965. By the early 1970s, Kushner's position in Leningrad had become uniquely advantageous, since his competitors had moved to Moscow (e.g., **Evgeny Reyn**), emigrated (e.g., **Joseph Brodsky**), or were unable to publish (e.g., Viktor Krivulin [1944–2001]). As John Elsworth stated, "During the Soviet period [Kushner] avoided confrontation with the authorities, and never lost the possibility of publishing his work, although its uncommitted and non-ideological nature nevertheless gave rise to official condemnation on occasion." A 1962 lampoon in *Crocodile* (*Krokodil*) and a 1985 article against Kushner in *Pravda* delivered a calculated message but also made Kushner into a hero of the moderate Soviet intelligentsia (and their émigré counterparts).

By the 1970s, Kushner's traditionalist formal agenda had placed him in opposition to the official (e.g., Andrey Voznesensky) and the unofficial (e.g., **Genrikh Sapgir**) Moscow avant-garde. A masterfully versified discourse on language and beauty, Kushner's poetry lacks both the double irony and the confessional bitterness of his poetic icon, Innokenty Annensky (1856–1909). As a literary critic, Kushner himself denies the existence of "Soviet" poetry; he nonetheless exemplifies a prescriptively classical trajectory of postwar Soviet Russian poetry.

Prolific and hardworking, Kushner has published a new Russian poetry collection every two to three years since the early 1970s. Among his books are *Letter* (1974), *Direct Speech* (1975, cf. **Joseph Brodsky**'s 1977 *A Part of Speech*), *Tavrichesky Garden* (1984), *Day Dreams* (1986), *Flautist* (1990), *On a Gloomy Star* (1994), *A Flying Bank [of Clouds]* (2000), *Shrubbery* (2002), *Wave and Stone* (2003), *Anapest Has Been Chosen by Clouds* (2008), *With Chalk and Charcoal* (2010), *Between Fontanka and Moyka* (2016), and others. Selected editions of his poetry include *Poems* (1986), introduced by his official champion, academician Dmitry Likhachev, *Poems: Four Decades* (2000), and *Selected Poems* (2016). Kushner has published essays on poetry, *Apollo in the Snow: Notes in the Margins* (St. Petersburg, 1991) and volumes combining essays and poetry, e.g., *One Thousand Leaves: Poems and Essays* (1998, the title appealing to Annensky's 1910 *A Cypress Chest* with its "trifolia" of poems). Kushner has written children's books and published essays and literary translations.

A Jew and not a Party member, Kushner never behaved dishonorably as a public figure and never signed oaths of loyalty to the Soviet regime. Nor has Kushner ever sought to emigrate. He lives in his native St. Petersburg with his second wife, the critic Elena Nevzglyadova. Kushner's laurels are but one measure of his enduring success: Russian State Prize (1995), Northern Palmyra Prize (1995), *Novy Mir* Prize (1997), the "Poet" Prize (2005), and so forth. Translations of his poetry have come out in many languages. The reception of Kushner's recent book, *Wave and Stone: Poetry and Prose* (2003), suggests the trappings of a literary cult. "The essays of Aleksandr Kushner," Sergey Arutyunov wrote in April 2004, "and needless to say, his poetry, are healing and elevating."

* * *

Aleksandr Kushner has occasionally responded to Jewish subjects, including antisemitism, the Shoah, and the exodus of Soviet Jews, in a fashion that highlights his social and cultural identity. Featured in the volume *One Thousand Leaves* (1998), Kushner's poem "There is no Jewish chess! There cannot be an Aryan one! . . ." articulates an assimilationist rhetoric on Jewish selfhood, simultaneously striking down both a stereotype of Jewish pride and a stereotype of antisemitic xenophobia. Kushner seems to be polemicizing here with **Vassily Aksyonov**'s dramatization of "Jewish chess" in "Victory" (1965; in this anthology), where the following exchange occurs on the train between a habitual antisemite and his fellow traveler, a non-Jewish chessmaster:

"'I wonder: why are all the chess players Jewish?' G.O. asked. 'Why all?' said the grandmaster, 'for example, I'm not Jewish.'"

Both of Kushner's Jewish poems featured below were composed in 1966 and appeared in Kushner's third collection, *Omens* (1969).

* * *

When that teacher in Poland, so as not
To abandon the orphans, accompanied
Them down into hell, and the new Herod
Could exult in his villainous feat,
Where was this God that you love?
Or is he, as Berdyaev thought, weaker
Than the weakest of scoundrels, a bit of smoke
Behind the clouds, a mere puff?

Just a shade, then, among the shades,
An eccentric—frankly, a loser; and any
Of those red-haired German machine-gunner lads
Is stronger and more dependable than he.
And as for innocents slaughtered,
Bible stories are teeming with them.
No one, you can be sure, in that time
Gave them a second thought.

But no lesson from philosophy
Can damp down my distress,
And such an unearthly coolness
Arouses only loathing in me.
The only permissible God
Goes with the children into the chambers,
Evil hiked high on his shoulder,
Like that old teacher in Poland.[5]

1966

---

5   The poem is referring to Janusz Korczak (1878–1942), born Henryk Goldszmit, Jewish-
Polish pedagogue, doctor, and author, who in 1912 founded an orphanage for Jewish children
in Warsaw. On 5 August 1942, Korczak and the staff of his orphanage chose to share the fate of
a group of two hundred children who were sent to Treblinka, where they were all murdered.

LETTERS

As you can see, in Latin typescript,
The hills of Rome are depicted,
And lambcurls of Mediterranean whitecaps,
A tangle of scales and ringlets—the herd will
Have already started to climb while
The shepherd sucks wine from a handflask.

But the Georgian alphabet was shattered
Into small shards by a sword,
Or dropped itself from some steep
Shelf. The morning mist gives a
Slight shiver—Titsian, Paolo, and Ilya[6]
Gather up each little round chip.

But in the Russian *zhe* and *sha*
The soul lives as a soul should,
A blizzard, roaring and foaming, sweeps through,
And a spry coachman, red-cheeked, daring, and tipsy,
With a hand at each hip of his
Caftan, steers the little horse through.

And here is High German letterpress
Where the characters' Gothic thickness
Makes it hard to tell one from another,
Huddled there like the rooftops
Of Marburg. Calls in the night, sound of steps.
Careful, don't rouse them! Softer! Softer!

A Jewish letter takes to the air—
Where to?—How should it know where?—

---

6   Titsian—Titsian Tabidze (1895–1937), Georgian poet, a leader of the Georgian symbol-
    ist movement; Paolo—Paolo Iashvili (1895–1937), Georgian poet, the founder of the
    Georgian symbolist group Blue Horns; T. Tabidze was purged, and P. Iashvili committed
    suicide during the Great Terror; Ilya—probably Ilya Chavchavadze (1837–1907), major
    Georgian political leader, educator, and author; assassinated by political opponents.

When the words are all written like notes.
So, take up, then, the old violin,
Press the handkerchief against your chin
And don't wail, just play . . . There, there, what's the matter, what is it?

1966

Translated from the Russian by Carol Ueland and Robert Carnevale

GENRIKH SAPGIR

Genrikh Sapgir (1928–1999), poet, screenwriter, children's author, fiction writer, translator, and essayist, was born in Biysk, in Altay Region, where his father worked in shoe manufacturing during the period of the New Economic Policy (NEP). Sapgir's parents came from Vitebsk; his father had possibly descended from the Karaites, and his mother was related to Marc Chagall. Soon after Sapgir's birth, his family moved to Moscow, where he grew up and spent most of his life. Sapgir started composing verse at the age of eight, and his first teacher of poetry was Arseny Alving (Smirnov), a follower of the major Silver Age poet Innokenty Annensky. In 1944, the teenaged Sapgir met the poet, visual artist, and composer Evgeny Kropivnitsky (1893–1978), who became his aesthetic mentor, his "Teacher," as Sapgir always referred to him. In 1952, after military service in the Urals, where he narrowly escaped arrest for writing verses about Soviet camp prisoners, Sapgir returned to Moscow. In 1953–60, he worked in the sculpture studios of the Moscow Art Foundation, where he befriended a number of avant-garde sculptors, including Ernst Neizvestny, Vladimir Lempert, Nikolay Silis, and Vadim Sidur.

In the 1950s–60s, Sapgir was a member of the underground "Lianozovo" group (named after the small town outside Moscow where members of the group congregated), whose guru was Evgeny Kropivnitsky and whose members included Oskar Rabin, Valentina Kropivnitskaya, Igor Kholin, **Yan Satunovsky**, Vsevolod Nekrasov, and others. Performative and vibrant, marked by idiomaticity, absurdism, and grotesqueness, Sapgir's poems of the time expose the social, aesthetic, and political aberrations of Soviet society.

Throughout Sapgir life, experimental visual artists—among them Ely Belyutin, Aleksandr Kharitonov, Vladimir Nemukhin, Viktor Pivovarov, Oskar Rabin, Eduard Shteynberg, Ülo Sooster, Anatoly Zverev, and others—were his closest comrades, and he consistently aimed in his own poetry for a synthesis of the verbal and the pictorial. Sapgir liked to paraphrase and reverse the words of Pablo Picasso: "'We and our poets,' said Picasso. And I will say, 'We and our painters.'" (Sapgir's own "sonnets on shirts"—sonnets that were literally drawn with a marker on white shirts—were exhibited at several shows of unofficial Soviet art in the 1970s.)

Sapgir destroyed nearly all his works written prior to 1958. He considered his "book" *Voices* his poetic birth. Written between 1958 and 1962 and circulated in Soviet samizdat, the poems from *Voices* did not appear in the USSR until 1989. In 1959–60, Sapgir became one of the writers publicly ostracized in the Soviet press and blacklisted for participating in Aleksandr Ginzburg's samizdat review *Syntax* (*Sintaksis*). Sapgir was unable to publish any of his original work for "adults" in the USSR until 1989. At the same time, he was one of the most famous underground poets of the Soviet 1960s–80s. Following the palliative advice of **Boris Slutsky**, Sapgir applied his profuse formal gifts and mytho-poetic imagination to writing for young readers, becoming one of the USSR's most beloved authors for children, with numerous books and forty animation screenplays to his credit (his works for children have remained immensely popular in post-Soviet Russia).

Sapgir's only preperestroika collection, *Sonnets on Shirts*, came out in 1978 in Paris, which Sapgir first visited in 1987. In the 1960s–80s, Sapgir's poetry and prose "not for children" appeared in the West in Russian émigré periodicals and also in translation, mainly into German and French (in 1979, a selection was featured in the scandalous collective *Metropol*; see **Vassily Aksyonov**). The ban on Sapgir's adult poetry was lifted in the Soviet Union in 1988, when his poems appeared in *Novy mir*. Between 1989 and 1999, over twenty volumes and chapbooks of Sapgir's poetry and prose were published, including *Moscow Myths* (1989), *Pushkin, Bufarev and Others* (1992), *Selected Works* (1993), and *Levitating and Sleeping* (1997). After Sapgir's "adult" work finally appeared in the USSR during perestroika, he spent his last decade as a patriarch of Moscow avant-garde letters and a mentor to younger poets, in whose "new freedom" from Soviet ethics and aesthetics Sapgir put stock—perhaps wishfully.

In 1998, under the influence of his then ailing third wife, Lyudmila Rodovskaya, Sapgir was baptized as a Russian Orthodox in Paris, his second favorite city after Moscow. In October 1999, at the height of his fame and acclaim, Sapgir died in Moscow in his wife's arms while riding on a trolleybus to a poetry reading in which he was to participate.

Sapgir's last summer was the most prolific in his life. The volume *Summer with the Angels*, comprised mainly Sapgir's works composed in the summer of 1999, appeared posthumously in 2000. It included the ground-breaking book *Tactile Instruments* (1999), whose significance and formal innovativeness can be compared to that of *Tender Buttons* (1914) by Gertrude Stein (1874–1946), with whom Genrikh Sapgir shared much more than his initials. The first academic edition of Sapgir's work, edited by Maxim D. Shrayer and **David Shrayer-Petrov**, was published by the New Poet's Library in St. Petersburg in 2004. That year Shrayer and **Shrayer-Petrov** also published the first book about Sapgir.

* * *

Besides his writings for children, Sapgir's published oeuvres include over six hundred poems and eleven long poems. From the late 1950s, Jewish and Judaic themes permeated Sapgir's works. Written under the impact of Sapgir's close friendship with the talented Yiddish writer for both children and adults Ovsey Driz (Shike Driz, 1908–1971), whose works he masterfully translated into Russian, the book *Psalms* (written in 1965–66) is Sapgir's most important Jewish text. Sapgir's Psalms are transpositions of and meditations on the themes and events of the Biblical Psalms. The scale of the radical transmogrification of Judaic sacred texts, as well as the degree to which Sapgir infused into his Psalms the vestiges of his contemporary history, politics, ideology, and everyday life, make Sapgir's book a Jewish-Russian text akin to Allen Ginsberg's *Kaddish* (1959). The setting of Sapgir's Psalms is the Soviet Union, and Sapgir's contemporary Soviet Jews act in place of the ancient Hebrews. The Psalmist himself may well be a *shiker* (drunk), a Yiddish poet-prophet living and writing in a country that by the 1950s had cut off the blood supply to its Jewish culture.

IN MEMORY OF MY FATHER

And no more time remained . . .
That is not news.
That often happens—
According to St. John the Divine's views
And the notations of Ecclesiastes.

Beneath the blue sky of Vostryakovo[7]
What
Had been
My
Father
Was a white
Unrecognizable face.

---

7   Vostryakovo—cemetery in the southwest of Moscow named after the former village of the same name.

For us
There's time.
For him?
No thing?

To keep from extra jolts
They placed the coffin on a sledge,
Without hurrying
They pulled it
To the gravesite edge.
The rabbi
Constantly addressed you: —Benjamin
Son of Fayvish!
But the body remained
Restrained.
No name?
No tribe or nation?
No time remained?

1962

PSALM 3[8]

1. Lord I am running!

2. Glancing around I see
how my enemies multiply—
or do their ugly faces burn in me?
A mania—
run run

---

8 Sapgir follows the numbering of the Psalms in the Orthodox Christian and Catholic Bibles, both of which follow the Greek translation (Septuagint); the latter differs slightly from the numbering of the Psalms in the Hebrew Bible and the Protestant Bible, which follow the Masoretic Text. Thus, Sapgir's Psalm 116 corresponds to Psalm 117 in the Jewish and Protestant Bibles; Psalm 132, to 133; Psalm 136, to 137; but Psalms 3 and 150 in both the Orthodox and the Catholic Bibles correspond to the same respective numbers in the Jewish and Protestant Bibles. Parenthetical numbers have been added in the titles of the Psalms where the numbering differs.

3. Spain Germany
Poland Russia
What scorches my unshod
heels so?
These ashes
are still warm
Lord release me!

4. —There is no salvation for him in God!
—There is no salvation for him in God!
—There is no salvation for him in God!
But for you—zip zero nyet
I run

5. And I laugh and I cry
but do not shy away

6. Here I lay down and slept
and God protected my sleep

7. I will not shy away
let there be more of you
ten thousand more of you
for He—my shield—
will crack your jaw—will break your teeth—

8. Lord I relie but I run
for
I cannot not run
I run like a hare holding the flaps of my coat
I run from my very own home
from my son (the louse)
Absalom
from my bothers and wife I run

9. I run and think on the run

1965–66

PSALM 116 (117)

1. Praise the Lord all you nations:
id'n and od'n, radas and vedas

2. Glorify him all tribes
beginning in O
and in U
and in A
and in I

3. For His kindness
even His kindness
even for nothing—
Halleluiah!

4. Desiring nothing
Halleluiah
lying drunk polluted
Halleluiah
and in me—through me
all nations all times
howl:
God—take me!
Take me! Take me! Take me!
Halleluiah!

1965–66

PSALM 132 (133)

1. It's good on a summer evening sunny
in the country
for two condolent souls

2. Leaves—and boards—and light and the grass
and thoughts—an absence of thoughts
shines through and breathes
warms and caresses
and lowers its shadows

3. *This*—like a precious balm upon the head
running down the beard
the beard of Aaron

4. Like the dew of Hermon
that falls upon the mountains of Zion
a blessing and life forever

1965–66

PSALM 136 (137)

To Ovsey Driz

1. By the streams of Babylon we sat and wept
—O nori—nora!
—O nori—nora ruolo![9]
—Juden juden sing sing! More joyfully!—
our captors laughed
—Er zangt vi di einige Nachtigal[10]

—Veili bashar! Veili baion!
—Juden juden dance! Hop—hop!

2. They stood with hands on automatics
—O Yahweh!
their dogs—the killers—looked at us
                              with interest
—O leivi baaram batsy Tsion
in a foreign land!

---

9 Most likely, Sapgir did not know Hebrew, as opposed to Yiddish, which he, like many other Jews of his generation, knew passively since childhood. A number of possible sources—dictionaries, speakers of Hebrew, the Jewish liturgy?—may have contributed to the making of the phrases and lines that are meant to communicate to the reader a vaguely recognizable sense of the Hebrew of the Psalms and also of the dialogue taking place in the poem between the Babylonians and the captive Jews, which would have been conducted in Aramaic. Three main factors, etymology, the text of the Hebrew Bible, and Sapgir's structural composition of the poem, influenced the shape and the sound of these phrases: "O nori—nora!"; "O nori—nora ruolo"; "Veili bashar! Veili baion!"; and "O leivi baaram batsy Tsion." From the etymological point of view, besides the obvious "Tsion" = "Zion," the word "nori" may be a partial anagram of the Hebrew "kinor" = "harp" (which points to the text of the Hebrew Psalm 137). Also, "baaram" should probably be interpreted here as the Hebrew "ba aram" = "in Aram" (in Babylon, which could also refer to other places of exile). In Leonid Katsis's reading, "batsy Zion" suggests the Hebrew "daughters of Zion." "Leivi" points to "levi" (Levite) and the Jewish tribe. Thus, O leivi baaram batsy Tsion" may be interpreted as "O Jews in Babylon, daughters [of Zion] [sing us one of the songs] of Zion," that is, in keeping with the corresponding lines in the Hebrew Psalm. One also finds a structural parallel between "Juden juden [German for 'Jews'] sing sing! More joyfully [. . .] Juden juden dance!" and "O leivi baaram batsy Tsion." Finally, the word "veili" in "Veili bashar! Veili baion!" is an anagram of "leivi." Sapgir's meaningful "imitations" of Hebrew and Aramaic are much more than a brilliant use of onomatopoeia and word/sound play.

10 Er zangt vi di einige Nachtigal (Yidd.) = He sings like some nightingale.

3. The fatty soot of our children
settled on their faces
as we departed
up the crematory chimney
as smoke—to the sky

4. Remember o Lord against the children of Edom
the day of Jerusalem
When they said
—Zerstören! Order No. 125
—Vernichten! Order No. 126
—Vernichten! No. 127[11]

5. The daughters of Babylon walked among us
scraping their lacquered boots—
six-month-old lambkins
with German shepherds
—O nori—nora! ruolo!
Whip! whip!—
Erschiessen[12]

6. Happy the man who shall seize and smash
your little ones against a rock

1965–66

---

11 Zerstören (Ger.) = to annilhilate; vernichten (Ger.) = to destroy, to erase from the face of
the earth.
12 Erschiessen (Ger.) = to shoot dead.

PSALM 150

1. Praise the Lord with timbrels
with drums
. . . . (three loud beats)

2. Praise Him in the assembly of drunkards
. . . . (swearing obscenely)

3. Praise Him in the weekly factory meetings
. . . . (two or three phrases from the newspaper)

4. Inarticulately
. . . . (childish babble adamic language)

5. With a clapping of hands
. . . . (clap hands three times)

6. Praise Him like a dog
. . . . (bark three times)

7. Like a wolf
. . . . (howl three times)

8. Silently exulting
. . . .(silence)

9. Let everything that has breath praise the Lord
. . . . shout cry wail knock—
                complete
(liberation)
Halleluiah!
(12 times in all keys)

1965–66

A POLE RODE

A Pole rode
Over plains
To hounds, with his knights:
Drzbrzbrzewski, Pszpszpszewski,
And a monk.

Hastened he to Krakow town
To select from among all Poles—
Rzyrzka pszyszka pszbrze goodski[13]—
A new king.

On the way he met a Yid,
Who was fleeing Krakow,
Gertel-mertel, zuchter-nachter,[14]
Family in tow.

Take pity on us, Sir!
Let us go, I'll give you all we have:
Gelt'n-velt'n, nitkes-latkes,[15]
I know what!

---

13 In line 3 of stanza 2, as well as in line 3 of stanza 5, Sapgir plays on the way Russians stereotypically perceive and imitate Polish speech, with its characteristic sibilants, and thereby creates a series of nonsense "Polish" words rendered in Russian transliteration as though they were real words: *Żyżka pszyszka pszbrze dobrze; Matka boska bryśka pryśka*. However, at the end of the former of these two lines and at the beginning of the latter, Sapgir uses genuine Polish words and expressions that the Russian reader understands owing to the similarity of the Russian and Polish roots in those instances: *dobrze* ("well" or "good") and *Matka Boska* ("Mother of God"). To render a comparable effect, the translator has created Polish-English synthetic words by combining English roots with Polish suffixes: *goodski* from "good" and the Polish suffix "ski"; *godski* from "god" and "ska." In "britely spritely" the translator creates a phonetic effect similar to that of the nonsensical Polish *bryśka pryśka*.
14 Zucher-nachter: cf. *zuchen* (Yiddish) = to seek; *nacht* (Yiddish) = night.
15 *Gelt'n* (Yiddish) = money; *velt'n* (Yiddish) = worlds; *nitkes* = probably from the Russian *nitki* = threads; *latkes* (Yiddish) = potato pancakes.

Barks and shouts, and all is lost . . .
From the coach a lady comes,
Mother of Godska, britely spritely,
Pretty she.

The lady cried out, "Father!
Remember Malka, get off your knees!"
Now geshtorbn, oy geborgn,[16]
Ouch he'll whip!

Gertsel-shmertsel[17] his own daughter,
His own blood, a Yidess
He didn't recognize.

1985

Translated from the Russian by Gerald Janecek

---

16 *Geshtorbn* (Yiddish) = past participle of "to die"; *geborgn* (Yiddish) = past participle of "to save, to rescue."
17 *Shmerts* (Yiddish) = death.

ALEKSANDR ARONOV

Aleksandr Aronov (1934–2001), poet, journalist, and translator, was born in Moscow in a Jewish family. After graduating from the Moscow City Pedagogical Institute, he worked as a schoolteacher in the environs of Moscow and later in the city itself. Aronov subsequently received a candidate's degree from the Institute of Artistic Education and conducted research in the field of mathematical linguistics. For over thirty years, Aronov was a special correspondent at the *Moscow Komsomol Member* (*Moskovskii Komsomolets* [*MK*]), a popular daily that managed to preserve some of its Thaw-era intellectual rigor during the years of "stagnation."

Even though Aronov was a published poet since the late 1950s, he was unable to place a collection of his verse until 1987. Five of his poems were featured in issue 1 of Aleksandr Ginzburg's samizdat magazine *Syntax* in 1959, among them "Ballad of Streetcar Painting." Circulating in the Moscow underground of the 1960s–80s, his poems occasionally made it through the hurdles of blacklisting and appeared in Soviet periodicals and collectives, including *Youth* (1964) and *Poetry Day Moscow* (1980). Aronov's poems of the Thaw displayed an affinity with those of **Boris Slutsky** and Leonid Martynov (1905–1980); the poet identified with the critique of philistinism by the émigré **Vladislav Khodasevich**. At *MK* Aronov sometimes published his poems, although in the 1970s and 1980s he did little to promote them, pushing instead for younger poets, among them Oleg Khlebnikov and Evgeny Bunimovich. Where his poetic texts reached a massive mainstream audience, it was in the form of song lyrics, including the song "If You Don't Have an Aunt" (music Mikael Tariverdiev), sung by actor Andrey Myagkov in Eldar Ryazanov's film *The Irony of Fate* (1975).

As both a columnist for the relatively liberal *MK* and a vastly underpublished poet, Aronov enjoyed a legendary status among the younger Moscow poetry lovers. When Aronov's poems finally appeared widely in the reform-era Soviet Union, the results were more disappointing than they might have been: unlike some of his peers, such as **Genrikh Sapgir**, who was also unpublished in the USSR until perestroika, Aronov's 1960s verse aesthetics had remained virtually unchanged. Aronov's first poetry book, *Safety Island*, was released by Soviet Writer publishing house in 1987, followed by *Texts* (1989), the chapbook *First Life* (1989), and *Rain of Uninhabited Planets,* a book-length section in the poetry annual *Sources* (*Istoki,* 1997), all published in Moscow. Aleksandr Aronov died in 2001 in Moscow, after a long illness.

* * *

From his earliest poems, the subject of his dual, Jewish-Soviet identity preoccupied Aronov. "How can I connect these two stars—/The five pointed and the six pointed?" he wrote in "Juvenilia." Later in the same poem from the 1950s (unpublished until the 1980s), recalling the famous lines from the civil war epic poem *Tripolie Three-Field* by Boris Kornilov (1907–1938), Aronov wrote, "Yids and Communists, step forward!/I'm stepping forward. Shoot me twice!" Aronov contributed two translations of Yaakov Fichman (1881–1958) to the anthology *Poets of Israel* (Moscow, 1963), edited by **Boris Slutsky**. The experience, as well as inevitable thoughts of emigration, informed his powerful poem "Haifa. Refugee Camp," about a Jewish-Polish woman who lost her family in the Shoah and is learning Hebrew in Haifa.

"That raving blatherskite . . . ," the second of the two poems selected below, testifies to Aronov's identification with the Biblical Aaron, brother of—and principal spokesman for—the tongue-tied Moses. The first poem in the selection, "Ghetto. 1943," also from the 1960s, was familiar to the readers of the Soviet literary underground before its publication at home. The argument of Aronov's poem juxtaposes the events of the Warsaw Ghetto Uprising (1943) with those of the Warsaw Uprising (1944) and does so in a way that both decries the inaction of the Polish underground during the former and offers an apologetic perspective on the inaction of the Soviet Army during the latter. It also suggests that Warsaw's non-Jewish population was not particularly sympathetic toward the victims of the Warsaw Ghetto. (The Anglo-American readers would have found a similar authorial perspective in Louis Begley's novel *Wartime Lies* [1991], set in Poland during the Shoah and told from the point of view of a Jewish boy living in hiding and passing himself off as a Polish Christian; the boy relates the prevalent sentiment of the Warsaw residents in 1943: "But now Germans were teaching the Jews a final lesson, and at the end of every afternoon, the weather being mild, we all went to the roof under Pani Z.'s direction to watch what she called our fireworks. She claimed it [the shelling and burning of the Jewish Ghetto by the Nazis] was the first real entertainment the Germans had provided in all this sad time.")

In the Warsaw Ghetto Uprising (19 April–16 May 1943), a force of about seven hundred fifty members of the Jewish Fighting Organization, assisted by the Jewish Military Union, fiercely opposed Nazi troops for almost a month before being crushed and annihilated. The fighters in the Warsaw Ghetto Uprising enjoyed limited private support from Warsaw residents. However, despite the efforts by the Jewish underground to persuade members of the Polish guerilla forces to join arms and rise together, they refused.

In the Warsaw Uprising (1 August–2 October 1944), about 40,000 guerrilla fighters of the Polish Home Army, hoping to liberate Warsaw, fought superior Nazi forces while Soviet troops waited nearby across the Wisła (Vistula), refusing to render substantial military assistance and not allowing the Allies to drop ammunition and supplies. As a result, 85 percent of Warsaw was razed.

Aleksandr Aronov's "Ghetto. 1943" represents a striking example of a vision of history by a Jewish-Russian poet that is both Judeocentric and Russocentric or, perhaps more accurately put, both Judeocentric and Sovietocentric.

GHETTO. 1943

There was the ghetto burning,
There was the ghetto burning,
And Warsaw was delighted
Throughout those four long days.
As loud as dynamite,
That crackling fire was bright,
And people watching said,
"Bedbugs ablaze!"

And twenty-five years later
A very sharp debater
Met with me over a bottle
Of wine for his tirade.
This Janusz, my good friend,
Began, "You can't defend
Your monstrous Russian guilt.
My Poland was betrayed.

In '45, you Russians
Ignored the repercussions
And stayed across the Wisła.
Why? You let Warsaw fall."
And I replied, "Well, first
Our strength was at its worst,
And then there was no way
To help you, after all."

"So our Warsaw Uprising
Is blasted and capsizing.
So our Warsaw Uprising
Is drowned in that bloodshed."
And with a quavering sigh,
"Before my brothers die,
I'd rather die myself,"
My friend and colleague said.

I said to him, returning,
"There was the ghetto burning,
There was the ghetto burning
Throughout those four long days.
As loud as dynamite,
That crackling fire was bright,
And all of you just said,
"Bedbugs ablaze!"

1960s

* * *

That raving blatherskite,
Hysterical and brittle,
That Moses was a fright,
Wheezing and spraying spittle.

Aaron, my ancestor,
Whom destiny had humbled,
Would courteously defer
And listen as he mumbled.

He didn't roll his eyes.
He didn't quake and quiver.
He'd merely verbalize
Moans Moses would deliver.

Who saw the Promised Land
And freedom for his nation?
I think I understand
Aaron's fierce supplication:

"Lord, why should I expend
Intelligence in sadness?
Why should my talents lend
Authority to madness?

Why should, when people seem
To make mature decisions,
A holy fool's mad dream
Defeat the truth with visions?

O prophet, blowhard, freak,
Your younger brother's risen.
Stand here, and I will speak
And free us from our prison."

1960s

Translated from the Russian by Maxim D. Shrayer and J. B. Sisson

SEMYON LIPKIN

Semyon Lipkin (1911–2003), poet, translator, novelist, and memoirist, was born in Odessa to the family of a Jewish tailor active in the Menshevik movement. Lipkin's father took him to Odessa's Main Synagogue, where he would go to "talk politics." One of his strong childhood memories was observing Hayyim Nahman Bialik engrossed in conversation with Lipkin's father, in the courtyard of the synagogue. Parallel to studying at a gymnasium, Lipkin received Hebrew and Torah instruction at a heder for one and a half years.

Lipkin published poems as a teenager in Odessa. In 1929, he moved to Moscow, where his poems appeared in literary journals in 1929–30. A protégé of fellow Odessan **Eduard Bagritsky**, Lipkin unfairly judged him in his memoirs, published in 1997. Lipkin got to know **Osip Mandelstam** and subsequently wrote an admiring memoir about him.

After 1931, Lipkin had a difficult time placing poetry and turned instead to literary translation. Lipkin became a member of the Union of Soviet Writers in 1934. In 1937, he graduated from the Moscow Institute of Engineering and Economics. The project that put him on the map was his Russian translation of the Kalmyk national epic *Dzhangar* (1940). In his prolific career, Lipkin translated and adapted classical and modern poets and heroic epics of republics and ethnic regions in Central Asia, the Volga basin, the Caucasus, and the Far East, including *Manas* (Kyrgyz) and *Narts* (Kabarda-Balkar), as well as ancient epics, including *Gilgamesh* and *Mahabharata*. After studying Tajik-Farsi, Lipkin translated the works of Firdousi and Rudaki. Lipkin's translations from the Yiddish included works by Perets Markish, Itsik Fefer, Shmuel Halkin, Moyshe Kulbak, and others. Having forgotten the alphabet, Lipkin relied on Latin transcriptions of the Yiddish originals.

Lipkin was a military journalist during World War II and fought at Stalingrad. His original poems did not appear until the Thaw. His poems published in 1956 in *Novy mir* were immediately attacked as "album verse." While Lipkin enjoyed a sterling career as a top Soviet translator (poet, translator, and memoirist Anatoly Nayman labeled Lipkin the "emperor of translating the peoples of the USSR"), he had a more difficult time publishing poetry. *Eyewitness*, Lipkin's first collection of poems, appeared in Moscow in 1967, followed by *Eternal Day* (1975) and *Notebook of Being: Poems and Translations* (Dushanbe, Tajikistan, 1977).

In the 1970s, Lipkin began to contribute to émigré publications. In 1980, he and his second wife, **Inna Lisnyanskaya**, resigned from the Writers' Union to protest the expulsion of two cocontributors to the *Metropol* collective (1979; see **Vassily Aksyonov**). He was blacklisted in the USSR, but his books appeared in Russian in the United States, cementing Lipkin's reputation abroad. *Freedom* [or *Will*] (1981), a retrospective of Lipkin's poetry, was edited by **Joseph Brodsky**.

In October 1986, Lipkin was restored to the Writers' Union, and his works began to appear in the USSR. His books published in Russia include *Lyre. Poems of Different Years* (1989), *Moonlight. Long Poems* (1991), and others. *Quadriga* (1997) includes Lipkin's fiction and memoirs. Lipkin, who had safeguarded a copy of **Vassily Grossman**'s *Life and Fate*, edited Grossman's four-volume *Works* (1998).

Traditionalists admire Lipkin's verse, which was composed in the classical vein but occasionally betrayed the Soviet modernist winds of his youth. Lipkin considered his "main" poetical work to be the narrative poem *Technical Supplies Officer* (1961). Lipkin was hailed in post-Soviet Russia as a minor classic and an emblem of Jewish artists who had not emigrated and, Russian by culture as they were, have preserved a Jewish spirit. In 1995, Lipkin received the Pushkin Prize (Germany). He died in Moscow at age ninety-two.

"I cannot part with [the Jewish theme]," Lipkin told the editor of this anthology in January 2000. Lipkin turned to Jewish topics during the Shoah, and some of Lipkin's Shoah poems were gathered in his collection *Will*; his Jewish poems were featured in *Ancient Letters* (1991) and *Seven Decades* (2000). One of Lipkin's most powerful poems, "Ashes," dated 1967 and published, notably, in the Moscow annual collection *Poetry Day* (*Den' poezii*), speaks in the first person about a victim of the Shoah. Having been burned in a concentration camp crematorium, Lipkin's poetic protagonist "whispers": "They've incinerated me./ How can I now reach Odessa?"

The poem selected below dates to the 1970s, when Jewish motifs resurged in Lipkin's lyrics. That Lipkin was writing Judaic religious poetry in Moscow in the late Soviet period is in itself remarkable. His cycle "Abraham's Last Night" (1981) belongs to a series of Lipkin's meditations on episodes of the Torah. In several Jewish poems, such as "Khaim (Hayim)," which Lipkin contributed to *Metropol* (1979), he resorted to historical analogy and Aesopian language.

Decades of translating the poetry and epics of different ethnic groups, including such victims of Stalinist genocidal repressions and collective punishment as Crimean Tatars, Kalmyks, and Chechens, made Lipkin exceptionally attuned to the persecution of smaller nations. At the same time, Lipkin's writings about the Jews display an obsession with demonstrating that Jews are just as capable of wrongdoing as are non-Jews—as though such a truism requires proof. This tendency, displayed, for instance, in Lipkin's novel *Notes of a Resident* (published 1992), amounts to Lipkin's compulsion to persuade the Russian majority that he is not a Jewish nationalist.

Lipkin has resorted to Christian imagery in memorializing victims of Nazism and Stalinism. Discussing his own identity and what defines a Jewish writer in Russia, Lipkin stated in January 2000, "The important thing is how a person perceives himself . . . . Not for a single moment have I felt myself to be *not* Jewish. But I love Christ . . . consider him the greatest Jewish prophet. I cannot perceive him as the son of God; for me from the Jewish point of view this is impossible. God is one and unknowable. For God to pass his sperm via Archangel Gabriel [. . .] [t]his to me is wild fantasy . . . a concession to paganism. But I love Christ . . . as the one who authored the greatest books."

KHAIM

Where once speeded the host of Geser,[18]
And in later years—a gendarme colonel,
Where to this day an Old Believer
Keeps in his hut a prayer-filled journal,
Where the yellowed Buryat Buddhist books
Have been scattered across remote aimáks,[19]
There, silver tinted, voluminous,
Flows a river that's called Khaím.[20]

---

18 Geser—man-deity of extraordinary prowess, protagonist of the national Buryat-Mongolian heroic epic; Geser (Bukhe Beligte) embodies the Buryat-Mongolian shamanistic ideal of (super)man living in balance with nature and his own mission. A number of sacred sites devoted to Geser and his cult are found in Buryatia, including its capital, Ulan-Ude. Lipkin translated *Geser* into Russian (published Moscow, 1973).

19 Aimak (Turkic, Mongolian)—a tribal unit of Turkic or Mongolian ethnic groups; in modern Russian, *aimák* refers to an administrative center in the Buryat Autonomous Republic and the Republic of Mongolia.

20 A play on words and historical associations engenders this poem, built around the coincidence of Khaím, the name of an actual river and a mountain pass in Eastern Siberia, and the Jewish name Kháim (*Hayim* [Heb.] = life). In the poem "Union," Lipkin wrote about the Yi, an ethnic group from southern China. Lipkin was taken with the fact that in Chinese

We may doubt those tales of old:
How homeward he trekked across the taiga,
He was stopped and was slain for a pocket of gold
By a roving criminal gang.
Or how he sheltered those runaway
Convicts in his roadside inn,
And his generous nature was rewarded . . .
There's a river and mountain pass: Khaím.

The eternal spirit dwells in an idol of stone,
An ancient scroll, and a little cross.
In Siberia, Khaim, were you content
With your river flow and mountain pass?
What's that silvery sparkling I've seen?
Who is smiling in the taiga? The one
Who once confused the Benarian[21] wise men
And saved his kin in the hot desert sun?

1973

Translated from the Russian by Amelia Glaser

---

just one character and in Russian just one letter (*i*) captures the name of an entire people.
A scandal erupted after the publication of "Union" in 1968: as the "anti-Zionist" campaign
gained speed in the Soviet Union, many took the poem to be a coded tribute to Israel and
the Jewish people.

21 Varanasi (Banaras, Benaras)—one of India's most ancient cities, a religious center and major
site of pilgrimages; located about eight miles from Sarnath, where Buddha preached his first
sermon.

YURY KARABCHIEVSKY

Yury Karabchievsky (1938–1992), fiction writer, essayist, and poet, was born and grew up in Moscow. After graduating from the Moscow Energy Institute, he worked as a researcher in biomedical laboratories. Karabchievsky was employed as a repairman at Moscow's Etalon factory servicing electronic equipment from 1974 to 1989. Karabchievsky debuted as a poet during the Thaw but published only a few poems in the Soviet press, in 1961 in *Youth* (*Yunost'*) and in 1965 in *Rainbow* (*Raduga*). Karabchievsky's poetry was later collected in *A Farewell to Friends* (Moscow, 1992). Demoralized by the 1968 Prague events, Karabchievsky stopped pursuing a Soviet literary career. After 1972, he turned to prose and began to send his works abroad, where in the 1970s and 1980s they appeared in émigré periodicals. Published in *Facets* (*Grani*) in 1980, Karabchievsky's meditative short novel *Longing for Armenia* developed the Armenian theme of **Osip Mandelstam, Vasily Grossman**, and Andrey Bitov (b. 1935). The KGB kept Karabchievsky under a "hood" (Karabchievsky's wording); he described the harassment in the novel *Unforgettable Mishunya*, first published in Israel in 1989.

Karabchievsky participated as a poet in the *Metropol* collective (1979; see **Vassily Aksyonov**). He later spoke of the *Metropol* scandal as his "legitimization": "I had been completely unknown, and I now joined a well-known group of authors." *Mayakovsky's Resurrection*, a scathingly personal treatment of Vladimir Mayakovsky, brought Karabchievsky recognition. Published in Munich in 1985, the book received the 1986 Dahl Prize (Paris). Disseminated in the underground, Karabchievsky's book touched a raw nerve of the Soviet intelligentsia, whose members were divided on Mayakovsky: some nostalgic for youthful Soviet illusions, some truly appreciating Mayakovsky's peerless contribution to Russian and Soviet culture, and many (including some dissidents and refuseniks) dismissing Mayakovsky on simplistic if principled ideological grounds.

Having received permission to emigrate during the reform years, Karabchievsky chose to stay in the USSR, anxious about his future in Israel and tempted by the new publishing opportunities. Karabchievsky's return to the Soviet press occurred in 1988, and in 1988–90, the leading magazines, including *Novy mir*, *October* (*Oktiabr'*), and *People's Friendship* (*Druzhba narodov*), printed his poetry, fiction, and essays. Karabchievsky's works, previously published abroad, were reprinted, and he enjoyed favor with the critics. Three books of his prose appeared in Moscow in 1990–91.

In 1991–92, Karabchievsky spent periods of time in Israel, where he had close family. He never made aliyah; in April 1992, having returned from his third visit, he spoke both of the hardships of living in Israel and of his "great attachment" to it, of Israel's "familial [. . .] very warm, cozy" atmosphere. In the same interview with Sergey Shapovalov, Karabchievsky described Russian ultranationalists standing in Moscow's underground passes with antisemitic slogans. Of his conflicted feelings as a Russian Jew, Karabchievsky said, "I think today not one Russian Jew steeped in Russian culture, living in it, can escape the sensation of living out the rest of his days [*dozhivanie*]. In all likelihood, Russian Jewry is coming to an end. [. . .] I, as a person living out the rest of his days, have no other place to live out those remaining days, [and so] I must and will live here, unless, of course, something totally extreme happens. It's a heavy, bitter sensation, and it's hard to come to terms with it [. . .]. Yury Karabchievsky took his own life in the summer of 1992 in Moscow.

* * *

Students of Jewish-Russian writing will find intriguing Karabchievsky's essays "**Mandelstam** Street" (published 1974), "God's Mistake [cf. **Isaak Babel**'s phrase in the story "How It Was Done in Odessa"] or a Russian Jew's Reflections on Russian Jews" (published 1991), and "On [**Samuil**] **Marshak**" (published 1993). One of Karabchievsky's most provocative essays was titled "Struggle with a Jew." First published in 1989, it examined the 1986 epistolary confrontation between Natan Eidelman (1930–1989), a prominent Moscow cultural historian, and Viktor Astafiev (1924–2001), a major representative of Russian Village Prose. Karabchievsky's discursive writings were collected in *Mayakovsky's Resurrection. Essays* (Moscow, 2000).

In April 1992, Karabchievsky stated, "I actually do not like it when they say that in my prose I'm preoccupied with the Jewish theme. My theme is life, people, circumstances, relationships. But I write only about what I know well. In the end, only about myself, even when it's not about me [. . .]." Fiction and creative nonfiction were, for Karabchievsky, both a métier and an outlet for venting his biographical and cultural frustrations and as such a mélange of beautifully sensitive and hysterically uncontrolled pages.

Those interested in reading about antisemitic taunting in the postwar USSR—a rite of passage for many Jews growing up there—will be well served by turning to the opening of Karabchievsky's most accomplished fiction, the autobiographical novel *The Life of Alexander Zilber* (1974–75). Originally serialized in 1980 in *Time and We* (*Vremya i my*), it was reprinted several times in the reform-era USSR. An excerpt from the opening chapter follows below.

FROM *THE LIFE OF ALEXANDER ZILBER*[*]

Chapter 1

3

[...] Alik darts into his building, I walk on alone. A long, long line of mottled sheds with roofs that jump up and down. The smell of hay and rabbit droppings. I open *our* gate, I'm still breathing heavily, and my legs can't keep up with me, my hands are black with tree sap, and my face is swollen from crying. And I know that I shouldn't say anything, and at the same time I know that I'll tell everything, and even embellish some, even add a few tears to the sighs and lamentations of my family. The two-tongued murmuring will envelop me like a warm wall, and I'll be thinking that these Jewish exhortations do not replicate the Russian ones but carry within them something all their own, truly important and comforting.

Mama's already home from work, she's standing by the door to the terrace in that green crepe-de-chine dress of hers, and upon seeing her, I quicken my step, but my sadness, ready to burst out in a stream of heart-rending words, is driven back inside by another, incomparably greater sadness. My mother's beautiful, black eyes, slightly arched, look straight at me, beyond me, through me, further, further, into infinity. Her bright lips part, and . . . .

"Sashenka!" she says joyfully. "You know, don't you, that tomorrow morning we're going to camp!"

Samoylov sits two rows behind me, around him—the veterans from the month before, and he raises his head, our eyes meet, and he's not singing anymore, not Samoylov, he's *looking*. God, how I know that look, it's always the same! The astonishing inevitability of it, that for every twenty-five indifferent looks you'll find at least one such look–just like Samoylov's. There isn't even

---

[*]   The text has been abridged.

anger there; more like joy: he's found me, my Samoylov. Everything was going just fine for him, only I was missing, and now I've appeared, made to order. I'm still moving, quivering, I'm still trying to turn my eyes from this terrible crossroads, I'm still pretending that nothing has happened, although I know all too well that I'm doomed. If just once, I think, if just once it wouldn't happen! Couldn't there be one exception, just one, if only once, oh please! . . . "Ah, there he is, just look at his kinky hair," says Samoylov. That's it. Here we go.

4

Of all the digs the one that worked best was the most primitive and the most widespread at the time.

It's raining, the counselors are in their room, we're sitting on our neatly made bunks in the cabin, waiting for the lunch bell. The conversation is about our fathers—who does what. Naturally, the ones who speak up are those whose fathers have colorful and tangible jobs: chauffeur, military officer, lathe operator. Savitsky's father, I know, is a boss, some sort of big shot in the People's Commissariat, but Savitsky keeps quiet: what could he say, after all, boss isn't a job. All of a sudden somebody says, "Mine was killed in the war." I climb on board too, "Yeah, and mine was killed too," although nobody had really asked me. But now comes Samoylov's turn.

"Killed?" he drawls with pleasure, jutting his lower lip forward. "Get outta h-e-e-e-re! Killed too. More likely kicked the bucket from the runs."

Everyone likes the joke, they're all laughing. Tears cloud my eyes and choke my throat.

"What do you mean!" I say, my voice cracking. "What, what do you mean!"

"I don't mean nothing! Just that the Jews, if you want to know, weren't even at the front, they stayed home, sitting on their warm stoves. Hey, Edik, tell us, did the Jews fight in the war?"

Edik, so smart, so neat, and bespectacled, our "professor," or as they would say now, our intellectual, peers at us with a sober, unseeing gaze.

"Yes, I'd say it's a fact, there's no way around it. There were very few Jews at the front."

"You could even say there weren't any at all, couldn't you?"

"Well . . . yes, you could say that . . . ."

Samoylov is ecstatic.

"Aha, you see, Zilber! Edik wouldn't say so for nothing. Edik knows for sure, Edik says so—so you can stuff it!"

"Edik!" I finally blurt out. "Edik, how can you say that, he was killed in '42, I get a pension because of him!"

"Well, now. A pension!" Samoylov guffaws and makes a great show of spitting out the window. "Goldilocks!" he yells out to Goldfarb. "Goldilocks, is your father Jewish?

"Yeah, he's Jewish," Goldfarb says softly, swallowing the vowel: "Jwish."

"Listen, stop it!" our group leader, Simonenko, suddenly speaks up. "You got nothing better to do?" But he clams up straight away and even looks in the other direction. Samoylov makes out like he doesn't hear him.

"Well, tell us, Goldilocks," Samoylov continues peaceably. "Was he at the front?"

"No, he wasn't," Goldfarb answers just as softly. "He worked in a factory during the war."

Samoylov looks at Goldfarb tenderly. Right now he practically loves him, although at other times he digs at him almost as much as he does at me.

"You see, worked in a factory. Goldilocks at least doesn't lie. Now where was yours, Zilber? Keeping shop in a kiosk? Where did Papa Zilber work? Come on, tell us, don't be afraid, nothing will happen to you . . . ."

The bugle hits a wrong note and cleans everyone out of the cabin. "Take a spoon, take some bread . . . ." Lunch.

I lie face down on my bunk, and my most acute desire is to become a blanket, just as flat and gray as the one that now lies under me, so that Vera the counselor doesn't notice me when she walks into the cabin and doesn't call me.

"What is it, what's the matter with you, Sashenka?" she says in a hearty voice. "Did someone hurt your feelings? Come on now. Let's go, let's go and get in line quickly now or else you'll let the whole troop down . . ."

5

Many years later I read about an American boy who would get sick when he saw the nape of the person standing in front of him. I was struck by the exactness of the sensation but felt that for me something was missing. And only with time did I understand: it was the dining hall that was missing. For me the nape of the person standing in front is also linked to nausea—but only in the dining hall. At Young Pioneer camp I never wanted to eat. All food was disgusting to me, and the uninterrupted torture of life at camp would reach its peak four times a day, like clockwork.

So here we all are, standing together in line, and I see the nape of the person standing in front of me, and then we're all walking together, and I see the nape of the person walking ahead of me, I see a lot of napes ahead of me, and there's plenty of foreheads behind me as well. Someone pokes me in the back, somebody hits my legs with a twig. Some fun and games before feeding time, venting some healthy impatience. Let's get going already, into the dining hall although it would be better if there wasn't any dining hall at all . . .

[. . .] The smell of the dining hall is a symbol of my loneliness, an image of my helplessness.

The dining hall—it's—such a big, open but at the same time enclosed space, where there's absolutely nowhere to hide, where anyone can get at you, "like an elephant in a zoo, like a fly in a glass, like a goose on a platter," where you can't walk away, move to another place, turn away . . .

I sit down with everyone else, I start to eat, fighting the nausea. The bowl is big, it's quite a way to the bottom. And now Samoylov's happy gaze crosses the distance between us, a jolly freshly rolled ball of bread flies along the same trajectory and deftly plops into my plate. All right, here we go. Now I'm simply obliged to roll up one of my own and throw it at Samoylov. But nothing good will come of it. In the first place, I'm bound to miss him and hit Rogov who's sitting next to him, and Rogov won't let me forget it. Second, Samoylov tosses with ease and a light touch, while I throw with a lot of noise and fuss, swinging my whole body and waving my arms about. This means that the troop counselor won't even see him, but I'll get chewed out, to the delight and exultation of twenty bystanders. But the most important thing is this: I don't even want to throw anything, and Samoylov wants to. For me it's a tiresome duty, for him a pleasant way to amuse himself; for me an obligation and a waste of time, for him life itself and pleasure. And so we exchange throws back and forth, and he gets happier and happier, while I just feel more and more miserable. I'm worn out by this stupid work, I'm only throwing out of pride, and later for no reason at all, it's just inertia. I'm not even aiming anymore, just throwing blindly, hitting one kid, then another, and they all make a big noisy show of getting upset, promising me all sorts of joys. My bowl is already full of bread balls, sticky gray balls covered with Samoylov's fingerprints. Fleetingly, I sweep a glance over the faces of my companions, timidly searching for sympathy—there isn't any on those faces. Joy, curiosity, indifference—but no sympathy. In any case, now I don't have time for observation, I can't allow myself the luxury. I look right in front of me, into the disgusting, nauseating bowl that has long ceased to be mine and that has been transformed into yet another instrument of torture, an extension and mutation of that loathsome Samoylov into his round and liquid incarnation . . .

"Zilber, you're not eating again! You're not sick, are you? Look, you're all red. No, your forehead's not hot. What, you're not talking to me? Nikolay Ivanych! Nikolay Ivanych! I've got a boy here . . ."

And now it's not just my three companions at the table, not just the entire sixth troop—now it's the whole dining hall, the whole camp, counselors and head counselors, the rank and file, the whole camp has torn itself away from its gulping and gobbling to look at me, waiting for my final irreparable act of foolishness. And I commit this act of foolishness. Sobbing loudly, I leap up from the table and run to the exit. I run across the endless hall, covering my face with my arm bent at the elbow. This must be a really funny sight, I hear noise, laughter apparently, through the small crook of my arm I see only the painted floor boards and legs of the chairs; someone sticks a leg out in my way–not a chair's but his own–but I don't fall, what incredible luck, and I run out finally through the open door. I run across the campground; plywood signs tremble on either side of me, faded signs with slogans and lines of poetry, pink Young Pioneer boys and girls with toothpaste instead of teeth give me their eternal plywood salute; I run past them to wherever my feet will carry me, at least that's how it seems to me, although in reality my path leads to that same, already familiar cabin, to my strange, cold bunk with the prickly blanket and hard pillow. But that still isn't the end of it. There's no limit to my humiliation, no limit! Behind me I hear the approach of stomping feet: the counselor has sent the best runners, and among them, of course, is Samoylov. They block my path, grab me by the arms with strong, callous fingers. Everyone is silent, only Samoylov has a big grin on his face:

"Whe-er-re do you think you're going? Ba-ack, ba-ack!"

I resist, they drag me, restrain me, give me a few light punches, but without anger. Without anger—but not without pleasure. They're not fighting, they're taking the necessary measures, just following orders . . . Finally, almost at the entrance to the dining hall, Vera comes over to us and sets me free; I'm covered in tears and my nose is running, and she takes me by the shoulders and leads me to the troop counselors' room—for some compote and a heart-to-heart.

6

I try to be around the grownups as much as possible–I pester them with my offers of help, ingratiating myself with everyone, and though I completely annoy everybody, still I start to feel right at home. It seems to me that in contrast to the chaos and confusion of the children's world, calm, order, and balance hold sway here. Of course, these aren't real adults either, the sea of childhood washes and laps all around this isle of benevolence and common sense, yet it never floods it entirely. A Young Pioneer dashes in and out only when he must, but otherwise there's no reason for *normal* kids to be here.

Larisa Arkhipova, the editor-in-chief, spatters a piece of drawing paper with a wet toothbrush, turning it blue before our eyes.

"Zilber," Larisa says sternly, "write a short piece for us. There's some space left right there."

"About what?" I ask eagerly.

"Oh, it doesn't matter, about whatever you want."

"Like what?"

"Look, what's the matter with you. If I knew, I'd write it myself. Why don't you write about your hike to the river?"

"*The river?!* All right, that's what I'll write about."

I take a pencil, sit down at the table and confidently write on a piece of notebook paper:

Our Trip to the River

"In the morning, right after breakfast, troop counselor Vera informed us . . ."

I cross out "informed" and write "announced." "Troop counselor Vera announced to us . . ." Or maybe "informed" was better after all? "We were all very excited and with a cheerful song . . ."

In the morning, right after breakfast, troop counselor Vera had us line up in front of our cabin and said to us:

Whoever can't swim—take one step forward!"

I stayed put.

About eight people calmly stepped out, and if I had done so too, it wouldn't have been a big deal. But this time I stayed put. I just couldn't do it again. Every time it was the same story: who can't—I can't; who has never—I have never; who wants to stay behind—me again, me once more, it's always me! And now it's as if some hidden mechanism, maybe an instinctive sense of rhythm, stopped me from taking that small step. Come what may, somehow I'll get out of it.

But I didn't get out of it.

While all of us who *could* swim were filing down to the river, arguing about which was faster, the crawl or the overarm stroke, I without cease offered a silent prayer. The word "Lord" was not in my lexicon, so instead I said "if only." "If only," I prayed. "If only everything would come out all right! I'll go home and every day—every day!—I'll go down to the river and learn how to swim better than anyone, well no, not better than anyone, but good and fast. Then I'll go to camp . . . What, again—! Well, okay, I'm even willing to do that, but right now, just now, if only! . . ."

And so we line up at the water's edge—now it's just us swimmers, the non-swimming spectators—lucky people!—sit on a little hill, plucking at the grass and watching us with studied indifference.

"Listen up," Vera says. "We're going to get ready for the BGTO national fitness test. Today we're swimming ten meters, to the other side and back. It's shallow, you won't drown (a good thing, that . . .)."

"One!" Vera orders spiritedly.

We are all standing up to our waists in the water, the other shore is an arm's length away, it's probably so easy to swim over there, if only you know how . . .

"Two!" Vera orders. We all bend down, waiting. But what am I bending down for, stupid idiot! The water is warm, but I'm shaking all over. "Vera!" I say, without moving my lips. "I don't feel so good!"

"Three," Vera orders, and everybody, except me, works their arms and legs whichever way they can. Well, and what am I supposed to do? Here's what I do. I lower myself into the water up to my neck and start shuffling my feet along the bottom. This way I creep forward a little ways on all fours, with my chin touching the water. The bottom here is sandy, you can see everything as in a glass, and I only stop when the heart-rending guffaws of the spectators reach me.

"Look at him go!" they shout. "He's taking the lead!"

I stop, turn around, and see that serious, stern Vera is laughing, lying face down on the grass, covering her face with her hands. Nobody is swimming anymore, everyone is standing and laughing.

"He's doing the Jewish stroke," Samoylov says suddenly.

"Yeah, yeah, the Jewish stroke," the others repeat after him cheerfully.

"Stop it, boys," Vera mumbles through her tears, but everyone knows that she's not angry, just keeping up appearances.

"Well," Samoylov says loudly, looking straight at me and laughing, "and now let's all race along the shore as fast as we can doing the Zilber stroke!..."

"It's nice to spend a hot day by the river!" I write my last sentence.

"Well done!" Larisa says, "you've got a real talent for this sort of thing. Just like in *The Young Pioneer's Pravda*..." [...]

8

And though its march seems to keep slowing and slowing, time still crawls on toward the final week. Breakfast, lunch, snack, dinner, breakfast, lunch, snack, dinner, and only three days left. The camp's closing ceremony, a star-shaped campfire at the edge of the forest—I'm reading poetry, of course. "And sent the German soldiers to kill the people Soviet..." Samoylov and Losev support Edik on their knees, two others pull them by the elbows from either side—a shaky pyramid to thunderous applause; the fifth troop dances the "Apple," and a girl from the third troop does a Ukrainian dance. For the finale we all sing a chorus of "Who is there?..." The mosquitoes are biting; it's the latest we've ever stayed out. "You will always meet the sun of the Motherland with a young pioneer's salute!" That's it. "No wandering off, no wandering off, get in line, in line! Straight to bed, no running off!" That's it, now we're almost there. I walk alone; I couldn't care less about their getting in line, you can't see anything anyway. I'm leaving a day early; my mother is coming to get me on Sunday. I'll take my suitcase out of the closet, crackers from the side table, I won't talk to anyone, won't talk to... "Ow-ow-ow!" A sharp blow to the jaw knocks me off my feet. I fly somewhere off to the side, but I don't fall because I get a fist in the ribs; they grab me and keep a firm hold on me by the arms. Why? What have I done? Samoylov's face, that finest of faces, emerges from the darkness and moves toward me.

"What, you sonofabitch, thought you could just take off like that? You thought you could give me the slip. You thought.... Oh, getta look at that filthy Jewish mug!"

He twists my nose with his sweaty fingers, then wipes them off on my face squeamishly.

"Well, don't they all just make you sick," he says, stepping back a bit, and suddenly I feel his foul spit hit my cheek and begin to roll slowly down toward my chin.

"Here, wipe you face," I hear section leader Simonenko's voice coming from my right, and my right arm is released. I wipe my face, feeling that the grip on my left arm has also relaxed.

"Anyone else want a go?" Samoylov asks. "Well. Come on, guys, think about it, settle your score, today's your last chance. Don't worry, he won't say anything, he knows what'll happen to him . . ."

"Ye-ah-ah, he knows," Simonenko drawls, and here I lunge to the right and run in the direction opposite of where Samoylov's voice is coming from. It's stupid to run, of course, I'm surrounded by *our gang*, but someone I run into almost immediately, who could easily stop me, doesn't, he even steps aside, letting me pass through freely. And I run and keep running, howling, with bloody snot streaming down my face . . .

I try not to fall asleep at night, but nobody touches me. It looks as though they've decided I'd had enough. One way or another, I escape the fate of those smeared in toothpaste and shoe polish, or wrapped up in blankets and tossed outside, showered with urine, or burned with bits of flaming paper between their toes, what they call the bicycle.

In the morning, I walk all over the campground, praying and conjuring, "If only she'd come! If only she'd come. If only she'd come!" The spell works. And now I'm already walking along the wooded path, *outside* the camp, *not* in line, and I'm not afraid of anybody in the world, I squeak out my tall tales, and my young, beautiful mother carries my hideous suitcase.

1974–75

Translated from the Russian by Natalia Ermolaev, Sergey Levchin, Ronald Meyer,
Jonathan Platt, and Timothy Williams

INNA LISNYANSKAYA

Inna Lisnyanskaya (1928–2014), poet, translator, and prose writer, was born in Baku, Azerbaijan's multiethnic capital, where Russian was the lingua franca. Lisnyanskaya's Jewish father was a doctor; her Armenian mother, an engineer. Lisnyanskaya's maternal grandparents spoke Yiddish to each other, and her Jewish grandfather was observant, but Lisnyanskaya received no Judaic upbringing. Baptized as an infant in an Armenian church by her maternal grandmother, Lisnyanskaya later went to Russian Orthodox services.

In 1944, Lisnyanskaya registered her nationality as Jewish. She had just heard about Babi Yar and learned from her father about the antisemitic policies in the Soviet Army. "And I thought ... if I'm baptized as a Christian, then I must register as a Jew, because so many have been annihilated. . . ," Lisnyanskaya explained to the editor of this anthology in January 2000. "And so I went and chose this nationality for myself, and I had many [troubles] on its account."

Lisnyanskaya's first publications date to 1948. Her first husband was the poet Grigory Korin (Godel Korenberg), and their daughter Elena was born in 1951. (In Israel since 1990, Elena Makarova writes poignantly about cultural life in Teresienstadt, including the artist Fridl Dicker-Brandeis). *This Happened to Me*, Lisnyanskaya's debut collection, appeared in 1957 in Baku. During the Thaw, the editor of *Novy mir*, Aleksandr Tvardovsky, published her poetry. Lisnyanskaya became a member of the Union of Soviet Writers in 1957. Her second collection, *Loyalty*, came out in 1958 in Moscow, where she moved in 1961. Two unremarkable collections followed in the 1960s.

In 1967, Lisnyanskaya met the poet and translator **Semyon Lipkin**. They were together from 1968 until Lipkin's death in 2003, and she herself acknowledges Lipkin's influence on the formal aspects of her poetry. Soviet editors-cum-censors objected to her religious lyrics, central to Lisnyanskaya's poetic identity; as a consequence, Lisnyanskaya's volume *Grape Light* (1978) appeared after a hiatus of eleven years. Following the publication of *Metropol* in 1979 and the selective repressions that ensued (see **Vassily Aksyonov** and **Semyon Lipkin**), Lisnyanskaya and Lipkin resigned from the Writers' Union in protest. As Ron Meyer commented, "the *succès de scandale* of [. . .] *Metropol* [. . .] decided the course not only of [Lisnyanskaya's] writing career [. . .] but also of the nature of the writing itself." Unable to publish in the USSR, Lisnyanskaya sent her work abroad, and it appeared in *Continent, Time and We* and other émigré journals. Two Russian-language collections of Lisnyanskaya's poetry were published in the West in the 1980s.

In 1987, Lisnyanskaya's membership in the Writers' Union was restored and her writings returned to print. She was a prominent contributor to the cultural life of reform-era and post-Soviet Russia. Her collections include *Air Stratum* (1990), *Solitary Gift* (1995), *Without You* (2003), and others. Lisnyanskaya was a recipient of several awards, notably the Aleksandr Solzhenitsyn Prize (1999).

* * *

Lisnyanskaya told the editor of this anthology that, after hearing her read, **Boris Pasternak** commented, "Whence such Russian music in Jewish-Armenian blood raised on Azeri soil? . . ." Born to two peoples whose very history in the twentieth century is synonymous with the Holocaust, Lisnyanskaya became a Russian poet who identified herself as a Jew and as a Christian. In Lisnyanskaya's case, this double duality of self stems both from her origins and from her conscious desire to advance a Judeo-Christian platform. Lisnyanskaya told the editor that she believed in the possibility of Judeo-Christianity and "loved the Old and New Testaments equally." Perhaps not surprisingly, of the Jewish prophets she identified most intimately with Ruth.

The topic of antisemitism, both ethnic and religious, features prominently in Lisnyanskaya's poetry, as the two poems below illustrate. In her confessional lyric, where the dramatic effects are sometimes overdone, Lisnyanskaya writes about feeling like an alien and an "outcast" amid Russians and Christians in Russia. Her lyrical arguments go against the aspirations of those Jews who expect to assimilate through conversion. Lisnyanskaya speaks of "unpleasant Jews" who converted and tried to act more "orthodox" than the Russian Orthodox themselves in the hope of gaining acceptance.

To many Russian churchgoers, Lisnyanskaya remains a Jew; being an alien to them is the subject of Lisnyanskaya's bitterest lyric, "An Incident" (1981), based on a real-life occurrence. After the "incident," Lisnyanskaya confirmed, she nearly stopped going to services. "I stopped going to church when everybody started going [. . .] all the Komsomol members [in the 1970s]. [. . .] And now [in post-Soviet Russia] that the church has become [. . .] a state institution, I'm even less inclined [to go]."

In the end, the language of her poetry is the only place where she does not feel alienated. "My motherland is Russian speech," Lisnyanskaya stated in

January 2000. "My daughter [emigrated] [...] but I cannot." Inna Lisnyanskaya spent the last few years of her life in Israel. She died in Haifa in 2014.

* * *

My father, a military doctor,
Chest dense with wounds.
Fiddler, play for him
A lament for Israel!
For music with a thread-like
Pulse, lacking in tone,
I swear he spent it all,
His veteran's pension.
As you see he was no dodger—
Decorations abound,
But about the motherland,
Fiddler, nothing from your bow.
For yet another night,
He speaks in a delirium,
Telling of gas chambers,
Instructing me, "Daughter,
Don't sign on as a Jew."
Oh play, fiddler, play!
When the war is over and won,
Let him see her in a dream—
The Promised Land.
Wasn't it for her he gave his life,
So wicked and sweet?
Play to the end, fiddler,
And say a prayer at his grave.

1975

AN INCIDENT

To go to church around here is futile—
I feel ashamed; I don't want to.
I lit a candle to the Mother of God—
Someone blew my candle out.

They blew it out because of my eyes,
They're dark, and my face is swarthy,
They blew the flame out while the Divine
Liturgy was going on.

Now I'll walk past, I'll pause at the door—
But what if someone suddenly again,
Cruelly hurting the one who bore God,
Were to bend and extinguish it once more?

1981

Translated from the Russian by Larissa Szporluk

BORIS SLUTSKY

(See the introduction to Boris Slutsky and his poems in the section "The Thaw: 1950s–1960s.")

Slutsky returned to the themes of the Shoah and antisemitism in the late 1960s and 1970s. He was able to publish a few of the poems with Jewish themes, including "Now Auschwitz Frequently Appears in My Dreams..." (in *Contemporary Stories* [or *Histories*], 1969) and "Addressing me by first name and patronymic..." (in *The Year [Clock] Hand*, 1971). These elegiac poems were marked by a new, gaping historical skepticism. In "Christ's Relatives" (1977), a diary poem not published until 1989, Slutsky decried the implacable irony of Christian antisemitism.

A quintessence of Slutsky's Jewish concerns, the three poems that follow appeared in the USSR during the reform years. The third, "The rabbis came down to the valley ...," belongs with the greatest poems about the Shoah, and translation does but partial justice to Slutsky's clairvoyance of diction and verbal artistry. Only a poet of God's grace could hear in the paronomastic collision of the rhyming pair *ravviny* (rabbis)–*ravniny* (valleys) the double tragedy of Soviet Jewry. Here Slutsky discarded his ideological armor, towering above most of his contemporaries as an heir to the multilingual voices of Russia's greatest Jewish poets.

* * *

Let's cross out the Pale. All the ashes have settled:
The poorest of buyers and the wealthiest of sellers
Have vanished. A train rushed them off to the land
Of spectral pleasure and phantomous pain.
Queen Herring, a holiday's glory and pride,
Queen Herring now swims in the Lethean tide.

The world was extinguished in the Auschwitz furnace:
White tablecloth of shabbes, the buzz of lekhayim.
It's greasy. It's black. It's a sickly sweet smoke.
But I can remember when this world was still young.
And I can recall it in holiday silks,
The folds so crisp, they rustled like thunder;

And also the workdays, when down on its luck
It tightened its belt and prayed for a wonder.
Queen Herring, a holiday's glory and pride,
Queen Herring now swims in the Lethean tide.

A planet. Good or bad? I don't know.
So how can I give it a "yes" or a "no"?
I know very little. I know one thing for sure:
This planet had burned to the core long ago.
Melameds burned down in their threadbare coats,
Their something turned nothing, what *was* is no more.
Burned Party officials and railway workers,
The beggars, the buggers, the backward and forward,
Burned down and drowned in Lethean waters,
Excised like the families Mstislavsky and Shuysky.[22]
Queen Herring, a holiday's glory and pride,
Queen Herring now swims in the Lethean tide.

1970s

* * *

I love the antisemites, they reward
me with tireless lessons dedicated
to detailing all my shortcomings as fated,
and readily appointing the day that
they'll finally drive me to the psych ward.
I don't believe the schedules they assemble—
the run of time will tear them all apart,
and that is why I love the antisemites—
where reason fails, I love them with all my heart.

before 1977

---

22 The Mstislavskys and the Shuyskys were families of pre-Petrine aristocracy whose repre-
sentatives played a particularly prominent role in Russia's political history of the sixteenth
and early seventeenth centuries; from the Shuysky family came Tsar Vasily Shuysky (1552–
1612; ruled 1606–10). The Mstislavsky and Shuysky families ceased to exist with the deaths
of their last representatives in 1622 and 1638, respectively.

* * *

The rabbis came down to the valley,
it was, perhaps, their first time,
for rabbis look on Nature rarely,
and now, before they were to die,

an hour before the thick black smoke
rose up to scatter the rabbis' ashes,
they, for the first time, saw the precious
white apple bows in April smoke.

before 1977

Translated from the Russian by Sergey Levchin and Maxim D. Shrayer

ANATOLY RYBAKOV

Anatoly Rybakov (1911–1998), novelist, screenwriter, and memoirist, was born to an educated Jewish family in Chernigov, a provincial capital in north-central Ukraine. Rybakov's father moved his family to Moscow in 1919. In 1933, in his last year at the Moscow Institute of Transportation Engineers (MIIT), Rybakov was arrested; in 1934 he was charged with counterrevolutionary propaganda and agitation (Article 58-10). After serving his three years of administrative exile, Rybakov spent three itinerant years working at various odd jobs.

Drafted in 1941 as a driver-private, Ryvakov ended the war as a decorated major. In 1945, a military tribunal found Rybakov innocent of the 1934 charges, but he was not rehabilitated until 1960. In 1946, Rybakov returned to Moscow with an invalid veteran's pension (cf. **Boris Slutsky**). He turned to writing, adopting his mother's last name, Rybakov (literally, "son of a fisherman," inconspicuous compared to his father's markedly Jewish Aronov, "son of Aaron"). Rybakov's short adventure novel *Dirk*, published in 1948, became a Soviet teenage bestseller. By some accounts the book's total printings have exceeded ten million copies. *Dirk* formed a trilogy with two other novels, *A Bronze Bird* (1956) and *The Shot* (1975). Rybakov received a Russian Federation State Prize for *Minute of Silence* (1971), a screenplay based on his teenage novel *The Unknown Soldier* (1970).

After Rybakov's debut adult novel *Drivers* (1950), which garnered a Stalin Prize in 1951, came *Ekaterina Voronina* (1955). In his early fiction, Rybakov reproduced the formulaic designs of the postwar Soviet novel: a positive hero, an idealist, struggles and succeeds in exposing individual aberrations, such as corruption, profiteering, or dishonesty, within the fundamentally good Soviet system. Rybakov's timid anti-Stalinist novel *Summer in Sosnyaki* appeared in 1964.

Jewish themes did not take center stage in Rybakov's writing until *Heavy Sand*, written in 1975–77 (excerpt below). Published in 1978, *Heavy Sand* made Rybakov famous; in the first months after its publication, twenty-six countries reportedly contracted to publish the novel. However, in his *Novel-Memoir* (1997), Rybakov deemed not *Heavy Sand* but *Children of the Arbat*, a histrionic trilogy of novels about Stalinism, his principal work. Rybakov has emphasized the importance of his decision to publish the novel in the USSR rather than abroad, presumably placing himself in contrast to such famous cases as **Boris Pasternak**'s *Doctor Zhivago*, Andrey Sinyavsky and **Yuly Daniel**, the 1979 *Metropol* collective (see **Vassily Aksyonov**), or works by dissident and refusenik writers published abroad in the 1970s and 1980s. Interviewed at his dacha for the CBS special *The Soviet Union: Seven Days in May* (1987), Rybakov told then CBS anchorman Dan Rather that he "never" considered emigrating. "Many times I was offered to publish [the novel *Children of the Arbat*] in the West," Rybakov commented. "But I didn't give it to the West, because this novel is needed by my people, is needed by my country, and must be published at home. [. . .] Then I will tell the people the truth about themselves, about their history." The American documentary contrasted Rybakov's comments with those by two refuseniks: a pianist, Vladimir Feltsman, then still waiting for permission, and a writer, **David Shrayer-Petrov**, about to emigrate. Rybakov traveled to the United States on official lecture tours in 1986, when Jewish emigration was at a dead low, and again in 1987, as the emigration door reopened.

John Schillinger labeled *Children of the Arbat*, along with its sequels, *Fear: '35 and Other Years* (published 1988–90) and *Dust and Ashes* (published 1994), an "anti-Stalinist blockbuster." Completed in 1967, Rybakov's *Children of the Arbat* was first announced as forthcoming in 1969 but was not published until 1988. It has appeared in dozens of languages, landing Rybakov on the cover of *Time* magazine in 1988. Rybakov divided his last years between Moscow and New York, where he had family. He died in New York in December 1998 and was buried in Moscow.

* * *

In an interview published in the New York daily *New Russian Word* (*Novoye russkoe sloe*) in January 1997, Rybakov spoke of the time when he wrote *Heavy Sand*: "In the 1970s, state-sponsored antisemitism had resumed [*sic*] in the USSR under the disguise of fighting Zionism. All sorts of nefarious books were being published about the Zionists; they trampled Israel, and I was proud of it [i.e., Israel]. My people had returned to its country." (In the 1987 interview with Dan Rather, Rybakov had used the expression "my people" in reference to the "Soviet people.")

The title *Heavy Sand* hints at a verse from the book of Job: "It would be heavier than the sand of the sea" (Job 6:3). Gary Rosenshield concluded his thoughtful 1996 rereading of Rybakov's novel by suggesting that "all that is left of Rybakov's assimilationist ideal may be the traces of heavy sand." However one (re)reads *Heavy Sand*, the sand in Rybakov's best novel is soaked with the blood of the murdered Jews and heavy with the compromistic legacy of its composition and publication.

Heavy Sand is set in a small town in Rybakov's native Chernigov Province, where the Jews had not settled in significant numbers until after the third partition of Poland in 1795; chronologically, the novel opens at the beginning of the twentieth century, taking the reader through the last tsarist years and early Soviet decades to conclude in 1972; the novel focuses on the events of World War II and the Shoah. The narrator's father, Yakov (Jakob) Ivanovsky, a Jewish-Swiss-German young man from Basel, a professor's son, whose grandfather had emigrated to Switzerland from the Ukrainian town of Ivanovka, visits his ancestors' home in the Pale and falls in love and marries the narrator's mother, Rakhil (Rachel) Rakhlenko, the novel's matriarch (note the Biblical names of the narrator's parents). The narrator, Boris Ivanovsky, is a self-professed "internationalist" who was "raised" that way by "the Soviet system" ("Russian, Jew, Belorussian—it's all the same to me"). When he tells his story in the early 1970s, he is married to an ethnic Russian woman with whom he has three Russified sons who all married non-Jewish women, "so my grandchildren are Russian, too, and for all of us our motherland is Soviet Russia."

The novel appeared serially in the moderately conservative Moscow monthly *October* (*Oktiabr'*) in 1978 (nos. 7–9); at the time of the serialization, the magazine claimed a print run of 218,000 copies. It was published as a book the following year by a leading Moscow publisher, the print run totaling 150,000 copies; the novel was subsequently reprinted in book form. The English translation, excerpted below, appeared in 1981.

According to the critic Vladimir Kardin, after agreeing in principle to publish *Heavy Sand*, the editor of *October*, Anatoly Ananiev, took the manuscript to the Central Committee of the Communist Party. The officials asked for revisions that concerned both the treatment of the Stalinist 1930s and the Jewish theme, and Rybakov made numerous changes, ranging from radical changes to superficial grafting. Although in the post-Soviet years Rybakov published an "authoritative" edition, which restored some censored passages, the 1978 published version of *Heavy Sand* is likely to remain both the standard translated text and a monument to its time and epoch.

The issue of whether or not Rybakov had been directly prompted by the powers that be to carry out an ideological commission—to write a heroic novel about the Soviet Jews—is not that fascinating to a student of Jewish literature. One day a conscientious biographer may investigate the novel's genesis and archeology. That the official Jew Rybakov cooperated over the novel's revisions is hardly surprising. Much more important is that by writing *Heavy Sand* Rybakov infused the Soviet popular imagination of the late Brezhnev era with a threefold ideological agenda: he created positive and inspiring images of Soviet Jews; he overcame the official Soviet obfuscation of the Shoah; and, third and finally, he attempted an antidote for the massive Jewish emigration.

Both the timing and the concept of his novel suggest a connection with the wave of exodus of Soviet Jewry: its numbers reached about 30,000 in both 1972 and 1973, dropped to about 14,000–16,000 in 1975–77, when Rybakov was working on *Heavy Sand*; but rose again by 1978, when his novel was first published and reached its peak in 1979, about 51,000 emigrants, when it first came out in book form. Is it a coincidence or a rhetorical reversal of history that in *Heavy Sand* a Jew returns from the West (Switzerland) to regain his roots while so many of Rybakov's Jewish contemporaries were uprooting themselves in the 1970s? Was the Party's imprimatur of Rybakov's depiction of the Shoah a carefully calculated concession both to the wavering Soviet Jews and to the watchful West? Hinting at a possible link between Rybakov's treatment of the Shoah and the historical context of the Soviet 1970s, Maurice Friedberg went as far as to suggest, in 1984, that although *Heavy Sand* "dealt, it is true, at length and with much sympathy, with the subject of the Holocaust [. . .] in the final analysis, it, too, by implication merely advanced the thesis of the desirability of a complete disappearance in the USSR of the Jews as a distinct group."

Indeed, some of the novel's Western readers—and not all of them writing for conservative publications—were critical of it. Both Walter Laqueur (in 1979 in *Commentary*) and Josephine Wall (in 1981 in *The New Republic*) took issue with *Heavy Sand*; Paul Abelman called his 1981 review in *The Spectator* "Propaganda." Others wrote admiringly of *Heavy Sand* and exaggerated its importance. Harold Shukman has stated that "in 1978 [Rybakov] was the first Russian writer of Jewish origin to approach the subject of the Russian Jewish past and of the Holocaust in the USSR [. . .]." A consideration of the prose and poetry that **Vasily Grossman, Ilya Ehrenburg, Boris Yampolsky, Lev Ozerov**, and **Boris Slutsky**, to take five examples, published in the mainstream Soviet press during and after World War II, should convince one that Rybakov was hardly the "first" to "approach" the subject. (It is ironic that **Grossman**'s *Life and Fate* [excerpt in this anthology], with its central Shoah sequence, appeared in the West in 1980 [English translation 1985] but in the USSR not until 1989.)

Rybakov wrote with power and passion of the Jewish Holocaust (without using this term) in occupied Ukraine. Although he presented the majority of the local population in the occupied Soviet territories as actively assisting the Jews and resisting the Nazis, he did write of the collaboration of the local non-Jewish population with the Nazis (cf. **Vasily Grossman** and **Lev Ginzburg**). Additionally, he hinted at furrows and wrinkles on the face of official Soviet historiography, such as the fact that some of the anti-Nazi guerilla units in Ukraine and Belorussia avoided merging with the Jewish partisans. Given the introduction of a de facto taboo, by the late 1960s, on the presentation of the Shoah apart from the unspecified losses of the Soviet people, *Heavy Sand* was an achievement, albeit a limited one. Do its main shortcomings stem less from what Gary Rosenshield links with the "ethos of socialist realism" and much more from Rybakov's lip service to the Soviet rhetoric on the Jewish question?

Rybakov's ambition was to alter the popular Soviet perception of the Jews and of the Shoah. In assessing *Heavy Sand*, one must be clear about the ideological climate of the 1970s and the restrictions on what even the officially favored writers (including the official Jews) were permitted to say in print. It bears acknowledging that, limitations aside, many of Rybakov's pages about Jewish life in the Pale are moving, and the concluding chapters of *Heavy Sand* (see the excerpt below) describing the death of the narrator's mother, Rakhil Rakhlenko, truly inspiring. For many of Rybakov's Jewish readers at home, especially those bent on staying in the USSR when many others tried to leave, Rybakov's token use of Hebrew in the novel's last lines amounted to something small, albeit real, to sustain those staying in their Jewish lives of self-denial.

FROM *HEAVY SAND*

[...]

Six hundred people left the ghetto, the rest stayed behind. Those who had barricaded themselves in remained behind, as well as many who had come out but had fled back inside when the machine-gun on the watch-tower opened up and the streets ran with blood. And, of course, cripples and invalids stayed behind, and the sick, the feeble, old men and women, and anyone who was unable to move, as there were no stretchers to carry them on.

Grisha urged the people to move fast, the Germans would quickly collect themselves, their units would arrive, they would organize the pursuit, it was essential to get to the forest, to a particular place where two men were waiting with a machine gun, and where it would be possible to organize some defense to hold off the enemy, though, as a matter of fact, it was nearly eight miles to that point. Now, Grisha hadn't expected that, while his men were assembling to leave, many of the young people wouldn't come out of their positions but would go on firing from cover, in order to kill as many SS and police as possible. What did they know, these boys and girls? They had enough courage to attack, but they didn't have the know-how to get out in time, they thought they were holding up the Germans, but in fact they were no longer doing any good where they were, it was all over. They were needed on the march, but they had stayed behind, and now they couldn't get out, either they were killed, or they joined the others in the barricaded houses.

Every fighter was important to Grisha—six hundred people make a long column, not a military column, a column of fugitives, seized with terror. He needed a large defense force for so many people, but what he had was a dozen partisans and a few boys and girls with guns.

Nevertheless, Grisha posted escorts ahead, on the flank, and in the rear, in the regular way. He left their first covering force at the cemetery, and a second one two miles further on, each of them to meet the pursuing forces on its own ridge. Of course, they would be slaughtered, of course, it was a death sentence, but, still, they would delay the enemy for a few precious minutes. Grisha couldn't spare extra men for the covering positions, it was necessary to protect the helpless, terrified people, who were heading for the unknown, with death behind them and in front of them, each one thinking only of his own salvation. At the first sign of panic, they would run in all directions, or rather shuffle—they were far too weak to run. The stronger of them were walking faster, hurrying to reach the forest. The weaker ones tried to keep up with them, but they hadn't the strength. They sat down at the side of the path, or they fell down and had to be picked up and pulled along, because to leave them for the enemy to defile would mean to turn the column into a herd of animals—animals don't carry their wounded with them, only human beings do that, as long as they remain human beings. They left behind only those who were already dead. There was no time to bury the dead and not enough strength to carry them. What strength there was, was needed by the living. The column stretched out further and further, a long line of shuffling skeletons, falling down and getting up again, or not getting up, each one shuffling along on his own.

Suddenly, the people stopped. They heard shooting behind them and saw tongues of flame leaping up into the sky. It was the ghetto burning and being destroyed.

Of course, the Germans could have waited to deal with it later, the ghetto wasn't going to fly away, they ought to have flung themselves into the pursuit. But fury and the thirst for revenge overcame them, and they vented their rage on those who had stayed behind. The SS platoon that had come in by truck surrounded the rebellious ghetto and set about exterminating it right there, on the spot, in the streets. The SS tried to break into the barricaded houses where shots were being fired; they tossed in grenades, and when the people came running out, they mowed them down with machine guns, and Sand Street and Hospital Street ran with blood. Yet people still tried to break through the cordon with whatever weapons they could find, but not one of them succeeded. When the resistance was broken and the fighters ran out of ammunition and were all killed, and the sound of shooting was no longer drowned by the cries and screams of the wounded, the avengers burst into the houses and finished off the cripples, the sick and the old; the dogs sniffed round the yards and the SS picked off the children who had hidden there. It was all over in a few hours, the ghetto liquidated and nearly two thousand people found their graves in the ditch in the forest clearing. But they hadn't gone there themselves, they hadn't lain down in the ditch! Their corpses had been loaded on to trucks, driven into the forest, and thrown into the ditch. It had been necessary to exterminate the inhabitants of the ghetto in their own houses, the ghetto had put up resistance, it had exacted a price for its life, and it was wiped off the face of the earth. The Nazis never mentioned it, this shame and defeat of theirs, it is not even in the list of the fifty ghettoes we know about. But it did exist, it did fight, and it perished with honor.

Once they had finished with the ghetto, the Germans set off in pursuit of the fugitives, who were already getting close to the forest. The two covering forces had left their ambush and rejoined the main force, where they took up defense positions at the edge of the forest. They now had a machine gun. The soldiers soon arrived, too, as they had no need to look for the path, which was marked out for them with corpses. But when they approached the forest, they were met by machine-gun, submachine gun, and rifle fire.

Meanwhile, the fugitives went deeper into the forest. They were led by two partisans, Yevsey Kuznetsov and Kolya Gorodetsky, who were supposed to take them further, to the dense Bryansk forest, where Sidorov's partisans were waiting, and where the Germans wouldn't dare to poke their noses. There were not more than four hundred of them left; the fighters stayed behind at the edge of the forest, and the others, who hadn't been able to survive the march, littered the melancholy scene with their bodies. But the forest, which they had to get through, was also big, over six miles across, and these people had already come eight and could go no further, especially as they had now left the open ground and so felt safe to a certain extent. They'd been told, "The forest, we must get to the forest," and now they'd got there, they were told they mustn't stop.

Mother said to Yevsey Kuznetsov, "The people must rest. They can't go on."

"No," Yevsey replied. "Grisha won't wait for long. And if they sit down, they won't get up."

So they carried on, but more and more people kept falling down on the forest path, or stopping to lean against the trees.

So then mother said to Yevsey, "You go on with those who can, and I'll stay with those who need at least a short break. Leave Kolya to show us the way, and in half an hour I'll get them going again."

Those who still had the strength went on with Yevsey, the rest sat down in a clearing, and mother went back for those who had fallen behind and brought them to the clearing.

Then in the presence of Kolya Gorodetsky, mother said to Olya, "Ask Uncle Sidorov to send you to Chernigov to a lawyer called Tereshchenko. Tell Tereshchenko that you're Rakhil Rakhlenko's granddaughter. Kolya, will you tell Sidorov?"

"We'll tell him," Kolya replied.

Mother then said to the people, "Come on, get up, we can't stay here any longer, we must go on." A few of them got up, but most of them hadn't the strength.

Then mother said, "You hear those shots? That's your children dying to save you! You're not slaves any more, you're free, you're going to revenge the blood of your families and friends, you're going to make these monsters pay for your suffering, you're going to destroy them, like the mad dogs they are, because that's what you have to do with mad dogs. Find the strength to go on, come! Kolya, lead them!"

And the people found the strength in themselves to get up and shuffle along further. But mother didn't move, they shuffled past her, while she stood there and inspired strength in every one of them. It was hard to recognize the earlier Rakhil Rakhlenko in this woman, though she was only forty-nine. Only the height and bearing of the original Rakhil remained. Tall and straight, she stood without moving or leaving her place, but she was receding deeper into the forest for each person who went by her, her image faded, and she seemed to melt into the air and gradually disappear. And when the people looked back, she was no longer there. Nobody heard the sound of her footsteps or the crunch of twigs under her feet, she simply dissolved into the forest amid the motionless pines, she melted into the air, which was saturated with the sharp scent of resin, just as it had been when, as a girl of sixteen, she had sat in the forest with her Jakob, a boy with blue eyes, from Basel, Switzerland.

You think it's fantasy, or mysticism? Maybe. But, even so, nobody ever saw my mother again, alive or dead. She vanished, melted, dissolved into thin air in the pine forest, near the little town where she was born, where she'd lived her life, where she had loved and been loved, where, in spite of all the misfortunes, she'd been happy, where she'd brought up her children, raised her grandchildren and watched their terrible deaths, where she had endured more than any human heart can endure. But her heart did endure, and in the last minutes of her life she was able to be a mother to those wretched and unfortunate people, and to put them on the path of struggle and a dignified death.

Meanwhile, the battle at the edge of the forest continued. The Germans had no idea of their enemy's strength, so they took cover, fired off some shots at intervals, and waited for reinforcements. After an hour, Grisha sent on ten men and had twenty fighters left, then an hour later, he sent on another twelve, and that left him with eight.

When the SS arrived, the troops rose to the attack. The SS men were tall and strong. They were drunk, had no hats, and were wearing black shirts with rolled-up sleeves, bearing the skull and cross-bones. They ran at full height, and the machine gun massacred the first rank. The second rank stepped over the dead, the third rank stepped over the second and reached our boys, who went into hand-to-hand fighting with them. There were many Germans and the *Polizei*, and Grisha had all of eight men. They all died in the unequal battle. But the SS lost more than half their contingent and didn't go any further into the forest. Trucks came and carted off their dead and wounded, but the bodies of Grisha, his sons, Venya and Tolya, and five other fighters remained in the clearing. Next morning, the partisans collected them and took them away to the distant forest, where they buried them to a salute of twenty rifle salvoes.

About four hundred people arrived at Sidorov's. For many of them the dreadful march had been their last effort, their last hope had been fulfilled, and many were buried in the first week. Those who survived were either attached to Sidorov's partisan unit or sent to join others, and the old and the sick were hidden away on farms by people who could be trusted, and there they lived out their last days. As mother had wanted, Olya was sent to Tereshchenko in Chernigov, and Tereshchenko took her in and became her father, she bears his name, Olga

Tereshchenko. She now has two children of her own and, like her adoptive father, she is a lawyer, too. It was from Olya that I learned so much about the life and death of our family. She is the only witness left out of all of them.

The ghetto ceased to exist in September 1942, and the war ended in May 1945. Very few of those who got out of the ghetto are still alive; they either died in partisan battles, or later on in the army, when the partisans merged with our regular units, and those who survived have settled all over the country, scattered throughout the land; practically nobody went home, there was no home to go to.

Still, I did manage to discover a few partisans who were able to add some details to Olya's account, which she couldn't have known about. And these tough, brave men, who had been through just about everything a man can go through, confirmed that, before their eyes, my mother really did dissolve in the forest, she had simply melted away into thin air. They swore they had seen it with their own eyes. Maybe they didn't see it happen with their own eyes, maybe this legend arose like a hallucination in the minds of people who had reached their limit. The exodus from the ghetto had been a miracle, and when one miracle has been performed, another can occur, so the legend became rooted in people's minds as though it were reality, a fact.

But even Sidorov, who is still alive and whom I often see, even an old Communist like him, a man of sober mind and free of any superstition, when I asked him about mother, was not definite.

"I didn't see it myself, as your mother didn't reach us, but people say that's how it happened." And he lowered his eyes. You see, as an old member of the Communist Party, the commander of a partisan regiment, a man who doesn't believe in God or the devil, he didn't like to admit that he believed in mother's mysterious disappearance, so he gave an indefinite reply and looked away.

Before the war, there were several thousand Jews living in our town, now there are no more than two hundred. You already know what happened to those who remained under the Germans, and those who didn't either died in other battles or left with the evacuation and settled down in new places. It was mainly old people who came back, among them our barber, Bernard Semyonovich, still cheerful, grey-haired, but neat and fine-looking.

For many days, the old men wandered around the yards, the wasteland, along the roads, and through the woods and fields, collecting the remains of the dead in sacks. The corpses had decomposed, but Bernard Semyonovich could identify some of them by the hair—it seems the hair doesn't fall out after death.

They also identified the remains of my sister, Dina. The SS had tied her to the cross with some old electric wire, which had remained on her bones, and that's how they knew it was Dina. They buried the remains of those they could identify at the cemetery, and the others they buried in a communal grave, the one the Nazis had dug in the forest. The old men wanted to move the communal grave to the cemetery, but it was impossible, several thousand had been killed, and in fact the cemetery no longer existed as, on the commandant's orders, the headstones had been pulled away, and the whole area ploughed over.

The remains of all ten Stashenkos[23] were found, lying together, the way they had hanged together. I cabled Olesya, that is, Alexandrina Afanasyevna Stashenko, and she came, Maksim, her nephew, Andrey Stashenko's son, came, and we buried the remains of their family. Petrus, Stashenko's second son, couldn't attend the mournful ceremony, as he had been killed, fighting on the northern Donets.

We didn't find the remains of my father, Yakov Ivanovsky, though the neighbors pointed out exactly where he had been buried, a wasteland not far from our street, on the way to the river. I even found the man the police had ordered to dig the grave. But there was no grave to be found, only clean sand. We dug over the whole wasteland and found nothing but sand, clean, dry, heavy sand. My father's remains had vanished without a trace. Strange, isn't it?

I made frequent visits to the town, nearly every time I had time off, and I helped as much as I could. There was quite a bit to do, you know, to restore the old cemetery, to put the communal grave in order, to collect money for a memorial, to rebuild the fences. Alexandrina Afanasyevna Stashenko would come over, too, and we went together to the district committee of the Party and to the town soviet, where, of course, they were sympathetic but had enough problems of their own. They had to rehabilitate the town and the factories and get the agriculture going again, as everything had been smashed and destroyed. It is important to consider the living, that's true, but we cannot forget the dead, either, they won't be resurrected, they will live on only in our memories, and we have no right to deny them that, or to deprive them of it. I'd come, walk around, try and get something done, and when I got back to Moscow, I would write to Sidorov. He had retired by then, he had time, and he also did what he could to help—he had lived and worked and made war together with these people.

Then, I must admit, I started to go less often. My sons were growing up and demanding more of my attention, and at my age I had to have medical

---

23 Members of a Ukrainian family executed for assisting the town's Jews.

treatment from time to time, and my wife needed a rest. The last time I was there was 1972, September, the thirtieth anniversary of the uprising and destruction of the ghetto.

Sidorov came with me to the cemetery. The fields all round were turning into autumn gold, we went by the path, along which they used to carry the dead from the ghetto, and along which my mother, Rakhil, and my Uncle Grisha had led the living. They had rehabilitated the cemetery and fenced it off and, where the graves had been, they had planted young silver birches, which had already grown tall, standing in straight lines and rustling their leaves above the unnamed graves. Inside the fence was space for new graves, where they would bury those who would die in their own time.

It was a sad picture, the deserted cemetery, almost without headstones, without monuments, without inscriptions, without flowers. Where were the graves of my forefathers? Where lay grandmother, Uncle Lazar, my brother Sasha, my little nephew Igor?

Sidorov and I stood for a while in silence, then we went to the communal grave, in the pine wood, near [an] old veranda, where he used to sell kefir and ice cream, where people used to relax in their hammocks, and where, once upon a time, my young father and mother had sat and tried to speak to each other in different languages, and where they were able to understand each other in only one language, the great language of love.

There were some other people at the communal grave, a few locals, some old men, some middle-aged, and some young people who had grown up here since the war. Some of them knew my mother, Rakhil, my father, Yakov, my brave grandfather Avraam Rakhlenko, some of them didn't. But their grandmothers and grandfathers, and their fathers and mothers and sisters and brothers, were lying here, too, lying in this vast ditch where, unarmed and helpless, they had been massacred by machine guns.

A large slab of black granite had been erected above the grave, and on it was engraved, in Russian: "To the eternal memory of the victims of the German Fascist invaders." Below it was an inscription in Hebrew.[24]

Next to me stood Sidorov, an ex-miner, then manager of the shoe factory, then a partisan commander, and now a pensioner. He had been born in the

---

24 In Rybakov's Russian, "an inscription in Jewish" (*nadpis' na evreiskom*), as opposed to *na drevneevreiskom* ("in ancient Jewish") or *na ivrite* ("in Hebrew"), which would have been the correct standard Russian terms for "Hebrew." Rybakov made no changes in the usage in the "restored" edition.

Donbass, but he'd lived here a long time, he knew everything, understood everything through and through.

He pointed to the inscription in Russian and Hebrew and asked me, quietly, "Tell me, Boris, did they translate the Russian text right?"

As a child, probably until I was eight or nine, I had gone to cheder, then I transferred to a Russian school, and I'd long ago forgotten the Hebrew characters.

Yet, nearly sixty years later, those letters and those words came back to me from the unknown and eternal depths of my memory, I remembered them, and I read:

"Venikoisi domom loi nikoisi."[25]

The meaning of those words is "Everything is forgiven, but those who have spilled innocent blood shall never be forgiven."

Seeing that I was slow to reply, Sidorov gave me a look, he understood [everything], and again he asked,

"Well, did they get it right?"

"Yes," I said. "It's right, it's exact."

1975–77

Translated from the Russian by Harold Shukman

---

25 This is a transliteration of Rybakov's Ashkenzaic phonetic reproduction, rendered in Cyrillic characters, of the Hebrew of Joel 4:21 (the last verses of Joel): "Thus I will treat as innocent their blood/Which I have not treated as innocent;/And the Lord shall dwell in Zion." Many readers are more familiar with an emendation of the first two lines of Joel 21, which, footnoted in the JPS translation of the *Tanakh*, used throughout this anthology, reads as "their unavenged blood shall be avenged." In Rybakov's Soviet novel, the last clause ("And the Lord shall dwell in Zion") is omitted. These lines from Joel are traditionally recited in the Sabbath service as part of the prayer in memory of the departed and martyrs, which explains their choice for the Hebrew inscription commemorating the memory of Shoah victims. In his essay "Socialist Realism and the Holocaust: Jewish Life and Death in Anatoly Rybakov's *Heavy Sand*" (1996), Gary Rosenshield exposes some of the tensions stemming from the discrepancy between the inscription in Russian and the Hebrew inscription, which does not "translate" it or correspond to it but rather quotes a passage from Joel, truncated and censored in such a way as to omit the reference to God and to Zion and obliterate the meaning and significance of the reference for those readers who are not familiar with the Bible or with Hebrew.

YURY TRIFONOV

Yury Trifonov (1925–1981), prose writer and playwright, was born in 1925 and grew up in Moscow. His father, Valentin Trifonov, an old Bolshevik of Don Cossack stock, a Red Army hero, and later a Soviet official, was executed in 1938; the future writer's Jewish mother, Evgenia Lurie, paid with a sentence of eight years for her refusal to denounce her husband. Trifonov's privileged childhood ended abruptly; he and his sister were raised by their Jewish grandmother Tatyana Slovatinskaya, herself a stern old Bolshevik. After spending 1941–42 in Tashkent, Trifonov returned to Moscow in 1943 and worked in factory jobs. In 1944, concealing his father's identity, Trifonov entered the Moscow Institute of Literature, which he attended until 1949 while working at night. Trifonov's mother was allowed to return to Moscow in 1946.

Trifonov debuted in *Moscow Komsomol Member* (*Moskovskii komsomolets*) with a feuilleton in 1947; his first stories appeared in 1948. Since the 1940s one of his closest friends was the translator and nonfiction writer **Lev Ginzburg**. Trifonov's graduation novel *Students*, a fervently formulaic Soviet work that the British scholar David Gillespie called a "typical product of socialist realism," was published in *Novy mir* in 1950. In 1951, Trifonov became the youngest Soviet writer to receive a Stalin Prize. He applied to join the Union of Soviet Writers, again hiding his past, but the deception was discovered. Trifonov was not granted membership until 1957, two years after his father's official rehabilitation.

Following his conformist success and first difficulties, Trifonov spent over a decade retrenching. His 1953 play, *Guarantee of Success*, explored an artist's quest, one of Trifonov's principal themes, which would culminate in his novel *Time and Place* (1981). Trifonov's trips to Central Asia—and especially his travels in Turkmenistan—yielded journalistic writings and short stories, some of which were gathered in *Under the Sun* (1959). Trifonov also wrote about sports (he was a passionate soccer fan) for magazines and newspapers. Collected in *At the End of the Season* (1961), *Torches on Flaminio* (1965), and other volumes, much of Trifonov's sportswriting was a form of escapism. Trifonov's next novel, *Thirst Quenched* (1963), utilized the material gathered at the construction of the Kara Kum Canal and was reminiscent of the much better novel about Central Asia by the purged Jewish-Polish, later Jewish-Russian, writer Bruno Yasensky (Jasieński, 1901–1938), *A Man Changes His Skin* (1934). Thaw-era readers saw in Trifonov's production novel an allegory of irrigating post-Stalinist Russia with truth.

In 1965, Trifonov published the documentary novel *Fireglow* (1966, expanded edition). Incorporating personal reminiscences, interviews, and archival and historical research, Trifonov sought to tell the story of his father so as to memorialize and exonerate his generation of revolutionaries. According to Trifonov's palliative historical argument, most of the old Bolsheviks were idealists whom Stalin annihilated. Apologetics became another central dilemma of Trifonov's career.

The 1969 collection *Derby with a Large Visor* included some of Trifonov's finest stories. The turning point in Trifonov's career came in 1969–71, with the publication in *Novy mir* of the first three of his short novels of the "Moscow cycle": *The Exchange* (1969), *Preliminary Stocktaking* (1970), and *The Long Goodbye* (1971). *Another Life* appeared in *Novy mir* in 1975, while the last two parts of the cycle appeared in what was then the more liberal monthly *People's Friendship* (*Druzhba narodov*): *House on the Embankment* (1976; Hebrew translation 1991) and the long novel *The Old Man* (1978). Trifonov was unequalled in Russian Soviet literature of the 1970s and 1980s in unerringly capturing the embourgeoisement and moral compromises of the middle echelon of the Soviet elite, whose privileged circles included not only Brezhnevite cynics and careerists but also surviving members of the old guard.

The "Moscow cycle" brought Trifonov domestic and international fame and admiration, resulting in translations of his works into many languages. He occupied what was perhaps a unique position in Soviet culture: careful not to overstep the shifting boundaries separating official writers from dissidents, he declined to participate in *Metropol* (1979; see **Vassily Aksyonov**), yet he never partook in denunciatory actions against fellow writers despite official pressure. As Gillespie put it, "[. . .] dissident Soviet writers of the 1970s were wary of Trifonov, who managed to remain a Soviet writer in good standing with officialdom even as he published works that would have been denounced as anti-Soviet had they rolled off underground or Western presses." Trifonov's diaries reveal that he had an increasingly hard time being macro- and micromanaged by Communist Party officials.

Trifonov's interest in shifting time frames and split narrative voices, especially in *House on the Embankment*, invited a comparison with Vladimir Nabokov's exploration of the "texture of time." The mellifluous prose of Trifonov's "novel of consciousness" (his own term), studded with multiple

ironies, cultivated a fruitful authorial ambiguity. The liberal Soviet intelligen-
tsia adored Trifonov despite the ideological seams and wrinkled corners of his
prose, while orthodox Communist critics attacked him for his refusal to judge
his characters. The details of Trifonov's compromises came to light in his dia-
ries and notebooks, which his widow and third wife, the writer Olga Trifonova
(b. 1938, née Miroshnichenko) published with her commentary in *People's
Friendship* in 1998–99 (she published her memoirs of Trifonov in 2003 under
the same cover with a selection of Trifonov's memoiristic prose).

Trifonov's outwardly calm demeanor masked his turmoil. "I am, as always,
somehow between Scylla and Charybdis," Trifonov recorded in his diary in
1980. "Western journalists push me to make extreme statements, to make it
more 'interesting.' [. . .] And I want to live here, publish here, and write what I
want. 'Ours' can't wait for me to be blown up, so that that Trifonov would be
removed from circulation, which means one less rival. [. . .]" Trifonov strug-
gled to remain silent as the USSR invaded Afghanistan. In connection with the
introduction of military rule in Poland in 1980, he wrote down, "This is the
beginning of the disintegration of the [Eastern Bloc] and perhaps [the USSR].
Actually this corpse will take a long time to rot." Trifonov died in March 1981
in Moscow of a pulmonary embolism following surgery to remove a kidney. In
1981, he was considered a close contender for the Nobel Prize in Literature.

Two works appeared right after Trifonov's death: the novel-like cycle of sto-
ries *The Overturned House* (1981), based on his travel abroad; and the novel *Time
and Place* (1981), a metafictional examination of the anxieties of a Soviet writer.
In 1987, Trifonov's widow published *Disappearance*, a novel he had composed in
the 1970s, returning to the subject of the Great Terror. Trifonov's four-volume
Collected Works appeared in Moscow in 1985–97. Trifonov is one of the very few
authors among the prosaists of the late Soviet period whose published works
have endured political change without losing much of their originality.

* * *

Jewish themes are not central to Trifonov's published prose, in which Jewish
and partly Jewish characters flit by for reasons of verisimilitude and only occa-
sionally take center stage. The three cases that expose Trifonov's subterranean
interest in the Jewish question were *Impatience* (1973), *The Old Man* (1978),
and *The Overturned House* (1981). In *The Old Man*, Trifonov the historian
disproportionately represented—and Trifonov the fictionist drew unflattering
portraits of—Jewish commissars, including one Braslavsky (cf. Ilya Bratslavsky

in **Isaac Babel**'s "The Rabbi's Son" [1924]). Some Jewish acquaintances reproached Trifonov, the son of a Jewish mother, for making "bloodthirsty commissars Jewish," to which Trifonov, according to his widow, replied that "[. . .] really among the commissars there were many Jews. There were also Latvians, and Hungarians, and Austrians. My Bychin [a character in *The Old Man*] is a Russian [. . .]." We will probably never know whether Trifonov sincerely believed he was reflecting a historical truth about Jews in the Revolution. (Trifonov's historical novel *Impatience* dealt with the People's Will organization and their assassination of Alexander II in 1881 and described the historical Jewish-Russian terrorist Grigory Goldenberg. Trifonov also left an unfinished novel about the revolutionary and tsarist secret police agent Evno Azef (cf. the belletristic essay *Azef* by **Mark Aldanov**, as well as the 1962 historical novel *Azef* by the émigré Roman Gul and the 1926 play *Azef: Heads or Tails* by Aleksey Tolstoy and Pavel Shchegolev). At the same time, in Trifonov's diaries and notebooks, his reflections on his Jewish origins and the role Jews had played in history and culture are apparent, as is also Trifonov's ambivalence toward the Jewish commissars of yore.

Trifonov's close friends included a number of Jewish or half-Jewish writers, and he was especially devastated by the death of **Lev Ginzburg**. In one of his last diary entries, on February 1981, Trifonov wrote, "Olya [Trifonov's wife] once said [. . .] this person elicits the vilest feelings and human qualities. Yes, there are such people. Robert Cohn from Hemingway's *Fiesta*." Cutting both ways, Trifonov's remark suggests that he harbored unresolved feelings toward his own ethnic identity. Diaries record Trifonov's equal irritation with some of the recent Jewish-Soviet émigrés he got to know during his two-month official visit to the United States in 1977 and with instances of antisemitism among non-Jewish Russian émigrés in America. Trifonov was painfully sensitive to private overtures of those who perceived him as a true-blue Russian. And he was not unaware of being courted by writers of the nationalist Russian wing of the Writers' Union. Yet Trifonov's widow reported that behind Trifonov's back some Russian writers spoke of his writing as "Jewish whining" and of Trifonov as a "kikish idol."

Featured below, "A Visit with Marc Chagall" appeared posthumously as a chapter-story in *The Overturned House*. One of Trifonov's finest stories, it fictionalizes his impressions of seeing the ninety-two-year-old Marc Chagall in the summer of 1980 in the company of his wife and his French translator Lily Denis. Trifonov admired Chagall. In his diary he wrote of his extreme agitation before meeting Chagall, as well as of the "distrusting manner of a shtetl dweller" with which the artist queried his Soviet visitors. The encounter gave Trifonov an opportunity to remember Amshey Nyurnberg (1897–1979), the father of his first wife, the singer Nina Nelina, who died in 1966. In the 1910s, Nyurnberg lived in Paris and was friendly with Chaim Soutine, Amedeo Modigliani, and Marc Chagall. Later in life he painted official portraits of Soviet leaders while remaining faithful, in the privacy of his studio, to the modernist experiments of his youth. Fictionalizing his late father-in-law and concealing his Jewish name, Trifonov gave him the poignant first name Iona—the Russian equivalent of the name Jonah.

FROM *THE OVERTURNED HOUSE*

A Visit with Marc Chagal

We had been invited for five o'clock. Lily picked us up at Rocquefort-la-Pen, and we sped along a looping road, which now dived into the overheated gorges that were tucked in between the hills, now burst free and climbed the mountains, and on the edge of the transparent expanse some dilapidated, foggy skeletons became visible that circled on flaky air looking like city ruins and getting farther from us, while the breath of the rather distant sea was wafting into the car. I was thinking not only of the artist whom we were going to see, of his simpleton cows, crippled wood huts, one-eyed muzhiks wearing peaked caps, his green and pink dreamy Jews aflight in the ultramarine sky, his shade of the color blue, the Ulysses, the slow and permanent flooding of the world with his mysterious fame—but also of another old man who had died two years ago in a home for the elderly on the bank of the canal[26] past the River Terminal—he, this other old man, would have given everything to be sitting in a car, wind blowing through him, and riding to St. Paul! I thought of Iona Alexandrovich. They were peers. One called the other Marc, the other addressed him as Iona. In 1910, fate brought them together in Paris; later they met there in the twenties, when Iona Alexandrovich was living in Paris on some assignment or other, I'm not sure. I couldn't help remembering him. He so trembled when he spoke about Chagall; he would mix up words, and his hands would shake when he

---

26 Moscow-Volga Canal.

had occasion to hear about Chagall or speak of him. Once in that house on Maslovka Street[27] he hit the painter Tsarenko, who said Chagall was a hacker who couldn't draw—no, he didn't exactly hit him, but in a paroxysm of wrath he softly exclaimed, "You lie!" and with the tips of his fingers lightly slapped Tsarenko on his face—but even this was for him a desperate act revealing Iona Alexandrovich's adoration of Chagall, which he had been carefully concealing for a long time; Tsarenko responded with a mighty whack that knocked the old man off his feet and a joyous scream, "It's you who lies!" I was living on Maslovka Street at the time. It was during the summer of '51 or perhaps '52. I was married to Iona Alexandrovich's daughter. She and I were together for fifteen years until her sudden death at a Lithuanian resort where she dashed off alone for unknown reasons. Chagall's levitating lovers—those are all of us who swim in the blue sky of fate. I guessed this later. At first Iona Alexandrovich loved me, later hated me. And I too at different times felt differently about him. He changed like a landscape throughout the day—at dusk, in the sun, in fog, under moonlight. He was a short-legged, stocky fellow; his face, more peasant than Odessan, had powerful cheekbones; he combed the fringe of his gray hair to the side and while speaking had the habit of making smacking noises as though he were cleaning his teeth with his tongue after a meal. In him, Parisian salons and seaport taverns of his native Odessa were ridiculously commingled. From a mythologically remote past, a self-portrait of young Chagall had landed and survived in his studio, hanging in a safe spot; a lithograph signed in pencil. The face was round, with mad bemusement in the eyes, and contorted after a strange fashion: it seemed unnaturally crooked, as though resting on a broken neck and yet somehow endlessly alive. The face of a person caught by surprise. A person mortally stricken with something. Iona Alexandrovich treasured this lithograph more than any of the other works he owned, and he had etudes by Korovin and Levitan, drawings by Grigoriev, canvases by Osmerkin, Feshin, Falk, and a large painting that depicted a monastery courtyard on the day of a church holiday and was attributed to Myasoedov. Oh, I forgot: there were also Bogaevsky, Malyutin, Kostandi, and some Frenchman, maybe Fantin-Latour, maybe somebody else, although the authorship was questionable. But to all of this he preferred Chagall's ephemeral drawing. In those days, when he liked me, he would frequently and verbosely speculate about the self-portrait, which collectors were trying to tempt him into selling, offering big money, which he cer-

---

27 Maslovka—a street northwest of the old center of Moscow.

tainly needed. Who among the artists living on Maslovka didn't need money in those days! He spoke, swaying me in the direction of thoughts about my own torments and convulsions—I was at the time agonizing in quest of some turn, some new key, as my old writing was making me sick—about the authentic in art always being a bit off kilter, slightly slanted, a bit disjointed, slightly unfinished and unstarted, and then it all pulsates with the magic of life. And now this extraordinary lithograph—its yellowish mat manufactured in Paris, framed, and put under glass—disappeared from his studio. Iona Alexandrovich didn't brag about the lithograph and showed it to few people, only to the ones he could trust and to experts. Only a few people had he told about meeting Chagall in 1910, never mind their meetings in 1927. Those were almost a secret. Of course, it was quite impossible to obliterate his ties to the intolerable antirealist, since everyone did remember that in the early '30s Iona Alexandrovich was lashed during public discussions and in the press—the critic Kugelman, one of the leaders of the ArtFront, incorruptible and furious, distinguished himself in this regard before vanishing in the purges five years later—for pernicious *Chagallism* (Kugelman's term), and poor Iona Alexandrovich repented and denounced and as proof of his sincerity even destroyed some of his own early works, in which *Chagallism* had blossomed most poisonously. Much had transpired in twenty years: war, evacuation, famine, death of loved ones, anxiety about his daughter, old enemies gone, new ones born, and insensibly, like night snowfall, old age had descended, and still his fear of Kugelman and *Chagallism* lingered ceaselessly, like children's strangled fear of darkness. This is why Iona Alexandrovich decided not to make noise over the picture's disappearance. He suffered in silence, wracking his brain over what to do. His wife ranted. The old man, she believed, was entirely to blame. Hadn't he said no to Boris Edgarovich, the doctor of homeopathy, who had offered five thousand for the picture, refused due to his own stupid pride and incomprehension of life? And now he had neither picture nor money. At times Yanina Vladimirovna considered Iona Alexandrovich a fool and declared it firmly and clearly. At other times she considered him a highly intelligent person. She would say, "Everyone knows that you're a fool and easy to deceive." And sometimes, "Iona, why do you get involved in arguments? They're not worthy of your pinkie. You're the smartest one in this building."

All this came back to me on the way to St. Paul. I now rarely recall the house on Maslovka Street. It happened too long ago. It was at the time when . . . .

Nodding at a villa that flashed white through green verdure behind an egg-yellow fence, Lily said,

"Russians who'd settled in Provence after your revolution used to live here. They raised chickens."

And so: it was a time when TV antennas weren't jutting from rooftops; when women wore *trois-quarts* coats with padded shoulders and men walked around in gabardine coats, and some in trench coats; when Luzhniki Stadium hadn't been built and all the games took place at the Dynamo, and from morning till night a crowd milled about the northern gate, some leaving, others coming, the whole soccer commotion bubbling with excitement; when the impressionists were considered suspect and alien to realism; when they hadn't invented the antiroach chemical Prima and in fact there were no cockroaches—they had disappeared during World War II; when Italian films hadn't yet been shown in Moscow and everyone watched German trophy pictures that played not in movie theaters but in clubs; when the Grand Hotel still existed, and it was fashionable to go to the Actor's House restaurant where the Beard was the maitre d'; when the entire area east of Dynamo Stadium was strewn with decrepit wooden houses and resembled a big village with lots of trees, dogs, mud in autumn, poplar fuzz in summer, snowdrifts in winter. And I, too, was living in that strange house on Maslovka that had been built in the '30s with the expectation that the friendly, lifeloving creators of proletarian art would settle there, unperturbed by anything besides their main task of rushing forth into the bright future, and hence it was like living at a train station: one toilet and one faucet for each floor of about twenty people. They lived as though it was all in preparation for something, hastily painting rough drafts of life, and, God-willing, one way or another they would create their main canvas! But the amazing thing is that artists truly paid no attention to life's nonsensical matters such as having to wait in line to go to the toilet or running down the corridor with pails of water. They buried themselves in their canvases, pasteboards, stretchers, tubes of paint, in working rabidly for a deadline, and in the evening they drank vodka, philosophized about their craft, argued fiercely over the devil knows what. On the third floor, where I lived and where Iona Alexandrovich's studio was located, once every three months an important event would take place—a meeting of the purchasing commission. Anxiously the artists would start preparing in advance, finding out by roundabout ways—one day prior to the fateful trial—who had been appointed to the commission, whose voice would weigh more heavily; the meeting of the commission really was fateful, as it determined one's life for the year or even years to come. The artists would lug their paintings from all over Moscow, placing them in the corridor against the wall and writing their names in charcoal on the frame, and sleep badly the night before. In the morning, the spectacle that in its mercilessness resembled Michaelangelo's *Final Judgment* would begin: with one motion of the hand somebody's creations were lifted into paradisal spheres, with another gesture they fell into the inferno. Iona Alexandrovich had been stricken once: two years prior to the disappearance of his Chagall, on the night before the meeting of the commission, a work painted jointly by Iona Alexandrovich and his friend Palatnikov had vanished, a large portrait of the great leader painted square by square. But the thing quickly turned up at the Exhibition of Agriculture: it had already been packed and was about to be shipped to a collective farm in the Kuban region. The plotters who had sold other people's labor were also found; they were two boozers, Glotov and Purizhansky, who had long since forgotten how to paint and were spending their days in a little snack bar on Maslovka Street, which was commonly known as Kudinovka after its regular, the old Pasha Kudinov, one of the last surviving members of the Itinerants.[28] The two boozers were easy to find. They went over to Kudinovka, and the trail revealed itself right away: of course Glotov and Purizhansky had been babbling about the heist. And Fedya Palatnikov roused such terrible screaming! Now one couldn't scream, and complaining was risky. Distraught, Iona Alexandrovich asked my advice, "And what if we should file a formal complaint to the law enforcement organs? To them Marc's name means nothing, doesn't it? But they'll start questioning witnesses, neighbors . . . Marc's name will surface . . . You have no idea how much of an irritant it is . . . ." But occasionally he would exclaim with desperate recklessness, "Oh, damn it! I've had it! I'll tell them all what I think about Marc, about his blue color, his inimitable imagination. This lithograph has no equals, you see . . . He gave me this lithograph when things were difficult in his life . . . Can I forget that? And the times, thank God, are different: '51 is no '31 . . ." The times were of course different, but the word *Chagallism* still sounded ominous: something between *shamanism* and *cabbalism*. And here Afanasy turned up. Actually, Afanasy had always been there, loafing around artists' studios even before the war; but only later did he acquire the specialty for which the artists nicknamed him "Ear." It's a known fact that it's

---

28 The Itinerants (peredvizhniki) was a movement of Russian artists who organized traveling exhibitions, starting with 1871.

difficult to paint ears and particularly the ears of important people known to the world, and in this connection an impressive point of interest was discovered on the modest Afanasy Fedorovich Dymtsov: his ear was a precise copy of the ear of the great leader. Afanasy, hardly an Apollo, a whiny and rather unintelligent person, was considered an average model with whom few wanted to deal, and then suddenly his little Roman head with small curls, a low forehead, and a protruding lower jaw was in great demand, all due to his ear. Afanasy started earning a lot of money, bought himself a suit, became haughty and capricious, and although everything was being kept a secret and his remarkable specialty wasn't talked about openly—because who knew how *they* would feel if *they* heard about it—Afanasy gave one the impression that he now had special connections and opportunities, which he said he preferred not to reveal but at the right moment would put to use. He used this to scare the artists, forcing them to pay a double fee. Then he got so brazen that he began to borrow money from the artists; he also demanded that they feed him and serve him beer during their sessions and coerced one artist into lending him a fur coat that he never returned even after winter was over. People were afraid of messing with him. A rumor went around that he had been summoned somewhere and that he received *permission*. Once he showed up in a military cap and stood outside in front of the house, one leg set back at ease, a cigarette in his mouth, chatting with the super, and the artists walked around the two trying not to look at Afanasy. There was something creepy in his whole appearance. One sculptor reprimanded Afanasy for being late to a session. Afanasy gave the sculptor a wild stare and burst out: "You can wait, God-damned aristocrat!" The sculptor froze, hands down his sides, and didn't say anything. And now, at the height of Afanasy's terrifying powers, somebody informed Iona Alexandrovich that he had seen Chagall's self-lithograph in Afanasy's home, thumbtacked to the wall. Iona Alexandrovich was astonished: Why Afanasy all of a sudden? *And how dare he hang it with thumbtacks?* What occurred after that I remember poorly. After all, it's been almost thirty years. I don't recall how the lithograph got into Afanasy's hands: I rather think he simply snatched it after having decided to become a collector. Somebody had given him the idea to start with Chagall. The owner, they said, wouldn't make noise over it. Indeed, Iona's negotiations with Afanasy proceeded nervously but not noisily: Afanasy swore that he didn't have the lithograph, demanded a search with witnesses present and also a court of public opinion, pretended to be deeply insulted, while in a whisper, almost in tears, Iona begged him to return the treasure. He had gone to an extreme, offering Afanasy a Levitan or a Korovin in exchange for the lithograph. He also tried to put some different pressure on Afanasy, telling him that with him, Iona Alexandrovich, one shouldn't joke around, that in 1918 he had been a commissar of the arts in Odessa, that he once spent five days detained by General Denikin's counterintelligence, that he was nearly taken prisoner by Makhno's troops had Budyony's Red Cavalrymen not rescued him, and so he, too, had connections. But Afanasy obdurately stood his ground: he didn't know anything about it, he didn't have the lithograph. For some reason or other he had set his teeth into Chagall, and now he wasn't going to return it for anything in the world. As is the case with stupid manipulators, his obduracy was senseless but had an insidious core. "Sue me!" he offered. "Write to the district attorney!" This was precisely what Iona Alexandrovich couldn't do. Old fear, like a hernia, tormented him unrelentingly. I remember him in a moment of dejection, sitting, old and forlorn, on an oak bench in his studio. "What can be done? I'm unarmed, and the criminal is armed head to toe . . ." His wife consoled him, "The devil with him, with Chagall. Haven't you suffered enough because of him? It's a good thing you got rid of him. I'm very glad."

Later everything was somehow resolved. In the mid '50s, after an exhibition of French painting had shaken up Moscow marking the collapse of an epoch, I remember Chagall in his previous place in Iona Alexandrovich's studio. But how did he return? By what means did Iona manage to wrest it from stupid Afanasy, who had mystified everyone into fearing him? Oh, it all worked out, it seems, by itself: the ear had ceased to be in demand, the impressionists were no longer considered ideologically suspect, Chagall was now mentioned without insults, Afanasy died. His wife returned the lithograph to Iona, who on that day got terribly drunk, the way he hadn't since his Parisian days, since café La Rotonde, out of which his friends would carry him—Marc Chagall, Kisling, Kremen, Paskin, Soutine, Modigliani, Toulouse-Lautrec, Bastienne-Lepage, Renoir, Courbet, Millet, and Ingres, the resplendent master of the line.

Many years have gone by, all who lived on Maslovka Street at the time have vanished: the boozers Glotov and Purizhansky, the itinerant Kudinov, the savvy businessman Palatnikov, who managed to get commissions for painting portraits square by square; both the wife and the daughter of Iona Alexandrovich have vanished, and he was the last to go at the age of ninety-two at a home for the elderly beyond the River Terminal; only Marc Chagall remained, and I was now on a mountain road on my way to see him.

At first I mistook a stiff old gentleman with gray hair and a long face for Chagall; he was in the sitting room talking with a German pastor visiting from Mainz. Chagall had made stained-glass windows for a cathedral in Mainz, and now the pastor brought color photographs and postcards with views of the cathedral and the windows. Everybody was looking at them; it was a salutary activity for the first few minutes after we arrived. The old gentleman whom I had mistaken for Chagall cast tepid and absent glances at the postcards, the way a creative artist ought to be gazing. And all the while I would look at him from the corner of my eye, thinking, "If you only knew how much Iona Alexandrovich suffered on your account!" Suddenly the old gentleman started saying good bye. I got worried and whispered to Vava, Chagall's wife:

"I'd like to ask Marc Chagall about a few things . . ."

"He'll be here shortly. He's with a doctor. In a couple of minutes."

Vava and I were whispering in Russian. And suddenly, instead of the stiff and tepid man, another one burst into the room—short, quicksilver, tanned, dressed casually, with bald spots in his messed-up hair, and a sincere enchantment in his eyes, which had been slightly discolored by nearly a century of living—this was the real Chagall. And the other one was a wealthy businessman, the founder of the St. Paul museum where we had just been and where I had bought a few Chagall reproductions. The real one attacked us with questions. He was hungry for a conversation. He had interrupted his work after spending several hours upstairs alone in his studio painting a grand piano or a harpsichord, and now he couldn't wait to talk to us.

"You're a writer? You can write anything you want? When are you going back home? She's beautiful! Your wife or just . . . ? They still remember me in Moscow? Haven't forgotten me? You don't say! Have you really been to Vitebsk? No, really, have you been to Vitebsk? You're mistaken, that street is next to a cemetery. Thank God, I remember. You don't need to teach me Vitebsk. Is she your wife or just . . . ? I knew Mayakovsky, Esenin, many others, they're all dead. They died young. Why do you think my sister keeps sending me monographs by Soviet artists? Don't they cost a lot? She spends so much money! I write her: don't spend, don't send! You want names? Hmm, well, let's see, Borisov-Musatov. Yes, yes, Borisov-Musatov. Then, hmm, well, let's see, Levitan . . . and Vrubel . . . yes, Vrubel, Vrubel! Well, I don't know whom else to name for you. I used to like one thing by Serov—remember?—boys standing on a wooden bridge. I loved it in my youth. In your youth you like one thing, in your old age another. In two years I will be ninety-three. Is this really your wife or just something . . . ? You say you like this work? Where could you have seen it? Where? This cannot be true! In Moscow you couldn't have seen it! Vava, who has this work? Ah, Ida. That's different." In a whisper he tells me like a secret, "She's my daughter with Bella. Bella was my wife. She didn't want to come here." And loudly again, "Then you're right; you could've seen this work in Moscow . . ."

My wife stuck in front of him a reproduction that we had just bought at the museum. Against a dark brown background, an old grandfather clock in a wooden case stands slightly tilting to the side. He studied the reproduction silently. Holding it at a distance from his eyes, he looked at it for a while, closely, as if it were a work by somebody else. And suddenly he whispered barely audibly, not to us but to himself, "How miserable one must be to have painted this . . ."

I thought: he had whispered off the very essence of it. To havebeen miserable in order to paint. Later you can be anything, but at first—miserable. The clock in a wooden case tilts to the side. One must overcome tilting time, which tosses people all over: some it keeps in Vitebsk, others it throws to Paris, and others yet to Maslovka Street, to that old constructivist house now inhabited by people I don't know. Probably, as in the old days, the purchasing committee holds its meeting on the third floor. I started asking, did Chagall remember such and such? I named artists who came from Russia, whose names I had once heard from Iona Alexandrovich. For some reason I was afraid to ask about Iona Alexandrovich himself. I felt it would be the same as to ask if my old life had existed, the life that had forever vanished. Chagall remembered everyone but didn't say much about anyone, only responding with a half-question: "Yes, yes. Has he died?"

It seems that everyone I asked about had died, and it was to be expected. Chagall was used to it. Finally I gathered enough spirit to ask, did he remember Iona Alexandrovich? I mentioned the name and waited with trepidation.

"Yes, yes," Chagall said. "Has he died?"

"He died two years ago. And you know . . ."

I wanted to tell him about his life in the home for the elderly on the bank of the canal, where he brought his books, his cardboards, his paints, the Parisian trunk, some of the paintings—the majority he had given to a museum—and in the most visible place he hung Chagall's self-portrait with a strangely contorted face; how he worked until his last day drawing old people, calling them into his room, forcing them to sit on his bed; obediently they would sit, some dozing off, while he would tell them the same thing about Chagall he had told me before, sometimes dozing off at his easel so that occasionally the two of them would both be snoozing. Suddenly he decided to marry nurse Natasha, a pretty young woman with rosy cheeks who wasn't from Moscow and was hoping to get a residence permit for his room on Maslovka Street. Later he became jealous of a certain doctor with whom he would speak in an intolerable fashion while refusing to take medications the doctor had prescribed, fearful that the doctor would try to get rid of him so he could have Natasha. At the city hall office they were dragging it on and on, having suspected that Natasha couldn't possibly love such an old man—he was ninety-two, Natasha twenty-four—and he was determined to fight it, write letters to various places and achieve his goal, but unexpectedly he died at the beginning of the summer, and no one could figure out why: he was in good health. But I didn't get a chance to talk about it because Chagall looked at his watch and asked:

"Vava, I should probably be going?"

"Stay a little longer," Vava said.

In a short while he glanced at his watch again and said he must go to work. Mincing as fast as when he had burst into the sitting room, he now ran off upstairs to the second floor.

On the way back we drove along the coast, and the sea lay in the dusk like a huge sheet of dark and light blue under which one could hide all, all, all.

1980

Translated from the Russian by Maxim D. Shrayer

LEV GINZBURG

Lev Ginzburg (1921–1980), translator, prose writer, and investigative journalist, was born in Moscow, in a family of Jewish intelligentsia, on his mother's side originally from Courland (Kurland). Studying German and writing poetry since childhood, Ginzburg attended the literary seminar at the Moscow Palace of Young Pioneers, directed by the Jewish-Soviet poet Mikhail Svetlov (1904–1964). Ginzburg entered the Moscow Institute of Philosophy, Literature, and History (IFLI) in the fall of 1939 but a month later was drafted into the army, serving for six years in the Far East and joining the Communist Party in 1945. After the war, he studied at the Philology Faculty of Moscow State University (MGU). One of his closest friends since the late 1940s was the writer **Yury Trifonov**.

By the late 1950s–early 1960s, Ginzburg had emerged as a major translator from German. Ginzburg's contributions included exemplary translations of Wolfram von Eschenbach's *Parzival*, German baroque poetry (especially Martin Opitz, Paul Fleming, and Andreas Gryphius), Schiller's drama *Wallenstein's Camp*, German *clerici vagantes* poetry, and German folklore (*Reineke Fox*). His translations were collected in a number of books, including *Words of Mourning and Consolations: German Poetry of the Thirty-Year War, 1618–1648, translated by L. Ginzburg* (1963). In 1969, he received the Johannes Becher Prize in the German Democratic Republic (GDR), whose poets he also translated, sometimes exaggerating their significance. In 1967, Ginzburg wrote an introduction to *Passages of Time* (*Sroki vremeni*), an important anthology of younger German-language poets from the FRG, Austria, Switzerland, and West Berlin, to which he contributed the first Russian translation of Paul Celan's "Death Fugue."

Ginzburg devoted much of his energies to investigating and writing about Nazi atrocities and neo-Nazism. Contemporaries offer diverging accounts of Ginzburg's position in the Soviet establishment, some charging him with being an official Jew and a functionary carrying out missions abroad, others suggesting that the choices Ginzburg made as a translator (e.g., his obsession with the Thirty-Year War) and as a writer about Nazism and Fascism were forms of protest against totalitarianism and antisemitism not in Germany alone but also at home. Some of Ginzburg's optimistic pages about the German Democratic Republic read like propagandistic journalism and lack the wisdom and depth of the best pages of his prose.

Among Ginzburg's books about Nazism were *The Ratcatcher's Pipe: Writer's Sketches, 1956–1959* (1960) and *The Price of Ashes: German Sketches* (1962), where a long chapter titled "The Eichmann Dossier" forms the book's moral center, and two other chapters concern aspects of Eichmann's life and trial. In 1939, Karl Adolf Eichmann (1906–1962) was appointed by Hitler as head of the Reich Central Office of Jewish Emigration and in 1942, following the Wannsee Conference, Eichmann took charge of the Final Solution. Agents of the Mossad (Israeli secret service) located Eichmann in Argentina, where he had fled, and abducted him to Israel in 1960. At his trial in Jerusalem (11 April–14 August 1961), Eichmann argued that he was "following orders." Found guilty of crimes against humanity and the Jewish people and of war crimes, Eichmann was sentenced to death on 15 December 1961 and executed on 31 May 1962. Ginzburg's book was "signed into print" (according to the information printed in *The Price of Ashes*) on the same date, symbolically, that Eichmann was executed. Despite criticism of the handling of the trial by the Israeli government and of Israeli relations with the Federal Republic of Germany ("Ben-Gurion committed an act of betrayal not only in respect to the cause of peace but also in respect to the Jewish people"), Ginzburg wrote of the details of the Eichmann trial, of the Israeli Holocaust memorial Yad Vashem, and of the address to the court, in the name of "six million accusers," by Israel's attorney general Gideon Hausner (at the time, the USSR still maintained diplomatic relations with Israel, which it revoked in June 1967, following the Six-Day War). Ginzburg wrote one of the first lengthy literary treatments of the Eichmann trial, inviting a comparison with Hannah Arendt's *Eichmann in Jerusalem: A Report on the Banality of Evil* (1963), originally serialized in *The New Yorker* in 1963 and published as a book. Ginzburg's report on the October 1963 Krasnodar trial of Nazi collaborators in the Soviet Union (all nine defendants, all of them former auxiliaries of Sonderkommando 10A of Einsatzgruppe D, were found guilty of war crimes, sentenced to death, and executed) was published as *Abyss: A Narrative Based on Documents* (Moscow, 1966).

Ginzburg gave his next book, *Otherworldly Encounters*, the subtitle *From a Munich Notebook*. *Otherworldly Encounters* grew out of *Abyss*, and Ginzburg's ambition was to meet face to face with and interview some of the surviving Nazi leaders and those who knew them intimately. The specific Nazi criminal that bridged *Abyss* and *Otherworldly Encounters* was the former commander of SS Sonderkommando 10A Kurt Christmann. The book was serialized in *Novy mir* at the end of 1969; Soviet Writer publishing house was scheduled to issue it as a book. On 13 April 1970, writing in *Pravda*, the deputy chief of the Propaganda Section of the Central Committee of the Communist Party, A. Dmitriuk, zeroed in on Ginzburg in a defamatory passage: "reek[s] of sick sensationalism." The book was withdrawn from publication, and Ginzburg was blacklisted for a few years as a writer of prose.

Ginzburg died in Moscow in September 1980, a few months after completing his greatest achievement in prose, the posthumously published *"Only My Heart Was Broken . . ." : A Novel-Essay*, published in *Novy mir* in 1981 and as a book in 1983. A volume of Ginzburg's *Selected Works* (1985) included chapters from *The Price of Ashes* and the entire texts of *Abyss* and *Only My Heart Was Broken*. In 1990, *Abyss* and *Otherworldly Encounters* were reprinted as a single volume, and in it *Abyss, Otherworldly Encounters,* and *"Only My Heart Was Broken . . ."* came out as a trilogy. In today's Russia, Ginzburg is remembered as a talented translator from German but largely forgotten as an anti-Fascist polemicist and a talented prose writer. Students of Jewish culure and Shoah historians have yet to recognize Lev Ginzburg and his contribution.

* * *

"Only My Heart Was Broken" is the second half of the last line of Heinrich Heine's poem "Lost Child" (*Enfant Perdu*, 1851): "[. . .] Nur mein Herze brach." The first Jew to become a German national poet, Heine converted to Protestantism to skirt restrictions but never came to terms with his apostasy. He has been popular with Russian poet-translators, such as Afanasy Fet. Jewish writers have identified with Heine differently, depending on their own degree of acculturation and/or Christianization; antisemites have targeted Heine as an example of a Jew who allegedly penetrated Aryan culture to corrupt it. Initially contemplating the title *Confession of a Poetry Translator*, Ginzburg changed it to one that evokes profound historical and cultural associations.

This excerpt from "Wheel of Fortune," the fourth of the book's six chapters, features some of Ginzburg's narrative strategies, here conjoining reportage and autobiographical digressions. Ginzburg interspersed pages about the investigation of Nazi crimes with reflections on the German poetry he had so lovingly translated. "Novel-essay" underscores the hybrid genre of Ginzburg's book, where the personal blends with the historical and the literary with the political. It sprouts out of the ashes and memories of the Shoah and writes itself the way Soviet life composes the Jewish author's biography. Having entered

Russian from the French, in Russian *roman* means both "novel" and "love affair." "*Only My Heart Was Broken . . .*" is Ginzburg's novelistic meditation on his enduring if tortured love for Germany and its culture.

FROM *ONLY MY HEART WAS BROKEN . . .*

[. . .]

O fortune! . . . It's difficult to unravel the riddles of fate, to learn *what will be*. And to learn what *was*? I recall a car trip to the Baltic Sea . . .

. . . This thing looked like the backyard of a fire station, with plywood garage doors painted green, a deserted yard with a solitary soldier on duty walking back and forth. From behind the fence you saw a jail with rusty awnings over the windows.

Smetanin[29] wasn't in; he had gone out to lunch. Then a young man in plain clothes entered from the street, studied me with the wrathless air of a true professional, and inquired what I was doing there. That was Smetanin. Without issuing me a pass he led me to his ventilated office . . .

Actually, I had stopped there on the way to the seacoast, although the pretext was hardly suitable for a family vacation. I wanted to record the history of the local ghetto in connection with the fact that in West Germany they had found both the ghetto's former administrator and the *Gebietskommissar*; supposedly they were going to put them on trial, and even the surviving witnesses were being summoned. I had heard all this on the fly, at the editorial office of the *Literary Gazette* in Moscow, but they suggested I gather the details on location with the assistance of Smetanin, who was investigating this whole matter.

And yet I had one more reason—an intimate one, one might say—to visit this town where I hadn't been before and where my mother had been born and married my father; a town that had given birth to much of the family lore. Since my childhood I would hear from my mother, my father, my grandparents about this town, where before World War I (or, as they put it back then, "during the time of peace"), they had been living on Schilder Street until the German offensive of 1915 had forced them to move to Moscow and to settle there permanently, six years before I was born. It seems strange now, but in early childhood I used to envision Moscow as a place much smaller than this provincial Baltic town, which in my imagination was limitless like the world itself. And in

---

29   The last name Smetanin derives from the Russian noun *smetana* = sour cream.

fact it had been a world of sorts, the beguiling world of family traditions, legends, holidays, and various events that had remained forever beyond a boundary of history.

There I was, in the summer of 1966, when none of the former inhabitants of Schidler Street were alive, there I was stepping behind this boundary of history—or rather driving over it—having brought with me my wife and kids whom I also wanted to introduce to the family lore. But for some reason my children weren't moved by any of this. Fenced off from everything that had once been there by the comfortable lives of their milieu and generation, they only thought of hopping over this town as quickly as possible and driving to the sea; sitting behind my back in our Pobeda,[30] they hardly even looked around, burying themselves in *Quiet Flows the Don*[31] (he) and *A Farewell to Arms* (she).

In the meantime, having left behind Smolensk, we passed through the places and former shtetls whence our three lives had taken their sources—mine and my two children's—and where in the past, a hundred years or so ago, the great-grandfather and great-grandmothers whom we never knew had initiated our biography. Straining my imagination, I ventured to picture their shadows, their dim images, but it didn't work, and all I saw in front of my eyes was a long asphalt highway running through pine forests, and then district centers with standard architecture appeared, all of them resembling one another: the past hadn't been overgrown—it simply didn't exist; it had been built over like a vacant lot.

We had stopped for the night at a provincial capital, where long before my father had been brought to attend secondary school, but even there nothing intimately familiar had descended upon me: it was a modern city, with universities and junior colleges, with factories and the philharmonic; the playbills announced that a symphony orchestra from the capital was performing that evening, and in the vestibule of the hotel I ran into a famous Moscow conductor wearing tails . . .

We were getting nearer and nearer to the town where my mother had been born and where my grandfather had been director of an insurance company or insurance bank of some sort. In our Moscow apartment, located on the first floor, the bathroom window used to be reinforced with a metal sign, "Insurance

---

30 Pobeda—make of a Soviet family car designed and tested during World War II, apparently after what was then the fashion of American automobiles, and introduced in 1946 as a symbol of Red Army victory (in Russian *pobeda* means "victory").

31 Famous novel by Mikhail Sholokhov (1905–1984).

Society 'Salamander,'" to protect it from burglars, and this metal sign, along with my grandfather's old business cards printed on solid handsome paper, surviving in a desk drawer, and a plush-bound photo album with pictures of men in starched stand-up collars and goatees and women in wide-brimmed hats with ostrich feathers, had constituted to me as a child *prerevolutionary times.*

Occasionally my grandfather would get a visit from friends and people he grew up with, who had also moved to Moscow with their sons, daughters, and sons-in-law. One of these old men had a winter coat lined with the fluffy fur of a little animal called a *lyre*, another a walking stick with a handle made of ivory, yet another one wore a pince-nez on a string—this is how I remember them. They would come together in the evening and play sixty-six; gradually there were fewer and fewer of them. My grandfather had survived them all and was the last one to die; on his deathbed, half-delirious, scratching the wall with his fingers, he uttered, "The old guard is leaving."

Meanwhile their children had set deep roots into the Moscow soil; one of them had become a deputy people's commissar, [32] and in my grandfather's circle this man's father was believed to be the biggest left-winger. He would arrive in his son's official vehicle and get angry when the others—while they were playing cards—would now and then curse the new times and regime. As if wishing to reeducate his peers in the spirit of the new times, he would tell them about the benefits of industrialization and also what a wonderful thing the metro, which was then being built in Moscow, was: "It's a miracle, a true miracle! . . ." An argument would ignite, and occasionally, losing his temper, one of the old men would leave, loudly slamming the door; but a few days later he would show up again, settle at the table, shuffle the cards, and start again . . .

To confess, I always felt a little sorry for all these old men, as I also felt sorry for the town that seemed abandoned and orphaned without them. Who lived here now? Who strolled along the dike, near the fortress, where they used to walk in the evening, arm in arm with their wives, to hear military music? Where had all this collapsed? Gradually in our family (and especially after the deaths of my grandfather and grandmother) memories of this town petered out until they were finally gone. After twenty years of being considered foreign, since it had been part of Latvia, when the town became Soviet again, Soviet and therefore open for free entry, neither my mother nor my father even thought of taking advantage of the opportunity to visit the place, once so dear to their hearts. No traces whatsoever

---

32 *Narkom* in a standard abbreviation for *narodnyi komissar* (people's commissar), an earlier Soviet term for "(cabinet) minister."

remained: no metal sign, no business cards; and during the years of war and evac-
uation, the porcelain dishes "from the previous life" with blue flowers on them,
the dishes that, while my grandfather was still alive, would go on the table only on
special festive occasions, were now all broken; only one soup bowl survived, and
we were now using it every day, routinely . . .

"So we'll arrange it for you," said Smetanin after he understood the upshot
of my request, and he made a small chuckle. "We have here a specialist in all
these things, the denture maker, Mindlin Simon Abramovich. I'll connect you
with him now."

Without consulting his address book, Smetanin dialed the number and
asked for Mindlin. Mindlin and I agreed to meet at my hotel the next day. He
came as we had agreed, an old man of about seventy, with a spotty bald head
brown from being suntanned, in a jersey with sleeves rolled up to the elbows;
his fingers were blackened from work. Something about him made you think
of an old American farmer, and his "*kar*" was parked at the entrance to the
hotel—a blue new Volga.[33]

Later, sitting next to him, I observed the confidence with which he oper-
ated his car and talked, talked, talked. He knew his town well, and everyone in
this town knew him, was a little afraid of him, and respected him for reasons
that apparently differed from individual to individual. For some he was a skill-
ful denture master, for others a persona connected with the authorities, for yet
others an officially recognized and thus legitimized *victim of Fascism*, veteran
of the ghetto, who "in this connection" even traveled abroad and appeared on
television with his reminiscences.

He would peek inside stores as if he was their owner, exchange a word or
two with managers or salespersons, and they would right away bring out the
things he needed; at the main hotel, which bore the name "Moscow," the con-
cierge greeted him with a smile, and when, looking for surviving witnesses, he
brought me to a house of prayer, the congregants grew silent and surrounded
him, as though awaiting his next instruction. Driving me around town, he
would now and then stop his vehicle and go in "for a minute"—to the court-
house, the pharmacy, the post office: he just had to be everywhere.

He delved right into his account as soon as he pushed the gas pedal, and
off he went without letting up: "To be frank, everyone had it bad here. These
ones," he nodded at the house on the opposite side of the street, "were taken to

---

33 Volga—make of a Soviet car frequently used by Soviet executives and officials.

the fortress one year later, and they worked as shoemakers there, and then the Aizsargi[34] killed them. Well, I located one of the scumbags in '49, his name's Rokpelins, an Aizsargi member, I recognized him in the street, ran after him losing my breath, but I managed to catch up with him near the factory entrance booth; they call law enforcement, I telephone Riga, the deputy minister, with my connections it's not hard to do, all of Latvia wears my jaws, it was the same before the war back when Ulmanis was still in power, and later, and I've just made the lower jaw for the regional director of the OBKhSS,[35] so, yes, so I immediately get in touch with the deputy minister, then a prosecutor arrives from Riga, an investigator, they arrest him, put him on trial, and sentence him to twenty-five years . . . And now we're driving down Rainis Street; what can I tell you, you can see how beautiful it is! And before the war none of this was here, it's all new construction, and our town Party secretary is a remarkable man: very cultured, never raises his voice, never screams; he received me in his office and even helped me on with my coat . . ."

"So, where was I? Since '49 I've been on the hunt for them—I've got a whole archive, two hundred forty-five index cards; naturally I work in contact with the authorities, and it all began after a dream I had. I dreamt of my wife and daughter, a fourteen-year-old, a beauty; I'm sleeping, and I hear their voices calling for me: 'Papa, we're here, open the door! . . .' I scream and fall off the bed. My wife's terrified: 'What's the matter? . . .' This was my second wife, also from the ghetto, we met after the war; she'd also lost everybody: her daughter, husband . . . So, as I was saying, my late wife (the poor thing died last year—so much emotional baggage, who could bear it?) tells me, 'You know what, go to Poland, to Stutthof, they're calling for you, find their grave . . .' And you know, I did it: through the same deputy minister I got my passport, a visa, all the right papers, and here I am going to Stutthof, and, of course, I find no traces at all. What traces? A monument, a common grave—that's all. But after that I became a little calmer and set to work . . ."

Like all Baltic towns, the town around which we were driving was green, quiet, and neat. At the time it was being rebuilt and expanded: many streets were dug up—here they were laying tramway tracks, there removing them.

---

34 Aizsargi (Latvian) = land guard—Latvian paramilitary organization whose members actively participated in the destruction of Latvian Jews during the Shoah, both independently and alongside the Nazi forces; the post-Soviet era witnessed a rebirth of Aizsargi organizations in independent Latvia.

35 Abbreviation for Society for Fighting the Theft of Socialist Property.

Hidden among flowers and green branches were englassed cafés of the new sort. But Schilder Street (now renamed Yury Gagarin[36] Street) had retained its image: here the buildings were old, three storied, and in my mind I immediately populated them with people from the old family album. I almost literally *saw* my grandfather heading over to his bank, a gold chain across his vest, a top hat, a walking stick, and my mother, a little girl with braidlets and a bow, wearing a school uniform and tall laced-up boots. Meanwhile Mindlin had brought me to a red brick house and started telling me that it was from here that he and his wife and daughter were taken to the ghetto, to the fortress, which he and I were about to visit.

I stated earlier that as a child I used to hear a lot about this fortress as one of the town's landmarks and major points of interest—I used to hear it a lot, and the fortress would loom in my imagination as some sort of medieval castle. Incidentally, it was also mentioned in connection with the events of 1905: demonstrators would go there with red flags and demand the release of prisoners. This fortress, built at the beginning of the nineteenth century to protect the western boundaries of the Russian Empire, had never actually been used for its direct purpose. Nicholas I turned it into a jail and kept the Decembrists here; later, participants of peasant rebellions served time here; then members of the People's Will; later the social-democrats; then, during the first German occupation, hostages; and during the years of bourgeois Latvia, the communists; under Hitler's occupation the ghetto was here . . .

"And so they gathered us here, fifteen thousand people," Mindlin was telling me. "We were lying on the ground in the courtyard, all cramped up, and the heat was awful—August!—and besides they'd turned off the water, and people were dying of thirst under the scorching sun. Can you imagine the shouting, especially the poor little children. We were no longer expecting anything for ourselves, thinking we would die here just like that, and suddenly—rescue, a miracle! An officer arrives, a dandy: '*Ordnung! Rühe!* Stop this calamity! Those who wish will be sent to Peski[37] (this is a vacation area, who hadn't gone to Peski in the summer?)—there we'll quarter you in a decent fashion.'

---

36 Gagarin, Yury (1934–1968)—Soviet cosmonaut, first man to fly in space and orbit the Earth (1961).

37 Peski (Rus.) = sands; Mindlin is using the Russian translation of the Latvian Skede, an area of dunes on the Baltic coast north of the Latvian city of Liepaja, where executions of the Jews of Liepaja took place in 1941; on 14–17 December 1941, over twenty-seven hundred local Jews were murdered by the Nazi mobile killing units and their Latvian collaborators. Ginzburg does not identify the town where his family came from and where Mindlin was

"Of course everyone wanted to go, people started pushing each other, lists of those interested in going were being compiled, and everyone was trying to get on the list, and even volunteers had turned up, as in any queue, to keep order and make sure no one, God forbid, would get on the list before their turn. In a word, why beat around the bush, we never got on the list, we and ten or fifteen other families stayed in the fortress, and the other 'lucky ones' were driven away. Do you know where they took them? Have you ever been to Peski? There two and a half thousand children were executed right away, now there are just little bones scattered all around; if you start digging, the soil will scream in horror, you and I will definitely drive there . . . But why am I telling you this? This is why: that dandy officer was *Gebietskommissar* Schwung himself, the one for whom I once made gold dentures, and in connection with his trial they invited me to Germany last year, to testify as a witness. No, I truly believe life's full of miracles, and one can never tell in advance how and where things will turn. Well, can you imagine what Schwung would've felt if back in August 1941 someone had pointed at me, or whispered, that this miserable Jew, this scarecrow from the ghetto, this doomed goner would not only survive but twenty years later would come as a witness from the Union of Soviet Socialist Republics to Germany, which would, by the way, not be Germany at all, as it used to be, but something a little different—*West* Germany (I'm not touching the Germany Democratic Republic), and he, Schwung, would tremble at the thought that I would be able to identify him and cry out, "That's him, Schwung!"

"But back then neither he nor I could even think about it, it would've seemed sheer fantasy. They kept me at the ghetto, and for two years I was professionally employed by them. I don't want to lie: I had the opportunity to get by and feed my family, and German clients would even come to see me from Riga . . .

"You probably find this strange, but in the ghetto there was a life of its own, and the people, who were all doomed to compulsory death, occupied different positions, as in real life. There were those at the top and those at the bottom, and some of them were even doing classified work for the Germans. Every morning they would take them somewhere, and in the evening they would bring them

---

living at the time the episode took place, but he is clearly referring to Liepaja (Rus. Libava; Ger. Libau), Latvia's third largest city, over two hundred kilometers west of Riga on the west coast of Latvia (in Courland Province of the Russian Empire). Over seven hundred Jews lived in Libava prior to the Nazi invasion of the USSR; about two hundred survived the Nazi occupation. Libava was the birthplace of the poet Anna Prismanova.

back, and of course no one knew what sort of services they performed, and I only learned about one of them by accident. He was the former owner of a haberdashery store, Averbukh, my former client. So you want to know *what* his job was? He worked as a *comforter*. When those about to die would arrive at the station, soon to be loaded off the trains and marched to the edge of the town where they killed them, Averbukh would stand on the platform, well dressed, wearing a nice suit, clean shaven and neatly combed, and greet the new arrivals; and along with the others charged with the same task, he would accompany them right to the place of execution. And when people got agitated and panicked, he would tell them, 'But what are you worried about? See, I'm a Jew like you, and they didn't do anything bad to me, and the conditions are quite agreeable, look at me and tell me, do I resemble a victim? So stop being silly and calm down...' And then, after they were brought to their destination, he would return his suit to the warehouse, change into his rags with the yellow star, and go back to the fortress. And like that every day, until it was his turn to die. And you know, Averbukh didn't think he acted reprehensibly; he believed he was doing good because people needed moral support, and the *Gebietskommissar* Schwung and the ghetto *Kommandant* Tauberg were happy they were managing to avoid the panic. Yes, I got sidetracked, and you're probably interested in what happened when I went to West Germany, since you write about revanchism.

"We arrived in Dortmund, seven of us. Well, what can I say: a fancy city, and they treated us splendidly. When we started giving testimony, the secretary sobbed, and the investigator clasped his head: '*Mein Gott!* What scoundrels! ...' I say to him, 'Why are you clasping your head? Better you tell me what will happen to these bandits. Where are they? Let me look at them, I'll recognize their faces, and if you have detained Tauberg or Schwung, Schwung has my teeth, and if I made the teeth, trust me, he's still wearing them, and I'll identify my work...'

"'*Nein, nein,* no,' they say. 'It's not allowed. It can interfere with the investigation...' *Warum*? Why interfere? Well, it's clear why, they're all in it together, why would they want me to identify the criminals; it was enough that they invite us, take our testimony, and feed us like meat cows: fifty marks[38] of daily allowance, that's big bucks, and multiply fifty by seven—three hundred fifty marks! We dressed ourselves from head to toe... 'So, how's our investigation proceeding?' we ask. The investigator makes a serious face: '*Kommt Zeit, kommt*

---

38 In 1982, 50 DM equaled about US$22.50.

Rat,' which means in time all will be well. Two years we've been waiting now, no trial yet, of course. I must have written them thousands of letters; I wrote to New York, to the UN, same answer: the investigation continues. Since when, I ask you, have they become such legalists? What sort of investigation do they need? Or are they trying to get them all an amnesty? Or waiting for them to have a heart attack as a result of nervous exhaustion, and then they'll be unfit to stand trial?! This is what you should write about; this is what the sirens should be sounded for! Perhaps I myself should turn to Sergey Sergeevich Smirnov?[39] To Ehrenburg? Or perhaps Yevtushenko[40] could write a poem about it? . . ."

I hadn't even noticed that several listeners had gathered around us: a lieutenant and two privates. When Mindlin had finally finished and started wiping his bald spot with a handkerchief, they looked at him with empathy, and the lieutenant asked if Mindlin would agree to address the soldiers during political training, because in their lesson plan there was the subject of neo-Nazism . . .

We drove to Peski across the dike, the same dike along which my grandfather and grandmother liked to walk, and even now there were many people strolling, mainly young people. About fifteen kilometers from the town lay the boundary of a little beach village that I knew from family stories: I'd heard of Peski in my childhood.

"Yes, all around here were summer cottages, many summer cottages," Mindlin said. "And *your* folks probably used to come out here. Here lived engineer Glinternik, here doctor Lurie, here attorney Ratner . . . This here is a golden spot, wonderful, especially for people with hypertension; I recommend you come here some time with your family for a vacation . . . Now, you see this monument?"

Behind the village a sculptural group was visible through the woods. Mindlin stopped the car and, shifting all of his weight forward as if someone were pushing him from behind, approached the monument. For the first time I thought of how old he was.

"This is where they brought them."

He grew silent, reliving everything again.

---

39 Smirnov, Sergey (1915–1976)—writer and Soviet literary functionary, author of the novel *The Brest Fortress* (originally published as *Fortress at the Frontier*, 1956).

40 Yevtushenko, Yevgeny (1933–2017)—famous, and formerly official Soviet, Russian poet and novelist, author of the poem "Babi Yar" (1961; see **Vasily Grossman, Lev Ozerov, Ilya Ehrenburg**).

"In '54 I was able to get the authorities to erect this monument; it had taken a lot—architects worked on it, a local sculptor, a special committee oversaw it, but I don't like the monument. Something isn't right here; these are some superhumans, you see? Why no children and tormented people, the kind they had executed here? I consider this monument unfortunate, and if you're going to write something, hint at it: why aren't there any depictions of children?"

He was now closely studying the surroundings, covered with patches of thick green grass. He peered closely at hillocks and mounds while having a conversation with them, a conversation *they* alone could understand . . . After walking for some time around the mounds, Mindlin returned to the car. He looked a little subdued, having lost his previously cheerful spirit, but after settling behind the wheel, he took a few deep breaths, and as we drove back past the summer cottages, he had regained his strength.

"See this cottage," he asked, turning his head. "This used to be my cottage, I'd built it myself before the war, for my wife and daughter, but later I felt that I couldn't return here, although the cottage had remained intact and I had the papers and there were witnesses as well. So I could get it back any time. No, it was unbearable, too many bitter memories . . ."

And he once again returned to the subject of his occupation-time Odyssey; he was living in the ghetto then, at the cost of incredible efforts and a huge bribe he moved to the town with his family, reasonably expecting that the ghetto would soon be liquidated, because the frontline was getting closer and it was perfectly clear to all that the Germans were going to leave . . .

"And when our rescue was almost there, when we already thought we were saved, one vile woman, our former neighbor, saw us and right away started yelling at the top of her voice calling the police. I, of course, later found her and exposed her; she has served a five-year sentence and now returned home—what's going to happen to her? She's a bull, not a woman. Yes, she's still living, and we were captured and—no questions asked—sent under convoy to the railroad station, where they were forming a train to Stutthof, the death camp. We were separated, pushed apart, and in this squash I was able to hide, dart out of the crowd, rip off the yellow patches and by way of the back streets—no one was stopping me, they had other things to do, one could already hear the artillery nearby—sneak out of town . . ."

Mindlin asked what else we would like to see: there were many points of interest, one couldn't see them all in one day; we could, of course, visit the museum or go to the park or to the old cemetery where Mindlin's second wife was buried; he had built the best gravestone for her at the cemetery. With this cemetery he had one more connection, something that happened after he escaped from the ghetto and then for a while couldn't find shelter in town. Then he came to the old cemetery guard, asking him to help him find shelter or give some sort of advice.

"So this little old man says, 'You know, Simon, I've got some poison, and since they'll kill you anyway, why don't you take some poison, and I'll bury you in a decent way, and for that you'll give me this suit of yours. What do you need it for, if you're going to be dead?' And I thought to myself, maybe I should really do it? But then I didn't do it after all. A man will always have the chance to die, whereas life is given only once. Once only is life given to a person, but how many times they try to take it away! Every step of the way! It's terrifying!"

The cemetery through which we were walking was very old, with many abandoned and overgrown graves: sections of ancient gravestones with rubbed-off lettering had taken root and sunk into the earth, resembling stakes. Apparently under one such gravestone lay my great-grandfather, and from direct contact with this earth I felt as though an electrical shock was going through me: for the first time in my life I really, physically felt the linkage of generations, that greatest mystery of being, binding my ancestors with me, and me—through my children—with my unknown successors . . .

Having guessed what I was feeling, Mindlin began to speak, drawing on numerous details, like an experienced tour guide, about the history of the local families, in turn addressing me and my children. And they stood there, tired of the excursion, of Mindlin's stories. Languid from having been in the sun that was getting hotter and hotter, they pulled me by the sleeve, quietly urging, "Let's go to the beach . . ."

That long, distant life is over . . .

1980

Translated from the Russian by Maxim D. Shrayer

EVGENY REYN

Evgeny Reyn (b. 1935), poet, screenwriter, translator, and memoirist, was born in Leningrad to a family of the Jewish intelligentsia. Reyn's father, an architect, perished in World War II; his mother was an instructor of German. Reyn entered the Leningrad Technological Institute in 1953, but in 1956 a scandal broke out over a student poster, and Reyn became the target of a denunciatory article published in *Komsomol Truth* (*Komsomol'skaia pravda*). He was expelled in 1957 and spent six months as part of a geological expedition on the Kamchatka. He graduated from the Leningrad Institute of the Refrigeration Industry in 1959.

By the late 1950s, his poems still unpublished, Reyn had become famous on the Leningrad literary scene. He struck his audience with the vivacity of his verse, in which early Soviet modernism came alive (**Eduard Bagritsky, Ilya Selvinsky**, and others). He composed poems of great formal sophistication, possessing a starkly recognizable voice when his peers were still searching for one. In 1955–59, Reyn was a member of the literary seminar (*lito*) at the House of Culture of Industrial Cooperation, known as *Promka*. Other members included Reyn's classmates Dmitry Bobyshev and Anatoly Nayman; the medical students **Vassily Aksyonov**, Ilya Averbakh, and **David Shrayer-Petrov**; Sergey Volf; and others. Around 1959–60, a new literary formation later to be known as "Akhmatova's orphans" emerged on the ruins of *Promka* as Bobyshev, Nayman, and Reyn, along with the younger **Joseph Brodsky**, gravitated to Anna Akhmatova (1889–1966) and fell under her mesmerizing influence (Reyn to a lesser degree than the others). Reyn "discovered" and mentored young **Brodsky** and ceded to him the Leningrad poetry crown in the early 1960s. Reyn studied at the Higher Courses of Screenwriting in Moscow and wrote over twenty documentary screenplays. In 1972, he settled permanently in Moscow.

Reyn's poems were first published in the early 1960s, and over the next two decades only a handful appeared in the USSR. The main reason for Reyn's blacklisting was his friendship with **Brodsky**, which continued after **Brodsky**'s trial (1964) and emigration (1972). Reyn's hyperrealistic poems, many composed as though he were filming them with a hand-held camera, seemed unsafe to editors, and his efforts to publish his first collection in Leningrad failed; in the 1970s he continued these efforts in Moscow. Influential authors promoted

Reyn—Yevgeny Yevtushenko, **Aleksandr Mezhirov**, **Yury Trifonov**—but to little avail. The disastrous publication of the collective *Metropol* (1979; see **Vassily Aksyonov**), to which Reyn contributed poems, caused a major setback. *Names of Bridges*, Reyn's first collection, finally appeared in 1984.

In 1987, Reyn was admitted to the Writers' Union. Leading magazines finally opened their doors to him, and in the next five years, he triumphantly rose to the top of the Russian literary establishment. Several collections appeared in Russia in a short time, including *Coastline* (1989) and *Darkness of Mirrors* (1990). Reyn has published over twenty books in the post-Soviet period, including two volumes of chatty memoirs. His most recent poetry books include *After Our Common Era* (2004) and *Labyrinth* (2013). In the 1990s and 2000s, he has garnered more prizes than, perhaps, any contemporary Russian poet, among them a Russian State Prize (1996). Reyn insists that his recent poem "I've grown to love the NKVD—with a late and reciprocated love..." is ironic, but it could be read as unironic. Was **Joseph Brodsky** correct, in his half-hearted introduction to Reyn's collection *Counterclockwise* (1991), that "[Reyn's] main theme is the end of things [...] of the world order that [is] dear—or at least acceptable—to him"?

Reyn's best poems are lyrical compendia of authorial imperfections: confessional, denuding accounts of his own lost youth, broken marriages, warped friendships, regrets and cavils, and of the poet's brushes with History. Having gained a distinct, almost peerless manner by the 1960s, Reyn has remained frozen in his time and his own literary aesthetics.

* * *

Reyn never sought to emigrate. Although he was reportedly baptized, secretly, as an infant by his Russian peasant nanny, he has never played at conversion and holds a skeptical view of Jewish apostasy. In *Anecdotal Notes of a Marathoner* (2003), Reyn discussed his Jewish-Russian identity and Israel most explicitly.

The Jewish theme holds a modest place in Reyn's poetry. Memorializing Reyn's grandparents, his "Preobrazhenskoe Cemetery in Leningrad" echoes **Brodsky**'s "Jewish graveyard near Leningrad" (in this anthology). Reyn's long poem *Nanny Tanya* takes its epigraph from **Vladislav Khodasevich**'s "Not my mother but a Tula peasant woman..." (1917; 1922; in this anthology). In Reyn's poem, however, the intonation is not anguished but falsely comforting, reminiscent of another Jewish-Soviet nanny poem—"Serpukhov" by **Aleksandr Mezhirov**. Reyn's poem ends "SO, GOODBYE, NANNY. Sleep now, until/Louis Armstrong, the black-skinned archangel./Starts playing the reveille over/American, Russian, and Jewish land . . ."

Published for the first time in *People's Friendship* (*Druzhba narodov*) in 1988, "For the Last Time" describes his first visit with the great Anna Akhmatova and the impact of this visit on a young Russian poet from an assimilated Jewish family.

FOR THE LAST TIME

I learned that life is riddled with partitions
when I was hiking down into the valley
and, as in some extensive renovation,
plywood debris was tumbling all around me,
revealing the original apartments
before all those communal subdivisions.
Suddenly everything became apparent.
A Jewish boy who earned straight As since childhood,
winner of hundreds of scholastic honors,
a cavalier who took a silver medal,
this high achiever always on the dean's list,
who has already tasted ash and cinders
and drunk the rotgut wine of Khrushchev's vineyard,
who's written light and nervous youthful poems
sprung with a backbeat syncopated rhythm,
blood mixed with Leningrad's malignant water
during the time when narrow Western labels
were sewn again on Soviet cheviot woolens,
though not with poetry but with flimsy stitches
piecing the mundane scraps of life together—
this boy plucked from the wheel of sleepy fortune,
from *Info Leningrad*, a slip of paper
on which his future lot in life was written:
"Red Cavalry Street," then a string of numbers.
He found the door, and everything was different.
How marvelous to meet the Muse of Russia,
tall and grown heavy since three heart infarctions,

the one who had dictated "God," and "Prophet,"[41]
"Premature Child," and "Trefoil in the Garden."
She mumbles to herself the latest poems.
You take her hand, still feminine though withered,
and her handshake is bracing and almighty.
She offers you a chair, hands you a teacup
full of a brick-red brew that leaves you sleepless.
Here is the sugar bowl, poor sugar lumps,
so go ahead and sweeten the first poison
and take a little sip, then drink it all,
and she will never slight you with her pity.[42]

1987

Translated from the Russian by J. B. Sisson and Maxim D. Shrayer

---

41 Perhaps a reference to Anna Akhmatova's poem "Muse" (1924), in which Akhmatova's lyr-ical self asks the Muse if she was the one who "dictated to Dante/The pages of Hell," and the Muse replies, "Yes." The list of titles that follows is a list of poems by major Russian poets of the late eighteenth through early twentieth centuries who have been important in Akhmatova's literary pedigree and also bear on the meaning and significance of Reyn's poem: "God" by Gavrila Derzhavin (1743–1816), "Prophet" by Aleksandr Pushkin (1799–1837), "Prematurly Born] Child" by Evgeny Baratynsky (1800–1844), and "Trefoil in the Park" by Innokenty Annensky (1856–1909).

42 Reyn had first met Anna Akhmatova in 1947 at a party given for her by Reyn's Moscow aunt, the distinguished Soviet chemist Valeria Poznanskaya, at a hotel during one of Poznanskaya's visits to Leningrad. Eleven years later, in 1958, he looked up Akhmatova and resumed their acquaintance.

SARA POGREB

Sara Pogreb (b. 1921), poet, was born Sara Bronisman to a Jewish family in Zaporozhye, a provincial capital in southeastern Ukraine. Pogreb studied philology at Kazakhstan State University in Alma-Ata (Almaty) during World War II; she took her husband's last name. Like many poets of her generation, in her youth Pogreb was influenced by Vladimir Mayakovsky and **Boris Pasternak**. Returning to Ukraine after the war, Pogreb attended graduate school at Zaporozhye Pedagogical Institute. Her dissertation focused on the postromantic Fyodor Tyutchev (1803–1873). As the anticosmopolitan campaign gained speed, Pogreb took to heart the dictum that Tyutchev articulated in his 1830 poem "Silentium": "How can a heart express itself?/How can the other understand you?/Will he understand by what you live?/An uttered thought is a lie." Pogreb was expelled from graduate school in 1949 without having defended her dissertation. The openly antisemitic climate in Ukrainian universities and magazines prevented her from continuing her academic career and publishing. Pogreb became a high-school teacher of Russian language and literature, living in Zaporozhye and later in the Crimea.

Pogreb returned to writing in the early 1980s, after a hiatus of nearly four decades. Instrumental in bringing her poems to readers was Zinovy Gerdt (1916–1996), a famous Soviet actor of Jewish origin. Gerdt showed Pogreb's poems to his friends, well-known poets Yury Levitansky and David Samoylov, who recognized her gift and unusual circumstances. Sara Pogreb moved to Moscow in 1985, and her verse began to appear in Soviet magazines, including *People's Friendship* (*Druzhba narodov*) and *Youth* (*Iunost'*). Samoylov wrote a preface to Pogreb's first collection, *I've Kept Silent until Verses*, published in Moscow in 1990, the year Pogreb made aliyah.

In Israel Pogreb settled in Ariel, founded on the West Bank in 1978 and connected with Jerusalem by the Trans-Samaria Highway. In Israel she gained an audience among the large Russian community, especially those who made aliyah in the 1990s. Pogreb's second collection, *Under the Eaves of the Sky* (Tel Aviv, 1996, with an afterword by her former classmate, the author Dora Shturman), won a prize from the Union of Israeli Writers in 1997. The second part of the collection is titled "From Ariel to Jerusalem." Writing about becoming an Israeli at an advanced age, Pogreb employs delicate irony when she identifies everyday parallels between Biblical and contemporary themes ("We're Samaritans now . . ."). *Ariel*, a volume of Pogreb's selected poetry, appeared in 2003.

* * *

Written in the 1980s, both poems chosen here appeared in Sara Pogreb's debut collection, *I've Kept Silent until Verses* (1990). Formally unadventurous, they illustrate a common feature of Pogreb's Jewish poetry: a lyrical clash of autobiographical *Dichtung* with historical *Wahrheit*. In the first poem, "I'm going to see my grandparents . . . ," Pogreb reminisces about a journey in the Ukrainian steppe, weaving into her recollection references to the 1932–33 Great Famine and to the destruction of Jewish rural life as her ancestors knew it, first during the prewar Soviet decades and then during the Nazi and Romanian occupation.

In "I'm bidding farewell to the slush . . ." (1989), a poem of leave-taking, Pogreb links her decision to emigrate, after nearly seven decades of living in Ukraine and Russia, with the rise of unabashed antisemitism in the reform-era Russian press. Igor Shafarevich (b. 1923), the first of the two figures whom Pogreb mentions in the poem, is a well-known Russian mathematician, dissident essayist during the Soviet years, and author of openly and virulently antisemitic writings, including his treatise *Russophobia*. Widely circulated in Soviet samizdat in the mid-1980s, *Russophobia* first appeared in the USSR in the Moscow monthly *Our Contemporary* (*Nash sovremennik*). After assuming the editorship of *Our Contemporary* during the years of transition, poet and essayist Stanislav Kunyaev (b. 1932) emerged as one of the leaders of post-Soviet Russian cultural chauvinism. Kunyaev first publicly stated his position in an address during the panel discussion "The Classics and We" held at the Central House of Writers in Moscow on 21 December 1977, with almost a thousand people attending. Targeting **Eduard Bagritsky**, Kunyaev interpreted the career of the great Odessan poet as emblematic of everything that supposedly went wrong with Russian culture in Jewish hands after the Bolshevik Revolution. In his memoir *Poetry. Destiny. Russia* (book edition Moscow, 2001–2), Kunyaev called "The Classics and We" discussion "our first rebellion"—the pronoun "our" pointing to the emergence of the Russian ultra-nationalist movement within the ranks of official Soviet writers.

In her collection *Under the Eaves of the Sky* (1996), Pogreb included a different version of the last six lines of the poem. Pogreb made the changes in 1992, after having immigrated to Israel. In reworking the poem, Pogreb refocused the ending on the inspiration her lyrical self had drawn from Israel. Having left behind her previous (and some might say Quixotic) polemic with Russian literary antisemites, Pogreb called on the same notes that **Samuil Marshak** and Leyb Jaffe had introduced eight decades before Pogreb in their early Zionist poetry.

* * *

I'm going to see my grandparents. The cart
Is piled full of sweet hay. Beneath the sack
It pricks against my legs. I must be four,
Or maybe older—one whole lifetime back.

From Golta to Yuzefpol's no quick drive;[43]
My scarf keeps sliding back and slipping off,
And there above me is the low, low sky,
Like a ceiling, whitewashed with one bluing drop.

The horses whip their tails and stomp their hooves,
Our driver's kind although he holds a knout.
The heat has passed. We drive between the roofs,
And there's the old house, first one on the right.

My Grandma poured warm water in a trough
And gave me baths. Her hand was big and hard,
Scrubbing my back. She combed out my rough shock
Of hair and wove bright ribbons in the braid.

Gloomy in public. Chary with her words.
But what did I know, fidget that I was,
Although the people whispered, "Avrum's girl,"
Not trying to hide the moisture in their eyes.

These verses are too long. They should be cut.
But what I'm getting to is what is always
With me, the main thing: There, beside the wattles,
Along the sloping path we both go walking.

---

43 Golta—a town that is now part of Pervomaisk, a distinct center in Nikolaev (Mykolaiv)
Province in the steppe area of south-central Ukraine; most of Golta's Jews were herded
to the Bogdanovka camp in Transnistria and murdered in the course of the *Aktion* by the
Romanian troops, Ukrainian police, and members of the local ethnic German population
(*Volksdeutsche*) in late December 1941. Yuzefpol (Ukr. Yosypivka)—a village north of Golta
in the direction of Uman, lost its Jewish population during the Shoah.

Below, such green—it almost hurts your eyes.
A deep stream flowing past. The water's dark.
And poplar trees, tall marching poplar trees,
Head for the distance, who knows where they march.

How many times I've had dreams of this place!
And still I dream of it. The grief keeps glowing.
Mama would tell me, "See, that is his grave."
Grandma kept silent, sparing her granddaughter.

Because in all the world they had just me.
The neighbors gladly would have helped, but couldn't,
And so that hungry year, in '33,
They passed away, in the Odessa poorhouse.[44]

Don't soothe your conscience thinking you were much
Too weak to help, too little on your own.
Ask yourself rather, did you always rush—
Quick! Quick!—to help, as soon as you were grown.

1986

* * *

I'm bidding farewell to the slush.
     In October's first days
Over Moscow fine snow drifts down, sifting through sieves until dusk,
I hurry to breathe in my fill of the slippery moisture,
Dip the hooves of my autumnal footgear into these puddles,
And the fibrousness of those clouds,
      their so Russian dawdle—
For me there's no dawn in the world that it couldn't outblaze.

This depth, firmament—a world written as my fate solely,
Brothers in common graves.
     Sickly willows above our ancestors.
And the regional wind grown so dear to us, with all its gusts,

---

44 In the original, "V odesskoi bogadel'ne"; compare the title of Isaac Babel's short story "The
  End of an Almshouse" ("Konets bogadel'ni," published in 1932)

The vistas we paged through like children's books, till they were holey.

Shafarevich expounded,
                                    Kunyaev stamped it with his seal—
About me, Russophobic,
                                    the verdict is much reproduced.
If they do throw you out on your ear, with a curse at your heels
                                              —let's invest
All of our speech's silver,
                                    And gold of that grove in the frost
(How absently shining, surprised by a day of bad weather!),
To hide it more deeply. To cover it.
                          Then to bequeath it.[45]

1989

Translated from the Russian by Sibelan Forrester

---

45 Compare the last six lines in the modified version of the poem in Pogreb's *Under the Eaves of the Sky* (1996):

[...] And so what then? Still not one of *us*. Not ours—so go on!
Come together, my people—a great people too—for tomorrow,
There's a country for labor. For love. And for our Jewish sorrow.
For a high wave—we shook it up, and was it for nothing?
And over Jerusalem this radiant light is primordial.
And Biblical mountains. And blueness—from dawn until dawn. (Trans. Sibelan Forrester)

ISRAEL METTER

Israel (Izrail') Metter (1909–1996), fiction writer, playwright, screenwriter, and memoirist, was born in Kharkov (see excerpt below). A portrait of Theodor Herzl hung in his parents' home, and Metter was a member of the Maccabi Zionist youth organization. Metter first read works by such Jewish writers as Bialik and Frug in his father's library and attended a Hebrew high school until it was closed by the Bolsheviks in 1920.

After finishing secondary school, Metter worked in construction to obtain the proletarian status he needed to attend university. He studied at the Kharkov Institute of People's Education in 1926–29, and then, without taking a degree, he moved to Leningrad, where he taught mathematics in the 1930s. A member of the Ukrainian group Avant-Garde, Metter published his first fiction in Ukrainian, in 1929 in the magazine *New Generation* (*Nova generatsia*), signed Es. Metter. (Both the group leader, Valerian Poleshchuk, and the magazine editor, Mikhail Semenko, were purged in 1937.)

In the 1930s, Metter's Russian-language stories appeared in *Crocodile* (*Krokodil*), *Leningrad*, and other magazines. His semiautobiographical short novel *End of Childhood*, about a Jewish family on the eve and during the 1917 revolutions, came out in 1935. **Veniamin Kaverin** edited Metter's short novel *Apart* (1940). Metter worked on the Leningrad Radio Committee in 1941–42 writing anti-Nazi satires for the radio chronicle that boosted the morale of the besieged population. Evacuated to Perm in the Urals, Metter cowrote two plays about the war.

Metter is remembered for his knightly conduct at the beginning of Zhdanovshchina. The 14 August 1946 Declaration of the Central Committee of the Communist Party attacked the writers Mikhail Zoshchenko and Anna Akhmatova, who were further vilified by Andrey Zhdanov, the Party secretary for ideology, in his Leningrad speeches. Zoshchenko and Akhmatova were expelled from the Union of Soviet Writers in September 1946. After Zoshchenko's courageous remarks at an official meeting of Leningrad writers, Metter applauded Zoshchenko in what witnesses reported was dead silence. Thereafter until 1952 Metter had difficulties publishing.

Metter's prose began to appear in *Novy mir* in the 1950s. His collections of stories included *The Teacher* (1954), *The Meeting* (1957), and others. Aleksandr Tvardovsky's publishing of Metter's short novel *Mukhtar* (1960;

alternative title *Murat*) in *Novy mir* brought Metter popularity and success (he also wrote the screenplay for the film version). This story of an injured search dog and a rank-and-file law-enforcement officer venturing to save his partner from "retirement" offered a Chekhovian alternative to the epic-heroic images of police dogs in Soviet fiction and cinema. Metter led literary seminars at the Writers' Union in the 1960s and 1970s and helped younger authors (such as Sergei Dovlatov). He served as a defense witness in 1964 during the trial of **Joseph Brodsky**.

Much to his chagrin, until perestroika Metter was mainly known as a "militia writer" ("militia" is the name of the regular Soviet police). His fiction was collected and reprinted in a number of volumes, among them *Offense* (1960; reprinted 1962), *Different Destinies* (1973), *Among the People* (1979), and *Meetings and Partings* (1984). In 1987, Metter published *Weekdays*, a volume of fiction, essays, and memoirs (of Anna Akhmatova, **Yury German**, and other writers). The volume included *Homestead Notes* (1975–85), in which Metter described visiting his parents' graves at the Jewish cemetery outside Leningrad. In 1989, *Neva* magazine printed *The Fifth Corner*, Metter's only long novel, which he had unsuccessfully tried publishing in the 1960s. Metter was awarded the 1992 Premio Grinzane Cavour for the Italian translation.

Following Metter's death in St. Petersburg in 1996, two volumes of his prose appeared there, prepared with the assistance of his widow, the former Kirov ballerina Ksenia Zlatkovskaya: *Interrogation* (1998) and *Selected Works* (1999).

* * *

"Nowhere do I feel so much a Jew as at a Jewish cemetery," Metter stated in *Homestead Notes*, originally written for the desk drawer. "My memory has long been Russified, but only in its depths, like lava in the core of the earth, memories of my ethnic group heave. [. . .] I write in Russian, think in Russian, live the destiny of my country's people [. . .] but I am a Jew, my soul suffers doubly [. . .]." In his autobiographical prose published during the reform and post-Soviet years, Metter articulated the notion—familiar to Jewish historians and anthropologists—of Russian Jews as a unique entity with unique ethnic, historical, and cultural parameters (see general introduction).

Metter concluded the long autobiographical essay *Pedigree* (opening section below) with a parable. His mother appeared before a Soviet judge after the death of her husband so as to ensure that she receive his pension. Having demanded documentary proof that Metter's parents had indeed been married, the judge declared a *ketubah* (wedding contract) signed by a Minsk government rabbi in 1903 "invalid" without an "official seal."

PEDIGREE

I was born a long time ago.

The date is of no importance. In and of itself, it lacks color. The past gets its texture not from the calendar but from the earmarks of a bygone epoch.

I was born so long ago that in the years of my early youth people still said "water closet." Actually, what they said was even more familiar—simply "WC," so "water closet" sounded somewhat official, like a name and patronymic. This word came to us from the West or, as we used to say, from Europe. That provided a certain cachet not subject to challenge even in 1949.[46] If I had any intention of plunging into this serious linguistic theme, I would be obliged to report that the common people called the WC a "can," whereas the petty bourgeoisie bashfully said, "Where the tsar goes on foot."

Thus, I was born a very long time ago—so much so that in my childhood the women in the wretched courtyard of our building were addressed as *madame*; that is, my mother was also addressed as Madame, and my father as Mister.

What's more, if I kept reading as it was getting dark, Motya, our most dear and honest servant, reared in Mtsensk, would order me to "turn up the light," which meant that I should turn on the electric light. Motya was strict with my parents—she addressed them by the familiar *ty*, while they addressed her by the formal *vy*.

Mother gave birth to me under the supervision of an obstetrician named Dr. Arie. He had a private clinic downtown, on Pushkin Street.

"I gave birth at Arie's" was a phrase heard often from the women in our neighborhood. The matter was also discussed in the future tense:

"Where are you going to give birth?"

"At Arie's."

And for a long time I had no idea what an Arie was. With my sister the whole thing was much simpler. Mama gave birth to her at home on the big

---

46 Metter is referring to the years of the so-called anticosmopolitan campaign in the Soviet Union, in 1948–53, when native Russian terms were being forcefully privileged over Western borrowings.

dining room table. In 1918 this Arie vanished. As for me, I never really saw him, though he was the first man on the entire planet whom I was supposed to have seen. I read the sign by the door of his clinic many times—it was as big as a painting—and I even remember the sensation of a mysterious, living connection with that sign and the high folding ceremonial door beside which I slowed down when I was walking past. Visible through the thick mirrored panes of glass in the door was a marble stairway. Down those wide steps, tightly swaddled, I was carried by my father.

All of this I remembered or invented when I was visiting Kharkov several years ago. I found the Arie home without having a plan of action—like an old eel swimming upstream to perish at its birthplace. On both sides of the peeled, sagging folding door, repainted a hundred times, refusing to close, were signs beyond reckoning, and each of them was covered all over with letters of the Russian alphabet, but in a bizarrely abbreviated combination as if a dozen tribes of some future civilization had seized that building and tried to live in it together.

Father completed four grades of the municipal high school in Minsk. This may not be exact—maybe it was only three grades. He made grammatical mistakes both in speaking and in writing—such fanciful stresses that nowadays would have permitted one to suppose that he had studied by correspondence and graduated from one of our institutions of higher learning and worked as a Party official.

About twenty years ago, when I was already nearly sixty, I suddenly got interested in my family tree. The impulse for this new development was provided by a photograph of my great-grandfather. A melancholy, pensive old man, with an abundant gray beard, in a peaked cap and a long kaftan, is sitting in a chair. One hand is on his knee, the other on a thick open book. It was the book that inflamed my imagination.

Quickly counting up the previous generations, I calculated that the photograph of my great-grandfather had been taken no later than the middle of the nineteenth century. And the book meant that my family had been literate for time out of mind. And that burdened my young soul with a pride not to be compared to the ironic sadness with which I remember the pathetic certificate attesting to my own education. During the one hundred fifty years that separate me from the photograph of my great-grandfather, I could have acquired a grasp of many fields of learning. But I never managed to get my hands on the baton—great-grandfather carried it in the back pocket of his kaftan.

Persistently and insistently, childhood memories invade my old age. It is incomprehensible how they succeeded in remaining intact under the pressure of reality—not just to remain intact but to soar above it.

A deaf-mute used to visit our courtyard. He would ask for an oblation—there was such a word then. Thin, his dark, bare body covered with rags, his face immobile, he made the rounds of the huge oval courtyard, with a fenced-in garden in the middle; he would walk under the windows, under the balconies, and drawl in a sonorous voice, "N n n n a a a a ... N n n a a a ..."

This moan scared me to death. At the time I was only two, though the accuracy of the dates involved is hard to verify.

Memories lie like a bird's eggs in a nest. The soul warms them for years on end until they chaotically and relentlessly peck their way out.

The courtyard came back to life. Over it, as in a theater, rose the curtain of memory.

Out of nowhere appears a puny Chinese man in a blue jacket and voluminous blue pants. He smiles incessantly and chatters something in his quick, finely chopped language. His name is Ho Da. When he had placed a little rug in the front garden, he covered it with fans, little boxes, and little lanterns made of gay colored paper. These were all for sale. Most importantly, though, Ho Da would extract from the bottomless pockets of his voluminous pants little balls the size of a big cherry. He would swallow ten of them one after another, and then, showing us his empty palms, he would remove those little balls from our ears, our open mouths, our armpits.

My first funeral. My grandmother died, my mother's mother—a tall, straight, proud old lady, constantly at odds with someone in the family. It was easy for her to sustain this state of affairs since she had children without number—about twelve. I could not begin to list them all. What's more, she had on her hands a depressing irritant—my grandfather. In my child's view of the matter, he was afraid of her, but she behaved as though he threatened at any minute to erupt in despotism and rebellion.

Actually, neither Grandma nor Granddad spoiled us with their tender attention. It even seemed to me that they weren't completely certain about my name.

Granddad didn't visit us very often. Immediately upon arriving, he would down half a samovar of unsweetened tea, drawn into his mouth through a deposit of finely chopped sugar. Sometimes he would wordlessly summon me, beckoning with an enormous yellow index finger that smelled of carpenter's glue—Granddad was a bookbinder—and he would roughly put me between his knees, thoughtfully scrutinize my bored face, then ask:

"Well?"

I would answer, "Fine, thanks."

He would nod with approval and start speaking in "jargon" (as the Jews in Kharkov referred to Yiddish).[47] He would say in jargon always the same two words:

"Zei a mentsh!"

I understood that phrase in Russian to mean, "Be a human being."

From my point of view at the time, the wish made no sense at all: It was ridiculous that I, already a human being, should wish to become one.

We could not have a more substantive conversation: my comprehension of jargon was limited, and Granddad used his meager supply of Russian words only as a last resort.

Many years later, when both he and Grandma had long since ceased to be among the living, I found out by accident that the quiet, boring old man in whose company I languished in childhood bore no resemblance to the wild young Jew who had pooled his meager savings to buy a modest bookbinder's shop. Having thus transformed himself into a proprietor, he immediately submitted himself to all the iron laws of developed capitalism through the genius of the German Jew Karl Marx. Whenever he encountered his competitors on the streets of Minsk, Granddad invariably got into a bitter fight.

And more often than not, he would return home with a scratched face and a bloody nose. And since these fights usually took place on Sabbath, when a devout Jew is forbidden by his religion to carry any burden whatsoever, including even a handkerchief, Granddad had no chance to wipe his nose.

Grandma would wash his face and smear the scratches with iodine, but at the same time she would tyrannize his soul with endless nagging. The list of her reproaches was known to Granddad from the very first days of their nuptials. Grandma's family lived on Zakharevskaya Street, the best street in Minsk, a provincial capital. Grandpa's family eked out their existence on Rakovskaya Street. When it rained, galoshes—for the few who had them!— were sucked into the mud. The head of Grandma's family would, from generation to generation, each year buy the most expensive seats in the second row of the stalls in the best choral synagogue that Minsk had to offer. Granddad's

---

47 Not just in Kharkov, of course, but all over Russia, scores of acculturated Jews commonly referred to Yiddish as a "jargon."

family prayed standing behind the rickety chairs of the synagogue in the marketplace. Grandma's family celebrated holidays by drinking a fine kosher wine from the famous Zheverzheev Emporium on Gubernatorskaya Square. As for Granddad's family, well, Granddad himself made wine all year round out of small seedless grapes and hops, and, to top it off, Grandma once secretly watched as Granddad, being with her at a party, drank three indecently large glasses of Passover kosher vodka and then proceeded to pinch the hostess on her fat backside, and she, in turn, gasping for breath in her corset, smiled at him with her gold teeth. Granddad was patient, to the extent that his supply of patience lasted, but with each new provocation his patience diminished. He would bellow in Russian the foulest curses, long familiar to him from the *balagoleh*[48]—on Zakharevskaya Street. Grandma didn't know those words, but she calmed down, satisfied: she had managed to infuriate him.

I used to visit my grandparents. I loved that distant journey into a different realm—they lived on the outskirts of Kharkov—this was no longer the city. To get there, you had to travel first of all in a gaily ringing horse-drawn train in a little through car without any side panels. It was pulled along the rails by two dear, affable, hard-working horses. We glimpsed the motley display windows of the stores; we saw the fire engines racing along with a clatter of bells; we heard the thunder of the silver trumpets of bands in front of the valiant ranks of soldiers—I was transported by a world of discoveries. All the trifles registered then have now suddenly grown to such dimensions that I occasionally take refuge in them to shield myself from the disturbances of the present.

After the train I had a long, dusty walk down a wide unpaved street. Behind a fence, one-story wooden houses stood every which way in the middle of empty courtyards. In the most lopsided house lived my old people.

I remember the kitchen, whose outlandishly large oven ran the whole length of the bleached wall. Into its mysterious cavern Grandma would wedge the upper half of her long body as she manipulated a long paddle to pull out an enormous cast-iron pot of food quivering with heat. Only in that place did I relish food, food that was utterly unprecedented. The cast-iron pot was hermetically sealed with an equally heavy black lid. And when Grandma, her hands swathed in a rag, lifted the lid, a holiday smell so brilliant that it actually seemed

---

48 *Balagoleh* (Yiddish) = wagoner, teamster, coachman; the word has entered the Russian language as *balagur* to refer to a coarsely charismatic man without much in the way of manners or culture.

to glow wafted throughout the entire kitchen, from the cracked floor to the crooked ceiling.

I stayed there on Sabbath, greedily devouring that holiday food. It was called *cholent*,[49] a word unknown to me to this day. The main ingredient of *cholent* was ordinary potatoes. But, dear Lord, is it really possible that potatoes were the main thing? The taste of that dish was determined by a quivering piece of Grandma's soul, added to the mixture along with a piece of kosher beef.

If not I, then who would now have the strength to disclose to the world the secret ingredients used to prepare that ritual Sabbath food consumed by indigent religious Jews?

On a Friday afternoon, absolutely before sunset, while it is still not a sin to work, Grandma would go outside and select pieces of firewood. Gradually, she would deposit them in the maw of the stove, arranging them in a certain way known only to her. Meanwhile, outside the window the sunlight would grow dim, but Grandma didn't have to look at the clock—the Friday sunset accelerated the beating of her devout heart.

The courtyard harbored one other individual who passionately awaited that moment. With the last ray of the departing sun, who should appear on the threshold of the kitchen but the caretaker, in whose fist was clutched a box of matches. Silently and efficiently he headed first to the table where candle stubs stuck out in the menorah. Having lit them from one match, he went over to the oven. The skillfully laid firewood called forth his flattering admiration: "How is it that you people know how to do everything! Our Russian fool doesn't know his ass from a hole in the ground."

On the corner of the table lay a five-kopeck piece—payment for the sin for which a *shabes goy*—the Sabbath person of another faith—absolved my old people: to light a fire on Friday evening and during the day on Saturday is forbidden by the terrible Jahweh. Quickly brushing the copper into his spacious claw, the caretaker hurried to the neighboring houses, where he was also awaited by a devout clientele—on Fridays he served the entire block.

And the firewood in the oven burned for a long time. What remained was a heap of powerfully glowing charcoal. And in that scorching heat, with her face turned to the side, Grandma shoved in, on a paddle, the cast-iron pot with the future *cholent*. First it boiled furiously, straining to burst out from under the

---

49 *Cholent*—traditional Jewish stew with beef, potatoes, and beans.

heavy lid; then, exhausted, submissively and tenderly steeped around the clock in the closed stove, its cavern tightly shut by an iron plate.

Granddad ate this dish in his own peculiar way—not as Grandma and I did. Right next to his plate stood a cup of water, into which he crumbled stale brown bread and ate this hodgepodge with the aromatic cholent. He used a spoon to draw this mixture from the cup . . . How could I have guessed then that the base was not water but vodka? This mixture enabled him to overcome Grandma's vigilance. I did notice that he came to life after eating and evinced toward me a sudden interest, not provoked by our blood ties but by a strongly felt urge for self-expression. He led me into the shed, into his moribund book-binder's workshop. He could no longer work, but he still filled the small orders that occasionally came his way, say, for prayer books. With an enthusiasm verging on rapture, he would pull up his workbench and spread out before me his books, respectfully stroking the velvet bindings, pale blue and navy blue: the names of the owners of the prayer books were stamped in gold letters on the velvet, and the pages were edged in gold.

Granddad did not pester me with his devoutness. Even as a young kid, I understood that the main thing for him at the time was to show me his work. Having shown me what there was to see, he would promptly disconnect himself, drifting off to a state of postprandial never-never land, and, no matter how hard I tried, I could never anticipate that split second when he would fly away from me. His big head and his silk yarmulke continued to crown his broad-shouldered body even when his eyes were at half-mast, but then Granddad seemed to exist in two worlds at the same time: in his current world, numbed and blinded, and in another world, unknown to everyone—perhaps in the distant past, perhaps in the future.

. . . These old people, indifferent to me in childhood, had disappeared from my consciousness forever. Why have they suddenly revived now, at the worst possible time for them and for me? Their shifting outlines sway in my memory like the plants at the bottom of a river. It doesn't enter my mind either to be proud of them or to experience a feeling of shame. But there is the unexplainable impression that they are *mine*, that I came forth out of them, that they are my *family*. I feel enriched by the continuity of existence, by a sense of the divine.

The history of the family, the details of my ancestors' lives, the customs and rituals of their faith—all this I could have related incomparably better if I had made inquiries of experts on ethnic and religious traditions. Not having done so, I understand that I'm making, and will continue to make, unspeakable mistakes. They will probably seem offensive to many of my coreligionists. But I beg them to forgive me. I set out on this false path deliberately, because I'm intentionally proceeding only from my own extant memories, devoured by the moth of time and twisted by the turbid shroud of oblivion. It is precisely for this reason that they are essential to me, though, I confess, at times I am sure that all this happened not to me and not in my presence, so visible is the incomparability in the life of all *that* and the life of all *this*. According to the laws of biology, either all of me should have been torn out or all *that* should have been torn out.

I'm used to the shaky balance of my ethnic self-consciousness. And if malicious peripheral forces do not shake it, this indefiniteness actually suits me. Behind me always remains the right of continual choice. And I choose differently, depending on where my thought process and participation are more needed. Should the world become more peaceful, it would probably be possible to number me in the ranks of the assimilated, though the lexical meaning of that concept—assimilation—sickens me. Likening oneself to others, whoever they may be, is a little respected occupation.

My beloved homeland, Russia, incessantly shudders from the din of national threats and the howl of hatred toward aliens.

Well, so much for my assimilation, then.

I'm a Jew.

A Russian Jew—there's no getting around that.

1980s

Translated from the Russian by Richard Sheldon

ALEKSANDR MEZHIROV

Aleksandr Mezhirov (1923–2009; b. 1921 according to Mezhirov), poet, translator, and critic, was born in Moscow to an educated Jewish family: his father was a jurist, and one of his grandfathers was a rabbi. Drafted as a private in July 1941, Mezhirov was demobilized as a lieutenant in 1943 due to a serious injury. That same year he joined the Communist Party. A published poet since 1941, Mezhirov studied at the Literary Institute. In 1944, he married Elena Yashchenko; their daughter, the writer Zoya Velikhova, was born in 1949.

Mezhirov's first collection, *The Road Is Long*, appeared in 1947 in Moscow, edited by **Pavel Antokolsky**. Mezhirov published the poem *Communists, Ahead!* (*Kommunisty, vpered!*) in 1948. Reprinted in his second collection, *New Encounters* (1949), and in countless volumes, anthologies, and samplers, this poem served as a safe conduct for the rest of his Soviet career. "Mezhirov is a ravenous emulator," Ilya Falikov wrote in 1997. In the title of this poem, Mezhirov took credit for a line that had previously been featured in the epic poem *Tripolie Three-Field* by Boris Kornilov (1907–1938), who died in the Great Purge. In Kornilov's poem, set in Ukraine during the civil war, a band of marauders orders the captured Red Army troops: "Five steps,/communists,/Russians/and kikes! . . ./ Communists,/ahead—/step ahead! . . ."

Mezhirov has a special gift for seamlessly incorporating into his verse the voices of his predecessors from the 1900s–1930s and of his contemporaries; for instance, the bones of **Eduard Bagritsky**'s "Origin" (in this anthology) gleam through the poem "Some smells of childhood remain . . ." in Mezhirov's collection *Farewell to the Snow* (1964). In his once famous war poems (e.g., "Memories of Infantry"), Mezhirov alchemized a poetic intonation that was intimate, anti-heroic, and dissonant, resembling, if anything, Erich Maria Remarque's narrator in *All Quiet on the Western Front* (1929). Mezhirov some-times sang from the song sheets of Anna Akhmatova, Aleksandr Blok, **Vladislav Khodasevich**, Mikhail Kuzmin, Vladimir Lugovskoy, David Samoylov, and Arseny Tarkovsky, to name just a few predecessors and contemporaries, but he was nobody's epigone. Knowing poetry like the back of his hand, the aes-thetically moderate Mezhirov was capable of controversial opinions, such as his comment, in a 1990 essay about **Evgeny Reyn**, that "**Bagritsky**'s natural, original talent exceeded [**Osip**] **Mandelstam**'s."

Celebrated for his war lyrics, Mezhirov published over thirty books of poetry in the Soviet years alone during his long successful career, among them *Communists, Ahead!* (1950; reprinted 1952), *Windshield* (1961), *Ice of Lake Ladoga* (1965), *Under the Old Sky* (1976), *Selected Works* (2 volumes, 1981), *Prose in Verse* (1982 USSR State Prize), *Moonshine Mutter* (1991), and others. The output of his books diminished in the post-Soviet years. Mezhirov was a virtuosic translator, especially recognized for his renditions of Georgian and Lithuanian poetry.

Prominent in the Soviet literary establishment, Mezhirov was a figure of polyvalent allegiances, at different points close to writers of disparate orientations: the Jewish-Russian Rabelaisian **Boris Yampolsky**; the Kazakh pan-Asiatic nationalist writer Olzhas Suleimenov; and the éminence grise of Russian cultural ultranationalism, critic Vadim Kozhinov. Of the younger poets, Mezhirov protéged and favored the official liberal poet Yevgeny Yevtushenko; the poet Tatyana Glushkova, who espoused extreme nationalist views in the mid-1980s; and **Evgeny Reyn**, who was blacklisted in the USSR until the mid-1980s.

In 1992, Mezhirov suddenly left Russia and moved to the United States, first living in New York and later settling in Portland, Oregon. He died in New York in 2009, without having visited Russia.

Mezhirov used to be a passionate pool player, cultivating friendships with professional billiardists and excelling at other games. "My whole life I have played, accustomed to calculating the [winning] exit move with one or even two decks [in mind]. This trains the memory. [. . .] Now memory only gets in the way," Mezhirov wrote in 1996.

* * *

Mezhirov went out of his way to make it publicly known how much he loved his Russian motherland and also, as Jewish emigration in the USSR reached mass proportions, that he could not imagine living apart from it. Admiring **Vladislav Khodasevich**, Mezhirov used Khodasevich's "Not my mother but a Tula peasant woman . . ." (in this anthology) as a point of departure for "Serpukhov" (name of a town south of Moscow), a funeral poem about his Russian nanny first published in 1965. In advancing a thesis that no Jews or very few Jews can be truly Russian writers or true Russians, a former member of Mezhirov's inner circle Stanislav Kunyaev, a leader of the post-Soviet Russian cultural right, readily quotes the ending of "Serpukhov": "Motherland mine, Russia,/Nanny

. . . Dunya . . . Evdokia . . . ." Russian ultranationalists took Mezhirov's emigration as an emblematic sign of a Jewish–Russian divorce, if not of a Jewish betrayal of Russia, and exploited it to their advantage.

Mezhirov introduced Jewish questions into his poetry during the reform period, and his long poem *Blizzard* has been a subject of debate. He started it in 1988, originally setting it during World War II. He subsequently rewrote it several times, first publishing it in the émigré *Time and We* in 1992 and in Russia in 1996 and arriving at what he thought would be the final version in 1997 (it was not).

Featured below is the concluding section of *Blizzard* as it appeared in Mezhirov's collection *Apologia of the Circus* (St. Petersburg, 1997). The poem's argument might be summarized as follows: (1) Russian Christian antisemitism, like any Christian antisemitism, is absurd as it undercuts the very foundation of the Christian faith; (2) Mezhirov did not anticipate that fellow Russian writers with whom he had been close would embrace antisemitic rhetoric; (3) Mezhirov is getting what he deserves for having deluded himself with false hopes of a harmonious assimilation.

Mezhirov radically altered the polemical thrust of *Blizzard* after the publication, in 1991–92, of overtly antisemitic poems by Nikolay Tryapkin (1918–1999), with whom he had been friendly. A talented poet in the peasant-folkloric vein, Tryapkin reacted viscerally to the economic reforms and the disintegration of the USSR. "[. . .] Kettledrums roar, drums thunder,/ Near the Trinity Monastery—a kikish tavern,/Let us sing./Huge lice get fatter and fatter in the ground/And Hassids shit in the Moscow Kremlin,/Let us sing [. . .] ," wrote Tryapkin. Tryapkin's paroxysms of despair appeared in *Our Contemporary* (*Nash sovremennik*) and the newspapers *Day* (*Den'*) and *Tomorrow* (*Zavtra*), all three promoting a Russian ultranationalist platform. In one of the versions of *Blizzard*, Mezhirov refers to a "white" cover of a magazine that he "came across," to find in it "your [i.e., Tryapkin's] 'Damnation'"—pointing to the June 1991 issue of *Our Contemporary* featuring Tryapkin's poems. The elderly and sick Tryapkin, who had not been known to profess antisemitic beliefs, was probably manipulated by the leaders of the Russian cultural right so as to give their movement greater legitimacy in the eyes of the lovers of Russian folk heritage. This is not to defend Tryapkin but to emphasize the shocking effect of Tryapkin's wild attacks. Apparently realizing that he had committed acts of open intolerance, Tryapkin subsequently published two poems lovingly addressed to specific Jews. Tryapkin's "Address to Mark Sobol" (written for the son of **Andrey Sobol**) and "Verses about **Pavel Antokolsky**" suggest, in their internal logic, that he sought to differentiate between Jews who allegedly destroy Russia (the "kikes" of his defamatory verses) and Jews who remain her loyal sons. Should one be comforted by such a distinction?

One of the most intriguing aspects of *Blizzard* is the number of its existing versions (see the bibliography of primary sources) and the changes Mezhirov kept introducing. Even after the publication of Mezhirov's collection *Blizzard* (Moscow, 1997), where the poem's text was billed as "final" and the concluding section differed only slightly from the text featured below, Mezhirov contin-ued to rewrite it, altering it as late as 2002. He agonized over the inclusion of references to Nikolay Tryapkin. In the first two published versions (1992 and 1996), Tryapkin was identified by name, whereas in the subsequent published versions his presence was reduced to a hint. In the unpublished versions dated 2000–2002, Tryapkin's presence virtually evaporated. "[...] In torments I had reached the conclusion that engaging in a struggle with antisemitism is a sense-less activity," Mezhirov told the editor of this anthology on 2 March 1998. And he added, "Any people in diaspora that does not assimilate becomes an object of hatred." In the course of the same conversation, Mezhirov explained that the new changes followed his realization that "it should be as in [Hayyim Nahman] Bialik's *The Tale of the Pogrom* [see **Vladimir Jabotinsky**] [...] where not Bialik but God speaks."

Mezhirov also sought to erase the presence of Andrey Platonov (1899–1951), whom he had initially introduced to counterbalance Tryapkin. One of the greatest twentieth-century Russian prose writers, Platonov was ostracized after the war following the publication, in 1946 in *Novy mir*, of his short story "Ivanov's Family" (also known as "The Return"), where the Jewish theme and the Shoah play a major role. In early 1947, the official critic Vladimir Ermilov (1904–1965) vilified Platonov in *Literary Gazette* in the article "A Slanderous Story by A. Platonov." Platonov died in poverty and isolation.

Featured as a character in the earlier versions of *Blizzard*, Platonov is oblit-erated in the unpublished versions from 2000–2002 and a nameless "somebody" acts in his stead. The version of *Blizzard* that follows is the only one to take as an epigraph—and to paraphrase in the text—a line from Andrey Platonov's short story "The Old Mechanic": "And without me the people is incomplete!" (Mezhirov had previously used the line as an epigraph to "Dedication," from the 1961 collection *Windshield*.)

"I'm capable of neither lies nor sincerity," Mezhirov told the editor on 4 February 1998. In a feverish note dated 20 January 2001, Mezhirov wrote to the editor that Tryapkin and Platonov should not be in *Blizzard*, that it was a "grave error. Failure of taste. And worse than that. It was falsity, double profiting." The editor disagreed, believing that literary history is always in part literary mythology and holding in the highest esteem the 1997 version from *Apologia of the Circus*, where Mezhirov's personal and historical motivations and arguments attain their most genuinely palpable outlines.

FROM *BLIZZARD*

11

Leagues remote from my location
Dwell the folk of mighty nation.
Within its bounds a small one lives
Bearing a scapegoat's imputation—
Guilty as charged, since sinful man
Requires a clan for expiation.

But one exception carved its traces,
Buried them deep in memory.
So just in case this too erases
I pen it for posterity,
An incident well worth a printer,
Simple as it may first appear,
Unforgettable, that winter
Of a long-departed prewar year.
Nikitskaya Street—snow gusts were blowing
As colleagues came to a writer's place
Where vodka, straight, not tea was flowing,
To share a meal and party in peace,
Speaking of all but politics,
Interrupting by fits and starts,
To try the single words that flicks
The gateway switch to others' hearts,
To drop a tear upon the table,

Where no one moves to wipe it off.
And there to join this scribblers' babel
Came also Andrey Platonov.

Below a bright Venetian luster
Looms a board of winter delights,
Smoked and salted goods in clusters
Arranged to pique all appetites.
The tablecloth is starched for traffic,
On the walls Kustodiev, Chagall[50]
Replace the Stalin iconographic.

Suddenly someone with fellow feeling
For those with whom he shared the meal
Said, "Don't you find it most appealing
That among us there's not a single Jew?"
Silence under the smoke-blue ceiling;
No one answered him "yes" or "no."

But Platonov stood up abruptly,
Eyed a spot somewhere on the floor;
Lids still down he left the supper,
Walked slowly toward the frosted door,
Lingered a moment as if awaiting
In a daze or dream what he would do,
Then to the guests, still seated, gaping,
Said slowly, "Goodbye. I am a Jew."

They rose at last to stop his going,
But he melted into the whiteout street;
They lost him in their agitation
As, strained against the ground-wind blowing,
He moved on slowly toward the nation
That is, without him, incomplete.

---

50 Kustodiev, Boris (1878–1927)—major Russian painter; about Marc Chagall, see **Yury Trifonov**.

Even if this fragile story
Will not survive the centuries' strife,
Where a truth of words lays claim to glory
And subjugates the truth of life,

Even if I were not inclining
To trust this tale upon its face,
Ermine sparkling, crystal shining,
Snowflakes drift through my window case,
Blown by the wind of my motherland,
My little hut's near lost from view.
Snowflakes swirl through the window case
I've thrown wide open and broken, too.

1986–2000

Translated from the Russian by Maxim D. Shrayer and Andrew Von Hendy

BELLA ULANOVSKAYA

Bella Ulanovskaya (1943–2005), fiction writer and essayist, was born Isabella Ulanovskaya in Sverdlovsk (Ekaterinburg) to a family of the Jewish intelligentsia and spent her early childhood in the Uralian town of Irbit, returning to Leningrad from the evacuation after the end of the war. Ulanovskaya's father taught in an agricultural college outside Leningrad; her mother was a pianist.

Ulanovskaya graduated from the Philology Faculty of Leningrad University in 1967. She did a great deal of traveling around the country in her youth, trekking from one fishing village to another along the coast of the White Sea. (Ulanovskaya's hunting experience and her knowledge of nature and rural living informed her writing, including the essay "Voluntary Seclusion: The Life of a Lonely Old Woman in a Deserted Village" [published 1992].) After Ulanovskaya graduated, she worked as a reporter at the local-circulation newspaper *Leningrad Metro Builder* (*Leningradskii metrostroitel'*). In 1969, she became one of the founding researchers at the Literary-Memorial Museum of Fyodor Dostoevsky, located in Dostoevsky's last St. Petersburg apartment on Kuznechny Lane. Ulanovskaya presented and published a number of articles on literary subjects, including, in 1969, an important discovery of a historical prototype behind the protagonist of Fyodor Sologub's novel *Petty Demon* (1907).

Writing fiction from her student years, Ulanovskaya benefited from her friendship with the talented writer Yury Kazakov (1927–1982), some of whose finest stories are set in the White Sea region. Her first stories appeared in 1966 in the samizdat journal *Chain Links* (*Zven'ia*). In the early 1970s, Ulanovskaya was part of a seminar of young prose authors under the aegis of the Leningrad branch of the Union of Soviet Writers led by the novelist and critic Viktor Bakinsky, but until 1985 her works appeared only in Leningrad's underground publications, such as *Hours* (*Chasy*) and *Obvodny Canal*, not in official Soviet ones.

In 1985, her story "A'lbinos" was included in the collective *Circle* (*Krug*), published by the Leningrad branch of the Sovetskii pisatel' (Soviet Writer) publishing house. Featuring works by thirty-four authors, many of them hardly "young" or "beginners" and a number of them Jewish, *Circle* was a breakthrough for underground culture. In 1985, Ulanovskaya contributed fiction to *Echo* (*Ekho*) and in 1990 to *Syntax* (*Sintaksis*), both Parisian émigré magazines.

Her short novel *Autumnal March of Frogs* appeared in *Neva* in 1987, and her fiction slowly made its way to the pages of Moscow's "thick" journals (*Banner* [*Znamia*] in 1992, *Novy mir* in 1992, and others). Ulanovskaya's first Russian-language book, the collection of five novellas and three stories *Autumnal March of Frogs* (named for the novella of the same title) came out in 1992 in St. Petersburg. Ulanovskaya was a slow and self-discriminating writer who shunned self-promotion; the volume of her published oeuvre is small. Her second book of fiction, *The Peacock's Personal Immodesty*, appeared only in 2004, in Moscow.

Lidia Ginzburg (1902–1990), the last survivor of the 1920s Russian formalist movement, commended Ulanovskaya's "combination of a refined depiction of the quotidian with an intellectual tension in the authorial reflection." Reviewers have spoken of Ulanovskaya as an existential writer and a student of Japanese prose. One could identify traces of Fyodor Sologub in her imagery; something of Yury Kazakov, Boris Pilnyak, and Mikhail Prishvin in her description technique; and something of Western authors, echoes of late Hermann Hesse and of Haldor Laxness, in her narrative voice. But Ulanovskaya's intonation is most of all uniquely her own, as are her themes and her treatment of landscape elements as prominent characters in her fiction. In 1994, Ulanovskaya received the Tsarskoe Selo Prize.

Ulanovskaya lived in St. Petersburg on Vasilievsky Ostrov with her husband and collaborator, the critic Vladimir Novoselov. She died of cancer on 12 October 2005 and was buried at St. Peterburg's Preobrazhenskoe Jewish cemetery. *A Lonely Letter*, a memorial volume of writings by and about Ulanovskaya, appeared in 2009 in Moscow.

* * *

Below is Bella Ulanovskaya's novella (*povest'*) *Journey to Kashgar*, composed in the 1970s but first published only in 1990 and subsequently reprinted and translated, more recently in Ulanovskaya's Italian-language collection *Viaggio a Kasgar e altre storie* (2003). The intricate design of Ulanovskaya's narrative, as well as her tribute to the sections of Vladimir Nabokov's *The Gift* describing the Central Asian explorations of Fyodor Godunov-Cherdyntsev's father, will emerge from the reading, but one authorial decision merits a brief explication at this point. The name Lieutenant Tatyana Levina readily signals the Jewish origins of Ulanovskaya's heroine. Certain aspects of Ulanovskaya's narrative probably teeter on the verge of the absurd(ist). Yet, the self-conscious nature of her name choice lies not in its violation of verisimilitude—surely there must have been a lieutenant with a Jewish last name in all of the enormous Soviet military—but in its deliberate emphasis of the unspoken postwar official taboo on making Jews heroines and heroes of Soviet works of literature and art. Doubly marked as a female military officer (a linguist serving as a military interpreter) and a Jew, Lieutenant Levina would have been unpalatable to the official Soviet editors-cum-censors. In choosing to name her protagonist Levina, Ulanovskaya also tipped her hat to her late Leningrad colleague **Yury German**, whose remarkable novel *Lieutenant Colonel of the Medical Corps,* banned in 1949 and first published in full in 1956, featured the character of a Jewish naval physician, Aleksandr Levin.

JOURNEY TO KASHGAR[*]

We marched to the Eastern mountains.

The Shitszin[51]

After a fire, when the earth has been left so charred that you would think nothing could live there again, or not for years afterwards, you can sometimes see strange toadstools sprouting, their long fragile stalks ending in small sooty caps. Condemned, by an extraordinary stroke of fate, to live in places of extinction, under impossible conditions, these blackened toadstools can only grow on scorched and burned soil; they cannot tolerate soft living. A whole generation of carbon-loving plants grows up on the ashes of catastrophe, preparing the soil and renewing it for the rush of life that will follow.

I have begun this sketch for a biography without knowing whether I shall manage to finish it, to draw events to their concluding point—a wall in Kashgar[52] with the dawn chill still on it. See, there I am, deliberately running ahead, saying the last words first—describing the morning of Tatyana Levina's execution in Xinjiang.[53] [...]

---

[*]   The text has been abridged in consultation with the author. Here and hereafter, the notes by Catriona Kelly have been slightly expanded or modified.

51   *The Shitszin*—an anthology of Chinese classical poetry from the eleventh to the sixth centuries BCE; the title dates from the twelfth century CE.

52   Kashgar—an ancient city in Eastern (Chinese) Turkestan, on the Kashgar River, near the Tian-Shan mountain range; the name Kashgar (or Kashgaria) is also given to the region where the city is located.

53   Xinjiang (Sin-Kiang)—the Chinese name for Eastern Turkestan.

[. . .] I have the feeling that I am destined to do something with the tale of her heroic death. No, it's not a question of destiny: I just don't want to give up at this stage, when I have already collected all the material that I can about her life, when I know more about her than anyone else. More than that: I haven't the right to give up. I procrastinated over writing up what I had gathered, hoping that I would be able to hand it on to someone else and that they would use it to better effect than I could, that they would make a novel or story out of her life. But it turned out that no one else could do it, or would do it. Friends would stop listening the minute I started talking bout Tatyana Levina. You can't still be fussing round with that, they would say, you must be sick to death of it by now, it's so boring, and isn't there enough of that kind of thing around anyway?

Should I change her name? If I did that I could make up imaginary conversations, describe the journeys she must have made, or the first time she fell in love—give me a free hand, and I could tell you just what was going on inside her head. [. . .] Just recently, though, in fact exactly at the stage when I was beginning to amass material about Tatyana Levina's life, something odd happened. People stopped talking about her; you read about her less and less often in the newspapers. Eventually she sank without a trace.

We won't change her name, then.

The stuff that used to get trotted out about her, though! Her parents were the first culprits, with those awful speeches of theirs, and those visits to Young Pioneer meetings, and the like. Do all your homework, and then you'll get good marks, like Tatyana Levina did! Be brave, like she was, then you might grow up to be a heroine, like her! And when the children heard about the streets of Kashgar, they all burst out crying; but they held their heads proudly, and flashed their eyes, feeling their sandy hair blow in the breeze, feeling the rope noose tight round their necks. (A red-haired girl, leggy as a young goat, is led through town on the end of a rope—and not one Jewish face, not one Russian face, not one European face in sight.)

But I keep leaping ahead, rushing on to the end. We have a long way to travel with Tatyana before that, and I know that we shall travel it in style. Yet I keep going back (if you can go back to what lies ahead), back to Tatyana's last hours. Not a face that she knew—did she think about that?

It's odd, that instinct to surround ourselves with familiar faces. At weddings, birthdays, important meetings, farewell parties, we gather them round us. Do we need people to chronicle our lives, is that it?

Whom would she have wanted to witness her last hours?

I'm not a blood relation of hers, but mine is the only face left that she knows. Suppose I had been fated to show my face for a second in that hostile crowd, amongst all those people with their bristly hair, like black wires? Perhaps Tatyana would have seen me, and turned away. It's pointless to think about that, though, that's like imagining what, say, Dostoevsky would have wanted. Imagine if he rose from the dead and visited the Dostoevsky museum, imagine what he'd do to the lot of us then, when he saw us all goggling at the exhibits, why, he'd kick us all straight out for sure. And imagine how red our faces would be if he went round and looked at the memorial flat we'd tricked out for him, every stick of it bogus—what right did we have to do that? Imagine him reading what was written on the captions, let alone joining (heaven help us!) one of the guided tours . . .

[. . .] So what is a poor chronicler to do? Come on, get a move on, do your best—there's a lot to get through. We need as accurate an account as possible of what happened. I won't say as good an account as possible, because that way we'd just end up with flowers that would never set fruit, so we'd have to nip them all out in any case.

The Atrocities in Korea

Forty-five black pinafores[54]–worsted, rayon, sateen—were squeezed together shoulder to shoulder, in four rows. The sateen pinafores were the ones that couldn't read at all, the rayon pinafores (this was the largest group) were the ones that muddled through somehow, but the worsted ones could rattle along at top speed, without pausing for breath.

When the photograph had been taken, the top row—who might have been picked out for their bad marks and for not having any collars as well as for their height—jumped down off the bench (it had been brought in from the music-room), and the bottom row got up off the sticky polished floor; the third row clambered out from behind the chairs—their chins would be masked in the photograph by the heads of the [third] row. Last to get up was Stalinka[55] the general's daughter, who'd been sitting at teacher's right hand. She was wearing a white band round her sleeve, with a red cross made out of a bit of old red felt hat stitched to it: her mother had sewn it for her.

---

54 The uniform dress of Russian schoolgirls has, since well before the Revolution, been a woolen dress with detachable collar, worn with a pinafore.

55 Stalinka—the diminutive of Stalina, a first name derived from the Soviet leader's surname that was quite commonly given to girls in the 1930s and 1940s.

A lot of the girls dreamt of making friends with Stalinka; they kept telling you how pretty she was, and how lovely her parents' flat was, really big, all full of wonderful German things, and with this huge dog wandering about all over the place, but the dog wasn't fierce with children at all, and one day they'd tied it to Stalinka's toboggan, and it had dragged her all down Baskov Lane,[56] Kuraeva had seen it, the tall girl, she'd visited them several times and met Stalinka's father; he was a general in the MGB[57] you know—and although that sounded funny when Kuraeva said it, smacking her lips over the unfamiliar sounds, no one laughed.

"I woke up and heard the dogs barking in alarm . . ."

You had to write the rest of the story yourself.

Miss Sirotkina, the teacher's copper-plate handwriting flowed neatly over the black board; the top classes had dark brown boards, that made you think of something solid and respectable, like the sepia-tinted photographs—not those vulgar colored snaps, heaven help us!—that were appropriate to the status of our famous, highly respectable girls' school. Before the Revolution it had been a girl's *gymnasium*; Lenin's "wife, friend and faithful helper"[58] had studied here, and won a gold medal in her leaving exam. We all detested anything gaudy. All the hair-ribbons wound round girls' bed-ends at night were brown or black. The ends got creased if you were too lazy to iron them, but it wasn't half so bad to have creased ends as it was to wear a blue ribbon or worst of all, a scarlet one. Any girl stupid enough to wear a scarlet ribbon might even find herself in for a thrashing from her schoolmates. [. . .]

Of course, everyone was going to write a story about a wolf, about him coming running out of the forest and creeping up to the dark byre where the sheep were sleeping, and scraping off the thatch, leaping down, and snatching a warm soft lamb. Uncle takes his gun down from a nail on the wall, puts on his padded coat, and rushes out to the porch. He sees the fields white in the moon, and the forest dark in the distance, and a speck of black moving slowly toward the trees. In their pen, the sheep press closely together, and a dark track of blood runs across the snow-sprinkled field (time those gaps in the fence were stopped up). He takes a crust sprinkled with salt from his pocket—he left it there yesterday by mistake—then opens the lower door and goes in to

---

56   Baskov Lane—Russian *Baskov pereulok*, a side street just east of Liteiny Prospekt and north of Nevsky, in the center of Leningrad/St. Petersburg.

57   MGB—Ministry of State Security, the Soviet secret police force (predecessor of the KGB).

58   Krupskaya, Nadezhda K. (1869–1939)—the pedagogue and Party activist, who had studied at the Princess Obolenskaya Gymnasium in the 1870s.

the sheep. Their little hooves clatter on the frozen floor as they start backward. In the narrow window the glass glimmers, white with hoar-frost. Dogs are still barking somewhere at the edge of the village.

Tatyana Levina looked round. Everyone was writing, listening hard to the barking of the dogs. [...]

In the distance you could hear the sound of men singing in harmony. That was our soldiers, marching from Nekrasov Bathhouse,[59] guarding our sleep.

I'll write something bold and heroic, Tatyana Levina decided.

A sabattur[60] has just landed. He made a parachute jump in the night—see the silvery-white globe cascading down over his shoulders—and now he starts running, running over the potato-field, away from boring old uncle with his gun. That was what uncle said in his letter. "I arrested a sabattur and took him to the pollis in the morning." Boasting.

That was the end of lessons, but they had to stay for an hour of political education. Miss Sirotkina was telling them about the American atrocities in Korea. The forty-four sateen, rayon, and worsted pinafores, and the one silk pinafore, froze in delighted horror and indignation. The Americans had burnt villages, stuck needles under people's fingernails, chopped their tongues out, and plastered them with napalm. Then they had dropped an atom bomb on Korea.

The leaving-bell had still to sound, but Form IB had already lined up and marched out of the classroom, and now they were going down the main staircase. You were supposed to walk as quietly as you could, "like mice," in single file, as close to the wall as you could get without touching it, stopping at every landing as soon as you were given the word.

At last the orderly line of young ladies reached the cloakroom, breaking up by the wire coat-racks. Immediately teacher was surrounded by a throng of parents. She talked to them for a while, looking over her shoulder every now and again. Eventually the girls had all put their coats on and left, and all the parents except Stalina's mother had gone. Stalina's mother was the head of the parents' committee.

Tatyana Levina crept up behind the two and stood for a long time, not sure whether she should say anything. Eventually she asked:

"Did the Americans really drop the atom bomb on Korea?"

---

59 Nekrasov Bathhouse—public baths on Nekrasov Street, a long thoroughfare running east–west to the south of Baskov Lane.

60 I.e., saboteur

But at the same moment the general's wife said: "I'd like you to show me Stalina's marks."

Fat little Stalinka already had her coat on, and was waiting for her mother in the dimly lit passage outside. Just then the bell went; the noise from overhead grew louder and louder. Stalinka began pretending to be very interested in the huge memorial board with its names in gold letters. Tatyana Levina was still standing about, not sure what to do. At that moment some older girls, bold and fearless Amazons from the second form—or maybe even the third, some of them—came down the stairs. When they saw Stalinka, they all shouted at the tops of their voices, "There she is! There she is! Tell-tale!" and went straight for her. Stalinka shot a glance upwards—no sign of her mother—and rushed outside. Run, Stalinka! They all went after Stalinka, the whole of Form 2A, not stopping for their coats, they chased her up Baskov Lane, tripping her up with their cases. Past the school she rushed, then straight across the road—the house where she lived was opposite. There was a bus just coming round the corner into the street, and all the girls shouted at her to wait, but too late! She'd reached her home front doorstep already.

The next morning Tatyana Levina went off to school, dragging her heavy briefcase behind her. She was late; Baskov Lane was deserted. Black flags hung from the poles at first-floor level; it was the anniversary of Kirov's murder.[61]

Tatyana Levina walked the length of the brick barracks, thinking about Kirov, the boy from Urzhum, and staring through all the windows. The gates where the sentry stood weren't completely shut, and inside she could see a narrow yard with a cannon standing inside it. The sentry stared after her and said, "You got legs like a piano's." She was astonished: how did he know that she was having music lessons?

She didn't like her music lessons. It wasn't just the lessons themselves, or the terror of playing at concerts, it was the sense that she was missing out on life. She had the feeling that there were only two sorts of people in the world, those who were forced to have music lessons, and those who were spared them. Most of the girls in her class, in the district where she lived, and the books she'd read, seemed happier and freer than her. Feeling that real life, in all its rough vitality, was passing her by, she became ever more obsessed with descriptions of life. She never left home, never went anywhere, she never even went to Young Pioneer camp, though she was often asked to. Instead, she became more and

---

61 The anniversary of Kirov's murder—the anniversary of the murder, at Stalin's instigation, of Sergey Kirov, the Leningrad Party leader, on 1 December 1934.

more addicted to reading. "That's right, you go and get some fresh air," her parents would say, seeing her going off to her music lessons—and she did, three gulps of it, between the door of the house where she lived and the door of the music school five yards down the street.

"I'm finished," Tatyana Levina would often think, "My goody-goody life is dragging along in the dust like a music case." She enjoyed tormenting herself with thoughts like this, trailing the hated case along the ground as she walked.

One day at school, she said something so dreadful that everyone stopped speaking to her. For some reason she couldn't stop herself lying to the whole class, telling them that her father was Gaydar[62] the writer. In fact Gaydar had been killed well before she was born—indeed, before anyone in Form IB was born. Not that anyone did the sums; they simply walked away from her in silence.

It's an oddly significant incident. By substituting an imaginary life for a real one, Tatyana had moved deep into the territory of art; yet she had felt compelled to lean on a father's strong arm to do it, not trusting in her own frail fictions. Imagine saying that about your parents, though! You sometimes see something like that happen with a hunting dog: it suddenly leaves its owners and goes off with a visitor, as though it had sensed a real hunter in this total stranger.

There was almost no one around outside school, and lessons had started. A lame girl whom Tatyana Levina didn't know was rushing toward the doors as fast as she could. Her mother was with her, carrying her briefcase. Tatyana Levina made to run too, but then she stopped, not wanting to barge in front of the lame girl; she stepped back, staring fixedly at her from behind. The girl was in baggy trousers; they were tucked into felt boots that had become pink, from the school polish. What on earth were they thinking of? The headmistress, Miss Surepka,[63] had said that the girls were to wear shoes, not boots, to school.

"Stop, they won't let you in!" cried Tatyana Levina, rushing after them. "Not in those felt boots!"

---

62 Gaydar—pen name of Arkady Golikov (1904–1941), a very popular children's writer who was also, significantly for this story, a military hero. He joined the Red Army at fourteen and fought valorously in the civil war; he was killed in battle during the first months of World War II.

63 Surepka—probably a nickname for some surname such as Surepina, since this is the common name of *Sinapis arvensis*, charlock, a straggly yellow-flowered weed belonging to the mustard family.

No one in Form IB had ever seen Miss Surepka; some people said that she always wore a yellow dress, but that was all anyone knew. She was as hard to spot as a single stem of charlock in a tidy, monotonous ploughed field.

But everyone knew, loved, feared, and respected Kseniya Alekseevna, the black-haired director of studies for the lower school. She was so tall and thin, so neat in her severe black dress, cut in the pre-Revolutionary way; the girls must have loved her just as much then too, and when she went up to the main *gymnasium* staircase they'd all greeted her politely, inclining their heads just so—like that.

When Tatyana Levina came into the classroom, she stood and waited by the door, expecting she'd have to apologize and make her excuses. But everyone ignored her, so she went and sat down.

Something strange was happening. Tall Kuraeva had been standing at her desk and sounding off something.

Suddenly she stopped speaking.

"Go on," said Miss Sirotkina.

"Tatyana doesn't pull her weight, she doesn't make any contribution to the collective."

"Don't worry." Tatyana's neighbor whispered. "It's not you they're arresting, only your parents."

It was her that Kuraeva was talking about. She was calling her by her full name, Tatyana this, Tatyana that, just as if she were some newspaper reporter. And suddenly she brought up Gaydar, and it was clear that had really done it, there was no saving Tatyana now.

The door opened, and a grown-up pioneer no one knew came in and said loudly, "I'm to take Tatyana Levina to see the headmistress."

Tatyana got up, walked along the rows of desks and out into the corridor, then down the stairs, following the pioneer girl, who walked in stony silence.

The huge mirrors of the former girls' *gimnaziia* glimmered in the half-light. A strange cleaner was scrubbing the steps. On the second floor, there was no mirror: a big picture in a frame hung there instead. The picture was of Stalin, with a little Central Asian girl called Mamlakat in his arms: she was holding out a bouquet to him, and had her other arm wrapped round his neck.

At that point Tatyana Levina's nerves gave way and she burst out sobbing. In stern indifference, the pioneer girl waited for her to stop crying, and then they walked on.

"There she is, that's the one, the one who made those big bullies push Stalina under the bus."

It was the general's wife, sitting slumped on a sofa. Miss Surepka, in yellow, and Kseniya Alekseevna, in black, were sitting at a desk.

"They'd actually grabbed hold of her, you know," said Stalinka's mother. "Fortunately she managed to struggle free, but they tore a great lump of fur out of her coat first."

She leaned against the oilcloth back of the headmistress's sofa, and dropped her voice.

"My husband shot twenty hares last autumn, twenty, so that our little girl could have a proper winter coat. Now they go and grab her by the coat. Here, I'll show you!"

She began rootling in a shopping-bag that was standing by her on the sofa; the black and dun fox tippet round her neck slid sideways, leering with its red glass eyes.

So I find myself acting as a chronicler for Tatyana after all. It's a thankless task, and I'd appreciate the chance to say something about it. To date, all the chroniclers that ever existed—in Russia and everywhere else—have been men. There isn't a female equivalent of the role, and I think that's a pity. Women chroniclers have some advantages, if you like to put it that way. I seem to remember that Tolstoy got his wife to dress his heroines—that is, to tell him about her own clothes, so he knew what to put them in. Conversely, we women chroniclers have no trouble in dressing the bride all by ourselves, but we have to consult some retired officer we know about whether a detachment's position was really all that hopeless, and how it got into the mess in the first place. The officer I consulted had served in the Far East; he could answer all my questions about Tatyana perfectly.

Whose advice carries more weight, then, Sofya Andreevna's or my friend the retired pilot's? I think both kinds are equally important; I also think they relate to similar questions, that is, to questions of kit. There are times when it's more important how you kit yourself out at a ball than it is on a battlefield. Comparisons between the two situations are by no means fortuitous: in both cases victory depends on well-designed and reliable equipment just as much as it does on a well-though-out strategy. A battleship's effectiveness often hangs on the quality of its rigging, I can tell you. [. . .]

Woman is a chronicler by nature. Name me one headmistress or school-teacher who can resist telling her husband every detail of the latest staff meeting the minute she gets home. More: I am absolutely convinced that many Soviet families only stay together because the husbands indulge their wives, and let them chatter on about work. If a wife is deprived of this, she'll go straight off to wail to her friends about her miserable life. And what joy when harmony is restored once more, when her husband is back home, and sober, and listening to her again, and even asking every so often, "And how's that colleague of yours, what's her name, Arsefeatures, or whatever you call her?" [. . .]

In any case, you can say what you like: I'm not letting anyone else get hold of Tatyana Levina's story.

So you're wondering what women know about war? No one asked that when they were made to do military subjects as part of their university courses, when all language graduates were forced to do "military interpreting" as a subsidiary, and women were given military rankings—not to speak of being made to serve in the armed forces, if you please.[64] Tatyana Levina herself understood as much about war as anyone could be expected to, and when she rushed into the reeds to save "everyone," then that's exactly what she thought she was doing, "saving everyone."

And that's how I saw it too, though I did have quite a few arguments with my informant about things; he insisted that she shouldn't have done what she did at all, she shouldn't have got stuck in those wretched thickets to start with. It was her commanding officer's fault that she got stuck. Well, we can all understand that much. If they were going to go chasing after the partisans into the forest, then they should have had at least two motor launches equipped with machine-guns, and half-a-dozen grenade throwers, and they should have been sure to keep in radio contact all the time. But the radio contact was the strangest bit of the whole story, and neither I nor my informant understand much of what was going on there. In time, though, more may be discovered, so that we have a clearer picture of that last tragic battle.

Well, if I live long enough myself, I'll get hold of that bastard on the lakeshore post who called out "Keep left." She did what he said; after all, she was the messenger, and how was she to know that the post was in enemy hands? And the bastard spoke to her in Russian, how did they get him to do that? He called out to her, "Over here, it's OK." Did they use force? Well, they may have done, perhaps he even thought they'd shoot him, but in that case, why did he have to shout out so cheerfully? Surely they can't have made him do that, after all, why should they have wanted to? What was so threat-

---

64   As a general rule, in the USSR mandatory military draft only applied to men.

ening in seeing some damn fool of a woman a few feet away, quite obviously lost? Say what you like, but I'm sure he could have managed to drop her a hint. Actually, what I really think is this. He did it on purpose. After all, he had some sort of a funny name, didn't he? Bavyka, or Bavyakin, something like that. Not a Russian name, anyway. A good man to leave as a guard, I don't think! I've even heard he went out to welcome the partisans himself; well, he'd had plenty of time waiting around to think of how he'd give them the hospitality treatment! Anyway, I hope that when this essay is published someone who knew him well will come forward. They wouldn't give me his case papers—there must have been classified information of some kind in them. He had the radio, and when they asked him to pass a message on, he said it was broken. I'm sure he was responsible for what happened to Tatyana Levina—and for the fact that the whole detachment was surrounded, wiped out. No, it's a clear case of treachery, and I'm astonished that the responsible authorities, as they say, haven't dealt with it yet.

If I ever get to him, the bastard, I'll make sure everyone in the country knows who he is, and I'll put a curse on his whole family. Unto the seventh generation.

War isn't the place for delicate young girls and high-minded chroniclers. Quite true. But if people like us happen to get mixed up in it, what can we do? After all, we see what we see.

When the general mobilization was announced, we were all given three hours to reach base. We were given bowls, mugs, toothbrushes and a day's supply of food. Soon we were on our way east.

I don't need to go into the details of what happened next, it's all too well known. But in due course our unit was disbanded, and we all ended up in different places. I was sent to the capital, and Tatyana Levina, the heroine-to-be, ended up in a village in the provinces, way up in the mountains. [...]

Our forces soon moved on to the far east, leaving the detachment with which Tatyana Levina was stationed far behind in the rearguard. She was given a billet in a mud hut on the outskirts of the village; her quarters were in the best part of the hut, and the large family to whom the hut belonged was left crammed together in one corner.

HQ was set up in what had been the local Party headquarters, at one corner of the village market square.

There was a lot to do in the first few days. The military commandant's address to the local people had to be translated. He told them that a government that genuinely reflected the wishes of the people would be introduced, and that the norms of Party authority would be restored. Then there was a bit about the sincere friendship that had always subsisted between fraternal nations, before the commandant rounded off by ordering that all firearms be surrendered within twenty-four hours, and decreeing that a curfew was to be instituted throughout the district.

Some of the old men did duly hand in their guns, ancient Soviet weapons of long obsolete design, and some of our men dragged in a heavy machine-gun which they had found lying in a thicket somewhere (now someone needed to check what the name of the place was).

One day a prisoner of war was brought in to HQ. The colonel himself acted as interrogator, and Tatyana as translator.

The prisoner had been wounded whilst the rebel forces were in retreat. The local teacher's daughter had found him a hiding-place somewhere over by Southern Mountain. He had a slim, fine-featured face, and spoke like a man with an education. His pronunciation indicated that he was from the capital; from the few things that he was prepared to say, it seemed likely that he had been exiled here, to the wilds of the country, as part of a "re-education program." He soon began refusing to answer any questions, though Tatyana tried to convey to him as gently as possible the colonel's assurances that the teacher's daughter had nothing to fear, and that the only sensible course was for the prisoner to co-operate, especially as no one was going to rush him into a decision.

A few days later, Tatyana was asked to go out with a hunting party. The path into the hills led through orchards of green apricots and pomegranates that had just set fruit; beyond lay fields of flax, white with blossom, and a plantation of opium poppy. I have not been able to establish in detail what happened during the hunt, but I know for certain that Tatyana shot a lynx, a splendid specimen, apparently—accounts are consistent on that. I also know that on the way back, Tatyana's companions let off a few rounds at some jackdaws which had been feeding on the poppy seeds, and which were perched on the poplars round about stoned out of their heads—some of them were so far gone that they had given up any attempt to perch, and were sprawling on the ground below the trees. [...]

Tatyana had told Captain Tarasenko several times how awkward she felt that she should be occupying the greater part of the hut where she was billeted, whilst its owners slept crammed into one corner. Every time she made a cup of coffee or opened a tin of milk she was seized by embarrassment; she knew perfectly well that the locals were severely short of food, and had been for some time. Officers' rations included a generous supply of tins of sprat paste and sticks of soy meat; Tatyana would try to catch one of the children in the courtyard whenever she got the chance, and press a tin of food, or a sweet, on him or her.

We found out that the war had begun on a Sunday morning.

It was a wonderful morning in March. Tatyana was getting ready to go for a trip into the forest; she was waxing her skis, whilst Taipi, her setter, bounded around impatiently.

Did she sense, when she gave her dog that name (which means both "decadence" and "rebirth," I think), how soon she would be face to face with the people whose ancient culture she so respected?

"I sit indoors during the wine-making season"—this was the title which she gave to a tristich that she had composed in imitation of Far Eastern poetry:

> An autumn moon.
> Bubbles escape from the bottles.
> Time for a walk to the hay.

She was going down to the lake, by a path she had used often before. If she was lucky, she would get a glimpse of the quail, flying up from their roosting places under the snow, and on the way back she would be able to cross a broad glade in the woodland. It freezes hard in the mornings there, making a crust of snow you can ski over fast without fear of falling through, light and swift as a bird.

Tatyana switched on the radio for the weather forecast. She needed to know what kind of wax to use on her skis, and the thermometer outside the window was in full sun, so that there was no relying on it. Suddenly the forecast was interrupted; first came the schoolmarmy voice of an announcer, then the calling signal, then a famous voice. Levitan's.[65] "Attention, all stations," he said. She was expecting to hear that they'd just launched a new space-rocket or something like that, but instead she learned that war had been declared.

Outwardly nothing had changed; Taipi still leapt at her feet, and the smell of resin hung on the air; but she would be following different paths from now on.

---

65 Levitan, Yury (1914–1983)—Soviet radio announcer legendary for his deep, big basso voice, in which Levitan chronicled the events of World War II in the daily broadcasts of *Sovinformburo*.

Tatyana had long been trying to talk to the old man in the family where she was staying, but it was clear that he was avoiding her; if she ever did run into him and start talking about the old days—she was particularly interested in hearing about any antiquities there might be nearby—he would pretend that he couldn't understand what she was saying.

In HQ everyone was talking about one thing. Partisans had appeared up in the hills; they had attacked a shed where food was stored, and blown up a bridge.

That night Tatyana woke up, with the sensation that something had just run across her face. She sat up in bed. It was dark, and dogs were barking somewhere in the distance. She would have to get the torch. Usually she tried not to walk barefoot on the earth floor, but there was no use thinking of that now. She found the torch in the pocket of her uniform jacket, and flashed it at the bed; there, right on her pillow, was an enormous scorpion, long hooked tail upraised. She took one corner of the pillow and shooed it gently, but the creature didn't even twitch; and so she placed the flat of her hand under the pillow, picked it up as delicately as a fresh iced cake, took it to the window, and flung it, and its marzipan decoration, straight out into the yard.

She lay down, head on the bare, damp, rice-straw mattress, from which a vile stink was wafting. The air was dense and thick. [. . .]

Tatyana managed to get back to sleep in the small hours. She dreamt that she had taken it into her head to go and look at a shamisen, a kind of ancient Oriental instrument that geishas play.

So here she was, in the Hermitage. The lights were out, the shadows in the corners were growing longer, the vistas of worn marquetry floors down the halls shorter. Outside the huge chilly windows glimmered the dark-blue expanses of Palace Square and the Neva. There was no one about, and the air smelt faintly of New Year tangerines.

At last came a distant, capricious shine: the gold of pipes, the silver of flutes; she was walking past case after case of strange instruments when she suddenly heard the sound of a Chinese song.

In a corner at the other side of the room stood a piano; a musician was sitting at it and playing superbly (what, a Chinese song on a piano? From sheet music?). She went closer, and saw that the man was Chinese, and breathtakingly handsome. And he was reading from music, ordinary music, except that the word "Sonata" was picked out in red. Who was he playing for? No one ever came to this room, it was too far off the beaten track; and in any case the whole Winter Palace was empty by now.

He had stopped playing. How could she show him how enraptured \she was? She put her right hand on her heart and made a low, respectful bow. He kissed her hand.

"Comrade Lieutenant!" Someone was knocking at the door.

"What do you want?" Tatyana leapt from her bed, awake at once.

In a low voice the messenger told her: "The commandant is asking for you. The sentry's been stabbed, and the prisoner has escaped."

Tatyana threw on her clothes, and went with the messenger to the market square. It was just getting light. The whole village was still asleep, or pretending to be.

How could she ever pass on to anyone the sound of that music? It was still ringing in her ears. She would never see that face again, he would never take her hand, and she would never feel gratitude like that again.

Was he a famous pianist whose hands had been beaten to pulp? Was that his soul, finding a last audience?

From the poplars came the sounds of dawn stirrings. The crows were cawing faintly. The officers walked to HQ in silence. Outside in the corridor, Tatyana used a tin mug to scoop some tepid water from a bucket and drank it down quickly. Who had that been out with the teacher's daughter? What was going on? Who had killed the sentry?

The Punitive Detachment

A few days later, Tatyana Levina is one of a group taking part in a special operation. The motor-launch chugs down the lake, patrolling down empty banks, nosing into winding creeks. The occasional scattered villages have been deserted by their Muslim inhabitants. According to all available information, they are in the heart of partisan country.

One evening at sunset, when the patrol boat was in Shaidan Cove, the look-out spotted some dots moving about on the bank to starboard side. On closer inspection, however, all that was found was a herd of horses; no sign of human habitation was visible nearby, at any rate from the boat.

The commanding officer gave the order to drop anchor beyond the peninsula and dispatch a search party from there once darkness had fallen, in order to establish whether there might be a nomadic settlement anywhere around, and if so, whether it was a large one. He also ordered that one of the locals was to be brought in for questioning.

The next morning, when she came out of the tent, Tatyana noticed the marks of bare feet on the sand by the lake shore. They were so small they could have been a woman's, even her own, had it not been for the fact that nothing would have induced her to go barefoot on this terrain. She was always wary of poisonous creatures, scorpions, phalanges, and karakurts, especially when she reached for her boots in the mornings—she had to leave them by the tent flap overnight, getting soaked through with dew. So if she hadn't been sleep-walking through the moonlit fields, the marks must have been made by a stranger.

She followed the tracks, and they went from the sand into the water— he had been walking through the shallows—and back again. The heel was touchingly round, the toes straight, with hardly a trace of instep between—this spy certainly didn't have flat feet. The traces vanished in the reeds, next to an inlet—here the walker had swum away.

So he'd swum away. Fine. Time for a wash. Tatyana scooped up a mugfull of the salty water, and hung her towel on a tuft of salt reeds; she reached for the soap, but the dish slid out of her hands and went bounding over the scalloped sand, into a pool of lake water that had filled up during a recent storm. The dish rolled over and over, then floated away on a blue wavelet.

Two herons flew by. The sun was up; it was high time to be going back. But suddenly Tatyana heard an echoing splash, as though someone had just dived heavily into the water.

She froze. Was it a flock of geese settling on the lake? No, it was too loud for that—it was more likely to be wild boar taking their young for a splash. She imagined them all, screwing up their eyes and plunging in. In that case, though, better move on. She'd got used to seeing their narrow tracks on the sand, and the paths they battered down in the reeds, she'd even seen the hollows once or twice where they'd been lying, but she wouldn't exactly have liked to meet one close to. But then she stopped: best have a look after all. She crept up as quietly as she could. Not a boar in sight. Could it be that barefoot Chinese fox? Suddenly she heard another splash, and then saw spreading ripples in the water. A glossy black back showed for an instant above the water—what could it be? Then she saw another, this time in the shallows. Tatyana ran up: so that's what it was, a huge fish. The water was knee-deep, but the fish was stranded; it lay trapped, thrashing by her legs. She tried to pick it up, but it was impossible; each time it slipped from her hands.

Tatyana ran for her towel; the fish was still lying there when she returned, so she wrapped it gently in the towel, picked it up, and carried it in triumph back to the camp.

It was still too early for reveille. Tatyana opened the tent-flap quietly and threw the fish in. It thrashed about wildly in the small, close space; the soldiers woke up and leapt from their beds. *Allah akbar!*[66] Drop your weapons! Good for you, Lieutenant!

The soldiers rushed to the water, and began catching the fish with anything that came to hand. It was a whole shoal of carp spawning, it turned out. A cauldron of water was soon boiling; now all that remained was to cook the gutted fish. Gulls and crows were wheeling overhead. Bubbles of fish's breath rushed over the lake surface; every ripple brought up more and more of them.

But there was no time even to taste the fish soup. The commanding officer divided the detachment in two. One group was to stay here, another to track along the channel.

"That channel's a maze, no sense in trying to follow it," thought Tatyana. She'd noticed that even the local fishermen made marks so that they could take their bearings and find their way back. They'd bend a tuft of salt reeds or make a knot in one, or leave a stick standing upright on the tallest dune.

The captain studied the map. If they kept to the left of the channel all the way, they were bound to come back into Shaidan Cove eventually.

Exactly as she had thought. They'd got lost amongst all those endless lakes, with their thousands of channels and inlets; not only had they not been able to keep track of the enemy, they hadn't even been able to find their way out. Now they were coming under hostile fire from the opposite bank, and their position was dangerously exposed. Strange whistling noises were coming from the radio: it looked as though it had packed up altogether. The radio mast was at base camp. Two launches had sunk.

Someone had to go back for help. Why shouldn't she do it? They didn't seem likely to need a translator at the moment. She'd find her way, of course she would.

"At least let me try, comrade captain."

"Very well then, off you go. Be sure to take enough water, and a rifle. Leave the dictionary behind."

---

66 *Allah Akbar* (Arabic) = Great God!

This was a new adventure, the most interesting she had had so far. She would find her way back to Shaidan Cove. What was the meaning of "Shaidan," incidentally? It meant a martyrs' burial ground, or something like that. Not bad.

She saw herself as someone who found, not someone who lost. What hadn't she found? Knives on forest paths, lots of them, one a real bandit knife with a blade that sprang out the minute you pressed a red button on the handle. Once she had found a huge watermelon floating along a river, God knew from where. On Nevsky she'd found a piece of lapus lazuli—it had probably fallen out of somebody's ring. She'd been cutting up a Hungarian cockerel to make a celebration meal, and in its thawing giblets she'd found a big pink pearl. Either some woman worker in the food factory had dropped it in, or else the Hungarian cockerel itself had grubbed up the pearl at some stage during its free-range existence, on a river-bank somewhere.

She wouldn't get lost in this jungle either. All she needed was a cork helmet. The rest was in order. The more so since she'd already covered a lot of the way back. Maybe she'd even end up with a cork helmet. How? It would float to her downriver, that's how.

She walked the path to Shaidan Cove convinced of her own invulnerability.

She'd soon be back to base camp, and they'd send out the helicopters. Congratulations. Lieutenant! She'd always known she was destined to do something extraordinary. Even if the detachment was surrounded, it would be possible to hold out for a long time, but breaking out would be much more difficult. They'd probably be ambushed: there was only one route through from the lakes, only one channel led back to deep water, the rest led nowhere. But she would save them.

If only someone could see her. This was what she had lived for, this was why she'd learnt the language. How far had she got down the boar path, she wondered?

Every now and again she would come up against a huge spider's web, binding the panicles of the reeds so tightly that the fat stems had given slightly, leaning one toward the other. At one corner lurked the spider itself. At first she tried to skirt the webs, but she soon forgot about them. Sticky strands clung to her sweaty face and damp neck.

A black column of smoke was blowing about on the horizon somewhere, and if you looked carefully you could see flames, though these were almost transparent in the bright spring air. It was perfectly normal, she assured herself. You often got fires. What a lot of game there was round here, and all paired off already.

A cormorant flew by, black as a cinder, looking like something you might find at the bottom of a careless housewife's frying pan. There was a smell of smoke. She was nearer the fire now. It was upwind of her.

So what was she to do when the fire reached here? Wade up to her neck in water, or climb out of the reeds and up on to high ground—on to one of those volcanic hills there? Hell, now it was turning, coming at her from the other side too—that barefoot fox would smoke her out like a hare.

Better make for the high ground all the same. Damn, now she'd cut her hand, there was blood all over the yellow stalks.

Suppose those leaflets were right, the ones they had posted on the gates and walls of the village? We told the soldiers they were nothing to worry about, nothing interesting at all, prophecies, New Year greetings. They were messages from the partisans, though. They said the enemy forces were suffering heavy losses; soon the People's Army would liberate Sin-Kiang.

At last she had scrambled out of the steamy rushes and was up on the sandy bank. A fresh wind had dried her sweaty face.

Up here on the dune, that barefoot man could pick her off as easy as pie. Better lie down behind that bush and reconnoiter. She had a look round. Beyond the sea of rushes rose a line of sandy hills.

What huge expanses. The fire had scorched all the lower ground, circling all the hidden lakes and channels; now it was racing onwards, leaving a line of black smoking bristles behind it.

It couldn't reach this land beyond the dunes, though. There was nothing here but sand, and the odd bush, and clumps of Tangut rhubarb. A broad leaf spread under her hand. She snapped off its stalk and peeled the pink skin. It tasted just like the ordinary stuff.

Below her, holes gaped black in the sand, and grey lizards were scuttling about. What were they called? Hang on, hang on—look at that one bending its tail, like a peeled rhubarb stalk. A huge open mouth. Hi, Big Ears. I got a real fright when I saw your slit-eyed mug.

She'd run from the fire, so had all the creatures that could. The ones that lived high up were safe, all the ones that nested lower down had been burnt. Better look what had happened to her brood, though: after all, they nested on the ground, too. She could see a faint trace of smoke rising.

It all looked so tidy: only a few shriveled leaves of rhubarb were left, like shreds of burnt newspaper.

A wolf ran by the shores of the lake, throwing up dust.

The fire had vanished behind the hills. Time she vanished as well. She must cross those blackened tracts of ground as quickly as possible and get back in the sheltering clumps of reeds. Quickly, quickly. The sun shone dully. She felt the heat seep through her boots, black clouds rose with every step she took, like exploding puffballs. It had all changed in the space of minutes. As though there had never been rustling jungles of reeds and nests and herds of wild boar, as though she herself had never forced her way through. She was running as fast as the wolf—let the ground burn under the enemy's feet—she wasn't anyone's enemy, how could she be, she'd never hit anyone, she'd never had an enemy, she was kind and pretty and that was all, her face was covered in soot, so who did she think she was anyway, and she did have an enemy, a deadly enemy, oh now she was finished. She stuck out like a white winter hare on a black footpath.

Bloody hell, she'd left the water bottle over on the sand-hill, now she had nothing to drink, too bad, you can drink salt water if you have to. She was nearly at the end of her strength, but she still pressed on, going further and further north. She must be getting to the big lake by now, provided she hadn't got lost, of course. She had to skirt lake after lake. The sound of the shooting seemed no further away; the water made it carry, so you couldn't tell where it was.

Then she saw a pole on one of the dunes. Good, somewhere over there the channel goes into the Great Lake, that's where base camp is. She thought she could hear the waves, but it could just have been the air beating in her ears.

Another creek blocked her path, a small one. She didn't want to have to go all round it. She waded into the water: it couldn't be more than ten paces across. Couldn't she just follow the creek's winding bank? You could see the water vanish there into the thickets, and that narrow channel could perfectly well broaden out into another lake. There were white traces of salt here on the banks, that meant the water level was low, so it must be shallow here.

She trudged through the water, scooping it up in her hands and splashing it on her face. Then suddenly her foot slipped and she fell flat in the water. She tried to get up, but her feet were stuck fast in the mud. She hauled out her boots and staggered backwards, sending a shoal of bubbles from the bottom.

She flopped down on her belly and tried to swim; every now and then one of her feet caught the treacherous bottom. Swirls of the mud she had disturbed rose into the water. At last she reached the bank, but she had struck a wall of reeds on which she could make no impression. She should never have left the boar path. She tried to edge along the fringes of the creek, but she soon lost her footing, her feet sank back into the sticky mud. She seized hold of the thick reeds and hauled out each foot in turn.

"Hey! I'm stu-uck!" she yelled, just in case. After all, camp should be quite close by now.

She heard a noise ahead, then the sound of someone moving. A voice called: "Who goes there?"

"It's me! Lieutenant Levina!"

She could hear the voice shouting again, and she thought she caught the words "Keep to the left, to the left!" She moved to the left, but the wall of reeds was just as thick there.

"I can't get out!" But now she could hear people forcing their way toward her, splashing through the water. The reeds next to her parted, and two men came out.

"Hans uh!" they shouted, training their machine-guns on her.

When the allied forces liberated Kashgar, the Uigurs[67] told them that they had seen a tall girl being led through the town with a rope round her neck. But whether that girl was Tatyana or not is hard to say.

1973–89

Translated from the Russian and with notes by Catriona Kelly

Bella Ulanovskaya, *Puteshestvie v Kashgar*. Copyright © by the Estate of Bella Ulanovskaya. Reprinted from *An Anthology of Women's Writing, 1777–1992*, edited by Catriona Kelly (1994), by permission of Oxford University Press and Catriona Kelly. English translation copyright © by Catriona Kelly. Notes copyright © by Catriona Kelly and Maxim D. Shrayer. Introduction copyright © by Maxim D. Shrayer.

---

67 Uigurs—a Turkic-speaking ethnic group who presently inhabit mainly Western China (Eastern Turkestan). The Uigur, who are Sunni Muslims, constitute about half of the population of the Xinjiang (the Xinjiang Uigur Autonomous Region).

ALEKSANDR MELIKHOV

Aleksandr Melikhov (b. 1947), prose writer and critic, was born Aleksandr Meylakhs in Rossosh, Voronezh Province. Soon after World War II, Melikhov's Jewish father, a historian, fearing a second arrest (he had been arrested previously), fled and settled in the small town of Stepnyak in northern Kazakhstan. In Kazakhstan, he met Melikhov's mother, a descendant of Ukrainians exiled to Kazakhstan in the nineteenth century, a physics teacher by profession. In a brief "Autobiography," which Melikhov sent to the editor of this anthology, he wrote that in Kazakhstan his father "taught foreign languages, geography, and history, becoming for several generations a symbol of a Teacher."

A science prodigy, Melikhov studied at the Mechanical-Mathematical Faculty of Leningrad University. Upon graduation in 1967, he sought employment at Arsamas-16, the classified nuclear research center, but his application was denied because of his Jewish name. In 1969, Melikhov joined the research staff of Leningrad University's Institute of Applied Mathematics, obtaining a candidate's degree in 1974. In Melikhov's own words, "For a half-cast [*dlia polukrovki*], my scientific career progressed bearably, although with all the expected humiliations." By the early 1990s, when he left the shrinking academic field, Melikhov had published sixty papers on mathematics. During perestroika, Melikhov "shuffled" goods from abroad for resale at home; the experience informed his *Novel with Prostatitis* (published 1997).

Writing since his late twenties, Melikhov debuted with the story "Incident" in the magazine *North* (*Sever*) in 1979 under his real name. He took the pen name Aleksandr Melikhov after an editor suggested that "the publication of an author with your name might be interpreted as an anti-Russian act." Melikhov's *Treatise on Bathhouses*, published in *Aurora* (*Avrora*) in 1982, was deemed a "political error" by the Leningrad Province Party Committee. This delayed publication of his collection, *The Provincial*, until 1986, when it finally appeared with censorial interventions. *Scales for Goodness*, a volume of Melikhov's fiction, came out in 1989 in what was still Leningrad.

Melikhov gained recognition after the publication of his fictional works and polemical essays during the reform and early post-Soviet years: the short novel *Events and Discoveries* (*Aurora*, 1987), the novel *Thus Spoke Saburov* (*Neva*, 1992), the short novel *Gifts of the Pauper* (*Star*, 1993), and the novels *Eros and Tanatos, or a Rewarded Obedience* (*Neva*, 1993) and *Banishment from Eden. The Confession of a Jew* (excerpt below; *Novy mir*, 1994). His other works have included the short novel *Lofty Malady* (its title echoing **Pasternak**; *October*, 1997), the novel *The Plague* (*Novy mir*, 2003), and others fiction. All too visibly, the titles of Melikhov's works mimic the well-known works of philosophy and literature by Friedrich Nietzsche, O'Henry, M. Ageev, Albert Camus, and others. Melikhhov's books also include *Hunchbacked Atlantes, or the New Don Quixote* (1995), *The World to Us Is Foreign* (2003), and others. He is a recipient of the 1993 Nabokov Prize of the St. Petersburg Writers' Union and other prizes.

In the late 1980s, Melikhov founded the voluntary society Circle (Krug), which, before its closing, provided support to potential suicide victims. Melikhov has been a regular contributor to *The Teacher's Paper* (*Uchitel'skaia gazeta*) and to Russia's monthly magazines as an essayist and book critic. He writes on the subjects of political extremism and nationalism. "The Will to Simplicity," his essay about Hitler and vulgarity, appeared in 2000 in *People's Friendship.* His doubly polemical analysis of the reception of volume 1 of Aleksandr Solzhenitsyn's tendentious study of Jewish-Russian relations, *Two Hundred Years Together* (2001), appeared in 2002, also in *People's Friendship.* In 2003–4, after a hiatus of almost ten years, Melikhov returned to Jewish topics in fiction: the short novel *In the Valley of the Blessed* (2005); and in longer nonfiction bordering on fiction, the book *Red Zion* (2005), the latter published under the name "Aleksandr Meylakhs (Melikhov)." Melikhov's recent books include *Drifting Idols* (2011), *Immortal Valka* (2013), and *Rendezvous with Quasimodo* (2016).

* * *

Featured below is an excerpt from Aleksandr Melikhov's autobiographical novel *The Confession of a Jew* (book edition St. Petersburg, 1994; reprinted 2004), which some critics consider his most scandalous work. Melikhov's novel takes its title from *The Confession of One Jew*, a remarkable book about Avraam-Uria Kovner by Leonid Grossman (1888–1965). Published in Russia in 1924, Grossman's book became well known in the West but was suppressed in the USSR (it was finally reprinted in Russia in 1999).

In his "Autobiography," Melikhov suggests a pairing of two works: "Both novels—perhaps not by accident—together form some contradictory unity: *The Confession of a Jew* expresses terror at human unanimity, and *Hunchbacked Atlantes*, at human disjointedness." He expounded on his previous comment in a 2004 interview: "I think that the problem of Jewishness is only an entrance into the problem of loneliness, of being cast away from something, which is immeasurably more powerful and more eternal than one's own self. To withstand, to preserve loyalty to one's goals alone is incredibly hard (this also applies to the question of suicides). Jewishness as a cause of alienation I took from my own experience, but I strongly exaggerated everything so as to stretch it toward being a symbol."

FROM *THE CONFESSION OF A JEW*

I try to conjure up my dear Stepnogorsk[68] through the eyes of my dad driving into this paradise on somebody else's one-and-a-half-ton truck (forty kilometers from the railway), but nothing happens—his feet have frozen too much in canvas plimsolls (pumps?) in the middle of the West-Siberian winter. Now if there were a forest of orchids teeming all around . . .

In Grandfather Avrum's house it was considered a frivolous and I dare say even a sinful matter *to feast one's eyes* on anything, whatever it was—this world was not a place for diversions (not a temple but a workshop. Or a kiosk). All right then, the Marxist aesthetic of the workers' continuing-education colleges amounted even more so to utility, utility, utility: everything that could not be eaten and shot from incurred contempt. Father began to notice "nature" only with the arrival of his first grey hairs. And even then he used it like medicine, at set times, in set doses . . .

So the supreme artist of Russian nature, Izzie Levitan,[69] had quite clearly robbed the Russian people, having sucked his fill from them with that penetrating, pinching, crushing, stabbing, cutting love: only a vampire could burst into tears at the sight of hoarfrost on the windowpanes.

I recall: father was surprised by the flat, earth-strewn roofs of our peasant shanties—among the Ukrainian Yids any ragamuffin nevertheless had a double-sloped roof, even if it was a straw one. All the same, three whole two-story buildings offered encouragement. And the main thing was, gold mining held out the promise of keeping food on the table.

---

68 Stepnogorsk—both an altered form of Stepnyak, a town in Kokchetav Province of northern Kazakhstan, the area that borders with Omsk Province, Siberia, and a real town in the Akmolinsk Province of northern Kazakhstan.

69 Levitan, Isaac (1860–1900)—great Russian landscape painter of Jewish origin.

Yet in me, a young lad of five or six, my breath would be taken away, as if it was on a swing, when this divine panorama opened up before me after the summer holidays: the blackened pit-head frames scattered among the knolls like little pyramids in a disorderly gigantic country graveyard. The plain was so enormous that, in spite of every effort of the knolls to undulate it, it still remained a plain.

It is only from those times that I remember how one can love the *land*.

Then the three majestic two-story buildings unfold to the view: the district committee and town soviet, the I. V. Stalin School, and my paramount pride, the Club—concrete steps ascending to an unattainable five-meter height, where there are lanterns and voluted columns . . . The Club was preternaturally beautiful, an indisputable masterpiece of Stalin's empire style— the most supranational style in our century, like the whole of Stalin's regime. Grishka, who was given to patriotism and roguery in equal measure, counted as many as five floors in the Club, including the basement, the attic, and, unless I'm much mistaken, the stage as well.

After the sights of the town, one could make out the small wretched houses scattered higgledy-piggledy. Grandpa Kovalchuk had once snorted contemptuously, "We're Voroshilov[70] No. 19, and Voroshilov No. 21 is somewhere over there," and he gave a wide sweep of his arm into the unknown. "Where's Voroshilov No. 21?" an old woman who had got lost once asked me, and I repeated with the same magisterial annoyance, "We're Voroshilov No. 19, and Voroshilov No. 21 is somewhere over there," and sent the old woman off into unknown areas with an expansive, disdainful gesture, and no one ever saw her again after that.

Had she almost certainly not got lost in the boundless expanses of Irmovka, where no white man ever voluntarily set foot: "they've been taken to Irmovka" meant "they've been taken to a hospital"—a whitewashed infectious-diseases ward a couple or three kilometers from the town boundary, a distance deemed insuperable, because among us no one went anywhere without cause. We'd have been taken aback if we'd been told that we could just go, just like that, for a stroll—that was called "loafing."

The constellations of houses were divided by the knolls (three hundred meters measured along the curve) into isolated and often mutually hostile mini-Edens—the areas (twenty years later I did not have time to be astonished

---

70 Voroshilov, Kliment (1881–1969)—Soviet military and state leader, marshall of the Soviet Union (1935), one of Stalin's closest henchmen.

when piercing my way through the town from area to area, from steppe to steppe, in a quarter of an hour).

Each knoll was surmounted, as with a frontier sign, by a nesting box of a latrine open to the four winds. The chairman of the town soviet, and for this he went down in history, erected them on the most visible sites in order to observe from his balcony who visited them and how often. And those visiting them were not just anybody but the aristocracy who lived in government-funded housing; the more ordinary people had nesting boxes in their own vegetable gardens. And between the knolls, around the pit-head frames, were the mountains, mountains, mountains of broken rock that was hauled day and night in buckets out of the mines and dragged along an elevated stone tramway in ore cars to the ore-dressing plant: the silhouettes of horses everlastingly stooping above our heads and nodding dejectedly in time with their steps.

It was there also, to the factory, that the hard water from the mines was pumped—overhead the rusty pipes extended, snaked, and leaked a spray at the joints (the Little Sun fountain at Petergof).[71] After I had been accepted by the miners as one of their own, I made a habit of walking along those pipes, balancing between life and death, from the source to the outfall.

When after twenty years I looked at my paradise through the eyes of a stranger, my first thought was: "Do people really live here? . . ." A rust-colored foliated stone, with artemisia clinging to it here and there, obtruded itself from every quarter—there was not a part unaffected; absolutely everything was strewn with broken stone chippings (if you came a cropper while running, you would take your skin off down to the flesh—and I used to actually, I used to . . .). The red-hot summer steppe, visible everywhere between the little houses, was also generously peppered with stone chippings and seasoned with glaucous torpefying artemisia. At the same time, like the air above a bonfire, the lilac horizon was constantly streaming, and that airy precious inlay upon it, Mount Sinyukha [Mount Blue], was a transparent blue. The water in the wells was saline, fit only for washing clothes; if you washed your head in the bathhouse, your hair stood on end like an American Indian's feathers. Drinking water was brought round by a water-carrier on a nag. In winter, shrouded in hoar-frost along with his horse, he looked like a ghost on his frosted-glass water cask.

---

71 Petergof (Peterhof)—site of the summer residence of the Russian tsars located about seven miles west of St. Petersburg, famous for its fountains; during the Soviet period it was renamed Petrodvorets.

Not one of the latrines raised up so high on its summit had a single hook—you were lucky if there was a wire hanging there. It was just hold on as tight as you could if you found a place to get settled: the floor was littered with piles of coarse artillery gunpowder that were in fact over-roasted excrement. That was in summer. In winter, however, there was the heaped-up multiflorality of the ice-covered mounds, and if you sat too long (though the frost would not let you: more than −30°C was the norm), you risked having to stay sitting there till spring. Everything became snowbound before your very eyes, behind the smallest mound there would drift an enormously long snow . . . shadow as it were, trying to rise from the ground. It rose up against each post like a membrane, turning it into a sundial of snow. The shanties were snowbound to their roofs—concave hyperbolas soared up to their eaves, just like on the Space Explorers Monument.

Yet in this Eden everything becomes a source of happiness: the many-tiered snow corridors opened up with plywood shovels, through which one had to pick one's way to the privy; the anthill-like labyrinths into which we urchins tunneled the thickness of the compacted snow (and in the center was a little den with an oil lamp); the water-carrier's ice-encrusted roof, seemingly cast in frosted glass; the frenzied streams from the knolls in spring—and one had to erect dam after dam with maniacal haste, launch toy boats and be swept along with them in imagination into lustrous tunnels and grottoes, which would have outshone all the wonders of nature with their awesome beauty if we had only been about five hundred times shorter.

In spring everyone was seized by an arsonist's itch—they would go and set fire to old grass in the steppe, heaven knows why, like everything that happens in paradise—only because everybody does it: you would even see some demure girl, an outstanding student and leader of a Young Pioneer unit, squatting and striking matches swiped from her dad. And they would achieve their aim in the end: the reddish glow of fires would be reflected over a huge expanse of the night sky!

I swear I don't know a more beautiful place! And when, as an exile and turncoat, I despairingly look through and shower kisses upon stone after stone, ice lump after ice lump, excremental powder grain after powder grain in the proud latrines open on all four sides, I feel like weeping from happiness and pain, but the tears have dried up in me, and any half-sensitive tomcat could weep a more generous amount . . .

My father, bumping up and down on the flattened seat of that one-and-a-half-ton truck of his that reeked of rubbishy fuel, was even less inclined to tears.

On the road (the iron, merciless road) he earned extra money as a loader, doing such a phenomenal job that he was soon offered bed and board, but the guiding finger of the state was leading him to my mother: Soviet power was preparing a dubious gift for me—life.

Father was nurturing the resourceful Jewish design to get fixed up as a loader in the Consumers' Union, but IT (the People's Education Department)[72] got in his way every time: the provincial-*it*, the district-*it*, the town-*it*, the Eden-*it*— and he would blush in front of the reproachful signboard, although, as someone taken away from school under escort in full view of his pupils, he already considered himself free from the chimera called conscience. However, after the first ingratiating plea of the cowed school half-principal—"But won't you help us?"—he quickly returned to his former disposition and became again what he was, a person born to *help*: her pleading, aggrieved tone galvanized him into action as irresistibly as the battle trumpet did the old regimental warhorse.

Even after twenty years, very old women teacherlettes could not recall without tears his endless good deeds and preternatural refinement—in our earthly Eden, Huns-to-be[73] were already luminaries of culture. He even put out his back in the field of charity work, unloading firewood for one of the innumerable widowed mothers of pupils: that's not the same as exalting socialism under convoy in exchange for a prison-camp ration—disinterestedness is contraindicated for Jews. Since then the stink of exotic embrocations has not been eliminated among us: just think—snake venom, some sort of African "*Bom bengue*" (Good bhang)![74] Yet the eternal gratitude of widows and orphans was as useless as a poultice to a dead man.

For the Russian people it was simply dangerous, after all: the great, revived Vasily Vasilievich Rozanov, whose greatness it is not given to foreigners to comprehend, pointed out quite rightly that Jews are most dangerous in that they are sincerely obliging and disposed to be devoted—that is why each of them finds protectors (traitors) among the Russians.[75]

---

72 In Russian, the abbreviation *ono* (*otdel narodnogo obrazovaniia*, People's Education Department) coincides with the neutral singular pronoun *ono* (it), hence the humor and wordplay.

73 Reference to "Griadushchie gunny" (1904–5), a programmatic poem by the symbolist Valery Bryusov (1873–1924).

74 *Bom bengue, bom bangue, bom bango* (Portuguese) = good cannabis, especially as a drug. (Trans.)

75 Rozanov, Vasily (1856–1919)—gifted Russian writer and thinker obsessed with the Jews and Judaism; his works include the antisemitic treatise *The Olfactory and Tactile Attitude of*

I will correct myself as regards Huns: if you seize and devour any book that has come your way for fifteen or so years running, you will pick up something notwithstanding: father was accepted as one of their own by the circle of the out-in-the-sticks Siberian intelligentsia, who included, thanks to the prison and exile policy of the Soviet government, some far from commonplace characters: one had graduated from Liège University, another played chess with Lasker[76] himself, a third sat with such a straight back on her chair that other women preferred not to sit down at all in her presence...

True, her more long-standing friends sat out their time somewhere very steadfastly, for many years each—but on the other hand the children of these outcasts now include plenty of well-known men of letters, prominent engineers, and all without exception simply estimable people.

Their main wealth—aspirations—these insects took away with them into exile and passed on to their children without payment of an inheritance tax.

Father was fixed up in lodgings with a local trade-union little panjandrum, Deryuchenko, who was considered a hero of the civil war on account of his having only one arm. For the Deryuchenkos, husband and wife, father would transport water in a barrel up the ice-covered mountain, would feed the cows and pigs, from which he was allowed to take a few small unpealed boiled potatoes, and would fetch firewood and light the stove—not in his own room, of course. In return for this he was accorded a door laid on two boxes and covered with two sacks of straw; the sheepskin coat thrown on top of this he was forbidden to remove from the premises. One-off services—let's say transporting a stack of hay from the steppe under cover of night (as far as possible from envious eyes) and nearly freezing to death in the process—were not specially stipulated for.

Yet what kind of antisemitism among the people are we talking about if the head of the district-*it*, Valentina Nikolaevna Korzun, after closely observing him, soon issued my father with a coupon for socks—prior to this he used to wrap his feet inside his canvas plimsolls in some sort of rags. What's more, after some time the district committee entrusted him in particular, of three people who knew German, with the task of translating for Party activists the Fascist propaganda pamphlets sent to acquaint them with the ideas of the enemy. Everything that related to the Jews in these pamphlets met with

---

Jews to Blood (1914).

76 Lasker, Emanuel (1868–1941)—dintinguished German chess player. Lasker won the world championship in 1894 and held it until he was defeated by Capablanca in 1921.

complete approval among the activists. And it was a real treat for father to encounter the content of these pamphlets once again—memories of youth!— almost unchanged in the perestroika publications of the journals *Their Contemporary* and *The Old Guard*.[77]

The Deryuchenkos also used to afford him the opportunity of keeping the Sabbath in a distinctive way: together with the head of Food Supply, they would settle down at the table in the evening with vodka and indescribable and undispatchable chow, and at the same time invite their industrious lodger as well. While he ceremoniously cut off a piece of this or that, the masters of life would gobble, drink, and then launch into a mad dance—as if they were trying to break through ice first with one heel, then with the other—and after that collapse and fall asleep anywhere they landed.

And at this point the great guzzling would begin! Father would leave just exactly as many leftovers for the pigs as they left him on weekdays. Even by Monday he was still boasting in the teachers' common room about his well-stuffed belly. Everyone roared with laughter, and only the young woman who taught physics, mathematics, and astronomy appealed to his self-respect with ineffable disgust: "How on earth can you tell people such a thing?!"

That was my mother. When she was perched on a stepladder adjusting the Leader's portrait, father was struck by her ankles, which were bandaged on account of famine-induced boils. "Like Voroshilov's horse," he thought. But on the other hand, during the "All for the Front!" voluntary-assistance haymaking on the collective farm, she wielded a pitchfork better than anyone, while all in all he made Herculean efforts, it being precisely there that he laid the foundation of his pedagogical reputation.

For about forty years the pupils of that time wrote to him and traveled to see him (at Yasnaya Polyana,[78] I almost wrote in my increasing haste). We eliminated religion in vain; they shared their insights, and some took their talk so far as to argue that we had built the wrong sort of socialism. Father remonstrated for the sake of appearances but was secretly overjoyed at the late sprouting of his seeds.

---

77 Puns on the names of two magazines, *Nash Sovremennik* (*Our Contemporary*) and *Molodaia gvardiia* (*Young Guard*), both of which had held Communist-Russian chauvinist positions during the Soviet period and became openly and staunchly ultranationalistic and antisemitic in the post-Soviet era.

78 Yasnaya Polyana—former estate of Lev Tolstoy, where he is buried, in Tula Province, south of Moscow; now a museum.

The best workers for the front, for victory, were the offspring of dispossessed kulaks, the "*dzhyukoyaks*,"[79] resettled to our parts from somewhere or other in central Russia. The word *dzhyukoyak* apparently meant "wooden foot"—bast shoes had not been seen in our part of the world up to then. Although they started with dug-out houses—pits covered with poles (their area was called Diggings for this reason)—after ten years the *dzhyukoyaks* were already living in good houses and sending their kids to college. They, too, could not be deprived of their main wealth—their aspirations; eternal justice is attainable only through killing.

Each pupil who entered college was a source of pride for my parents: their memory was peopled with dozens of groups of graduating students, and to the end of their days they argued passionately over who was the more able, Petrusha Vanyushin or Vanyusha Petrushin.

It seemed to me that father was always and invariably the general favorite and merely had time to acknowledge the cheerful shouts of greeting from all sides: "How d'ye do, Yakov Abramovich!" Only quite by chance, many years later, did I learn that some teenager too old to qualify for the part (and at that time they included the most dreadful types) had yelled at him behind his back: "Kike!" Enlightened tongues did turn up even in such backwaters.

Father gave him such a shake by the lapels that the back of his head hit his shoulder-blades; then, regaining his composure, he flung the youth away from him, almost splitting his skull open on the radiator—and this instead of humbly begging the unfortunate youth's pardon for the wrongs that no doubt some other Jews had done him.

"Aha!" I thought, "the brigand's blood will out even in you, my pretty darling." Again I confirm that you are correct, dear phagocytes: Jewish meekness cannot be trusted, even if it has been sustained for thirty years running—after all, even I could have sworn that father was incapable of laying a finger on anyone. And more grist to your mill: he was also a closet Zionist, because Father would never have grabbed someone by the lapels out of any *personal* affront. To tell the truth, don't expect any excesses from me, inasmuch as I don't expect anything good from you: I've already forgotten when I last felt like hitting someone or wishing them ill—I want only to hide in a corner so as not to see you.

---

79 *Dzhyukoyak*—probably from the Kazakh *dzhyuke* = lime, bast + *ayaq* = foot. (Trans.)

My parents, who had become friends in the course of their feats of labor, went out walking in the steppe together every evening. Gradually father gained such trust in mother that he made up his mind to share with her his innermost insight: that Stalin had borrowed the industrialization plan from Trotsky. This news made no great impact. Expecting to be arrested again at any moment, father did not dare even to contemplate marriage, but there will always be women who take great pains over that in your stead. I don't know how father legalized it formally: after the camp, Grandpa Avrum asked him why he wasn't marrying, and he almost burned up with shame: one's own father and on such indelicate matters (a sample of Jewish prudishness). For mother, though, it was a mental effort beyond her powers to realize that she was throwing in her lot with a deportee and a Jew at one and the same time; she always had difficulty in managing to see in a person something else besides the person—a nationality maybe, or a rank... But then during her wedding at the registry office in the city hall she could not pronounce her infernal new surname.

In the drinking line father was a great disappointment to Grandpa Kovalchuk, but to make up for it he was so good at *kizyak* (among us it was used as a solid fuel—bricks of dried dung kneaded beforehand by bare feet), he glided so easily from the well with four pails of water at once, he so effortlessly manhandled a five-pood[80] sack of flour from the market—three versts after all ... Incidentally, he most likely won over Grandma with just the thing in which he disappointed grandpa.

An ice-cold wretched barrack room containing only a bed is to my mind the ideal accommodation for newlyweds (and this at a time when the Russian people were bleeding to death on the battlefields—not a single Jew has the right to sleep with his wife while even a single Russian is suffering—let the Deryuchenkos alone live in clover!). Right up till Grishka's birth, mother continued to address father formally, even calling him by first name and patronymic, Yakov Abramovich.

With Grishka already a babe in arms (the war had ended by this time), my parents made their exodus to Voronezh Province[81]—by some miracle, work had turned up at a teachers' college—nearer to the Learning they worshipped. There father was reunited for a brief period with Grandpa Avrum and Grandma Dvoira. It was there, too, that my mother finally realized that the word "Jew," wherewith people in the know had tried to forewarn her, really did

---

80 A pood (obsolete Russian unit of weight) = sixteen kilos.
81 Voronezh is a provincial capital in south-central Russia, in the "black soil" region.

mean something. Some sort of oddish people addressed her husband: *kalia-balia* (that is how the Kazakh language was represented among us in our Eden), and to her amazement he suddenly replied likewise: *kalia-balia, kalia-balia*...

My appearance in the world; the nocturnal vigils over a new dissertation; the clandestine trips to Moscow libraries (father was not entitled to stop too long in large cities); the ongoing lecturer's triumph (when he read something interesting in a book, father could hardly wait until morning to tell his students); the undergraduates wearing their decorations and round *kubanka* hats (when they bent over their notebooks, their medals would jingle and lie flat on the paper, father used to recall in delight).

A vigilant informer (father mentioned in a lecture that some cosmopolitan Turks or other had had the idea for the Volga–Don canal before Stalin); the rector, a former commander of a partisan detachment, who shut the base informer's trap by declaring that Katzenelenbogen had long ago been rehabilitated—the chutzpah was so risky that it never entered anyone's head to check (and it never entered father's head to consider the informer just as much a Russian as his savior: he remained convinced that the Russian people were only ever his saviors).

Arrests of "second-rounders"; the local state security boss—a correspondence student of father's, who held him all night and the next morning also risked his neck by personally procuring him a ticket back to Akmolinsk [now Tselinograd] Province to save the morons from low grades and the hooligans from prison (there were always some lowlife ugly customers or other knocking about in our house—but for me these were very alluring acquaintances).

When he got away a month before defending a new dissertation, father no longer dreamed of anything more than delivering mother and the children into the calloused hands of Grandpa Kovalchuk and setting off somewhere to join with gold-diggers or loggers, but he was pressed to come back to school, first to the disastrous Irmovka and then to the central staff—just give a Jew an inch. In 1950 perhaps it was, the Party activist Razorenov, who had arrived back from the capital, expressed indignation in the district Party committee that Jews were being put away everywhere—we alone were keeping aloof from progress. We had two Jews. The director of the machine works, Goldin, was in fact put away for arranging for water to be delivered round to the workers on a stud horse. Father, however, was simply removed from teaching the Party science of logic and the Party science of geography—but even an alien could be left in *languages*.

Yet how could father be angry about such trifles if his decorated students waited all night for him outside the state security building in the darkness beneath the trees? For the sake of these wartime buddies, father, also after the manner of a swarm from the mother hive, did not take even Razorenov and the like seriously: the phagocytes, those most naturally occurring products and most essential defenses of any nation, seemed to him a load of untypical scoundrels. They got to him properly only through his children, that is, through Grishka and me.

The word "career" evoked in father a look of squeamish bewilderment, but the fact that the state firmly refused to acknowledge his unsullied and gifted sons as *its own*, with the virtually complete approval or indifference of his colleagues, was possibly the severest shock in his turbulent life. And sometime in the 1970s he rebelled—a rebellion on his knees: with a great many precautions (the very intention was utterly seditious!) he set about collecting proof that Jews are in fact none other than people. Over a period of some ten years, resting his cheek on the page and doing his mischief martyr-like with his pen right under his eye, father assembled the most enormous card index, which presented irrefutable evidence that Jews weep too when they lose relatives or loved ones, that there are occasions when they show courage and magnanimity, that they sometimes perish in war or else perpetrate thoughtless deeds, that they include not only Bolsheviks but also Mensheviks and even Constitutional Democrats, not only members of the Cheka[82] but also their opponents, and so on, and so on. He exasperated us by reading out yet more and more new evidence that we, too, are people. He so sought out and looked out everything in every quarter concerning Jews that it began to infuriate me: as if there was nothing else to be interested in apart from his precious Jews. I didn't understand that I was the very person he was trying to defend.

What difference did it make, I seethed, how many Heroes of the Soviet Union, physicists, and poets or how many cutthroats and opportunists there were among the Jews—I did not desire either Kafka's crown or Yagoda's[83] stigma—everyone must answer only for himself; besides, I was making an attempt on the life of Unity, the mainstay of which is the principle "one for all

---

82 Cheka—abbreviation of the executive commission (*Chrezvychainaia komissiia*), the early Soviet precursor of the GPU–KGB.

83 Yagoda, Genrikh (1891–1938)—Soviet leader, minister of state security (1935), minister of internal affairs (1934–36), instrumental in organizing and effecting mass repressions and purges of the 1930s; executed in 1938 during the purge of the state security apparatus.

and all for one." Father, however, was trying to convince himself that antisemitism is the fruit of sincere delusion, which can be dispelled by the facts. But then again, I cannot even now lift a hand to consign to the waste paper basket the world's most complete body of evidence, collected with selfless devotion in ant- and bee-like fashion, which, if faced with, not a single court could reject as proof that a Jew is cold in the frost and hot in the heat.

Yet even toward Jews father became unusually strict, because after all they actually give ammunition to antisemites, bring grist to the enemy's mill: while tirelessly demonstrating that Jews, too, are people, he wanted them to turn into angels (he didn't guess that even this would not help them). He denounced the state of Israel for its double-standard policy toward the Arabs—he was confident that any terrorist could be disarmed by magnanimity and indulgence: look, there was a Kalmyk murderer in the camp with them, and father finally made friends with him all the same! Father condemned Jewish dissidents for their arrogant behavior in the courts and at investigations—they were supposed to arouse sympathy and repentance in the judges and investigators, not irritation.

Manifestations of every kind of national exclusiveness in all manner of different peoples provoked in father a derisive smile. The national exclusivities of Russians made this derision bitter. As a historian and a man of the world, oh what a Russophobic card index he could have compiled at their expense: after all, the truth is always the most vicious calumny against a people—"just to look for such a thing is shameful, disgraceful!" But examples of Jewish exclusivism simply made him ill. "I say to her: what a clever boy you have, and she says: what do you expect—he's a Jewish child! What a thing to say!" Episodes like that seemed to undermine his whole life's work. The dialectic academicians Yudin and Mitin[84] he called nothing but "two lousy kikes."

I was firmly convinced that socialism, like any dominion of falsehood and boorishness, would never come to an end, but father was certain that everything based on a lie is transient. This had once been explained to him by his Jewish dad, Grandpa Avrum (when he freed himself from Jewish Marxism, father once again fell under the influence of shtetl prejudices), so that of the two of us only I was surprised by perestroika. Yet national movements, too, left

---

84 Yudin, Pavel (1899–1968)—Soviet Marxist philosopher, academician, in 1938–44 director of the Institute of Philosophy of the Soviet Academy of Sciences; Mitin, Mark (1901– 1987)—Soviet Marxist philosopher, academician, laureate of the Stalin Prize (1943); both Yudin and Mitin were Jews.

him astonished—their mass character, which often came to light in the most unpleasant way.

In order to leave the People unsullied, father everywhere looked for the intrigues of a small band of educated nationalist careerists, always asking himself the purely teacherly question: "Who taught them?"—"But, you know, they were taught all their lives not to steal, not to loaf about, not to guzzle vodka, not . . . And they didn't take a blind bit of notice. But thousands learned straight away how to carry out a pogrom." Yet that millions of the most *ordinary* people there are find inspiration simply in opposing foreigners and aliens, Father wouldn't even hear of it. With tears in his eyes, leaving not the slightest gap for a word of truth, he would begin to lament in a tremulous voice, without letting up, that Grandpa Avrum never made any distinction between Russians and Jews, that ordinary women not only hid him during pogroms (who organized these pogroms he passed over in silence) but also asked him "what he could ea-at," that Grandpa Kovalchuk had many Kazakh friends, that students waited for him at the gates of the State Security Services, that . . .

Sometimes he rose to the level of his own grandson's convictions: there are no nations, there are only individual people, bad and good (there's no forest, there're individual trees). The hallowed words "our land" plunged him into sorrow: the land belongs to everyone, and *that* language is good which everyone knows, and if because of that the Jewish nation will one day have to dissolve and disappear, let it go, there's no need to feel sorry—just so long as individual people live in the world.

Father even occasionally used to forget about his sacred modesty and allude to the universal love for him of all the peoples of the world with whom he had dealings. This was almost true, though into this nearly universal love for him there often crept the condescension with which worldly-wise adults look upon a charming child. In old age, when he had become the ultimate handsome man, he continued to cut his prophetic grey hair in a short back and sides; his innocent bare ears stuck out like a baby's. All the same, his international fame was not a patch on the shtetl authority of his father: Grandpa Avrum was even trusted to pass the local policeman the communal bribe, which, as everybody knows, is handed over without a receipt.

Once, we were landed with a policeman catastrophically resistant to bribes and therefore able to discern who was dealing in what, who was sewing with how many others in a group, and who was paying how much tax. So grandpa appealed to his conscience until he threw open his uniform: "You see, I haven't even a shirt!" Grandpa promptly lugged in a length of madapollam[85] sufficient for a shirt and underpants—and the economy of the shtetl was saved, while the economy of the Russian state was undermined.

As long ago as the 1960s, I unexpectedly saw Grandpa among other elders sitting formally along the synagogue wall in a documentary film about the hydra of Zionism. Yet as a true representative of a "little nation," Grandpa Avrum, in spite of his listed crimes against the "Great Nation," had no doubt at all that he would go to Paradise.

For all that, if I were the Jewish God I would have also taken there my father, who spent his whole life serving the goyim. I would have heeded their voices, too. When, already manifestly a bird of passage in designer blue jeans—my articles had begun to be translated in England and the States—I paid a visit to that Eden sealed up by the Angel of Death, a middle-aged lush struck up a conversation with me at the station. When he discovered that I hailed from Stepnogorsk, his first reaction was curiosity to know whether I remembered Yakov Abramovich—"Now there was a real man for you!" I shattered his last illusion by not concealing the fact that such a man's son had become an undisguised alien—and after all, the apple doesn't fall far from the tree . . .

In the Jewish heaven father will really miss the goyim—widows cleaning toilets and orphaned hooligans, although even so—a Jew is a Jew—he will miss his own wife and children more. Consequently I have an earnest request for Great Yahweh to disregard the formalities of the fifth point and let my Russian mother through to father—let her, too, feast in eternity on the gefilte fish named Leviathan, although she was never enthusiastic about Jewish cuisine. As for me, I make no claim—I have not merited a place alongside my father.

1993

Translated from the Russian by Brian Cooper

Aleksandr Melikhov, *Ispoved' evreia*. Copyright © by Limbus Press. Translated and reprinted by permission of Limbus Press. English translation copyright © by Brian Cooper. Introduction and notes copyright © by Maxim D. Shrayer.

---

85 Madapollam—a kind of cotton cloth originally manufactured at Madhava-palam, a suburb of Narsapur in Madras, India. (Trans.)

LUDMILA ULITSKAYA

Ludmila Ulitskaya (b. 1943), fiction writer, playwright, and screenwriter, was born in Davlekanovo, Bashkir Autonomous Republic (Bashkortostan), to a Jewish family evacuated there during the war, and grew up in Moscow. Her father was a biochemist and her mother an agricultural engineer. In 1967, Ulitskaya graduated from Moscow University's Biology Faculty. In 1970, she was fired from the Research Institute of General Genetics, where she had pursued an advanced degree, for reading samizdat literature. Ulitskaya remained unemployed until 1979, raising two children. Her interest in Jewish history and culture landed her a job as literary director of the Chamber Jewish Musical Theater (KEMT, 1977–85), headed by Yury Sherling. Nominally based in the Jewish Autonomous Province (EAO; see **Viktor Fink**) but rehearsing in Moscow, KEMT was a token Jewish-Soviet cultural institution. Ulitskaya stayed at KEMT until 1982, soon after which she became a freelancer, writing children's books and animation scripts and doing other literary work.

Ulitskaya was first noticed in 1992, when *Novy mir* published her novella *Sonechka*. *Poor Relatives*, Ulitskaya's first collection of stories, appeared in 1994, first in France and then in Russia. In 1996, Ulitskaya received the Prix Médicis étranger for the French translation of *Sonechka*. Her subsequent books and reprintings of her works have been very successful in the post-Soviet literary marketplace. To quote the critic Maria Litovskaya, "Ulitskaya invariably affirms in her fiction the significance of the 'private' lives of people who for a variety of reasons [...] do not take active roles in shaping the world [...]." Otherworldly spheres whose configurations hint at an influence of Jewish mysticism frequently exist parallel with or adjacent to the quotidian worlds of Ulitskaya's characters. Ulitskaya's shorter fiction constitutes her most original contribution; several, including *Sonechka* and "The Happy Ones," are small gems of post-Soviet Jewish-Russian fiction. Ulitskaya's novel *Funeral Party* (1998), its protagonist informed by Ulitskaya's first husband, the oceanographer Yury Taits, depicts the last days of a Jewish-Russian émigré painter dying in New York and bringing together at his deathbed a carnivalesque gathering, including a rabbi and an Orthodox priest. Ulitskaya received the 2001 Smirnoff–Booker Prize and the 2006 Penne Prize for her novel *The Kukotsky Enigma* (2000). Her works have garnered other prizes, appeared in over twenty languages, and been made into motion pictures. *Jacob's Ladder*, her most recent novel, came out in

2015. A critic of the Putin regime who lends her voice to Russia's opposition politics, Ulitskaya is outspoken about her fears of living in Russia. "But then, why don't you leave?" Yury Zubtsov asked her in a March 2002 interview. "You know, I've already [made the choice] to stay here," Ulitskaya replied. "[. . .] And I hope that I'll get to finish my life here. [. . .] Although in actuality there is one very cruel historical example—Nazi Germany. [. . .] So I take the risk by living here." Married to the Moscow artist Andrey Krasulin, Ulitskaya divides her time between Russia and Italy. An active voice in Russia's cultural-philanthropic and educational initiatives, in 2007 she established the Ludmila Ulitskaya Foundation, which selects books for Russian libraries. Ulitskaya is presently one of the most successful Russian authors in translation.

* * *

From the late 1960s, Ulitskaya's great spiritual influence has been Father Aleksandr Men (1935–1990), a charismatic Jewish-born priest and theologian. Men's preaching of the "double consciousness" of "Jewish" Christians attracted into the Russian Orthodox Church a number of Jewish-Russian intellectuals and artists, a number of whom he personally baptized. (See the section "Apostasy, Assimilation, and the Changing Types of Duality" in the editor's general introduction.) Aleksandr Men, who was brutally murdered in 1990, remains Ulitskaya's personal "saint." "Church diehard conservatives and nationalists hated Father Alexander," Ulitskaya stated in 2001. "He had a difficult life task: to be a Jew and an Orthodox priest in an antisemitic country, hardly touched by Christianity. He knew to what extent today's Russian Orthodoxy has been infected with idolatry and did endlessly much to liberate souls from a pagan captivity."

With a neophyte's zeal reminiscent of the Moscow-based poet and fiction writer Anatoly Nayman (b. 1936), who has written about his conversion to Russian Orthodoxy, Ulitskaya speaks of Christianity: "A Christian is not merely a person who has taken baptism, but a person who has accepted Christ's teachings as a rule of life. There are very few such people" (a 2003 interview). Ulitskaya admires the Jewish-born Simone Weil (1909–1943), a philosopher who considered herself a Christian but never formally went through a baptism, refusing it even on her deathbed. "But actually Christianity is a very inconvenient thing. Very," Ulitskaya remarked in a 2004 interview. "The moment it becomes convenient, it ceases to be itself." When the editor of this anthology queried Ulitskaya, "when and under what circumstances she took baptism," she replied, in an e-mail dated 22 October 2004, "The question is completely personal; I do not reply to such questions." In the short story "My Favorite Arab" from her recent collection *The People of Our Tsar* (2005), Ulitskaya wrote: "[...] I'm Russian by culture, Jewish by blood, and a Christian by confession."

The trajectory of Ulitskaya's religious quest is summed up by her remarks from an address, "Neopaganism and We," given at the Fourteenth International Aleksandr Men Conference (2004): "Having encountered Christianity in the '60s, for several decades I've been living with the happy sensation that in my hands is a universal key that opens all locks. The circumstances were exceptionally favorable—I found myself within the sphere of gravity of several remarkable individuals who professed Christianity. [. . .] But there were other wonderful people who did not profess Christianity— atheists, skeptics, scientists—whose behavior toward their loved ones was impeccable. Later I encountered several [practitioners of Judaism] who also displayed remarkable examples of beauty, dignity, and moral stature. And now I no longer believe that specifically and only Christians possess the completeness of the truth." Ulitskaya's ideal of spirituality is embodied most fully in her novel *Daniel Stein, Translator* (2006). Its protagonist is based on Oswald Rufeisen (1922–1998), a Polish Jew who survived the Shoah, helped rescue Jews from death, and became a Catholic and a Carmelite friar. Rufeisen, known as Brother Daniel, OCD, later moved to Israel, where he had to fight for his right to qualify for citizenship under the Law of Return. He lived at the Stella Maris Carmelite Monastery in Haifa, seeking to advance the controversial idea of Jews as doubly chosen to be followers of Jesus Christ. The example of Ulitskaya, a Jewish-born Christian, a Russophone writer who keenly features Jewish characters and entertaining Jewish questions, challenges us to understand the outer boundaries of modern Jewish culture.

* * *

"Genele the Purse Lady" (1993), the story that follows below, may have been informed by Ulitskaya's paternal grandmother, of whom she said in 2001, "Her poverty was jolly and light. Everything excessive she called philistinism. She was a very lofty creature. And with that, scared down to her marrow." The editor's experience at teaching "Genele the Purse Lady" to an audience of American college students indicates that readers are divided as to whether it offers a bitter view of Jewish survival in Diaspora (even if Jews possess material wealth, it does not buy them safety) or an inspiring parable (the ancient Jewish traditions endure against all odds). "Literature, of course, owes nothing to anybody," Ulitskaya said in a 2004 interview. "'Heroics' in general is not my thing."

GENELE THE PURSE LADY

Aunt Genele had the temperament of a public figure. Life's larger tasks hadn't turned up on her path, so she applied herself to relatively small issues; in particular, she made sure that the northwest corner of our building's landscaped courtyard would remain clean. Her zeal would have actually sufficed for the entire courtyard, but she preferred to focus on a smaller area and achieve total perfection. Aunt Genele loved perfection.

After the mud dried up a bit, Aunt Genele, her boots sinking in puddles camouflaged with postwinter rubbish, would drag herself to her post—a peeling bench beside a dilapidated fountain. There she would sit down to await the transgressors.

The spring cleanup that usually preceded the May holidays[86] hadn't begun, and the alleys were strewn with faded candy wrappers, swollen cigarette butts, and small, hastily procured accouterments of homeless lovemaking.

It was still low season and few visitors showed up at the yard, but Genele had started her own duties early, beating the first visitor by a day or two. This time her first visitor was a man with a briefcase. He sat down a short distance away, lit up a cigarette, and tossed a match over his back. Genele shuddered like a hunting dog and, smiling sweetly, took aim:

"Citizen, the trashcan is only two steps away; is this so hard?"

Absently, the citizen looked at her; he had anxious eyes.

"Excuse me, did you say something?"

"Yes, I did," Genele pronounced slowly and authoritatively. "The trashcan is two steps away from you, and you throw a match right on the ground!"

He laughed unexpectedly, got up, picked up the match—fresh white amid the dark-gray dirt—and tossed it in the trashcan. The old woman turned away in disappointment; the game she intended to play wasn't real. The man stood smoking for a while and then left, tossing the cigarette butt where he was supposed to.

---

86 International Workers' Days, 1 May, and the Day of Victory over Germany, 9 May, were national holidays in the USSR.

"That's the way," contemptuously she said to his back; she was convinced that away from under her vigilant eyes he would again bypass the trashcan.

Later she was visited by three pigeons, ragged and distended. They looked hung over. From a small shopping bag Genele removed a jar with bread she had soaked in water; she collected old bread from her neighbors since she never let her own bread go stale. Genele mashed the bread and divided it into three even portions, but the foolish birds didn't understand fairness, or perhaps they were committed collectivists. Pushing one another, all three of them attacked the little mound of bread nearest to them and greedily pecked at it, while leaving the other two untouched. Genele tried to direct them to the food, but now, as always, they didn't understand her.

Waiting until lunchtime, when the feeble sun began to push through the clouds, she got up and headed home, mincing her little bowlegs. She was in a fabulous mood; the melancholy interlude separating winter from spring was over, and she felt her spirits surging. And after lunch came the time when she carried out the most important of her life's tasks: seeing relatives. She visited them according to a schedule. Sister Marusya, niece Vera, niece Galya, grand-niece Tamara, and nephew Viktor formed one cycle, while the other was headed by her brother Naum, who lived with his unmarried and mildly retarded son Grigory. After them came nephew Aleksandr and niece Raya. There were also two unmarried sisters, Motya and Nusya, and this family circle would be concluded with Anna Markovna, a distant relative whom nonetheless she deemed worthy of her visits.

Because she had quite a few relatives, Genele ended up visiting each one of them about once a month. And all of them put up with such frequency, conscious of the fact that she served as some sort of cement binding the family and preventing it from falling apart.

Small, neatly dressed, curly white, she would enter a home and deliver a line that had the ring of a compliment, something like this:

"Marusya, the last time I saw you, you looked so wonderful . . ."

She was a genius in this practice: she would never say anything unpleasant to anyone, but her compliments somehow came out a bit off . . .

"Oh, if you only knew what a wonderful son Shura has! Straight A's in school, nothing but *excellent*! But you do understand, don't you, what sort of standards they have at school these days?"

"Oh, Galya, a great pie! Very tasty! If you only knew what cabbage pies Raya makes, delicious!" she would exclaim, finishing a piece of pie that Galya, not Raya, had baked.

She would enter an apartment loaded with multiple shopping bags, and under her left elbow she firmly held a large purse with which she never parted. Because of that she got her nickname—the Purse Lady.

The purse had been brought from Switzerland before World War I by her affluent aunt who had been studying dentistry in Zurich. Originally the purse was dark brown, with a rich purple sheen and a silky glitter. Over the years the purse grew darker and darker, becoming almost black, and later it turned gray and acquired an indescribably refined yellowish-gray tint. Several times the purse had gone in and out of fashion. On its back façade there was a large cut, thoroughly stitched together by the hand of its owner; once in '44 the purse had been attacked by a robber's knife and injured. Wilted art nouveau leaves were dying on the lock; Genele's thin gnarly fingers would weave themselves into the lock's withered ornament, and it looked as though both her skin and the purse's leather came from the same ancient animal, now extinct.

In public Genele never opened her precious purse, but from one of her numerous other bags she would take out a homemade treat—coleslaw Provençal, which she made according to some unimaginable recipe from seventeen ingredients, including several odd ones: parsley root, raisins, and lemon peel. There were relatives who thought that her famous slaw was sheer poison, but it would never occur to anyone to refuse the offering, which Genele usually made with a mysterious and agitated face.

Everyone knew that Genele's pension was ridiculously miniscule. For her part, she never complained of a shortage of money, instead behaving with the dignity of a wealthy relative. She instructed her nieces, and later their daughters, in the fine principles of housekeeping, considering herself a learned master of this lofty métier.

"You should buy in small amounts but always the very best," she enlightened her impractical nieces, and once she even gave Galya an unforgettable master class in food shopping. Genele brought her to the Tishinsky Farmers' Market on a Sunday, when business was slowing down, about an hour before closing.

"First you need to walk around all the stalls and have a good look. Take mental notes: who has the best wares. The second time around—you already know who has the finest stuff—now you inquire about the prices. And on the third round you do your buying, and you will never, ever go wrong."

With flaming eyes Genele sped across the market, peeking and peering, criticizing the quality of wares, praising the weather, wishing years of health and wealth to a fat Ukrainian woman who was hurrying to catch a train, and managing—on the fly—to call a sullen long-faced Oriental man "totally crazy in the head." She waved her hands, fingered parsley, pointing out to Galya that she should only pick out carrots with round tips, and massaged a wilted eggplant. With her sharp nose she sniffed cucumbers "with little warts," as she called them, then insulted somebody's cabbage brine, then churned a drop of honey between her thumb and index finger while whispering to her niece:

"Pure honey is absorbed completely, and if something remains, then it's not pure!"

From a simple old woman, a resident of a village outside Moscow, she bought carrots, beets, and two turnips for half the price that had already been lowered, also taking the last white squash, a crooked specimen, which she placed in her bag, considering it a legitimate commission on the purchases for which Galya was paying.

"I need one hundred fifty grams," she demanded, but the woman behind the counter, not accustomed to such small quantities, shook a thin slab of flaky farmer's cheese off her knife. The slab of cheese weighed almost three hundred grams.

"Why are you giving me all this, I only need a hundred and fifty! Why can't I just buy what I need?" she insisted while the unfazed saleswoman wrapped the farmer's cheese into white paper.

"Oh just leave it alone," the saleswoman said derisively. "I won't go broke."

And Genele gave Galya a victorious look and whispered more instructions.

"So, you understand? Use you brain! Yes, your brain. I can see it by the way she's standing she's lazy, that she would be too lazy to put it back. And they can never cut a hundred and fifty grams, always more!"

Galya's pale face was covered in red blots of nervousness; she was imploring Genele to leave, but it was too late. Excited, Genele wanted to showcase the brilliance of her talent as she tried to talk a woman at the takeout foods counter into knocking fifty kopecks off the government-priced goulash.

For the rest of her life Galya would demur when recalling this trip for her daughter. Aunt Genele's antics from that market day had entered the annals of family jokes. When carrots were mentioned, one of her family members would be sure to ask, "With a round tip?" Cucumbers were divided into those "with little warts" and those "without little warts."

And all the while Genele was living in dire poverty. Actually, if someone were to hint at it, she would be surprised. This was because she lived the way she chose to live. In contrast to a countless number of individuals clinging to their relatives and friends for help and sustenance, she was so independently lonely that even visits to relatives were for her an obligation to those people who required her company, her advice and instruction.

There was something joyful and monastic in her poverty. Her pencil box of a room, eleven meters long, looked jubilant and even defiant. A white cloth napkin was starched so hard that it stood up on a little side table with wax-polished legs, a white hospital-style spread lay on top of the bed, and the coarse covers on her white chairs made one feel like a welcome visitor to a small museum.

In her proud destitution she unfailingly followed her main principle: to buy only the best. This is why she was never too lazy to go to the Filippov bakery every other day, where she bought the best *kalach* in the world, and this soft white bread would last her two days. After that she would stop by the Eliseev food store and buy one hundred grams of Swiss cheese. In regards to cheese, she harbored a suspicion that there were better cheeses in the world. But here, in Russia, the best cheese was the Swiss from Eliseev's. The rest of her diet consisted of buckwheat meal and millet porridge, which, as she liked to put it, no one cooked better than she. This was probably true. She flavored them with sunflower oil bought at the farmer's market, and with lunch she would eat a quarter of an apple or onion or else a small carrot with a round tip.

Only once a year, at Passover, she bought a chicken. In actuality, the chicken *was* her Passover. On the day of buying the chicken, she would get up at the crack of dawn, slowly and thoroughly prepare for the trip, put some black twine and a stack of newspapers into a sturdy bag woven from silk thread, and leave at five in the morning. She would catch the first tram at Pokrovsky Boulevard, get off at Tsvetnoy Boulevard, and arrive at the Central Farmers' Market some twenty minutes before the opening. For a while, sometimes for as long as two hours, she would wait for "her" guy, a one-eyed rusty-brown old Jew who dealt in what had become a rare commodity—live cackling goods. It seemed that, like Genele herself, the chicken salesman lived according to his own uncompromising principles. For instance, he didn't like to put out on the counter more than one chicken. Genele, for her part, obeyed her own law, which stated that she could never buy a chicken, even the most spectacular one, without having groped all the others thoroughly.

She would stand and wait as the old Jew unhurriedly cut the seam that attached a thick gray cloth cover to the top of his large oblong basket, put his hand into the opening without looking, and removed the first chicken with tied feet. Genele would rest her elbow on the counter and say in the casual tone of a person who just happened to be walking by, "So, there you are, as good as new . . . and what do you have there, a chicken?"

The one-eyed Jew wouldn't honor her with a reply.

Genele, pressing her antique purse to her side with the elbow of her left arm, would begin to examine the chicken. More than anything, her manipulations resembled a physical. She looked the chicken in its frozen eyes, opened her beak, felt her neck, squeezed her breast and rear end. Spreading the wings, she appeared to be x-raying the bird's soul. Then she would push the chicken away as unworthy of her time.

"That's all you got?" she would ask contemptuously.

The one-eyed Jew would silently dip his hand into the basket and remove the next chicken.

"What do you think you're showing me? Put that away!" Genele took umbrage. And the salesman, pressing his narrow lips even tighter, picked up another chicken from under the counter.

She would choose the chicken the way a mother picks a bride for her only son. Fretfully aware of her grave responsibility, she was fearful of making the wrong choice. Knowing her own penchant for black chickens with gray speckles, she aspired to remain impartial, so that her bias wouldn't influence her scientific choice. She knew very well that a white or a rusty-brown chicken could end up as the chosen one.

Toward his picky customer the old man felt vexation mixed with ever growing respect. He was also a chicken expert, an expert in the very best, the esteemed Passover chickens that were raised on pure grain. He knew that the old woman always chose the very best one and wondered whether it would happen again. In all the years he had known her, she had never made a mistake.

The chosen chicken would finally be determined. They would bargain for a long time. Finally Genele removed new bills from her treasured purse, and the *tsar's bride* still unnaturally suspended head down, would be passed into Genele's hands. Genele would wrap her in multiple layers of newspaper, then in a clean white cloth, then place her into a silk-woven net, and finally into a shopping bag.

After all these arcane manipulations, Genele would journey to Malakhovka, a Moscow suburb, to see a *shoykhet*. She would wait in line, surrounded by two dozen women from her tribe, behind a shed attached to the back of a stately two-story house. She would surrender her dumbfounded ward to a short fat

Jew wearing a yarmulke and wait for the *shoykhet* to recite the brief apologetic prayer over the chicken and then release the bird's stupid soul, which resided, as it was believed, in the small amount of blood that was trickling onto a zinc tray for as long as the heart continued to pulse.

All of the complex beliefs of her ancestors, all the numerous restrictions and prohibitions that over the millennia had lost their rational sense, were linked in Genele's mind to this brainless, clean little bird symbolizing the paschal lamb.

But actually this is where all religious associations would end, yielding to Genele's fussy culinary magic. In her experienced hands this one and only chicken would be transmogrified into a number of dishes: bouillon with matzo balls that were known as *kneydlekh*, stuffed chicken neck, chicken cutlets, liver pâté, and even chicken meat in aspic. How did she manage it? She just did. And in between her chicken tricks, gefilte fish would somehow emerge out of thin air, and also little doughnuts cooked in honey.

And then she packed it all in jars and little pots. What had to be kept warm she wrapped very carefully. She tied it all together, stuffing rolls of newspaper in between so nothing would spill, and took it to her brother's to celebrate Passover. Her brother Naum usually bought a bottle of sweet wine.

He was twice a widower and a hopeless loser. After the death of his first wife, who passed when she was young, he remarried so that the new wife would raise his children. But soon she developed a particularly nasty and slow-growing form of cancer and was taking years to die, being of no use to the family and instead forcing Naum to expend his remaining strength on fruitless compassion. His children inherited Naum's lucklessness, especially his son Grigory, who was born nice and healthy but suffered an electric shock and became feebleminded.

Such was the home to which Genele brought her Passover offerings. There she would hear the well-known story of the exodus from Egypt, which her brother Naum read hastily, and then sit unhurriedly at the festive table, enjoying this wisely conceived universe where both the daily hustle-bustle and this ceremonial meal are assigned a place and where the one and only Lord, accompanied by his messenger angel, goes around the homes of his chosen people like a mail carrier, while the feebleminded Grigory joyfully smiles, his large face glistening with chicken fat.

On that particular day, Genele came out of her apartment building burdened by three bags. She was heading for Naum's but turned the wrong way.

She reached the corner, her eyes searched for the tram stop, but there was none in sight. She couldn't recognize the intersection she had probably known since her childhood.

"My God! How did I end up in a strange city?" she uttered as she began to fall in slow motion, pressing her brown purse firmly to her side while also clutching the precious bags she had in her clingy hands.

This is how the medics brought her—bags, purse, and all—to the Petrovsky Gates, to the emergency room of the former Catherine's Hospital.

Something terrible had happened to Genele: her entire world, simply, firmly, and cleverly put together, had lost its inner links and become unrecognizable. She saw the rainbow iris of the greenish-speckled eye of the doctor who was bending over her, the brightly starched sheen of his white coat, his swarthy cheek overgrown with stubble after attending on the wards for twenty-four hours. She saw the rough spots on a white painted wall, the flank of a medicine cabinet, and the windowsill, but these details were all disjointed and didn't add up to the whole picture.

Genele made a mental effort to put into words the thought that was slipping away, but she couldn't. All that remained was the feeling that she, a little girl, had lost her way and had to hurry someplace on some incredibly urgent matter. They had taken away her bags, and the fingers of her left hand stirred; her hand felt that it was missing something.

Hurt and robbed, little Genele lay in a narrow spring bed, tormented by her confusion. She didn't hear the questions they were asking. An old nurse opened her brown purse and felt inside it with the long fingers of her creepy hands. Genele's gaze fell on her purse, and tears slowly welled up in her eyes.

The nurse removed from the purse a hand-cream container wrapped in dark paper, an assortment of little keys on a chain, and a worn-out passport. Genele was identified.

She was moved to the neurological ward, to a single room. Her anxiety grew. Genele couldn't recognize anything, as though she had all at once forgotten her entire life. When a nurse's aid brought her water, she couldn't at first remember how to swallow. With her mouth full of water, she halted and didn't know what to do next. The nurse's aid had seen this before and tapped on her throat, and then Genele was able to swallow.

At the call room two doctors were discussing which particular section of the brain had been affected. One of them believed that this was a case of a hemorrhage in the brain stem, while the other one thought there was no hemorrhage at all, and instead they were looking at a strong spasm of the arteries, which had disrupted the blood circulation in her brain.

While the young doctors were discussing this medical mystery, Genele's head became clearer, the unconnected pictures both inside and outside her head had slowed down their torturous horseplay, and one single image emerged together with the word that referred to it. Her purse. Not the idea of a purse but that very one, her brown purse. She said rather loudly,

"Purse! Purse!" Genele's eyes implored.

"I told you it was a spasm," one of the doctors said triumphantly. "She hasn't lost her speech!"

Until the darkest and deafest hour of night, she screamed the one word she still knew. She tried getting out of the bed and escaping. She tossed and jerked her limbs. To prevent her from falling off the bed and hurting herself, they put a net around her.

She was acting as though the purse was in her hands. She didn't want to surrender it and kept screaming, "Purse! Purse!"

She knew that the louder she screamed, the greater would be her claim of ownership to this decrepit leather thing with the winding ornament on the tortoise-shell lock.

And a tender and rueful voice belonging to someone she knew kept telling her the same thing,

"Come on, come on, let it be!"

But Genele refused to give up until the end. She died this way, curving her left arm and curling her fingers, clutching an invisible lock.

In the morning, her grieving nieces Galya and Raya and her older brother Naum, whose wide trousers were too short in the ankles, received her belongings listed in the hospital inventory. Galya took the brown purse containing a small sum of money, which was listed separately; Naum took the Passover treats, which had reached him after a delay.

Later, at home, when he opens the bundles, he will discover that the bouillon was still warm in the thermos, and it will be placed on the funeral table along with the other dishes that Genele made. This last meal will be a severe violation of Jewish custom, because it had long been a tradition to fast after the funeral of a loved one and not to gorge on delicious food.

Raya went to several funereal institutions to take care of the paperwork, while Galya went to Vostryakovo, to the cemetery, to find out what sort of documents they would need in order to put the deceased Genele to rest next to her sisters, brothers, and parents.

In the evening Galya came over to her Uncle Naum's place. Raya had come over earlier. A little lamp was burning, the one he lit on the *yortsayten* of his family members. They sat around a rickety table. With a joyous smile, Grigory went to put on the kettle. After he left the room, Naum said solemnly to his nieces, mainly addressing the smart and slightly pedantic Galya.

"My daughters! Genele is dead. And she didn't suffer. May she rest in peace. Now go over to her place and look carefully before the neighbors have robbed it and the management has sealed off her room."

"What's to look for, Uncle Naum?" Raya asked in disbelief.

"First, her will." Raya shrugged her shoulders as Naum continued. "And second, Genele had inherited diamond earrings from our grandmother. Huge rocks!" He locked his thumb and index finger into a ring the size of a walnut.

"What diamonds? Uncle Naum, you're imagining things!" Galya said with astonishment. "We were always poor as church mice!"

"That's what happened. She did have the earrings. Spanish settings. Something out of this world!" Naum kissed the tips of his fingers. "I should live like that! Genele took care of grandmother when she was dying. And Genele was a clever little girl, so she took them. When her sisters asked about the earrings, she said, 'I don't know what you're talking about! I looked after grandmother, I fed her, I did the wash, this much I know. But the diamonds, I don't know anything about it!' You see what I mean, right?" Naum kept insisting. "Look in her underwear, her stockings; do I know where women hide things?"

Frowning, Galya looked out the dark window. Then she got up. "I'll be going, Uncle Naum. Sasha is away on a business trip, and the kids are home alone." And she left.

Late into the evening, with a precise and mechanical thoughtlessness, Galya did various women's chores around the house, the sort that never seem to end.

And then she sat down, took out Genele's purse, and looked at it with sadness. Then she opened it. In the purse were some old prescriptions, a bunch of small keys on a chain, and a little hand-cream container wrapped in parchment. She took off the parchment wrapping. Inside the container was something that looked like Vaseline; on top of the Vaseline there was a thick oxidized patina.

"Poor little Genele!" Galya thought as she emptied the contents of the old purse onto a newspaper. "What can I do for her now? Nothing."

And then it dawned on her. She tossed the old junk back into the purse. She realized there was something nice she could do for Genele. At the funeral, she would slip the purse into her casket.

And so it was: the feeble gray smoke dispersed over the chimney of the Donskoy crematorium, and up the celestial path hurried Genele, ever more brittle and transparent, pressing to her left side the shadow of her purse, in which the shadows of her diamonds would be stored for eternity, the fragile shadows of the diamonds she had concealed from the authorities and from her own family.

1993

Translated from the Russian by Maxim D. Shrayer

The Jewish Exodus:
1970s–1990s

Editor's Introduction

For the twelve writers chosen for this section, a distribution by year of departure corresponds to a studied pattern of Jewish emigration: two in 1972, two in 1974, one in 1976, one in 1978, one in 1980, one in 1981, one in 1982, one in 1987, one in 1989, and one in 1990.

The total number of Jews and their families who emigrated from the former USSR on exit visas to Israel as well as to all destinations in 1970–88 was 290,800 (50,400 from the Russian Federation).[1] The Jewish Exodus accorded the Third Wave of emigration from the USSR (in the 1970s and 1980s) its distinctive ideological and cultural parameters. The Jewish emigration from the USSR crested in 1977–79 and had come to a near standstill by the middle 1980s, not resuming until the reform years 1987–88, when many of the veteran refuseniks were finally allowed to emigrate (in this anthology, **David Shrayer-Petrov** [b. 1936; immigrated to the United States in 1987]). There is some disagreement as to when the Third Wave actually ended, but a reasonable upper boundary might be placed on the years 1987–88, several years prior to the collapse of the USSR in 1991. The Third Wave as a cultural community was formed when various official obstacles stood in the way of the Jewish Exodus from the USSR.

Five writers in this section immigrated to Israel, five to the United States, and two to Germany. While Israel and the United States loom large on the literary globe of the Jewish Exodus, Canada, Germany, Great Britain, and France also figure as cultural communities, especially as countries of authors' secondary emigrations. Notable examples of such a second (and secondary)

---

1   See Mark Tolts, "Demography of the Jews in the Former Soviet Union: Yesterday and Today," in *Jewish Life after the USSR*, ed. Zvi Gitelman, Musya Glants, and Marshall I. Goldman, 173–206 (Bloomington: Indiana University Press, 2003); Mikaella Kagan analyzed the specifics of the 1970s–1990s Jewish emigration from the Soviet Union to the United States in *Evreiskaia emigratsiia iz byvshego SSSR v SShA: obzor izmenii za 70–90-e gody* (Moscow: Institut etnologii i antropologii RAN, 1996). Kagan cites the statistics of the Hebrew Immigrant Aid Society (HIAS), according to which 308,600 Soviet Jews entered the United States as refugees from 1970 to 1993.

emigration from Israel to Germany are the poet Henri Volohonsky (1936–2017, immigrated to Israel in 1973 and to Germany in 1985) and Leonid Girshovich, another former Leningrader (b. 1948; immigrated to Israel in 1973 and to Germany in 1979).

Prior to having emigrated, some of the writers in this section already had established literary careers in the USSR (e.g., **Ruth Zernova** [1919–2004; emigrated in 1976]), but emigration accorded opportunities to bring out previously unpublished Jewish-conscious works (for example, consider the short story "The Last Rabbi" by the Odessan writer Arkady Lvov [b. 1927; immigrated to the United States in 1976], written in the 1960s but first published in 1978). Some émigrés had developed strong literary reputations abroad prior to having left the USSR on Israeli visas. The case of **Joseph Brodsky** (1940–1996; emigrated in 1972, in the section "The Thaw: 1950s–1960s") is especially noteworthy, not only because of his literary stardom as an American author but also because of his translingualism. Other writers came to Israel and the West without having published in the official Soviet press (e.g., **Ilia Bokstein** [1937–1999; emigrated in 1972]). Some writers brought with them or smuggled out their principal works, which saw publication in the émigré press and in translation. At the same time, the success of the literary careers of several Jewish-Russian writers (in this section, especially **Michael B. Kreps** [1940–1994; emigrated in 1974], **Philip Isaac Berman** [b. 1936; emigrated in 1981], and **Marina Temkina** [b. 1948; emigrated in 1978]) owed itself to emigration. Especially intriguing is the career of Igor Mikhalevich-Kaplan (b. 1943), who emigrated from Lvov (Lviv) in 1979 and already in America switched from writing in Ukrainian to writing mainly in Russian while also exploring Jewish themes in his works.

In addition to contributing to the Russian periodicals and publishing houses established by the émigrés of the First Wave (post–1917 revolutions and the Russian Civil War) and the Second Wave (mainly so-called displaced persons, who found themselves abroad during and immediately after World War II), Jewish-Russian writers started publications of their own in the 1970s and 1980s, some with markedly Jewish concerns, such as the magazines *Twenty-Two* (*Dvadtsat' dva*) and *Time and We* (*Vremia i my*). In Israel, America, and Western Europe, Jewish-Russian writers of the Third Wave enjoyed vastly new opportunities that were free of censorship but that also encouraged self-publishing. Like their American literary colleagues, few immigrants could make a living as writers in the United States. Some turned to journalism; others supported themselves and their families by working in other professional capacities. The book-publishing boom in the former USSR in the early 1990s resulted in the closing of a number of Third-Wave publishing houses and magazines. While the literary culture of the Third Wave has lost much of its distinct character in the post-Soviet world, a strong group of Third-Wave Jewish-Russian writers continues to work in emigration. These writers still define their cultural identities in terms of their experience of being part of the Jewish Exodus. This, however, in no way means that the writers' attempts at emigration, especially the traumatic years as the Jewish disenfranchised stuck in the USSR in the 1970s and 1980s, form a central thematic core of their writings. The latter is particularly true for the younger generation of Third-Wave writers in the United States and Canada. Calling for greater critical attention are Pavel Lembersky (b. 1956, immigrated to the United States in 1977) and Anna Halberstadt (b. in 1949, immigrated to the United States in 1979), both of whom have written in Russian and English about the experience of Jewish-Russian immigrants.

In 1989–98, 769,900 Jews and their relatives came to Israel from the Soviet Union and its successor states (230,500 from the Russian Federation) and 290,000 (70,900 from the Russian Federation) to the United States. Additionally, about 115,000 Jews and their families immigrated to Germany.[2] Some of the writers who left during the very last Soviet and the first post-Soviet years had already been formed as literary professionals or even enjoyed professional careers there. This was the case of the poet and translator Ilya Kutik (b. 1961), who first immigrated to Sweden and subsequently moved to the United States in 1995. For the poet and translator Ian Probstein (b. 1953), immigration to the United States in 1989 opened new publishing opportunities and transcultural horizons.

The literary careers of some of the Fourth-Wave authors who left in their thirties and forties took off already after emigration—consider the examples of the poet and essayist Gennady Katsov (b. 1956; immigrated to the United States in 1989) and the poet and translator Vladimir Gandelsman (b. 1948; immigrated to the United States in 1990). Of the younger Fourth-Wave Jewish-Russian immigrants to the United States, not many developed Russian-language literary careers, and even fewer wrote in Russian about their Jewish

---

2   Tolts, "Demography of Jews in the Former Soviet Union: Yesterday and Today," 177–78.

and immigrant experiences. In this regard, the careers of both Liana Alaverdova (b. 1959; immigrated to the United States in 1993) and Katia Kapovich (b. 1960; immigrated in 1990 to Israel and in 1992 to the United States) are exceptional.

The Russian-language literature in Israel benefited greatly from the great outflux of Jews and their family members from the former USSR in the late 1980s and early 1990s, and it continues to benefit from the arrival of new *olim* from Russia and the republics of the former USSR. (See also the section "In Israel" of the editor's general introduction.) Alexander Ilichevsky (b. 1970), one of the best-known Jewish-Russian prose writers of his generation, made Israel his home in 2014. The Israeli scholar Roman Katsman speaks of the demarginalization of Russian-language writing in Israel as a result of the influx of the 1990s: "Russophone writers in Israel find a way to overwhelm both the traditional Jewish-Russian poetics and the ghetto mentality." In this anthology, the prose writer **Dina Rubina** (b. 1953; immigrated to Israel in 1990) and the poet **Anna Gorenko** (pseudonym of Anna Karpa, 1972–1999; immigrated to Israel in 1989) represent some of the forces and trends that transformed the Russophone literary landscape of today's Israel.

Finally, a group of those who left the USSR as children or young people have built up careers in the languages of their new countries, becoming writers and pop-entertainment figures with a Jewish-Russian pedigree, authors whose cultural patrimony should probably be defined as Jewish-American (such as the prose writers Gary Shteyngart [b. 1972; immigrated to the United States in 1977] and Anya Ulinich [b. 1973; immigrated to the United States in 1991] and the poets Genya Turovskaya [born 1973; immigrated to the United States in 1979] and Ilya Kaminsky [born 1977; immigrated to the United States in 1993]), Jewish-Canadian (such as the prose writer and filmmaker David Bermozgis [born 1974; immigrated to Canada in 1980]), and Jewish-German (such as the writer and entertainer Wladimir Kaminer [b. 1967; immigrated to Germany in 1990]). The creative lives of Hebrew-language authors, who were born in the Soviet Union and as children or young people made aliyah with their families, call for a separate conversation and a separate anthology. These new Russian-Israeli authors, among them the prose writers Alona Kimhi (born 1963; immigrated to Israel in 1972) and Alex Epstein (born 1971; immigrated to Israel in 1979), have brought Jewish-Russian traditions into the Israeli literary mainstream.

LEV MAK

Lev Mak (b. 1939), poet and screenwriter, was born Leonid Mark to an Odessan Jewish family. Mak's father was a professor at the Odessa Polytechnic Institute; his mother was a teacher of Russian. In his youth, Mak was a weightlifting champion of Ukraine. He entered the Odessa Polytechnic after high school but left after two years to apply himself to writing. He worked at a factory and participated in expeditions to the Pamir. For a year he attended the Geography Faculty of Leningrad University but unenrolled in 1962 after he, as a Jewish student, was turned down for an overseas oceonographic expedition. In Leningrad he became friendly with the writers Sergei Dovlatov, **Evgeny Reyn**, and **Joseph Brodsky**. Mak did a stint as a reporter for a local television station in Vorkuta, a coal-mining city north of the Arctic Circle, where some of the worst gulag camps had been set up in the 1930s. Returning to Odessa, Mak graduated as a mechanical engineer in 1965 and worked in his field. He tried placing his poems but nothing came of it. Samizdat activities resulted in Mak's first troubles with the authorities.

Mak studied at the Higher Courses of Screenwriting in Moscow in 1968–70. He subsequently worked at the Odessa Film Studios, running into further trouble with the authorities for his poems, which were suffused with religious imagery and critical of the Soviet system. He worked a number of odd jobs, including those of a longshoreman at the Odessa seaport, an ambulance medic, and a loader at a candy factory. In September 1974, an article vilifying Mak appeared in *Evening Odessa* (*Vecherniaia Odessa*). Titled "Renegades," in its tone and thrust the article was reminiscent of the infamous article "A Paraliterary Drone," which had appeared in *Evening Leningrad* (*Vechernii Leningrad*) in 1963 and led to the arrest and trial of **Joseph Brodsky**. The KGB confiscated his personal papers and gave Mak the choice between serving a sentence for anti-Soviet activity or leaving the country. He was forced to immigrate to Israel in November 1974.

After six months in Israel, Mak was hired by Occidental Petroleum to work in London as a technical translator and later was transferred to Kansas City, Missouri. He was able to restore from memory many of the poems confiscated by the KGB. During his first decade and a half abroad, Mak's poetry appeared in *Continent* (*Kontinent*, in 1975), *Time and We* (*Vremia i my*, in 1983), and *The New Review* (*Novyi zhurnal*, in 1988). In 1976, a small American publisher in Kansas City released his Russian-language poetry collection, *From the Night*.

In 1978, the University of Iowa Writing Program's Translation Series and Ardis Publishers copublished a collection of Mak's poems in English, *From the*

Night and Other Poems. The volume was edited and cotranslated by Daniel Weissbort, whose introduction to it remains the principal English-language source of information about Mak. When Mak's poems were published in *Time and We* in 1983, his biographical sketch indicated that Mak was living in Los Angeles, California. Thereafter, information about Mak becomes ever more scant. From Lev Mak, the editor of this anthology subsequently learned that in the late 1970s, after failed attempts to sell a screenplay about Alexander the Great and to complete a novel, Mak became a real-estate broker. In Mak's own words, "Much to my amazement, I started making decent money and soon bought a big expensive house on one of the most prestigious lakes outside Los Angeles. I married again, we had children, and for nineteen years I stopped dreaming about professional literary work. But I did continue to write, albeit in snatches and sporadically."

Until quite recently, students of poetry know of Mak mainly from his poems featured in Konstantin K. Kuzminsky and Gregory L. Kovalev's *The Blue Lagoon Anthology of Modern Russian Poetry*, published in 1980–86 in the United States, as well as his four poems reprinted in *Samizdat of the Century* (Minsk–Moscow, 1997), an anthology coedited by **Genrikh Sapgir**. Occasional references to Mak wind up in poems and memoirs. **Evgeny Reyn** included recollections of Mak in *Notes of a Marathoner: Uncanonical Memoirs* (2003), remembering young Mak as a "superman" who sought to convince everyone that he "was the strongest, most manly, most talented one." For **Reyn** the memoirist, Mak was an occasion to relate an anecdote about **Joseph Brodsky**, whom Mak (as assistant director) had unsuccessfully employed at the Odessa Film Studios in the filming of *Train to a Distant August* (directed by Vadim Lysenko, 1972).

Retired, Lev Mak lives in Venice Beach, California, and now devotes himself full time to literary work. In 2009, a large retrospective collection of his verse, *Waiting to Inhale*, was published in Moscow with a preface by the writer Aleksandr Volodarsky.

* * *

"We have in Lev Mak a poet almost drunk with poetry, with a love of words and, above all, of sights and sounds that one is tempted (knowing of his Odessan origins) to call 'Southern,'" Daniel Weissbort wrote. Indeed, the Odessan Mak fused the traditions of the Southwestern school (which included **Eduard Bagritsky**, Arkady Shteynberg, Mark Tarlovsky, and other Jewish-Russian authors) and postacmeist St. Petersburg poetry. Buttressed by Biblical and classical mythopoetics, Mak's vision of the world (kindred to surrealist political poetry, especially

Louis Aragon) communicates a Soviet Jew's despair and longing for the age of innocence (see poems below). Weissbort has deemed Mak's *From the Night and Other Poems* a "[. . .] book of nightmares, nightmares not so much of actuality as of potentiality—post-Auschwitz, post-Stalin nightmares [. . .]."

A FAREWELL TO RUSSIA

The apartment is empty.
My wife's nightie hangs weightlessly over a chair,
Sprawling, a rag doll embraces a potty.
A sad teddy bear sits on my suitcase. Soon
I'll be leaving my house and never come back.

The children have gone to the zoo to look at the zebra.

In Odessa it's hard being a zebra. But only a fraction better
In Russia to be a Jew and understand how things are,
To accept each day, each second,
your chastisement—
Oppressed by the heat, to await the rattle and howl of the hunt,
Throat on fire, to drink the foul liquid that trickles
From the rusty faucet in your place of refuge! Scorn!
Scorn! Scorn!

The hunting dog hates his quarry, the hunter has fun,
And only the beater's afraid.

Now, in the Jewish quarter, they're being recruited.
Worldly wisdom,
Fear, and Darwin, all studied at school,
Have made the choice easy for them. In the evening paper
There's a picture of a wolf, gnawing the hide
Of the ill-fated sheep he's sprung from that morning . . .

Suitcases line the wall.
The children, the mother and wife, remain.
It may be forever . . .

What makes us good, what evil,
Wise, base, blessed? Is it that force which molds
The clouds and hills, which fold back the bristling red sabers
Of grasshoppers, so as not to inhibit their leap,
Which has given to man his omnivorous stomach and delicate soul,
And allowed him to live, satisfying the one and the other . . .

You get used to anguish, like the sharp smell of fish
That the neighbors are frying.

No, I don't want to, I am unable
To grasp what the chief of the Kremlin's death experts is grunting
As he smacks down the map of the Med on the dissection table,
Disemboweling Palestine, just like Poland before,
So the Jews might be
Salted and dead, like the Dead Sea, their pitiful lake.
To become the chosen of fate, the personal, intimate friend of Nemesis,
To confirm sentences, confirming, perfecting myself by so doing,
To know who is fated to part with his loved one, and when,
What the bullets will twitter and chirp, as they pass one another,
Who will roll in the grass with a goalkeeper's cry on his lips,
As he grips an invisible ball,
Whose eyes will be shut tight forever, and who'll weep . . .
To become the betrayer of brothers, hermetically sealed in
                                       foul-smelling barracks,
With only the leavings of camp-kitchen harpies to eat,
To make rags out of pine bark, to live from letter to letter!

Farewell, Russia! Forgive me my tearful goodbye.
Do not weep over me. Behind you, even now,
Lurks the spy with the barbed Tatar noose
Who's both eunuch, and husband, and impotent rapist!

Lousy Jew!—he cries through your lips.
In a whisper, I answer—Farewell, Mother!

1974

Translated from the Russian by Daniel Weissbort

AUGUST IN ODESSA

Onto the town, stars dropped
Like sapphires into a safe.
The street-lamp rocked
Above the murdered thief.
By impregnable houses
Hemmed about,
The Milky Way ploughs its
Illumined moat.

Guttural speech emerges
From behind milky furrows.
Menora starlight
The Jewish boroughs:
In the August night
Jehova condemns his children
To hunger and the plight
Of post offices unopened.

With night a lottery, you
Stick a hand in the sack—
The God of Soviet Jews
Bends like a quack,
Over your soul. At that, far off
Loom, twinkling, aglow,
The slatternly earth.
The merciful snow.

1974

Translated from the Russian by Daniel Weissbort and Maxim D. Shrayer

BORIS KHAZANOV

Boris Khazanov (b. 1928, German spelling: Boris Chasanow), fiction writer and essayist, was born Gieronim Faybusovich (Gennady Faibussowitsch) in Leningrad. His father, originally from Novozybkov (now in Russia's Bryansk Province), came to Petrograd as a young man. In 1932, the family moved to Moscow, where Khazanov grew up. Khazanov's mother, a pianist, died at the age of thirty-three, when Khazanov was six. "I was raised by my father, practically without Jewish religious traditions, and in Russian," Khazanov wrote to the editor of this anthology in 2004. "Older relatives spoke Yiddish when they wanted to conceal something from me. As an adult, I studied a little Hebrew."

Khazanov spent part of the war in Tatarstan, later entering the Philological Faculty of Leningrad University. Arrested as a fifth-year student in 1949, he was sentenced to eight years at a labor camp for anti-Soviet activity. The main charge was based on the observations he had shared with close friends, one of whom was a KGB informer, after reading the Russian translation of *Each Dies Alone* (1947), an anti-Nazi novel by Hans Fallada (1893–1947). Khazanov was shocked that Soviet censorship had overlooked the fact that the Hitlerite atmosphere depicted by Fallada was strikingly akin to that of Stalinist Russia.

Released in 1955 without the right to reside in Moscow, Khazanov graduated from the medical school in Kalinin (now Tver) in 1961. He worked as a physician in the country, later in Moscow, defending a candidate's degree in medical science. Khazanov subsequently left the medical field and in 1976–81 worked as a science editor at the magazine *Chemistry and Life* (*Khimiia i zhizn'*). Under the pen name Gennady Shingaryov, he published books for teenagers.

As Boris Khazanov, his literary name (from the Hebrew *hazzan* = cantor), he began to circulate his writings in samizdat, in particular in the magazine *Jews in the USSR* (*Evrei v SSSR*; 1972–79), whose last editor, Viktor Brailovsky, received a sentence for his activities. Khazanov's works appeared abroad. A collection of his fiction, *Scent of Stars*, came out in Israel in 1977, followed in 1981 by *I, Sunday, and Life*. Khazanov was subjected to harassment by the KGB. In 1982, he immigrated to Germany.

Khazanov's fiction and nonfiction, much of it touching on Jewish and Judaic topics, appeared frequently in *Time and We* (*Vremia i my*), but also in *Syntax* (*Sintaksis*), *Twenty-Two* (*Dvadtsat' dva*), and other émigré reviews.

He cofounded, with Etan Finkelshteyn and Kronid Lubarsky, the magazine and publishing house *Country and World* (*Strana i mir; Das Land und die Welt*, 1984–92), based in Germany. Serving as one of its editors, he was instrumental in publishing *The Psalm* by **Friedrich Gorenstein**. Three of Khazanov's best-known novels appeared under the same cover as *The King's Hour: The King's Hour; I, Sunday, and Life;* and *Anti-Time: A Moscow Novel* (New York, 1985). He published books of nonfiction, including *The Russia Myth. An Essay in Romantic Political Science* (New York, 1986).

Khazanov's works were returned to Russia in 1990–91. *Fear,* a collection of Khazanov's stories, appeared in Moscow in 1990. Other books have followed, including the collection *The City and Dreams* (2001), *To the North of the Future: A Russian-German Novel* (2004), *After Us the Deluge* (2010), *Let the Night Fall* (2013). Khazanov is an active contributor to post-Soviet periodicals, particularly as an essayist and reviewer for *Banner* (*Znamia*) and *October* (*Octiabr'*). A number of his books have appeared in German. In 1998, Khazanov and his translator, Annelore Nitschke, received the Hilde Domin "Literatur im Exil" Prize. Khazanov lives in Munich.

* * *

Featured below is the conclusion of Khazanov's short novel *The King's Hour.* Composed in Moscow in 1968–69, *The King's Hour* appeared in the samizdat magazine *Jews in the USSR* in 1975. It was reprinted in 1976 by *Time and We,* then appeared in Israel, and has been included in several volumes of Khazanov's fiction.

The King's Hour fictionalizes the latter years of Denmark's beloved King Christian X (1870–1947), who appears under the name Cedric X, and the history of Denmark's occupation. Denmark surrendered to Nazi Germany on 19 April 1940. The episode depicted below is Khazanov's version of a popular legend. According to the historian Richard Petrow, as early as October 1943 the British press reported an alleged comment by the Danish king that, in case of a Nazi *aktion* against his Jewish subjects, he would wear a yellow star "as a sign of the highest distinction." Other writers, including Leon Uris in *Exodus* (1958), have fictionalized the episode, and it made its way into the Soviet press. In 1962, in the nonfictional *The Price of Ashes,* **Lev Ginzburg** referred to the Danish king "who, as they say, wore an armband with a yellow star on his arm as a sign of protest." No such thing apparently took place. What is true, however, is that the majority of Denmark's roughly eight thousand Jews escaped to Sweden, thanks largely to the rescue efforts of the Danish population. Responding to the editor's query, Khazanov stressed, in an email dated 25 July 2004, that his short novel is a work of fiction and that it takes place not in Denmark but in a fictitious small country in northern Europe.

It is fitting to conclude with an excerpt from a poem by Khazanov's contemporary, the Leningrad poet Vladimir Livshits (1913–1978), father of the émigré poet and Joseph Brodsky scholar Lev Loseff (1937–2009). Titled "A Danish Legend," it appeared in Livshits's collection *The Appointed Day* (Moscow, 1968): "And on the appointed day, the one that is now becoming a fairy tale/The king emerged from the palace for a stroll around town/And unhurriedly he walked with a yellow armband./The residents of Copenhagen understood this silent signal/And the Gestapo chief raced his inconspicuous Volkswagen/Up and down Market Street, to the train station, the town hall, the seaport, along the canal,/All of Copenhagen already walked around with armbands! . . ./Maybe this happened, or maybe not at all,/But I didn't tell you this legend in vain,/For the golden Andersonian light shines through it,/And in the twentieth century, like hope, it's beautiful."

FROM *THE KING'S HOUR*

Chapter 18

The morning of the following day, mild and overcast, was uneventful apart from the fact that, immediately after the usual work in his study, the king had that thing brought to him. He even asked for two specimens at once. His secretary heard the order and puzzled over what this might mean. Then, in the queen's apartments (Amalia had followed these preparations with horror), Cedric dispatched a lady's maid with a request for everything necessary to be left on the small table in front of the mirror. In the end he was a surgeon and an old soldier and was quite capable of coping with the threads himself, but he considered it important that Amalia should do this. There was a need to make haste, for the King's Hour was drawing near, and Cedric could not permit himself to be even a minute late.

He had time to change—as always he was wearing the green and blue uniform of the royal guard squadron, of which he was accounted chief; however, the Chevalier star had had to be removed, since regulations prescribed wearing the hexagram on the same side, that is, on the left. And now he was standing patiently at attention with his arms by his sides and his chin raised while Amalia, who scarcely reached his shoulder with the last coil of her copious yellow-grey chignon, busied herself with the needle and bit off the thread with her teeth, like some mailman's wife sewing on a button for her husband just before sending him off to work. But they both, in the end, resembled nothing so much as an elderly provincial couple. On his instructions, she did the sewing also on herself. There ensued something of an elderly lady's embarrassment, almost dismay, at being obliged to remove her dress in the presence of a man. The thimble rolled under the table. In a word, it all took bags of time.

And then some striker in the clock tower began to beat a copper sledgehammer on a copper plate. Twelve strikes. And something turned over in the antiquated mechanism, and the chimes began to ring out a hymn solemnly and with a twang. The sentry in a costume recalling the days of d'Artagnan[3] respectfully opened the gates. As tall as a beanpole, Cedric walked along the avenue with the hurriedly mincing Amalia on his arm. An unheard-of break with tradition was occurring, for the chevalier's horse was vainly pawing the ground with anger in the cool half-light of its stall. The king had set off on foot.

Passers-by were nonplussed at seeing the king for the first time out of the saddle and arm in arm with his wife, but principally they were scandalized by the unexpected and quite inappropriate detail that adorned the costumes of this most august parading couple. Just before they turned into the boulevard, the couple came upon a short weak-sighted man who was trudging along toward them, burdened with wearing that same sign. People tried not to notice him, just as it is not done to stare at a cripple or a freak of nature with a disfigured face; in return, everyone's gaze was riveted all the more inevitably, as if hypnotized, on the large, yellow, hexagrammoid star on the chest of Cedric X and the small star on the queen's ceremonial dress.

This star seemed an insane vision, a fantastic symbol of evil; it was impossible to believe that it was real, and sense could not be made of it at first. Some decided that the old king had gone off his head. The Reichkommissar's order stood out black on the playbill posts and corners of houses.

Close one's eyes. Turn away quickly. But these two were still walking . . .

---

3 D'Artagnan is one of the main characters of *The Three Musketeers*, a novel by Alexandre Dumas set in seventeenth-century France; *The Three Musketeers* and the other novels in the cycle chronicling the adventures of the king's elite Musketeers Athos, Porthos, Aramis (and d'Artagnan, who eventually joins the elite unit) are vastly popular in Russia and belong (in translation) to a teenager's standard reading list.

Parents led their children away.

There can be no doubt that at that very minute an alarm-sounding telephone was already jangling in the office of the *Ortskommissar*. From there the unprecedented news flew along the telephone wires further and higher, into the mystic realms of authority. It was impossible to comprehend how one should react to what had happened.

Meanwhile the sun came out, its weak rays filtering through the grey cotton wool of the clouds, and the wet boughs of the linden trees on the boulevard began to glisten. The road surface gleamed brightly . . . The reader may have noticed how atmospheric phenomena sometimes unexpectedly resolve difficult psychological problems. Suddenly everything became simple and cheerful, like the sight of these two elderly people. The king more and more often raised his military cap in response to someone's greeting; Amalia nodded the lackluster bell of her hair and smiled her dry smile. The king looked round in search of the librarian. The librarian was nowhere to be seen.

With an old man's gallantry, the king touched the peak of his cap in response to the greeting of a lady who was walking quickly past holding a child's hand. Both had yellow stars on their chest. This could be considered a rare coincidence: according to church statistics, there were no more than fifteen hundred people living in the town who had the right to this sign.

Then he noticed that the number of passers-by with the hexagram seemed to be becoming larger. Cedric cast a sidelong glance at Amalia, who was mincing along next to him—three of Her Majesty's small steps were needed for every step of his. Amalia had pursed her lips; her face had adopted an unusually prim and proper expression. It looked as if these fifteen hundred people had actually arranged to come out and meet them; these outcasts, excommunicated from humanity, had crept out of their burrows into God's world and were parading in company with them through the town, walking about the streets with no other aim but to show they were still alive! However, there were somehow already too many of them. They kept growing in number. Some people were emerging from doorways with yellow scraps of rag hurriedly pinned to their coats, children were running out of gateways with misshapen likenesses of stars cut from cardboard, some had pinned on colored pieces of newspaper. On Sankt-Andreas Market, on the other side of the boulevard, a policeman controlling traffic with a striped baton in his outstretched hand saluted the king. A canary-colored star stood out vividly on his dark-blue uniform. He too was one of those fifteen hundred! And so the statistics were discredited, or else it was necessary to assume that his subjects had assigned themselves to two nationalities at the same time, and this properly speaking meant nothing but that the statistics had come to grief.

The queen was tired from the long walk, and the king was also fatigued, mainly by the necessity of keeping in check emotions which would have been difficult to describe; at any rate, it was a long time since he had experienced anything similar. For it was a happy day, a happy ending with which we shall conclude our tale about the king. On the way home, Cedric refrained from discussing everything they had seen, fancying that comment in this regard was premature or, conversely, rather late in the day. He merely drew Amalia's attention to the fact that the lindens had lost their leaves early that year. They successfully crossed the bridge leading to the Island and skirted the palace square. A musketeer with a sword at his side and a yellow star on his chest threw open the iron-bound gates before them.

1968–69

Translated from the Russian by Brian Cooper

ILIA BOKSTEIN

Ilia Bokstein (1937–1999), poet and essayist, was born in Moscow to a Jewish family. Before the 1941 Nazi invasion, Bokstein developed tuberculosis of the bones and was placed in a children's sanatorium, which was soon evacuated. He recovered and returned to Moscow in 1948.

Bokstein studied at the Technical College of Communications in 1956–58, although, as he reminisced, he "had no technical aptitude whatsoever." He spent most of his time at research libraries, pursuing his interests in literature and philosophy. In 1960, Bokstein became a low-residency student at the Moscow Institute of Culture, majoring in library science. In June 1961, Bokstein gave a two-hour speech, "Forty-Four Years of the Bloody Path to Communism," in front of the monument to Vladimir Mayakovsky in the center of Moscow, where poetry lovers used to gather to hear poets. Bokstein repeated his speech and received a warning from law enforcement. After thirty minutes of his third public speech about reforming Soviet society, the KGB arrested him. Bokstein was sentenced to five years, which he served in Dubrovlag in Mordovia. In a 1993 interview with Yury Apter, Bokstein reminisced that he was "content with camp living—content because one didn't have to be hypocritical, didn't have to listen to all that Soviet 'newspeak,' which has nothing to do with the Russian language."

Bokstein composed his first poem in 1965. In Moscow, Bokstein regularly studied in the Library of Foreign Literature in order to feel like a person "living in Western society." He avoided Soviet life by not reading Soviet newspapers or following contemporary literature. When Bokstein immigrated to Israel in 1972, he brought with him "three suitcases with notes and drafts, and also thirty finished poems." In Israel he devoted himself fully to writing. Bokstein's poetry was featured in many émigré magazines, including *Alef, Gnosis* (*Gnozis*), *Time and We,* and *Twenty-Two.*

Bokstein mainly worked in free or polymetric verse. His only lifetime book, *Glints of the Wave,* a facsimile reproduction of almost three hundred fifty pages of Bokstein's handwritten texts illuminated with his drawings, appeared in 1986 in Bat Yam. In 1984, *Notebook,* a collector's chapbook of Bokstein's verses, appeared in Brooklyn, New York. Bokstein's verses lose some of their aesthetic and spiritual wholeness when set in standard type and bereft of what accompanies them in his manuscripts: drawings, diagrams, hieroglyphs, and mystical symbols. His poetry, both original and innovative, transcends conventional divisions into genres and branches of knowledge, and Bokstein believed his main contribution to be the esoteric concept of "logocreativity" (*logotvorchestvo*), a theory of the thought process that he advanced in discursive prose and verse. Central to Bokstein's creativity—in verse and in prose—was the invention of neologisms, often based on non-Slavic roots and forms. Bokstein summed up the principles of logocreativity in his *Extremic Dictionary*, which, like many of his discursive writings, remains unpublished.

Bokstein did not master Hebrew, convinced that he would not be able to write "seriously" in it. In Israel he lived like a hermit, only occasionally participating in literary events and readings. He died suddenly in Tel Aviv in 1999, from an abscess of the brain. In a tribute to Bokstein, the poet Konstantin K. Kuzminsky (1940–2015) called him "holy fool, dervish, saint." Bokstein's cousin and executrix Minna Lein, who lives in Haifa, has dedicated herself to the preservation of his legacy. She has edited three volumes of his verses, essays, and interviews, published in Jerusalem as *I Wanted to Be Loved* (2001), *The Star Speaks with the Moon* (2002), and *An Avant-Gardist Has Come Out onto the Roof* (2003). Students of avant-garde poetry in Russia discovered Bokstein in the 1990s. Bokstein's contribution as an ecologist of culture is also gaining acceptance.

* * *

Answering the question "Do you consider Jews a God-chosen people?" Bokstein stated, "This depends on how one understands God-chosenness. I think that God-chosenness expresses itself in the consciousness not only of some definite, striking ideas but in the creation of a culturological complex. Jews gave us monotheistic religion, which served as a basis of Christianity and Islam. But religion only serves as a basis of culture—it's not yet culture. Religion is the culture of the masses. [. . .] Culture is a personification of spirituality in consciousness, a personification of God in art."

Bokstein is one of the most manifestly Jewish metaphysical poets of the modern era, and how harmoniously his unswerving Judaic identity coexists with the broad-mindedness of a sage who learns from other traditions! When the Jewish poet Bokstein speaks of "the overlooked principle of supernatural urban civilization" as the "basis of his faith," in the final part of the cycle "Afánta-Utóma" [4] ("Fantasia-Judaica," from *Glints of the Wave*), in his worship of world culture he reminds one of **Osip Mandelstam**, whom **Joseph Brodsky** called "the child of civilization."

---

4   "Afánta-Utóma" is a term of Bokstein's own esoteric coinage given in his own Latin spelling; Bokstein explained the word "afánta" to mean "fantasy." He assigned the present "afánta" the designation "A-57," presumably the fifty-seventh in a series.

FROM *GLINTS OF THE WAVE*

Part IV: "Afánta-Utóma" ("Fantasia-Judaica")

1.

I—a Jew
not by Madonna born
not to a cross nailed
nor for me to express all my longing
chains of the tribe on me
grief of the people in me
I have frozen at the speechless doors

2.

I was like everyone
I tended herds of sheep and goats
but when all the shepherds were resting
I thought about God
and God entered
one of my souls
to console the innocent
sheep and goats

3.

I'm both slave and master
a redeemer of humanity
and a pupil of the heavenly teacher
whom one time
in the desert I overpowered
and lamed,
so I await the one
who's been here before

4.

I did not look like anyone,
I served an unseen truth
discovered for humanity
the One Redeemer
but in me the truth invisible
is weeping in my flesh
from nondisclosure

5.

I was jealous
of the One overseer Yhwh
I destroyed the pagan temples
I broke the idols
though some of them
afterward would get to me
they were quite beautiful
and in distress at the belated
aesthetization
of their rhinocery
they forced all
sculptors to bow
to an invisible
and colossal
fish

6.

If you should see
my path to the sky
my spirit on you
will doubly repose
you will
raise the dead up
not giving them
your breath

I saw only a chariot
and a fiery whirlwind
that had rushed upward
and I gave its breathing over
to all the living
and the whole day the earth rejoiced
and the widow's son
I had resurrected
covered it

7.

A godly man was walking
and met some little children:
go away, old baldhead,
and don't kick up the dust.
hee-hee, hah-hah!—
the village idiot, look!—
run after the scarecrow,
and turning around, Elijah
cursed them like early Zeus—
to face the little taunters.
from the forest two frightful she-bears
came out to eat their supper.
o superenlightened person!
be afraid of pagan Gods
long since forgotten
they are immortal
just like miracles

8. Reb Akiva[5]

I was an ordinary shepherd,
but I devotedly studied the Law
and then became a teacher,
acquired pupils
and created my own

---

5   Akiva Ben Joseph—ca. 40–135 CE, great Talmudic scholar, Jewish leader, and martyr.

school of philosophy,
and, finally, decided to decipher
the secret structure of the universe
and started on my search for words.
but God, I see, has punished me—
I lost the falsity
of living sight
and ordinary language I forgot
in place of warm and human eyes
I see a firework of stones—the stars.

9. Jacob and Rachel

for fourteen years you
served for my sake
and they were for you—
as a single day.
but having received me, Jacob,
you cooled toward me within a month.
have I really managed
to age in a month?
—not at all, Rachel,
but you were my dream,
and since I didn't notice
how the time came
for its fulfillment,
now I dream
about the time that passed unnoticed.

10. A Cabbalist

to bring order to my system
of concepts of the Universe
into the canon of the Holy Law
I introduce the Graeco-Roman
pantheon of Gods
I have surrendered my people
to the protection of Saturn—
ruler of the earth and time

and human paths
so that the earth recalls
with invisible attention
on the table in the room
researching the meanings
of the words I've thought up
from my body I fly to the stars.

11.

The basis of my faith is
the overlooked principle
of supernatural urban
civilization—
the replacement of the sun's love
by verbal elegance
But our civilization
is still pterodactylian
and that's why I am—
a pre–Ice Age behemoth
at its feet
and from above I'm studied
by our joint visage.
And on its huge
red tongue
a small black
monkey—
thus do I see from earth
the hotel of my
future city—
ballerina missive
that had torn up words.

late 1960s–1970s

Translated from the Russian by Gerald J. Janecek

DAVID MARKISH

David Markish (b. 1938), prose writer, poet, and translator, was born in Moscow. In 1952, his father, the Yiddish writer Perets Markish (1895–1952), was executed with other leaders of the Jewish Antifascist Committee (see John D. Klier's "Outline of Jewish-Russian History"). In February 1953, Markish, his mother and sister, and his brother Shimon Markish (1931–2004), subsequently a leading scholar of Jewish-Russian literature, were exiled to Kazakhstan for ten years. In a brief English-language "Autobiography," submitted upon the request of the editor of this anthology, Markish wrote, "The sharpest adventures of my life were the exile to Kazakhstan at the age of fourteen where I played cymbals [...] in the undertakers' orchestra for food at funeral repast; six ascents in summer and in winter [...] to the greatest Pamir Mountains Fedchenko Glacier." In the summer of 1955, the members of the Markish family were allowed to return to Moscow.

Markish started out as a poet and studied at the Literary Institute in Moscow. As a student he began to publish journalism in *Ogonyok* (*Little Flame*) and later attended the Higher Courses of Screenwriting (see also **Friedrich Gorenstein**, **Evgeny Reyn**, and **Lev Mak**). Markish's poetry appeared twice in Soviet periodicals. By the late 1960s, Markish's Zionist poems circulated in samizdat. In 1972, he repatriated to Israel.

The experience of exile to Kazakhstan informed Markish's first novel, *Story Embellishment* (*Priskazka*), known in its American edition as *A New World for Simon Ashkenazy*. Written in 1970–71, it appeared first in English (1976) and then in Russian (Israel, 1978). Alice Nakhimovsky characterized it as "interesting for its straightforward identification with Jews, linked with the romantic belief in a Jewish future outside of the Soviet Union." In Israel, Markish gradually gave up writing poetry. His Russian novels, most of them translated into Hebrew, include *The Dog* (1984), *In the Shadow of the Big Rock* (1986), *The Donor* (1987), and others. Markish's short fiction was collected in *My Enemy the Cat and Other Stories, 1958–1988* (1990). He described fighting in the 1973 Arab–Israeli war in a book of nonfiction, *Follow Me!* (1984; cf. the Jewish-Russian poetry of Mikhail Grobman and Yuri Leving about serving in the Israeli Defense Forces).

Markish's works began to appear in the former Soviet Union in the 1990s. His book *To Become Lyutov: Free Fantasies from the Life of the Writer Isaac*

Emmanuilovich Babel (St. Petersburg, 2001) attracted attention at the time of a post-Soviet critical reevaluation of **Isaac Babel**'s career. Two of Markish's books have been published in Bishkek, Kyrgyzstan, one of them reflecting his lifelong fascination with Central Asia: *Shadows and Others: Asian Prose* (2003). Markish's novel *White Circle* (2003) is devoted to the destiny of the Russian avant-garde artist Sergey Kalmykov (1891–1967).

In Israel, Markish has held several editorial positions, was president of the Union of Russian-Language Writers of Israel in 1982–85, and served as an adviser on the Russian Diaspora to Prime Minister Yitzchak Rabin. In the article "Russian-Jewish Literature in Israel" (1984), David Markish thus characterized himself and his fellow writers: "Our feet still in the stirrups of our native Russian-Jewish literary tradition, we prefer to call ourselves Israeli-Russian writers." In a March 2004 interview, Markish did not mince words in describing his identity: "I'm a Jew connected, through my spiritual interests, with the Jewish people, its customs, its history above all. And one writing in the Russian language . . ."

* * *

Found below is a fragment from Chapter 8 ("The Appearance of Prophet Elijah. 1714") of Markish's novel *The Jesters: or Chronicle of the Lives of Itinerant People, 1689–1738*, composed in 1981–82 and first published in Israel in 1983 (Hebrew translation 1985; first English translation 1988; below is a new translation). The novel was reprinted in St. Petersburg in 2001 under a revised title: *The Jew of Peter the Great, or Chronicle of the Lives of Itinerant People*.

Markish's novel focuses on three prominent Jews in the court and government of Peter the Great (see John D. Klier's "Outline of Jewish-Russian History"). The novel's principal Jewish characters are Pyotr Shafirov (1669–1739), Antoine Divier (Devier; 1682–1745), and Ian d'Acosta (known in Russia as Lacosta; 16??–1740s?). The son of Jewish converts, Baron Pyotr Shafirov was one of Peter's closest associates, a privy councilor, senator, and vice-chancellor, one of Russia's top diplomats. Both Divier and Lacosta were descendants of Portuguese Jews. Peter met Divier in Holland and brought him back to Russia. Divier later became a count and a senator and held the post of St. Petersburg's police chief (*general-politsmeister*). Lacosta came to Russia from Hamburg. A great wit, he became a jester at Peter's court around 1714; Peter reportedly enjoyed having long philosophical conversations with his Jewish jester.

Dark historical irony abets Markish's literary imagination. In the epilogue to *The Jesters*, Markish describes Ian Lacosta's return from Russia to

Hamburg in 1738. The last sentence of the epilogue—and of the entire novel—traces Lacosta's family line down to its annihilation in the Shoah: "On the fifth of August 1943, Ian Lacosta's direct descendants: males Josef, Johann, and Heinrich, females Hilda and Rosalinda, children Hans, Hubert, and Minna, were murdered in a gas chamber and burned in a crematorium of the Buchenwald concentration camp, in Germany."

FROM *THE JESTERS*

Chapter 8. The Appearance of Prophet Elijah, 1714

Shafirov decided to celebrate Pesah at home.

This decision came to him the moment he learned there would be no fireworks, no allegorical arch. Well, all right then, how marvelous! There it was, the reward for faithful service—for a Yid's brainbox, for a Yid's tongue, for three years' sitting near the stake, almost impaled on the stake! There was nothing for which to thank God's anointed sovereign Pyotr Alekseevich, let us then render thanks to God for His mercy, at His seder . . .

Thoughts of arranging a secret seder at Lacosta's behind closed shutters fell away by themselves. No, no, Pesah should be celebrated openly and without fear, in Shafirov's palace, in the main hall. And let all Petersburg talk about the fact that the vice-chancellor of Russia, Pyotr Shafirov, was praising his Jewish God for bringing him out of the domain of the infidel Turk with His strong hand . . . Following some reflection, Shafirov decided after all to move downstairs from the main hall to the windowless basement, which was also comfortable and almost luxurious, and arrange everything there: having escaped one mortal danger by a miracle, there was no call to go exposing oneself to another by openly provoking the Most Holy Synod, which even as things were was eyeing Shafirov very mistrustfully and askance. And what's more, Lacosta would very likely not venture to nibble matzah and chant Jewish prayers in full view of the whole world, while Divier would most certainly not risk it. It was immaterial, in the end, on what floor one celebrated Pesah, the ground floor or the basement. And, anyway, Shafirov's basement was much more reliable than Lacosta's place, which anyone who was curious could enter uninvited. The main dining table would need to be taken down into the basement and the walls hung with tapestries. And there must be no forgetting to put a velvet chair there for the prophet Elijah. It was always so touching: right to the end of the evening to expect that at any moment the door would open and the prophet Elijah would enter and sit in the chair. To know that no prophet Elijah would come but to expect him all the same. There was something childlike, innocent in it. A pale-blue velvet chair for the prophet Elijah.

As inviting Anna Danilovna Menshikova to an underground seder would be senseless, Shafirov decided to manage without any of the household at his celebration; there was no need for it, and they would not understand. The company would therefore be male: the host himself, Divier, Lacosta and that Borokh Leybov[6] from Zveryatichi. Well, why not, if it's to be Borokh then let it be Borokh! When else should one perform a mitzvah if not on a paschal evening? What's more, according to Divier, Borokh Leybov was a quick-witted fellow and would not go blabbing idly about whose basement he had passed this seder in.

The table was brought downstairs, the tapestries hung, the velvet chair arranged. As he paced about the spacious basement, Shafirov reflected festively on where his path had led, which had begun in Egypt in times immemorial. And this was where: to the mercers' stalls in Moscow's Kitay-gorod;[7] it was from there that everything had begun, from that brawl with Aleksashka Menshikov.[8] And just like Joseph the Goodly under Pharaoh, so he, Shafirov, had become under Pyotr[9] . . . The windowless basement, decorated with oriental tapestries, was reminiscent of a mysterious cavern, and it was sweet and joyous for Shafirov to feel himself Joseph—an alien Jew who, thanks to his intellect and native wit, had risen high and saved the tsar and Russia. And as for the fireworks and allegorical arch—well, so what: probably even Joseph, after all, had remained a lousy kike for the envious Egyptians and

---

6   Borokh Leybov (16??–1738)—a Jew from Smolensk Province who made a number of trips to St. Petersburg in the 1700s. Leybov was charged with spreading the "Jewish heresy" and "converting" the retired Naval officer Aleksandr Voznitsyn to Judaism; both were publicly burned at the stake on 15 July 1738 in St. Petersburg during the rule of Empress Anna Ioanovna.

7   Kitay-gorod—an area in the center of old Moscow where wealthy merchants formerly resided (hence the legacy of richly decorated churches and mansions). In the nineteenth century, it became the heart of pre-Revolutionary Moscow's financial life. Although *Kitay-gorod* literally means "Chinatown," its origins are not connected with China or the Chinese in any obvious way. One of the theories of the origin of the name links it with the old Russian word for "middle"; surrounded by the "middle" walls (the outer walls being the Kremlin, the inner walls being *Belyi gorod*), Kitay-gorod was thus the middle part of Moscow.

8   Peter's favorite Prince Aleksandr Menshikov (1672–1729); Divier married his sister Anna Menshikova against her brother's wishes but with Peter's approval.

9   That is, Peter the Great, Pyotr (Peter), Shafirov's namesake.

prayed in secret to his God, perhaps in just such a basement of his palace. And as to whether he had taken or not taken Pharaoh's wife somewhere—that was another question; it had been called for, so he would have taken her. And the fact that there was not a single syllable about it in the Bible—that was understandable: they would hardly be likely to write about that night on the river Pruth in the books, either.[10] "Her Majesty sacrificed her jewels for Russia"—that sounded much more noble and literary. He, Shafirov, knew what she had sacrificed; it would be as well if he were the only one. As the late Mehmet said at the time, "Secrets are kept in an iron chest, but even iron will not withstand the ravages of time" . . . And Pharaoh's wife was also presumably a beauty, no worse than Catherine, only to a particular taste.

Catching himself in this naughty thought, Shafirov shook his head in its cumbersome curled wig. Wouldn't that just come to mind, honestly, and on an evening like this too! . . . Yet even Joseph the Goodly had probably found it nice to come together with his own kind at least once a year, without any Egyptians there. Well, twice a year then, but no more. One can have too much of a good thing.

Divier turned up first, looked round observantly, and gave a "hmm" of satisfaction. In place of a greeting, he said, "You've arranged it all here perfectly, Pyotr Pavlovich. And the main thing is, no one can ever guess . . ."

"Apart from the prophet Elijah!" Shafirov added, warming to the theme. "There's the chair for him."

"In his case it's: you're most welcome!" smirked Divier. "But should my dear kinsman Aleksandr Danilych get wind of it, you'll face a sea of troubles."

"There's an envious man!" said Shafirov and shook his head despondently. "If his envy were converted into heat, everyone close to the tsar would long

---

10 In an earlier section of the novel, set during the unsuccessful 1711 Pruth expedition of the Russian troops against the Ottoman Empire and taking fictional liberties at presenting its historical events, Shafirov, who is Russia's chief diplomat, brokers an armistice deal with the Turkish commander Grand Vizier Mehmet. In Markish's novel, for one night with Empress Catherine I (wife of Peter the Great), Mehmet agrees to allow the surrounded Russian troops to cross the river Pruth and retreat unharmed. Shafirov claims that his successful negotiations "saved Russia." Shafirov's skillful diplomacy did in fact save Peter the Great and his small army from a humiliating surrender and captivity; prepared to cede more of its territory, Russia ended up ceding only Azov. Shafirov ended up spending two and a half years in Istanbul as a guarantor of the deal and upon his return was awarded Russia's highest decoration, St. Andrew's Star. Mehmet was impaled in punishment for his conduct.

since have been shriveled to cinders by it. He, Menshikov I mean, is like a beetle eating away the tree in which he lives! I told him so to his face."

"Wrong!" responded Divier laconically.

"Nothing's wrong!" pouted Shafirov with a frown. "I know for a fact that in many battles he looked on from afar through a spyglass, like Neptune from the Thracian hills at the battle of the Trojans with the Greeks."

"You told him that, too?" asked Divier.

"Yes!" Shafirov raised his voice. "That too! To his face!"

"Doubly wrong," said Divier, narrowing his eyes.

"I know it's a mistake," admitted Shafirov with a sigh. "But it can't be taken back now: what's said can't be unsaid . . . Yet on the other hand, what pleasure I felt as I was looking into his insolent mug! He went as red as a boiled lobster."

"Well, if that's the case . . ." Divier inclined his head slightly. "It must be enjoyable, that's true."

"You'll see, he'll be his own demise!" continued Shafirov, rubbing his hands. "The envious bastard!"

"It's best to be rid of people like that at once," said Divier in an even voice, "or not touch them at all, even if that's to your own disadvantage. Prince Menshikov is a very grudge-bearing man, Pyotr Pavlovich."

"I know, I know!" agreed Shafirov with a wave of his hand. "But we shall still put up a fight! Truth will win its way!"

"Truth?" asked Divier in surprise, and his thin motionless eyebrows crept up his forehead. "Are you serious?"

"And why not . . ." Shafirov lowered his shoulders. "If we are lucky . . ."

"Well, yes," said Divier and ran his small swarthy palms heavily over his face, from forehead to chin, as if to put back in place the eyebrows that had gone up without permission. "Lucky, that's just it, lucky, but where will it lead . . . I prefer not to believe in this luck, and so far I have not been mistaken once."

"But in isolated happy instances . . ." Shafirov defended himself listlessly.

"I'm not talking about my department," said Divier with authority, wishing to put an end to this senseless conversation, "but let's take yours, the diplomatic. What is diplomacy?" And he voiced the words as if he had cut them off with a broadsword: "The art of falsehood!"

"Yes, yes," Shafirov concurred absentmindedly. "A great art . . ." And he lapsed into silence, to Divier's gratification.

"And you, Pyotr Pavlovich, the high priest of this great art," Divier went on more gently now. "Your position does not allow you to stay in the shade, and you have no desire to . . . But truth—what is truth? Here truth begins and ends with Tsar Pyotr Alekseevich, and that is right: were it not for this royal truth, everything would start to slip and slide as if on wet clay: circumstances, ideas, supporting beams. And we," Divier raised his voice at his host's gesture of objection, "you and I would be the first to be crushed by these beams."

"You would know better," said Shafirov with a bored look.

"Perhaps!" admitted Divier readily. "Let's at least once a year, at least on this day, not lie . . . Truth! Truth is a divine matter, and each of us fabricates his own truth, either by calculation or by failure to think things through."

"And the tsar?" asked Shafirov, arching his eyebrows.

"The tsar, fortunately, doesn't think about that," said Divier. "What he does is for him the only truth, the heavenly truth. And then we remove it piece by piece, each to our own corner, like jackals. You're not going to try to persuade me that what you do is your, Shafirov's, heavenly truth."

"Let's assume not," remarked Shafirov evasively. "But look, you yourself say that the tsar . . ."

"After the Pruth the tsar became a different man," interrupted Divier, snapping his fingers in vexation, "given to looking over his shoulder, paranoid. But to be frank I like that: you won't achieve great things in innocence of mind and with helpers like his. You must keep a constant eye on things, believe me!"

"Why after the Pruth in particular?" asked Shafirov in a subdued voice and looked at Divier with a sharp eye.

"He grew up," said Divier with a scarcely perceptible grin. "Matured. Found a new truth . . . But it should not be of any concern to you and me."

"You don't think so?" Shafirov sounded him out warily.

"I'm certain," said Divier firmly, "provided only that we render conscientious service for the money that the tsar pays us. We must do as we are told. And chatter as little as possible about our new homeland—it makes no difference, no one believes us. We remain for everyone what we have always been: Yids, outsiders. A homeland is not a spoon after all; there is no obligation to carry it about with one all over the world. Russia is the homeland for the Russians, Pyotr Pavlovich. And a Russian thinks for himself; the higher he stands, the stronger is his desire to change direction in his own way, even by an inch, but in his own way. And to do so in such a way that he definitely feels warmer as a result. Would that we were only talking about money—but in fact, you know, it's about the system of government, about the order! . . . Yet for us it's a different matter; we are hirelings, birds of passage, not to say fly-by-nights. His

Highness Prince Aleksandr Danilych Menshikov, my brother-in-law, is a fly-by-night of a much purer kind than you and I put together, but he is *one of their own*: he may, we may not. The tsar trusts us as long as we do not go poking into high politics of our own accord. It's our job, Pyotr Pavlovich, not to push ourselves forward!"

Throwing back the tapestry door curtain, Lacosta strode into the basement. He was followed by Borokh Leybov, holding up the skirts of his black festival cloak and bending his head, on which he was wearing a pointed black hat. Borokh had a small canvas bag in his hand. After he had looked exactingly over the basement setting and shaken his head more in censure than enthusiasm, he made for his host.

"Peace be unto you and your house, Reb Shapir!" he said loudly.

Shafirov made a wry face as if struck by a sudden pang of toothache. "Reb Shapir" to Baron Shafirov, the vice-chancellor of Russia, the privy councillor running the Ambassadorial Department, a Knight of the Orders of the Polish White Eagle and Prussian Magnanimity—this was too much even for a Passover seder! Yet Borokh Leybov was not in the least discomfited by the pained reaction of his host; on the contrary, it even amused him: he half-closed his eyes and smiled with a contented and imposing air.

"Take your seats at table, gentlemen!" exclaimed Shafirov, wishing to smooth over the awkwardness. "Otherwise we shall probably miss the great Exodus from Egypt." Pulling out of his pocket a gold watch about the size of a snuffbox, he flicked open the lid, on which his baronial arms were inlaid in diamonds and rubies. "Five to nine . . . And that is for the prophet Elijah!" Shafirov pointed so that Borokh Leybov should not mix things up and sit in the velvet chair.

The guests took their seats; only Borokh remained standing behind his chair. Shafirov looked at him with some apprehension.

"Well then . . . ," said Borokh, with a stern look. "You'll have to remove your little wigs."

Lacosta and Divier obediently pulled off their wigs, but Shafirov dawdled as if it had been suggested that he should take off his trousers.

"Wigs are worn by our married Jewish women," Borokh Leybov explained to his host in exasperation, as to a child who is slow on the uptake. "Jewish men wear skullcaps." He thrust his hand deep into his canvas bag and drew out of it three black silk skullcaps.

With an imperceptible sigh Shafirov took off his wig and pulled the yarmulke onto his balding dome-like head. Borokh followed his movements attentively. Under the restless, piercing gaze of his guest, almost nothing remained in Shafirov of the vice-chancellor and knight of those orders; he suddenly became like an elderly, not wholly healthy Jew—a shopkeeper or innkeeper. He felt no antipathy to Borokh Leybov, only bewilderment half mixed with fear, as if facing an uncontrollable person wildly excited by something, who was about to do goodness knows what: let out a yell or pounce.

But Borokh was now praying aloud rapidly, swaying the upper part of his body back and forth jerkily.

When he had finished praying, he finally sat down and, surveying the rich table, asked, "Is the food kosher?"

"There is no suckling-pig today," Shafirov hastened to inform him. "But you know yourself, I can't give a complete guarantee . . ."

Divier, glancing to and fro between Borokh and Shafirov, smiled without parting his lips. He was not at all afraid of the exacting guest. Lacosta, on the other hand, was serious and slightly despondent.

"Is there any leaven in the house?" Borokh interrupted impatiently. "Leavened bread? Beer?"

"Yes, there is," said Shafirov and, with a sigh, shrugged his shoulders apologetically.

"And you call yourselves Jews!" said Borokh Leybov reproachfully. "*Reboine Shel Oilem*,[11] Reb Shapir . . . Well then!" He resolutely pushed the place setting away from him, turned up the tablecloth and, once again thrusting his hands deep into the canvas bag, extracted from it his food: balls of gefilte-fish, a piece of meat, horseradish in a jar, salt, apple butter,[12] a square one-liter bottle, and a small pile of matzoth. After he had spread all this out in front of him on the bare polished tabletop, he looked defiantly askance at the host.

"We have matzah," declared Shafirov, abashed, looking at Borokh Leybov's meagre provisions. "Wonderful matzah . . . Look!" He pointed to a silver dish covered with a white silk cloth on which the Star of David and lions were embroidered in gold.

"You eat your wonderful matzah, and I'll eat my wonderful matzah," said Borokh Leybov stubbornly. "A Jew should eat matzah at Pesah even if it isn't kosher. It's better than nothing." Stretching out his hand, he flicked the edge of the silver dish with his nail and lent an attentive ear of encouragement to the

---

11 *Reboine Shel Oilem* (Heb.) = Lord of the Universe, here used as an exclamation of disapproval.
12 This is in fact *horosis*, a traditional component of a Passover seder meal.

long dulcet ringing. "Pure silver. Good stuff. Its place is in a synagogue or on the table of a tzaddik."

Shafirov grew uncomfortable. "There now, I feel awkward," he thought agitatedly. "Who could ever have imagined it: some nutcase, a fanatic, has put me to the blush. Very likely my grandfather Shafir was the same sort of person, and he was also from near Smolensk[13] . . . I shall have to donate that dish to the synagogue, incognito of course."

Divier had grown bored with Borokh Leybov. Leaning back on his chair and half-closing his eyes, he began quietly singing the Passover song about a white goat:

> Ehat gadya, ehat gadya,
> Ehat gadya![14]

"Stop!" shouted Borokh, waving his arms. "Don't you know the order?! I'll say when to sing." Shafirov and Lacosta looked reproachfully at Divier who, irritatedly surprised at himself, fell silent in the middle of his sentence and, not knowing what action to take, fixed his eyes on the bottle that Borokh had brought.

"It's kosher vodka for Passover," said Borokh Leybov, lifting the square bottle with both hands, "we'll all drink it. At Pesah a Jew must drink kosher vodka. The question arises: where will kosher vodka come from at Reb Shapir's house? It is said: if leaven is not cleared out of a house before Pesah, give that house a wide berth . . . Well now: you are bad Jews, but you are Jews all the same. A bad Jew is better than a good goy. And I have come to do a mitzvah and participate in the seder with you."

Shafirov began to breathe heavily, bending forward low with his elbows on the table. Certain that it was he who had done the mitzvah by inviting a poor Jew from Zveryatichi to the Passover seder, Shafirov was not about to part with this pleasing certainty of his.

"Now all of you repeat together after me," went on Borokh Leybov, "and then, when I say, each of you repeat separately . . ." He took a well-worn book from his canvas bag, opened it and, almost without looking at the text, began:

---

13 Smolensk—provincial capital in the west of the Russian Federation, about 225 miles west southwest of Moscow and bordering with Belarus. First mentioned in the chronicle in 863 CE, Smolensk became the capital of Smolensk Province of the Russian Empire in 1708.

14 Traditional song about "the only kid" sung in Aramaic at the Passover seder.

"Well then. We were slaves in the land of Egypt and the Lord our God brought us out from there with a strong hand."

He read for a long time, and in the course of reading he took onto his tongue now a pinch of salt, now a sliver of horseradish, now a drop of apple butter. When he had finished reading, he moved the book aside and said:

"Now we can drink a mouthful each."

The kosher vodka proved to be very strong and this imbued the hungry Divier with pleasant expectations. Shafirov also brightened up after his drink, grunted with relish, and reached for a bite to eat with it, but Borokh Leybov leaned across the table and slapped his hand.

"It's not time for eating yet!" said Borokh, pulling a face as if he had tasted something bitter. "Be patient! A Jew must be patient, and then he will know that he is a real Jew."

"Yes, we must be patient," echoed Lacosta and adjusted the yarmulke which had slipped to one side on his head. "There's nothing else for it . . ."

"Those rebelling against patience are like unto sheep and goats," said Borokh in support of Lacosta and, lifting up his hands in his habitual way, he put them against his head like horns. "Rebellion is permitted only against the persecutors of our faith, and that is a mitzvah."

"And you are rebelling?" asked Divier inquisitively.

"And I am rebelling, with God's help," confirmed Borokh Leybov, casting an unfriendly glance at Divier. "I'm going to open a heder to God's glory among us in Zveryatichi, and Jews," at this point he shifted his searching gaze to Shafirov, "all Jews must help me!"

"Well of course, of course!' with great relief exclaimed Shafirov, who had at last received the expected request from his austere guest and immediately felt more confident. "We will help you with money—anonymously, of course—and you open a heder there in your village near Smolensk."

Borokh Leybov did not show any increase in warmth, however; his voice sounded as dry as before:

"It is said: a nameless donor is more pleasing to God than a named one . . . Well then: repeat after me, Reb Shapir: And the Lord our God sent down a murrain upon the Egyptians, the children of Pharaoh . . ."

The distinct sound of approaching footsteps could be heard in the corridor leading to the basement.

"Who is that?" asked Divier quickly.

"The prophet Elijah," joked Shafirov uneasily, turning his head.

The tapestry door curtain flew open with a crash. On the threshold, rubbing his forehead, which had bumped against the low lintel, stood Pyotr. From beneath his fist he surveyed the men who had jumped up from the table one after the other in horror. He grinned contentedly at the confusion he had caused. Then, stepping heavily over the carpets, he crossed to the pale-blue velvet chair, sank deep into it, and comfortably spread out his long legs.

Shafirov, with his mouth open but unable to speak, stared at the tsar in the chair. Divier was biting his thin lips, the muscles of his cheekbones bobbing under his skin as he did so. Lacosta and Borokh Leybov, looking in different directions, were whispering prayers.

"What's this, you're enjoying yourselves here celebrating your Yids' *Pashka*, and you forgot to invite me!" said Pyotr in mock reproach. "But I'm very curious to have a look at your Passover, and it's actually useful for general knowledge . . . Come now, pour me some of that, baron!" With finger extended, Pyotr pointed to the square bottle.

Shafirov poured off some of the kosher vodka into a silver goblet with an unsteady hand and passed it to the tsar. Pyotr breathed out, crossed himself, and tipped back the vodka into his mouth in a single long draught.

"It's good!" complimented Pyotr, after clearing his throat with a snort, and then his eyes searched across the table, and he seized the piece of meat that was lying in front of Borokh on a bit of cloth, sank his teeth into it, and began to chew. "But why have you stopped? Carry on!"

Slowly, with an effort, Borokh Leybov bent over his bag, fished out of it a black yarmulke, and held this out in silence to the tsar. Shafirov turned pale; suddenly he couldn't breathe. Continuing to chew, Pyotr turned the headgear over in his hands with interest, looked inside it, and, discovering nothing there but grease and dandruff, put it on his head.

"Well then," said Borokh Leybov, after glancing warily at the tsar, "anyone who wishes can repeat after me: And the Lord our God sent a murrain upon the Egyptians, the children of Pharaoh . . ."

More than ever Shafirov did not want Borokh Leybov to call him Reb Shapir now.

1981–82

Translated from the Russian by Brian Cooper

MICHAEL KREPS

Michael (Mikhail) **Kreps** (1940–1994), poet, critic, and essayist, was born in Leningrad (St. Petersburg), to a Jewish family. After high school, he worked at a factory, then served for three years in the military. Kreps graduated from the Philology Faculty of Leningrad State University, where he subsequently received a candidate's advanced degree. Kreps taught at the Leningrad State Pedagogical Institute in 1967–73.

In 1974, Kreps, his wife, Marina, and their son immigrated to the United States. In 1974–77, Kreps taught Russian at the Defense Language Institute in Monterey, California, and he subsequently pursued doctoral studies at the University of California–Berkeley. In 1981, Kreps moved to Boston and became a professor of Russian and Polish language and literature at Boston College. For many years Kreps also taught at the Summer Russian School at Middlebury College. He died of cancer on 8 December 1994. In 1997, The Michael B. Kreps Memorial Readings (*Krepsovskie chteniia*) were inaugurated at Boston College to feature Russian émigré writers.

Writing poetry since college, Kreps started publishing in the West. His first poem appeared in *The New Review* (*Novyi zhurnal*) in 1976, and he contributed there as well as to *Continent* (*Kontinent*), *Time and We* (*Vremia i my*), *Encounters* (*Vstrechi*), and other émigré periodicals and collectives. His first collection, *Interview with the Bird Phoenix*, appeared in 1986 in New York, its poems composed in free verse. His next collection, *Budd of the Head* (Philadelphia, 1987) included *vers libres* written in 1985–87 and stemming from *Interview with the Bird Phoenix*, as well as Kreps's early poems (1963–73) and works of the first émigré years, written under the influence of **Joseph Brodsky**. Kreps's poems not in free verse display sophisticated rhyming and wordplay, in places too deliberate and distracting. One of his achievements was the witty and formally virtuosic long poem *Princess-Frog*, published in 1990 in *The New Review*.

Kreps began to publish in Moscow and St. Petersburg literary journals in the early 1990s. He visited Russia twice and gathered large audiences. In his lifetime, the long poem *The Russian Pygmalion* appeared as a chapbook in St. Petersburg (1992), followed by the book *Flies and Their Intelligence* (1993). In 1995, a group of Kreps's friends in Boston published *Cosmos, Petersburg, Shoulder*, a retrospective volume with an introduction by **Alexander Kushner**.

It included a number of poems from the 1990s, in which Kreps revisited postromantic Russian verse and tipped his hat to **Osip Mandelstam** and Nikolay Zabolotsky.

Kreps is known for three monographs: *Pasternak and Bulgakov as Novelists* (1984); *On Brodsky's Poetry* (1984), which was the first book about **Joseph Brodsky**; and *Zoshchenko's Technique of the Comical* (1986). Kreps approached the subjects of his research as both a critic and an artist—as a scholar-poet. This is why such aphoristic formulations as "Parrotry and Nightingaleship" (a chapter in his **Brodsky** book) have their antecedents in Kreps's poetry. The distinction between poets-imitators (parrots) and poets with original voices (nightingales) goes back to the poem "Thus Talk Parrots," based on a word-play with names of famous Russian authors: "From the age of twenty-five/A person begins to turn into a parrot/Repeating thoughts, habits, words of others [. . .]./They usually talk this way: /Pushkin, Peshkov!/Peshkin, Pushkov!/ Mandelstam, Pasternak!/Pasterstam, Mandelnak!/Fool! Fool!"

Reading Kreps's palindromes in Russian is a literary fête; translating them seems next to impossible. The palindromes were Kreps's crowning achievement, and his collection *Mukhi i ikh um* (*Flies and Their Intelligence*) has few equivalents in terms of the complexity of the palindromes' design and the subtle elegance and grace of their versification. The editor of this anthology remembers stopping by Kreps's summer apartment in Middlebury, Vermont, to find him engrossed in composition, jotting down lists of words and clusters of sounds. Like his predecessor, the futurist genius Velimir Khlebnikov, Kreps the master of palindromes was fascinated by the notions of the reversibility, recurrence, and comprehensibility of time. Why palindromes? Did Kreps's sec-ularized Judaic self manifest itself through these poems that can also be read from right to left like Hebrew verse?

* * *

Jewishness was by no means a central concern for Kreps the poet, although in several free-verse poems in *Interview with the Bird Phoenix* (1986) the subjects of antisemitism and Jewish assimilation take center stage, as do stories of the Jewish Bible.

Michael B. Kreps admired the émigré Orpheus **Vladislav Khodasevich** for his stoicism, his critique of philistinism, and the anatomical precision of his descriptions. There is a fatidic parallelism in the lives of Kreps and Khodasevich, who died of cancer in 1939 at the age of fifty-three. "Only a genius could have come up with this," Kreps once told the editor of this anthology, quoting a short 1922 poem: "Happy is the one who falls head down: /If only for a moment, the world looks different to him."

CHILDHOOD

In a grey hat resembling a pregnant cat,
In a ginger fake fur coat, threadbare and thin,
I remember you, mama.

At the time women still wore muffs.
(No one remembers this now.)
In Ramenskoe there was no power at night,
And you would switch on your little flashlight—
Snugly wrapped in your muff—
Run by two batteries,
A present from father on your anniversary.

At the time you were almost twenty-five, mama.
In thirty years you would die of lung cancer,
And now you're only twenty-five
Or twenty-six.

There you are, on your way home,
Tired after work,
In one hand—a purse, in the other—a grocery bag.
In the bag, besides bread, are treats for me:
Sometimes a chocolate bunny, sometimes fruit wafers.

All day I run around,
Amuse myself with a piece of iron rod, my makeshift hockey stick.
(No one remembers this today.)
Or I tease Dingo, the orphanage dog,
Or munch on oil cakes—a treat from Aunt Frosya,
Or pull a silver ribbon
From an old abandoned condenser—
It flutters splendidly in the wind,
And with it you can make birds and frogs.

In this unusually warm November,
There's isn't any snow to make snow balls
Or to ski on—too early for ice skates.

I'm a small Russian boy.
In two years I'll become a Jew.
In twenty-seven—an American.
And now I'm only five
Or six.

Tired after running around with other boys,
I come back home in the evening, to the warmth.
(Aunt Frosya has already fired up the stove.)
I make paper cut-outs with scissors,
Play with the cat, listen to the radio, look out the window.
And when a little light begins to flicker in the darkness,
I'm happy: here comes mama.

1980s

THE CAT WITH A YELLOW STAR

Someone has tied to the tail of a cat
A tin can.
The cat runs,
The can rings,
The boys laugh.

Passersby take notice—
Some approve, some disapprove.
The cat runs,
The can rings,
The boys laugh.

The cat with the can resembles a man
With a yellow star on the front pocket of his shirt.
The man ran, the star smoldered,
The passersby took notice and pointed fingers—
Some approved, some disapproved,
The boys laughed.

Where does this strange comparison come from?
The man with the star looks nothing like a cat.
Can you force a cat
To tie a can
To his own tail?

The cat runs,
The can rings,
The boys laugh.

1980s

CALL OF THE ANCESTORS

Within me live all of my numerous ancestors:
Grandfather—a watchmaker (on my mother's side),
Who received a permit to live in St. Petersburg,
And grandfather—a doctor (on my father's side),
Who was educated in Paris and Vienna,
Great-grandfather—a merchant, owner of steamships in the Crimea,
And great-grandfather—a rabbi, owner of hearts in a Belorussian schtetl,
Great-great-grandfather—a judge, a Pole of Mosaic confession,
And great-great-grandfather—a Marrano, importer of oranges from Andalucía.

Within me live all of my numerous ancestors:
>   Doctors and artisans,
>   Actors and jewelers,
>   Philosophers and traders,
>   Interpreters and money changers,
>   Sephardim and Ashkenazim,
>   Rote memorizers and Talmudists,[15]
>   Shepherds and farmers,
>   Bookworms and Pharisees,
>   The first Jews and the first Christians.

---

15 Kreps ironically is making strange and reversing the word order of the Russian, *talmudisty i
nachetchiki* (literally, "Talmudists and rote memorizers"), an expression that Stalin had orig-
inally used in the context of Marxist theory ("Talmudic [interpreters] and rote memorizers
of Marxist thought"); during the anticosmopolitan campaign, that expression acquired a
coded, distinctly anti-Jewish flavor.

They reach out their bony hands
From deep inside my body.
Locked in this prison, they flash at me
Their bitter almond-shaped eyes.

Give us the gift of speech!
Raise us from the dead!
Why are you silent?

If I tell them,
Why I am silent,
They won't believe me.

1980s

Translated from the Russian by Emelye Crehore

PHILIP ISAAC BERMAN

Philip Isaac Berman (b. 1936), fiction writer, essayist, and playwright, was born in Moscow to a Jewish family. Berman's mother was a homemaker; his father held a variety of managerial jobs. Berman and his mother and sister spent the war evacuated to Kazakhstan while his father fought at the front. In the morning before work, Berman's father prayed at the Moscow Choral Synagogue. In stark contrast to the vast majority of Jewish-Russian writers of his generation who grew up in large cities outside the former Pale, the ex-Muscovite Berman understands and speaks Yiddish and naturally infuses his prose with Yiddish words and expressions.

In 1959, Berman graduated from the Moscow Institute of Railroad Transport Engineers. He subsequently worked as an engineer at a Moscow factory. In 1972, Berman, already working as a researcher, defended a candidate's advanced degree in solid-body mechanics and thereafter headed a laboratory at one of Moscow's research institutes.

Berman started writing fiction in 1959. His first short stories appeared in the early 1960s in small Moscow newspapers. In the 1960s and 1970s, Berman's stories and essays occasionally appeared in newspapers and magazines, including *Moscow Truth (Moskovskaia pravda)*, *Youth (Iunost')*, and *Man and Nature (Chelovek i priroda)*. His Jewish name stood in the way of more publications; despite editors' overtures to adopt a Russian pen name, Berman refused to do it. In the 1970s, Berman was a member of literary seminars at the Union of Soviet Writers led by Sergey Antonov (1915–1995) and **Yury Trifonov**. Both writers thought highly of Berman's prose, and Antonov compared Berman's treatment of humanity to that of Andrey Platonov (see **Aleksandr Mezhirov**'s *Blizzard*). In 1978, the central newspaper *Literary Russia (Literaturnaia Rossiia)* printed Berman's story "White Fuzz" (1975) with a flattering preface by Yury Nagibin (1920–1994), another powerful figure in the Soviet literary pantheon. Despite endorsements by leading prose writers, all of Berman's efforts to publish a book of fiction came to naught, bringing him to the Moscow literary underground, where his work was disseminated.

In the summer of 1980, Berman and six other Moscow writers, Evgeny Kharitonov, Nikolay Klimontovich, Evgeny Kozlovsky, Vladimir Kormer, Evgeny Popov, and Dmitry Prigov, founded the literary group Catalogue (*Katalog*). On 18 November 1980, they notified the Moscow city government and the Central Committee of the Communist Party of the creation of "an independent club of writers in Russia" and asked to be allowed to publish a collective volume. The same day, in the evening, four members of Catalogue, Berman among them, were detained, and a copy of their collective was confiscated. The group's members faced further repressions.

Philip Berman immigrated to the United States in 1981, and a year later he edited the volume *Catalogue* for publication in Russian by Ardis, then the leading publisher of Russian books in America. Settling in Philadelphia, Berman worked as a mechanical and structural engineer for a number of American companies and continued to write prolifically. Composed in the late 1970s and first published in *Time and We* (*Vremia i my*) in 1981, Berman's short novel *Registrar* appeared as a separate book in 1984. Some critics believe *Registrar* to be Berman's best work, and the experience of reading this metaphysical narrative may be likened to watching Andrey Tarkovsky's remarkable film *Mirror* (1975). In the West, Berman's fiction and philosophical creative prose have been featured in a number of periodicals, including *Continent* (*Kontinent*) and *Third Wave* (*Tret'ia volna*). From its founding in 1991, Berman has been a regular contributor to Philadelphia's Russian literary annual *The Coast* (*Poberezh'e*), where several of his best Jewish stories and a play have appeared. Less successful, from a literary standpoint, are Berman's political-philosophical allegories (e.g., "Courtyard of the Empire").

Now retired from his duties as an engineer, Berman lives outside Philadelphia and in Florida, devoting himself full-time to writing. His literary return to Russia has been slower as compared to other Third-Wave writers. Since 2016, he has been contributing blogs to the popular Russian site Snob. ru. In 2014, a retrospective volume of Berman's prose, titled *The Celestial-Wooden Road*, came out in Philadelphia.

* * *

Jewish questions are also central to *Registrar*, Berman's play *Overpass above the Ravine* (ca. 1973; published 1996), and many of his short stories ("Aza Diamant," "We're All Big Fools," "Hung above Herb Roots," and others). The problematic of a dual, Jewish-Russian identity consumes Berman's literary imagination. Written in emigration, Berman's short story "Sarah and the Rooster" (1988; published 1991) belongs among the best works of postwar Jewish-Russian fiction, and its author's achievement deserves wider recognition by non-Russian readers. Set in late Stalinist Russia in 1953—at a critical point in the history of

Soviet Jews (see John D. Klier's "Outline of Jewish-Russian History"), "Sarah and the Rooster" masterfully captures the public intimacy of a Moscow communal apartment where Jews and Russians (re)enact the battles of modern history—and eternal battles of humankind.

SARAH AND THE ROOSTER*

I'd like to tell you my story. You know what means Russia?

First there were Jewish pogroms, then revolution, then again pogroms, then again revolution. Then again Jewish pogroms. Then there were the Reds, then there were the Whites, then there were the Greens. Who knows how many others. And who's to blame? You already know the answer. The Jews.

So you know already you're that kind of people, so don't get in the way. We are always to blame. We should know that and mind our own business. That's our fate. You don't want it to get better, *so lig in drerd*, you know, lie in the ground.[16]

One of my brothers, Israel, Izya they called him, he was a handsome guy. You should have seen him, and what an excellent tailor he was. When he made a coat, you could kiss each of his fingers, it fit so well. You know how some women are. They would come in just to look at him, to have him touch them somewhere. When a revolution happened in Russia, the Whites threw him in jail. The Bolsheviks got him out of jail. This is how Izya became a Red.

My other brother, Yesif, a real nut, ran away from home when he was fourteen. He was tall and handsome, too. Wherever he is, may he rest in peace. I hope what I say does him no harm.

In Odessa he became a *balagoleh*.[17] He could carry a piano on his back to the fourth floor.

And who do you think it worried most? Mama.

When one son becomes a Red and the other a bum, mama has what to worry about.

My father was a *huhim*, a brilliant man. He said, Esther, that's life, Esther, life is a hurricane, Esther. My father had a beard this long; you should've seen him walk. And my mother! She had blue, blue eyes and long braids, down to here. We were very poor, of course, but not like my husband Abram's father. We

---

*   The text has been abridged and modified by the author for this anthology. Some of the notes are based on the author's explanations in the Russian text.

16   *Lig in drerd* (Yiddish) = (literally) lie in a grave; means "get lost."

17   *Balagoleh* (Yiddish) = a coachman/mover; see Naum Korzhavin's poems.

had one cow. But we always had a sack of sugar and a sack of flour in the house. That we always had. And we were never without meat, like under the Soviets. Of course we didn't have TV, but no food? Never. Nobody knew from standing and pushing in lines. Nobody grabbed stuff from your hands. *Abi gezunt,* which means, just be healthy and the rest will work itself out.[18]

Then came Stalin, the criminal of all nations, and said that we Jews had poisoned all the Soviet leaders! That the Jewish doctors had poisoned all the big shots, the *balebosim*! That was the famous Doctors' Plot.[19] And so when I opened the newspaper, it became dark in front of my eyes: I read famous Jewish doctors: Vovsi, Kogan, Feldman, all our Jews there. So I ask you, how can I look anybody in the eyes? If we can do this, poison people, then we were not beaten enough, not called "dirty Jews" enough, may the earth not carry us! Because we have the commandment: Thou shallt not kill! *Oy Gotenu!*[20] I say to myself, what for did you send it to us! What did we do to deserve this, who would do this against you? Who? My father, my grandfather? Who? No, they couldn't have done this. So who then? Not my father, not my grandfather, not my mother. What did we know? Pogroms. They were honest Jews, worked hard all their lives, raised their children, dreamed of a better life for their children, and prayed to God that their children and grandchildren should have it a little easier. No, impossible, I said to myself. That Jews should do this, no way! This is the Beilis trial all over again.[21] We've had this before. It's not the first time. We just have to wait and see, whatever God has in store for us. We just have to wait and see.

When Marusya brought me the morning paper, she said, look what you Jews did. I said: Marusya, you know me, you know Abram, we have shared everything with you, always. Then she broke down and wept: I don't understand a thing. I've lived with Jews all my life, I've never heard anything like it. She went back to her room. You should've seen what followed! In the morning

---

18 *Abi gezunt* (Yiddish) = just to be healthy.

19 The so-called Doctors' Plot of 1953, in which a group of predominantly Jewish physicians was falsely accused of poisoning Soviet leaders. It is believed, although documentary evidence has not proven it, that Stalin's plan was to arouse the population's wrath against the Jews and to use a threat of pogroms as a pretext for massive deportations of the Jews to Kazakhstan and Siberia.

20 *Oy Gotenu* (Yiddish) = God (vocative).

21 Beilis trial—famous antisemitic trial of 1913; a Jewish man named Mendel Beilis was falsely accused of a ritual murder of a Christian child (the so-called "blood libel"); Beilis was found not guilty.

it began with the Jews and in the evening it ended with the Jews. You'd think that if it weren't for the Jews, there would be meat in the stores. If there were no Jews in Russia, the Soviet power would give the Russians a good life!

I couldn't go to the kitchen to make dinner. We shared one apartment with two other neighbors. And we had a common kitchen. This is how most people lived in Moscow. One of our neighbors was Marusya. Whenever her son Tolya got sick, I'd be there to help, when my kid got sick, she'd do the same. Whenever I cooked something nice, Abram would say: Did you give Marusya a taste? So when she said look what you Jews did, it hurt. After all, she's not Jewish, and when it hurts you, it hurts only you. For her it is somebody else's pain. And what about us? We are the same way. When it is your own pain it feels deep inside, when it is your own! No matter what! Marusya did a lot of good for us. When Abram went to fight the Germans in 1941, I was left alone with two kids on my hands. I don't know what I would have done without Marusya. The Germans bombed the city, to get some food was impossible, there was no food! There was panic in Moscow on October 16 in 1941, the Germans were very close, maybe twenty miles from the downtown! Marusya got us a horse and a wagon. We left in a freight train for Kazakhstan. Marusya stayed in our room and paid the rent. You know what a room in Moscow means? Now one has to pay thousands and thousands to get one in the city. So when we returned in 1943 we had a place to live in. I had left her as much money as I could. What was money then? Nothing, *gornit*! A *shtikel* paper![22] In the cupboard I had left a jar of strawberry jam. She did not eat it, she thought that the war would end soon, we would return, and then we would eat it. She said to me: You better run away from here, what we Russians can take, you won't. Take your kids and save yourselves.

When I returned, I see, there is the jar of strawberry jam on the shelf. It was all dried up, just sugar, but still good. I said, Marusya why didn't you eat it? And then she told me why. I kissed her and cried. We both cried. We cried, happy that God got us through the war, that Abram had come back alive. Her husband also came back alive, but he didn't come back to Marusya. He returned to his new girlfriend.

I said, that's okay, when the war's over, we'll make two pails of jam, one for her and one for me. We'll make a big party. That was Marusya.

---

22 A *shtikel* paper (Yiddish) = a bit of paper.

The other neighbor was a *banditka*![23] When all that stuff about the Jews was printed in the newspaper, she said: Now all you Jews will get your throats cut! So that you don't go around poisoning our leaders. Thank God, Stalin is still alive. He'll show you what's what! And all the Jews who're still alive, whose throats haven't yet been cut, she said, will be sent to Siberia to saw down the forest trees. That's so you Jews can kill one another there. Because you Jews know nothing about cutting down trees! And when the trees fall, they will all fall down on you. You'll all be killed because you don't know nothing about work. That's the kind of death she thought up for us.

She said: Why doesn't your Jewish God save you? Where's your God? Why doesn't he save you?! Hitler didn't strangle all of you. We'll finish you off. Where's your God to save you! Now you won't be cooking your chicken soup in our kitchen any more. You Jews have got too much freedom! Some of you cook your Jewish chicken soup, the others fry chicken! Now you won't fry your chicken in our Russian frost!

I said, you *banditka*, you lousy bitch! You slut! Go ahead, eat us up, eat and choke on our bones. When you swallow us you'll choke on our bones, you and your *banditen*! I said, our bones will rip your stomachs open. You'll drown in your own blood, you bitch! You better *lig in drerd, banditka*! You better think about God, he sees everything, he sees everything what you are doing!

She yelled: Why didn't your God save you? Why doesn't he save you? Where is your Jewish God? Where is your God? Where is your Jewish God? Why doesn't he save you, your kikish God? Because there isn't any! Where is he? Where is he, your Jewish God? Where is he? Show him to me, *Sarochka*, show him to me, *Sarochka*, your Jewish God![24] Show him, *Sarochka*, the Jewish God! There she stood, shouting her head off, screaming like a nut. And every minute she was yelling, *Sarochka, Sarochka*!

I said, I'll show you *banditka* how to scream *Sarochka*! I will show you our Jewish God, the Almighty God. When she began to scream like crazy: *Sarochka, Sarochka*, I didn't know what to do.

Than I grabbed my heavy cast iron pan. My *kugel* was in it, it was cooling off for when Abram would get home from work.[25] I grabbed that pot and hit the bitch over the head. I said, That's for *Sarochka*. That's for Hitler didn't

---

23 *Banditka* (Rus., used in Yiddish) = lit., a female bandit; a crude, dangerous, amoral woman.

24 *Sarochka* (Rus.) = diminutive of Sara; used in Russia as a derogatory name for a Jewish woman.

25 *Kugel* (Yiddish)—a traditional Jewish dish of baked noodles with different ingredients.

finish you off. That's for our Jewish God. Eat us Jews and eat our Jewish *kugel*. Here are our bones, I said, you bitch, you lousy slut! You bitch, I said, you sleep around with a bunch of Armenians from the grocery store, you stinker you! I said, take this, eat it. Eat my cast iron pot over your ugly face! You will now finish us off and swallow our bones. But remember that you'll choke on them, you slut. This is how I gave her a bang over the head. And so she collapsed. I see on the floor lies the *banditka*. I see pieces of my *kugel* all around her. I didn't know what to do. The *banditka* was lying there, quiet, not a word. I didn't know whether I killed her or she was alive.

Marusya came running in. She said, you handled her just right. She'll remember this for the rest of her life. Lousy whore. Marusya didn't give it another thought, dead or not dead. The bitch got what she deserves. She picks on people because nobody hit her over the head lately.

I thought: God whatever there's in store for me, let it be, but don't abandon me. Help me, God. Help me. Scare me, God; only don't punish me. *Shreck mir, Gotenu,* but don't punish me.[26] In my whole life, I never hurt anyone.

Can you imagine what state I was in, to pick up a heavy pot and bang this tramp over the head? I don't know what had to happen to make me want to kill her! What a *banditka* she must be to make me pick up a pot and bang her over the head! What kind of a life it has to be for a Jew to be able to kill another human being!

At that moment the *banditka*, thank God, jumped up and opened her mouth and let out a scream, the likes of which I'd never heard before. Jews killed me! she screamed. Jews killed me! Jews poisoned me! I was poisoned by the Jews, hey people! She started with such a voice, she could've sung at the Bolshoy Opera! She screamed so loud that the walls shook. I bent down to pick up my heavy pot again, just in case. If she attacks, I want to defend myself. I said, thank you, *Gotenu,* that I didn't kill the louse.

You can imagine her screaming if I had really killed her, let the bitch be alive and well. And so I stood there, pot in hand, thanking God that I didn't kill her. Thank you God, thank you God, thank you, dear God! If it's her fate to be killed, let it not be at my hands. Because we were not brought up to kill anyone. We were not raised to knock someone over the head with a cast iron pot. We were not raised to poison anyone. Even if there are such criminals around who deserve to be poisoned.

---

26 *Shrek mir, Gotenu* (Yiddish) = scare me, God.

I stood there praying to God. I was so happy that I hadn't killed her. My hands were trembling. I was still holding the cast iron pot just in case. The *banditka* didn't attack me. Instead, she backed away to my kerosene stove screaming at the top of her opera voice. She just stood there and screamed: The Jews killed me! The Jews killed me! The Jews killed me! She takes another deep breath and screams near the kerosene stove all over again: The Jews killed me! The Jews killed me! Dear Comrade Stalin, she screams. Dear general secretary of the Communist Party of the U S-S-R! The Jews killed me. The Jews knocked me over the head. Dear Comrade Stalin! The Jews knocked me over the head, Comrade Stalin, protect us from the Jews! She went crazy, I thought. My hands trembled. There she was, standing near the kerosene stove screaming.

I thought: What if, God forbid, she turns over my pot of chicken soup and scalds her legs. Then I'll have *tsores*, real trouble.[27]

Marusya guessed my thoughts. She said, you better stop acting, don't put on a show here! You better move your ass away from that stove. She said to the *banditka*: you better get away from Pearl Fridelevna's kerosene stove. Get your ass away otherwise you are going to scald your sweet tail; the Armenians will stop coming to you.

Then the *banditka* turns to Marusya. *Banditka* says, Jealous the Armenians like me, huh! Jealous that the Armenians come to me and not to you! They come to me and not to you, so you're jealous! Now the bitch forgot that the Jews killed her. She forgot about Comrade Stalin too. She said to Marusya: See, you're young, but nobody wants you, nobody makes a pass at you. And to me they come and will keep coming, Armenians and Jews! Both! Because my tail is sweeter. I have what it takes. This is why they come to me! And you, you thief, you Jewish ass kisser! You'll never have anybody. You just sing with the Jews whatever they sing, you brown nose! So that you can get a fatter bone, the *banditka* said. What they don't need they throw to you! To give you some of their chicken soup so that you serve them better!

Marusya gave it to her: Look who's talking. You lousy whore! You lousy slut! I am just doing you a favor, I'm telling you to move your sweet tail away from the kerosene stove to preserve it for your Armenians and Jews and you're not listening! Why did you attack Pearl Fridelevna? Why do you attack people, slut? Because they are Jewish? She did the right thing to hit you over the head. Marusya said: It's too bad she didn't finish you off, lousy bitch. If I'd started

---

27 *Tsores* (Yiddish) = troubles.

beating you up I'd beat the living crap out of you! I'm not Pearl Fridelevna. I'm not Jewish. I would've put an end to you. She just felt sorry for you, you lousy slut! And listen what she felt sorry for! You should thank her, instead you stand there screaming and shouting over the whole street that Jews killed you, you lousy bitch! You fucking whore! If they had only killed you, you wouldn't be screaming around like crazy! Why do you pick on them? Marusya said. Why do you keep screaming, I'm Russian, you are Jews! So what? You may be Russian, but your soul is not Russian!

You say: Men come to me, but men don't go to you! If I only wanted to, there would be a line from Red Square to Nikitsky Gate to see me! They would be taking numbers and writing them down on their hands like in the bread lines during the war! Only I don't sleep around! I won't lay with everybody! Because my queen is not like a piece of junk! You can't pick it up in a garbage can! She is not available! Admission is not free, by a special pass only! Like to a military parade on Red Square!

My queen is visited only by special permission! My queen requires courting and hard work, she's not for everybody! Mine's not yours, we're in different categories! Yours is there for anyone: an Armenian, a Jew, or our own Ivan the fool! Mine's not from a grocery store! Not for public use, not for all who feel like having it. You give it to one, you give it to another. What a fucking giver! Like there ain't nobody else to give! Like we got only one of those Zoykas in all of Russia, one for everybody, the unequaled little bitch! Don't you worry. There are plenty of flat backs screwing around, better than you! So you say I steal! Did you hear that? Because I bring home some flour for the kids. And you don't? And when you come home from the store with bags full of groceries? That's not stealing? That's only screwing the bakery manager, that's not stealing. Me, said Marusya, I worked behind the wheel, delivering flour, fortyeight-hour shifts in the truck to feed the kids, I worked my ass off, two days and two nights in a row on that god-damned truck, while you, dirt bag, were screwing with Armenians and stuffing bags with food in the manager's storage!

Look at her, said Marusya! Hot cakes, hot cakes! Hot cakes, you yell, but it's all ice, permafrost! That's because you can't love no more, that's why. Sure, I would also rather be lying with a boyfriend like you than working and stealing. And instead I steal and bust my buns. A louse, that's what you are. Scum and a whore. And you won't admit it. That's what's driving you so crazy, because it's true!

The *banditka* was listening in order to know what to say back. For a moment I thought she was going to wack Marusya. She jumped away from my kerosene stove to grab something. That's when I yelled, stop right there, bitch! If you hurt her, I will give it to you. I'll beat or stab you, whatever I can! Nothing will stop me then. That's when you will really find out what *Sarochka* can do. I talk to her as if I'm calm, but all my guts are trembling! She looked at us and saw she was one against two. She kicked the door and ran outside. I wish I had her health; nothing gets her. She almost tore the door off the hinges. Just look at her. After I had hit her with a cast iron pot! She was down and out, but soon she was on her feet again! I couldn't have gotten up. But her, she lay a little, got up, and started screaming again. And then she almost tore the door off the hinges.

In the evening her husband, Kolya, came home from work. She danced around him but said nothing. She had taken a walk outside before he came. Now she came in and was silent like a grave.

Her Kolya was a quiet kind of guy. An electrician. He liked to drink. Why not? It comes with the territory.

So he came home and said to me: Hello, Pearl Fridelevna. And I said: Hello. He said hello so I said hello too. It doesn't cost me money to answer.

I don't know if he knew about the Armenians or not. Everybody used to visit her. She slept around with Russian guys, too. You think Jewish guys didn't come? You better believe it. She slept around with Jewish guys too. For sure. A little scrawny Jew used to come around. I told him: Why do you come to her? You're so skinny your trousers are almost falling off. The men who came most frequently were the Armenians. They lived next door to the grocery store near Nikitsky Gates on a side street. There's also a store there called Three Little Pigs.

That night we were fast asleep, everything was quiet, thank God. Enough living like on a volcano, I thought to myself. Soon we heard a knocking on the kitchen door. I said, Abram, maybe you'll go and open the door? And he said, like hell I will. Let the plague open the door! Our kids are home sleeping. Whoever it's for can go and open it. I should have known, when Abram sleeps, he sleeps. Cannon fire can't wake him up. When the Germans bombed Moscow, everyone ran to the shelters, not Abram. He went to bed. If, he said, it's my fate to die, I'll die, but not before. If my fate is not to die, I'll not die. No bomb will get me. He said, if God doesn't betray you no pig will eat you! He said, you can only die once. No one has ever managed to die twice, I won't either. He said, let the plague open the door. He turned over and went back to sleep.

I heard Kolya go to open the door. He opened the door and went out to talk to someone who knocked at the kitchen door. It was *banditka's* boyfriend. He got Kolya's shifts mixed up. He thought Kolya was on the night shift, she explained afterward. Kolya returned to his room quietly. I guess he didn't want to disturb us. Then I heard a loud thud like thunder, as if a wardrobe or a sofa had fallen. Zoyka the *banditka* ran out and began banging on our door, so loud that even Abram jumped.

She shouted: Let me in, Pearl Fridelevna, let me in. Kolya will kill me. He's got a knife. He's going to kill me!

You see, when Kolya went after her, she pushed the wardrobe on him. While he was crawling out from under it, she ran and began banging on our door, just as she was, in her nightgown. She's so hefty she can push a wardrobe onto her husband. What to do? Of course she's a whore, but when somebody is about to be killed and you can save her, how can you not save her? If I don't open the door, the neighbors on the street will say that we killed her.

When I told this to Abram, be said I was right. He said, open the door and let her *lig in drerd*, which means in Yiddish what you, of course, already know, let her lie in a coffin! Or let her lie in the grave! There isn't a big difference, grave or coffin. It's almost the same!

Abram said: Tell me, Pearl, who gave us this *melukhe*, this government, these neighbors, knives, prostitutes, knocking on doors for us to take them in?![28] Why does God punish us so?

I'd seen something earlier. Zoyka the whore made a barrel of homemade salt cabbage. She put it in our common kitchen near the door. A barrel with homemade salt cabbage. Kolya came home after work and sat in a barrel of homemade salt cabbage. I'll tell you how. He had returned from work. He was a little bit under the influence. He made a pass at Marusya. He tried to hug her. When he gets drunk, he goes after her. He said, my darling neighbor, I love you.

Marusya said to him, you have a lawful wife, go put your arms around her. She has a sweeter tail. Go to your lawful wife, she said, and started laughing. But Kolya embraced her again. He said, I love only you. Maybe her tail is sweeter, but I love only you. She's sweeter, but you're younger. I want younger not sweeter. I love just you. It doesn't matter what kind of tail she has.

Marusya said: See, he wants someone younger. But someone else wants someone older! Do you hear that, Pearl, she said to me, he wants me better than his own lawful wife.

---

28 *Melukhe* (Yiddish) = sarcastic expression for government, here for "Soviet power."

You have a lawful wife so go to her. And she gave him a slight push. And that's how he landed in the barrel of salt cabbage. The barrel was still half full. Kolya sat into it and he couldn't get out. He liked it that Marusya pushed him. He figured he'd go after her again when he got out of the barrel. He wanted to hug her again.

Marusya was a strong woman. She worked as a truck driver.

Her husband was also a truck driver, handsome, blond, broad shouldered, a real village peasant. Where he worked there was a young bitch, a secretary. You know how women are nowadays? They see a pair of trousers, they go after the trousers, and no pair of trousers can escape them. And you know how men are nowadays? They see a skirt, they go after the skirt. They're after every skirt they see. This is how her husband and the secretary got together, he went after her skirt and she went after his trousers. That's life for you. One person makes salt cabbage in a barrel, another is a bum and has nothing to himself, and a third is a scrawny Jew.

And Marusya, beautiful, young, but unhappy. She's all alone.

When Kolya drinks a little, he always goes to hug her. He used to bring her hard candy on a stick, the kind you suck on all day. They used to make lollypop suckers shaped like roosters, perched on a wooden stick. He bought her red roosters on a wooden stick. After the war they used to sell them in the street near movie theaters. He would bring Marusya a sucker on a stick. He would stand outside the door and say to her: I want you to have it, Marusya. I want you to taste it.

Zoyka the *banditka* saw Kolya with Marusya just as she was helping him out of the barrel. She saw them both joking and laughing. She went back to her room. She slammed the door so hard it would've woken the dead. That's when Kolya heard her. He climbed out of the barrel and shook off the cabbage. He said, first take the lollypop, then I'll go home. You see he wasn't going to miss out on anything. Marusya took the red rooster and held it up to the light. Maybe it's a fake. Lots of fake suckerroosters were floating around. She looked at the red rooster and smiled and Kolya went to his room where the *banditka* was. Marusya stood there smiling, with her gift, the red rooster. And the light went through the rooster into her eyes.

The next morning I was looking out of the window. The sky was blue, the way I like it. Two white clouds were sailing by. I said to Marusya: Look up at the sky. I'm washing clothes. Then I will hang them out to dry. They will dry quickly. I will iron the clothes while I'm waiting for my man. I will spread fresh sheets on the bed when he comes. The sheets will smell of fresh air. I'll put dinner on the table. I will set his food on a clean white tablecloth. I will set my food on a clean white tablecloth.

Marusya said: Pearl, you are a lucky women. You are so lucky, Pearl. Because when you do the laundry, you have such weather. You have such a sky and you have such air. She said, Pearl, look up at the sky!

I went to finish my laundry. I had a new wash board. I hate taking clothes to be washed. They always come back gray. My wash in such air comes out white as snow. My wash under such a sky comes out white as snow.

As I was saying, we let the *banditka* in, all trembling in her nightgown. That's the way she came in, nothing on but a nightgown. She threw her arms around me. For God's sake save me. I say to her, you're here already, so stay. We have no other choice. *Ver geleymt.*[29] Look at yourself standing there in a night-gown in front of my husband. And she says, be grateful I put something on. I always sleep naked with him. So what if I ran in naked?

Of course, what else can you expect from her, a slut is a slut.

At that moment Kolya began drumming on our door after he picked him-self up from under the wardrobe or a couch, who knows. He shouted: Hey Zoyka, bitch. If you are going to hide yourself there with the Jews, don't even bother coming home. I'll cut your fucking throat, you whore. If not today, then tomorrow. Together with your Jews.

So the bitch pressed herself against Abram, like she's afraid she's going to be killed and only Abram can save her. She put her arms around him and whis-pered in his ear: Don't be afraid, Abramchik. He'll be like jelly tomorrow.

Abram spoke to Kolya through the closed door: God gave me this life and when the time is right God will take it away. And he won't need the help of a fool like you. Abram said: at war I blew up German tanks, you know that. You and I we've drunk many bottles together. And you have even seen the hole in my neck. Someone is always trying to kill Abram. Just because he's Abram! And Abram is still alive. Someone is always trying to kill me. And I'm still alive! And those who wanted to kill me are long in *drerd*, dead. And I'm still here.

If you don't want others to screw your wife, lock her up and put her on a chain.

Life is a hurricane! You're in a hurricane, and I'm in that hurricane.

---

29 *Ver geleymt* (Yiddish) = I wish you were dead.

But life is happiness. You're in this happiness, and I'm in this happiness. It's bad only for those who are in *drerd*, dead. We are both alive.

The hurricane carries us about with its sorrows and its joys, but it carries life.

Maybe God wants your wife to sleep with the one she sleeps with and not with the one she doesn't sleep with. Maybe God wants your wife to be here with me with her arms around me in a nightshirt with you standing outside the door ready to kill us.

Knives, that's bad, knives, that's prison. Get knives out of your head. Come, let's make up and be friends. Tomorrow we'll drink *lekhayim*.[30]

We let the bitch sleep in the dining room on the sofa. Our kids slept there, may they live to be a hundred and twenty. We had just two tiny rooms. A dining room and a bedroom. And now we had a very important guest, our *banditka*, and we put her on the sofa. In the daytime we fight and at night we sleep together. But you see, God gave us this life, no other, and so we live the life we were given.

When Kolya was yelling he was going to kill her, I let her in. I gave Zoyka, the bitch, my old red quilt. I couldn't put her up in our bedroom. It's only thirty square feet, barely enough for the two of us. I'm not complaining. But to bring her into the same room and to put her next to our bed, she'd be in bed with my husband in the morning.

Zoyka got up in the morning and went to her room. She said Kolya would be like jelly in the morning. So she crawled naked into her jelly under the blanket with Kolya.

My father, may he rest in peace, he was a *huhim*, he said to my mother: This is life, Esther, this is a hurricane, Esther. Life is like a hurricane.

One is in one jelly, the other one is in a different jelly! Each one is in his own jelly. Because life floats over us, we don't float over life. Life floats like white clouds in the sky, and we cannot reach it. Like a white cloud in the blue sky, and we only sense the fragrance in the air. Marusya came out. She put a jar of water on her table. She stuck the red lollypop in a jar of water, wooden stick down. Maybe it will turn into a flower, she said laughing. Maybe the rooster will turn into a flower.

Kolya came out and went up to Abram and said, you're a good guy, Abram. Even though you're Jews, you're good people. We've drunk together, and

---

30 *Lekhayim* (Yiddish from Hebrew) = To life!

we'll have many more drinks. Please forget the row we had. It can happen to anybody. And my wife will come out and apologize to Pearl.

Whomever your Jewish doctors poisoned is not our business. You didn't poison anybody. Now if they'd also poisoned my boss, I would take my hat off and thank them. But no such luck. They're just a little bit off. You, Abram, blew up German tanks, you shed blood for our country. You weren't in Tashkent eating dried apricots like some other Jews.[31] And you didn't poison any Party leaders.

Then the *banditka* also came up to me and said: Pearl Fridelevna, forgive me. You saved me from a knife. You're good people, even though you're Jews. But please, do not save me again. We live our life, you live your own. It's nobody's business. It's our life. If he kills me, I'll put him in jail. If I die, others will put him in jail .We love each other. I have never loved him more than after what happened yesterday. He wanted to kill me because he loves me.

I want to apologize. When you need anything in the way of food, I'll get it for you. I have connections, you know. Bakery goods, meat, whatever you need. Though I know you can get stuff, you are Jews, you know how to get around, but anyway, just let me know, I'll get you anything you need. We'll be friends.

Afterward, after such an awful day, I had a terrible dream. When I think of it, I get goose bumps. I got up early and began to bake. Why I decided to bake I'll tell you later after you know what happened. In our small town there was an old woman. Jewish. Her name was Rakhil. As far back as I can remember, she was always old. And it so happened that in Moscow she also lived close by, and at that time she must've been a hundred years old.

Whoever had a bad dream would go to her. People used to say she could tell you everything that's going to happen to you. I baked a Jewish honey cake, a *lekekh*, and went to talk to her. I said, Rakhil, I had a terrible dream. I'd like to talk to you about it. She said, what did you dream about, my darling Pearl? She liked me very much when I was little. She lived right across the street from where *Yankel Der Blinder* lived.[32] I remember once when I was little she said to me: Do you know what a *pearl* is, Pearl dear? She pulled me closer and said: A pearl is a jewel.

When I grew up and had to get my passport, the *goyka* in the office asked me,[33] What shall I put down? Pelageya? In our language it would be Pelageya,

---

31 Tashkent—capital of Uzbekistan; hundreds of thousands of Soviet people were evacuated to Tashkent during World War II.

32 *Yankel Der Blinder* (Yiddish) = Jacob the Blind.

33 *Goyka* (Rus.-Yiddish) = a non-Jewish woman (Yiddish *goy* plus Russian feminine ending-ka).

right? And I said: Nope. You write down Pearl, the name was given when I was born. I want to die with the same name. You put down my Jewish name, Pearl, the name I was given, not Pelageya.

Rakhil asked me: So, Pearl, what was your dream about? Then I plucked up my courage and said: All right, I'll tell you my dream, but it must be buried in your stomach. Then Rakhil said: I knew your mother Esther. She used to tell me her dreams. I knew your father Friedl. He used to tell me his dreams. And you, Pearl, used to tell me your dreams.

So I unwrapped my *lekekh* and gave it to her. She said: This is the kind of cake we've eaten all our life. It's dark because life is dark. It's sweet because life is sweet.

So I tell her my dream. I dreamed that the sky was black—not a single star, not a single cloud. It's dark because it's night, nothing terrible about that. But it became so quiet, so quiet. I could hear my own heart beating. Marusya appears, and we both keep looking up at the sky, we want to see something. Instead we are in Red Square. There're cobblestones everywhere, and we keep stumbling on them.

An empty dovecote stands on the Lenin Mausoleum. Not a single bird in the house. All of a sudden I see Stalin, forgive me, as you will forgive your own mother, in long johns. He has a rope around his neck as if he were going to hang out my laundry. I got scared. Ours may be the best country in the world, but for such a dream in this paradise, you can get ten years in prison, and you might even disappear.

Why, I think, should God punish me with such a dream? Better let the *banditka* have such a dream. She already sleeps with Armenians and Jews. Let her have a Georgian also.

Who could I tell such a dream to? So I came to Rakhil.

And then I see, Stalin is climbing up on the Lenin Mausoleum. The rope around his neck begins to swing like a pendulum, this way, that way. He almost caught me in it. It swings as he walks. His belly is round like a football, and still he climbs. I am shaking all over. He climbs and I stand and tremble. Finally, thank God, he reaches the top. May *he* tremble in his grave like I trembled. He stood quietly there near the dovecote. To tell you the truth I never thought it was in him to be so quiet. He stood there next to the dovecote, a rope hanging from his neck. May my enemies all see him that way. In my dream I hear myself think: what will be when I wake up? Better not to wake up at all, because when you open your eyes you realize that it was only a dream, *puste khaloymes*.[34]

---

34 *Puste khaloymes* (Yiddish) = pipe dreams, empty dreams.

All sorts of thoughts kept running through my head, like on the way to the bakery the janitor is going to hit me with her shovel. Someone else is going to push me. Another one is going to shout, hey, you kike. And another, that we poisoned the whole Soviet *melukhe.*

The *Balebos* stood there like a lamppost on the mausoleum with a rope around his neck.[35] And when he climbed to the top, he stood next to the dovecote where the pigeons used to live.

And what do I see? Stalin is sucking on Marusya's lollypop. Standing belly and all in long johns, sucking Marusya's red rooster. May he suck on *geshvolne makes.*[36] He has everything already, the whole country, still not enough. He needs a lollypop. A red rooster. May the plague strike you!

As soon as Rakhil heard the dream, she screamed: *Oy!*

What's the *oy* for? I asked.

She didn't say a word. She went to bolt the door. You already know she was a hundred years old. It took her a whole lifetime to get to the door. And it took her a whole lifetime to get back.

My whole life in the shtetl passed before me, how I was born, how I married Abram, how blue the sky was. How we were beaten, how they shouted kike, how my children were born, how the war started, how when it was over Abram returned alive and well.

It took her a lifetime to close the door and a lifetime to get back. When she had closed the door and had come back to me she said: Pearl, I screamed *oy* because I have had the very same dream! So far I have had six Jews come to me with the same dream. You are, thank God, the seventh one.

When she said that, I got goose bumps, I shivered.

She said, to see that place in your dream is a bad omen.

Why? I asked. Why is that a bad omen?

Because in that Kremlin wall lie the dead. Their ashes.

Because in that Kremlin ground lie dead bodies. Their bones. And where *that man* climbed, as he licked the red rooster, also lies a dead body. And he's a stuffed doll! They think that from there life begins, but life ends from there! When night falls, they all crawl out from their graves and begin to talk who killed who. There they sit in a circle talking. And they drink tea. And they divide us up.

---

35 *Balebos* (Yiddish) = landlord, owner, boss; Soviet Jews privately referred to Stalin this way.
36 *Geshvolne makes* (Yiddish) = swollen sores.

Sometimes they quarrel and fight, who gets what. They don't know how to distribute us. Then they drink tea with our *lekekh*. Quietly they sit talking of what bone to throw into our broth. Which bone not to throw into our broth. What bone should they saw off their leg to add to our *esik fleysh*.[37] And no one wants to donate his leg. Then they start to kill each other again. Because of us Jews they start to kill each other. Then they sit down in a neat circle and talk quietly. And they drink tea. And when the first star disappears from the sky, they get up to dance *freylekhs*.[38] And the stuffed doll lies there as before, and they keep on dancing around it. And when the second star disappears from the sky, they leave. Some back into the wall, others back into the earth.

When a dream like this comes to someone, it's always a bad sign. When Abraham lived, God came to him one day.

You see, in Abraham's day everyone made a little god for himself from wood or from clay. It became their god. They went to bed with it and woke up with it.

After Abraham saw God, he realized that a piece of wood cannot be God.

So he took his wife Sarah and his nephew and left. He went to a place pointed out by God.

Now when he got up in the morning, he saw his God, not a clay doll.

And when the day came to an end, he saw his God, not a clay doll.

He walked in front of his sheep and not behind them. They followed him because he led them.

May he sleep in peace wherever he is, and his children and grandchildren and their children and grandchildren.

I asked her: Tell me, Rakhil, what does it mean that he got up on Lenin's tomb, the Mausoleum? I asked her.

It means that he has one foot in the grave already.

Then I asked her again: And why does he have a rope round his neck?

I asked and feared when I asked her.

It means that his other foot is in the grave also, she said.

Forgive me, Rakhil, as you would your own daughter, why was he standing there in his long johns? When I saw this I almost went crazy.

Because, she said, when he dies, everything will come off. People will strip him naked. He'll be left only in his long johns so that nobody sees his rotten *shmuck*!

---

37 *Esik fleysh* (Yiddish) = sweet-and-sour Jewish stew.
38 *Freylekhs* (Yiddish) = joyful Jewish dance.

That place will be forgotten. People will go there to remember their past sorrows. But who wants to remember grief?

I said: But whenever there's a holiday, we go there, we run there.

No you don't, you don't run there. You don't go there. You are led there. You do not go there, you are taken there.

That is what she said to me: You are led there, you are brought there. She said: Do you think you know where it is you are hurrying? Do you think I know where it is I am hurrying? Everybody goes there, so I go there too. People run and run and then everybody comes to the same place. Everybody ends up in the same place. They dance and make merry and when their time comes, it turns out that they are all dancing at their own funerals. They think they are going to a great celebration, and instead they have come to their own graves.

She said: We don't know where we are going. We walk and we run, but we don't know where we walk, and we don't know where we run. We walk and we run. Jews, stop for a second, don't rush, where are you running to, Jews? But who can stop them? Nobody can stop them. And Jews go and go. And they get killed over and over again. Stop, Jews, where you are rushing, Jews? What's the rush? *Vuss? Ven?* Why? What, when, why? Who knows this? Nobody knows this. God knows this: what, when, why. Why we go. Why we run. Why they kill us.

Who knows this? Nobody knows. I only want to ask God that the years allotted to me should be lived without the person I saw in my dream.

Without the person you, Pearl, saw in your dream. And six other Jews saw in their dream. Without that person with the red rooster, the sucker! So that we can dance at my grandchildren's weddings. So that you, Pearl, will be able to dance at the weddings of your children and the weddings of your grandchildren. So that we can die in our own beds, when the time comes, and not in the street or in jail.

In times of trouble, you mature. As I walked down the street after I left Rakhil, I looked at the people coming my way. I saw people. I didn't know who they were, I didn't know what would happen to me tomorrow. I did not know what would happen to them tomorrow. I thought they could kill me, but somebody will always be with us. He will be watching from up there.

And something else I saw. As if something was above us. First a blue sky, then two clouds flying. They parted, and I saw his face. He was flying toward us and falling on us. His face held us all: me, and Abram, and our children, and our home, and me.

And everybody was in Him who was under Him.

And we rose and flew to Him, and he flew toward us.

We were in Him, and He was in us.

When we came together, we felt pain, joy, and sorrow. And we knew that we were in Him and He was in us and was everywhere outside us to the day of our own death, which would never happen.

I was returning from the bakery. The janitor took a swing at me with her shovel, hey, you lousy kike! I was carrying bread in my bag. The bread was both bitter and sweet. Then my heart grew heavy. I thought, dear God, do you really exist in the world? I put the bag with bread down on the earth. The bread was on this earth. And I was standing on this earth. Why was I born from my mother's womb? Why didn't my mother's milk dry up as she nursed me? Why did I see the light of day? I should've seen the night only, so that I should never see the daylight.

Are you there, Lord, for us? Are you there, Lord, in the world for our father Abraham and for all his children?

But He was flying toward us and falling down on us. And in His face we saw ourselves, Abram and the children and me. When we came together, there was pain, joy, and sadness. But I saw Him flying, and us flying up to meet Him, and when I disappeared, so did everything else.

When will water wash away all the mountains and there will be no mountains?

As long as your soul remains alive, water will never wash away the mountains.

And when the wind stops blowing, and leaves no longer appear on the trees, and when the rains stop falling from the sky?

The mountains will stand, the wind will continue to bring us white clouds, as long as your soul is alive. Then you will fly up to meet him.

I was in the hospital for two weeks after the janitor knocked me over the head with her shovel. There's Jewish luck for you. In order to see God, you have to have your block knocked off, only then do you think of him. By that time you have forgotten what happened. I forgot all about my dream as I lay there.

Spring came while I was in the hospital. It was March already. I looked out of the window. There was the blue sky and two white clouds. I looked at the clouds and the sky. When I looked at them, I remembered something. I don't know what. It was kind of scary, like I hadn't been born yet, but I knew that I would be born. What would happen after, I didn't know. I was daydreaming, looking out of the window. At that moment, the door opens and in comes

Zoyka, the *banditka*, bringing me goodies in a large shopping bag. Here, Pearl Fridelevna, for you. She takes out some pink and yellow candy with white and green around the edges.

She said: Here's something my husband Kolya sent, and she holds up a red rooster on a wooden stick. I began to cry. Why, I don't know, fool that I am.

That's our life, the life we live. And we have no other life. And we live the life God gave us. And why, we don't know. When the door opens again, that scrawny Jew Yasha comes in. He came to see Zoyka while Kolya was at work. I said to him, shame on you. You can't even keep your pants on.

She said: Kolya was working second shift yesterday, Yasha came to see me. I told him I was going to see you in the hospital and so he followed me, like a tail, wherever I go, he follows me. We can't go to the movies, we'll be seen. His wife would give him hell, and Kolya would kill me. And so we decided at least to go together to the hospital.

Look what a beautiful sky, she said, look at that sun! You will definitely get better with such fine weather. It's March, one more month till spring. Yasha, why don't you take me to see *Swan Lake*? I bet you took your wife. Such gorgeous weather!

Yasha said to her: I had no idea you liked such dancing. I really didn't know that. If you want to go to the Bolshoy Theater, I will get you tickets to the Bolshoy Theater. No problem. Right, Pearl Fridelevna? When a woman wants something, you must give a woman what she wants. It's a rule with me, to give a woman whatever she wants. And that's why women love me. She wants this, I give her this. She wants that, I give her that. I will get two tickets so you and Kolya can see whatever you like. You want the theater, you get the theater. *Swan Lake, Goose Lake.* See whatever you want. Enjoy. My pleasure. Go with Kolya, go with Shmolya. That's what you want? You got it. Is there something in the world that I wouldn't get for you?

And then she says: No, you don't understand, Yasha. I want to go with you. Yes, I want to go with you. You will wear the new suit we got you at the Central Department Store. And I will put on the new dress you gave me for a present. The white dress.

I hid it in the sofa, so Kolya wouldn't find it. You know what he would say. Where did you get this dress? We can hardly make it from paycheck to paycheck, and here, this dress.

You know the big white columns in the theater, we'll walk past them together. We'll sit in our red velvet seats in the box, and on the stage we will see white swans. We'll sit there side by side looking at the dancers. Right, Pearl Fridelevna?

What could I say? Who knows what is right and what is wrong.

I said: He's married, Zoyka.

She said: So am I. I love Yasha because I don't love anyone else. Even though he's Jewish. Nobody really knows him. None of you know what he says to me when we are alone. If you knew, you would love him, too. But you don't know that. Just look at that sky. Look at that sun!

As she spoke something wonderful happened. The sky walked into my room. And Rakhil appeared. It took her one hundred years to walk to me, reaching me no longer as Rakhil but as the sky. She had on the same dress that she wore when I brought her my *lekekh*. Rakhil said: When darkness falls they all come out of their graves and they all begin talking about who killed whom. They all sit around in a circle talking and drinking tea. He will get up and walk to the dovecote and feed the pigeons breadcrumbs. Another time he will bring them water. They get thirsty at night. Soon there will be lots of water. Spring will come. Water will flow over the streets, and water will flow over the squares, water will be everywhere. There will be enough to drown everybody. Then everybody will get their turn to drink. And everybody will get their turn to drown. That's the kind of spring we are going to have. That's the kind of spring because of such a blue sky. Because of such a sky and such a sun everyone may drown.

When I looked up, I saw Rakhil and Abram sitting. And Rakhil is holding the *lekekh* in her hands. And Abram is holding the Torah in his hands. Rakhil says to me, the *lekekh* is dark because life is dark. The *lekekh* is sweet because life is sweet. Eat and all your *veytik* will disappear.[39] Abram will pray to God for you, for me, and for your children. For all our children.

The door opens again and in walks Marusya in tears. Make Abram pray for us, she says, for all the Russian people. Stalin died. Ask Abram to pray for us, Pearl, for my children, and for your children, our great dear father is dead!

Rakhil says: Water will flood the squares. Nearly everybody will drown because of such sun. Because of such spring. That's because our sky is so blue and we live under it.

I ask Rakhil: What will be with us? What will be with the Jews?

---

39 *Veytik* (Yiddish) = pain, disease.

Abram says: When a bandit is born, that's bad, but when a bandit dies, it becomes twice as bad. When Stalin dies, that's a disaster. It's an *umglik* for everyone when somebody like that dies.[40] Who knows what criminal will take his place.

Abram says, Marusya, you are crying? Why? You don't even know. You didn't cry during the war. Sorrow and trouble dried up your tears. Now you weep.

And he began to soothe her and kiss her, saying it's an *umglik*, Pearl, an *umglik*, Pearl. In Yiddish it means a disaster, it means misfortune, it means a lot of things. He says, who knows, tomorrow they will say that it was us who killed Stalin. He says, last time we poisoned everybody, and now we've killed Stalin. And tomorrow at sunup, we're all going to kill Stalin's falcons, his trusted followers.

Now there will be water enough for everybody when they begin to drown in their own tears, old Rakhil said. There will be plenty of water for all of us. Oh God! We will get what we deserve.

And Marusya says: What's going to happen with us, o Lord?

I see a blue sky, the likes of which I have never seen before. I see such a blue light, I've never seen in all my life before. Because life floats over us, not under us. Life moves above us like the white clouds across the sky, and we cannot reach it.

I say to Abram: When death will come to us, at the brink of death we will love each other. When death calls me to her, I shall go to you. We shall love each other unto death. The *banditka* appears leading Kolya by the hand. He follows her like a blind man, quietly.

She says: Now we all have what we always wished for. And I have what I always wanted.

She says to Kolya: Take a knife. You may need it, it's yours. I've loved Abram all my life.

She tells Abram: Put your Israel on my belly. I'm blinded by you. Put your leg on my leg, put your lips on my lips. Crush my breasts with your hands. Let me hug you before I die. I will wind my legs around your waist. I will hug your back with my legs.

And Abram says to her: Come here Zoyka, I've wanted you all my life. I have loved you all my life.

---

40 *Umglik* (Yiddish) = disaster.

Voices of Jewish-Russian Literature

And he says to Kolya: Knives are bad. Throw knives out of your head. Chain up your wife. And barricade the doors and windows with timber trucks.

Then my children walk in, and their children, and the children of their children.

Then we all sat down around the table.

Abram sat down, the *banditka* sat down, and Kolya with the knife, and Marusya. And my children with their children, and the children of their children.

I sat down at the table.

Rakhil cut slices of *lekekh*, the Jewish honey cake, for everybody. A slice for me. And a slice for Abram. And a slice for the *banditka*. And a slice for Marusya. She gave *lekekh* to my children and to their children and grandchildren.

And everyone ate his piece of *lekekh*.

I looked at the sky.

Hey, life, where are you flying, passing us by?

There, we don't know where.

There, where there is life we do not know.

Hey, life! Where are you flying, passing us by?

1988

Translated from the Russian by Yelena Lebedinsky and the author

Philip Isaac Berman, "Sarra i Petushok." Copyright © by Philip Isaac Berman. English translation copyright © by Yelena Lebedinsky and Philip Isaac Berman. Introduction and notes copyright © by Maxim D. Shrayer.

RUTH ZERNOVA

Ruth (Ruf') **Zernova** (1919–2004), prose writer and translator, was born Ruth Zemina in Tiraspol (now in Moldova) to an educated Jewish family and grew up in Odessa. In 1936, Zernova left home to attend the Leningrad Institute of Philosophy, Literature, and Culture (LIFLI, soon merged with Leningrad University), where she studied French. The Spanish Civil War changed Zernova's life. She was put through a course of intensive Spanish and, in May 1938, given a new name, Zernova, and sent to Spain as a translator for Soviet civilian and military personnel. Upon returning from Spain, Zernova was assigned to the Soviet Naval Office as a translator. Zernova worked in Moscow until 1941, when her office was evacuated to Ulyanovsk (Simbirsk) on the Volga. She made her way to Tashkent, reuniting with her family. In Tashkent Zernova worked for the Soviet press agency TASS as a translator and editor. She met and married the Vitebsk-born Ilya Serman (1913–2010), a wounded military officer and a graduate student in philology. Their daughter Nina was born in Tashkent and their son Mark after their return to Leningrad. Zernova received her university diploma in Leningrad in 1947, defending a thesis on Prosper Mérimée.

In the late 1940s, Zernova contributed book reviews to *Star* (*Zvezda*) and published a translation of a novella by Charles Nodier (1870–1944). Like many Jewish-Russian intellectuals of her generation, Zernova and Serman woke up from the Stalinist anesthesia while also experiencing a post-Holocaust reawakening of Jewish selfhood. In 1949, both Serman and Zernova were arrested and sentenced for "anti-Soviet agitation." First kept at a Leningrad jail, they were sent to different labor camps, Zernova to Boksitogorsk (east of Leningrad), Altay, and finally Amur Region, Serman to Kolyma. Both were released in 1954.

From the camps Zernova brought her first story, "Tonechka." In the story the protagonist overhears a raw love story told by one fellow female prisoner to another. The influential writer Vera Panova (1905–1973) selected Zernova's story for an anthology of new Soviet writing. The anthology was derailed as part of the political crackdown following the suppression of the 1956 Hungarian uprising, and Zernova's story did not appear until 1963. The breakthrough occurred in 1960, when Zernova's story "Scorpion Berries" appeared in the mass-produced magazine *Little Flame* (*Ogonyok*), winning its literary prize. The literary monthlies opened their pages to Zernova: *Novy mir*, *Star*, *Neva*, and others. Three collections appeared in succession in Moscow: *Scorpion Berries* (1961), *Baccalao* (1963), and *Light and Shadow* (1963). Privileging the individual and unique over the collective and epic, some of Zernova's stories related the historical experiences of the Spanish Civil War, World War II, and Stalinism, while others dealt with the eternal anguishes of love. Zernova's storytelling manner and her fascination with uneducated women possessing a nobleness of the heart connects her with the stories of her better-known contemporary Yury Kazakov (1927–1982). Zernova published three more collections in the USSR: *A Long, Long Summer* (1967), *The Sunny Side* (1968), and *Mute Phone Calls* (1974), as well as a volume of stories for children. She also edited *Leningraders in Spain, 1936–1939* (Leningrad, 1967), a memorial volume. In the 1960s and early 1970s, Zernova's collections appeared in translation in Poland, Romania, and Czechoslovakia.

In 1976, Zernova and her family repatriated to Israel. Serman, previously a researcher at the Institute of Russian Literature, became a professor at Hebrew University. Zernova's fiction and nonfiction appeared in a number of émigré reviews, including *Echo* (*Ekho*), *The New Russian Word* (*Novoe russkoe slovo*), and *Time and We* (*Vremia i my*). Zernova published three representative collections of Russian-language fiction, *Women's Stories* (Ann Arbor, MI, 1981), *Long Shadows* (Jerusalem, 1995), and *To the Seashore and Back* (Jerusalem, 1998). A retrospective of Zernova's stories, *Mute Phone Calls and Other Stories*, appeared in English, edited by Helen Reeve, Zernova's principal western student and translator. Two books containing Zernova's essays, reminiscences, and fictionalized memoirs also appeared: *This Was in Our Time* (Jerusalem, 1988) and *Israel and Its Environs* (Jerusalem, 1990). One of their central topics is a revaluation of the Jewish-Russian cultural identity. Zernova's Russian translation of Golda Meir's *My Life* (1975) came out in Jerusalem in 1983. Ruth Zernova died in Jerusalem in 2004.

* * *

Zernova's stories of the 1980s transcend the conventional boundaries of fiction and memoir as they continue to fashion strong, opinionated, spirited female characters and narrators. Zernova included "All Vows" in her book *Israel and Its Environs* (1990). As the warm rays of Zernova's Odessan childhood shine through the pages of her prose, they highlight Zernova's links to the Odessan theme in Russian prose. The focus of Zernova's story on music and the romantic pathos of its ending bring to mind "Gambrinus" (1907), Aleksandr Kuprin's famous novella about a Jewish musician in Odessa at the time of World War I—and about art's survival and endurance.

ALL VOWS

Recently I heard over the radio an interview with a young *hazzan*[41] from Tashkent.

It occurred to me that the time had come for me to recall something I had put away in my treasure box, the one with my "cherries from Japan." Each one of us has many "cherries" stuffed in our root cellar.

This story has to do with an Odessan family: Milka and her mother and grandfather.

That's the kind of family it was (there were quite a few like them in the twenties and thirties): their men had been wiped out, by wars, divorces, arrests. At first, no one thought that when a man was arrested his better half could be taken, too.

Milka lived in a one-story house, on the corner of the street that our windows faced, the windows of our large, beautiful, high, four-story house on Preobrazhenskaya Street. Now it's Soviet Army Street. Milka and I, classmates in Six B, would walk along this street, walk and walk, seeing each other home. Milka was one of those to whom my mama had taken a dislike. So we walked the streets, since for a long time Milka didn't invite me in. When she finally did ask me, I considered it an honor. And it never dawned on me—I think it did so just now—that she was embarrassed by her place: they had just one room for the three of them, and a toilet outdoors.

Milka was older than me. She had turned thirteen long ago. She was very small—under five feet—swarthy, with a dark complexion, but very light hair and eyes. What's more, she sang.

True, her voice seemed strange to us: it was low, with no luster, somehow grown-up. Our music teacher listened to her attentively but had nothing complimentary to say (she did place her immediately in with the second voices, but they had no solo parts). But Milka had her own repertory. She made me pick out songs on their upright (I had trouble reading music). A friend of mine

---

41 *Hazzan* (Heb.) = cantor; *Hazzanut* = term usually referring to the art, technique, and traditions of Ashkenazic cantorial singing.

from before who had older sisters knew the repertory of the NEP period well.[42] Milka, however, had no sisters, just a mother.

How old could Milka's mother be? She was a bit taller than Milka and maybe a bit thinner. She had a small head, a Bubenkopf, as it was called then (fashions came from Germany to the Soviet Union), a very short boy's haircut with bangs on a slant; round brown eyes, high cheek bones, a straight short nose. If it weren't for her faded complexion, she'd have resembled our camp counselor a bit (our camp counselors came from the Technical College). With us, Milka's friends, she behaved as if she were one of us: she was up on everything, gave advice, liked to talk about things . . .

I didn't care for her stories or her advice and conversation. Everything in her seemed out of place, even her looks. I preferred my own mother, tall and haughty, who never inquired about anything with sympathy and who mercilessly dismissed all my girl friends, one after another. If she ever said about one of them that "she seemed to be a good girl," it was cause for celebration. Milka's mother, however . . . I kept thinking that she was putting on an act, that our matters could not possibly interest her. Why was she constantly with us, like some sort of an aging girl?

"Milochka has a voice," she'd say. "I, too, used to have a voice. But I smoked too much, shouted too much."

She'd laugh. Her teeth were not white, like Milka's, but brownish, from smoking. And her complexion, too; her skin had large pores. When girls would say, "Milka's mother is pretty," I wouldn't argue but would be surprised inwardly.

"Today, on an empty stomach, I ate a bellyfull of Mayakovsky!" she once announced to us.[43]

It looked to me like they never had dinner, even though there was a kerosene stove in their room. Also, in that one room of theirs there was a large table, but, as far as I could tell, no one ever ate at the table; Grandfather sat at that table.

Grandfather never talked to anyone. And no one talked to him. Milka's mother would sometimes ask him, "Papa, will you have some dinner?" He would mumble something like "no," and leave. I once saw him sitting in the corner, eating bread with salt . . . Did he notice me, did he ever notice Milka's other friends?

---

42 NEP—acronym for the New Economic Policy in Soviet Russia in the 1920s.
43 Mayakovsky, Vladimir (1893–1930)—major Russian and Soviet poet and playwright.

He had his own guest, one for the whole time that I visited them, only one. Tall, skinny, with a long neck. He would come in and unwind from his neck a narrow, dark *cache-nez*. *Cache-nez*! One of the forgotten words. Later they called it *sharfik*. Still later this diminutive form—intolerable to the Russian ear—vanished, and people began calling it a *sharf*. And so, he unwound his *cache-nez*, or *sharfik*, and politely gave his greeting, though he saw no one aside from Grandfather. And Grandfather smiled at him and said something. I couldn't make out his Yiddish speech; I understood only when it resembled German.

And so he spoke, and the other one answered. The silent film went on for several minutes: the unwinding of the *sharfik*, the rubbing of his frozen reddened hands, very large and bony. The winter winds in Odessa are fierce, cutting; and when we lost our last gloves (one could not buy new ones!), we had to walk around forever with frozen hands. They talked a bit, then Grandfather smiled again. Then the tall man would finally stuff his *cache-nez* into his trouser pocket, sit down at the table, and unwrap the package he had brought with him: it looked like sheet music. At this point the silent film was over, and the singing began, or rather, the chanting.

The young man took up a sad chant, and Grandfather droned along. At times Grandfather would stop droning, and the young man would fall silent immediately and listen respectfully. Grandfather said something briefly. No doubt, he himself wanted to sing a bit but couldn't. He droned something, like a bumble bee, which I couldn't understand at all. But the other one did understand—shook his head, repeated; and Grandfather no longer interrupted him.

All the while Milka and I kept talking softly about our own affairs, with our feet on her *topchan*. It was from her that I heard for the first time the word *topchan*—a futon of sorts. At home, we had sofas, a couch, and beds, but no *topchan*. So here we are, sitting on her *topchan*, talking in soft voices, not loudly, but not whispering either—because we are not bothering them, and they are not bothering us. Between us is an imaginary wall of mutual respectful inattention toward each other. I, at any rate, was completely convinced that the young man, from the minute he unwound his scarf and sat down at the table, no longer saw us; as for Grandfather, I cannot say anything. I think that he never saw me at all. As for us . . . But still, even though I never looked and didn't understand and didn't ask, I've preserved under my eyelids, in the memory banks of a child's perception, the image of the two of them at the forever bare dinner table.

In fact, I never asked who it was who was visiting them. It was a side of grown-up life of which one didn't speak. Actually, the first time the guest appeared, I looked at Milka questioningly and in answer got a dismissive gesture—oh, well, pay no attention. And so I didn't pay attention. I didn't, and not once, never, nowhere did I ever mention it—not in school, nor to girl-friends, not even at home. Not that I was afraid that telling this little fact might hurt Milka aesthetically (because her grandfather and his visitor with his *sharfik* and their morose singing at quarter voice impressed me as ugly, ridiculous, and somewhat shameful)—whereas I delighted in Milka with all my heart and wanted everybody to share in my delight—no, the reason here was different. It was political. I couldn't, for example, stand up in my social studies class and say, "My nanny says that Nicholas II was a drunkard, and under him everybody drank and ate; but nowadays, even though people don't drink, they . . ."

But I used to visit Milka every day, and almost every day that tall, young fellow would come . . . This continued into the spring, then was interrupted for a while, and in the summer he appeared again, in the same *sharfik* but no over-coat. And—now I remember—in the summer he would take from his pocket a skullcap and put it on his head before starting to sing. (In the winter he got along without this; he simply never took off his hat.) He sang so you could just barely hear him, because the window, their only window, was open; it was hot. But I was not at all curious about him.

And then once, when Milka and I were discussing something important . . . Yes, it was summertime, and I remember distinctly Milka's mother's sunburned brown arms. For some reason, the window was shut. And so, suddenly—Milka and I were whispering and not bothering anyone—Milka's mother abruptly said something to her father in Yiddish, out of the blue: she interrupted their singing, all in a rush came up to them and sang a brief passage. Her voice was muffled and dulled from tobacco, but probably what she sang was something very apt, because Grandfather turned serious right away, stopped her with a gesture, appeared to listen to something within himself, suddenly nodded, and said some appropriate words to the young man. The young man shrugged his shoulders, and with his face expressed, I don't think so, but if you insist . . . He asked Milka's mother something, threw his head back so that I saw his Adam's apple moving, and began to sing exuberantly.

Right off he began singing, passionately hitting a hugely high note. I felt that he was not trying to creep up to it, not weighing his strength, which he had held back and held down for so many hours, so many days and nights. Was he able to sing at full voice at least in his house, from a full soul? Or, there too, did he have to hold back by its feet the huge silver bird that was so powerfully breaking free now and beginning to claw at our hearts and tenderly to lick our wounds, all at the same time? And then, as if it were flapping its wings, it struggled upward, in ever tighter circles, strewing notes all around—and broke away . . .

Later, after many years had passed, when I read Mandelstam's phrase "God's name, like a large bird . . . ," I saw that white throat with the melody splashing around in it; it was precisely that bird that I saw in my mind then, and also that it was silver.[44] Milka looked at her mother and said, "Have him sing some more." Her mother answered, "He won't; he was only showing us that he could. What's the matter? In the fall he'll sing in the synagogue, you'll be able to go listen to him there."

I moved on the *topchan* over to the window and looked out onto the street. People stood there, maybe five or six, with their heads raised. His voice had burst out of the room for barely a minute, and already . . .

"You have an operatic voice! A voice for opera! You have to train it!" we exclaimed emphatically, in spite of our agitation.

He looked at us sorrowfully, with a kind of regret, then past us, and said, "Thank you."

Grandfather kept looking at him and smiling, and the young man smiled back at him; then he left.

"Mama, how do you know this melody?" asked Milka.

"That is Kol Nidrei," she said, "a prayer, 'All Vows.' It's sung in the synagogue on the Day of Atonement."

An operatic voice! I wasn't quite sure what kind of a thing that was; I gathered it was some epithet. "Just think," I said, "what this is. He should go and study, he'd get accepted at the conservatory—but he's here." Milka certainly agreed with me. And Milka's mother, too.

"Uneducated, uncivilized people," she said, pursing her lips so that dimples formed below her cheekbones. "It seems that for them, there was no Revolution. You think he is the only one to think so, this young man? There are lots of them now in Odessa. I'm not talking about some place like Balta or Tulchin. This one has just come from Tulchin. Came to the big city. Well, then go and study, if your social background is in order. But no. He found himself an

---

44 "God's name, like a large bird . . ." ("Bozh'e imia, kak bol'shaia ptitsa . . .")—from the poem "Obraz tvoi, muchitel'nyi zybkii . . ." ("Your image, torturous and fleeting . . . ," 1912) by **Osip Mandelstam**.

old man and is learning from him the *hazzanut*. To be a cantor in a synagogue. Humph! Cantor! Do you know what that is? It's like a choir boy, a soloist, so to speak—cantor."

"Cantor—I've heard that word."

"Well, thank God, at least this word you've heard. What can I tell you, girls, I don't even feel sorry for him, this fellow. He grew up so blind and deaf, he can't see that life is different now . . . The synagogue! All but a few have been shut down. And who needs them? Have you even once been to a synagogue? Milochka has never been either. A whole generation's growing up now without hearing a thing about it."

She fired herself up with her own words. We quite agreed with her, but she needed an antagonist, an opponent. She turned to Grandfather with a tirade in Yiddish. He heard her out, smiled, and answered her calmly. I made out the word *shansonetkes*.[45] She raised her voice. He bent over a book and signed off.

"He says, 'Better God than *shansonetkes* . . .' And I say to him, '*Shansonetkes* are at least live women, and what about your God? Where is he?'"

* * *

I never thought of him again, ever. I remembered him but didn't think of him. A few stills: him standing by the empty table, rumpling the end of a long, twisted *cache-nez*; him sitting at the same table, very close to Grandfather (a grey beard, Grandfather's beard, flashed as soon as I recalled that picture in my memory!), his face down, he seems either to be mumbling or to be humming something; at times he glances—not at us, but to the side, or down. And, of course, the image of him, his head thrust back, as if he were gargling, of him standing not in a usual place, his Adam's apple moving . . . But now comes something else: a sound at the same high level of memory, a musical phrase, struggling to escape, tearing your heart out, and, at the same time, soothing it with its beauty—or maybe, many voices?—all in all, what he sang comes up in my memory and, not so much by sound and, of course, not by melody, which I don't know, but by the spasm of my heart, always so unexpected. And after several minutes, the last still imprinted exactly and for a long time: thick eyebrows raised in woe, heavy red-rimmed eyelids lowered, and a corner of his mouth twisted—an image of vexed disdain, maybe, or scornful sympathy for us. That was when we,

---

45 *Shansonetkes* (Yiddish) = female popular singer, corruption of the French *chansonnette*, which denotes a light or satirical song; *chansonnier(e)* (French) = a male (female) performer of *chansonnettes*.

stunned, exalted (but I don't see us), were exclaiming about his voice and that he must study . . . Why disdain for us? Why no joy, not even a suppressed smile at our excitement? Arrogant pride? Or humility? Ah yes, humility! He looked down at us when he wasn't looking to the side!

Maybe that was the reason I didn't think of him, because of this woeful and disdainful expression. My conscious memory keeps and cherishes agreeable memories. That is why I left this out; I could not erase it, but I left it out, put it away.

I remembered him only recently, only now, in Jerusalem, after a radio interview with a *hazzan* who recently arrived from Tashkent.

"Art?" he asked in surprise. "One has to have a Hassidic soul, and knowledge of style. Words limit singing; when a song is based on words, it means less, it's worth less. One can also improvise, why not? But, of course, there are also melodies—Kol Nidrei, for example, and a few others—where one cannot improvise; they are transmitted from generation to generation without change."

And I remembered.

That phrase! From Kol Nidrei. I already knew that it was not a prayer but a "form of renunciation," a renunciation of all imposed vows and sworn testimonies, probably formulated in Spain under Visigothic kings. And one mustn't change anything in it? So that since those times, this melody has been passed from generation to generation? And that is why Milka's mother was able to correct him—she remembered. And Grandfather then agreed with her immediately. She had, in fact, a very precise ear, perhaps even perfect pitch.

"You lived in Russia for twenty years," the interviewer said. "Your era is the era of the guitar. Why did everybody sing to the guitar, but you . . ."

"Because of the family, of course," answered the *hazzan*. "My family is traditional. And I knew. I was trying hard, but of course, I haven't accomplished it yet . . . You see, when I was little, back in Tashkent, I heard a *hazzan*. I don't even know where he came from. He didn't stay long. I followed him everywhere. He soon left, I don't know where. At that time I was too timid to ask, and then there was no one to ask. And this man . . . I don't even know what there was in him . . . His voice, probably—a 'spinto'—a dramatic tenor, like mine, but he could sing everything, also things for a lyrical tenor . . . but this is probably not the main point. To this day I can still hear him. He sang the Kol Nidrei in a way I never heard in my life again. He sang—and everybody was on tiptoes, trying to reach his voice . . . No, there is no way to describe it."

Later, when they played a recording of this Tashkent singer, I kept waiting to hear again . . . No, I didn't hear it. His voice was cautious, soft, and did not rush headlong up and up; it glided, playing the middle ranges. And I listened and waited: will he? will he?

I didn't listen to the end. Well, so what? From an Odessa day, shriveled, dried out, deadened, turned, or almost turned, into a husk, there unfurled, emerged, sounded forth an almost uninterrupted, an almost undamaged spool of memories. Student and teacher, next to each other, at the same table, elbow to elbow, absorbed by the same book; they breathe in unison, they are doing what they were born into this world to do—it was like love. On Grandfather's lips plays something like a smile; maybe he is shaping his lips this way to sing, but maybe he is simply happy about his returning courage, the courage of a creator, a sower, who finally has found a fertile soil that will preserve and grow his crops, will make his life not irrelevant. The soil is attentive, sensitive, and given into his hands, and the soil is grateful and responsive. Never again did I see such full agreement between student and teacher. I have had occasion to see mesmerized student audiences, hushed with exultation; but that was different, there was a professor-artist and a public; there was no secret and fertile equality between two people.

Don't try to stop me! I want to think that that young cantor whose name I don't even know once turned up in Tashkent. And it was him that the Hassidic singer from Tashkent attempted to equal for many years. He, too, after all, was facing the same dilemma: God or *shansonetkes*?

1988

Translated from the Russian by Helen Reeve with Martha Kitchen

DAVID SHRAYER-PETROV

David Shrayer-Petrov (b. 1936), poet, fiction writer, translator, essayist, and memoirist, was born to a Jewish family and grew up in Leningrad (St. Petersburg). Descended from Lithuanian rabbis and Podolian millers, Shrayer-Petrov heard Yiddish in the traditional home of his paternal grandparents. Both of Shrayer-Petrov's parents (father an engineer, mother a chemist) made the transition from the former Pale to Leningrad (St. Petersburg) in the 1920s. Evacuated from Leningrad in 1941, Shrayer-Petrov spent three years in a Russian village in the Urals.

Shrayer-Petrov entered the literary scene as a poet and translator in the mid-to-late 1950s. He was a founding member of a literary seminar (*lito*) at the House of Culture of Industrial Cooperation (known as *Promka*); the group's gatherings were attended by **Vassily Aksyonov**, Ilya Averbakh, **Evgeny Reyn**, and others who were then young literary lights. Upon the suggestion of **Boris Slutsky**, he adopted the pen name David Petrov, derived from Pyotr—a Russianized form of his father's first name, Peysakh. This assimilatory gesture did not ease the publication of Shrayer-Petrov's poetry in the USSR, and he made a name for himself largely as a translator of verse. After graduating from Leningrad First Medical School in 1959, Shrayer-Petrov served as a military physician in Belorussia. In 1964, two years after marrying the philologist and translator Emilia Polyak, Shrayer-Petrov moved to Moscow, where his son, Maxim D. Shrayer, was born in 1967. Shrayer-Petrov received a candidate's advanced degree from the Leningrad Institute of Tuberculosis in 1966, and he worked as a researcher at the Gamaleya Institute of Microbiology in Moscow from 1967 to 1978. At the Gamaleya Institute Shrayer-Petrov defended another advanced degree—doctor of medical science.

From his earliest verses, Shrayer-Petrov explored the nature of Jewish identity. Although he managed to publish a collection of poems (*Canvasses*, 1967, with an introduction by **Lev Ozerov**) and two books of essays in the 1970s, most of his writings were too controversial for Soviet officialdom to allow their publication. Shrayer-Petrov's occasional flights into official Soviet subjects (e.g., space exploration, the Baikal–Amur Railroad) in poetry, essays, and song lyrics earned him no trust on the part of the regime. Despite recommendations by such prominent writers as **Viktor Shklovsky**, Shrayer-Petrov was only admitted to the Union of Soviet Writers in 1976 after a long battle.

His second poetry collection, *Winter Ship*, moved up the frozen straights of the Sovetskii pisatel' (Soviet Writer) publishing house with discouraging slowness and was finally never published. By the early 1970s, the relations between Jews and Gentiles became a principal concern of Shrayer-Petrov's writing.

In January 1979, Shrayer-Petrov and his family applied for exit visas. Fired from his academic position and expelled from the Union of Soviet Writers (three of his books derailed, one of them already set in galleys and illustrated), Shrayer-Petrov became a refusenik. He was unable to publish in the Soviet Union throughout the years of a refusenik's limbo. In 1979–80, while driving an illegal cab at night and working in a hospital emergency room, Shrayer-Petrov wrote the first part of what would become a trilogy of novels about refuseniks: *Doctor Levitin, May You Be Cursed, Don't Die*, and *The Third Life*. In documenting with anatomical precision the mutually unbreachable contradictions of a mixed Jewish-Russian marriage, Shrayer-Petrov also treats the story of Doctor Herbert Levitin as an allegory of Jewish-Russian history. Part one was completed in 1980, part two in 1983. In 1986, an abridged version of part one appeared in Israel under the title *Being Refused*; in 1992, the first two parts came out in Moscow under the title *Herbert and Nelly*, which was longlisted for the 1993 Russian Booker Prize. Two revised editions of *Herbert and Nelly* have since come out in Russia: in 2005 in St. Petersburg and in 2014 in Moscow. Written in the United States following Shrayer-Petrov's emigration, part three of the refusenik trilogy, *The Third Life*, was published in 2009. *Doctor Levitin*, part one of the refusenik trilogy, appered in the United States in English translation in 2018. In spite of persecution and arrests by the KGB, Shrayer-Petrov's last Soviet decade was prolific; he wrote two novels, several plays, a memoir, and many stories and verses. The refusenik's isolation from the rest of Soviet society, coupled with the absurdity of being a Jewish writer who is both silenced by and shackled to Russia, led to Shrayer-Petrov's discovery of the form he calls *fantella* (perhaps decipherable as "*fant*astic nov*ella*"?). In 1982–87, Shrayer-Petrov and his wife hosted a salon for refuseniks, where a number of Jewish writers, including **Yury Karabchievsky** and **Genrikh Sapgir**, gave readings.

Shrayer-Petrov was finally granted permission to emigrate in April 1987. Leaving the Soviet Union on 7 June 1987, Shrayer-Petrov and his wife, Emilia Shrayer, settled in Providence, Rhode Island, after a summer in Austria and Italy. Arriving on the tail end of the Third Wave, the writer began to sign his literary publications with the hyphenated Shrayer-Petrov—a dual name that betokens his literary career. Since emigrating, Shrayer-Petrov has published twelve books of poetry (among them *Petersburg Doge* [St. Petersburg, 1999] and *Drums of Fortune* [Moscow, 2002]), ten novels, six collections of short stories, and four volumes of memoirs. In several of his works, notably the novel *French Cottage* (Providence, RI, 1999), scientific interests dovetail with those of a fiction writer, not surprising since for twenty years Shrayer-Petrov divided his time between writing and cancer research. Published in Moscow in 2004, his book *Those Strange Russian Jews* was composed of two novels, *Savely Ronkin* and the autobiographical *Strange Danya Rayev*. Three volumes of Shrayer-Petrov's fiction have appeared in English translation: *Jonah and Sarah: Jewish Stories of Russia and America* (2003), *Autumn in Yalta: A Novel and Three Stories* (2006), and *Dinner with Stalin and Other Stories* (2014; finalist of the Wallant Prize), all edited by Maxim D. Shrayer. Now retired from research, Shrayer-Petrov lives in Brookline, Massachusetts, with his wife of over fifty-five years and devotes himself to full-time writing.

Jews and Russians are the "two peoples [who] are the closest to me in flesh (genes) and spirit (language)," Shrayer-Petrov wrote in 1985, less than two years before emigrating from Russia. In a 2014 interview, Shrayer-Petrov commented on his experience as an immigrant writer: "Most of [my recent] stories fashion Russian—Jewish-Russian—characters living in America. In this sense, I've become an American writer. . . . I think that I've rooted myself in New England. It has become my second—now my main—habitat." In 2015, the Moscow-based publisher of Jewish books Knizhniki, which had previously reprinted *Herbert and Nelly*, published a volume of Shrayer-Petrov's selected short stories, *Around-the-Globe Happiness*. His collection of selected long poems, *Village Orchestra*, came out in 2016 in St. Petersburg.

* * *

In 1975–76, Shrayer-Petrov composed poems where disharmonies of his Russian and Jewish selves adumbrate his conflict with the Soviet regime. "Chagall's Self-Portrait with Wife," "My Slavic Soul," and "Early Morning in Moscow" were published in the writer's first émigré collection, *Song about a Blue Elephant* (1990). Read in April 1978 at the televised closing ceremony of the Spring Festival of Poetry in Vilnius, Lithuania, "My Slavic Soul" brought forth repressive measures against the author and finalized his decision to emigrate. Shrayer-Petrov started "Villa Borghese" in June 1987 in Rome, three weeks after leaving Moscow, and completed it after his arrival in the United States. Part dirge, part confession of a Jew's expired love for Russia, "Villa Borghese" bridges Shrayer-Petrov's poetry of the Russian and the émigré years.

Marriages between Jews and non-Jews continue to fascinate Shrayer-Petrov in his outwardly unturbulent life as a Jewish-Russian-American writer in New England. Rooting into his adopted land and its culture, Shrayer-Petrov features a greater variety of American characters in his fiction as he continues to inscribe (autobiographical) émigré writers into the landscapes and culturescapes of his adopted America. Composed in 1999, the story that follows was featured in Shrayer-Petrov's English-language collection *Jonah and Sarah: Jewish Stories of Russia and America* (2003) and in his Russian-language collection *Carp for Gefilte Fish: Jewish Stories* (2005).

CHAGALL'S SELF-PORTRAIT WITH WIFE

for Boris Bernstein[46]

Bella, why did you fly out
With Marc over the old hut?
There are no coins in his purse,
He doesn't belong in Russia.
Better if in that little church
You'd had a fling with the deacon,
Together you could steal the kopecks
From the poor village plate.
But look there, you are flying—the bride
In white over the white countryside.
What? Isn't there space enough
In that one-room hut to press
Your tired wings
Against his seething brushes,
And love this country painlessly
All your life?

1975

Translated from the Russian by Edwin Honig and Maxim D. Shrayer

---

46 Bernstein, Boris (1924–2015)—art historian and critic, originally from Odessa, lived and taught in Tallinn, Estonia, from the early 1950s until 1995; subsequently moved to California. In 1973–87, Shrayer-Petrov's family were friendly with Bernstein and his wife, the pianist Bella Bernstein (née Pribluda), and socialized with them every summer at the Estonian resort of Pärnu.

MY SLAVIC SOUL

My Slavic soul trapped in the shell of a familiar Jewish wrapping,
Forswearing the daily strife that suffocates me all my life,
One day will outsmart its lot, turn a clever somersault,
And dashingly escape to burn like anthracite, the wondrous stone.
I'll chase her: Wait! What shall I do alone amid this grove of birches
In my perennial, banal, so typically Jewish wrapping?
The ruts and roadside ditches that have viewed me as a solid fellow
Will realize that I'm barren, like an abandoned charabanc.

Come back, my soul, you're my guide; a blind cripple, I'm helpless.
I don't have the wild expanse of those generous Slavic cheeks,
Come back, my soul, come back to me! I once resembled a human being,
And once the people weren't loathe to share with me their drunken joy.
Hiding from me in someone's barn, where in the hayloft she took refuge,
Bulging her bare-naked eyes as though she were an octopus,
My soul said: I'd rather be with those who have lost their riches,
Than shatter myself, a teardrop that falls into the icy night.

1975

Translated from the Russian by Maxim D. Shrayer

VILLA BORGHESE

These dogs copulating at Villa Borghese,
Copulating, the casual bitches and males,
Taking over the place, blaring out Brothellaise,
Blatantly wagging their tails—oh, details!

The concrete music of dog bodies rustling,
Of dogs' scrawny bodies, a low street ballet.
The concrete tears for the anguish of Russia.
The weeping ballet has flown, rushed away.

Like a stray with the Roman dogs of the Villa,
Like a gasping fish on the banks of the Tiber,
Forget the purging, the crushing, the spilling,
Forget the evil caress of the empire.

At Villa Borghese, on Italianate evenings,
In grandeur, the lap of luxurious Rome,
A stray is still howling for his Russian leavings,
The lost, irretrievable things of his home.

To wake and feel pressed by tails to the railing,
To wake and feel grass intertwining with hair,
Beneath skies of Rome, to go madly on mumbling
Oh, Nádenka, Nádya—a stumbling prayer—

Oh Véra, Verúnchik . . . Oh, Lyúbushka, Lyúba,
Valyúsha, Marína, Katyúsha, and Zína.[47]
Here the soberest New England winters
Offer their lips to me, cool and serene.

When my time comes to die, when I'm barely alive,
Half-dead lips will whisper, like never before:
For you and us, Russia, no closeness survives,
We, sons of Yehudah, who used to be yours.

To lie here embracing—perhaps it's a laugh—
Last bottle, last letter, whatever remains.
At Villa Borghese, like an old photograph
On history's dump. Along with the frame.

At Villa Borghese, hang out with the gang
Of roaming wild dogs, an antique mosaic.
How much can you care, oh my Lord, for the paining
Soul and how much for the marble, anemic

---

47 Russian female names, some of them affectionate and diminutive forms; stresses have been
    added to preserve the amphibrachic tetrameter.

Creatures arranged among columns of wood.
Like Petersburg's Summer Gardens. We walked
A sweet winding path, lovers' lane, and we stood
All night beneath skies that would never grow dark.

Those archangels blaring their trumpets of exile,
Those animals hounding us, shunned and banned,
Those judases killing with kindness and smiles.
And yet, despite all, we still loved that land

That cast us away like inferior stuff,
Aborted like something conceived out of error,
All that wasn't all, it was never enough,
Until they were rid of us cursed ones forever,

Until I came here to this barbarous Villa
Where statuesque maidens and dogs crowd my sight,
Out walking the dear little paths, like my darling
Remember, back home, how we walked those white nights?

1987–90

Translated from the Russian by Dolores Stewart and Maxim D. Shrayer

HÄNDE HOCH![48]

We were visiting the Wassers in Athol, a small town in rural north-central Massachusetts. We had met the Wassers—Ernest and Judith—during a trip to Spain. On the first day of the tour, their seats happened to be next to ours on the bus. We hit it off with them, so for the rest of the trip we sat together, chatting. We talked a lot about Russia. They asked many questions. We reminisced. The Wassers turned out to be great admirers of Jewish memoir literature. Both of them loved to read reminiscences of Jewish writers, philosophers, and scientists. Even recollections of those from the inner circle of our people's greats fascinated the Wassers. And accounts by survivors of Nazi concentration camps they held in the highest esteem. After we told them that Mila (my wife) and I had waited for almost nine years to emigrate, that is, had been refuseniks[48] during those years,

---

48 Refusenik—the Russian term *otkaznik* means "one who was refused, denied permission" to

the number of their questions about living in Russia rose so dramatically that we could no longer concentrate on the tour guide's explanations. We could only follow with our eyes along the hills on which olive trees stood like chess pieces. Or else we could guess, from the silhouettes of windmills, that the melancholy knight Don Quixote had galloped across these valleys and mountain passes. Of course, Don Quixote had inherited his eternal sadness from the Jews of Spain.

I've observed that American Jews like to talk about Russia. This is especially true of the ones whose ancestors came from Eastern Europe. They often speak of it with such excitement and enthusiasm as if Russia, and not Israel, was their forefathers' ancient homeland. But the Wassers truly shared a connection to the vast expanse of fields and great forests where Mila and I had been born and lived until the late 1980s. As children, both of the Wassers were taken to Siberia. In 1939, their parents, Polish Jews from Lublin, had miraculously escaped from the Nazis and fled to the Soviet Union. Together their families had lived through evacuation to Siberia. Together they returned to Poland after the war only to flee again, this time to America. The rescuing hand belonged to a Jew from their old neighborhood in Lublin who had settled in the American town of Athol, Massachusetts, a few years before the outbreak of the war. He was searching for his relatives in Lublin. All of them had been killed, and the letter was forwarded to the Wassers, Ernest's parents. Because Judith's parents, the Zolotowskis, were their only friends and fellow survivors, both families replied with one letter, composed in the Aesopian language of hints and allusions. But their fellow countrymen were able to figure it out, and the new American from Athol sent both families an invitation with an affidavit, recognizing them as blood relatives. Ernest and Judith—now the American teenagers "Ernie" and "Judy"—went to school in the small New England town.

Ernie became a salesman in the furniture showroom his father had opened. Judy worked in a bakery. They got married. Judy stayed home with the children. By the time we met the Wassers in Spain, Ernie had retired, leaving the business to his son. Their daughter was living in Providence, Rhode Island, with her husband, a professor of sociology at Brown, and a five-year-old son . . .

"Tomorrow you'll meet the whole *mishpokhe*," Ernie promised me on the phone.[49] "Do you know how to get here? And I want you and Mila to come

---

leave the Soviet Union. In its literal English translation-cum-calque, the term "refusenik" has acquired an ambiguity whose irony was hardly intentional: the Soviet authorities, not the Jews, were doing the refusing, unless, of course, you also consider the fact that the refuseniks themselves had refused the ticket to Soviet paradise.

49 *Mishpokhe* (Yiddish) = family.

early. We'll have an unrushed dinner, talk awhile. You know how your pockets are always full of interesting news about Russia. Remember, in the evening we're all going to shul to see a play?"

How could I forget?! Ernie was talking about a play that was being put on by the Jewish Theatrical Society. The Jewish Theatrical Society of Athol was well known in the area for its productions of plays translated from the Yiddish. They also staged plays based on the works of Jewish fiction writers, Sholem Aleichem, Isaac Bashevis Singer, and others. Along with the invitation to attend the opening performance, I had received a letter from the local rabbi (also the director of the play). The rabbi-director wrote that if the nature and style of the production appealed to me, they would commission from me a play based on my novel about refuseniks, *Herbert and Nelly*. Writing a play based on my own novel—what could be better!

Early spring. The beginning of April. A Massachusetts of fir trees. We drive north, then west, then turn north again. The woods become denser and dimmer. Dark wet branches of the firs reach down to the pink-and-gray granite clefts. The roads here are winding and narrow, slithering along like black asphalt snakes. By five o'clock our Subaru swallows the last twists and turns off the road, and we're in Athol.

We drive up the main street past the gray ferro-concrete building of the bank, a redbrick fire station, and a lemon-colored hotel with false columns and a bright white trim. The town's only stoplight winks at us: here we turn right. We cross a bridge over an uproarious stream. The red neon sign of the local paper, *The Athol Times*, is also in the directions Ernie Wasser gave me over the phone. And here's the final landmark: a painted sign of a furniture store and a section of a bedroom in the store window. Two more minutes, and we turn into the Wassers' long driveway.

Their house is a large Victorian with a wraparound porch. Ornate cast-iron railings. Cast-iron grates on the first-floor windows. A solid, stately house where the Wassers have been living since the 1950s. The house is flanked on one side by an apple orchard. Lilac trees mark off the boundaries of the property on the other side. Rhododendrons are planted in the front; they are swollen, ready to burst into bloom. A Teutonic-looking giant strolls in the garden with a boy of five or six. The boy is clutching a baseball bat in his right hand. The giant turns out to be Wilhelm (Willy), the Wassers' son-in-law, and the quick-eyed and mischievous boy is his son, Mark, their grandson.

We learn all this immediately after parking our Subaru near the gates of the carriage house now used as a garage. We park our car, remove our weekend bag from the trunk, and fall into the hands of Ernie Wasser, kissing and hugging him, petting King the chocolate spaniel on his fluffy ears, being introduced to Willy, little Mark, and also Jessica, the Wassers' daughter.

Our arrival has inadvertently distracted Willy and Mark from an important activity. The giant apologizes and leads Mark away into the far corner of the garden, from where we soon hear guttural sounds of foreign speech.

"Our son-in-law is teaching our grandson German," Ernie explains and takes us inside to say hello to Judy, who is in the kitchen. We go up to the guest room to drop off our bag. Mila hurries back down to help Judy and Jessica. I linger in the room, examining a pyramid of books on the night stand between the two twin beds. Many of the books are on Jewish history: Jews in Morocco, the Inquisition, the destiny of Poland's Jews. I leaf through a book of photographs from Auschwitz: stacks of corpses, smoking chimneys, piles of footwear that belonged to the people gassed alive . . .

The ellipsoidal table is set for eight: the Wassers (Ernie and Judy), the Hoffmanns (Willy, Jessica, and Mark), Mila and myself, and also another gentleman whom Ernie introduces to us as a "very dear guest." While making the introductions, Ernie gently nods, licks his dry lips, and timidly smiles. I know his mannerisms, his timid smile that accompanies the welling up of tears in his eyes.

"A very dear guest. A special guest," Ernie repeats. The Wassers' special guest sits across from me. His name is Jan Silberstadt. He is well over eighty. The coat of his black two-piece suit hangs on the back of his chair. He is silent, concentrating on the meal.

We're served a standard Jewish-American dinner: lettuce dressed with oil and vinegar, chicken broth with egg noodles, roast chicken with white rice and carrots, and prune compote. The traditional Jewish compote! My grandmother Freyda used to make it every week: prunes plump like Odessan women, water, sugar, and a drop of starch for thickness. Sweet with a barely tangible bitterness, like a Jewish wedding song. And a freshly baked *babka* with raspberry jam. A bottle of Shiraz stands in the middle of the table. At the beginning of dinner, Ernie offers everyone some wine; only Mila and I accept.

"Is there any vodka?" Willy asks loudly.

The master of the house nervously licks his lips and removes a bottle of Stoli from a glass cabinet. The bottle is nearly full. Mila and I each drink a glass of wine. Willy downs two shots of vodka in a row. "Russian vodka is very good!" he says and smiles at us. The elderly guest lowers his gaze into the bowl of chicken broth with noodles. Ernie stops offering drinks. He even puts the wine and vodka away into the glass cabinet. However tempting, it would be *inaccurate* to attribute to inebriation a certain argumentative brashness that both Mila and Willy show during the dinner, since neither one of them has had much to drink. Inaccurate versus accurate . . . the English language here displays a proclivity to evaluate the method employed in the presentation of a given piece of information. The English language assesses the method rather than the underlying ethic, as would my native Russian language, in which I would be inclined to say *dishonest* instead of *inaccurate*. Dishonest versus honest . . .

For some reason the dinner conversation turns to the subject of automobile license plates.

"In many European countries, including Russia, things are much easier," Mila says. "License plates tell you in which city or which county center the car is registered. Someplace in Belgium, at a gas station or in a hotel parking lot, you see a car whose license plates say it's from Amsterdam. And you just happen to be driving to Amsterdam from Paris. So you strike up a conversation with the owner of the car. You find out something that you cannot extract from any guide book."

"But not everyone wishes to inform the whole world where he or she lives," Willy retorts. "I prefer the American system with the name of the state and a combination of numbers and letters on the license plates."

"What's to hide? Amsterdam, St. Petersburg, Venice! The names alone possess their own charm, their own flavor and color. They evoke so much— the lace of canals, the necklaces of bridges. It's not like it says Dachau on the plate!"

Ernie drops his fork. It's good that the average American doesn't use both knife and fork simultaneously. Otherwise it would have sounded like the entrance of the percussion instruments at the culmination of an orchestral piece. I mean, if you take a dinner conversation to be a symphony with its adagio, its andante, and its strong finale with a crescendo. Ernie picks up his fork and puts in his lap his grandson, Mark, who is happily consuming chicken with rice. They say the protective centers of the brains of children and animals are much more sensitive as compared to adult humans.

"So what, so what about Dachau?" Willy attacks my wife. "Say I was born in Dachau. And if I continued to live there, and not in this country, the license plate on my Volkswagen would reveal the name 'Dachau.'"

Ernie looks guiltily at his special guest Jan Silberstadt, who continues to eat, unperturbed by the agitation. I try to calm Mila, stroking her right hand, in which she holds an old silver-plated knife. Sometimes it helps, but not now. Mila pays no attention to my preemptive patting of her hand. Her gray-blue eyes turn the steely color of a thunderous sky.

"If I had the misfortune of being born in Dachau," she burst out, "I would run as far as I could from there at the first opportunity. Which, I suppose, you did."

"My husband didn't need to run from any place or to any place. Wilhelm was invited to Brown University because of his world-renowned research on the social psychology of populations living near sites of massive executions," Jessica weighs in. Everything about her is impressive: head, bosom, hips.

Willy takes over from his wife after biting into and swallowing some chicken from a drumstick. "I was able to discover many similarities among the Poles, Germans, and Latvians residing in the vicinities of Oświęcim, Dachau, Salaspils, and other places bearing the burden of sorrowful memories."

"A sense of shame?" Mila asks, to clarify his point.

"Actually, more of a sense of bitterness," the Brown professor replies.

"And I would die of shame at the mere thought that I'm a native of Dachau!" Mila shakes my calming hand off of hers. That's what she's like in wrath, my darling lifelong companion.

"And what about the natives of Vinnitsa, in Ukraine, where officers of the NKVD shot thousands of their fellow citizens right within the boundaries of the city? Or the residents of Petersburg with their infamous 'Big House'? Or take the Muscovites with their Lubyanka? You're from Moscow, aren't you? Weren't you ashamed to shop at Detsky Mir, the "Children's World" department store in Dzerzhinsky Square? It stands right next to the KBG headquarters in whose underground cells they interrogated, even in your times, yes, interrogated the dissidents and Jewish refuseniks? No, I believe the only acceptable responses to such situations are bitterness, sorrow, and deep regret that such evil crimes have been committed," says Willy and sighs, looking over his shoulder at the glass cabinet where Ernie stored away the alcohol. What can one say? This professor is no dummy.

Throughout the entire discussion, the Wassers' special guest Jan Silberstadt hasn't uttered a single word . . .

The synagogue is filled with congregants and their guests. It was only built a year ago. Inside, the smell of fresh varnish on the rafters and woodwork is laced with the aroma of freshly brewed coffee. Along the walls, narrow tables stand heavy with coffee thermoses and trays with the uncomplicated New England desserts: cookies, brownies, apple pies. From a distance, platters of fruit resemble exotic oriental ornaments. Each family has contributed something.

The Jews of Athol are dressed in their best clothes. Men wear suits (many of them three piece). A number of women wear heavy long dresses with sequins. Necklaces and bracelets; costume jewelry, gold, precious stones. The congregants are excited to attend the new production at their shul. But they also pay handsome tribute to the coffee and desserts, each of which follows its own family recipe. The people stand near the long tables or mill around, saying hello to each other. Children snatch away pieces of desert and cavort around the hall. They don't care about the play. Their peers and the holiday atmosphere is entertainment enough for them.

From time to time we can see through the doors of the main sanctuary a costumed actress or actor sticking their heads through a chink in the middle of the curtain and smiling at someone in the audience. Besides the Wassers, we don't know a single soul in Athol. We're being introduced left and right. Some people have heard about my refusenik novel, most likely from the Wassers. Many here are concerned about the future of the Jews still living in Russia. We can see it in the way they speak to us. We're touched. We're grateful to the Wassers for their invitation.

The people are filling the sanctuary and sitting down. A crowd's hum metamorphoses into whispering. Everyone awaits the beginning of the play. The curtain heaves like a sail caressed by gentle breeze. Now and then a baby's crying interrupts the quiet that precedes the miracle of a performance. Finally the rabbi-director comes on stage. He describes the play that the members of the Jewish Theatrical Society are about to perform. The play is based on a memoir by Jan Silberstadt, a former inmate of Dachau. The director explains that his play faithfully follows the events of the love story that Jan Silberstadt describes in his memoir. Everything has been preserved: the real names and even the turn of the plot that brings about the final scene. The director comes down from the stage and approaches the front row. We're all sitting in the same row with Jan: Ernie, Judy, Mila and I, Willy with Mark in his lap, and Jessica. The rabbi shakes the hand of the Wassers' solemn guest and asks him to stand on stage. The Athol community greets the survivor with big applause. The play begins.

The set depicts a Jewish ghetto in a Polish city occupied by the Nazis. A stone archway; an overgrown courtyard with a desolate chestnut tree; a room with an old upright piano. This is the meeting place of the ill-fated young lovers, Anka and Jan. The Nazi administration has announced, through the local Judenrat, the upcoming deportations of the ghetto residents. From books and films about the Holocaust, the audience knows that "deportation" means transport to concentration camps where the Jews (mothers, wives, daughters separated from fathers, husbands, brothers) will be gassed alive and then burned in crematoria. Reminded of the horrors, the audience expects a tragic ending to the love story. Start the final scene.

Anka's room. Outside the windows—the whistles of policemen, the barking of guard dogs, shooting. Anka is at the piano. Jan sits beside her with his cello. They play Mendelssohn's "Song without Words." The banging of fists and the clattering of heavy boots resound across the room. Anka and Jan continue playing. Nazi soldiers break the door. Their machine guns are aimed at Anka and Jan. The soldiers yell, "*Hände hoch! Hände hoch!*" The piano gives out a plaintive sound. The cello drops to the floor. The curtain falls. A screen descends from the ceiling. Rays of the slide projector bring to the screen the brick chimneys of the crematoria. Heavy smoke. The camp's gates. A solitary figure of an inmate in a striped uniform. Chimneys. Smoke. Smoke. Smoke. The screen is pulled up. Lights go out, and the curtain is raised again. Everyone applauds the actors, the director, the Wassers' guest Jan Silberstadt.

To preserve the fullness of all the events, I should add that when the Nazi soldiers broke into Anka's room and rabidly shouted, "*Hände hoch! Hände hoch!*" many in the audience were shaken. The tragedy of European Jewry came alive before their eyes. At that point Willy whispered "Excuse me" and left to put Mark to bed. Jessica followed them.

The success of the play has exceeded all expectations. Actors and actresses, especially the two who played the lead parts of Anka and Jan, are surrounded by relatives and friends. In Athol all the Jews are friends or relatives, usually both. The members of the audience come up to congratulate the cast and director, discuss the most memorable episodes, ask the director when he plans to start working on the next production.

Old Jan Silberstadt looks tired, spent. At first the people approach him with questions: "Where can we buy or order your memoir? How close is the play to real life? What are you working on now?" He replies reluctantly, dryly, disallowing any hearty conversation. They finally leave him alone.

The thespian rabbi now takes me to his study at the opposite end of the synagogue. The walls are adorned with works of Israeli artists, including David Sharir.[50]

---

50 Sharir, David (b. 1938)—Israeli artist and set designer, Shrayer-Petrov's first cousin. Sharir is a Hebrew version of the last name Shrayer, which the Israeli branch of the family took after emigrating from Russia to Palestine in the 1920s.

"I love his work!" the rabbi exclaims. "He lives in Old Jaffa."

"Yes, I know his paintings very well," I reply. "He's my cousin."

"By the way, what did you think of the production?" asks the rabbi.

"Excellent set, very good directing, fine acting," I answer. "Very professional."

"Do you have anyone in mind we could commission to do the sets for your play?"

"I would recommend Boris Sheynes.[51] He's a former refusenik. Knows the specifics of the period."

"Excellent! Excellent! You're the author, you know what's best," the director replies.

We discuss the terms: number of characters, deadline for the play, honorarium. Then the rabbi walks me back to the sanctuary, now empty except for Ernie, Judy, Jan, and Mila, who are all waiting for me. We drive back to the Wassers' house . . .

Neither of us can fall asleep. We turn on the TV. Scraps of thrillers, hackneyed game shows, beauty pageants don't help chase away the burdensome thoughts. What's changed? Hundreds of thousands tortured or expelled by the Inquisition. Six million turned to tears and ashes by the Nazis. Tens of thousands herded by the Soviets into the ghettos of refusenik isolation and persecution. And once again, just a few weeks ago, in California: burned synagogues and murdered children. When will this stop? Will it ever?

Mila and I discuss the play. We both wonder if the performers, the director, the set designer have been completely successful in preserving the character of Silberstadt's memoir.

"You know, the final scene, the very last episode, did you think it was a bit too simplistic, with the soldiers shouting their '*Hände hoch!*'? A little formulaic, like those Soviet war movies?" Mila asks me.

I hesitate to respond. I also think that something in the final episode was off. Had it really happened like this? And even if it had, should a reflection of the past be a mere copy of the original? And the most important: in my future play, do I want now, many years later, to see the things we lived through as refuseniks with the same eyes as I did in my novel?

I go downstairs and find Willy in the dining room; a bottle of vodka stands in front of him on the table.

"Would you like some Stoli?" he asks.

---

51 Sheynes, Boris (b. 1935)—Russian-American artist, former refusenik, emigrated in 1985 and lives in Chicago.

We have a drink together and talk about the weather. It turns out Willy is a passionate fisherman, just like me. He keeps a motor boat down in Narragansett Bay. We discuss the weather, fishing, his preference for Stoli over Smirnoff and my preference for Absolut over Stoli. We have another drink and chat, chat, chat about the weather, fishing, Stoli, Smirnoff, Absolut . . . About anything under the sun, anything except the play. It's getting late. I get up to go to bed.

"Did you like the performance?" Willy asks and looks at me, expecting an answer.

"On the whole, yes," I answer. "Good night." I don't want to discuss it with him.

"In reality everything was just like that—" Willy's words catch up with me on the stairs, "—and wasn't."

Next morning Mila wakes me up. "Wake up, sleepy head! We'll take a walk before breakfast. Don't you want to see the town?"

We go out to the front porch. It has rained overnight. Shiny drops hang on the white and amethyst clusters of lilacs. A large blue-winged bird swings on a long fir branch, getting ready to continue on his journey. Where to? Old Jan Silberstadt sits on a cast-iron bench near the porch, reading the Sunday paper. We go up to him to say hello.

"There you go, look: Germans protecting Albanians from Serbs. The world is going mad!" says the old man and shows us a photo from the news-paper. Burly lads in military uniforms and helmets ride on tanks into Kosovo.

Before we've had a chance to reply to him, we see Willy running out of the apple orchard and onto the front lawn. He is laughing as he raises his arms and bends his elbows. Armed with a toy machine gun, little Mark chases him across the lawn. Ecstatic, the boy doesn't even notice us. Laughing the happiest of laughs, he pursues the giant Willy. At the top of his lungs, Mark screams, "Surrender, daddy! Please surrender, daddy! *Hände hoch! Hände hoch! Hände hoch!*"

1999

Translated from the Russian by Maxim D. Shrayer

MARINA TEMKINA

Marina Temkina (b. 1948), poet, critic, translator, and mixed-media artist, was born in Leningrad (St. Petersburg). Both her parents come from Rechitsa, a county seat in Minsk Province (now in Gomel Province of Belarus). A late child, Temkina lost her father in 1951. Jewish traditions survived in their family and in their communal apartment, where other Jewish families lived. Temkina recalls first experiencing antisemitism in kindergarten.

As a teenager, Temkina gained inspiration from the novels of Lion Feuchtwanger and Thomas Mann's *Joseph and His Brothers* (in Russian translation). She attended dissident gatherings from the age of fifteen. After failing to gain admission to three universities in Moscow, Temkina studied art history at Leningrad University, graduating in 1976 with a thesis on the Russian avant-garde. Although Temkina wrote poetry since the age of twenty-four, she did not seek its publication.

In 1978, Temkina emigrated with her husband, the musician and visual artist Sergei Blumin (the marriage ended in divorce), and their son. After a year and a half in Europe, they arrived in New York, where she lives today. Temkina contributed to émigré periodicals: *Archer* (*Strelets*), *Continent* (*Kontinent*), *Twenty-Two* (*Dvadtsat' dva*), Sergei Dovaltov's *The New American* (*Novy ameri-kanets*), and others. Her first and second collections, *A Part of a Part* (1985) and *In the Opposite Direction* (1989), were published in Paris by *Syntax* (*Sintaksis*), which was run by Maria Rozanova, Andrey Sinyavsky's wife (see **Yuly Daniel**). *Observatoire geomnesique*, Temkina's trilingual collection, was illustrated by her partner, the artist Michel Gerard, and appeared in France in 1990.

In the 1990s, Temkina's writing underwent a radical transformation. As Temkina explains in her third collection, *Water Tower: Gendered Lyric* (New York, 1995), "Since leaving in 1973, living in emigration for one third of my life, I have turned into a person of whom I had only a vague notion before emigrating." Temkina's works began to appear in Russia in the 1990s; a volume of her selected poetry, *Canto Immigranto*, apppeared in Moscow in 2005. She has embraced visual poetry and mixed media and has had a number of exhibits.

Temkina has worked as a translator and taught at American universities. In 1996–98, she conducted interviews for the Survivors of the Shoah Visual History Foundation. She was the cofounder and president of The Archive for Jewish Immigrant Culture, established in New York City in 1996.

* * *

"One of the personal motivations to emigrate," Temkina wrote to the editor of this anthology in 2002, "[. . .] was a desire to show [poems] to **Brodsky** and to hear his critique [. . .]. [W]e became rather close [. . .], and I prepared for publication [**Brodsky**'s] *New Stanzas to Augusta* and *Marbles*, without my name being acknowledged, and translated his essays [two from English into Russian]." **Joseph Brodsky** entered Temkina's pre-1990s poems as an influence, a subject, and an addressee. Her title *A Part of a Part* bows, above all else, to **Joseph Brodsky**'s *A Part of Speech*.

Unlike the poems in Temkina's first two collections, the verses written in the early 1990s and collected in *Water Tower* explode with originality of voice and freedom from conventions. Monologues, recitatives, manifestoes, free-verse satires—these are some of the terms that describe Temkina's project. The subtitle "gendered lyric" maps out only part of Temkina's program. The poems in *Water Tower* negotiate the multiple identity of their maker, an identity that Temkina articulated in "Postcard to Alfred C.," written in English for the American poet Alfred Corn: "I am a Russian-Jewish-immigrant-female-poet/and I speak Babylonian, my native language."

Temkina's *Water Tower* opens with the poem chosen below. The editor regrets being unable to include "Comics on Ethnic Subjects" (1994), the book's longest text (over 500 lines), deserving of study by historians of Jewish writing. Starting as a discourse on both the all-inclusiveness and the uniqueness of the category "Jew," Temkina's poem advances to the subject of Russian Jewry: "[. . .] From two components this identity originates,/you cannot extract one without damaging the other,/the previous division either–or here doesn't apply,/here the method of inclusiveness is required: both Russians we are and Jews/together, the former and the latter are conjoined in us,/all mixed together and inseparable, ethnic with cultural [. . .]." Concluding that "after such a turnout of events in us, Russian Jews,/very little Jewish remains, nothing but a museum/collectible, too rare to discard all this, but/preserving it is also problematic," Temkina finds herself ill at ease to define "Russian Jews" and skeptical of their long-term survival, which might explain her motivation for founding The Archive for Jewish Immigrant Culture. Jewish topics in *Water Tower* give a voice to a trebly marked poet in quest of both self-liberation and self-conservation. "For me," Temkina wrote to the editor, "Marcel Proust is (also) Jewish literature, a creation of minority, including sexual."

1995: HAPPY NEW YEAR!

I imagine myself dressed in a chiffon gown
dancing with Kurt Waldheim[52] at a charity ball;
he wears an elegant Nazi uniform; we waltz
around the room full of blown-up photos:
open pits with excavated bodies of Dachau inmates,
streets of the Warsaw ghetto lined with the Jewish dead.
I imagine myself dancing in a white tuxedo
with Leni Riefenstahl;[53] she wears a slimming dress
with wide shoulders and a small waist,
her hair sleek and blond; everyone watches us tango,
cheek to cheek, while projectors roll her glorious footage
of Nazi conventions, those clean-shaven young men,
their delicate necks, their soft hands saluting the Führer.

---

52 Waldheim, Kurt (b. 1918)—Austrian and international political leader, secretary-general of
    the United Nations from 1971 to 1981. In 1986 Waldheim was elected president of Austria
    and served until 1992 amid a scandal surrounding his service as a propaganda officer in the
    German army, in a unit that committed mass atrocities in the former Yugoslavia in 1944.
    Waldheim's conduct and concealment became the subject of much discussion, including a
    book, *Betrayal: The Untold Story of the Kurt Waldheim Investigation and Cover-Up* (1992),
    by Eli M. Rosenbaum and William Hoffer. The State Department placed Waldheim on its
    list denying entrance to the United States to "any foreign national who assisted or otherwise
    participated in activities amounting to persecution during World War II."

53 Riefenstahl, Leni (1902–2003)—German innovative film director and photographer,
    author of such major statements of Nazi artistic propaganda as "Triumph of Will" (1934)
    and "Olympia" (1936). Declared a Nazi sympathizer following the end of World War II, to
    the end of her long life L. Riefenstahl insisted that her films of the Nazi era were first and
    foremost works of art, that in making them she was not "selling out" to Hitler's regime, and
    that she was not complicit with the Nazi crimes.

I imagine myself dancing in glittering pumps
with Eddie Limonov,[54] tan, lithe, and slender,
a charming provincial with an AK-47 behind his back,
a swastika on his sleeve, cross-belts, steel, and leather,
we dance in perfect harmony to the ecstatic tunes
of the '50s big bands; we glide past the images of
dismembered Bosnian bodies, crowds of women,
pregnant, screaming, herded like cattle, raped.

I imagine myself as a sixteen-year-old dancing
in a sparkling mini skirt and a see-through blouse,
clinging to Vladimir Volfovich Zhirinovsky[55]
at his open-air election party, Russia's new president
looks thinner after everything he's been through,
he wears a suit from the House of Dior, he smirks
as the jubilant crowds shout "Vo-la-re-oo,"
floodlights illumine the giant TV screens,
which show in continuous fashion bodies
being unloaded from gas chambers, women and children
being buried alive, Chechnya being bombed, and casualties
mounting on both sides as the European leaders raise their glasses,
and we say to each other, "Happy New . . ."

1995

Translated from the Russian by Maxim D. Shrayer

Marina Temkina, "Vmesto predisloviia: s novym 1995-m godom!"
Copyright © by Marina Temkina. English translation, introduction, and notes
copyright © by Maxim D. Shrayer.

---

54 Limonov, Eduard (b. 1943)—pseudonym of Eduard Savenko, Russian author and extremist political activist. Limonov left the Soviet Union in 1974, spent time in the United States, and moved to France, where he enjoyed a successful literary career. In 1991, he returned to live in the Russian Federation, where he founded the National-Bolshevik Party (NBP) and published its newspaper, *Limonka*. The title of Limonov's best-known novel is *Eto ia— Edichka* (1976; Eng. translation, *It's Me. Eddie: A Fictional Memoir*, 1983).

55 Zhirinovsky, Vladimir (b. 1946)—contemporary Russian politician, founder and leader of the Russian Liberal-Democratic Party, which, despite its name, advocates an ultrapatriotic Russian platform. Zhirinovsky became internationally known after the success of his party at the 1993 Russian parliamentary election. The son of a Jewish father and a non-Jewish mother, the Russian nationalist Zhirinovsky has made anti-Jewish and xenophobic statements of various sorts and applauded Hitler's national-socialist ideology.

DINA RUBINA

Dina Rubina (b. 1953), prose writer, playwright, screenwriter, and translator, was born in Tashkent, Uzbekistan. Rubina's parents, both Ukrainian Jews, met in Tashkent after World War II; her father was a visual artist, and her mother was a history teacher. Rubina studied piano from 1972 to 1977 at the Tashkent Conservatory; she taught at the Tashkent Institute of Culture in 1977–79. In 1971, Rubina debuted in *Youth* (*Iunost'*) with a humorous piece, "Restless Temper"; her fiction continued to appear in this magazine. A youthful Soviet sentimentality distinguished Rubina's stories and short novels of the 1970s to early 1980s. In 1979, Rubina became a member of the Union of Soviet Writers. Her play, based on the title of the short novel in her first book, *When Will It Start Snowing . . .* ? (Tashkent, 1980), was staged several times. Rubina's next two collections, *House behind a Green Fence* (1982) and *Open the Window* (1987), appeared in Tashkent. Her literary activities included translating from Uzbek and writing radio plays. In 1984, a film based on her short novel *Tomorrow as Usual* (which Rubina calls "unsuccessful") was produced at Uzbekfilm. Although Rubina wrote the script, she now refers to the film *Our Grandson Works in Law Enforcement* as "horrible." She met her second husband, the painter Boris Karafelov (b. 1946), during the filming; she moved to Moscow to be with him.

Jewish motifs surfaced in Rubina's fiction in the late 1980s. In her story "Lyubka" (1989; cf. "Lyubka Kazak" by **Isaac Babel**), a leader of a gang of thieves shows kindness to a young Jewish doctor during the Doctors' Plot. Rubina's collection *A Dual Name* came out in Moscow in 1990, the year she immigrated to Israel. In the early 1990s, Rubina began to publish fictions of her repatriate experience in the leading Moscow periodicals, including *Novy mir*, where *At Thy Gates* appeared in 1993. The list of her books, exceeding forty titles, includes *One Intellectual Slumped Down on the Road* (Jerusalem, 1994; reprinted St. Petersburg, 2000), *Lessons of Music* (Jerusalem, 1996; reprinted Moscow, 1998), *Under the Sign of the Carnival* (Ekaterinburg, 2000), and *A Few Hasty Words of Love* (Moscow, 2003).

In some of her most hilarious fictions about Russian Israelis interacting with other Israelis, especially non-Ashkenazi Jews, Rubina lays bare the extent to which the former are "burdened by some legacy of Russian culture" (to borrow Anna P. Ronell's recent formulation), and the latter are not. Conjoining semiautobiographical lyricism and journalistic sensationalism, Rubina's prose enjoys popularity among Russian readers the world over. A gifted self-promoter (few Russian writers operate a webpage like www.dinarubina.com), Rubina toured the Russian Diaspora in 2004 with her new book, *Syndicate*, a "novel-comic." In *Syndicate*, Rubina explosively fictionalized her experience of serving in Moscow in 2000–2003 as head of the department of cultural ties of the Russian branch of the World Jewish Agency Sohnut. Rubina's career is increasingly taking her away from artistic prose and in the direction of popular entertainment.

Rubina strongly identifies as an Israeli and a Zionist. When asked during a 2004 interview with Yury Vasiliev how she feels about Russia, she responded, "I left Russia. [. . .] Now it is already a completely different country, toward which I no longer feel social or civil obligations." Rubina does not shy away from voicing her hawkish political views. After having lived in Maale-Adumim, a West Bank settlement outside East Jerusalem in the Judean Desert, Rubina and her family moved to Mavaseret Zion, a suburb of Jerusalem. She is one of the most commercially successful authors in today's Russian literary marketplace, with almost thirty books published in Russia in the 2000s–2010s. The protagonist of her best-selling novel *White Dove of Cordoba* (2009), the art forger Zakhar Kordovin, is an ex-Soviet Jew living in Jerusalem.

In a 1999 interview, answering Dmitry Golovanov's question about Russian literary life in Jerusalem, Rubina remarked: "[. . .] the recipe of the Russian literary Israeli cocktail is this: we take the Jewish national temperament, add a large measure of Soviet mentality, dump into the thick of it a full spoon of zesty immigrant problems, a pinch of normal human vanity, half a cup of the existential prophetic itch, then pour in, without measure, sincere love for the Russian word and culture, heat it up in the scorching Jerusalem sun, shake well, and empty this mixture into various large and small forms."

* * *

Rubina's novel *Here Comes the Messiah!* was serialized in *People's Friendship* (*Druzhba narodov*) in 1996; the first book edition appeared in Israel in 1996, followed by several reprints in Russia. For a period of time, Rubina served as a literary editor at *Friday* (*Piatnitsa*), a supplement to the Russian-Israeli newspaper *Our Country* (*Nasha strana*), and her work there informed the novel. Set in the 1990s in Israel, *Here Comes the Messiah!* tells the story of Zyama, a formerly Soviet Israeli, and of the female writer N., also a Jewish-Russian

Israeli who is writing Zyama's story; both lives are captured and locked into a double-parallel frame of the overarching narrative by the novel's implied author. What is new in Rubina's contribution to Russophone literature—fresh, amusing, and moving—is the theme of the 1990s massive wave of Soviet Jews assimilating to their new lives in Israel. Rubina's novel offers both a reversal of and a rebuttal to the stories of Jewish conversion to Christianity in contemporary literature (e.g., the writing of Anatoly Nayman and **Ludmila Ulitskaya**). In the section of the novel featured below (and forming an insert story in its own right), Rubina zooms in on an individual case of an ethnic Russian choosing to become a Jew.

FROM *HERE COMES THE MESSIAH!*

Throughout the history of the State of Israel, a great many people have deserted it. Moreover, as a rule, it was the ardent patriots. There's nothing incredible about this: in all ages and in all countries, it is precisely the ardent patriots whose testimony rarely bears up against that of their own people.

Uri Bar-Hanina felt that the whole of the Jewish people—from babies to those steeped in old age—must gather in the Holy Land of their ancestors so that, having perfected a righteous life, they would become increasingly pure and lofty and would point—as is, in fact, written in the Book of Books—the path to a bright future for the peoples of the earth.

Borya Kagan loved to repeat that all the kikes, the whole entire gang, should sit on their little patch of dirt, gobble up their own shit, and not pry into the rest of the nations' souls.

Both he and the other, without question, were staunch Zionists.

It's no secret that sometimes one encounters mad Judeophiles. As a general matter, one encounters a bit of everything in nature; for example, a bearded woman—if I'm not mistaken, in an eighth-grade textbook. An unexplainable phenomenon.

From childhood (when he was still an ethnic Russian), Uri Bar-Hanina, born Yurik Baranov, distinguished himself as one such unexplainable, congenital Judeophile. This goes to show that you can never tell where danger is lying in wait to pounce upon you. Yury's parents, Mama and Papa Baranov, were normal people, without deviations; his older brother and sister were also absolutely healthy in the sense that, after a few good drinks in good company, they'd even tell jokes like "Abram goes in unto Sara" and would sometimes gripe that Jews were encroaching upon their native laboratory on all sides.

But Yurik was born the way he was.

It began in kindergarten, when strong, handsome Yurik began to trail behind freckle-faced, sniveling Borya Kagan everywhere, as if attached, hanging on his every word and not allowing anyone to touch him. The scrofulous Borya had a talent—one wishes to write "as a storyteller," but he wasn't any sort of storyteller; on the contrary, he had marbles in his mouth his whole life, and stuttered to boot . . . but all he had to do was open his mouth and others would cling to him. Borya affected Yurik like an absolute siren. He bewitched him . . . . "And he gave him a . . . punch! A-and a ppunch—in the ppuss!" Borya would say. "And the other guy, the sppy . . . took out his ppistol, aimed, and b-b-bam!"

In the kindergarten's older group, Yurik twice beat Kolya Solovyov with a wooden bowling pin because he'd taunted Borya, calling him a "kike." The teacher noted this incident as a phenomenal occurrence in her long years of pedagogical practice. Having received, after the scandal with the bowling pin, a terrible scolding from the directress, teacher Marina explained, crying, "I tell him, 'Yurik, my child, what on Earth is this Kagan to you; get away from him!' But he looks up from under his brows with those little eyes, clenches his fists, and says, 'Just let anybody say that word to him once more . . .'"

A calamity!

Wait—there's more. It is well-known that in Soviet schools many "D-minus" roughnecks would protect weakling Jewish Four-Eyes who let them copy tests or who whispered to them at the blackboard. But the incident, which may arbitrarily be called "The Yurik Baranov Phenomenon," overturned every shape of existing stereotype.

In the first place, Yurik displayed an outstanding ability for the hard sciences, languages, and, yes, actually, for all the rest. He drew beautifully, although he hadn't studied how. And after hearing an opera once, "Aida" for example (a fifth-grade group field trip to the Bolshoy Theater), he was easily able to hum the leitmotif of any aria.

As for his friend and classmate Borya Kagan—he developed into an unfortunate boy. Borya's father left the family when his son was eight and his sister Zinochka was five. When Borya entered seventh grade, his Mama died of cancer. Borya and Zina were left to live with their grandmother.

Borya smoked, swore, and was rude to his grandmother. Whatever it was that the mature, well-read, and successful Yurik Baranov found for himself, got out of his friendship with him, remained a mystery to all without exception. But all Borya Kagan had to do was open his mouth and begin to recite any sort of obscene nonsense ("Then we'll take some port, horse-piss vodka, and a pack of BT smokes and go to that hustler's dacha, he's got a neighbor-girl there—a real hot piece of ass with legs . . ."), and Yurik, for some reason, would silently lend an ear to this puny, red-headed fool.

Borya managed to finish school only thanks to Yurik, to his talent for cramming before exams. On the whole, it can be said without exaggeration that all the worries about this ungainly household lay entirely on Yurik's shoulders. He went to the store for groceries, attended parents' meetings in Zinochka's classes, signed her notebook under "Parents' signature," and corrected her lessons.

Yes, to everyone around, first and foremost to his own family, he came across as an awfully strange boy, but all the same, no one, not even in his wildest of conjectures, could have guessed how everything would turn out.

Of course, he got into Moscow State University like a shot. A talented, handsome, well-bred young man, unburdened, thank God, by an ethnicity problem—could it have been otherwise? As is typically written in biographies, "The pride of two academic departments, the soul of any circle of friends, he very soon became a desired guest in a great number of prestigious homes."

And so? This class pet discovered, with surprise and bitterness, that his kindergarten bowling pin would hardly prove handy in all these high-ranking households.

However, joking aside, Yurik could no longer bring himself to be a puss-basher. He understood that other, more basic, more convincing arguments were needed here.

The final step along this path turned out to be a pamphlet, as famous and immortal as the Wandering Jew, a pamphlet hotly discussed by the whole class, one about the conspiracy of the Elders of Zion.

The next day, his former classmate Sashka Rabinovich brought Yurik to a certain apartment near the Kirovskaya Metro Station where underground lessons in Judaism were being carried on. Sashka vouched for Yurik as for himself. It was no joking matter. For such innocent inquisitiveness at that time, one could get a respectable prison term.

The lessons were led by Petya Kravtsov (for secrecy's sake, everyone was ordered to call him Dima)—a young man who knew Hebrew perfectly. Petya read aloud and commented on the Torah and the Talmud and, in passing, would shower his pupils with various tidbits from Jewish history. He bubbled while explaining every passage of the weekly chapter, and when giving commentary, he spoke of long-dead forefathers as about real, fully alive people. Sometimes he was unable to restrain his tears. The pupils looked from one to another. This was such a fervent heart, possessed by the idea of national rebirth, the righteous man of a generation, one of those at whom God's finger was pointing.

Petya traveled from city to city, knocked together underground study circles where, for a month or two, he avidly and hurriedly taught Hebrew and rendered historical pictures. He called all this "The Basics of Judaism" and said that he was striving to liquidate—at least partially—the ethnic illiteracy of Soviet Jews.

The KGB followed him, so Petya changed his first and last names in every city—no one has ever yet been insured against stool pigeons. Never mind, Petya Kravtsov said, when we finally find ourselves in the country of our ancestors, we won't have to change our names any longer.

(When, five years later, Petya repatriated to Israel, he changed his first and last names to Peretz Kravetz.)

Is it even necessary to say that Yurik Baranov's exceptional linguistic and mathematical abilities, his splendid logical faculties, and brilliant skill at conceptualizing turned out as well-suited to the study of Torah, Talmudic tracts, and works of the Halakha's codifiers, as—we turn to elevated style—the blade of a Damascus steel dagger is suited to a jewel-encrusted sheath, as Guarneri's cello to its velvet case, and the bare bodies of trembling lovers to the making of endless love.

After just a few months, he and Petya could, for hours on end, argue to the point of hoarseness about a Talmudic problem or discuss Rashi's commentaries on this or that phrase from the *Tanakh*.

Borya, meanwhile, succeeded in getting mixed up in some kind of scam involving the re-sale of Altay folk medicine. The scam fell through, Borya owed the "Boss" a sizeable amount of money. To pay off Borya's debt, Yurik managed, before his university classes, to work with some drunks unloading a pair of trucks. After classes he'd rush to the apartment near the Kirovskaya Station.

By that time, he was already perfectly prepared for any dispute with the Judeophobes in his class. At his disposal were convincing arguments in the field of theology as well as in the field of philosophy and history. But right then and there, all of a sudden something surprising came to light: Yurik had lost interest in polemicizing with Judeophobes. The abyss of their ignorance and blind hatred turned out to be so apparent and mind-bogglingly fathomless, existential, senseless, and downright stinky, and so offensive was it to him to look at it anew and waste precious strength of soul on pointless efforts to smother it, that Yurik Baranov could experience nothing except the desire to recoil from that stagnant abyss—to hell with it!—and no longer even bothered.

He swung to the other side and walked, walked, not glancing back, not turning at the puzzled, sorrowful calls from his family, kept taking one step after another along that path.

In springtime, on an overcast Moscow day covered by quilted clouds, at the dinner table in Petya Kravtsov's apartment, Rabbi Yeshua Parkhomovsky, come especially from Vilnius, pronounced over Yury the holy ritual of foreskin circumcision. Yury Baranov, henceforward one of God's children, was introduced into the bosom of Abraham and was bestowed with the name Uri Bar-Hanina.[56]

That day, Yurik nearly perished from loss of blood. His Jewishness had been achieved through such profound suffering that every year to this day he observes the day with a twenty-four-hour fast.

When Borya's grandmother died, Yurik arranged everything himself, and he himself read the mourner's kaddish, to the shock of the cemetery beggars (rich old Jews who made an industry out of reading prayers for those who didn't know how). With holy horror they gazed "at this goy," who quickly and fluidly came out in Aramaic with "Magnified and sanctified be His great Name in the world which He hath created according to His will. May He establish His kingdom during your life and during your days and during the life of all the house of Israel, even speedily and at a near time, and say ye, Amen."

The poor old woman, who long ago had made her peace with the fact that for the past seventy years she'd been celebrating International Labor Day with the entire country instead of Pesach, couldn't even have dreamt that they'd bury her like a real person.

When according to law the traditional *shloshim*, the thirty-day period after his grandmother's death, had passed, Uri Bar-Hanina asked Zinochka to be his wife.[57]

---

56 The Hebraized name of Rubina's converted Russian character Yury Baranin (Baranin is derived from *baran* = "ram") may point to the name of the late fourth-century Jewish scholar Bar-Hanina. The identification is not free of double irony as the ancient Jewish scholar was a teacher of St. Jerome and may have had an impact on the Vulgate translation of the Bible; see also notes to **Vladimir Jabotinsky**'s "In Memory of Herzl" in this anthology.

57 *Shloshim* (Heb.) = thirty [days]; *shloshim* is the stage of mourning that follows *shiva* (seven [days]).

And here's where Borya reared up on his hind legs.

Not on your life, he screamed, except over my dead body! You've lost your mind, he screamed at his sister; what's the matter with you, can't you see that this one's a religious fanatic? He'll force you to go to a *mikvah* and give birth to one after another!

Yes, Yurik said to this, a Jewish family must have lots of children.

You'll get all tangled up with that idiotic kosher business, the inconsolable Borya appealed to his sister. You won't be able to stick ham on a slice of bread!

Certainly she won't, said Yurik, such an abomination.

They, of course, registered at the Kirovsky regional marriage bureau so as to divert the eyes of the police and the Visas and Registrations Department, but the real Jewish wedding under the *chupah*, ratified by a *ketubah*, the traditional marriage contract, took place in the old dacha of Petya's father-in-law, on the banks of the Klyazma one bright summer's day.

They were married by Rabbi Yeshua Parkhomovsky, come especially from Vilnius.

All their friends from their underground circle were there—Petya, Sashka Rabinovich, a certain talented physicist-bard with the Russian surname of Sokolov (a friend of Rabinovich's), an artist—the husband of famous writer N.

And when Yurik, entangling his cold fingers with Zina's slender ones, finally put on the ring, all his former life started to roll past, whirling like a carousel . . . He recalled how, when she was little, he'd tie her shoe-laces, and how during a parent–teacher meeting when she was in seventh grade he was scolded for her having lagged behind in the hard sciences.

Something squeaked in his throat and, in a trembling, wheezing voice he stated, "Behold, thou art consecrated unto me by this ring, according to the Law of Moses and of Israel."

Well, at just that time, Borya managed to hook up with a certain dark crowd in Maryina Roshcha.[58] He began disappearing somewhere for weeks on end, resurfacing somehow strangely excited and cheerful but not smelling of alcohol.

---

58 Maryina Roshcha (literally "Mary's Grove")—neighborhood in Moscow, which used to have the reputation of being a center of shady and criminal activities; also a historic area of Jewish life in old Moscow. Presently Maryina Roshdha is a hotbed of Jewish religion and communal life in Russia.

When they figured out what was what and what misfortune had befallen, Zinochka fell into a state of prostration and cried for days on end, kept saying that it was all over for Borya and that the only good thing was that Mama and Grandma hadn't lived to see it.

Carrying heavily now in her third month, it was dangerous for her to keep worrying.

Then Yurik decided: it's all or nothing. He recalled kindergarten bowling.

For starters, overcoming his revulsion, he gave Borya a methodical and proper beating. The latter fell several times, Yurik picked him up and smashed him again, not feeling the slightest pang of conscience for it—after all, now he was free of the Russian intelligentsia's demands to stand up for the aggrieved Jew regardless of why others were beating him up.

Then he poured a pot of cold water all over the snotty, bloodied Borya, dragged him to the bedroom, and tied him spread-eagled on the bed. After which he took his accumulated vacation time from work and hired a famous narcotics specialist, who agreed to come and treat Borya at home. They used up all the money given to them at the wedding by friends and acquaintances.

For some reason, Yurik was convinced that he must not untie Borya; therefore, not permitting pregnant Zina near him, he himself hand fed him with a spoon, unbuttoned his pants, set him on the bedpan.

He lost twenty pounds that month.

He and Zina slept in the dining room, on the floor, since the arrested Borya was being detained in the bedroom.

In a word, Yurik saved this idiot yet again. It was one of those rare occasions when a person kicked the habit as if "jumping up from the point of a pin without a scratch." More precisely, he didn't jump; Yurik yanked him up from the pin, like a butterfly already stuck to cardboard yet then set to fly free. That is, Borya sort of flew within, of course, the confines of the apartment but with his arms already untied and in a completely stabilized condition.

He watched television for days on end, every program in turn—from deputies' fights in the Duma to "Good Night, My Child."

And here's when a rather curious thing became clear: Borya turned out to be a genuine, consistent antisemite. Jews altogether irritated him, their stereotypical traits, their manner of speaking Russian too animatedly and too correctly, of thoroughly investigating every issue and of easily manipulating details, their habit of using a gesture to emphasize an already spoken word.

Psychopathology even has a special term for instances like this, a certain kind of syndrome there. But does it explain anything for real?

"I used to think," said Borya Kagan, "that antisemitism was ignorance. Now I regard it as a point of view, including that of an intellectual."

And so, from morning to night, Borya, regaining strength bit by bit, watched television programs; and, as luck would have it, Jews participated in each one. They argued about Russia's fate, foretold something, stood up against something, defended something . . . in a word, with exceptional fervor, they shored up the social and cultural life of the country. For those three months Borya watched television without a break. Jews succeeded in plaguing him to death. He swore terribly and said that, once more, this wouldn't end well.

It was during those very days that Yurik and Zina received an invitation for permanent residence in Israel. As it happens, Borya was listed on the invitation as well; they simply wouldn't go without him. Yurik kept procrastinating with the explanation that he feared even to imagine what storm of indignation, what onslaught, what violent outburst that conversation would elicit. And so one week passed, another . . .

One of those days, Yurik returned home all worked up: they'd seen off Petya Kravtsov and Sashka Rabinovich. These two had gone to Israel on the eve of the Persian Gulf War. The ultimatum had already been declared to Saddam, and everyone had to wait for things to happen day by day. And everyone just had to sit here because of that cretin.

Yurik poured himself some tea and took his cup into the dining room. Borya was sitting there, in front of the television, as usual, acting all indignant. Then he jumped up, started running around the room, and suddenly said, "Listen up—yes, you. You're inconsistent, old man! Three times a day, damn it, you read prayers; you don't let me swallow a piece of pork like a normal person; you torture everybody with your *kashrut* . . . The question is—so what are you doing here: after all, you're a Jew, right? A dirty kike. With your sweet new world view, it would be more honest to shove off for your fucking shtetl Israel."

Yurik gagged on a gulp of tea and, after clearing his throat, said, "I won't go without you. And you know that, you scum."

Borya threw himself into a chair, snapped his fingers in his own face, and exclaimed in irritation, "So who the hell am I, Prince Golitsyn?[59] Let's go

---

59 The Golitsyns were a prominent family of the pre-Petrine Russian aristocracy.

already, you defendants on trial, before they beat you to a pulp! I suggest clearing off the premises! You've got to do what's right . . ."

Two months later, at Ben-Gurion Airport, a Russian-speaking soldier boy was handing them gas masks and showing them how to use them. At that point, very appropriately, an air-raid siren started to wail, sending Yurik to the height of ecstasy. Zina looked very funny in a gas mask, with her huge belly. Borya twirled around in his rubber snout, guffawed, and cried, "You look perfect, Mr. and Mrs. Russophobe!"

And a week later, in Hadassah Hospital's delivery ward, a new Israeli of three kilos, seven hundred grams began to bawl loudly and insistently in Yurik's arms, as he shook, now overwhelmed with the horror of childbirth. She was a little copy of her father, with wet, light brown ringlets and the cloudy gaze of her Vologda[60] ancestors. Uri Bar-Hanina lifted his daughter to the window and said to her, "Look: it's Yerushalaim!"

In honor of his late grandmother, they named the girl Rivka. Rivka Bar-Hanina.

And if anyone is able, without flinching, to state that he understands this entire story, then we offer him our hearty congratulations.

1996

Translated from the Russian by Daniel M. Jaffe

Dina Rubina, *Vot idet messiia!* English translation copyright © 2000 by Zephyr Press. Reprinted by permission of Zephyr Press. Introduction and notes copyright © by Maxim D. Shrayer.

---

60 Vologda—ancient city in the north of Russia, founded by the Novgorodians in the twelfth century; historically Russia's gate to the north; more often than not blond and blue eyed, residents of the Vologda region are believed to have retained the original Russian phenotype predating the Tatar-Mongol invasion.

FRIEDRICH GORENSTEIN

Friedrich Gorenstein (1932–2002), fiction writer, playwright, screenwriter, and essayist, was born in Kiev to the family of a professor of political economy, who was arrested in 1935 and perished in jail. Gorenstein's mother died at the beginning of the war, and he spent part of his childhood in orphanages. After graduating in 1955 from the Dnepropetrovsk Mining Institute, Gorenstein worked as an engineer until 1961.

The Higher Courses of Screenwriting in Moscow was Gorenstein's ticket to a professional career in writing. Between 1963 and 1980, he wrote and cowrote sixteen scripts, although he did not always receive proper credit. He coauthored the scripts of two major films: *Solaris* (1972) with director Andrey Tarkovsky, and *Slave of Love* (1975, directed by Nikita Mikhalkov) with Andrey Mikhalkov-Konchalovsky. Prior to emigration, only one story by Gorenstein, "House with a Turret," was published in the USSR, in *Youth* (*Iunost'*) in 1964. Gorenstein's writings began to appear in the West in the late 1970s. He contributed the short novel *Steps* to the unsanctioned collective *Metropol* (1979; see **Vassily Aksyonov**).

After emigrating in 1980, Gorenstein settled in West Berlin. His fiction and polemical essays adorned the pages of *Continent* (*Kontinent*), *Facets* (*Grani*), *Syntax* (*Sintaksis*), and other émigré magazines. Students of the Jewish question will appreciate Gorenstein's essay "The Sixth Point of the Red Star: A Literary Analysis of the *Protocols of the Elders of Zion*" (*Time and We* [*Vremia i my*], 1982), which traced the history of the forgery and its reincarnation in Soviet anti-Zionist (read: antisemitic) rhetoric.

Gorenstein's émigré books of fiction included *Redemption* (1984), *Traveling Companions* (1989; English translation, 1991), *Dresden Passions* (1993), and others. *Three Plays* (1988) included *Arguments about Dostoevsky*, *Berdichev*, and *Child-Murderer*. *Berdichev* (written 1975) belongs with the best works of postwar Russian-language theater. Dramatizing provincial Jewish life in Ukraine, whose mores and languages he knew so intimately, Gorenstein staked a claim on being an heir to **Isaac Babel**'s plays.

In 1989–90, Gorenstein's writings appeared in *Little Flame* (*Ogonyok*), *Theater* (*Teatr*), and other magazines in Russia. In 1992, he received the literary prize of *October* (*Oktiabr'*) magazine. Gorenstein's three-volume *Selected*

Works came out in 1991–93 in Moscow, followed by other books, and two of his plays were staged by leading theaters. In 1996, *October* published Gorenstein's *The Airplane Feels Like Flying: A Fantasy on the Motifs of Marc Chagall* (book editions: New York, 2000; Moscow, 2003).

Some critics recognize Gorenstein's *The Psalm: Novel-Reflection about the Lord's Four Punishments* (1974–75) as his most important work. *The Psalm* emblematizes the oversized dimensions of Gorenstein's talent and his wide-angle vision of Jewish history. Originally published in 1986 and reprinted in post-Soviet Russia, *The Psalm* is set in the 1930s–70s in Ukraine, the Volga region, and Moscow. The novel's protagonist is Antichrist, a Jew by the name of Dan (Gorenstein subsequently named his son Dan). In Gorenstein's conception, Antichrist is a representative of God, who, along with his brother Jesus, is said to do God's will—not through love and forgiveness but through damnation and punishment. To quote Dan: "For the oppressors Christ is the savior, for the oppressed Antichrist is the savior." Gorenstein's Antichrist comes not to engineer the end of time but to infuse Soviet history with Biblical mythopoetics and to punish the enemies of the Jews—not a Christian apocalyptic but a Judeocentric sui generis scenario. Antisemites in Gorenstein's *The Psalm* (cf. **Genrikh Sapgir**'s *Psalms*) are persecuted, while the marriage of Jews to Russia is doomed. In Russia the critics reacted to *The Psalm* with a mixture of awkward silence and circumspection. Some accusations of Russophobia emerged from the right. Gorenstein's Jewish readers were divided in their response. In post-Soviet Russia, Gorenstein's writings touched raw nerves and forced readers to remember what many had pushed under the affordable rug of post-Soviet amnesia. "As a true Jewish creator, [Gorenstein] suffered not from the lack of memory but from the surplus of it [...]," Marat Grinberg observed in 2002.

Besides *Berdichev*, Gorenstein's best works include the short novel *Redemption* (1967), set in a small southern Russian town after the Shoah, and the tale *The Last Summer on the Volga* (1988), the Jewish writer's "valediction forbidding mourning." Set in 1973, his tale "Champagne with Bile" depicts with heartrending accuracy a Jewish reawakening of a Soviet *intelligent*. Gorenstein's epic novels suffer from their cardboard structure, as do his historical plays. Be that as it may, of Jewish-Russian writers, Gorenstein might have come the closest to Dostoevskian moments of prophetic rage beyond literary form and convention. Perhaps echoing Vyacheslav Ivanov's notion of Dostoevsky's "novel-tragedy," **Boris Khazanov** lovingly called Gorenstein's superb play *Berdichev* a "novel for the stage."

Gorenstein died of cancer in West Berlin on 2 March 2002. According to Mina Polyanskaya, Gorenstein's émigré biographer, not long before his death he had completed a long novel, *Book Hanging on Ropes*, and had been preparing to write a play about Hitler. Since his death, Gorenstein has been the subject of several books and a documentary film, *Gorenstein's Space*, by the Berlin-based journalist Yury Vekster. The writer and theater director Mikhail Levitin may have said it best: "As whom did Friedrich perceive himself—a writer, a play-wright? I'll answer: No. A Jew. [...] A Jew defying a nightmare [...]."

* * *

In October 2001, the editor of this anthology participated in a Dostoevsky symposium in Germany and spoke with Gorenstein, who sounded on the phone like a composite image of the Jewish characters he had brilliantly captured in his play *Berdichev*. It was agreed that Gorenstein would come to the United States to appear in the **Michael B. Kreps** Memorial Readings at Boston College. Gorenstein offered for translation into English what was then an unpublished story, "The Arrest of an Antisemite," one of the lightest by contrast to most of his work. Life made different arrangements. Gorenstein never visited Boston or saw his story in print, either in Russian or in English translation.

THE ARREST OF AN ANTISEMITE

(A True Story)⁶¹

*To Olga Iurgens*⁶²

There are fragments that are stored in your memory as a whole.

You don't recall such nuggets so much as you pick them up, polish and grind them, especially if they involve something unusual, almost unheard of. They used to arrest the rootless cosmopolitans, the Zionist murderers in white lab coats, the Trotskyites, the Zinoviev–Kamenevites, the Bukharinites, and so on. Everyone knows about that. But the arrest of an antisemite–not many people, if any at all, had ever heard of that. But I not only heard about it, I saw it with my own eyes, and, you could even say, participated in it. True, it happened only once in my life, when I was ten years old—in 1942.

---

61 The subtitle in the original is *byl'*, which refers to a belletrized (and perhaps fictionalized) account of a true event or occurrence.

62 Iurgens, Olga—a visual artist, a friend of Gorenstein's.

We were in the Uzbek city of Namangan. It was summertime, June or July. No, I think it was August, because the German army had already reached Stalingrad. I heard about it from our neighbor, the mother of my nine-year-old school friend. This neighbor played the main part in the unusual story I'm about to tell, but I don't remember her name. What was it, Sofiya Semyonovna? Rafa Moiseevna? Aunt Betya? I don't remember the name of her nine-year-old daughter, either. Fanya? Manya? Funny that I remember the minutiae of everyday life in detail, but don't remember names. I remember that "Aunt Betya" told me about Stalingrad as she drew water into a bucket from the irrigation ditch that ran through the courtyard: "They reported intense fighting near Stalingrad, in the Stalingrad sector. *Oy veyz mir!*" The *aryk*, or irrigation ditch, was thickly over-grown with grass on which the dragonflies used to sit, sometimes coupled, and you especially wished you could catch those mating pairs. The usual scorching Asiatic heat was bearable because of the irrigation ditches and the shady rows of trees lining the streets. It was only in the narrow clay labyrinths of the old *kishlak*[63] streets that the heat was oven like and unbearable. But we only went there out of necessity, to try our luck at stealing grapes or apples. The Uzbeks, if they caught children, didn't beat them, only took away their loot. And they might swear, "*Ana nekutegeskay.*" Or you could get badly bitten by a dog. If they caught you, you had to bow slightly, holding your right hand to your heart, and say, "I won't do it again, I swear on my mother." However, the dogs didn't accept this oath. That's why some preferred to steal at the bazaar, where there were no dogs. You would just grab and run. If they caught you, they would take your loot and swear at you. And you would say, pressing your hand to your heart, "I swear by my mother, it's the last time." We only stole from the Uzbeks. We were afraid to steal from the Russian women who sold lard, milk, and farmer's cheese—we were scared of them and didn't steal because those women would have beaten us. They were sturdy, bony, and almost all of them blue eyed—deportees most of them, dispossessed kulaks. The local Uzbek kulaks had been dispossessed and sent to Siberia, and those from Siberia, Vologda, and others like them were sent to Central Asia. But with their tenacious kulak cunning they contrived even here, on the parched ground, to set up shop to the very limits of what the law allowed, and they vigilantly watched over their property. When you went past their stalls with their tempting wares, you would eat the lard and cheese with your eyes and drink the milk with your eyes, and the women would guard the produce with

---

63 *Kishlak*—a small village in Central Asia.

their eyes. They guarded with their eyes while they talked among themselves. "That one," they would say, "he's Jewish, and that one—a Jewess. But that other one over there—he doesn't look Jewish." If they saw that you had overheard, they would look straight at you and smirk in their peasant way. Or they would express themselves even more provocatively, openly, and viscerally in front of everyone, in an antisemitic vein. Sometimes the Uzbeks would do it, too, especially the young ones, but not so nastily, more light-heartedly. I remember, they would point at an old man and say, laughing: "*Dzhugut, dzhugut.*" The first time I heard it, I was surprised: why call an old man *dzhigit*, a warrior? But it turned out it wasn't *dzhigit*, but *dzhugut.* "*Dzhugut*" means Jew in Uzbek. And you understand, of course, that no arrests were made among the Russians or the Uzbeks. And suddenly, this development—an arrest on charges of antisemitism. Who was this antisemitic victim of repression? Not far from where we were living in evacuation, on Isparkhan Street (for some reason I remember the name of the street—street names are more material than the names of people), there was some government office—a long abbreviated name, the Regional Bureau of Construction, Water, and Cotton Works, Land Improvement and so on, or something like that. The chief accountant of this Regional Bureau of Construction, Water Works and so on was a colorful personality. Whenever I saw him, I always followed him with my eyes. He was tall, with sloping, sculpted shoulders and an imposing air about him. If I saw him now I would describe him as a "*Römerkopf*"—a Roman head straight out of a textbook of Latin history. And a profile like the ones you would see on ancient Germanic or Slavic coins. On the Slavic ones it was ruler number such-and-such. The man was already going gray. His face was clean shaven, without a moustache or beard, and his gray, silvery hair was cut short around his *Römerkopf.* The chief accountant also dressed unusually. Those around him wore Uzbek striped robes and *tyubeteykas,*[64] or else dressed in a quasi-military style: greatcoats, soldiers' shirts, peaked caps. But he wore white, gray, or pink shirts embroidered with Russian satin-stitch or little cockerels, and when it was cold, he donned an old-fashioned overcoat and hat of the sort that Pushkin would have had his Troekurov wear.[65] His post as chief accountant at the Regional Bureau was, of course, one he was given after deportation; he, too, had been disenfranchised. Even his chief adversary—Aunt Betya, who worked as an accountant at the same institution—said that he had formerly occupied a very high position in Moscow. He belonged to what she called "old regime aristocracy," from the former ranks

---

64 *Tyubeteyka*—traditional Central Asian head wear, similar to a beanie.
65 Troekurov—a wealthy and tyrannical aristocrat, one of the main characters of Aleksandr Pushkin's short novel *Dubrovsky.*

of landowners and capitalists. Aunt Betya was talking about the chief accountant to her friend, a local Tatar woman, and I overheard them because I was over at Aunt Betya's house, visiting my classmate. Aunt Betya's husband "gave his life for his country," and she wasn't even thirty yet. On Sunday evenings, she and her Tatar girlfriend used to dress up and perfume themselves with Carmen or Red Moscow and then go strolling in the park. At that time, there was a terrible dearth of men. Even the maimed ones were a high commodity, especially those who had only a moderate infirmity whether congenital or earned in battle. The lame, the one-armed, the wall-eyed, and even the more mutilated ones enjoyed success. A joke from that time went: A schoolteacher gives a riddle: "What has no legs or arms but jumps onto your mom?" The correct answer was "A yoke," but a student answered, "A veteran of the Great Patriotic War." It was not often that you saw a young, healthy man, unless he was one of the criminals in the park, who commanded the streets and the respect of all the young boys. In the park by the lake, next to plaster statues in the shade of the plane trees, these well-groomed young men played cards or basked, stretching their legs and slippered feet, always surrounded by young hussies. But that was a different world. During Stalin's rule, it was, I think, the only tolerated form of opposition, and it had its own laws. Against the background of this dearth of men, the chief accountant understandably made a big splash, especially with the women. He wasn't young, but he was still strikingly handsome and had the figure of a guardsman. Moreover, according to Aunt Betya, he was "a bachelor," or a divorcé but had, of course, many mistresses, one of whom he wanted to set up in the relatively well-paid position of accountant. And because of this he tried to drive out Aunt Betya, who had a degree from the College of Finance and Economics. All the more so because he was also the acting director of the bureau. The conflicts flared often, but one of them brought the situation to a head: things heated up to a white-hot pitch and then suddenly boiled over and burst out into the open.

Once I was coming home from somewhere when I saw the courtyard in total chaos. In the center of the yard, next to the arch, stood Aunt Betya with a red, tear-stained face. The neighbors were talking among themselves, and the children were running onto the street in great excitement, trying to track down something or other. My classmate, Aunt Betya's daughter, merrily informed me that the chief accountant was yelling at mama and cursing all the Jews, and that now they were coming to arrest him. He had begun the row at the office and then had come out onto the street and into the courtyard after Aunt Betya. "I was afraid he was going to hit me," Aunt Betya said tearfully. "That's why I ran out, so that he would hit me in front of witnesses." The chief accountant did not hit Aunt Betya, but apparently he said in front of witnesses, "Read the newspapers, Yids, listen to the radio. Soon it will all be over for you. You ran here, but where will you run next?" This was a serious problem. Lately I had been getting up early and going to the town square to listen to the radio. It was almost always the same people who gathered in a group there, most of them Jews. "The minyan is convening," they joked bitterly. "The boy always comes, too." They would discuss the news, sigh, and talk of planning their escape to Iran.

Several evacuated families lived in the buildings overlooking the courtyard. But there was also a family of Bukharan Jews. "That doesn't concern us," said the head of the family, a Bukharan Jew who had recently been mobilized but had returned soon after with a conveniently injured right hand. "We lived here in peace with the Uzbeks for centuries. And then you Russian Jews had to come and ruin our good life." The Bukharan Jew had two young boys, brothers, almost my age. I once squabbled with one of the sons, and he said to me: "You Russian Jew."

"And you're a Bukharan Jew," I replied.

"Bukharan Jew is better. Russian Jew comes out and looks up like this at the mountains."

That was how he expressed himself. Look where? What mountains? Actually, they were kind of dull, on a par with their parents, and not very apt students of Russian. I think their names were Mikhail and Daniil. I remember those names. Memory is a mysterious thing that still holds many amazing discoveries. Maybe if we could understand the mechanisms of memory, we could understand the psychology of an entire era. Time, after all, is not a continuum but is woven together from broken, individual pieces that are by no means equal in value and are often absolutely superfluous. But then again, who knows what is superfluous in this world and what is necessary.

Those vignettes of waiting for the authorities to arrive and arrest the antisemite chief accountant . . . I remember them as though I had recorded them on video back then and had watched them many times over since then. Aunt Betya called the authorities, and they responded right away. People said afterward that apparently Aunt Betya knew one of the investigators at the local police station—a Jew, they said. And that the head of the law-enforcement department was an Armenian. Whether that was true, I don't know. In any case, within about twenty minutes an officer did appear, because the station was nearby, just around the corner, near the bank. And what an officer he was! I have already described the colorful appearance of the head accountant, the handsome antisemite, but the law-enforcement officer who came to arrest him was no less colorful, although he had different racial features. You could read about such a face in Herodotus's description of Scythia, or in al-Biruni's description of ancient Khorassan. You could see a face like that on vases excavated from old Scythian and Sarmatian cities. You could find such profiles on coins from Khorassan, the predatory profile of a man with an aquiline nose. Emperor number such-and-such. Except that instead of a Scythian tiara, covered with scales of little silver plates, he had a peaked cap on his gray head. The officer was not a young man, either. His Turkic-Mongolian, Genghiside face with its high cheekbones was adorned with a large gray moustache, which came down almost to the end of his chin, in the manner of a Zaporozhian Cossack or a Ukrainian bandura player. Keep in mind that the look of the Zaporozhian Cossacks was borrowed from the Turks, including the wide trousers and the *osseledets*—the forelock of hair on a shaved head. In all other respects, the officer's appearance was Soviet. His chest was decorated with badges such as "Voroshilov's Marksman," "OSOAVIAKHIM," "GTO,"[66] as well as the badge "Outstanding Officer of the NKVD"—a shield with crossed swords, a symbol of successful work. There were also two older decorations—not arranged in bars, as is the custom now with mass military insignia, but screwed onto his soldier's tunic. Those were probably earned either in the civil war or during the suppression of the Central Asian nationalist insurrections in the 1920s and 1930s.

"Who is the victim here?" the officer asked and read out the last name.

"That's me," answered Aunt Betya.

"And where is he?" the policeman asked.

"He's over there," said Aunt Betya. "He locked himself in his office. He wanted to beat me up," she added and started to cry. "He infringed upon the great friendship of nations guaranteed by the great Stalin Constitution," she added through her tears.

The chief accountant was not in his office. "He ran off," said Aunt Betya, "he went out the back way."

"No, look, he jumped out the window," I said, obsessed as I was with Sherlock Holmes books at the time. "The window latch is up and the plants on the window sill have been moved."

"He went to the barber's," explained the Uzbek cleaning woman. Next to the bureau, near the *chaikhana*, or Uzbek teashop, was a barbershop.

---

66 Osoaviakhim—abbreviation for *Obshchestvo sodeistviia oborone i aviatsionno-khimich-eskomu stroitel'stvu* (literally, Society for the Support of Defense and Aviation-Chemical Construction); GTO—abbreviation for *Gotov k trudu i oborone* (literally, Ready for Labor and Defense, a set of athletic and fitness tests that Soviet youths were expected to pass).

And sure enough, the chief accountant was sitting there in a chair with thick shaving cream on his face. The policeman went into the barbershop, and we children followed.

"You kids—go away," said the policeman. "This is none of your business."

We went, but not very far—we stayed behind the half-closed door and listened to the policeman as he informed the accountant of his arrest. But he allowed him to finish having his shave. Then the officer came out and went into the *chaikhana*, where he settled himself on the wooden platform covered with a rug and crossed his legs, Uzbek style, in his official-issue boots. And so, sitting and holding a shallow bowl of steaming green tea served from a beaten-up little teapot, he carried on a leisurely conversation with the other Uzbeks, most of them old men, who were sitting in the same pose in their long robes and *tyubeteykas*. At the *chaikhana*, in the shade of an enormous, tent-like mulberry tree, you could even order lunch if you had the money. Of course, you couldn't use your cafeteria ration cards because they charged you commercial prices. But then you got real meat instead of bones and skins in your lunch. They had soups on the menu: *kurma-shurpa, kafta-shurpa, kaima-shurpa, shurpa-chaban*. There was *shavulia* meat, and rice pilaf with spiced lamb, and *kysym*, little sausages; there was *zharkop* (stewed meat) and *daliak-chichva* (Uzbek dumplings). Once, when my classmate turned nine, Aunt Betya took the two of us to the *chaikhana* and treated us: we had *shur-pa-chaban* (soup with potatoes and tomatoes), *chachvara* (dumplings stuffed with *tayshimerpu*, that is, meat and spiced chopped onions). But the officer who was on duty ordered only hot tea and a hot *samsa*–an Uigur patty filled with lamb and sheep's tail fat. The Uigurs, unlike the Uzbeks, like to drink their tea with peppered meat and sheep's tail fat instead of with sweet dried apricots or seedless grapes. It's possible that the policeman was an Uigur. So he sat there, drinking the hot tea with the greasy *samsa* and talking, but all the while vigilantly watching the door of the barbershop, waiting for the accountant to come out. Half an hour went by, and more—and still he didn't emerge. Then the officer went to the barbershop himself, and we kids, of course, followed him up to the half-open door. And there we saw the accountant, clean shaven, sitting in front of a fan and reading the newspaper. Without a word, the officer took away the paper—or rather, ripped it away—he was obviously angry, and putting his hands on the accountant's shoulders, lifted him up with a whoop. But here the accountant resisted arrest. He didn't throw himself at the officer and start a fist fight with him, and it didn't quite happen as in

Conan Doyle, whom I still love but whom I especially adored back then, in the unspoiled, fresh, chaste readings of childhood.

"Holmes crouched back against the wall, and I did the same, my hand closing upon the handle of my revolver. Peering through the gloom, I saw the vague outline of a man, a shade blacker than the blackness of the open door. He stood for an instant, and then he crept forward, crouching, menacing, into the room. At that instant Holmes sprang like a tiger on to the marksman's back, and hurled him flat upon his face. He was up again in a moment, and with convulsive strength he seized Holmes by the throat . . ."[67]

No, it was not like that. The accountant just dug his heels in, like a goat or a sheep or a donkey who resists being led against his will. And, I remind you, the accountant was a tall man with the stature of a guardsman and sloping, sculpted shoulders. But the law-enforcement officer, although he was a head shorter than the accountant and more wiry, obviously possessed the strength and endurance of his nomadic Genghiside ancestors. So they stood without speaking, trembling with agitation, with flushed, red faces, and all those around them stood in silence as they observed the scene. Finally the officer succeeded in overcoming the accountant's resistance and shoving him out of the door of the barbershop. As soon as the chief accountant crossed the threshold of the cool barbershop and stepped into the heat outside, it was as if something broke in him, and he gave up and went quietly, led by the shoulders by the officer. We children followed them at some distance. When he had brought the prisoner to the corner of Isparkhan Street and Bank Street, at the end of which stood the station, the officer led the prisoner along the middle of the road at gunpoint, in accordance with protocol, and followed two paces behind him. We kids followed in a gang on the sidewalk. The people on the sidewalk watched but didn't ask questions. Such processions were common at the time—deserters with overgrown faces and greatcoats without half-belts, thieves, black marketeers who illicitly traded in loaves of bread, and other shady types. When we reached the station, the prisoner and arresting officer disappeared from our view behind the door.

A few days later, when I came over to see my classmate, Aunt Betya asked me, "Did you hear what that scoundrel was yelling in the courtyard?"

"No, I didn't–I wasn't there."

---

67 The translator has identified the passage as originating from Arthur Conan Doyle's "The Adventure of the Empty House" (1903) in *The Return of Sherlock Holmes*.

"But you'll still go as a witness. We need more witnesses. Who knows which children were in the courtyard. So you'll tell them about how that scoundrel was yelling."

"But what was he yelling?"

"She'll tell you in her kid's way so that you'll understand better and remember. Tell him."

"He was yelling that all the Jews should be billed," said my classmate.

"Not billed, *killed*, you dimwit. All the Jews should be killed, that's what the antisemite was yelling. And that Hitler was doing the right thing. That's what you should say to the investigator. Here, take a pencil and an apple."

I had plenty of pencils and you could steal as many apples as you wanted at the cemetery, but I agreed to perjure myself because Aunt Betya was the mother of my classmate, whom I loved with all the innocence of a child's first love. And besides, it was probably true that the accountant had yelled those things—I just hadn't heard it because I wasn't in the courtyard at that moment. When the policeman was leading the accountant out of the barbershop, I stood not far away, in front of the other children, and the accountant looked at me. I saw him up close for the first time. "It was a tremendously virile and yet sinister face which was turned toward us. With the brow of a philosopher above and the jaw of a sensualist below, the man must have started with great capacities for good or for evil. But one could not look upon his cruel blue eyes, with their drooping, cynical lids, or upon the fierce, aggressive nose and the threatening, deep-lined brow, without reading Nature's plainest danger-signals."[68] That's how it was in Conan Doyle. Encouraged and fortified by Conan Doyle, I was ready to bear witness against this man, even if it was in principle perjury. Thus I was calm as I entered the investigator's office, with its portrait of Akhunbabaev, the Uzbek Communist-Internationalist who was the boss in Uzbekistan at that time. However, the investigator had barely laid eyes on me before he said to Aunt Betya, "No, this little one, he won't do as a witness." And he sent me away along with all the other children. There were, however, enough witnesses against the antisemitic chief accountant. Not everyone from the evacuated Jewish families agreed to go and, of course, not the local Bukharan Jew with the conveniently injured right hand, but many others did: the Uzbek cleaning woman, the Tatar night watchman, the Russian schoolteacher evacuated from Kiev, and the chemistry professor's widow—she was, incidentally, an ethnic German, and the chief accountant had insulted her as well; to him all of the evacuees were Jews. There

---

68   This quotation, too, is from "The Adventure of the Empty House" (see previous note).

were enough witnesses, apparently, because after that I never again saw the colorful chief accountant in his Russian embroidered shirt. And they sent a new head accountant to the bureau—an Uzbek whose only noteworthy feature was his lame leg. But after a time Aunt Betya and my classmate left Namangan and went to live with her sister in Andidzhan. And I said farewell to my first love, whose name I can't remember today—such are the caprices of memory. Although Andidzhan was also in the Fergana Valley, not far from Namangan, and my classmate promised to write, she never did, and I never saw her or heard from her again. If she's still alive, she must be a grandmother by now.

More than half a century has passed; and now that the passing of time has changed some things beyond recognition and left others unchangeably recognizable, I have remembered this anecdote, which resembles a broadcast of the "Armenian radio":[69] "According to the sources of Armenian Radio, an antisemite was arrested in the town of Namangan." I listened to the radio every day back then—not "Armenian" but Soviet. I used to get up in the morning and go to the square expressly for that purpose. I must say, I was already a most refined weaver of fictions even then, not only in real life but also in dreams. Maybe it was the influence of adventure novels and the frustrated desires of the flesh. And so I dream that I'm listening to the Sovinformburo's news summary: "Over the past several days the enemy continued his offensive in the Stalingrad region. All of the enemy's attacks were rebuffed with heavy losses for the enemy. Over forty airplanes were shot down and over fifity tanks were destroyed in the battle. In the region of Krasnovodsk a parachute landing force was destroyed. In the region of Namangan in the Uzbek SSR a dangerous antisemite was arrested for attempting to subvert the great friendship of nations of the USSR guaranteed by the great Stalin Constitution. There have been no significant changes on other parts of the front."

1998

Translated from the Russian by Alexandra Kirilcuk

---

69 Jokes about a fictional Armenian Radio Service were among the most popular series of jokes during the Soviet period. By and large, the humor was not that of ethnic jokes at the expense of the Armenians, as was the case with the anti-Polish or anti-Jewish jokes familiar to Americans. In these Armenian jokes, citizens would submit various questions and the Armenian Radio Service would offer witty responses, often with sexual innuendoes.

ANNA GORENKO

Anna Gorenko (1972–1999), poet, translator, and essayist, was born Anna Karpa in Bendery, Moldovia (Moldova), to a Jewish family. She started writing in 1987–88. In 1989, Gorenko repatriated to Israel, living at first in Jerusalem and then settling in Tel Aviv. Gorenko, who spent much time in the company of other drug users, died of a heroine overdose on 4 April 1999. She was twenty-seven and left behind a young son. She was buried in Tel Aviv at the Yarkon Cemetery.

Anna Gorenko was "one of the most intriguing figures of the Russian literary bohemian circles in Israel," wrote the Israeli-Russian author Evgeny Soshkin, who edited a posthumous collection of Gorenko's poetry. In 1990, soon after having arrived in Israel, the poet adopted the pen name Anna Gorenko, which is the birth name of the great Russian poet Anna Akhmatova (1889–1966), who was born in Odessa and grew up in Tsarskoe Selo outside St. Petersburg. Young Akhmatova took the Tatar last name of her maternal great-grandmother as her nom de plume after her father asked her not to embarrass the family name Gorenko with her verses. Anna Karpa's taking upon herself the real name of the great Akhmatova was an act of fatidic double irony.

Gorenko's first poems appeared in 1991 in the Jerusalem-based *Inhabited Island* (*Obitaemyi ostrov*). In her lifetime, selections of Gorenko's work appeared only five times in Israeli Russian-language magazines and collectives. She never put together a final version of her first collection, although, as Evgeny Soshkin, with whom she was friendly, reported, she talked "readily" about it but "procrastinated, preparing it, hesitating between different possibilities of [arranging the contents], unable to find a title, and simply afraid of making the important move." Gorenko was also making plans for a second collection when she passed on.

Two of Gorenko's posthumous collections appeared in 2000 in Jerusalem: *Verses*, edited by Evgeny Soshkin, and *Small Collection*, edited by the Israeli-Russian writer Vladimir Tarasov (printed on the cover of this edition is the name "Anechka," a diminutive of Anna with which Gorenko liked to introduce herself). Since her death, Gorenko's poems have appeared in Hebrew translation. In 2003, a larger collection of her poetry was brought out by *NLO* in Moscow. Bearing the title *Feast of Unripe Bread*, it was a joint labor of the Israelis Soshkin and Tarasov and the Moscow critic Ilya Kukulin. Danila Davydov, a leading herald of the post-Soviet generation of younger Russian writers, wrote an introductory, homiletic essay, "The Poetics of Consistent

Departure." Since her premature death, Anna Gorenko has become some-thing of a cult figure among the new wave of Russian-Israeli authors, and the first festival of Russian-language Israeli poets in Peta Tikvah, near Tel Aviv, was dedicated to her memory. Thanks to the 2003 Moscow edition and the positive reception it has generated, readers in Russia are starting to appreciate Gorenko's poetry.

* * *

Critics have indicated the influence of postwar Israeli poetry on Gorenko, partic-ularly of Yona Volach (1944–1985), whom Gorenko admired, identified as her poetic "sister," and translated into Russian. Gorenko, who came to Israel when she was seventeen, spoke of herself not as a "Russian poet" but rather an "Israeli poet writing in Russian." In her verses, written in first person, Gorenko sought to live out an Israeli postmodern version of the poetic experience of Russian acmeism, especially **Osip Mandelstam**'s lyrical self-refashioning. Gorenko's diction fluctu-ates between lyrical-confessional and ironic modes (she spared no irony at the expense of literary authorities and political and ideological "-isms").

On the not-so-tall horizon of the new Russian-Israeli poetry of the 1990s, Gorenko shone like a bright star because of the freedom with which she manip-ulated language into submission—bending syntax, disrupting meters, employ-ing surrealist and primitivist techniques as she wrote about unloving, vulgarity, the human body, childhood, her oneiric visions. But her playfulness and light-ness have something foreboding and unsettling about them, a disturbing quality that might have prompted the Moscow critic Evgeny Lesin to remark, in a review published in August 2003, "This is not little Israeli poetry for big Russians but big children's poetry for little adults."

Of the three texts that follow below, "The Golem" constitutes part two of Gorenko's four-part cycle "Songs of Dead Children." "Translating from the European," written in April 1999 during the last days of Gorenko's life, carries a dedication to "A. G." The Russian *perevod* means both "translating," that is the act of translation, and "translation," the product of this act. Both connotations illumine the poem's afterlife. Although one of the commentators, Vladimir Tarasov, has revealed the addressee of the dedication to be Andrey Glikman, a friend of Gorenko's, it is so difficult not to think of A. G., the birth initials of Anna Akhmatova as well, as the initials of the poet's own self—which self? Gorenko put the words "Terezinstadt, April 1943" at the bottom of the poem, inviting her future readers to historicize and—challenging them to rethink again—Theodor Adorno's dictum about writing poetry "after Auschwitz."

* * *

wake up all the poets all died overnight
in the hospital basement they fill three big shelves
some are swollen up horribly,
others have shriveled up,
and one stinks so much even the orderlies
drop hints to each other about it

get dressed let's go see
sixteen prigovs alone[70]
they still haven't counted the aigis[71]
they're giving their false teeth out to the blind kiddies
for the Jewish carnival

or instead, you know, let's stay home
they say there are firemen there and police
I'm afraid of police
you're afraid of firemen
Natalia is afraid of wolves
let's stay and drink lemonade
remembering
how the poets walked in the parade–ta-rum-pum-pum! Taroo!

1995

---

70 Prigovs—reference to Dmitrii Aleksandrovich Prigov (1940–2007), author and visual and
performance artist, one of the leading representatives of Moscow conceptualism.

71 Aigis—reference to Gennady Aigi (1934–2006), Russian and Chuvash poet and transla-
tor, whose avant-garde Russian-language poems are considered by some critics to be high
achievements of Russian postwar free verse. Gorenko does not capitalize the names of
Prigov and Aigi in the original.

FROM *SONGS OF DEAD CHILDREN*

The Golem

Where life is fulfilled with a wearying hope
The foliage sated with thick blueness
Return me there—
There's a dome a cross and a weathervane
They graze in a puff of fusible shame

But here I'm a crumbly stone embryo
Washed off with rock dust
The importunate world will refuse me won't help me
And the fish in its throat a clawed number

                              You

fed the lepers with raspberry
placed half a desert on its rib
led the quiet livestock to look at mirages
as if into your own leonine bowels.

                           Return me!

I never will
spy on how sweetly you sing,
wrapped in a household chill
as if a fire clad in rain.

In my mouth a dry drop of god's flattery,
with itself in stony arms:
On the streets of Prague crafty Jews
Saw me in hellish childhood dreams,

where life is fulfilled with a wearying hope
the ski-track of heaven gleams before me
Return me devoted and tender to hold a child
                          over the dead crowd.

1997

TRANSLATING FROM THE EUROPEAN

to A. G.

As if some England some France
Our country at the hour of dawn
The birds go blind, flowers and trees go deaf
And today the Lord himself told me something scabrous

Either I'm holy
or else, more likely
our Lord is like unto a taxi driver
He whispers such a word to every maiden
who comes out on a Sunday morning
to feed a sparrow an ant and a lame cat from a motley bowl

But on good days our Lord's a great commander
And to a square full of clerks, uhlans, bartenders
In a language foreign, heavenly and splendid,
he utters such a word that their ears burn

Lord, give me not forever but from now on
a soft suit, ordered in the summer in Warsaw
there are small sweets, bypassing rhyme
a raisin, for example, from the pockets, and other crumbs.

Terezinstadt
April 1943

1999

Translated from the Russian by Sibelan Forrester

Outline of
Jewish-Russian History

By John D. Klier[*]

The Jews did not come to Russia; Russia came to the Jews during the partitions of 1772, 1793, and 1795. Through the forcible annexation of large portions of the Polish–Lithuanian Commonwealth—the lands that today comprise all or part of the states of Poland, Belarus, Ukraine, and Lithuania—the Russian Empire acquired the largest Jewish population in the world, almost one million people. Bessarabia, the present state of Moldova, was acquired in 1815. Before 1772, Jews had been barred from even entering the Russian Empire, as the Russian empress Elizabeth Petrovna perceived them as "the enemies of Christ," who would work spiritual and physical harm upon her subjects. Ironically, one of the foremost servitors of her father, Peter the Great, was Baron Pyotr Shafirov, the scion of a converted Jewish family. Settlements of Jews in classical times actually predated the Slav presence in eastern Europe. The first Slavic state, Kievan Rus, had paid tribute to the Khazars, a Turkic people who were converts to Judaism and who participated in the legendary debate surrounding the choice of a higher religion, Orthodox Christianity, by Kiev's Grand Prince Vladimir in 988.

At the time of the late-eighteenth-century annexations, Russia was ruled by the tolerant Empress Catherine II ("The Great"). In her first act regarding the Jews in 1772, Empress Catherine recognized their usefulness as a mercantile population by guaranteeing them all the rights they had enjoyed under Polish rule. The key to Jewish life in Poland–Lithuania was the exercise of communal autonomy. As long as it fulfilled its fiscal obligations to the state, each legally constituted local Jewish community, or *kahal*, was allowed extensive self-government. Jewish society within the *kahal* was governed by religious traditions and cultural values that had evolved over centuries and were safeguarded and enforced by voluntary bodies known as brotherhoods

---

[*] The distinguished historian **John D. Klier** (1944–2007) was Sidney and Elizabeth Corob Professor of Modern Jewish History in the Department of Hebrew and Jewish Studies at University College London. Among his numerous publications on the history of Russian Jewry are *Russia Gathers Her Jews: The Origins of the Jewish Question in Russia, 1772–1825* (Dekalb, IL, 1986) and *Imperial Russia's Jewish Question, 1855–1881* (Cambridge, 1996).

(the *hevrah*; pl. *hevrot*). The *hevrot* oversaw communal welfare, such as assistance to the poor, and religious devotion, such as the upkeep of synagogues and study houses. The variety and importance of these institutions were without equal elsewhere in Europe.

Judaism assigned distinct roles to women and men, awarding a higher status to the latter in terms of worship and in the central obligation to study Torah—broadly conceived, the body of Jewish sacred texts and commentaries written in Hebrew and Aramaic. A network of private schools (the heder), each led by a teacher (the melamed), provided primary religious instruction for all Jewish males. A community with higher aspirations might also have supported a center for more advanced study, a yeshiva, and the Lithuanian lands became famous for theirs. While women were not educated to study the sacred texts, many were literate. A body of secular and religious materials in the Yiddish vernacular served their needs.

The period of the partitions witnessed the rise of a mass religious movement, Hassidism, inspired by the semi-legendary religious leader Israel ben Eliezer, the Ba'al Shem Tov (the *BeShT*, c. 1700–1760). Hassidic doctrine emphasized ecstatic prayer and the leading role of a religious leader known as a tzaddik, whose status was determined not by his learning and legal skills but by his charismatic personality. At the turn of the eighteenth century, east European Jewry was plagued by a religious civil war between the adherents of Hassidism and their opponents, the so-called Mitnagdim. Hassidism had the largest number of adherents in Ukraine and Belorussia, while its strongest foes were in Lithuania.

Jews had initially been invited to settle in the region in the Middle Ages by Polish kings who hoped to benefit from their trade and commercial acumen. After 1569, Polish noblemen received large landholdings in the newly colonized Ukraine. They succeeded in binding the peasantry to the land and imposing a feudal economy in which Jews played a major role as agents, serving in the capacity of estate managers and leaseholders of the numerous feudal privileges possessed by the nobility, in particular the monopoly on the distillation and sale of spirits. The large landowners (the magnates) offered land to Jews for settlement. The typical settlement became the small Jewish market town, or shtetl, a distinctive feature of Jewish life in eastern Europe.

Jewish prosperity was tied to the welfare of Poland–Lithuania as a whole. Jews thrived during the buoyant years of the sixteenth and early seventeenth centuries, when east European grain was an important resource for the rest of

Europe, and in turn experienced economic distress when the Polish–Lithuanian Commonwealth suffered political and economic decline due to the rise of powerful and aggressive neighbors such as Russia, Sweden, and Prussia.

When Russian rulers first encountered the Jews in 1772, they sought to use their mercantile abilities and granted them extensive trade and commercial rights. Gradually, Russian officials became aware of the additional role played by Jews as middlemen in the village, especially as tavern keepers, which they identified as exploitation of the peasantry. The perception of the Jews as a harmful economic force caused the Russian state to restrict Jewish movement within the empire through laws that created a Jewish "Pale of Settlement" in the northwestern and southwestern provinces and barred most Jews from residence in the Russian interior. The Pale was variously strengthened and relaxed throughout the nineteenth century, but it endured until the outbreak of war in 1914.

Russian administrators also looked to the experience of western states. The dominant assumption of eighteenth-century Enlightenment thinkers was that the Jews were religious fanatics whose beliefs alienated them from all non-Jews. It was said that Jews employed their mercantile skills to deceive and exploit their peasant neighbors. The western solution to the "Jewish Question" thus lay in reducing Jewish fanaticism through education and eliminating exploitation by directing the Jews into productive work. Russian officials sought to follow this western lead, most famously through the work of the Jewish Committee of 1802–4 and in the Statute for the Jews of 1804. Falling short of extending all civil liberties to the Jews, the 1804 statute allowed them to enter all Russian state educational institutions and offered various privileges to Jews who undertook agriculture or manufacturing. The statute also attempted to resettle Jews from the countryside into nearby towns, an initiative that was unsuccessful but that nonetheless caused much economic dislocation and distress for the Jews.

Russian attempts to reform the Jewish population were aided by a small group of Jews eager to assist. These were the followers of the Haskalah, the Jewish version of the European-wide Enlightenment movement of the eighteenth century. The Haskalah took many forms, but its key element in eastern Europe was a belief in the need for Jews to move away from the exclusive study of Jewish texts. By learning from the "wisdom of the Gentiles," they believed, Jews could engage with the modern world. The followers of Haskalah, known as the maskilim, hoped to turn the Jews into a productive class, especially by directing them into agriculture. The language of the western Haskalah was German; forced by necessity, east European maskilim had to use the language of the masses, Yiddish, a Germanic language with Hebrew, Slavic, and Romance additions that was derided by intellectuals as a nonliterary "jargon." Maskilim in eastern Europe, such as Isaac Baer Levinson (1788–1860) were confident, with some justification, that Russian officials shared their goals. The mass of east European Jews, on the contrary, scorned the maskilim and considered the government initiatives to be little more than attempts at conversion or persecution.

Jewish traditionalists saw this view validated by the policies that marked the reign of Tsar Nicholas I. Nicholas ordered the drafting of Jews into the Russian army in 1827, ending a previous exemption. Jewish communities were required to choose the recruits themselves and were allowed to draft boys between the ages of 11 and 17; community officials who did not meet their recruitment targets could be drafted themselves. These boys entered special "cantonist schools" for preliminary training before beginning their twenty-five-year term of active service. Although not the original intent of the policy— Nicholas believed the harsh discipline of the army could correct the perceived shortcomings of the Jews—military commanders conducted missionary activity among the recruits, often using coercive methods, and it is estimated that one-third, about 25,000, of Jewish recruits were converted to Christianity. Military recruitment was just part of a wider scheme to "make the Jews more productive." Nicholas also encouraged agricultural colonization (without much success) and imposed restrictions upon those he saw as "unproductive" Jews. Nicholas abolished the *kahal* system in 1844, ostensibly to promote Jewish integration, but this goal might have been better served by abolishing the Pale of Settlement. Nicholas also placed restrictions on traditional Jewish dress.

One of Nicholas's most interesting reforms was motivated by a desire to wean the Jews from what Russians saw as "religious fanaticism." This reform was devised by a high-level committee, headed by Count P. D. Kiselev after its creation in 1840, called the Committee to Develop Measures for a Fundamental Transformation of the Jews. In 1844, Nicholas ordered the creation of a state-sponsored Jewish school system designed to rival the traditional heders and yeshivas. The state Jewish school system, which numbered about one hundred institutions, met great resistance in the Jewish communities, which viewed it as a direct threat to Judaism and its traditions, and only enrolled some five thousand students. The schools nevertheless opened the way for some Jews to enter the mainstream of Russian culture and society, with graduates moving into journalism and the legal and medical professions.

The system educated the pioneer creators and consumers of Jewish literature in Russian, who may collectively be called the Jewish-Russian intelligentsia. The same drive toward modernity led other writers to create a modern Jewish literature in other languages: Avraham Mapu, Perets Smolenskin, and Reuben Braudes in modern Hebrew; S. Y. Abramovitsh (Mendele Moykher-Sforim) in Hebrew and Yiddish; and Shalom Rabinovich (Sholem Aleichem) and Isaac Leib Peretz in Yiddish.

The reality of acculturation, symbolized by the Jewish-Russian intelligentsia, was mirrored in the Jewish population as a whole; it was not motivated by ideology but was generated by the processes of modernization. The decisive date was 1861, when the Russian serfs—peasants who were bound to the land and virtually the slaves of the landowners—were emancipated. The social changes associated with emergent capitalism produced new ideologies, variously calling for liberal democracy or socialism. The Russian government was slow to respond to the need to create new political and legal systems, resulting in the rise of political dissent and revolutionary activism, including terrorism.

Jews were directly influenced by the social, economic, and political changes that were taking place around them. The abolition of serfdom made superfluous the role of Jews as middlemen; the creation of a rail network put many Jewish teamsters and innkeepers out of work; the reorganization of the spirit trade reduced the role of the Jewish tavern keeper. At the same time, industrialization created jobs for Jewish factory workers, although often under brutal conditions. These changes encouraged a movement of Jews from the countryside and the shtetl to the new industrial centers of Odessa, Warsaw, and Lodz. But Jews, like non-Jews, found that industry did not grow rapidly enough to absorb Russia's surplus labor. The Jewish population of the Russian Empire in particular increased fivefold between 1800 and 1900, numbering over five million in the first national Russian census of 1897.

In 1881, in the unsettled atmosphere following the assassination of Emperor Alexander II, a series of anti-Jewish riots, or pogroms, broke out in the southwestern provinces of the empire in major centers like Kiev and Elizavetgrad (later renamed Kirovohrad and presently Kropyvnytskyi). In its efforts to control this popular violence, the government reversed the policies designed to promote Jewish integration that it had followed for over seventy-five years: the so-called May Laws of 1882 endeavored to restrict Jews from residence in the countryside, and quotas were imposed upon Jewish access to higher education and to the professions. The pogroms and legal restrictions intensified the trend of Jewish out-migration already generated by poverty, and by 1914 over two million Jews had left the empire to settle in the Americas, Europe, South Africa, and Palestine.

Some acculturated Jews, such as the sculptor Mark Antokolsky, the painter Isaac Levitan, and the composer Anton Rubinstein, made notable contributions to modern Russian culture. Yet no phenomenon reveals the extent of Jewish acculturation in the late empire as much as the participation of Jews in the Russian revolutionary movement. Specialists differ as to why Jews were overrepresented in all branches of the movement, even as the mass of Jews remained politically quiescent. Revolutionaries of Jewish descent played active, even leadership roles in the revolutionary struggle: the populist (*narodnik*) theoretician Mark Natanson, the Socialist-Revolutionary Party leader Gregory Gershuni, the Menshevik leader Yuly Martov, the Bundists Arkady Kremer and Vladimir Medem, and, most famously, Leon Trotsky, who became one of Lenin's closest collaborators, the director of the revolution in Petrograd, and the founder of the Red Army. Before 1917, the tsarist government depicted the Jews as the carriers of revolution into Russia and encouraged the extremist Right to make Jews the target of physical and verbal attacks. In contrast to Jewish socialists, a tiny number of Jews, such as the banker Horace Günzberg and the railway contractor Samuel Poliakov, became immensely rich capitalists. Playing to the right-wing obsession with Jewish conspiracies, officials of the Russian secret police fabricated the infamous "Protocols of the Learned Elders of Zion" (first published in 1903), purporting to reveal an international Jewish plot for world domination. After the Revolution of 1905, antisemitic groups, known collectively as the "Black Hundreds," carried out violent attacks on Jews.

The early twentieth century saw no improvement in the situation of the Jews. They were the target of pogroms in Kishinev in 1903 and throughout the revolutionary period of 1905–6. Jews derived little benefit from the creation of a constitutional monarchy following the October Manifesto (dated 17 October and issued by Nicholas II on 30 October 1905). There was little improvement in their legal position, and they were the object of hostile propaganda and provocations, most notably the trial of the Jew Mendel Beilis on a trumped-up charge of ritual murder in 1913. In contrast, liberal parties such as the Constitutional Democrats, some of whose leading members, notably Maxim Vinaver and Iosif Gessen, were Jewish, called for the grant of full civil rights to the Jews.

The immediate causes of the revolution that forced the abdication of Nicholas II on 15 March 1917 were the social and economic strains of the Great War and Russia's inability to capitalize on its natural advantages in manpower and resources. The Provisional Government that came to power in February/March 1917 attempted to reform the empire by promising land to the peasantry and satisfying the aspirations of national minorities, and one of its first actions was to remove all restrictions on the Jews, including restrictions on residence and education. The Provisional Government also actively—and unsuccessfully—continued the war. The failure of Russian arms and the delay of promised reforms undermined the Provisional Government's position and facilitated the October/November coup led by V. I. Lenin's Bolsheviks.

The Bolsheviks acted quickly to withdraw Russia from the war, to announce the distribution of land to the peasants, and to permit dissident national groups to secede from the empire. When the Great War ended in November 1918, Russia was consumed by a fierce civil war whose major participants were the Reds (the Bolsheviks and their left-wing allies), the Whites (the monarchist Volunteer Army), the Greens (peasant anarchists), as well as bandits, brigands, and various national armies (primarily in Ukraine). In the midst of the civil war, the new Soviet state also fought a war with Poland.

The Great War and the civil war were disastrous for the empire's Jewish population. Major Jewish settlements were located in the middle of the zone of conflict. Early in the war, Russian military commanders evicted large numbers of Jews, forcing them to move into the Russian interior. The civil war marked the complete breakdown of state authority. Marauding armies terrorized both Jews and non-Jews with pogroms, arson, and looting. For this reason, some Jews in the Pale welcomed the victory of the Red Army, while tens of thousands fled the country altogether. When the Reds triumphed in 1921–22, all the citizens of the Russian state, Jews and non-Jews, confronted a state whose economy was crippled and that was led by a small party of political radicals who were isolated from the rest of the world.

To paraphrase the famous joke, Soviet rule up to 1945 may be characterized as "good for the Jew, but bad for the Jews." In other words, Jews as individuals were able to participate in the economic development of the Soviet state and were offered sweeping opportunities for educational and social advancement. On the other hand, Judaism as a religion was almost destroyed, and traditional Jewish culture was demolished. The new Soviet state desperately needed personnel, or "cadres" in Soviet terminology, a resource that the Jews could provide. Any servitor of the old regime (bureaucrats, educators, and police and army personnel) was considered politically unreliable. Jews, a target of tsarist discrimination, were viewed as reliable simply by virtue of being Jewish. This implicit loyalty was reinforced by the Whites' use of antisemitic propaganda against the Communists. Conveniently, many Jews possessed high levels of literacy and education, which were in short supply among the workers and peasants, the core supporters of the new Soviet state. Some Jews from other revolutionary parties, especially the Bund, were willing to throw in their lot with the victorious Bolsheviks. In the early twenties, therefore, Jews were well represented in the Communist Party, in the Soviet bureaucracy, in the officer corps of the Red Army, and in the ranks of the security forces and secret police. Many members of Lenin's first government, such as Lev Kamenev, Grigory Zinoviev, Yakov Sverdlov, and Leon Trotsky, were of Jewish descent. Their attitude to this "accident of birth" was well illustrated by a legendary meeting of Trotsky with a Jewish delegation that appealed to him for help on the basis of his Jewish origins. Trotsky corrected them: He was not a "Jew" but a "Social Democrat." In the future, antisemites would attribute Jewish support for the regime to Russophobia or to an alleged destructive, revolutionary spirit in Judaism. A more reasonable and unbiased explanation was that Jews, like other Soviet citizens, sought a livelihood in troubled times, since the war and revolution left the majority of Jews destitute.

Despite his own origins, Karl Marx had scant respect for the Jews, and classic Marxist dogma considered the Jews as little more than ethnic debris whose identity was created by discrimination and persecution. Once these disabilities were removed, it was assumed that Jews would assimilate into the majority population, and the "Jewish Question" would disappear. Reality intruded into this wishful thinking. In 1918, Russia had a Jewish population of over two and a half million persons. Jewish political parties, such as the socialist Bund and the vigorous Zionist parties, sought to mobilize Jewish identity. The new Soviet state responded by co-opting or abolishing these rivals and by granting the Jews the same prerogatives as the other national minorities that comprised the new Union of Soviet Socialist Republics created in 1923. The Jews were assigned an identity, *evrei*, defined as an east European national group (there being no such thing as "world Jewry" in Soviet eyes) with a common historical experience, a common Germanic language, Yiddish, and a common folk culture, expressed in music, art, and literature. The term *evrei* (Jew) is used in modern literary Russian primarily in reference to the ethnic and historical origin of the Jews, whereas *iudei* (Hebrew, "Judean") is used primarily in reference to the religious tradition of Judaism. Other segments of the Jewish population of the USSR, such as the Georgian-speaking Jews of the Caucasus, were either erroneously assigned to the same category as the Ashkenazic, Yiddish-speaking Jews or given a separate national identity altogether, as in the case of the so-called Mountain Jews, who spoke Judeo-Tat, a Hebrew-Persian language. Judaism and anything linked to it, such as the Bible and the Hebrew language, were decried as nonessential and counterrevolutionary. The recognition of the Jews as a national minority was of vital importance, for nationality was a central organizing principle of the new regime. Yet while *evrei* (ethnic Jews) were officially tolerated as a national minority, Judaism, Hebrew, and the millennia-old religious culture of the Jews was increasingly persecuted.

The regime recruited Jewish cadres "to bring the revolution to the Jewish street" by implementing the ideological program of communism among the Jewish masses. For this purpose, special Jewish sections were created in the party (the *Evsektsii*) and the state bureaucracy (the *Evkomy*). These institutions combated Jewish religious culture and created a network of Yiddish-language schools organized along the communist principle of "national in form, socialist in content," which meant that, whatever the language, Soviet ideological guidelines had to be followed. Sympathetic writers were encouraged to publish in Yiddish, and a substantial body of Soviet Yiddish poetry and prose appeared, while Yiddish theatres operated in Moscow and major provincial centers. In the economic realm, the Soviet state sought to make the Jews more "productive" by encouraging agricultural colonization, largely with the assistance of foreign Jewish bodies such as Agro-Joint and ORT. By 1930, such programs had moved over 5 percent of the Soviet Jewish population into agriculture, most notably in Crimea and Ukraine.

Perhaps the most idiosyncratic move of the Soviet state in regard to the Jews as an ethnic group was the creation, in 1930, of a national territory for them in Birobidzhan, a remote and undeveloped territory on the Soviet–Chinese frontier. Despite efforts to resettle Jews in this region, Jews never constituted a majority of Birobidzhan's population, and the Jewish Autonomous Region always functioned more as an illusory Jewish "Potemkin village" than a Soviet Zion.

Having won the battle for leadership of the Communist Party in 1928, Stalin presided over a dramatic new program, later known as the First Five-Year Plan. It is best summarized as a program to modernize the national economy through total state control in order to produce unprecedented rates of growth. A parallel change was the forced reorganization of all peasants into collective farms, where they could be easily controlled and exploited by the regime. Economic centralization placed unprecedented power in the hands of the

Communist Party, and Stalin used this accumulated power to purge all real or potential rivals within the party through a series of dramatic show trials. The so-called Great Terror was extended to the general population. Tens of thousands were executed, while millions more were sent to corrective labor camps—the gulags.

Jews, like the Soviet population as a whole, were significantly transformed during the period from 1929 to 1939. The economic aspects of the tsarist-era "Jewish Question" were resolved, as Jews moved into all sectors of the USSR's modernizing economy. Culturally, a new generation of Soviet Jews emerged, well-acculturated Soviet citizens who also maintained a distinct Jewish identity, albeit one largely stripped of religious culture. In fact, Jews increasingly abandoned Yiddish and displayed high rates of intermarriage. By law, antisemitism was illegal, but it remained widespread among the general population.

During the 1930s, Stalin consolidated total political control over the Communist Party, the army, and the secret police. Although a number of prominent individuals of Jewish origin perished in the purges of high-ranking officials, including former party leaders Lev Kamenev, Grigory Zinoviev, former secret police chief Genrikh Yagoda, and Red Army general Yona Yakir, the Great Terror of 1937–38 did not have a specifically anti-Jewish coloration.

The USSR was able to postpone war with Nazi Germany by signing a nonaggression pact with Hitler in 1939. The pact effectively divided eastern Europe into spheres of influence and allowed the USSR to occupy or annex eastern Poland, the Baltic states, and parts of Romania and Finland, all but the last of which had substantial Jewish populations. When Nazi Germany invaded the USSR in June 1941, the Jewish population in Soviet-controlled territories numbered over five million.

The war was a disaster for the Soviet population, and approximately twenty-five million Soviet citizens perished. The war was even more catastrophic for the Jews, as it provided the opportunity for the Nazis to implement their Final Solution—a high-priority effort to murder all the Jews of Europe. The Nazi program of mass shootings and mechanized slaughter numbered as many as two million Soviet Jews among the estimated six million Jewish victims of the Shoah. There was a substantial degree of participation in the mass murder by collaborators in the German-occupied territories, especially the Baltic states and the Ukraine.

Soviet Jews, however, were not merely passive victims. They served with distinction in the Red Army, and Jews were fifth among Soviet nationalities in the total number of wartime decorations received, far in excess of their percentage of the Soviet population. Jews also played a role on the propaganda front as journalists (**Ilya Ehrenburg, Vasily Grossman**) and broadcasters. Particularly successful was the Jewish Antifascist Committee (JAC), composed of prominent Jewish-Soviet cultural leaders, including the writers Dovid Bergelson, Der Nister (Pinhas Kahanovich), Perets Markish, and Itsik Fefer, and headed by the celebrated Yiddish actor Solomon (Shloyme) Mikhoels. The JAC publicized the Soviet war effort among Jewish groups abroad, sought support for a second front, and advocated financial and material aid to the USSR. The JAC accidentally became the "Jewish address" in the USSR, as Jews contacted its headquarters to seek help, to search for missing family members, or to report events on the home front, especially incidents of antisemitism.

At the end of the war, Jews, like the rest of the population, expected the party to deliver on its war-time promises of reconstruction, the end of political repression, and a higher standard of living. Instead, the outbreak of political and ideological rivalry between the USSR and its western allies gave rise to the cold war. The Soviet government tightened ideological controls and censorship (particularly directed against anything Western), renewed political repression, and returned to the worst excesses of state economic planning.

The period of late Stalinism was especially ominous for Soviet Jews. The JAC, with its numerous links to the West, fell under suspicion. Mikhoels was murdered by the secret police in 1948, while the JAC was closed down and many of its leading members arrested. The Soviet anti-Western campaign made a special target of "rootless cosmopolitans," who lacked ideological loyalty and were not to be trusted. Jews were increasingly placed in this category, and many Jewish writers and critics working in Yiddish, Russian, and Ukrainian were repressed.

The Soviet Union had supported the partition of Palestine and the creation of the state of Israel in 1948. But the subsequent orientation of Israel to the West and the public support for the new Jewish state voiced by many Soviet Jews compromised them in the eyes of Stalin. Many Jews had responded to the Shoah with a heightened sense of their Jewish identity and called for the rebuilding of Jewish communal life in the USSR. In the atmosphere of the late 1940s, the secret police easily depicted such activity as "bourgeois nationalism." Stalin apparently came to question the loyalty and political reliability of all Soviet Jews despite their almost total removal from most of the higher echelons of the Party, with the exception of a few symbolic figures such as Lazar Kaganovich.

In 1952, the leaders of the JAC, under arrest since 1948, were tried on charges of spying for the West and Israel and for bourgeois nationalist deviations. A total of fourteen defendants were secretly tried and all but one, Dr. Lina Shtern, were executed on 12 August 1952, the "Night of the Murdered Poets." This judicial murder of many of the leaders of modern Yiddish literature, including Markish, Fefer, Leyb Kvitko, and Bergelson, was a devastating blow to Yiddish culture. The attack on Soviet Jews began to spread wider. On 13 January 1953, it was announced that a number of prominent Soviet physicians who staffed the elite medical clinic in the Kremlin that served the Soviet leadership were "assassins in white coats" linked to foreign intelligence operations. Most of the accused at the center of this Doctors' Plot, such as Professor Miron Vovsi, were Jews. Rumors were rife in Moscow and Leningrad, the veracity of which is still debated by scholars, that the trial of the doctors would provide the pretext for a massive anti-Jewish pogrom, which would be followed by the exile of much of the Jewish population of the USSR to camps in Soviet Central Asia. At this juncture, Stalin suffered a stroke and died on 5 March 1953. One of the first actions of the new collective leadership was to denounce the Doctors' Plot as a provocation and to release all the accused. Jews, even more than other Soviet citizens, viewed this as a miraculous escape. Nonetheless, the legacy of war, the Shoah, and the purges put paid to the claim that Soviet Russia was ruled by Jews.

The death of Joseph Stalin on 5 March 1953 produced extraordinary reactions in the Soviet Union. On the street, people wept openly at the death of the man who had presided over the greatest triumphs and tragedies of Soviet history. Scores of people were suffocated in the crush of the huge crowds that stood for days to pay their respects at Stalin's lying in state before he was interred next to V. I. Lenin in the mausoleum on Red Square. Not all the tears were signs of grief. It was said that, of the Politburo members, only Stalin's old comrade Vyacheslav Molotov wept sincerely. Others, including the head of state security, Lavrenty Beria, were breathing sighs of relief, for they were almost certainly the targets of a new purge of the Communist Party leadership that Stalin was quite openly planning. The relatives of Stalin's many victims secretly rejoiced.

Among those pleased to see the end of the old dictator were many Soviet Jews. The cultural leadership of Soviet Jewry had been executed in 1952, variously charged with espionage activities, and the looming purge had an unmistakably anti-Jewish coloration. Jews were increasingly identified as the "rootless cosmopolitans" against whom a major ideological campaign was being waged.

A special feature of this campaign was the publication of the "Jewish" names of those who wrote under pseudonyms. The majority of those accused in the Doctors' Plot, announced on 13 January 1953, were Jews. Jewish centers throughout the USSR were rife with rumors that a huge pogrom was being organized by the state security forces, one that would culminate in the forced exile of masses of Soviet Jews to Siberia or Central Asia. For those of a religious bent, it was as though the plans of a modern-day Haman, the implacable enemy of the Jews in the Biblical story of Esther, had been foiled. Indeed, Stalin's death was appropriately close to Purim, the Jewish holiday that recalled this event.

Stalin bequeathed a troubled legacy to his successors. The great-power competition of the Cold War put great demands on the Soviet economy, which was slow to recover from the enormous human and physical destruction of the war against Nazi Germany. The political system still relied on a high degree of coercion in response to the disappointed aspirations of Soviet citizens, who had been promised a better life after the sacrifices of the war. The Soviet Union itself, enlarged as a result of the postwar territorial settlement, was faced with the task of mollifying discontented national groups within its new borders. Moreover, it had acquired an empire of satellite states, including Poland, Czechoslovakia, and East Germany, that chafed under Soviet rule. A crucial decision had to be made as to whether or not to continue with the system that bore the late ruler's name—Stalinism.

In an effort to prevent the emergence of another Stalin, with his capricious control over lives and careers, his successors declared an era of "collective leadership," with shared power. They quickly disposed of the dangerous Beria, who was blamed for the excesses of late Stalinism. As a result of power struggles within the collective leadership, Communist Party chief Nikita Khrushchev emerged as the overall leader, but he never enjoyed the power of a Stalin and was always constrained by his Politburo colleagues. However, until his own political fall in 1964, he was able to determine foreign and domestic policies. He pursued a variety of dynamic—and often eccentric—projects designed to transform the Stalinist state.

The most obvious, albeit dangerous, reform initiative was to attack the status of Stalin himself, the dominant symbol of Communism in the USSR for over a quarter of a century. The worst aspects of late Stalinism—"vigilance campaigns," a stress on military production rather than consumer goods, the continued exploitation of collective farmers—were gradually relaxed in a period that came to be known as the Thaw, after the title of a novel by Ilya Ehrenburg. The central event was a speech delivered behind closed doors by Khrushchev to the Twentieth Congress of the Communist Party on 25 February 1956, the so-called Secret Speech. In attacking the Stalin myth, Khrushchev pursued the difficult task of differentiating the good and the bad in Stalin's policies. Accordingly, Khrushchev argued that when Stalin followed the legacy of Lenin and the guiding hand of the Communist Party, he accomplished great tasks, such as the five-year plans and the collectivization of agriculture. When he allowed his arrogance and pride to dominate, he was guilty of criminal excesses, exemplified by the horrific purges of Party, state, and military personnel in the 1930s. Stalin was a gifted wartime leader when he followed the lead of the Communist Party and encouraged the sacrificial exploits of the Soviet people. On the other hand, he created a ludicrous myth around himself as a brilliant military strategist, "Generalissimo Stalin."

After the war, Stalin became remote from postwar realities, consumed by his own exaggerated reputation and distrustful of his Party colleagues. Khrushchev thus credited all the successes of Stalin to the Communist Party, while his numerous crimes—euphemistically called "the cult of personality"— were attributed to Stalin's character defects. The general policy of dismantling the Stalin myth became known as de-Stalinization. One of its most significant features was the process of political rehabilitation, whereby the criminal charges made against Stalin's purge victims, living and dead, were reexamined and miscarriages of justice remedied.

Dissatisfaction with Khrushchev's policies culminated in an unsuccessful attempt to remove him from his position as general secretary of the Party in 1957. Khrushchev branded his opponents an "anti-Party group," claiming that his opponents sought to end de-Stalinization. This was a dubious claim, since there were many aspects of Khrushchev's policies that merited criticism: his continual and chaotic reorganization of the Party and state apparatus; agricultural reforms, such as the Virgin Lands Campaign and his command that corn be widely planted irrespective of environmental conditions; foreign adventurism that would later lead to the Berlin Crisis of 1961 and the Cuban Missile Crisis of 1962. Nonetheless, Khrushchev's depiction of his victory as an affirmation of de-Stalinization encouraged many Soviet intellectuals to believe that a turning point had been reached and that the Soviet Union would create a longed-for "socialism with a human face."

While de-Stalinization did bring an end to mass terror, it did not end the stigmatization of Jews as an ethnic group that had been collectively menaced in 1953. The doctors accused of the Doctors' Plot were released, but the Jewish cultural leaders who had been shot as spies and nationalists in 1952 were not immediately rehabilitated. The increasingly hostile attitude of the Soviet Union toward the state of Israel reflected badly on Soviet Jewry. In contrast to the period at the end of the war, when writers spoke openly of the special suffering of Jews at the hands of the Nazis, the Shoah was never specifically acknowledged by the Soviet state. Instead, the fate of the Jews was submerged in the category of the twenty million victims of Fascism. Efforts to recall or commemorate the special victimization of the Jews were discouraged or condemned as a manifestation of "bourgeois nationalism."

This official silence underlay a number of subsequent controversies, most notably Yevgeny Yevtushenko's 1961 poem "Babi Yar," protesting that no memorial stood at this site of mass murder. The same theme was the focus of Anatoly Kuznetsov's documentary novel *Babi Yar*, published in 1966 (in full only after Kuznetsov's 1969 defection to the West). Neglect of the role of Jews in the war was especially galling because of the enduring canard that Jews had avoided military service. Popular antisemitism accepted the claim that Jews had "fought the war in Tashkent," irrespective of the actual war record, which showed that Soviet Jews had won military decorations far in excess of their percentage in the Soviet population.

Jews now became the target of unacknowledged quotas in employment and access to higher education. They were removed from positions in the national republics in a program of affirmative action designed to promote local cadres. Despite these efforts, Jews still occupied a prominent position in many areas, including the academic and scientific worlds. A Khrushchev-sponsored antireligious campaign was especially onerous for the small number of religiously observant Jews.

In 1964, the erratic Khrushchev was removed from power. The new leadership, dominated by Leonid Brezhnev, aimed to maintain domestic stability, especially through continuity of Party cadres. This particular policy was especially successful: the increasingly decrepit Brezhnev ruled until 1982; he was replaced by the terminally ill Yuri Andropov, who died in 1984, followed by Konstantin Chernenko, who lasted barely a year. Only with the advent to power of Mikhail Gorbachev in 1985 did a generation of younger leaders claim authority in the USSR.

Under Brezhnev, reformist change in the Soviet satellites was quashed by military intervention (Czechoslovakia in 1968) or the implementation of martial law (Poland in 1981). At the same time, efforts were made to normalize relations with the USSR's cold war adversaries. This policy, known as détente, featured nuclear weapons control treaties and increased economic relations.

Détente endured until the USSR sent troops into Afghanistan at the end of 1979.

Some feared that the abandonment of Khrushchev's chaotic domestic policies might also bring an end to de-Stalinization. In 1964, the brilliant young Leningrad poet **Joseph Brodsky** was sentenced to internal exile on a spurious charge of "parasitism," that is, not holding a full-time job. There was further confirmation in that same year when two writers, Abram Tertz and Nikolay Arzhak (the doubly ironic pen names of the ethnic Russian Andrey Sinyavsky and the Jew **Yuly Daniel**) were arrested and charged with "anti-Soviet propaganda" for sending their stories abroad to be published. Their show trial appeared to be a return to the repressive methods of Stalinism. In response, a small group of Soviet intellectuals began to circulate documents relating to this trial and other forms of political repression. This action ushered in a period of political dissidence that came to be known as the Democratic Movement. Numerically small, it nonetheless attracted a number of outstanding Soviet intellectuals to its side, most notably the nuclear physicist Andrey Sakharov. The movement quickly caught the attention of the West, and the treatment of dissidents became an important factor in Soviet–Western relations. Many of the first dissidents were of Jewish descent, such as Pavel Litvinov, Aleksandr Ginzburg, and Elena Bonner (who was later to marry Andrey Sakharov), although the mainstream dissident movement itself was not Jewish.

Both external and internal factors encouraged Soviet Jews to become more assertive. The Six-Day War in 1967, which saw Israel's crushing victory over Soviet-sponsored and -armed Arab states, engendered pride and self-confidence among many Jews. At the same time, Israel's victory led to a sundering of Soviet–Israeli diplomatic relations and the unleashing of a torrent of anti-Zionist rhetoric, publications, and caricatures that evoked some of the worst examples of prerevolutionary tsarist antisemitism.

It was against this background that the Jewish national movement arose in the last three decades of the existence of the Soviet Union. The movement had two dominant tendencies. There were proponents of emigration—those who wished to leave the Soviet Union, usually to the state of Israel. These activists sought to lead a more authentic Jewish life, to escape discrimination, or to improve their lives. They were balanced by advocates of a cultural revival among those who sought either to rebuild a secular Jewish life in the Soviet Union or simply to assert a Jewish identity with pride rather than shame or fear. Those who wished to leave were assisted by a 1964 decision of the Soviet leadership that members of selected national minorities (Armenians, Germans,

Greeks, Jews) should be allowed to emigrate from the Soviet Union, under the pretext of the "reunification of families." It was hoped that this humanitarian gesture would help to improve relations with the West. In 1975, the Soviets signed the Helsinki Accords, which recognized existing postwar boundaries and also committed the signatories to respect human rights, including the right to move freely between countries.

Adherents of these two tendencies inevitably cooperated, despite the difference of their ultimate objectives, since a revivified Jewish identity was important whether one planned to go or stay. An unofficial cultural movement evolved, offering classes in Hebrew language, Jewish history and culture, and information about Israel. The Jewish national movement won the support of the leaders of the broader Democratic Movement. The "Zionists"—both those who sought to leave for Israel and those who desired a Western destination, especially the United States—accepted this support but remained aloof from the movement as a whole; those who planned to stay participated more closely in the activities of the broader dissident movement. Often the boundaries between the two groups were blurred and hard to discern. An "official," limited, Yiddish-based culture also survived, grouped around the journal *The Soviet Homeland* (*Sovetish heymland*).

As Jews began to apply for permission to leave the Soviet Union, a new phenomenon emerged, that of the refuseniks. These were individuals who had been refused permission to leave on various pretexts (the word "refuse-nik" derives from the Russian slang term *otkaznik*, which means "one who was refused, denied permission"). Refusenik families lived in a legal no-man's land since their members were unable to secure specialized employment or to pursue higher education. Their plight came to the attention of the West. A worldwide movement to "save Soviet Jewry" proved a continual embarrassment to the Soviet leadership and complicated East–West relations. In 1974, for example, a Soviet–American trade treaty was scuppered when the United States congress passed the Jackson–Vanik Amendment, which linked ratification to increased emigration from the USSR. Unable to differentiate easily between those who wished to go and those who planned to stay, the Soviet authorities repressed all activists of the Jewish national movement. This reinforced the image of the Soviet Union as a militantly antisemitic state. With the waning of détente after the Soviet invasion of Afghanistan in late 1979, the USSR no longer had a motive to permit Jewish emigration. It had averaged about 19,000 persons in the 1970s (with a high of 51,320 in 1979) but slipped to an average of 5,000 a year in the seven years before 1987, with 1980 representing the high point of 21,471 and 1984 the low point of 876. Between 1970 and 1987, approximately 125,000 Jews had emigrated from the USSR mainly to Israel and the United States.

With the naming of Mikhail Gorbachev as general secretary of the Communist Party in 1985, a new political generation came to power in the USSR. Gorbachev gradually implemented a program of internal reform that was known as perestroika (literally, restructuring). It ultimately envisioned the democratization of the Party, the relaxing of central economic controls, the cultivation of better relations with the Soviet satellites, and improvement of relations with the West, especially the United States. Arms-control agreements, it was hoped, would ease pressure on the overburdened Soviet economy. To expedite the task of reform, Gorbachev introduced a policy of *glasnost* (literally, publicity, openness), expressed as a relaxation of censorship, examination of the "blank spots" in Soviet history, and toleration of more diverse cultural policies.

In 1987, the Jewish national movement, like other dissident and democratic groups that benefited from the liberal atmosphere surrounding Gorbachev's reforms, began to grow in size and self-confidence. Fully legal and quasi-legal Jewish newspapers appeared, along with unofficial educational activities. Most significantly, Gorbachev relaxed emigration controls. Scores of veteran refuseniks, such as Ida Nudel and Vladimir and Masha Slepak, were allowed to leave in 1987–88. They were followed by a growing number of Jews who made no secret of the fact that were motivated not so much by the ideals of the founders of the Jewish national movement as by a desire for a materially better, freer life. Increasing numbers of emigrating Soviet Jews sought to settle in the United States rather than Israel.

It was not only democrats and national minorities who took advantage of Gorbachev's liberalization. An aggressive, antidemocratic, ultranationalist movement, relatively small in numbers but noisy in action, emerged. It was typified by a group known as Pamyat' ("Memory"). Pamyat' began as an unofficial movement to preserve the Russian national heritage and evolved into a network of chauvinistic and antisemitic organizations. It benefited from the support of a number of prominent, right-wing Russian writers and cultural figures, who combined Russian nationalism with the traditions of pre-Revolutionary antisemitism and Soviet anti-Zionist rhetoric. The mathematician and publicist Igor Shafarevich popularized the term "Russophobia" and depicted the Jews as a "little nation" of anti-Russian extremists who had brought on the Revolution and all its subsequent misery for the Russian people. This fit neatly with the timeworn notion that contemporary Jews were part of a "Judeo-Masonic conspiracy" intent on subjugating and exploiting the Russian people. While groups like Pamyat', with their militant antisemitic rhetoric, never succeeded in mobilizing significant public support, they created an atmosphere of unease and fear in major Jewish centers such as Moscow and Leningrad. They were probably responsible for recurrent rumors in late 1989 and throughout 1990 predicting anti-Jewish riots, or pogroms.

The Gorbachev reforms represented the last unsuccessful attempt to reform and preserve the Soviet Union. A half-hearted plot by Communist Party officials to remove Gorbachev from power in October 1991 led to the final collapse of the Communist Party as a ruling institution. Gorbachev's political rival, Boris Yeltsin, the president of the Russian Federation, used the opportunity to join with other republic-level presidents to dissolve the structures of the Soviet state. On 1 January 1992, the USSR formally ceased to exist.

This eventful period of Jewish-Russian history has had lasting consequences. A variety of factors had caused the diminution of the Jewish population since 1939. Most important was the Shoah, to which were added the phenomena of an aging Jewish population, extensive intermarriage, and small family size. The period of détente saw the beginning of out-migration, which reached massive proportions under Gorbachev: between 1986 and 1991, nearly a half-million Jews left the Soviet Union. As a consequence, self-conscious Russian-Jewish communities are now to be found around the world, often maintaining physical and cultural ties with the states of origin. The demographic decline of the Jewish population in the former Soviet Union has been dramatic. There are an estimated 265,000 Jews in Russia, 100,000 in Ukriane, and 28,000 in Belarus.[1] Yet the remaining population remains active: there are a growing number of Jewish cultural, educational, welfare, and religious institutions, many of them supported by outside sources. Many of the so-called oligarchs who dominated the Russian economy under President Boris Yeltsin were of Jewish descent, rekindling the antisemitic theme of the Jewish domination of Russia.

The aliyah of Jews from eastern Europe has had a significant impact on the State of Israel, where "Russians," as they are collectively known, number over

---

1   As of 2018, about 160,000 Jews remain in the Russian Federation, under 60,000 in Ukraine, and under 10,000 in Belarus. (Ed.)

900,000 and represent approximately 14 percent of the total population.[2] In Israel there are a wide variety of cultural institutions that operate in the Russian language. There are two political parties identified with this population, one headed by former refusenik Natan Sharansky and the other by Avigdor Lieberman, both of whom have served in Israeli cabinets. In North America—especially in New York but also in large urban centers such as Boston, Chicago, Los Angeles, Philadelphia, and Toronto—numerous Third- and Fourth-Wave Jewish-Russian cultural institutions sprouted up in the 1980s–1990s and continue to serve local communities.

It is therefore probable that "Soviet" or "Russian" Jewry will endure in some form as a cultural community scattered about the world. At the same time, the rebirth of Jewish institutions in eastern Europe suggests that some Jews are determined that the long and creative presence of the Jews in Russia and eastern Europe should not be allowed to disappear without a trace.

London, UK
2007
Copyright © by John D. Klier

---

2   Over 1 million Russian-speaking Jews live in Israel, about 500,000 Russian-speaking Jews live in North America, and about 120,000 Russian-speaking Jews live in Germany. (Ed.)

The Jews in Russia and The Soviet Union, 1772–2000: A Selected Bibliography*

Jews in Tsarist Russia: 1772-1917

Aronson, I. Michael. *Troubled Waters: The Origins of the 1881 Anti-Jewish Pogroms in Russia.* Pittsburgh: University of Pittsburgh Press, 1990.

Berk, Stephen M. *Year of Crisis, Year of Hope: Russian Jewry and the Pogroms of 1881–1882.* Westport, CT: Greenwood Press, 1985.

Frankel, Jonathan. *Prophecy and Politics: Socialism, Nationalism, and the Russian Jews, 1862–1917.* Cambridge: Cambridge University Press, 1981.

Hundert, Gershon, ed. *The YIVO Encyclopedia of Jews in Eastern Europe.* 2 vols. New Haven: Yale University Press, 2008.

Judge, Edward H. *Easter in Kishinev: Anatomy of a Pogrom.* New York: New York University Press, 1992.

Klier, John D. *Imperial Russia's Jewish Question, 1855–1881.* Cambridge: Cambridge University Press, 1996.

_____. *Russia Gathers Her Jews: The Origins of the Jewish Question in Russia, 1772–1825.* DeKalb: Northern Illinois University Press, 1986.

Klier, John D., and Lambroza, Shlomo, eds. *Pogroms: Anti-Jewish Violence in Modern Russian History.* Cambridge: Cambridge University Press, 1991.

Levitats, Isaac. *The Jewish Community in Russia, 1844–1917.* Jerusalem: Posner, 1981.

Mendelsohn, Ezra. *Class Struggle in the Pale: The Formative Years of the Jewish Workers' Movement in Tsarist Russia.* Cambridge: Cambridge University Press, 1970.

Nathans, Benjamin. *Beyond the Pale: The Jewish Encounter with Late Imperial Russia.* Berkeley: University of California Press, 2002.

Polonsky, Antony. *Jews in Poland and Russia: A Short History.* Liverpool: Littman Library of Jewish Civilization; Liverpool University Press, 2013.

Rogger, Hans. *Jewish Policies and Right-Wing Politics in Imperial Russia.* London: Macmillan, 1986.

Shchedrin, Vasily. *Jewish Bureaucracy in Late Imperial Russia: The Phenomenon of Expert Jews. 1850–1917.* Detroit: Wayne State University Press, 2011.

Stanislawski, Michael. *Tsar Nicholas I and the Jews: The Transformation of Jewish Society: 1825–1855.* Philadelphia: The Jewish Publication Society of America, 1983.

---

* The bibliography has been updated with some of the titles published after John D. Klier's death. (Ed.)

Zipperstein, Steven J. *The Jews of Odessa: A Cultural History, 1794–1881*. Stanford: Stanford University Press, 1985.

Jews in the Soviet Union: 1917–1945

Abramson, Henry. *A Prayer for the Government: Ukrainians and Jews in Revolutionary Times, 1917–1920*. Cambridge, MA: Harvard University Press, 1999.

Altshuler, Mordechai. *Soviet Jewry on the Eve of the Holocaust: A Social and Demographic Profile*. Jerusalem: Hebrew University Centre for Research of East European Jewry, 1998.

Aronson, Gregor, ed. *Russian Jewry, 1917–1967*. Trans. Joel Carmichael. New York: Thomas Yoseloff, 1969.

Baron, Salo Wittmayer. *The Russian Jew under Tsars and Soviets*. New York: Macmillan, 1976.

Bemporad, Elissa. *Becoming Soviet Jews: The Bolshevik Experiment in Minsk*. Bloomington: Indiana University Press, 2013.

Emiot, Israel. *The Birobidzhan Affair: A Yiddish Writer in Siberia*. Philadelphia: The Jewish Publication Society of America, 1981.

Gilboa, Yehoshua A. *A Language Silenced: The Suppression of Hebrew Literature and Culture in the Soviet Union*. New York: Associated University Presses, 1982.

Gitelman, Zvi. *Jewish Nationality and Soviet Politics: The Jewish Sections of the CPSU*. Princeton, NJ: Princeton University Press, 1972.

Goldman, Guido G. *Zionism under Soviet Rule (1917–1928)*. New York: Herzl Press, 1960.

Gurevitz, Baruch. *National Communism in the Soviet Union, 1918–28*. Pittsburgh: University of Pittsburgh Press, 1980.

Kagedan, Allan Laine. *Soviet Zion: The Quest for a Russian Jewish Homeland*. Houndmills: Macmillan, 1994.

Klier, John D. "Russian Jews and the Soviet Agenda." In *Reinterpreting Russia*, ed. Geoffrey Hosking and Robert Service, 183–97. London: Arnold, 1999.

Kochan, Lionel, ed. *The Jews in Soviet Russia since 1917*. 3d ed., rev. Oxford: Oxford University Press, 1978.

Levin, Nora. *The Jews in the Soviet Union since 1917: Paradox of Survival*. 2 vols. New York: I.B. Tauris, 1988.

Moss, Kenneth. *Jewish Renaissance in the Russian Revolution*. Cambridge, MA: Harvard University Press, 2009.

Miller, Jack, ed. *Jews in Soviet Culture*. New Brunswick, NJ: Transaction Books, 1984.

Pinkus, Benjamin. *The Jews of the Soviet Union: The History of a National Minority*. Cambridge: Cambridge University Press, 1988.

———. *The Soviet Government and the Jews, 1948–1967: A Documented Study*. Cambridge: Cambridge University Press, 1984.

Ro'i, Yaacov, ed. *Jews and Jewish Life in Russia and the Soviet Union*. Ilford: Frank Cass, 1995.

Rabinovich, Simon. *Jewish Rights, National Rites: Nationalism and Autonomy in Late Imperial and Revolutionary Russia*. Stanford, CA: Stanford University Press, 2014.

Rothenberg, Joshua. *The Jewish Religion in the Soviet Union*. New York: Ktav, 1971.

Sawyer, Thomas E. *The Jewish Minority in the Soviet Union*. Boulder, CO: Westview Press, 1979.

Shternshis, Anna. *When Sonia Met Boris: An Oral History of Jewish Life under Stalin*. New York: Oxford University Press, 2017.

Weinberg, Robert. *Stalin's Forgotten Zion: Birobidzhan and the Making of a Soviet Jewish Homeland. An Illustrated History, 1928–1996*. Berkeley: University of California Press, 1998.

The Shoah: 1941–1945

Arad, Yitzhak. *The Holocaust in the Soviet Union*. Lincoln: University of Nebraska Press, 2009.

Dawidowicz, Lucy. *The War against the Jews, 1933–1945*. New York: Holt, Rinehart and Winston, 1975.

Dobroszycki, L., and Gurock, J., eds. *The Holocaust in the Soviet Union: Studies and Sources on the Destruction of the Jews in Nazi-Occupied Territories of the USSR, 1941–1945*. Armonk, NY: M.E. Sharpe, 1993.

Ehrenburg, Ilya, and Grossman, Vasily, eds. *The Complete Black Book of Russian Jewry*. Tran. and ed. David Patterson. New Brunswick, NJ: Transaction Publishers, 2002.

Garrard, John, and Garrard, Carol. *The Bones of Berdichev: The Life and Fate of Vasily Grossman*. New York: Free Press, 1996.

Gilbert, Martin. *The Holocaust. A History of the Jews During the Second World War*. London: Fontana, 1986.

Gitelman, Zvi, ed. *Bitter Legacy: Confronting the Holocaust in the USSR*. Bloomington: Indiana University Press, 1997.

Hilberg, Raul. *The Destruction of the European Jews*. 3 vols. New York: Holmes and Meier, 1985.

Levin, Nora. *The Destruction of European Jewry, 1933–1945*. New York: Schocken, 1973.

Porter, Jack Nusan, ed. *Jewish Partisans: A Documentary of Jewish Resistance in the Soviet Union During World War II*. 2 vols. Washington, DC: University Press of America, 1982.

The Jews and Post-War Stalinism: 1945–1953

Gilboa, Yehoshua A. *The Black Years of Soviet Jewry, 1935–1953*. Boston: Little, Brown and Company, 1971.

Kostyrchenko, Gennadi V. *Out of Red Shadows: Antisemitism in Stalin's Russia*. Amherst, NY: Prometheus Books, 1995.

Krammer, Arnold. *The Forgotten Friendship: Israel and the Soviet Bloc, 1947–53*. Champaign: University of Illinois Press, 1974.

Rapoport, Louis. *Stalin's War against the Jews: The Doctors' Plot and the Soviet Solution*. New York: Free Press, 1990.

Redlich, Shimon. *Propaganda and Nationalism in Wartime Russia: The Jewish Anti-Fascist Committee in the USSR, 1941–1948.* Boulder, CO: Eastern European Monographs, 1982.

_____. *War, Holocaust and Stalinism. A Documented History of the Jewish Anti-Fascist Committee in the USSR.* Luxembourg: Harwood Academic Publishers, 1995.

Vaksberg, Arkady. *Stalin against the Jews.* New York: Knopf, 1994.

The Khrushchev Period and De-Stalinization: 1953–1964

Altshuler, Mordechai. *Soviet Jewry since the Second World War: Population and Social Structure.* New York: Greenwood Press, 1987.

Dagan, Avigdor. *Moscow and Jerusalem: Twenty Years of Relations between Israel and the Soviet Union.* New York: Abelard-Shuman, 1970.

Gitelman, Zvi. *A Century of Ambivalence: The Jews of Russia and the Soviet Union, 1881 to the Present.* 2nd expanded ed. Bloomington: Indiana University Press, 2001.

Pinkus, Benjamin. *The Soviet Government and the Jews, 1948–1967.* Cambridge: Cambridge University Press, 1984.

Ro'i, Yaacov, ed. *Jews and Jewish Life in Russia and the Soviet Union.* Portland, OR: Frank Cass, 1995.

Rubin, Ronald, ed. *The Unredeemed: Antisemitism in the Soviet Union.* Chicago: Quadrangel, 1968.

Wiesel, Elie. *The Jews of Silence: A Personal Report on Soviet Jewry.* Translated from the Hebrew and with a historical afterword by Neal Kozodoy. New York, Holt, Rinehart and Winston, 1966.

The Brezhnev Period, Jewish Emigration, and the Dissident Movement: 1964–1985

Alexeyeva, Ludmilla. *Soviet Dissent: Contemporary Movements for National, Religious, and Human Rights.* Middleton, CT: Wesleyan University Press, 1985.

Barghorn, Frederick C. *Détente and the Democratic Movement in the USSR.* New York: Free Press, 1976.

Buwalda, Petrus. *They Did Not Dwell Alone: Jewish Emigration from the Soviet Union, 1967–1990.* Washington and Baltimore: Woodrow Wilson Centre and Johns Hopkins University Press, 1997.

Cohen, Richard, ed. *Let My People Go: Today's Documentary Story of Soviet Jewry's Struggle to Be Free.* New York: Popular Library, 1971.

Cohen, Stephen F., ed. *An End to Silence: Uncensored Opinion in the Soviet Union.* New York: Norton, 1982.

Korey, William. *The Soviet Cage: Antisemitism in Russia.* New York: Viking, 1973.

Kornblatt, Judith Deutsch. *Doubly Chosen: Jewish Identity, the Soviet Intelligentsia, and the Russian Orthodox Church.* Madison: University of Wisconsin Press, 2004.

Orbach, William. *The American Movement to Aid Soviet Jews.* Amherst: University of Massachusetts Press, 1979.

Prital, David, ed. *In Search of Self: The Soviet Jewish Intelligentsia and the Exodus.* Jerusalem: Scientists Committee of the Israel Public Council for Soviet Jewry: Mt. Scopus Publications, 1982.

Ro'i, Yaacov. *The Struggle for Soviet Jewish Emigration, 1948–1967*. Cambridge: Cambridge University Press, 1991.

Rothberg, Abram. *Heirs of Stalin: Dissidence and the Soviet Regime (1953–1970)*. Ithaca: Cornell University Press, 1972.

Rubenstein, Joshua. *Soviet Dissidents: Their Struggle for Human Rights*. Boston: Beacon Press, 1980.

Sharansky, Natan. *Fear No Evil*. New York: Random House, 1988.

Shrayer, Maxim D. *Leaving Russia: A Jewish Story*. Syracuse: Syracuse University Press, 2013.

Gorbachev and the Era of Perestroika: 1985–1991

Brown, Archie. *The Gorbachev Factor*. Oxford: Oxford University Press, 1996.

Brudny, Yitzhak M. *Reinventing Russia: Russian Nationalism and the Soviet State, 1953–1991*. Cambridge, MA: Harvard University Press, 1998.

Klier, John D., "The Dog That Didn't Bark: Antisemitism in Post-Communist Russia." In *Russian Nationalism, Past and Present*, ed. G. Hosking and R. Service, 129–47. Houndmills: Macmillan, 1998.

Korey, William. *Russian Antisemitism, Pamyat, and the Demonology of Zionism*. Chur, Switzerland: Harwood Academic Publishers, 1995.

Shrayer, Maxim D. *Waiting for America: A Story of Emigration*. Syracuse: Syracuse University Press, 2006.

White, Stephen. *Gorbachev and After*. 3rd ed. Cambridge: Cambridge University Press, 1992.

After the Soviet Union

Gitelman, Zvi, ed. *The New Jewish Diaspora: Russian-Speaking Immigrants in the United States, Israel, and Germany*. New Brunswick, NJ: Rutgers University Press, 2016.

Gitelman, Zvi, et al., eds. *Jewish Life after the USSR*. Bloomington: Indiana University Press, 2003.

Shrayer, Maxim D. *With or Without You: The Prospect for Jews in Today's Russia*. Boston: Academic Studies Press, 2017.

Bibliography of Primary Sources

The sources of the Russian originals are listed below in the same order as their English translations appear in the anthology and chronologically within each entry. In cases of excerpts from longer texts, the inclusive pages refer only to the parts used in this anthology. The textual sources from which the translations were drawn are printed in boldface type. Where there are several sources listed, it is the source in boldface that provided the text from which our entry was translated.

This bibliography is not meant to be an exhaustive listing of all appearances of the anthologized texts in periodicals, individual collections and editions, and collective edited volumes. Of the numerous editions of some of the works, only the sources the editor consulted *de visu* are included below. While any previously unpublished original works have been excluded from this anthology by its selection criteria, alternative manuscript versions have been consulted, in several cases with the authors' assistance, where it was deemed necessary.

The textological challenges of works published under conditions of Soviet censorship have been dealt with in scholarship (e.g., in Herman Ermolaev's ground-breaking work), and they can be boundless. Those challenges, as demonstrated by post-Soviet scholarship (e.g., Arlen Blyum's illuminating research), can be especially prohibitive for a historian of Jewish writing in the Soviet period. This is why, however helpful they may be, no Soviet-era academic editions of works by Jewish-Russian authors are fully reliable and/or complete. At the same time, while most works by émigré authors were not subjected to government censorship, the very limited conditions of their publication and distribution frequently doomed them to obscurity. In seeking to represent the history of a given work's publication or to date the work, the editor in some cases had to check the later, modified versions against the original publications; significant differences have been accounted for in the notes to the texts. The editor frequently consulted the original publications, whether in periodical or in book form. Such consultation was not always possible as this information may not be available, and the editor welcomes any suggestions and additions. The editor's task was made less arduous by the appearance in the 1990s of a number of reliable academic editions of Jewish-Russian works, both in the former Soviet Union and abroad, and by the generous help of the individuals listed in the acknowledgments.

If an English translation included in the anthology has appeared pre-
viously, the information about it follows the information about the Russian
original.

A standard Library of Congress system of transliterating the Russian
alphabet (without diacritical marks) is used throughout bibliographical
references.

EARLY VOICES: 1800s–1850s

Leyba Nevakhovich

From *Lament of the Daughter of Judah*: Vopl' dshcheri iudeiskoi, sochinenie Leiby
Nevakhovicha, 27–43. St. Petersburg: pechatano v privilegirovannoi Breitkopfovoi
Tipografii, 1803.

English translation by Brian Cooper, in *An Anthology of Jewish-Russian Literature: Two Centuries
of Dual Identity in Prose and Poetry, 1801–2001*, ed. Maxim D. Shrayer, vol. 1, 7–11. Armonk,
NY and London: M. E. Sharpe, 2007.

Leon Mandelstam

From "The People": "Narod," in L. I. Mandel'shtam, *Stikhotvoreniia*, 67–72. Moscow: V
universitetskoi tipografii, 1841.

English translations by Alyssa Dinega Gillespie, in *An Anthology of Jewish-Russian Literature: Two
Centuries of Dual Identity in Prose and Poetry, 1801–2001*, ed. Maxim D. Shrayer, vol. 1, 17–19.
Armonk, NY and London: M. E. Sharpe, 2007.

Ruvim Kulisher

From *An Answer to the Slav*: Otvet slavianinu, Perezhitoe 3 (St. Petersburg, 1911): 365–77.
(Published, with introduction, by S. M. Ginzburg.)

English translation by Maxim D. Shrayer, in *An Anthology of Jewish-Russian Literature: Two
Centuries of Dual Identity in Prose and Poetry, 1801–2001*, ed. Maxim D. Shrayer, vol. 1, 28–32.
Armonk, NY and London: M. E. Sharpe, 2007.

Osip Rabinovich

From *The Penal Recruit: Shtrafnoi*, in *Russkii vestnik* 6 (1859): 510–21; in Osip Rabinovich,
Izbrannoe, ed. M. Vainshtein, 21–43. Jerusalem: Institut rossiikogo evreistva, 1985.

English translation by Brian Horowitz, in *An Anthology of Jewish-Russian Literature: Two Centuries of Dual Identity in Prose and Poetry, 1801–2001*, ed. Maxim D. Shrayer, vol. 1, 35–43. Armonk, NY and London: M. E. Sharpe, 2007.

SEETHING TIMES: 1860s–1880s

Lev Levanda

From *Seething Times: Goriachee vremia. Roman,* "Chast' pervaia. Na pravo ili na levo?" *Evreiskaia biblioteka*, vol. 1 (1871): 13–15; 22–25; 36; 50–55; 66–68; in Lev Levanda, *Goriachee vremia: roman iz poslednego pol'skogo vosstaniia*, 14–16; 24–27; 40–41; 57–59; 59–63; 76–78. St. Petersburg: A. E. Landau, 1875.

English translation by Maxim D. Shrayer, in *Polin* 20 (2007): 459–72; English translation by Maxim D. Shrayer, in *An Anthology of Jewish-Russian Literature: Two Centuries of Dual Identity in Prose and Poetry, 1801–2001*, ed. Maxim D. Shrayer, vol. 1, 47–59. Armonk, NY and London: M. E. Sharpe, 2007.

Grigory Bogrov

From *Notes of a Jew: Zapiski evreia*, in G. Bogrov, *Sobranie sochinenii*, 2nd ed., vol. 1, 55–81. Odessa: Knigoizdatel'stvo Shermana, 1912.

English translation by Gabriella Safran, in *An Anthology of Jewish-Russian Literature: Two Centuries of Dual Identity in Prose and Poetry, 1801–2001*, ed. Maxim D. Shrayer, vol. 1, 62–70. Armonk, NY and London: M. E. Sharpe, 2007.

Rashel Khin

From *The Misfit: Ne ko dvoru*, in R. M. Khin, *Siluety*, 203–10. Moscow: T-vo skoropechatni A. A. Levenson, 1895; in Rashel' Khin, *Ne ko dvoru*, ed. M. B. Averbukh and L. I. Berdnikov, 63–187. St. Petersburg: Alleteia, 2017.

English translation by Emily Tall, in *An Anthology of Jewish-Russian Literature: Two Centuries of Dual Identity in Prose and Poetry, 1801–2001*, ed. Maxim D. Shrayer, vol. 1, 75–78. Armonk, NY and London: M. E. Sharpe, 2007.

Semyon Nadson

From "The Woman": "Zhenshchina" (part 2: "Ros odinoko ia. Menia ne ograzhdala . . ."); "I grew up shunning you, O most degraded nation . . .": "Ia ros tebe chuzhim, otverzhennyi narod . . .";

both in S. Ia. Nadson, Stikhotvoreniia, ed. F. I. Shushovskaia, 184–85, 262. Leningrad: Sovetskii pisatel', 1957.

English translations by Alyssa Dinega Gillespie, in *An Anthology of Jewish-Russian Literature: Two Centuries of Dual Identity in Prose and Poetry, 1801–2001*, ed. Maxim D. Shrayer, vol. 1, 81–82. Armonk, NY and London: M. E. Sharpe, 2007.

ON THE EVE: 1890s–1910s

Ben-Ami

Author's Preface to vol. 1 of *Collected Stories and Sketches*: "Ot avtora," in Ben-Ami, *Sobranie rasskazov i ocherkov*, vol. 1, v–viii. Odessa: Tipografiia G. M. Levinsona, 1898.
English translation by Maxim D. Shrayer, in *An Anthology of Jewish-Russian Literature: Two Centuries of Dual Identity in Prose and Poetry, 1801–2001*, ed. Maxim D. Shrayer, vol. 1, 97–99. Armonk, NY and London: M. E. Sharpe, 2007.

David Aizman

"The Countrymen": "Zemliaki," in D. Aizman, *Zemliaki. Rasskazy*, 201–44. Moscow: Priboi, 1929; in D. Aizman, *Krovavyi razliv i drugie proizvedeniia*, ed. M. Vainshtein, 2 vols. Vol. 1, 230–65. [Jerusalem], 1991.
English translation by Maxim D. Shrayer, in *Commentary* 6 (2003): 30–40; English translation by Maxim D. Shrayer, in *An Anthology of Jewish-Russian Literature: Two Centuries of Dual Identity in Prose and Poetry, 1801–2001*, ed. Maxim D. Shrayer, vol. 1, 115–32. Armonk, NY and London: M. E. Sharpe, 2007.

Semyon Yushkevich

From *The Jews: Evrei*, in Semen Iushkevich, *Evrei: povest'*, 188–204. Munich: Verlag Dr. J. Marchlewski, 1904; in Semen Iushkevich, *Evrei*, 158–69. St. Petersburg: Izdanie tovarishchestva "Znanie," 1906; in Semen Iushkevich, *Evrei*, 203–16. Leningrad–Moscow: Kniga, 1928.
English translation by Ruth Rischin, in *An Anthology of Jewish-Russian Literature: Two Centuries of Dual Identity in Prose and Poetry, 1801–2001*, ed. Maxim D. Shrayer, vol. 1, 135–41. Armonk, NY and London: M. E. Sharpe, 2007.

Vladimir Jabotinsky

"In Memory of Herzl": "Pamiati Gertslia," under the title "Hespêd," in *Evreiskaia zhizn'* 6 (1904): 8–10; in Vladimir Zhabotinskii, *Doktor Gertsl'*, 3–4. Odessa: Knigoizdatel'stvo "Kadima," 1905; in Vladimir (Ze'ev) Zhabotinskii, *Izbrannoe*, 7–8. Jerusalem: Biblioteka "Aliia," 1978 (with minor variations).
English translation by Jaime Goodrich and Maxim D. Shrayer, in *An Anthology of Jewish-Russian Literature: Two Centuries of Dual Identity in Prose and Poetry, 1801–2001*, ed. Maxim D. Shrayer, vol. 1, 148–50. Armonk, NY and London: M. E. Sharpe, 2007.

Sasha Cherny

"The Jewish Question": "Evreiskii vopros";

"Judeophobes": "Iudofoby";

both in *Satirikon* 47 (1909): 2–3 ("Spetsial'nyi evreiskii nomer"); **both in Sasha Chernyi, *Sobranie sochinenii v piati tomakh*, ed. A. S. Ivanov, vol. 1, 335–37. Moscow: "Ellis Lak," 1996.**

English translations by Catriona Kelly, in *An Anthology of Jewish-Russian Literature: Two Centuries of Dual Identity in Prose and Poetry, 1801–2001*, ed. Maxim D. Shrayer, vol. 1, 166–67. Armonk, NY and London: M. E. Sharpe, 2007.

S. An-sky

"The Book": "Kniga," in *Evreiskii mir* 5 (4 February 1910): 60–64; **in S. An-skii, *Sobranie sochinenii*, vol. 1, 94–102. St. Petersburg: T-vo "Prosveshchenie," 1911.**

English translation by Gabriella Safran, in *An Anthology of Jewish-Russian Literature: Two Centuries of Dual Identity in Prose and Poetry, 1801–2001*, ed. Maxim D. Shrayer, vol. 1, 176–79. Armonk, NY and London: M. E. Sharpe, 2007.

Samuil Marshak

"Palestine": "Palestina," in *U rek vavilonskikh: natsional'no-evreiskaia lirika v mirovoi poezii*, ed. L[ev] Iaffe, 129–35. Moscow: Safrut, 1917.

English translation by Andrew Von Hendy and Maxim D. Shrayer, in *An Anthology of Jewish-Russian Literature: Two Centuries of Dual Identity in Prose and Poetry, 1801–2001*, ed. Maxim D. Shrayer, vol. 1, 194–98. Armonk, NY and London: M. E. Sharpe, 2007.

Sofia Parnok

"My anguish does the Lord not heed . . .": "Ne vnial toske moei Gospod'. . . ," in *Liricheskii krug: stranitsy poezii i kritiki*, vol. 1, 19. Moscow: Severnye dni, 1922 (third of four-poem cycle numbered 1–4); **in Sofiia Parnok, *Loza*, 30. Moscow, 1923;** in *Novyi zhurnal* 138 (March 1980): 86 (incorrectly identified as "previously unpublished");

"Hagar": "Agar'"; "Not for safekeeping for awhile . . .":

"Ne na khranen'e do pory . . .";

all three in Sofiia Parnok, *Sobranie stikhotvorenii*, ed. S. Poliakova, 250, 286, 291. St. Petersburg: Inapress, 1998.

English translations by Diana L. Burgin, in *An Anthology of Jewish-Russian Literature: Two Centuries of Dual Identity in Prose and Poetry, 1801–2001*, ed. Maxim D. Shrayer, vol. 1, 201–2. Armonk, NY and London: M. E. Sharpe, 2007.

Leonid Kannegiser

"A Jewish Wedding": "Evreiskoe venchanie";

"Regimental Inspection": "Smotr";

both in *Leonid Kannegiser*; stat'i Georgiia Adamovicha, M. A. Aldanova, Georgiia Ivanova; iz posmertnykh stikhov Leonida Kannegisera, 77, 80–81. Paris, 1928.

English translations by J. B. Sisson and Maxim D. Shrayer, in *An Anthology of Jewish-Russian Literature: Two Centuries of Dual Identity in Prose and Poetry, 1801–2001*, ed. Maxim D. Shrayer, vol. 1, 211–12. Armonk, NY and London: M. E. Sharpe, 2007.

REVOLUTION AND EMIGRATION: 1920s–1930s

Veniamin Kaverin

"Shields (and Candles)": "Schity (i svechi)," in Veniamin Kaverin, *Mastera i podmaster'ia*, 37–47. Moscow–Petersburg: Krug, 1923.

English translation by Gary Kern in *Russian Literature of the Twenties: An Anthology*, ed. Carl R. Proffer et al., 141–48. Ann Arbor, MI: Ardis, 1987; English translation by Gary Kern, in *An Anthology of Jewish-Russian Literature: Two Centuries of Dual Identity in Prose and Poetry, 1801– 2001*, ed. Maxim D. Shrayer, vol. 1, 270–76. Armonk, NY and London: M. E. Sharpe, 2007.

Lev Lunts

"Native Land": "Rodina," in *Evreiskii al'manakh*, ed. B. I. Kaufman and I. A. Kleinman, 27–43. Petrograd–Moscow: Knigoizdatel'stvo Petrograd, 1923; in Lev Lunts, *Vne zakona*, ed. M. Vainshtein, 13–24. St. Petersburg: Kompozitor, 1994.

English translation by Gary Kern in *The Serapion Brothers: A Critical Anthology*, ed. Gary Kern and Christopher Collins, 35–45. Ann Arbor, MI: Ardis, 1975; English translation by Gary Kern, in *An Anthology of Jewish-Russian Literature: Two Centuries of Dual Identity in Prose and Poetry, 1801– 2001*, ed. Maxim D. Shrayer, vol. 1, 257–67. Armonk, NY and London: M. E. Sharpe, 2007.

Vladislav Khodasevich

"Not my mother but a Tula peasant woman . . .": "Ne mater'iu, no tul'skuiu krest'iankoi . . . ," in Vladislav Khodasevich, *Tiazhelaia lira: Chetvertaia kniga stikhov, 1920–1922*, 21–22. Moscow–Petrograd: Gosudarstvennoe izdatel'stvo, 1922; in Vladislav Khodasevich, *Tiazhelaia lira: Chetvertaia kniga stikhov*, 10–11. Berlin–Petrograd: Izdatel'stvo Z. I. Grzhebina, 1923; in Vladislav Khodasevich, *Sobranie stikhov*, 68–69. Paris: Vozrozhdenie, 1927; in Vladislav Khodasevich, *Sobranie stikhov (1913–1939)*, ed. Nina Berberova, 66. New Haven, CT: N. Berberova, 1961; in Vladislav Khodasevich, *Sobranie stikhov v dvukh tomakh*, ed. Iurii Kolker, vol. 1, 134–35. Paris: La Presse Libre, 1983;

"In Moscow I was born. I never . . .": "Ia rodilsia v Moskve. Ia dyma . . .";
both in Vladislav Khodasevich, *Sobranie stikhov v drukh tomakh,* ed. Iurii Kolker, vol. 2, 78.
Paris: La Presse Libre, 1983 (incomplete version of second poem); **both in Vladislav
Khodasevich, *Sobranie stikhov,* ed. A. Dorofeev and A. Lavrin, 158–59, 365. Moscow:
Tsenturion Interpaks, 1992**; both in Vladislav Khodasevich, *Stikhotvoreniia,* ed. Dzhon
[John] Malmstad, 85–86, 163–64. St. Petersburg: Akademicheskii proekt, 2001.
English translations by Alyssa Dinegie Gillespie, in *An Anthology of Jewish-Russian Literature:
Two Centuries of Dual Identity in Prose and Poetry, 1801–2001,* ed. Maxim D. Shrayer, vol. 1,
423–25. Armonk, NY and London: M. E. Sharpe, 2007.

Andrey Sobol

"The Count": "Schet," in Andrei Sobol', *Kniga malen'kikh rasskazov: 1922–1925 gg.,*
51–61. Moscow: Moskovskoe tovarishchestvo pisatelei, 1925.
English translation by *Natalia Ermolaev, Sergey Levchin, Ronald Meyer, Jonathan Platt, and
Timothy Williams,* in *An Anthology of Jewish-Russian Literature: Two Centuries of Dual Identity
in Prose and Poetry, 1801–2001,* ed. Maxim D. Shrayer, vol. 1, 285–88. Armonk, NY and
London: M. E. Sharpe, 2007.

Ilya Ehrenburg

From *Julio Jurenito*: Il'ia Erenburg, *Neobychainye pokhozhdeniia Khulio Khurenito i ego
uchenikov . . . ,* 121–27. Moscow–Berlin: Gelikon, 1922.
English translation by Anna Bostock in collaboration with Yvonne Kapp, in Ilya Ehrenburg, *Julio
Jurenito,* 110–16. London: McGibbon and Kee, 1958; English translation by Anna Bostock in
collaboration with Yvonne Kapp, in *An Anthology of Jewish-Russian Literature: Two Centuries
of Dual Identity in Prose and Poetry, 1801–2001,* ed. Maxim D. Shrayer, vol. 1, 278–82.
Armonk, NY and London: M. E. Sharpe, 2007.

Viktor Shklovsky

From *Zoo, or Letters Not about Love*: in Viktor Shklovskii, *Zoo, ili pis'ma ne o liubvi,* 33–36,
50–52, 93–95. Berlin: Gelikon, 1923.
English translation by Richard Sheldon in *Zoo, or Letters Not about Love,* 27–30, 44–46, 90–93.
Ithaca: Cornell University Press, 1971; English translation by Richard Sheldon, in *An Anthology
of Jewish-Russian Literature: Two Centuries of Dual Identity in Prose and Poetry, 1801–2001,* ed.
Maxim D. Shrayer, vol. 1, 292–98. Armonk, NY and London: M. E. Sharpe, 2007.

Matvey Royzman

"Kol Nidrei": "Kol Nidrei," in Matvei Roizman, *Khevronskoe vino,* 3–12. Moscow:
Vserossiiskii soiuz poetov, 1923; in *Poety-imazhinisty,* ed. E. M. Shneiderman, 375–79. St.
Petersburg: Peterburgskii pisatel', 1997; Moscow: Agraf, 1997.

English translation by J. B. Sisson and Maxim D. Shrayer, in *An Anthology of Jewish-Russian Literature: Two Centuries of Dual Identity in Prose and Poetry, 1801–2001*, ed. Maxim D. Shrayer, vol. 1, 301–6. Armonk, NY and London: M. E. Sharpe, 2007.

Mark Aldanov

"The Assassination of Uritsky": "Ubiistvo Uritskogo," in *Leonid Kannegiser*, 7–37. Paris, 1928; in M. A. Aldanov, *Sobranie sochinenii v shesti tomakh*, ed. Andrei Chernyshev, 486–516. Moscow: Pravda, 1991 (significantly longer version).

English translation by C. Nicholas Lee, in *An Anthology of Jewish-Russian Literature: Two Centuries of Dual Identity in Prose and Poetry, 1801–2001*, ed. Maxim D. Shrayer, vol. 1, 428–41. Armonk, NY and London: M. E. Sharpe, 2007.

Osip Mandelstam

"Judaic Chaos": "Khaos iudeiskii," in *Shum vremeni*, O. E. Mandel'shtam, *Sobranie sochinenii*, ed. G. P. Struve and B. A. Filippov, vol. 2, 65–71. Moscow: Terra, 1991.

English translation by Amelia Glaser and Alexander Zeyliger, in *An Anthology of Jewish-Russian Literature: Two Centuries of Dual Identity in Prose and Poetry, 1801–2001*, ed. Maxim D. Shrayer, vol. 1, 243–47. Armonk, NY and London: M. E. Sharpe, 2007.

"One Alexander Herzovich . . .": "Zhil Aleksandr Gertsevich, evreiskii muzykant . . .";
"Say, desert geometer, shaper . . .": "Skazhi mne, chertezhnik pustyni . . .";
both in O.E. Mandel'shtam, *Sobranie sochinenii*, ed. G. P. Struve and B. A. Filippov, vol. 1, 162–63, 201. Moscow: Terra, 1991; both in O. Mandel'shtam, *Polnoe sobranie stikhotvorenii*, ed. A. G. Mets, 198, 229. St. Petersburg: Akedemicheskii proekt, 1997.

English translation by Maxim D. Shrayer and J. B. Sisson, *AGNI* 55 (Spring 2002): 172–74; English translations by Maxim D. Shrayer and J. B. Sisson, in *An Anthology of Jewish-Russian Literature: Two Centuries of Dual Identity in Prose and Poetry, 1801–2001*, ed. Maxim D. Shrayer, vol. 1, 241–43. Armonk, NY and London: M. E. Sharpe, 2007.

Evgeny Shklyar

"Shield of David, crescent or ikon . . .": "Pred shchitom li Davida, pred sviatoi li ikonoi . . . ," in Evgenii Shkliar, *Ogni na vershinakh. Tret'ia kniga liriki*, 14. Berlin: Otto Kirschner, 1923;
"Where's Home?": "Gde dom?" in Evgenii Shkliar, *Posokh. V sbornik stikhov*, 48. Riga, 1925.

English translations by Andrew Von Hendy and Maxim D. Shrayer in *Bee Museum* 3 (2005): 83–85; English translations by Maxim D. Shrayer and Andrew Von Hendy, in *An Anthology of Jewish-Russian Literature: Two Centuries of Dual Identity in Prose and Poetry, 1801–2001*, ed. Maxim D. Shrayer, vol. 1, 444–45. Armonk, NY and London: M. E. Sharpe, 2007.

Dovid Knut

"I, Dovid-Ari Ben Meir . . .": "Ia, Dovid-Ari ben Meir . . . ," in Dovid Knut, *Moikh tysiacheletii*, 7–10. Paris: K-vo Ptitselov, [1925];

"A Kishinev Burial": "Kishinevskie pokhorony," in Dovid Knut, *Parizhskie nochi*, 35–39. Paris: Izd-vo "Rodnik," 1932 (published as untitled);

"The Land of Israel": "Zemlia izrail'skaia";

all three in Dovid Knut, *Izbrannye stikhi*, 9–11; 107–10; 181–82. Paris, 1949; **all three in Dovid Knut, *Sobranie sochinenii v dvukh tomakh*, ed. V[ladimir] Khazan, vol. 1, 77–78, 159–61, 202–3. Jerusalem: The Hebrew University of Jerusalem, 1997.**

English translations by Ruth Rischin, in *An Anthology of Jewish-Russian Literature: Two Centuries of Dual Identity in Prose and Poetry, 1801–2001*, ed. Maxim D. Shrayer, vol. 1, 440–54, 457. Armonk, NY and London: M. E. Sharpe, 2007.

Isaac Babel

"The Rabbi Son": "Syn rabbi," *Krasnaia nov'* 1 (1924): 69–71;

"Awakening": "Probuzhdenie," in *Molodaia gvardiia* 17–18 (1931): 13–16;

both in Isaak Babel', *Sochineniia*, ed. A. N. Pirozhkova, 2 vols. Vol. 2, 128–29, 171–78. Moscow: Khudohestvennaia literatura, 1991–92.

English translation by Maxim D. Shrayer, *Tablet Magazine*, 1 May 2018.

Vera Inber

"The Nightingale and the Rose": "Solovei i roza," in *Prozhektor* 11 (1925): 15–18; **in Vera Inber, *Solovei i roza. Rasskazy*, 7–18. Kharkov: Proletarii, 1928;** Vera Inber, *Izbrannye proizvedeniia*, 2 vols. Vol. 2, 7–13. Moscow: Gosudarstvennoe izdatel'stvo khudozhestvennoi literatury, 1955.

English translation by Catriona Kelly, in *An Anthology of Jewish-Russian Literature: Two Centuries of Dual Identity in Prose and Poetry, 1801–2001*, ed. Maxim D. Shrayer, vol. 1, 340–45. Armonk, NY and London: M. E. Sharpe, 2007.

Elizaveta Polonskaya

"Encounter": "Vstrecha," in Elizaveta Polonskaia, *Upriamyi kalendar'*, 87–89. Leningrad: Izdatel'stvo pisatelei, 1929; "Encounter," untitled in *Goda. Izbrannye stikhi*, 89–91. Leningrad: Izdatel'stvo pisatelei, 1935.

English translations by Larissa Szporluk, in *An Anthology of Jewish-Russian Literature: Two Centuries of Dual Identity in Prose and Poetry, 1801–2001*, ed. Maxim D. Shrayer, vol. 1, 325–27. Armonk, NY and London: M. E. Sharpe, 2007.

Viktor Fink

"The Preachers" and "The New Culture," from *Jews on the Land*: "Propovedniki" and "Novaia kul'tura," both in Viktor Fink, *Evrei na zemle*, 176–96. Moscow–Leningrad: Gosudarstvennoe izdatel'stvo, 1929.

English translation by Richard Sheldon, in *An Anthology of Jewish-Russian Literature: Two Centuries of Dual Identity in Prose and Poetry, 1801–2001*, ed. Maxim D. Shrayer, vol. 1, 365–69. Armonk, NY and London: M. E. Sharpe, 2007.

Semyon Kirsanov

"R": "Bukva R," in Semen Kirsanov, *Slovo predostavliaetsia Kirsanovu*. Moscow: Gosudarstvennoe izdatel'stvo, 1930; in Semen Kirsanov, *Iskaniia*, 14–16. Moscow: Khudozhestvennaia literatura, 1967.

English translation by Maxim D. Shrayer and J. B. Sisson, "The Letter 'R'," *Sí Señor*, 2 (Winter 2003): 40–43; English translation by Maxim D. Shrayer and J. B. Sisson, in *An Anthology of Jewish-Russian Literature: Two Centuries of Dual Identity in Prose and Poetry, 1801–2001*, ed. Maxim D. Shrayer, vol. 1, 372–74. Armonk, NY and London: M. E. Sharpe, 2007.

Eduard Bagritsky

"Origin": "Proiskhozhdenie," *Novyi mir* 11 (1930): 108; in Eduard Bagritskii, *Pobediteli*, 3. Moscow: GIKhL, 1930; in Eduard Bagritskii, *Stikhotvoreniia i poemy*, ed. E. P. Liubareva and S. A. Kovalenko, 107–8. Moscow: Sovetskii pisatel', 1964; **in Eduard Bagritskii, *Stikhotvoreniia*, ed. G. A. Morev, 88–90. St. Petersburg: Akademicheskii proekt, 2000**.

English translation by Maxim D. Shrayer, "Origin," *AGNI* 52 (2000), 221–23; English translation by Maxim D. Shrayer, in Maxim D. Shrayer, *Russian Poet/Soviet Jew: The Legacy of Eduard Bagritskii*, 21–23. Lanham, MD: Rowman and Littlefield, 2000; English translations by Maxim D. Shrayer, in *An Anthology of Jewish-Russian Literature: Two Centuries of Dual Identity in Prose and Poetry, 1801–2001*, ed. Maxim D. Shrayer, vol. 1, 377–79. Armonk, NY and London: M. E. Sharpe, 2007.

From *February*: *Fevral'*, in Eduard Bagritskii. *Al'manakh*, ed. Vladimir Narbut, 123–44. Moscow: Sovetskii pisatel', 1936; in Eduard Bagritskii, *Stikhotvoreniia i poemy*, ed. E. P. Liubareva and S. A. Kovalenko, 203–21. Moscow: Sovetskii pisatel', 1964; in Eduard Bagritskii, *Stikhotvoreniia*, ed. G. A. Morev, 151–74. St. Petersburg: Akedemicheskii proekt, 2000.

English translation by Maxim D. Shrayer, in Maxim D. Shrayer, *Russian Poet/Soviet Jew: The Legacy of Eduard Bagritskii*, 25; 27–30; 36–36. Lanham, MD: Rowman and Littlefield, 2000; English translation by Maxim D. Shrayer, in *An Anthology of Jewish-Russian Literature: Two*

Centuries of Dual Identity in Prose and Poetry, 1801–2001, ed. Maxim D. Shrayer, vol. 1, 379–84. Armonk, NY and London: M. E. Sharpe, 2007.

Mark Egart

From *The Scorched Land*: *Opalennaia zemlia*, in Mark Egart, *Opalennaia zemlia: kniga vto-raia*, 25–40. Moscow: **Sovetskii pisatel', 1934**; Mark Egart, *Opalennaia zemlia* (Moscow: Sovetskii pisatel', 1937): 171–186 (with significant modifications).

English translation by Margarit Tadevosyan Ordykhanyan and Maxim D. Shrayer, in *An Anthology of Jewish-Russian Literature: Two Centuries of Dual Identity in Prose and Poetry, 1801–2001*, ed. Maxim D. Shrayer, vol. 1, 400–412. Armonk, NY and London: M. E. Sharpe, 2007.

Ilya Ilf

"The Prodigal Son Retuns Home": **"Bludnyi syn vozvrashchaetsia domoi,"** *Ogonek* 2 (15 January 1930): 10; in Il'ia Il'f and Evgenii Petrov, *Neobyknovennye istorii iz zhizni goroda Kololanska*, ed. **Mikhail Dolinskii, 209–11. Moscow: Knizhnaia palata, 1989.**

English translation by Alice Nakhimovsky, in *An Anthology of Jewish-Russian Literature: Two Centuries of Dual Identity in Prose and Poetry, 1801–2001*, ed. Maxim D. Shrayer, vol. 1, 388–90. Armonk, NY and London: M. E. Sharpe, 2007.

Ilya Ilf and Evgeny Petrov

From *The Little Golden Calf* : **"Zolotoi telenok,"** in Il'ia Il'f, Evgeni Petrov, *Novye pok-hozhdeniia Ostapa Bendera: kniga vtoraia romana "Zolotoi telenok,"* **140–152. Riga: Zhizn' i kul'tura, 1931**; Il'ia Il'f, Evgenii Petrov, *Dvenadtsat' stul'ev. Zolotoi telenok,* 566–76. Kiev: Radian'skii pis'mennik, 1957; Il'ia Il'f i Evgenii Petrov, *Zolotoi telenok,* ed. M. Odesskii and D. Fel'dman, 299–307. Moscow: Vagrius, 2000.

English translation by Margarit Tadevosyan Ordukhanya, in collaboration with Maxim D. Shrayer, in *An Anthology of Jewish-Russian Literature: Two Centuries of Dual Identity in Prose and Poetry, 1801–2001*, ed. Maxim D. Shrayer, vol. 1, 392–97. Armonk, NY and London: M. E. Sharpe, 2007.

Raisa Blokh

"A snatch of speech came floating on the air . . .": **"Prinesla sluchainaia molva . . . ,"** in Raisa Blokh, *Zdes' shumiat chuzhie goroda,* 90. Moscow: Izograf, 1996; in Raisa Blokh, Mikhail Gorlin, *Izbrannye stikhotvoreniia,* 39. Paris: Rifma/Izdatel'stvo imeni Iriny Iassen, 1959;

"Remember, father would stand . . .": **"Pomnish', otets, byvalo . . . ,"** in *Nevod. Tretii sbornik stikhov berlinskikh poetov,* 63. Berlin: Slovo, 1933; in Raisa Blokh, *Zdes' shumiat chuzhie goroda,* 89. Moscow: Izograf, 1996;

both in Raisa Blokh, *Tishina: Stikhi* 1928–1934, 47, 52. Berlin: Petropilis, 1935.

English translations by Catriona Kelly, in *An Anthology of Jewish-Russian Literature: Two Centuries of Dual Identity in Prose and Poetry, 1801–2001*, ed. Maxim D. Shrayer, vol. 1, 464–65. Armonk, NY and London: M. E. Sharpe, 2007.

WAR AND SHOAH: 1940s

Boris Yampolsky

From *Country Fair*: "Mr. Dykhes and Others": "Gospodin Dykhes i drugie," in Boris Iampol'skii, *Iarmarka, Krasnaia nov'* 3 (March) 1941: 34–87; in Boris Iampol'skii, *Iarmarka*, 128–54. Moscow: Sovetskii pisatel', 1942; in Boris Iampol'skii, *Arbat, rezhimnaia ulitsa*, ed. Vladimir Prikhod'ko, 321–41. Moscow: Vagrius, 1997.

English translation by Richard Sheldon, in *An Anthology of Jewish-Russian Literature: Two Centuries of Dual Identity in Prose and Poetry, 1801–2001*, ed. Maxim D. Shrayer, vol. 1, 515–28. Armonk, NY and London: M. E. Sharpe, 2007.

Ilya Ehrenburg

"To the Jews": "Evreiam," in *Izvestiia*, 26 August 1941; in Il'ia Erenburg, *Staryi skorniak i drugie proizvedeniia*, ed. M. Vainshtein, 2 vols. Vol. 2, 251–52. Jerusalem, 1983.

English translation by Joshua Rubenstein, in *An Anthology of Jewish-Russian Literature: Two Centuries of Dual Identity in Prose and Poetry, 1801–2001*, ed. Maxim D. Shrayer, vol. 1, 532–33. Armonk, NY and London: M. E. Sharpe, 2007; English translation by Joshua Rubenstein, in *Soviet Jews in World War II: Fighting, Witnessing, Remembering*, ed. Harriet Murav and Gennady Estraikh, 39–40. Boston: Academic Studies Press, 2014.

"Six Poems" (The January 1945 *Novy mir* cycle): "Stikhi," in *Novyi mir* 1 (1945): 16; in Il'ia Erenburg, *Stikhotvoreniia*, ed. B. Ia. Frezinskii, 512 (as "Babii Iar"), 518, 518, 519, 519, 520. St. Petersburg: Akademicheskii proekt, 2000 (not published as a cycle).

English translation by Maxim D. Shrayer, in *Eastern European Jewish Literature of the 20th and 21st Centuries: Identity and Poetics*, ed. Klavdia Smola, 207–9. Munich-Berlin: Die Welt der Slaven Sammelbände, Verlag Otto Sagner, 2013.

Ilya Selvinsky

"I Saw It!": "Ia eto videl!" in *Krasnaia zvezda*, 27 February 1942, 3; in *Oktiabr'* 1–2 (1942): 65–66; in Il'ia Sel'vinskii, *Ballady, plakaty i pesni*, 87–92. Krasnodar: Kraevoe izdatel'stvo, 1942; in *Zverstva nemetskikh fashistov v Kerchi. Sbornik rasskazov postradavshikh i ochevidtsev*, 33–38. Sukhumi: Krasnyi Krym, 1943; in Il'ia Sel'vinskii, *Voennaia lirika*, 18–22. Tashkent: Gosudarstvennoe izdatel'stvo UzSSR, 1943; in Il'ia Sel'vinskii, *Ballady i pesni*, 42–45. Moscow: Goslitizdat, 1943; in Il'ia Sel'vinskii, *Krym Kavkaz Kuban'. Stikhi*, 7–12. Moscow: Sovetskii pisa-

tel', 1947; in Il'ia Sel'vinskii, *Lirika i dramy*, 51–55. Moscow: Gosudarstvennoe izdatel'stvo khu-
dozhestvennoi literatury, 1947; in Il'ia Sel'vinskii, *Izbrannye proizvedeniia*, 2 vols. Vol. 1, 162–65.
Moscow: Gosudarstvennoe izdatel'stvo khudozhestvennoi literatury, 1956; in Il'ia Sel'vinskii,
in *Lirika*, 249–53. Moscow: Khudozhestvennaia literatura, 1964; in Il'ia Sel'vinskii, *Sobranie
sochinenii v shesti tomakh*. Vol. 1. *Stikhotvoreniia*, 352–55. Moscow: Khudozhestvennaia litera-
tura, 1971; in Il'ia Sel'vinskii, *Izbrannye proizvedeniia*, ed. I. L. Mikhailov and N. G. Zakharenko,
206–9. Leningrad: Sovetskii pisatel' [Biblioteka poeta], 1972; in Il'ia Sel'vinskii, *Stikhotvoreniia.
Tsarevna-lebed': tragediia*, ed. Ts. Voskresenskaia, 111–14. Moscow: Khudozhestvennaia
literatura, 1984; in Il'ia Sel'vinskii, *Izbrannye proizvedeniia v dvukh tomakh*, 2 vols., ed. Ts.
Voskresenskaia. Vol. 1, 176–79. Moscow: Khudozhestvennaia literatura, 1989; in Il'ia Sel'vinskii,
Iz pepla, iz poem, iz snovidenii, ed. A. M. Revich, 139–44. Moscow: Vremia, 2004.

"Kerch": **"Kerch",** *Znamia* 2 **(1945): 78–79;** in Il'ia Sel'vinskii, *Stikhotvoreniia. Tsarevna-lebed':
tragediia*, ed. Ts. Voskresenskaia, 108–11. Moscow: Khudozhestvennaia literatura, 1984; in
Il'ia Sel'vinskii, *Izbrannye proizvedeniia v dvukh tomakh*, 2 vols., ed. Ts. Voskresenskaia. Vol. 1,
193–96. Moscow: Khudozhestvennaia literatura, 1989; in Il'ia Sel'vinskii, *Iz pepla, iz poem, iz
snovidenii*, ed. A. M. Revich, 150–54. Moscow: Vremia, 2004.

English translations by Maxim D. Shrayer, in *Four Centuries: Russian Poetry in Translation* 4 (2013):
29–37; English translations by Maxim D. Shrayer, in Shrayer, *I SAW IT: Ilya Selvinsky and the
Legacy of Bearing Witness to the Shoah*, 266–69; 274–77. Boston: Academic Studies Press, 2013.

Sofia Dubnova-Erlikh

"Shtetl": "Mestechko," *Novosel'e* 3 (1943): 64–67.
"Scorched Hearth": "Na pepelishche," *Novosel'e* 11 (1944): 70–73.
English translation by Helen Reeve and Martha Kitchen, in *An Anthology of Jewish-Russian
Literature: Two Centuries of Dual Identity in Prose and Poetry, 1801–2001*, ed. Maxim D.
Shrayer, vol. 1, 473–75, 476–78. Armonk, NY and London: M. E. Sharpe, 2007.

Vasily Grossman

"The Hell of Treblinka": "Treblinskii ad," in *Znamia* 11 (1944): 121–44; in Vasilii
Grossman, *Treblinskii ad*. Moscow: Voenizdat, 1945; in Vasilii Grossman, *Na evreiskie temy*,
ed. Shimon Markish, 2 vols. Vol. 1, 144–90. Jerusalem: Biblioteka-Aliia, 1985; **in Vasilii
Grossman, *Sobranie sochinenii v chetyrekh tomakh*, ed. S. I. Lipkin, 4 vols. Vol. 4, 380–
410. Moscow: Vagrius-Agraf, 1998.**

Lev Ozerov

"Babii Iar": "Baby Yar," in *Oktaibr'*, 3–4 (1946): 160–63; **in Lev Ozerov, *Liven'*, ed. P.
Antokol'skii, 25–32. Moscow: Molodaia gvardiia, 1947;** in Lev Ozerov, *Lirika: Izbannye
stikhotvoreniia*, 25–32, Moscow: Sovetskii pisatel', 1966.

English translation by Richard Sheldon, in *An Anthology of Jewish-Russian Literature: Two Centuries of Dual Identity in Prose and Poetry, 1801–2001,* ed. Maxim D. Shrayer, vol. 1, 575–79. Armonk, NY and London: M. E. Sharpe, 2007.

Pavel Antokolsky

"Death Camp": "Lager' unichtozheniia," *Znamia* 10 (1945): 34; **in Pavel Antokol'skii, *Izbrannoe,* 174–76. Moscow: Molodaia gvardiia, 1946**; in Pavel Antokol'skii, *Sobranie sochinenii,* 4 vols. Vol. 2, 81–82. Moscow: Khudozhestvennaia literatura, 1971.
English translation by Maxim D. Shrayer and J. B. Sisson, in *An Anthology of Jewish-Russian Literature: Two Centuries of Dual Identity in Prose and Poetry, 1801–2001,* ed. Maxim D. Shrayer, vol. 1, 582–83. Armonk, NY and London: M. E. Sharpe, 2007.

Yury German

From *Lieutenant Colonel of the Medical Corps: Podpolkovnik meditsinskoi sluzhby,* in Iurii German, *Podpolkovnik meditsinskoi sluzhby,* 109–116. Leningrad: Sovetskii pisatel', 1956; in Iurii German, *Podpolkovnik meditisnskoi sluzhby. Nachalo. Butsefal. Lapshin. Zhmakin. Vospominaniia,* 110–17. Leningrad: Sovetskii pisatel', 1968; **in Iurii German, *Podpolkovnik meditsinskoi sluzhby,* 107–14. Moscow: Sovetskii pisatel', 1972**; in Iurii German, *Podpolkovnik meditsinskoi sluzhby,* 110–16. Moscow: ACT/Olimp, 2001.
English translation by Helen Reeve with Martha Kitchen, in *An Anthology of Jewish-Russian Literature: Two Centuries of Dual Identity in Prose and Poetry, 1801–2001,* ed. Maxim D. Shrayer, vol. 1, 586–90. Armonk, NY and London: M. E. Sharpe, 2007.

Boris Pasternak

"In the Lowlands": "V nizov'iakh," in Boris Pasternak, *Zemnoi prostor: stikhi,* 41. Moscow: Sovetskii pisatel', 1945;
"Odessa";
both in Boris Pasternak, *Stikhotvoreniia i poemy,* ed. L. A. Ozerov, 422–23, 568–69. (Moscow–Leningrad: Sovetskii pisatel', 1965.
English translations by Andrew Von Hendy and Maxim D. Shrayer, in *An Anthology of Jewish-Russian Literature: Two Centuries of Dual Identity in Prose and Poetry, 1801–2001,* ed. Maxim D. Shrayer, vol. 1, 594–97. Armonk, NY and London: M. E. Sharpe, 2007.
From *Doctor Zhivago*: in Boris Pasternak, *Doktor Zhivago: roman,* 19–24, 140–45. Paris: Société d'Edition et d'Impression Mondiale, 1959. English translation by Max Hayward and Manya Harari, in Boris Pasternak, *Doctor Zhivago,* 12–16, 118–23. New York: Pantheon, 1958; English translation by Max Hayward and Manya Harari, corrected by Maxim D. Shrayer, in *An Anthology of Jewish-Russian Literature: Two Centuries of Dual Identity in Prose and Poetry, 1801–2001,* ed. Maxim D. Shrayer, vol. 1, 598–605. Armonk, NY and London: M. E. Sharpe, 2007.

THE THAW: 1950s–1960s

Boris Slutsky

"These Abrám, Isák and Yákov . . .": "U Abrama, Isaka i Iakova . . . ," in *God za godom* 5 (1989): 92–93; in Boris Slutskii, *Sobranie sochinenii v trekh tomakh*, ed. Iu. Boldyrev, vol. 1, 71. Moscow: Khudozhestvennaia literatura, 1991; in Boris Slutskii, *Teper' Osventsim chasto snitsia mne . . .* , ed. P. Z. Gorelik, 30. St. Petersburg: Zhurnal Neva, 1999;

"Of the Jews": "Pro evreev," in *Sovetskaia potaennaia muza; Iz stikhov sovetskikh poetov, napisannykh ne dlia pechati*, ed. Boris Filippov, 135 [anonymously and without a title as part 1 of a two-poem cycle]. Munich: I. Baschkirzew Verlag, 1961; in *Modern Russian Poetry: An Anthology with Verse Translations*, ed. Vladmir Markov and Merrill Sparks, 812 [anonymously]. Indianapolis, IN: The Bobbs-Merrill Company, Inc., 1966; in *Neopalimaia kupina: Evreiskie siuzhety v russkoi poezii. Antologiia*, ed. Aleksandr Donat, 420 [anonymously]. New York: New York University Press, 1973; in *Na odnoi volne: Evreiskie motivy v russkoi poezii*, ed. Tamar Dolzhanskaia, 207 [anonymously]. Tel Aviv: Biblioteka "Aliia," 1974; in *Novyi mir* 10 (1987): 175; in Boris Slutskii, *Sobranie sochinenii v trekh tomakh*, ed. Iu. Boldyrev, vol. 1, 165. Moscow: Khudozhestvennaia literatura, 1991; in Boris Slutskii, *Teper' Osventsim chasto snitsia mne . . .* , ed. P. Z. Gorelik, 31. St. Petersburg: Zhurnal Neva, 1999; in Boris Slutskii, *Zapiski o voine*, ed. P[etr] Gorelik, 298. St. Petersburg: Logos, 2000;

"Horses in the Ocean": "Loshadi v okeane," in *Pioner* 3 (1956): 61; in *Moskva* 2 (1957): 44–45; in Boris Slutskii, *Pamiat'*, 79–80. Moscow: Sovetskii pisatel', 1957; in Boris Slutskii, *Sobranie sochinenii v trekh tomakh*, ed. Iu. Boldyrev, vol. 1, 126–27. Moscow: Khudozhestvennaia literatura, 1991; in Boris Slutskii, *Teper' Osventsim chasto snitsia mne . . .* , ed. P. Z. Gorelik, 55. St. Petersburg: Zhurnal Neva, 1999; in Boris Slutskii, *Zapiski o voine*, ed. P[etr] Gorelik, 239–40. St. Petersburg: Logos, 2000;

"Prodigal Son": "Bludnyi syn," in Boris Slutskii, *Pamiat'*, 91. Moscow: Sovetskii pisatel', 1957; in Boris Slutskii, *Pamiat'. Stikhi 1944–1968*, 184–85. Moscow: Khudozhestvennaia literatura, 1969; in Boris Slutskii, *Sobranie sochinenii v trekh tomakh*, ed. Iu. Boldyrev, vol. 1, 132. Moscow: Khudozhestvennaia literatura, 1991;

"Puny Jewish children . . .": "Evreiskim khilym detiam," in *God za godom* 5 (1989): 96; in Boris Slutskii, *Sobranie sochinenii v trekh tomakh*, ed. Iu. Boldyrev, vol. 1, 297. Moscow: Khudozhestvennaia literatura, 1991; in Boris Slutskii, *Teper' Osventsim chasto snitsia mne . . .* , ed. P. Z. Gorelik, 37. St. Petersburg: Zhurnal Neva, 1999.

English translations by Sergey Levchin and Maxim D. Shrayer, "These Abrám, Isák and Yákov..."; "Horses in the Ocean"; "Prodigal Son"; "Puny Jewish Children," in *Absinthe: New European Writing* 5 (2006): 34–40; English translations by Sergey Levchin and Maxim D. Shrayer, in *An Anthology of Jewish-Russian Literature: Two Centuries of Dual Identity in Prose and Poetry, 1801–2001*, ed. Maxim D. Shrayer, vol. 2, 643–47. Armonk, NY and London: M. E. Sharpe, 2007.

Vasily Grossman

From *Life and Fate*: *Zhizn' i sud'ba*, in Vasilii Grossman, *Na evreiskie temy: Izbrannoe v dvukh tomakh*, vol. 1, 264–79. Jerusalem: Biblioteka "Aliia," 1985; **in Vasilii Grossman, *Sobrannie sochinenii v 4kh tomakh*, ed. S. I. Lipkin, vol. 2, 404–15. Moscow: Agraf, 1998.**

English translation by John Garrard, in *An Anthology of Jewish-Russian Literature: Two Centuries of Dual Identity in Prose and Poetry, 1801–2001*, ed. Maxim D. Shrayer, vol. 2, 649–60. Armonk, NY and London: M. E. Sharpe, 2007.

Joseph Brodsky

"Jewish graveyard near Leningrad...": "Evreiskoe kladbishche okolo Leningrada...," in *Grani* 58 (1965): 163 [reprint of issue 3 of the Moscow samizdat magazine *Sintaksis*]; in Iosif Brodskii, *Stikhotvoreniia i poemy*, 54–55. Washington, DC: Inter-Language Literary Associates, 1965;

"I'm not asking death for immortality...": "Bessmertiia u smerti ne proshu...";
both in Iosif Brodskii, *Sochineniia Iosifa Brodskogo*, ed. G. F. Komarov, vol. 1, 21, 153. St. Petersburg: Pushkinskii Fond, 1992.

English translations by Joanna Trzeciak, in *An Anthology of Jewish-Russian Literature: Two Centuries of Dual Identity in Prose and Poetry, 1801–2001*, ed. Maxim D. Shrayer, vol. 2, 670–72. Armonk, NY and London: M. E. Sharpe, 2007.

Vladimir Britanishsky

"A German Girl": "Nemka," in Vladimir Britanishskii, *Starye fotografii*, 45–46. Moscow: Literaturno-khudozhestvennoe agentstvo "LIRA," 1993.

English translation by J. B. Sisson and Maxim D. Shrayer, *Bee Museum* 3 (2005): 113–14; English translation by J. B. Sisson and Maxim D. Shrayer, in *An Anthology of Jewish-Russian Literature: Two Centuries of Dual Identity in Prose and Poetry, 1801–2001*, ed. Maxim D. Shrayer, vol. 2, 929–30. Armonk, NY and London: M. E. Sharpe, 2007.

Yuly Daniel

From *This Is Moscow Speaking*: *Govorit Moskva*, in Nikolai Arzhak [pseudonym of Yu. Daniel], *Govorit Moskva: Povesti i rasskazy*, 11–23. Washington, DC: Inter-Language Literary Associates, 1966; in Iulii Daniel, *Govorit Moskva*, ed. I. Uvarova et al., 71–78. Moscow: Moskovskii rabochii, 1991.

English translation by John Richardson, in *Dissonant Voices in Soviet Literature*, ed. Patricia Blake and Max Hayward, 262–73. New York: Pantheon, 1962; English translation by John Richardson, in *An Anthology of Jewish-Russian Literature: Two Centuries of Dual Identity in Prose and Poetry, 1801–2001*, ed. Maxim D. Shrayer, vol. 2, 675–80. Armonk, NY and London: M. E. Sharpe, 2007.

Emmanuil Kazakevich

"Enemies": "Vragi," in *Izvestiia*, 21 April 1962: 6; in Em. Kazakevich, *Siniaia tetrad': povest', rasskaz, ocherk*, 142–58 (modified text). Moscow: Sovetskii pisatel', 1991.

English translation by Mary Ann Szporluk, in *An Anthology of Jewish-Russian Literature: Two Centuries of Dual Identity in Prose and Poetry, 1801–2001*, ed. Maxim D. Shrayer, vol. 2, 683–93. Armonk, NY and London: M. E. Sharpe, 2007.

Yan Satunovsky

"In the country that has nearly forgotten . . .": "V otvykshei bit' zhidov strane . . . ," in Ian Satunovskii, *Rublenaia proza*, ed. Vol'fgang Kazak [Wolfgang Kasack], 43. Munich: Verlag Otto Sagner in Kommission, 1994;

"Who are you, repatriated widows? . . .": "Kto vy—repatriirovannye vdovy . . . ," in Ian Satunovskii, *Rublenaia proza*, ed. Vol'fgang Kazak, 36. Munich: Verlag Otto Sagner in Kommission, 1994;

"Girls with golden eyes . . .": "Devushki s zolotymi glazami . . . ," in Ian Satunovskii, *Rublenaia proza*, ed. Vol'fgang Kazak, 48. Munich: Verlag Otto Sagner in Kommission, 1994;

"You're mistaken . . .": "Vy oshibaetes' . . . ," in Ian Satunovskii, *Rublenaia proza*, ed. Vol'fgang Kazak, 92. Munich: Verlag Otto Sagner in Kommission, 1994;

"It's the end of our nation . . .": "Konchaetsia nasha natsiia . . . ," in Ian Satunovskii, *Khochu li ia posmertnoi slavy*, ed. P. Satunovskii and I. Akhmet'ev, 32. Moscow: Biblioteka al'manakha "Vesy," 1992;

"My Slavic language is Russian . . .": "Moi iazyk slavianskii—russkii . . . ," in Ian Satunovskii, *Khochu li ia posmertnoi slavy*, ed. P. Satunovskii and I. Akhmet'ev, 39. Moscow: Biblioteka al'manakha "Vesy," 1992;

"I'm Moyshe from Berdichev . . .": "Ia Moisha iz Berdycheva . . . ," in Ian Satunovskii, *Khochu li ia posmertnoi slavy*, ed. P. Satunovskii and I. Akhmet'ev, 40. Moscow: Biblioteka al'manakha "Vesy," 1992;

"Eve, a civilized Jewess . . .": "Eva, tsivilizovannaia evreika . . . ," in Ian Satunovskii, *Khochu li ia posmertnoi slavy*, ed. P. Satunovskii and I. Akhmet'ev, 40. Moscow: Biblioteka al'manakha "Vesy," 1992;

"Expressionism-Zionism . . .": "Ekspressionizm-Sionizm . . . ," in Ian Satunovskii, *Khochu li ia posmertnoi slavy*, ed. P. Satunovskii and I. Akhmet'ev, 54. Moscow: Biblioteka al'manakha "Vesy," 1992;

"Blessed be the ill fate . . .": "Blagoslovenno zlopoluchie . . . ," in Ian Satunovskii, *Khochu li ia posmernoi slavy*, ed. P. Satunovskii and I. Akhmet'ev, 71. Moscow: Biblioteka al'manakha "Vesy," 1992;

"Gate slamming, shelter closing . . .": "Zakhlopnulas' kalitka . . . ," in Ian Satunovskii, *Rublenaia proza*, ed. Vol'fgang Kazak, 14. Munich: Verlag Otto Sagner in Kommission, 1994;

"There are antisemites, and antisemites . . .": "Antisemit antisemitu rozn'. . . ," in Ian Satunovskii, *Khochu li ia posmernoi slavy*, ed. P. Satunovskii and I. Akhmet'ev, 106. Moscow: Biblioteka al'manakha "Vesy," 1992;

"Some say: in Solzhenitsyn's time . . .": "Odni govoriat: v epokhu Solzhenitsyna . . . ," in Ian Satunovskii, *Khochu li ia posmernoi slavy*, ed. P. Satunovskii and I. Akhmet'ev, 106. Moscow: Biblioteka al'manakha "Vesy," 1992.

English translations by Maxim D. Shrayer, in *An Anthology of Jewish-Russian Literature: Two Centuries of Dual Identity in Prose and Poetry, 1801–2001*, ed. Maxim D. Shrayer, vol. 2, 746–52. Armonk, NY and London: M. E. Sharpe, 2007.

LATE SOVIET EMPIRE: 1960s–1980s

Vassily Aksyonov

"Victory": "Pobeda," in *Iunost'* 6 (1965): 28–30; in Vasilii Aksenov, *Sobranie sochinenii*, vol. 2, 403–8. Moscow; Izdatel'skii dom "Iunost'," 1995.

English translation by Greta Slobin, in *The Ardis Anthology of Recent Russian Literature*, ed. Carl Proffer and Ellendea Proffer, 191–95. Ann Arbor: Ardis, 1973; English translation by Greta Slobin, in *An Anthology of Jewish-Russian Literature: Two Centuries of Dual Identity in Prose and Poetry, 1801–2001*, ed. Maxim D. Shrayer, vol. 2, 730–35. Armonk, NY and London: M. E. Sharpe, 2007.

Aleksandr Kushner

"When that teacher in Poland, so as not . . .": "Kogda tot pol'skii pedagog . . . ," in Aleksandr Kushner, *Primety*, 25–26. Leningrad: Sovetskii pisatel', 1969;

"Letters": "Bukvy," in Aleksandr Kushner, *Primety*, 91–92. Leningrad: Sovetskii pisatel', 1969; both poems in Aleksandr Kushner, *Izbrannoe*, 64, 83. St. Petersburg: Khudozhestvennaia literatura, 1997.

English translations by Carol Ueland and Robert Carnevale, in *An Anthology of Jewish-Russian Literature: Two Centuries of Dual Identity in Prose and Poetry, 1801–2001*, ed. Maxim D. Shrayer, vol. 2, 755–56. Armonk, NY and London: M. E. Sharpe, 2007.

Genrikh Sapgir

"In Memory of My Father": "Pamiati ottsa";

"Psalm 3": "Psalom 3," in *Tret'ia volna* 6 (1979): 12–13; in *Russkii evrei* 1 (1998): 17;

"Psalm 116 (117)": "Psalom 116," in *Tret'ia volna* 6 (1979): 17; in *Russkii evrei* 1 (1998): 17;

"Psalm 132 (133)": "Psalom 132," in *Russkii evrei* 1 (1988): 17;

"Psalm 136 (137)": "Psalom 136";

"Psalm 150": "Psalom 150";

all but "Pamiati ottsa" in Genrikh Sapgir, *Izbrannye stikhi* [*Izbrannoe* on the cover], 65–66, 75, 76, 77–78, 83. Moscow–Paris–New York: Tret'ia volna, 1993; all in Genrikh Sapgir, *Sobranie sochinenii*, [2 vols. of 4 published to date], vol. 1, 121–22, 179–80, 188, 189, 190–91, 196. New York–Moscow–Paris: Tret'ia volna, 1999; **all in Genrikh Sapgir, *Stikhotvoreniia i poemy*, ed. David Shrayer-Petrov and Maxim D. Shrayer, 121–22, 154–55, 155–56, 156–57, 160–61. St. Petersburg: Akademicheskii proekt, 2004;**
"A Pole Rode": "Ekhal liakh," in Genrikh Sapgir, *Pushkin, Bufarev i drugie*, 153–54. Moscow: S. A. Nitochkin, 1992.
English translations by Gerald Janecek, in *An Anthology of Jewish-Russian Literature: Two Centuries of Dual Identity in Prose and Poetry, 1801–2001*, ed. Maxim D. Shrayer, vol. 2, 713–22. Armonk, NY and London: M. E. Sharpe, 2007.

Aleksandr Aronov

"Ghetto. 1943": "Getto. 1943," in Aleksandr Aronov, *Teksty: stikhi*, 17–18. Moscow: Knizhnaia palata, 1989; in Aleksandr Aronov, *Pervaia zhizn'*, 10. Moscow: Biblioteka "Ogonek," 1989;
"That raving blatherskite . . .": "Nevniatitseiu vsei . . . ," in *Menora: Evreiskie motivy v russkoi poezii*, ed. Ada Kolganova, 78. Moscow: Evreiskii universitet v Moskve, 1993.
English translations by Maxim D. Shrayer and J. B. Sisson, in *An Anthology of Jewish-Russian Literature: Two Centuries of Dual Identity in Prose and Poetry, 1801–2001*, ed. Maxim D. Shrayer, vol. 2, 725–27. Armonk, NY and London: M. E. Sharpe, 2007.

Semyon Lipkin

"Khaim," in "Khaim," *Metropol'. Literaturny al'manakh*, ed. V. Aksenov, A. Bitov, et al., 322. Ann Arbor: Ardis, 1979; in Semen Lipkin, *Sem' desiatiletii*, 197, 232–33. Moscow: Vozvrashchenie, 2000.
English translation by Amelia Glaser, in *An Anthology of Jewish-Russian Literature: Two Centuries of Dual Identity in Prose and Poetry, 1801–2001*, ed. Maxim D. Shrayer, vol. 2, 775–76. Armonk, NY and London: M. E. Sharpe, 2007.

Yury Karabchievsky

From *The Life of Alexander Zilber*: *Zhizn' Aleksandra Zil'bera*, in *Vremia i my* 55 (1980): 5–27; in Iurii Karabchievskii, *Toska po domu. Roman, povesti*, 9–17. Moscow: Ex Libris/ Izdaniia knizhnoi red. sov.-britanskogo sovmestnogo predpriiatiia "Slovo," 1991.
English translation by *Natalia Ermolaev, Sergey Levchin, Ronald Meyer, Jonathan Platt, and Timothy Williams*, in *An Anthology of Jewish-Russian Literature: Two Centuries of Dual Identity*

in Prose and Poetry, 1801–2001, ed. Maxim D. Shrayer, vol. 2, 781–88. Armonk, NY and London: M. E. Sharpe, 2007.

Inna Lisnyanskaya

"My father a military doctor . . .": **"Moi otets—voennyi vrach,"** in *Vremia i my* 49 (**1980**): **71–72**; in Inna Lisnianskaia, *Dozhdi i zerkala. Stikhi*, 100. Paris: YMCA-Press, 1983; in *Svet dvuedinyi. Evrei i Rossiia v sovremennoi poezii*, ed. M. Grozovskii and E. Vitkovskii, 96. Moscow: Izdatel'stvo AO "Kh.G.S.," 1996; in Inna Lisnianskaia, *Odinokii dar*, 80. Moscow: OGI, 2003;

"An Incident": **"Sluchai,"** in Inna Lisnianskaia, *Dozhdi i zerkala. Stikhi*, 224. Paris: YMCA-Press, 1983; **in *Svet dvuedinyi. Evrei i Rossiia v sovremennoi poezii*, ed. M. Grozovskii and E. Vitkovskii, 102. Moscow: Izdatel'stvo AO "Kh.G.S.," 1996**; in Inna Lisnianskaia, *Odinokii dar*, 140. Moscow: OGI, 2003.

English translations by Larissa Szporluk, in *An Anthology of Jewish-Russian Literature: Two Centuries of Dual Identity in Prose and Poetry, 1801–2001*, ed. Maxim D. Shrayer, vol. 2, 791–93. Armonk, NY and London: M. E. Sharpe, 2007.

Boris Slutsky

"Let's cross out the Pale . . .": **"Cherta pod chertoiu. Propala osedlost'. . . ,"** in *Literaturnaia Gruziia* 2 (1985): 38–39 [incomplete text under the title "Anafema vragam mira na zemle"]; **in Boris Slutskii, *Sobranie sochinenii v trekh tomakh*, ed. Iu. Boldyrev, vol. 2, 340. Moscow: Khudozhestvennaia literatura, 1991;** in Boris Slutskii, *Teper' Osventsim chasto snitsia mne . . .*, ed. P. Z. Gorelik, 8. St. Petersburg: Zhurnal Neva, 1999;

"I love the antisemites . . .": **"Liubliu antisemitov, zadarma . . . ,"** in *Znamia* 1 (1988): 74; **in Boris Slutskii, *Sobranie sochinenii v trekh tomakh*, ed. Iu. Boldyrev, vol. 2, 311. Moscow: Khudozhestvennaia literatura, 1991;** in Boris Slutskii, *Teper' Osventsim chasto snitsia mne . . .*, ed. P. Z. Gorelik, 33. St. Petersburg: Zhurnal Neva, 1999;

"The rabbis came down to the valley . . .": **"Ravviny vyshli na ravniny . . . "** **all in *God za godom* [Moscow] 5 (1989): 87, 93, 95.**

"The rabbis came down to the valley . . .": English translations by Sergey Levchin and Maxim D. Shrayer, in *Absinthe: New European Writing* 5 (2006): 40; all English translations by Sergey Levchin and Maxim D. Shrayer, in *An Anthology of Jewish-Russian Literature: Two Centuries of Dual Identity in Prose and Poetry, 1801–2001*, ed. Maxim D. Shrayer, vol. 2, 795–96. Armonk, NY and London: M. E. Sharpe, 2007.

Anatoly Rybakov

From *Heavy Sand*: *Tiazhelyi pesok*, in *Druzhba narodov* 9 (1978): 142–47; **in Anatolii Rybakov, *Tiazhelyi pesok*, 296–304. Moscow: Sovetskii pisatel', 1979**; modified version in Anatolii Rybakov, *Tiazhelyi pesok. Roman*, vol. 4 of *Sobranie sochinenii v semi tomakh*, 293–302. Moscow: Terra, 1995.

English translation by Harold Shukman, in Anatoly Rybakov, *Heavy Sand*, 371–81. Harmondsworth: Penguin, 1981; English translation by Harold Shukman, in *An Anthology of Jewish-Russian Literature: Two Centuries of Dual Identity in Prose and Poetry, 1801–2001*, ed. Maxim D. Shrayer, vol. 2, 819–25. Armonk, NY and London: M. E. Sharpe, 2007.

Yury Trifonov

"A Visit with Marc Chagall": **"Poseshchenie Marka Shagala,"** in *Novyi mir* 7 (1981): 58–87; **in Iurii Trifonov, *Vechnye temy*, 619–28 (chapter of *Oprokinutyi dom*). Moscow: Sovetskii pisatel', 1984**; in *Iurii i Ol'ga Trifonova vspominaiut*, 228–37. Moscow: Kollektsiia "Sovershenno sekretno," 2003.

English translation by Maxim D. Shrayer, *AGNI* 61 (Spring 2005): 156–65; English translation by Maxim D. Shrayer, in *An Anthology of Jewish-Russian Literature: Two Centuries of Dual Identity in Prose and Poetry, 1801–2001*, ed. Maxim D. Shrayer, vol. 2, 841–49. Armonk, NY and London: M. E. Sharpe, 2007.

Lev Ginzburg

From *"Only My Heart Was Broken"*: **"Razbilos' lish' serdtse moe,"** in *Novyi mir* 8 (1981): 107–14; **in Lev Ginzburg, *"Razbilos' lish' serdtse moe: roman-esse,"* 172–82. Moscow: Sovetskii pisatel', 1983**; in Lev Ginzburg, *"Razbilos' lish' serdtse moe: roman-esse,"* in Lev Ginzburg, *Izbrannoe*, 363–70. Moscow: Sovetskii pisatel', 1985; in Lev Ginzburg, *Koleso fortuny*, 651–64. Moscow: AST Zebra E, 2008.

English translation by Maxim D. Shrayer, *Descant* 35, 1 (Spring 2004): 225–36. Special issue: *In Latvia, Observed/Abroad/In Memory*; English translation by Maxim D. Shrayer, in *An Anthology of Jewish-Russian Literature: Two Centuries of Dual Identity in Prose and Poetry, 1801–2001*, ed. Maxim D. Shrayer, vol. 2, 828–37. Armonk, NY and London: M. E. Sharpe, 2007.

Evgeny Reyn

"For the Last Time": **"V poslednii raz,"** in *Druzhba narodov* 10 (1988): 5–6; in Evgenii Rein, *Beregovaia polosa*, 27–29. Moscow: Sovremennik, 1989; **in Evgenii Rein, *Izbrannoe*, 184–85. Moscow–Paris–New York: Tret'ia volna, 1992;** in Evgenii Rein, *Izbrannye stikhotvoreniia i poemy*, 314–15. Moscow–St. Petersburg: Letnii Sad, 2001.

English translation by Maxim D. Shrayer and J. B. Sisson, *Bee Museum* 2 (Summer 2002): 36–37; English translation by Maxim D. Shrayer and J. B. Sisson, in *An Anthology of Jewish-Russian Literature: Two Centuries of Dual Identity in Prose and Poetry, 1801–2001*, ed. Maxim D. Shrayer, vol. 2, 887–88. Armonk, NY and London: M. E. Sharpe, 2007.

Sara Pogreb

"I'm going to see my grandparents . . .": "Ia edu k dedu s babushkoi. Podvoda . . . ," in Sara Pogreb, *Ia domolchalas' do stikhov*, 44. Moscow: Knizhnaia palata, 1990;

"I'm bidding farewell to the slush . . .": "Ia proshchaius' so sliakot'iu. V pervye dni oktiabria . . . ," in Sara Pogreb, *Ia domolchalas' do stikhov*, 129. Moscow: Knizhnaia palata, 1990; in Sara Pogreb, *Pod oknom nebosvoda*, 148 [modified version]. Tel Aviv: Skopus, 1996.

English translations by Silebal Forrester, in *An Anthology of Jewish-Russian Literature: Two Centuries of Dual Identity in Prose and Poetry, 1801–2001*, ed. Maxim D. Shrayer, vol. 2, 891–93. Armonk, NY and London: M. E. Sharpe, 2007.

Israel (Izrail') Metter

From "Pedigree": "Rodoslovnaia," in *Sintaksis* 28 (1990): 168–75 [as "Avtobiografiia"] *Neva* 1 (1992): 12–18; in Izrail' Metter, *Dopros*, 3–11. St. Petersburg: Biblioteka al'manakha "Petropol"/Fond russkoi poezii/Zhurnal "Zvezda," 1998; in Izrail' Metter, *Izbrannoe*, 12–27. St. Petersburg: Russko-baltiiskii informatsionnyi tsentr BLITs, 1999.

English translation by Richard Sheldon, in *An Anthology of Jewish-Russian Literature: Two Centuries of Dual Identity in Prose and Poetry, 1801–2001*, ed. Maxim D. Shrayer, vol. 2, 896–902. Armonk, NY and London: M. E. Sharpe, 2007.

Aleksandr Mezhirov

From *Blizzard*: *Pozemka*, in Aleksandr Mezhirov, *Apologiia tsirka*, 95–97. St. Petersburg: Izd-vo Al'manakha "Petrpol'," 1997; alternative versions of the section, both earlier and later, published in *To—chemu nazvan'ia net*, in *Vremia i my* 117 (1992): 129–32; *Pozemka*, in *Svet dvuedinyi. Evrei i Rossiia v sovremennoi poezii*, ed. M. Grozovskii and E. Vitkovskii, 412–16. Moscow: Izdatel'stvo AO "Kh.G.S., 1996; in Aleksandr Mezhirov, *Pozemka*, ed. Tat'iana Bek, 171–72. Moscow: Glagol, 1997.

English translation by Maxim D. Shrayer and Andrew Von Hendy, in *An Anthology of Jewish-Russian Literature: Two Centuries of Dual Identity in Prose and Poetry, 1801–2001*, ed. Maxim D. Shrayer, vol. 2, 882–84. Armonk, NY and London: M. E. Sharpe, 2007.

Bella Ulanovskaya

Journey to Kashgar: Puteshestvie v Kashgar, in *Sintaksis* 28 (1990): 137–165; *Neva* 2 (1991): 69–81; in Bella Ulanovskaia, *Osennii pokhod liagushek*, 3–31. St. Petersburg: Sovetskii pisatel', 1992; in Bella Ulanovakaia, *Lichnaia neskromnost' pavlina: povesti i rasskazy*, 3–43. Moscow; Agraf, 2004.

English translation by Catriona Kelly, in *An Anthology of Russian Women's Writing, 1777–1992,* ed. Catriona Kelly, 360–89. Oxford: Oxford University Press, 1994; English translation by Catriona Kelly, in *An Anthology of Jewish-Russian Literature: Two Centuries of Dual Identity in Prose and Poetry, 1801–2001,* ed. Maxim D. Shrayer, vol. 2, 909–26. Armonk, NY and London: M. E. Sharpe, 2007.

Aleksandr Melikhov

From The Confession of a Jew: Ispoved' evreia, as Izgnanie iz Edema: Ispoved' evreiia (Banishment from Eden: Confession of a Jew), in Novyi mir 1 (1994): 27–33; **in Aleksandr Melikhov, *Ispoved' evreia. Roman, povest',* 63–75. St. Petersburg: Izdatel'stvo Novyi Gelikon, 1994.**

English translation by Brian Cooper, in *An Anthology of Jewish-Russian Literature: Two Centuries of Dual Identity in Prose and Poetry, 1801–2001,* ed. Maxim D. Shrayer, vol. 2, 1125–36. Armonk, NY and London: M. E. Sharpe, 2007.

Ludmila Ulitskaya

"Genele the Purse Lady": "Genele-sumochnitsa," in Liudmila Ulitskaia, Bednye rodstven-niki, 34–45. Moscow: Slovo, 1993.

English translation by Maxim D. Shrayer, in *Absinthe: New European Writing* 3 (2004): 70–80; English translation by Maxim D. Shrayer, in *An Anthology of Jewish-Russian Literature: Two Centuries of Dual Identity in Prose and Poetry, 1801–2001,* ed. Maxim D. Shrayer, vol. 2, 1105–13. Armonk, NY and London: M. E. Sharpe, 2007.

THE JEWISH EXODUS: 1970s–1990s

Lev Mak

"A Farewell to Russia": "Proshchanie s Rossiei," in Lev Mak, *Iz nochi/From the Night,* 5–6. Kansas City, MO: BkMk, 1976;

"August in Odessa": "Avgust v Odesse," in *Vremia i my* 73 (1983): 100; in The Blue Lagoon Anthology of Modern Russian Poetry, ed. Konstantin K. Kuzminsky and Grigory L. Kovalev, vol. 3B, 706. Newtonville, MA: Oriental Research Partners, [1980s]; in Lev Mak, *V ozhidanii vdokha,* 84. Moscow: Aspekt Press, 2009.

English translations by Daniel Weissbort, and by Daniel Weissbort and Maxim D. Shrayer, in *An Anthology of Jewish-Russian Literature: Two Centuries of Dual Identity in Prose and Poetry, 1801–2001,* ed. Maxim D. Shrayer, vol. 2, 939–41. Armonk, NY and London: M. E. Sharpe, 2007.

Boris Khazanov

From *The King's Hour*: **Chas korolia,** in *Evrei v SSSR* 9 (1975?), reprinted, *Evreiskii samiz-dat/Jewish Samizdat* 11 (1976), 92–129. Jerusalem: The Hebrew University of Jerusalem/ The Centre for Research and Documentation of East European Jewry, n.d.; in *Vremia i my* 6 (April 1976): 64–71; in Boris Khazanov, *Zapakh zvezd*, 87–91. Tel Aviv: Vremia i my, 1977; **in Boris Khazanov, *Chas korolia. Ia, voskresenie i zhizn'. Antivremia: moskovskii roman,* 65–68. New York: Vremia i my, 1985**; in Boris Khazanov, *Chas korolia. Antivremia. Moskovskii roman*, 79–82. Moscow: Ex Libris. Slovo/Slovo, 1991.

English translation by Brian Cooper, in *An Anthology of Jewish-Russian Literature: Two Centuries of Dual Identity in Prose and Poetry, 1801–2001*, ed. Maxim D. Shrayer, vol. 2, 988–90. Armonk, NY and London: M. E. Sharpe, 2007.

Ilia Bokstein

"Afánta-Utóma" ("Fantasia-Judaica"): "Afánta-Iutóma" ("Fantaziia-Iudaika"), in Il'ia Bokshtein, *Bliki volny. Kniga stikhov* (faksimil'noe izdanie), 83–91. Bat-Yam: Moria, 1986; parts 1, 8, 9, in Il'ia Bokshtein, *Byt' ia liubimym khotel*, ed. Mina Lein, 3, 41, 16. Jerusalem: Biblioteka Ierusalimskogo zhurnala, 2001; part 5 in Il'ia Bokshtein, *Govorit zvezda s lunoi*, ed. Mina Lein, 12. Jerusalem: Biblioteka Ierusalimskogo zhurnala, 2002).

English translation by Gerald Janecek, in *An Anthology of Jewish-Russian Literature: Two Centuries of Dual Identity in Prose and Poetry, 1801–2001*, ed. Maxim D. Shrayer, vol. 2, 964–69. Armonk, NY and London: M. E. Sharpe, 2007.

David Markish

From *Jesters: Shuty*, **in David Markish, *Shuty, ili khronika iz zhizni prokhozhikh liudei* (1689–1738), 161–72. Tel Aviv: Izdatel'stvo Avtora, 1991.**
English translation by Brian Cooper, in *An Anthology of Jewish-Russian Literature: Two Centuries of Dual Identity in Prose and Poetry, 1801–2001*, ed. Maxim D. Shrayer, vol. 2, 972–80. Armonk, NY and London: M. E. Sharpe, 2007.

Michael Kreps

"Childhood": "Detstvo";
"The Cat with a Yellow Star": "Koshka s zheltoi zvezdoi," in *Vremia i my* 91 (1986): 98–99;
"Call of the Ancestors": "Zov predkov," in *Vremia i my* 91 (1986): 103–4;
all in Mikhail Kreps, *Interv'iu s ptitsei Feniks*, 19–20, 95–96, 116. Paris–New York: Tret'ia volna, 1986.

English translations by Emelye Crehore, in *An Anthology of Jewish-Russian Literature: Two Centuries of Dual Identity in Prose and Poetry, 1801–2001*, ed. Maxim D. Shrayer, vol. 2, 1023–26. Armonk, NY and London: M. E. Sharpe, 2007.

Philip Isaac Berman

"**Sarah and the Rooster**": "**Sarra i Petushok**," in *Al'manakh-91 Klub russkikh pisatelei*, 99–129. New York: The Russian Writers' Club, 1991; **in *Poberezh'e* 4 (1995): 23–41**; in *Filadel'fiiskie stranitsy. Antologiia*, ed. Igor' Mikhalevich-Kaplan and Valentina Sinkevich, 25–47. Philadelphia: Poberezh'e, 1998; in Filipp Isaak Berman, *Nebesno-dereviannaia doroga*, 77–108. Philadelphia: Poberezh'e, 2014.

English translation by Yelena Lebedinsky and the author, in *An Anthology of Jewish-Russian Literature: Two Centuries of Dual Identity in Prose and Poetry, 1801–2001*, ed. Maxim D. Shrayer, vol. 2, 1029–46. Armonk, NY and London: M. E. Sharpe, 2007.

Ruth Zernova

"**All Vows**": "**Vse obety**," in Ruf' Zernova, *Izrail' i okrestnosti*, 47–57. **Jerusalem: Biblioteka "Aliia," 1990.**

English translation by Helen Reeve with Martha Kitchen, in *An Anthology of Jewish-Russian Literature: Two Centuries of Dual Identity in Prose and Poetry, 1801–2001*, ed. Maxim D. Shrayer, vol. 2, 1049–55. Armonk, NY and London: M. E. Sharpe, 2007.

David Shrayer-Petrov

"**Chagall's Self-Portrait with Wife**": "**K avtoportretu Shagala s zhenoi**";
"**My Slavic Soul**": "**Moia slavianskaia dusha**";
"**Villa Borghese**": "**Villa Borgeze**," in David Shrayer-Petrov, *Villa Borgeze*, 57–58. Holyoke, MA: New England Publishing Co., 1992;
in *Poberezh'e* 1 (1992): 54–55; *in Svet dvuedinyi. Evrei i Rossiia v sovremennoi poezii*, ed. M. Grozovskii and E. Vitkovskii, 444–45. Moscow: Izdatel'stvo AO "Kh.G.S.," 1996; in David Shrayer-Petrov, *Propashchaia dusha*, 6–8. Providence, RI: APKA Publishers, 1997; in David Shrayer-Petrov, *Derevenskii orkestr*, 57–60. St. Petersburg: Ostrovitianin, 2016; **all in David Shrayer-Petrov, *Forma liubvi*, 49–52, 84–85. Moscow: Izdatel'skii dom "Iunost'," 2003.**

English translation of "Chagall's Portrait with Wife" by Edwin Honig and Maxim D. Shrayer, in "*Bee Museum* 3 (2005): 27; English translation of "Villa Borghese" by Dolores Stewart and Maxim D. Shrayer, *Salmagundi* 101–2 (Winter–Spring 1994): 151–53; English translation of "My Slavic Soul" by Maxim D. Shrayer, in *Bee Museum* 3 (2005); 27; English translations by Edwin Honig and Maxim D. Shrayer, and by Dolores Stewart and Maxim D. Shrayer, in *Four Centuries: Russian Poetry in Translation* 2 (2012): 15–26; English translations by Edwin Honig and Maxim D. Shrayer, and by Dolores Stewart and Maxim D. Shrayer, in *An Anthology of Jewish-Russian Literature: Two Centuries of Dual Identity in Prose and Poetry, 1801–2001,* ed. Maxim D. Shrayer, vol. 2, 1058–61. Armonk, NY and London: M. E. Sharpe, 2007.

"Hände Hoch!": **"Hände Hoch!"** *Forverts* 218 (14–20 January 2000): 10; *Nasha ulitsa* 9 (2000): 88–95; **in David Shrayer-Petrov.** *Karp dlia farshirovannoi ryby,* **150–80. Moscow: Raduga, 2005;**

English translation by Maxim D. Shrayer, in David Shrayer-Petrov, *Jonah and Sarah: Jewish Stories of Russia and America,* ed. Maxim D. Shrayer, 140–52. Syracuse: Syracuse University Press, 2003; English translation by Maxim D. Shrayer, in *An Anthology of Jewish-Russian Literature: Two Centuries of Dual Identity in Prose and Poetry, 1801–2001,* ed. Maxim D. Shrayer, vol. 2, 1062–70. Armonk, NY and London: M. E. Sharpe, 2007.

Marina Temkina

"1995: Happy New Year!": **"Vmesto predisloviia: s novym 1995-m godom!"** in Marina Temkina, *Kalancha: Gendernaia lirika,* **6. New York: Slovo-Word, 1995.**

English translation by Maxim D. Shrayer, in *An Anthology of Jewish-Russian Literature: Two Centuries of Dual Identity in Prose and Poetry, 1801–2001,* ed. Maxim D. Shrayer, vol. 2, 1078–79. Armonk, NY and London: M. E. Sharpe, 2007.

Dina Rubina

From *Here Comes the Messiah!*: *Vot idet messiia!* in *Druzhba narodov* 9–10 (1996): 129–34; **in Dina Rubina,** *Vot idet Messiia!* **123–32. Moscow: Podkova, 1999.**

English translation by Daniel Jaffe, in Dina Rubina, *Here Comes the Messiah!* 134–143. Brookline, MA: Zephyr Press, 2000; English translation by Daniel Jaffe, in *An Anthology of Jewish-Russian Literature: Two Centuries of Dual Identity in Prose and Poetry, 1801–2001,* ed. Maxim D. Shrayer, vol. 2, 1170–76. Armonk, NY and London: M. E. Sharpe, 2007.

Friedrich Gorenstein

"The Arrest of an Antisemite" (a true story): **"Arest antisemita"** (byl'); **in** *Slovo-Word* **34 (2002): 16–20.**

English translation by Alexandra Kirilcuk, in *An Anthology of Jewish-Russian Literature: Two Centuries of Dual Identity in Prose and Poetry, 1801–2001,* ed. Maxim D. Shrayer, vol. 2, 1082–90. Armonk, NY and London: M. E. Sharpe, 2007.

Anna Gorenko

"wake up all the poets all died overnight . . .": **"prosypaisia umerli noch'iu poety vse-vse . . .";**

"The Golem": "Golem" [part 2 of "Pesni mertvykh detei"];

"Translating from the European": "Perevod s evropeiskogo";

all in Anna Gorenko, *Stikhi*, ed. Evgenii Soshkin, 33, 45–46, 74. Jerusalem: Beseder, 2000; all in Anna Gorenko, *Maloe sobranie* [dedication to Andriusha Glikman], ed. Vladimir Tarasov, 42, 60–61, 88. Jerusalem: Alphabet Publishers, 2000; all in Anna Gorenko, *Prazdnik nespelogo khleba*, ed. E[vgenii] Soshkin et al., 53, 69–70, 99. Moscow: Novoe literaturnoe obozrenie, 2003.

English translation by Sibelan Forrester, in *An Anthology of Jewish-Russian Literature: Two Centuries of Dual Identity in Prose and Poetry, 1801–2001*, ed. Maxim D. Shrayer, vol. 2, 1165–67. Armonk, NY and London: M. E. Sharpe, 2007.

Index of Authors

Index of Translators
(with names of authors' translated)

Index of Names, Works, and Subjects

Items in bold indicate authors and texts featured in this Anthology.

About the Editor

The bilingual author and scholar Maxim D. Shrayer was born in Moscow in 1967 to a Jewish-Russian family and spent almost nine years as a refusenik. He and his parents, the writer and doctor David Shrayer-Petrov and the translator Emilia Shrayer, left the USSR and immigrated to the United States in 1987 after spending a summer in Austria and Italy. Shrayer attended Moscow University, Brown University, and Rutgers University and received a Ph.D. at Yale University in 1995. He is professor of Russian, English, and Jewish studies at Boston College, where he cofounded the Jewish Studies Program, and an associate at Harvard University's Davis Center, where he directs the Project on Russian and Eurasian Jewry.

Maxim D. Shrayer has authored and edited over fifteen books of criticism, biography, nonfiction, fiction, poetry, and translation, among them the critical studies *The World of Nabokov's Stories* and *Russian Poet/Soviet Jew*. He is the author of the acclaimed literary memoirs *Waiting for America: A Story of Emigration* and *Leaving Russia: A Jewish Story* (finalist of the 2013 National Jewish Book Awards), of the story collection *Yom Kippur in Amsterdam*, and of three collections of Russian-language poetry. He has also edited and cotranslated four books of fiction by his father, David Shrayer-Petrov, most recently the novel *Doctor Levitin*. Shrayer's book *I Saw It: Ilya Selvinsky and the Legacy of Bearing Witness to the Shoah* appeared in 2013. Shrayer's book *Bunin and Nabokov: A History of Rivalry* was published in 2014 in Moscow and became a national bestseller. His recent books include *Zalman's Disappearance*, a collection of Russian-language short stories, and *With or Without You: The Prospect for Jews in Today's Russia*.

Shrayer's works have been translated into nine languages. Shrayer is the recipient of a number of awards and fellowships, including those from the Guggenheim Foundation, the National Endowment for the Humanities, the Rockefeller Foundation, and the Bogliasco Foundation. He lectures widely on topics ranging from the legacy of the refusenik movement and the experience of ex-Soviet Jews in America to Shoah literature and Jewish-Russian culture. Shrayer lives in Massachusetts with his wife, Dr. Karen E. Lasser, a medical researcher and physician, and their two daughters. They divide their time between Brookline and South Chatham, Massachusetts.

For more information, visit Shrayer's literary website at *www.shrayer.com*.

PRAISE FOR *VOICES OF JEWISH-RUSSIAN LITERATURE*

"This is an enlightening, well-edited anthology, a partial answer to an eternally vexed question: what does it mean to be a writer with talent and Jewish blood in Russia? A kind of triple consciousness emerges from the biographies and works included. The surprise is that the problem of identity for Jewish writers began so early and persisted so long, whether under tsar or commissar or gangster capitalism.

The attitudes of these writers of two centuries are varied and complex, but their experiences of anti-Semitism are the same. A valuable contribution to the study of Russian literature."

—Ellendea Proffer Teasley, MacArthur Fellow and co-founder of Ardis Publishers

"Jewish literature is an essential element of the Russian and Ukrainian historical experience. This meticulously assembled rich collection of nineteenth-through twentieth-century works, some freshly translated, is sure to appeal to historians and literary scholars alike. Biographical portraits, an historical essay, and an extensive bibliography make this rich literary oeuvre accessible to graduate and undergraduate students. For scholars of Jewish and Russian literature, *Voices of Jewish-Russian Literature* is an indispensable vademecum."

—Patricia Herlihy, Professor Emerita of History, Brown University and author of *Odessa: A History, 1794–1914*

"Stunning work, Maxim D. Shrayer's *Voices of Jewish-Russian Literature* brings center stage the rich contribution of Jewish-Russian writers. Selections in all genres of writing from writers such as Mandelstam, Shklovsky, Babel and Ehrenburg focus on Jewish issues and happenings directly or indirectly. Equally stunning is the way *Voices of Jewish-Russian Literature*—through its selection and network of superb commentary—provides the groundwork for an exploration of the esthetic and psychological ambiguities of adaptation that from time immemorial have marked the Jewish response to non-Jewish languages and cultures. The inspiration, design and intellectual crafting of the stellar scholar and author, Maxim D. Shrayer, *Voices of Jewish-Russian Literature* is not to be missed by anyone interested in the meeting of the Jewish and Russian spirit."

—Robert Louis Jackson, B. E. Bensinger Professor Emeritus of Slavic Languages and Literatures, Yale University and author of *Dialogues with Dostoevsky*

"This anthology creates closure for the two-hundred-year history of Jewish-Russian literature which, by transforming its basic properties and habitat at the turn of the twentieth century, becomes Russian-Israeli literature, Russian-American, and so forth. Moving beyond all essentialist and cultural definitions, Maxim D. Shrayer points to the elusive quality that makes this literature specifically Jewish and this anthology required reading for any Russianist. The quality Shrayer identifies lies in the truth this literature tells about Jewish history and life—the truth which a religious Jew may not look for and a non-Jew may not see."

—Roman Katsman, Professor of Literature of the Jewish People, Bar Ilan University and author of *Nostalgia for a Foreign Land: Studies in Russian-Language Literature in Israel*

"With the publication of this critical literary anthology, Maxim D. Shrayer seeks to transparently and inclusively represent traditional and experimental movements, thematic trends, many genres and forms of prose and poetry—leading to a broad anatomy of two centuries of the Jewish-Russian literary heritage. There is no living scholar better-equipped to examine the legacy of Jewish-Russian literature than Shrayer. His creative and editorial work in this field has both sustained and re-vivified its legacy for future generations. His reconstruction of the canon through the publication of the anthology includes a distinctly defined concept of a Jewish poetics born at the intersection of the author's identity and aesthetics—a most useful addition to ongoing conversations about Jewish-hyphenate literary identity more generally. Readers will be astounded by the depth and breadth of the contributions, including the editor's notes, and general, editorial, and author introductions. It must be said that while the content is presented in a most inviting state for all readers, teachers will find within the text productive pedagogical tools to knowledgeably teach the literature and its legacy. It offers a full measure of a political- ideological and cultural-linguistic poetics that will contribute a thousandfold to our understanding of the Jewish-Russian literary legacy."

—Holli Levitsky, Professor of English and Director of Jewish Studies Program, Loyola Marymount University and editor of *Literature of Exile and Displacement*

"This anthology is a major contribution to our understanding of key role played by Russian Jews in both Russian and Jewish culture. It is absolutely indispensable for anyone with a serious interest in the subject."

—Samuel D Kassow, Charles H. Northam Professor of History, Trinity College and author of *The Distinctive Life of East European Jewry*

CPSIA information can be obtained
at www.ICGtesting.com
Printed in the USA
LVHW031520030221
678278LV00001B/1